THE CLASSIC Fantasy COLLECTION

THE CLASSIC Fantasy COLLECTION

SIRIUS

SIRIUS

This edition published in 2025 by Sirius Publishing, a division of
Arcturus Publishing Limited,
26/27 Bickels Yard, 151–153 Bermondsey Street,
London SE1 3HA

Cover design: Peter Ridley
Cover illustration: Tithi Luadthong

ISBN: 978-1-3988-6101-5
AD005941US

Printed in China

CONTENTS

The Phoenix on the Sword by Robert E. Howard 11

The Scarlet Citadel by Robert E. Howard 33

Rogues in the House by Robert E. Howard 69

The Tower of the Elephant by Robert E. Howard 93

The Queen of the Black Coast by Robert E. Howard 117

The Dunwich Horror by H. P. Lovecraft 145

The Call of Cthulhu by H. P. Lovecraft 185

The Color out of Space by H. P. Lovecraft 213

Werewolf of the Sahara by G. G. Pendarves 239

The Magic Shop by H. G. Wells 271

The Man Who Could Work Miracles by H. G. Wells 283

Mr Skelmersdale in Fairyland by H. G. Wells 299

The Story of the Inexperienced Ghost by H. G. Wells 313

The Wood Beyond the World by William Morris 327

The Soul of the Great Bell by Lafcadio Hearn 431

The Return of Yen-Tchin-King by Lafcadio Hearn 437

The Tale of the Porcelain-God by Lafcadio Hearn 443

The Dream of Akinosuke by Lafcadio Hearn 453

Rokuro-Kubi by Lafcadio Hearn 460

The Moon Pool by Abraham Merritt 471

The People of the Pit by Abraham Merritt 509

The Great God Pan by Arthur Machen 527

The Inmost Light by Arthur Machen 575

The Transmutation of Ling by Ernest Bramah 601

The Story of Yung Chang by Ernest Bramah 673

The Probation of Sen Heng by Ernest Bramah 685

The Experiment of the Mandarin Chan Hung
by Ernest Bramah 703

The Confession of Kai Lung by Ernest Bramah 721

The Vengeance of Tung Fel by Ernest Bramah 737

The Career of the Charitable Quen-Ki-Tong
by Ernest Bramah 757

The Vision of Yin, the Son of Yat Huang
by Ernest Bramah 777

The Ill-Regulated Destiny of Kin Yen, the Picture Maker
by Ernest Bramah 791

The Repairer of Reputations by Robert W. Chambers 803

The Mask by Robert W. Chambers 833

In the Court of the Dragon by Robert W. Chambers 849

The Yellow Sign by Robert W. Chambers 859

The Shadows by George MacDonald 877

The Golden Key by George MacDonald 903

INTRODUCTION

Most people believe that the modern fantasy genre began with J. R. R. Tolkien and his epic novels *The Hobbit* and *The Lord of the Rings*. Fantasy has reached new heights in the 21st century as hundreds of new writers have burst on to the scene, some following in Tolkien's tradition, others denying it utterly, and television, film and even video games have embraced the genre as their own. Yet by the time Tolkien was putting the finishing touches on *The Lord of the Rings* in 1954, fantasy was already a well-established genre, with masterful writers telling fascinating tales that showcased their extensive imagination.

This collection brings together a selection of those who practiced their craft before the genre became synonymous with a single individual and a singular style. It ranges from the classical epic romances of William Morris to the terrifying tales of the master of horror, H. P. Lovecraft. Some draw on Norse mythologies and the history of medieval Europe while others turn to East Asia, to Japan and China, for inspiration. Some blur the lines between horror, fantasy and science fiction. The tone of the writing is sometimes whimsical, sometimes dreamlike and sometimes epic. It is a hard genre to define. There is no simple archetype which makes a fantasy novel "fantasy". Even today, some writers are uncomfortable with their work being labelled as "fantasy fiction" despite possessing several fantastic elements, while others embrace the genre enthusiastically. The number of sub-genres can be bewildering – epic, gothic, sword & sorcery, urban, alternate history, magical realism, weird fiction – it is an almost endless list, reflecting the genre's vast range of possibilities.

Yet all these stories share a common thread. They bring together the impossible and they make it seem both plausible and natural. They are set in alternate universes, some very similar to our own, others utterly alien, and draw us in to the fascinating worlds that exist between the author's words. Many use the device of alternate worlds to address important contemporary political or social issues, engaging powerful magic or strange creatures as cyphers for present-day concerns.

None of this is to say that there has always been a distinctive fantasy genre. While mythical tales involving gods, magic, heroes and fearsome creatures like dragons have been around since the dawn of oral tradition, these tales were often believed to be true. Fairytales, folklore and legends are not quite the same thing as the fantasy stories collected here – though they often provided essential inspiration. The fantasy genre, in its modern form, emerged in the last few decades of the 19th century. Writers like George MacDonald, Edgar Allan Poe, Abraham Merritt at the end of the century targeted their fantastic writings at an adult audience. They sought to tell tales involving elements of the impossible that were clearly distinguishable from the fairytales and myths that had gone before.

George MacDonald's *Phantastes*, first published in 1858, is widely credited as the first fantasy novel ever written. He was the writer most admired by C.S. Lewis and had a fundamental influence on the many fantasy writers that followed. MacDonald was a deeply religious man, a Calvinist minister and a Celtic scholar. For MacDonald, as it would be for countless generations, fantasy was for both escapism – for "the child-like, whether they be of five, or fifty, or seventy-five" years of age – and for exploring the human condition in a different way. By the turn of the century, several more writers had followed in MacDonald's footsteps. H. G. Wells is best known for his classic science fiction novels, but in his short fiction he turned his hand to fantasy, too. He embraced several supernatural motifs, including themes of spiritual possession, dreaming, and ghosts. It was William Morris, though, the poet, textile designer and novelist, who truly established the form of the alternate world epic. Awash with fanciful language, taking their inspiration equally from classical romances and mythology, Morris is one of the unacknowledged masters of the genre.

At the same time, an entirely different tradition of fantasy literature was emerging. For some writers, it was the fairytales of Asia that captured the imagination. Lafcadio Hearn (1850–1904), born in Greece, American resident and Japanese enthusiast, wrote a number of traditional Japanese legends and ghost stories in the style of modern fiction after marrying a Japanese woman and moving to Matsue in western Japan. Ernest Bramah (1868–1942) was an English author whose works ranged from comedy to science fiction to the supernatural. His greatest work was *The Wallet of Kai Lung*, the collection of short stories contained in this volume that feature the nominal ancient Chinese storyteller, Kai Lung. The narrator undergoes several fantastic encounters with dragons, demons and gods and the character has obtained a cult-like status amongst fantasy connoisseurs.

Others sought to combine the sensibilities of gothic horror with a newfound interest in the supernatural. The American writer and illustrator Robert William Chambers (1865–1933) created in *The King in Yellow*, the collection from which many of the stories in this volume are taken, a landmark statement in weird fiction. He turned away from the tropes of werewolves, vampires and ghosts towards an altogether more alien, cosmic horror. He was not the only one to do so. Arthur Machen (1863–1947), the Welsh writer, took his inspiration from pagan ritual. In his controversial novella, *The Great God Pan*, described by Stephen King as "maybe the best [horror story] in the English language", a young girl is forced to see the terrifying truth behind the Devil, known as Pan. These authors set the stage for a new generation of fantasy writers.

Between the First and Second World Wars a new style of writing took hold. Pulp magazines had grown rapidly in popularity from their emergence at the turn of the century. Cheaply produced, and cheaply sold, they were short fiction magazines that garnered a wide audience and were often ridiculed by literary critics. Nonetheless, they provided an essential medium for developing fantasy writers. Pulps such as *Argosy* and *Weird Tales* helped stimulate young writers who found their work rejected by publishers more interested in maintaining the status quo. G. G. Pendarves, the pseudonym of the English author Gladys Gordon Trenery, published a number of supernatural stories for *Weird Tales* and in the "Werewolf of the Sahara" she wrote an evocative tale of horror that characterized the strengths of the genre.

The two most successful pulp writers of this period were H.P. Lovecraft (1890–1937) and Robert E. Howard (1906–1936). Both lived short, unhappy yet extraordinarily productive lives. Lovecraft was a prolific writer best known for his creation of the Cthulhu universe. Profoundly affected by the death of his grandfather in 1904, he turned to an isolated existence where he honed his literary craft.

Born an only son in a dysfunctional Texan family and first-hand witness to the violence of the day through his father's career as a doctor, Howard turned to fiction for an escape. A voracious reader, he soon aspired towards creating his own fiction. Over the course of his career, Howard wrote more than 100 stories. Included here are several featuring his most famous character, Conan the Cimmerian. There is perhaps no more iconic character in the history of sword & sorcery than the powerful, sullen barbarian who roamed the Hyborian world saving princesses, fighting wizards and acting at times as thief, mercenary, pirate and even king.

Neither writer managed to achieve commercial success during their own lifetimes, but their influence on their respective genres has been profound. Lovecraft has been cited as the key inspiration for writers as diverse as Stephen King, Neil Gaiman and China Miéville, while there is hardly a fantasy writer working today that does not acknowledge a debt to Robert E. Howard.

THE PHOENIX ON THE SWORD

ROBERT E. HOWARD

I

"Know, oh prince, that between the years when the oceans drank Atlantis and the gleaming cities, and the years of the rise of the Sons of Aryas, there was an Age undreamed of, when shining kingdoms lay spread across the world like blue mantles beneath the stars—Nemedia, Ophir, Brythunia, Hyperborea, Zamora with its dark-haired women and towers of spider-haunted mystery, Zingara with its chivalry, Koth that bordered on the pastoral lands of Shem, Stygia with its shadow-guarded tombs, Hyrkania whose riders wore steel and silk and gold. But the proudest kingdom of the world was Aquilonia, reigning supreme in the dreaming west. Hither came Conan, the Cimmerian, black-haired, sullen-eyed, sword in hand, a thief, a reaver, a slayer, with gigantic melancholies and gigantic mirth, to tread the jeweled thrones of the Earth under his sandalled feet."

—The Nemedian Chronicles

Over shadowy spires and gleaming towers lay the ghostly darkness and silence that runs before dawn. Into a dim alley, one of a veritable labyrinth of mysterious winding ways, four masked figures came hurriedly from a door, which a dusky hand furtively opened. They spoke not but went swiftly into the gloom, cloaks wrapped closely about them; as silently as the ghosts of murdered men they disappeared in the darkness. Behind them a sardonic countenance was framed in the partly opened door; a pair of evil eyes glittered malevolently in the gloom.

"Go into the night, creatures of the night," a voice mocked. "Oh, fools, your doom hounds your heels like a blind dog, and you know it not."

The speaker closed the door and bolted it, then turned and went up the corridor, candle in hand. He was a somber giant, whose dusky skin revealed his Stygian blood. He came into an inner chamber, where a tall, lean man in worn velvet lounged like a great lazy cat on a silken couch, sipping wine from a huge golden goblet.

"Well, Ascalante," said the Stygian, setting down the candle, "your dupes have slunk into the streets like rats from their burrows. You work with strange tools."

"Tools?" replied Ascalante. "Why, they consider me that. For months now, ever since the Rebel Four summoned me from the southern desert, I have been living in the very heart of my enemies, hiding by day in this obscure house, skulking through dark alleys and darker corridors at night. And I have accomplished what those rebellious nobles could not. Working through them, and through other agents, many of whom have never seen my face, I have honeycombed the empire with sedition and unrest. In short I, working in the shadows, have paved the downfall of the king who sits throned in the sun. By Mitra, I was a statesman before I was an outlaw."

"And these dupes who deem themselves your masters?"

"They will continue to think that I serve them, until our present task is completed. Who are they to match wits with Ascalante? Volmana, the dwarfish count of Karaban; Gromel, the giant commander of the Black Legion; Dion, the fat baron of Attalus; Rinaldo, the hare-brained minstrel. I am the force which has welded together the steel in each, and by the clay in each, I will crush them when the time comes. But that lies in the future; tonight the king dies."

"Days ago I saw the imperial squadrons ride from the city," said the Stygian.

"They rode to the frontier which the heathen Picts assail—thanks to the strong liquor which I've smuggled over the borders to madden them. Dion's great wealth made that possible. And Volmana made it possible to dispose of the rest of the imperial troops which remained in the city. Through his princely kin in Nemedia, it was easy to persuade King Numa to request the presence of Count Trocero of Poitain, seneschal of Aquilonia; and of course, to do him honor, he'll be accompanied by an imperial escort, as well as his own troops, and Prospero, King Conan's righthand man. That leaves only the king's personal bodyguard in the city—beside the Black Legion. Through Gromel I've corrupted a spendthrift officer of that guard, and bribed him to lead his men away from the king's door at midnight.

"Then, with sixteen desperate rogues of mine, we enter the palace by a secret tunnel. After the deed is done, even if the people do not rise to welcome us, Gromel's Black Legion will be sufficient to hold the city and the crown."

"And Dion thinks that crown will be given to him?"

"Yes. The fat fool claims it by reason of a trace of royal blood. Conan makes a bad mistake in letting men live who still boast descent from the old dynasty, from which he tore the crown of Aquilonia.

"Volmana wishes to be reinstated in royal favor as he was under the old regime, so that he may lift his poverty-ridden estates to their former grandeur. Gromel hates Pallantides, commander of the Black Dragons, and desires the command of the whole army, with all the stubbornness of the Bossonian. Alone of us all, Rinaldo has no personal ambition. He sees in Conan a red-handed, rough-footed barbarian who came out of the north to plunder a civilized land. He idealizes the king whom Conan killed to get the crown, remembering only that he occasionally patronized the arts, and forgetting the evils of his reign, and he is making the people forget. Already they openly sing *The Lament for the King* in which Rinaldo lauds the sainted villain and denounces Conan as 'that black-hearted savage from the abyss.' Conan laughs, but the people snarl."

"Why does he hate Conan?"

"Poets always hate those in power. To them perfection is always just behind the last corner, or beyond the next. They escape the present in dreams of the past and future. Rinaldo is a flaming torch of idealism, rising, as he thinks, to overthrow a tyrant and liberate the people. As for me—well, a few months ago I had lost all ambition but to raid the caravans for the rest of my life; now old dreams stir. Conan will die; Dion will mount the throne. Then he, too, will die. One by one, all who oppose me will die—by fire, or steel, or those deadly wines you know so well how to brew. Ascalante, king of Aquilonia! How like you the sound of it?"

The Stygian shrugged his broad shoulders.

"There was a time," he said with unconcealed bitterness, "when I, too, had my ambitions, beside which yours seem tawdry and childish. To what a state I have fallen! My old-time peers and rivals would stare indeed could they see Thoth-amon of the Ring serving as the slave of an outlander, and an outlaw at that; and aiding in the petty ambitions of barons and kings!"

"You laid your trust in magic and mummery," answered Ascalante carelessly. "I trust my wits and my sword."

"Wits and swords are as straws against the wisdom of the Darkness," growled the Stygian, his dark eyes flickering with menacing lights and shadows. "Had I not lost the Ring, our positions might be reversed."

"Nevertheless," answered the outlaw impatiently, "you wear the stripes of my whip on your back, and are likely to continue to wear them."

"Be not so sure!" the fiendish hatred of the Stygian glittered for an instant redly in his eyes. "Some day, somehow, I will find the Ring again, and when I do, by the serpent-fangs of Set, you shall pay—"

The hot-tempered Aquilonian started up and struck him heavily across the mouth. Thoth reeled back, blood starting from his lips.

"You grow over-bold, dog," growled the outlaw. "Have a care; I am still your master who knows your dark secret. Go upon the housetops and shout that Ascalante is in the city plotting against the king—if you dare."

"I dare not," muttered the Stygian, wiping the blood from his lips.

"No, you do not dare," Ascalante grinned bleakly. "For if I die by your stealth or treachery, a hermit priest in the southern desert will know of it, and will break the seal of a manuscript I left in his hands. And having read, a word will be whispered in Stygia, and a wind will creep up from the south by midnight. And where will you hide your head, Thoth-amon?"

The slave shuddered and his dusky face went ashen.

"Enough!" Ascalante changed his tone peremptorily. "I have work for you. I do not trust Dion. I bade him ride to his country estate and remain there until the work tonight is done. The fat fool could never conceal his nervousness before the king today. Ride after him, and if you do not overtake him on the road, proceed to his estate and remain with him until we send for him. Don't let him out of your sight. He is mazed with fear, and might bolt—might even rush to Conan in a panic, and reveal the whole plot, hoping thus to save his own hide. Go!"

The slave bowed, hiding the hate in his eyes, and did as he was bidden. Ascalante turned again to his wine. Over the jeweled spires was rising a dawn crimson as blood.

II

When I was a fighting-man, the kettle-drums they beat,
The people scattered gold-dust before my horses' feet;
But now I am a great king, the people hound my track
With poison in my wine-cup, and daggers at my back.

—*The Road of Kings*

The room was large and ornate, with rich tapestries on the polished, panelled walls, deep rugs on the ivory floor, and with the lofty ceiling adorned with intricate carvings and silver scrollwork. Behind an ivory, gold-inlaid writing-table sat a man whose broad shoulders and sun-browned skin seemed out of place among those luxuriant surroundings. He seemed more a part of the sun and winds and high places of the outlands. His slightest movement spoke of steel-spring muscles knit to a keen brain with the co-ordination of a born fighting-man. There was nothing deliberate or measured about his actions. Either he was perfectly at rest—still as a bronze statue—or else he was in motion, not with the jerky quickness of over-tense nerves, but with a cat-like speed that blurred the sight that tried to follow him.

His garments were of rich fabric, but simply made. He wore no ring or ornaments, and his square-cut black mane was confined merely by a cloth-of-silver band about his head.

Now he laid down the golden stylus with which he had been laboriously scrawling on waxed papyrus, rested his chin on his fist, and fixed his smoldering blue eyes enviously on the man who stood before him. This person was occupied in his own affairs at the moment, for he was taking up the laces of his gold-chased armor, and abstractedly whistling—a rather unconventional performance, considering that he was in the presence of a king.

"Prospero," said the man at the table, "these matters of statecraft weary me as all the fighting I have done never did."

"All part of the game, Conan," answered the dark-eyed Poitainian. "You are king—you must play the part."

"I wish I might ride with you to Nemedia," said Conan enviously. "It seems ages since I had a horse between my knees—but Publius says that affairs in the city require my presence. Curse him!

"When I overthrew the old dynasty," he continued, speaking with the easy familiarity which existed only between the Poitainian and himself, "it was easy enough, though it seemed bitter hard at the time. Looking back now over the wild path I followed, all those days of toil, intrigue, slaughter and tribulation seem like a dream.

"I did not dream far enough, Prospero. When King Numedides lay dead at my feet and I tore the crown from his gory head and set it on my own, I had reached the ultimate border of my dreams. I had prepared myself to take the crown, not to hold it. In the old free days all I wanted was a sharp sword and a straight path to my enemies. Now no paths are straight and my sword is useless.

"When I overthrew Numedides, then I was the Liberator—now they spit at my shadow. They have put a statue of that swine in the temple of Mitra, and people go and wail before it, hailing it as the holy effigy of a saintly monarch who was done to death by a red-handed barbarian. When I led her armies to victory as a mercenary, Aquilonia overlooked the fact that I was a foreigner, but now she cannot forgive me.

"Now in Mitra's temple there come to burn incense to Numedides' memory, men whom his hangmen maimed and blinded, men whose sons died in his dungeons, whose wives and daughters were dragged into his seraglio. The fickle fools!"

"Rinaldo is largely responsible," answered Prospero, drawing up his sword-belt another notch. "He sings songs that make men mad. Hang him in his jester's garb to the highest tower in the city. Let him make rimes for the vultures."

Conan shook his lion head. "No, Prospero, he's beyond my reach. A great poet is greater than any king. His songs are mightier than my scepter; for he has near ripped the heart from my breast when he chose to sing for me. I shall die and be forgotten, but Rinaldo's songs will live for ever.

"No, Prospero," the king continued, a somber look of doubt shadowing his eyes, "there is something hidden, some undercurrent of which we are not aware. I sense it as in my youth I sensed the tiger hidden in the tall grass. There is a nameless unrest throughout the kingdom. I am like a hunter who crouches by his small fire amid the forest, and hears stealthy feet padding in the darkness, and almost sees the glimmer of burning eyes. If I could but come to grips with something tangible, that I could cleave with my sword! I tell you, it's not by chance that the Picts have of late so fiercely assailed the frontiers, so that the Bossonians have called for aid to beat them back. I should have ridden with the troops."

"Publius feared a plot to trap and slay you beyond the frontier," replied Prospero, smoothing his silken surcoat over his shining mail, and admiring his tall lithe figure in a silver mirror. "That's why he urged you to remain in the city. These doubts are born of your barbarian instincts. Let the people snarl! The mercenaries are ours, and the Black Dragons, and every rogue in Poitain swears by you. Your only danger is assassination, and that's impossible, with men of the imperial troops guarding you day and night. What are you working at there?"

"A map," Conan answered with pride. "The maps of the court show well the countries of south, east and west, but in the north they are vague and faulty. I am adding the northern lands myself. Here is Cimmeria, where I was born. And—"

"Asgard and Vanaheim," Prospero scanned the map. "By Mitra, I had almost believed those countries to have been fabulous."

Conan grinned savagely, involuntarily touching the scars on his dark face. "You had known otherwise, had you spent your youth on the northern frontiers of Cimmeria! Asgard lies to the north, and Vanaheim to the northwest of Cimmeria, and there is continual war along the borders."

"What manner of men are these northern folk?" asked Prospero.

"Tall and fair and blue-eyed. Their god is Ymir, the frost-giant, and each tribe has its own king. They are wayward and fierce. They fight all day and drink ale and roar their wild songs all night."

"Then I think you are like them," laughed Prospero. "You laugh greatly, drink deep and bellow good songs; though I never saw another Cimmerian who drank aught but water, or who ever laughed, or ever sang save to chant dismal dirges."

"Perhaps it's the land they live in," answered the king. "A gloomier land never was—all of hills, darkly wooded, under skies nearly always gray, with winds moaning drearily down the valleys."

"Little wonder men grow moody there," quoth Prospero with a shrug of his shoulders, thinking of the smiling sun-washed plains and blue lazy rivers of Poitain, Aquilonia's southernmost province.

"They have no hope here or hereafter," answered Conan. "Their gods are Crom and his dark race, who rule over a sunless place of everlasting mist, which is the world of the dead. Mitra! The ways of the Æsir were more to my liking."

"Well," grinned Prospero, "the dark hills of Cimmeria are far behind you. And now I go. I'll quaff a goblet of white Nemedian wine for you at Numa's court."

"Good," grunted the king, "but kiss Numa's dancing-girls for yourself only, lest you involve the states!"

His gusty laughter followed Prospero out of the chamber.

III

Under the caverned pyramids great Set coils asleep;
Among the shadows of the tombs his dusky people creep.
I speak the Word from the hidden gulfs that never knew the sun
Send me a servant for my hate, oh scaled and shining One!

The sun was setting, etching the green and hazy blue of the forest in brief gold. The waning beams glinted on the thick golden chain which Dion of Attalus twisted continually in his pudgy hand as he sat in the flaming riot of blossoms and flower-trees which was his garden. He shifted his fat body on his marble seat and glanced furtively about, as if in quest of a lurking enemy. He sat within a circular grove of slender trees, whose interlapping branches cast a thick shade over him. Near at hand a fountain tinkled silverly, and other unseen fountains in various parts of the great garden whispered an everlasting symphony.

Dion was alone except for the great dusky figure which lounged on a marble bench close at hand, watching the baron with deep somber eyes. Dion gave little thought to Thoth-amon. He vaguely knew that he was a slave in whom Ascalante reposed much trust, but like so many rich men, Dion paid scant heed to men below his own station in life.

"You need not be so nervous," said Thoth. "The plot cannot fail."

"Ascalante can make mistakes as well as another," snapped Dion, sweating at the mere thought of failure.

"Not he," grinned the Stygian savagely, "else I had not been his slave, but his master."

"What talk is this?" peevishly returned Dion, with only half a mind on the conversation.

Thoth-amon's eyes narrowed. For all his iron self-control, he was near bursting with long pent-up shame, hate and rage, ready to take any sort of a desperate chance. What he did not reckon on was the fact that Dion saw him, not as a human being with a brain and a wit, but simply a slave, and as such, a creature beneath notice.

"Listen to me," said Thoth. "You will be king. But you little know the mind of Ascalante. You can not trust him, once Conan is slain. I can help you. If you will protect me when you come to power, I will aid you.

"Listen, my lord. I was a great sorcerer in the south. Men spoke of Thoth-amon as they spoke of Rammon. King Ctesphon of Stygia gave me great honor, casting down the magicians from the high places to exalt me above them. They hated me, but they feared me, for I controlled beings from outside which came at my call and did my bidding. By Set, mine enemy knew not the hour when he might awake at midnight to feel the taloned fingers of a nameless horror at his throat! I did dark and terrible magic with the Serpent Ring of Set, which I found in a nighted tomb a league beneath the earth, forgotten before the first man crawled out of the slimy sea.

"But a thief stole the Ring and my power was broken. The magicians rose up to slay me, and I fled. Disguised as a camel-driver, I was traveling in a caravan in the land of Koth, when Ascalante's reavers fell upon us. All in the caravan were slain except myself; I saved my life by revealing my identity to Ascalante and swearing to serve him. Bitter has been that bondage!

"To hold me fast, he wrote of me in a manuscript, and sealed it and gave it into the hands of a hermit who dwells on the southern borders of Koth. I dare not strike a dagger into him while he sleeps, or betray him to his enemies, for then the hermit would open the manuscript and read—thus Ascalante instructed him. And he would speak a word in Stygia—"

Again Thoth shuddered and an ashen hue tinged his dusky skin.

"Men knew me not in Aquilonia," he said. "But should my enemies in Stygia learn my whereabouts, not the width of half a world between us would suffice to save me from such a doom as would blast the soul of a bronze statue. Only a king with castles and hosts of swordsmen could protect me. So I have told you my secret, and urge that you make a pact with me. I can aid you with my wisdom, and you can protect me. And some day I will find the Ring—"

"Ring? Ring?" Thoth had underestimated the man's utter egoism. Dion had not even been listening to the slave's words, so completely engrossed was he in his own thoughts, but the final word stirred a ripple in his self-centeredness.

"Ring?" he repeated. "That makes me remember—my ring of good fortune. I had it from a Shemitish thief who swore he stole it from a wizard far to the south, and that it would bring me luck. I paid him enough, Mitra knows. By the gods, I need all the luck I can have, what with Volmana and Ascalante dragging me into their bloody plots—I'll see to the ring."

Thoth sprang up, blood mounting darkly to his face, while his eyes flamed with the stunned fury of a man who suddenly realizes the full depths of a fool's swinish stupidity. Dion never heeded him. Lifting a secret lid in the marble seat, he fumbled for a moment among a heap of gewgaws of various kinds—barbaric charms, bits of bones, pieces of tawdry jewelry—luck-pieces and conjures which the man's superstitious nature had prompted him to collect.

"Ah, here it is!" He triumphantly lifted a ring of curious make. It was of a metal like copper, and was made in the form of a scaled serpent, coiled in three loops, with its tail in its mouth. Its eyes were yellow gems which glittered balefully. Thoth-amon cried out as if he had been struck, and Dion wheeled and gaped, his face suddenly bloodless. The slave's eyes were blazing, his mouth wide, his huge dusky hands outstretched like talons.

"The Ring! By Set! The Ring!" he shrieked. "My Ring—stolen from me—" Steel glittered in the Stygian's hand and with a heave of his great dusky shoulders he drove the dagger into the baron's fat body. Dion's high thin squeal broke in a strangled gurgle and his whole flabby frame collapsed like melted butter. A fool to the end, he died in mad terror, not knowing why. Flinging aside the crumpled corpse, already forgetful of it, Thoth grasped the ring in both hands, his dark eyes blazing with a fearful avidness.

"My Ring!" he whispered in terrible exultation. "My power!"

How long he crouched over the baleful thing, motionless as a statue, drinking the evil aura of it into his dark soul, not even the Stygian knew.

When he shook himself from his reverie and drew back his mind from the nighted abysses where it had been questing, the moon was rising, casting long shadows across the smooth marble back of the garden-seat, at the foot of which sprawled the darker shadow which had been the lord of Attalus.

"No more, Ascalante, no more!" whispered the Stygian, and his eyes burned red as a vampire's in the gloom. Stooping, he cupped a handful of congealing blood from the sluggish pool in which his victim sprawled, and rubbed it in the copper serpent's eyes until the yellow sparks were covered by a crimson mask.

"Blind your eyes, mystic serpent," he chanted in a blood-freezing whisper. "Blind your eyes to the moonlight and open them on darker gulfs! What do you see, oh serpent of Set? Whom do you call from the gulfs of the Night? Whose shadow falls on the waning Light? Call him to me, oh serpent of Set!"

Stroking the scales with a peculiar circular motion of his fingers, a motion which always carried the fingers back to their starting place, his voice sank still lower as he whispered dark names and grisly incantations forgotten the world over save in the grim hinterlands of dark Stygia, where monstrous shapes move in the dusk of the tombs.

There was a movement in the air about him, such a swirl as is made in water when some creature rises to the surface. A nameless, freezing wind blew on him briefly, as if from an opened door. Thoth felt a presence at his back, but he did not look about. He kept his eyes fixed on the moonlit space of marble, on which a tenuous shadow hovered. As he continued his whispered incantations, this shadow grew in size and clarity, until it stood out distinct and horrific. Its outline was not unlike that of a gigantic baboon, but no such baboon ever walked the earth, not even in Stygia. Still Thoth did not look, but drawing from his girdle a sandal of his master—always carried in the dim hope that he might be able to put it to such use—he cast it behind him.

"Know it well, slave of the Ring!" he exclaimed. "Find him who wore it and destroy him! Look into his eyes and blast his soul, before you tear out his throat! Kill him! Aye," in a blind burst of passion, "and all with him!"

Etched on the moonlit wall Thoth saw the horror lower its misshapen head and take the scent like some hideous hound. Then the grisly head was thrown back and the thing wheeled and was gone like a wind through the trees. The Stygian flung up his arms in maddened exultation, and his teeth and eyes gleamed in the moonlight.

A soldier on guard without the walls yelled in startled horror as a great loping black shadow with flaming eyes cleared the wall and swept by him with a swirling rush of wind. But it was gone so swiftly that the bewildered warrior was left wondering whether it had been a dream or a hallucination.

IV

When the world was young and men were weak, and the fiends of the night
walked free,
I strove with Set by fire and steel and the juice of the upas tree;
Now that I sleep in the mount's black heart, and the ages take their toll,
Forget ye him who fought with the Snake to save the human soul?

Alone in the great sleeping-chamber with its high golden dome King Conan slumbered and dreamed. Through swirling gray mists he heard a curious call, faint and far, and though he did not understand it, it seemed not within his power to ignore it. Sword in hand he went through the gray mist, as a man might walk through clouds, and the voice grew more distinct as he proceeded until he understood the word it spoke—it was his own name that was being called across the gulfs of Space or Time.

Now the mists grew lighter and he saw that he was in a great dark corridor that seemed to be cut in solid black stone. It was unlighted, but by some magic he could see plainly. The floor, ceiling and walls were highly polished and gleamed dull, and they were carved with the figures of ancient heroes and half-forgotten gods. He shuddered to see the vast shadowy outlines of the Nameless Old Ones, and he knew somehow that mortal feet had not traversed the corridor for centuries.

He came upon a wide stair carved in the solid rock, and the sides of the shaft were adorned with esoteric symbols so ancient and horrific that King Conan's skin crawled. The steps were carven each with the abhorrent figure of the Old Serpent, Set, so that at each step he planted his heel on the head of the Snake, as it was intended from old times. But he was none the less at ease for all that.

But the voice called him on, and at last, in darkness that would have been impenetrable to his material eyes, he came into a strange crypt, and saw a vague white-bearded figure sitting on a tomb. Conan's hair rose up and he grasped his sword, but the figure spoke in sepulchral tones.

"Oh man, do you know me?"

"Not I, by Crom!" swore the king.

"Man," said the ancient, "I am Epemitreus."

"But Epemitreus the Sage has been dead for fifteen hundred years!" stammered Conan.

"Harken!" spoke the other commandingly. "As a pebble cast into a dark lake sends ripples to the further shores, happenings in the Unseen world have broken like waves on my slumber. I have marked you well, Conan of Cimmeria, and the stamp of mighty happenings and great deeds is upon you. But dooms are loose in the land, against which your sword cannot aid you."

"You speak in riddles," said Conan uneasily. "Let me see my foe and I'll cleave his skull to the teeth."

"Loose your barbarian fury against your foes of flesh and blood," answered the ancient. "It is not against men I must shield you. There are dark worlds barely guessed by man, wherein formless monsters stalk—fiends which may be drawn from the Outer Voids to take material shape and rend and devour at the bidding of evil magicians. There is a serpent in your house, oh king—an adder in your kingdom, come up from Stygia, with the dark wisdom of the shadows in his murky soul. As a sleeping man dreams of the serpent which crawls near him, I have felt the foul presence of Set's neophyte. He is drunk with terrible power, and the blows he strikes at his enemy may well bring down the kingdom. I have called you to me, to give you a weapon against him and his hell-hound pack."

"But why?" bewilderedly asked Conan. "Men say you sleep in the black heart of Golamira, whence you send forth your ghost on unseen wings to aid Aquilonia in times of need, but I—I am an outlander and a barbarian."

"Peace!" the ghostly tones reverberated through the great shadowy cavern. "Your destiny is one with Aquilonia. Gigantic happenings are forming in the web and the womb of Fate, and a blood-mad sorcerer shall not stand in the path of imperial destiny. Ages ago Set coiled about the world like a python about its prey. All my life, which was as the lives of three common men, I fought him. I drove him into the shadows of the mysterious south, but in dark Stygia men still worship him who to us is the arch-demon. As I fought Set, I fight his worshipers and his votaries and his acolytes. Hold out your sword."

Wondering, Conan did so, and on the great blade, close to the heavy silver guard, the ancient traced with a bony finger a strange symbol that glowed like white fire in the shadows. And on the instant crypt, tomb and ancient vanished, and Conan, bewildered, sprang from his couch in the great golden-domed chamber. And as he stood, bewildered at the strangeness of his dream, he realized that he was gripping his sword in his hand. And his hair prickled at the nape of his neck, for on the broad blade was carven a symbol—the outline of a phoenix. And he remembered that on the tomb in the crypt he had seen what he had thought to be a similar figure, carven of stone. Now he wondered if it had been but a stone figure, and his skin crawled at the strangeness of it all.

Then as he stood, a stealthy sound in the corridor outside brought him to life, and without stopping to investigate, he began to don his armor; again he was the barbarian, suspicious and alert as a gray wolf at bay.

V

What do I know of cultured ways, the gilt, the craft and the lie?
I, who was born in a naked land and bred in the open sky.
The subtle tongue, the sophist guile, they fail when the broadswords sing;
Rush in and die, dogs—I was a man before I was a king.

—*The Road of Kings*

Through the silence which shrouded the corridor of the royal palace stole twenty furtive figures. Their stealthy feet, bare or cased in soft leather, made no sound either on thick carpet or bare marble tile. The torches which stood in niches along the halls gleamed red on dagger, sword and keen-edged ax.

"Easy all!" hissed Ascalante. "Stop that cursed loud breathing, whoever it is! The officer of the night-guard has removed most of the sentries from these halls and made the rest drunk, but we must be careful, just the same. Back! Here come the guard!"

They crowded back behind a cluster of carven pillars, and almost immediately ten giants in black armor swung by at a measured pace. Their faces showed doubt as they glanced at the officer who was leading them away from their post of duty. This officer was rather pale; as the guard passed the hiding-places of the conspirators, he was seen to wipe the sweat from his brow with a shaky hand. He was young, and this betrayal of a king did not come easy to him. He mentally cursed the vainglorious extravagance which had put him in debt to the money-lenders and made him a pawn of scheming politicians.

The guardsmen clanked by and disappeared up the corridor.

"Good!" grinned Ascalante. "Conan sleeps unguarded. Haste! If they catch us killing him, we're undone—but few men will espouse the cause of a dead king."

"Aye, haste!" cried Rinaldo, his blue eyes matching the gleam of the sword he swung above his head. "My blade is thirsty! I hear the gathering of the vultures! On!"

They hurried down the corridor with reckless speed and stopped before a gilded door which bore the royal dragon symbol of Aquilonia.

"Gromel!" snapped Ascalante. "Break me this door open!"

The giant drew a deep breath and launched his mighty frame against the panels, which groaned and bent at the impact. Again he crouched and plunged. With a snapping of bolts and a rending crash of wood, the door splintered and burst inward.

"In!" roared Ascalante, on fire with the spirit of the deed.

"In!" yelled Rinaldo. "Death to the tyrant!"

They stopped short. Conan faced them, not a naked man roused mazed and unarmed out of deep sleep to be butchered like a sheep, but a barbarian wide-awake and at bay, partly armored, and with his long sword in his hand.

For an instant the tableau held—the four rebel noblemen in the broken door, and the horde of wild hairy faces crowding behind them—all held momentarily frozen by the sight of the blazing-eyed giant standing sword in hand in the middle of the candle-lighted chamber. In that instant Ascalante beheld, on a small table near the royal couch, the silver scepter and the slender gold circlet which was the crown of Aquilonia, and the sight maddened him with desire.

"In, rogues!" yelled the outlaw. "He is one to twenty and he has no helmet!"

True; there had been lack of time to don the heavy plumed casque, or to lace in place the side-plates of the cuirass, nor was there now time to snatch the great shield from the wall. Still, Conan was better protected than any of his foes except Volmana and Gromel, who were in full armor.

The king glared, puzzled as to their identity. Ascalante he did not know; he could not see through the closed vizors of the armored conspirators, and Rinaldo had pulled his slouch cap down above his eyes. But there was no time for surmise. With a yell that rang to the roof, the killers flooded into the room, Gromel first. He came like a charging bull, head down, sword low for the disemboweling thrust. Conan sprang to meet him, and all his tigerish strength went into the arm that swung the sword. In a whistling arc the great blade flashed through the air and crashed on the Bossonian's helmet. Blade and casque shivered together and Gromel rolled lifeless on the floor. Conan bounded back, still gripping the broken hilt.

"Gromel!" he spat, his eyes blazing in amazement, as the shattered helmet disclosed the shattered head; then the rest of the pack were upon him. A dagger point raked along his ribs between breastplate and backplate, a sword-edge flashed before his eyes. He flung aside the dagger-wielder with his left arm, and smashed his broken hilt like a cestus into the swordsman's temple. The man's brains spattered in his face.

"Watch the door, five of you!" screamed Ascalante, dancing about the edge of the singing steel whirlpool, for he feared that Conan might smash through their midst and escape. The rogues drew back momentarily, as their leader seized several and thrust them toward the single door, and in that brief respite Conan leaped to the wall and tore therefrom an ancient battle-ax which, untouched by time, had hung there for half a century.

With his back to the wall he faced the closing ring for a flashing instant, then leaped into the thick of them. He was no defensive fighter; even in the teeth of overwhelming odds he always carried the war to the enemy. Any other man would have already died there, and Conan himself did not hope to survive, but he did ferociously wish to inflict as much damage as he could before he fell. His barbaric soul was ablaze, and the chants of old heroes were singing in his ears.

As he sprang from the wall his ax dropped an outlaw with a severed shoulder, and the terrible back-hand return crushed the skull of another. Swords whined venomously about him, but death passed him by breathless margins. The Cimmerian moved in, a blur of blinding speed. He was like a tiger among baboons as he leaped, side-stepped and spun, offering an ever-moving target, while his ax wove a shining wheel of death about him.

For a brief space the assassins crowded him fiercely, raining blows blindly and hampered by their own numbers; then they gave back suddenly—two corpses on the floor gave mute evidence of the king's fury, though Conan himself was bleeding from wounds on arm, neck and legs.

"Knaves!" screamed Rinaldo, dashing off his feathered cap, his wild eyes glaring. "Do ye shrink from the combat? Shall the despot live? Out on it!"

He rushed in, hacking madly, but Conan, recognizing him, shattered his sword with a short terrific chop and with a powerful push of his open hand sent him reeling to the floor. The king took Ascalante's point in his left arm, and the outlaw barely saved his life by ducking and springing backward from the swinging ax. Again the wolves swirled in and Conan's ax sang and crushed. A hairy rascal stooped beneath its stroke and dived at the king's legs, but after wrestling for a brief instant at what seemed a solid iron tower, glanced up in time to see the ax falling, but not in time to avoid it. In the interim, one of his comrades lifted a broadsword with both hands and hewed through the king's left shoulder-plate, wounding the shoulder beneath. In an instant Conan's cuirass was full of blood.

Volmana, flinging the attackers right and left in his savage impatience, came plowing through and hacked murderously at Conan's unprotected head. The king ducked deeply and the sword shaved off a lock of his black hair as it whistled above him. Conan pivoted on his heel and struck in from the side. The ax crunched through the steel cuirass and Volmana crumpled with his whole left side caved in.

"Volmana!" gasped Conan breathlessly. "I'll know that dwarf in Hell—" He straightened to meet the maddened rush of Rinaldo, who charged in wild and wide open, armed only with a dagger. Conan leaped back, lifting his ax.

"Rinaldo!" his voice was strident with desperate urgency. "Back! I would not slay you—"

"Die, tyrant!" screamed the mad minstrel, hurling himself headlong on the king. Conan delayed the blow he was loth to deliver, until it was too late. Only when he felt the bite of the steel in his unprotected side did he strike, in a frenzy of blind desperation.

Rinaldo dropped with his skull shattered, and Conan reeled back against the wall, blood spurting from between the fingers which gripped his wound.

"In, now, and slay him!" yelled Ascalante.

Conan put his back against the wall and lifted his ax. He stood like an image of the unconquerable primordial—legs braced far apart, head thrust forward, one hand clutching the wall for support, the other gripping the ax on high, with the great corded muscles standing out in iron ridges, and his features frozen in a death snarl of fury—his eyes blazing terribly through the mist of blood which veiled them. The men faltered—wild, criminal and dissolute though they were, yet they came of a breed men called civilized, with a civilized background; here was the barbarian—the natural killer. They shrank back—the dying tiger could still deal death.

Conan sensed their uncertainty and grinned mirthlessly and ferociously. "Who dies first?" he mumbled through smashed and bloody lips.

Ascalante leaped like a wolf, halted almost in midair with incredible quickness and fell prostrate to avoid the death which was hissing toward him. He frantically whirled his feet out of the way and rolled clear as Conan recovered from his missed blow and struck again. This time the ax sank inches deep into the polished floor close to Ascalante's revolving legs.

Another misguided desperado chose this instant to charge, followed half-heartedly by his fellows. He intended killing Conan before the Cimmerian could wrench his ax from the floor, but his judgment was faulty. The red ax lurched up and crashed down and a crimson caricature of a man catapulted back against the legs of the attackers.

At that instant a fearful scream burst from the rogues at the door as a black misshapen shadow fell across the wall. All but Ascalante wheeled at that cry, and then, howling like dogs, they burst blindly through the door in a raving, blaspheming mob, and scattered through the corridors in screaming flight.

Ascalante did not look toward the door; he had eyes only for the wounded king. He supposed that the noise of the fray had at last roused the palace, and that the loyal guards were upon him, though even in that moment it seemed strange that his hardened rogues should scream so terribly in their flight. Conan did not look toward the door because he was watching the outlaw with the burning eyes of a dying wolf. In this extremity Ascalante's cynical philosophy did not desert him.

"All seems to be lost, particularly honor," he murmured. "However, the king is dying on his feet—and—" Whatever other cogitation might have passed through his mind is not to be known; for, leaving the sentence uncompleted, he ran lightly at Conan just as the Cimmerian was perforce employing his ax-arm to wipe the blood from his blinded eyes.

But even as he began his charge, there was a strange rushing in the air and a heavy weight struck terrifically between his shoulders. He was dashed headlong and great talons sank agonizingly in his flesh. Writhing desperately beneath his attacker, he twisted his head about and stared into the face of Nightmare and lunacy. Upon him crouched a great black thing which he knew was born in no sane or human world. Its slavering black fangs were near his throat and the glare of its yellow eyes shrivelled his limbs as a killing wind shrivels young corn.

The hideousness of its face transcended mere bestiality. It might have been the face of an ancient, evil mummy, quickened with demoniac life. In those abhorrent features the outlaw's dilated eyes seemed to see, like a shadow in the madness that enveloped him, a faint and terrible resemblance to the slave Thoth-amon. Then Ascalante's cynical and all-sufficient philosophy deserted him, and with a ghastly cry he gave up the ghost before those slavering fangs touched him.

Conan, shaking the blood-drops from his eyes, stared frozen. At first he thought it was a great black hound which stood above Ascalante's distorted body; then as his sight cleared he saw that it was neither a hound nor a baboon.

With a cry that was like an echo of Ascalante's death-shriek, he reeled away from the wall and met the leaping horror with a cast of his ax that had behind it all the desperate power of his electrified nerves. The flying weapon glanced singing from the slanting skull it should have crushed, and the king was hurled half-way across the chamber by the impact of the giant body.

The slavering jaws closed on the arm Conan flung up to guard his throat, but the monster made no effort to secure a death-grip. Over his mangled arm it glared fiendishly into the king's eyes, in which there began to be mirrored a likeness of the horror which stared from the dead eyes of Ascalante. Conan felt his soul shrivel and begin to be drawn out of his body, to drown in the yellow wells of cosmic horror which glimmered spectrally in the formless chaos that was growing about him and engulfing all life and sanity. Those eyes grew and became gigantic, and in them the Cimmerian glimpsed the reality of all the abysmal and blasphemous horrors that lurk in the outer darkness of formless voids and nighted gulfs. He opened his bloody lips to shriek his hate and loathing, but only a dry rattle burst from his throat.

But the horror that paralyzed and destroyed Ascalante roused in the Cimmerian a frenzied fury akin to madness. With a volcanic wrench of his whole body he plunged backward, heedless of the agony of his torn arm, dragging the monster bodily with him. And his outflung hand struck something his dazed fighting-brain recognized as the hilt of his broken sword. Instinctively he gripped it and struck with all the power of nerve and thew, as a man stabs with a dagger. The broken blade sank deep and Conan's arm was released as the abhorrent mouth gaped as in agony. The king was hurled violently aside, and lifting himself on one hand he saw, as one mazed, the terrible convulsions of the monster from which thick blood was gushing through the great wound his broken blade had torn. And as he watched, its struggles ceased and it lay jerking spasmodically, staring upward with its grisly dead eyes. Conan blinked and shook the blood from his own eyes; it seemed to him that the thing was melting and disintegrating into a slimy unstable mass.

Then a medley of voices reached his ears, and the room was thronged with the finally roused people of the court—knights, peers, ladies, men-at-arms, councillors—all babbling and shouting and getting in one another's way. The Black Dragons were on hand, wild with rage, swearing and ruffling, with their hands on their hilts and foreign oaths in their teeth. Of the young officer of the door-guard nothing was seen, nor was he found then or later, though earnestly sought after.

"Gromel! Volmana! Rinaldo!" exclaimed Publius, the high councillor, wringing his fat hands among the corpses. "Black treachery! Someone shall dance for this! Call the guard."

"The guard is here, you old fool!" cavalierly snapped Pallantides, commander of the Black Dragons, forgetting Publius' rank in the stress of the moment. "Best stop your caterwauling and aid us to bind the king's wounds. He's like to bleed to death."

"Yes, yes!" cried Publius, who was a man of plans rather than action. "We must bind his wounds. Send for every leech of the court! Oh, my lord, what a black shame on the city! Are you entirely slain?"

"Wine!" gasped the king from the couch where they had laid him. They put a goblet to his bloody lips and he drank like a man half dead of thirst.

"Good!" he grunted, falling back. "Slaying is cursed dry work."

They had stanched the flow of blood, and the innate vitality of the barbarian was asserting itself.

"See first to the dagger-wound in my side," he bade the court physicians.

"Rinaldo wrote me a deathly song there, and keen was the stylus."

"We should have hanged him long ago," gibbered Publius. "No good can come of poets—who is this?"

He nervously touched Ascalante's body with his sandaled toe.

"By Mitra!" ejaculated the commander. "It is Ascalante, once count of Thune! What devil's work brought him up from his desert haunts?"

"But why does he stare so?" whispered Publius, drawing away, his own eyes wide and a peculiar prickling among the short hairs at the back of his fat neck. The others fell silent as they gazed at the dead outlaw.

"Had you seen what he and I saw," growled the king, sitting up despite the protests of the leeches, "you had not wondered. Blast your own gaze by looking at—" He stopped short, his mouth gaping, his finger pointing fruitlessly. Where the monster had died, only the bare floor met his eyes.

"Crom!" he swore. "The thing's melted back into the foulness which bore it!"

"The king is delirious," whispered a noble. Conan heard and swore with barbaric oaths.

"By Badb, Morrigan, Macha and Nemain!" he concluded wrathfully. "I am sane! It was like a cross between a Stygian mummy and a baboon. It came through the door, and Ascalante's rogues fled before it. It slew Ascalante, who was about to run me through. Then it came upon me and I slew it—how I know not, for my ax glanced from it as from a rack. But I think that the Sage Epemitreus had a hand in it—"

"Hark how he names Epemitreus, dead for fifteen hundred years!" they whispered to each other.

"By Ymir!" thundered the king. "This night I talked with Epemitreus! He called to me in my dreams, and I walked down a black stone corridor carved with old gods, to a stone stair on the steps of which were the outlines of Set, until I came to a crypt, and a tomb with a phœnix carved on it—"

"In Mitra's name, lord king, be silent!" It was the high-priest of Mitra who cried out, and his countenance was ashen.

Conan threw up his head like a lion tossing back its mane, and his voice was thick with the growl of the angry lion.

"Am I a slave, to shut my mouth at your command?"

"Nay, nay, my lord!" The high-priest was trembling, but not through fear of the royal wrath. "I meant no offense." He bent his head close to the king and spoke in a whisper that carried only to Conan's ears.

"My lord, this is a matter beyond human understanding. Only the inner circle of the priestcraft know of the black stone corridor carved in the black heart of Mount Golamira, by unknown hands, or of the phoenix-guarded tomb where Epemitreus was laid to rest fifteen hundred years ago. And since that time no living man has entered it, for his chosen priests, after placing the Sage in the crypt, blocked up the outer entrance of the corridor so that no man could find it, and today not even the high-priests know where it is. Only by word of mouth, handed down by the high-priests to the chosen few, and jealously guarded, does the inner circle of Mitra's acolytes know of the resting-place of Epemitreus in the black heart of Golamira. It is one of the Mysteries, on which Mitra's cult stands."

"I cannot say by what magic Epemitreus brought me to him," answered Conan. "But I talked with him, and he made a mark on my sword. Why that mark made it deadly to demons, or what magic lay behind the mark, I know not; but though the blade broke on Gromel's helmet, yet the fragment was long enough to kill the horror."

"Let me see your sword," whispered the high-priest from a throat gone suddenly dry.

Conan held out the broken weapon and the high-priest cried out and fell to his knees.

"Mitra guard us against the powers of darkness!" he gasped. "The king has indeed talked with Epemitreus this night! There on the sword—it is the secret sign none might make but him—the emblem of the immortal phoenix which broods forever over his tomb! A candle, quick! Look again at the spot where the king said the goblin died!"

It lay in the shade of a broken screen. They threw the screen aside and bathed the floor in a flood of candlelight. And a shuddering silence fell over the people as they looked. Then some fell on their knees calling on Mitra, and some fled screaming from the chamber.

There on the floor where the monster had died, there lay, like a tangible shadow, a broad dark stain that could not be washed out; the thing had left its outline clearly etched in its blood, and that outline was of no being of a sane and normal world. Grim and horrific it brooded there, like the shadow cast by one of the apish gods that squat on the shadowy altars of dim temples in the dark land of Stygia.

THE SCARLET CITADEL

ROBERT E. HOWARD

I

They trapped the Lion on Shamu's plain;
They weighted his limbs with an iron chain;
They cried aloud in the trumpet-blast,
They cried, "The lion is caged at last!"
Woe to the Cities of river and plain
If ever the Lion stalks again!

—*Old Ballad*

The roar of battle had died away; the shout of victory mingled with the cries of the dying. Like gay-hued leaves after an autumn storm, the fallen littered the plain; the sinking sun shimmered on burnished helmets, gilt-worked mail, silver breastplates, broken swords and the heavy regal folds of silken standards, overthrown in pools of curdling crimson. In silent heaps lay warhorses and their steel-clad riders, flowing manes and blowing plumes stained alike in the red tide. About them and among them, like the drift of a storm, were strewn slashed and trampled bodies in steel caps and leather jerkins—archers and pikemen.

The oliphants sounded a fanfare of triumph all over the plain, and the hoofs of the victors crunched in the breasts of the vanquished as all the straggling, shining lines converged inward like the spokes of a glittering wheel, to the spot where the last survivor still waged unequal strife.

That day Conan, king of Aquilonia, had seen the pick of his chivalry cut to pieces, smashed and hammered to bits, and swept into eternity. With five thousand knights he had crossed the south-eastern border of Aquilonia and ridden into the grassy meadowlands of Ophir, to find his former ally, King Amalrus of Ophir, drawn up against him with the hosts of Strabonus, king of Koth. Too late he had seen the trap. All that a man might do he had done with his five thousand cavalrymen against the thirty thousand knights, archers and spearmen of the conspirators.

Without bowmen or infantry, he had hurled his armored horsemen against the oncoming host, had seen the knights of his foes in their shining mail go down before his lances, had torn the opposing center to bits, driving the riven ranks headlong before him, only to find himself caught in a vise as the untouched wings closed in. Strabonus' Shemitish bowmen had wrought havoc among his knights, feathering them with shafts that found every crevice in their armor, shooting down the horses, the Kothian pikemen rushing in to spear the fallen riders. The mailed lancers of the routed center had re-formed, reinforced by the riders from the wings, and had charged again and again, sweeping the field by sheer weight of numbers.

The Aquilonians had not fled; they had died on the field, and of the five thousand knights who had followed Conan southward, not one left the field alive. And now the king himself stood at bay among the slashed bodies of his house-troops, his back against a heap of dead horses and men. Ophirean knights in gilded mail leaped their horses over mounds of corpses to slash at the solitary figure; squat Shemites with blue-black beards, and dark-faced Kothian knights ringed him on foot. The clangor of steel rose deafeningly; the black-mailed figure of the western king loomed among his swarming foes, dealing blows like a butcher wielding a great cleaver. Riderless horses raced down the field; about his iron-clad feet grew a ring of mangled corpses. His attackers drew back from his desperate savagery, panting and livid.

Now through the yelling, cursing lines rode the lords of the conquerors Strabonus, with his broad dark face and crafty eyes; Amalrus, slender, fastidious, treacherous, dangerous as a cobra; and the lean vulture Tsothalanti, clad only in silken robes, his great black eyes glittering from a face that was like that of a bird of prey. Of this Kothian wizard dark tales were told; tousle-headed women in northern and western villages frightened children with his name, and rebellious slaves were brought to abased submission quicker than by the lash, with threat of being sold to him. Men said that he had a whole library of dark works bound in skin flayed from living human victims, and that in nameless pits below the hill whereon his palace sat, he trafficked with the powers of darkness, trading screaming girl slaves for unholy secrets. He was the real ruler of Koth.

Now he grinned bleakly as the kings reined back a safe distance from the grim iron-clad figure looming among the dead. Before the savage blue eyes blazing murderously from beneath the crested, dented helmet, the boldest shrank. Conan's dark scarred face was darker yet with passion; his black armor was hacked to tatters and splashed with blood; his great sword red to the cross-piece. In this stress all the veneer of civilization had faded; it was a barbarian who faced his conquerors. Conan was a Cimmerian by birth, one of those fierce moody hillmen who dwelt in their gloomy, cloudy land in the north. His saga, which had led him to the throne of Aquilonia, was the basis of a whole cycle of hero-tales.

So now the kings kept their distance, and Strabonus called on his Shemitish archers to loose their arrows at his foe from a distance; his captains had fallen like ripe grain before the Cimmerian's broadsword, and Strabonus, penurious of his knights as of his coins, was frothing with fury. But Tsotha shook his head.

"Take him alive."

"Easy to say!" snarled Strabonus, uneasy lest in some way the black-mailed giant might hew a path to them through the spears. "Who can take a man-eating tiger alive? By Ishtar, his heel is on the necks of my finest swordsmen! It took seven years and stacks of gold to train each, and there they lie, so much kite's meat. Arrows, I say!"

"Again, nay!" snapped Tsotha, swinging down from his horse. He laughed coldly. "Have you not learned by this time that my brain is mightier than any sword?"

He passed through the lines of the pikemen, and the giants in their steel caps and mail brigandines shrank back fearfully, lest they so much as touch the skirts of his robe. Nor were the plumed knights slower in making room for him. He stepped over the corpses and came face to face with the grim king. The hosts watched in tense silence, holding their breath. The black-armored figure loomed in terrible menace over the lean, silk-robed shape, the notched, dripping sword hovering on high.

"I offer you life, Conan," said Tsotha, a cruel mirth bubbling at the back of his voice.

"I give you death, wizard," snarled the king, and backed by iron muscles and ferocious hate the great sword swung in a stroke meant to shear Tsotha's lean torso in half. But even as the hosts cried out, the wizard stepped in, too quick for the eye to follow, and apparently merely laid an open hand on Conan's left forearm, from the ridged muscles of which the mail had been hacked away. The whistling blade veered from its arc and the mailed giant crashed heavily to earth, to lie motionless. Tsotha laughed silently.

"Take him up and fear not; the lion's fangs are drawn."

The kings reined in and gazed in awe at the fallen lion. Conan lay stiffly, like a dead man, but his eyes glared up at them, wide open, and blazing with helpless fury. "What have you done to him?" asked Amalrus uneasily.

Tsotha displayed a broad ring of curious design on his finger. He pressed his fingers together and on the inner side of the ring a tiny steel fang darted out like a snake's tongue.

"It is steeped in the juice of the purple lotus, which grows in the ghost-haunted swamps of southern Stygia," said the magician. "Its touch produces temporary paralysis. Put him in chains and lay him in a chariot. The sun sets and it is time we were on the road for Khorshemish."

Strabonus turned to his general Arbanus.

"We return to Khorshemish with the wounded. Only a troop of the royal cavalry will accompany us. Your orders are to march at dawn to the Aquilonian border, and invest the city of Shamar. The Ophireans will supply you with food along the march. We will rejoin you as soon as possible, with reinforcements."

So the host, with its steel-sheathed knights, its pikemen and archers and campservants, went into camp in the meadowlands near the battlefield. And through the starry night the two kings and the sorcerer, who was greater than any king, rode to the capital of Strabonus, in the midst of the glittering palace troop, and accompanied by a long line of chariots, loaded with the wounded. In one of these chariots lay Conan, king of Aquilonia, weighted with chains, the tang of defeat in his mouth, the blind fury of a trapped tiger in his soul.

The poison which had frozen his mighty limbs to helplessness had not paralyzed his brain. As the chariot in which he lay rumbled over the meadowlands, his mind revolved maddeningly about his defeat. Amalrus had sent an emissary imploring aid against Strabonus, who, he said, was ravaging his western domain, which lay like a tapering wedge between the border of Aquilonia and the vast southern kingdom of Koth. He asked only a thousand horsemen and the presence of Conan, to hearten his demoralized subjects. Conan now mentally blasphemed. In his generosity he had come with five times the number the treacherous monarch had asked. In good faith he had ridden into Ophir, and had been confronted by the supposed rivals allied against him. It spoke significantly of his prowess that they had brought up a whole host to trap him and his five thousand.

A red cloud veiled his vision; his veins swelled with fury and in his temples a pulse throbbed maddeningly. In all his life he had never known greater and more helpless wrath. In swift-moving scenes the pageant of his life passed fleetingly before his mental eye—a panorama wherein moved shadowy figures which were himself, in many guises and conditions—a skin-clad barbarian; a mercenary swordsman in horned helmet and scale-mail corselet; a corsair in a dragon-prowed galley that trailed a crimson wake of blood and pillage along southern coasts; a captain of hosts in burnished steel, on a rearing black charger; a king on a golden throne with the lion banner flowing above, and throngs of gay-hued courtiers and ladies on their knees. But always the jouncing and rumbling of the chariot brought his thoughts back to revolve with maddening monotony about the treachery of Amalrus and the sorcery of Tsotha. The veins nearly burst in his temples and cries of the wounded in the chariots filled him with ferocious satisfaction.

Before midnight they crossed the Ophirean border and at dawn the spires of Khorshemish stood up gleaming and rose-tinted on the south-eastern horizon, the slim towers overawed by the grim scarlet citadel that at a distance was like a splash of bright blood in the sky. That was the castle of Tsotha. Only one narrow street, paved with marble and guarded by heavy iron gates, led up to it, where it crowned the hill dominating the city. The sides of that hill were too sheer to be climbed elsewhere. From the walls of the citadel one could look down on the broad white streets of the city, on minaretted mosques, shops, temples, mansions, and markets. One could look down, too, on the palaces of the king, set in broad gardens, highwalled, luxurious riots of fruit trees and blossoms, through which artificial streams murmured, and silvery fountains rippled incessantly. Over all brooded the citadel, like a condor stooping above its prey, intent on its own dark meditations.

The mighty gates between the huge towers of the outer wall clanged open, and the king rode into his capital between lines of glittering spearmen, while fifty trumpets pealed salute. But no throngs swarmed the white-paved streets to fling roses before the conqueror's hoofs. Strabonus had raced ahead of news of the battle, and the people, just rousing to the occupations of the day, gaped to see their king returning with a small retinue, and were in doubt as to whether it portended victory or defeat.

Conan, life sluggishly moving in his veins again, craned his neck from the chariot floor to view the wonders of this city which men called the Queen of the South. He had thought to ride some day through these golden-chased gates at the head of his steel-clad squadrons, with the great lion banner flowing over his helmeted head. Instead, he entered in chains, stripped of his armor and thrown like a captive slave on the bronze floor of his conqueror's chariot. A wayward devilish mirth of mockery rose above his fury, but to the nervous soldiers who drove the chariot his laughter sounded like the muttering of a rousing lion.

II

Gleaming shell of an outworn lie; fable of Right divine
You gained your crowns by heritage, but Blood was the price of mine.
The throne that I won by blood and sweat, by Crom, I will not sell
For promise of valleys filled with gold, or threat of the Halls of Hell!

—*The Road of Kings*

In the citadel, in a chamber with a domed ceiling of carven jet, and the fretted arches of doorways glimmering with strange dark jewels, a strange conclave came to pass. Conan of Aquilonia, blood from unbandaged wounds caking his huge limbs, faced his captors. On either side of him stood a dozen black giants, grasping their long-shafted axes. In front of him stood Tsotha, and on divans lounged Strabonus and Amalrus in their silks and gold, gleaming with jewels, naked slave boys beside them pouring wine into cups carved of a single sapphire. In strong contrast stood Conan, grim, blood-stained, naked but for a loin-cloth, shackles on his mighty limbs, his blue eyes blazing beneath the tangled black mane which fell over his low broad forehead. He dominated the scene, turning to tinsel the pomp of the conquerors by the sheer vitality of his elemental personality, and the kings in their pride and splendor were aware of it each in his secret heart, and were not at ease. Only Tsotha was not disturbed.

"Our desires are quickly spoken, king of Aquilonia," said Tsotha. "It is our wish to extend our empire."

"And so you want to swine my kingdom," rasped Conan.

"What are you but an adventurer, seizing a crown to which you had no more claim than any other wandering barbarian?" parried Amalrus. "We are prepared to offer you suitable compensation—"

"Compensation!" It was a gust of deep laughter from Conan's mighty chest. "The price of infamy and treachery! I am a barbarian, so I shall sell my kingdom and its people for life and your filthy gold? Ha! How did you come to your crown, you and that black-faced pig beside you? Your fathers did the fighting and the suffering, and handed their crowns to you on golden platters. What you inherited without lifting a finger—except to poison a few brothers—I fought for.

"You sit on satin and guzzle wine the people sweat for, and talk of divine rights of sovereignty—bah! I climbed out of the abyss of naked barbarism to the throne and in that climb I spilt my blood as freely as I spilt that of others. If either of us has the right to rule men, by Crom, it is I! How have you proved yourselves my superiors?

"I found Aquilonia in the grip of a pig like you—one who traced his genealogy for a thousand years. The land was torn with the wars of the barons, and the people cried out under oppression and taxation. Today no Aquilonian noble dares maltreat the humblest of my subjects, and the taxes of the people are lighter than anywhere else in the world.

"What of you? Your brother, Amalrus, holds the eastern half of your kingdom, and defies you. And you, Strabonus, your soldiers are even now besieging castles of a dozen or more rebellious barons. The people of both your kingdoms are crushed into the earth by tyrannous taxes and levies. And you would loot mine—ha! Free my hands and I'll varnish this floor with your brains!"

Tsotha grinned bleakly to see the rage of his kingly companions.

"All this, truthful though it be, is beside the point. Our plans are no concern of yours. Your responsibility is at an end when you sign this parchment, which is an abdication in favor of Prince Arpello of Pellia. We will give you arms and horse, and five thousand golden lunas, and escort you to the eastern frontier."

"Setting me adrift where I was when I rode into Aquilonia to take service in her armies, except with the added burden of a traitor's name!" Conan's laugh was like the deep short bark of a timber wolf. "Arpello, eh? I've had suspicions of that butcher of Pellia. Can you not even steal and pillage frankly and honestly, but you must have an excuse, however thin? Arpello claims a trace of royal blood; so you use him as an excuse for theft, and a satrap to rule through. I'll see you in hell first."

"You're a fool!" exclaimed Amalrus. "You are in our hands, and we can take both crown and life at our pleasure!"

Conan's answer was neither kingly nor dignified, but characteristically instinctive in the man, whose barbaric nature had never been submerged in his adopted culture. He spat full in Amalrus' eyes. The king of Ophir leaped up with a scream of outraged fury, groping for his slender sword. Drawing it, he rushed at the Cimmerian, but Tsotha intervened.

"Wait, your majesty; this man is my prisoner."

"Aside, wizard!" shrieked Amalrus, maddened by the glare in the Cimmerian's blue eyes.

"Back, I say!" roared Tsotha, roused to awesome wrath. His lean hand came from his wide sleeve and cast a shower of dust into the Ophirean's contorted face. Amalrus cried out and staggered back, clutching at his eyes, the sword falling from his hand. He dropped limply on the divan, while the Kothian guards looked on stolidly and King Strabonus hurriedly gulped another goblet of wine, holding it with hands that trembled. Amalrus lowered his hands and shook his head violently, intelligence slowly sifting back into his gray eyes.

"I went blind," he growled. "What did you do to me, wizard?"

"Merely a gesture to convince you who was the real master," snapped Tsotha, the mask of his formal pretense dropped, revealing the naked evil personality of the man. "Strabonus has learned his lesson—let you learn yours. It was but a dust I found in a Stygian tomb which I flung into your eyes—if I brush out their sight again, I will leave you to grope in darkness for the rest of your life."

Amalrus shrugged his shoulders, smiled whimsically and reached for a goblet, dissembling his fear and fury. A polished diplomat, he was quick to regain his poise. Tsotha turned to Conan, who had stood imperturbably during the episode. At the wizard's gesture, the blacks laid hold of their prisoner and marched him behind Tsotha, who led the way out of the chamber through an arched doorway into a winding corridor, whose floor was of many-hued mosaics, whose walls were inlaid with gold tissue and silver chasing, and from whose fretted arched ceiling swung golden censers, filling the corridor with dreamy perfumed clouds. They turned down a smaller corridor, done in jet and black jade, gloomy and awful, which ended at a brass door, over whose arch a human skull grinned horrifically. At this door stood a fat repellent figure, dangling a bunch of keys—Tsotha's chief eunuch, Shukeli, of whom grisly tales were whispered—a man with whom a bestial lust for torture took the place of normal human passions.

The brass door let onto a narrow stair that seemed to wind down into the very bowels of the hill on which the citadel stood. Down these stairs went the band, to halt at last at an iron door, the strength of which seemed unnecessary. Evidently it did not open on outer air, yet it was built as if to withstand the battering of mangonels and rams. Shukeli opened it, and as he swung back the ponderous portal, Conan noted the evident uneasiness among the black giants who guarded him; nor did Shukeli seem altogether devoid of nervousness as he peered into the darkness beyond. Inside the great door there was a second barrier, composed of heavy steel bars. It was fastened by an ingenious bolt which had no lock and could be worked only from the outside; this bolt shot back, the grille slid into the wall. They passed through, into a broad corridor, the floor, walls and arched ceiling of which seemed to be cut out of solid stone. Conan knew he was far underground, even below the hill itself. The darkness pressed in on the guardsmen's torches like a sentient, animate thing.

They made the king fast to a ring in the stone wall. Above his head in a niche in the wall they placed a torch, so that he stood in a dim semicircle of light. The blacks were anxious to be gone; they muttered among themselves, and cast fearful glances at the darkness. Tsotha motioned them out, and they filed through the door in stumbling haste, as if fearing that the darkness might take tangible form and spring upon their backs. Tsotha turned toward Conan, and the king noticed uneasily that the wizard's eyes shone in the semi-darkness, and that his teeth much resembled the fangs of a wolf, gleaming whitely in the shadows.

"And so, farewell, barbarian," mocked the sorcerer. "I must ride to Shamar, and the siege. In ten days I will be in your palace in Tamar, with my warriors. What word from you shall I say to your women, before I flay their dainty skins for scrolls whereon to chronicle the triumphs of Tsotha-lanti?"

Conan answered with a searing Cimmerian curse that would have burst the eardrums of an ordinary man, and Tsotha laughed thinly and withdrew. Conan had a glimpse of his vulture-like figure through the thick-set bars, as he slid home the grate; then the heavy outer door clanged, and silence fell like a pall.

III

The Lion strode through the Halls of Hell;
Across his path grim shadows fell
Of many a mowing, nameless shape
Monsters with dripping jaws agape.
The darkness shuddered with scream and yell
When the Lion stalked through the Halls of Hell.

—*Old Ballad*

King Conan tested the ring in the wall and the chain that bound him. His limbs were free, but he knew that his shackles were beyond even his iron strength. The links of the chain were as thick as his thumb and were fastened to a band of steel about his waist—a band broad as his hand and half an inch thick. The sheer weight of his shackles would have slain a lesser man with exhaustion. The locks that held band and chain were massive affairs that a sledge-hammer could hardly have dinted. As for the ring, evidently it went clear through the wall and was clinched on the other side.

Conan cursed and panic surged through him as he glared into the darkness that pressed against the half-circle of light. All the superstitious dread of the barbarian slept in his soul, untouched by civilized logic. His primitive imagination peopled the subterranean darkness with grisly shapes. Besides, his reason told him that he had not been placed there merely for confinement. His captors had no reason to spare him. He had been placed in these pits for a definite doom. He cursed himself for his refusal of their offer, even while his stubborn manhood revolted at the thought, and he knew that were he taken forth and given another chance, his reply would be the same. He would not sell his subjects to the butcher. And yet it had been with no thought of anyone's gain but his own that he had seized the kingdom originally. Thus subtly does the instinct of sovereign responsibility enter even a red-handed plunderer sometimes.

Conan thought of Tsotha's last abominable threat, and groaned in sick fury, knowing it was no idle boast. Men and women were to the wizard no more than the writhing insect is to the scientist. Soft white hands that had caressed him, red lips that had been pressed to his, dainty white bosoms that had quivered to his hot fierce kisses, to be stripped of their delicate skin, white as ivory and pink as young petals—from Conan's lips burst a yell so frightful and inhuman in its mad fury that a listener would have stared in horror to know that it came from a human throat.

The shuddering echoes made him start and brought back his own situation vividly to the king. He glared fearsomely at the outer gloom, and thought of the grisly tales he had heard of Tsotha's necromantic cruelty, and it was with an icy sensation down his spine that he realized that these must be the very Halls of Horror named in shuddering legendry: the tunnels and dungeons wherein Tsotha performed horrible experiments with beings human, bestial, and, it was whispered, demoniac, tampering blasphemously with the naked basic elements of life itself. Rumor said that the mad poet Rinaldo had visited these pits, and been shown horrors by the wizard, and that the nameless monstrosities of which he hinted in his awful poem *The Song of the Pit* were no mere fantasies of a disordered brain. That brain had crashed to dust beneath Conan's battle-ax on the night the king had fought for his life with the assassins the mad rhymer had led into the betrayed palace, but the shuddersome words of that grisly song still rang in the king's ears as he stood there in his chains.

Even with the thought the Cimmerian was frozen by a soft rustling sound, blood-freezing in its implication. He tensed in an attitude of listening, painful in its intensity. An icy hand stroked his spine. It was the unmistakable sound of pliant scales slithering softly over stone. Cold sweat beaded his skin, as beyond the ring of dim light he saw a vague and colossal form, awful even in its indistinctness. It reared upright, swaying slightly, and yellow eyes burned icily on him from the shadows. Slowly a huge, hideous, wedge-shaped head took form before his dilated eyes, and from the darkness oozed, in flowing scaly coils, the ultimate horror of reptilian development.

It was a snake that dwarfed all Conan's previous ideas of snakes. Eighty feet it stretched from its pointed tail to its triangular head, which was bigger than that of a horse. In the dim light its scales glistened coldly, white as hoarfrost. Surely this reptile was one born and grown in darkness, yet its eyes were full of evil and sure sight. It looped its titan coils in front of the captive, and the great head on the arching neck swayed a matter of inches from his face. Its forked tongue almost brushed his lips as it darted in and out, and its fetid odor made his senses reel with nausea. The great yellow eyes burned into his, and Conan gave back the glare of a trapped wolf. He fought against the mad impulse to grasp the great arching neck in his tearing hands. Strong beyond the comprehension of civilized man, he had broken the neck of a python in a fiendish battle on the Stygian coast in his corsair days. But this reptile was venomous; he saw the great fangs, a foot long, curved like scimitars. From them dripped a colorless liquid that he instinctively knew was death. He might conceivably crush that wedge-shaped skull with a desperate clenched fist, but he knew that at his first hint of movement, the monster would strike like lightning.

It was not because of any logical reasoning process that Conan remained motionless, since reason might have told him—since he was doomed anyway—to goad the snake into striking and get it over with; it was the blind black instinct of self-preservation that held him rigid as a statue blasted out of iron. Now the great barrel reared up and the head was poised high above his own, as the monster investigated the torch. A drop of venom fell on his naked thigh, and the feel of it was like a white-hot dagger driven into his flesh. Red jets of agony shot through Conan's brain, yet he held himself immovable; not by the twitching of a muscle or the flicker of an eyelash did he betray the pain of the hurt that left a scar he bore to the day of his death.

The serpent swayed above him, as if seeking to ascertain whether there were in truth life in this figure which stood so death-like still. Then suddenly, unexpectedly, the outer door, all but invisible in the shadows, clanged stridently. The serpent, suspicious as all its kind, whipped about with a quickness incredible for its bulk, and vanished with a long-drawn slithering down the corridor. The door swung open and remained open. The grille was withdrawn and a huge dark figure was framed in the glow of torches outside. The figure glided in, pulling the grille partly to behind it, leaving the bolt poised. As it moved into the light of the torch over Conan's head, the king saw that it was a gigantic black man, stark naked, bearing in one hand a huge sword and in the other a bunch of keys. The black spoke in a sea-coast dialect, and Conan replied; he had learned the jargon while a corsair on the coasts of Kush.

"Long have I wished to meet you, Amra," the black gave Conan the name Amra, the Lion—by which the Cimmerian had been known to the Kushites in his piratical days. The slave's skull split in an animal-like grin, showing white tusks, but his eyes glinted redly in the torchlight. "I have dared much for this meeting! Look! The keys to your chains! I stole them from Shukeli. What will you give me for them?"

He dangled the keys in front of Conan's eyes.

"Ten thousand golden lunas," answered the king quickly, new hope surging fiercely in his breast.

"Not enough!" cried the black, a ferocious exultation shining on his ebon countenance. "Not enough for the risks I take. Tsotha's pets might come out of the dark and eat me, and if Shukeli finds out I stole his keys, he'll hang me up by my—well, what will you give me?"

"Fifteen thousand lunas and a palace in Poitain," offered the king.

The black yelled and stamped in a frenzy of barbaric gratification. "More!" he cried. "Offer me more! What will you give me?"

"You black dog!" A red mist of fury swept across Conan's eyes. "Were I free I'd give you a broken back! Did Shukeli send you here to mock me?"

"Shukeli knows nothing of my coming, white man," answered the black, craning his thick neck to peer into Conan's savage eyes. "I know you from of old, since the days when I was a chief among a free people, before the Stygians took me and sold me into the north. Do you not remember the sack of Abombi, when your sea-wolves swarmed in? Before the palace of King Ajaga you slew a chief and a chief fled from you. It was my brother who died; it was I who fled. I demand of you a blood-price, Amra!"

"Free me and I'll pay you your weight in gold pieces," growled Conan.

The red eyes glittered, the white teeth flashed wolfishly in the torchlight. "Aye, you white dog, you are like all your race; but to a black man gold can never pay for blood. The price I ask is—your head!"

The last word was a maniacal shriek that sent the echoes shivering. Conan tensed, unconsciously straining against his shackles in his abhorrence of dying like a sheep; then he was frozen by a greater horror. Over the black's shoulder he saw a vague horrific form swaying in the darkness.

"Tsotha will never know!" laughed the black fiendishly, too engrossed in his gloating triumph to take heed of anything else, too drunk with hate to know that Death swayed behind his shoulder. "He will not come into the vaults until the demons have torn your bones from their chains. I will have your head, Amra!"

He braced his knotted legs like ebon columns and swung up the massive sword in both hands, his great black muscles rolling and cracking in the torchlight. And at that instant the titanic shadow behind him darted down and out, and the wedge-shaped head smote with an impact that re-echoed down the tunnels. Not a sound came from the thick blubbery lips that flew wide in fleeting agony. With the thud of the stroke, Conan saw the life go out of the wide black eyes with the suddenness of a candle blown out. The blow knocked the great black body clear across the corridor and horribly the gigantic sinuous shape whipped around it in glistening coils that hid it from view, and the snap and splintering of bones came plainly to Conan's ears. Then something made his heart leap madly. The sword and the keys had flown from the black's hands to crash and jangle on the stone—and the keys lay almost at the king's feet.

He tried to bend to them, but the chain was too short; almost suffocated by the mad pounding of his heart, he slipped one foot from its sandal, and gripped them with his toes; drawing his foot up, he grasped them fiercely, barely stifling the yell of ferocious exultation that rose instinctively to his lips.

An instant's fumbling with the huge locks and he was free. He caught up the fallen sword and glared about. Only empty darkness met his eyes, into which the serpent had dragged a mangled, tattered object that only faintly resembled a human body. Conan turned to the open door. A few quick strides brought him to the threshold—a squeal of high-pitched laughter shrilled through the vaults, and the grille shot home under his very fingers, the bolt crashed down. Through the bars peered a face like a fiendishly mocking carven gargoyle—Shukeli the eunuch, who had followed his stolen keys. Surely he did not, in his gloating, see the sword in the prisoner's hand. With a terrible curse Conan struck as a cobra strikes; the great blade hissed between the bars and Shukeli's laughter broke in a death-scream. The fat eunuch bent at the middle, as if bowing to his killer, and crumpled like tallow, his pudgy hands clutching vainly at his spilling entrails.

Conan snarled in savage satisfaction; but he was still a prisoner. His keys were futile against the bolt which could be worked only from the outside. His experienced touch told him the bars were hard as the sword; an attempt to hew his way to freedom would only splinter his one weapon. Yet he found dents on those adamantine bars, like the marks of incredible fangs, and wondered with an involuntary shudder what nameless monsters had so terribly assailed the barriers. Regardless, there was but one thing for him to do, and that was to seek some other outlet. Taking the torch from the niche, he set off down the corridor, sword in hand. He saw no sign of the serpent or its victim, only a great smear of blood on the stone floor.

Darkness stalked on noiseless feet about him, scarcely driven back by his flickering torch. On either hand he saw dark openings, but he kept to the main corridor, watching the floor ahead of him carefully, lest he fall into some pit. And suddenly he heard the sound of a woman, weeping piteously. Another of Tsotha's victims, he thought, cursing the wizard anew, and turning aside, followed the sound down a smaller tunnel, dank and damp.

The weeping grew nearer as he advanced, and lifting his torch he made out a vague shape in the shadows. Stepping closer, he halted in sudden horror at the amorphic bulk which sprawled before him. Its unstable outlines somewhat suggested an octopus, but its malformed tentacles were too short for its size, and its substance was a quaking, jelly-like stuff which made him physically sick to look at. From among this loathsome gelid mass reared up a frog-like head, and he was frozen with nauseated horror to realize that the sound of weeping was coming from those obscene blubbery lips. The noise changed to an abominable high-pitched tittering as the great unstable eyes of the monstrosity rested on him, and it hitched its quaking bulk toward him. He backed away and fled up the tunnel, not trusting his sword. The creature might be composed of terrestrial matter, but it shook his very soul to look upon it, and he doubted the power of man-made weapons to harm it. For a short distance he heard it flopping and floundering after him, screaming with horrible laughter. The unmistakably human note in its mirth almost staggered his reason. It was exactly such laughter as he had heard bubble obscenely from the fat lips of the salacious women of Shadizar, City of Wickedness, when captive girls were stripped naked on the public auction block. By what hellish arts had Tsotha brought this unnatural being into life? Conan felt vaguely that he had looked on blasphemy against the eternal laws of nature.

He ran toward the main corridor, but before he reached it he crossed a sort of small square chamber, where two tunnels crossed. As he reached this chamber, he was flashingly aware of some small squat bulk on the floor ahead of him; then before he could check his flight or swerve aside, his foot struck something yielding that squalled shrilly, and he was precipitated headlong, the torch flying from his hand and being extinguished as it struck the stone floor. Half stunned by his fall, Conan rose and groped in the darkness. His sense of direction was confused, and he was unable to decide in which direction lay the main corridor. He did not look for the torch, as he had no means of rekindling it. His groping hands found the openings of the tunnels, and he chose one at random. How long he traversed it in utter darkness, he never knew, but suddenly his barbarian's instinct of near peril halted him short.

He had the same feeling he had had when standing on the brink of great precipices in the darkness. Dropping to all fours, he edged forward, and presently his outflung hand encountered the edge of a well, into which the tunnel floor dropped abruptly. As far down as he could reach the sides fell away sheerly, dank and slimy to his touch. He stretched out an arm in the darkness and could barely touch the opposite edge with the point of his sword. He could leap across it, then, but there was no point in that. He had taken the wrong tunnel and the main corridor lay somewhere behind him.

Even as he thought this, he felt a faint movement of air; a shadowy wind, rising from the well, stirred his black mane. Conan's skin crawled. He tried to tell himself that this well connected somehow with the outer world, but his instincts told him it was a thing unnatural. He was not merely inside the hill; he was below it, far below the level of the city streets. How then could an outer wind find its way into the pits and blow up from below? A faint throbbing pulsed on that ghostly wind, like drums beating, far, far below. A strong shudder shook the king of Aquilonia.

He rose to his feet and backed away, and as he did something floated up out of the well. What it was, Conan did not know. He could see nothing in the darkness, but he distinctly felt a presence—an invisible, intangible intelligence which hovered malignly near him. Turning, he fled the way he had come. Far ahead he saw a tiny red spark. He headed for it, and long before he thought to have reached it, he caromed headlong into a solid wall, and saw the spark at his feet. It was his torch, the flame extinguished, but the end a glowing coal. Carefully he took it up and blew upon it, fanning it into flame again. He gave a sigh as the tiny blaze leaped up. He was back in the chamber where the tunnels crossed, and his sense of direction came back.

He located the tunnel by which he had left the main corridor, and even as he started toward it, his torch flame flickered wildly as if blown upon by unseen lips. Again he felt a presence, and he lifted his torch, glaring about.

He saw nothing; yet he sensed, somehow, an invisible, bodiless thing that hovered in the air, dripping slimily and mouthing obscenities that he could not hear but was in some instinctive way aware of. He swung viciously with his sword and it felt as if he were cleaving cobwebs. A cold horror shook him then, and he fled down the tunnel, feeling a foul burning breath on his naked back as he ran.

But when he came out into the broad corridor, he was no longer aware of any presence, visible or invisible. Down it he went, momentarily expecting fanged and taloned fiends to leap at him from the darkness. The tunnels were not silent. From the bowels of the earth in all directions came sounds that did not belong in a sane world. There were titterings, squeals of demoniac mirth, long shuddering howls, and once the unmistakable squalling laughter of a hyena ended awfully in human words of shrieking blasphemy. He heard the pad of stealthy feet, and in the mouths of the tunnels caught glimpses of shadowy forms, monstrous and abnormal in outline.

It was as if he had wandered into hell—a hell of Tsotha-lanti's making. But the shadowy things did not come into the great corridor, though he distinctly heard the greedy sucking-in of slavering lips, and felt the burning glare of hungry eyes. And presently he knew why. A slithering sound behind him electrified him, and he leaped to the darkness of a near-by tunnel, shaking out his torch. Down the corridor he heard the great serpent crawling, sluggish from its recent grisly meal. From his very side something whimpered in fear and slunk away in the darkness. Evidently the main corridor was the great snake's hunting-ground and the other monsters gave it room.

To Conan the serpent was the least horror of them; he almost felt a kinship with it when he remembered the weeping, tittering obscenity, and the dripping, mouthing thing that came out of the well. At least it was of earthly matter; it was a crawling death, but it threatened only physical extinction, whereas these other horrors menaced mind and soul as well.

After it had passed on down the corridor he followed, at what he hoped was a safe distance, blowing his torch into flame again. He had not gone far when he heard a low moan that seemed to emanate from the black entrance of a tunnel nearby. Caution warned him on, but curiosity drove him to the tunnel, holding high the torch that was now little more than a stump. He was braced for the sight of anything, yet what he saw was what he had least expected. He was looking into a broad cell, and a space of this was caged off with closely set bars extending from floor to ceiling, set firmly in the stone. Within these bars lay a figure, which, as he approached, he saw was either a man, or the exact likeness of a man, twined and bound about with the tendrils of a thick vine which seemed to grow through the solid stone of the floor. It was covered with strangely pointed leaves and crimson blossoms—not the satiny red of natural petals, but a livid, unnatural crimson, like a perversity of flower-life. Its clinging, pliant branches wound about the man's naked body and limbs, seeming to caress his shrinking flesh with lustful avid kisses. One great blossom hovered exactly over his mouth. A low bestial moaning drooled from the loose lips; the head rolled as if in unbearable agony, and the eyes looked full at Conan. But there was no light of intelligence in them; they were blank, glassy, the eyes of an idiot.

Now the great crimson blossom dipped and pressed its petals over the writhing lips. The limbs of the wretch twisted in anguish; the tendrils of the plant quivered as if in ecstasy, vibrating their full snaky lengths. Waves of changing hues surged over them; their color grew deeper, more venomous.

Conan did not understand what he saw, but he knew that he looked on horror of some kind. Man or demon, the suffering of the captive touched Conan's wayward and impulsive heart. He sought for entrance and found a grille-like door in the bars, fastened with a heavy lock, for which he found a key among the keys he carried, and entered. Instantly the petals of the livid blossoms spread like the hood of a cobra, the tendrils reared menacingly and the whole plant shook and swayed toward him. Here was no blind growth of natural vegetation. Conan sensed a malignant intelligence; the plant could see him, and he felt its hate emanate from it in almost tangible waves. Stepping warily nearer, he marked the root-stem, a repulsively supple stalk thicker than his thigh, and even as the long tendrils arched toward him with a rattle of leaves and hiss, he swung his sword and cut through the stem with a single stroke.

Instantly the wretch in its clutches was thrown violently aside as the great vine lashed and knotted like a beheaded serpent, rolling into a huge irregular ball. The tendrils thrashed and writhed, the leaves shook and rattled like castanets, and the petals opened and closed convulsively; then the whole length straightened out limply, the vivid colors paled and dimmed, and a reeking white liquid oozed from the severed stump.

Conan stared, spellbound; then a sound brought him round, sword lifted. The freed man was on his feet, surveying him. Conan gaped in wonder. No longer were the eyes in the worn face expressionless. Dark and meditative, they were alive with intelligence, and the expression of imbecility had dropped from the face like a mask. The head was narrow and well-formed, with a high splendid forehead. The whole build of the man was aristocratic, evident no less in his tall slender frame than in his small trim feet and hands. His first words were strange and startling.

"What year is this?" he asked, speaking Kothic.

"Today is the tenth day of the month Yuluk, of the year of the Gazelle," answered Conan.

"Yagkoolan Ishtar!" murmured the stranger. "Ten years!" He drew a hand across his brow, shaking his head as if to clear his brain of cobwebs. "All is dim yet. After a ten-year emptiness, the mind cannot be expected to begin functioning clearly at once. Who are you?"

"Conan, once of Cimmeria. Now king of Aquilonia."

The other's eyes showed surprize.

"Indeed? And Namedides?"

"I strangled him on his throne the night I took the royal city," answered Conan.

A certain naiveté in the king's reply twitched the stranger's lips.

"Pardon, your majesty. I should have thanked you for the service you have done me. I am like a man woken suddenly from sleep deeper than death and shot with nightmares of agony more fierce than hell, but I understand that you delivered me. Tell me—why did you cut the stem of the plant Yothga instead of tearing it up by the roots?"

"Because I learned long ago to avoid touching with my flesh that which I do not understand," answered the Cimmerian.

"Well for you," said the stranger. "Had you been able to tear it up, you might have found things clinging to the roots against which not even your sword would prevail. Yothga's roots are set in hell."

"But who are you?" demanded Conan.

"Men called me Pelias."

"What!" cried the king. "Pelias the sorcerer, Tsotha-lanti's rival, who vanished from the earth ten years ago?"

"Not entirely from the earth," answered Pelias with a wry smile. "Tsotha preferred to keep me alive, in shackles more grim than rusted iron. He pent me in here with this devil-flower whose seeds drifted down through the black cosmos from Yag the Accursed, and found fertile field only in the maggot-writhing corruption that seethes on the floors of hell.

"I could not remember my sorcery and the words and symbols of my power, with that cursed thing gripping me and drinking my soul with its loathsome caresses. It sucked the contents of my mind day and night, leaving my brain as empty as a broken wine-jug. Ten years! Ishtar preserve us!"

Conan found no reply, but stood holding the stump of the torch, and trailing his great sword. Surely the man was mad—yet there was no madness in the dark eyes that rested so calmly on him.

"Tell me, is the black wizard in Khorshemish? But no—you need not reply. My powers begin to wake, and I sense in your mind a great battle and a king trapped by treachery. And I see Tsotha-lanti riding hard for the Tybor with Strabonus and the king of Ophir. So much the better. My art is too frail from the long slumber to face Tsotha yet. I need time to recruit my strength, to assemble my powers. Let us go forth from these pits."

Conan jangled his keys discouragedly.

"The grille to the outer door is made fast by a bolt which can be worked only from the outside. Is there no other exit from these tunnels?"

"Only one, which neither of us would care to use, seeing that it goes down and not up," laughed Pelias. "But no matter. Let us see to the grille."

He moved toward the corridor with uncertain steps, as of long-unused limbs, which gradually became more sure. As he followed, Conan remarked uneasily, "There is a cursed big snake creeping about this tunnel. Let us be wary lest we step into his mouth."

"I remember him of old," answered Pelias grimly, "the more as I was forced to watch while ten of my acolytes were fed to him. He is Satha, the Old One, chiefest of Tsotha's pets."

"Did Tsotha dig these pits for no other reason than to house his cursed monstrosities?" asked Conan.

"He did not dig them. when the city was founded three thousand years ago there were ruins of an earlier city on and about this hill. King Khossus V, the founder, built his palace on the hill, and digging cellars beneath it, came upon a walled-up doorway, which he broke into and discovered the pits, which were about as we see them now. But his grand vizier came to such a grisly end in them that Khossus in a fright walled up the entrance again. He said the vizier fell into a well—but he had the cellars filled in, and later abandoned the palace itself, and built himself another in the suburbs, from which he fled in a panic on discovering some black mold scattered on the marble floor of his palace one morning.

"He then departed with his whole court to the eastern corner of the kingdom and built a new city. The palace on the hill was not used and fell into ruins. When Akkutho I revived the lost glories of Khorshemish, he built a fortress there. It remained for Tsotha-lanti to rear the scarlet citadel and open the way to the pits again. Whatever fate overtook the grand vizier of Khossus, Tsotha avoided it. He fell into no well, though he did descend into a well he found, and came out with a strange expression which has not since left his eyes.

"I have seen that well, but I do not care to seek in it for wisdom. I am a sorcerer, and older than men reckon, but I am human. As for Tsotha—men say that a dancing-girl of Shadizar slept too near the pre-human ruins on Dagoth Hill and woke in the grip of a black demon; from that unholy union was spawned an accursed hybrid men call Tsotha-lanti—"

Conan cried out sharply and recoiled, thrusting his companion back. Before them rose the great shimmering white form of Satha, an ageless hate in its eyes. Conan tensed himself for one mad berserker onslaught—to thrust the glowing fagot into that fiendish countenance and throw his life into the ripping sword-stroke. But the snake was not looking at him. It was glaring over his shoulder at the man called Pelias, who stood with his arms folded, smiling. And in the great cold yellow eyes slowly the hate died out in a glitter of pure fear—the only time Conan ever saw such an expression in a reptile's eyes. With a swirling rush like the sweep of a strong wind, the great snake was gone.

"What did he see to frighten him?" asked Conan, eyeing his companion uneasily.

"The scaled people see what escapes the mortal eye," answered Pelias, cryptically. "You see my fleshly guise; he saw my naked soul."

An icy trickle disturbed Conan's spine, and he wondered if, after all, Pelias were a man, or merely another demon of the pits in a mask of humanity. He contemplated the advisability of driving his sword through his companion's back without further hesitation. But while he pondered, they came to the steel grille, etched blackly in the torches beyond, and the body of Shukeli, still slumped against the bars in a curdled welter of crimson.

Pelias laughed, and his laugh was not pleasant to hear.

"By the ivory hips of Ishtar, who is our doorman? Lo, it is no less than the noble Shukeli, who hanged my young men by their feet and skinned them with squeals of laughter! Do you sleep, Shukeli? Why do you lie so stiffly, with your fat belly sunk in like a dressed pig's?"

"He is dead," muttered Conan, ill at ease to hear these wild words.

"Dead or alive," laughed Pelias, "he shall open the door for us."

He clapped his hands sharply and cried, "Rise, Shukeli! Rise from hell and rise from the bloody floor and open the door for your masters! Rise, I say!"

An awful groan reverberated through the vaults. Conan's hair stood on end and he felt clammy sweat bead his hide. For the body of Shukeli stirred and moved, with infantile gropings of the fat hands. The laughter of Pelias was merciless as a flint hatchet, as the form of the eunuch reeled upright, clutching at the bars of the grille. Conan, glaring at him, felt his blood turn to ice, and the marrow of his bones to water; for Shukeli's wide-open eyes were glassy and empty, and from the great gash in his belly his entrails hung limply to the floor. The eunuch's feet stumbled among his entrails as he worked the bolt, moving like a brainless automaton. When he had first stirred, Conan had thought that by some incredible chance the eunuch was alive; but the man was dead—had been dead for hours.

Pelias sauntered through the opened grille, and Conan crowded through behind him, sweat pouring from his body, shrinking away from the awful shape that slumped on sagging legs against the grate it held open. Pelias passed on without a backward glance, and Conan followed him, in the grip of nightmare and nausea. He had not taken half a dozen strides when a sodden thud brought him round. Shukeli's corpse lay limply at the foot of the grille.

"His task is done, and hell gapes for him again," remarked Pelias pleasantly; politely affecting not to notice the strong shudder which shook Conan's mighty frame.

He led the way up the long stairs, and through the brass skull-crowned door at the top. Conan gripped his sword, expecting a rush of slaves, but silence gripped the citadel. They passed through the black corridor and came into that in which the censers swung, billowing forth their everlasting incense. Still they saw no one.

"The slaves and soldiers are quartered in another part of the citadel," remarked Pelias. "Tonight, their master being away, they doubtless lie drunk on wine or lotus-juice."

Conan glanced through an arched, golden-silled window that let out upon a broad balcony, and swore in surprise to see the dark-blue, star-flecked sky. It had been shortly after sunrise when he was thrown into the pits. Now it was past midnight. He could scarcely realize he had been so long underground. He was suddenly aware of thirst and a ravenous appetite. Pelias led the way into a gold-domed chamber, floored with silver, its lapis lazuli walls pierced by the fretted arches of many doors.

With a sigh Pelias sank onto a silken divan.

"Gold and silks again," he sighed. "Tsotha affects to be above the pleasures of the flesh, but he is half devil. I am human, despite my black arts. I love ease and good cheer—that's how Tsotha trapped me. He caught me helpless with drink. Wine is a curse—by the ivory bosom of Ishtar, even as I speak of it, the traitor is here! Friend, please pour me a goblet—hold! I forgot that you are a king. I will pour."

"The devil with that," growled Conan, filling a crystal goblet and proffering it to Pelias. Then, lifting the jug, he drank deeply from the mouth, echoing Pelias' sigh of satisfaction.

"The dog knows good wine," said Conan, wiping his mouth with the back of his hand. "But by Crom, Pelias, are we to sit here until his soldiers awake and cut our throats?"

"No fear," answered Pelias. "Would you like to see how fortune holds with Strabonus?"

Blue fire burned in Conan's eyes, and he gripped his sword until his knuckles showed blue. "Oh, to be at sword-points with him!" he rumbled.

Pelias lifted a great shimmering globe from an ebony table.

"Tsotha's crystal. A childish toy, but useful when there is lack of time for higher science. Look in, your majesty."

He laid it on the table before Conan's eyes. The king looked into cloudy depths which deepened and expanded. Slowly images crystallized out of mist and shadows. He was looking on a familiar landscape. Broad plains ran to a wide winding river, beyond which the level lands ran up quickly into a maze of low hills. On the northern bank of the river stood a walled town, guarded by a moat connected at each end with the river.

"By Crom!" ejaculated Conan. "It's Shamar! The dogs besiege it!"

The invaders had crossed the river; their pavilions stood in the narrow plain between the city and the hills. Their warriors swarmed about the walls, their mail gleaming palely under the moon. Arrows and stones rained on them from the towers and they staggered back, but came on again.

Even as Conan cursed, the scene changed. Tall spires and gleaming domes stood up in the mist, and he looked on his own capital of Tamar, where all was confusion. He saw the steel-clad knights of Poitain, his staunchest supporters, riding out of the gate, hooted and hissed by the multitude which swarmed the streets. He saw looting and rioting, and men-at-arms whose shields bore the insignia of Pellia, manning the towers and swaggering through the markets. Over all, like a fantasmal mirage, he saw the dark, triumphant face of Prince Arpello of Pellia. The images faded.

"So!" raved Conan. "My people turn on me the moment my back is turned—"

"Not entirely," broke in Pelias. "They have heard that you are dead. There is no one to protect them from outer enemies and civil war, they think. Naturally, they turn to the strongest noble, to avoid the horrors of anarchy. They do not trust the Poitanians, remembering former wars. But Arpello is on hand, and the strongest prince of the central provinces."

"When I come to Aquilonia again he will be but a headless corpse rotting on Traitor's Common," Conan ground his teeth.

"Yet before you can reach your capital," reminded Pelias, "Strabonus may be before you. At least his riders will be ravaging your kingdom."

"True!" Conan paced the chamber like a caged lion. "With the fastest horse I could not reach Shamar before midday. Even there I could do no good except to die with the people, when the town falls—as fall it will in a few days at most. From Shamar to Tamar is five days' ride, even if you kill your horses on the road. Before I could reach my capital and raise an army, Strabonus would be hammering at the gates; because raising an army is going to be hell—all my damnable nobles will have scattered to their own cursed fiefs at the word of my death. And since the people have driven out Trocero of Poitain, there's none to keep Arpello's greedy hands off the crown—and the crown treasure. He'll hand the country over to Strabonus, in return for a mock throne—and as soon as Strabonus' back is turned, he'll stir up revolt. But the nobles won't support him, and it will only give Strabonus excuse for annexing the kingdom openly. Oh Crom, Ymir, and Set! If I but had wings to fly like lightning to Tamar!"

Pelias, who sat tapping the jade table top with his fingernails, halted suddenly, and rose as with a definite purpose, beckoning Conan to follow. The king complied, sunk in moody thoughts, and Pelias led the way out of the chamber and up a flight of marble, gold-worked stairs that let out on the pinnacle of the citadel, the roof of the tallest tower. It was night, and a strong wind was blowing through the star-filled skies, stirring Conan's black mane. Far below them twinkled the lights of Khorshemish, seemingly farther away than the stars above them. Pelias seemed withdrawn and aloof here, one in cold unhuman greatness with the company of the stars.

"There are creatures," said Pelias, "not alone of earth and sea, but of air and the far reaches of the skies as well, dwelling apart, unguessed of men. Yet to him who holds the Master-words and Signs and the Knowledge underlying all, they are not malignant nor inaccessible. Watch, and fear not."

He lifted his hands to the skies and sounded a long weird call that seemed to shudder endlessly out into space, dwindling and fading, yet never dying out, only receding farther and farther into some unreckoned cosmos. In the silence that followed, Conan heard a sudden beat of wings in the stars, and recoiled as a huge bat-like creature alighted beside him. He saw its great calm eyes regarding him in the starlight; he saw the forty-foot spread of its giant wings. And he saw it was neither bat nor bird.

"Mount and ride," said Pelias. "By dawn it will bring you to Tamar."

"By Crom!" muttered Conan. "Is this all a nightmare from which I shall presently awaken in my palace at Tamar? What of you? I would not leave you alone among your enemies."

"Be at ease regarding me," answered Pelias. "At dawn the people of Khorshemish will know they have a new master. Doubt not what the gods have sent you. I will meet you in the plain by Shamar."

Doubtfully Conan clambered upon the ridged back, gripping the arched neck, still convinced that he was in the grasp of a fantastic nightmare. With a great rush and thunder of titan wings, the creature took the air, and the king grew dizzy as he saw the lights of the city dwindle far below him.

IV

"The sword that slays the king cuts the cords of the empire."
—Aquilonian proverb

The streets of Tamar swarmed with howling mobs, shaking fists and rusty pikes. It was the hour before dawn of the second day after the battle of Shamu, and events had occurred so swiftly as to daze the mind. By means known only to Tsotha-lanti, word had reached Tamar of the king's death, within half a dozen hours after the battle. Chaos had resulted. The barons had deserted the royal capital, galloping away to secure their castles against marauding neighbors. The well-knit kingdom Conan had built up seemed tottering on the edge of dissolution, and commoners and merchants trembled at the imminence of a return of the feudalistic regime. The people howled for a king to protect them against their own aristocracy no less than foreign foes. Count Trocero, left by Conan in charge of the city, tried to reassure them, but in their unreasoning terror they remembered old civil wars, and how this same count had besieged Tamar fifteen years before. It was shouted in the streets that Trocero had betrayed the king; that he planned to plunder the city. The mercenaries began looting the quarters, dragging forth screaming merchants and terrified women.

Trocero swept down on the looters, littered the streets with their corpses, drove them back into their quarter in confusion, and arrested their leaders. Still the people rushed wildly about, with brainless squawks, screaming that the count had incited the riot for his own purposes.

Prince Arpello came before the distracted council and announced himself ready to take over the government of the city until a new king could be decided upon, Conan having no son. While they debated, his agents stole subtly among the people, who snatched at a shred of royalty. The council heard the storm outside the palace windows, where the multitude roared for Arpello the Rescuer. The council surrendered.

Trocero at first refused the order to give up his baton of authority, but the people swarmed about him, hissing and howling, hurling stones and offal at his knights. Seeing the futility of a pitched battle in the streets with

Arpello's retainers, under such conditions, Trocero hurled the baton in his rival's face, hanged the leaders of the mercenaries in the market square as his last official act, and rode out of the southern gate at the head of his fifteen hundred steel-clad knights. The gates slammed behind him and Arpello's suave mask fell away to reveal the grim visage of the hungry wolf.

With the mercenaries cut to pieces or hiding in their barracks, his were the only soldiers in Tamar. Sitting his warhorse in the great square, Arpello proclaimed himself king of Aquilonia, amid the clamor of the deluded multitude.

Publius the Chancellor, who opposed this move, was thrown into prison. The merchants, who had greeted the proclamation of a king with relief, now found with consternation that the new monarch's first act was to levy a staggering tax on them. Six rich merchants, sent as a delegation of protest, were seized and their heads slashed off without ceremony. A shocked and stunned silence followed this execution. The merchants, confronted by a power they could not control with money, fell on their fat bellies and licked their oppressor's boots.

The common people were not perturbed at the fate of the merchants, but they began to murmur when they found that the swaggering Pellian soldiery, pretending to maintain order, were as bad as Turanian bandits. Complaints of extortion, murder and rape poured in to Arpello, who had taken up his quarters in Publius' palace, because the desperate councillors, doomed by his order, were holding the royal palace against his soldiers. He had taken possession of the pleasure-palace, however, and Conan's girls were dragged to his quarters. The people muttered at the sight of the royal beauties writhing in the brutal hands of the iron-clad retainers—dark-eyed damsels of Poitain, slim black-haired wenches from Zamora, Zingara and Hyrkania, Brythunian girls with tousled yellow heads, all weeping with fright and shame, unused to brutality.

Night fell on a city of bewilderment and turmoil, and before midnight word spread mysteriously in the street that the Kothians had followed up their victory and were hammering at the walls of Shamar. Somebody in Tsotha's mysterious secret service had babbled. Fear shook the people like an earthquake, and they did not even pause to wonder at the witchcraft by which the news had been so swiftly transmitted. They stormed at Arpello's doors, demanding that he march southward and drive the enemy back over the Tybor. He might have subtly pointed out that his force was not sufficient, and that he could not raise an army until the barons recognized his claim to the crown. But he was drunk with power, and laughed in their faces.

A young student, Athemides, mounted a column in the market, and with burning words accused Arpello of being a cat's-paw for Strabonus, painting a vivid picture of existence under Kothian rule, with Arpello as satrap. Before he finished, the multitude was screaming with fear and howling with rage. Arpello sent his soldiers to arrest the youth, but the people caught him up and fled with him, deluging the pursuing retainers with stones and dead cats. A volley of crossbow quarrels routed the mob, and a charge of horsemen littered the market with bodies, but Athemides was smuggled out of the city to plead with Trocero to retake Tamar, and march to aid Shamar.

Athemides found Trocero breaking his camp outside the walls, ready to march to Poitain, in the far southwestern corner of the kingdom. To the youth's urgent pleas he answered that he had neither the force necessary to storm Tamar, even with the aid of the mob inside, nor to face Strabonus. Besides, avaricious nobles would plunder Poitain behind his back, while he was fighting the Kothians. With the king dead, each man must protect his own. He was riding to Poitain, there to defend it as best he might against Arpello and his foreign allies.

While Athemides pleaded with Trocero, the mob still raved in the city with helpless fury. Under the great tower beside the royal palace the people swirled and milled, screaming their hate at Arpello, who stood on the turrets and laughed down at them while his archers ranged the parapets, bolts drawn and fingers on the triggers of their arbalests.

The prince of Pellia was a broad-built man of medium height, with a dark stern face. He was an intriguer, but he was also a fighter. Under his silken jupon with its gilt-braided skirts and jagged sleeves, glimmered burnished steel. His long black hair was curled and scented, and bound back with a cloth-of-silver band, but at his hip hung a broadsword the jeweled hilt of which was worn with battles and campaigns.

"Fools! Howl as you will! Conan is dead and Arpello is king!"

What if all Aquilonia were leagued against him? He had men enough to hold the mighty walls until Strabonus came up. But Aquilonia was divided against itself. Already the barons were girding themselves each to seize his neighbor's treasure. Arpello had only the helpless mob to deal with. Strabonus would carve through the loose lines of the warring barons as a galley-ram through foam and, until his coming, Arpello had only to hold the royal capital.

"Fools! Arpello is king!"

The sun was rising over the eastern towers. Out of the crimson dawn came a flying speck that grew to a bat, then to an eagle. Then all who saw screamed in amazement, for over the walls of Tamar swooped a shape such as men knew only in half-forgotten legends, and from between its titan-wings sprang a human form as it roared over the great tower. Then with a deafening thunder of wings it was gone, and the folk blinked, wondering if they dreamed. But on the turret stood a wild barbaric figure, half naked, blood-stained, brandishing a great sword. And from the multitude rose a roar that rocked the towers, "The king! It is the king!"

Arpello stood transfixed; then with a cry he drew and leaped at Conan. With a lion-like roar the Cimmerian parried the whistling blade, then dropping his own sword, gripped the prince and heaved him high above his head by crotch and neck.

"Take your plots to hell with you!" he roared, and like a sack of salt, he hurled the prince of Pellia far out, to fall through empty space for a hundred and fifty feet. The people gave back as the body came hurtling down, to smash on the marble pave, spattering blood and brains, and lie crushed in its splintered armor, like a mangled beetle.

The archers on the tower shrank back, their nerve broken. They fled, and the beleaguered councilmen sallied from the palace and hewed into them with joyous abandon. Pellian knights and men-at-arms sought safety in the streets, and the crowd tore them to pieces. In the streets the fighting milled and eddied, plumed helmets and steel caps tossed among the tousled heads and then vanished; swords hacked madly in a heaving forest of pikes, and over all rose the roar of the mob, shouts of acclaim mingling with screams of blood-lust and howls of agony. And high above all, the naked figure of the king rocked and swayed on the dizzy battlements, mighty arms brandished, roaring with gargantuan laughter that mocked all mobs and princes, even himself.

V

A long bow and a strong bow, and let the sky grow dark!
The cord to the nock, the shaft to the ear, and the king of Koth for a mark!
—Song of the Bossonian Archers

The mid-afternoon sun glinted on the placid waters of the Tybor, washing the southern bastions of Shamar. The haggard defenders knew that few of them would see that sun rise again. The pavilions of the besiegers dotted the plain. The people of Shamar had not been able successfully to dispute the crossing of the river, outnumbered as they were. Barges, chained together, made a bridge over which the invader poured his hordes. Strabonus had not dared march on into Aquilonia with Shamar, unsubdued, at his back. He had sent his light riders, his spahis, inland to ravage the country, and had reared up his siege engines in the plain. He had anchored a flotilla of boats, furnished him by Amalrus, in the middle of the stream, over against the river-wall. Some of these boats had been sunk by stones from the city's ballistas, which crashed through their decks and ripped out their planking, but the rest held their places and from their bows and mastheads, protected by mandets, archers raked the riverward turrets. These were Shemites, born with bows in their hands, not to be matched by Aquilonian archers.

On the landward side, mangonels rained boulders and tree trunks among the defenders, shattering through roofs and crushing humans like beetles; rams pounded incessantly at the stones; sappers burrowed like moles in the earth, sinking their mines beneath the towers. The moat had been dammed at the upper end, and emptied of its water, had been filled up with boulders, earth and dead horses and men. Under the walls the mailed figures swarmed, battering at the gates, rearing up scaling ladders, pushing storming towers, thronged with spearmen, against the turrets.

Hope had been abandoned in the city, where a bare fifteen hundred men resisted forty thousand warriors. No word had come from the kingdom whose outpost the city was. Conan was dead, so the invaders shouted exultantly. Only the strong walls and the desperate courage of the defenders had kept them so long at bay, and that could not suffice forever. The western wall was a mass of rubbish on which the defenders stumbled in hand-to-hand conflict with the invaders. The other walls were buckling from the mines beneath them, the towers leaning drunkenly.

Now the attackers were massing for a storm. The oliphants sounded, the steel-clad ranks drew up on the plain. The storming towers, covered with raw bull-hides, rumbled forward. The people of Shamar saw the banners of Koth and Ophir, flying side by side in the center, and made out, among their gleaming knights, the slim lethal figure of the golden-mailed Amalrus, and the squat black-armored form of Strabonus. And between them was a shape that made the bravest blench with horror—a lean vulture figure in a filmy robe. The pikemen moved forward, flowing over the ground like the glinting waves of a river of molten steel; the knights cantered forward, lances lifted, guidons streaming. The warriors on the walls drew a long breath, consigned their souls to Mitra, and gripped their notched and red-stained weapons.

Then, without warning, a bugle-call cut the din. A drum of hoofs rose above the rumble of the approaching host. North of the plain across which the army moved, rose ranges of low hills, mounting northward and westward like giant stair-steps. Now down out of these hills, like spume blown before a storm, shot the spahis who had been laying waste the countryside, riding low and spurring hard, and behind them sun shimmered on moving ranks of steel. They moved into full view, out of the defiles—mailed horsemen, the great lion banner of Aquilonia floating over them.

From the electrified watchers on the towers, a great shout rent the skies. In ecstasy warriors clashed their notched swords on their riven shields, and the people of the town, ragged beggars and rich merchants, harlots in red kirtles and dames in silks and satins, fell to their knees and cried out for joy to Mitra, tears of gratitude streaming down their faces.

Strabonus, frantically shouting orders, with Arbanus, that would wheel around the ponderous lines to meet this unexpected menace, grunted, "We still outnumber them, unless they have reserves hidden in the hills. The men on the battle towers can mask any sorties from the city. These are Poitanians—we might have guessed Trocero would try some such mad gallantry."

Amalrus cried out in unbelief.

"I see Trocero and his captain Prospero—but who rides between them?"

"Ishtar preserve us!" shrieked Strabonus, paling. "It is King Conan!"

"You are mad!" squalled Tsotha, starting convulsively. "Conan has been in Satha's belly for days!" He stopped short, glaring wildly at the host which was dropping down, file by file, into the plain. He could not mistake the giant figure in black, gilt-worked armor on the great black stallion, riding beneath the billowing silken folds of the great banner. A scream of feline fury burst from Tsotha's lips, flecking his beard with foam. For the first time in his life, Strabonus saw the wizard completely upset, and shrank from the sight.

"Here is sorcery!" screamed Tsotha, clawing madly at his beard. "How could he have escaped and reached his kingdom in time to return with an army so quickly? This is the work of Pelias, curse him! I feel his hand in this! May I be cursed for not killing him when I had the power!"

The kings gaped at the mention of a man they believed ten years dead, and panic, emanating from the leaders, shook the host. All recognized the rider on the black stallion. Tsotha felt the superstitious dread of his men, and fury made a hellish mask of his face.

"Strike home!" he screamed, brandishing his lean arms madly. "We are still the stronger! Charge and crush these dogs! We shall yet feast in the ruins of Shamar tonight! Oh, Set!" he lifted his hands and invoked the serpent-god to even Strabonus' horror, "grant us victory and I swear I will offer up to thee five hundred virgins of Shamar, writhing in their blood!"

Meanwhile, the opposing host had debouched onto the plain. With the knights came what seemed a second, irregular army on tough swift ponies. These dismounted and formed their ranks on foot—stolid Bossonian archers, and keen pikemen from Gunderland, their tawny locks blowing from under their steel caps.

It was a motley army Conan had assembled, in the wild hours following his return to his capital. He had beaten the frothing mob away from the Pellian soldiers who held the outer walls of Tamar, and impressed them into his service. He had sent a swift rider after Trocero to bring him back. With these as a nucleus of an army he had raced southward, sweeping the countryside for recruits and for mounts. Nobles of Tamar and the surrounding countryside had augmented his forces, and he had levied recruits from every village and castle along his road. Yet it was but a paltry force he had gathered to dash against the invading hosts, though of the quality of tempered steel.

Nineteen hundred armored horsemen followed him, the main bulk of which consisted of the Poitanian knights. The remnants of the mercenaries and professional soldiers in the trains of loyal noblemen made up his infantry—five thousand archers and four thousand pikemen. This host now came on in good order—first the archers, then the pikemen, behind them the knights, moving at a walk.

Over against them Arbanus ordered his lines, and the allied army moved forward like a shimmering ocean of steel. The watchers on the city walls shook to see that vast host, which overshadowed the powers of the rescuers. First marched the Shemitish archers, then the Kothian spearmen, then the mailed knights of Strabonus and Amalrus. Arbanus' intent was obvious—to employ his footmen to sweep away the infantry of Conan, and open the way for an overpowering charge of his heavy cavalry.

The Shemites opened fire at five hundred yards, and arrows flew like hail between the hosts, darkening the sun. The western archers, trained by a thousand years of merciless warfare with the Pictish savages, came stolidly on, closing their ranks as their comrades fell. They were far outnumbered, and the Shemitish bow had the longer range, but in accuracy the Bossonians were equal to their foes, and they balanced sheer skill in archery by superiority in morale, and in excellency of armor. Within good range they loosed, and the Shemites went down by whole ranks. The blue-bearded warriors in their light mail shirts could not endure punishment as could the heavier-armored Bossonians. They broke, throwing away their bows, and their flight disordered the ranks of the Kothian spearmen behind them.

Without the support of the archers, these men-at-arms fell by the hundreds before the shafts of the Bossonians, and charging madly into close quarters, they were met by the spears of the pikemen. No infantry was a match for the wild Gundermen, whose homeland, the northern-most province of Aquilonia, was but a day's ride across the Bossonian marches from the borders of Cimmeria, and who, born and bred to battle, were the purest blood of all the Hyborian peoples. The Kothian spearmen, dazed by their losses from arrows, were cut to pieces and fell back in disorder.

Strabonus roared in fury as he saw his infantry repulsed, and shouted for a general charge. Arbanus demurred, pointing out the Bossonians re-forming in good order before the Aquilonian knights, who had sat their steeds motionless during the melee. The general advised a temporary retirement, to draw the western knights out of the cover of the bows, but Strabonus was mad with rage. He looked at the long shimmering ranks of his knights, he glared at the handful of mailed figures over against him, and he commanded Arbanus to give the order to charge.

The general commended his soul to Ishtar and sounded the golden oliphant. With a thunderous roar the forest of lances dipped, and the great host rolled across the plain, gaining momentum as it came. The whole plain shook to the rumbling avalanche of hoofs, and the shimmer of gold and steel dazzled the watchers on the towers of Shamar.

The squadrons clave the loose ranks of the spearmen, riding down friend and foe alike, and rushed into the teeth of a blast of arrows from the Bossonians. Across the plain they thundered, grimly riding the storm that scattered their way with gleaming knights like autumn leaves. Another hundred paces and they would ride among the Bossonians and cut them down like corn; but flesh and blood could not endure the rain of death that now ripped and howled among them. Shoulder to shoulder, feet braced wide, stood the archers, drawing shaft to ear and loosing as one man, with deep, short shouts.

The whole front rank of the knights melted away, and over the pin-cushioned corpses of horses and riders, their comrades stumbled and fell headlong. Arbanus was down, an arrow through his throat, his skull smashed by the hoofs of his dying warhorse, and confusion ran through the disordered host. Strabonus was screaming an order, Amalrus another, and through all ran the superstitious dread the sight of Conan had awakened.

And while the gleaming ranks milled in confusion, the trumpets of Conan sounded, and through the opening ranks of the archers crashed the terrible charge of the Aquilonian knights.

The hosts met with a shock like that of an earthquake, that shook the tottering towers of Shamar. The disorganized squadrons of the invaders could not withstand the solid steel wedge, bristling with spears, that rushed like a thunderbolt against them. The long lances of the attackers ripped their ranks to pieces, and into the heart of their host rode the knights of Poitain, swinging their terrible two-handed swords.

The clash and clangor of steel was as that of a million sledges on as many anvils. The watchers on the walls were stunned and deafened by the thunder as they gripped the battlements and watched the steel maelstrom swirl and eddy, where plumes tossed high among the flashing swords, and standards dipped and reeled.

Amalrus went down, dying beneath the trampling hoofs, his shoulder-bone hewn in twain by Prospero's two-handed sword. The invaders' numbers had engulfed the nineteen hundred knights of Conan, but about this compact wedge, which hewed deeper and deeper into the looser formation of their foes, the knights of Koth and Ophir swirled and smote in vain. They could not break the wedge.

Archers and pikemen, having disposed of the Kothian infantry which was strewn in flight across the plain, came to the edges of the fight, loosing their arrows point-blank, running in to slash at girths and horses' bellies with their knives, thrusting upward to spit the riders on their long pikes.

At the tip of the steel wedge Conan roared his heathen battle-cry and swung his great sword in glittering arcs that made naught of steel burgonet or mail habergeon. Straight through a thundering waste of foes he rode, and the knights of Koth closed in behind him, cutting him off from his warriors. As a thunderbolt strikes, Conan struck, hurtling through the ranks by sheer power and velocity, until he came to Strabonus, livid among his palace troops. Now here the battle hung in balance, for with his superior numbers, Strabonus still had opportunity to pluck victory from the knees of the gods.

But he screamed when he saw his arch-foe within arm's length at last, and lashed out wildly with his ax. It clanged on Conan's helmet, striking fire, and the Cimmerian reeled and struck back. The five-foot blade crushed Strabonus' casque and skull, and the king's charger reared screaming, hurling a limp and sprawling corpse from the saddle. A great cry went up from the host, which faltered and gave back. Trocero and his house troops, hewing desperately, cut their way to Conan's side, and the great banner of Koth went down. Then behind the dazed and stricken invaders went up a mighty clamor and the blaze of a huge conflagration. The defenders of Shamar had made a desperate sortie, cut down the men masking the gates, and were raging among the tents of the besiegers, cutting down the camp followers, burning the pavilions, and destroying the siege engines. It was the last straw. The gleaming army melted away in flight, and the furious conquerors cut them down as they ran.

The fugitives raced for the river, but the men on the flotilla, harried sorely by the stones and shafts of the revived citizens, cast loose and pulled for the southern shore, leaving their comrades to their fate. Of these many gained the shore, racing across the barges that served as a bridge, until the men of Shamar cut these adrift and severed them from the shore. Then the fight became a slaughter. Driven into the river to drown in their armor, or hacked down along the bank, the invaders perished by the thousands. No quarter they had promised; no quarter they got.

From the foot of the low hills to the shores of the Tybor, the plain was littered with corpses, and the river whose tide ran red, floated thick with the dead. Of the nineteen hundred knights who had ridden south with Conan, scarcely five hundred lived to boast of their scars, and the slaughter among the archers and pikemen was ghastly. But the great and shining host of Strabonus and Amalrus was hacked out of existence, and those that fled were less than those that died.

While the slaughter yet went on along the river, the final act of a grim drama was being played out in the meadow land beyond. Among those who had crossed the barge bridge before it was destroyed was Tsotha, riding like the wind on a gaunt weird-looking steed whose stride no natural horse could match. Ruthlessly riding down friend and foe, he gained the southern bank, and then a glance backward showed him a grim figure on a great black stallion in pursuit. The lashings had already been cut, and the barges were drifting apart, but Conan came recklessly on, leaping his steed from boat to boat as a man might leap from one cake of floating ice to another. Tsotha screamed a curse, but the great stallion took the last leap with a straining groan, and gained the southern bank. Then the wizard fled away into the empty meadowland, and on his trail came the king, riding hard, swinging the great sword that spattered his trail with crimson drops.

On they fled, the hunted and the hunter, and not a foot could the black stallion gain, though he strained each nerve and thew. Through a sunset land of dim and illusive shadows they fled, till sight and sound of the slaughter died out behind them. Then in the sky appeared a dot, that grew into a huge eagle as it approached. Swooping down from the sky, it drove at the head of Tsotha's steed, which screamed and reared, throwing its rider.

Old Tsotha rose and faced his pursuer, his eyes those of a maddened serpent, his face an inhuman mask. In each hand he held something that shimmered, and Conan knew he held death there.

The king dismounted and strode toward his foe, his armor clanking, his great sword gripped high.

"Again we meet, wizard!" he grinned savagely.

"Keep off!" screamed Tsotha like a blood-mad jackal. "I'll blast the flesh from your bones! You cannot conquer me—if you hack me in pieces, the bits of flesh and bone will reunite and haunt you to your doom! I see the hand of Pelias in this, but I defy ye both! I am Tsotha, son of—"

Conan rushed, sword gleaming, eyes slits of wariness. Tsotha's right hand came back and forward, and the king ducked quickly. Something passed by his helmeted head and exploded behind him, searing the very sands with a flash of hellish fire. Before Tsotha could toss the globe in his left hand, Conan's sword sheared through his lean neck. The wizard's head shot from his shoulders on an arching fount of blood, and the robed figure staggered and crumpled drunkenly. Yet the mad black eyes glared up at Conan with no dimming of their feral light, the lips writhed awfully, and the hands groped, as if searching for the severed head. Then with a swift rush of wings, something swooped from the sky—the eagle which had attacked Tsotha's horse. In its mighty talons it snatched up the dripping head and soared skyward, and Conan stood struck dumb, for from the eagle's throat boomed human laughter, in the voice of Pelias the sorcerer.

Then a hideous thing came to pass, for the headless body reared up from the sand, and staggered away in awful flight on stiffening legs, hands blindly outstretched toward the dot speeding and dwindling in the dusky sky. Conan stood like one turned to stone, watching until the swift reeling figure faded in the dusk that purpled the meadows.

"Crom!" his mighty shoulders twitched. "A murrain on these wizardly feuds! Pelias has dealt well with me, but I care not if I see him no more. Give me a clean sword and a clean foe to flesh it in. Damnation! What would I not give for a flagon of wine!"

ROGUES IN THE HOUSE

ROBERT E. HOWARD

I

At a court festival, Nabonidus, the Red Priest, who was the real ruler of the city, touched Murilo, the young aristocrat, courteously on the arm. Murilo turned to meet the priest's enigmatic gaze, and to wonder at the hidden meaning therein. No words passed between them, but Nabonidus bowed and handed Murilo a small gold cask. The young nobleman, knowing that Nabonidus did nothing without reason, excused himself at the first opportunity and returned hastily to his chamber. There he opened the cask and found within a human ear, which he recognized by a peculiar scar upon it. He broke into a profuse sweat and was no longer in doubt about the meaning in the Red Priest's glance.

But Murilo, for all his scented black curls and foppish apparel was no weakling to bend his neck to the knife without a struggle. He did not know whether Nabonidus was merely playing with him or giving him a chance to go into voluntary exile, but the fact that he was still alive and at liberty proved that he was to be given at least a few hours, probably for meditation. However, he needed no meditation for decision; what he needed was a tool. And Fate furnished that tool, working among the dives and brothels of the squalid quarters even while the young nobleman shivered and pondered in the part of the city occupied by the purple-towered marble and ivory palaces of the aristocracy.

There was a priest of Anu whose temple, rising at the fringe of the slum district, was the scene of more than devotions. The priest was fat and full-fed, and he was at once a fence for stolen articles and a spy for the police. He worked a thriving trade both ways, because the district on which he bordered was the Maze, a tangle of muddy, winding alleys and sordid dens, frequented by the bolder thieves in the kingdom. Daring above all were a Gunderman deserter from the mercenaries and a barbaric Cimmerian. Because of the priest of Anu, the Gunderman was taken and hanged in the market square. But the Cimmerian fled, and learning in devious ways of the priest's treachery, he entered the temple of Anu by night and cut off the priest's head. There followed a great turmoil in the city, but the search for the killer proved fruitless until a woman betrayed him to the authorities and led a captain of the guard and his squad to the hidden chamber where the barbarian lay drunk.

Waking to stupefied but ferocious life when they seized him, he disemboweled the captain, burst through his assailants, and would have escaped but for the liquor that still clouded his senses. Bewildered and half blinded, he missed the open door in his headlong flight and dashed his head against the stone wall so terrifically that he knocked himself senseless. When he came to, he was in the strongest dungeon in the city, shackled to the wall with chains not even his barbaric thews could break.

To this cell came Murilo, masked and wrapped in a wide black cloak. The Cimmerian surveyed him with interest, thinking him the executioner sent to dispatch him. Murilo set him at rights and regarded him with no less interest. Even in the dim light of the dungeon, with his limbs loaded with chains, the primitive power of the man was evident. His mighty body and thick-muscled limbs combined the strength of a grizzly with the quickness of a panther. Under his tangled black mane his blue eyes blazed with unquenchable savagery.

"Would you like to live?" asked Murilo. The barbarian grunted, new interest glinting in his eyes.

"If I arrange for your escape, will you do a favor for me?" the aristocrat asked.

The Cimmerian did not speak, but the intentness of his gaze answered for him.

"I want you to kill a man for me."

"Who?"

Murilo's voice sank to a whisper. "Nabonidus, the king's priest!"

The Cimmerian showed no sign of surprise or perturbation. He had none of the fear or reverence for authority that civilization instills in men. King or beggar, it was all one to him. Nor did he ask why Murilo had come to him, when the quarters were full of cutthroats outside prisons.

"When am I to escape?" he demanded.

"Within the hour. There is but one guard in this part of the dungeon at night. He can be bribed; he has been bribed. See, here are the keys to your chains. I'll remove them and, after I have been gone an hour, the guard, Athicus, will unlock the door to your cell. You will bind him with strips torn from your tunic; so when he is found, the authorities will think you were rescued from the outside and will not suspect him. Go at once to the house of the Red Priest and kill him. Then go to the Rats' Den, where a man will meet you and give you a pouch of gold and a horse. With those you can escape from the city and flee the country."

"Take off these cursed chains now," demanded the Cimmerian. "And have the guard bring me food. By Crom, I have lived on moldy bread and water for a whole day, and I am nigh to famishing."

"It shall be done; but remember—you are not to escape until I have had time to reach my home."

Freed of his chains, the barbarian stood up and stretched his heavy arms, enormous in the gloom of the dungeon. Murilo again felt that if any man in the world could accomplish the task he had set, this Cimmerian could. With a few repeated instructions he left the prison, first directing Athicus to take a platter of beef and ale in to the prisoner. He knew he could trust the guard, not only because of the money he had paid, but also because of certain information he possessed regarding the man.

When he returned to his chamber, Murilo was in full control of his fears. Nabonidus would strike through the king—of that he was certain. And since the royal guardsmen were not knocking at his door, it was certain that the priest had said nothing to the king, so far. Tomorrow he would speak, beyond a doubt—if he lived to see tomorrow.

Murilo believed the Cimmerian would keep faith with him. Whether the man would be able to carry out his purpose remained to be seen. Men had attempted to assassinate the Red Priest before, and they had died in hideous and nameless ways. But they had been products of the cities of men, lacking the wolfish instincts of the barbarian. The instant that Murilo, turning the gold cask with its severed ear in his hands, had learned through his secret channels that the Cimmerian had been captured, he had seen a solution of his problem.

In his chamber again, he drank a toast to the man, whose name was Conan, and to his success that night. And while he was drinking, one of his spies brought him the news that Athicus had been arrested and thrown into prison. The Cimmerian had not escaped.

Murilo felt his blood turn to ice again. He could see in this twist of fate only the sinister hand of Nabonidus, and an eery obsession began to grow on him that the Red Priest was more than human—a sorcerer who read the minds of his victims and pulled strings on which they danced like puppets. With despair came desperation. Girding a sword beneath his black cloak, he left his house by a hidden way and hurried through the deserted streets. It was just at midnight when he came to the house of Nabonidus, looming blackly among the walled gardens that separated it from the surrounding estates.

The wall was high but not impossible to negotiate. Nabonidus did not put his trust in mere barriers of stone. It was what was inside the wall that was to be feared. What these things were Murilo did not know precisely. He knew there was at least a huge savage dog that roamed the gardens and had on occasion torn an intruder to pieces as a hound rends a rabbit. What else there might be he did not care to conjecture. Men who had been allowed to enter the house on brief, legitimate business, reported that Nabonidus dwelt among rich furnishings, yet simply, attended by a surprisingly small number of servants. Indeed, they mentioned only one as having been visible—a tall, silent man called Joka. Someone else, presumably a slave, had been heard moving about in the recesses of the house, but this person no one had ever seen. The greatest mystery of the mysterious house was Nabonidus himself, whose power of intrigue and grasp on international politics had made him the strongest man in the kingdom. People, chancellor and king moved puppet-like on the strings he worked.

Murilo scaled the wall and dropped down into the gardens, which were expanses of shadow, darkened by clumps of shrubbery and waving foliage. No light shone in the windows of the house, which loomed so blackly among the trees. The young nobleman stole stealthily yet swiftly through the shrubs. Momentarily he expected to hear the baying of the great dog and to see its giant body hurtle through the shadows. He doubted the effectiveness of his sword against such an attack, but he did not hesitate. As well die beneath the fangs of a beast as of the headsman.

He stumbled over something bulky and yielding. Bending close in the dim starlight, he made out a limp shape on the ground. It was the dog that guarded the gardens, and it was dead. Its neck was broken and it bore what seemed to be the marks of great fangs. Murilo felt that no human being had done this. The beast had met a monster more savage than itself. Murilo glared nervously at the cryptic masses of bush and shrub; then with a shrug of his shoulders, he approached the silent house.

The first door he tried proved to be unlocked. He entered warily, sword in hand, and found himself in a long, shadowy hallway dimly illuminated by a light that gleamed through the hangings at the other end. Complete silence hung over the whole house. Murilo glided along the hall and halted to peer through the hangings. He looked into a lighted room, over the windows of which velvet curtains were drawn so closely as to allow no beam to shine through. The room was empty, in so far as human life was concerned, but it had a grisly occupant, nevertheless: in the midst of a wreckage of furniture and torn hangings that told of a fearful struggle, lay the body of a man. The form lay on its belly, but the head was twisted about so that the chin rested behind a shoulder. The features, contorted into an awful grin, seemed to leer at the horrified nobleman.

For the first time that night, Murilo's resolution wavered. He cast an uncertain glance back the way he had come. Then the memory of the headsman's block and axe steeled him, and he crossed the room, swerving to avoid the grinning horror sprawled in its midst. Though he had never seen the man before, he knew from former descriptions that it was Joka, Nabonidus' saturnine servant.

He peered through a curtained door into a broad circular chamber, banded by a gallery half-way between the polished floor and the lofty ceiling. This chamber was furnished as if for a king. In the midst of it stood an ornate mahogany table, loaded with vessels of wine and rich viands. And Murilo stiffened. In a great chair whose broad back was toward him, he saw a figure whose habiliments were familiar. He glimpsed an arm in a red sleeve resting on the arm of the chair; the head, clad in the familiar scarlet hood of the gown, was bent forward as if in meditation. Just so had Murilo seen Nabonidus sit a hundred times in the royal court.

Cursing the pounding of his own heart, the young nobleman stole across the chamber, sword extended, his whole frame poised for the thrust. His prey did not move, nor seem to hear his cautious advance. Was the Red Priest asleep, or was it a corpse which slumped in that great chair? The length of a single stride separated Murilo from his enemy, when suddenly the man in the chair rose and faced him.

The blood went suddenly from Murilo's features. His sword fell from his fingers and rang on the polished floor. A terrible cry broke from his livid lips; it was followed by the thud of a falling body. Then once more silence reigned over the house of the Red Priest.

II

Shortly after Murilo left the dungeon where Conan the Cimmerian was confined, Athicus brought the prisoner a platter of food which included, among other things, a huge joint of beef and a tankard of ale. Conan fell to voraciously, and Athicus made a final round of the cells, to see that all was in order, and that none should witness the pretended prison break. It was while he was so occupied that a squad of guardsmen marched into the prison and placed him under arrest. Murilo had been mistaken when he assumed this arrest denoted discovery of Conan's planned escape. It was another matter; Athicus had become careless in his dealings with the underworld, and one of his past sins had caught up with him.

Another jailer took his place, a stolid, dependable creature whom no amount of bribery could have shaken from his duty. He was unimaginative, but he had an exalted idea of the importance of his job.

After Athicus had been marched away to be formally arraigned before a magistrate, this jailer made the rounds of the cell as a matter of routine. As he passed that of Conan, his sense of propriety was shocked and outraged to see the prisoner free of his chains and in the act of gnawing the last shreds of meat from a huge beefbone. The jailer was so upset that he made the mistake of entering the cell alone, without calling guards from the other parts of the prison. It was his first mistake in the line of duty, and his last. Conan brained him with the beef bone, took his poniard and his keys, and made a leisurely departure. As Murilo had said, only one guard was on duty there at night. The Cimmerian passed himself outside the walls by means of the keys he had taken and presently emerged into the outer air, as free as if Murilo's plan had been successful.

In the shadows of the prison walls, Conan paused to decide his next course of action. It occurred to him that since he had escaped through his own actions, he owed nothing to Murilo; yet it had been the young nobleman who had removed his chains and had the food sent to him, without either of which his escape would have been impossible. Conan decided that he was indebted to Murilo and, since he was a man who discharged his obligations eventually, he determined to carry out his promise to the young aristocrat. But first he had some business of his own to attend to.

He discarded his ragged tunic and moved off through the night naked but for a loincloth. As he went he fingered the poniard he had captured—a murderous weapon with a broad, double-edged blade nineteen inches long. He slunk along alleys and shadowed plazas until he came to the district which was his destination—the Maze. Along its labyrinthian ways he went with the certainty of familiarity. It was indeed a maze of black alleys and enclosed courts and devious ways; of furtive sounds, and stenches. There was no paving on the streets; mud and filth mingled in an unsavory mess. Sewers were unknown; refuse was dumped into the alleys to form reeking heaps and puddles. Unless a man walked with care he was likely to lose his footing and plunge waist-deep into nauseous pools. Nor was it uncommon to stumble over a corpse lying with its throat cut or its head knocked in, in the mud. Honest folk shunned the Maze with good reason.

Conan reached his destination without being seen, just as one he wished fervently to meet was leaving it. As the Cimmerian slunk into the courtyard below, the girl who had sold him to the police was taking leave of her new lover in a chamber one flight up. This young thug, her door closed behind him, groped his way down a creaking flight of stairs, intent on his own meditations, which, like those of most of the denizens of the Maze, had to do with the unlawful acquirement of property. Part-way down the stairs, he halted suddenly, his hair standing up. A vague bulk crouched in the darkness before him, a pair of eyes blazed like the eyes of a hunting beast. A beast-like snarl was the last thing he heard in life, as the monster lurched against him and a keen blade ripped through his belly. He gave one gasping cry and slumped down limply on the stairway.

The barbarian loomed above him for an instant, ghoul-like, his eyes burning in the gloom. He knew the sound was heard, but the people in the Maze were careful to attend to their own business. A death cry on darkened stairs was nothing unusual. Later, someone would venture to investigate, but only after a reasonable lapse of time.

Conan went up the stairs and halted at a door he knew well of old. It was fastened within, but his blade passed between the door and the jamb and lifted the bar. He stepped inside, closing the door after him, and faced the girl who had betrayed him to the police.

The wench was sitting cross-legged in her shift on her unkempt bed. She turned white and stared at him as if at a ghost. She had heard the cry from the stairs, and she saw the red stain on the poniard in his hand. But she was too filled with terror on her own account to waste any time lamenting the evident fate of her lover. She began to beg for her life, almost incoherent with terror. Conan did not reply; he merely stood and glared at her with his burning eyes, testing the edge of his poniard with a callused thumb.

At last he crossed the chamber, while she cowered back against the wall, sobbing frantic pleas for mercy. Grasping her yellow locks with no gentle hand, he dragged her off the bed. Thrusting his blade in the sheath, he tucked his squirming captive under his left arm and strode to the window. As in most houses of that type, a ledge encircled each story, caused by the continuance of the window ledges. Conan kicked the window open and stepped out on that narrow band. If any had been near or awake, they would have witnessed the bizarre sight of a man moving carefully along the ledge, carrying a kicking, half-naked wench under his arm. They would have been no more puzzled than the girl.

Reaching the spot he sought, Conan halted, gripping the wall with his free hand. Inside the building rose a sudden clamor, showing that the body had at last been discovered. His captive whimpered and twisted, renewing her importunities. Conan glanced down into the muck and slime of the alleys below; he listened briefly to the clamor inside and the pleas of the wench; then he dropped her with great accuracy into a cesspool. He enjoyed her kickings and flounderings and the concentrated venom of her profanity for a few seconds, and even allowed himself a low rumble of laughter. Then he lifted his head, listened to the growing tumult within the building, and decided it was time for him to kill Nabonidus.

III

It was a reverberating clang of metal that roused Murilo. He groaned and struggled dazedly to a sitting position. About him all was silence and darkness, and for an instant he was sickened with the fear that he was blind. Then he remembered what had gone before, and his flesh crawled. By the sense of touch he found that he was lying on a floor of evenly joined stone slabs. Further groping discovered a wall of the same material. He rose and leaned against it, trying in vain to orient himself. That he was in some sort of a prison seemed certain, but where and how long he was unable to guess. He remembered dimly a clashing noise and wondered if it had been the iron door of his dungeon closing on him, or if it betokened the entrance of an executioner.

At this thought he shuddered profoundly and began to feel his way along the wall. Momentarily he expected to encounter the limits of his prison, but after a while he came to the conclusion that he was traveling down a corridor. He kept to the wall, fearful of pits of other traps, and was presently aware of something near him in the blackness. He could see nothing, but either his ears had caught a stealthy sound, or some subconscious sense warned him. He stopped short, his hair standing on end; as surely as he lived, he felt the presence of some living creature crouching in the darkness in front of him.

He thought his heart would stop when a voice hissed in a barbaric accent: "Murilo! Is it you?"

"Conan!" Limp from the reaction, the young nobleman groped in the darkness, and his hands encountered a pair of great naked shoulders.

"A good thing I recognized you," grunted the barbarian. "I was about to stick you like a fattened pig."

"Where are we, in Mitra's name?"

"In the pits under the Red Priest's house; but why—"

"What is the time?"

"Not long after midnight."

Murilo shook his head, trying to assemble his scattered wits.

"What are you doing here?" demanded the Cimmerian.

"I came to kill Nabonidus. I heard they had changed the guard at your prison—"

"They did," growled Conan. "I broke the new jailer's head and walked out. I would have been here hours agone, but I had some personal business to attend to. Well, shall we hunt for Nabonidus?"

Murilo shuddered. "Conan, we are in the house of the archfiend! I came seeking a human enemy; I found a hairy devil out of hell!"

Conan grunted uncertainly; fearless as a wounded tiger as far as human foes were concerned, he had all the superstitious dreads of the primitive.

"I gained access to the house," whispered Murilo, as if the darkness were full of listening ears. "In the outer gardens I found Nabonidus' dog mauled to death. Within the house I came upon Joka, the servant. His neck had been broken. Then I saw Nabonidus himself seated in his chair, clad in his accustomed garb. At first I thought he, too, was dead. I stole up to stab him. He rose and faced me. God!" The memory of that horror struck the young nobleman momentarily speechless as he re-lived that awful instant.

"Conan," he whispered, "it was no man that stood before me! In body and posture it was not unlike a man, but from the scarlet hood of the priest grinned a face of madness and nightmare! It was covered with black hair, from which small pig-like eyes glared redly; its nose was flat, with great flaring nostrils; its loose lips writhed back, disclosing huge yellow fangs, like the teeth of a dog. The hands that hung from the scarlet sleeves were misshapen and likewise covered with black hair. All this I saw in one glance, and then I was overcome with horror; my senses left me and I swooned."

"What then?" muttered the Cimmerian uneasily.

"I recovered consciousness only a short time ago; the monster must have thrown me into these pits. Conan, I have suspected that Nabonidus was not wholly human! He is a demon—a were-thing! By day he moves among humanity in the guise of men, and by night he takes on his true aspect."

"That's evident," answered Conan. "Everyone knows there are men who take the form of wolves at will. But why did he kill his servants?"

"Who can delve the mind of a devil?" replied Murilo. "Our present interest is in getting out of this place. Human weapons cannot harm a were-man. How did you get in here?"

"Through the sewer. I reckoned on the gardens being guarded. The sewers connect with a tunnel that lets into these pits. I thought to find some door leading up into the house unbolted."

"Then let us escape by the way you came!" exclaimed Murilo. "To the devil with it! Once out of this snake-den, we'll take our chances with the king's guardsmen and risk a flight from the city. Lead on!"

"Useless," grunted the Cimmerian. "The way to the sewers is barred. As I entered the tunnel, an iron grille crashed down from the roof. If I had not moved quicker than a flash of lightning, its spearheads would have pinned me to the floor like a worm. When I tried to lift it, it wouldn't move. An elephant couldn't shake it. Nor could anything bigger than a rabbit squirm between the bars."

Murilo cursed, an icy hand playing up and down his spine. He might have known Nabonidus would not leave any entrance into his house unguarded. Had Conan not possessed the steel-spring quickness of a wild thing, that falling portcullis would have skewered him. Doubtless his walking through the tunnel had sprung some hidden catch that released it from the roof. As it was, both were trapped living.

"There's but one thing to do," said Murilo, sweating profusely. "That's to search for some other exit; doubtless they're all set with traps, but we have no other choice."

The barbarian grunted agreement, and the companions began groping their way at random down the corridor. Even at that moment, something occurred to Murilo.

"How did you recognize me in this blackness?" he demanded.

"I smelled the perfume you put on your hair, when you came to my cell," answered Conan. "I smelled it again a while ago, when I was crouching in the dark and preparing to rip you open."

Murilo put a lock of his black hair to his nostrils; even so the scent was barely apparent to his civilized senses, and he realized how keen must be the organs of the barbarian.

Instinctively his hand went to his scabbard as they groped onward, and he cursed to find it empty. At that moment a faint glow became apparent ahead of them, and presently they came to a sharp bend in the corridor, about which the light filtered grayly. Together they peered around the corner, and Murilo, leaning against his companion, felt his huge frame stiffen. The young nobleman had also seen it—the body of a man, half naked, lying limply in the corridor beyond the bend, vaguely illumined by a radiance which seemed to emanate from a broad silver disk on the farther wall. A strange familiarity about the recumbent figure, which lay face down, stirred Murilo with inexplicable and monstrous conjectures. Motioning the Cimmerian to follow him, he stole forward and bent above the body. Overcoming a certain repugnance, he grasped it and turned it on its back. An incredulous oath escaped him; the Cimmerian grunted explosively.

"Nabonidus! The Red Priest!" ejaculated Murilo, his brain a dizzy vortex of whirling amazement. "Then who—what—?"

The priest groaned and stirred. With cat-like quickness Conan bent over him, poniard poised above his heart. Murilo caught his wrist.

"Wait! Don't kill him yet—"

"Why not?" demanded the Cimmerian. "He has cast off his were-guise, and sleeps. Will you awaken him to tear us to pieces?"

"No, wait!" urged Murilo, trying to collect his jumbled wits. "Look! He is not sleeping—see that great blue welt on his shaven temple? He has been knocked senseless. He may have been lying here for hours."

"I thought you swore you saw him in beastly shape in the house above," said Conan.

"I did! Or else—he's coming to! Keep back your blade, Conan; there is a mystery here even darker than I thought. I must have words with this priest, before we kill him."

Nabonidus lifted a hand vaguely to his bruised temple, mumbled, and opened his eyes. For an instant they were blank and empty of intelligence; then life came back to them with a jerk, and he sat up, staring at the companions. Whatever terrific jolt had temporarily addled his razor-keen brain, it was functioning with its accustomed vigor again. His eyes shot swiftly about him, then came back to rest on Murilo's face.

"You honor my poor house, young sir," he laughed coolly, glancing at the great figure that loomed behind the young nobleman's shoulder. "You have brought a bravo, I see. Was your sword not sufficient to sever the life of my humble self?"

"Enough of this," impatiently returned Murilo. "How long have you lain here?"

"A peculiar question to put to a man just recovering consciousness," answered the priest. "I do not know what time it now is. But it lacked an hour or so of midnight when I was set upon."

"Then who is it that masquerades in your own gown in the house above?" demanded Murilo.

"That will be Thak," answered Nabonidus, ruefully fingering his bruises. "Yes, that will be Thak. And in my own gown? The dog!"

Conan, who comprehended none of this, stirred restlessly, and growled something in his own tongue. Nabonidus glanced at him whimsically.

"Your bully's knife yearns for my heart, Murilo," he said. "I thought you might be wise enough to take my warning and leave the city."

"How was I to know that was to be granted me?" returned Murilo. "At any rate, my interests are here."

"You are in good company with that cutthroat," murmured Nabonidus. "I had suspected you for some time. That was why I caused that pallid court secretary to disappear. Before he died he told me many things, among others the name of the young nobleman who bribed him to filch state secrets, which the nobleman in turn sold to rival powers. Are you not ashamed of yourself, Murilo, you white-handed thief?"

"I have no more cause for shame than you, you vulture-hearted plunderer," answered Murilo promptly. "You exploit a whole kingdom for your personal greed; and, under the guise of disinterested statesmanship, you swindle the king, beggar the rich, oppress the poor, and sacrifice the whole future of the nation for your ruthless ambition. You are no more than a fat hog with his snout in the trough. You are a greater thief than I am. This Cimmerian is the most honest man of the three of us, because he steals and murders openly."

"Well, then, we are all rogues together," agreed Nabonidus equably. "And what now? My life?"

"When I saw the ear of the secretary that had disappeared, I knew I was doomed," said Murilo abruptly, "and I believed you would invoke the authority of the king. Was I right?"

"Quite so," answered the priest. "A court secretary is easy to do away with, but you are a bit too prominent. I had intended telling the king a jest about you in the morning."

"A jest that would have cost me my head," muttered Murilo. "Then the king is unaware of my foreign enterprises?"

"As yet," sighed Nabonidus. "And now, since I see your companion has his knife, I fear that jest will never be told."

"You should know how to get out of these rat-dens," said Murilo. "Suppose I agree to spare your life. Will you help us to escape, and swear to keep silent about my thievery?"

"When did a priest keep an oath?" complained Conan, comprehending the trend of the conversation. "Let me cut his throat; I want to see what color his blood is. They say in the Maze that his heart is black, so his blood must be black, too—"

"Be quiet," whispered Murilo. "If he does not show us the way out of these pits, we may rot here. Well, Nabonidus, what do you say?"

"What does a wolf with his leg in the trap say?" laughed the priest. "I am in your power and, if we are to escape, we must aid one another. I swear, if we survive this adventure, to forget all your shifty dealings. I swear by the soul of Mitra!"

"I am satisfied," muttered Murilo. "Even the Red Priest would not break that oath. Now to get out of here. My friend here entered by way of the tunnel, but a grille fell behind him and blocked the way. Can you cause it to be lifted?"

"Not from these pits," answered the priest. "The control lever is in the chamber above the tunnel. There is only one other way out of these pits, which I will show you. But tell me, how did you come here?"

Murilo told him in a few words, and Nabonidus nodded, rising stiffly. He limped down the corridor, which here widened into a sort of vast chamber, and approached the distant silver disk. As they advanced the light increased, though it never became anything but a dim shadowy radiance. Near the disk they saw a narrow stair leading upward.

"That is the other exit," said Nabonidus. "And I strongly doubt if the door at the head is bolted. But I have an idea that he who would go through that door had better cut his own throat first. Look into the disk."

What had seemed a silver plate was in reality a great mirror set in the wall. A confusing system of copper-like tubes jutted out from the wall above it, bending down toward it at right angles. Glancing into these tubes, Murilo saw a bewildering array of smaller mirrors. He turned his attention to the larger mirror in the wall, and ejaculated in amazement. Peering over his shoulder, Conan grunted.

They seemed to be looking through a broad window into a well-lighted chamber. There were broad mirrors on the walls, with velvet hangings between; there were silken couches, chairs of ebony and ivory, and curtained doorways leading off from the chamber. And before one doorway, which was not curtained, sat a bulky black object that contrasted grotesquely with the richness of the chamber.

Murilo felt his blood freeze again as he looked at the horror which seemed to be staring directly into his eyes. Involuntarily he recoiled from the mirror, while Conan thrust his head truculently forward, till his jaws almost touched the surface, growling some threat or defiance in his own barbaric tongue.

"In Mitra's name, Nabonidus," gasped Murilo, shaken, "what is it?"

"That is Thak," answered the priest, caressing his temple. "Some would call him an ape, but he is almost as different from a real ape as he is different from a real man. His people dwell far to the east, in the mountains that fringe the eastern frontiers of Zamora. There are not many of them; but, if they are not exterminated, I believe they will become human beings in perhaps a hundred thousand years. They are in the formative stage; they are neither apes, as their remote ancestors were, nor men, as their remote descendants may be. They dwell in the high crags of well-nigh inaccessible mountains, knowing nothing of fire or the making of shelter or garments, or the use of weapons. Yet they have a language of a sort, consisting mainly of grunts and clicks.

"I took Thak when he was a cub, and he learned what I taught him much more swiftly and thoroughly than any true animal could have done. He was at once bodyguard and servant. But I forgot that being partly a man, he could not be submerged into a mere shadow of myself, like a true animal. Apparently his semi-brain retained impressions of hate, resentment and some sort of bestial ambition of its own.

"At any rate, he struck when I least expected it. Last night he appeared to go suddenly mad. His actions had all the appearance of bestial insanity, yet I know that they must have been the result of long and careful planning.

"I heard a sound of fighting in the garden, and going to investigate—for I believed it was yourself, being dragged down by my watchdog—I saw Thak emerge from the shrubbery dripping with blood. Before I was aware of his intention, he sprang at me with an awful scream and struck me senseless. I remember no more, but can only surmise that, following some whim of his semi-human brain, he stripped me of my gown and cast me still living into the pits—for what reason, only the gods can guess. He must have killed the dog when he came from the garden, and after he struck me down, he evidently killed Joka, as you saw the man lying dead in the house. Joka would have come to my aid, even against Thak, who he always hated."

Murilo stared in the mirror at the creature which sat with such monstrous patience before the closed door. He shuddered at the sight of the great black hands, thickly grown with hair that was almost furlike. The body was thick, broad, and stooped. The unnaturally wide shoulders had burst the scarlet gown, and on these shoulders Murilo noted the same thick growth of black hair. The face peering from the scarlet hood was utterly bestial, and yet Murilo realized that Nabonidus spoke truth when he said that Thak was not wholly a beast. There was something in the red murky eyes, something in the creature's clumsy posture, something in the whole appearance of the thing that set it apart from the truly animal. That monstrous body housed a brain and soul that were just budding awfully into something vaguely human. Murilo stood aghast as he recognized a faint and hideous kinship between his kind and that squatting monstrosity, and he was nauseated by a fleeting realization of the abysses of bellowing bestiality up through which humanity had painfully toiled.

"Surely he sees us," muttered Conan. "Why does he not charge us? He could break this window with ease."

Murilo realized that Conan supposed the mirror to be a window through which they were looking.

"He does not see us," answered the priest. "We are looking into the chamber above us. That door that Thak is guarding is the one at the head of these stairs. It is simply an arrangement of mirrors. Do you see those mirrors on the walls? They transmit the reflection of the room into these tubes, down which other mirrors carry it to reflect it at last on an enlarged scale in this great mirror."

Murilo realized that the priest must be centuries ahead of his generation, to perfect such an invention; but Conan put it down to witchcraft and troubled his head no more about it.

"I constructed these pits for a place of refuge as well as a dungeon," the priest was saying. "There are times when I have taken refuge here and, through these mirrors, watched doom fall upon those who sought me with ill intent."

"But why is Thak watching that door?" demanded Murilo.

"He must have heard the falling of the grating in the tunnel. It is connected with bells in the chambers above. He knows someone is in the pits, and he is waiting for him to come up the stairs. Oh, he has learned well the lessons I taught him. He has seen what happened to men who come through that door, when I tugged at the rope that hangs on yonder wall, and he waits to mimic me."

"And while he waits, what are we to do?" demanded Murilo.

"There is naught we can do, except watch him. As long as he is in that chamber, we dare not ascend the stairs. He has the strength of a true gorilla and could easily tear us all to pieces. But he does not need to exert his muscles; if we open that door he has but to tug that rope, and blast us into eternity."

"How?"

"I bargained to help you escape," answered the priest; "not to betray my secrets."

Murilo started to reply, then stiffened suddenly. A stealthy hand had parted the curtains of one of the doorways. Between them appeared a dark face whose glittering eyes fixed menacingly on the squat form in the scarlet robe.

"Petreus!" hissed Nabonidus. "Mitra, what a gathering of vultures this night is!"

The face remained framed between the parted curtains. Over the intruder's shoulder other faces peered—dark, thin faces, alight with sinister eagerness.

"What do they here?" muttered Murilo, unconsciously lowering his voice, although he knew they could not hear him.

"Why, what would Petreus and his ardent young nationalists be doing in the house of the Red Priest?" laughed Nabonidus. "Look how eagerly they glare at the figure they think is their arch-enemy. They have fallen into your error; it should be amusing to watch their expressions when they are disillusioned."

Murilo did not reply. The whole affair had a distinctly unreal atmosphere. He felt as if he were watching the play of puppets, or as a disembodied ghost himself, impersonally viewing the actions of the living, his presence unseen and unsuspected.

He saw Petreus put his finger warningly to his lips, and nod to his fellow conspirators. The young nobleman could not tell if Thak was aware of the intruders. The ape-man's position had not changed, as he sat with his back toward the door through which the men were gliding.

"They had the same idea you had," Nabonidus was muttering at his ear. "Only their reasons were patriotic rather than selfish. Easy to gain access to my house, now that the dog is dead. Oh, what a chance to rid myself of their menace once and for all! If I were sitting where Thak sits—a leap to the wall—a tug on that rope—"

Petreus had placed one foot lightly over the threshold of the chamber; his fellows were at his heels, their daggers glinting dully. Suddenly, Thak rose and wheeled toward him. The unexpected horror of his appearance, where they had thought to behold the hated but familiar countenance of Nabonidus, wrought havoc with their nerves, as the same spectacle had wrought upon Murilo. With a shriek Petreus recoiled, carrying his companions backward with him. They stumbled and floundered over each other; and in that instant Thak, covering the distance in one prodigious, grotesque leap, caught and jerked powerfully at a thick velvet rope which hung near the doorway.

Instantly the curtains whipped back on either hand, leaving the door clear, and down across it something flashed with a peculiar silvery blur.

"He remembered!" Nabonidus was exulting. "The beast is half a man! He had seen the doom performed, and he remembered! Watch, now! Watch! Watch!"

Murilo saw that it was a panel of heavy glass that had fallen across the doorway. Through it he saw the pallid faces of the conspirators. Petreus, throwing out his hands as if to ward off a charge from Thak, encountered the transparent barrier, and from his gestures, said something to his companions. Now that the curtains were drawn back, the men in the pits could see all that took place in the chamber that contained the nationalists. Completely unnerved, these ran across the chamber toward the door by which they had apparently entered, only to halt suddenly, as if stopped by an invisible wall.

"The jerk of the rope sealed that chamber," laughed Nabonidus. "It is simple; the glass panels work in grooves in the doorways. Jerking the rope trips the spring that holds them. They slide down and lock in place, and can only be worked from outside. The glass is unbreakable; a man with a mallet could not shatter it. Ah!"

The trapped men were in a hysteria of fright; they ran wildly from one door to another, beating vainly at the crystal walls, shaking their fists wildly at the implacable black shape which squatted outside. Then one threw back his head, glared upward, and began to scream, to judge from the working of his lips, while he pointed toward the ceiling.

"The fall of the panels released the clouds of doom," said the Red Priest with a wild laugh. "The dust of the gray lotus, from the Swamps of the Dead, beyond the land of Khitai."

In the middle of the ceiling hung a cluster of gold buds; these had opened like the petals of a great carven rose, and from them billowed a gray mist that swiftly filled the chamber. Instantly the scene changed from one of hysteria to onc of madness and horror. The trapped men began to stagger; they ran in drunken circles. Froth dripped from their lips, which twisted as in awful laughter. Raging, they fell upon one another with daggers and teeth, slashing, tearing, slaying in a holocaust of madness. Murilo turned sick as he watched and was glad that he could not hear the screams and howls with which that doomed chamber must be ringing. Like pictures thrown on a screen, it was silent.

Outside the chamber of horror Thak was leaping up and down in brutish glee, tossing his long hairy arms on high. At Murilo's shoulder, Nabonidus was laughing like a fiend.

"Ah, a good stroke, Petreus! That fairly disemboweled him! Now one for you, my patriotic friend! So! They are all down, and the living tear the flesh of the dead with their slavering teeth."

Murilo shuddered. Behind him the Cimmerian swore softly in his uncouth tongue. Only death was to be seen in the chamber of the gray mist; torn, gashed, and mangled, the conspirators lay in a red heap, gaping mouths and blood-dabbled faces staring blankly upward through the slowly swirling eddies of gray.

Thak, stooping like a giant gnome, approached the wall where the rope hung, and gave it a peculiar sidewise pull.

"He is opening the farther door," said Nabonidus. "By Mitra, he is more of a human than even I had guessed! See, the mist swirls out of the chamber and is dissipated. He waits, to be safe. Now he raises the other panel. He is cautious—he knows the doom of the gray lotus, which brings madness and death. By Mitra!"

Murilo jerked about at the electric quality of the exclamation.

"Our one chance!" exclaimed Nabonidus. "If he leaves the chamber above for a few minutes, we will risk a dash up those stairs."

Suddenly tense, they watched the monster waddle through the doorway and vanish. With the lifting of the glass panel, the curtains had fallen again, hiding the chamber of death.

"We must chance it!" gasped Nabonidus, and Murilo saw perspiration break out on his face. "Perhaps he will be disposing of the bodies as he has seen me do. Quick! Follow me up those stairs!"

He ran toward the steps and up them with an agility that amazed Murilo. The young nobleman and the barbarian were close at his heels, and they heard his gusty sigh of relief as he threw open the door at the top of the stairs. They burst into the broad chamber they had seen mirrored below. Thak was nowhere to be seen.

"He's in that chamber with the corpses!" exclaimed Murilo. "Why not trap him there as he trapped them?"

"No, no!" gasped Nabonidus, an unaccustomed pallor tingeing his features. "We do not know that he is in there. He might emerge before we could reach the trap rope, anyway! Follow me into the corridor; I must reach my chamber and obtain weapons which will destroy him. This corridor is the only one opening from this chamber which is not set with a trap of some kind."

They followed him swiftly through a curtained doorway opposite the door of the death chamber and came into a corridor, into which various chambers opened. With fumbling haste Nabonidus began to try the doors on each side. They were locked, as was the door at the other end of the corridor.

"My god!" The Red Priest leaned against the wall, his skin ashen. "The doors are locked, and Thak took my keys from me. We are trapped, after all."

Murilo stared appalled to see the man in such a state of nerves, and Nabonidus pulled himself together with an effort.

"The beast has me in a panic," he said. "If you had seen him tear men as I have seen—well, Mitra aid us, but we must fight him now with what the gods have given us. Come!"

He led them back to the curtained doorway, and peered into the great chamber in time to see Thak emerge from the opposite doorway. It was apparent that the beast-man had suspected something. His small, close-set ears twitched; he glared angrily about him and, approaching the nearest doorway, tore aside the curtains to look behind them.

Nabonidus drew back, shaking like a leaf. He gripped Conan's shoulder. "Man, do you dare pit your knife against his fangs?"

The Cimmerian's eyes blazed in answer.

"Quick!" the Red Priest whispered, thrusting him behind the curtains, close against the wall. "As he will find us soon enough, we will draw him to us. As he rushes past you, sink your blade in his back if you can. You, Murilo, show yourself to him and then flee up the corridor. Mitra knows, we have no chance with him in hand-to-hand combat, but we are doomed anyway when he finds us."

Murilo felt his blood congeal in his veins, but he steeled himself and stepped outside the doorway. Instantly Thak, on the other side of the chamber, wheeled, glared, and charged with a thunderous roar. His scarlet hood had fallen back, revealing his black misshapen head; his black hands and red robe were splashed with a brighter red. He was like a crimson and black nightmare as he rushed across the chamber, fangs barred, his bowed legs hurtling his enormous body along at a terrifying gait.

Murilo turned and ran back into the corridor and, quick as he was, the shaggy horror was almost at his heels. Then as the monster rushed past the curtains, from among them catapulted a great form that struck full on the ape-man's shoulders, at the same instant driving the poniard into the brutish back. Thak screamed horribly as the impact knocked him off his feet, and the combatants hit the floor together. Instantly there began a whirl and thrash of limbs, the tearing and rending of a fiendish battle.

Murilo saw that the barbarian had locked his legs about the ape-man's torso and was striving to maintain his position on the monster's back while he butchered it with his poniard. Thak, on the other hand, was striving to dislodge his clinging foe, to drag him around within reach of the giant fangs that gaped for his flesh. In a whirlwind of blows and scarlet tatters they rolled along the corridor, revolving so swiftly that Murilo dared not use the chair he had caught up, lest he strike the Cimmerian. And he saw that in spite of the handicap of Conan's first hold, and the voluminous robe that lashed and wrapped about the ape-man's limbs and body, Thak's giant strength was swiftly prevailing. Inexorably he was dragging the Cimmerian around in front of him. The ape-man had taken punishment enough to have killed a dozen men. Conan's poniard had sunk again and again into his torso, shoulders, and bull-like neck; he was streaming blood from a score of wounds; but, unless the blade quickly reached some absolutely vital spot, Thak's inhuman vitality would survive to finish the Cimmerian and, after him, Conan's companions.

Conan was fighting like a wild beast himself, in silence except for his gasps of effort. The black talons of the monster and the awful grasp of those misshapen hands ripped and tore at him, the grinning jaws gaped for his throat. Then Murilo, seeing an opening, sprang and swung the chair with all his power, and with force enough to have brained a human being. The chair glanced from Thak's slanted black skull; but the stunned monster momentarily relaxed his rending grasp, and in that instant Conan, gasping and streaming blood, plunged forward and sank his poniard to the hilt in the ape-man's heart.

With a convulsive shudder, the beast-man started from the floor, then sank limply back. His fierce eyes set and glazed, his thick limbs quivered and became rigid.

Conan staggered dizzily up, shaking the sweat and blood out of his eyes. Blood dripped from his poniard and fingers, and trickled in rivulets down his thighs, arms, and breast. Murilo caught at him to support him, but the barbarian shook him off impatiently.

"When I cannot stand alone, it will be time to die," he mumbled, through mashed lips. "But I'd like a flagon of wine."

Nabonidus was staring down at the still figure as if he could not believe his own eyes. Black, hairy, abhorrent, the monster lay, grotesque in the tatters of the scarlet robe; yet more human than bestial, even so, and possessed somehow of a vague and terrible pathos.

Even the Cimmerian sensed this, for he panted: "I have slain a man tonight, not a beast. I will count him among the chiefs whose souls I've sent into the dark, and my women will sing of him."

Nabonidus stooped and picked up a bunch of keys on a golden chain. They had fallen from the ape-man's girdle during the battle. Motioning his companions to follow him, he led them to a chamber, unlocked the door, and led the way inside. It was illumined like the others. The Red Priest took a vessel of wine from a table and filled crystal beakers. As his companions drank thirstily, he murmured: "What a night! It is nearly dawn, now. What of you, my friends?"

"I'll dress Conan's hurts, if you will fetch me bandages and the like," said Murilo, and Nabonidus nodded, and moved toward the door that led into the corridor. Something about his bowed head caused Murilo to watch him sharply. At the door the Red Priest wheeled suddenly. His face had undergone a transformation. His eyes gleamed with his old fire, his lips laughed soundlessly.

"Rogues together!" his voice rang with its accustomed mockery. "But not fools together. You are the fool, Murilo!"

"What do you mean?" The young nobleman started forward.

"Back!" Nabonidus' voice cracked like a whip. "Another step and I will blast you!"

Murilo's blood turned cold as he saw that the Red Priest's hand grasped a thick velvet rope, which hung among the curtains just outside the door.

"What treachery is this?" cried Murilo. "You swore—"

"I swore I would not tell the king a jest concerning you! I did not swear not to take matters into my own hands if I could. Do you think I would pass up such an opportunity? Under ordinary circumstances I would not dare to kill you myself, without sanction of the king, but now none will ever know. You will go into the acid vats along with Thak and the nationalist fools, and none will be the wiser. What a night this has been for me! If I have lost some valuable servants, I have nevertheless rid myself of various dangerous enemies. Stand back! I am over the threshold, and you cannot possibly reach me before I tug this cord and send you to Hell. Not the gray lotus, this time, but something just as effective. Nearly every chamber in my house is a trap. And so, Murilo, fool that you are—"

Too quickly for the sight to follow, Conan caught up a stool and hurled it. Nabonidus instinctively threw up his arm with a cry, but not in time. The missile crunched against his head, and the Red Priest swayed and fell facedown in a slowly widening pool of dark crimson.

"His blood was red, after all," grunted Conan.

Murilo raked back his sweat-plastered hair with a shaky hand as he leaned against the table, weak from the reaction of relief.

"It is dawn," he said. "Let us get out of here, before we fall afoul of some other doom. If we can climb the outer wall without being seen, we shall not be connected with this night's work. Let the police write their own explanation."

He glanced at the body of the Red Priest where it lay etched in crimson, and shrugged his shoulders.

"He was the fool, after all; had he not paused to taunt us, he could have trapped us easily."

"Well," said the Cimmerian tranquilly, "he's traveled the road all rogues must walk at last. I'd like to loot the house, but I suppose we'd best go."

As they emerged from the dimness of the dawn-whitened garden, Murilo said: "The Red Priest has gone into the dark, so my road is clear in the city, and I have nothing to fear. But what of you? There is still the matter of that priest in the Maze, and—"

"I'm tired of this city anyway," grinned the Cimmerian. "You mentioned a horse waiting at the Rats' Den. I'm curious to see how fast that horse can carry me into another kingdom. There's many a highway I want to travel before I walk the road Nabonidus walked this night."

THE TOWER OF THE ELEPHANT

ROBERT E. HOWARD

I

Torches flared murkily on the revels in the Maul, where the thieves of the east held carnival by night. In the Maul they could carouse and roar as they liked, for honest people shunned the quarters, and watchmen, well paid with stained coins, did not interfere with their sport. Along the crooked, unpaved streets with their heaps of refuse and sloppy puddles, drunken roisterers staggered, roaring. Steel glinted in the shadows where wolf preyed on wolf, and from the darkness rose the shrill laughter of women and the sounds of scufflings and strugglings. Torchlight licked luridly from broken windows and wide-thrown doors, and out of those doors, stale smells of wine and rank, sweaty bodies, clamor of drinking-jacks and fists hammered on rough tables, snatches of obscene songs, rushed like a blow in the face.

In one of these dens merriment thundered to the low smoke-stained roof, where rascals gathered in every stage of rags and tatters—furtive cut-purses, leering kidnappers, quick-fingered thieves, swaggering bravoes with their wenches, strident-voiced women clad in tawdry finery. Native rogues were the dominant element—dark-skinned, dark-eyed Zamorians, with daggers at their girdles and guile in their hearts. But there were wolves of half a dozen outland nations there as well. There was a giant Hyperborean renegade, taciturn, dangerous, with a broadsword strapped to his great gaunt frame—for men wore steel openly in the Maul. There was a Shemitish counterfeiter, with his hook nose and curled blueblack beard. There was a bold-eyed Brythunian wench, sitting on the knee of a tawny-haired Gunderman—a wandering mercenary soldier, a deserter from some defeated army. And the fat, gross rogue whose bawdy jests were causing all the shouts of mirth was a professional kidnapper come up from distant Koth to teach woman-stealing to Zamorians who were born with more knowledge of the art than he could ever attain.

This man halted in his description of an intended victim's charms, and thrust his muzzle into a huge tankard of frothing ale. Then, blowing the foam from his fat lips, he said, "By Bel, god of all thieves, I'll show them how to steal wenches: I'll have her over the Zamorian border before dawn, and there'll be a caravan waiting to receive her. Three hundred pieces of silver, a count of Ophir promised me for a sleek young Brythunian of the better class. It took me weeks, wandering among the border cities as a beggar, to find one I knew would suit. And is she a pretty baggage!"

He blew a slobbery kiss in the air.

"I know lords in Shem who would trade the secret of the Elephant Tower for her," he said, returning to his ale.

A touch on his tunic sleeve made him turn his head, scowling at the interruption. He saw a tall, strongly made youth standing beside him. This person was as much out of place in that den as a gray wolf among mangy rats of the gutters. His cheap tunic could not conceal the hard, rangy lines of his powerful frame, the broad, heavy shoulders, the massive chest, lean waist, and heavy arms. His skin was brown from outland suns, his eyes blue and smoldering; a shock of tousled black hair crowned his broad forehead. From his girdle hung a sword in a worn leather scabbard.

The Kothian involuntarily drew back; for the man was not one of any civilized race he knew.

"You spoke of the Elephant Tower," said the stranger, speaking Zamorian with an alien accent. "I've heard much of this tower; what is its secret?"

The fellow's attitude did not seem threatening, and the Kothian's courage was bolstered up by the ale, and the evident approval of his audience. He swelled with self-importance.

"The secret of the Elephant Tower?" he exclaimed. "Why, any fool knows that Yara the priest dwells there with the great jewel men call the Elephant's Heart, that is the secret of his magic."

The barbarian digested this for a space.

"I have seen this tower," he said. "It is set in a great garden above the level of the city, surrounded by high walls. I have seen no guards. The walls would be easy to climb. Why has not somebody stolen this secret gem?"

The Kothian stared wide-mouthed at the other's simplicity, then burst into a roar of derisive mirth, in which the others joined.

"Harken to this heathen!" he bellowed. "He would steal the jewel of Yara! Harken, fellow," he said, turning portentously to the other, "I suppose you are some sort of a northern barbarian—"

"I am a Cimmerian," the outlander answered, in no friendly tone. The reply and the manner of it meant little to the Kothian; of a kingdom that lay far to the south, on the borders of Shem, he knew only vaguely of the northern races.

"Then give ear and learn wisdom, fellow," said he, pointing his drinking jack at the discomfited youth. "Know that in Zamora, and more especially in this city, there are more bold thieves than anywhere else in the world, even Koth. If mortal man could have stolen the gem, be sure it would have been filched long ago. You speak of climbing the walls, but once having climbed, you would quickly wish yourself back again. There are no guards in the gardens at night for a very good reason—that is, no human guards. But in the watch-chamber, in the lower part of the tower, are armed men, and even if you passed those who roam the gardens by night, you must still pass through the soldiers, for the gem is kept somewhere in the tower above."

"But if a man could pass through the gardens," argued the Cimmerian, "why could he not come at the gem through the upper part of the tower and thus avoid the soldiers?"

Again the Kothian gaped at him.

"Listen to him!" he shouted jeeringly. "The barbarian is an eagle who would fly to the jeweled rim of the tower, which is only a hundred and fifty feet above the earth, with rounded sides slicker than polished glass!"

The Cimmerian glared about, embarrassed at the roar of mocking laughter that greeted this remark. He saw no particular humor in it, and was too new to civilization to understand its discourtesies. Civilized men are more discourteous than savages because they know they can be impolite without having their skulls split, as a general thing. He was bewildered and chagrined, and doubtless would have slunk away, abashed, but the Kothian chose to goad him further.

"Come, come!" he shouted. "Tell these poor fellows, who have only been thieves since before you were spawned, tell them how you would steal the gem!"

"There is always a way, if the desire be coupled with courage," answered the Cimmerian shortly, nettled.

The Kothian chose to take this as a personal slur. His face grew purple with anger.

"What!" he roared. "You dare tell us our business, and intimate that we are cowards? Get along; get out of my sight!" And he pushed the Cimmerian violently.

"Will you mock me and then lay hands on me?" grated the barbarian, his quick rage leaping up; and he returned the push with an open-handed blow that knocked his tormenter back against the rude-hewn table. Ale splashed over the jack's lip, and the Kothian roared in fury, dragging at his sword.

"Heathen dog!" he bellowed. "I'll have your heart for that!"

Steel flashed and the throng surged wildly back out of the way. In their flight they knocked over the single candle and the den was plunged into darkness, broken by the crash of upset benches, drum of flying feet, shouts, oaths of people tumbling over one another and a single strident yell of agony that cut the din like a knife. When a candle was relighted, most of the guests had gone out by doors and broken windows, and the rest huddled behind stacks of wine kegs and under tables. The barbarian was gone; the center of the room was deserted except for the gashed body of the Kothian. The Cimmerian, with the unerring instinct of the barbarian, had killed his man in the darkness and confusion.

II

The lurid lights and drunken revelry fell away behind the Cimmerian. He had discarded his torn tunic, and walked through the night naked except for a loincloth and his high-strapped sandals. He moved with the supple ease of a great tiger, his steely muscles rippling under his brown skin.

He had entered the part of the city reserved for the temples. On all sides of him they glittered white in the starlight—snowy marble pillars and golden domes and silver arches, shrines of Zamora's myriad strange gods. He did not trouble his head about them; he knew that Zamora's religion, like all things of a civilized, long-settled people, was intricate and complex, and had lost most of the pristine essence in a maze of formulas and rituals. He had squatted for hours in the courtyards of the philosophers, listening to the arguments of theologians and teachers, and come away in a haze of bewilderment, sure of only one thing, and that, that they were all touched in the head.

His gods were simple and understandable; Crom was their chief, and he lived on a great mountain, whence he sent forth dooms and death. It was useless to call on Crom, because he was a gloomy, savage god and he hated weaklings. But he gave a man courage at birth, and the will and might to kill his enemies, which, in the Cimmerian's mind, was all any god should be expected to do.

His sandaled feet made no sound on the gleaming pave. No watchmen passed, for even the thieves of the Maul shunned the temples, where strange dooms had been known to fall on violators. Ahead of him he saw, looming against the sky, the Tower of the Elephant. He mused, wondering why it was so named. No one seemed to know. He had never seen an elephant, but he vaguely understood that it was a monstrous animal, with a tail in front as well as behind. This a wandering Shemite had told him, swearing that he had seen such beasts by the thousands in the country of the Hyrkanians; but all men knew what liars were the men of Shem. At any rate, there were no elephants in Zamora.

The shimmering shaft of the tower rose frostily in the stars. In the sunlight it shone so dazzlingly that few could bear its glare, and men said it was built of silver. It was round, a slim perfect cylinder, a hundred and fifty feet in height, and its rim glittered in the starlight with the great jewels which crusted it. The tower stood among the waving exotic trees of a garden raised high above the general level of the city. A high wall enclosed this garden, and outside the wall was a lower level, likewise enclosed by a wall. No lights shone forth; there seemed to be no windows in the tower—at least not above the level of the inner wall. Only the gems high above sparkled frostily in the starlight.

Shrubbery grew thick outside the lower or outer wall. The Cimmerian crept close and stood beside the barrier, measuring it with his eye. It was high, but he could leap and catch the coping with his fingers. Then it would be child's play to swing himself up and over, and he did not doubt that he could pass the inner wall in the same manner. But he hesitated at the thought of the strange perils which were said to await within. These people were strange and mysterious to him; they were not of his kind—not even of the same blood as the more westerly Brythunians, Nemedians, Kothians and Aquilonians, whose civilized mysteries had awed him in times past. The people of Zamora were very ancient and, from what he had seen of them, very evil.

He thought of Yara, the high priest, who worked strange dooms from this jeweled tower, and the Cimmerian's hair prickled as he remembered a tale told by a drunken page of the court—how Yara had laughed in the face of a hostile prince, and held up a glowing, evil gem before him, and how rays shot blindingly from that unholy jewel to envelop the prince, who screamed and fell down and shrank to a withered blackened lump that changed to a black spider which scampered wildly about the chamber until Yara set his heel upon it.

Yara came not often from his tower of magic, and always to work evil on some man or some nation. The king of Zamora feared him more than he feared death, and kept himself drunk all the time because that fear was more than he could endure sober. Yara was very old—centuries old, men said, and added that he would live forever because of the magic of his gem, which men called the Heart of the Elephant, for no better reason than they named his hold the Elephant's Tower.

The Cimmerian, engrossed in these thoughts, shrank quickly against the wall. Within the garden someone was passing, who walked with a measured stride. The listener heard the clink of steel. So after all a guard did pace those gardens. The Cimmerian waited, expected to hear him pass again on the next round, but silence rested over the mysterious gardens.

At last curiosity overcame him. Leaping lightly he grasped the wall and swung himself up to the top with one arm. Lying flat on the broad coping, he looked down into the wide space between the walls. No shrubbery grew near him, though he saw some carefully trimmed bushes near the inner wall. The starlight fell on the even sward and somewhere a fountain tinkled.

The Cimmerian cautiously lowered himself down on the inside and drew his sword, staring about him. He was shaken by the nervousness of the wild at standing thus unprotected in the naked starlight, and he moved lightly around the curve of the wall, hugging its shadow, until he was even with the shrubbery he had noticed. Then he ran quickly toward it, crouching low, and almost tripped over a form that lay crumpled near the edges of the bushes.

A quick look to right and left showed him no enemy in sight at least, and he bent close to investigate. His keen eyes, even in the dim starlight, showed him a strongly built man in the silvered armor and crested helmet of the Zamorian royal guard. A shield and a spear lay near him and it took but an instant's examination to show that he had been strangled. The barbarian glanced about uneasily. He knew that this man must be the guard he had heard pass his hiding place by the wall. Only a short time had passed, yet in that interval nameless hands had reached out of the dark and choked out the soldier's life.

Straining his eyes in the gloom, he saw a hint of motion through the shrubs near the wall. Thither he glided, gripping his sword. He made no more noise than a panther stealing through the night, yet the man he was stalking heard. The Cimmerian had a dim glimpse of a huge bulk close to the wall, felt relief that it was at least human; then the fellow wheeled quickly with a gasp that sounded like panic, made the first motion of a forward plunge, hands clutching, then recoiled as the Cimmerian's blade caught the starlight. For a tense instant neither spoke, standing ready for anything.

"You are no soldier," hissed the stranger at last. "You are a thief like myself."

"And who are you?" asked the Cimmerian in a suspicious whisper.

"Taurus of Nemedia."

The Cimmerian lowered his sword.

"I've heard of you. Men call you a prince of thieves."

A low laugh answered him. Taurus was tall as the Cimmerian, and heavier; he was big-bellied and fat, but his every movement betokened a subtle dynamic magnetism, which was reflected in the keen eyes that glinted vitally, even in the starlight. He was barefooted and carried a coil of what looked like a thin, strong rope, knotted at regular intervals.

"Who are you?" he whispered.

"Conan, a Cimmerian," answered the other. "I came seeking a way to steal Yara's jewel, that men call the Elephant's Heart."

Conan sensed the man's great belly shaking in laughter, but it was not derisive. "By Bel, god of thieves!" hissed Taurus. "I had thought only myself had courage to attempt that poaching. These Zamorians call themselves thieves—bah! Conan, I like your grit. I never shared an adventure with anyone but, by Bel, we'll attempt this together if you're willing."

"Then you are after the gem, too?"

"What else? I've had my plans laid for months, but you, I think, have acted on sudden impulse, my friend."

"You killed the soldier?"

"Of course. I slid over the wall when he was on the other side of the garden. I hid in the bushes; he heard me, or thought he heard something. When he came blundering over, it was no trick at all to get behind him and suddenly grip his neck and choke out his fool's life. He was like most men, half-blind in the dark. A good thief should have eyes like a cat."

"You made one mistake," said Conan.

Taurus' eyes flashed angrily.

"I? I, a mistake? Impossible!"

"You should have dragged the body into the bushes."

"Said the novice to the master of the art. They will not change the guard until past midnight. Should any come searching for him now and find his body, they would flee at once to Yara, bellowing the news, and give us time to escape. Were they not to find it, they'd go beating up the bushes and catch us like rats in a trap."

"You are right," agreed Conan.

"So. Now attend. We waste time in this cursed discussion. There are no guards in the inner garden—human guards, I mean, though there are sentinels even more deadly. It was their presence which baffled me for so long, but I finally discovered a way to circumvent them."

"What of the soldiers in the lower part of the tower?"

"Old Yara dwells in the chambers above. By that route we will come—and go, I hope. Never mind asking me how. I have arranged a way. We'll steal down through the top of the tower and strangle old Yara before he can cast any of his accursed spells on us. At least we'll try; it's the chance of being turned into a spider or a toad, against the wealth and power of the world. All good thieves must know how to take risks."

"I'll go as far as any man," said Conan, slipping off his sandals.

"Then follow me." And turning, Taurus leaped up, caught the wall and drew himself up. The man's suppleness was amazing, considering his bulk; he seemed almost to glide up over the edge of the coping. Conan followed him, and lying flat on the broad top, they spoke in wary whispers.

"I see no light," Conan muttered. The lower part of the tower seemed much like that portion visible from outside the garden—a perfect, gleaming cylinder, with no apparent openings.

"There are cleverly constructed doors and windows," answered Taurus, "but they are closed. The soldiers breathe air that comes from above."

The garden was a vague pool of shadows, where feathery bushes and low-spreading trees waved darkly in the starlight. Conan's wary soul felt the aura of waiting menace that brooded over it. He felt the burning glare of unseen eyes, and he caught a subtle scent that made the short hairs on his neck instinctively bristle as a hunting dog bristles at the scent of an ancient enemy.

"Follow me," whispered Taurus, "keep behind me, as you value your life."

Taking what looked like a copper tube from his girdle, the Nemedian dropped lightly to the sward inside the wall. Conan was close behind him, sword ready, but Taurus pushed him back, close to the wall, and showed no inclination to advance himself. His whole attitude was of tense expectancy, and his gaze, like Conan's, was fixed on the shadowy mass of shrubbery a few yards away. This shrubbery was shaken, although the breeze had died down. Then two great eyes blazed from the waving shadows and behind them other sparks of fire glinted in the darkness.

"Lions!" muttered Conan.

"Aye. By day they are kept in subterranean caverns below the tower. That's why there are no guards in this garden."

Conan counted the eyes rapidly.

"Five in sight; maybe more back in the bushes. They'll charge in a moment—"

"Be silent!" hissed Taurus, and he moved out from the wall cautiously, as if treading on razors, lifting the slender tube. Low rumblings rose from the shadows and the blazing eyes moved forward. Conan could sense the great slavering jaws, the tufted tails lashing tawny sides. The air grew tense—the Cimmerian gripped his sword, expecting the charge and the irresistible hurtling of giant bodies. Then Taurus brought the mouth of the tube to his lips and blew powerfully. A long jet of yellowish powder shot from the other end of the tube and billowed out instantly in a thick green-yellow cloud that settled over the shrubbery, blotting out the glaring eyes.

Taurus ran back hastily to the wall. Conan glared without understanding. The thick cloud hid the shrubbery, and from it no sound came.

"What is that mist?" the Cimmerian asked uneasily.

"Death!" hissed the Nemedian. "If a wind springs up and blows it back upon us, we must flee over the wall. But no, the wind is still, and now it is dissipating. Wait until it vanishes entirely. To breathe it is death."

Presently only yellowish shreds hung ghostily in the air; then they were gone, and Taurus motioned his companion forward. They stole toward the bushes, and Conan gasped. Stretched out in the shadows lay five great tawny shapes, the fire of their grim eyes dimmed forever. A sweetish cloying scent lingered in the atmosphere.

"They died without a sound!" muttered the Cimmerian. "Taurus, what was that powder?"

"It was made from the black lotus, whose blossoms wave in the lost jungles of Khitai, where only the yellow-skulled priests of Yun dwell. Those blossoms strike dead any who smell of them."

Conan knelt beside the great forms, assuring himself that they were indeed beyond power of harm. He shook his head; the magic of the exotic lands was mysterious and terrible to the barbarians of the north.

"Why can you not slay the soldiers in the tower in the same way?" he asked.

"Because that was all the powder I possessed. The obtaining of it was a feat which in itself was enough to make me famous among the thieves of the world. I stole it out of a caravan bound for Stygia, and I lifted it, in its cloth-of-gold bag, out of the coils of the great serpent which guarded it, without awaking him. But come, in Bel's name! Are we to waste the night in discussion?"

They glided through the shrubbery to the gleaming foot of the tower, and there, with a motion enjoining silence, Taurus unwound his knotted cord, on one end of which was a strong steel hook. Conan saw his plan, and asked no questions as the Nemedian gripped the line a short distance below the hook, and began to swing it about his head. Conan laid his ear to the smooth wall and listened, but could hear nothing. Evidently the soldiers within did not suspect the presence of intruders, who had made no more sound than the night wind blowing through the trees. But a strange nervousness was on the barbarian; perhaps it was the lion-smell which was over everything.

Taurus threw the line with a smooth, ripping motion of his mighty arm. The hook curved upward and inward in a peculiar manner, hard to describe, and vanished over the jeweled rim. It apparently caught firmly, for cautious jerking and then hard pulling did not result in any slipping or giving.

"Luck the first cast," murmured Taurus. "I—"

It was Conan's savage instinct which made him wheel suddenly; for the death that was upon them made no sound. A fleeting glimpse showed the Cimmerian the giant tawny shape, rearing upright against the stars, towering over him for the death-stroke. No civilized man could have moved half so quickly as the barbarian moved. His sword flashed frostily in the starlight with every ounce of desperate nerve and thew behind it, and man and beast went down together.

Cursing incoherently beneath his breath, Taurus bent above the mass, and saw his companion's limbs move as he strove to drag himself from under the great weight that lay limply upon him. A glance showed the startled Nemedian that the lion was dead, its slanting skull split in half. He laid hold of the carcass and, by his aid, Conan thrust it aside and clambered up, still gripping his dripping sword.

"Are you hurt, man?" gasped Taurus, still bewildered by the stunning swiftness of that touch-and-go episode.

"No, by Crom!" answered the barbarian. "But that was as close a call as I've had in a life no-ways tame. Why did not the cursed beast roar as he charged?"

"All things are strange in this garden," said Taurus. "The lions strike silently—and so do other deaths. But come—little sound was made in that slaying, but the soldiers might have heard, if they are not asleep or drunk. That beast was in some other part of the garden and escaped the death of the flowers, but surely there are no more. We must climb this cord—little need to ask a Cimmerian if he can."

"If it will bear my weight," grunted Conan, cleansing his sword on the grass. "It will bear thrice my own," answered Taurus. "It was woven from the tresses of dead women, which I took from their tombs at midnight, and steeped in the deadly wine of the upas tree, to give it strength. I will go first—then follow me closely."

The Nemedian gripped the rope and crooking a knee about it, began the ascent; he went up like a cat, belying the apparent clumsiness of his bulk. The Cimmerian followed. The cord swayed and turned on itself, but the climbers were not hindered; both had made more difficult climbs before. The jeweled rim glittered high above them, jutting out from the perpendicular of the wall, so that the cord hung perhaps a foot from the side of the tower—a fact which added greatly to the ease of the ascent.

Up and up they went, silently, the lights of the city spreading out further and further to their sight as they climbed, the stars above them more and more dimmed by the glitter of the jewels along the rim. Now Taurus reached up a hand and gripped the rim itself, pulling himself up and over. Conan paused a moment on the very edge, fascinated by the great frosty jewels whose gleams dazzled his eyes—diamonds, rubies, emeralds, sapphires, turquoises, moonstones, set thick as stars in the shimmering silver. At a distance their different gleams had seemed to merge into a pulsing white glare; but now, at close range, they shimmered with a million rainbow tints and lights, hypnotizing him with their scintillations.

"There is a fabulous fortune here, Taurus," he whispered; but the Nemedian answered impatiently, "Come on! If we secure the Heart, these and all other things shall be ours."

Conan climbed over the sparkling rim. The level of the tower's top was some feet below the gemmed ledge. It was flat, composed of some dark blue substance, set with gold that caught the starlight, so that the whole looked like a wide sapphire flecked with shining gold dust. Across from the point where they had entered there seemed to be a sort of chamber, built upon the roof. It was of the same silvery material as the walls of the tower, adorned with designs worked in smaller gems; its single door was of gold, its surface cut in scales, and crusted with jewels that gleamed like ice.

Conan cast a glance at the pulsing ocean of lights which spread far below them, then glanced at Taurus. The Nemedian was drawing up his cord and coiling it. He showed Conan where the hook had caught—a fraction of an inch of the point had sunk under a great blazing jewel on the inner side of the rim.

"Luck was with us again," he muttered. "One would think that our combined weight would have torn that stone out. Follow me; the real risks of the venture begin now. We are in the serpent's lair, and we know not where he lies hidden."

Like stalking tigers they crept across the darkly gleaming floor and halted outside the sparkling door. With a deft and cautious hand Taurus tried it.

It gave without resistance, and the companions looked in, tensed for anything. Over the Nemedian's shoulder Conan had a glimpse of a glittering chamber, the walls, ceiling and floor of which were crusted with great white jewels which lighted it brightly, and which seemed its only illumination. It seemed empty of life.

"Before we cut off our last retreat," hissed Taurus, "go you to the rim and look over on all sides; if you see any soldiers moving in the gardens, or anything suspicious, return and tell me. I will await you within this chamber."

Conan saw scant reason in this, and a faint suspicion of his companion touched his wary soul, but he did as Taurus requested. As he turned away, the Nemedian slipped inside the door and drew it shut behind him. Conan crept about the rim of the tower, returning to his starting-point without having seen any suspicious movement in the vaguely waving sea of leaves below. He turned toward the door—suddenly from within the chamber there sounded a strangled cry.

The Cimmerian leaped forward, electrified—the gleaming door swung open and Taurus stood framed in the cold blaze behind him. He swayed and his lips parted, but only a dry rattle burst from his throat. Catching at the golden door for support, he lurched out upon the roof, then fell headlong, clutching at his throat. The door swung to behind him.

Conan, crouching like a panther at bay, saw nothing in the room behind the stricken Nemedian, in the brief instant the door was partly open—unless it was not a trick of the light which made it seem as if a shadow darted across the gleaming floor. Nothing followed Taurus out on the roof, and Conan bent above the man.

The Nemedian stared up with dilated, glazing eyes, that somehow held a terrible bewilderment. His hands clawed at his throat, his lips slobbered and gurgled; then suddenly he stiffened, and the astounded Cimmerian knew that he was dead. And he felt that Taurus had died without knowing what manner of death had stricken him. Conan glared bewilderedly at the cryptic golden door. In that empty room, with its glittering jeweled walls, death had come to the prince of thieves as swiftly and mysteriously as he had dealt doom to the lions in the gardens below.

Gingerly the barbarian ran his hands over the man's half-naked body, seeking a wound. But the only marks of violence were between his shoulders, high up near the base of his bull-neck—three small wounds, which looked as if three nails had been driven deep in the flesh and withdrawn. The edges of these wounds were black, and a faint smell as of putrefaction was evident. Poisoned darts? thought Conan—but in that case the missiles should be still in the wounds.

Cautiously he stole toward the golden door, pushed it open, and looked inside. The chamber lay empty, bathed in the cold, pulsing glow of the myriad jewels. In the very center of the ceiling he idly noted a curious design—a black eight-sided pattern, in the center of which four gems glittered with a red flame unlike the white blaze of the other jewels. Across the room there was another door, like the one in which he stood, except that it was not carved in the scale pattern. Was it from that door that death had come?—And having struck down its victim, had it retreated by the same way?

Closing the door behind him, the Cimmerian advanced into the chamber. His bare feet made no sound on the crystal floor. There were no chairs or tables in the chamber, only three or four silken couches, embroidered with gold and worked in strange serpentine designs, and several silver-bound mahogany chests. Some were sealed with heavy golden locks; others lay open, their carven lids thrown back, revealing heaps of jewels in a careless riot of splendor to the Cimmerian's astounded eyes. Conan swore beneath his breath; already he had looked upon more wealth that night than he had ever dreamed existed in all the world, and he grew dizzy thinking of what must be the value of the jewel he sought.

He was in the center of the room now, going stooped forward, head thrust out warily, sword advanced, when again death struck at him soundlessly. A flying shadow that swept across the gleaming floor was his only warning, and his instinctive sidelong leap all that saved his life. He had a flashing glimpse of a hairy black horror that swung past him with a clashing of frothing fangs, and something splashed on his bare shoulder that burned like drops of liquid hell-fire. Springing back, sword high, he saw the horror strike the floor, wheel and scuttle toward him with appalling speed—a gigantic black spider, such as men see only in nightmare dreams.

It was as large as a pig, and its eight thick hairy legs drove its ogreish body over the floor at headlong pace; its four evilly gleaming eyes shone with a horrible intelligence, and its fangs dripped venom that Conan knew, from the burning of his shoulder where only a few drops had splashed as the thing struck and missed, was laden with swift death. This was the killer that had dropped from its perch in the middle of the ceiling on a strand of its web, on the neck of the Nemedian. Fools that they were not to have suspected that the upper chambers would be guarded as well as the lower!

These thoughts flashed briefly through Conan's mind as the monster rushed. He leaped high, and it passed beneath him, wheeled and charged back. This time he evaded its rush with a sideways leap, and struck back like a cat. His sword severed one of the hairy legs, and again he barely saved himself as the monstrosity swerved at him, fangs clicking fiendishly. But the creature did not press the pursuit; turning, it scuttled across the crystal floor and ran up the wall to the ceiling, where it crouched for an instant, glaring down at him with its fiendish red eyes. Then without warning it launched itself through space, trailing a strand of slimy grayish stuff.

Conan stepped back to avoid the hurtling body—then ducked frantically, just in time to escape being snared by the flying web-rope. He saw the monster's intent and sprang toward the door, but it was quicker, and a sticky strand cast across the door made him a prisoner. He dared not try to cut it with his sword; he knew the stuff would cling to the blade, and before he could shake it loose, the fiend would be sinking its fangs into his back.

Then began a desperate game, the wits and quickness of the man matched against the fiendish craft and speed of the giant spider. It no longer scuttled across the floor in a direct charge, or swung its body through the air at him. It raced about the ceiling and the walls, seeking to snare him in the long loops of sticky gray web-strands, which it flung with a devilish accuracy. These strands were thick as ropes, and Conan knew that once they were coiled about him, his desperate strength would not be enough to tear him free before the monster struck.

All over the chamber went on that devil's dance, in utter silence except for the quick breathing of the man, the low scuff of his bare feet on the shining floor, the castanet rattle of the monstrosity's fangs. The gray strands lay in coils on the floor; they were looped along the walls; they overlaid the jewel chests and silken couches, and hung in dusky festoons from the jeweled ceiling. Conan's steel-trap quickness of eye and muscle had kept him untouched, though the sticky loops had passed him so close they rasped his naked hide. He knew he could not always avoid them; he not only had to watch the strands swinging from the ceiling, but to keep his eye on the floor, lest he trip in the coils that lay there. Sooner or later a gummy loop would writhe about him, python-like, and then, wrapped like a cocoon, he would lie at the monster's mercy.

The spider raced across the chamber floor, the gray rope waving out behind it. Conan leaped high, clearing a couch—with a quick wheel the fiend ran up the wall, and the strand, leaping off the floor like a live thing, whipped about the Cimmerian's ankle. He caught himself on his hands as he fell, jerking frantically at the web which held him like a pliant vise, or the coil of a python. The hairy devil was racing down the wall to complete its capture. Stung to frenzy, Conan caught up a jewel chest and hurled it with all his strength. It was a move the monster was not expecting. Full in the midst of the branching black legs the massive missile struck, smashing against the wall with a muffled sickening crunch. Blood and greenish slime spattered, and the shattered mass fell with the burst gem-chest to the floor. The crushed black body lay among the flaming riot of jewels that spilled over it; the hairy legs moved aimlessly, the dying eyes glittered redly among the twinkling gems.

Conan glared about, but no other horror appeared, and he set himself to working free of the web. The substance clung tenaciously to his ankle and his hands, but at last he was free and, taking up his sword, he picked his way among the gray coils and loops to the inner door. What horrors lay within he did not know. The Cimmerian's blood was up, and since he had come so far, and overcome so much peril, he was determined to go through to the grim finish of the adventure, whatever that might be. And he felt that the jewel he sought was not among the many so carelessly strewn about the gleaming chamber.

Stripping off the loops that fouled the inner door, he found that it, like the other, was not locked. He wondered if the soldiers below were still unaware of his presence. Well, he was high above their heads, and if tales were to be believed, they were used to strange noises in the tower above them—sinister sounds, and screams of agony and horror.

Yara was on his mind, and he was not altogether comfortable as he opened the golden door. But he saw only a flight of silver steps leading down, dimly lighted by what means he could not ascertain. Down these he went silently, gripping his sword. He heard no sound, and came presently to an ivory door, set with blood stones. He listened, but no sound came from within; only thin wisps of smoke drifted lazily from beneath the door, bearing a curious exotic odor unfamiliar to the Cimmerian. Below him the silver stair wound down to vanish in the dimness, and up that shadowy well no sound floated; he had an eery feeling that he was alone in a tower occupied only by ghosts and phantoms.

III

Cautiously he pressed against the ivory door and it swung silently inward. On the shimmering threshold Conan stared like a wolf in strange surroundings, ready to fight or flee on the instant. He was looking into a large chamber with a domed golden ceiling; the walls were of green jade, the floor of ivory, partly covered by thick rugs. Smoke and exotic scent of incense floated up from a brazier on a golden tripod, and behind it sat an idol on a sort of marble couch. Conan stared aghast; the image had the body of a man, naked and green in color; but the head was one of nightmare and madness. Too large for the human body, it had no attributes of humanity. Conan stared at the wide flaring ears, the curling proboscis, on either side of which stood white tusks tipped with round golden balls. The eyes were closed, as if in sleep.

This then, was the reason for the name, the Tower of the Elephant, for the head of the thing was much like that of the beasts described by the Shemitish wanderer. This was Yara's god; where then should the gem be, but concealed in the idol, since the stone was called the Elephant's Heart?

As Conan came forward, his eyes fixed on the motionless idol, the eyes of the thing opened suddenly! The Cimmerian froze in his tracks. It was no image—it was a living thing, and he was trapped in its chamber!

That he did not instantly explode in a burst of murderous frenzy is a fact that measures his horror, which paralyzed him where he stood. A civilized man in his position would have sought doubtful refuge in the conclusion that he was insane; it did not occur to the Cimmerian to doubt his senses. He knew he was face to face with a demon of the Elder World, and the realization robbed him of all his faculties except sight.

The trunk of the horror was lifted and quested about, the topaz eyes stared unseeingly, and Conan knew the monster was blind. With the thought came a thawing of his frozen nerves, and he began to back silently toward the door. But the creature heard. The sensitive trunk stretched toward him, and Conan's horror froze him again when the being spoke, in a strange, stammering voice that never changed its key or timbre. The Cimmerian knew that those jaws were never built or intended for human speech.

"Who is here? Have you come to torture me again, Yara? Will you never be done? Oh, Yag-kosha, is there no end to agony?"

Tears rolled from the sightless eyes, and Conan's gaze strayed to the limbs stretched on the marble couch. And he knew the monster would not rise to attack him. He knew the marks of the rack, and the searing brand of the flame, and tough-souled as he was, he stood aghast at the ruined deformities which his reason told him had once been limbs as comely as his own. And suddenly all fear and repulsion went from him, to be replaced by a great pity. What this monster was, Conan could not know, but the evidence of its sufferings was so terrible and pathetic that a strange aching sadness came over the Cimmerian, he knew not why. He only felt that he was looking upon a cosmic tragedy, and he shrank with shame, as if the guilt of a whole race were laid upon him.

"I am not Yara," he said. "I am only a thief. I will not harm you."

"Come near that I may touch you," the creature faltered, and Conan came near unfearingly, his sword hanging forgotten in his hand. The sensitive trunk came out and groped over his face and shoulders, as a blind man gropes, and its touch was light as a girl's hand.

"You are not of Yara's race of devils," sighed the creature. "The clean, lean fierceness of the wastelands marks you. I know your people from of old, whom I knew by another name in the long, long ago when another world lifted its jeweled spires to the stars. There is blood on your fingers."

"A spider in the chamber above and a lion in the garden," muttered Conan.

"You have slain a man too, this night," answered the other. "And there is death in the tower above. I feel; I know."

"Aye," muttered Conan. "The prince of all thieves lies there dead from the bite of a vermin."

"So—and so!" the strange inhuman voice rose in a sort of low chant. "A slaying in the tavern and a slaying on the roof—I know; I feel. And the third will make the magic of which not even Yara dreams—oh, magic of deliverance, green gods of Yag!"

Again tears fell as the tortured body was rocked to and fro in the grip of varied emotions. Conan looked on, bewildered.

Then the convulsions ceased; the soft, sightless eyes were turned toward the Cimmerian, the trunk beckoned.

"Oh man, listen," said the strange being. "I am foul and monstrous to you, am I not? Nay, do not answer; I know. But you would seem as strange to me, could I see you. There are many worlds besides this earth, and life takes many shapes. I am neither god nor demon, but flesh and blood like yourself, though the substance differ in part, and the form be cast in different mold.

"I am very old, oh man of the waste countries; long and long ago I came to this planet with others of my world, from the green planet Yag, which circles forever in the outer fringe of this universe. We swept through Space on mighty wings that drove us through the cosmos quicker than light, because we had warred with the kings of Yag and were defeated and outcast. But we could never return, for on earth our wings withered from our shoulders. Here we abode apart from earthly life. We fought the strange and terrible forms of life which then walked the earth, so that we became feared, and were not molested in the dim jungles of the east, where we had our abode.

"We saw men grow from the ape and build the shining cities of Valusia, Kamelia, Commoria, and their sisters. We saw them reel before the thrusts of the heathen Atlanteans and Picts and Lemurians. We saw the oceans rise and engulf Atlantis and Lemuria, and the isles of the Picts and the shining cities of civilization. We saw the survivors of Pictdom and Atlantis build their stone-age empires, and go down to ruin, locked in bloody wars. We saw the Picts sink into abysmal savagery, the Atlanteans into apedom again. We saw new savages drift southward in conquering waves from the Arctic Circle to build a new civilization, with new kingdoms called Nemedia, and Koth, and Aquilonia and their sisters. We saw your people rise under a new name from the jungles of the apes that had been Atlanteans. We saw the descendants of the Lemurians who had survived the cataclysm, rise again through savagery and ride westward, as Hyrkanians. And we saw this race of devils, survivors of the ancient civilization that was before Atlantis sank, come once more into culture and power—this accursed kingdom of Zamora.

"All this we saw, neither aiding nor hindering the immutable cosmic law, and one by one we died; for we of Yag are not immortal, though our lives are as the lives of planets and constellations. At last I alone was left, dreaming of old times among the ruined temples of jungle-lost Khitai, worshiped as a god by an ancient yellow-skinned race. Then came Yara, versed in dark knowledge handed down through the days of barbarism, since before Atlantis sank.

"First he sat at my feet and learned wisdom. But he was not satisfied with what I taught him, for it was white magic, and he wished evil lore, to enslave kings and glut a fiendish ambition. I would teach him none of the black secrets I had gained, through no wish of mine, through the eons.

"But his wisdom was deeper than I had guessed; with guile gotten among the dusky tombs of dark Stygia, he trapped me into divulging a secret I had not intended to bare; and turning my own power upon me, he enslaved me. Ah, gods of Yag, my cup has been bitter since that hour!

"He brought me up from the lost jungles of Khitai where the gray apes danced to the pipes of the yellow priests, and offerings of fruit and wine heaped my broken altars. No more was I a god to kindly jungle-folk—I was slave to a devil in human form."

Again tears stole from the unseeing eyes.

"He pent me in this tower, which at his command I built for him in a single night. By fire and rack he mastered me, and by strange unearthly tortures you would not understand. In agony I would long ago have taken my own life, if I could. But he kept me alive—mangled, blinded, and broken—to do his foul bidding. And for three hundred years I have done his bidding, from this marble couch, blackening my soul with cosmic sins, and staining my wisdom with crimes, because I had no other choice. Yet not all my ancient secrets has he wrested from me, and my last gift shall be the sorcery of the Blood and the Jewel.

"For I feel the end of time draw near. You are the hand of Fate. I beg of you, take the gem you will find on yonder altar."

Conan turned to the gold and ivory altar indicated, and took up a great round jewel, clear as crimson crystal; and he knew that this was the Heart of the Elephant.

"Now for the great magic, the mighty magic, such as earth has not seen before and shall not see again, through a million million of millenniums. By my life-blood I conjure it, by blood born on the green breast of Yag, dreaming far-poised in the great blue vastness of Space.

"Take your sword, man, and cut out my heart; then squeeze it so that the blood will flow over the red stone. Then go you down these stairs and enter the ebony chamber where Yara sits wrapped in lotus-dreams of evil. Speak his name and he will awaken. Then lay this gem before him, and say, 'Yag-kosha gives you a last gift and a last enchantment.' Then get you from the tower quickly; fear not, your way shall be made clear. The life of man is not the life of Yag, nor is human death the death of Yag. Let me be free of this cage of broken, blind flesh, and I will once more be Yogah of Yag, morning-crowned and shining, with wings to fly, and feet to dance, and eyes to see, and hands to break."

Uncertainly Conan approached, and Yag-kosha, or Yogah, as if sensing his uncertainty, indicated where he should strike. Conan set his teeth and drove the sword deep. Blood streamed over the blade and his hand, and the monster started convulsively, then lay back quite still. Sure that life had fled, at least life as he understood it, Conan set to work on his grisly task and quickly brought forth something that he felt must be the strange being's heart, though it differed curiously from any he had ever seen. Holding the still pulsing organ over the blazing jewel, he pressed it with both hands, and a rain of blood fell on the stone. To his surprise, it did not run off, but soaked into the gem, as water is absorbed by a sponge.

Holding the jewel gingerly, he went out of the fantastic chamber and came upon the silver steps. He did not look back; he instinctively felt that some sort of transmutation was taking place in the body on the marble couch, and he further felt that it was of a sort not to be witnessed by human eyes.

He closed the ivory door behind him, and without hesitation descended the silver steps. It did not occur to him to ignore the instructions given him. He halted at an ebony door, in the center of which was a grinning silver skull, and pushed it open. He looked into a chamber of ebony and jet, and saw, on a black silken couch, a tall, spare form reclining. Yara the priest and sorcerer lay before him, his eyes open and dilated with the fumes of the yellow lotus, far-staring, as if fixed on gulfs and nighted abysses beyond human ken.

"Yara!" said Conan, like a judge pronouncing doom. "Awaken!"

The eyes cleared instantly and became cold and cruel as a vulture's. The tall, silken-clad form lifted erect, and towered gauntly above the Cimmerian.

"Dog!" His hiss was like the voice of a cobra. "What do you here?"

Conan laid the jewel on the great ebony table.

"He who sent this gem bade me say, 'Yag-kosha gives a last gift and a last enchantment.'"

Yara recoiled, his dark face ashy. The jewel was no longer crystal-clear; its murky depths pulsed and throbbed, and curious smoky waves of changing color passed over its smooth surface. As if drawn hypnotically, Yara bent over the table and gripped the gem in his hands, staring into its shadowed depths, as if it were a magnet to draw the shuddering soul from his body. And as Conan looked, he thought that his eyes must be playing him tricks. For when Yara had risen up from his couch, the priest had seemed gigantically tall; yet now he saw that Yara's head would scarcely come to his shoulder. He blinked, puzzled, and for the first time that night, doubted his own senses. Then with a shock he realized that the priest was shrinking in stature—was growing smaller before his very gaze.

With a detached feeling he watched, as a man might watch a play; immersed in a feeling of overpowering unreality, the Cimmerian was no longer sure of his own identity; he only knew that he was looking upon the external evidence of the unseen play of vast Outer forces, beyond his understanding.

Now Yara was no bigger than a child; now like an infant he sprawled on the table, still grasping the jewel. And now the sorcerer suddenly realized his fate, and he sprang up, releasing the gem. But still he dwindled, and Conan saw a tiny, pigmy figure rushing wildly about the ebony table-top, waving tiny arms and shrieking in a voice that was like the squeak of an insect.

Now he had shrunk until the great jewel towered above him like a hill, and Conan saw him cover his eyes with his hands, as if to shield them from the glare, as he staggered about like a madman. Conan sensed that some unseen magnetic force was pulling Yara to the gem. Thrice he raced wildly about it in a narrowing circle, thrice he strove to turn and run out across the table; then with a scream that echoed faintly in the ears of the watcher, the priest threw up his arms and ran straight toward the blazing globe.

Bending close, Conan saw Yara clamber up the smooth, curving surface, impossibly, like a man climbing a glass mountain. Now the priest stood on the top, still with tossing arms, invoking what grisly names only the gods know. And suddenly he sank into the very heart of the jewel, as a man sinks into a sea, and Conan saw the smoky waves close over his head. Now he saw him in the crimson heart of the jewel, once more crystal-clear, as a man sees a scene far away, tiny with great distance. And into the heart came a green, shining winged figure with the body of a man and the head of an elephant—no longer blind or crippled. Yara threw up his arms and fled as a madman flees, and on his heels came the avenger. Then, like the bursting of a bubble, the great jewel vanished in a rainbow burst of iridescent gleams, and the ebony table-top lay bare and deserted—as bare, Conan somehow knew, as the marble couch in the chamber above, where the body of that strange transcosmic being called Yag-kosha and Yogah had lain.

The Cimmerian turned and fled from the chamber, down the silver stairs. So amazed was he that it did not occur to him to escape from the tower by the way he had entered it. Down that winding, shadowy silver well he ran, and came into a large chamber at the foot of the gleaming stairs. There he halted for an instant; he had come into the room of the soldiers. He saw the glitter of their silver corselets, the sheen of their jeweled sword-hilts. They sat slumped at the banquet board, their dusky plumes waving somberly above their drooping helmeted heads; they lay among their dice and fallen goblets on the wine-stained lapis-lazuli floor. And he knew that they were dead. The promise had been made, the word kept; whether sorcery or magic or the falling shadow of great green wings had stilled the revelry, Conan could not know, but his way had been made clear. And a silver door stood open, framed in the whiteness of dawn.

Into the waving green gardens came the Cimmerian, and as the dawn wind blew upon him with the cool fragrance of luxuriant growths, he started like a man waking from a dream. He turned back uncertainly, to stare at the cryptic tower he had just left. Was he bewitched and enchanted? Had he dreamed all that had seemed to have passed? As he looked he saw the gleaming tower sway against the crimson dawn, its jewel-crusted rim sparkling in the growing light, and crash into shining shards.

QUEEN OF THE BLACK COAST

• • • • •

ROBERT E. HOWARD

I

Believe green buds awaken in the spring,
That autumn paints the leaves with somber fire;
Believe I held my heart inviolate
To lavish on one man my hot desire.

The Song of Belît

Hoofs drummed down the street that sloped to the wharfs. The folk that yelled and scattered had only a fleeting glimpse of a mailed figure on a black stallion, a wide scarlet cloak flowing out on the wind. Far up the street came the shout and clatter of pursuit, but the horseman did not look back. He swept out onto the wharfs and jerked the plunging stallion back on its haunches at the very lip of the pier. Seamen gaped up at him, as they stood to the sweep and striped sail of a high-prowed, broadwaisted galley. The master, sturdy and black-bearded, stood in the bows, easing her away from the piles with a boat-hook. He yelled angrily as the horseman sprang from the saddle and with a long leap landed squarely on the mid-deck.

"Who invited you aboard?"

"Get under way!" roared the intruder with a fierce gesture that spattered red drops from his broadsword.

"But we're bound for the coasts of Kush!" expostulated the master.

"Then I'm for Kush! Push off, I tell you!" The other cast a quick glance up the street, along which a squad of horsemen were galloping; far behind them toiled a group of archers, crossbows on their shoulders.

"Can you pay for your passage?" demanded the master.

"I pay my way with steel!" roared the man in armor, brandishing the great sword that glittered bluely in the sun. "By Crom, man, if you don't get under way, I'll drench this galley in the blood of its crew!"

The shipmaster was a good judge of men. One glance at the dark scarred face of the swordsman, hardened with passion, and he shouted a quick order, thrusting strongly against the piles. The galley wallowed out into clear water, the oars began to clack rhythmically; then a puff of wind filled the shimmering sail, the light ship heeled to the gust, then took her course like a swan, gathering headway as she skimmed along.

On the wharfs the riders were shaking their swords and shouting threats and commands that the ship put about, and yelling for the bowmen to hasten before the craft was out of arbalest range.

"Let them rave," grinned the swordsman hardily. "Do you keep her on her course, master steersman."

The master descended from the small deck between the bows, made his way between the rows of oarsmen, and mounted the mid-deck. The stranger stood there with his back to the mast, eyes narrowed alertly, sword ready. The shipman eyed him steadily, careful not to make any move toward the long knife in his belt. He saw a tall powerfully built figure in a black scale-mail hauberk, burnished greaves and a blue-steel helmet from which jutted bull's horns highly polished. From the mailed shoulders fell the scarlet cloak, blowing in the sea-wind. A broad shagreen belt with a golden buckle held the scabbard of the broadsword he bore. Under the horned helmet a square-cut black mane contrasted with smoldering blue eyes.

"If we must travel together," said the master, "we may as well be at peace with each other. My name is Tito, licensed mastershipman of the ports of Argos. I am bound for Kush, to trade beads and silks and sugar and brass-hilted swords to the black kings for ivory, copra, copper ore, slaves and pearls."

The swordsman glanced back at the rapidly receding docks, where the figures still gesticulated helplessly, evidently having trouble in finding a boat swift enough to overhaul the fast-sailing galley.

"I am Conan, a Cimmerian," he answered. "I came into Argos seeking employment, but with no wars forward, there was nothing to which I might turn my hand."

"Why do the guardsman pursue you?" asked Tito. "Not that it's any of my business, but I thought perhaps—"

"I've nothing to conceal," replied the Cimmerian. "By Crom, though I've spent considerable time among you civilized peoples, your ways are still beyond my comprehension.

"Well, last night in a tavern, a captain in the king's guard offered violence to the sweetheart of a young soldier, who naturally ran him through. But it seems there is some cursed law against killing guardsmen, and the boy and his girl fled away. It was bruited about that I was seen with them, and so today I was hauled into court, and a judge asked me where the lad had gone. I replied that since he was a friend of mine, I could not betray him. Then the court waxed wroth, and the judge talked a great deal about my duty to the state and society, and other things I did not understand, and bade me tell where my friend had flown. By this time I was becoming wrathful myself, for I had explained my position.

"But I choked my ire and held my peace, and the judge squalled that I had shown contempt for the court, and that I should be hurled into a dungeon to rot until I betrayed my friend. So then, seeing they were all mad, I drew my sword and cleft the judge's skull; then I cut my way out of the court and, seeing the high constable's stallion tied near by, I rode for the wharfs, where I thought to find a ship bound for foreign parts."

"Well," said Tito hardily, "the courts have fleeced me too often in suits with rich merchants for me to owe them any love. I'll have questions to answer if I ever anchor in that port again, but I can prove I acted under compulsion. You may as well put up your sword. We're peaceable sailors, and have nothing against you. Besides, it's as well to have a fighting-man like yourself on board. Come up to the poop-deck and we'll have a tankard of ale."

"Good enough," readily responded the Cimmerian, sheathing his sword.

The *Argus* was a small, sturdy ship, typical of those trading-craft which ply between the ports of Zingara and Argos and the southern coasts, hugging the shoreline and seldom venturing far into the open ocean. It was high of stern, with a tall curving prow; broad in the waist, sloping beautifully to stem and stern. It was guided by the long sweep from the poop, and propulsion was furnished mainly by the broad striped silk sail, aided by a jib sail. The oars were for use in tacking out of creeks and bays, and during calms. There were ten to the side, five fore and five aft of the small mid-deck. The most precious part of the cargo was lashed under this deck, and under the foredeck. The men slept on deck or between the rowers' benches, protected in bad weather by canopies. With twenty men at the oars, three at the sweep, and the shipmaster, the crew was complete.

So the *Argus* pushed steadily southward, with consistently fair weather. The sun beat down from day to day with fiercer heat, and the canopies were run up—striped silken cloths that matched the shimmering sail and the shining goldwork on the prow and along the gunwales.

They sighted the coast of Shem—long, rolling meadowlands with the white crowns of the towers of cities in the distance, and horsemen with blue-black beards and hooked noses, who sat their steeds along the shore and eyed the galley with suspicion. She did not put in; there was scant profit in trade with the sons of Shem.

Nor did master Tito pull into the broad bay where the Styx river emptied its gigantic flood into the ocean, and the massive black castles of Khemi loomed over the blue waters. Ships did not put unasked into this port, where dusky sorcerers wove awful spells in the murk of sacrificial smoke mounting eternally from blood-stained altars where naked women screamed, and where Set, the Old Serpent, arch-demon of the Hyborians but god of the Stygians, was said to writhe his shining coils among his worshipers.

Master Tito gave that dreamy, glass-floored bay a wide berth, even when a serpent-prowed gondola shot from behind a castellated point of land, and naked dusky women, with great red blossoms in their hair, stood and called to his sailors, and posed and postured brazenly.

Now no more shining towers rose inland. They had passed the southern borders of Stygia and were cruising along the coasts of Kush. The sea and the ways of the sea were never-ending mysteries to Conan, whose homeland was among the high hills of the northern uplands. The wanderer was no less of interest to the sturdy seamen, few of whom had ever seen one of his race.

They were characteristic Argosean sailors, short and stockily built. Conan towered above them, and no two of them could match his strength. They were hardy and robust, but his was the endurance and vitality of a wolf, his thews steeled and his nerves whetted by the hardness of his life in the world's wastelands. He was quick to laugh, quick and terrible in his wrath. He was a valiant trencherman, and strong drink was a passion and a weakness with him. Naive as a child in many ways, unfamiliar with the sophistry of civilization, he was naturally intelligent, jealous of his rights, and dangerous as a hungry tiger. Young in years, he was hardened in warfare and wandering, and his sojourns in many lands were evident in his apparel. His horned helmet was such as was worn by the golden-haired AEsir of Nordheim; his hauberk and greaves were of the finest workmanship of Koth; the fine ring-mail which sheathed his arms and legs was of Nemedia; the blade at his girdle was a great Aquilonian broadsword; and his gorgeous scarlet cloak could have been spun nowhere but in Ophir.

So they beat southward, and master Tito began to look for the high-walled villages of the black people. But they found only smoking ruins on the shore of a bay, littered with naked black bodies. Tito swore.

"I had good trade here, aforetime. This is the work of pirates."

"And if we meet them?" Conan loosened his great blade in its scabbard.

"Mine is no warship. We run, not fight. Yet if it came to a pinch, we have beaten off reavers before and might do it again; unless it were Belît's Tigress."

"Who is Belît?"

"The wildest she-devil unhanged. Unless I read the signs awrong, it was her butchers who destroyed that village on the bay. May I some day see her dangling from the yardarm! She is called the queen of the black coast. She is a Shemite woman, who leads black raiders. They harry the shipping and have sent many a good tradesman to the bottom."

From under the poop-deck Tito brought out quilted jerkins, steel caps, bows and arrows.

"Little use to resist if we're run down," he grunted. "But it rasps the soul to give up life without a struggle."

It was just at sunrise when the lookout shouted a warning. Around the long point of an island, off the starboard bow, glided a long lethal shape, a slender serpentine galley, with a raised deck that ran from stem to stern. Forty oars on each side drove her swiftly through the water, and the low rail swarmed with naked blacks who chanted and clashed spears on oval shields. From the masthead floated a long crimson pennon.

"Belît!" yelled Tito, paling. "Yare! Put her about! Into that creek-mouth! If we can beach her before they run us down, we have a chance to escape with our lives!"

So, veering sharply, the *Argus* ran for the line of surf that boomed along the palm-fringed shore, Tito striding back and forth, exhorting the panting rowers to greater efforts. The master's black beard bristled, his eyes glared.

"Give me a bow," requested Conan. "It's not my idea of a manly weapon, but I learned archery among the Hyrkanians, and it will go hard if I can't feather a man or so on yonder deck."

Standing on the poop, he watched the serpent-like ship skimming lightly over the waters, and landsman though he was, it was evident to him that the *Argus* would never win that race. Already arrows, arching from the pirate's deck, were falling with a hiss into the sea, not twenty paces astern.

"We'd best stand to it," growled the Cimmerian; "else we'll all die with shafts in our backs, and not a blow dealt."

"Bend to it, dogs!" roared Tito with a passionate gesture of his brawny fist. The bearded rowers grunted, heaved at the oars, while their muscles coiled and knotted, and sweat started out on their hides. The timbers of the stout little galley creaked and groaned as the men fairly ripped her through the water. The wind had fallen; the sail hung limp. Nearer crept the inexorable raiders, and they were still a good mile from the surf when one of the steersmen fell gagging across a sweep, a long arrow through his neck. Tito sprang to take his place, and Conan, bracing his feet wide on the heaving poop-deck, lifted his bow. He could see the details of the pirate plainly now. The rowers were protected by a line of raised mantelets along the sides, but the warriors dancing on the narrow deck were in full view. These were painted and plumed, and mostly naked, brandishing spears and spotted shields.

On the raised platform in the bow stood a slim figure whose white skin glistened in dazzling contrast to the glossy ebon hides about it. Belît, without a doubt. Conan drew the shaft to his ear—then some whim or qualm stayed his hand and sent the arrow through the body of a tall plumed spearman beside her.

Hand over hand the pirate galley was overhauling the lighter ship. Arrows fell in a rain about the *Argus*, and men cried out. All the steersmen were down, pincushioned, and Tito was handling the massive sweep alone, gasping black curses, his braced legs knots of straining thews. Then with a sob he sank down, a long shaft quivering in his sturdy heart. The *Argus* lost headway and rolled in the swell. The men shouted in confusion, and Conan took command in characteristic fashion.

"Up, lads!" he roared, loosing with a vicious twang of cord. "Grab your steel and give these dogs a few knocks before they cut our throats! Useless to bend your backs any more: they'll board us ere we can row another fifty paces!"

In desperation the sailors abandoned their oars and snatched up their weapons. It was valiant, but useless. They had time for one flight of arrows before the pirate was upon them. With no one at the sweep, the *Argus* rolled broadside, and the steel-baked prow of the raider crashed into her amidships. Grappling-irons crunched into the side. From the lofty gunwales, the black pirates drove down a volley of shafts that tore through the quilted jackets of the doomed sailormen, then sprang down spear in hand to complete the slaughter. On the deck of the pirate lay half a dozen bodies, an earnest of Conan's archery.

The fight on the *Argus* was short and bloody. The stocky sailors, no match for the tall barbarians, were cut down to a man. Elsewhere the battle had taken a peculiar turn. Conan, on the high-pitched poop, was on a level with the pirate's deck. As the steel prow slashed into the *Argus*, he braced himself and kept his feet under the shock, casting away his bow. A tall corsair, bounding over the rail, was met in mid-air by the Cimmerian's great sword, which sheared him cleanly through the torso, so that his body fell one way and his legs another. Then, with a burst of fury that left a heap of mangled corpses along the gunwales, Conan was over the rail and on the deck of the *Tigress*.

In an instant he was the center of a hurricane of stabbing spears and lashing clubs. But he moved in a blinding blur of steel. Spears bent on his armor or swished empty air, and his sword sang its death-song. The fighting-madness of his race was upon him, and with a red mist of unreasoning fury wavering before his blazing eyes, he cleft skulls, smashed breasts, severed limbs, ripped out entrails and littered the deck like a shambles with a ghastly harvest of brains and blood.

Invulnerable in his armor, his back against the mast, he heaped mangled corpses at his feet until his enemies gave back panting in rage and fear. Then as they lifted their spears to cast them, and he tensed himself to leap and die in the midst of them, a shrill cry froze the lifted arms. They stood like statues, the black giants poised for the spearcasts, the mailed swordsman with his dripping blade.

Belît sprang before the blacks, beating down their spears. She turned toward Conan, her bosom heaving, her eyes flashing. Fierce fingers of wonder caught at his heart. She was slender, yet formed like a goddess: at once lithe and voluptuous. Her only garment was a broad silken girdle. Her white ivory limbs and the ivory globes of her breasts drove a beat of fierce passion through the Cimmerian's pulse, even in the panting fury of battle. Her rich black hair, black as a Stygian night, fell in rippling burnished clusters down her supple back. Her dark eyes burned on the Cimmerian.

She was untamed as a desert wind, supple and dangerous as a she-panther. She came close to him, heedless of his great blade, dripping with blood of her warriors. Her supple thigh brushed against it, so close she came to the tall warrior. Her red lips parted as she stared up into his somber menacing eyes.

"Who are you?" she demanded. "By Ishtar, I have never seen your like, though I have ranged the sea from the coasts of Zingara to the fires of the ultimate south. Whence come you?"

"From Argos," he answered shortly, alert for treachery. Let her slim hand move toward the jeweled dagger in her girdle, and a buffet of his open hand would stretch her senseless on the deck. Yet in his heart he did not fear; he had held too many women, civilized or barbaric, in his iron-thewed arms, not to recognize the light that burned in the eyes of this one.

"You are no soft Hyborian!" she exclaimed. "You are fierce and hard as a gray wolf. Those eyes were never dimmed by city lights; those thews were never softened by life amid marble walls."

"I am Conan, a Cimmerian," he answered.

To the people of the exotic climes, the north was a mazy, half-mythical realm, peopled with ferocious blue-eyed giants who occasionally descended from their icy fastnesses with torch and sword. Their raids had never taken them as far south as Shem, and this daughter of Shem made no distinction between Aesir, Vanir or Cimmerian. With the unerring instinct of the elemental feminine, she knew she had found her lover, and his race meant naught, save as it invested him with the glamor of far lands.

"And I am Belît," she cried, as one might say, "I am queen."

"Look at me, Conan!" She threw wide her arms. "I am Belît, queen of the black coast. Oh, tiger of the North, you are cold as the snowy mountains which bred you. Take me and crush me with your fierce love! Go with me to the ends of the earth and the ends of the sea! I am a queen by fire and steel and slaughter—be thou my king!"

His eyes swept the blood-stained ranks, seeking expressions of wrath or jealousy. He saw none. The fury was gone from the ebon faces. He realized that to these men Belît was more than a woman: a goddess whose will was unquestioned. He glanced at the Argus, wallowing in the crimson sea-wash, heeling far over, her decks awash, held up by the grappling-irons. He glanced at the blue-fringed shore, at the far green hazes of the ocean, at the vibrant figure which stood before him; and his barbaric soul stirred within him. To quest these shining blue realms with that white-skinned young tiger-cat—to love, laugh, wander and pillage—"I'll sail with you," he grunted, shaking the red drops from his blade.

"Ho, N'Yaga!" her voice twanged like a bowstring. "Fetch herbs and dress your master's wounds! The rest of you bring aboard the plunder and cast off."

As Conan sat with his back against the poop-rail, while the old shaman attended to the cuts on his hands and limbs, the cargo of the ill-fated *Argus* was quickly shifted aboard the *Tigress* and stored in small cabins below deck. Bodies of the crew and of fallen pirates were cast overboard to the swarming sharks, while wounded blacks were laid in the waist to be bandaged. Then the grappling-irons were cast off, and as the *Argus* sank silently into the blood-flecked waters, the *Tigress* moved off southward to the rhythmic clack of the oars.

As they moved out over the glassy blue deep, Belît came to the poop. Her eyes were burning like those of a she-panther in the dark as she tore off her ornaments, her sandals and her silken girdle and cast them at his feet. Rising on tiptoe, arms stretched upward, a quivering line of naked white, she cried to the desperate horde: "Wolves of the blue sea, behold ye now the dance—the mating-dance of Belît, whose fathers were kings of Askalon!"

And she danced, like the spin of a desert whirlwind, like the leaping of a quenchless flame, like the urge of creation and the urge of death. Her white feet spurned the blood-stained deck and dying men forgot death as they gazed frozen at her. Then, as the white stars glimmered through the blue velvet dusk, making her whirling body a blur of ivory fire, with a wild cry she threw herself at Conan's feet, and the blind flood of the Cimmerian's desire swept all else away as he crushed her panting form against the black plates of his corseleted breast.

II

In that dead citadel of crumbling stone.
Her eyes were snared by that unholy sheen,
And curious madness took me by the throat,
As of a rival lover thrust between.

The Song of Belît

The *Tigress* ranged the sea, and the black villages shuddered. Tom-toms beat in the night, with a tale that the she-devil of the sea had found a mate, an iron man whose wrath was as that of a wounded lion. And survivors of butchered Stygian ships named Belît with curses, and a white warrior with fierce blue eyes; so the Stygian princes remembered this man long and long, and their memory was a bitter tree which bore crimson fruit in the years to come.

But heedless as a vagrant wind, the *Tigress* cruised the southern coasts, until she anchored at the mouth of a broad sullen river, whose banks were jungle-clouded walls of mystery.

"This is the river Zarkheba, which is Death," said Belît. "Its waters are poisonous. See how dark and murky they run? Only venomous reptiles live in that river. The black people shun it. Once a Stygian galley, fleeing from me, fled up the river and vanished. I anchored in this very spot, and days later, the galley came floating down the dark waters, its decks blood-stained and deserted. Only one man was on board, and he was mad and died gibbering. The cargo was intact, but the crew had vanished into silence and mystery.

"My lover, I believe there is a city somewhere on that river. I have heard tales of giant towers and walls glimpsed afar off by sailors who dared go part-way up the river. We fear nothing: Conan, let us go and sack that city."

Conan agreed. He generally agreed to her plans. Hers was the mind that directed their raids, his the arm that carried out her ideas. It mattered little to him where they sailed or whom they fought, so long as they sailed and fought. He found the life good.

Battle and raid had thinned their crew; only some eighty spear-men remained, scarcely enough to work the long galley. But Belît would not take the time to make the long cruise southward to the island kingdoms where she recruited her buccaneers. She was afire with eagerness for her latest venture; so the *Tigress* swung into the river mouth, the oarsmen pulling strongly as she breasted the broad current.

They rounded the mysterious bend that shut out the sight of the sea, and sunset found them forging steadily against the sluggish flow, avoiding sandbars where strange reptiles coiled. Not even a crocodile did they see, nor any four-legged beast or winged bird coming down to the water's edge to drink. On through the blackness that preceded moonrise they drove, between banks that were solid palisades of darkness, whence came mysterious rustlings and stealthy footfalls, and the gleam of grim eyes. And once an inhuman voice was lifted in awful mockery the cry of an ape, Belît said, adding that the souls of evil men were imprisoned in these man-like animals as punishment for past crimes. But Conan doubted, for once, in a gold-barred cage in an Hyrkanian city, he had seen an abysmal sad-eyed beast which men told him was an ape, and there had been about it naught of the demoniac malevolence which vibrated in the shrieking laughter that echoed from the black jungle.

Then the moon rose, a splash of blood, ebony-barred, and the jungle awoke in horrific bedlam to greet it. Roars and howls and yells set the black warriors to trembling, but all this noise, Conan noted, came from farther back in the jungle, as if the beasts no less than men shunned the black waters of Zarkheba.

Rising above the black denseness of the trees and above the waving fronds, the moon silvered the river, and their wake became a rippling scintillation of phosphorescent bubbles that widened like a shining road of bursting jewels. The oars dipped into the shining water and came up sheathed in frosty silver. The plumes on the warrior's head-piece nodded in the wind, and the gems on sword-hilts and harness sparkled frostily.

The cold light struck icy fire from the jewels in Belît's clustered black locks as she stretched her lithe figure on a leopard-skin thrown on the deck. Supported on her elbows, her chin resting on her slim hands, she gazed up into the face of Conan, who lounged beside her, his black mane stirring in the faint breeze. Belît's eyes were dark jewels burning in the moonlight.

"Mystery and terror are about us, Conan, and we glide into the realm of horror and death," she said. "Are you afraid?"

A shrug of his mailed shoulders was his only answer.

"I am not afraid either," she said meditatively. "I was never afraid. I have looked into the naked fangs of Death too often. Conan, do you fear the gods?"

"I would not tread on their shadow," answered the barbarian conservatively. "Some gods are strong to harm, others, to aid; at least so say their priests. Mitra of the Hyborians must be a strong god, because his people have built their cities over the world. But even the Hyborians fear Set. And Bel, god of thieves, is a good god. When I was a thief in Zamora I learned of him."

"What of your own gods? I have never heard you call on them."

"Their chief is Crom. He dwells on a great mountain. What use to call on him? Little he cares if men live or die. Better to be silent than to call his attention to you; he will send you dooms, not fortune! He is grim and loveless, but at birth he breathes power to strive and slay into a man's soul. What else shall men ask of the gods?"

"But what of the worlds beyond the river of death?" she persisted.

"There is no hope here or hereafter in the cult of my people," answered Conan. "In this world men struggle and suffer vainly, finding pleasure only in the bright madness of battle; dying, their souls enter a gray misty realm of clouds and icy winds, to wander cheerlessly throughout eternity."

Belît shuddered. "Life, bad as it is, is better than such a destiny. What do you believe, Conan?"

He shrugged his shoulders. "I have known many gods. He who denies them is as blind as he who trusts them too deeply. I seek not beyond death. It may be the blackness averred by the Nemedian skeptics, or Crom's realm of ice and cloud, or the snowy plains and vaulted halls of the Nordheimer's Valhalla. I know not, nor do I care. Let me live deep while I live; let me know the rich juices of red meat and stinging wine on my palate, the hot embrace of white arms, the mad exultation of battle when the blue blades flame and crimson, and I am content. Let teachers and priests and philosophers brood over questions of reality and illusion. I know this: if life is illusion, then I am no less an illusion, and being thus, the illusion is real to me. I live, I burn with life, I love, I slay, and am content."

"But the gods are real," she said, pursuing her own line of thought. "And above all are the gods of the Shemites—Ishtar and Ashtoreth and Derketo and Adonis. Bel, too, is Shemitish, for he was born in ancient Shumir, long, long ago and went forth laughing, with curled beard and impish wise eyes, to steal the gems of the kings of old times."

"There is life beyond death, I know, and I know this, too, Conan of Cimmeria—" she rose lithely to her knees and caught him in a pantherish embrace—"my love is stronger than any death! I have lain in your arms, panting with the violence of our love; you have held and crushed and conquered me, drawing my soul to your lips with the fierceness of your bruising kisses. My heart is welded to your heart, my soul is part of your soul! Were I still in death and you fighting for life, I would come back from the abyss to aid you—aye, whether my spirit floated with the purple sails on the crystal sea of paradise, or writhed in the molten flames of hell! I am yours, and all the gods and all their eternities shall not sever us!"

A scream rang from the lookout in the bows. Thrusting Belît aside, Conan bounded up, his sword a long silver glitter in the moonlight, his hair bristling at what he saw. The black warrior dangled above the deck, supported by what seemed a dark pliant tree trunk arching over the rail. Then he realized that it was a gigantic serpent, which had writhed its glistening length up the side of the bow and gripped the luckless warrior in its jaws. Its dripping scales shone leprously in the moonlight as it reared its form high above the deck, while the stricken man screamed and writhed like a mouse in the fangs of a python. Conan rushed into the bows, and swinging his great sword, hewed nearly through the giant trunk, which was thicker than a man's body. Blood drenched the rails as the dying monster swayed far out, still gripping its victim, and sank into the river, coil by coil, lashing the water to bloody foam, in which man and reptile vanished together.

Thereafter Conan kept the lookout watch himself, but no other horror came crawling up from the murky depths, and as dawn whitened over the jungle, he sighted the black fangs of towers jutting up among the trees. He called Belît, who slept on the deck, wrapped in his scarlet cloak; and she sprang to his side, eyes blazing. Her lips were parted to call orders to her warriors to take up bows and spears; then her lovely eyes widened.

It was but the ghost of a city on which they looked when they cleared a jutting jungle-clad point and swung in toward the incurving shore. Weeds and rank river grass grew between the stones of broken piers and shattered paves that had once been streets and spacious plazas and broad courts. From all sides except that toward the river, the jungle crept in, masking fallen columns and crumbling mounds with poisonous green. Here and there buckling towers reeled drunkenly against the morning sky, and broken pillars jutted up among the decaying walls. In the center space a marble pyramid was spired by a slim column, and on its pinnacle sat or squatted something that Conan supposed to be an image until his keen eyes detected life in it.

"It is a great bird," said one of the warriors, standing in the bow.

"It is a monster bat," insisted another.

"It is an ape," said Belît.

Just then the creature spread broad wings and flapped off into the jungle.

"A winged ape," said old N'Yaga uneasily. "Better we had cut our throats than come to this place. It is haunted."

Belît mocked at his superstitions and ordered the galley run inshore and tied to the crumbling wharfs. She was the first to spring ashore, closely followed by Conan, and after them trooped the ebon-skinned pirates, white plumes waving in the morning wind, spears ready, eyes rolling dubiously at the surrounding jungle.

Over all brooded a silence as sinister as that of a sleeping serpent. Belît posed picturesquely among the ruins, the vibrant life in her lithe figure contrasting strangely with the desolation and decay about her. The sun flamed up slowly, sullenly, above the jungle, flooding the towers with a dull gold that left shadows lurking beneath the tottering walls. Belît pointed to a slim, round tower that reeled on its rotting base. A broad expanse of cracked, grass-grown slabs led up to it, flanked by fallen columns, and before it stood a massive altar. Belît went swiftly along the ancient floor and stood before it.

"This was the temple of the old ones," she said. "Look—you can see the channels for the blood along the sides of the altar, and the rains of ten thousand years have not washed the dark stains from them. The walls have all fallen away, but this stone block defies time and the elements."

"But who were these old ones?" demanded Conan.

She spread her slim hands helplessly. "Not even in legend is this city mentioned. But look at the hand-holes at either end of the altar! Priests often conceal their treasures beneath their altars. Four of you lay hold and see if you can lift it."

She stepped back to make room for them, glancing up at the tower which loomed drunkenly above them. Three of the strongest blacks had gripped the hand-holes, cut into the stone curiously unsuited to human hands—when Belît sprang back with a sharp cry. They froze in their places and Conan, bending to aid them, wheeled with a startled curse.

"A snake in the grass," she said, backing away. "Come and slay it; the rest of you bend your backs to the stone."

Conan came quickly toward her, another taking his place. As he impatiently scanned the grass for the reptile, the giant blacks braced their feet, grunted and heaved with their huge muscles coiling and straining under their ebon skin. The altar did not come off the ground, but it revolved suddenly on its side. And simultaneously there was a grinding rumble above and the tower came crashing down, covering the four black men with broken masonry.

A cry of horror rose from their comrades. Belît's slim fingers dug into Conan's arm-muscles. "There was no serpent," she whispered. "It was but a ruse to call you away. I feared; the old ones guarded their treasure well. Let us clear away the stones."

With herculean labor they did so, and lifted out the mangled bodies of the four men. And under them, stained with their blood, the pirates found a crypt carved in the solid stone. The altar, hinged curiously with stone rods and sockets on one side, had served as its lid. And at first glance the crypt seemed brimming with liquid fire, catching the early light with a million blazing facets. Undreamable wealth lay before the eyes of the gaping pirates: diamonds, rubies, bloodstones, sapphires, turquoises, moonstones, opals, emeralds, amethysts, unknown gems that shone like the eyes of evil women. The crypt was filled to the brim with bright stones that the morning sun struck into lambent flame.

With a cry Belît dropped to her knees among the bloodstained rubble on the brink and thrust her white arms shoulder-deep into that pool of splendor. She withdrew them, clutching something that brought another cry to her lips—a long string of crimson stones that were like clots of frozen blood strung on a thick gold wire. In their glow the golden sunlight changed to bloody haze.

Belît's eyes were like a woman's in a trance. The Shemite soul finds a bright drunkenness in riches and material splendor, and the sight of this treasure might have shaken the soul of a sated emperor of Shushan.

"Take up the jewels, dogs!" her voice was shrill with her emotions.

"Look!" A muscular black arm stabbed toward the *Tigress*, and Belît wheeled, her crimson lips a-snarl, as if she expected to see a rival corsair sweeping in to despoil her of her plunder. But from the gunwales of the ship a dark shape rose, soaring away over the jungle.

"The devil-ape has been investigating the ship," muttered the blacks uneasily.

"What matter?" cried Belît with a curse, raking back a rebellious lock with an impatient hand. "Make a litter of spears and mantles to bear these jewels—where the devil are you going?"

"To look to the galley," grunted Conan. "That bat-thing might have knocked a hole in the bottom, for all we know."

He ran swiftly down the cracked wharf and sprang aboard. A moment's swift examination below decks, and he swore heartily, casting a clouded glance in the direction the bat-being had vanished. He returned hastily to Belît, superintending the plundering of the crypt. She had looped the necklace about her neck, and on her naked white bosom the red clots glimmered darkly. A huge naked black stood crotch-deep in the jewel-brimming crypt, scooping up great handfuls of splendor to pass them to eager hands above. Strings of frozen iridescence hung between his dusky fingers; drops of red fire dripped from his hands, piled high with starlight and rainbow. It was as if a black titan stood straddle-legged in the bright pits of hell, his lifted hands full of stars.

"That flying devil has staved in the water-casks," said Conan. "If we hadn't been so dazed by these stones we'd have heard the noise. We were fools not to have left a man on guard. We can't drink this river water. I'll take twenty men and search for fresh water in the jungle."

She looked at him vaguely, in her eyes the blank blaze of her strange passion, her fingers working at the gems on her breast.

"Very well," she said absently, hardly heeding him. "I'll get the loot aboard."

The jungle closed quickly about them, changing the light from gold to gray. From the arching green branches creepers dangled like pythons. The warriors fell into single file, creeping through the primordial twilights like black phantoms following a white ghost.

The underbrush was not so thick as Conan had anticipated. The ground was spongy but not slushy. Away from the river, it sloped gradually upward. Deeper and deeper they plunged into the green waving depths, and still there was no sign of water, either running stream or stagnant pool. Conan halted suddenly, his warriors freezing into basaltic statues. In the tense silence that followed, the Cimmerian shook his head irritably.

"Go ahead," he grunted to a sub-chief, N'Gora. "March straight on until you can no longer see me; then stop and wait for me. I believe we're being followed. I heard something."

The blacks shuffled their feet uneasily, but did as they were told. As they swung onward, Conan stepped quickly behind a great tree, glaring back along the way they had come. From that leafy fastness anything might emerge. Nothing occurred; the faint sounds of the marching spearmen faded in the distance. Conan suddenly realized that the air was impregnated with an alien and exotic scent. Something gently brushed his temple. He turned quickly. From a cluster of green, curiously leafed stalks, great black blossoms nodded at him. One of these had touched him. They seemed to beckon him, to arch their pliant stems toward him. They spread and rustled, though no wind blew.

He recoiled, recognizing the black lotus, whose juice was death, and whose scent brought dream-haunted slumber. But already he felt a subtle lethargy stealing over him. He sought to lift his sword, to hew down the serpentine stalks, but his arm hung lifeless at his side. He opened his mouth to shout to his warriors, but only a faint rattle issued. The next instant, with appalling suddenness, the jungle waved and dimmed before his eyes; he did not hear the screams that burst out awfully not far away, as his knees collapsed, letting him pitch limply to the earth. Above his prostrate form the great black blossoms nodded in the windless air.

III

Was it a dream the nighted lotus brought?
Then curst the dream that bought my sluggish life;
And curst each laggard hour that does not see
Hot blood drip blackly from the crimsoned knife.

The Song of Belît

First there was the blackness of an utter void, with the cold winds of cosmic space blowing through it. Then shapes, vague, monstrous and evanescent, rolled in dim panorama through the expanse of nothingness, as if the darkness were taking material form. The winds blew and a vortex formed, a whirling pyramid of roaring blackness. From it grew Shape and Dimension;

then suddenly, like clouds dispersing, the darkness rolled away on either hand and a huge city of dark green stone rose on the bank of a wide river, flowing through an illimitable plain. Through this city moved beings of alien configuration.

Cast in the mold of humanity, they were distinctly not men. They were winged and of heroic proportions; not a branch on the mysterious stalk of evolution that culminated in man, but the ripe blossom on an alien tree, separate and apart from that stalk. Aside from their wings, in physical appearance they resembled man only as man in his highest form resembles the great apes. In spiritual, esthetic and intellectual development they were superior to man as man is superior to the gorilla. But when they reared their colossal city, man's primal ancestors had not yet risen from the slime of the primordial seas.

These beings were mortal, as are all things built of flesh and blood. They lived, loved and died, though the individual span of life was enormous. Then, after uncounted millions of years, the Change began. The vista shimmered and wavered, like a picture thrown on a windblown curtain. Over the city and the land the ages flowed as waves flow over a beach, and each wave brought alterations. Somewhere on the planet the magnetic centers were shifting; the great glaciers and ice-fields were withdrawing toward the new poles.

The littoral of the great river altered. Plains turned into swamps that stank with reptilian life. Where fertile meadows had rolled, forests reared up, growing into dank jungles. The changing ages wrought on the inhabitants of the city as well. They did not migrate to fresher lands. Reasons inexplicable to humanity held them to the ancient city and their doom. And as that once rich and mighty land sank deeper and deeper into the black mire of the sunless jungle, so into the chaos of squalling jungle life sank the people of the city. Terrific convulsions shook the earth; the nights were lurid with spouting volcanoes that fringed the dark horizons with red pillars.

After an earthquake that shook down the outer walls and highest towers of the city, and caused the river to run black for days with some lethal substance spewed up from the subterranean depths, a frightful chemical change became apparent in the waters the folk had drunk for millenniums uncountable.

Many died who drank of it; and in those who lived, the drinking wrought change, subtle, gradual and grisly. In adapting themselves to the changing conditions, they had sunk far below their original level. But the lethal waters altered them even more horribly, from generation to more bestial generation. They who had been winged gods became pinioned demons, with all that remained of their ancestors' vast knowledge distorted and perverted and twisted into ghastly paths. As they had risen higher than mankind might dream, so they sank lower than man's maddest nightmares reach. They died fast, by cannibalism, and horrible feuds fought out in the murk of the midnight jungle. And at last, among the lichen-grown ruins of their city, only a single shape lurked, a stunted abhorrent perversion of nature.

Then for the first time humans appeared: dark-skinned, hawk-faced men in copper and leather harness, bearing bows—the warriors of pre-historic Stygia. There were only fifty of them, and they were haggard and gaunt with starvation and prolonged effort, stained and scratched with jungle-wandering, with blood-crusted bandages that told of fierce fighting. In their minds was a tale of warfare and defeat, and flight before a stronger tribe which drove them ever southward, until they lost themselves in the green ocean of jungle and river.

Exhausted they lay down among the ruins where red blossoms that bloom but once in a century waved in the full moon, and sleep fell upon them. And as they slept, a hideous shape crept red-eyed from the shadows and performed weird and awful rites about and above each sleeper. The moon hung in the shadowy sky, painting the jungle red and black; above the sleepers glimmered the crimson blossoms, like splashes of blood. Then the moon went down and the eyes of the necromancer were red jewels set in the ebony of night.

When dawn spread its white veil over the river, there were no men to be seen: only a hairy, winged horror that squatted in the center of a ring of fifty great spotted hyenas that pointed quivering muzzles to the ghastly sky and howled like souls in hell.

Then scene followed scene so swiftly that each tripped over the heels of its predecessor. There was a confusion of movement, a writhing and melting of lights and shadows, against a background of black jungle, green stone ruins and murky river. Black men came up the river in long boats with skulls grinning on the prows, or stole stooping through the trees, spear in hand. They fled screaming through the dark from red eyes and slavering fangs. Howls of dying men shook the shadows; stealthy feet padded through the gloom, vampire eyes blazed redly. There were grisly feasts beneath the moon, across whose red disk a bat-like shadow incessantly swept.

Then abruptly, etched clearly in contrast to these impressionistic glimpses, around the jungled point in the whitening dawn swept a long galley, thronged with shining ebon figures, and in the bows stood a white-skinned ghost in blue steel.

It was at this point that Conan first realized that he was dreaming. Until that instant he had had no consciousness of individual existence. But as he saw himself treading the boards of the *Tigress*, he recognized both the existence and the dream, although he did not awaken.

Even as he wondered, the scene shifted abruptly to a jungle glade where N'Gora and nineteen black spearmen stood, as if awaiting someone. Even as he realized that it was he for whom they waited, a horror swooped down from the skies and their stolidity was broken by yells of fear. Like men maddened by terror, they threw away their weapons and raced wildly through the jungle, pressed close by the slavering monstrosity that flapped its wings above them.

Chaos and confusion followed this vision, during which Conan feebly struggled to awake. Dimly he seemed to see himself lying under a nodding cluster of black blossoms, while from the bushes a hideous shape crept toward him. With a savage effort he broke the unseen bonds which held him to his dreams, and started upright.

Bewilderment was in the glare he cast about him. Near him swayed the dusky lotus, and he hastened to draw away from it.

In the spongy soil nearby there was a track as if an animal had put out a foot, preparatory to emerging from the bushes, then had withdrawn it. It looked like the spoor of an unbelievably large hyena.

He yelled for N'Gora. Primordial silence brooded over the jungle, in which his yells sounded brittle and hollow as mockery. He could not see the sun, but his wilderness-trained instinct told him the day was near its end. A panic rose in him at the thought that he had lain senseless for hours. He hastily followed the tracks of the spearmen, which lay plain in the damp loam before him. They ran in single file, and he soon emerged into a glade—to stop short, the skin crawling between his shoulders as he recognized it as the glade he had seen in his lotus-drugged dream. Shields and spears lay scattered about as if dropped in headlong flight.

And from the tracks which led out of the glade and deeper into the fastnesses, Conan knew that the spearmen had fled, wildly. The footprints overlay one another; they weaved blindly among the trees. And with startling suddenness the hastening Cimmerian came out of the jungle onto a hill-like rock which sloped steeply, to break off abruptly in a sheer precipice forty feet high. And something crouched on the brink.

At first Conan thought it to be a great black gorilla. Then he saw that it was a giant black man that crouched ape-like, long arms dangling, froth dripping from the loose lips. It was not until, with a sobbing cry, the creature lifted huge hands and rushed towards him, that Conan recognized N'Gora. The black man gave no heed to Conan's shout as he charged, eyes rolled up to display the whites, teeth gleaming, face an inhuman mask.

With his skin crawling with the horror that madness always instils in the sane, Conan passed his sword through the black man's body; then, avoiding the hooked hands that clawed at him as N'Gora sank down, he strode to the edge of the cliff.

For an instant he stood looking down into the jagged rocks below, where lay N'Gora's spearmen, in limp, distorted attitudes that told of crushed limbs and splintered bones. Not one moved. A cloud of huge black flies buzzed loudly above the blood-splashed stones; the ants had already begun to gnaw at the corpses. On the trees about sat birds of prey, and a jackal, looking up and seeing the man on the cliff, slunk furtively away.

For a little space Conan stood motionless. Then he wheeled and ran back the way he had come, flinging himself with reckless haste through the tall grass and bushes, hurdling creepers that sprawled snake-like across his path. His sword swung low in his right hand, and an unaccustomed pallor tinged his dark face.

The silence that reigned in the jungle was not broken. The sun had set and great shadows rushed upward from the slime of the black earth. Through the gigantic shades of lurking death and grim desolation Conan was a speeding glimmer of scarlet and blue steel. No sound in all the solitude was heard except his own quick panting as he burst from the shadows into the dim twilight of the river-shore.

He saw the galley shouldering the rotten wharf, the ruins reeling drunkenly in the gray half-light.

And here and there among the stones were spots of raw bright color, as if a careless hand had splashed with a crimson brush.

Again Conan looked on death and destruction. Before him lay his spearmen, nor did they rise to salute him. From the jungle edge to the riverbank, among the rotting pillars and along the broken piers they lay, torn and mangled and half devoured, chewed travesties of men.

All about the bodies and pieces of bodies were swarms of huge footprints, like those of hyenas.

Conan came silently upon the pier, approaching the galley above whose deck was suspended something that glimmered ivory-white in the faint twilight. Speechless, the Cimmerian looked on the Queen of the Black Coast as she hung from the yard-arm of her own galley. Between the yard and her white throat stretched a line of crimson clots that shone like blood in the gray light.

IV

The shadows were black around him,
The dripping jaws gaped wide,
Thicker than rain the red drops fell;
But my love was fiercer than Death's black spell,
Nor all the iron walls of hell
Could keep me from his side.

The Song of Belît

The jungle was a black colossus that locked the ruin-littered glade in ebon arms. The moon had not risen; the stars were flecks of hot amber in a breathless sky that reeked of death. On the pyramid among the fallen towers sat Conan the Cimmerian like an iron statue, chin propped on massive fists. Out in the black shadows stealthy feet padded and red eyes glimmered. The dead lay as they had fallen. But on the deck of the *Tigress*, on a pyre of broken benches, spear-shafts and leopard-skins, lay the Queen of the Black Coast in her last sleep, wrapped in Conan's scarlet cloak. Like a true queen she lay, with her plunder heaped high about her: silks, cloth-of-gold, silver braid, casks of gems and golden coins, silver ingots, jeweled daggers and teocallis of gold wedges.

But of the plunder of the accursed city, only the sullen waters of Zarkheba could tell where Conan had thrown it with a heathen curse. Now he sat grimly on the pyramid, waiting for his unseen foes. The black fury in his soul drove out all fear. What shapes would emerge from the blackness he knew not, nor did he care.

He no longer doubted the visions of the black lotus. He understood that while waiting for him in the glade, N'Gora and his comrades had been terror-stricken by the winged monster swooping upon them from the sky, and fleeing in blind panic, had fallen over the cliff, all except their chief, who had somehow escaped their fate, though not madness.

Meanwhile, or immediately after, or perhaps before, the destruction of those on the riverbank had been accomplished. Conan did not doubt that the slaughter along the river had been massacre rather than battle. Already unmanned by their superstitious fears, the blacks might well have died without striking a blow in their own defense when attacked by their inhuman foes.

Why he had been spared so long, he did not understand, unless the malign entity which ruled the river meant to keep him alive to torture him with grief and fear. All pointed to a human or superhuman intelligence—the breaking of the watercasks to divide the forces, the driving of the blacks over the cliff, and last and greatest, the grim jest of the crimson necklace knotted like a hangman's noose about Belît's white neck.

Having apparently saved the Cimmerian for the choicest victim, and extracted the last ounce of exquisite mental torture, it was likely that the unknown enemy would conclude the drama by sending him after the other victims. No smile bent Conan's grim lips at the thought, but his eyes were lit with iron laughter.

The moon rose, striking fire from the Cimmerian's horned helmet. No call awoke the echoes; yet suddenly the night grew tense and the jungle held its breath. Instinctively Conan loosened the great sword in its sheath. The pyramid on which he rested was four-sided, one—the side toward the jungle carved in broad steps. In his hand was a Shemite bow, such as Belît had taught her pirates to use. A heap of arrows lay at his feet, feathered ends towards him, as he rested on one knee.

Something moved in the blackness under the trees. Etched abruptly in the rising moon, Conan saw a darkly blocked-out head and shoulders, brutish in outline. And now from the shadows dark shapes came silently, swiftly, running low—twenty great spotted hyenas. Their slavering fangs flashed in the moonlight, their eyes blazed as no true beast's eyes ever blazed.

Twenty: then the spears of the pirates had taken toll of the pack, after all. Even as he thought this, Conan drew nock to ear, and at the twang of the string a flame-eyed shadow bounded high and fell writhing. The rest did not falter; on they came, and like a rain of death among them fell the arrows of the Cimmerian, driven with all the force and accuracy of steely thews backed by a hate hot as the slag-heaps of hell.

In his berserk fury he did not miss; the air was filled with feathered destruction. The havoc wrought among the on-rushing pack was breathtaking. Less than half of them reached the foot of the pyramid. Others dropped upon the broad steps. Glaring down into the blazing eyes, Conan knew these creatures were not beasts; it was not merely in their unnatural size that he sensed a blasphemous difference. They exuded an aura tangible as the black mist rising from a corpse-littered swamp. By what godless alchemy these beings had been brought into existence, he could not guess; but he knew he faced diabolism blacker than the Well of Skelos.

Springing to his feet, he bent his bow powerfully and drove his last shaft point blank at a great hairy shape that soared up at his throat. The arrow was a flying beam of moonlight that flashed onward with but a blur in its course, but the were-beast plunged convulsively in mid-air and crashed headlong, shot through and through.

Then the rest were on him, in a nightmare rush of blazing eyes and dripping fangs. His fiercely driven sword sheared the first asunder; then the desperate impact of the others bore him down. He crushed a narrow skull with the pommel of his hilt, feeling the bone splinter and blood and brains gush over his hand; then, dropping the sword, useless at such deadly close quarters, he caught at the throats of the two horrors which were ripping and tearing at him in silent fury. A foul acrid scent almost stifled him, his own sweat blinded him. Only his mail saved him from being ripped to ribbons in an instant. The next, his naked right hand locked on a hairy throat and tore it open. His left hand, missing the throat of the other beast, caught and broke its foreleg. A short yelp, the only cry in that grim battle, and hideously human-like, burst from the maimed beast. At the sick horror of that cry from a bestial throat, Conan involuntarily relaxed his grip.

One, blood gushing from its torn jugular, lunged at him in a last spasm of ferocity, and fastened its fangs on his throat—to fall back dead, even as Conan felt the tearing agony of its grip.

The other, springing forward on three legs, was slashing at his belly as a wolf slashes, actually rending the links of his mail. Flinging aside the dying beast, Conan grappled the crippled horror and, with a muscular effort that brought a groan from his blood-flecked lips, he heaved upright, gripping the struggling, bearing fiend in his arms. An instant he reeled off balance, its fetid breath hot on his nostrils; its jaws snapping at his neck; then he hurled it from him, to crash with bone-splintering force down the marble steps.

As he reeled on wide-braced legs, sobbing for breath, the jungle and the moon swimming bloodily to his sight, the thrash of bat-wings was loud in his ears. Stooping, he groped for his sword, and swaying upright, braced his feet drunkenly and heaved the great blade above his head with both hands, shaking the blood from his eyes as he sought the air above him for his foe.

Instead of attack from the air, the pyramid staggered suddenly and awfully beneath his feet. He heard a rumbling crackle and saw the tall column above him wave like a wand. Stung to galvanized life, he bounded far out; his feet hit a step, halfway down, which rocked beneath him, and his next desperate leap carried him clear. But even as his heels hit the earth, with a shattering crash like a breaking mountain the pyramid crumpled, the column came thundering down in bursting fragments. For a blind cataclysmic instant the sky seemed to rain shards of marble. Then a rubble of shattered stone lay whitely under the moon.

Conan stirred, throwing off the splinters that half covered him. A glancing blow had knocked off his helmet and momentarily stunned him. Across his legs lay a great piece of the column, pinning him down. He was not sure that his legs were unbroken. His black locks were plastered with sweat; blood trickled from the wounds in his throat and hands. He hitched up on one arm, struggling with the debris that prisoned him.

Then something swept down across the stars and struck the sward near him. Twisting about, he saw it—the winged one!

With fearful speed it was rushing upon him, and in that instant Conan had only a confused impression of a gigantic man-like shape hurtling along on bowed and stunted legs; of huge hairy arms outstretching misshapen black-nailed paws; of a malformed head, in whose broad face the only features recognizable as such were a pair of blood-red eyes. It was a thing neither man, beast, nor devil, imbued with characteristics subhuman as well as characteristics superhuman.

But Conan had no time for conscious consecutive thought. He threw himself toward his fallen sword, and his clawing fingers missed it by inches. Desperately he grasped the shard which pinned his legs, and the veins swelled in his temples as he strove to thrust it off him. It gave slowly, but he knew that before he could free himself the monster would be upon him, and he knew that those black-taloned hands were death.

The headlong rush of the winged one had not wavered. It towered over the prostrate Cimmerian like a black shadow, arms thrown wide—a glimmer of white flashed between it and its victim.

In one mad instant she was there—a tense white shape, vibrant with love fierce as a she-panther's. The dazed Cimmerian saw between him and the on-rushing death, her lithe figure, shimmering like ivory beneath the moon; he saw the blaze of her dark eyes, the thick cluster of her burnished hair; her bosom heaved, her red lips were parted, she cried out sharp and ringing at the ring of steel as she thrust at the winged monster's breast.

"Belît!" screamed Conan. She flashed a quick glance at him, and in her dark eyes he saw her love flaming, a naked elemental thing of raw fire and molten lava. Then she was gone, and the Cimmerian saw only the winged fiend which had staggered back in unwonted fear, arms lifted as if to fend off attack. And he knew that Belît in truth lay on her pyre on the *Tigress*'s deck. In his ears rang her passionate cry: "Were I still in death and you fighting for life I would come back from the abyss—"

With a terrible cry he heaved upward hurling the stone aside. The winged one came on again, and Conan sprang to meet it, his veins on fire with madness. The thews started out like cords on his forearms as he swung his great sword, pivoting on his heel with the force of the sweeping arc. Just above the hips it caught the hurtling shape, and the knotted legs fell one way, the torso another as the blade sheared clear through its hairy body.

Conan stood in the moonlit silence, the dripping sword sagging in his hand, staring down at the remnants of his enemy. The red eyes glared up at him with awful life, then glazed and set; the great hands knotted spasmodically and stiffened. And the oldest race in the world was extinct.

Conan lifted his head, mechanically searching for the beast-things that had been its slaves and executioners. None met his gaze. The bodies he saw littering the moon-splashed grass were of men, not beasts: hawk-faced, dark-skinned men, naked, transfixed by arrows or mangled by sword-strokes. And they were crumbling into dust before his eyes.

Why had not the winged master come to the aid of its slaves when he struggled with them? Had it feared to come within reach of fangs that might turn and rend it? Craft and caution had lurked in that misshapen skull, but had not availed in the end.

Turning on his heel, the Cimmerian strode down the rotting wharfs and stepped aboard the galley. A few strokes of his sword cut her adrift, and he went to the sweep-head. The *Tigress* rocked slowly in the sullen water, sliding out sluggishly toward the middle of the river, until the broad current caught her. Conan leaned on the sweep, his somber gaze fixed on the cloak-wrapped shape that lay in state on the pyre the richness of which was equal to the ransom of an empress.

V

Now we are done with roaming, evermore;
No more the oars, the windy harp's refrain;
Nor crimson pennon frights the dusky shore;
Blue girdle of the world, receive again
Her whom thou gavest me.

The Song of Belît

Again dawn tinged the ocean. A redder glow lit the river-mouth. Conan of Cimmeria leaned on his great sword upon the white beach, watching the *Tigress* swinging out on her last voyage. There was no light in his eyes that contemplated the glassy swells. Out of the rolling blue wastes all glory and wonder had gone. A fierce revulsion shook him as he gazed at the green surges that deepened into purple hazes of mystery.

Belît had been of the sea; she had lent it splendor and allure. Without her it rolled a barren, dreary and desolate waste from pole to pole. She belonged to the sea; to its everlasting mystery he returned her. He could do no more. For himself, its glittering blue splendor was more repellent than the leafy fronds which rustled and whispered behind him of vast mysterious wilds beyond them, and into which he must plunge.

No hand was at the sweep of the *Tigress*, no oars drove her through the green water. But a clean tanging wind bellied her silken sail, and as a wild swan cleaves the sky to her nest, she sped seaward, flames mounting higher and higher from her deck to lick at the mast and envelop the figure that lay lapped in scarlet on the shining pyre.

So passed the Queen of the Black Coast, and leaning on his red-stained sword, Conan stood silently until the red glow had faded far out in the blue hazes and dawn splashed its rose and gold over the ocean.

THE DUNWICH HORROR

H. P. LOVECRAFT

Gorgons and Hydras and Chimaeras—dire stories of Celaeno and the Harpies—may reproduce themselves in the brain of superstition—*but they were there before.* They are transcripts, types—the archetypes are in us, and eternal. How else should the recital of that which we know in a waking sense to be false come to affect us at all? Is it that we naturally conceive terror from such objects, considered in their capacity of being able to inflict upon us bodily injury? O, least of all! *These terrors are of older standing. They date beyond body*—or without the body, they would have been the same... That the kind of fear here treated is purely spiritual—that it is strong in proportion as it is objectless on earth, that it predominates in the period of our sinless infancy—are difficulties the solution of which might afford some probable insight into our ante-mundane condition, and a peep at least into the shadowland of pre-existence.

—Charles Lamb: *Witches and Other Night-Fears*

I

When a traveler in north central Massachusetts takes the wrong fork at the junction of the Aylesbury pike just beyond Dean's Corners he comes upon a lonely and curious country. The ground gets higher, and the brier-bordered stone walls press closer and closer against the ruts of the dusty, curving road. The trees of the frequent forest belts seem too large, and the wild weeds, brambles and grasses attain a luxuriance not often found in settled regions. At the same time, the planted fields appear singularly few and barren; while the sparsely scattered houses wear a surprisingly uniform aspect of age, squalor, and dilapidation. Without knowing why, one hesitates to ask directions from the gnarled, solitary figures spied now and then on crumbling doorsteps or on the sloping, rock-strewn meadows. Those figures are so silent and furtive that one feels somehow confronted by forbidden things, with which it would be better to have nothing to do. When a rise in the road brings the mountains in view above the deep woods, the feeling of strange uneasiness is increased. The summits are too rounded and symmetrical to give a sense of comfort and naturalness, and sometimes the sky silhouettes with especial clearness the queer circles of tall stone pillars with which most of them are crowned.

Gorges and ravines of problematical depth intersect the way, and the crude wooden bridges always seem of dubious safety. When the road dips again there are stretches of marshland that one instinctively dislikes, and indeed almost fears at evening when unseen whippoorwills chatter and the fireflies come out in abnormal profusion to dance to the raucous, creepily insistent rhythms of stridently piping bull-frogs. The thin, shining line of the Miskatonic's upper reaches has an oddly serpent-like suggestion as it winds close to the feet of the domed hills among which it rises.

As the hills draw nearer, one heeds their wooded sides more than their stone-crowned tops. Those sides loom up so darkly and precipitously that one wishes they would keep their distance, but there is no road by which to escape them. Across a covered bridge one sees a small village huddled between the stream and the vertical slope of Round Mountain, and wonders at the cluster of rotting gambrel roofs bespeaking an earlier architectural period than that of the neighboring region. It is not reassuring to see, on a closer glance, that most of the houses are deserted and falling to ruin, and that the broken-steepled church now harbors the one slovenly mercantile establishment of the hamlet. One dreads to trust the tenebrous tunnel of the bridge, yet there is no way to avoid it. Once across, it is hard to prevent the impression of a faint, malign odor about the village street, as of the massed mold and decay of centuries. It is always a relief to get clear of the place, and to follow the narrow road around the base of the hills and across the level country beyond till it rejoins the Aylesbury pike. Afterward one sometimes learns that one has been through Dunwich.

Outsiders visit Dunwich as seldom as possible, and since a certain season of horror all the signboards pointing toward it have been taken down. The scenery, judged by any ordinary aesthetic canon, is more than commonly beautiful; yet there is no influx of artists or summer tourists. Two centuries ago, when talk of witch-blood, Satan-worship and strange forest presences was not laughed at, it was the custom to give reasons for avoiding the locality. In our sensible age—since the Dunwich horror of 1928 was hushed up by those who had the town's and the world's welfare at heart—people shun it without knowing exactly why. Perhaps one reason—though it cannot apply to uninformed strangers—is that the natives are now repellently decadent, having gone far along that path of retrogression so common in many New England backwaters. They have come to form a race by themselves, with the well-defined mental and physical stigmata of degeneracy and inbreeding. The average of their intelligence is woefully low, whilst their annals reek of overt viciousness and of half-hidden murders, incests, and deeds of almost unnamable violence and perversity. The old gentry, representing the two or three armigerous families which came from Salem in 1692, have kept somewhat above the general level of decay; though many branches are sunk into the sordid populace so deeply that only their names remain as a key to the origin they disgrace. Some of the Whateleys and Bishops still send their eldest sons to Harvard and Miskatonic, though those sons seldom return to the moldering gambrel roofs under which they and their ancestors were born.

No one, even those who have the facts concerning the recent horror, can say just what is the matter with Dunwich; though old legends speak of unhallowed rites and conclaves of the Indians, amidst which they called forbidden shapes of shadow out of the great rounded hills, and made wild orgiastic prayers that were answered by loud crackings and rumblings from the ground below. In 1747 the Reverend Abijah Hoadley, newly come to the Congregational Church at Dunwich Village, preached a memorable sermon on the close presence of Satan and his imps; in which he said:

> *It must be allow'd, that these Blasphemies of an infernall Train of Daemons are Matters of too common Knowledge to be deny'd; the cursed Voices of Azazel and Buzrael, of Beelzebub and Belial, being heard now from under Ground by above a Score of credible Witnesses now living. I myself did not more than a Fortnight ago catch a very plain Discourse of evill Powers in the Hill behind my House; wherein there were a Rattling and Rolling, Groaning, Screeching, and Hissing, such as no Things of this Earth cou'd raise up, and which must needs have come from those Caves that only black Magick can discover, and only the Divell unlock.*

Mr Hoadley disappeared soon after delivering this sermon; but the text, printed in Springfield, is still extant. Noises in the hills continued to be reported from year to year, and still form a puzzle to geologists and physiographers.

Other traditions tell of foul odors near the hill-crowning circles of stone pillars, and of rushing airy presences to be heard faintly at certain hours from stated points at the bottom of the great ravines; while still others try to explain the Devil's Hop Yard—a bleak, blasted hillside where no tree, shrub or grass-blade will grow. Then too, the natives are mortally afraid of the numerous whippoorwills which grow vocal on warm nights. It is vowed that the birds are psychopomps lying in wait for the souls of the dying, and that they time their eerie cries in unison with the sufferer's struggling breath. If they can catch the fleeing soul when it leaves the body, they instantly flutter away chittering in daemoniac laughter; but if they fail, they subside gradually into a disappointed silence.

These tales, of course, are obsolete and ridiculous; because they come down from very old times. Dunwich is indeed ridiculously old—older by far than any of the communities within thirty miles of it. South of the village one may still spy the cellar walls and chimney of the ancient Bishop house, which was built before 1700; whilst the ruins of the mill at the falls, built in 1806, form the most modern piece of architecture to be seen. Industry did not flourish here, and the nineteenth-century factory movement proved short-lived. Oldest of all are the great rings of rough-hewn stone columns on the hilltops, but these are more generally attributed to the Indians than to the settlers. Deposits of skulls and bones, found within these circles and around the sizeable table-like rock on Sentinel Hill, sustain the popular belief that such spots were once the burial-places of the Pocumtucks; even though many ethnologists, disregarding the absurd improbability of such a theory, persist in believing the remains Caucasian.

II

It was in the township of Dunwich, in a large and partly inhabited farmhouse set against a hillside four miles from the village and a mile and a half from any other dwelling, that Wilbur Whateley was born at 5 a.m. on Sunday, February 2nd, 1913. This date was recalled because it was Candlemas, which people in Dunwich curiously observe under another name; and because the noises in the hills had sounded, and all the dogs of the countryside had barked persistently, throughout the night before. Less worthy of notice was the fact that the mother was one of the decadent Whateleys, a somewhat deformed, unattractive albino woman of thirty-five, living with an aged and half-insane father about whom the most frightful tales of wizardry had been whispered in his youth. Lavinia Whateley had no known husband, but according to the custom of the region made no attempt to disavow the child; concerning the other side of whose ancestry the country folk might—and did—speculate as widely as they chose. On the contrary, she seemed strangely proud of the dark, goatish-looking infant who formed such a contrast to her own sickly and pink-eyed albinism, and was heard to mutter many curious prophecies about its unusual powers and tremendous future.

Lavinia was one who would be apt to mutter such things, for she was a lone creature given to wandering amidst thunderstorms in the hills and trying to read the great odorous books which her father had inherited through two centuries of Whateleys, and which were fast falling to pieces with age and worm-holes. She had never been to school, but was filled with disjointed scraps of ancient lore that Old Whateley had taught her. The remote farmhouse had always been feared because of Old Whateley's reputation for black magic, and the unexplained death by violence of Mrs Whateley when Lavinia was twelve years old had not helped to make the place popular. Isolated among strange influences, Lavinia was fond of wild and grandiose daydreams and singular occupations; nor was her leisure much taken up by household cares in a home from which all standards of order and cleanliness had long since disappeared.

There was a hideous screaming which echoed above even the hill noises and the dogs' barking on the night Wilbur was born, but no known doctor or midwife presided at his coming. Neighbors knew nothing of him till a week afterward, when Old Whateley drove his sleigh through the snow into Dunwich Village and discoursed incoherently to the group of loungers at Osborn's general store. There seemed to be a change in the old man—an added element of furtiveness in the clouded brain which subtly transformed him from an object to a subject of fear—though he was not one to be perturbed by any common family event. Amidst it all he showed some trace of the pride later noticed in his daughter, and what he said of the child's paternity was remembered by many of his hearers years afterward.

"I dun't keer what folks think—ef Lavinny's boy looked like his pa, he wouldn't look like nothin' ye expeck. Ye needn't think the only folks is the folks hereabaouts. Lavinny's read some, an' has seed some things the most o' ye only tell abaout. I calc'late her man is as good a husban' as ye kin find this side of Aylesbury; an' ef ye knowed as much abaout the hills as I dew, ye wouldn't ast no better church weddin' nor her'n. Let me tell ye suthin'—*some day yew folks'll hear a child o' Lavinny's a-callin' its father's name on the top o' Sentinel Hill!*"

The only persons who saw Wilbur during the first month of his life were old Zechariah Whateley, of the undecayed Whateleys, and Earl Sawyer's common-law wife, Mamie Bishop. Mamie's visit was frankly one of curiosity, and her subsequent tales did justice to her observations; but Zechariah came to lead a pair of Alderney cows which Old Whateley had bought of his son Curtis. This marked the beginning of a course of cattle-buying on the part of small Wilbur's family which ended only in 1928, when the Dunwich horror came and went; yet at no time did the ramshackle Whateley barn seem overcrowded with livestock. There came a period when people were curious enough to steal up and count the herd that grazed precariously on the steep hillside above the old farmhouse, and they could never find more than ten or twelve anemic, bloodless-looking specimens. Evidently some blight or distemper, perhaps sprung from the unwholesome pasturage or the diseased fungi and timbers of the filthy barn, caused a heavy mortality amongst the Whateley animals. Odd wounds or sores, having something of the aspect of incisions, seemed to afflict the visible cattle; and once or twice during the earlier months certain callers fancied they could discern similar sores about the throats of the gray, unshaven old man and his slatternly, crinkly-haired albino daughter.

In the spring after Wilbur's birth Lavinia resumed her customary rambles in the hills, bearing in her misproportioned arms the swarthy child. Public interest in the Whateleys subsided after most of the country folk had seen the baby, and no one bothered to comment on the swift development which that newcomer seemed every day to exhibit. Wilbur's growth was indeed phenomenal, for within three months of his birth he had attained a size and muscular power not usually found in infants under a full year of age. His motions and even his vocal sounds showed a restraint and deliberateness highly peculiar in an infant, and no one was really unprepared when, at seven months, he began to walk unassisted, with falterings which another month was sufficient to remove.

It was somewhat after this time—on Hallowe'en—that a great blaze was seen at midnight on the top of Sentinel Hill where the old table-like stone stands amidst its tumulus of ancient bones. Considerable talk was started when Silas Bishop—of the undecayed Bishops—mentioned having seen the boy running sturdily up that hill ahead of his mother about an hour before the blaze was remarked. Silas was rounding up a stray heifer, but he nearly forgot his mission when he fleetingly spied the two figures in the dim light of his lantern. They darted almost noiselessly through the underbrush, and the astonished watcher seemed to think they were entirely unclothed. Afterward he could not be sure about the boy, who may have had some kind of a fringed belt and a pair of dark trunks or trousers on. Wilbur was never subsequently seen alive and conscious without complete and tightly buttoned attire, the disarrangement or threatened disarrangement of which always seemed to fill him with anger and alarm. His contrast with his squalid mother and grandfather in this respect was thought very notable until the horror of 1928 suggested the most valid of reasons.

The next January gossips were mildly interested in the fact that "Lavinny's black brat" had commenced to talk, and at the age of only eleven months. His speech was somewhat remarkable both because of its difference from the ordinary accents of the region, and because it displayed a freedom from infantile lisping of which many children of three or four might well be proud. The boy was not talkative, yet when he spoke he seemed to reflect some elusive element wholly unpossessed by Dunwich and its denizens. The strangeness did not reside in what he said, or even in the simple idioms he used; but seemed vaguely linked with his intonation or with the internal organs that produced the spoken sounds. His facial aspect, too, was remarkable for its maturity; for though he shared his mother's and grandfather's chinlessness, his firm and precociously shaped nose united with the expression of his large, dark, almost Latin eyes to give him an air of quasi-adulthood and well-nigh preternatural intelligence. He was, however, exceedingly ugly despite his appearance of brilliancy; there being something almost goatish or animalistic about his thick lips, large-pored, yellowish skin, coarse crinkly hair, and oddly elongated ears. He was soon disliked even more decidedly than his mother and grandsire, and all conjectures about him were spiced with references to the bygone magic of Old Whateley, and how the hills once shook when he shrieked the dreadful name of *Yog-Sothoth* in the midst of a circle of stones with a great book open in his arms before him. Dogs abhorred the boy, and he was always obliged to take various defensive measures against their barking menace.

III

Meanwhile Old Whateley continued to buy cattle without measurably increasing the size of his herd. He also cut timber and began to repair the unused parts of his house—a spacious, peaked-roofed affair whose rear end was buried entirely in the rocky hillside, and whose three least-ruined ground-floor rooms had always been sufficient for himself and his daughter.

There must have been prodigious reserves of strength in the old man to enable him to accomplish so much hard labor; and though he still babbled dementedly at times, his carpentry seemed to show the effects of sound calculation. It had already begun as soon as Wilbur was born, when one of the many toolsheds had been put suddenly in order, clapboarded, and fitted with a stout fresh lock. Now, in restoring the abandoned upper story of the house, he was a no less thorough craftsman. His mania showed itself only in his tight boarding-up of all the windows in the reclaimed section—though many declared that it was a crazy thing to bother with the reclamation at all.

Less inexplicable was his fitting up of another downstairs room for his new grandson—a room which several callers saw, though no one was ever admitted to the closely boarded upper story. This chamber he lined with tall, firm shelving; along which he began gradually to arrange, in apparently careful order, all the rotting ancient books and parts of books which during his own day had been heaped promiscuously in odd corners of the various rooms.

"I made some use of 'em," he would say as he tried to mend a torn black-letter page with paste prepared on the rusty kitchen stove, "but the boy's fitten to make better use of 'em. He'd orter hev 'em as well sot as he kin, for they're goin' to be all of his larnin'."

When Wilbur was a year and seven months old—in September of 1914—his size and accomplishments were almost alarming. He had grown as large as a child of four, and was a fluent and incredibly intelligent talker. He ran freely about the fields and hills, and accompanied his mother on all her wanderings. At home he would pore diligently over the queer pictures and charts in his grandfather's books, while Old Whateley would instruct and catechize him through long, hushed afternoons. By this time the restoration of the house was finished, and those who watched it wondered why one of the upper windows had been made into a solid plank door. It was a window in the rear of the east gable end, close against the hill; and no one could imagine why a cleated wooden runway was built up to it from the ground. About the period of this work's completion people noticed that the old tool-house, tightly locked and windowlessly clapboarded since Wilbur's birth, had been abandoned again. The door swung listlessly open, and when Earl Sawyer once stepped within after a cattle-selling call on Old Whateley he was quite discomposed by the singular odor he encountered—such a stench, he averred, as he had never before smelled in all his life except near the Indian circles on the hills, and which could not come from anything sane or of this earth. But then, the homes and sheds of Dunwich folk have never been remarkable for olfactory immaculateness.

The following months were void of visible events, save that everyone swore to a slow but steady increase in the mysterious hill noises. On May Eve of 1915 there were tremors which even the Aylesbury people felt, whilst the following Hallowe'en produced an underground rumbling queerly synchronized with bursts of flame—"them witch Whateleys' doin's"—from the summit of Sentinel Hill. Wilbur was growing up uncannily, so that he looked like a boy of ten as he entered his fourth year. He read avidly by himself now; but talked much less than formerly. A settled taciturnity was absorbing him, and for the first time people began to speak specifically of the dawning look of evil in his goatish face. He would sometimes mutter an unfamiliar jargon, and chant in bizarre rhythms which chilled the listener with a sense of unexplainable terror. The aversion displayed toward him by dogs had now become a matter of wide remark, and he was obliged to carry a pistol in order to traverse the countryside in safety. His occasional use of the weapon did not enhance his popularity amongst the owners of canine guardians.

The few callers at the house would often find Lavinia alone on the ground floor, while odd cries and footsteps resounded in the boarded-up second story. She would never tell what her father and the boy were doing up there, though once she turned pale and displayed an abnormal degree of fear when a jocose fish-peddler tried the locked door leading to the stairway. That peddler told the store loungers at Dunwich Village that he thought he heard a horse stamping on that floor above. The loungers reflected, thinking of the door and runway, and of the cattle that so swiftly disappeared. Then they shuddered as they recalled tales of Old Whateley's youth, and of the strange things that are called out of the earth when a bullock is sacrificed at the proper time to certain heathen gods. It had for some time been noticed that dogs had begun to hate and fear the whole Whateley place as violently as they hated and feared young Wilbur personally.

In 1917 the war came, and Squire Sawyer Whateley, as chairman of the local draft board, had hard work finding a quota of young Dunwich men fit even to be sent to a development camp. The government, alarmed at such signs of wholesale regional decadence, sent several officers and medical experts to investigate; conducting a survey which New England newspaper readers may still recall. It was the publicity attending this investigation which set reporters on the track of the Whateleys, and caused the *Boston Globe* and *Arkham Advertiser* to print flamboyant Sunday stories of young Wilbur's precociousness, Old Whateley's black magic, the shelves of strange books, the sealed second story of the ancient farmhouse, and the weirdness of the whole region and its hill noises. Wilbur was four and a half then, and looked like a lad of fifteen. His lips and cheeks were fuzzy with a coarse dark down, and his voice had begun to break.

Earl Sawyer went out to the Whateley place with both sets of reporters and camera men, and called their attention to the queer stench which now seemed to trickle down from the sealed upper spaces. It was, he said, exactly like a smell he had found in the toolshed abandoned when the house was finally repaired; and like the faint odors which he sometimes thought he caught near the stone circles on the mountains. Dunwich folk read the stories when they appeared, and grinned over the obvious mistakes. They wondered, too, why the writers made so much of the fact that Old Whateley always paid for his cattle in gold pieces of extremely ancient date. The Whateleys had received their visitors with ill-concealed distaste, though they did not dare court further publicity by a violent resistance or refusal to talk.

IV

For a decade the annals of the Whateleys sink indistinguishably into the general life of a morbid community used to their queer ways and hardened to their May Eve and All-Hallows orgies. Twice a year they would light fires on the top of Sentinel Hill, at which times the mountain rumblings would recur with greater and greater violence; while at all seasons there were strange and portentous doings at the lonely farmhouse. In the course of time callers professed to hear sounds in the sealed upper story even when all the family were downstairs, and they wondered how swiftly or how lingeringly a cow or bullock was usually sacrificed. There was talk of a complaint to the Society for the Prevention of Cruelty to Animals; but nothing ever came of it, since Dunwich folk are never anxious to call the outside world's attention to themselves.

About 1923, when Wilbur was a boy of ten whose mind, voice, stature, and bearded face gave all the impressions of maturity, a second great siege of carpentry went on at the old house. It was all inside the sealed upper part, and from bits of discarded lumber people concluded that the youth and his grandfather had knocked out all the partitions and even removed the attic floor, leaving only one vast open void between the ground story and the peaked roof. They had torn down the great central chimney, too, and fitted the rusty range with a flimsy outside tin stovepipe.

In the spring after this event Old Whateley noticed the growing number of whippoorwills that would come out of Cold Spring Glen to chirp under his window at night. He seemed to regard the circumstance as one of great significance, and told the loungers at Osborn's that he thought his time had almost come.

"They whistle jest in tune with my breathin' naow," he said, "an' I guess they're gittin' ready to ketch my soul. They know it's a-goin' aout, an' dun't calc'late to miss it. Yew'll know, boys, arter I'm gone, whether they git me er not. Ef they dew, they'll keep up a-singin' an' laffin' till break o' day. Ef they dun't they'll kinder quiet daown like. I expeck them an' the souls they hunts fer hev some pretty tough tussles sometimes."

On Lammas Night, 1924, Dr Houghton of Aylesbury was hastily summoned by Wilbur Whateley, who had lashed his one remaining horse through the darkness and telephoned from Osborn's in the village. He found Old Whateley in a very grave state, with a cardiac action and stertorous breathing that told of an end not far off. The shapeless albino daughter and oddly bearded grandson stood by the bedside, whilst from the vacant abyss overhead there came a disquieting suggestion of rhythmical surging or lapping, as of the waves on some level beach. The doctor, though, was chiefly disturbed by the chattering night birds outside; a seemingly limitless legion of whippoorwills that cried their endless message in repetitions timed diabolically to the wheezing gasps of the dying man.

It was uncanny and unnatural—too much, thought Dr Houghton, like the whole of the region he had entered so reluctantly in response to the urgent call.

Toward one o'clock Old Whateley gained consciousness, and interrupted his wheezing to choke out a few words to his grandson.

"More space, Willy, more space soon. Yew grows—an' *that* grows faster. It'll be ready to sarve ye soon, boy. Open up the gates to Yog-Sothoth with the long chant that ye'll find on page 751 *of the complete edition,* an' *then* put a match to the prison. Fire from airth can't burn it nohaow."

He was obviously quite mad. After a pause, during which the flock of whippoorwills outside adjusted their cries to the altered tempo while some indications of the strange hill noises came from afar off, he added another sentence or two.

"Feed it reg'lar, Willy, an' mind the quantity; but dun't let it grow too fast fer the place, fer ef it busts quarters or gits aout afore ye opens to Yog-Sothoth, it's all over an' no use. Only them from beyont kin make it multiply an' work.... Only them, the old uns as wants to come back...."

But speech gave place to gasps again, and Lavinia screamed at the way the whippoorwills followed the change. It was the same for more than an hour, when the final throaty rattle came. Dr Houghton drew shrunken lids over the glazing gray eyes as the tumult of birds faded imperceptibly to silence. Lavinia sobbed, but Wilbur only chuckled whilst the hill noises rumbled faintly.

"They didn't git him," he muttered in his heavy bass voice.

Wilbur was by this time a scholar of really tremendous erudition in his one-sided way, and was quietly known by correspondence to many librarians in distant places where rare and forbidden books of old days are kept. He was more and more hated and dreaded around Dunwich because of certain youthful disappearances which suspicion laid vaguely at his door; but was always able to silence inquiry through fear or through use of that fund of old-time gold which still, as in his grandfather's time, went forth regularly and increasingly for cattle-buying. He was now tremendously mature of aspect, and his height, having reached the normal adult limit, seemed inclined to wax beyond that figure. In 1925, when a scholarly correspondent from Miskatonic University called upon him one day and departed pale and puzzled, he was fully six-and-three-quarters feet tall.

Through all the years Wilbur had treated his half-deformed albino mother with a growing contempt, finally forbidding her to go to the hills with him on May Eve and Hallowmass; and in 1926 the poor creature complained to Mamie Bishop of being afraid of him.

"They's more abaout him as I knows than I kin tell ye, Mamie," she said, "an' naowadays they's more nor what I know myself. I vaow afur Gawd, I dun't know what he wants nor what he's a-tryin' to dew."

That Hallowe'en the hill noises sounded louder than ever, and fire burned on Sentinel Hill as usual; but people paid more attention to the rhythmical screaming of vast flocks of unnaturally belated whippoorwills which seemed to be assembled near the unlighted Whateley farmhouse. After midnight their shrill notes burst into a kind of pandemoniac cachinnation which filled all the countryside, and not until dawn did they finally quiet down. Then they vanished, hurrying southward where they were fully a month overdue. What this meant, no one could quite be certain till later. None of the country folk seemed to have died—but poor Lavinia Whateley, the twisted albino, was never seen again.

In the summer of 1927 Wilbur repaired two sheds in the farmyard and began moving his books and effects out to them. Soon afterward Earl Sawyer told the loungers at Osborn's that more carpentry was going on in the Whateley farmhouse. Wilbur was closing all the doors and windows on the ground floor, and seemed to be taking out partitions as he and his grandfather had done upstairs four years before. He was living in one of the sheds, and Sawyer thought he seemed unusually worried and tremulous. People generally suspected him of knowing something about his mother's disappearance, and very few ever approached his neighborhood now. His height had increased to more than seven feet, and showed no signs of ceasing its development.

V

The following winter brought an event no less strange than Wilbur's first trip outside the Dunwich region. Correspondence with the Widener Library at Harvard, the Bibliothèque Nationale in Paris, the British Museum, the University of Buenos Aires and the Library of Miskatonic University of Arkham had failed to get him the loan of a book he desperately wanted; so at length he set out in person, shabby, dirty, bearded and uncouth of dialect, to consult the copy at Miskatonic, which was the nearest to him geographically. Almost eight feet tall, and carrying a cheap new valise from

Osborn's general store, this dark and goatish gargoyle appeared one day in Arkham in quest of the dreaded volume kept under lock and key at the college library—the hideous *Necronomicon* of the mad Arab Abdul Alhazred in Olaus Wormius's Latin version, as printed in Spain in the seventeenth century. He had never seen a city before, but had no thought save to find his way to the university grounds; where, indeed, he passed heedlessly by the great white-fanged watchdog that barked with unnatural fury and enmity, and tugged frantically at its stout chain.

Wilbur had with him the priceless but imperfect copy of Dr Dee's English version which his grandfather had bequeathed him, and upon receiving access to the Latin copy he at once began to collate the two texts with the aim of discovering a certain passage which would have come on the 751st page of his own defective volume. This much he could not civilly refrain from telling the librarian—the same erudite Henry Armitage (A.M. Miskatonic, Ph. D. Princeton, Litt. D. Johns Hopkins) who had once called at the farm, and who now politely plied him with questions. He was looking, he had to admit, for a kind of formula or incantation containing the frightful name *Yog-Sothoth*, and it puzzled him to find discrepancies, duplications, and ambiguities which made the matter of determination far from easy. As he copied the formula he finally chose, Dr Armitage looked involuntarily over his shoulder at the open pages; the left-hand one of which, in the Latin version, contained such monstrous threats to the peace and sanity of the world.

> *Nor is it to be thought* [ran the text as Armitage mentally translated it] *that man is either the oldest or the last of earth's masters, or that the common bulk of life and substance walks alone. The Old Ones were, the Old Ones are, and the Old Ones shall be. Not in the spaces we know, but between them, They walk serene and primal, undimensioned and to us unseen. Yog-Sothoth knows the gate. Yog-Sothoth is the gate. Yog-Sothoth is the key and guardian of the gate. Past, present, future, all are one in Yog-Sothoth. He knows where the Old Ones broke through of old, and where They shall break through again. He knows where They have trod earth's fields, and where They still tread them, and why no one can behold Them as They tread. By Their smell can men sometimes know Them near, but of Their semblance can no man know, saving only in the features of those They have begotten on mankind; and of those are there many sorts, differing in likeness from man's truest eidolon to that shape without sight or substance which is Them. They walk unseen and foul in lonely places*

where the Words have been spoken and the Rites howled through at their Seasons. The wind gibbers with Their voices, and the earth mutters with Their consciousness. They bend the forest and crush the city, yet may not forest or city behold the hand that smites. Kadath in the cold waste hath known Them, and what man knows Kadath? The ice desert of the South and the sunken isles of Ocean hold stones whereon Their seal is engraven, but who hath seen the deep frozen city or the sealed tower long garlanded with seaweed and barnacles? Great Cthulhu is Their cousin, yet can he spy Them only dimly. Iä! Shub-Niggurath! As a foulness shall ye know Them. Their hand is at your throats, yet ye see Them not; and Their habitation is even one with your guarded threshold. Yog-Sothoth is the key to the gate, whereby the spheres meet. Man rules now where They ruled once; They shall soon rule where man rules now. After summer is winter, and after winter summer. They wait patient and potent, for here shall They reign again.

Dr Armitage, associating what he was reading with what he had heard of Dunwich and its brooding presences, and of Wilbur Whateley and his dim, hideous aura that stretched from a dubious birth to a cloud of probable matricide, felt a wave of fright as tangible as a draft of the tomb's cold clamminess. The bent, goatish giant before him seemed like the spawn of another planet or dimension; like something only partly of mankind, and linked to black gulfs of essence and entity that stretch like titan phantasms beyond all spheres of force and matter, space and time. Presently Wilbur raised his head and began speaking in that strange, resonant fashion which hinted at sound-producing organs unlike the run of mankind's.

"Mr Armitage," he said, "I calc'late I've got to take that book home. They's things in it I've got to try under sarten conditions that I can't git here, an' it 'ud be a mortal sin to let a red-tape rule hold me up. Let me take it along, Sir, an' I'll swar they wun't nobody know the difference. I dun't need to tell ye I'll take good keer of it. It wa'n't me that put this Dee copy in the shape it is...."

He stopped as he saw firm denial on the librarian's face, and his own goatish features grew crafty. Armitage, half-ready to tell him he might make a copy of what parts he needed, thought suddenly of the possible consequences and checked himself. There was too much responsibility in giving such a being the key to such blasphemous outer spheres. Whateley saw how things stood, and tried to answer lightly.

"Wal, all right, ef ye feel that way abaout it. Maybe Harvard wun't be so fussy as yew be." And without saying more he rose and strode out of the building, stooping at each doorway.

Armitage heard the savage yelping of the great watchdog, and studied Whateley's gorilla-like lope as he crossed the bit of campus visible from the window. He thought of the wild tales he had heard, and recalled the old Sunday stories in the *Advertiser;* these things, and the lore he had picked up from Dunwich rustics and villagers during his one visit there. Unseen things not of earth—or at least not of tri-dimensional earth—rushed fetid and horrible through New England's glens, and brooded obscenely on the mountain tops. Of this he had long felt certain. Now he seemed to sense the close presence of some terrible part of the intruding horror, and to glimpse a hellish advance in the black dominion of the ancient and once passive nightmare. He locked away the *Necronomicon* with a shudder of disgust, but the room still reeked with an unholy and unidentifiable stench. "As a foulness shall ye know them," he quoted. Yes—the odor was the same as that which had sickened him at the Whateley farmhouse less than three years before. He thought of Wilbur, goatish and ominous, once again, and laughed mockingly at the village rumors of his parentage.

"Inbreeding?" Armitage muttered half-aloud to himself. "Great God, what simpletons! Show them Arthur Machen's *The Great God Pan* and they'll think it a common Dunwich scandal! But what thing—what cursed shapeless influence on or off this three-dimensioned earth—was Wilbur Whateley's father? Born on Candlemas—nine months after May Eve of 1912, when the talk about the queer earth noises reached clear to Arkham—what walked on the mountains that May-Night? What Roodmas horror fastened itself on the world in half-human flesh and blood?"

During the ensuing weeks Dr Armitage set about to collect all possible data on Wilbur Whateley and the formless presences around Dunwich. He got in communication with Dr Houghton of Aylesbury, who had attended Old Whateley in his last illness, and found much to ponder over in the grandfather's last words as quoted by the physician. A visit to Dunwich Village failed to bring out much that was new; but a close survey of the *Necronomicon,* in those parts which Wilbur had sought so avidly, seemed to supply new and terrible clues to the nature, methods, and desires of the strange evil so vaguely threatening this planet. Talks with several students of archaic lore in Boston, and letters to many others elsewhere, gave him a growing amazement which passed slowly through varied degrees of alarm to a state of really acute spiritual fear. As the summer drew on he felt dimly that something ought to be done about the lurking terrors of the upper Miskatonic valley, and about the monstrous being known to the human world as Wilbur Whateley.

VI

The Dunwich horror itself came between Lammas and the equinox in 1928, and Dr Armitage was among those who witnessed its monstrous prologue. He had heard, meanwhile, of Whateley's grotesque trip to Cambridge, and of his frantic efforts to borrow or copy from the *Necronomicon* at the Widener Library. Those efforts had been in vain, since Armitage had issued warnings of the keenest intensity to all librarians having charge of the dreaded volume. Wilbur had been shockingly nervous at Cambridge; anxious for the book, yet almost equally anxious to get home again, as if he feared the results of being away long.

Early in August the half-expected outcome developed, and in the small hours of the 3rd Dr Armitage was awakened suddenly by the wild, fierce cries of the savage watchdog on the college campus. Deep and terrible, the snarling, half-mad growls and barks continued; always in mounting volume, but with hideously significant pauses. Then there rang out a scream from a wholly different throat—such a scream as roused half the sleepers of Arkham and haunted their dreams ever afterward—such a scream as could come from no being born of earth, or wholly of earth.

Armitage, hastening into some clothing and rushing across the street and lawn to the college buildings, saw that others were ahead of him; and heard the echoes of a burglar-alarm still shrilling from the library. An open window showed black and gaping in the moonlight. What had come had indeed completed its entrance; for the barking and the screaming, now fast fading into a mixed low growling and moaning, proceeded unmistakably from within. Some instinct warned Armitage that what was taking place was not a thing for unfortified eyes to see, so he brushed back the crowd with authority as he unlocked the vestibule door. Among the others he saw Professor Warren Rice and Dr Francis Morgan, men to whom he had told some of his conjectures and misgivings; and these two he motioned to accompany him inside. The inward sounds, except for a watchful, droning whine from the dog, had by this time quite subsided; but Armitage now perceived with a sudden start that a loud chorus of whippoorwills among the shrubbery had commenced a damnably rhythmical piping, as if in unison with the last breaths of a dying man.

The building was full of a frightful stench which Dr Armitage knew too well, and the three men rushed across the hall to the small genealogical reading-room whence the low whining came. For a second nobody dared to turn on the light, then Armitage summoned up his courage and snapped the switch. One of the three—it is not certain which—shrieked aloud at what sprawled before them among disordered tables and overturned chairs. Professor Rice declares that he wholly lost consciousness for an instant, though he did not stumble or fall.

The thing that lay half-bent on its side in a fetid pool of greenish-yellow ichor and tarry stickiness was almost nine feet tall, and the dog had torn off all the clothing and some of the skin. It was not quite dead, but twitched silently and spasmodically while its chest heaved in monstrous unison with the mad piping of the expectant whippoorwills outside. Bits of shoe leather and fragments of apparel were scattered about the room, and just inside the window an empty canvas sack lay where it had evidently been thrown. Near the central desk a revolver had fallen, a dented but undischarged cartridge later explaining why it had not been fired. The thing itself, however, crowded out all other images at the time. It would be trite and not wholly accurate to say that no human pen could describe it, but one may properly say that it could not be vividly visualized by anyone whose ideas of aspect and contour are too closely bound up with the common life-forms of this planet and of the three known dimensions. It was partly human, beyond a doubt, with very man-like hands and head, and the goatish, chinless face had the stamp of the Whateleys upon it. But the torso and lower parts of the body were teratologically fabulous, so that only generous clothing could ever have enabled it to walk on earth unchallenged or uneradicated.

Above the waist it was semi-anthropomorphic; though its chest, where the dog's rending paws still rested watchfully, had the leathery, reticulated hide of a crocodile or alligator. The back was piebald with yellow and black, and dimly suggested the squamous covering of certain snakes. Below the waist, though, it was the worst; for here all human resemblance left off and sheer fantasy began. The skin was thickly covered with coarse black fur, and from the abdomen a score of long greenish-gray tentacles with red sucking mouths protruded limply. Their arrangement was odd, and seemed to follow the symmetries of some cosmic geometry unknown to earth or the solar system. On each of the hips, deep set in a kind of pinkish, ciliated orbit, was what seemed to be a rudimentary eye; whilst in lieu of a tail there depended a kind of trunk or feeler with purple annular markings, and with many evidences of being an undeveloped mouth or throat. The limbs, save for their black fur, roughly resembled the hind legs of prehistoric earth's giant saurians; and terminated in ridgy-veined pads that were neither hooves nor claws. When the thing breathed, its tail and tentacles rhythmically changed color, as if from some circulatory cause normal to the non-human side of its ancestry. In the tentacles this was observable as a deepening of the greenish tinge, whilst in the tail it was manifest as a yellowish appearance which alternated with a sickly grayish-white in the spaces between the purple rings. Of genuine blood there was none; only the fetid greenish-yellow ichor which trickled along the painted floor beyond the radius of the stickiness, and left a curious discoloration behind it.

As the presence of the three men seemed to rouse the dying thing, it began to mumble without turning or raising its head. Dr Armitage made no written record of its mouthings, but asserts confidently that nothing in English was uttered. At first the syllables defied all correlation with any speech of earth, but toward the last there came some disjointed fragments evidently taken from the *Necronomicon*, that monstrous blasphemy in quest of which the thing had perished. These fragments, as Armitage recalls them, ran something like: "*N'gai, n'gha'ghaa, bugg-shoggog, y'hah; Yog-Sothoth, Yog-Sothoth....*" They trailed off into nothingness as the whippoorwills shrieked in rhythmical crescendos of unholy anticipation.

Then came a halt in the gasping, and the dog raised its head in a long, lugubrious howl. A change came over the yellow, goatish face of the prostrate thing, and the great black eyes fell in appallingly. Outside the window the shrilling of the whippoorwills had suddenly ceased, and above the murmurs of the gathering crowd there came the sound of a panic-struck whirring and fluttering. Against the moon vast clouds of feathery watchers rose and raced from sight, frantic at that which they had sought for prey.

All at once the dog started up abruptly, gave a frightened bark, and leaped nervously out of the window by which it had entered. A cry rose from the crowd, and Dr Armitage shouted to the men outside that no one must be admitted till the police or medical examiner came. He was thankful that the windows were just too high to permit of peering in, and drew the dark curtains carefully down over each one. By this time two policemen had arrived; and Dr Morgan, meeting them in the vestibule, was urging them for their own sakes to postpone entrance to the stench-filled reading-room till the examiner came and the prostrate thing could be covered up.

Meanwhile frightful changes were taking place on the floor. One need not describe the kind and rate of shrinkage and disintegration that occurred before the eyes of Dr Armitage and Professor Rice; but it is permissible to say that, aside from the external appearance of face and hands, the really human element in Wilbur Whateley must have been very small. When the medical examiner came, there was only a sticky whitish mass on the painted boards, and the monstrous odor had nearly disappeared. Apparently Whateley had had no skull or bony skeleton; at least, in any true or stable sense. He had taken somewhat after his unknown father.

VII

Yet all this was only the prologue of the actual Dunwich horror. Formalities were gone through by bewildered officials, abnormal details were duly kept from press and public, and men were sent to Dunwich and Aylesbury to look up property and notify any who might be heirs of the late Wilbur Whateley. They found the countryside in great agitation, both because of the growing rumblings beneath the domed hills, and because of the unwonted stench and the surging, lapping sounds which came increasingly from the great empty shell formed by Whateley's boarded-up farmhouse. Earl Sawyer, who tended the horse and cattle during Wilbur's absence, had developed a woefully acute case of nerves. The officials devised excuses not to enter the noisome boarded place; and were glad to confine their survey of the deceased's living quarters, the newly mended sheds, to a single visit. They filed a ponderous report at the courthouse in Aylesbury, and litigations concerning heirship are said to be still in progress amongst the innumerable Whateleys, decayed and undecayed, of the upper Miskatonic valley.

An almost interminable manuscript in strange characters, written in a huge ledger and adjudged a sort of diary because of the spacing and the variations in ink and penmanship, presented a baffling puzzle to those who found it on the old bureau which served as its owner's desk. After a week of debate it was sent to Miskatonic University, together with the deceased's collection of strange books, for study and possible translation; but even the best linguists soon saw that it was not likely to be unriddled with ease. No trace of the ancient gold with which Wilbur and Old Whateley always paid their debts has yet been discovered.

It was in the dark of September 9th that the horror broke loose. The hill noises had been very pronounced during the evening, and dogs barked frantically all night. Early risers on the 10th noticed a peculiar stench in the air. About seven o'clock Luther Brown, the hired boy at George Corey's, between Cold Spring Glen and the village, rushed frenziedly back from his morning trip to Ten-Acre Meadow with the cows. He was almost convulsed with fright as he stumbled into the kitchen; and in the yard outside the no less frightened herd were pawing and lowing pitifully, having followed the boy back in the panic they shared with him. Between gasps Luther tried to stammer out his tale to Mrs Corey.

"Up thar in the rud beyont the glen, Mis' Corey—they's suthin' ben thar! It smells like thunder, an' all the bushes an' little trees is pushed back from the rud like they'd a haouse ben moved along of it. An' that ain't the wust, nuther. They's *prints* in the rud, Mis' Corey—great raound prints as big as barrel-heads, all sunk daown deep like a elephant had ben along, *only they's a sight more nor four feet could make!* I looked at one or two afore I run, an' I see every one was covered with lines spreadin' aout from one place, like as if big palm-leaf fans—twict or three times as big as any they is—hed of ben paounded daown into the rud. An' the smell was awful, like what it is araound Wizard Whateley's ol' haouse...."

Here he faltered, and seemed to shiver afresh with the fright that had sent him flying home. Mrs Corey, unable to extract more information, began telephoning the neighbors; thus starting on its rounds the overture of panic that heralded the major terrors. When she got Sally Sawyer, housekeeper at Seth Bishop's, the nearest place to Whateley's, it became her turn to listen instead of transmit; for Sally's boy Chauncey, who slept poorly, had been up on the hill toward Whateley's, and had dashed back in terror after one look at the place, and at the pasturage where Mr Bishop's cows had been left out all night.

"Yes, Mis' Corey," came Sally's tremulous voice over the party wire, "Cha'ncey he just come back a-postin', and couldn't haff talk fer bein' scairt! He says Ol' Whateley's haouse is all blowed up, with the timbers scattered raound like they'd ben dynamite inside; only the bottom floor ain't through, but is all covered with a kind o' tar-like stuff that smells awful an' drips daown offen the aidges onto the graoun' whar the side timbers is blown away. An' they's awful kinder marks in the yard, tew—great raound marks bigger raound than a hogshead, an' all sticky with stuff like is on the blowed-up haouse. Cha'ncey he says they leads off into the medders, whar a great swath wider'n a barn is matted daown, an' all the stun walls tumbled every whichway wherever it goes.

"An' he says, says he, Mis' Corey, as haow he sot to look fer Seth's caows, frighted ez he was; an' faound 'em in the upper pasture nigh the Devil's Hop Yard in an awful shape. Haff on 'em's clean gone, an' nigh haff o' them that's left is sucked most dry o' blood, with sores on 'em like they's ben on Whateley's cattle ever senct Lavinny's black brat was born. Seth he's gone aout naow to look at 'em, though I'll vaow he wun't keer ter git very nigh Wizard Whateley's! Cha'ncey didn't look keerful ter see whar the big matted-daown swath led arter it leff the pasturage, but he says he thinks it p'inted towards the glen rud to the village.

"I tell ye, Mis' Corey, they's suthin' abroad as hadn't orter be abroad, an' I for one think that black Wilbur Whateley, as come to the bad eend he desarved, is at the bottom of the breedin' of it. He wa'n't all human hisself, I allus says to everybody; an' I think he an' Ol' Whateley must a raised suthin' in that there nailed-up haouse as ain't even so human as he was. They's allus ben unseen things araound Dunwich—livin' things—as ain't human an' ain't good fer human folks.

"The graoun' was a-talkin' lass night, an' towards mornin' Cha'ncey he heerd the whippoorwills so laoud in Col' Spring Glen he couldn't sleep nun. Then he thought he heerd another faint-like saound over towards Wizard Whateley's—a kinder rippin' or tearin' o' wood, like some big box er crate was bein' opened fur off. What with this an' that, he didn't git to sleep at all till sunup, an' no sooner was he up this mornin', but he's got to go over to Whateley's an' see what's the matter. He see enough, I tell ye, Mis' Corey! This dun't mean no good, an' I think as all the men-folks ought to git up a party an' do suthin'. I know suthin' awful's abaout, an' feel my time is nigh, though only Gawd knows jest what it is.

"Did your Luther take accaount o' whar them big tracks led tew? No? Wal, Mis' Corey, ef they was on the glen rud this side o' the glen, an' ain't got to your haouse yet, I calc'late they must go into the glen itself. They would do that. I allus says Col' Spring Glen ain't no healthy nor decent place. The whippoorwills an' fireflies there never did act like they was creaters o' Gawd, an' they's them as says ye kin hear strange things a-rushin' an' a-talkin' in the air daown thar ef ye stand in the right place, atween the rock falls an' Bear's Den."

By that noon fully three-quarters of the men and boys of Dunwich were trooping over the roads and meadows between the new-made Whateley ruins and Cold Spring Glen, examining in horror the vast, monstrous prints, the maimed Bishop cattle, the strange, noisome wreck of the farmhouse, and the bruised, matted vegetation of the fields and roadsides. Whatever had burst loose upon the world had assuredly gone down into the great sinister ravine; for all the trees on the banks were bent and broken, and a great avenue had been gouged in the precipice-hanging underbrush. It was as though a house, launched by an avalanche, had slid down through the tangled growths of the almost vertical slope. From below no sound came, but only a distant, undefinable fetor; and it is not to be wondered at that the men preferred to stay on the edge and argue, rather than descend and beard the unknown Cyclopean horror in its lair. Three dogs that were with the party had barked furiously at first, but seemed cowed and reluctant when near the glen. Someone telephoned the news to the *Aylesbury Transcript;* but the editor, accustomed to wild tales from Dunwich, did no more than concoct a humorous paragraph about it; an item soon afterward reproduced by the Associated Press.

That night everyone went home, and every house and barn was barricaded as stoutly as possible. Needless to say, no cattle were allowed to remain in open pasturage. About two in the morning a frightful stench and the savage barking of the dogs awakened the household at Elmer Frye's, on the eastern edge of Cold Spring Glen, and all agreed that they could hear a sort of muffled swishing or lapping sound from somewhere outside. Mrs Frye proposed telephoning the neighbors, and Elmer was about to agree when the noise of splintering wood burst in upon their deliberations. It came, apparently, from the barn; and was quickly followed by a hideous screaming and stamping amongst the cattle. The dogs slavered and crouched close to the feet of the fear-numbed family. Frye lit a lantern through force of habit, but knew it would be death to go out into that black farmyard. The children and the womenfolk whimpered, kept from screaming by some obscure, vestigial instinct of defense which told them their lives depended on silence. At last the noise of the cattle subsided to a pitiful moaning, and a great snapping, crashing, and crackling ensued. The Fryes, huddled together in the sitting-room, did not dare to move until the last echoes died away far down in Cold Spring Glen. Then, amidst the dismal moans from the stable and the daemoniac piping of late whippoorwills in the glen, Selina Frye tottered to the telephone and spread what news she could of the second phase of the horror.

The next day all the countryside was in a panic; and cowed, uncommunicative groups came and went where the fiendish thing had occurred. Two titan swaths of destruction stretched from the glen to the Frye farmyard, monstrous prints covered the bare patches of ground and one side of the old red barn had completely caved in. Of the cattle, only a quarter could be found and identified. Some of these were in curious fragments, and all that survived had to be shot. Earl Sawyer suggested that help be asked from Aylesbury or Arkham, but others maintained it would be of no use. Old Zebulon Whateley, of a branch that hovered about half way between soundness and decadence, made darkly wild suggestions about rites that ought to be practiced on the hilltops. He came of a line where tradition ran strong, and his memories of chantings in the great stone circles were not altogether connected with Wilbur and his grandfather.

Darkness fell upon a stricken countryside too passive to organize for real defense. In a few cases closely related families would band together and watch in the gloom under one roof; but in general there was only a repetition of the barricading of the night before, and a futile, ineffective gesture of loading muskets and setting pitchforks handily about. Nothing, however, occurred except some hill noises; and when the day came there were many who hoped that the new horror had gone as swiftly as it had come. There were even bold souls who proposed an offensive expedition down in the glen, though they did not venture to set an actual example to the still reluctant majority.

When night came again the barricading was repeated, though there was less huddling together of families. In the morning, both the Frye and the Seth Bishop households reported excitement among the dogs and vague sounds and stenches from afar, while early explorers noted with horror a fresh set of the monstrous tracks in the road skirting Sentinel Hill. As before, the sides of the road showed a bruising indicative of the blasphemously stupendous bulk of the horror; whilst the conformation of the tracks seemed to argue a passage in two directions, as if the moving mountain had come from Cold Spring Glen and returned to it along the same path. At the base of the hill a thirty-foot swath of crushed shrubbery saplings led steeply upward, and the seekers gasped when they saw that even the most perpendicular places did not deflect the inexorable trail. Whatever the horror was, it could scale a sheer stony cliff of almost complete verticality; and as the investigators climbed around to the hill's summit by safer routes they saw that the trail ended—or rather, reversed—there.

It was here that the Whateleys used to build their hellish fires and chant their hellish rituals by the table-like stone on May Eve and Hallowmass. Now that very stone formed the center of a vast space thrashed around by the mountainous horror, whilst upon its slightly concave surface was a thick and fetid deposit of the same tarry stickiness observed on the floor of the ruined Whateley farmhouse when the horror escaped. Men looked at one another and muttered. Then they looked down the hill. Apparently the horror had descended by a route much the same as that of its ascent. To speculate was futile. Reason, logic and normal ideas of motivation stood confounded. Only old Zebulon, who was not with the group, could have done justice to the situation or suggested a plausible explanation.

Thursday night began much like the others, but it ended less happily. The whippoorwills in the glen had screamed with such unusual persistence that many could not sleep, and about 3 a.m. all the party telephones rang tremulously. Those who took down their receivers heard a fright-mad voice shriek out, "Help, oh, my Gawd!..." and some thought a crashing sound followed the breaking off of the exclamation. There was nothing more. No one dared do anything, and no one knew till morning whence the call came. Then those who had heard it called everyone on the line, and found that only the Fryes did not reply. The truth appeared an hour later, when a hastily assembled group of armed men trudged out to the Frye place at the head of the glen. It was horrible, yet hardly a surprise. There were more swaths and monstrous prints, but there was no longer any house. It had caved in like an eggshell, and amongst the ruins nothing living or dead could be discovered. Only a stench and a tarry stickiness. The Elmer Fryes had been erased from Dunwich.

VIII

In the meantime, a quieter yet even more spiritually poignant phase of the horror had been blackly unwinding itself behind the closed door of a shelf-lined room in Arkham. The curious manuscript record or diary of Wilbur Whateley, delivered to Miskatonic University for translation, had caused much worry and bafflement among the experts in languages both ancient and modern; its very alphabet, notwithstanding a general resemblance to the heavily shaded Arabic used in Mesopotamia, being absolutely unknown to any available authority. The final conclusion of the linguists was that the text represented an artificial alphabet, giving the effect of a cipher; though none of the usual methods of cryptographic solution seemed to furnish any clue, even when applied on the basis of every tongue the writer might conceivably have used. The ancient books taken from Whateley's quarters, while absorbingly interesting and in several cases promising to open up new and terrible lines of research among philosophers and men of science, were of no assistance whatever in this matter. One of them, a heavy tome with an iron clasp, was in another unknown alphabet—this one of a very different cast, and resembling Sanskrit more than anything else. The old ledger was at length given wholly into the charge of Dr Armitage, both because of his peculiar interest in the Whateley matter, and because of his wide linguistic learning and skill in the mystical formulae of antiquity and the Middle Ages.

Armitage had an idea that the alphabet might be something esoterically used by certain forbidden cults which have come down from old times, and which have inherited many forms and traditions from the wizards of the Saracenic world. That question, however, he did not deem vital; since it would be unnecessary to know the origin of the symbols if, as he suspected, they were used as a cipher in a modern language. It was his belief that, considering the great amount of text involved, the writer would scarcely have wished the trouble of using another speech than his own, save perhaps in certain special formulae and incantations. Accordingly he attacked the manuscript with the preliminary assumption that the bulk of it was in English.

Dr Armitage knew, from the repeated failures of his colleagues, that the riddle was a deep and complex one; and that no simple mode of solution could merit even a trial. All through late August he fortified himself with the massed lore of cryptography; drawing upon the fullest resources of his own library, and wading night after night amidst the arcana of Trithemius's *Poligraphia,* Giambattista Porta's *De Furtivis Literarum Notis,* De Vigenère's *Traité des Chiffres,* Falconer's *Cryptomenysis Patefacta,* Davys's and Thicknesse's eighteenth-century treatises, and such fairly modern authorities as Blair, von Marten, and Klüber's *Kryptographik.* He interspersed his study of the books with attacks on the manuscript itself, and in time became convinced that he had to deal with one of those subtlest and most ingenious of cryptograms, in which many separate lists of corresponding letters are arranged like the multiplication table, and the message built up with arbitrary key-words known only to the initiated. The older authorities seemed rather more helpful than the newer ones, and Armitage concluded that the code of the manuscript was one of great antiquity, no doubt handed down through a long line of mystical experimenters. Several times he seemed near daylight, only to be set back by some unforeseen obstacle. Then, as September approached, the clouds began to clear. Certain letters, as used in certain parts of the manuscript, emerged definitely and unmistakably; and it became obvious that the text was indeed in English.

On the evening of September 2nd the last major barrier gave way, and Dr Armitage read for the first time a continuous passage of Wilbur Whateley's annals. It was in truth a diary, as all had thought; and it was couched in a style clearly showing the mixed occult erudition and general illiteracy of the strange being who wrote it. Almost the first long passage that Armitage deciphered, an entry dated November 26th, 1916, proved highly startling and disquieting. It was written, he remembered, by a child of three and a half who looked like a lad of twelve or thirteen.

> *Today learned the Aklo for the Sabaoth* [it ran], *which did not like, it being answerable from the hill and not from the air. That upstairs more ahead of me than I had thought it would be, and is not like to have much earth brain. Shot Elam Hutchins's collie Jack when he went to bite me, and Elam says he would kill me if he dast. I guess he won't. Grandfather kept me saying the Dho formula last night, and I think I saw the inner city at the 2 magnetic poles. I shall go to those poles when the earth is cleared off, if I can't break through with the Dho-Hna formula when I commit it. They from the air told me at Sabbat that it will be years before I can clear off the earth, and I guess grandfather will be dead then, so I shall have to learn all the angles of the planes and all the formulas between the Yr and the Nhhngr. They from outside will help, but they cannot take body without human blood. That upstairs looks it will have the right cast. I can see it a little when I make the Voorish sign or blow the powder of Ibn Ghazi at it, and it is near like them at May Eve on the Hill. The other face may wear off some. I wonder how I shall look when the earth is cleared and there are no earth beings on it. He that came with the Aklo Sabaoth said I may be transfigured, there being much of outside to work on.*

Morning found Dr Armitage in a cold sweat of terror and a frenzy of wakeful concentration. He had not left the manuscript all night, but sat at his table under the electric light turning page after page with shaking hands as fast as he could decipher the cryptic text. He had nervously telephoned his wife he would not be home, and when she brought him a breakfast from the house he could scarcely dispose of a mouthful. All that day he read on, now and then halted maddeningly as a reapplication of the complex key became necessary. Lunch and dinner were brought him, but he ate only the smallest fraction of either. Toward the middle of the next night he drowsed off in his chair, but soon woke out of a tangle of nightmares almost as hideous as the truths and menaces to man's existence that he had uncovered.

On the morning of September 4th, Professor Rice and Dr Morgan insisted on seeing him for a while, and departed trembling and ashen-gray. That evening he went to bed, but slept only fitfully. Wednesday—the next day—he was back at the manuscript, and began to take copious notes both from the current sections and from those he had already deciphered. In the small hours of that night he slept a little in an easy chair in his office, but was at the manuscript again before dawn. Some time before noon his physician, Dr Hartwell, called to see him and insisted that he cease work. He refused; intimating that it was of the most vital importance for him to complete the reading of the diary, and promising an explanation in due course of time. That evening, just as twilight fell, he finished his terrible perusal and sank back exhausted. His wife, bringing his dinner, found him in a half-comatose state; but he was conscious enough to warn her off with a sharp cry when he saw her eyes wander toward the notes he had taken. Weakly rising, he gathered up the scribbled papers and sealed them all in a great envelope, which he immediately placed in his inside coat pocket. He had sufficient strength to get home, but was so clearly in need of medical aid that Dr Hartwell was summoned at once. As the doctor put him to bed he could only mutter over and over again, "*But what, in God's name, can we do?*"

Dr Armitage slept, but was partly delirious the next day. He made no explanations to Hartwell, but in his calmer moments spoke of the imperative need of a long conference with Rice and Morgan. His wilder wanderings were very startling indeed, including frantic appeals that something in a boarded-up farmhouse be destroyed, and fantastic references to some plan for the extirpation of the entire human race and all animal and vegetable life from the earth by some terrible elder race of beings from another dimension. He would shout that the world was in danger, since the Elder Things wished to strip it and drag it away from the solar system and cosmos of matter into some other plane or phase of entity from which it had once fallen, vigintillions of eons ago. At other times he would call for the dreaded *Necronomicon* and the *Daemonolatreia* of Remigius, in which he seemed hopeful of finding some formula to check the peril he conjured up.

"Stop them, stop them!" he would shout. "Those Whateleys meant to let them in, and the worst of all is left! Tell Rice and Morgan we must do something—it's a blind business, but I know how to make the powder.... It hasn't been fed since the second of August, when Wilbur came here to his death, and at that rate...."

But Armitage had a sound physique despite his seventy-three years, and slept off his disorder that night without developing any real fever. He woke late Friday, clear of head, though sober with a gnawing fear and tremendous sense of responsibility. Saturday afternoon he felt able to go over to the library and summon Rice and Morgan for a conference, and the rest of that day and evening the three men tortured their brains in the wildest speculation and the most desperate debate. Strange and terrible books were drawn voluminously from the stack shelves and from secure places of storage; and diagrams and formulae were copied with feverish haste and in bewildering abundance. Of skepticism there was none. All three had seen the body of Wilbur Whateley as it lay on the floor in a room of that very building, and after that not one of them could feel even slightly inclined to treat the diary as a madman's raving.

Opinions were divided as to notifying the Massachusetts State Police, and the negative finally won. There were things involved which simply could not be believed by those who had not seen a sample, as indeed was made clear during certain subsequent investigations. Late at night the conference disbanded without having developed a definite plan, but all day Sunday Armitage was busy comparing formulae and mixing chemicals obtained from the college laboratory. The more he reflected on the hellish diary, the more he was inclined to doubt the efficacy of any material agent in stamping out the entity which Wilbur Whateley had left behind him—the earth-threatening entity which, unknown to him, was to burst forth in a few hours and become the memorable Dunwich horror.

Monday was a repetition of Sunday with Dr Armitage, for the task in hand required an infinity of research and experiment. Further consultations of the monstrous diary brought about various changes of plan, and he knew that even in the end a large amount of uncertainty must remain. By Tuesday he had a definite line of action mapped out, and believed he would try a trip to Dunwich within a week. Then, on Wednesday, the great shock came. Tucked obscurely away in a corner of the *Arkham Advertiser* was a facetious little item from the Associated Press, telling what a record-breaking monster the bootleg whiskey of Dunwich had raised up. Armitage, half stunned, could only telephone for Rice and Morgan. Far into the night they discussed, and the next day was a whirlwind of preparation on the part of them all.

Armitage knew he would be meddling with terrible powers, yet saw that there was no other way to annul the deeper and more malign meddling which others had done before him.

IX

Friday morning Armitage, Rice, and Morgan set out by motor for Dunwich, arriving at the village about one in the afternoon. The day was pleasant, but even in the brightest sunlight a kind of quiet dread and portent seemed to hover about the strangely domed hills and the deep, shadowy ravines of the stricken region. Now and then on some mountain-top a gaunt circle of stones could be glimpsed against the sky. From the air of hushed fright at Osborn's store they knew something hideous had happened, and soon learned of the annihilation of the Elmer Frye house and family. Throughout that afternoon they rode around Dunwich; questioning the natives concerning all that had occurred, and seeing for themselves with rising pangs of horror the drear Frye ruins with their lingering traces of the tarry stickiness, the blasphemous tracks in the Frye yard, the wounded Seth Bishop cattle, and the enormous swaths of disturbed vegetation in various places. The trail up and down Sentinel Hill seemed to Armitage of almost cataclysmic significance, and he looked long at the sinister altar-like stone on the summit.

At length the visitors, apprised of a party of State Police which had come from Aylesbury that morning in response to the first telephone reports of the Frye tragedy, decided to seek out the officers and compare notes as far as practicable. This, however, they found more easily planned than performed; since no sign of the party could be found in any direction. There had been five of them in a car, but now the car stood empty near the ruins in the Frye yard. The natives, all of whom had talked with the policemen, seemed at first as perplexed as Armitage and his companions. Then old Sam Hutchins thought of something and turned pale, nudging Fred Farr and pointing to the dank, deep hollow that yawned close by.

"Gawd," he gasped, "I telled 'em not ter go daown into the glen, an' I never thought nobody'd dew it with them tracks an' that smell an' the whippoorwills a-screechin' daown thar in the dark o' noonday...."

A cold shudder ran through natives and visitors alike, and every ear seemed strained in a kind of instinctive, unconscious listening. Armitage, now that he had actually come upon the horror and its monstrous work, trembled with the responsibility he felt to be his. Night would soon fall, and it was then that the mountainous blasphemy lumbered upon its eldritch course. *Negotium perambulans in tenebris....* The old librarian rehearsed the formulae he had memorized, and clutched the paper containing the alternative one he had not memorized. He saw that his electric flashlight was in working order. Rice, beside him, took from a valise a metal sprayer of the sort used in combating insects; whilst Morgan uncased the big-game rifle on which he relied, despite his colleague's warnings that no material weapon would be of help.

Armitage, having read the hideous diary, knew painfully well what kind of a manifestation to expect; but he did not add to the fright of the Dunwich people by giving any hints or clues. He hoped that it might be conquered without any revelation to the world of the monstrous thing it had escaped. As the shadows gathered, the natives commenced to disperse homeward, anxious to bar themselves indoors despite the present evidence that all human locks and bolts were useless before a force that could bend trees and crush houses when it chose. They shook their heads at the visitors' plan to stand guard at the Frye ruins near the glen; and as they left, had little expectancy of ever seeing the watchers again.

There were rumblings under the hills that night, and the whippoorwills piped threateningly. Once in a while a wind, sweeping up out of Cold Spring Glen, would bring a touch of ineffable fetor to the heavy night air; such a fetor as all three of the watchers had smelled once before, when they stood above a dying thing that had passed for fifteen years and a half as a human being. But the looked-for terror did not appear. Whatever was down there in the glen was biding its time, and Armitage told his colleagues it would be suicidal to try to attack it in the dark.

Morning came wanly, and the night-sounds ceased. It was a gray, bleak day, with now and then a drizzle of rain; and heavier and heavier clouds seemed to be piling themselves up beyond the hills to the northwest. The men from Arkham were undecided what to do. Seeking shelter from the increasing rainfall beneath one of the few undestroyed Frye outbuildings, they debated the wisdom of waiting, or of taking the aggressive role and going down into the glen in quest of their nameless, monstrous quarry. The downpour waxed in heaviness, and distant peals of thunder sounded from far horizons. Sheet lightning shimmered, and then a forky bolt flashed near at hand, as if descending into the accursed glen itself. The sky grew very dark, and the watchers hoped that the storm would prove a short, sharp one followed by clear weather.

It was still gruesomely dark when, not much over an hour later, a confused babel of voices sounded down the road. Another moment brought to view a frightened group of more than a dozen men, running, shouting, and even whimpering hysterically. Someone in the lead began sobbing out words, and the Arkham men started violently when those words developed a coherent form.

"Oh, my Gawd, my Gawd," the voice choked out. "It's a-goin' agin, *an' this time by day!* It's aout—it's aout an' a-movin' this very minute, an' only the Lord knows when it'll be on us all!"

The speaker panted into silence, but another took up his message.

"Nigh on a haour ago Zeb Whateley here heerd the 'phone a-ringin', an' it was Mis' Corey, George's wife, that lives daown by the junction. She says the hired boy Luther was aout drivin' in the caows from the storm arter the big bolt, when he see all the trees a-bendin' at the maouth o' the glen—opposite side ter this—an' smelt the same awful smell like he smelt when he faound the big tracks las' Monday mornin'. An' she says he says they was a swishin', lappin' saound, more nor what the bendin' trees an' bushes could make, an' all on a suddent the trees along the rud begun ter git pushed one side, an' they was a awful stompin' an' splashin' in the mud. But mind ye, Luther he didn't see nothin' at all, only just the bendin' trees an' underbrush.

"Then fur ahead where Bishop's Brook goes under the rud he heerd a awful creakin' an' strainin' on the bridge, an' says he could tell the saound o' wood a-startin' to crack an' split. An' all the whiles he never see a thing, only them trees an' bushes a-bendin'. An' when the swishin' saound got very fur off—on the rud towards Wizard Whateley's an' Sentinel Hill—Luther he had the guts ter step up whar he'd heerd it furst an' look at the graound. It was all mud an' water, an' the sky was dark, an' the rain was wipin' aout all tracks abaout as fast as could be; but beginnin' at the glen maouth, whar the trees had moved, they was still some o' them awful prints big as bar'ls like he seen Monday."

At this point the first excited speaker interrupted.

"But *that* ain't the trouble naow—that was only the start. Zeb here was callin' folks up an' everybody was a-listenin' in when a call from Seth Bishop's cut in. His haousekeeper Sally was carryin' on fit ter kill—she'd jest seed the trees a-bendin' beside the rud, an' says they was a kind o' mushy saound, like a elephant puffin' an' treadin', a-headin' fer the haouse. Then she up an' spoke suddent of a fearful smell, an' says her boy Cha'ncey was a-screamin' as haow it was jest like what he smelt up to the Whateley rewins Monday mornin'. An' the dogs was all barkin' an' whinin' awful.

"An' then she let aout a turrible yell, an' says the shed daown the rud had jest caved in like the storm hed blowed it over, only the wind wa'n't strong enough to dew that. Everybody was a-listenin', an' we could hear lots o' folks on the wire a-gaspin'. All 't once Sally she yelled agin, an' says the front yard picket fence hed just crumbled up, though they wa'n't no sign o' what done it. Then everybody on the line could hear Cha'ncey an' ol' Seth Bishop a-yellin' tew, an' Sally was shriekin' aout that suthin' heavy hed struck the haouse—not lightnin' nor nothin', but suthin' heavy agin the front, that kep' a-launchin' itself agin an' agin, though ye couldn't see nothin' aout the front winders. An' then... an' then..."

Lines of fright deepened on every face; and Armitage, shaken as he was, had barely poise enough to prompt the speaker.

"An' then... Sally she yelled aout, 'O help, the haouse is a-cavin' in'... an' on the wire we could hear a turrible crashin', an' a hull flock o' screamin'... jest like when Elmer Frye's place was took, only wuss...."

The man paused, and another of the crowd spoke.

"That's all—not a saound nor squeak over the 'phone arter that. Jest still-like. We that heerd it got aout Fords an' wagons an' raounded up as many able-bodied menfolks as we could git, at Corey's place, an' come up here ter see what yew thought best ter dew. Not but what I think it's the Lord's jedgment fer our iniquities, that no mortal kin ever set aside."

Armitage saw that the time for positive action had come, and spoke decisively to the faltering group of frightened rustics.

"We must follow it, boys." He made his voice as reassuring as possible. "I believe there's a chance of putting it out of business. You men know that those Whateleys were wizards—well, this thing is a thing of wizardry, and must be put down by the same means. I've seen Wilbur Whateley's diary and read some of the strange old books he used to read; and I think I know the right kind of spell to recite to make the thing fade away. Of course, one can't be sure, but we can always take a chance. It's invisible—I knew it would be—but there's a powder in this long-distance sprayer that might make it show up for a second. Later on we'll try it. It's a frightful thing to have alive, but it isn't as bad as what Wilbur would have let in if he'd lived longer. You'll never know what the world has escaped. Now we've only this one thing to fight, and it can't multiply. It can, though, do a lot of harm; so we mustn't hesitate to rid the community of it.

"We must follow it—and the way to begin is to go to the place that has just been wrecked. Let somebody lead the way—I don't know your roads very well, but I've an idea there might be a shorter cut across lots. How about it?"

The men shuffled about a moment, and then Earl Sawyer spoke softly, pointing with a grimy finger through the steadily lessening rain.

"I guess ye kin git to Seth Bishop's quickest by cuttin' acrost the lower medder here, wadin' the brook at the low place, an' climbin' through Carrier's mowin' and the timber-lot beyont. That comes aout on the upper rud mighty nigh Seth's—a leetle t'other side."

Armitage, with Rice and Morgan, started to walk in the direction indicated; and most of the natives followed slowly. The sky was growing lighter, and there were signs that the storm had worn itself away. When Armitage inadvertently took a wrong direction, Joe Osborn warned him and walked ahead to show the right one. Courage and confidence were mounting; though the twilight of the almost perpendicular wooded hill which lay toward the end of their short cut, and among whose fantastic ancient trees they had to scramble as if up a ladder, put these qualities to a severe test.

At length they emerged on a muddy road to find the sun coming out. They were a little beyond the Seth Bishop place, but bent trees and hideously unmistakable tracks showed what had passed by. Only a few moments were consumed in surveying the ruins just around the bend. It was the Frye incident all over again, and nothing dead or living was found in either of the collapsed shells which had been the Bishop house and barn. No one cared to remain there amidst the stench and tarry stickiness, but all turned instinctively to the line of horrible prints leading on toward the wrecked Whateley farmhouse and the altar-crowned slopes of Sentinel Hill.

As the men passed the site of Wilbur Whateley's abode they shuddered visibly, and seemed again to mix hesitancy with their zeal. It was no joke tracking down something as big as a house that one could not see, but that had all the vicious malevolence of a daemon. Opposite the base of Sentinel Hill the tracks left the road, and there was a fresh bending and matting visible along the broad swath marking the monster's former route to and from the summit.

Armitage produced a pocket telescope of considerable power and scanned the steep green side of the hill. Then he handed the instrument to Morgan, whose sight was keener. After a moment of gazing Morgan cried out sharply, passing the glass to Earl Sawyer and indicating a certain spot on the slope with his finger. Sawyer, as clumsy as most non-users of optical devices are, fumbled a while; but eventually focused the lenses with Armitage's aid. When he did so his cry was less restrained than Morgan's had been.

"Gawd almighty, the grass an' bushes is a-movin'! It's a-goin' up—slow-like—creepin' up ter the top this minute, heaven only knows what fur!"

Then the germ of panic seemed to spread among the seekers. It was one thing to chase the nameless entity, but quite another to find it. Spells might be all right—but suppose they weren't? Voices began questioning Armitage about what he knew of the thing, and no reply seemed quite to satisfy. Everyone seemed to feel himself in close proximity to phases of Nature and of being utterly forbidden, and wholly outside the sane experience of mankind.

X

In the end, the three men from Arkham—old, white-bearded Dr Armitage, stocky, iron-gray Professor Rice, and lean, youngish Dr Morgan—ascended the mountain alone. After much patient instruction regarding its focusing and use, they left the telescope with the frightened group that remained in the road; and as they climbed they were watched closely by those among whom the glass was passed around. It was hard going, and Armitage had to be helped more than once. High above the toiling group the great swath trembled as its hellish maker re-passed with snail-like deliberateness. Then it was obvious that the pursuers were gaining.

Curtis Whateley—of the undecayed branch—was holding the telescope when the Arkham party detoured radically from the swath. He told the crowd that the men were evidently trying to get to a subordinate peak which overlooked the swath at a point considerably ahead of where the shrubbery was now bending. This, indeed, proved to be true; and the party were seen to gain the minor elevation only a short time after the invisible blasphemy had passed it.

Then Wesley Corey, who had taken the glass, cried out that Armitage was adjusting the sprayer which Rice held, and that something must be about to happen. The crowd stirred uneasily, recalling that this sprayer was expected to give the unseen horror a moment of visibility. Two or three men shut their eyes, but Curtis Whateley snatched back the telescope and strained his vision to the utmost. He saw that Rice, from the party's point of vantage above and behind the entity, had an excellent chance of spreading the potent powder with marvelous effect.

Those without the telescope saw only an instant's flash of gray cloud—a cloud about the size of a moderately large building—near the top of the mountain. Curtis, who had held the instrument, dropped it with a piercing shriek into the ankle-deep mud of the road. He reeled, and would have crumpled to the ground had not two or three others seized and steadied him. All he could do was moan half-inaudibly.

"Oh, oh, great Gawd... that... that..."

There was a pandemonium of questioning, and only Henry Wheeler thought to rescue the fallen telescope and wipe it clean of mud. Curtis was past all coherence, and even isolated replies were almost too much for him.

"Bigger'n a barn... all made o' squirmin' ropes... hull thing sort o' shaped like a hen's egg bigger'n anything, with dozens o' legs like hogsheads that haff shut up when they step... nothin' solid abaout it—all like jelly, an' made o' sep'rit wrigglin' ropes pushed clost together... great bulgin' eyes all over it... ten or twenty maouths or trunks a-stickin' aout all along the sides, big as stovepipes, an' all a-tossin' an' openin' an' shuttin'... all gray, with kinder blue or purple rings... *an' Gawd in heaven—that haff face on top!...*"

This final memory, whatever it was, proved too much for poor Curtis; and he collapsed completely before he could say more. Fred Farr and Will Hutchins carried him to the roadside and laid him on the damp grass. Henry Wheeler, trembling, turned the rescued telescope on the mountain to see what he might. Through the lenses were discernible three tiny figures, apparently running toward the summit as fast as the steep incline allowed. Only these—nothing more. Then everyone noticed a strangely unseasonable noise in the deep valley behind, and even in the underbrush of Sentinel Hill itself. It was the piping of unnumbered whippoorwills, and in their shrill chorus there seemed to lurk a note of tense and evil expectancy.

Earl Sawyer now took the telescope and reported the three figures as standing on the topmost ridge, virtually level with the altar-stone but at a considerable distance from it. One figure, he said, seemed to be raising its hands above its head at rhythmic intervals; and as Sawyer mentioned the circumstance the crowd seemed to hear a faint, half-musical sound from the distance, as if a loud chant were accompanying the gestures. The weird silhouette on that remote peak must have been a spectacle of infinite grotesqueness and impressiveness, but no observer was in a mood for aesthetic appreciation. "I guess he's sayin' the spell," whispered Wheeler as he snatched back the telescope. The whippoorwills were piping wildly, and in a singularly curious irregular rhythm quite unlike that of the visible ritual.

Suddenly the sunshine seemed to lessen without the intervention of any discernible cloud. It was a very peculiar phenomenon, and was plainly marked by all. A rumbling sound seemed brewing beneath the hills, mixed strangely with a concordant rumbling which clearly came from the sky. Lightning flashed aloft, and the wondering crowd looked in vain for the portents of storm. The chanting of the men from Arkham now became unmistakable, and Wheeler saw through the glass that they were all raising their arms in the rhythmic incantation. From some farmhouse far away came the frantic barking of dogs.

The change in the quality of the daylight increased, and the crowd gazed about the horizon in wonder. A purplish darkness, born of nothing more than a spectral deepening of the sky's blue, pressed down upon the rumbling hills. Then the lightning flashed again, somewhat brighter than before, and the crowd fancied that it had showed a certain mistiness around the altar-stone on the distant height. No one, however, had been using the telescope at that instant. The whippoorwills continued their irregular pulsation, and the men of Dunwich braced themselves tensely against some imponderable menace with which the atmosphere seemed surcharged.

Without warning came those deep, cracked, raucous vocal sounds which will never leave the memory of the stricken group who heard them. Not from any human throat were they born, for the organs of man can yield no such acoustic perversions. Rather would one have said they came from the pit itself, had not their source been so unmistakably the altar-stone on the peak. It is almost erroneous to call them *sounds* at all, since so much of their ghastly, infra-bass timbre spoke to dim seats of consciousness and terror far subtler than the ear; yet one must do so, since their form was indisputably though vaguely that of half-articulate *words*. They were loud—loud as the rumblings and the thunder above which they echoed—yet did they come from no visible being. And because imagination might suggest a conjectural source in the world of non-visible beings, the huddled crowd at the mountain's base huddled still closer, and winced as if in expectation of a blow.

"*Ygnaiih... ygnaiih... thflthkh'ngha... Yog-Sothoth...*" rang the hideous croaking out of space. "*Y'bthnk... h'ehye—n'grkdl'lh....*"

The speaking impulse seemed to falter here, as if some frightful psychic struggle were going on. Henry Wheeler strained his eye at the telescope, but saw only the three grotesquely silhouetted human figures on the peak, all moving their arms furiously in strange gestures as their incantation drew near its culmination. From what black wells of Acherontic fear or feeling, from what unplumbed gulfs of extra-cosmic consciousness or obscure, long-latent heredity, were those half-articulate thunder-croakings drawn? Presently they began to gather renewed force and coherence as they grew in stark, utter, ultimate frenzy.

"Eh-ya-ya-ya-yahaah—e'yayayayaaaa... ngh'aaaaa... ngh'aaaa... h'yuh... h'yuh... HELP! HELP!... ff—ff—ff—FATHER! FATHER! YOG-SOTHOTH!..."

But that was all. The pallid group in the road, still reeling at the *indisputably English* syllables that had poured thickly and thunderously down from the frantic vacancy beside that shocking altar-stone, were never to hear such syllables again. Instead, they jumped violently at the terrific report which seemed to rend the hills; the deafening, cataclysmic peal whose source, be it inner earth or sky, no hearer was ever able to place. A single lightning bolt shot from the purple zenith to the altar-stone, and a great tidal wave of viewless force and indescribable stench swept down from the hill to all the countryside. Trees, grass, and underbrush were whipped into a fury; and the frightened crowd at the mountain's base, weakened by the lethal fetor that seemed about to asphyxiate them, were almost hurled off their feet. Dogs howled from the distance, green grass and foliage wilted to a curious, sickly yellow-gray, and over field and forest were scattered the bodies of dead whippoorwills.

The stench left quickly, but the vegetation never came right again. To this day there is something queer and unholy about the growths on and around that fearsome hill. Curtis Whateley was only just regaining consciousness when the Arkham men came slowly down the mountain in the beams of a sunlight once more brilliant and untainted. They were grave and quiet, and seemed shaken by memories and reflections even more terrible than those which had reduced the group of natives to a state of cowed quivering. In reply to a jumble of questions they only shook their heads and reaffirmed one vital fact.

"The thing has gone forever," Armitage said. "It has been split up into what it was originally made of, and can never exist again. It was an impossibility in a normal world. Only the least fraction was really matter in any sense we know. It was like its father—and most of it has gone back to him in some vague realm or dimension outside our material universe; some vague abyss out of which only the most accursed rites of human blasphemy could ever have called him for a moment on the hills."

There was a brief silence, and in that pause the scattered senses of poor Curtis Whateley began to knit back into a sort of continuity; so that he put his hands to his head with a moan. Memory seemed to pick itself up where it had left off, and the horror of the sight that had prostrated him burst in upon him again.

"Oh, oh, my Gawd, that haff face—that haff face on top of it... that face with the red eyes an' crinkly albino hair, an' no chin, like the Whateleys... It was a octopus, centipede, spider kind o' thing, but they was a haff-shaped man's face on top of it, an' it looked like Wizard Whateley's, only it was yards an' yards acrost..."

He paused exhausted, as the whole group of natives stared in a bewilderment not quite crystallized into fresh terror. Only old Zebulon Whateley, who wanderingly remembered ancient things but who had been silent heretofore, spoke aloud.

"Fifteen year' gone," he rambled, "I heerd Ol' Whateley say as haow some day we'd hear a child o' Lavinny's a-callin' its father's name on the top o' Sentinel Hill..."

But Joe Osborn interrupted him to question the Arkham men anew.

"What was it anyhaow, an' haowever did young Wizard Whateley call it aout o' the air it come from?"

Armitage chose his words very carefully.

"It was—well, it was mostly a kind of force that doesn't belong in our part of space; a kind of force that acts and grows and shapes itself by other laws than those of our sort of Nature. We have no business calling in such things from outside, and only very wicked people and very wicked cults ever try to. There was some of it in Wilbur Whateley himself—enough to make a devil and a precocious monster of him, and to make his passing out a pretty terrible sight. I'm going to burn his accursed diary, and if you men are wise you'll dynamite that altar-stone up there, and pull down all the rings of standing stones on the other hills. Things like that brought down the beings those Whateleys were so fond of—the beings they were going to let in tangibly to wipe out the human race and drag the earth off to some nameless place for some nameless purpose.

"But as to this thing we've just sent back—the Whateleys raised it for a terrible part in the doings that were to come. It grew fast and big from the same reason that Wilbur grew fast and big—but it beat him because it had a greater share of the outsideness in it. You needn't ask how Wilbur called it out of the air. He didn't call it out. *It was his twin brother, but it looked more like the father than he did.*"

THE CALL OF CTHULHU

H. P. LOVECRAFT

(Found Among the Papers of the Late
Francis Wayland Thurston, of Boston)

Of such great powers or beings there may be conceivably a survival... a survival of a hugely remote period when... consciousness was manifested, perhaps, in shapes and forms long since withdrawn before the tide of advancing humanity... forms of which poetry and legend alone have caught a flying memory and called them gods, monsters, mythical beings of all sorts and kinds....

—*Algernon Blackwood*

I

The most merciful thing in the world, I think, is the inability of the human mind to correlate all its contents. We live on a placid island of ignorance in the midst of black seas of infinity, and it was not meant that we should voyage far. The sciences, each straining in its own direction, have hitherto harmed us little; but some day the piecing together of dissociated knowledge will open up such terrifying vistas of reality, and of our frightful position therein, that we shall either go mad from the revelation or flee from the deadly light into the peace and safety of a new dark age.

Theosophists have guessed at the awesome grandeur of the cosmic cycle wherein our world and human race form transient incidents. They have hinted at strange survivals in terms which would freeze the blood if not masked by a bland optimism. But it is not from them that there came the single glimpse of forbidden eons which chills me when I think of it and maddens me when I dream of it. That glimpse, like all dread glimpses of truth, flashed out from an accidental piecing together of separated things—in this case an old newspaper item and the notes of a dead professor. I hope that no one else will accomplish this piecing out; certainly, if I live, I shall never knowingly supply a link in so hideous a chain. I think that the professor, too, intended to keep silent regarding the part he knew, and that he would have destroyed his notes had not sudden death seized him.

My knowledge of the thing began in the winter of 1926–27 with the death of my great-uncle George Gammell Angell, Professor Emeritus of Semitic Languages in Brown University, Providence, Rhode Island. Professor Angell was widely known as an authority on ancient inscriptions, and had frequently been resorted to by the heads of prominent museums; so that his passing at the age of ninety-two may be recalled by many. Locally, interest was intensified by the obscurity of the cause of death. The professor had been stricken whilst returning from the Newport boat; falling suddenly, as witnesses said, after having been jostled by a nautical-looking negro who had come from one of the queer dark courts on the precipitous hillside which formed a short cut from the waterfront to the deceased's home in Williams Street. Physicians were unable to find any visible disorder, but concluded after perplexed debate that some obscure lesion of the heart, induced by the brisk ascent of so steep a hill by so elderly a man, was responsible for the end. At the time I saw no reason to dissent from this dictum, but latterly I am inclined to wonder—and more than wonder.

As my grand-uncle's heir and executor, for he died a childless widower, I was expected to go over his papers with some thoroughness; and for that purpose moved his entire set of files and boxes to my quarters in Boston. Much of the material which I correlated will be later published by the American Archaeological Society, but there was one box which I found exceedingly puzzling, and which I felt much averse from showing to other eyes. It had been locked, and I did not find the key till it occurred to me to examine the personal ring which the professor carried always in his pocket. Then indeed I succeeded in opening it, but when I did so seemed only to be confronted by a greater and more closely locked barrier. For what could be the meaning of the queer clay bas-relief and the disjointed jottings, ramblings, and cuttings which I found? Had my uncle, in his latter years, become credulous of the most superficial impostures? I resolved to search out the eccentric sculptor responsible for this apparent disturbance of an old man's peace of mind.

The bas-relief was a rough rectangle less than an inch thick and about five by six inches in area; obviously of modern origin. Its designs, however, were far from modern in atmosphere and suggestion; for although the vagaries of cubism and futurism are many and wild, they do not often reproduce that cryptic regularity which lurks in prehistoric writing. And writing of some kind the bulk of these designs seemed certainly to be; though my memory, despite much familiarity with the papers and collections of my uncle, failed in any way to identify this particular species, or even to hint at its remotest affiliations.

Above these apparent hieroglyphics was a figure of evidently pictorial intent, though its impressionistic execution forbade a very clear idea of its nature. It seemed to be a sort of monster, or symbol representing a monster, of a form which only a diseased fancy could conceive. If I say that my somewhat extravagant imagination yielded simultaneous pictures of an octopus, a dragon, and a human caricature, I shall not be unfaithful to the spirit of the thing. A pulpy, tentacled head surmounted a grotesque and scaly body with rudimentary wings; but it was the *general outline* of the whole which made it most shockingly frightful. Behind the figure was a vague suggestion of a Cyclopean architectural background.

The writing accompanying this oddity was, aside from a stack of press cuttings, in Professor Angell's most recent hand; and made no pretence to literary style. What seemed to be the main document was headed "CTHULHU

CULT" in characters painstakingly printed to avoid the erroneous reading of a word so unheard-of. The manuscript was divided into two sections, the first of which was headed "1925—Dream and Dream Work of H. A. Wilcox, 7 Thomas St, Providence, RI" and the second, "Narrative of Inspector John R. Legrasse, 121 Bienville St, New Orleans, La, at 1908 A. A. S. Mtg—Notes on Same, & Prof. Webb's Acct". The other manuscript papers were all brief notes, some of them accounts of the queer dreams of different persons, some of them citations from theosophical books and magazines (notably W. Scott-Elliot's *Atlantis and the Lost Lemuria*), and the rest comments on long-surviving secret societies and hidden cults, with references to passages in such mythological and anthropological source-books as Frazer's *Golden Bough* and Miss Murray's *Witch-Cult in Western Europe.* The cuttings largely alluded to *outré* mental illnesses and outbreaks of group folly or mania in the spring of 1925.

The first half of the principal manuscript told a very peculiar tale. It appears that on March 1st, 1925, a thin, dark young man of neurotic and excited aspect had called upon Professor Angell bearing the singular clay bas-relief, which was then exceedingly damp and fresh. His card bore the name of Henry Anthony Wilcox, and my uncle had recognized him as the youngest son of an excellent family slightly known to him, who had latterly been studying sculpture at the Rhode Island School of Design and living alone at the Fleur-de-Lys Building near that institution. Wilcox was a precocious youth of known genius but great eccentricity, and had from childhood excited attention through the strange stories and odd dreams he was in the habit of relating. He called himself "psychically hypersensitive," but the staid folk of the ancient commercial city dismissed him as merely "queer." Never mingling much with his kind, he had dropped gradually from social visibility, and was now known only to a small group of aesthetes from other towns. Even the Providence Art Club, anxious to preserve its conservatism, had found him quite hopeless.

On the occasion of the visit, ran the professor's manuscript, the sculptor abruptly asked for the benefit of his host's archeological knowledge in identifying the hieroglyphics on the bas-relief. He spoke in a dreamy, stilted manner which suggested pose and alienated sympathy; and my uncle showed some sharpness in replying, for the conspicuous freshness of the tablet implied kinship with anything but archeology. Young Wilcox's rejoinder, which impressed my uncle enough to make him recall and record it verbatim, was of a fantastically poetic cast which must have typified his whole conversation, and which I have since found highly characteristic of him. He said, "It is new, indeed, for I made it last night in a dream of strange cities; and dreams are older than brooding Tyre, or the contemplative Sphinx, or garden-girdled Babylon."

It was then that he began that rambling tale which suddenly played upon a sleeping memory and won the fevered interest of my uncle. There had been a slight earthquake tremor the night before, the most considerable felt in New England for some years; and Wilcox's imagination had been keenly affected. Upon retiring, he had had an unprecedented dream of great Cyclopean cities of titan blocks and sky-flung monoliths, all dripping with green ooze and sinister with latent horror. Hieroglyphics had covered the walls and pillars, and from some undetermined point below had come a voice that was not a voice; a chaotic sensation which only fancy could transmute into sound, but which he attempted to render by the almost unpronounceable jumble of letters "*Cthulhu fhtagn.*"

This verbal jumble was the key to the recollection which excited and disturbed Professor Angell. He questioned the sculptor with scientific minuteness; and studied with almost frantic intensity the bas-relief on which the youth had found himself working, chilled and clad only in his night-clothes, when waking had stolen bewilderingly over him. My uncle blamed his old age, Wilcox afterward said, for his slowness in recognizing both hieroglyphics and pictorial design. Many of his questions seemed highly out-of-place to his visitor, especially those which tried to connect the latter with strange cults or societies; and Wilcox could not understand the repeated promises of silence which he was offered in exchange for an admission of membership in some widespread mystical or paganly religious body. When Professor Angell became convinced that the sculptor was indeed ignorant of any cult or system of cryptic lore, he besieged his visitor with demands for future reports of dreams. This bore regular fruit, for after the first interview the manuscript records daily calls of the young man, during which he related startling fragments of nocturnal imagery whose burden was always some terrible Cyclopean vista of dark and dripping stone, with a subterrene voice or intelligence shouting monotonously in enigmatical sense-impacts uninscribable save as gibberish. The two sounds most frequently repeated are those rendered by the letters "*Cthulhu*" and "*R'lyeh.*"

On March 23rd, the manuscript continued, Wilcox failed to appear; and inquiries at his quarters revealed that he had been stricken with an obscure sort of fever and taken to the home of his family in Waterman Street. He had cried out in the night, arousing several other artists in the building, and had manifested since then only alternations of unconsciousness and delirium. My uncle at once telephoned the family, and from that time forward kept close watch of the case; calling often at the Thayer Street office of Dr Tobey, whom he learned to be in charge. The youth's febrile mind, apparently, was dwelling on strange things; and the doctor shuddered now and then as he spoke of them. They included not only a repetition of what he had formerly dreamed, but touched wildly on a gigantic thing "miles high" which walked or lumbered about.

He at no time fully described this object, but occasional frantic words, as repeated by Dr Tobey, convinced the professor that it must be identical with the nameless monstrosity he had sought to depict in his dream-sculpture. Reference to this object, the doctor added, was invariably a prelude to the young man's subsidence into lethargy. His temperature, oddly enough, was not greatly above normal; but his whole condition was otherwise such as to suggest true fever rather than mental disorder.

On April 2nd at about 3 p.m. every trace of Wilcox's malady suddenly ceased. He sat upright in bed, astonished to find himself at home and completely ignorant of what had happened in dream or reality since the night of March 22nd. Pronounced well by his physician, he returned to his quarters in three days; but to Professor Angell he was of no further assistance. All traces of strange dreaming had vanished with his recovery, and my uncle kept no record of his night thoughts after a week of pointless and irrelevant accounts of thoroughly usual visions.

Here the first part of the manuscript ended, but references to certain of the scattered notes gave me much material for thought—so much, in fact, that only the ingrained skepticism then forming my philosophy can account for my continued distrust of the artist. The notes in question were those descriptive of the dreams of various persons covering the same period as that in which young Wilcox had had his strange visitations. My uncle, it seems, had quickly instituted a prodigiously far-flung body of inquiries amongst nearly all the friends whom he could question without impertinence, asking for nightly reports of their dreams, and the dates of any notable visions for some time past. The reception of his request seems to have been varied; but he must, at the very least, have received more responses than any ordinary man could have handled without a secretary. This original correspondence was not preserved, but his notes formed a thorough and really significant digest. Average people in society and business—New England's traditional "salt of the earth"—gave an almost completely negative result, though scattered cases of uneasy but formless nocturnal impressions appear here and there, always between March 23rd and April 2nd—the period of young Wilcox's delirium. Scientific men were little more affected, though four cases of vague description suggest fugitive glimpses of strange landscapes, and in one case there is mentioned a dread of something abnormal.

It was from the artists and poets that the pertinent answers came, and I know that panic would have broken loose had they been able to compare notes. As it was, lacking their original letters, I half suspected the compiler of having asked leading questions, or of having edited the correspondence in corroboration of what he had latently resolved to see. That is why I continued to feel that Wilcox, somehow cognizant of the old data which my uncle had possessed, had been imposing on the veteran scientist. These responses from aesthetes told a disturbing tale. From February 28th to April 2nd a large proportion of them had dreamed very bizarre things, the intensity of the dreams being immeasurably the stronger during the period of the sculptor's delirium. Over a fourth of those who reported anything, reported scenes and half-sounds not unlike those which Wilcox had described; and some of the dreamers confessed acute fear of the gigantic nameless thing visible toward the last. One case, which the note describes with emphasis, was very sad. The subject, a widely known architect with leanings toward theosophy and occultism, went violently insane on the date of young Wilcox's seizure, and expired several months later after incessant screamings to be saved from some escaped denizen of hell. Had my uncle referred to these cases by name instead of merely by number, I should have attempted some corroboration and personal investigation; but as it was, I succeeded in tracing down only a few. All of these, however, bore out the notes in full. I have often wondered if all the objects of the professor's questioning felt as puzzled as did this fraction. It is well that no explanation shall ever reach them.

The press cuttings, as I have intimated, touched on cases of panic, mania, and eccentricity during the given period. Professor Angell must have employed a cutting bureau, for the number of extracts was tremendous and the sources scattered throughout the globe. Here was a nocturnal suicide in London, where a lone sleeper had leaped from a window after a shocking cry. Here likewise a rambling letter to the editor of a paper in South America, where a fanatic deduces a dire future from visions he has seen. A dispatch from California describes a theosophist colony as donning white robes en masse for some "glorious fulfillment" which never arrives, whilst items from India speak guardedly of serious native unrest toward the end of March. Voodoo orgies multiply in Haiti, and African outposts report ominous mutterings. American officers in the Philippines find certain tribes bothersome about this time, and New York policemen are mobbed by hysterical

Levantines on the night of March 22nd–23rd. The west of Ireland, too, is full of wild rumor and legendry, and a fantastic painter named Ardois-Bonnot hangs a blasphemous "Dream Landscape" in the Paris spring salon of 1926. And so numerous are the recorded troubles in insane asylums, that only a miracle can have stopped the medical fraternity from noting strange parallelisms and drawing mystified conclusions. A weird bunch of cuttings, all told; and I can at this date scarcely envisage the callous rationalism with which I set them aside. But I was then convinced that young Wilcox had known of the older matters mentioned by the professor.

II

The older matters which had made the sculptor's dream and bas-relief so significant to my uncle formed the subject of the second half of his long manuscript. Once before, it appears, Professor Angell had seen the hellish outlines of the nameless monstrosity, puzzled over the unknown hieroglyphics, and heard the ominous syllables which can be rendered only as "*Cthulhu*"; and all this in so stirring and horrible a connection that it is small wonder he pursued young Wilcox with queries and demands for data.

The earlier experience had come in 1908, seventeen years before, when the American Archaeological Society held its annual meeting in St Louis. Professor Angell, as befitted one of his authority and attainments, had had a prominent part in all the deliberations; and was one of the first to be approached by the several outsiders who took advantage of the convocation to offer questions for correct answering and problems for expert solution.

The chief of these outsiders, and in a short time the focus of interest for the entire meeting, was a commonplace-looking middle-aged man who had traveled all the way from New Orleans for certain special information unobtainable from any local source. His name was John Raymond Legrasse, and he was by profession an Inspector of Police. With him he bore the subject of his visit, a grotesque, repulsive, and apparently very ancient stone statuette whose origin he was at a loss to determine. It must not be fancied that Inspector Legrasse had the least interest in archeology. On the contrary, his wish for enlightenment was prompted by purely professional considerations. The statuette, idol, fetish, or whatever it was, had been captured some months before in the wooded swamps south of New Orleans during a raid on a supposed voodoo meeting; and so singular and hideous were the rites connected with it, that the police could not but realize that they had stumbled on a dark cult totally unknown to them, and infinitely more diabolic than even the blackest of the African voodoo circles. Of its origin, apart from the erratic and unbelievable tales extorted from the captured members, absolutely nothing was to be discovered; hence the anxiety of the police for any antiquarian lore which might help them to place the frightful symbol, and through it track down the cult to its fountain-head.

Inspector Legrasse was scarcely prepared for the sensation which his offering created. One sight of the thing had been enough to throw the assembled men of science into a state of tense excitement, and they lost no time in crowding around him to gaze at the diminutive figure whose utter strangeness and air of genuinely abysmal antiquity hinted so potently at unopened and archaic vistas. No recognized school of sculpture had animated this terrible object, yet centuries and even thousands of years seemed recorded in its dim and greenish surface of unplaceable stone.

The figure, which was finally passed slowly from man to man for close and careful study, was between seven and eight inches in height, and of exquisitely artistic workmanship. It represented a monster of vaguely anthropoid outline, but with an octopus-like head whose face was a mass of feelers, a scaly, rubbery-looking body, prodigious claws on hind and fore feet, and long, narrow wings behind. This thing, which seemed instilled with a fearsome and unnatural malignancy, was of a somewhat bloated corpulence, and squatted evilly on a rectangular block or pedestal covered with indecipherable characters. The tips of the wings touched the back edge of the block, the seat occupied the center, whilst the long, curved claws of the doubled-up, crouching hind legs gripped the front edge and extended a quarter of the way down toward the bottom of the pedestal. The cephalopod head was bent forward, so that the ends of the facial feelers brushed the backs of huge forepaws which clasped the croucher's elevated knees. The aspect of the whole was abnormally life-like, and the more subtly fearful because its source was so totally unknown. Its vast, awesome, and incalculable age was unmistakable; yet not one link did it show with any known type of art belonging to civilization's youth—or indeed to any other time. Totally separate and apart, its very material was a mystery; for the soapy, greenish-black stone with its golden or iridescent flecks and striations resembled nothing familiar to geology or mineralogy. The characters along the base were equally baffling; and no member present, despite a representation of half the world's expert learning in this field, could form the least notion of even their remotest linguistic kinship. They, like the subject and material, belonged to something horribly remote and distinct from mankind as we know it; something frightfully suggestive of old and unhallowed cycles of life in which our world and our conceptions have no part.

And yet, as the members severally shook their heads and confessed defeat at the Inspector's problem, there was one man in that gathering who suspected a touch of bizarre familiarity in the monstrous shape and writing, and who presently told with some diffidence of the odd trifle he knew. This person was the late William Channing Webb, Professor of Anthropology in Princeton University, and an explorer of no slight note. Professor Webb had been engaged, forty-eight years before, in a tour of Greenland and Iceland in search of some Runic inscriptions which he failed to unearth; and whilst high up on the West Greenland coast had encountered a singular tribe or cult of degenerate Eskimos whose religion, a curious form of devil worship, chilled him with its deliberate bloodthirstiness and repulsiveness. It was a faith of which other Eskimos knew little, and which they mentioned only with shudders, saying that it had come down from horribly ancient eons before ever the world was made. Besides nameless rites and human sacrifices there were certain queer hereditary rituals addressed to a supreme elder devil or *tornasuk;* and of this Professor Webb had taken a careful phonetic copy from an aged *angekok* or wizard-priest, expressing the sounds in Roman letters as best he knew how. But just now of prime significance was the fetish which this cult had cherished, and around which they danced when the aurora leaped high over the ice cliffs. It was, the professor stated, a very crude bas-relief of stone, comprising a hideous picture and some cryptic writing. And so far as he could tell, it was a rough parallel in all essential features of the bestial thing now lying before the meeting.

This data, received with suspense and astonishment by the assembled members, proved doubly exciting to Inspector Legrasse; and he began at once to ply his informant with questions. Having noted and copied an oral ritual among the swamp cult-worshipers his men had arrested, he besought the professor to remember as best he might the syllables taken down amongst the diabolist Eskimos. There then followed an exhaustive comparison of details, and a moment of really awed silence when both detective and scientist agreed on the virtual identity of the phrase common to two hellish rituals so many worlds of distance apart. What, in substance, both the Eskimo wizards and the Louisiana swamp-priests had chanted to their kindred idols was something very like this—the word-divisions being guessed at from traditional breaks in the phrase as chanted aloud:

Ph'nglui mglw'nafh Cthulhu R'lyeh wgah'nagl fhtagn.

Legrasse had one point in advance of Professor Webb, for several among his mongrel prisoners had repeated to him what older celebrants had told them the words meant. This text, as given, ran something like this:

"In his house at R'lyeh dead Cthulhu waits dreaming."

And now, in response to a general and urgent demand, Inspector Legrasse related as fully as possible his experience with the swamp worshipers; telling a story to which I could see my uncle attached profound significance. It savored of the wildest dreams of myth-maker and theosophist, and disclosed an astonishing degree of cosmic imagination among such half-castes and pariahs as might be least expected to possess it.

On November 1st, 1907, there had come to the New Orleans police a frantic summons from the swamp and lagoon country to the south. The squatters there, mostly primitive but good-natured descendants of Lafitte's men, were in the grip of stark terror from an unknown thing which had stolen upon them in the night. It was voodoo, apparently, but voodoo of a more terrible sort than they had ever known; and some of their women and children had disappeared since the malevolent tom-tom had begun its incessant beating far within the black haunted woods where no dweller ventured. There were insane shouts and harrowing screams, soul-chilling chants and dancing devil-flames; and, the frightened messenger added, the people could stand it no more.

So a body of twenty police, filling two carriages and an automobile, had set out in the late afternoon with the shivering squatter as a guide. At the end of the passable road they alighted, and for miles splashed on in silence through the terrible cypress woods where day never came. Ugly roots and malignant hanging nooses of Spanish moss beset them, and now and then a pile of dank stones or fragment of a rotting wall intensified by its hint of morbid habitation a depression which every malformed tree and every fungous islet combined to create. At length the squatter settlement, a miserable huddle of huts, hove in sight; and hysterical dwellers ran out to cluster around the group of bobbing lanterns. The muffled beat of tom-toms was now faintly audible far, far ahead; and a curdling shriek came at infrequent intervals when the wind shifted. A reddish glare, too, seemed to filter through the pale undergrowth beyond endless avenues of forest night. Reluctant even to be left alone again, each one of the cowed squatters refused point-blank to advance another inch toward the scene of unholy worship, so Inspector Legrasse and his nineteen colleagues plunged on unguided into black arcades of horror that none of them had ever trod before.

The region now entered by the police was one of traditionally evil repute, substantially unknown and untraversed by white men. There were legends of a hidden lake unglimpsed by mortal sight, in which dwelt a huge, formless white polypous thing with luminous eyes; and squatters whispered that bat-winged devils flew up out of caverns in inner earth to worship it at midnight. They said it had been there before D'Iberville, before La Salle, before the Indians, and before even the wholesome beasts and birds of the woods. It was nightmare itself, and to see it was to die. But it made men dream, and so they knew enough to keep away. The present voodoo orgy was, indeed, on the merest fringe of this abhorred area, but that location was bad enough; hence perhaps the very place of the worship had terrified the squatters more than the shocking sounds and incidents.

Only poetry or madness could do justice to the noises heard by Legrasse's men as they plowed on through the black morass toward the red glare and the muffled tom-toms. There are vocal qualities peculiar to men, and vocal qualities peculiar to beasts; and it is terrible to hear the one when the source should yield the other. Animal fury and orgiastic license here whipped themselves to daemoniac heights by howls and squawking ecstasies that tore and reverberated through those nighted woods like pestilential tempests from the gulfs of hell. Now and then the less organized ululation would cease, and from what seemed a well-drilled chorus of hoarse voices would rise in sing-song chant that hideous phrase or ritual:

Ph'nglui mglw'nafh Cthulhu R'lyeh wgah'nagl fhtagn.

Then the men, having reached a spot where the trees were thinner, came suddenly in sight of the spectacle itself. Four of them reeled, one fainted and two were shaken into a frantic cry, which the mad cacophony of the orgy fortunately deadened. Legrasse dashed swamp water on the face of the fainting man, and all stood trembling and nearly hypnotized with horror.

In a natural glade of the swamp stood a grassy island of perhaps an acre's extent, clear of trees and tolerably dry. On this now leaped and twisted a more indescribable horde of human abnormality than any but a Sime or an Angarola could paint. Void of clothing, this hybrid spawn were braying, bellowing, and writhing about a monstrous ring-shaped bonfire; in the center of which, revealed by occasional rifts in the curtain of flame, stood a great granite monolith some eight feet in height; on top of which, incongruous with its diminutiveness, rested the noxious carven statuette. From a wide circle of ten scaffolds set up at regular intervals with the flame-girt monolith as a center hung, head downward, the oddly marred bodies of the helpless squatters who had disappeared. It was inside this circle that the ring of worshipers jumped and roared, the general direction of the mass motion being from left to right in endless Bacchanal between the ring of bodies and the ring of fire.

It may have been only imagination and it may have been only echoes which induced one of the men, an excitable Spaniard, to fancy he heard antiphonal responses to the ritual from some far and unillumined spot deeper within the wood of ancient legendry and horror. This man, Joseph D. Galvez, I later met and questioned; and he proved distractingly imaginative. He indeed went so far as to hint of the faint beating of great wings, and of a glimpse of shining eyes and a mountainous white bulk beyond the remotest trees—but I suppose he had been hearing too much native superstition.

Actually, the horrified pause of the men was of comparatively brief duration. Duty came first; and although there must have been nearly a hundred mongrel celebrants in the throng, the police relied on their firearms and plunged determinedly into the nauseous rout. For five minutes the resultant din and chaos were beyond description. Wild blows were struck, shots were fired, and escapes were made; but in the end Legrasse was able to count some forty-seven sullen prisoners, whom he forced to dress in haste and fall into line between two rows of policemen. Five of the worshipers lay dead, and two severely wounded ones were carried away on improvised stretchers by their fellow-prisoners. The image on the monolith, of course, was carefully removed and carried back by Legrasse.

Examined at headquarters after a trip of intense strain and weariness, the prisoners all proved to be men of a very low, mixed-blooded, and mentally aberrant type. Most were seamen, and a sprinkling of negroes and mulattoes, largely West Indians or Brava Portuguese from the Cape Verde Islands, gave a coloring of voodooism to the heterogeneous cult. But before many questions were asked, it became manifest that something far deeper and older than negro fetishism was involved. Degraded and ignorant as they were, the creatures held with surprising consistency to the central idea of their loathsome faith.

They worshiped, so they said, the Great Old Ones who lived ages before there were any men, and who came to the young world out of the sky. Those Old Ones were gone now, inside the earth and under the sea; but their dead bodies had told their secrets in dreams to the first men, who formed a cult which had never died. This was that cult, and the prisoners said it had always existed and always would exist, hidden in distant wastes and dark places all over the world until the time when the great priest Cthulhu, from his dark house in the mighty city of R'lyeh under the waters, should rise and bring the earth again beneath his sway. Some day he would call, when the stars were ready, and the secret cult would always be waiting to liberate him.

Meanwhile, no more must be told. There was a secret which even torture could not extract. Mankind was not absolutely alone among the conscious things of earth, for shapes came out of the dark to visit the faithful few. But these were not the Great Old Ones. No man had ever seen the Old Ones. The carven idol was great Cthulhu, but none might say whether or not the others were precisely like him. No one could read the old writing now, but things were told by word of mouth. The chanted ritual was not the secret—that was never spoken aloud, only whispered. The chant meant only this: *in his house at R'lyeh dead Cthulhu waits dreaming.*

Only two of the prisoners were found sane enough to be hanged, and the rest were committed to various institutions. All denied a part in the ritual murders, and averred that the killing had been done by Black Winged Ones which had come to them from their immemorial meeting-place in the haunted wood. But of those mysterious allies no coherent account could ever be gained. What the police did extract, came mainly from an immensely aged mestizo named Castro, who claimed to have sailed to strange ports and talked with undying leaders of the cult in the mountains of China.

Old Castro remembered bits of hideous legend that paled the speculations of theosophists and made man and the world seem recent and transient indeed. There had been eons when other Things ruled on the earth, and They had had great cities. Remains of Them, he said the deathless Chinamen had told him, were still to be found as Cyclopean stones on islands in the Pacific. They all died vast epochs of time before men came, but there were arts which could revive Them when the stars had come round again to the right positions in the cycle of eternity. They had, indeed, come themselves from the stars, and brought Their images with Them.

These Great Old Ones, Castro continued, were not composed altogether of flesh and blood. They had shape—for did not this star-fashioned image prove it?—but that shape was not made of matter. When the stars were right, They could plunge from world to world through the sky; but when the stars were wrong, They could not live. But although They no longer lived, They would never really die. They all lay in stone houses in Their great city of R'lyeh, preserved by the spells of mighty Cthulhu for a glorious resurrection when the stars and the earth might once more be ready for Them. But at that time some force from outside must serve to liberate Their bodies. The spells that preserved Them intact likewise prevented Them from making an initial move, and They could only lie awake in the dark and think whilst uncounted millions of years rolled by. They knew all that was occurring in the universe, but Their mode of speech was transmitted thought. Even now They talked in Their tombs. When, after infinities of chaos, the first men came, the Great Old Ones spoke to the sensitive among them by molding their dreams; for only thus could Their language reach the fleshly minds of mammals.

Then, whispered Castro, those first men formed the cult around small idols which the Great Ones showed them; idols brought in dim eras from dark stars. That cult would never die till the stars came right again, and the secret priests would take great Cthulhu from His tomb to revive His subjects and resume His rule of earth. The time would be easy to know, for then mankind would have become as the Great Old Ones; free and wild and beyond good and evil, with laws and morals thrown aside and all men shouting and killing and reveling in joy. Then the liberated Old Ones would teach them new ways to shout and kill and revel and enjoy themselves, and all the earth would flame with a holocaust of ecstasy and freedom. Meanwhile the cult, by appropriate rites, must keep alive the memory of those ancient ways and shadow forth the prophecy of their return.

In the elder time chosen men had talked with the entombed Old Ones in dreams, but then something had happened. The great stone city R'lyeh, with its monoliths and sepulchers, had sunk beneath the waves; and the deep waters, full of the one primal mystery through which not even thought can pass, had cut off the spectral intercourse. But memory never died, and high-priests said that the city would rise again when the stars were right. Then came out of the earth the black spirits of earth, moldy and shadowy, and full of dim rumors picked up in caverns beneath forgotten sea-bottoms. But of them old Castro dared not speak much. He cut himself off hurriedly, and no amount of persuasion or subtlety could elicit more in this direction. The *size* of the Old Ones, too, he curiously declined to mention. Of the cult, he said that he thought the center lay amid the pathless deserts of Arabia, where Irem, the City of Pillars, dreams hidden and untouched. It was not allied to the European witch-cult, and was virtually unknown beyond its members. No book had ever really hinted of it, though the deathless Chinamen said that there were double meanings in the *Necronomicon* of the mad Arab Abdul Alhazred which the initiated might read as they chose, especially the much-discussed couplet:

That is not dead which can eternal lie,
  And with strange eons even death may die.

Legrasse, deeply impressed and not a little bewildered, had inquired in vain concerning the historic affiliations of the cult. Castro, apparently, had told the truth when he said that it was wholly secret. The authorities at Tulane University could shed no light upon either cult or image, and now the detective had come to the highest authorities in the country and met with no more than the Greenland tale of Professor Webb.

The feverish interest aroused at the meeting by Legrasse's tale, corroborated as it was by the statuette, is echoed in the subsequent correspondence of those who attended; although scant mention occurs in the formal publications of the society. Caution is the first care of those accustomed to face occasional charlatanry and imposture. Legrasse for some time lent the image to Professor Webb, but at the latter's death it was returned to him and remains in his possession, where I viewed it not long ago. It is truly a terrible thing, and unmistakably akin to the dream-sculpture of young Wilcox.

That my uncle was excited by the tale of the sculptor I did not wonder, for what thoughts must arise upon hearing, after a knowledge of what Legrasse had learned of the cult, of a sensitive young man who had *dreamed* not only the figure and exact hieroglyphics of the swamp-found image and the Greenland devil tablet, but had come *in his dreams* upon at least three of the precise words of the formula uttered alike by Eskimo diabolists and mongrel Louisianans? Professor Angell's instant start on an investigation of the utmost thoroughness was eminently natural; though privately I suspected young Wilcox of having heard of the cult in some indirect way, and of having invented a series of dreams to heighten and continue the mystery at my uncle's expense. The dream-narratives and cuttings collected by the professor were, of course, strong corroboration; but the rationalism of my mind and the extravagance of the whole subject led me to adopt what I thought the most sensible conclusions. So, after thoroughly studying the manuscript again and correlating the theosophical and anthropological notes with the cult narrative of Legrasse, I made a trip to Providence to see the sculptor and give him the rebuke I thought proper for so boldly imposing upon a learned and aged man.

Wilcox still lived alone in the Fleur-de-Lys Building in Thomas Street, a hideous Victorian imitation of seventeenth-century Breton architecture which flaunts its stuccoed front amidst the lovely colonial houses on the ancient hill, and under the very shadow of the finest Georgian steeple in America. I found him at work in his rooms, and at once conceded from the specimens scattered about that his genius is indeed profound and authentic. He will, I believe, sometime be heard from as one of the great decadents; for he has crystallized in clay and will one day mirror in marble those nightmares and fantasies which Arthur Machen evokes in prose, and Clark Ashton Smith makes visible in verse and in painting.

Dark, frail, and somewhat unkempt in aspect, he turned languidly at my knock and asked me my business without rising. When I told him who I was, he displayed some interest; for my uncle had excited his curiosity in probing his strange dreams, yet had never explained the reason for the study. I did not enlarge his knowledge in this regard, but sought with some subtlety to draw him out. In a short time I became convinced of his absolute sincerity, for he spoke of the dreams in a manner none could mistake. They and their subconscious residuum had influenced his art profoundly, and he showed me a morbid statue whose contours almost made me shake with the potency of its black suggestion. He could not recall having seen the original of this thing except in his own dream bas-relief, but the outlines had formed themselves insensibly under his hands. It was, no doubt, the giant shape he had raved of in delirium. That he really knew nothing of the hidden cult, save from what my uncle's relentless catechism had let fall, he soon made clear; and again I strove to think of some way in which he could possibly have received the weird impressions.

He talked of his dreams in a strangely poetic fashion; making me see with terrible vividness the damp Cyclopean city of slimy green stone—whose *geometry*, he oddly said, was *all wrong*—and hear with frightened expectancy the ceaseless, half-mental calling from underground: *Cthulhu fhtagn*, *Cthulhu fhtagn*.

These words had formed part of that dread ritual which told of dead Cthulhu's dream-vigil in his stone vault at R'lyeh, and I felt deeply moved despite my rational beliefs. Wilcox, I was sure, had heard of the cult in some casual way, and had soon forgotten it amidst the mass of his equally weird reading and imagining. Later, by virtue of its sheer impressiveness, it had found subconscious expression in dreams, in the bas-relief, and in the terrible statue I now beheld; so that his imposture upon my uncle had been a very innocent one. The youth was of a type, at once slightly affected and slightly ill-mannered, which I could never like; but I was willing enough now to admit both his genius and his honesty. I took leave of him amicably, and wish him all the success his talent promises.

The matter of the cult still remained to fascinate me, and at times I had visions of personal fame from researches into its origin and connections. I visited New Orleans, talked with Legrasse and others of that old-time raiding-party, saw the frightful image, and even questioned such of the mongrel prisoners as still survived. Old Castro, unfortunately, had been dead for some years. What I now heard so graphically at first-hand, though it was really no more than a detailed confirmation of what my uncle had written, excited me afresh; for I felt sure that I was on the track of a very real, very secret, and very ancient religion whose discovery would make me an anthropologist of note. My attitude was still one of absolute materialism, as I wish it still were, and I discounted with almost inexplicable perversity the coincidence of the dream notes and odd cuttings collected by Professor Angell.

One thing I began to suspect, and which I now fear I *know,* is that my uncle's death was far from natural. He fell on a narrow hill street leading up from an ancient waterfront swarming with foreign mongrels, after a careless push from a negro sailor. I did not forget the mixed blood and marine pursuits of the cult-members in Louisiana, and would not be surprised to learn of secret methods and poison needles as ruthless and as anciently known as the cryptic rites and beliefs. Legrasse and his men, it is true, have been let alone; but in Norway a certain seaman who saw things is dead. Might not the deeper inquiries of my uncle after encountering the sculptor's data have come to sinister ears? I think Professor Angell died because he knew too much, or because he was likely to learn too much. Whether I shall go as he did remains to be seen, for I have learned much now.

III

If heaven ever wishes to grant me a boon, it will be a total effacing of the results of a mere chance which fixed my eye on a certain stray piece of shelf-paper. It was nothing on which I would naturally have stumbled in the course of my daily round, for it was an old number of an Australian journal, the *Sydney Bulletin* for April 18th, 1925. It had escaped even the cutting bureau which had at the time of its issuance been avidly collecting material for my uncle's research.

I had largely given over my inquiries into what Professor Angell called the "Cthulhu Cult," and was visiting a learned friend in Paterson, New Jersey; the curator of a local museum and a mineralogist of note. Examining one day the reserve specimens roughly set on the storage shelves in a rear room of the museum, my eye was caught by an odd picture in one of the old papers spread beneath the stones. It was the *Sydney Bulletin* I have mentioned, for my friend has wide affiliations in all conceivable foreign parts; and the picture was a half-tone cut of a hideous stone image almost identical with that which Legrasse had found in the swamp.

Eagerly clearing the sheet of its precious contents, I scanned the item in detail; and was disappointed to find it of only moderate length. What it suggested, however, was of portentous significance to my flagging quest; and I carefully tore it out for immediate action. It read as follows:

MYSTERY DERELICT FOUND AT SEA
Vigilant Arrives With Helpless Armed New Zealand Yacht in Tow.
One Survivor and Dead Man Found Aboard.
Tale of Desperate Battle and Deaths at Sea.
Rescued Seaman Refuses Particulars of Strange Experience.
Odd Idol Found in His Possession. Inquiry to Follow.

The Morrison Co.'s freighter *Vigilant*, bound from Valparaiso, arrived this morning at its wharf in Darling Harbour, having in tow the battled and disabled but heavily armed steam yacht *Alert* of Dunedin, NZ, which was sighted April 12th in S. Latitude 34° 21', W. Longitude 152° 17' with one living and one dead man aboard.

The *Vigilant* left Valparaiso March 25th, and on April 2nd was driven considerably south of her course by exceptionally heavy storms and monster waves. On April 12th the derelict was sighted; and though apparently deserted, was found upon boarding to contain one survivor in a half-delirious condition and one man who had evidently been dead for more than a week. The living man was clutching a horrible stone idol of unknown origin, about a foot in height, regarding whose nature authorities at Sydney University, the Royal Society, and the Museum in College Street all profess complete bafflement, and which the survivor says he found in the cabin of the yacht, in a small carved shrine of common pattern.

This man, after recovering his senses, told an exceedingly strange story of piracy and slaughter. He is Gustaf Johansen, a Norwegian of some intelligence, and had been second mate of the two-masted schooner *Emma* of Auckland, which sailed for Callao February 20th with a complement of eleven men. The *Emma*, he says, was delayed and thrown widely south of her course by the great storm of March 1st, and on March 22nd, in S. Latitude 49° 51', W. Longitude 128° 34', encountered the *Alert*, manned by a queer and evil-looking crew of Kanakas and half-castes. Being ordered peremptorily to turn back,

> Capt. Collins refused; whereupon the strange crew began to fire savagely and without warning upon the schooner with a peculiarly heavy battery of brass cannon forming part of the yacht's equipment. The *Emma*'s men showed fight, says the survivor, and though the schooner began to sink from shots beneath the waterline they managed to heave alongside their enemy and board her, grappling with the savage crew on the yacht's deck, and being forced to kill them all, the number being slightly superior, because of their particularly abhorrent and desperate though rather clumsy mode of fighting.
>
> Three of the *Emma*'s men, including Capt. Collins and First Mate Green, were killed; and the remaining eight under Second Mate Johansen proceeded to navigate the captured yacht, going ahead in their original direction to see if any reason for their ordering back had existed. The next day, it appears, they raised and landed on a small island, although none is known to exist in that part of the ocean; and six of the men somehow died ashore, though Johansen is queerly reticent about this part of his story, and speaks only of their falling into a rock chasm. Later, it seems, he and one companion boarded the yacht and tried to manage her, but were beaten about by the storm of April 2nd. From that time till his rescue on the 12th the man remembers little, and he does not even recall when William Briden, his companion, died. Briden's death reveals no apparent cause, and was probably due to excitement or exposure. Cable advices from Dunedin report that the *Alert* was well known there as an island trader, and bore an evil reputation along the waterfront. It was owned by a curious group of half-castes whose frequent meetings and night trips to the woods attracted no little curiosity; and it had set sail in great haste just after the storm and earth tremors of March 1st. Our Auckland correspondent gives the *Emma* and her crew an excellent reputation, and Johansen is described as a sober and worthy man. The admiralty will institute an inquiry on the whole matter beginning tomorrow, at which every effort will be made to induce Johansen to speak more freely than he has done hitherto.

This was all, together with the picture of the hellish image; but what a train of ideas it started in my mind! Here were new treasuries of data on the Cthulhu Cult, and evidence that it had strange interests at sea as well as on land. What motive prompted the hybrid crew to order back the *Emma* as they sailed about with their hideous idol? What was the unknown island on which six of the *Emma*'s crew had died, and about which the mate

Johansen was so secretive? What had the vice-admiralty's investigation brought out, and what was known of the noxious cult in Dunedin? And most marvelous of all, what deep and more than natural linkage of dates was this which gave a malign and now undeniable significance to the various turns of events so carefully noted by my uncle?

March 1st—our February 28th according to the International Date Line—the earthquake and storm had come. From Dunedin the *Alert* and her noisome crew had darted eagerly forth as if imperiously summoned, and on the other side of the earth poets and artists had begun to dream of a strange, dank Cyclopean city whilst a young sculptor had molded in his sleep the form of the dreaded Cthulhu. March 23rd the crew of the *Emma* landed on an unknown island and left six men dead; and on that date the dreams of sensitive men assumed a heightened vividness and darkened with dread of a giant monster's malign pursuit, whilst an architect had gone mad and a sculptor had lapsed suddenly into delirium! And what of this storm of April 2nd—the date on which all dreams of the dank city ceased, and Wilcox emerged unharmed from the bondage of strange fever? What of all this—and of those hints of old Castro about the sunken, star-born Old Ones and their coming reign; their faithful cult *and their mastery of dreams?* Was I tottering on the brink of cosmic horrors beyond man's power to bear? If so, they must be horrors of the mind alone, for in some way April 2nd had put a stop to whatever monstrous menace had begun its siege of mankind's soul.

That evening, after a day of hurried cabling and arranging, I bade my host adieu and took a train for San Francisco. In less than a month I was in Dunedin; where, however, I found that little was known of the strange cult-members who had lingered in the old sea-taverns. Waterfront scum was far too common for special mention; though there was vague talk about one inland trip these mongrels had made, during which faint drumming and red flame were noted on the distant hills. In Auckland I learned that Johansen had returned *with yellow hair turned white* after a perfunctory and inconclusive questioning at Sydney, and had thereafter sold his cottage in West Street and sailed with his wife to his old home in Oslo. Of his stirring experience he would tell his friends no more than he had told the admiralty officials, and all they could do was to give me his Oslo address.

After that I went to Sydney and talked profitlessly with seamen and members of the vice-admiralty court. I saw the *Alert*, now sold and in commercial use, at Circular Quay in Sydney Cove, but gained nothing from its non-committal bulk. The crouching image, with its cuttlefish head, dragon body, scaly wings, and hieroglyphed pedestal, was preserved in the Museum at Hyde Park; and I studied it long and well, finding it a thing of balefully exquisite workmanship, and with the same utter mystery, terrible antiquity, and unearthly strangeness of material which I had noted in Legrasse's smaller specimen. Geologists, the curator told me, had found it a monstrous puzzle; for they vowed that the world held no rock like it. Then I thought with a shudder of what old Castro had told Legrasse about the primal Great Ones: "They had come from the stars, and had brought Their images with Them."

Shaken with such a mental revolution as I had never before known, I now resolved to visit Mate Johansen in Oslo. Sailing for London, I re-embarked at once for the Norwegian capital; and one autumn day landed at the trim wharves in the shadow of the Egeberg. Johansen's address, I discovered, lay in the Old Town of King Harold Haardrada, which kept alive the name of Oslo during all the centuries that the greater city masqueraded as "Christiana." I made the brief trip by taxicab, and knocked with palpitant heart at the door of a neat and ancient building with plastered front. A sad-faced woman in black answered my summons, and I was stung with disappointment when she told me in halting English that Gustaf Johansen was no more.

He had not survived his return, said his wife, for the doings at sea in 1925 had broken him. He had told her no more than he had told the public, but had left a long manuscript—of "technical matters" as he said—written in English, evidently in order to safeguard her from the peril of casual perusal. During a walk through a narrow lane near the Gothenburg dock, a bundle of papers falling from an attic window had knocked him down. Two Lascar sailors at once helped him to his feet, but before the ambulance could reach him he was dead. Physicians found no adequate cause for the end, and laid it to heart trouble and a weakened constitution.

I now felt gnawing at my vitals that dark terror which will never leave me till I, too, am at rest; "accidentally" or otherwise. Persuading the widow that my connection with her husband's "technical matters" was sufficient to entitle me to his manuscript, I bore the document away and began to read it on the London boat. It was a simple, rambling thing—a naive sailor's effort at a *post-facto* diary—and strove to recall day by day that last awful voyage. I cannot attempt to transcribe it verbatim in all its cloudiness and redundance, but I will tell its gist enough to show why the sound of the water against the vessel's sides became so unendurable to me that I stopped my ears with cotton.

Johansen, thank God, did not know quite all, even though he saw the city and the Thing, but I shall never sleep calmly again when I think of the horrors that lurk ceaselessly behind life in time and in space, and of those unhallowed blasphemies from elder stars which dream beneath the sea, known and favored by a nightmare cult ready and eager to loose them on the world whenever another earthquake shall heave their monstrous stone city again to the sun and air.

Johansen's voyage had begun just as he told it to the vice-admiralty. The *Emma,* in ballast, had cleared Auckland on February 20th, and had felt the full force of that earthquake-born tempest which must have heaved up from the sea-bottom the horrors that filled men's dreams. Once more under control, the ship was making good progress when held up by the *Alert* on March 22nd, and I could feel the mate's regret as he wrote of her bombardment and sinking. Of the swarthy cult-fiends on the *Alert* he speaks with significant horror. There was some peculiarly abominable quality about them which made their destruction seem almost a duty, and Johansen shows ingenuous wonder at the charge of ruthlessness brought against his party during the proceedings of the court of inquiry. Then, driven ahead by curiosity in their captured yacht under Johansen's command, the men sight a great stone pillar sticking out of the sea, and in S. Latitude 47° 9', W. Longitude 123° 43' come upon a coastline of mingled mud, ooze, and weedy Cyclopean masonry which can be nothing less than the tangible substance of earth's supreme terror—the nightmare corpse-city of R'lyeh, that was built in measureless eons behind history by the vast, loathsome shapes that seeped down from the dark stars. There lay great Cthulhu and his hordes, hidden in green slimy vaults and sending out at last, after cycles incalculable, the thoughts that spread fear to the dreams of the sensitive and called imperiously to the faithful to come on a pilgrimage of liberation and restoration. All this Johansen did not suspect, but God knows he soon saw enough!

I suppose that only a single mountaintop, the hideous monolith-crowned citadel whereon great Cthulhu was buried, actually emerged from the waters. When I think of the extent of all that may be brooding down there I almost wish to kill myself forthwith. Johansen and his men were awed by the cosmic majesty of this dripping Babylon of elder daemons, and must have guessed without guidance that it was nothing of this or of any sane planet. Awe at the unbelievable size of the greenish stone blocks, at the dizzying height of the great carven monolith, and at the stupefying identity of the colossal statues and bas-reliefs with the queer image found in the shrine on the *Alert,* is poignantly visible in every line of the mate's frightened description.

Without knowing what futurism is like, Johansen achieved something very close to it when he spoke of the city; for instead of describing any definite structure or building, he dwells only on broad impressions of vast angles and stone surfaces—surfaces too great to belong to any thing right or proper for this earth, and impious with horrible images and hieroglyphs. I mention his talk about *angles* because it suggests something Wilcox had told me of his awful dreams. He had said that the *geometry* of the dream-place he saw was abnormal, non-Euclidean, and loathsomely redolent of spheres and dimensions apart from ours. Now an unlettered seaman felt the same thing whilst gazing at the terrible reality.

Johansen and his men landed at a sloping mud-bank on this monstrous Acropolis, and clambered slipperily up over titan oozy blocks which could have been no mortal staircase. The very sun of heaven seemed distorted when viewed through the polarizing miasma welling out from this sea-soaked perversion, and twisted menace and suspense lurked leeringly in those crazily elusive angles of carven rock where a second glance showed concavity after the first showed convexity.

Something very like fright had come over all the explorers before anything more definite than rock and ooze and weed was seen. Each would have fled had he not feared the scorn of the others, and it was only half-heartedly that they searched—vainly, as it proved—for some portable souvenir to bear away.

It was Rodriguez the Portuguese who climbed up the foot of the monolith and shouted of what he had found. The rest followed him, and looked curiously at the immense carved door with the now familiar squid-dragon bas-relief. It was, Johansen said, like a great barn-door; and they all felt that it was a door because of the ornate lintel, threshold, and jambs around it, though they could not decide whether it lay flat like a trap-door or slantwise like an outside cellar door. As Wilcox would have said, the geometry of the place was all wrong. One could not be sure that the sea and the ground were horizontal, hence the relative position of everything else seemed phantasmally variable.

Briden pushed at the stone in several places without result. Then Donovan felt over it delicately around the edge, pressing each point separately as he went. He climbed interminably along the grotesque stone molding—that is, one would call it climbing if the thing was not after all horizontal—and the men wondered how any door in the universe could be so vast. Then, very softly and slowly, the acre-great panel began to give inward at the top; and they saw that it was balanced. Donovan slid or somehow propelled himself down or along the jamb and rejoined his fellows, and everyone watched the queer recession of the monstrously carven portal. In this fantasy of prismatic distortion it moved anomalously in a diagonal way, so that all the rules of matter and perspective seemed upset.

The aperture was black with a darkness almost material. That tenebrousness was indeed a *positive quality;* for it obscured such parts of the inner walls as ought to have been revealed, and actually burst forth like smoke from its eon-long imprisonment, visibly darkening the sun as it slunk away into the shrunken and gibbous sky on flapping membranous wings. The odor arising from the newly opened depths was intolerable, and at length the quick-eared Hawkins thought he heard a nasty, slopping sound down there. Everyone listened, and everyone was listening still when It lumbered slobberingly into sight and gropingly squeezed Its gelatinous green immensity through the black doorway into the tainted outside air of that poison city of madness.

Poor Johansen's handwriting almost gave out when he wrote of this. Of the six men who never reached the ship, he thinks two perished of pure fright in that accursed instant. The Thing cannot be described—there is no language for such abysms of shrieking and immemorial lunacy, such eldritch contradictions of all matter, force, and cosmic order. A mountain walked or stumbled. God! What wonder that across the earth a great architect went mad, and poor Wilcox raved with fever in that telepathic instant? The Thing of the idols, the green, sticky spawn of the stars, had awaked to claim his own. The stars were right again, and what an age-old cult had failed to do by design, a band of innocent sailors had done by accident. After vigintillions of years great Cthulhu was loose again, and ravening for delight.

Three men were swept up by the flabby claws before anybody turned. God rest them, if there be any rest in the universe. They were Donovan, Guerrera, and Ångstrom. Parker slipped as the other three were plunging frenziedly over endless vistas of green-crusted rock to the boat, and Johansen swears he was swallowed up by an angle of masonry which shouldn't have been there; an angle which was acute, but behaved as if it were obtuse. So only Briden and Johansen reached the boat, and pulled desperately for the *Alert* as the mountainous monstrosity flopped down the slimy stones and hesitated floundering at the edge of the water.

Steam had not been suffered to go down entirely, despite the departure of all hands for the shore; and it was the work of only a few moments of feverish rushing up and down between wheel and engines to get the *Alert* under way. Slowly, amidst the distorted horrors of that indescribable scene, she began to churn the lethal waters; whilst on the masonry of that charnel shore that was not of earth, the titan Thing from the stars slavered and gibbered like Polypheme cursing the fleeing ship of Odysseus. Then, bolder than the storied Cyclops, great Cthulhu slid greasily into the water and began to pursue with vast wave-raising strokes of cosmic potency. Briden looked back and went mad, laughing shrilly as he kept on laughing at intervals till death found him one night in the cabin, whilst Johansen was wandering deliriously.

But Johansen had not given out yet. Knowing that the Thing could surely overtake the *Alert* until steam was fully up, he resolved on a desperate chance; and, setting the engine for full speed, ran lightning-like on deck and reversed the wheel. There was a mighty eddying and foaming in the noisome brine, and as the steam mounted higher and higher the brave Norwegian drove his vessel head on against the pursuing jelly which rose above the unclean froth like the stern of a daemon galleon. The awful squid-head with writhing feelers came nearly up to the bowsprit of the sturdy yacht, but Johansen drove on relentlessly. There was a bursting as of an exploding bladder, a slushy nastiness as of a cloven sunfish, a stench as of a thousand opened graves, and a sound that the chronicler would not put on paper. For an instant the ship was befouled by an acrid and blinding green cloud, and then there was only a venomous seething astern; where—God in heaven!—the scattered plasticity of that nameless sky-spawn was nebulously *recombining* in its hateful original form, whilst its distance widened every second as the *Alert* gained impetus from its mounting steam.

That was all. After that Johansen only brooded over the idol in the cabin and attended to a few matters of food for himself and the laughing maniac by his side. He did not try to navigate after the first bold flight, for the reaction had taken something out of his soul. Then came the storm of April 2nd, and a gathering of the clouds about his consciousness. There is a sense of spectral whirling through liquid gulfs of infinity, of dizzying rides through reeling universes on a comet's tail, and of hysterical plunges from the pit to the moon and from the moon back again to the pit, all livened by a cachinnating chorus of the distorted, hilarious elder gods and the green, bat-winged mocking imps of Tartarus.

Out of that dream came rescue—the *Vigilant,* the vice-admiralty court, the streets of Dunedin and the long voyage back home to the old house by the Egeberg. He could not tell—they would think him mad. He would write of what he knew before death came, but his wife must not guess. Death would be a boon if only it could blot out the memories.

That was the document I read, and now I have placed it in the tin box beside the bas-relief and the papers of Professor Angell. With it shall go this record of mine—this test of my own sanity, wherein is pieced together that which I hope may never be pieced together again. I have looked upon all that the universe has to hold of horror, and even the skies of spring and the flowers of summer must ever afterward be poison to me. But I do not think my life will be long. As my uncle went, as poor Johansen went, so I shall go. I know too much, and the cult still lives.

Cthulhu still lives, too, I suppose, again in that chasm of stone which has shielded him since the sun was young. His accursed city is sunken once more, for the *Vigilant* sailed over the spot after the April storm; but his ministers on earth still bellow and prance and slay around idol-capped monoliths in lonely places. He must have been trapped by the sinking whilst within his black abyss, or else the world would by now be screaming with fright and frenzy. Who knows the end? What has risen may sink, and what has sunk may rise. Loathsomeness waits and dreams in the deep, and decay spreads over the tottering cities of men. A time will come—but I must not and cannot think! Let me pray that, if I do not survive this manuscript, my executors may put caution before audacity and see that it meets no other eye.

THE COLOR OUT OF SPACE

• • • • •

H. P. LOVECRAFT

West of Arkham the hills rise wild, and there are valleys with deep woods that no axe has ever cut. There are dark narrow glens where the trees slope fantastically, and where thin brooklets trickle without ever having caught the glint of sunlight. On the gentler slopes there are farms, ancient and rocky, with squat, moss-coated cottages brooding eternally over old New England secrets in the lee of great ledges; but these are all vacant now, the wide chimneys crumbling and the shingled sides bulging perilously beneath low gambrel roofs.

The old folk have gone away, and foreigners do not like to live there. French-Canadians have tried it, Italians have tried it, and the Poles have come and departed. It is not because of anything that can be seen or heard or handled, but because of something that is imagined. The place is not good for the imagination, and does not bring restful dreams at night. It must be this which keeps the foreigners away, for old Ammi Pierce has never told them of anything he recalls from the strange days. Ammi, whose head has been a little queer for years, is the only one who still remains, or who ever talks of the strange days; and he dares to do this because his house is so near the open fields and the traveled roads around Arkham.

There was once a road over the hills and through the valleys, that ran straight where the blasted heath is now; but people ceased to use it and a new road was laid curving far toward the south. Traces of the old one can still be found amidst the weeds of a returning wilderness, and some of them will doubtless linger even when half the hollows are flooded for the new reservoir. Then the dark woods will be cut down and the blasted heath will slumber far below blue waters whose surface will mirror the sky and ripple in the sun. And the secrets of the strange days will be one with the deep's secrets; one with the hidden lore of old ocean, and all the mystery of primal earth.

When I went into the hills and vales to survey for the new reservoir they told me the place was evil. They told me this in Arkham, and because that is a very old town full of witch legends I thought the evil must be something which grandams had whispered to children through centuries. The name "blasted heath" seemed to me very odd and theatrical, and I wondered how it had come into the folklore of a Puritan people. Then I saw that dark westward tangle of glens and slopes for myself, and ceased to wonder at anything besides its own elder mystery. It was morning when I saw it, but shadow lurked always there. The trees grew too thickly, and their trunks were too big for any healthy New England wood. There was too much silence in the dim alleys between them, and the floor was too soft with the dank moss and mattings of infinite years of decay.

In the open spaces, mostly along the line of the old road, there were little hillside farms; sometimes with all the buildings standing, sometimes with only one or two, and sometimes with only a lone chimney or fast-filling cellar. Weeds and briers reigned, and furtive wild things rustled in the undergrowth. Upon everything was a haze of restlessness and oppression; a touch of the unreal and the grotesque, as if some vital element of perspective or chiaroscuro were awry. I did not wonder that the foreigners would not stay, for this was no region to sleep in. It was too much like a landscape of Salvator Rosa; too much like some forbidden woodcut in a tale of terror.

But even all this was not so bad as the blasted heath. I knew it the moment I came upon it at the bottom of a spacious valley; for no other name could fit such a thing, or any other thing fit such a name. It was as if the poet had coined the phrase from having seen this one particular region. It must, I thought as I viewed it, be the outcome of a fire; but why had nothing new ever grown over those five acres of gray desolation that sprawled open to the sky like a great spot eaten by acid in the woods and fields? It lay largely to the north of the ancient road line, but encroached a little on the other side. I felt an odd reluctance about approaching, and did so at last only because my business took me through and past it. There was no vegetation of any kind on that broad expanse, but only a fine gray dust or ash which no wind seemed ever to blow about. The trees near it were sickly and stunted, and many dead trunks stood or lay rotting at the rim. As I walked hurriedly by I saw the tumbled bricks and stones of an old chimney and cellar on my right, and the yawning black maw of an abandoned well whose stagnant vapors played strange tricks with the hues of the sunlight. Even the long, dark woodland climb beyond seemed welcome in contrast, and I marveled no more at the frightened whispers of Arkham people. There had been no house or ruin near; even in the old days the place must have been lonely and remote. And at twilight, dreading to repass that ominous spot, I walked circuitously back to the town by the curving road on the south. I vaguely wished some clouds would gather, for an odd timidity about the deep skyey voids above had crept into my soul.

In the evening I asked old people in Arkham about the blasted heath, and what was meant by that phrase "strange days" which so many evasively muttered. I could not, however, get any good answers, except that all the mystery was much more recent than I had dreamed. It was not a matter of old legendry at all, but something within the lifetime of those who spoke. It had happened in the 'eighties, and a family had disappeared or was killed. Speakers would not be exact; and because they all told me to pay no attention to old Ammi Pierce's crazy tales, I sought him out the next morning, having heard that he lived alone in the ancient tottering cottage where the trees first begin to get very thick. It was a fearsomely archaic place, and had begun to exude the faint miasmal odor which clings about houses that have stood too long. Only with persistent knocking could I rouse the aged man, and when he shuffled timidly to the door I could tell he was not glad to see me. He was not so feeble as I had expected; but his eyes drooped in a curious way, and his unkempt clothing and white beard made him seem very worn and dismal. Not knowing just how he could best be launched on his tales, I feigned a matter of business; told him of my surveying, and asked vague questions about the district. He was far brighter and more educated than I had been led to think, and before I knew it had grasped quite as much of the subject as any man I had talked with in Arkham. He was not like other rustics I had known in the sections where reservoirs were to be. From him there were no protests at the miles of old wood and farmland to be blotted out, though perhaps there would have been had not his home lain outside the bounds of the future lake. Relief was all that he shewed; relief at the doom of the dark ancient valleys through which he had roamed all his life. They were better under water now—better under water since the strange days. And with this opening his husky voice sank low, while his body leaned forward and his right forefinger began to point shakily and impressively.

It was then that I heard the story, and as the rambling voice scraped and whispered on I shivered again and again despite the summer day. Often I had to recall the speaker from ramblings, piece out scientific points which he knew only by a fading parrot memory of professors' talk, or bridge over gaps where his sense of logic and continuity broke down. When he was done I did not wonder that his mind had snapped a trifle, or that the folk of Arkham would not speak much of the blasted heath. I hurried back before sunset to my hotel, unwilling to have the stars come out above me in the open; and the next day returned to Boston to give up my position. I could not go into that dim chaos of old forest and slope again, or face another time that gray blasted heath where the black well yawned deep beside the tumbled bricks and stones. The reservoir will soon be built now, and all those elder secrets will be safe forever under watery fathoms. But even then I do not believe I would like to visit that country by night—at least, not when the sinister stars are out; and nothing could bribe me to drink the new city water of Arkham.

It all began, old Ammi said, with the meteorite. Before that time there had been no wild legends at all since the witch trials, and even then these western woods were not feared half so much as the small island in the Miskatonic where the devil held court beside a curious stone altar older than the Indians. These were not haunted woods, and their fantastic dusk was never terrible till the strange days. Then there had come that white noontide cloud, that string of explosions in the air, and that pillar of smoke from the valley far in the wood. And by night all Arkham had heard of the great rock that fell out of the sky and bedded itself in the ground beside the well at the Nahum Gardner place. That was the house which had stood where the blasted heath was to come—the trim white Nahum Gardner house amidst its fertile gardens and orchards.

Nahum had come to town to tell people about the stone, and had dropped in at Ammi Pierce's on the way. Ammi was forty then, and all the queer things were fixed very strongly in his mind. He and his wife had gone with the three professors from Miskatonic University who hastened out the next morning to see the weird visitor from unknown stellar space, and had wondered why Nahum had called it so large the day before. It had shrunk, Nahum said as he pointed out the big brownish mound above the ripped earth and charred grass near the archaic well-sweep in his front yard; but the wise men answered that stones do not shrink. Its heat lingered persistently, and Nahum declared it had glowed faintly in the night. The professors tried it with a geologist's hammer and found it was oddly soft. It was, in truth, so soft as to be almost plastic; and they gouged rather than chipped a specimen to take back to the college for testing. They took it in an old pail borrowed from Nahum's kitchen, for even the small piece refused to grow cool. On the trip back they stopped at Ammi's to rest, and seemed thoughtful when Mrs Pierce remarked that the fragment was growing smaller and burning the bottom of the pail. Truly, it was not large, but perhaps they had taken less than they thought.

The day after that—all this was in June of '82—the professors had trooped out again in a great excitement. As they passed Ammi's they told him what queer things the specimen had done, and how it had faded wholly away when they put it in a glass beaker. The beaker had gone, too, and the wise men talked of the strange stone's affinity for silicon. It had acted quite unbelievably in that well-ordered laboratory; doing nothing at all and shewing no occluded gases when heated on charcoal, being wholly negative in the borax bead, and soon proving itself absolutely non-volatile at any producible temperature, including that of the oxy-hydrogen blowpipe. On an anvil it appeared highly malleable, and in the dark its luminosity was very marked. Stubbornly refusing to grow cool, it soon had the college in a state of real excitement; and when upon heating before the spectroscope it displayed shining bands unlike any known colors of the normal spectrum there was much breathless talk of new elements, bizarre optical properties, and other things which puzzled men of science are wont to say when faced by the unknown.

Hot as it was, they tested it in a crucible with all the proper reagents. Water did nothing. Hydrochloric acid was the same. Nitric acid and even aqua regia merely hissed and spattered against its torrid invulnerability. Ammi had difficulty in recalling all these things, but recognized some solvents as I mentioned them in the usual order of use. There were ammonia and caustic soda, alcohol and ether, nauseous carbon disulphide and a dozen others; but although the weight grew steadily less as time passed, and the fragment seemed to be slightly cooling, there was no change in the solvents to shew that they had attacked the substance at all. It was a metal, though, beyond a doubt. It was magnetic, for one thing; and after its immersion in the acid solvents there seemed to be faint traces of the Widmannstätten figures found on meteoric iron. When the cooling had grown very considerable, the testing was carried on in glass; and it was in a glass beaker that they left all the chips made of the original fragment during the work. The next morning both chips and beaker were gone without trace, and only a charred spot marked the place on the wooden shelf where they had been.

All this the professors told Ammi as they paused at his door, and once more he went with them to see the stony messenger from the stars, though this time his wife did not accompany him. It had now most certainly shrunk, and even the sober professors could not doubt the truth of what they saw. All around the dwindling brown lump near the well was a vacant space, except where the earth had caved in; and whereas it had been a good seven feet across the day before, it was now scarcely five. It was still hot, and the sages studied its surface curiously as they detached another and larger piece with hammer and chisel. They gouged deeply this time, and as they pried away the smaller mass they saw that the core of the thing was not quite homogeneous.

They had uncovered what seemed to be the side of a large colored globule imbedded in the substance. The color, which resembled some of the bands in the meteor's strange spectrum, was almost impossible to describe; and it was only by analogy that they called it color at all. Its texture was glossy, and upon tapping it appeared to promise both brittleness and hollowness. One of the professors gave it a smart blow with a hammer, and it burst with a nervous little pop. Nothing was emitted, and all trace of the thing vanished with the puncturing. It left behind a hollow spherical space about three inches across, and all thought it probable that others would be discovered as the enclosing substance wasted away.

Conjecture was vain; so after a futile attempt to find additional globules by drilling, the seekers left again with their new specimen—which proved, however, as baffling in the laboratory as its predecessor had been. Aside from being almost plastic, having heat, magnetism, and slight luminosity, cooling slightly in powerful acids, possessing an unknown spectrum, wasting away in air, and attacking silicon compounds with mutual destruction as a result, it presented no identifying features whatsoever; and at the end of the tests the college scientists were forced to own that they could not place it. It was nothing of this earth, but a piece of the great outside; and as such dowered with outside properties and obedient to outside laws.

That night there was a thunderstorm, and when the professors went out to Nahum's the next day they met with a bitter disappointment. The stone, magnetic as it had been, must have had some peculiar electrical property; for it had "drawn the lightning," as Nahum said, with a singular persistence. Six times within an hour the farmer saw the lightning strike the furrow in the front yard, and when the storm was over nothing remained but a ragged pit by the ancient well-sweep, half-choked with caved-in earth. Digging had borne no fruit, and the scientists verified the fact of the utter vanishment. The failure was total; so that nothing was left to do but go back to the laboratory and test again the disappearing fragment left carefully cased in lead. That fragment lasted a week, at the end of which nothing of value had been learned of it. When it had gone, no residue was left behind, and in time the professors felt scarcely sure they had indeed seen with waking eyes that cryptic vestige of the fathomless gulfs outside; that lone, weird message from other universes and other realms of matter, force, and entity.

As was natural, the Arkham papers made much of the incident with its collegiate sponsoring, and sent reporters to talk with Nahum Gardner and his family. At least one Boston daily also sent a scribe, and Nahum quickly became a kind of local celebrity. He was a lean, genial person of about fifty, living with his wife and three sons on the pleasant farmstead in the valley. He and Ammi exchanged visits frequently, as did their wives; and Ammi had nothing but praise for him after all these years. He seemed slightly proud of the notice his place had attracted, and talked often of the meteorite in the succeeding weeks. That July and August were hot, and Nahum worked hard at his haying in the ten-acre pasture across Chapman's Brook; his rattling wain wearing deep ruts in the shadowy lanes between. The labor tired him more than it had in other years, and he felt that age was beginning to tell on him.

Then fell the time of fruit and harvest. The pears and apples slowly ripened, and Nahum vowed that his orchards were prospering as never before. The fruit was growing to phenomenal size and unwonted gloss, and in such abundance that extra barrels were ordered to handle the future crop. But with the ripening came sore disappointment; for of all that gorgeous array of specious lusciousness not one single jot was fit to eat. Into the fine flavor of the pears and apples had crept a stealthy bitterness and sickishness, so that even the smallest of bites induced a lasting disgust. It was the same with the melons and tomatoes, and Nahum sadly saw that his entire crop was lost. Quick to connect events, he declared that the meteorite had poisoned the soil, and thanked heaven that most of the other crops were in the upland lot along the road.

Winter came early, and was very cold. Ammi saw Nahum less often than usual, and observed that he had begun to look worried. The rest of his family, too, seemed to have grown taciturn; and were far from steady in their church-going or their attendance at the various social events of the countryside. For this reserve or melancholy no cause could be found, though all the household confessed now and then to poorer health and a feeling of vague disquiet. Nahum himself gave the most definite statement of anyone when he said he was disturbed about certain footprints in the snow. They were the usual winter prints of red squirrels, white rabbits, and foxes, but the brooding farmer professed to see something not quite right about their nature and arrangement. He was never specific, but appeared to think that they were not as characteristic of the anatomy and habits of squirrels and rabbits and foxes as they ought to be. Ammi listened without interest to this talk until one night when he drove past Nahum's house in his sleigh on the way back from Clark's Corners. There had been a moon, and a rabbit had run across the road, and the leaps of that rabbit were longer than either Ammi or his horse liked. The latter, indeed, had almost run away when brought up by a firm rein. Thereafter Ammi gave Nahum's tales more respect, and wondered why the Gardner dogs seemed so cowed and quivering every morning. They had, it developed, nearly lost the spirit to bark.

In February the McGregor boys from Meadow Hill were out shooting woodchucks, and not far from the Gardner place bagged a very peculiar specimen. The proportions of its body seemed slightly altered in a queer way impossible to describe, while its face had taken on an expression which no one ever saw in a woodchuck before. The boys were genuinely frightened, and threw the thing away at once, so that only their grotesque tales of it ever reached the people of the countryside. But the shying of the horses near Nahum's house had now become an acknowledged thing, and all the basis for a cycle of whispered legend was fast taking form.

People vowed that the snow melted faster around Nahum's than it did anywhere else, and early in March there was an awed discussion in Potter's general store at Clark's Corners. Stephen Rice had driven past Gardner's in the morning, and had noticed the skunk-cabbages coming up through the mud by the woods across the road. Never were things of such size seen before, and they held strange colors that could not be put into any words. Their shapes were monstrous, and the horse had snorted at an odor which struck Stephen as wholly unprecedented. That afternoon several persons drove past to see the abnormal growth, and all agreed that plants of that kind ought never to sprout in a healthy world. The bad fruit of the fall before was freely mentioned, and it went from mouth to mouth that there was poison in Nahum's ground. Of course it was the meteorite; and remembering how strange the men from the college had found that stone to be, several farmers spoke about the matter to them.

One day they paid Nahum a visit; but having no love of wild tales and folklore were very conservative in what they inferred. The plants were certainly odd, but all skunk-cabbages are more or less odd in shape and odor and hue. Perhaps some mineral element from the stone had entered the soil, but it would soon be washed away. And as for the footprints and frightened horses—of course this was mere country talk which such a phenomenon as the aërolite would be certain to start. There was really nothing for serious men to do in cases of wild gossip, for superstitious rustics will say and believe anything. And so all through the strange days the professors stayed away in contempt. Only one of them, when given two phials of dust for analysis in a police job over a year and a half later, recalled that the queer color of that skunk-cabbage had been very like one of the anomalous bands of light shewn by the meteor fragment in the college spectroscope, and like the brittle globule found imbedded in the stone from the abyss. The samples in this analysis case gave the same odd bands at first, though later they lost the property.

The trees budded prematurely around Nahum's, and at night they swayed ominously in the wind. Nahum's second son Thaddeus, a lad of fifteen, swore that they swayed also when there was no wind; but even the gossips would not credit this. Certainly, however, restlessness was in the air. The entire Gardner family developed the habit of stealthy listening, though not for any sound which they could consciously name. The listening was, indeed, rather a product of moments when consciousness seemed half to slip away. Unfortunately such moments increased week by week, till it became common speech that "something was wrong with all Nahum's folks." When the early saxifrage came out it had another strange color; not quite like that of the skunk-cabbage, but plainly related and equally unknown to anyone who saw it. Nahum took some blossoms to Arkham and shewed them to the editor of the *Gazette,* but that dignitary did no more than write a humorous article about them, in which the dark fears of rustics were held up to polite ridicule. It was a mistake of Nahum's to tell a stolid city man about the way the great, overgrown mourning-cloak butterflies behaved in connexion with these saxifrages.

April brought a kind of madness to the country folk, and began that disuse of the road past Nahum's which led to its ultimate abandonment. It was the vegetation. All the orchard trees blossomed forth in strange colors, and through the stony soil of the yard and adjacent pasturage there sprang up a bizarre growth which only a botanist could connect with the proper flora of the region. No sane wholesome colors were anywhere to be seen except in the green grass and leafage; but everywhere those hectic and prismatic variants of some diseased, underlying primary tone without a place among the known tints of earth. The Dutchman's breeches became a thing of sinister menace, and the bloodroots grew insolent in their chromatic perversion. Ammi and the Gardners thought that most of the colors had a sort of haunting familiarity, and decided that they reminded one of the brittle globule in the meteor. Nahum plowed and sowed the ten-acre pasture and the upland lot, but did nothing with the land around the house. He knew it would be of no use, and hoped that the summer's strange growths would draw all the poison from the soil. He was prepared for almost anything now, and had grown used to the sense of something near him waiting to be heard. The shunning of his house by neighbors told on him, of course; but it told on his wife more. The boys were better off, being at school each day; but they could not help being frightened by the gossip. Thaddeus, an especially sensitive youth, suffered the most.

In May the insects came, and Nahum's place became a nightmare of buzzing and crawling. Most of the creatures seemed not quite usual in their aspects and motions, and their nocturnal habits contradicted all former experience. The Gardners took to watching at night—watching in all directions at random for something... they could not tell what. It was then that they all owned that Thaddeus had been right about the trees. Mrs Gardner was the next to see it from the window as she watched the swollen boughs of a maple against a moonlit sky. The boughs surely moved, and there was no wind. It must be the sap. Strangeness had come into everything growing now. Yet it was none of Nahum's family at all who made the next discovery. Familiarity had dulled them, and what they could not see was glimpsed by a timid windmill salesman from Bolton who drove by one night in ignorance of the country legends. What he told in Arkham was given a short paragraph in the *Gazette;* and it was there that all the farmers, Nahum included, saw it first. The night had been dark and the buggy-lamps faint, but around a farm in the valley which everyone knew from the account must be Nahum's the darkness had been less thick. A dim though distinct luminosity seemed to inhere in all the vegetation, grass, leaves, and blossoms alike, while at one moment a detached piece of the phosphorescence appeared to stir furtively in the yard near the barn.

The grass had so far seemed untouched, and the cows were freely pastured in the lot near the house, but toward the end of May the milk began to be bad. Then Nahum had the cows driven to the uplands, after which the trouble ceased. Not long after this the change in grass and leaves became apparent to the eye. All the verdure was going gray, and was developing a highly singular quality of brittleness. Ammi was now the only person who ever visited the place, and his visits were becoming fewer and fewer. When school closed the Gardners were virtually cut off from the world, and sometimes let Ammi do their errands in town. They were failing curiously both physically and mentally, and no one was surprised when the news of Mrs Gardner's madness stole around.

It happened in June, about the anniversary of the meteor's fall, and the poor woman screamed about things in the air which she could not describe. In her raving there was not a single specific noun, but only verbs and pronouns. Things moved and changed and fluttered, and ears tingled to impulses which were not wholly sounds. Something was taken away—she was being drained of something—something was fastening itself on her that ought not to be—someone must make it keep off—nothing was ever still in the night—the walls and windows shifted. Nahum did not send her to the county asylum, but let her wander about the house as long as she was harmless to herself and others. Even when her expression changed he did nothing. But when the boys grew afraid of her, and Thaddeus nearly fainted at the way she made faces at him, he decided to keep her locked in the attic. By July she had ceased to speak and crawled on all fours, and before that month was over Nahum got the mad notion that she was slightly luminous in the dark, as he now clearly saw was the case with the nearby vegetation.

It was a little before this that the horses had stampeded. Something had aroused them in the night, and their neighing and kicking in their stalls had been terrible. There seemed virtually nothing to do to calm them, and when Nahum opened the stable door they all bolted out like frightened woodland deer. It took a week to track all four, and when found they were seen to be quite useless and unmanageable. Something had snapped in their brains, and each one had to be shot for its own good. Nahum borrowed a horse from Ammi for his haying, but found it would not approach the barn. It shied, balked, and whinnied, and in the end he could do nothing but drive it into the yard while the men used their own strength to get the heavy wagon near enough the hayloft for convenient pitching. And all the while the vegetation was turning gray and brittle. Even the flowers whose hues had been so strange were graying now, and the fruit was coming out gray and dwarfed and tasteless. The asters and goldenrod bloomed gray and distorted, and the roses and zinneas and hollyhocks in the front yard were such blasphemous-looking things that Nahum's oldest boy Zenas cut them down. The strangely puffed insects died about that time, even the bees that had left their hives and taken to the woods.

By September all the vegetation was fast crumbling to a grayish powder, and Nahum feared that the trees would die before the poison was out of the soil. His wife now had spells of terrific screaming, and he and the boys were in a constant state of nervous tension. They shunned people now, and when school opened the boys did not go. But it was Ammi, on one of his rare visits, who first realized that the well water was no longer good. It had an evil taste that was not exactly fetid nor exactly salty, and Ammi advised his friend to dig another well on higher ground to use till the soil was good again. Nahum, however, ignored the warning, for he had by that time become calloused to strange and unpleasant things. He and the boys continued to use the tainted supply, drinking it as listlessly and mechanically as they ate their meager and ill-cooked meals and did their thankless and monotonous chores through the aimless days. There was something of stolid resignation about them all, as if they walked half in another world between lines of nameless guards to a certain and familiar doom.

Thaddeus went mad in September after a visit to the well. He had gone with a pail and had come back empty-handed, shrieking and waving his arms, and sometimes lapsing into an inane titter or a whisper about "the moving colors down there." Two in one family was pretty bad, but Nahum was very brave about it. He let the boy run about for a week until he began stumbling and hurting himself, and then he shut him in an attic room across the hall from his mother's. The way they screamed at each other from behind their locked doors was very terrible, especially to little Merwin, who fancied they talked in some terrible language that was not of earth. Merwin was getting frightfully imaginative, and his restlessness was worse after the shutting away of the brother who had been his greatest playmate.

Almost at the same time the mortality among the livestock commenced. Poultry turned grayish and died very quickly, their meat being found dry and noisome upon cutting. Hogs grew inordinately fat, then suddenly began to undergo loathsome changes which no one could explain. Their meat was of course useless, and Nahum was at his wit's end. No rural veterinary would approach his place, and the city veterinary from Arkham was openly baffled. The swine began growing gray and brittle and falling to pieces before they died, and their eyes and muzzles developed singular alterations. It was very inexplicable, for they had never been fed from the tainted vegetation. Then something struck the cows. Certain areas or sometimes the whole body would be uncannily shriveled or compressed, and atrocious collapses or disintegrations were common. In the last stages—and death was always the result—there would be a graying and turning brittle like that which beset the hogs. There could be no question of poison, for all the cases occurred in a locked and undisturbed barn. No bites of prowling things could have brought the virus, for what live beast of earth can pass through solid obstacles? It must be only natural disease—yet what disease could wreak such results was beyond any mind's guessing. When the harvest came there was not an animal surviving on the place, for the stock and poultry were dead and the dogs had run away. These dogs, three in number, had all vanished one night and were never heard of again. The five cats had left some time before, but their going was scarcely noticed since there now seemed to be no mice, and only Mrs Gardner had made pets of the graceful felines.

On the nineteenth of October Nahum staggered into Ammi's house with hideous news. The death had come to poor Thaddeus in his attic room, and it had come in a way which could not be told. Nahum had dug a grave in the railed family plot behind the farm, and had put therein what he found. There could have been nothing from outside, for the small barred window and locked door were intact; but it was much as it had been in the barn. Ammi and his wife consoled the stricken man as best they could, but shuddered as they did so. Stark terror seemed to cling round the Gardners and all they touched, and the very presence of one in the house was a breath from regions unnamed and unnamable. Ammi accompanied Nahum home with the greatest reluctance, and did what he might to calm the hysterical sobbing of little Merwin. Zenas needed no calming. He had come of late to do nothing but stare into space and obey what his father told him; and Ammi thought that his fate was very merciful. Now and then Merwin's screams were answered faintly from the attic, and in response to an inquiring look Nahum said that his wife was getting very feeble. When night approached, Ammi managed to get away; for not even friendship could make him stay in that spot when the faint glow of the vegetation began and the trees may or may not have swayed without wind. It was really lucky for Ammi that he was not more imaginative. Even as things were, his mind was bent ever so slightly; but had he been able to connect and reflect upon all the portents around him he must inevitably have turned a total maniac. In the twilight he hastened home, the screams of the mad woman and the nervous child ringing horribly in his ears.

Three days later Nahum lurched into Ammi's kitchen in the early morning, and in the absence of his host stammered out a desperate tale once more, while Mrs Pierce listened in a clutching fright. It was little Merwin this time. He was gone. He had gone out late at night with a lantern and pail for water, and had never come back. He'd been going to pieces for days, and hardly knew what he was about. Screamed at everything. There had been a frantic shriek from the yard then, but before the father could get to the door, the boy was gone. There was no glow from the lantern he had taken, and of the child himself no trace. At the time Nahum thought the lantern and pail were gone too; but when dawn came, and the man had plodded back from his all-night search of the woods and fields, he had found some very curious things near the well. There was a crushed and apparently somewhat melted mass of iron which had certainly been the lantern; while a bent bail and twisted iron hoops beside it, both half-fused, seemed to hint at the remnants of the pail. That was all. Nahum was past imagining, Mrs Pierce was blank, and Ammi, when he had reached home and heard the tale, could give no guess. Merwin was gone, and there would be no use in telling the people around, who shunned all Gardners now. No use, either, in telling the city people at Arkham who laughed at everything. Thad was gone, and now Merwin was gone. Something was creeping and creeping and waiting to be seen and felt and heard. Nahum would go soon, and he wanted Ammi to look after his wife and Zenas if they survived him. It must all be a judgment of some sort; though he could not fancy what for, since he had always walked uprightly in the Lord's ways so far as he knew.

For over two weeks Ammi saw nothing of Nahum; and then, worried about what might have happened, he overcame his fears and paid the Gardner place a visit. There was no smoke from the great chimney, and for a moment the visitor was apprehensive of the worst. The aspect of the whole farm was shocking—grayish withered grass and leaves on the ground, vines falling in brittle wreckage from archaic walls and gables, and great bare trees clawing up at the gray November sky with a studied malevolence which Ammi could not but feel had come from some subtle change in the tilt of the branches. But Nahum was alive, after all. He was weak, and lying on a couch in the low-ceiled kitchen, but perfectly conscious and able to give simple orders to Zenas. The room was deadly cold; and as Ammi visibly shivered, the host shouted huskily to Zenas for more wood. Wood, indeed, was sorely needed; since the cavernous fireplace was unlit and empty, with a cloud of soot blowing about in the chill wind that came down the chimney. Presently Nahum asked him if the extra wood had made him any more comfortable, and then Ammi saw what had happened. The stoutest cord had broken at last, and the hapless farmer's mind was proof against more sorrow.

Questioning tactfully, Ammi could get no clear data at all about the missing Zenas. "In the well—he lives in the well—" was all that the clouded father would say. Then there flashed across the visitor's mind a sudden thought of the mad wife, and he changed his line of inquiry. "Nabby? Why, here she is!" was the surprised response of poor Nahum, and Ammi soon saw that he must search for himself. Leaving the harmless babbler on the couch, he took the keys from their nail beside the door and climbed the creaking stairs to the attic. It was very close and noisome up there, and no sound could be heard from any direction. Of the four doors in sight, only one was locked, and on this he tried various keys on the ring he had taken. The third key proved the right one, and after some fumbling Ammi threw open the low white door.

It was quite dark inside, for the window was small and half-obscured by the crude wooden bars; and Ammi could see nothing at all on the wide-planked floor. The stench was beyond enduring, and before proceeding further he had to retreat to another room and return with his lungs filled with breathable air. When he did enter he saw something dark in the corner, and upon seeing it more clearly he screamed outright. While he screamed he thought a momentary cloud eclipsed the window, and a second later he felt himself brushed as if by some hateful current of vapor. Strange colors danced before his eyes; and had not a present horror numbed him he would have thought of the globule in the meteor that the geologist's hammer had shattered, and of the morbid vegetation that had sprouted in the spring. As it was he thought only of the blasphemous monstrosity which confronted him, and which all too clearly had shared the nameless fate of young Thaddeus and the livestock. But the terrible thing about this horror was that it very slowly and perceptibly moved as it continued to crumble.

Ammi would give me no added particulars to this scene, but the shape in the corner does not reappear in his tale as a moving object. There are things which cannot be mentioned, and what is done in common humanity is sometimes cruelly judged by the law. I gathered that no moving thing was left in that attic room, and that to leave anything capable of motion there would have been a deed so monstrous as to damn any accountable being to eternal torment. Anyone but a stolid farmer would have fainted or gone mad, but Ammi walked conscious through that low doorway and locked the accursed secret behind him. There would be Nahum to deal with now; he must be fed and tended, and removed to some place where he could be cared for.

Commencing his descent of the dark stairs, Ammi heard a thud below him. He even thought a scream had been suddenly choked off, and recalled nervously the clammy vapor which had brushed by him in that frightful room above. What presence had his cry and entry started up? Halted by some vague fear, he heard still further sounds below. Indubitably there was a sort of heavy dragging, and a most detestably sticky noise as of some fiendish and unclean species of suction. With an associative sense goaded to feverish heights, he thought unaccountably of what he had seen upstairs. Good God! What eldritch dream-world was this into which he had blundered? He dared move neither backward nor forward, but stood there trembling at the black curve of the boxed-in staircase. Every trifle of the scene burned itself into his brain. The sounds, the sense of dread expectancy, the darkness, the steepness of the narrow steps—and merciful heaven!—the faint but unmistakable luminosity of all the woodwork in sight; steps, sides, exposed laths, and beams alike!

Then there burst forth a frantic whinny from Ammi's horse outside, followed at once by a clatter which told of a frenzied runaway. In another moment horse and buggy had gone beyond earshot, leaving the frightened man on the dark stairs to guess what had sent them. But that was not all. There had been another sound out there. A sort of liquid splash—water—it must have been the well. He had left Hero untied near it, and a buggy-wheel must have brushed the coping and knocked in a stone. And still the pale phosphorescence glowed in that detestably ancient woodwork. God! How old the house was! Most of it built before 1670, and the gambrel roof not later than 1730.

A feeble scratching on the floor downstairs now sounded distinctly, and Ammi's grip tightened on a heavy stick he had picked up in the attic for some purpose. Slowly nerving himself, he finished his descent and walked boldly toward the kitchen. But he did not complete the walk, because what he sought was no longer there. It had come to meet him, and it was still alive after a fashion. Whether it had crawled or whether it had been dragged by any external force, Ammi could not say; but the death had been at it. Everything had happened in the last half-hour, but collapse, graying, and disintegration were already far advanced. There was a horrible brittleness, and dry fragments were scaling off. Ammi could not touch it, but looked horrifiedly into the distorted parody that had been a face. "What was it,

Nahum—what was it?" he whispered, and the cleft, bulging lips were just able to crackle out a final answer.

"Nothin'... nothin'... the color... it burns... cold an' wet... but it burns... it lived in the well... I seen it... a kind o' smoke... jest like the flowers last spring... the well shone at night... Thad an' Mernie an' Zenas... everything alive... suckin' the life out of everything... in that stone... it must a' come in that stone... pizened the whole place... dun't know what it wants... that round thing them men from the college dug outen the stone... they smashed it... it was that same color... jest the same, like the flowers an' plants... must a' ben more of 'em... seeds... seeds... they growed... I seen it the fust time this week... must a' got strong on Zenas... he was a big boy, full o' life... it beats down your mind an' then gits ye... burns ye up... in the well water... you was right about that... evil water... Zenas never come back from the well... can't git away... draws ye... ye know summ'at's comin', but 'tain't no use... I seen it time an' agin senct Zenas was took... whar's Nabby, Ammi?... my head's no good... dun't know how long senct I fed her... it'll git her ef we ain't keerful... jest a color... her face is gettin' to hev that color sometimes towards night... an' it burns an' sucks... it come from some place whar things ain't as they is here... one o' them professors said so... he was right... look out, Ammi, it'll do suthin' more... sucks the life out...."

But that was all. That which spoke could speak no more because it had completely caved in. Ammi laid a red checked tablecloth over what was left and reeled out the back door into the fields. He climbed the slope to the ten-acre pasture and stumbled home by the north road and the woods. He could not pass that well from which his horse had run away. He had looked at it through the window, and had seen that no stone was missing from the rim. Then the lurching buggy had not dislodged anything after all—the splash had been something else—something which went into the well after it had done with poor Nahum....

When Ammi reached his house the horse and buggy had arrived before him and thrown his wife into fits of anxiety. Reassuring her without explanations, he set out at once for Arkham and notified the authorities that the Gardner family was no more. He indulged in no details, but merely told of the deaths of Nahum and Nabby, that of Thaddeus being already known, and mentioned that the cause seemed to be the same strange ailment which had killed the livestock. He also stated that Merwin and Zenas had disappeared. There was considerable questioning at the police station, and in the end Ammi was compelled to take three officers to the Gardner farm, together with the coroner, the medical examiner, and the veterinary who had treated the diseased animals. He went much against his will, for the afternoon was advancing and he feared the fall of night over that accursed place, but it was some comfort to have so many people with him.

The six men drove out in a democrat-wagon, following Ammi's buggy, and arrived at the pest-ridden farmhouse about four o'clock. Used as the officers were to gruesome experiences, not one remained unmoved at what was found in the attic and under the red checked tablecloth on the floor below. The whole aspect of the farm with its gray desolation was terrible enough, but those two crumbling objects were beyond all bounds. No one could look long at them, and even the medical examiner admitted that there was very little to examine. Specimens could be analyzed, of course, so he busied himself in obtaining them—and here it develops that a very puzzling aftermath occurred at the college laboratory where the two phials of dust were finally taken. Under the spectroscope both samples gave off an unknown spectrum, in which many of the baffling bands were precisely like those which the strange meteor had yielded in the previous year. The property of emitting this spectrum vanished in a month, the dust thereafter consisting mainly of alkaline phosphates and carbonates.

Ammi would not have told the men about the well if he had thought they meant to do anything then and there. It was getting toward sunset, and he was anxious to be away. But he could not help glancing nervously at the stony curb by the great sweep, and when a detective questioned him he admitted that Nahum had feared something down there—so much so that he had never even thought of searching it for Merwin or Zenas. After that nothing would do but that they empty and explore the well immediately, so Ammi had to wait trembling while pail after pail of rank water was hauled up and splashed on the soaking ground outside. The men sniffed in disgust at the fluid, and toward the last held their noses against the fetor they were uncovering. It was not so long a job as they had feared it would be, since the water was phenomenally low. There is no need to speak too exactly of what they found. Merwin and Zenas were both there, in part, though the vestiges were mainly skeletal. There were also a small deer and a large dog in about the same state, and a number of bones of smaller animals. The ooze and slime at the bottom seemed inexplicably porous and bubbling, and a man who descended on hand-holds with a long pole found that he could sink the wooden shaft to any depth in the mud of the floor without meeting any solid obstruction.

Twilight had now fallen, and lanterns were brought from the house. Then, when it was seen that nothing further could be gained from the well, everyone went indoors and conferred in the ancient sitting-room while the intermittent light of a spectral half-moon played wanly on the gray desolation outside. The men were frankly nonplussed by the entire case, and could find no convincing common element to link the strange vegetable conditions, the unknown disease of livestock and humans, and the unaccountable deaths of Merwin and Zenas in the tainted well. They had heard the common country talk, it is true; but could not believe that anything contrary to natural law had occurred. No doubt the meteor had poisoned the soil, but the illness of persons and animals who had eaten nothing grown in that soil was another matter. Was it the well water? Very possibly. It might be a good idea to analyze it. But what peculiar madness could have made both boys jump into the well? Their deeds were so similar—and the fragments shewed that they had both suffered from the gray brittle death. Why was everything so gray and brittle?

It was the coroner, seated near a window overlooking the yard, who first noticed the glow about the well. Night had fully set in, and all the abhorrent grounds seemed faintly luminous with more than the fitful moonbeams; but this new glow was something definite and distinct, and appeared to shoot up from the black pit like a softened ray from a searchlight, giving dull reflections in the little ground pools where the water had been emptied. It had a very queer color, and as all the men clustered round the window Ammi gave a violent start. For this strange beam of ghastly miasma was to him of no unfamiliar hue. He had seen that color before, and feared to think what it might mean. He had seen it in the nasty brittle globule in that aerolite two summers ago, had seen it in the crazy vegetation of the springtime, and had thought he had seen it for an instant that very morning against the small barred window of that terrible attic room where nameless things had happened. It had flashed there a second, and a clammy and hateful current of vapor had brushed past him—and then poor Nahum had been taken by something of that color. He had said so at the last—said it was the globule and the plants. After that had come the runaway in the yard and the splash in the well—and now that well was belching forth to the night a pale insidious beam of the same daemoniac tint.

It does credit to the alertness of Ammi's mind that he puzzled even at that tense moment over a point which was essentially scientific. He could not but wonder at his gleaning of the same impression from a vapor glimpsed in the daytime, against a window opening on the morning sky, and from a nocturnal exhalation seen as a phosphorescent mist against the black and blasted landscape. It wasn't right—it was against Nature—and he thought of those terrible last words of his stricken friend, "It come from some place whar things ain't as they is here... one o' them professors said so...."

All three horses outside, tied to a pair of shriveled saplings by the road, were now neighing and pawing frantically. The wagon driver started for the door to do something, but Ammi laid a shaky hand on his shoulder. "Dun't go out thar," he whispered. "They's more to this nor what we know. Nahum said somethin' lived in the well that sucks your life out. He said it must be some'at growed from a round ball like one we all seen in the meteor stone that fell a year ago June. Sucks an' burns, he said, an' is jest a cloud of color like that light out thar now, that ye can hardly see an' can't tell what it is. Nahum thought it feeds on everything livin' an' gits stronger all the time. He said he seen it this last week. It must be somethin' from away off in the sky like the men from the college last year says the meteor stone was. The way it's made an' the way it works ain't like no way o' God's world. It's some'at from beyond."

So the men paused indecisively as the light from the well grew stronger and the hitched horses pawed and whinnied in increasing frenzy. It was truly an awful moment; with terror in that ancient and accursed house itself, four monstrous sets of fragments—two from the house and two from the well—in the woodshed behind, and that shaft of unknown and unholy iridescence from the slimy depths in front. Ammi had restrained the driver on impulse, forgetting how uninjured he himself was after the clammy brushing of that colored vapor in the attic room, but perhaps it is just as well that he acted as he did. No one will ever know what was abroad that night; and though the blasphemy from beyond had not so far hurt any human of unweakened mind, there is no telling what it might not have done at that last moment, and with its seemingly increased strength and the special signs of purpose it was soon to display beneath the half-clouded moonlit sky.

All at once one of the detectives at the window gave a short, sharp gasp. The others looked at him, and then quickly followed his own gaze upward to the point at which its idle straying had been suddenly arrested. There was no need for words. What had been disputed in country gossip was disputable no longer, and it is because of the thing which every man of that party agreed in whispering later on that the strange days are never talked about in Arkham. It is necessary to premise that there was no wind at that hour of the evening. One did arise not long afterward, but there was absolutely none then. Even the dry tips of the lingering hedge-mustard, gray and blighted, and the fringe on the roof of the standing democrat-wagon were unstirred. And yet amid that tense, godless calm the high bare boughs of all the trees in the yard were moving. They were twitching morbidly and spasmodically, clawing in convulsive and epileptic madness at the moonlit clouds; scratching impotently in the noxious air as if jerked by some alien and bodiless line of linkage with subterrene horrors writhing and struggling below the black roots.

Not a man breathed for several seconds. Then a cloud of darker depth passed over the moon, and the silhouette of clutching branches faded out momentarily. At this there was a general cry; muffled with awe, but husky and almost identical from every throat. For the terror had not faded with the silhouette, and in a fearsome instant of deeper darkness the watchers saw wriggling at that treetop height a thousand tiny points of faint and unhallowed radiance, tipping each bough like the fire of St Elmo or the flames that came down on the apostles' heads at Pentecost. It was a monstrous constellation of unnatural light, like a glutted swarm of corpse-fed fireflies dancing hellish sarabands over an accursed marsh; and its color was that same nameless intrusion which Ammi had come to recognize and dread. All the while the shaft of phosphorescence from the well was getting brighter and brighter, bringing to the minds of the huddled men a sense of doom and abnormality which far outraced any image their conscious minds could form. It was no longer *shining* out, it was *pouring* out; and as the shapeless stream of unplaceable color left the well it seemed to flow directly into the sky.

The veterinary shivered, and walked to the front door to drop the heavy extra bar across it. Ammi shook no less, and had to tug and point for lack of a controllable voice when he wished to draw notice to the growing luminosity of the trees. The neighing and stamping of the horses had become utterly frightful, but not a soul of that group in the old house would have ventured forth for any earthly reward. With the moments the shining of the trees increased, while their restless branches seemed to strain more and more toward verticality. The wood of the well-sweep was shining now, and presently a policeman dumbly pointed to some wooden sheds and bee-hives near the stone wall on the west. They were commencing to shine, too, though the tethered vehicles of the visitors seemed so far unaffected. Then there was a wild commotion and clopping in the road, and as Ammi quenched the lamp for better seeing they realized that the span of frantic grays had broke their sapling and run off with the democrat-wagon.

The shock served to loosen several tongues, and embarrassed whispers were exchanged. "It spreads on everything organic that's been around here," muttered the medical examiner. No one replied, but the man who had been in the well gave a hint that his long pole must have stirred up something intangible. "It was awful," he added. "There was no bottom at all. Just ooze and bubbles and the feeling of something lurking under there." Ammi's horse still pawed and screamed deafeningly in the road outside, and nearly drowned its owner's faint quaver as he mumbled his formless reflections. "It come from that stone... it growed down thar... it got everything livin'... it fed itself on 'em, mind and body... Thad an' Mernie, Zenas an' Nabby... Nahum was the last... they all drunk the water... it got strong on 'em... it come from beyond, whar things ain't like they be here... now it's goin' home...."

At this point, as the column of unknown color flared suddenly stronger and began to weave itself into fantastic suggestions of shape which each spectator later described differently, there came from poor tethered Hero such a sound as no man before or since ever heard from a horse. Every person in that low-pitched sitting room stopped his ears, and Ammi turned away from the window in horror and nausea. Words could not convey it—when Ammi looked out again the hapless beast lay huddled inert on the moonlit ground between the splintered shafts of the buggy. That was the last of Hero till they buried him next day. But the present was no time to mourn, for almost at this instant a detective silently called attention to something terrible in the very room with them. In the absence of the lamplight it was clear that a faint phosphorescence had begun to pervade the entire apartment. It glowed on the broad-planked floor and the fragment of rag carpet, and shimmered over the sashes of the small-paned windows. It ran up and down the exposed corner-posts, coruscated about the shelf and mantel, and infected the very doors and furniture. Each minute saw it strengthen, and at last it was very plain that healthy living things must leave that house.

Ammi shewed them the back door and the path up through the fields to the ten-acre pasture. They walked and stumbled as in a dream, and did not dare look back till they were far away on the high ground. They were glad of the path, for they could not have gone the front way, by that well. It was bad enough passing the glowing barn and sheds, and those shining orchard trees with their gnarled, fiendish contours; but thank heaven the branches did their worst twisting high up. The moon went under some very black clouds as they crossed the rustic bridge over Chapman's Brook, and it was blind groping from there to the open meadows.

When they looked back toward the valley and the distant Gardner place at the bottom they saw a fearsome sight. All the farm was shining with the hideous unknown blend of color; trees, buildings, and even such grass and herbage as had not been wholly changed to lethal gray brittleness. The boughs were all straining skyward, tipped with tongues of foul flame, and lambent tricklings of the same monstrous fire were creeping about the ridgepoles of the house, barn, and sheds. It was a scene from a vision of Fuseli, and over all the rest reigned that riot of luminous amorphousness, that alien and undimensioned rainbow of cryptic poison from the well—seething, feeling, lapping, reaching, scintillating, straining, and malignly bubbling in its cosmic and unrecognizable chromaticism.

Then without warning the hideous thing shot vertically up toward the sky like a rocket or meteor, leaving behind no trail and disappearing through a round and curiously regular hole in the clouds before any man could gasp or cry out. No watcher can ever forget that sight, and Ammi stared blankly at the stars of Cygnus, Deneb twinkling above the others, where the unknown color had melted into the Milky Way. But his gaze was the next moment called swiftly to earth by the crackling in the valley. It was just that. Only a wooden ripping and crackling, and not an explosion, as so many others of the party vowed. Yet the outcome was the same, for in one feverish, kaleidoscopic instant there burst up from that doomed and accursed farm a gleamingly eruptive cataclysm of unnatural sparks and substance; blurring the glance of the few who saw it, and sending forth to the zenith a bombarding cloudburst of such colored and fantastic fragments as our universe must needs disown. Through quickly re-closing vapors they followed the great morbidity that had vanished, and in another second they had vanished too. Behind and below was only a darkness to which the men dared not return, and all about was a mounting wind which seemed to sweep down in black, frore gusts from interstellar space. It shrieked and howled, and lashed the fields and distorted woods in a mad cosmic frenzy, till soon the trembling party realized it would be no use waiting for the moon to shew what was left down there at Nahum's.

Too awed even to hint theories, the seven shaking men trudged back toward Arkham by the north road. Ammi was worse than his fellows, and begged them to see him inside his own kitchen, instead of keeping straight on to town. He did not wish to cross the nighted, wind-whipped woods alone to his home on the main road. For he had had an added shock that the others were spared, and was crushed forever with a brooding fear he dared not even mention for many years to come. As the rest of the watchers on that tempestuous hill had stolidly set their faces toward the road, Ammi had looked back an instant at the shadowed valley of desolation so lately sheltering his ill-starred friend. And from that stricken, far-away spot he had seen something feebly rise, only to sink down again upon the place from which the great shapeless horror had shot into the sky. It was just a color—but not any color of our earth or heavens. And because Ammi recognized that color, and knew that this last faint remnant must still lurk down there in the well, he has never been quite right since.

Ammi would never go near the place again. It is over half a century now since the horror happened, but he has never been there, and will be glad when the new reservoir blots it out. I shall be glad, too, for I do not like the way the sunlight changed color around the mouth of that abandoned well I passed. I hope the water will always be very deep—but even so, I shall never drink it. I do not think I shall visit the Arkham country hereafter. Three of the men who had been with Ammi returned the next morning to see the ruins by daylight, but there were not any real ruins. Only the bricks of the chimney, the stones of the cellar, some mineral and metallic litter here and there, and the rim of that nefandous well. Save for Ammi's dead horse, which they towed away and buried, and the buggy which they shortly returned to him, everything that had ever been living had gone. Five eldritch acres of dusty gray desert remained, nor has anything ever grown there since. To this day it sprawls open to the sky like a great spot eaten by acid in the woods and fields, and the few who have ever dared glimpse it in spite of the rural tales have named it "the blasted heath."

The rural tales are queer. They might be even queerer if city men and college chemists could be interested enough to analyze the water from that disused well, or the gray dust that no wind seems ever to disperse. Botanists, too, ought to study the stunted flora on the borders of that spot, for they might shed light on the country notion that the blight is spreading—little by little, perhaps an inch a year. People say the color of the neighboring herbage is not quite right in the spring, and that wild things leave queer prints in the light winter snow. Snow never seems quite so heavy on the blasted heath as it is elsewhere. Horses—the few that are left in this motor age—grow skittish in the silent valley; and hunters cannot depend on their dogs too near the splotch of grayish dust.

They say the mental influences are very bad, too. Numbers went queer in the years after Nahum's taking, and always they lacked the power to get away. Then the stronger-minded folk all left the region, and only the foreigners tried to live in the crumbling old homesteads. They could not stay, though; and one sometimes wonders what insight beyond ours their wild, weird stores of whispered magic have given them. Their dreams at night, they protest, are very horrible in that grotesque country; and surely the very look of the dark realm is enough to stir a morbid fancy. No traveler has ever escaped a sense of strangeness in those deep ravines, and artists shiver as they paint thick woods whose mystery is as much of the spirit as of the eye. I myself am curious about the sensation I derived from my one lone walk before Ammi told me his tale. When twilight came I had vaguely wished some clouds would gather, for an odd timidity about the deep skyey voids above had crept into my soul.

Do not ask me for my opinion. I do not know—that is all. There was no one but Ammi to question; for Arkham people will not talk about the strange days, and all three professors who saw the aërolite and its colored globule are dead. There were other globules—depend upon that. One must have fed itself and escaped, and probably there was another which was too late. No doubt it is still down the well—I know there was something wrong with the sunlight I saw above that miasmal brink. The rustics say the blight creeps an inch a year, so perhaps there is a kind of growth or nourishment even now. But whatever daemon hatchling is there, it must be tethered to something or else it would quickly spread. Is it fastened to the roots of those trees that claw the air? One of the current Arkham tales is about fat oaks that shine and move as they ought not to do at night.

What it is, only God knows. In terms of matter I suppose the thing Ammi described would be called a gas, but this gas obeyed laws that are not of our cosmos. This was no fruit of such worlds and suns as shine on the telescopes and photographic plates of our observatories. This was no breath from the skies whose motions and dimensions our astronomers measure or deem too vast to measure. It was just a color out of space—a frightful messenger from unformed realms of infinity beyond all Nature as we know it; from realms whose mere existence stuns the brain and numbs us with the black extra-cosmic gulfs it throws open before our frenzied eyes.

I doubt very much if Ammi consciously lied to me, and I do not think his tale was all a freak of madness as the townfolk had forewarned. Something terrible came to the hills and valleys on that meteor, and something terrible—though I know not in what proportion—still remains. I shall be glad to see the water come. Meanwhile I hope nothing will happen to Ammi. He saw so much of the thing—and its influence was so insidious. Why has he never been able to move away? How clearly he recalled those dying words of Nahum's—"can't git away... draws ye... ye know summ'at's comin', but 'tain't no use...." Ammi is such a good old man—when the reservoir gang gets to work I must write the chief engineer to keep a sharp watch on him. I would hate to think of him as the gray, twisted, brittle monstrosity which persists more and more in troubling my sleep.

WEREWOLF OF THE SAHARA

• • • • •

G. G. PENDARVES

A tremendous tale, depicted against the background of the great desert, about the evil Arab sheykh El Shabur, and dreadful occult forces that were unleashed in a desperate struggle for the soul of a beautiful girl.

The three of them were unusually silent that night over their after-dinner coffee. They were camping outside the little town of Sollum on the Libyan coast of North Africa. For three weeks they had been delayed here en route for the Siwa oasis. Two men and a girl.

"So we really start tomorrow," Merle Anthony blew a cloud of smoke toward the glittering night sky. "I'm almost sorry. Sollum's been fun. And I've done two of the best pictures I ever made here."

"Was that why you burned them up yesterday?" her cousin, Dale Fleming, inquired in his comfortable pleasant voice.

The girl's clear pallor slowly crimsoned. "Dale! What a—"

"It's all right, Merle," Gunnar Sven interrupted her. "Dale's quite right. Why pretend this delay has done you any good? And it's altogether my fault. I found that out today in the market. Overheard some Arabs discussing our expedition to Siwa."

"Your fault!" Merle's beautiful face, and eyes gray as a gull's wing, turned to him. "Why, you've simply slaved to get the caravan ready."

Gunnar got to his feet and walked out to the verge of the headland on which they were camped. Tall, straight as a pine he stood.

The cousins watched him; the girl with trouble and perplexity, the man more searchingly. His eyes, under straight upper lids, flatly contradicted the rest of his appearance. He was very fat, with fair hair and smooth unlined face despite his forty years. A sort of Pickwickian good humor radiated from him. Dale Fleming's really great intellectual power showed only in those three-cornered heavily lidded eyes of his.

"Why did you give me away?" Merle demanded.

His round moon face beamed on her.

"Why bluff?" he responded.

"Snooping about as usual. Why don't you go and be a real detective?" she retorted crossly.

He gave a comfortable chuckle, but his eyes were sad. It was devilishly hard to watch her falling for this Icelander. Ever since his parents had adopted her—an orphan of six—she had come first in Dale's affections. His love was far from Platonic. Gunnar Sven was a fine creature, but there was something wrong. Some mystery shadowed his life. What it was, Dale was determined to discover.

"Truth will out, my child! The natives are in terror of him. You know it as well as I do! They're all against helping you and me because he's our friend."

"Stop being an idiot. No one could be afraid of Gunnar. And he's particularly good with natives."

"Yes. He handles them well. I've never seen a young 'un do it better."

"Well, then?"

"There's something queer about him. These Arabs know it. We know it. It's about two months now since he joined forces with us. Just after my mother decamped and left us in Cairo. The cable summoning her home to Aunt Sue's death-bed arrived Wednesday, May 3rd. She sailed May 5th. Gunnar Sven turned up May 6th."

"All right. I'm not contradicting you. It's never any use."

"You refused to wait for Mother's return in Cairo, according to her schedule."

"Well! Cairo! Everyone paints Cairo and the Nile. I wanted subjects that every five-cent tourist hadn't raved over."

"You wanted Siwa oasis. Of all God-forsaken dangerous filthy places! And in the summer—"

"You know you're dying to see the oasis too," she accused. "Just trying to save your face as my guardian and protector. Hypocrite!"

He roared with laughter. The Arab cook and several other servants stopped singing round their cooking-pots to grin at the infectious sound.

"Touché! I'd sacrifice my flowing raven locks to go to Siwa. But"—his face grew surprisingly stern—"about Gunnar. Why does he take such enormous pains not to tell us the name of the man he's been working for?"

"I've never asked him."

"I haven't in so many words, of course. But I've led him up to the fence over and over again. He's steadily refused it. With good reason."

"Well?"

"He works for an Arab. A sheykh. A man notorious from Morocco to Cairo. His nickname's Sheykh El Afrit. The Magician! His real name is Sheykh Zura El Shabur."

"And what's so earth-shaking about that?" asked Merle, patting a dark curl into place behind her ear.

"He's a very—bad—hat! Black Magic's no joke in this country. This Sheykh El Shabur's gone far. Too far."

"I'm going to talk to Gunnar. He'll tell me. It's fantastic. Gunnar and Black Magic indeed!"

Dale watched her, amused and touched. How she loathed subtleties and mysteries and tangled situations!

"She'd waltz up to a lion and pull its whiskers if anyone told her they were false. As good at concealment as a searchlight."

Gunnar turned from the sea as Merle walked purposefully in his direction. He stood beside her—mountain pine overshadowing a little silver birch.

"H-m-m!" Dale threw away a freshly lighted cigarette and took another. "Merle and I wouldn't suggest that. More like Friar Tuck and Maid Marian."

He was startled to see Gunnar suddenly leap and turn. The man looked as if he'd had a tremendous shock. He stood peering across the wastelands stretching eastward, frozen into an attitude of utmost horror.

Dale ran across to Merle. She broke from his detaining hand and rushed to Gunnar's side.

"What is it? What do you see? Gunnar! Answer me, Gunnar!"

His tense muscles relaxed. He sighed, and brushed a hand across his eyes and wet forehead.

"He's found me. He's coming. I had hoped never—"

"Who? What are you talking about?"

She shook his arm in terror at his wild look and words.

"He said I was free! Free! I wouldn't have come near you if I'd known he lied. Now I've brought him into your life. Merle! Forgive me!"

He took her hands, kissed them frantically, then turned to Dale with burning haste and fairly pushed him away.

"Go! Go! Go! Now—before he comes. Leave everything! Ride for your lives. He'll force me to ... go! Go!"

"*Ma yarudd*! What means this, Gunnar—my servant?"

The deep guttural voice seemed to come up from the bowels of the earth. The three turned as if a bomb had exploded. A figure loomed up not ten feet away. Merle stared with wide startled eyes. A minute ago the level wasteland had shown bare, deserted. How had this tall Arab approached unseen?

Gunnar seemed to shrink and wither. His face was tragic. The newcomer fixed him for a long moment in silence, staring him down.

"What means this, Gunnar, my servant?" Once more the words vibrated through the still night.

The Icelander made a broken ineffectual movement of his hands, and began to speak. His voice died away into low, vague murmurings.

"For this you shall account to me later," promised the tall Arab.

He strode forward. His black burnoose rippled and swayed about him. Its peaked hood was drawn close. A long face with pointed black beard, proud curving nose, and eyes dark and secret as forest pools gleamed beneath the hood.

Merle shrank back. Her fingers clutched Gunnar's. They were cold and limp in her grasp.

Dale leaned forward, peering into the Arab's face as a connoisseur examines an etching of rare interest.

"You speak very good English, my friend. Or is it enemy?"

The whole demeanor of the Arab changed. His white teeth flashed. He held out welcoming hands, clasped Dale's in his own, and bowed low to the girl. He turned last to the Icelander.

"Present me!" he ordered.

Gunnar performed the small ceremony with white lips. His voice sounded as if he'd been running hard.

"Zura El Shabur. Zura of the Mist," translated the sheykh. "I am your friend. I have many friends of your Western world. The language! All languages are one to me!"

Dale beamed. "Ah! Good linguist and all that! Jolly good name yours, what! Gave us quite a scare, popping up out of the atmosphere like Aladdin's djinnee!"

El Shabur's thin lips again showed his teeth.

"Those that dwell in the desert's solitude and silence learn to reflect its qualities."

"Quite! Quite!" Dale gurgled happy agreement. "Neat little accomplishment Very convenient—for you!"

"Convenient on this occasion for you also, since my coming prevented the inhospitality of my servant from driving you away."

"No! You're wrong there. Gunnar's been our guardian angel for weeks past. Given us a wonderful time."

"Nevertheless, I heard that he urged you to go—to go quickly from Solium."

Dale burst into laughter; long, low gurgles that relieved tension all around. "I'm one of those fools that'd rather lose a pot of gold than alter my plans. One of the camel-drivers has made off with a few bits of loot. You heard the thrifty Gunnar imploring me to follow him."

Merle backed up the tale with quick wit. "Nothing of vast importance.

My silver toilet things, a leather bag and a camera. Annoying, but hardly worth wasting hours to retrieve."

She came forward, all anxiety to give Gunnar time to pull himself together.

El Shabur made her a second low obeisance and stared down into her upturned vivid face. "Such youth and beauty must be served. Shall I send Gunnar after the thief?"

The idea of separation gave her a shock. Intuition warned her to keep the Icelander at her side for his sake, and for her own. Together there seemed less danger.

Danger! From what? Why did the word drum through her brain like an S.O.S. signal? She glanced at Gunnar. His face was downbent.

"No." She met the Arab's eyes with effort and gave a valiant little smile. "No. Indeed not. We can't spare him. He's promised to come with us, to be our guide to the Siwa oasis."

"Hope this won't clash with your plans for him. We've got so dependent on his help now." Dale's cherubic face registered anxiety.

"So." The Arab put a hand on Gunnar's shoulder. "It is good. You have done well."

The young man shivered. His eyes met Merle's in warning.

El Shabur turned to reassure her and Dale.

"Now all goes well. I, too, will join your caravan. It is necessary for my—my work—that I should visit Siwa very soon. I go also."

Dale took the outstretched hand. "Fine! Fine! We'll make a record trip now."

In his tent, Dale slept after many hours of hard, concentrated thought and intellectual work—very pink, very tired, younger-looking than ever in his profound repose.

In her tent, Merle lay quiet too.

Native servants snored, shapeless cocoons in their blankets. Even the camels had stopped moaning and complaining, and couched peacefully, barracked in a semicircle. Great mounds of baggage within its wide curve lay ready for loading.

Moonlight silvered long miles of grass and rushes. Leagues of shining water swung in almost tideless rhythm half a mile from camp.

Gunnar looked out on the scene from his tent. What had roused him from sleep? Why was his heart thumping, and the blood drumming in his ears? He peered out into the hushed world.

Tents, men, camels and baggage showed still as things on a painted canvas. He left his tent, made a noiseless detour about the sleeping camp, then frowned and stared about in all directions.

A bird, rising on startled wing, made him look sharply at an old Turkish fort. It stood, grim and battered sentinel, on a near-by promontory of Solium Bay. Through its gaping ruined walls he caught a glint of fire—green, livid, wicked names that stained the night most evilly.

"El Shabur! Already! The Pentacle of Fire!"

His whisper was harsh as the faint drag of pebbles on the shore. For several minutes he stood as if chained. Fear and anger warred with dawning resolution and a wild anxiety. Then he stumbled over to Merle's tent and tore open its flap. Flashlight in hand, he went in and stared down at the sleeping girl. She lay white and rigid as if in a trance. Gunnar touched her forehead, took up a limp hand in his own. She gave no sign of life.

He stood looking down at the still, waxen features. The rather square, resolute little face was uniformly white, even to the curved, just-parted lips. The hair seemed wrought in metal, so black and heavy and lifeless did it wave above the broad, intelligent brow. Gunnar looked in awe. The girl's animated, sparkling face was changed to something remote and strange and exquisite. Half child, half priestess.

"And in a few short weeks or months," he muttered, "El Shabur will initiate her. This is the first step. She will rot—perish—as I am doing!"

He bent, in passionate horror, over the still face.

"No! No! Not for you! Dear lovely child!"

He clenched his hands. "But if I disturb him now!"

For minutes he stood irresolute. Fear took him by the throat. He could not—he could not interfere! At last his will steadied. He mastered the sick terror that made him tremble and shiver like a beaten dog. As he left the tent, he glanced back once more.

"Good-bye! I'll do all I can," he promised softly. "I'd give my soul to save you—if I still had one."

He ran to the headland where the old fort stood. If El Shabur's occupation was what he feared, he would neither hear nor see. Intensely concentrating on his rites, nothing in the visible world would reach him.

Gunnar's calculations were justified. He went boldly in through the arched entrance to an inner court where green fires burned in a great ring, five points of two interlacing triangles which showed black upon the gray dust of the floor. In the center of this cabalistic symbol stood El Shabur, clothed in black. The rod he held was of black ebony.

Gunnar drew breath. He listened to the toneless continuous muttering of the sheykh. What point had El Shabur reached in his conjurations? How long since he had drawn Merle's soul from the lovely quiet body lying in her tent? It was of vital importance to know. If the devilish business was only begun, he might free her. If El Shabur had reached the last stage, closed the door behind the soul he was luring from its habitation, then it was fatally late.

He listened, head thrust forward, trying to distinguish the rapidly muttered words.

"Shekinah! Aralim! Ophanim! Assist me in the name of Melek Taos, Ruler of wind and stars and sea, who commands the four elements in the might of Adonai and the Ancient Ones!"

"A-h-h-h!" Gunnar gave a deep gasping sigh of relief. He was not too late. Sheykh El Shabur called on his allies. Merle's spirit was not yet cut off from its home. Her will resisted the Arab's compulsion.

He leaped forward, oversetting all five braziers. Their fire spilled and died out instantly. In the cold clear moonlight, El Shabur loomed tall, menacing. He stood glaring across the courtyard at the intruder. His black-clad figure overshadowed the Icelander's by many inches, like a cloud, like a bird of prey. Malignant, implacable, he towered.

Gunnar's golden head sank. His strong, straight body seemed to shrink and crumple. Inch by inch he retreated, until he reached the wall. He tried to meet the Arab's unblinking stare and failed. Again his bright head sank. His eyes sought the dusty earth. But his whole frame trembled with a wild, fanatical excitement. He had succeeded so far—had brought El Shabur back from that void where Merle's spirit had so perilously wandered. She was free. Free to go back to that still white body lying in her tent.

"So! You love this girl. You would save her from me. You—who cannot save yourself!"

"You're right." The young man's voice shook. "Right as far as I'm concerned. But Miss Anthony's on a different plane. You're not going to play your filthy tricks on her."

"So! It would seem that, in spite of my teaching, you are not yet well disciplined. Have you forgotten your vow? Have you forgotten that a cabalist may never retreat one inch of the road he treads? Have you forgotten the punishment that overtakes the renegade?"

"I would die to save her from you."

The other showed white teeth in a mirthless sardonic grin.

"Die!" echoed his deep, mocking voice. "Death is not for us. Are you not initiated and under protection? What can bring death to such as you?"

"There must be a way of escape for me—and for her. I will defeat you yet, El Shabur!"

The Icelander's voice rose. His eyes were blazing. He stepped forward. Moonlight touched his shining hair, his passion-contorted features, his angry, bloodshot eyes. Control slipped from him. He strove in vain to recapture it, to use his reason. He knew that anger was delivering him bound and helpless into his enemy's hands. It had been so from their first encounter. Emotion versus reason. He knew his fatal weakness, and strove against it now—in vain. Long habit ruled. Anger made his will a thing of straw.

"You would defy me—the Power I serve—the Power that serves me?"

Gunnar felt the blood rushing to his head. His ears sang. Red mist obscured his sight.

"You are a devil! And you serve devils!" he shouted. "But you won't always win the game! Curse you, El Shabur! Curse you! Curse you!"

The Arab looked long into his angry eyes, and came closer. With an incredibly swift movement he clasped the shaking, furious figure.

Gunnar felt dry lips touch his ears and mouth and brow, heard a low quick mutter. Then El Shabur released him suddenly, and stood back.

"Ignorant and beast-like! Be what you are—slave to your own passion! You, yourself, create the devil that haunts you. Therefore are you mine—for all devils are subject to me. Be what you are! Out, beast! Howl and snarl with your own kind until the dawn."

For a moment something dark scuffled in the dust at El Shabur's feet. The courtyard rang with a long, desolate howl. A shadow, lean and swift, fled from the camp, far, far out across the empty wasteland.

At sunset, the next day, Dale Fleming and his caravan reached Bir Augerin, the first well on their march. They had delayed their start some hours. Merle had insisted in waiting for Gunnar, but he had not turned up.

"He will join us en route," the sheykh had assured her. "He is well used to desert travel, Mademoiselle!"

"But his camel?"

"We will take it. He can easily hire another."

"Have you no idea why he went off and left us without warning? It's so unlike him."

El Shabur gave his dark unmirthful smile.

"He is young. Young and careless and—undisciplined. He has—friends. Oh, he is popular! That golden hair of his—it has a fascination...."

Merle's face crimsoned and grew pale. Dale's round face concealed his thoughts. He glanced at the Arab's lean hands that twisted a stiff length of wire rope with such slow and vicious strength. He had learned how betraying hands may be.

Merle made no more objections, and at 3:30 p. m. the caravan set out. The natives were superstitious about a journey's start. Mondays, Thursdays and Saturdays were fortunate; and Saturday the luckiest of the week.

At Bir Augerin, camp was quickly made. The servants drew up water from the large rectangular tank in leather buckets. Merle sat disconsolate to watch, and smoke, and think of Gunnar. Dale joined her, leaving the sheykh to direct the men.

"I don't believe it!" Merle burst out.

"About our absent friend?"

"Gunnar's not that sort. I think they've had a quarrel, Dale!" She put a beseeching hand on his arm. "You don't think—he wouldn't kill Gunnar!"

"My prophetic bones tell me not." He patted the hand in brisk, business-like fashion. "He'll turn up and explain himself. Don't worry. This Sheykh of the Mist's a queer old josser. About as trustworthy as a black panther, but the boy's too useful to be killed off in a hurry. All the same—look here, Merle: keep this handy at night."

He put a small snub-nosed automatic in her hand.

"It's loaded. And I've taught you to use it. Listen! There are wolves on this trail. Heard 'em last night about the camp."

"Wolves? In the desert? Jackals, you mean."

"Don't speak out of turn. Wolves. You know—things that go off like this."

He threw back his head and gave a blood-curdling howl that electrified the camp. El Shabur spun on his heel, long knife drawn. The servants groveled, then ran to pluck brands from the fire.

Dale gave a rich, infectious gurgle. "Splendid! Must have done that jolly well. Now perhaps you'll recognize a wolf when you hear it. If you do—shoot!"

Soon after 4 a.m. the caravan set out again in the chill clear moonlight. In spite of grilling days, the nights remained cool and made travel easy. They reached their next halt, Bir Hamed, about eight o'clock. This cistern was the last before real desert began. They decided to give the camels a good day's grazing and watering and push off again in the small hours before dawn.

Cooking-pots were slung over crackling fires. Fragrance of wood smoke mingled with odor of frying sausages and onions. Dale went over and implored the cook to refrain from using last night's dish-water to brew coffee. El Shabur approached Merle and pointed to the east.

"He comes."

She dropped a camera and roll of film and jumped to her feet.

"Who? Gunnar? I see no one."

"He comes riding from over there."

Low rolling dunes to the east showed bare and smooth and empty of life. She stared, and frowned at the speaker. "I see nothing. Dale!" she called out. "The sheykh says Gunnar's coming from over there. Can you see him?"

Dale scrutinized the empty eastern horizon, then turned to El Shabur with a bland wide smile. "Ah, you wonderful Arabs! Putting one over on us, aren't you? You people have extra valve sets. Pick up things from the ether. It's enough to give me an inferiority complex."

He thrust an arm through Merle's. "If he says so, it is so! I'll tell cook to fry a few more sausages.

"Servants are all in a state of jim-jams this morning," he said as he returned from his hospitable errand. "Ilbrahaim's been handing out samples from the Thousand and One Nights' Entertainments. What d'you suppose he's started now?"

"They talk much," the sheykh's deep scornful voice replied. "And they say nothing."

"Ilbrahaim is a chatty little fellow. Be invaluable at a funeral, wouldn't he? Distract the mourners and all that! Unless he got on to vampires and ghouls. He's keen on cabalistic beliefs."

"Such things are childish; they have no interest for a cabalist."

"No—really! Well, you probably know. Is there a place called Bilad El Kelab?"

El Shabur's eyes glinted. His chin went up in a gesture of assent.

"There is? Ah, then Ilbrahaim tells the truth now and then. His brother went to this place. Country of the Dogs—suggestive name! The yarn is that all the men there turn to dogs at sunset. Like werewolves, you know."

"Bilad El Kelab is far away. South—far south in the Sudan. Ilbrahaim has no brother, moreover."

"No?"

"No. There are many foolish legends from the Sudan."

"Not so foolish. I'm interested in folklore and legend and primitive beliefs. That's why I'm going to Siwa, apart from looking after my little cousin here."

El Shabur's eyes smoldered. "It is unwise to be too curious about such things. That which feeds an eagle is no meat for a fish."

"Quite! Quite! Good that, isn't it, Merle? Meaning we Westerners are fish! Oh, definitely good! This Ilbrahaim, though—he swears our camp's being haunted. He thinks a weredog, or werewolf, has attached itself to us. Says he woke and saw it prowling about last night."

"A long trail from the Bilad El Kelab!"

"You're right, El Shabur. Still, what's a few hundred miles to a werewolf? And I suppose it travels on camel-back by day, if it's got its man's body in good repair. Have to be a new camel each morning—eh? Not likely a self-respecting mehari would trot hoof in paw with a wolf each night."

"Dale! Is it the same wolf you said was—"

A cousinly kick on the ankle, as Dale moved to replace a blazing branch on the fire, warned her.

"Is it the wolf-tale they talked about in Alexandria?" she switched off quickly.

"Dear child!" Dale beamed approval. "How your little wits do work! No! That wolf was a jackal that haunted the Valley of the Kings in Egypt."

El Shabur turned his head sharply. "The lost one arrives," he remarked.

In the distance, magnified and distorted by the hot desert air, a vast camel and rider loomed. Merle lighted a cigarette with slow, unsteady hands.

"It may be anyone. Impossible to tell yet."

The sheykh spread his hands. "Mademoiselle will soon discover."

In half an hour, Gunnar rode into Camp. A sorry figure, disheveled, unshaven, he looked as if he'd been across Africa with a minimum of food and sleep. Merle had meant to be unrelenting at first, to await explanation, but her heart betrayed her at the sight of this desperately weary man. She ran to meet him as he dismounted, and tried to lead him over to where Dale and the Arab sat smoking.

He stood swaying on his feet. "No. Not now." His cracked, parched lips could scarcely frame the words. "I must sleep. I—I could not help it. I was prevented—I was prevented," he croaked.

"Gunnar—of course!" She beckoned to a servant. "Take care of him. I'll send Dale effendi to give him medicine. He is ill."

* * *

In the late afternoon the camp was in more or less of an uproar. The camels were driven in from pasturage to drink once again. They would have preferred to go on grazing and, being camels, they expressed disapproval noisily, and gave much trouble to the cursing, sweating men.

Dale sauntered off from their vicinity. The sun was casting shadows that lengthened steadily. He stopped in the shadow of a huge boulder and stared thoughtfully out across the barren desert.

"Got his goat all right about that legend and the cabalists. Now, just why did that strike home? The pattern's there, but all in little moving bits. I can't get the confounded mosaic right. Cabalists! Werewolves! Gunnar and the Sheykh of the Mist! Haunted camp and all the rest of it! A very, very pretty little mix-up. I wonder now.... I wonder...."

His eyes, fixed in abstracted non-seeing gaze, suddenly became wary. His big body grew taut. Then, with the lightness of movement for which fat men are often remarkable, he vanished into a cleft of the great rock. His hearing was acute and voices carried far in the desert stillness.

"... until we reach Siwa. From sunrise to sunset I will be with her." Gunnar's bitterness was apparent. "If you interfere I will tell her what you are!"

"In return I will explain what you are—after sunset!" El Shabur's voice mocked. "Will the knowledge make her turn to you for protection?"

"You devil!"

"You fool! Do not meddle with power you cannot control. Until Siwa, then."

They passed out of earshot. Dale watched them return to camp.

"More bite of mosaic, nice lurid color, too. Looks as though Siwa's going to be even more promising than I imagined. Evil old city, enough to make one write another Book of Revelations?"

The sun cast long shadows, stretching grotesquely over pink-stained leagues of sand. Dale was anxious to watch Gunnar when the sun actually did set; he felt that phrase of the young Icelander's had been significant: From sunrise to sunset I will be with her. Rather an odd poetic reference to time! Taken in conjunction with his unexplained disappearance last night, it was specially odd.

Dale ambled slowly in the direction of camp, empty pipe between his teeth. He had stayed a long hour. From his rocky crevice, he had watched Gunnar and the Arab return, seen Gunnar start off again with Merle into the desert. The two were returning now—dark against the reddening sky.

He was curious to see how the young man was going to behave; what explanation, if any, he had given to Merle. He was overwhelmingly anxious to discover just how far she returned the love that burned so steadfastly in Gunnar's eyes. If it was serious—really serious—with her, the whole queer dangerous situation was going to be deadly.

She would go her own way. If her heart was given, it was given, for good or evil. It seemed entirely evil, in his judgment, if she had decided to link her fate with this Icelander.

And El Shabur! How dangerous was this notorious Arab magician? Men of his practises fairly haunted desert cities and oases. Mostly they were harmless, sometimes genuinely gifted in the matter of prophecy. Rarely, they were men of inexplicable and very terrible power; who were dedicated, brain and body, to the cause of evil—evil quite beyond the comprehension of normal people.

Dale's eyes were cold and implacable as he recollected one or two such men he had known: his pleasant face looked unbelievably austere and grim.

One way or another, Merle stood in imminent and pressing danger; from Gunnar, no less than from El Shabur; from Gunnar, not because he was of himself evil, but because he was a channel through which the Arab could reach her. She was vulnerable in proportion to her love. There were infinite sources of danger ahead. El Shabur had a definite plan regarding her, something that would mature at Siwa. Three days remained to discover the nature of that plan.

Three days! Perhaps not even that. Gunnar's relations with the Arab seemed dangerously explosive; a crisis might work up at any moment. Merle would then be implicated, for she would defend Gunnar with blind partisanship. All the odds were on El Shabur. It was his country; he could queer the expedition easily without any supernatural agency. And, if he were the deadly poisonous creature Dale began to suspect, then the lonely desert made a superb background for murder ... he called it murder to himself, unwilling to give a far more terrible name to what he suspected El Shabur might do.

The lovers, walking slowly, reluctantly back to camp, were completely absorbed in each other.

"If only I'd known you earlier!" The man's sunken eyes looked down on the erect, slim, lovely girl beside him with immense regret.

"The only thing we can do about it is to make up for lost time, darling."

He stopped, faced her, took both firm, rather square hands in his own. "Merle, you're being a miracle. But it's impossible. I oughtn't to have told you how much I cared."

"Poor dear! You hadn't any choice, really. I did the leap-year stunt before you could stop me; and, being a little gent, you simply had to say you loved me too!"

She rattled away, hardly knowing what she said. "I've got to alter that look in his eyes," she told herself. "I thought it was because of me, conceited little beast that I am. But it isn't—it isn't!

"Gunnar," she tackled him with characteristic impetuosity, "Is your fear of El Shabur the biggest thing in your life? Is it bigger than—than your love for me?"

The grip of his hands tightened. His face bent to hers. His haunted red-rimmed eyes looked into her candid gray ones, that shone with love and kindness and a steadfast unwavering trust that made him want to kiss her dusty shoes. Instead, he dropped her hands, pulled his hat down over his face, walked on with quickened stride toward the distant encampment.

"It's no use ... I can't go on with it. I'm in a tangle that no one on earth can straighten out. It's revolting to think of you being caught up in such a beastly mess. I went into this thing because I was a young inquisitive fool! I'd no idea what it involved, no idea at all that there was something behind it stronger ... stronger than death! I was blind, I was credulous, I was utterly ignorant; I walked into El Shabur's trap—and the door shut behind me!"

"Gunnar, darling, can't you explain? People don't have to go on serving masters they hate unless—unless—"

"Exactly! Unless they're slaves. Well, I am his slave."

"I don't understand you."

"Thank heaven for it, and don't try! It's because you must never, never understand such things that I wanted you and Dale to go away that night at Sollum."

"If you owe the sheykh your time, can't you buy him off? Surely any contract can be broken."

"Not the one that binds me to him. Listen, Merle, my own! I can't—I daren't say more than this. Think of him as a poison—as something that blackens and burns like vitriol. Will you do what may seem a very childish thing, will you do it to please me?"

"What is it?"

"Tie this across the entrance of your sleeping-tent at night." He held out a little colored plait, four threads of green, white, red, and black, from which a seal depended. "Once more, I daren't explain, but use it. Promise me!"

* * *

Taken aback by his tone and manner, she promised. What, she thought, had a bit of colored string to do with all this mystery about him and the sheykh? A fleeting doubt as to his sanity came to her.

"No," he answered the look. "I was never more sane than now—when it's too late. Too late for myself, at least. You—nothing shall happen to you!"

"Won't you talk to Dale? He's such a queer wise old thing, I'm sure he could help if only you'd explain things to him."

"No. Not yet, at any rate. Not until we get to Siwa. I'll explain everything then. Silence is the price I've paid to be with you on this trip."

"But, really Dale is—"

"If you don't want him to die suddenly, say nothing to him. Anyone that interferes with El Shabur gets rubbed out like this!"

Gunnar stamped a small pebble deep into the sand.

"All right," she promised with a shiver. That quick vicious little movement had given her a sudden horrid fear of the sheykh—more than all Gunnar's words. "I'll say nothing. But Dale is pretty hard to deceive. There never seems any need to tell him things; he just knows them. I expect he's burrowing away underground about El Shabur already, just like an old ferret! I happen to know he loathes him."

"Nobody'd think so to see them chin-wagging."

"He behaves like a garrulous moron when he's putting salt on anyone's tail, and I've seldom seen him wallowing quite so idiotically as now."

"Much more likely the sheykh's putting salt on his tail by pretending to believe Dale's a fool."

"You don't know Dale."

"You don't know El Shabur." Gunnar had the last word—it proved to be accurate.

They found the two in camp and deep in talk.

"Arguing about our pet werewolf." Dale was bland. "Will you sit up with me and try a pot shot at the beast, Gunnar?"

The tall Icelander stood in silence. His face was a gray mask, his sunken eyes stared hard and long into the other's blank smooth face. He turned to the sheykh at length.

"You suggested this?"

Merle shivered at his voice.

The Arab shrugged. "On the contrary. It would be wisdom to sleep before tomorrow's march. If the effendi desires to hunt it would be well to wait until we reach the hills of Siwa."

"Well," Dale seemed determined to prolong the discussion, "what do you vote for, old man? The werewolf tonight, or the Siwa hills later?"

"The hills—definitely, the hills," the young man's voice cracked on a laugh. "According to legend, you can't kill a werewolf. No use wasting our shots and a night's sleep too."

"Thwarted!" moaned Dale. "The hills of Siwa, then. You can promise good hunting there, Sheykh?"

"By my sacred *wasm*."

"*Wasm?*" Dale lighted a cigarette with casual air.

"My mark, my insignia, my tribal sign. It is like heraldry in your land."

"Heavens above! I must remember to call my little label a *wasm* in future. Intriguing word, that! And what is your mark?"

El Shabur leaned forward and traced it in the sand. Dale regarded it with a smile that masked deep uneasiness. He recognized the ghastly little sign; he was one of the very few who had the peculiar knowledge to do so. A smoke-screen from his eternal pipe shielded his face from the watchful Arab. Was El Shabur trying to trick him into exposing his very special and intimate knowledge of the occult; or did he make that deadly mark feeling sure that only an initiate would recognize it?

El Shabur was a Yezidee, a Satanist, and worshipped Melek Taos. The symbol was unmistakably the outspread tail of the Angel-Peacock. Dale recoiled inwardly at having his darkest fears confirmed; he knew of no tribe on earth more vicious and powerful than the Yezidees. Their name and their fame went back into the mists of time. Seldom did one of them leave his hills and rock-dwelling up beyond Damascus. Once in a century or so, throughout the ages, a priest of the Yezidees would stalk the earth like a black, destroying god to acquaint himself with the world and its conditions. He would return to teach his tribe. So they remained, a nucleus of evil power that never seemed to die out.

"Nice little design; looks like half a ray-fish," he commented. Impossible to fathom what was going on behind the sheykh's carven, immobile features. "*Wasm*—did you say? Wait, I must write that down."

The whites of the Arab's eyes glinted as he glanced at Merle. "Are you like your cousin in this—do you also suffer from loss of memory?"

"I—we—what do you mean?"

"You have a saying in your Book of Wisdom, 'Thy much learning doth turn thee to madness.' The effendi is like to that man, Paul. For who, after years and years of study, could forget so simple a thing as a *wasm*?"

Dale didn't move a muscle. His bluff was called. All right! On with the next dance! Too late he realized why the Arab had started the absorbing *wasm* topic. It had been intended to shock and distract his own thoughts from Gunnar—to prevent his keeping an eye on him.

The Icelander had got up and gone over to his tent a minute ago with a murmur about tobacco. He had not returned. Dale was on his feet and peering into Gunnar's tent in a flash. No one there. He looked at the western horizon—the sun had dipped beyond it. He scanned the desert. It offered no shelter for Gunnar's six feet of height. He looked into every tent; saw that only the servants crouched before their fires, that only baggage lay heaped upon the ground.

Shadows were melting into dusk. But one long shadow seemed to move over there among the dunes not far away! Were his own dark thoughts inventing the thing that fled across the desert?

The darkest thought of all came as he went back to Merle and the silent watchful Arab. Was he a match for this man?

"You needn't worry about Gunnar. The Arab's at the back of these nightly disappearances, I'm quite certain, although the reasons he gave were of his own invention."

"Then you think he'll come back?" Merle looked tired and anxious in the light of her small lamp.

"He'll come back," asserted the man. "Good night, old lady. If you feel nervous or want anything, just give a yelp. I'll be awake—got to finish a bit of research work."

She caught a look that belied his cheerful voice. "Why d'you look round my tent like that? Is there any special danger—that wolf?"

"Well, I don't mind telling you there is a spot of danger. You're not the sort that goes off like a repeating-rifie at being warned. But—have you got your doodah handy?"

She showed the automatic underneath her pillow. "Perhaps I ought to tell you that Gunnar warned me too. No. Not about the wolf, but El Shabur."

"Worse than a whole pack of wolves," he agreed. "Know where you are with those noisy brutes, but the sheykh's another cup of tea, entirely."

"He gave me this. Told me to tie up my tent with it. Queer, don't you think?"

He examined the plait of colored string with profound interest.

"Jerusalem the Golden! If we ever reach dry land again, this will be an heirloom for you to hand on. That is, unless you're hard up and want to sell it to some Croesus for a sack of diamonds. This, my dear Black-eyed Susan, is a relic dating back thousands of years. The seal, of course, not the threads. It's an emerald. And that's the Eye of Horus cut in it."

"Emerald! It must be fearfully valuable. How on earth d'you think Gunnar got it?"

"From his master the sheykh. It's the sort of thing he'd need, poor fellow! It's a safeguard—oh, quite infallible."

"I never know when you're serious or when you're just being idiotic. Protection from what? What does it mean?"

"It means that El Shabur's a cabalist. And that Gunnar is an initiate and pretty far advanced too, to be in possession of this very significant thing. He's gone a long, long way on the road—poor lad!"

"He's in danger?"

"Extreme and imminent danger; there's scarcely a chance to cut him free now. Better face the thing, dear. Gunnar's not in a position to love or marry any woman; he's tied body and soul to El Shabur. It's a hideous, deplorable, ghastly mess, the whole affair." He sat down beside her on the little truckle bed and took her hand. "This is my fault. I knew well enough even at Solium that there was something abnormal about Gunnar."

"I love him," she answered very quietly, "and nothing can ever alter that. Whatever he's done, or is—I love him."

He stared at her a long minute. "And that's the damndest part of the whole show," he remarked with immense gravity.

He turned back at the tent opening. "About that thing Gunnar gave you. Fasten the tent-flap with it if you value your soul; wear it under your dress by day, never let the sheykh catch a glimpse of it. We reach Siwa the day after tomorrow. Try not to let El Shabur know we suspect anything, meantime. Sure you're all right—not afraid?"

"Not for myself. I don't understand what it's all about. But I'm afraid for my poor Gunnar. He's the sort that can't stand alone. Not like you and me, we're too hard-headed old things!"

"You're a wonder. Any other girl stranded here with a half-mad native sorcerer would go right up the pole. Tie up your tent, though, d'you hear?"

"The moment you've gone. Cross my heart!"

Night wore swiftly on. Dale sat smoking in his own tent, fully dressed, alert and expectant. He felt convinced that something was in the wind tonight. The sound of shots far off across the desert took him outside, rifle in hand.

Sleep held the camp; not a man had stirred. The black Bedouin tent in which the sheykh slept was closed. No one seemed to have been disturbed except himself. Again came that queer little tug of his senses—a warning of danger near.

His grip tightened on his weapon. He went on more slowly. A shadow seemed to move round the great mass of rock which had sheltered him a few hours ago. He halted half-way between rock and camp. Should he go back and rouse the men? Or should he go closer and inspect for himself? He walked on.

A high, piping wind blew clouds across the sky. A black mass obscured the moon. He halted once more, turned back to camp in a sudden certainty of peril. Too late. A rush. A scuffle. An arm of steel clasped him from behind, a hand like a vise was clamped across his lips before he could call out. His big body was enormously muscular and he fought like a tiger, threw off his assailant, shouted loudly. The strong wind shouted louder, tore his voice to shreds. It swept the black cloud from the moon too, and he saw a small band of natives, their faces veiled, knives glinting, burnooses bellying out like sails as they shouted and ran at him.

They were too close to take aim. He made for the rock. Unencumbered, and a good sprinter, he reached it safely, stood with his back to it and coolly picked out one after another of his enemies. It was only a momentary advantage; they were too many for him, and ran in again with savage yells.

To his amazement, a dark long swift body flung itself upon his attackers. A great wolf, huge, shaggy, thin and sudden as a torpedo. In vain the men plunged their knives into its rough pelt. Again and again Dale saw the wicked twisted blades drop as the brute caught the wrists of the raiders in its teeth.

The fight was short. Not a man was killed, but none escaped a wound. Some had faces slashed so that blood ran down and blinded them; some dragged a maimed foot; some a mangled arm. In terror of the swift, silent punishing creature that stood between them and their victim, the raiders turned and fled.

The wolf itself had been damaged in the savage encounter; an ear was torn, and it limped as it ran at the heels of the raiders, chasing them to their camels behind the huge rock pile.

The great panting beast looked full at Dale as it passed by. The man felt his heart beat, beat, beat in slow painful thuds against his chest. The creature's yellow, bloodshot eyes turned on him with a glance that cut deeper than any raider's knife. He leaned back. He felt very sick. The vast desert seemed to heave.

Slowly, soberly he made his way back to camp. He did not so much as glance back at the wolf. He knew now. He knew!

Siwa! Actually Siwa at last! The strange fort-like city loomed before the thin line of camels and their dusty weary riders. Like a vast house of cards Siwa had risen up and up from the plain. On its foundation of rock, one generation after another had built; father for son, father for son again; one story on another, the sun-baked mud and salt of its walls almost indistinguishable from the rock itself.

Tiny windows flecked the massive precipitous piles. Vast hives of life, these buildings. Layer upon layer, narrowing from their rocky base into turrets and towers and minarets.

Dale's eyes were for Merle, however. She rode beside him, her face so white and strained, her eyes so anxious that he was torn with doubt. Ought he to have told her Gunnar's secret? He had not turned up since the desert fight. Merle was sick with anxiety. Sheykh El Shabur smiled in his beard as he saw her quivering underlip, her glance that looked about with ever increasing fear.

"Where is he? Where is he?" She turned upon the sheykh. "You said he would be here at Siwa, waiting for us. Where is he?" she demanded.

Dale could have laughed had the situation been less grave and horrible. She loved as she hated, with her whole strong vigorous soul and body. She tackled the sinister, haughty Arab, demanding of him the man she loved, with the fearlessness of untried youth.

She was worth dying for, his little Merle! And it looked as though he, and she too, would make a finish here in this old barbaric city. If he had to go, he would see to it that she was not left behind, to be a sacrifice on some blood-stained ancient altar hewn in the rock beneath the city, to die slowly and horribly that the lust of Melek Taos should be appeased, to die in body—to live on in soul, slave to Sheykh Zura El Shabur.

And Gunnar? It was unnerving to think what might be happening to him. Dale knew that Gunnar had saved his life as surely as that El Shabur had plotted to kill him two nights ago. It was not nice to consider how the cabalist might punish this second interference of his young disciple.

They rode on through an endless warren of twisting dark lanes. Dale dropped behind Merle and the Arab when only two could ride abreast; he liked to have El Shabur before his eyes when possible. He could see Merle talking earnestly. Her companion seemed interested, his hands moved in quick eloquent gesture, he seemed to be reassuring her on some point. Gunnar, surely! No other subject in common could exist between those two.

Past the date-markets, under the shadow of the square white tomb of Sidi Suliman, past palm-shaded gardens, until they reached a hill shaped like a sugar-loaf and honeycombed with tombs.

"The Hill of the Dead!" El Shabur waved a lean dark hand.

"Quite," replied Dale. "It looks like it."

The Arab pointed to the white Rest-House built on a level terrace cut in the hillside. "It is there that travelers stay—such as come to Siwa."

"Very appropriate. One does associate rest with tombs, after all."

Merle looked up at the remarkable hill with blank, uninterested gaze.

"Ilbrahaim will take your camels. If you will dismount here! The *jonduk* is on the other side of the city."

The sheykh dismounted as he spoke. He sent the servant off with the weary beasts, and left the cousins with a salaam to Dale and a deep mocking obeisance to the girl. They watched him out of sight. The hood of his black burnoose obscured head and face; its wide folds, dark and ominous as the sable wings of a bird of prey, swung to his proud free walk. They sighed with relief as the tall figure vanished in Siwa's gloomy narrow streets.

"What were you two chinning about on the way here?" Dale steered the exhausted girl up the steep rocky path. "You seemed to goad our friend to unusual eloquence."

"I was asking about Gunnar. What else is there to say to him? Oh, do look at that!"

Below stretched rolling sandy dunes, palm groves, distant ranges of ragged peaks, the silver glint of a salt lake, and a far-off village on the crest of a rocky summit in the east.

He looked, not at the extraordinary beauty of desert, hill and lake, but at Merle. She had switched the conversation abruptly. Also, she was gazing out over the desert with eyes that saw nothing before them. He was certain of that. She was keyed up—thinking, planning, anticipating something. What? He knew she'd made up her mind to action, and guessed it was concerned with Gunnar. Long experience had taught him the futility of questioning her.

They found the Rest-House surprisingly clean and cool. Ilbrahaim presently returned to look after them. No other guests were there.

It was getting on toward evening when Dale was summoned to appear before the Egyptian authorities and report on his visit. He knew the easily offended, touchy character of local rulers and authorities, and that it was wise to obey the summons. But about Merle!

He glanced at her over the top of a map he was pretending to study.

"Would you care to come along with me across the city? Or will you stay here with Ilbrahaim and watch the sunset? Famous here, I've read."

"Yes," she replied, her eyes on a pencil sketch she was making of the huddled roofs seen from an open window where she sat.

"My fault, I'll start again! A—Will you come with me? B—Will you stay with Ilbrahaim?"

"B." She looked up for a moment, then returned to her sketch.

He got the impression of peculiar and sudden relief in her eyes, as if the problem had solved itself.

"Wants to get me off the scene!" he told himself.

She stopped further uneasy speculation on his part by bringing her sketch across and plunging into technical details about it. He was a sound critic and was beguiled into an enthusiastic discourse on architecture. She listened and argued and discussed points with flattering deference, until the sun was low and vast and crimson in the west.

Then she casually remarked, "You needn't go now, surely?"

He started up. "I'd completely forgotten my little call. Sorry, dear, to leave you even for an hour. Etiquette's extremely stiff on these small formalities; better go, I think. 'Bye, old lady, don't go wandering about."

"Thank heaven, he's gone!" Merle thrust her drawings into a portfolio, put on a hat, scrutinized her pale face in her compact-mirror, applied lipstick and rouge with an artist's hand, and walked down the hill path.

At its junction with the dusty road, a tall black-clad figure joined her.

"You are punctual, Mademoiselle! That is well, for we must be there before sunset."

It seemed an interminable walk to her as they dived and twisted through a labyrinth of courtyards, flights of steps, and overshadowed narrow streets. She followed her silent guide closely. It would be unpleasant to lose even such a grim protector as El Shabur. She shrank from the filthy whining beggars with their rags and sores, from the bold evil faces of the young men who stood to stare at her. Even the children revolted her—pale unhealthy abnormal little creatures that they were.

The sheykh hurried on through the old town with its towering fort-like houses to newer Siwa. Here the dwellings were only of two or three stories with open roofs that looked like great stone boxes shoved hastily together in irregular blocks.

El Shabur looked at the sun, then turned to his companion with such malice in his black eyes that she shrank from him.

"He is here."

She looked up at the house-front with its tiny windows and fought back the premonition of horror that made her throat dry and her heart beat heavily. She despised her weakness. Inside this sinister house, behind one of those dark slits of windows, Gunnar was waiting for her.

Why he'd not come to her, why she must visit him secretly with El Shabur, she refused to ask herself. She loved him. She was going to be with him. The rest did not count at all.

She followed her guide through a low entrance door, stumbled up a narrow dark stairway, caught glimpses of bare, untenanted, low-ceilinged rooms. El Shabur opened a door at the top of the house, drew back with a flash of white teeth. She stooped to enter the low doorway.

"Gunnar!"

There was no answer in words, but from the shadows a figure limped, his face and head cut and bleeding, so gaunt, so shadow-like too, that she cried out again.

"Oh! Oh, my dear!"

He took her in his arms. She clasped him, drew his head down to hers, kissed the gray tortured face with passionate love and pity.

"Gunnar, I am here with you! Look at me! What is it?—tell me, darling, let me help you!"

His eyes met hers in such bitter despair and longing that she clutched him to her again, pressing her face against his shoulder. With gentle touch he put her from him.

"Listen to me, Merle, my darling. My beloved! Listen carefully. This is the last time I shall see you—touch you—for ever. I am lost—lost and damned. In a moment you will see for yourself. That is why he brought you here. Remember that I love you more than the soul I have lost—always—always, Merle!"

He pushed her from him, retreated to the shadows, stood there with head flung up and back pressed to the gray mud wall. Even as she would have gone to him, he changed, swiftly, dreadfully! Down—down in the dust—torn rough head and yellow wolf's eyes at her feet.

Merle sat up on the broad divan. Dale had returned to find her walking up and down, up and down the long main room of the Rest-House. For long he had been unable to distract her mind from the terrible inner picture that tormented her. She would answer his anxious questions with an impatient glance of wild distracted eyes, then begin her endless restless pacing again.

She had drunk the strong sedative he gave her as if her body were acting independently of her mind, but the drug had acted. She had slept. Now she was awake and turned to the man who watched beside her—large, protecting, compassionate. She tried to tell him, but her voice refused to put the thing into words.

"My dear child, don't! Don't! I know what you saw."

"You know! You've seen him when—when—" She covered her face, then slipped from the divan and stood erect before him.

"Dale! I'm all right now. It was so inhuman, such a monstrous unbelievable thing! But he has to bear it—live through it. And we must talk about it. We have to help him. Dale! Dale! Surely there is a way to free him?"

He took her hands in his, swallowed hard before he could command his voice. "My chi—" He broke off abruptly.

There was nothing left of the child! It was a very resolute woman whose white face and anguished eyes confronted him. She looked, she was in effect, ten years older. He could not insult her by anything but the whole unvarnished truth now. She must make the final decision herself. He must not, he dare not withhold his knowledge. It would be a betrayal. Of her. Of Gunnar. Of himself.

"Merle!"

At the tightening of his clasp, the new note in his voice, she looked up with a passion of renewed hope.

"There is—there is a way?"

He nodded, and drew her down beside him on the divan. He looked ill and shaken all at once. His tongue felt stiff, as if it would not frame words. It was like pushing her over a precipice, or into a blazing fire. How cruel love was! Hers for Gunnar. His for Merle. Love that counted—it was always a sharp sword in the heart.

"There is a way," his hoarse voice made effort. "It's a way that depends on your love and courage. Those two things alone—love and courage! It's a test of both, a most devilish test, so dangerous that the chances are you will not survive it. And if you don't—"

For a moment he bowed his head, put a hand up to shield his face from her wide eager gaze.

"Dear! It's a test, a trial of your will against that fiend, El Shabur. There are ancient records. It has been done. Only one or two survived the ordeal. The others perished—damned—lost as Gunnar is!"

"No." The low, softly breathed word was more impressive than a defiant blare of trumpets. "He is not lost, for I shall save him. Tell me what to do."

El Shabur listened in silence, looked from Merle's white worn face to Dale's maddening smile. He had not expected resistance. He had not thought this lovesick girl would try to win back her lover. The man was at the back of it, of course. Had taught her the formula, no doubt. Should he stoop to take up the gage to battle—with a woman?

"First time your bluff's ever been called, eh, Sheykh of the Mist? Are you meditating one of your famous disappearances? Am I trying you a peg too high? It is, of course, a perilous experiment—this trial of will between you and my little cousin!"

The Arab's white teeth gleamed in a mocking, mirthless smile. His eyes showed two dark flames that flared up hotly at the taunt.

"You cannot save him. He is mine, my creature, my slave."

"Not for long, Sheykh El Shabur," the girl spoke softly.

"For ever," he suavely corrected her. "And you also put yourself in my hands by this foolish test—which is no test!"

Dale stood watching near the door of the Rest-House. Could this be the child he had known so well, this resolute stern little figure, whose steadfast look never wavered from the Arab's face?—who spoke to him with authority on which his evil sneering contempt broke like waves on a rock?

"You think that you—a woman, can withstand me? A vain trifling woman, and one, moreover, who is overburdened by lust for my servant as a frail craft by heavy cargo. I will destroy you with your lover."

"I don't take your gloomy view of the situation," Dale interrupted. He watched the other intently from under drooped eyelids, saw that Merle's fearlessness and his own refusal to be serious were piercing the man's colossal self-esteem, goading him to accept the challenge to his power. El Shabur felt himself a god on earth. In so far as he was master of himself, he was a god! Dale had never met so disciplined and powerful a will. Few could boast so controlled and obedient an intellect. But he was proud, as the fallen Lucifer was proud!

It was the ultimate weakness of all who dabbled in occult powers. They were forced to take themselves with such profound seriousness that in the end the fine balance of sanity was lost.

Dale continued as if they were discussing a trifling matter that began to bore him. His mouth was so dry that he found difficulty in speaking at all. It was like stroking an asp.

"The point is that I have never seen our young friend take this extraordinary semblance of a—a werewolf. My cousin is, as you remark so emphatically, a woman. Not her fault, and all that, of course! But no doubt she was over-sensitive, imaginative, conjured up that peculiar vision of our absent Gunnar by reason of excessive anxiety."

"She saw my disobedient servant," the sheykh's deep voice rang like steel on an anvil, "undergoing punishment. It was no delusion of the senses."

"Ah! Good! Excellent! You mean she was not so weak, after all. That's one up to her, don't you think? I mean, seeing him as he really was. Rather penetrating, if you take me!"

"She saw what she saw, because it was my design that she should. She is no more than a woman because of it."

"Ah, I can't quite agree there." Dale was persuasive, anxious to prove his point politely. "I'll bet she didn't scream or faint. Just trotted home a bit wobbly at the knees, perhaps?"

"She is obstinate, as all women are obstinate." The sheykh's lean hands were hidden by flowing sleeves, to Dale's disgust; but a muscle twitched above the high cheek-bone, and the dark fire of his eyes glowed red.

"Since you desire to sacrifice yourself," the Arab turned to Merle, "Ilbrahaim shall bring you just before sundown to the house."

"Any objections to my coming along?" Dale spoke as if a supper-party were under discussion. "My interest in magic-ceremonial—"

El Shabur cut in. "You think to save her from me? Ah, do I not know of your learning, your researches, your study of occult mysteries! It will avail you nothing. No other cabalist has dared what I have dared. I—the High Priest of Melek Taos! Power is mine. No man clothed in flesh can stand against me."

He seemed, in the dim low-ceilinged room, to fill the place with wind and darkness and the sound of beating wings. Suddenly he was gone. Like a black cloud he was gone.

Dale looked after him for long tense minutes. "No man clothed in flesh," he quoted reflectively. "And there's quite a lot of clothing in my case, too."

Once more the grim stone house in the outskirts of the city. The cousins stood before it. Ilbrahaim, who had guided them, put a hand before his face in terror.

"Effendi, I go! This is an evil place." The whites of his eyes glinted between outspread fingers. "An abode of the shaitans!"

He turned, scuttled under a low archway. They heard the agitated clap-clap of his heelless slippers on hard-baked earth. Then silence closed round about them. They stood in the warm glow of approaching sunset.

Merle looked at the western sky and the great globe that was remorselessly bringing day to a close. Dale studied her grave, set face. He hoped against hope that she might even now turn back. Her eyes were on the round red sun as it sank.

He too stared as if hypnotized. If he could hold it—stop its slow fatal moving on ... on .... It was drawing Merle's life with it. It was vanishing into darkness and night. Merle too would vanish into darkness ... into awful night....

She turned and smiled at him. The glory of the sky touched her pale face with fire. Her eyes shone solemn and clear as altar lamps. He gave one last glance at the lovely earth and sky and glorious indifferent sun, then opened the low door for Merle to pass.

Gunnar, in the upper room, stood by the narrow slit of his solitary window, more gaunt, more shadowy than yesterday. He saw Merle, rushed across to her, pushed her violently back across the threshold.

"I will not have it! This monstrous sacrifice! Take her away—at once. Go! I refuse it. Take her away!"

He thrust her back into Dale's arms, tried to close the door in their faces. Once more a faint hope of rescuing Merle at the eleventh hour rose in Dale's mind. But the door was flung wide. El Shabur confronted them, led them into the room, imperiously motioned Gunnar aside.

"Ya! Now is it too late to turn back. My hour is come. My power is upon me. Let Melek Taos claim his own!"

Merle went over to Gunnar, took his hand in hers, looked up into his gray face with the same look of shining inner exaltation Dale had seen as they lingered at the outer door.

"Yes, it is too late now to turn back," she affirmed. "For this last time you must endure your agony. The last time, Gunnar—my beloved. It shall swiftly pass to me. Can I not bear for a brief moment what you have borne so long? Through my soul and body this devil that possesses you shall pass to El Shabur, who created it. Endure for my sake, as I for yours."

"No! No! You cannot guess the agony—the torture—"

Dale sprang forward at her gesture, and drew about them a circle with oil poured from a long-necked phial. Instantly the two were shut within a barrier of fire, blue as wood-hyacinths, that rose in curving, swaying, lovely pillars to the ceiling, transforming the gray salt mud to a night-sky lit with stars.

"*Ya gomâny*! O mine enemy!" El Shabur's deep voice held sudden anguish. "Is it thou? Through all the years thy coming has been known to me, yet till now I knew thee not. Who taught thee such power as this?"

He strode to the fiery circle, put out a hand, drew it back scorched and blackened to the bone. He turned in savage menace. Dale's hand flashed, poured oil in a swift practised fling about El Shabur's feet and touched it to leaping flame.

Within this second ring the Arab stood upright. His voice boomed out like a great metal gong.

"Melek Taos! Melek Taos! Have I not served thee truly? Give aid—give aid! Ruler of Wind and Stars and Fire! I am held in chains!"

Dale breathed in suffocating gasps, He was cold to the marrow of his bones. He lost all sense of time—of space. He was hanging somewhere in the vast gulf of eternity. Hell battled for dominion in earth and sea and sky.

"To me, Abeor! Aberer! Chavajoth! Aid—give aid!" Again the great voice called upon his demon-gods.

A sudden shock made the room quiver. Dale saw that the fires grew pale. "Was I too soon? Too soon?" he asked himself in agony. "If the oil burns out before sundown—"

There was a crash. On every hand the solid ancient walls were riven. Up—up leaped the blue fiery pillars.

A shout of awful appeal. "Melek Taos! Master! Give aid!"

With almost blinded eyes, Dale saw Gunnar drop at Merle's feet, saw in his stead a wolf-shape crouching, saw her stoop to it, kneel, kiss the great beast between the eyes, heard her clear, steady voice repeat the words of power, saw the flames sink and leap again.

The issue was joined. Now! Now! God or Demon! The Arab, devil-possessed, calling on his gods. Merle, fearless before the onrush of his malice. Hate, cruel as the grave. Love, stronger than death.

Dale's breath tore him. Cold! Cold! Cold to the blood in his veins! God! it was upon her!

Gunnar stood in his own body, staring with wild eyes at the beast which brushed against his knee. He collapsed beside it, blind and deaf to further agony.

And still El Shabur's will was undefeated. Still beside the unconscious Gunnar stood a wolf, its head flung up, its yellow lambent eyes fixed, remote, suffering.

Again Dale felt himself a tiny point of conscious life swung in the womb of time. Again the forces that bear up the earth, sun, moon, and stars were caught in chaos and destruction. Again he heard the roar of fire and flood and winds that drive the seas before them. Through all the tumult there rang a voice, rallying hell's legions, waking old dark gods, calling from planet to planet, from star to star, calling for aid!

Dale knew himself on earth again. Stillness was about him. In a dim and dusty room he saw Merle and Gunnar, handfast, looking into each other's eyes. About their feet a little trail of fire ran—blue as a border of gentian.

Another circle showed, its fires dead, black ash upon the dusty ground. Across it sprawled a body, its burnoose charred and smoldering. Servant of Melek Taos. Victim of his own dark spells. El Shabur destroyed by the demon that had tormented Gunnar. Driven forth, homeless, it returned to him who had created it.

THE MAGIC SHOP

H. G. WELLS

I had seen the Magic Shop from afar several times; I had passed it once or twice, a shop window of alluring little objects, magic balls, magic hens, wonderful cones, ventriloquist dolls, the material of the basket trick, packs of cards that looked all right, and all that sort of thing, but never had I thought of going in until one day, almost without warning, Gip hauled me by my finger right up to the window, and so conducted himself that there was nothing for it but to take him in. I had not thought the place was there, to tell the truth – a modest-sized frontage in Regent Street, between the picture shop and the place where the chicks run about just out of patent incubators – but there it was sure enough. I had fancied it was down nearer the Circus, or round the corner in Oxford Street, or even in Holborn; always over the way and a little inaccessible it had been, with something of the mirage in its position; but here it was now quite indisputably, and the fat end of Gip's pointing finger made a noise upon the glass.

"If I was rich," said Gip, dabbing a finger at the Disappearing Egg, "I'd buy myself that. And that," which was The Crying Baby, Very Human. "And that," which was a mystery, and called, so a neat card asserted, "Buy One and Astonish Your Friends".

"Anything," said Gip, "will disappear under one of those cones. I have read about it in a book.

"And there, Dadda, is the Vanishing Halfpenny – only they've put it this way up so's we can't see how it's done."

Gip, dear boy, inherits his mother's breeding, and he did not propose to enter the shop or worry in any way; only, you know, quite unconsciously, he lugged my finger doorward, and he made his interest clear.

"That," he said, and pointed to the Magic Bottle.

"If you had that?" I said; at which promising inquiry he looked up with a sudden radiance.

"I could show it to Jessie," he said, thoughtful as ever of others.

"It's less than a hundred days to your birthday, Gibbles," I said, and laid my hand on the door-handle.

Gip made no answer, but his grip tightened on my finger, and so we came into the shop.

It was no common shop this; it was a magic shop, and all the prancing precedence Gip would have taken in the matter of mere toys was wanting. He left the burthen of the conversation to me.

It was a little, narrow shop, not very well lit, and the door-bell pinged again with a plaintive note as we closed it behind us. For a moment or so we were alone and could glance about us. There was a tiger in papier-mâché on the glass case that covered the low counter – a grave, kind-eyed tiger that waggled his head in a methodical manner; there were several crystal spheres, a china hand holding magic cards, a stock of magic fish-bowls in various sizes, and an immodest magic hat that shamelessly displayed its springs. On the floor were magic mirrors; one to draw you out long and thin, one to swell your head and vanish your legs, and one to make you short and fat like a draught; and while, we were laughing at these the shopman, as I suppose, came in.

At any rate, there he was behind the counter – a curious, sallow, dark man, with one ear larger than the other and a chin like the toe-cap of a boot.

"What can we have the pleasure?" he said, spreading his long magic fingers on the glass case; and so with a start we were aware of him.

"I want," I said, "to buy my little boy a few simple tricks."

"Legerdemain?" he asked. "Mechanical? Domestic?"

"Anything amusing?" said I.

"Um!" said the shopman, and scratched his head for a moment as if thinking. Then, quite distinctly, he drew from his head a glass ball. "Something in this way?" he said, and held it out.

The action was unexpected. I had seen the trick done at entertainments endless times before – it's part of the common stock of conjurers – but I had not expected it here. "That's good," I said, with a laugh.

"Isn't it?" said the shopman.

Gip stretched out his disengaged hand to take this object and found merely a blank palm.

"It's in your pocket," said the shopman, and there it was!

"How much will that be?" I asked.

"We make no charge for glass balls," said the shopman politely. "We get them" – he picked one out of his elbow as he spoke – "free." He produced another from the back of his neck, and laid it beside its predecessor on the counter. Gip regarded his glass ball sagely, then directed a look of inquiry at the two on the counter, and finally brought his round-eyed scrutiny to the shopman, who smiled. "You may have those two," said the shopman, "and, if you don't mind one from my mouth. So!"

Gip counselled me mutely for a moment, and then in a profound silence put away the four balls, resumed my reassuring finger, and nerved himself for the next event.

"We get all our smaller tricks in that way," the shopman remarked.

I laughed in the manner of one who subscribes to a jest. "Instead of going to the wholesale shop," I said. "Of course, it's cheaper."

"In a way," the shopman said. "Though we pay in the end. But not so heavily as people suppose... Our larger tricks, and our daily provisions and all the other things we want, we get out of that hat... And you know, sir, if you'll excuse my saying it, there isn't a wholesale shop, not for Genuine Magic goods, sir. I don't know if you noticed our inscription – the Genuine Magic Shop." He drew a business card from his cheek and handed it to me. "Genuine," he said, with his finger on the word, and added, "There is absolutely no deception, sir."

He seemed to be carrying out the joke pretty thoroughly, I thought.

He turned to Gip with a smile of remarkable affability. "You, you know, are the Right Sort of Boy."

I was surprised at his knowing that, because, in the interests of discipline, we keep it rather a secret even at home; but Gip received it in unflinching silence, keeping a steadfast eye on him.

"It's only the Right Sort of Boy gets through that doorway."

And, as if by way of illustration, there came a rattling at the door, and a squeaking little voice could be faintly heard. "Nyar! I warn 'a go in there, Dadda, I WARN 'a go in there. Ny-a-a-ah!" and then the accents of a downtrodden parent, urging consolations and propitiations. "It's locked, Edward," he said.

"But it isn't," said I.

"It is, sir," said the shopman, "always—for that sort of child," and as he spoke we had a glimpse of the other youngster, a little, white face, pallid from sweet-eating and over-sapid food, and distorted by evil passions, a ruthless little egotist, pawing at the enchanted pane. "It's no good, sir," said the shopman, as I moved, with my natural helpfulness, doorward, and presently the spoilt child was carried off howling.

"How do you manage that?" I said, breathing a little more freely.

"Magic!" said the shopman, with a careless wave of the hand, and behold! sparks of coloured fire flew out of his fingers and vanished into the shadows of the shop.

"You were saying," he said, addressing himself to Gip, "before you came in, that you would like one of our 'Buy One and Astonish your Friends' boxes?"

Gip, after a gallant effort, said "Yes."

"It's in your pocket."

And leaning over the counter – he really had an extraordinary long body— this amazing person produced the article in the customary conjurer's manner. "Paper," he said, and took a sheet out of the empty hat with the springs; "string," and behold his mouth was a string box, from which he drew an unending thread, which when he had tied his parcel he bit off – and, it seemed to me, swallowed the ball of string. And then he lit a candle at the nose of one of the ventriloquist's dummies, stuck one of his fingers (which had become sealing-wax red) into the flame, and so sealed the parcel. "Then there was the Disappearing Egg," he remarked, and produced one from within my coat-breast and packed it, and also The Crying Baby, Very Human. I handed each parcel to Gip as it was ready, and he clasped them to his chest.

He said very little, but his eyes were eloquent; the clutch of his arms was eloquent. He was the playground of unspeakable emotions. These, you know, were real Magics.

Then, with a start, I discovered something moving about in my hat – something soft and jumpy. I whipped it off, and a ruffled pigeon – no doubt a confederate – dropped out and ran on the counter, and went, I fancy, into a cardboard box behind the papier-mâché tiger.

"Tut, tut!" said the shopman, dexterously relieving, me of my headdress; "careless bird, and – as I live – nesting!"

He shook my hat, and shook out into his extended hand, two or three eggs, a large marble, a watch, about half a dozen of the inevitable glass balls, and then crumpled, crinkled paper, more and more and more, talking all the time of the way in which people neglect to brush their hats inside as well as out – politely, of course, but with a certain personal application. "All sorts of things accumulate, sir... Not you, of course, in particular... Nearly every customer... Astonishing what they carry about with them..." The crumpled paper rose and billowed on the counter more and more and more, until he was nearly hidden from us, until he was altogether hidden, and still his voice went on and on. "We none of us know what the fair semblance of a human being may conceal, sir. Are we all then no better than brushed exteriors, whited sepulchres..."

His voice stopped – exactly like when you hit a neighbour's gramophone with a well-aimed brick, the same instant silence – and the rustle of the paper stopped, and everything was still...

"Have you done with my hat?" I said, after an interval.

There was no answer.

I stared at Gip, and Gip stared at me, and there were our distortions in the magic mirrors, looking very rum, and grave, and quiet...

"I think we'll go now," I said. "Will you tell me how much all this comes to?...

"I say," I said, on a rather louder note, "I want the bill; and my hat, please."

It might have been a sniff from behind the paper pile...

"Let's look behind the counter, Gip," I said. "He's making fun of us."

I led Gip round the head-wagging tiger, and what do you think there was behind the counter? No one at all! Only my hat on the floor, and a common conjurer's lop-eared white rabbit lost in meditation, and looking as stupid and crumpled as only a conjurer's rabbit can do. I resumed my hat, and the rabbit lolloped a lollop or so out of my way.

"Dadda!" said Gip, in a guilty whisper.

"What is it, Gip?" said I.

"I do like this shop, Dadda."

"So should I," I said to myself, "if the counter wouldn't suddenly extend itself to shut one off from the door." But I didn't call Gip's attention to that. "Pussy!" he said, with a hand out to the rabbit as it came lolloping past us; "Pussy, do Gip a magic!" and his eyes followed it as it squeezed through a door I had certainly not remarked a moment before. Then this door opened wider, and the man with one ear larger than the other appeared again. He was smiling still, but his eye met mine with something between amusement and defiance. "You'd like to see our showroom, sir," he said, with an innocent suavity. Gip tugged my finger forward. I glanced at the counter and met the shopman's eye again. I was beginning to think the magic just a little too genuine. "We haven't very much time," I said. But somehow we were inside the showroom before I could finish that.

"All goods of the same quality," said the shopman, rubbing his flexible hands together, "and that is the Best. Nothing in the place that isn't Genuine Magic, and warranted thoroughly rum. Excuse me, sir!"

I felt him pull at something that clung to my coat-sleeve, and then I saw he held a little, wriggling red demon by the tail – the little creature bit and fought and tried to get at his hand – and in a moment he tossed it carelessly behind a counter. No doubt the thing was only an image of twisted india rubber, but for the moment – ! And his gesture was exactly that of a man who handles some petty biting bit of vermin. I glanced at Gip, but Gip was looking at a magic rocking-horse. I was glad he hadn't seen the thing. "I say," I said, in an undertone, and indicating Gip and the red demon with my eyes, "you haven't many things like that about, have you?"

"None of ours! Probably brought it with you," said the shopman, also in an undertone, and with a more dazzling smile than ever. "Astonishing what people will, carry about with them unawares!" And then to Gip, "Do you see anything you fancy here?"

There were many things that Gip fancied there.

He turned to this astonishing tradesman with mingled confidence and respect. "Is that a Magic Sword?" he said.

"A Magic Toy Sword. It neither bends, breaks, nor cuts the fingers. It renders the bearer invincible in battle against any one under eighteen. Half a crown to seven and sixpence, according to size. These panoplies on cards are for juvenile knights-errant and very useful – shield of safety, sandals of swiftness, helmet of invisibility."

"Oh, Dadda!" gasped Gip.

I tried to find out what they cost, but the shopman did not heed me. He had got Gip now; he had got him away from my finger; he had embarked upon the exposition of all his confounded stock, and nothing was going to stop him. Presently I saw with a qualm of distrust and something very like jealousy that Gip had hold of this person's finger as usually he has hold of mine. No doubt the fellow was interesting, I thought, and had an interestingly faked lot of stuff, really good faked stuff, still...

I wandered after them, saying very little, but keeping an eye on this prestidigital fellow. After all, Gip was enjoying it. And no doubt when the time came to go we should be able to go quite easily.

It was a long, rambling place, that showroom, a gallery broken up by stands and stalls and pillars, with archways leading off to other departments, in which the queerest-looking assistants loafed and stared at one, and with perplexing mirrors and curtains. So perplexing, indeed, were these that I was presently unable to make out the door by which we had come.

The shopman showed Gip magic trains that ran without steam or clockwork, just as you set the signals, and then some very, very valuable boxes of soldiers that all came alive directly you took off the lid and said – I myself haven't a very quick ear, and it was a tongue-twisting sound, but Gip – he has his mother's ear – got it in no time. "Bravo!" said the shopman, putting the men back into the box unceremoniously and handing it to Gip. "Now," said the shopman, and in a moment Gip had made them all alive again.

"You'll take that box?" asked the shopman.

"We'll take that box," said I, "unless you charge its full value. In which case it would need a Trust Magnate..."

"Dear heart! No!" and the shopman swept the little men back again, shut the lid, waved the box in the air, and there it was, in brown paper, tied up and with Gip's full name and address on the paper!

The shopman laughed at my amazement.

"This is the Genuine Magic," he said. "The real thing."

"It's a little too genuine for my taste," I said again.

After that he fell to showing Gip tricks, odd tricks, and still odder the way they were done. He explained them, he turned them inside out, and there was the dear little chap nodding his busy bit of a head in the sagest manner.

I did not attend as well as I might. "Hey, presto!" said the Magic Shopman, and then would come the clear, small "Hey, presto!" of the boy. But I was distracted by other things. It was being borne in upon me just how tremendously rum this place was; it was, so to speak, inundated by a sense of rumness. There was something a little rum about the fixtures even, about the ceiling, about the floor, about the casually distributed chairs. I had a queer feeling that whenever I wasn't looking at them straight they went askew, and moved about, and played a noiseless puss-in-the-corner behind my back. And the cornice had a serpentine design with masks – masks altogether too expressive for proper plaster.

Then abruptly my attention was caught by one of the odd-looking assistants. He was some way off and evidently unaware of my presence – I saw a sort of three-quarter length of him over a pile of toys and through an arch – and, you know, he was leaning against a pillar in an idle sort of way doing the most horrid things with his features! The particular horrid thing he did was with his nose. He did it just as though he was idle and wanted to amuse himself. First of all it was a short, blobby nose, and then suddenly he shot it out like a telescope, and then out it flew and became thinner and thinner until it was like a long, red flexible whip. Like a thing in a nightmare it was! He flourished it about and flung it forth as a fly-fisher flings his line.

My instant thought was that Gip mustn't see him. I turned about, and there was Gip quite preoccupied with the shopman, and thinking no evil. They were whispering together and looking at me. Gip was standing on a little stool, and the shopman was holding a sort of big drum in his hand.

"Hide and seek, Dadda!" cried Gip. "You're He!"

And before I could do anything to prevent it, the shopman had clapped the big drum over him.

I saw what was up directly. "Take that off," I cried, "this instant! You'll frighten the boy. Take it off!"

The shopman with the unequal ears did so without a word, and held the big cylinder towards me to show its emptiness. And the little stool was vacant! In that instant my boy had utterly disappeared!...

You know, perhaps, that sinister something that comes like a hand out of the unseen and grips your heart about. You know it takes your common self away and leaves you tense and deliberate, neither slow nor hasty, neither angry nor afraid. So it was with me.

I came up to this grinning shopman and kicked his stool aside.

"Stop this folly!" I said. "Where is my boy?"

"You see," he said, still displaying the drum's interior, "there is no deception..."

I put out my hand to grip him, and he eluded me by a dexterous movement. I snatched again, and he turned from me and pushed open a door to escape. "Stop!" I said, and he laughed, receding. I leapt after him – into utter darkness.

Thud!

"Lor' bless my 'eart! I didn't see you coming, sir!"

I was in Regent Street, and I had collided with a decent-looking working man; and a yard away, perhaps, and looking a little perplexed with himself, was Gip. There was some sort of apology, and then Gip had turned and come to me with a bright little smile, as though for a moment he had missed me.

And he was carrying four parcels in his arm!

He secured immediate possession of my finger.

For the second I was rather at a loss. I stared round to see the door of the Magic Shop, and, behold, it was not there! There was no door, no shop, nothing, only the common pilaster between the shop where they sell pictures and the window with the chicks!

I did the only thing possible in that mental tumult; I walked straight to the kerbstone and held up my umbrella for a cab.

"'Ansoms," said Gip, in a note of culminating exultation.

I helped him in, recalled my address with an effort, and got in also. Something unusual proclaimed itself in my tail-coat pocket, and I felt and discovered a glass ball. With a petulant expression I flung it into the street.

Gip said nothing.

For a space neither of us spoke.

"Dadda!" said Gip, at last, "that was a proper shop!"

I came round with that to the problem of just how the whole thing had seemed to him. He looked completely undamaged – so far, good; he was neither scared nor unhinged, he was simply tremendously satisfied with the afternoon's entertainment, and there in his arms were the four parcels.

Confound it! What could be in them?

"Um!" I said. "Little boys can't go to shops like that every day."

He received this with his usual stoicism, and for a moment I was sorry I was his father and not his mother, and so couldn't suddenly there, coram publico, in our hansom, kiss him. After all, I thought, the thing wasn't so very bad.

But it was only when we opened the parcels that I really began to be reassured. Three of them contained boxes of soldiers, quite ordinary lead soldiers, but of so good a quality as to make Gip altogether forget that originally these parcels had been Magic Tricks of the only genuine sort, and the fourth contained a kitten, a little living white kitten, in excellent health and appetite and temper.

I saw this unpacking with a sort of provisional relief. I hung about in the nursery for quite an unconscionable time...

That happened six months ago. And now I am beginning to believe it is all right. The kitten had only the magic natural to all kittens, and the soldiers seemed as steady a company as any colonel could desire. And Gip...?

The intelligent parent will understand that I have to go cautiously with Gip.

But I went so far as this one day. I said, "How would you like your soldiers to come alive, Gip, and march about by themselves?"

"Mine do," said Gip. "I just have to say a word I know before I open the lid."

"Then they march about alone?"

"Oh, quite, Dadda. I shouldn't like them if they didn't do that."

I displayed no unbecoming surprise, and since then I have taken occasion to drop in upon him once or twice, unannounced, when the soldiers were about, but so far I have never discovered them performing in anything like a magical manner...

It's so difficult to tell.

There's also a question of finance. I have an incurable habit of paying bills. I have been up and down Regent Street several times looking for that shop. I am inclined to think, indeed, that in that matter honour is satisfied, and that, since Gip's name and address are known to them, I may very well leave it to these people, whoever they may be, to send in their bill in their own time.

THE MAN WHO COULD WORK MIRACLES

H. G. WELLS

A PANTOUM IN PROSE

It is doubtful whether the gift was innate. For my own part, I think it came to him suddenly. Indeed, until he was thirty he was a sceptic, and did not believe in miraculous powers. And here, since it is the most convenient place, I must mention that he was a little man, and had eyes of a hot brown, very erect red hair, a moustache with ends that he twisted up, and freckles. His name was George McWhirter Fotheringay – not the sort of name by any means to lead to any expectation of miracles – and he was clerk at Gomshott's. He was greatly addicted to assertive argument. It was while he was asserting the impossibility of miracles that he had his first intimation of his extraordinary powers. This particular argument was being held in the bar of the Long Dragon, and Toddy Beamish was conducting the opposition by a monotonous but effective "So you say," that drove Mr Fotheringay to the very limit of his patience.

There were present, besides these two, a very dusty cyclist, landlord Cox, and Miss Maybridge, the perfectly respectable and rather portly barmaid of the Dragon. Miss Maybridge was standing with her back to Mr Fotheringay, washing glasses; the others were watching him, more or less amused by the present ineffectiveness of the assertive method. Goaded by the Torres Vedras tactics of Mr Beamish, Mr Fotheringay determined to make an unusual rhetorical effort. "Looky here, Mr Beamish," said Mr Fotheringay. "Let us clearly understand what a miracle is. It's something contrariwise to the course of nature, done by power of will, something what couldn't happen without being specially willed."

"So you say," said Mr Beamish, repulsing him.

Mr Fotheringay appealed to the cyclist, who had hitherto been a silent auditor, and received his assent – given with a hesitating cough and a glance at Mr Beamish. The landlord would express no opinion, and Mr Fotheringay, returning to Mr Beamish, received the unexpected concession of a qualified assent to his definition of a miracle.

"For instance," said Mr Fotheringay, greatly encouraged. "Here would be a miracle. That lamp, in the natural course of nature, couldn't burn like that upsy-down, could it, Beamish?"

"You say it couldn't," said Beamish.

"And you?" said Fotheringay. "You don't mean to say – eh?"

"No," said Beamish reluctantly. "No, it couldn't."

"Very well," said Mr Fotheringay. "Then here comes someone, as it might be me, along here, and stands as it might be here, and says to that lamp, as I might do, collecting all my will, 'Turn upsy-down without breaking, and go on burning steady,' and – hullo!"

It was enough to make anyone say "Hullo!". The impossible, the incredible, was visible to them all. The lamp hung inverted in the air, burning quietly with its flame pointing down. It was as solid, as indisputable as ever a lamp was, the prosaic common lamp of the Long Dragon bar.

Mr Fotheringay stood with an extended forefinger and the knitted brows of one anticipating a catastrophic smash. The cyclist, who was sitting next the lamp, ducked and jumped across the bar. Everybody jumped, more or less. Miss Maybridge turned and screamed. For nearly three seconds the lamp remained still. A faint cry of mental distress came from Mr Fotheringay. "I can't keep it up," he said, "any longer." He staggered back, and the inverted lamp suddenly flared, fell against the corner of the bar, bounced aside, smashed upon the floor, and went out.

It was lucky it had a metal receiver, or the whole place would have been in a blaze. Mr Cox was the first to speak, and his remark, shorn of needless excrescences, was to the effect that Fotheringay was a fool. Fotheringay was beyond disputing even so fundamental a proposition as that! He was astonished beyond measure at the thing that had occurred. The subsequent conversation threw absolutely no light on the matter so far as Fotheringay was concerned; the general opinion not only followed Mr Cox very closely but very vehemently. Everyone accused Fotheringay of a silly trick, and presented him to himself as a foolish destroyer of comfort and security. His mind was in a tornado of perplexity, he was himself inclined to agree with them, and he made a remarkably ineffectual opposition to the proposal of his departure.

He went home flushed and heated, coat-collar crumpled, eyes smarting, and ears red. He watched each of the ten street lamps nervously as he passed it. It was only when he found himself alone in his little bedroom in Church Row that he was able to grapple seriously with his memories of the occurrence, and ask, "What on earth happened?"

He had removed his coat and boots, and was sitting on the bed with his hands in his pockets repeating the text of his defence for the seventeenth time, "I didn't want the confounded thing to upset," when it occurred to him that at the precise moment he had said the commanding words he had inadvertently willed the thing he said, and that when he had seen the lamp in the air he had felt that it depended on him to maintain it there without being clear how this was to be done. He had not a particularly complex mind, or he might have stuck for a time at that "inadvertently willed," embracing, as it does, the abstrusest problems of voluntary action; but as it was, the idea came to him with a quite acceptable haziness. And from that, following, as I must admit, no clear logical path, he came to the test of experiment.

He pointed resolutely to his candle and collected his mind, though he felt he did a foolish thing. "Be raised up," he said. But in a second that feeling vanished. The candle was raised, hung in the air one giddy moment, and as Mr Fotheringay gasped, fell with a smash on his toilet-table, leaving him in darkness save for the expiring glow of its wick.

For a time Mr Fotheringay sat in the darkness, perfectly still. "It did happen, after all," he said. "And 'ow I'm to explain it I don't know." He sighed heavily, and began feeling in his pockets for a match. He could find none, and he rose and groped about the toilet-table. "I wish I had a match," he said. He resorted to his coat, and there was none there, and then it dawned upon him that miracles were possible even with matches. He extended a hand and scowled at it in the dark. "Let there be a match in that hand," he said. He felt some light object fall across his palm and his fingers closed upon a match.

After several ineffectual attempts to light this, he discovered it was a safety match. He threw it down, and then it occurred to him that he might have willed it lit. He did, and perceived it burning in the midst of his toilet-table mat. He caught it up hastily, and it went out. His perception of possibilities enlarged, and he felt for and replaced the candle in its candlestick. "Here, you be lit," said Mr Fotheringay, and forthwith the candle was flaring, and he saw a little black hole in the toilet-cover, with a wisp of smoke rising from it. For a time he stared from this to the little flame and back, and then looked up and met his own gaze in the looking-glass. By this help he communed with himself in silence for a time.

"How about miracles now?" said Mr Fotheringay at last, addressing his reflection.

The subsequent meditations of Mr Fotheringay were of a severe but confused description. So far, he could see it was a case of pure willing with him. The nature of his experiences so far disinclined him for any further experiments, at least until he had reconsidered them. But he lifted a sheet of paper, and turned a glass of water pink and then green, and he created a snail, which he miraculously annihilated, and got himself a miraculous new tooth-brush. Somewhere in the small hours he had reached the fact that his will-power must be of a particularly rare and pungent quality, a fact of which he had indeed had inklings before, but no certain assurance. The scare and perplexity of his first discovery was now qualified by pride in this evidence of singularity and by vague intimations of advantage. He became aware that the church clock was striking one, and as it did not occur to him that his daily duties at Gomshott's might be miraculously dispensed with, he resumed undressing, in order to get to bed without further delay. As he struggled to get his shirt over his head, he was struck with a brilliant idea. "Let me be in bed," he said, and found himself so. "Undressed," he stipulated; and, finding the sheets cold, added hastily, "and in my nightshirt – ho, in a nice soft woollen nightshirt. Ah!" he said with immense enjoyment. "And now let me be comfortably asleep..."

He awoke at his usual hour and was pensive all through breakfast-time, wondering whether his over-night experience might not be a particularly vivid dream. At length his mind turned again to cautious experiments. For instance, he had three eggs for breakfast; two his landlady had supplied, good, but shoppy, and one was a delicious fresh goose-egg, laid, cooked, and served by his extraordinary will. He hurried off to Gomshott's in a state of profound but carefully concealed excitement, and only remembered the shell of the third egg when his landlady spoke of it that night. All day he could do no work because of this astonishing new self-knowledge, but this caused him no inconvenience, because he made up for it miraculously in his last ten minutes.

As the day wore on his state of mind passed from wonder to elation, albeit the circumstances of his dismissal from the Long Dragon were still disagreeable to recall, and a garbled account of the matter that had reached his colleagues led to some badinage. It was evident he must be careful how he lifted frangible articles, but in other ways his gift promised more and more as he turned it over in his mind. He intended among other things to increase his personal property by unostentatious acts of creation. He called into existence a pair of very splendid diamond studs, and hastily annihilated them again as young Gomshott came across the counting-house to his desk. He was afraid young Gomshott might wonder how he had come by them. He saw quite clearly the gift required caution and watchfulness in its exercise, but so far as he could judge the difficulties attending its mastery would be no greater than those he had already faced in the study of cycling. It was that analogy, perhaps, quite as much as the feeling that he would be unwelcome in the Long Dragon, that drove him out after supper into the lane beyond the gasworks, to rehearse a few miracles in private.

There was possibly a certain want of originality in his attempts, for, apart from his will-power, Mr Fotheringay was not a very exceptional man. The miracle of Moses's rod came to his mind, but the night was dark and unfavourable to the proper control of large miraculous snakes. Then he recollected the story of *Tannhäuser* that he had read on the back of the Philharmonic programme. That seemed to him singularly attractive and harmless. He stuck his walking-stick – a very nice Poona-Penang lawyer – into the turf that edged the footpath, and commanded the dry wood to blossom. The air was immediately full of the scent of roses, and by means of a match he saw for himself that this beautiful miracle was indeed accomplished. His satisfaction was ended by advancing footsteps. Afraid of a premature discovery of his powers, he addressed the blossoming stick hastily: "Go back." What he meant was "Change back;" but of course he was confused. The stick receded at a considerable velocity, and incontinently came a cry of anger and a bad word from the approaching person. "Who are you throwing brambles at, you fool?" cried a voice. "That got me on the shin."

"I'm sorry, old chap," said Mr Fotheringay, and then, realising the awkward nature of the explanation, caught nervously at his moustache. He saw Winch, one of the three Immering constables, advancing.

"What d'yer mean by it?" asked the constable. "Hullo! it's you, is it? The gent that broke the lamp at the Long Dragon!"

"I don't mean anything by it," said Mr Fotheringay. "Nothing at all."

"What d'yer do it for then?"

"Oh, bother!" said Mr Fotheringay.

"Bother indeed! D'yer know that stick hurt? What d'yer do it for, eh?"

For the moment Mr Fotheringay could not think what he had done it for. His silence seemed to irritate Mr Winch. "You've been assaulting the police, young man, this time. That's what you done."

"Look here, Mr Winch," said Mr Fotheringay, annoyed and confused, "I'm sorry, very. The fact is—"

"Well?"

He could think of no way but the truth. "I was working a miracle." He tried to speak in an off-hand way, but try as he would he couldn't.

"Working a—! 'Ere, don't you talk rot. Working a miracle, indeed! Miracle! Well, that's downright funny! Why, you's the chap that don't believe in miracles… Fact is, this is another of your silly conjuring tricks – that's what this is. Now, I tell you—"

But Mr Fotheringay never heard what Mr Winch was going to tell him. He realised he had given himself away, flung his valuable secret to all the winds of heaven. A violent gust of irritation swept him to action. He turned on the constable swiftly and fiercely. "Here," he said, "I've had enough of this, I have! I'll show you a silly conjuring trick, I will! Go to Hades! Go, now!"

He was alone!

Mr Fotheringay performed no more miracles that night, nor did he trouble to see what had become of his flowering stick. He returned to the town, scared and very quiet, and went to his bedroom. "Lord!" he said. "It's a powerful gift – an extremely powerful gift. I didn't hardly mean as much as that. Not really... I wonder what Hades is like!"

He sat on the bed taking off his boots. Struck by a happy thought he transferred the constable to San Francisco, and without any more interference with normal causation went soberly to bed. In the night he dreamt of the anger of Winch.

The next day Mr Fotheringay heard two interesting items of news. Someone had planted a most beautiful climbing rose against the elder Mr Gomshott's private house in the Lullaborough Road, and the river as far as Rawling's Mill was to be dragged for Constable Winch.

Mr Fotheringay was abstracted and thoughtful all that day, and performed no miracles except certain provisions for Winch, and the miracle of completing his day's work with punctual perfection in spite of all the bee-swarm of thoughts that hummed through his mind. And the extraordinary abstraction and meekness of his manner was remarked by several people, and made a matter for jesting. For the most part he was thinking of Winch.

On Sunday evening he went to chapel, and oddly enough, Mr Maydig, who took a certain interest in occult matters, preached about "things that are not lawful." Mr Fotheringay was not a regular chapelgoer, but the system of assertive scepticism, to which I have already alluded, was now very much shaken. The tenor of the sermon threw an entirely new light on these novel gifts, and he suddenly decided to consult Mr Maydig immediately after the service. So soon as that was determined, he found himself wondering why he had not done so before.

Mr Maydig, a lean, excitable man with quite remarkably long wrists and neck, was gratified at a request for a private conversation from a young man whose carelessness in religious matters was a subject for general remark in the town. After a few necessary delays, he conducted him to the study of the manse, which was contiguous to the chapel, seated him comfortably, and, standing in front of a cheerful fire – his legs threw a Rhodian arch of shadow on the opposite wall – requested Mr Fotheringay to state his business.

At first Mr Fotheringay was a little abashed, and found some difficulty in opening the matter. "You will scarcely believe me, Mr Maydig, I am afraid" – and so forth for some time. He tried a question at last, and asked Mr Maydig his opinion of miracles.

Mr Maydig was still saying "Well" in an extremely judicial tone, when Mr Fotheringay interrupted again: "You don't believe, I suppose, that some common sort of person – like myself, for instance – as it might be sitting here now, might have some sort of twist inside him that made him able to do things by his will."

"It's possible," said Mr Maydig. "Something of the sort, perhaps, is possible."

"If I might make free with something here, I think I might show you by a sort of experiment," said Mr Fotheringay. "Now, take that tobacco-jar on the table, for instance. What I want to know is whether what I am going to do with it is a miracle or not. Just half a minute, Mr Maydig, please."

He knitted his brows, pointed to the tobacco-jar and said: "Be a bowl of vi'lets."

The tobacco-jar did as it was ordered.

Mr Maydig started violently at the change, and stood looking from the thaumaturgist to the bowl of flowers. He said nothing. Presently he ventured to lean over the table and smell the violets; they were fresh-picked and very fine ones. Then he stared at Mr Fotheringay again.

"How did you do that?" he asked.

Mr Fotheringay pulled his moustache. "Just told it – and there you are. Is that a miracle, or is it black art, or what is it? And what do you think's the matter with me? That's what I want to ask."

"It's a most extraordinary occurrence."

"And this day last week I knew no more that I could do things like that than you did. It came quite sudden. It's something odd about my will, I suppose, and that's as far as I can see."

"Is that – the only thing. Could you do other things besides that?"

"Lord, yes!" said Mr Fotheringay. "Just anything." He thought, and suddenly recalled a conjuring entertainment he had seen. "Here!" he pointed, "change into a bowl of fish – no, not that – change into a glass bowl full of water with goldfish swimming in it. That's better! You see that, Mr Maydig?"

"It's astonishing. It's incredible. You are either a most extraordinary... But no..."

"I could change it into anything," said Mr Fotheringay. "Just anything. Here! Be a pigeon, will you?"

In another moment a blue pigeon was fluttering round the room and making Mr Maydig duck every time it came near him. "Stop there, will you?" said Mr Fotheringay; and the pigeon hung motionless in the air. "I could change it back to a bowl of flowers," he said, and after replacing the pigeon on the table worked that miracle. "I expect you will want your pipe in a bit," he said, and restored the tobacco-jar.

Mr Maydig had followed all these later changes in a sort of ejaculatory silence. He stared at Mr Fotheringay and in a very gingerly manner picked up the tobacco-jar, examined it, replaced it on the table. "Well!" was the only expression of his feelings.

"Now, after that it's easier to explain what I came about," said Mr Fotheringay; and proceeded to a lengthy and involved narrative of his strange experiences, beginning with the affair of the lamp in the Long Dragon and complicated by persistent allusions to Winch. As he went on, the transient pride Mr Maydig's consternation had caused passed away; he became the very ordinary Mr Fotheringay of everyday intercourse again. Mr Maydig listened intently, the tobacco-jar in his hand, and his bearing changed also with the course of the narrative. Presently, while Mr Fotheringay was dealing with the miracle of the third egg, the minister interrupted with a fluttering, extended hand.

"It is possible," he said. "It is credible. It is amazing, of course, but it reconciles a number of amazing difficulties. The power to work miracles is a gift – a peculiar quality like genius or second sight; hitherto it has come very rarely and to exceptional people. But in this case... I have always wondered at the miracles of Mahomet, and at Yogi's miracles, and the miracles of Madame Blavatsky. But, of course – yes, it is simply a gift! It carries out so beautifully the arguments of that great thinker" – Mr Maydig's voice sank – "his Grace the Duke of Argyll. Here we plumb some profounder law – deeper than the ordinary laws of nature. Yes – yes. Go on. Go on!"

Mr Fotheringay proceeded to tell of his misadventure with Winch, and Mr Maydig, no longer overawed or scared, began to jerk his limbs about and interject astonishment. "It's this what troubled me most," proceeded Mr Fotheringay; "it's this I'm most mijitly in want of advice for; of course he's at San Francisco – wherever San Francisco may be – but of course it's awkward for both of us, as you'll see, Mr Maydig. I don't see how he can understand what has happened, and I daresay he's scared and exasperated something tremendous, and trying to get at me. I daresay he keeps on starting off to come here. I send him back, by a miracle, every few hours, when I think of it. And, of course, that's a thing he won't be able to understand, and it's bound to annoy him; and, of course, if he takes a ticket every time it will cost him a lot of money. I done the best I could for him, but, of course, it's difficult for him to put himself in my place. I thought afterwards that his clothes might have got scorched, you know – if Hades is all it's supposed to be – before I shifted him. In that case I suppose they'd have locked him up in San Francisco. Of course I willed him a new suit of clothes on him directly I thought of it. But, you see, I'm already in a deuce of a tangle—"

Mr Maydig looked serious. "I see you are in a tangle. Yes, it's a difficult position. How you are to end it..." He became diffuse and inconclusive.

"However, we'll leave Winch for a little and discuss the larger question. I don't think this is a case of the black art or anything of the sort. I don't think there is any taint of criminality about it at all, Mr Fotheringay – none whatever, unless you are suppressing material facts. No, it's miracles – pure miracles – miracles, if I may say so, of the very highest class."

He began to pace the hearthrug and gesticulate, while Mr Fotheringay sat with his arm on the table and his head on his arm, looking worried. "I don't see how I'm to manage about Winch," he said.

"A gift of working miracles – apparently a very powerful gift," said Mr Maydig, "will find a way about Winch – never fear. My dear sir, you are a most important man – a man of the most astonishing possibilities. As evidence, for example! And in other ways, the things you may do..."

"Yes, I've thought of a thing or two," said Mr Fotheringay. "But – some of the things came a bit twisty. You saw that fish at first? Wrong sort of bowl and wrong sort of fish. And I thought I'd ask someone."

"A proper course," said Mr Maydig, "a very proper course – altogether the proper course." He stopped and looked at Mr Fotheringay. "It's practically an unlimited gift. Let us test your powers, for instance. If they really are... If they really are all they seem to be."

And so, incredible as it may seem, in the study of the little house behind the Congregational Chapel, on the evening of Sunday, Nov. 10, 1896, Mr Fotheringay, egged on and inspired by Mr Maydig, began to work miracles. The reader's attention is specially and definitely called to the date. He will object, probably has already objected, that certain points in this story are improbable, that if any things of the sort already described had indeed occurred, they would have been in all the papers at that time. The details immediately following he will find particularly hard to accept, because among other things they involve the conclusion that he or she, the reader in question, must have been killed in a violent and unprecedented manner more than a year ago. Now a miracle is nothing if not improbable, and as a matter of fact the reader was killed in a violent and unprecedented manner in 1896. In the subsequent course of this story that will become perfectly clear and credible, as every right-minded and reasonable reader will admit. But this is not the place for the end of the story, being but little beyond the hither side of the middle. And at first the miracles worked by Mr Fotheringay were timid little miracles – little things with the cups and parlour fitments, as feeble as the miracles of Theosophists, and, feeble as they were, they were received with awe by his collaborator. He would have preferred to settle the

Winch business out of hand, but Mr Maydig would not let him. But after they had worked a dozen of these domestic trivialities, their sense of power grew, their imagination began to show signs of stimulation, and their ambition enlarged. Their first larger enterprise was due to hunger and the negligence of Mrs Minchin, Mr Maydig's housekeeper. The meal to which the minister conducted Mr Fotheringay was certainly ill-laid and uninviting as refreshment for two industrious miracle-workers; but they were seated, and Mr Maydig was descanting in sorrow rather than in anger upon his housekeeper's shortcomings, before it occurred to Mr Fotheringay that an opportunity lay before him. "Don't you think, Mr Maydig," he said, "if it isn't a liberty, I—"

"My dear Mr Fotheringay! Of course! No – I didn't think."

Mr Fotheringay waved his hand. "What shall we have?" he said, in a large, inclusive spirit, and, at Mr Maydig's order, revised the supper very thoroughly. "As for me," he said, eyeing Mr Maydig's selection, "I am always particularly fond of a tankard of stout and a nice Welsh rarebit, and I'll order that. I ain't much given to Burgundy," and forthwith stout and Welsh rarebit promptly appeared at his command. They sat long at their supper, talking like equals, as Mr Fotheringay presently perceived, with a glow of surprise and gratification, of all the miracles they would presently do. "And, by-the-by, Mr Maydig," said Mr Fotheringay, "I might perhaps be able to help you – in a domestic way."

"Don't quite follow," said Mr Maydig, pouring out a glass of miraculous old Burgundy.

Mr Fotheringay helped himself to a second Welsh rarebit out of vacancy, and took a mouthful. "I was thinking," he said, "I might be able (chum, chum) to work (chum, chum) a miracle with Mrs Minchin (chum, chum) – make her a better woman."

Mr Maydig put down the glass and looked doubtful.

"She's... she strongly objects to interference, you know, Mr Fotheringay. And – as a matter of fact – it's well past eleven and she's probably in bed and asleep. Do you think, on the whole—"

Mr Fotheringay considered these objections. "I don't see that it shouldn't be done in her sleep."

For a time Mr Maydig opposed the idea, and then he yielded. Mr Fotheringay issued his orders, and a little less at their ease, perhaps, the two gentlemen proceeded with their repast. Mr Maydig was enlarging on the changes he might expect in his housekeeper next day, with an optimism, that seemed even to Mr Fotheringay's supper senses a little forced and hectic, when a series of confused noises from upstairs began. Their eyes exchanged interrogations, and Mr Maydig left the room hastily. Mr Fotheringay heard him calling up to his housekeeper and then his footsteps going softly up to her.

In a minute or so the minister returned, his step light, his face radiant. "Wonderful!" he said, "and touching! Most touching!"

He began pacing the hearthrug. "A repentance – a most touching repentance – through the crack of the door. Poor woman! A most wonderful change! She had got up. She must have got up at once. She had got up out of her sleep to smash a private bottle of brandy in her box. And to confess it too!... But this gives us – it opens – a most amazing vista of possibilities. If we can work this miraculous change in her..."

"The thing's unlimited seemingly," said Mr Fotheringay. "And about Mr Winch—"

"Altogether unlimited." And from the hearthrug Mr Maydig, waving the Winch difficulty aside, unfolded a series of wonderful proposals – proposals he invented as he went along.

Now what those proposals were does not concern the essentials of this story. Suffice it that they were designed in a spirit of infinite benevolence, the sort of benevolence that used to be called post-prandial. Suffice it, too, that the problem of Winch remained unsolved. Nor is it necessary to describe how far that series got to its fulfilment. There were astonishing changes. The small hours found Mr Maydig and Mr Fotheringay careering across the chilly market square under the still moon, in a sort of ecstasy of thaumaturgy, Mr Maydig all flap and gesture, Mr Fotheringay short and bristling, and no longer abashed at his greatness. They had reformed every drunkard in the Parliamentary division, changed all the beer and alcohol to water (Mr Maydig had overruled Mr Fotheringay on this point); they had, further, greatly improved the railway communication of the place, drained Flinder's swamp, improved the soil of One Tree Hill, and cured the vicar's wart. And they were going to see what could be done with the injured pier at South Bridge. "The place," gasped Mr Maydig, "won't be the same place tomorrow. How surprised and thankful everyone will be!" And just at that moment the church clock struck three.

"I say," said Mr Fotheringay, "that's three o'clock! I must be getting back. I've got to be at business by eight. And besides, Mrs Wimms—"

"We're only beginning," said Mr Maydig, full of the sweetness of unlimited power. "We're only beginning. Think of all the good we're doing. When people wake..."

"But—" said Mr Fotheringay.

Mr Maydig gripped his arm suddenly. His eyes were bright and wild. "My dear chap," he said, "there's no hurry. Look" – he pointed to the moon at the zenith – "Joshua!"

"Joshua?" said Mr Fotheringay.

"Joshua," said Mr Maydig. "Why not? Stop it."

Mr Fotheringay looked at the moon.

"That's a bit tall," he said, after a pause.

"Why not?" said Mr Maydig. "Of course it doesn't stop. You stop the rotation of the earth, you know. Time stops. It isn't as if we were doing harm."

"H'm!" said Mr Fotheringay. "Well," he sighed, "I'll try. Here!"

He buttoned up his jacket and addressed himself to the habitable globe, with as good an assumption of confidence as lay in his power. "Jest stop rotating, will you?" said Mr Fotheringay.

Incontinently he was flying head over heels through the air at the rate of dozens of miles a minute. In spite of the innumerable circles he was describing per second, he thought; for thought is wonderful—sometimes as sluggish as flowing pitch, sometimes as instantaneous as light. He thought in a second, and willed. "Let me come down safe and sound. Whatever else happens, let me down safe and sound."

He willed it only just in time, for his clothes, heated by his rapid flight through the air, were already beginning to singe. He came down with a forcible, but by no means injurious, bump in what appeared to be a mound of fresh-turned earth. A large mass of metal and masonry, extraordinarily like the clock-tower in the middle of the market square, hit the earth near him, ricochetted over him, and flew into stonework, bricks and cement, like a bursting bomb. A hurtling cow hit one of the larger blocks and smashed like an egg. There was a crash that made all the most violent crashes of his past life seem like the sound of falling dust, and this was followed by a descending series of lesser crashes. A vast wind roared throughout earth and heaven, so that he could scarcely lift his head to look. For a while he was too breathless and astonished even to see where he was or what had happened. And his first movement was to feel his head and reassure himself that his streaming hair was still his own.

"Lord!" gasped Mr Fotheringay, scarce able to speak for the gale, "I've had a squeak! What's gone wrong? Storms and thunder. And only a minute ago a fine night. It's Maydig set me on to this sort of thing. What a wind! If I go on fooling in this way I'm bound to have a thundering accident!...

"Where's Maydig?

"What a confounded mess everything's in!"

He looked about him so far as his flapping jacket would permit. The appearance of things was really extremely strange. "The sky's all right anyhow," said Mr Fotheringay. "And that's about all that is all right. And even there it looks like a terrific gale coming up. But there's the moon overhead. Just as it was just now. Bright as midday. But as for the rest... Where's the village? Where's – where's anything? And what on earth set this wind a-blowing? I didn't order no wind."

Mr Fotheringay struggled to get to his feet in vain, and after one failure, remained on all fours, holding on. He surveyed the moonlit world to leeward, with the tails of his jacket streaming over his head. "There's something seriously wrong," said Mr Fotheringay. "And what it is – goodness knows."

Far and wide nothing was visible in the white glare through the haze of dust that drove before a screaming gale but tumbled masses of earth and heaps of inchoate ruins, no trees, no houses, no familiar shapes, only a wilderness of disorder, vanishing at last into the darkness beneath the whirling columns and streamers, the lightnings and thunderings of a swiftly rising storm. Near him in the livid glare was something that might once have been an elm-tree, a smashed mass of splinters, shivered from boughs to base, and further a twisted mass of iron girders – only too evidently the viaduct – rose out of the piled confusion.

You see, when Mr Fotheringay had arrested the rotation of the solid globe, he had made no stipulation concerning the trifling movables upon its surface. And the earth spins so fast that the surface at its equator is travelling at rather more than a thousand miles an hour, and in these latitudes at more than half that pace. So that the village, and Mr Maydig, and Mr Fotheringay, and everybody and everything had been jerked violently forward at about nine miles per second – that is to say, much more violently than if they had been fired out of a cannon. And every human being, every living creature, every house, and every tree – all the world as we know it – had been so jerked and smashed and utterly destroyed. That was all.

These things Mr Fotheringay did not, of course, fully appreciate. But he perceived that his miracle had miscarried, and with that a great disgust of miracles came upon him. He was in darkness now, for the clouds had swept together and blotted out his momentary glimpse of the moon, and the air was full of fitful struggling tortured wraiths of hail. A great roaring of wind and waters filled earth and sky, and peering under his hand through the dust and sleet to windward, he saw by the play of the lightnings a vast wall of water pouring towards him.

"Maydig!" screamed Mr Fotheringay's feeble voice amid the elemental uproar. "Here! – Maydig!

"Stop!" cried Mr Fotheringay to the advancing water. "Oh, for goodness' sake, stop!

"Just a moment," said Mr Fotheringay to the lightnings and thunder. "Stop jest a moment while I collect my thoughts... And now what shall I do?" he said. "What shall I do? Lord! I wish Maydig was about."

"I know," said Mr Fotheringay. "And for goodness' sake let's have it right this time."

He remained on all fours, leaning against the wind, very intent to have everything right.

"Ah!" he said. "Let nothing what I'm going to order happen until I say 'Off!'... Lord! I wish I'd thought of that before!"

He lifted his little voice against the whirlwind, shouting louder and louder in the vain desire to hear himself speak. "Now then! – Here goes! Mind about that what I said just now. In the first place, when all I've got to say is done, let me lose my miraculous power, let my will become just like anybody else's will, and all these dangerous miracles be stopped. I don't like them. I'd rather I didn't work 'em. Ever so much. That's the first thing. And the second is – let me be back just before the miracles begin; let everything be just as it was before that blessed lamp turned up. It's a big job, but it's the last. Have you got it? No more miracles, everything as it was – me back in the Long Dragon just before I drank my half-pint. That's it! Yes."

He dug his fingers into the mould, closed his eyes, and said "Off!"

Everything became perfectly still. He perceived that he was standing erect.

"So you say," said a voice.

He opened his eyes. He was in the bar of the Long Dragon, arguing about miracles with Toddy Beamish. He had a vague sense of some great thing forgotten that instantaneously passed. You see that, except for the loss of his miraculous powers, everything was back as it had been, his mind and memory therefore were now just as they had been at the time when this story began. So that he knew absolutely nothing of all that is told here – knows nothing of all that is told here to this day. And among other things, of course, he still did not believe in miracles.

"I tell you that miracles, properly speaking, can't possibly happen," he said, "whatever you like to hold. And I'm prepared to prove it up to the hilt."

"That's what you think," said Toddy Beamish, and "Prove it if you can."

"Looky here, Mr Beamish," said Mr Fotheringay. "Let us clearly understand what a miracle is. It's something contrariwise to the course of nature done by power of Will..."

MR SKELMERSDALE IN FAIRYLAND

H. G. WELLS

"There's a man in that shop," said the Doctor, "who has been in Fairyland."

"Nonsense!" I said, and stared back at the shop. It was the usual village shop, post-office, telegraph wire on its brow, zinc pans and brushes outside, boots, shirtings and potted meats in the window. "Tell me about it," I said, after a pause.

"I don't know," said the Doctor. "He's an ordinary sort of lout – Skelmersdale is his name. But everybody about here believes it like Bible truth."

I reverted presently to the topic.

"I know nothing about it," said the Doctor, "and I don't want to know. I attended him for a broken finger – Married and Single cricket match – and that's when I struck the nonsense. That's all. But it shows you the sort of stuff I have to deal with, anyhow, eh? Nice to get modern sanitary ideas into a people like this!"

"Very," I said in a mildly sympathetic tone, and he went on to tell me about that business of the Bonham drain. Things of that kind, I observe, are apt to weigh on the minds of Medical Officers of Health. I was as sympathetic as I knew how, and when he called the Bonham people "asses," I said they were "thundering asses," but even that did not allay him.

Afterwards, later in the summer, an urgent desire to seclude myself, while finishing my chapter on Spiritual Pathology – it was really, I believe, stiffer to write than it is to read – took me to Bignor. I lodged at a farmhouse, and presently found myself outside that little general shop again, in search of tobacco. "Skelmersdale," said I to myself at the sight of it, and went in.

I was served by a short, but shapely, young man, with a fair downy complexion, good, small teeth, blue eyes and a languid manner. I scrutinised him curiously. Except for a touch of melancholy in his expression, he was nothing out of the common. He was in the shirt-sleeves and tucked-up apron of his trade, and a pencil was thrust behind his inoffensive ear. Athwart his black waistcoat was a gold chain, from which dangled a bent guinea.

"Nothing more today, sir?" he inquired. He leant forward over my bill as he spoke.

"Are you Mr Skelmersdale?" said I.

"I am, sir," he said, without looking up.

"Is it true that you have been in Fairyland?"

He looked up at me for a moment with wrinkled brows, with an aggrieved, exasperated face. "O shut it!" he said, and, after a moment of hostility, eye to eye, he went on adding up my bill. "Four, six and a half," he said, after a pause. "Thank you, sir."

So, unpropitiously, my acquaintance with Mr Skelmersdale began.

Well, I got from that to confidence – through a series of toilsome efforts. I picked him up again in the Village Room, where of a night I went to play billiards after my supper and mitigate the extreme seclusion from my kind that was so helpful to work during the day. I contrived to play with him and afterwards to talk with him. I found the one subject to avoid was Fairyland. On everything else he was open and amiable in a commonplace sort of way, but on that he had been worried – it was a manifest taboo. Only once in the room did I hear the slightest allusion to his experience in his presence, and that was by a cross-grained farm hand who was losing to him. Skelmersdale had run a break into double figures, which, by the Bignor standards, was uncommonly good play. "Steady on!" said his adversary. "None of your fairy flukes!"

Skelmersdale stared at him for a moment, cue in hand, then flung it down and walked out of the room.

"Why can't you leave 'im alone?" said a respectable elder who had been enjoying the game, and in the general murmur of disapproval the grin of satisfied wit faded from the ploughboy's face.

I scented my opportunity. "What's this joke," said I, "about Fairyland?"

"'Tain't no joke about Fairyland, not to young Skelmersdale," said the respectable elder, drinking. A little man with rosy cheeks was more communicative. "They do say, sir," he said, "that they took him into Aldington Knoll an' kep' him there a matter of three weeks."

And with that the gathering was well under way. Once one sheep had started, others were ready enough to follow, and in a little time I had at least the exterior aspect of the Skelmersdale affair. Formerly, before he came to Bignor, he had been in that very similar little shop at Aldington Corner, and there whatever it was did happen had taken place. The story was clear that he had stayed out late one night on the Knoll and vanished for three weeks from the sight of men, and had returned with "his cuffs as clean as when he started," and his pockets full of dust and ashes. He returned in a state of moody wretchedness that only slowly passed away, and for many days he would give no account of where it was he had been. The girl he was engaged to at Clapton Hill tried to get it out of him, and threw him over partly because he refused, and partly because, as she said, he fairly gave her the "'ump." And then when, some time after, he let out to someone carelessly that he had been in Fairyland and wanted to go back, and when the thing spread and the simple badinage of the countryside came into play, he threw up his situation abruptly, and came to Bignor to get out of the fuss. But as to what had happened in Fairyland none of these people knew. There the gathering in the Village Room went to pieces like a pack at fault. One said this, and another said that.

Their air in dealing with this marvel was ostensibly critical and sceptical, but I could see a considerable amount of belief showing through their guarded qualifications. I took a line of intelligent interest, tinged with a reasonable doubt of the whole story.

"If Fairyland's inside Aldington Knoll," I said, "why don't you dig it out?"

"That's what I says," said the young ploughboy.

"There's a-many have tried to dig on Aldington Knoll," said the respectable elder, solemnly, "one time and another. But there's none as goes about today to tell what they got by digging."

The unanimity of vague belief that surrounded me was rather impressive; I felt there must surely be something at the root of so much conviction, and the already pretty keen curiosity I felt about the real facts of the case was distinctly whetted. If these real facts were to be got from any one, they were to be got from Skelmersdale himself; and I set myself, therefore, still more assiduously to efface the first bad impression I had made and win his confidence to the pitch of voluntary speech. In that endeavour I had a social advantage. Being a person of affability and no apparent employment, and wearing tweeds and knickerbockers, I was naturally classed as an artist in Bignor, and in the remarkable code of social precedence prevalent in Bignor an artist ranks considerably higher than a grocer's assistant. Skelmersdale, like too many of his class, is something of a snob; he had told me to "shut it," only under sudden, excessive provocation, and with, I am certain, a subsequent repentance; he was, I knew, quite glad to be seen walking about the village with me. In due course, he accepted the proposal of a pipe and whisky in my rooms readily enough, and there, scenting by some happy instinct that there was trouble of the heart in this, and knowing that confidences beget confidences, I plied him with much of interest and suggestion from my real and fictitious past. And it was after the third whisky of the third visit of that sort, if I remember rightly, that *à propos* of some artless expansion of a little affair that had touched and left me in my teens, that he did at last, of his own free will and motion, break the ice. "It was like that with me," he said, "over there at Aldington. It's just that that's so rum. First I didn't care a bit and it was all her, and afterwards, when it was too late, it was, in a manner of speaking, all me."

I forbore to jump upon this allusion, and so he presently threw out another, and in a little while he was making it as plain as daylight that the one thing he wanted to talk about now was this Fairyland adventure he had sat tight upon for so long. You see, I'd done the trick with him, and from being just another half-incredulous, would-be facetious stranger, I had, by all my wealth of shameless self-exposure, become the possible confidant. He had been bitten by the desire to show that he, too, had lived and felt many things, and the fever was upon him.

He was certainly confoundedly allusive at first, and my eagerness to clear him up with a few precise questions was only equalled and controlled by my anxiety not to get to this sort of thing too soon. But in another meeting or so the basis of confidence was complete; and from first to last I think I got most of the items and aspects – indeed, I got quite a number of times over almost everything that Mr Skelmersdale, with his very limited powers of narration, will ever be able to tell. And so I come to the story of his adventure, and I piece it all together again. Whether it really happened, whether he imagined it or dreamt it, or fell upon it in some strange hallucinatory trance, I do not profess to say. But that he invented it I will not for one moment entertain. The man simply and honestly believes the thing happened as he says it happened; he is transparently incapable of any lie so elaborate and sustained, and in the belief of the simple, yet often keenly penetrating, rustic minds about him I find a very strong confirmation of his sincerity. He believes – and nobody can produce any positive fact to falsify his belief. As for me, with this much of endorsement, I transmit his story – I am a little old now to justify or explain.

He says he went to sleep on Aldington Knoll about ten o'clock one night – it was quite possibly Midsummer night, though he has never thought of the date, and he cannot be sure within a week or so – and it was a fine night and windless, with a rising moon. I have been at pains to visit this Knoll thrice since his story grew up under my persuasions, and once I went there in the twilight summer moonrise on what was, perhaps, a similar night to that of his adventure. Jupiter was great and splendid above the moon, and in the north and northwest the sky was green and vividly bright over the sunken sun. The Knoll stands out bare and bleak under the sky, but surrounded at a little distance by dark thickets, and as I went up towards it there was a mighty starting and scampering of ghostly or quite invisible rabbits. Just over the crown of the Knoll, but nowhere else, was a multitudinous thin trumpeting of midges. The Knoll is, I believe, an artificial mound, the tumulus of some great prehistoric chieftain, and surely no man ever chose a more spacious prospect for a sepulchre. Eastward one sees along the hills to Hythe, and thence across the Channel to where, thirty miles and more perhaps away, the great white lights by Gris Nez and Boulogne wink and pass and shine. Westward lies the whole tumbled valley of the Weald, visible as far as Hindhead and Leith Hill, and the valley of the Stour opens the Downs in the north to interminable hills beyond Wye. All Romney Marsh lies southward at one's feet, Dymchurch and Romney and Lydd, Hastings and its hill are in the middle distance, and the hills multiply vaguely far beyond where Eastbourne rolls up to Beachy Head.

And out upon all this it was that Skelmersdale wandered, being troubled in his earlier love affair, and as he says, "not caring where he went." And there he sat down to think it over, and so, sulking and grieving, was overtaken by sleep. And so he fell into the fairies' power.

The quarrel that had upset him was some trivial matter enough between himself and the girl at Clapton Hill to whom he was engaged. She was a farmer's daughter, said Skelmersdale, and "very respectable," and no doubt an excellent match for him; but both girl and lover were very young and with just that mutual jealousy, that intolerantly keen edge of criticism, that irrational hunger for a beautiful perfection, that life and wisdom do presently and most mercifully dull. What the precise matter of quarrel was I have no idea. She may have said she liked men in gaiters when he hadn't any gaiters on, or he may have said he liked her better in a different sort of hat, but however it began, it got by a series of clumsy stages to bitterness and tears. She no doubt got tearful and smeary, and he grew dusty and drooping, and she parted with invidious comparisons, grave doubts whether she ever had really cared for him, and a clear certainty she would never care again. And with this sort of thing upon his mind he came out upon Aldington Knoll grieving, and presently, after a long interval, perhaps, quite inexplicably, fell asleep.

He woke to find himself on a softer turf than ever he had slept on before, and under the shade of very dark trees that completely hid the sky. Always, indeed, in Fairyland the sky is hidden, it seems. Except for one night when the fairies were dancing, Mr Skelmersdale, during all his time with them, never saw a star. And of that night I am in doubt whether he was in Fairyland proper or out where the rings and rushes are, in those low meadows near the railway line at Smeeth.

But it was light under these trees for all that, and on the leaves and amidst the turf shone a multitude of glow-worms, very bright and fine. Mr Skelmersdale's first impression was that he was small, and the next that quite a number of people still smaller were standing all about him. For some reason, he says, he was neither surprised nor frightened, but sat up quite deliberately and rubbed the sleep out of his eyes. And there all about him stood the smiling elves who had caught him sleeping under their privileges and had brought him into Fairyland.

What these elves were like I have failed to gather, so vague and imperfect is his vocabulary, and so unobservant of all minor detail does he seem to have been. They were clothed in something very light and beautiful, that was neither wool, nor silk, nor leaves, nor the petals of flowers. They stood all about him as he sat and waked, and down the glade towards him, down a glow-worm avenue and fronted by a star, came at once that Fairy Lady who is the chief personage of his memory and tale. Of her I gathered more. She was clothed in filmy green, and about her little waist was a broad silver girdle. Her hair waved back from her forehead on either side; there were curls not too wayward and yet astray, and on her brow was a little tiara, set with a single star. Her sleeves were some sort of open sleeves that gave little glimpses of her arms; her throat, I think, was a little displayed, because he speaks of the beauty of her neck and chin. There was a necklace of coral about her white throat, and in her breast a coral-coloured flower. She had the soft lines of a little child in her chin and cheeks and throat. And her eyes, I gather, were of a kindled brown, very soft and straight and sweet under her level brows. You see by these particulars how greatly this lady must have loomed in Mr Skelmersdale's picture. Certain things he tried to express and could not express; "the way she moved", he said several times; and I fancy a sort of demure joyousness radiated from this Lady.

And it was in the company of this delightful person, as the guest and chosen companion of this delightful person, that Mr Skelmersdale set out to be taken into the intimacies of Fairyland. She welcomed him gladly and a little warmly – I suspect a pressure of his hand in both of hers and a lit face to his. After all, ten years ago young Skelmersdale may have been a very comely youth. And once she took his arm, and once, I think, she led him by the hand down the glade that the glow-worms lit.

Just how things chanced and happened there is no telling from Mr Skelmersdale's disarticulated skeleton of description. He gives little unsatisfactory glimpses of strange corners and doings, of places where there were many fairies together, of "toadstool things that shone pink", of fairy food, of which he could only say, "You should have tasted it!" and of fairy music, "like a little musical box", that came out of nodding flowers. There was a great open place where fairies rode and raced on "things", but what Mr Skelmersdale meant by "these here things they rode", there is no telling. Larvae, perhaps, or crickets, or the little beetles that elude us so abundantly. There was a place where water splashed and gigantic king-cups grew, and there in the hotter times the fairies bathed together. There were games being played and dancing and much elvish love-making, too, I think, among the moss-branch thickets. There can be no doubt that the Fairy Lady made love to Mr Skelmersdale, and no doubt either that this young man set himself to resist her. A time came, indeed, when she sat on a bank beside him, in a quiet, secluded place "all smelling of vi'lets", and talked to him of love.

"When her voice went low and she whispered," said Mr Skelmersdale, "and laid 'er 'and on my 'and, you know, and came close with a soft, warm friendly way she 'ad, it was as much as I could do to keep my 'ead."

It seems he kept his head to a certain limited unfortunate extent. He saw "'ow the wind was blowing", he says, and so, sitting there in a place all smelling of violets, with the touch of this lovely Fairy Lady about him, Mr Skelmersdale broke it to her gently – that he was engaged!

She had told him she loved him dearly, that he was a sweet human lad for her, and whatever he would ask of her he should have – even his heart's desire.

And Mr Skelmersdale, who, I fancy, tried hard to avoid looking at her little lips as they just dropped apart and came together, led up to the more intimate question by saying he would like enough capital to start a little shop. He'd just like to feel, he said, he had money enough to do that. I imagine a little surprise in those brown eyes he talked about, but she seemed sympathetic for all that, and she asked him many questions about the little shop, "laughing like" all the time. So he got to the complete statement of his affianced position, and told her all about Millie.

"All?" said I.

"Everything," said Mr Skelmersdale, "just who she was, and where she lived, and everything about her. I sort of felt I 'ad to all the time, I did."

"Whatever you want you shall have," said the Fairy Lady. "That's as good as done. You shall feel you have the money just as you wish. And now, you know – you must kiss me."

And Mr Skelmersdale pretended not to hear the latter part of her remark, and said she was very kind. That he really didn't deserve she should be so kind. And—

The Fairy Lady suddenly came quite close to him and whispered, "Kiss me!"

"And," said Mr Skelmersdale, "like a fool, I did."

There are kisses and kisses, I am told, and this must have been quite the other sort from Millie's resonant signals of regard. There was something magic in that kiss; assuredly it marked a turning point. At any rate, this is one of the passages that he thought sufficiently important to describe most at length. I have tried to get it right, I have tried to disentangle it from the hints and gestures through which it came to me, but I have no doubt that it was all different from my telling and far finer and sweeter, in the soft filtered light and the subtly stirring silences of the fairy glades. The Fairy Lady asked him more about Millie, and was she very lovely, and so on – a great many times. As to Millie's loveliness, I conceive him answering that she was "all right". And then, or on some such occasion, the Fairy Lady told him she had fallen in love with him as he slept in the moonlight, and so he had been brought into Fairyland, and she had thought, not knowing of Millie, that perhaps he might chance to love her. "But now you know you can't," she said, "so you must stop with me just a little while, and then you must go back to Millie." She told him that, and you know Skelmersdale was already in love with her, but the pure inertia of his mind kept him in the way he was going. I imagine him sitting in a sort of stupefaction amidst all these glowing beautiful things, answering about his Millie and the little shop he projected and the need of a horse and cart... And that absurd state of affairs must have gone on for days and days. I see this little lady, hovering about him and trying to amuse him, too dainty to understand his complexity and too tender to let him go. And he, you know, hypnotised as it were by his earthly position, went his way with her hither and thither, blind to everything in Fairyland but this wonderful intimacy that had come to him. It is hard, it is impossible, to give in print the effect of her radiant sweetness shining through the jungle of poor Skelmersdale's rough and broken sentences. To me, at least, she shone clear amidst the muddle of his story like a glow-worm in a tangle of weeds.

There must have been many days of things while all this was happening – and once, I say, they danced under the moonlight in the fairy rings that stud the meadows near Smeeth – but at last it all came to an end. She led him into a great cavernous place, lit by a red nightlight sort of thing, where there were coffers piled on coffers, and cups and golden boxes, and a great heap of what certainly seemed to all Mr Skelmersdale's senses – coined gold. There were little gnomes amidst this wealth, who saluted her at her coming, and stood aside. And suddenly she turned on him there with brightly shining eyes.

"And now," she said, "you have been kind to stay with me so long, and it is time I let you go. You must go back to your Millie. You must go back to your Millie, and here – just as I promised you – they will give you gold."

"She choked like," said Mr Skelmersdale. "At that, I had a sort of feeling" (he touched his breastbone) "as though I was fainting here. I felt pale, you know, and shivering, and even then – I 'adn't a thing to say."

He paused. "Yes," I said.

The scene was beyond his describing. But I know that she kissed him good-bye.

"And you said nothing?"

"Nothing," he said. "I stood like a stuffed calf. She just looked back once, you know, and stood smiling like and crying – I could see the shine of her eyes – and then she was gone, and there was all these little fellows bustling about me, stuffing my 'ands and my pockets and the back of my collar and everywhere with gold."

And then it was, when the Fairy Lady had vanished, that Mr Skelmersdale really understood and knew. He suddenly began plucking out the gold they were thrusting upon him, and shouting out at them to prevent their giving him more. "'I don't want yer gold,' I said. 'I 'aven't done yet. I'm not going. I want to speak to that Fairy Lady again.' I started off to go after her and they held me back. Yes, stuck their little 'ands against my middle and shoved me back. They kept giving me more and more gold until it was running all down my trouser legs and dropping out of my 'ands. 'I don't want yer gold,' I says to them, 'I want just to speak to the Fairy Lady again.'"

"And did you?"

"It came to a tussle."

"Before you saw her?"

"I didn't see her. When I got out from them she wasn't anywhere to be seen."

So he ran in search of her out of this red-lit cave, down a long grotto, seeking her, and thence he came out in a great and desolate place athwart which a swarm of will-o'-the-wisps were flying to and fro. And about him elves were dancing in derision, and the little gnomes came out of the cave after him, carrying gold in handfuls and casting it after him, shouting, "Fairy love and fairy gold! Fairy love and fairy gold!"

And when he heard these words, came a great fear that it was all over, and he lifted up his voice and called to her by her name, and suddenly set himself to run down the slope from the mouth of the cavern, through a place of thorns and briers, calling after her very loudly and often. The elves danced about him unheeded, pinching him and pricking him, and the will-o'-the-wisps circled round him and dashed into his face, and the gnomes pursued him shouting and pelting him with fairy gold. As he ran with all this strange rout about him and distracting him, suddenly he was knee-deep in a swamp, and suddenly he was amidst thick twisted roots, and he caught his foot in one and stumbled and fell...

He fell and he rolled over, and in that instant he found himself sprawling upon Aldington Knoll, all lonely under the stars.

He sat up sharply at once, he says, and found he was very stiff and cold, and his clothes were damp with dew. The first pallor of dawn and a chilly wind were coming up together. He could have believed the whole thing a strangely vivid dream until he thrust his hand into his side pocket and found it stuffed with ashes. Then he knew for certain it was fairy gold they had given him. He could feel all their pinches and pricks still, though there was never a bruise upon him. And in that manner, and so suddenly, Mr Skelmersdale came out of Fairyland back into this world of men. Even then he fancied the thing was but the matter of a night until he returned to the shop at Aldington Corner and discovered amidst their astonishment that he had been away three weeks.

"Lor'! the trouble I 'ad!" said Mr Skelmersdale.

"How?"

"Explaining. I suppose you've never had anything like that to explain."

"Never," I said, and he expatiated for a time on the behaviour of this person and that. One name he avoided for a space.

"And Millie?" said I at last.

"I didn't seem to care a bit for seeing Millie," he said.

"I expect she seemed changed?"

"Everyone was changed. Changed for good. Everyone seemed big, you know, and coarse. And their voices seemed loud. Why, the sun, when it rose in the morning, fair hit me in the eye!"

"And Millie?"

"I didn't want to see Millie."

"And when you did?"

"I came up against her Sunday, coming out of church. 'Where you been?' she said, and I saw there was a row. I didn't care if there was. I seemed to forget about her even while she was there a-talking to me. She was just nothing. I couldn't make out whatever I 'ad seen in 'er ever, or what there could 'ave been. Sometimes when she wasn't about, I did get back a little, but never when she was there. Then it was always the other came up and blotted her out... Anyow, it didn't break her heart."

"Married?" I asked.

"Married 'er cousin," said Mr Skelmersdale, and reflected on the pattern of the tablecloth for a space.

When he spoke again it was clear that his former sweetheart had clean vanished from his mind, and that the talk had brought back the Fairy Lady triumphant in his heart. He talked of her – soon he was letting out the oddest things, queer love secrets it would be treachery to repeat. I think, indeed, that was the queerest thing in the whole affair, to hear that neat little grocer man after his story was done, with a glass of whisky beside him and a cigar between his fingers, witnessing, with sorrow still, though now, indeed, with a time-blunted anguish, of the inappeasable hunger of the heart that presently came upon him. "I couldn't eat," he said, "I couldn't sleep. I made mistakes in orders and got mixed with change. There she was day and night, drawing me and drawing me. Oh, I wanted her. Lord! How I wanted her! I was up there, most evenings I was up there on the Knoll, often even when it rained. I used to walk over the Knoll and round it and round it, calling for them to let me in. Shouting. Near blubbering I was at times. Daft I was and miserable. I kept on saying it was all a mistake. And every Sunday afternoon I went up there, wet and fine, though I knew as well as you do it wasn't no good by day. And I've tried to go to sleep there."

He stopped sharply and decided to drink some whisky.

"I've tried to go to sleep there," he said, and I could swear his lips trembled. "I've tried to go to sleep there, often and often. And, you know, I couldn't, sir – never. I've thought if I could go to sleep there, there might be something. But I've sat up there and laid up there, and I couldn't – not for thinking and longing. It's the longing... I've tried—"

He blew, drank up the rest of his whisky spasmodically, stood up suddenly and buttoned his jacket, staring closely and critically at the cheap oleographs beside the mantel meanwhile. The little black notebook in which he recorded the orders of his daily round projected stiffly from his breast pocket. When all the buttons were quite done, he patted his chest and turned on me suddenly. "Well," he said, "I must be going."

There was something in his eyes and manner that was too difficult for him to express in words. "One gets talking," he said at last at the door, and smiled wanly, and so vanished from my eyes. And that is the tale of Mr Skelmersdale in Fairyland just as he told it to me.

THE STORY OF THE INEXPERIENCED GHOST

H. G. WELLS

The scene amidst which Clayton told his last story comes back very vividly to my mind. There he sat, for the greater part of the time, in the corner of the authentic settle by the spacious open fire, and Sanderson sat beside him smoking the Broseley clay that bore his name. There was Evans, and that marvel among actors, Wish, who is also a modest man. We had all come down to the Mermaid Club that Saturday morning, except Clayton, who had slept there overnight – which indeed gave him the opening of his story. We had golfed until golfing was invisible; we had dined, and we were in that mood of tranquil kindliness when men will suffer a story. When Clayton began to tell one, we naturally supposed he was lying. It may be that indeed he was lying – of that the reader will speedily be able to judge as well as I. He began, it is true, with an air of matter-of-fact anecdote, but that we thought was only the incurable artifice of the man.

"I say!" he remarked, after a long consideration of the upward rain of sparks from the log that Sanderson had thumped, "you know I was alone here last night?"

"Except for the domestics," said Wish.

"Who sleep in the other wing," said Clayton. "Yes. Well..." He pulled at his cigar for some little time as though he still hesitated about his confidence. Then he said, quite quietly, "I caught a ghost!"

"Caught a ghost, did you?" said Sanderson. "Where is it?"

And Evans, who admires Clayton immensely and has been four weeks in America, shouted, "Caught a ghost, did you, Clayton? I'm glad of it! Tell us all about it right now."

Clayton said he would in a minute, and asked him to shut the door.

He looked apologetically at me. "There's no eavesdropping of course, but we don't want to upset our very excellent service with any rumours of ghosts in the place. There's too much shadow and oak panelling to trifle with that. And this, you know, wasn't a regular ghost. I don't think it will come again – ever."

"You mean to say you didn't keep it?" said Sanderson.

"I hadn't the heart to," said Clayton.

And Sanderson said he was surprised.

We laughed, and Clayton looked aggrieved. "I know," he said, with the flicker of a smile, "but the fact is it really was a ghost, and I'm as sure of it as I am that I am talking to you now. I'm not joking. I mean what I say."

Sanderson drew deeply at his pipe, with one reddish eye on Clayton, and then emitted a thin jet of smoke more eloquent than many words.

Clayton ignored the comment. "It is the strangest thing that has ever happened in my life. You know, I never believed in ghosts or anything of the sort, before, ever; and then, you know, I bag one in a corner; and the whole business is in my hands."

He meditated still more profoundly, and produced and began to pierce a second cigar with a curious little stabber he affected.

"You talked to it?" asked Wish.

"For the space, probably, of an hour."

"Chatty?" I said, joining the party of the sceptics.

"The poor devil was in trouble," said Clayton, bowed over his cigar-end and with the very faintest note of reproof.

"Sobbing?" someone asked.

Clayton heaved a realistic sigh at the memory. "Good Lord!" he said; "Yes." And then, "Poor fellow! Yes."

"Where did you strike it?" asked Evans, in his best American accent.

"I never realised," said Clayton, ignoring him, "the poor sort of thing a ghost might be," and he hung us up again for a time, while he sought for matches in his pocket and lit and warmed to his cigar.

"I took an advantage," he reflected at last.

We were none of us in a hurry. "A character," he said, "remains just the same character for all that it's been disembodied. That's a thing we too often forget. People with a certain strength or fixity of purpose may have ghosts of a certain strength and fixity of purpose – most haunting ghosts, you know, must be as one-idea'd as monomaniacs and as obstinate as mules to come back again and again. This poor creature wasn't." He suddenly looked up rather queerly, and his eye went round the room. "I say it," he said, "in all kindliness, but that is the plain truth of the case. Even at the first glance he struck me as weak."

He punctuated with the help of his cigar.

"I came upon him, you know, in the long passage. His back was towards me and I saw him first. Right off I knew him for a ghost. He was transparent and whitish; clean through his chest I could see the glimmer of the little window at the end. And not only his physique but his attitude struck me as being weak. He looked, you know, as though he didn't know in the slightest whatever he meant to do. One hand was on the panelling and the other fluttered to his mouth. Like – SO!"

"What sort of physique?" said Sanderson.

"Lean. You know that sort of young man's neck that has two great flutings down the back, here and here – so! And a little, meanish head with scrubby hair – and rather bad ears. Shoulders bad, narrower than the hips; turn-down collar, ready-made short jacket, trousers baggy and a little frayed at the heels. That's how he took me. I came very quietly up the staircase. I did not carry a light, you know – the candles are on the landing table and there is that lamp – and I was in my list slippers, and I saw him as I came up. I stopped dead at that – taking him in. I wasn't a bit afraid. I think that in most of these affairs one is never nearly so afraid or excited as one imagines one would be. I was surprised and interested. I thought, 'Good Lord! Here's a ghost at last! And I haven't believed for a moment in ghosts during the last five-and-twenty years.'"

"Um," said Wish.

"I suppose I wasn't on the landing a moment before he found out I was there. He turned on me sharply, and I saw the face of an immature young man, a weak nose, a scrubby little moustache, a feeble chin. So for an instant we stood – he looking over his shoulder at me and regarded one another. Then he seemed to remember his high calling. He turned round, drew himself up, projected his face, raised his arms, spread his hands in approved ghost fashion – came towards me. As he did so his little jaw dropped, and he emitted a faint, drawn-out 'Boo'. No, it wasn't – not a bit dreadful. I'd dined. I'd had a bottle of champagne, and being all alone, perhaps two or three – perhaps even four or five – whiskies, so I was as solid as rocks and no more frightened than if I'd been assailed by a frog. 'Boo!' I said. 'Nonsense. You don't belong to this place. What are you doing here?'

"I could see him wince. 'Boo-oo,' he said.

"'Boo – be hanged! Are you a member?' I said; and just to show I didn't care a pin for him I stepped through a corner of him and made to light my candle. 'Are you a member?' I repeated, looking at him sideways.

"He moved a little so as to stand clear of me, and his bearing became crestfallen. 'No,' he said, in answer to the persistent interrogation of my eye; 'I'm not a member – I'm a ghost.'

"'Well, that doesn't give you the run of the Mermaid Club. Is there any one you want to see, or anything of that sort?' and doing it as steadily as possible for fear that he should mistake the carelessness of whisky for the distraction of fear, I got my candle alight. I turned on him, holding it. 'What are you doing here?' I said.

"He had dropped his hands and stopped his booing, and there he stood, abashed and awkward, the ghost of a weak, silly, aimless young man. 'I'm haunting,' he said.

"'You haven't any business to,' I said in a quiet voice.

"'I'm a ghost,' he said, as if in defence.

"'That may be, but you haven't any business to haunt here. This is a respectable private club; people often stop here with nursemaids and children, and, going about in the careless way you do, some poor little mite could easily come upon you and be scared out of her wits. I suppose you didn't think of that?'

"'No, sir,' he said, 'I didn't.'

"'You should have done. You haven't any claim on the place, have you? Weren't murdered here, or anything of that sort?'

"'None, sir; but I thought as it was old and oak-panelled—'

"'That's no excuse.' I regarded him firmly. 'Your coming here is a mistake,' I said, in a tone of friendly superiority. I feigned to see if I had my matches, and then looked up at him frankly. 'If I were you I wouldn't wait for cock-crow – I'd vanish right away.'

"He looked embarrassed. 'The fact is, sir—' he began.

"'I'd vanish,' I said, driving it home.

"'The fact is, sir, that – somehow – I can't.'

"'You can't?'

"'No, sir. There's something I've forgotten. I've been hanging about here since midnight last night, hiding in the cupboards of the empty bedrooms and things like that. I'm flurried. I've never come haunting before, and it seems to put me out.'

"'Put you out?'

"'Yes, sir. I've tried to do it several times, and it doesn't come off. There's some little thing has slipped me, and I can't get back.'

"That, you know, rather bowled me over. He looked at me in such an abject way that for the life of me I couldn't keep up quite the high, hectoring vein I had adopted. 'That's queer,' I said, and as I spoke I fancied I heard someone moving about down below. 'Come into my room and tell me more about it,' I said. I didn't, of course, understand this, and I tried to take him by the arm. But, of course, you might as well have tried to take hold of a puff of smoke! I had forgotten my number, I think; anyhow, I remember going into several bedrooms – it was lucky I was the only soul in that wing – until I saw my traps. 'Here we are,' I said, and sat down in the arm-chair; 'sit down and tell me all about it. It seems to me you have got yourself into a jolly awkward position, old chap.'

"Well, he said he wouldn't sit down! He'd prefer to flit up and down the room if it was all the same to me. And so he did, and in a little while we were deep in a long and serious talk. And presently, you know, something of those whiskies and sodas evaporated out of me, and I began to realise just a little what a thundering rum and weird business it was that I was in. There he was, semi-transparent – the proper conventional phantom, and noiseless except for his ghost of a voice – flitting to and fro in that nice, clean, chintz-hung old bedroom. You could see the gleam of the copper candlesticks through him, and the lights on the brass fender, and the corners of the framed engravings on the wall – and there he was telling me all about this wretched little life of his that had recently ended on earth. He hadn't a particularly honest face, you know, but being transparent, of course, he couldn't avoid telling the truth."

"Eh?" said Wish, suddenly sitting up in his chair.

"What?" said Clayton.

"Being transparent – couldn't avoid telling the truth – I don't see it," said Wish.

"I don't see it," said Clayton, with inimitable assurance. "But it is so, I can assure you nevertheless. I don't believe he got once a nail's breadth off the Bible truth. He told me how he had been killed – he went down into a London basement with a candle to look for a leakage of gas – and described himself as a senior English master in a London private school when that release occurred."

"Poor wretch!" said I.

"That's what I thought, and the more he talked the more I thought it. There he was, purposeless in life and purposeless out of it. He talked of his father and mother and his schoolmaster, and all who had ever been anything to him in the world, meanly. He had been too sensitive, too nervous; none of them had ever valued him properly or understood him, he said. He had never had a real friend in the world, I think; he had never had a success. He had shirked games and failed examinations. 'It's like that with some people,' he said; 'whenever I got into the examination-room or anywhere everything seemed to go.' Engaged to be married of course – to another over-sensitive person, I suppose – when the indiscretion with the gas escape ended his affairs. 'And where are you now?' I asked. 'Not in—?'

"He wasn't clear on that point at all. The impression he gave me was of a sort of vague, intermediate state, a special reserve for souls too non-existent for anything so positive as either sin or virtue. I don't know. He was much too egotistical and unobservant to give me any clear idea of the kind of place, kind of country, there is on the Other Side of Things. Wherever he was, he seems to have fallen in with a set of kindred spirits: ghosts of weak Cockney young men, who were on a footing of Christian names, and among these there was certainly a lot of talk about 'going haunting' and things like that. Yes – going haunting! They seemed to think 'haunting' a tremendous adventure, and most of them funked it all the time. And so primed, you know, he had come."

"But really!" said Wish to the fire.

"These are the impressions he gave me, anyhow," said Clayton, modestly. "I may, of course, have been in a rather uncritical state, but that was the sort of background he gave to himself. He kept flitting up and down, with his thin voice going talking, talking about his wretched self, and never a word of clear, firm statement from first to last. He was thinner and sillier and more pointless than if he had been real and alive. Only then, you know, he would not have been in my bedroom here – if he had been alive. I should have kicked him out."

"Of course," said Evans, "there are poor mortals like that."

"And there's just as much chance of their having ghosts as the rest of us," I admitted.

"What gave a sort of point to him, you know, was the fact that he did seem within limits to have found himself out. The mess he had made of haunting had depressed him terribly. He had been told it would be a 'lark'; he had come expecting it to be a 'lark,' and here it was, nothing but another failure added to his record! He proclaimed himself an utter out-and-out failure. He said, and I can quite believe it, that he had never tried to do anything all his life that he hadn't made a perfect mess of – and through all the wastes of eternity he never would. If he had had sympathy, perhaps... He paused at that, and stood regarding me. He remarked that, strange as it might seem to me, nobody, not any one, ever, had given him the amount of sympathy I was doing now. I could see what he wanted straight away, and I determined to head him off at once. I may be a brute, you know, but being the Only Real Friend, the recipient of the confidences of one of these egotistical weaklings, ghost or body, is beyond my physical endurance. I got up briskly. 'Don't you brood on these things too much,' I said. 'The thing you've got to do is to get out of this get out of this – sharp. You pull yourself together and try.' 'I can't,' he said. 'You try,' I said, and try he did."

"Try!" said Sanderson. "How?"

"Passes," said Clayton.

"Passes?"

"Complicated series of gestures and passes with the hands. That's how he had come in and that's how he had to get out again. Lord! what a business I had!"

"But how could any series of passes—?" I began.

"My dear man," said Clayton, turning on me and putting a great emphasis on certain words, "you want everything clear. I don't know how. All I know is that you do – that he did, anyhow, at least. After a fearful time, you know, he got his passes right and suddenly disappeared."

"Did you," said Sanderson, slowly, "observe the passes?"

"Yes," said Clayton, and seemed to think. "It was tremendously queer," he said. "There we were, I and this thin vague ghost, in that silent room, in this silent, empty inn, in this silent little Friday-night town. Not a sound except our voices and a faint panting he made when he swung. There was the bedroom candle, and one candle on the dressing-table alight, that was all – sometimes one or other would flare up into a tall, lean, astonished flame for a space. And queer things happened. 'I can't,' he said; 'I shall never—!' And suddenly he sat down on a little chair at the foot of the bed and began to sob and sob. Lord! what a harrowing, whimpering thing he seemed!

"'You pull yourself together,' I said, and tried to pat him on the back, and... my confounded hand went through him! By that time, you know, I wasn't nearly so – massive as I had been on the landing. I got the queerness of it full. I remember snatching back my hand out of him, as it were, with a little thrill, and walking over to the dressing-table. 'You pull yourself together,' I said to him, 'and try.' And in order to encourage and help him I began to try as well."

"What!" said Sanderson, "the passes?"

"Yes, the passes."

"But—" I said, moved by an idea that eluded me for a space.

"This is interesting," said Sanderson, with his finger in his pipe-bowl. "You mean to say this ghost of yours gave away—"

"Did his level best to give away the whole confounded barrier? Yes."

"He didn't," said Wish; "he couldn't. Or you'd have gone there too."

"That's precisely it," I said, finding my elusive idea put into words for me.

"That is precisely it," said Clayton, with thoughtful eyes upon the fire.

For just a little while there was silence.

"And at last he did it?" said Sanderson.

"At last he did it. I had to keep him up to it hard, but he did it at last – rather suddenly. He despaired, we had a scene, and then he got up abruptly and asked me to go through the whole performance, slowly, so that he might see. 'I believe,' he said, 'if I could see I should spot what was wrong at once.' And he did. 'I know,' he said. 'What do you know?' said I. 'I know,' he repeated. Then he said, peevishly, 'I can't do it if you look at me – I really can't; it's been that, partly, all along. I'm such a nervous fellow that you put me out.' Well, we had a bit of an argument. Naturally I wanted to see; but he was as obstinate as a mule, and suddenly I had come over as tired as a dog – he tired me out. 'All right,' I said, 'I won't look at you,' and turned towards the mirror, on the wardrobe, by the bed.

He started off very fast. I tried to follow him by looking in the looking-glass, to see just what it was had hung. Round went his arms and his hands, so, and so, and so, and then with a rush came to the last gesture of all – you stand erect and open out your arms – and so, don't you know, he stood. And then he didn't! He didn't! He wasn't! I wheeled round from the looking-glass to him. There was nothingl I was alone, with the flaring candles and a staggering mind. What had happened? Had anything happened? Had I been dreaming?... And then, with an absurd note of finality about it, the clock upon the landing discovered the moment was ripe for striking one. So! – Ping! And I was as grave and sober as a judge, with all my champagne and whisky gone into the vast serene. Feeling queer, you know – confoundedly queer! Queer! Good Lord!"

He regarded his cigar-ash for a moment. "That's all that happened," he said.

"And then you went to bed?" asked Evans.

"What else was there to do?"

I looked Wish in the eye. We wanted to scoff, and there was something, something perhaps in Clayton's voice and manner, that hampered our desire.

"And about these passes?" said Sanderson.

"I believe I could do them now."

"Oh!" said Sanderson, and produced a penknife and set himself to grub the dottel out of the bowl of his clay.

"Why don't you do them now?" said Sanderson, shutting his penknife with a click.

"That's what I'm going to do," said Clayton.

"They won't work," said Evans.

"If they do—" I suggested.

"You know, I'd rather you didn't," said Wish, stretching out his legs.

"Why?" asked Evans.

"I'd rather he didn't," said Wish.

"But he hasn't got 'em right," said Sanderson, plugging too much tobacco in his pipe.

"All the same, I'd rather he didn't," said Wish.

We argued with Wish. He said that for Clayton to go through those gestures was like mocking a serious matter. "But you don't believe—?" I said. Wish glanced at Clayton, who was staring into the fire, weighing something in his mind. "I do – more than half, anyhow, I do," said Wish.

"Clayton," said I, "you're too good a liar for us. Most of it was all right. But that disappearance... happened to be convincing. Tell us, it's a tale of cock and bull."

He stood up without heeding me, took the middle of the hearthrug, and faced me. For a moment he regarded his feet thoughtfully, and then for all the rest of the time his eyes were on the opposite wall, with an intent expression. He raised his two hands slowly to the level of his eyes and so began...

Now, Sanderson is a Freemason, a member of the lodge of the Four Kings, which devotes itself so ably to the study and elucidation of all the mysteries of Masonry past and present, and among the students of this lodge Sanderson is by no means the least. He followed Clayton's motions with a singular interest in his reddish eye. "That's not bad," he said, when it was done. "You really do, you know, put things together, Clayton, in a most amazing fashion. But there's one little detail out."

"I know," said Clayton. "I believe I could tell you which."

"Well?"

"This," said Clayton, and did a queer little twist and writhing and thrust of the hands.

"Yes."

"That, you know, was what he couldn't get right," said Clayton. "But how do you—?"

"Most of this business, and particularly how you invented it, I don't understand at all," said Sanderson, "but just that phase – I do." He reflected. "These happen to be a series of gestures – connected with a certain branch of esoteric Masonry. Probably you know. Or else – how?" He reflected still further. "I do not see I can do any harm in telling you just the proper twist. After all, if you know, you know; if you don't, you don't."

"I know nothing," said Clayton, "except what the poor devil let out last night."

"Well, anyhow," said Sanderson, and placed his churchwarden very carefully upon the shelf over the fireplace. Then very rapidly he gesticulated with his hands.

"So?" said Clayton, repeating.

"So," said Sanderson, and took his pipe in hand again.

"Ah, now," said Clayton, "I can do the whole thing – right."

He stood up before the waning fire and smiled at us all. But I think there was just a little hesitation in his smile. "If I begin—" he said.

"I wouldn't begin," said Wish.

"It's all right!" said Evans. "Matter is indestructible. You don't think any jiggery-pokery of this sort is going to snatch Clayton into the world of shades. Not it! You may try, Clayton, so far as I'm concerned, until your arms drop off at the wrists."

"I don't believe that," said Wish, and stood up and put his arm on Clayton's shoulder. "You've made me half believe in that story somehow, and I don't want to see the thing done!"

"Goodness!" said I, "here's Wish frightened!"

"I am," said Wish, with real or admirably feigned intensity. "I believe that if he goes through these motions right he'll go."

"He'll not do anything of the sort," I cried. "There's only one way out of this world for men, and Clayton is thirty years from that. Besides… And such a ghost! Do you think—?"

Wish interrupted me by moving. He walked out from among our chairs and stopped beside the tole and stood there. "Clayton," he said, "you're a fool."

Clayton, with a humorous light in his eyes, smiled back at him. "Wish," he said, "is right and all you others are wrong. I shall go. I shall get to the end of these passes, and as the last swish whistles through the air – presto! – this hearthrug will be vacant, the room will be blank amazement, and a respectably dressed gentleman of fifteen stone will plump into the world of shades. I'm certain. So will you be. I decline to argue further. Let the thing be tried."

"No," said Wish, and made a step and ceased, and Clayton raised his hands once more to repeat the spirit's passing.

By that time, you know, we were all in a state of tension – largely because of the behaviour of Wish. We sat all of us with our eyes on Clayton – I, at least, with a sort of tight, stiff feeling about me as though from the back of my skull to the middle of my thighs my body had been changed to steel. And there, with a gravity that was imperturbably serene, Clayton bowed and swayed and waved his hands and arms before us. As he drew towards the end one piled up, one tingled in one's teeth. The last gesture, I have said, was to swing the arms out wide open, with the face held up. And when at last he swung out to this closing gesture I ceased even to breathe. It was ridiculous, of course, but you know that ghost-story feeling. It was after dinner, in a queer, old shadowy house. Would he, after all...?

There he stood for one stupendous moment, with his arms open and his upturned face, assured and bright, in the glare of the hanging lamp. We hung through that moment as if it were an age, and then came from all of us something that was half a sigh of infinite relief and half a reassuring "No!" For visibly – he wasn't going. It was all nonsense. He had told an idle story, and carried it almost to conviction, that was all!... And then in that moment the face of Clayton changed.

It changed. It changed as a lit house changes when its lights are suddenly extinguished. His eyes were suddenly eyes that were fixed, his smile was frozen on his lips, and he stood there still. He stood there, very gently swaying.

That moment, too, was an age. And then, you know, chairs were scraping, things were falling, and we were all moving. His knees seemed to give, and he fell forward, and Evans rose and caught him in his arms...

It stunned us all. For a minute I suppose no one said a coherent thing. We believed it, yet could not believe it... I came out of a muddled stupefaction to find myself kneeling beside him, and his vest and shirt were torn open, and Sanderson's hand lay on his heart...

Well – the simple fact before us could very well wait our convenience; there was no hurry for us to comprehend. It lay there for an hour; it lies athwart my memory, black and amazing still, to this day. Clayton had, indeed, passed into the world that lies so near to and so far from our own, and he had gone thither by the only road that mortal man may take. But whether he did indeed pass there by that poor ghost's incantation, or whether he was stricken suddenly by apoplexy in the midst of an idle tale – as the coroner's jury would have us believe – is no matter for my judging; it is just one of those inexplicable riddles that must remain unsolved until the final solution of all things shall come. All I certainly know is that, in the very moment, in the very instant, of concluding those passes, he changed, and staggered, and fell down before us – dead!

THE WOOD BEYOND THE WORLD

WILLIAM MORRIS

I

Awhile ago there was a young man dwelling in a great and goodly city by the sea which had to name Langton on Holm. He was but of five and twenty winters, a fair-faced man, yellow-haired, tall and strong; rather wiser than foolisher than young men are mostly wont; a valiant youth, and a kind; not of many words but courteous of speech; no roisterer, nought masterful, but peaceable and knowing how to forbear: in a fray a perilous foe, and a trusty war-fellow. His father, with whom he was dwelling when this tale begins, was a great merchant, richer than a baron of the land, a head-man of the greatest of the Lineages of Langton, and a captain of the Porte; he was of the Lineage of the Goldings, therefore was he called Bartholomew Golden, and his son Golden Walter.

Now ye may well deem that such a youngling as this was looked upon by all as a lucky man without a lack; but there was this flaw in his lot, whereas he had fallen into the toils of love of a woman exceeding fair, and had taken her to wife, she nought unwilling as it seemed. But when they had been wedded some six months he found by manifest tokens, that his fairness was not so much to her but that she must seek to the foulness of one worser than he in all ways; wherefore his rest departed from him, whereas he hated her for her untruth and her hatred of him; yet would the sound of her voice, as she came and went in the house, make his heart beat; and the sight of her stirred desire within him, so that he longed for her to be sweet and kind with him, and deemed that, might it be so, he should forget all the evil gone by. But it was not so; for ever when she saw him, her face changed, and her hatred of him became manifest, and howsoever she were sweet with others, with him she was hard and sour.

So this went on a while till the chambers of his father's house, yea the very streets of the city, became loathsome to him; and yet he called to mind that the world was wide and he but a young man. So on a day as he sat with his father alone, he spake to him and said: Father, I was on the quays even now, and I looked on the ships that were nigh boun, and thy sign I saw on a tall ship that seemed to me nighest boun. Will it be long ere she sail?

Nay, said his father, that ship, which hight the *Katherine*, will they warp out of the haven in two days' time. But why askest thou of her?

The shortest word is best, father, said Walter, and this it is, that I would depart in the said ship and see other lands.

Yea and whither, son? said the merchant.

Whither she goeth, said Walter, for I am ill at ease at home, as thou wottest, father.

The merchant held his peace awhile, and looked hard on his son, for there was strong love between them; but at last he said: Well, son, maybe it were best for thee; but maybe also we shall not meet again.

Yet if we do meet, father, then shalt thou see a new man in me.

Well, said Bartholomew, at least I know on whom to lay the loss of thee, and when thou art gone, for thou shalt have thine own way herein, she shall no longer abide in my house. Nay, but it were for the strife that should arise thenceforth betwixt her kindred and ours, it should go somewhat worse with her than that.

Said Walter: I pray thee shame her not more than needs must be, lest, so doing, thou shame both me and thyself also.

Bartholomew held his peace again for a while; then he said: Goeth she with child, my son?

Walter reddened, and said: I wot not; nor of whom the child may be. Then they both sat silent, till Bartholomew spake, saying: The end of it is, son, that this is Monday, and that thou shalt go aboard in the small hours of Wednesday; and meanwhile I shall look to it that thou go not away empty-handed; the skipper of the *Katherine* is a good man and true, and knows the seas well; and my servant Robert the Low, who is clerk of the lading, is trustworthy and wise, and as myself in all matters that look towards chaffer. The *Katherine* is new and stout-builded, and should be lucky, whereas she is under the ward of her who is the saint called upon in the church where thou wert christened, and myself before thee; and thy mother, and my father and mother all lie under the chancel thereof, as thou wottest.

Therewith the elder rose up and went his ways about his business, and there was no more said betwixt him and his son on this matter.

II

When Walter went down to the *Katherine* next morning, there was the skipper Geoffrey, who did him reverence, and made him all cheer, and showed him his room aboard ship, and the plenteous goods which his father had sent down to the quays already, such haste as he had made. Walter thanked his father's love in his heart, but otherwise took little heed to his affairs, but wore away the time about the haven, gazing listlessly on the ships that were making them ready outward, or unlading, and the mariners and aliens coming and going: and all these were to him as the curious images woven on a tapestry.

At last, when he had well-nigh come back again to the *Katherine*, he saw there a tall ship, which he had scarce noted before, a ship all-boun, which had her boats out, and men sitting to the oars thereof ready to tow her outwards when the hawser should be cast off, and by seeming her mariners were but abiding for someone or other to come aboard.

So Walter stood idly watching the said ship, and as he looked, lo! folk passing him toward the gangway. These were three; first came a dwarf, dark-brown of hue and hideous, with long arms and ears exceeding great and dog-teeth that stuck out like the fangs of a wild beast. He was clad in a rich coat of yellow silk, and bare in his hand a crooked bow, and was girt with a broad sax.

After him came a maiden, young by seeming, of scarce twenty summers; fair of face as a flower; grey-eyed, brown-haired, with lips full and red, slim and gentle of body. Simple was her array, of a short and strait green gown, so that on her right ankle was clear to see an iron ring.

Last of the three was a lady, tall and stately, so radiant of visage and glorious of raiment, that it were hard to say what like she was; for scarce might the eye gaze steady upon her exceeding beauty; yet must every son of Adam who found himself anigh her, lift up his eyes again after he had dropped them, and look again on her, and yet again and yet again. Even so did Walter, and as the three passed by him, it seemed to him as if all the other folk there about had vanished and were nought; nor had he any vision before his eyes of any looking on them, save himself alone. They went over the gangway into the ship, and he saw them go along the deck till they came to the house on the poop, and entered it, and were gone from his sight.

There he stood staring, till little by little the thronging people of the quays came into his eye-shot again; then he saw how the hawser was cast off and the boats fell to tugging the big ship towards the harbour-mouth with hale and how of men. Then the sail fell down from the yard and was sheeted home and filled with the fair wind as the ship's bows ran up on the first green wave outside the haven. Even therewith the shipmen cast abroad a banner, whereon was done in a green field a grim wolf ramping up against a maiden, and so went the ship upon her way.

Walter stood awhile staring at her empty place where the waves ran into the haven-mouth, and then turned aside and toward the *Katherine*; and at first he was minded to go ask shipmaster Geoffrey of what he knew concerning the said ship and her alien wayfarers; but then it came into his mind, that all this was but an imagination or dream of the day, and that he were best to leave it untold to any. So therewith he went his way from the water-side, and through the streets unto his father's house; but when he was but a little way thence, and the door was before him, him-seemed for a moment of time that he beheld those three coming out down the steps of stone and into the street; to wit the dwarf, the maiden and the stately lady: but when he stood still to abide their coming, and looked toward them, lo! there was nothing before him save the goodly house of Bartholomew Golden, and three children and a cur dog playing about the steps thereof, and about him were four or five passers-by going about their business. Then was he all confused in his mind, and knew not what to make of it, whether those whom he had seemed to see pass aboard ship were but images of a dream, or children of Adam in very flesh.

Howsoever, he entered the house, and found his father in the chamber, and fell to speech with him about their matters; but for all that he loved his father, and worshipped him as a wise and valiant man, yet at that hour he might not hearken the words of his mouth, so much was his mind entangled in the thought of those three, and they were ever before his eyes, as if they had been painted on a table by the best of limners. And of the two women he thought exceeding much, and cast no wyte upon himself for running after the desire of strange women. For he said to himself that he desired not either of the twain; nay, he might not tell which of the twain, the maiden or the stately queen, were clearest to his eyes; but sore he desired to see both of them again, and to know what they were.

So wore the hours till the Wednesday morning, and it was time that he should bid farewell to his father and get aboard ship; but his father led him down to the quays and on to the *Katherine*, and there Walter embraced him, not without tears and forebodings; for his heart was full. Then presently the old man went aland; the gangway was unshipped, the hawsers cast off; the oars of the towing-boats splashed in the dark water, the sail fell down from the yard, and was sheeted home, and out plunged the *Katherine* into the misty sea and rolled up the grey slopes, casting abroad her ancient withal, whereon was beaten the token of Bartholomew Golden, to wit a B and a G to the right and the left, and thereabove a cross and a triangle rising from the midst.

Walter stood on the stern and beheld, yet more with the mind of him than with his eyes; for it all seemed but the double of what the other ship had done; and he thought of it as if the twain were as beads strung on one string and led away by it into the same place, and thence to go in the like order, and so on again and again, and never to draw nigher to each other.

III

Fast sailed the *Katherine* over the seas, and nought befell to tell of, either to herself or her crew. She came to one cheaping-town and then to another, and so on to a third and a fourth; and at each was buying and selling after the manner of chapmen; and Walter not only looked on the doings of his father's folk, but lent a hand, what he might, to help them in all matters, whether it were in seaman's craft, or in chaffer. And the further he went and the longer the time wore, the more he was eased of his old trouble wherein his wife and her treason had to do.

But as for the other trouble, to wit his desire and longing to come up with those three, it yet flickered before him; and though he had not seen them again as one sees people in the streets, and as if he might touch them if he would, yet were their images often before his mind's eye; and yet, as time wore, not so often, nor so troublously; and forsooth both to those about him and to himself, he seemed as a man well healed of his melancholy mood.

Now they left that fourth stead, and sailed over the seas and came to a fifth, a very great and fair city, which they had made more than seven months from Langton on Holm; and by this time was Walter taking heed and joyance in such things as were toward in that fair city, so far from his kindred, and especially he looked on the fair women there, and desired them, and loved them; but lightly, as befalleth young men.

Now this was the last country whereto the *Katherine* was boun; so there they abode some ten months in daily chaffer, and in pleasuring them in beholding all that there was of rare and goodly, and making merry with the merchants and the townsfolk, and the country-folk beyond the gates, and Walter was grown as busy and gay as a strong young man is like to be, and was as one who would fain be of some account amongst his own folk.

But at the end of this while, it befell on a day, as he was leaving his hostel for his booth in the market, and had the door in his hand, there stood before him three mariners in the guise of his own country, and with them was one of clerky aspect, whom he knew at once for his father's scrivener, Arnold Penstrong by name; and when Walter saw him his heart failed him and he cried out: Arnold, what tidings? Is all well with the folk at Langton?

Said Arnold: Evil tidings are come with me; matters are ill with thy folk; for I may not hide that thy father, Bartholomew Golden, is dead, God rest his soul.

At that word it was to Walter as if all that trouble which but now had sat so light upon him, was once again fresh and heavy, and that his past life of the last few months had never been; and it was to him as if he saw his father lying dead on his bed, and heard the folk lamenting about the house. He held his peace a while, and then he said in a voice as of an angry man: What, Arnold! And did he die in his bed, or how? For he was neither old nor ailing when we parted.

Said Arnold: Yea, in his bed he died: but first he was somewhat sword-bitten.

Yea, and how? quoth Walter.

Said Arnold: When thou wert gone, in a few days' wearing, thy father sent thy wife out of his house back to her kindred of the Reddings with no honour, and yet with no such shame as might have been, without blame to us of those who knew the tale of thee and her; which, God-a-mercy, will be pretty much the whole of the city.

Nevertheless, the Reddings took it amiss, and would have a mote with us Goldings to talk of booting. By ill-luck we yea-said that for the saving of the city's peace. But what betid? We met in our Gild-hall, and there befell the talk between us; and in that talk certain words could not be hidden, though they were none too seemly nor too meek. And the said words once spoken drew forth the whetted steel; and there then was the hewing and thrusting! Two of ours were slain outright on the floor, and four of theirs, and many were hurt on either side. Of these was thy father, for as thou mayst well deem, he was nought backward in the fray; but despite his hurts, two in the side and one on the arm, he went home on his own feet, and we deemed that we had come to our above. But well-a-way! It was an evil victory, whereas in ten days he died of his hurts.

God have his soul! But now, my master, thou mayst well wot that I am not come to tell thee this only, but moreover to bear the word of the kindred, to wit that thou come back with me straightway in the swift cutter which hath borne me and the tidings; and thou mayst look to it, that though she be swift and light, she is a keel full weatherly.

Then said Walter: This is a bidding of war. Come back will I, and the Reddings shall wot of my coming. Are ye all-boun?

Yea, said Arnold, we may up anchor this very day, or tomorrow morn at latest. But what aileth thee, master, that thou starest so wild over my shoulder? I pray thee take it not so much to heart! Ever it is the wont of fathers to depart this world before their sons.

But Walter's visage from wrathful red had become pale, and he pointed up street, and cried out: Look! Dost thou see?

See what, master? quoth Arnold:

What! Here cometh an ape in gay raiment; belike the beast of some jongleur. Nay, by God's wounds! 'Tis a man, though he be exceeding misshapen like a very devil. Yea and now there cometh a pretty maid going as if she were of his meney; and lo! Here, a most goodly and noble lady! Yea, I see; and doubtless she owneth both the two, and is of the greatest of the folk of this fair city; for on the maiden's ankle I saw an iron ring, which betokeneth thralldom amongst these aliens. But this is strange! For notest thou not how the folk in the street heed not this quaint show; nay not even the stately lady, though she be as lovely as a goddess of the gentiles, and beareth on her gems that would buy Langton twice over; surely they must be overwont to strange and gallant sights. But now, master, but now!

Yea, what is it? said Walter.

Why, master, they should not yet be gone out of eye-shot, yet gone they are.

What is become of them, are they sunk into the earth? Tush, man! said Walter, looking not on Arnold, but still staring down the street; they have gone into some house while thine eyes were turned from them a moment.

Nay, master, nay, said Arnold, mine eyes were not off them one instant of time. Well, said Walter, somewhat snappishly, they are gone now, and what have we to do to heed such toys, we with all this grief and strife on our hands? Now would I be alone to turn the matter of thine errand over in my mind. Meantime do thou tell the shipmaster Geoffrey and our other folk of these tidings, and thereafter get thee all ready; and come hither to me before sunrise tomorrow, and I shall be ready for my part; and so sail we back to Langton.

Therewith he turned him back into the house, and the others went their ways; but Walter sat alone in his chamber a long while, and pondered these things in his mind. And whiles he made up his mind that he would think no more of the vision of those three, but would fare back to Langton, and enter into the strife with the Reddings and quell them, or die else. But lo, when he was quite steady in this doom, and his heart was lightened thereby, he found that he thought no more of the Reddings and their strife, but as matters that were passed and done with, and that now he was thinking and devising if by any means he might find out in what land dwelt those three. And then again he strove to put that from him, saying that what he had seen was but meet for one brainsick, and a dreamer of dreams. But furthermore he thought, Yea, and was Arnold, who this last time had seen the images of those three, a dreamer of waking dreams? for he was nought wonted in such wise; then thought he: At least I am well content that he spake to me of their likeness, not I to him; for so I may tell that there was at least something before my eyes which grew not out of mine own brain. And yet again, why should I follow them; and what should I get by it; and indeed how shall I set about it?

Thus he turned the matter over and over; and at last, seeing that if he grew no foolisher over it, he grew no wiser, he became weary thereof, and bestirred him, and saw to the trussing up of his goods, and made all ready for his departure, and so wore the day and slept at nightfall; and at daybreak comes Arnold to lead him to their keel, which hight the *Bartholomew*. He tarried nought, and with few farewells went aboard ship, and an hour after they were in the open sea with the ship's head turned toward Langton on Holm.

IV

Now swift sailed the *Bartholomew* for four weeks toward the north-west with a fair wind, and all was well with ship and crew. Then the wind died out on even of a day, so that the ship scarce made way at all, though she rolled in a great swell of the sea, so great, that it seemed to ridge all the main athwart. Moreover, down in the west was a great bank of cloud huddled up in haze, whereas for twenty days past the sky had been clear, save for a few bright white clouds flying before the wind. Now the shipmaster, a man right cunning in his craft, looked long on sea and sky, and then turned and bade the mariners take in sail and be right heedful. And when Walter asked him what he looked for, and wherefore he spake not to him thereof, he said surlily: Why should I tell thee what any fool can see without telling, to wit that there is weather to hand?

So they abode what should befall, and Walter went to his room to sleep away the uneasy while, for the night was now fallen; and he knew no more till he was waked up by great hubbub and clamour of the shipmen, and the whipping of ropes, and thunder of flapping sails, and the tossing and weltering of the ship withal. But, being a very stout-hearted young man, he lay still in his room, partly because he was a landsman, and had no mind to tumble about amongst the shipmen and hinder them; and withal he said to himself: What matter whether I go down to the bottom of the sea, or come back to Langton, since either way my life or my death will take away from me the fulfilment of desire? Yet soothly if there hath been a shift of wind, that is not so ill; for then shall we be driven to other lands, and so at the least our home-coming shall be delayed, and other tidings may hap amidst of our tarrying. So let all be as it will.

So in a little while, in spite of the ship's wallowing and the tumult of the wind and waves, he fell asleep again, and woke no more till it was full daylight, and there was the shipmaster standing in the door of his room, the sea-water all streaming from his wet-weather raiment. He said to Walter: Young master, the sele of the day to thee! For by good hap we have gotten into another day. Now I shall tell thee that we have striven to beat, so as not to be driven off our course, but all would not avail, wherefore for these three hours we have been running before the wind; but, fair sir, so big hath been the sea that but for our ship being of the stoutest, and our men all yare, we had all grown exceeding wise concerning the ground of the mid-main. Praise be to St Nicholas and All Hallows! For though ye shall presently look upon a new sea, and maybe a new land to boot, yet is that better than looking on the ugly things down below.

Is all well with ship and crew then? said Walter.

Yea forsooth, said the shipmaster; verily the *Bartholomew* is the darling of Oak Woods; come up and look at it, how she is dealing with wind and waves all free from fear.

So Walter did on his foul-weather raiment, and went up on to the quarter-deck, and there indeed was a change of days; for the sea was dark and tumbling mountain-high, and the white-horses were running down the valleys thereof, and the clouds drave low over all, and bore a scud of rain along with them; and though there was but a rag of sail on her, the ship flew before the wind, rolling a great wash of water from bulwark to bulwark.

Walter stood looking on it all awhile, holding on by a stay-rope, and saying to himself that it was well that they were driving so fast toward new things.

Then the shipmaster came up to him and clapped him on the shoulder and said: Well, shipmate, cheer up! And now come below again and eat some meat, and drink a cup with me.

So Walter went down and ate and drank, and his heart was lighter than it had been since he had heard of his father's death, and the feud awaiting him at home, which forsooth he had deemed would stay his wanderings a weary while, and therewithal his hopes. But now it seemed as if he needs must wander, would he, would he not; and so it was that even this fed his hope; so sore his heart clung to that desire of his to seek home to those three that seemed to call him unto them.

V

Three days they drave before the wind, and on the fourth the clouds lifted, the sun shone out and the offing was clear; the wind had much abated, though it still blew a breeze, and was a headwind for sailing toward the country of Langton. So then the master said that, since they were bewildered, and the wind so ill to deal with, it were best to go still before the wind that they might make some land and get knowledge of their whereabouts from the folk thereof. Withal he said that he deemed the land not to be very far distant.

So did they, and sailed on pleasantly enough, for the weather kept on mending, and the wind fell till it was but a light breeze, yet still foul for Langton.

So wore three days, and on the eve of the third, the man from the topmast cried out that he saw land ahead; and so did they all before the sun was quite set, though it were but a cloud no bigger than a man's hand.

When night fell they struck not sail, but went forth toward the land fair and softly; for it was early summer, so that the nights were neither long nor dark.

But when it was broad daylight, they opened a land, a long shore of rocks and mountains, and nought else that they could see at first. Nevertheless, as day wore and they drew nigher, first they saw how the mountains fell away from the sea, and were behind a long wall of sheer cliff; and coming nigher yet, they beheld a green plain going up after a little in green bents and slopes to the feet of the said cliff-wall.

No city nor haven did they see there, not even when they were far nigher to the land; nevertheless, whereas they hankered for the peace of the green earth after all the tossing and unrest of the sea, and whereas also they doubted not to find at the least good and fresh water, and belike other bait in the plain under the mountains, they still sailed on not unmerrily; so that by nightfall they cast anchor in five-fathom water hard by the shore.

Next morning they found that they were lying a little way off the mouth of a river not right great; so they put out their boats and towed the ship up into the said river, and when they had gone up it for a mile or thereabouts they found the sea water failed, for little was the ebb and flow of the tide on that coast. Then was the river deep and clear, running between smooth grassy land like to meadows. Also on their left board they saw presently three head of neat cattle going, as if in a meadow of a homestead in their own land, and a few sheep; and thereafter, about a bow-draught from the river, they saw a little house of wood and straw-thatch under a wooded mound, and with orchard trees about it. They wondered little thereat, for they knew no cause why that land should not be builded, though it were in the far outlands. However, they drew their ship up to the bank, thinking that they would at least abide awhile and ask tidings and have some refreshing of the green plain, which was so lovely and pleasant.

But while they were busied herein they saw a man come out of the house, and down to the river to meet them; and they soon saw that he was tall and old, long-hoary of hair and beard, and clad mostly in the skins of beasts.

He drew nigh without any fear or mistrust, and coming close to them gave them the sele of the day in a kindly and pleasant voice. The shipmaster greeted him in his turn, and said withal: Old man, art thou the king of this country?

The elder laughed. It hath had none other a long while, said he; and at least there is no other son of Adam here to gainsay.

Thou art alone here then? said the master.

Yea, said the old man, save for the beasts of the field and the wood, and the creeping things, and fowl. Wherefore it is sweet to me to hear your voices.

Said the master: Where be the other houses of the town?

The old man laughed. Said he: When I said that I was alone, I meant that I was alone in the land and not only alone in this stead. There is no house save this betwixt the sea and the dwellings of the Bears, over the cliff-wall yonder, yea and a long way over it.

Yea, quoth the shipmaster grinning, and be the bears of thy country so man-like that they dwell in builded houses?

The old man shook his head. Sir, said he, as to their bodily fashion, it is altogether man like, save that they be one and all higher and bigger than most. For they be bears only in name; they be a nation of half wild men; for I have been told by them that there be many more than that tribe whose folk I have seen, and that they spread wide about behind these mountains from east to west. Now, sir, as to their souls and understandings I warrant them not; for miscreants they be, trowing neither in God nor his hallows.

Said the master: Trow they in Mahound then?

Nay, said the elder, I wot not for sure that they have so much as a false God; though I have it from them that they worship a certain woman with mickle worship.

Then spake Walter: Yea, good sir, and how knowest thou that? Dost thou deal with them at all?

Said the old man: Whiles some of that folk come hither and have of me what I can spare; a calf or two, or a half-dozen of lambs or hoggets; or a skin of wine or cyder of mine own making: and they give me in return such things as I can use, as skins of hart and bear and other peltries; for now I am old, I can but little of the hunting hereabout. Whiles, also, they bring little lumps of pure copper, and would give me gold also, but it is of little use in this lonely land. Sooth to say, to me they are not masterful or rough-handed; but glad am I that they have been here but of late, and are not like to come again this while; for terrible they are of aspect, and whereas ye be aliens, belike they would not hold their hands from off you; and moreover ye have weapons and other matters which they would covet sorely.

Quoth the master: Since thou dealest with these wild men, will ye not deal with us in chaffer? For whereas we are come from long travel, we hanker after fresh victual, and here aboard are many things which were for thine avail.

Said the old man: All that I have is yours, so that ye do but leave me enough till my next ingathering: of wine and cyder, such as it is, I have plenty for your service; ye may drink it till it is all gone, if ye will: a little corn and meal I have, but not much; yet are ye welcome thereto, since the standing corn in my garth is done blossoming, and I have other meat. Cheeses have I and dried fish; take what ye will thereof. But as to my neat and sheep, if ye have sore need of any, and will have them, I may not say you nay: but I pray you if ye may do without them, not to take my milch-beasts or their engenderers; for, as ye have heard me say, the Bear-folk have been here but of late, and they have had of me all I might spare: but now let me tell you, if ye long after flesh meat, that there is venison of hart and hind, yea, and of buck and doe, to be had on this plain, and about the little woods at the feet of the rock-wall yonder: neither are they exceeding wild; for since I may not take them, I scare them not, and no other man do they see to hurt them; for the Bear-folk come straight to my house, and fare straight home thence. But I will lead you the nighest way to where the venison is easiest to be gotten. As to the wares in your ship, if ye will give me aught I will take it with a good will; and chiefly if ye have a fair knife or two and a roll of linen cloth, that were a good refreshment to me. But in any case what I have to give is free to you and welcome.

The shipmaster laughed: Friend, said he, we can thee mickle thanks for all that thou biddest us. And wot well that we be no lifters or sea-thieves to take thy livelihood from thee. So tomorrow, if thou wilt, we will go with thee and upraise the hunt, and meanwhile we will come aland, and walk on the green grass, and water our ship with thy good fresh water.

So the old carle went back to his house to make them ready what cheer he might, and the shipmen, who were twenty and one, all told, what with the mariners and Arnold and Walter's servants, went ashore, all but two who watched the ship and abode their turn. They went well-weaponed, for both the master and Walter deemed wariness wisdom, lest all might not be so good as it seemed. They took of their sail-cloths ashore, and tilted them in on the meadow betwixt the house and the ship, and the carle brought them what he had for their avail, of fresh fruits, and cheeses, and milk, and wine, and cyder, and honey, and there they feasted nowise ill, and were right fain.

VI

But when they had done their meat and drink the master and the shipmen went about the watering of the ship, and the others strayed off along the meadow, so that presently Walter was left alone with the carle, and fell to speech with him and said: Father, me seemeth thou shouldest have some strange tale to tell, and as yet we have asked thee of nought save meat for our bellies: now if I ask thee concerning thy life, and how thou camest hither, and abided here, wilt thou tell me aught?

The old man smiled on him and said: Son, my tale were long to tell; and may happen concerning much thereof my memory should fail me; and withal there is grief therein, which I were loth to awaken: nevertheless if thou ask, I will answer as I may, and in any case will tell thee nought save the truth.

Said Walter: Well then, hast thou been long here?

Yea, said the carle, since I was a young man, and a stalwarth knight.

Said Walter: This house, didst thou build it, and raise these garths, and plant orchard and vineyard, and gather together the neat and the sheep, or did some other do all this for thee?

Said the carle: I did none of all this; there was one here before me, and I entered into his inheritance, as though this were a lordly manor, with a fair castle thereon, and all well stocked and plenished.

Said Walter: Didst thou find thy foregoer alive here?

Yea, said the elder, yet he lived but for a little while after I came to him.

He was silent a while, and then he said: I slew him: even so would he have it, though I bade him a better lot.

Said Walter: Didst thou come hither of thine own will?

Mayhappen, said the carle; who knoweth? Now have I no will to do either this or that. It is wont that maketh me do, or refrain.

Said Walter: Tell me this; why didst thou slay the man? Did he any scathe to thee?

Said the elder: When I slew him, I deemed that he was doing me all scathe: but now I know that it was not so. Thus it was; I would needs go where he had been before, and he stood in the path against me; and I overthrew him, and went on the way I would.

What came thereof? said Walter.

Evil came of it, said the carle.

Then was Walter silent a while, and the old man spake nothing; but there came a smile in his face that was both sly and somewhat sad. Walter looked on him and said: Was it from hence that thou wouldst go that road?

Yea, said the carle.

Said Walter: And now wilt thou tell me what that road was; whither it went and whereto it led, that thou must needs wend it, though thy first stride were over a dead man?

I will not tell thee, said the carle.

Then they held their peace, both of them, and thereafter got on to other talk of no import.

So wore the day till night came; and they slept safely, and on the morrow after they had broken their fast, the more part of them set off with the carle to the hunting, and they went, all of them, a three hours' faring towards the foot of the cliffs, which was all grown over with coppice, hazel and thorn, with here and there a big oak or ash-tree; there it was, said the old man, where the venison was most and best.

Of their hunting need nought be said, saving that when the carle had put them on the track of the deer and shown them what to do, he came back again with Walter, who had no great lust for the hunting, and sorely longed to have some more talk with the said carle. He for his part seemed nought loth thereto, and so led Walter to a mound or hillock amidst the clear of the plain, whence all was to be seen save where the wood covered it; but just before where they now lay down there was no wood, save low bushes, betwixt them and the rock-wall; and Walter noted that whereas otherwhere, save in one place whereto their eyes were turned, the cliffs seemed well-nigh or quite sheer, or indeed in some places beetling over, in that said place they fell away from each other on either side; and before this sinking was a slope or scree, that went gently up toward the sinking of the wall. Walter looked long and earnestly at this place, and spake nought, till the carle said: What! thou hast found something before thee to look on. What is it then?

Quoth Walter: Some would say that where yonder slopes run together up towards that sinking in the cliff-wall there will be a pass into the country beyond.

The carle smiled and said: Yea, son; nor, so saying, would they err; for that is the pass into the Bear-country, whereby those huge men come down to chaffer with me.

Yea, said Walter; and therewith he turned him a little, and scanned the rock-wall, and saw how a few miles from that pass it turned somewhat sharply toward the sea, narrowing the plain much there, till it made a bight, the face whereof looked well-nigh north, instead of west, as did the more part of the wall. And in the midst of that northern-looking bight was a dark place, which seemed to Walter like a downright shard in the cliff. For the face of the wall was a bleak grey, and it was but little furrowed.

So then Walter spake: Lo, old friend, there yonder is again a place that meseemeth is a pass; whereunto doth that one lead? And he pointed to it: but the old man did not follow the pointing of his finger, but, looking down on the ground, answered confusedly, and said:

Maybe: I wot not. I deem that it also leadeth into the Bear-country by a roundabout road. It leadeth into the far land.

Walter answered nought: for a strange thought had come uppermost in his mind, that the carle knew far more than he would say of that pass, and that he himself might be led thereby to find the wondrous three. He caught his breath hardly, and his heart knocked against his ribs; but he refrained from speaking for a long while; but at last he spake in a sharp hard voice, which he scarce knew for his own: Father, tell me, I adjure thee by God and All Hallows, was it through yonder shard that the road lay, when thou must needs make thy first stride over a dead man?

The old man spake not a while, then he raised his head, and looked Walter full in the eyes, and said in a steady voice: NO, IT WAS NOT. Thereafter they sat looking at each other a while; but at last Walter turned his eyes away, but knew not what they beheld nor where he was, but he was as one in a swoon. For he knew full well that the carle had lied to him, and that he might as well have said aye as no, and told him, that it verily was by that same shard that he had stridden over a dead man. Nevertheless he made as little semblance thereof as he might, and presently came to himself, and fell to talking of other matters, that had nought to do with the adventures of the land. But after a while he spake suddenly, and said: My master, I was thinking of a thing.

Yea, of what? said the carle.

Of this, said Walter; that here in this land be strange adventures toward, and that if we, and I in especial, were to turn our backs on them, and go home with nothing done, it were pity of our lives: for all will be dull and deedless there. I was deeming it were good if we tried the adventure.

What adventure? said the old man, rising up on his elbow and staring sternly on him.

Said Walter: The wending yonder pass to the eastward, whereby the huge men come to thee from out of the Bear-country; that we might see what should come thereof.

The carle leaned back again, and smiled and shook his head, and spake: That adventure were speedily proven: death would come of it, my son.

Yea, and how? said Walter.

The carle said: The big men would take thee, and offer thee up as a blood-offering to that woman, who is their Mawmet. And if ye go all, then shall they do the like with all of you.

Said Walter: Is that sure?

Dead sure, said the carle.

How knowest thou this? said Walter.

I have been there myself, said the carle.

Yea, said Walter, but thou camest away whole.

Art thou sure thereof? said the carle.

Thou art alive yet, old man, said Walter, for I have seen thee eat thy meat, which ghosts use not to do. And he laughed.

But the old man answered soberly: If I escaped, it was by this, that another woman saved me, and not often shall that befall. Nor wholly was I saved; my body escaped forsooth. But where is my soul? Where is my heart, and my life? Young man, I rede thee, try no such adventure; but go home to thy kindred if thou canst. Moreover, wouldst thou fare alone? The others shall hinder thee.

Said Walter: I am the master; they shall do as I bid them: besides, they will be well pleased to share my goods amongst them if I give them a writing to clear them of all charges which might be brought against them.

My son! my son! said the carle, I pray thee go not to thy death!

Walter heard him silently, but as if he were persuaded to refrain; and then the old man fell to, and told him much concerning this Bear-folk and their customs, speaking very freely of them; but Walter's ears were scarce open to this talk: whereas he deemed that he should have nought to do with those wild men; and he durst not ask again concerning the country whereto led the pass on the northward.

VII

As they were in converse thus, they heard the hunters blowing on their horns all together; whereon the old man arose, and said: I deem by the blowing that the hunt will be over and done, and that they be blowing on their fellows who have gone scatter-meal about the wood. It is now some five hours after noon, and thy men will be getting back with their venison, and will be fainest of the victuals they have caught; therefore will I hasten on before, and get ready fire and water and other matters for the cooking. Wilt thou come with me, young master, or abide thy men here?

Walter said lightly: I will rest and abide them here; since I cannot fail to see them hence as they go on their ways to thine house. And it may be well that I be at hand to command them and forbid, and put some order amongst them, for rough playmates they be, some of them, and now all heated with the hunting and the joy of the green earth. Thus he spoke, as if nought were toward save supper and bed; but inwardly hope and fear were contending in him, and again his heart beat so hard, that he deemed that the carle must surely hear it. But the old man took him but according to his outward seeming, and nodded his head, and went away quietly toward his house.

When he had been gone a little, Walter rose up heedfully; he had with him a scrip wherein was some cheese and hard fish, and a little flasket of wine; a short bow he had with him, and a quiver of arrows; and he was girt with a strong and good sword, and a wood knife withal. He looked to all this gear that it was nought amiss, and then speedily went down off the mound, and when he was come down, he found that it covered him from men coming out of the wood, if he went straight thence to that shard of the rock-wall where was the pass that led southward. Now it is no nay that thitherward he turned, and went wisely, lest the carle should make a backward cast and see him, or lest any straggler of his own folk might happen upon him.

For to say sooth, he deemed that did they wind him, they would be like to let him of his journey. He had noted the bearings of the cliffs nigh the shard, and whereas he could see their heads everywhere except from the depths of the thicket, he was not like to go astray.

He had made no great way ere he heard the horns blowing all together again in one place, and looking thitherward through the leafy boughs (for he was now amidst of a thicket) he saw his men thronging the mound, and had no doubt therefore that they were blowing on him; but being well under cover he heeded it nought, and lying still a little, saw them go down off the mound and go all of them toward the carle's house, still blowing as they went, but not faring scatter-meal. Wherefore it was clear that they were nought troubled about him.

So he went on his way to the shard; and there is nothing to say of his journey till he got before it with the last of the clear day, and entered it straightway. It was in sooth a downright breach or cleft in the rock-wall, and there was no hill or bent leading up to it, nothing but a tumble of stones before it, which was somewhat uneasy going, yet needed nought but labour to overcome it, and when he had got over this, and was in the very pass itself, he found it no ill going: forsooth at first it was little worse than a rough road betwixt two great stony slopes, though a little trickle of water ran down amidst of it. So, though it was so nigh nightfall, yet Walter pressed on, yea, and long after the very night was come. For the moon rose wide and bright a little after nightfall. But at last he had gone so long, and was so wearied, that he deemed it nought but wisdom to rest him, and so lay down on a piece of green-sward betwixt the stones, when he had eaten a morsel out of his satchel and drunk of the water of the stream. There as he lay, if he had any doubt of peril, his weariness soon made it all one to him, for presently he was sleeping as soundly as any man in Langton on Holm.

VIII

Day was yet young when he awoke: he leapt to his feet, and went down to the stream and drank of its waters, and washed the night off him in a pool thereof, and then set forth on his way again. When he had gone some three hours, the road, which had been going up all the way, but somewhat gently, grew steeper, and the bent on either side lowered, and lowered, till it sank at last altogether, and then was he on a rough mountain-neck with little grass and no water; save that now and again was a soft place with a flow amidst of it, and such places he must needs fetch a compass about, lest he be mired. He gave himself but little rest, eating what he needs must as he went. The day was bright and calm, so that the sun was never hidden, and he steered by it due south. All that day he went, and found no more change in that huge neck, save that whiles it was more and whiles less steep. A little before nightfall he happened on a shallow pool some twenty yards over; and he deemed it good to rest there, since there was water for his avail, though he might have made somewhat more out of the tail end of the day.

When dawn came again he awoke and arose, nor spent much time over his breakfast; but pressed on all he might; and now he said to himself, that whatsoever other peril were athwart his way, he was out of the danger of the chase of his own folk.

All this while he had seen no four-footed beast, save now and again a hill fox, and once some outlandish kind of hare; and of fowl but very few: a crow or two, a long-winged hawk and twice an eagle high up aloft.

Again, the third night, he slept in the stony wilderness, which still led him up and up. Only toward the end of the day, him-seemed that it had been less steep for a long while: otherwise nought was changed, on all sides it was nought but the endless neck, wherefrom nought could be seen, but some other part of itself. This fourth night withal he found no water whereby he might rest, so that he awoke parched, and longing to drink just when the dawn was at its coldest.

But on the fifth morrow the ground rose but little, and at last, when he had been going wearily a long while, and now, hard on noontide, his thirst grieved him sorely, he came on a spring welling out from under a high rock, the water wherefrom trickled feebly away. So eager was he to drink, that at first he heeded nought else; but when his thirst was fully quenched his eyes caught sight of the stream which flowed from the well, and he gave a shout, for lo! it was running south. Wherefore it was with a merry heart that he went on, and as he went, came on more streams, all running south or thereabouts. He hastened on all he might, but in despite of all the speed he made, and that he felt the land now going down southward, night overtook him in that same wilderness. Yet when he stayed at last for sheer weariness, he lay down in what he deemed by the moonlight to be a shallow valley, with a ridge at the southern end thereof.

He slept long, and when he awoke the sun was high in the heavens, and never was brighter or clearer morning on the earth than was that. He arose and ate of what little was yet left him, and drank of the water of a stream which he had followed the evening before, and beside which he had laid him down; and then set forth again with no great hope to come on new tidings that day. But yet when he was fairly afoot, him seemed that there was something new in the air which he breathed, that was soft and bore sweet scents home to him; whereas heretofore, and that especially for the last three or four days, it had been harsh and void, like the face of the desert itself.

So on he went, and presently was mounting the ridge aforesaid and, as oft happens when one climbs a steep place, he kept his eyes on the ground, till he felt he was on the top of the ridge. Then he stopped to take breath, and raised his head and looked, and lo! he was verily on the brow of the great mountain-neck, and down below him was the hanging of the great hill-slopes, which fell down, not slowly, as those he had been those days a-mounting, but speedily enough, though with little of broken places or sheer cliffs. But beyond this last of the desert there was before him a lovely land of wooded hills, green plains and little valleys, stretching out far and wide, till it ended at last in great blue mountains and white snowy peaks beyond them.

Then for very surprise of joy his spirit wavered, and he felt faint and dizzy, so that he was fain to sit down a while and cover his face with his hands. Presently he came to his sober mind again, and stood up and looked forth keenly, and saw no sign of any dwelling of man. But he said to himself that that might well be because the good and well-grassed land was still so far off, and that he might yet look to find men and their dwellings when he had left the mountain wilderness quite behind him. So therewith he fell to going his ways down the mountain, and lost little time therein, whereas he now had his livelihood to look to.

IX

What with one thing, what with another, as his having to turn out of his way for sheer rocks, or for slopes so steep that he might not try the peril of them, and again for bogs impassable, he was fully three days more before he had quite come out of the stony waste, and by that time, though he had never lacked water, his scanty victual was quite done, for all his careful husbandry thereof. But this troubled him little, whereas he looked to find wild fruits here and there, and to shoot some small deer, as hare or coney, and make a shift to cook the same, since he had with him flint and fire-steel. Moreover, the further he went, the surer he was that he should soon come across a dwelling, so smooth and fair as everything looked before him. And he had scant fear, save that he might happen on men who should enthrall him.

But when he was come down past the first green slopes, he was so worn, that he said to himself that rest was better than meat, so little as he had slept for the last three days; so he laid him down under an ash tree by a stream-side, nor asked what was o'clock, but had his fill of sleep, and even when he awoke in the fresh morning was little fain of rising, but lay betwixt sleeping and waking for some three hours more; then he arose, and went further down the next green bent, yet somewhat slowly because of his hunger weakness. And the scent of that fair land came up to him like the odour of one great nosegay.

So he came to where the land was level, and there were many trees, as oak and ash, and sweet-chestnut and wych-elm, and hornbeam and quicken-tree, not growing in a close wood or tangled thicket, but set as though in order on the flowery greensward, even as it might be in a great king's park.

So came he to a big bird-cherry, whereof many boughs hung low down laden with fruit: his belly rejoiced at the sight, and he caught hold of a bough, and fell to plucking and eating. But whiles he was amidst of this, he heard suddenly, close anigh him, a strange noise of roaring and braying, not very great, but exceeding fierce and terrible, and not like to the voice of any beast that he knew. As has been aforesaid, Walter was no faint-heart; but what with the weakness of his travail and hunger, what with the strangeness of his adventure and his loneliness, his spirit failed him; he turned round towards the noise, his knees shook and he trembled: this way and that he looked, and then gave a great cry and tumbled down in a swoon; for close before him, at his very feet, was the dwarf whose image he had seen before, clad in his yellow coat, and grinning up at him from his hideous hairy countenance.

How long he lay there as one dead, he knew not, but when he woke again there was the dwarf sitting on his hams close by him. And when he lifted up his head, the dwarf sent out that fearful harsh voice again; but this time Walter could make out words therein, and knew that the creature spoke and said:

How now! What art thou? Whence comest? What wantest?

Walter sat up and said: I am a man; I hight Golden Walter; I come from Langton; I want victual.

Said the dwarf, writhing his face grievously, and laughing forsooth: I know it all: I asked thee to see what wise thou wouldst lie. I was sent forth to look for thee; and I have brought thee loathsome bread with me, such as ye aliens must needs eat: take it!

Therewith he drew a loaf from a satchel which he bore, and thrust it towards Walter, who took it somewhat doubtfully for all his hunger.

The dwarf yelled at him: Art thou dainty, alien? Wouldst thou have flesh? Well, give me thy bow and an arrow or two, since thou art lazy-sick, and I will get thee a coney or a hare, or a quail maybe. Ah, I forgot; thou art dainty, and wilt not eat flesh as I do, blood and all together, but must needs half burn it in the fire, or mar it with hot water; as they say my Lady does: or as the Wretch, the Thing does; I know that, for I have seen It eating.

Nay, said Walter, this sufficeth; and he fell to eating the bread, which was sweet between his teeth. Then when he had eaten a while, for hunger compelled him, he said to the dwarf: But what meanest thou by the Wretch and the Thing? And what Lady is thy Lady?

The creature let out another wordless roar as of furious anger; and then the words came: It hath a face white and red, like to thine; and hands white as thine, yea, but whiter; and the like it is underneath its raiment, only whiter still: for I have seen It… yes, I have seen It; ah yes and yes and yes.

And therewith his words ran into gibber and yelling, and he rolled about and smote at the grass: but in a while he grew quiet again and sat still, and then fell to laughing horribly again, and then said: But thou, fool, wilt think It fair if thou fallest into It's hands, and wilt repent it thereafter, as I did. Oh, the mocking and gibes of It, and the tears and shrieks of It; and the knife! What! Sayest thou of my Lady?… What Lady? O alien, what other Lady is there? And what shall I tell thee of her? It is like that she made me, as she made the Bear men. But she made not the Wretch, the Thing; and she hateth It sorely, as I do. And some day to come…

Thereat he brake off and fell to wordless yelling a long while, and thereafter spake all panting: Now I have told thee overmuch, and O if my Lady come to hear thereof. Now I will go.

And therewith he took out two more loaves from his wallet, and tossed them to Walter, and so turned and went his ways; whiles walking upright, as Walter had seen his image on the quay of Langton; whiles bounding and rolling like a ball thrown by a lad; whiles scuttling along on all-fours like an evil beast, and ever and anon giving forth that harsh and evil cry.

Walter sat a while after he was out of sight, so stricken with horror and loathing and a fear of he knew not what, that he might not move. Then he plucked up a heart, and looked to his weapons and put the other loaves into his scrip.

Then he arose and went his ways wondering, yea and dreading, what kind of creature he should next fall in with. For soothly it seemed to him that it would be worse than death if they were all such as this one; and that if it were so, he must needs slay and be slain.

X

But as he went on through the fair and sweet land so bright and sun-litten, and he now rested and fed, the horror and fear ran off from him, and he wandered on merrily, neither did aught befall him save the coming of night, when he laid him down under a great spreading oak with his drawn sword ready to hand, and fell asleep at once, and woke not till the sun was high.

Then he arose and went on his way again; and the land was no worser than yesterday; but even better, it might be; the greensward more flowery, the oaks and chestnuts greater. Deer of diverse kinds he saw, and might easily have got his meat thereof; but he meddled not with them since he had his bread, and was timorous of lighting a fire. Withal he doubted little of having some entertainment; and that, might be, nought evil; since even that fearful dwarf had been courteous to him after his kind, and had done him good and not harm. But of the happening on the Wretch and the Thing, whereof the dwarf spake, he was yet somewhat afeard.

After he had gone a while and whenas the summer morn was at its brightest, he saw a little way ahead a grey rock rising up from amidst of a ring of oak trees; so he turned thither straightway; for in this plain land he had seen no rocks heretofore; and as he went he saw that there was a fountain gushing out from under the rock, which ran thence in a fair little stream. And when he had the rock and the fountain and the stream clear before him, lo! a child of Adam sitting beside the fountain under the shadow of the rock. He drew a little nigher, and then he saw that it was a woman, clad in green like the sward whereon she lay. She was playing with the welling out of the water, and she had trussed up her sleeves to the shoulder that she might thrust her bare arms therein. Her shoes of black leather lay on the grass beside her, and her feet and legs yet shone with the brook.

Belike amidst the splashing and clatter of the water she did not hear him drawing nigh, so that he was close to her before she lifted up her face and saw him, and he beheld her, that it was the maiden of the thrice-seen pageant. She reddened when she saw him, and hastily covered up her legs with her gown skirt, and drew down the sleeves over her arms, but otherwise stirred not. As for him, he stood still, striving to speak to her; but no word might he bring out, and his heart beat sorely.

But the maiden spake to him in a clear sweet voice, wherein was now no trouble: Thou art an alien, art thou not? For I have not seen thee before.

Yea, he said, I am an alien; wilt thou be good to me?

She said: And why not? I was afraid at first, for I thought it had been the King's Son. I looked to see none other; for of goodly men he has been the only one here in the land this long while, till thy coming.

He said: Didst thou look for my coming at about this time?

O nay, she said; how might I?

Said Walter: I wot not; but the other man seemed to be looking for me, and knew of me, and he brought me bread to eat.

She looked on him anxiously, and grew somewhat pale, as she said: What other one?

Now Walter did not know what the dwarf might be to her, fellow-servant or what not, so he would not show his loathing of him; but answered wisely: The little man in the yellow raiment.

But when she heard that word, she went suddenly very pale, and leaned her head aback and beat the air with her hands; but said presently in a faint voice: I pray thee talk not of that one while I am by, nor even think of him, if thou mayest forbear.

He spake not, and she was a little while before she came to herself again;

then she opened her eyes, and looked upon Walter and smiled kindly on him, as though to ask his pardon for having scared him. Then she rose up in her place, and stood before him; and they were nigh together, for the stream betwixt them was little.

But he still looked anxiously upon her and said: Have I hurt thee? I pray thy pardon.

She looked on him more sweetly still, and said: O nay; thou wouldst not hurt me, thou!

Then she blushed very red, and he in like wise; but afterwards she turned pale, and laid a hand on her breast, and Walter cried out hastily: O me! I have hurt thee again. Wherein have I done amiss?

In nought, in nought, she said; but I am troubled, I wot not wherefore; some thought hath taken hold of me, and I know it not. Mayhappen in a little while I shall know what troubles me. Now I bid thee depart from me a little, and I will abide here; and when thou comest back, it will either be that I have found it out or not; and in either case I will tell thee.

She spoke earnestly to him; but he said: How long shall I abide away? Her face was troubled as she answered him: For no long while.

He smiled on her and turned away, and went a space to the other side of the oak trees, whence she was still within eyeshot. There he abode until the time seemed long to him; but he schooled himself and forbore; for he said: Lest she send me away again. So he abided until again the time seemed long to him, and she called not to him: but once again he forbore to go; then at last he arose, and his heart beat and he trembled, and he walked back again speedily, and came to the maiden, who was still standing by the rock of the spring, her arms hanging down, her eyes downcast. She looked up at him as he drew nigh, and her face changed with eagerness as she said: I am glad thou art come back, though it be no long while since thy departure (sooth to say it was scarce half an hour in all). Nevertheless I have been thinking many things, and thereof will I now tell thee.

He said: Maiden, there is a river betwixt us, though it be no big one. Shall I not stride over, and come to thee, that we may sit down together side by side on the green grass?

Nay, she said, not yet; tarry a while till I have told thee of matters. I must now tell thee of my thoughts in order.

Her colour went and came now, and she plaited the folds of her gown with restless fingers. At last she said: Now the first thing is this; that though thou hast seen me first only within this hour, thou hast set thine heart upon me to have me for thy speech-friend and thy darling. And if this be not so, then is all my speech, yea and all my hope, come to an end at once.

O yea! said Walter, even so it is: but how thou hast found this out I wot not; since now for the first time I say it, that thou art indeed my love, and my dear and my darling.

Hush, she said, hush! lest the wood have ears, and thy speech is loud: abide, and I shall tell thee how I know it. Whether this thy love shall outlast the first time that thou holdest my body in thine arms, I wot not, nor dost thou. But sore is my hope that it may be so; for I also, though it be but scarce an hour since I set eyes on thee, have cast mine eyes on thee to have thee for my love and my darling, and my speech-friend. And this is how I wot that thou lovest me, my friend. Now is all this dear and joyful, and overflows my heart with sweetness. But now must I tell thee of the fear and the evil which lieth behind it.

Then Walter stretched out his hands to her, and cried out: Yea, yea! But whatever evil entangle us, now we both know these two things, to wit, that thou lovest me, and I thee. Wilt thou not come hither, that I may cast mine arms about thee and kiss thee, if not thy kind lips or thy friendly face at all, yet at least thy dear hand: yea, that I may touch thy body in some wise?

She looked on him steadily, and said softly: Nay, this above all things must not be; and that it may not be is a part of the evil which entangles us. But hearken, friend, once again I tell thee that thy voice is over-loud in this wilderness fruitful of evil. Now I have told thee, indeed, of two things whereof we both wot; but next I must needs tell thee of things whereof I wot, and thou wottest not. Yet this were better, that thou pledge thy word not to touch so much as one of my hands, and that we go together a little way hence away from these tumbled stones, and sit down upon the open greensward; whereas here is cover if there be spying abroad.

Again, as she spoke, she turned very pale; but Walter said: Since it must be so, I pledge thee my word to thee as I love thee.

And therewith she knelt down, and did on her foot-gear, and then sprang lightly over the rivulet; and then the twain of them went side by side some half a furlong thence, and sat down, shadowed by the boughs of a slim quicken-tree growing up out of the greensward, whereon for a good space around was neither bush nor brake.

There began the maiden to talk soberly, and said: This is what I must needs say to thee now, that thou art come into a land perilous for anyone that loveth aught of good; from which, forsooth, I were fain that thou wert gotten away safely, even though I should die of longing for thee. As for myself, my peril is, in a measure, less than thine; I mean the peril of death. But lo, thou, this iron on my foot is token that I am a thrall, and thou knowest in what wise thralls must pay for transgressions. Furthermore, of what I am, and how I came hither, time would fail me to tell; but somewhile, maybe, I shall tell thee. I serve an evil mistress, of whom I may say that scarce I wot if she be a woman or not; but by some creatures is she accounted for a god, and as a god is heried; and surely never god was crueller nor colder than she. Me she hateth sorely; yet if she hated me little or nought, small were the gain to me if it were her pleasure to deal hardly by me. But as things now are, and are like to be, it would not be for her pleasure, but for her pain and loss, to make an end of me, therefore, as I said e'en now, my mere life is not in peril with her; unless, perchance, some sudden passion get the better of her, and she slay me, and repent of it thereafter. For so it is, that if it be the least evil of her conditions that she is wanton, at least wanton she is to the letter. Many a time hath she cast the net for the catching of some goodly young man; and her latest prey (save it be thou) is the young man whom I named, when first I saw thee, by the name of the King's Son. He is with us yet, and I fear him; for of late hath he wearied of her, though it is but plain truth to say of her, that she is the wonder of all Beauties of the World. He hath wearied of her, I say, and hath cast his eyes upon me, and if I were heedless, he would betray me to the uttermost of the wrath of my mistress. For needs must I say of him, though he be a goodly man, and now fallen into thralldom, that he hath no bowels of compassion; but is a dastard, who for an hour's pleasure would undo me, and thereafter stand by smiling and taking my mistress's pardon with good cheer, while for me would be no pardon. Seest thou, therefore, how it is with me between these two cruel fools? And moreover there are others of whom I will not even speak to thee.

And therewith she put her hands before her face, and wept, and murmured: Who shall deliver me from this death in life?

But Walter cried out: For what else am I come hither, I, I?

And it was a near thing that he did not take her in his arms, but he remembered his pledged word, and drew aback from her in terror, whereas he had an inkling of why she would not suffer it; and he wept with her.

But suddenly the Maid left weeping, and said in a changed voice: Friend, whereas thou speakest of delivering me, it is more like that I shall deliver thee. And now I pray thy pardon for thus grieving thee with my grief, and that more especially because thou mayst not solace thy grief with kisses and caresses; but so it was, that for once I was smitten by the thought of the anguish of this land, and the joy of all the world besides.

Therewith she caught her breath in a half-sob, but refrained her and went on: Now dear friend and darling, take good heed to all that I shall say to thee, whereas thou must do after the teaching of my words. And first, I deem by the monster having met thee at the gates of the land, and refreshed thee, that the Mistress hath looked for thy coming; nay, by thy coming hither at all, that she hath cast her net and caught thee. Hast thou noted aught that might seem to make this more like?

Said Walter: Three times in full daylight have I seen go past me the images of the monster and thee and a glorious lady, even as if ye were alive.

And therewith he told her in few words how it had gone with him since that day on the quay at Langton.

She said: Then it is no longer perhaps, but certain, that thou art her latest catch; and even so I deemed from the first: and, dear friend, this is why I have not suffered thee to kiss or caress me, so sore as I longed for thee. For the Mistress will have thee for her only, and hath lured thee hither for nought else; and she is wise in wizardry (even as some deal am I), and wert thou to touch me with hand or mouth on my naked flesh, yea, or were it even my raiment, then would she scent the savour of thy love upon me, and then, though it may be she would spare thee, she would not spare me.

Then was she silent a little, and seemed very downcast, and Walter held his peace from grief and confusion and helplessness; for of wizardry he knew nought.

At last the Maid spake again, and said: Nevertheless we will not die redeless. Now thou must look to this, that from henceforward it is thee, and not the King's Son, whom she desireth, and that so much the more that she hath not set eyes on thee. Remember this, whatsoever her seeming may be to thee. Now, therefore, shall the King's Son be free, though he know it not, to cast his love on whomso he will; and, in a way, I also shall be free to yeasay him. Though, forsooth, so fulfilled is she with malice and spite, that even then she may turn round on me to punish me for doing that which she would have me do. Now let me think of it.

Then was she silent a good while, and spoke at last: Yea, all things are perilous, and a perilous rede I have thought of, whereof I will not tell thee as yet; so waste not the short while by asking me. At least the worst will be no worse than what shall come if we strive not against it. And now, my friend, amongst perils it is growing more and more perilous that we twain should be longer together. But I would say one thing yet; and maybe another thereafter. Thou hast cast thy love upon one who will be true to thee, whatsoever may befall; yet is she a guileful creature, and might not help it her life long, and now for thy very sake must needs be more guileful now than ever before. And as for me, the guileful, my love have I cast upon a lovely man, and one true and simple, and a stout-heart; but at such a pinch is he, that if he withstand all temptation, his withstanding may belike undo both him and me. Therefore swear we both of us, that by both of us shall all guile and all falling away be forgiven on the day when we shall be free to love each the other as our hearts will.

Walter cried out: O love, I swear it indeed! thou art my Hallow, and I will swear it as on the relics of a Hallow; on thy hands and thy feet I swear it.

The words seemed to her a dear caress; and she laughed, and blushed, and looked full kindly on him; and then her face grew solemn, and she said: On thy life I swear it!

Then she said: Now is there nought for thee to do but to go hence straight to the Golden House, which is my Mistress's house, and the only house in this land (save one which I may not see), and lieth southward no long way. How she will deal with thee, I wot not; but all I have said of her and thee and the King's Son is true. Therefore I say to thee, be wary and cold at heart, whatsoever outward semblance thou mayst make. If thou have to yield thee to her, then yield rather late than early, so as to gain time. Yet not so late as to seem shamed in yielding for fear's sake. Hold fast to thy life, my friend, for in warding that, thou wardest me from grief without remedy. Thou wilt see me ere long; it may be tomorrow, it may be some days hence. But forget not, that what I may do, that I am doing. Take heed also that thou pay no more heed to me, or rather less, than if thou wert meeting a maiden of no account in the streets of thine own town. O my love! Barren is this first farewell, as was our first meeting; but surely shall there be another meeting better than the first, and the last farewell may be long and long yet.

Therewith she stood up, and he knelt before her a little while without any word, and then arose and went his ways; but when he had gone a space he turned about, and saw her still standing in the same place; she stayed a moment when she saw him turn, and then herself turned about.

So he departed through the fair land, and his heart was full with hope and fear as he went.

XI

It was but a little after noon when Walter left the Maid behind: he steered south by the sun, as the Maid had bidden him, and went swiftly; for, as a good knight wending to battle, the time seemed long to him till he should meet the foe.

So an hour before sunset he saw something white and gay gleaming through the boles of the oak trees, and presently there was clear before him a most goodly house builded of white marble, carved all about with knots and imagery, and the carven folk were all painted of their lively colours, whether it were their raiment or their flesh, and the housings wherein they stood all done with gold and fair hues. Gay were the windows of the house; and there was a pillared porch before the great door, with images betwixt the pillars both of men and beasts: and when Walter looked up to the roof of the house, he saw that it gleamed and shone; for all the tiles were of yellow metal, which he deemed to be of very gold.

All this he saw as he went, and tarried not to gaze upon it; for he said, belike there will be time for me to look on all this before I die. But he said also, that, though the house was not of the greatest, it was beyond compare of all houses of the world.

Now he entered it by the porch, and came into a hall many-pillared, and vaulted over, the walls painted with gold and ultramarine, the floor dark and spangled with many colours, and the windows glazed with knots and pictures. Mid-most thereof was a fountain of gold, whence the water ran two ways in gold-lined runnels, spanned twice with little bridges of silver. Long was that hall, and now not very light, so that Walter was come past the fountain before he saw any folk therein: then he looked up toward the high-seat, and him-seemed that a great light shone thence, and dazzled his eyes; and he went on a little way, and then fell on his knees; for there before him on the high-seat sat that wondrous Lady, whose lively image had been shown to him thrice before; and she was clad in gold and jewels, as he had erst seen her. But now she was not alone; for by her side sat a young man, goodly enough, so far as Walter might see him, and most richly clad, with a jewelled sword by his side and a chaplet of gems on his head.

They held each other by the hand, and seemed to be in dear converse together; but they spake softly, so that Walter might not hear what they said, till at last the man spake aloud to the Lady: Seest thou not that there is a man in the hall?

Yea, she said, I see him yonder, kneeling on his knees; let him come nigher and give some account of himself.

So Walter stood up and drew nigh, and stood there, all shamefaced and confused, looking on those twain, and wondering at the beauty of the Lady. As for the man, who was slim, and black-haired, and straight-featured, for all his goodliness Walter accounted him little, and nowise deemed him to look chieftain-like.

Now the Lady spake not to Walter any more than erst; but at last the man said: Why doest thou not kneel as thou didst erewhile?

Walter was on the point of giving him back a fierce answer; but the Lady spake and said: Nay, friend, it matters not whether he kneel or stand; but he may say, if he will, what he would have of me, and wherefore he is come hither.

Then spake Walter, for as wroth and ashamed as he was: Lady, I have strayed into this land, and have come to thine house as I suppose, and if I be not welcome, I may well depart straightway, and seek a way out of thy land, if thou wouldst drive me thence, as well as out of thine house.

Thereat the Lady turned and looked on him, and when her eyes met his, he felt a pang of fear and desire mingled shoot through his heart. This time she spoke to him; but coldly, without either wrath or any thought of him: New-comer, she said, I have not bidden thee hither; but here mayst thou abide a while if thou wilt; nevertheless, take heed that here is no King's Court. There is, forsooth, a folk that serveth me (or, it may be, more than one), of whom thou wert best to know nought. Of others I have but two servants, whom thou wilt see; and the one is a strange creature, who should scare thee or scathe thee with a good will, but of a good will shall serve nought save me; the other is a woman, a thrall, of little avail, save that, being compelled, she will work woman's service for me, but whom none else shall compel… Yea, but what is all this to thee; or to me that I should tell it to thee? I will not drive thee away; but if thine entertainment please thee not, make no plaint thereof to me, but depart at thy will. Now is this talk betwixt us overlong, since, as thou seest, I and this King's Son are in converse together. Art thou a King's Son?

Nay, Lady, said Walter, I am but of the sons of the merchants.

It matters not, she said; go thy ways into one of the chambers.

And straightway she fell a-talking to the man who sat beside her concerning the singing of the birds beneath her window in the morning; and of how she had bathed her that day in a pool of the woodlands, when she had been heated with hunting, and so forth; and all as if there had been none there save her and the King's Son.

But Walter departed all ashamed, as though he had been a poor man thrust away from a rich kinsman's door; and he said to himself that this woman was hateful, and nought loveworthy, and that she was little like to tempt him, despite all the fairness of her body.

No one else he saw in the house that even: he found meat and drink duly served on a fair table, and thereafter he came on a goodly bed, and all things needful, but no child of Adam to do him service, or bid him welcome or warning. Nevertheless he ate and drank, and slept, and put off thought of all these things till the morrow, all the more as he hoped to see the kind maiden some time betwixt sunrise and sunset on that new day.

XII

He arose betimes, but found no one to greet him, neither was there any sound of folk moving within the fair house; so he but broke his fast, and then went forth and wandered amongst the trees, till he found him a stream to bathe in, and after he had washed the night off him he lay down under a tree thereby for a while, but soon turned back toward the house, lest perchance the Maid should come thither and he should miss her.

It should be said that half a bow-shot from the house on that side (i.e. due north thereof) was a little hazel-brake, and round about it the trees were smaller of kind than the oaks and chestnuts he had passed through before, being mostly of birch and quicken-beam and young ash, with small wood betwixt them; so now he passed through the thicket, and, coming to the edge thereof, beheld the Lady and the King's Son walking together hand in hand, full lovingly by seeming.

He deemed it unmeet to draw back and hide him, so he went forth past them toward the house. The King's Son scowled on him as he passed, but the Lady, over whose beauteous face flickered the joyous morning smiles, took no more heed of him than if he had been one of the trees of the wood. But she had been so high and disdainful with him the evening before, that he thought little of that. The twain went on, skirting the hazel-copse, and he could not choose but turn his eyes on them, so sorely did the Lady's beauty draw them. Then befell another thing; for behind them the boughs of the hazels parted, and there stood that little evil thing, he or another of his kind; for he was quite unclad, save by his fell of yellowy-brown hair, and that he was girt with a leathern girdle, wherein was stuck an ugly two-edged knife: he stood upright a moment, and cast his eyes at Walter and grinned, but not as if he knew him; and scarce could Walter say whether it were the one he had seen, or another: then he cast himself down on his belly, and fell to creeping through the long grass like a serpent, following the footsteps of the Lady and her lover; and now, as he crept, Walter deemed, in his loathing, that the creature was liker to a ferret than aught else. He crept on marvellous swiftly, and was soon clean out of sight. But Walter stood staring after him for a while, and then lay down by the copse-side, that he might watch the house and the entry thereof; for he thought, now perchance presently will the kind maiden come hither to comfort me with a word or two. But hour passed by hour, and still she came not; and still he lay there, and thought of the Maid, and longed for her kindness and wisdom, till he could not refrain his tears, and wept for the lack of her. Then he arose, and went and sat in the porch, and was very downcast of mood.

But as he sat there, back comes the Lady again, the King's Son leading her by the hand; they entered the porch, and she passed by him so close that the odour of her raiment filled all the air about him, and the sleekness of her side nigh touched him, so that he could not fail to note that her garments were somewhat disarrayed, and that she kept her right hand (for her left the King's Son held) to her bosom to hold the cloth together there, whereas the rich raiment had been torn off from her right shoulder. As they passed by him, the King's Son once more scowled on him, wordless, but even more fiercely than before; and again the Lady heeded him nought.

After they had gone on a while, he entered the hall, and found it empty from end to end, and no sound in it save the tinkling of the fountain; but there was victual set on the board. He ate and drank thereof to keep life lusty within him, and then went out again to the wood-side to watch and to long; and the time hung heavy on his hands because of the lack of the fair Maiden.

He was of mind not to go into the house to his rest that night, but to sleep under the boughs of the forest. But a little after sunset he saw a bright-clad image moving amidst the carven images of the porch, and the King's Son came forth and went straight to him, and said: Thou art to enter the house, and go into thy chamber forthwith, and by no means to go forth of it betwixt sunset and sunrise. My Lady will not away with thy prowling round the house in the night-tide.

Therewith he turned away, and went into the house again; and Walter followed him soberly, remembering how the Maid had bidden him forbear. So he went to his chamber, and slept.

But amidst of the night he awoke and deemed that he heard a voice not far off, so he crept out of his bed and peered around, lest, perchance, the Maid had come to speak with him; but his chamber was dusk and empty: then he went to the window and looked out, and saw the moon shining bright and white upon the greensward. And lo! the Lady walking with the King's Son, and he clad in thin and wanton raiment, but she in nought else save what God had given her of long, crispy yellow hair. Then was Walter ashamed to look on her, seeing that there was a man with her, and gat him back to his bed; but yet a long while ere he slept again he had the image before his eyes of the fair woman on the dewy moonlit grass.

The next day matters went much the same way, and the next also, save that his sorrow was increased, and he sickened sorely of hope deferred. On the fourth day also the forenoon wore as erst; but in the heat of the afternoon Walter sought to the hazel-copse, and laid him down there hard by a little clearing thereof, and slept from very weariness of grief. There, after a while, he woke with words still hanging in his ears, and he knew at once that it was they twain talking together.

The King's Son had just done his say, and now it was the Lady beginning in her honey-sweet voice, low but strong, wherein even was a little of huskiness; she said: Otto, belike it were well to have a little patience, till we find out what the man is, and whence he cometh; it will always be easy to rid us of him; it is but a word to our Dwarf-king, and it will be done in a few minutes.

Patience! said the King's Son, angrily; I wot not how to have patience with him; for I can see of him that he is rude and violent and headstrong, and a low-born wily one. Forsooth, he had patience enough with me the other even, when I rated him in, like the dog that he is, and he had no manhood to say one word to me. Soothly, as he followed after me, I had a mind to turn about and deal him a buffet on the face, to see if I could but draw one angry word from him.

The Lady laughed, and said: Well, Otto, I know not; that which thou deemest dastardy in him may be but prudence and wisdom, and he an alien, far from his friends and nigh to his foes. Perchance we shall yet try him what he is. Meanwhile, I rede thee try him not with buffets, save he be weaponless and with bounden hands; or else I deem that but a little while shalt thou be fain of thy blow.

Now when Walter heard her words and the voice wherein they were said, he might not forbear being stirred by them, and to him, all lonely there, they seemed friendly.

But he lay still, and the King's Son answered the Lady and said: I know not what is in thine heart concerning this runagate, that thou shouldst bemock me with his valiancy, whereof thou knowest nought. If thou deem me unworthy of thee, send me back safe to my father's country; I may look to have worship there; yea, and the love of fair women belike.

Therewith it seemed as if he had put forth his hand to the Lady to caress her, for she said: Nay, lay not thine hand on my shoulder, for today and now it is not the hand of love, but of pride and folly, and would-be mastery. Nay, neither shalt thou rise up and leave me until thy mood is softer and kinder to me. Then was there silence betwixt them a while, and thereafter the King's Son spake in a wheedling voice: My goddess, I pray thee pardon me! But canst thou wonder that I fear thy wearying of me, and am therefore peevish and jealous? Thou so far above the Queens of the World, and I a poor youth that without thee were nothing!

She answered nought, and he went on again: Was it not so, O goddess, that this man of the sons of the merchants was little heedful of thee, and thy loveliness and thy majesty?

She laughed and said: Maybe he deemed not that he had much to gain of us, seeing thee sitting by our side, and whereas we spake to him coldly and sternly and disdainfully. Withal, the poor youth was dazzled and shamefaced before us; that we could see in the eyes and the mien of him.

Now this she spoke so kindly and sweetly, that again was Walter all stirred thereat; and it came into his mind that it might be she knew he was anigh and hearing her, and that she spake as much for him as for the King's Son: but that one answered: Lady, didst thou not see somewhat else in his eyes, to wit, that they had but of late looked on some fair woman other than thee? As for me, I deem it not so unlike that on the way to thine hall he may have fallen in with thy Maid.

He spoke in a faltering voice, as if shrinking from some storm that might come. And forsooth the Lady's voice was changed as she answered, though there was no outward heat in it; rather it was sharp and eager and cold at once. She said: Yea, that is not ill thought of; but we may not always keep our thrall in mind. If it be so as thou deemest, we shall come to know it most like when we next fall in with her; or if she hath been shy this time, then shall she pay the heavier for it; for we will question her by the Fountain in the Hall as to what betid by the Fountain of the Rock.

Spake the King's Son, faltering yet more: Lady, were it not better to question the man himself? The Maid is stout-hearted, and will not be speedily quelled into a true tale; whereas the man I deem of no account.

No, no, said the Lady sharply, it shall not be.

Then was she silent a while; and then she said: How if the man should prove to be our master?

Nay, our Lady, said the King's Son, thou art jesting with me; thou and thy might and thy wisdom, and all that thy wisdom may command, to be over-mastered by a gangrel churl!

But how if I will not have it command, King's Son? said the Lady: I tell thee I know thine heart, but thou knowest not mine. But be at peace! For since thou hast prayed for this woman... nay, not with thy words, I wot, but with thy trembling hands, and thine anxious eyes, and knitted brow... I say, since thou hast prayed for her so earnestly, she shall escape this time. But whether it will be to her gain in the long run, I misdoubt me. See thou to that, Otto! Thou who hast held me in thine arms so oft. And now thou mayest depart if thou wilt.

It seemed to Walter as if the King's Son were dumbfoundered at her words: he answered nought, and presently he rose from the ground, and went his ways slowly toward the house. The Lady lay there a little while, and then went her ways also; but turned away from the house toward the wood at the other end thereof, whereby Walter had first come thither.

As for Walter, he was confused in mind and shaken in spirit; and withal he seemed to see guile and cruel deeds under the talk of those two, and waxed wrathful thereat. Yet he said to himself, that nought might he do, but was as one bound hand and foot, till he had seen the Maid again.

XIII

Next morning was he up betimes, but he was cast down and heavy of heart, not looking for aught else to betide than had betid those last four days. But otherwise it fell out; for when he came down into the hall, there was the Lady sitting on the high-seat all alone, clad but in a coat of white linen; and she turned her head when she heard his footsteps, and looked on him, and greeted him, and said: Come hither, guest.

So he went and stood before her, and she said: Though as yet thou hast had no welcome here, and no honour, it hath not entered into thine heart to flee from us; and to say sooth, that is well for thee, for flee away from our hand thou mightest not, nor mightest thou depart without our furtherance. But for this we can thee thank, that thou hast abided here our bidding, and eaten thine heart through the heavy wearing of four days, and made no plaint. Yet I cannot deem thee a dastard; thou so well knit and shapely of body, so clear-eyed and bold of visage. Wherefore now I ask thee, art thou willing to do me service, thereby to earn thy guesting?

Walter answered her, somewhat faltering at first, for he was astonished at the change which had come over her; for now she spoke to him in friendly wise, though indeed as a great lady would speak to a young man ready to serve her in all honour. Said he: Lady, I can thee thank humbly and heartily in that thou biddest me do thee service; for these days past I have loathed the emptiness of the hours, and nought better could I ask for than to serve so glorious a Mistress in all honour.

She frowned somewhat, and said: Thou shalt not call me Mistress; there is but one who so calleth me, that is my thrall; and thou art none such. Thou shalt call me Lady, and I shall be well pleased that thou be my squire, and for this present thou shalt serve me in the hunting. So get thy gear; take thy bow and arrows, and gird thee to thy sword. For in this fair land may one find beasts more perilous than be buck or hart. I go now to array me; we will depart while the day is yet young; for so make we the summer day the fairest.

He made obeisance to her, and she arose and went to her chamber, and Walter dight himself, and then abode her in the porch; and in less than an hour she came out of the hall, and Walter's heart beat when he saw that the Maid followed her hard at heel, and scarce might he school his eyes not to gaze over-eagerly at his dear friend. She was clad even as she was before, and was changed in no wise, save that love troubled her face when she first beheld him, and she had much ado to master it: howbeit the Mistress heeded not the trouble of her, or made no semblance of heeding it, till the Maiden's face was all according to its wont.

But this Walter found strange, that after all that disdain of the Maid's thralldom which he had heard of the Mistress, and after all the threats against her, now was the Mistress become mild and debonaire to her, as a good lady to her good maiden. When Walter bowed the knee to her, she turned unto the Maid, and said: Look thou, my Maid, at this fair new Squire that I have gotten! Will not he be valiant in the greenwood? And see whether he be well shapen or not. Doth he not touch thine heart, when thou thinkest of all the woe, and fear, and trouble of the Wood beyond the World, which he hath escaped, to dwell in this little land peaceably, and well-beloved both by the Mistress and the Maid? And thou, my Squire, look a little at this fair slim Maiden, and say if she pleaseth thee not: didst thou deem that we had any thing so fair in this lonely place?

Frank and kind was the smile on her radiant visage, nor did she seem to note any whit the trouble on Walter's face, nor how he strove to keep his eyes from the Maid. As for her, she had so wholly mastered her countenance, that belike she used her face guilefully, for she stood as one humble but happy, with a smile on her face, blushing, and with her head hung down as if shamefaced before a goodly young man, a stranger.

But the Lady looked upon her kindly and said: Come hither, child, and fear not this frank and free young man, who belike feareth thee a little, and full certainly feareth me; and yet only after the manner of men.

And therewith she took the Maid by the hand and drew her to her, and pressed her to her bosom, and kissed her cheeks and her lips, and undid the lacing of her gown and bared a shoulder of her, and swept away her skirt from her feet; and then turned to Walter and said: Lo thou, Squire! is not this a lovely thing to have grown up amongst our rough oak-boles? What! Art thou looking at the iron ring there? It is nought, save a token that she is mine, and that I may not be without her.

Then she took the Maid by the shoulders and turned her about as in sport, and said: Go thou now, and bring hither the good grey ones; for needs must we bring home some venison today, whereas this stout warrior may not feed on nought save manchets and honey.

So the Maid went her way, taking care, as Walter deemed, to give no side glance to him. But he stood there shamefaced, so confused with all this open-hearted kindness of the great Lady and with the fresh sight of the darling beauty of the Maid, that he went nigh to thinking that all he had heard since he had come to the porch of the house that first time was but a dream of evil.

But while he stood pondering these matters, and staring before him as one mazed, the Lady laughed out in his face, and touched him on the arm and said: Ah, our Squire, is it so that now thou hast seen my Maid thou wouldst with a good will abide behind to talk with her? But call to mind thy word pledged to me e'en now! And moreover I tell thee this for thy behoof now she is out of ear-shot, that I will above all things take thee away today: for there be other eyes, and they nought uncomely, that look at whiles on my fair-ankled thrall; and who knows but the swords might be out if I take not the better heed, and give thee not every whit of thy will.

As she spoke and moved forward, he turned a little, so that now the edge of that hazel coppice was within his eye-shot, and he deemed that once more he saw the yellow-brown evil thing crawling forth from the thicket; then, turning suddenly on the Lady, he met her eyes, and seemed in one moment of time to find a far other look in them than that of frankness and kindness; though in a flash they changed back again, and she said merrily and sweetly: So so, Sir Squire, now art thou awake again, and mayest for a little while look on me.

Now it came into his head, with that look of hers, all that might befall him and the Maid if he mastered not his passion, nor did what he might to dissemble; so he bent the knee to her, and spoke boldly to her in her own vein, and said: Nay, most gracious of ladies, never would I abide behind today since thou farest afield. But if my speech be hampered, or mine eyes stray, is it not because my mind is confused by thy beauty, and the honey of kind words which floweth from thy mouth?

She laughed outright at his word, but not disdainfully, and said: This is well spoken, Squire, and even what a squire should say to his liege lady, when the sun is up on a fair morning, and she and he and all the world are glad.

She stood quite near him as she spoke, her hand was on his shoulder, and her eyes shone and sparkled. Sooth to say, that excusing of his confusion was like enough in seeming to the truth; for sure never creature was fashioned fairer than she: clad she was for the greenwood as the hunting-goddess of the Gentiles, with her green gown gathered unto her girdle, and sandals on her feet; a bow in her hand and a quiver at her back: she was taller and bigger of fashion than the dear Maiden, whiter of flesh, and more glorious, and brighter of hair; as a flower of flowers for fairness and fragrance.

She said: Thou art verily a fair squire before the hunt is up, and if thou be as good in the hunting, all will be better than well, and the guest will be welcome. But lo! Here cometh our Maid with the good grey ones. Go meet her, and we will tarry no longer than for thy taking the leash in hand.

So Walter looked, and saw the Maid coming with two couple of great hounds in the leash straining against her as she came along. He ran lightly to meet her, wondering if he should have a look, or a half-whisper from her; but she let him take the white thongs from her hand, with the same half-smile of shamefacedness still set on her face and, going past him, came softly up to the Lady, swaying like a willow-branch in the wind, and stood before her, with her arms hanging down by her sides. Then the Lady turned to her, and said: Look to thyself, our Maid, while we are away. This fair young man thou needest not to fear indeed, for he is good and leal; but what thou shalt do with the King's Son I wot not. He is a hot lover forsooth, but a hard man; and whiles evil is his mood, and perilous both to thee and me. And if thou do his will, it shall be ill for thee; and if thou do it not, take heed of him, and let me, and me only, come between his wrath and thee. I may do somewhat for thee. Even yesterday he was instant with me to have thee chastised after the manner of thralls; but I bade him keep silence of such words, and jeered him and mocked him, till he went away from me peevish and in anger. So look to it that thou fall not into any trap of his contrivance.

Then the Maid cast herself at the Mistress's feet, and kissed and embraced them; and as she rose up, the Lady laid her hand lightly on her head, and then, turning to Walter, cried out: Now, Squire, let us leave all these troubles and wiles and desires behind us, and flit through the merry greenwood like the Gentiles of old days.

And therewith she drew up the laps of her gown till the whiteness of her knees was seen, and set off swiftly toward the wood that lay south of the house, and Walter followed, marvelling at her goodliness; nor durst he cast a look backward to the Maiden, for he knew that she desired him, and it was her only that he looked to for his deliverance from this house of guile and lies.

XIV

As they went, they found a change in the land, which grew emptier of big and wide-spreading trees, and more beset with thickets. From one of these they roused a hart, and Walter let slip his hounds thereafter, and he and the Lady followed running. Exceeding swift was she, and well-breathed withal, so that Walter wondered at her; and eager she was in the chase as the very hounds, heeding nothing the scratching of briars or the whipping of stiff twigs as she sped on. But for all their eager hunting, the quarry outran both dogs and folk, and gat him into a great thicket, amidmost whereof was a wide plash of water. Into the thicket they followed him, but he took to the water under their eyes and made land on the other side; and because of the tangle of underwood, he swam across much faster than they might have any hope to come round on him; and so were the hunters left undone for that time.

So the Lady cast herself down on the green grass anigh the water, while Walter blew the hounds in and coupled them up; then he turned round to her, and lo! she was weeping for despite that they had lost the quarry; and again did Walter wonder that so little a matter should raise a passion of tears in her. He durst not ask what ailed her, or proffer her solace, but was not ill apaid by beholding her loveliness as she lay.

Presently she raised up her head and turned to Walter, and spake to him angrily and said: Squire, why dost thou stand staring at me like a fool?

Yea, Lady, he said; but the sight of thee maketh me foolish to do aught else but to look on thee.

She said, in a peevish voice: Tush, Squire, the day is too far spent for soft and courtly speeches; what was good there is nought so good here. Withal, I know more of thine heart than thou deemest.

Walter hung down his head and reddened, and she looked on him, and her face changed, and she smiled and said, kindly this time: Look ye, Squire, I am hot and weary, and ill-content; but presently it will be better with me; for my knees have been telling my shoulders that the cold water of this little lake will be sweet and pleasant this summer noonday, and that I shall forget my foil when I have taken my pleasure therein. Wherefore, go thou with thine hounds without the thicket and there abide my coming. And I bid thee look not aback as thou goest, for therein were peril to thee: I shall not keep thee tarrying long alone.

He bowed his head to her, and turned and went his ways. And now, when he was a little space away from her, he deemed her indeed a marvel of women, and well-nigh forgat all his doubts and fears concerning her, whether she were a fair image fashioned out of lies and guile, or it might be but an evil thing in the shape of a goodly woman. Forsooth, when he saw her caressing the dear and friendly Maid, his heart all turned against her, despite what his eyes and his ears told his mind, and she seemed like as it were a serpent enfolding the simplicity of the body which he loved.

But now it was all changed, and he lay on the grass and longed for her coming; which was delayed for somewhat more than an hour. Then she came back to him, smiling and fresh and cheerful, her green gown let down to her heels.

He sprang up to meet her, and she came close to him, and spake from a laughing face: Squire, hast thou no meat in thy wallet? For, meseemeth, I fed thee when thou wert hungry the other day; do thou now the same by me.

He smiled, and louted to her, and took his wallet and brought out thence bread and flesh and wine, and spread them all out before her on the green grass, and then stood by humbly before her. But she said: Nay, my Squire, sit down by me and eat with me, for today are we both hunters together.

So he sat down by her trembling, but neither for awe of her greatness, nor for fear and horror of her guile and sorcery.

A while they sat there together after they had done their meat, and the Lady fell a-talking with Walter concerning the parts of the earth, and the manners of men, and of his journeyings to and fro.

At last she said: Thou hast told me much and answered all my questions wisely, and as my good Squire should, and that pleaseth me. But now tell me of the city wherein thou wert born and bred; a city whereof thou hast hitherto told me nought.

Lady, he said, it is a fair and a great city, and to many it seemeth lovely. But I have left it, and now it is nothing to me.

Hast thou not kindred there? said she.

Yea, said he, and foemen withal; and a false woman waylayeth my life there.

And what was she? said the Lady.

Said Walter: She was but my wife.

Was she fair? said the Lady.

Walter looked on her a while, and then said: I was going to say that she was well-nigh as fair as thou; but that may scarce be. Yet was she very fair. But now, kind and gracious Lady, I will say this word to thee: I marvel that thou askest so many things concerning the city of Langton on Holm, where I was born, and where are my kindred yet; for meseemeth that thou knowest it thyself.

I know it, I? said the Lady.

What, then! thou knowest it not? said Walter.

Spake the Lady, and some of her old disdain was in her words: Dost thou deem that I wander about the world and its cheaping-steads like one of the chapmen? Nay, I dwell in the Wood beyond the World, and nowhere else. What hath put this word into thy mouth?

He said: Pardon me, Lady, if I have misdone; but thus it was: Mine own eyes beheld thee going down the quays of our city, and thence a ship-board, and the ship sailed out of the haven. And first of all went a strange dwarf, whom I have seen here, and then thy Maid; and then went thy gracious and lovely body.

The Lady's face changed as he spoke, and she turned red and then pale, and set her teeth; but she refrained her, and said: Squire, I see of thee that thou art no liar, nor light of wit, therefore I suppose that thou hast verily seen some appearance of me; but never have I been in Langton, nor thought thereof, nor known that such a stead there was until thou namedst it e'en now. Wherefore, I deem that an enemy hath cast the shadow of me on the air of that land.

Yea, my Lady, said Walter; and what enemy mightest thou have to have done this?

She was slow of answer, but spake at last from a quivering mouth of anger: Knowest thou not the saw, that a man's foes are they of his own house? If I find out for a truth who hath done this, the said enemy shall have an evil hour with me.

Again she was silent, and she clenched her hands and strained her limbs in the heat of her anger; so that Walter was afraid of her, and all his misgivings came back to his heart again, and he repented that he had told her so much. But in a little while all that trouble and wrath seemed to flow off her, and again was she of good cheer, and kind and sweet to him; and she said: But in sooth, however it may be, I thank thee, my Squire and friend, for telling me hereof. And surely no wyte do I lay on thee. And, moreover, is it not this vision which hath brought thee hither?

So it is, Lady, said he.

Then have we to thank it, said the Lady, and thou art welcome to our land.

And therewith she held out her hand to him, and he took it on his knees and kissed it; and then it was as if a red-hot iron had run through his heart, and he felt faint, and bowed down his head. But he held her hand yet, and kissed it many times, and the wrist and the arm, and knew not where he was.

But she drew a little away from him, and arose and said: Now is the day wearing, and if we are to bear back any venison we must buckle to the work. So arise, Squire, and take the hounds and come with me; for not far off is a little thicket which mostly harbours foison of deer, great and small. Let us come our ways.

XV

So they walked on quietly thence some half a mile, and ever the Lady would have Walter to walk by her side, and not follow a little behind her, as was meet for a servant to do; and she touched his hand at whiles as she showed him beast and fowl and tree, and the sweetness of her body overcame him, so that for a while he thought of nothing save her.

Now when they were come to the thicket-side, she turned to him and said: Squire, I am no ill woodman, so that thou mayst trust me that we shall not be brought to shame the second time; and I shall do sagely: so nock an arrow to thy bow, and abide me here, and stir not hence; for I shall enter this thicket without the hounds, and arouse the quarry for thee; and see that thou be brisk and clean-shooting, and then shalt thou have a reward of me.

Therewith she drew up her skirts through her girdle again, took her bent bow in her hand and drew an arrow out of the quiver, and stepped lightly into the thicket, leaving him longing for the sight of her, as he hearkened to the tread of her feet on the dry leaves, and the rustling of the brake as she thrust through it.

Thus he stood for a few minutes, and then he heard a kind of gibbering cry without words, yet as of a woman, coming from the thicket, and while his heart was yet gathering the thought that something had gone amiss, he glided swiftly, but with little stir, into the brake.

He had gone but a little way ere he saw the Lady standing there in a narrow clearing, her face pale as death, her knees cleaving together, her body swaying and tottering, her hands hanging down, and the bow and arrow fallen to the ground; and ten yards before her a great-headed yellow creature crouching flat to the earth and slowly drawing nigher.

He stopped short; one arrow was already notched to the string, and another hung loose to the lesser fingers of his string-hand. He raised his right hand, and drew and loosed in a twinkling; the shaft flew close to the Lady's side, and straightway all the wood rung with a huge roar, as the yellow lion turned about to bite at the shaft which had sunk deep into him behind the shoulder, as if a bolt out of the heavens had smitten him. But straightway had Walter loosed again, and then, throwing down his bow, he ran forward with his drawn sword gleaming in his hand, while the lion weltered and rolled, but had no might to move forward. Then Walter went up to him warily and thrust him through to the heart, and leapt aback, lest the beast might yet have life in him to smite; but he left his struggling, his huge voice died out, and he lay there moveless before the hunter.

Walter abode a little, facing him, and then turned about to the Lady, and she had fallen down in a heap whereas she stood, and lay there all huddled up and voiceless. So he knelt down by her, and lifted up her head, and bade her arise, for the foe was slain. And after a little she stretched out her limbs, and turned about on the grass, and seemed to sleep, and the colour came into her face again, and it grew soft and a little smiling. Thus she lay awhile, and Walter sat by her watching her, till at last she opened her eyes and sat up, and knew him, and smiling on him said: What hath befallen, Squire, that I have slept and dreamed?

He answered nothing, till her memory came back to her, and then she arose, trembling and pale, and said: Let us leave this wood, for the Enemy is therein.

And she hastened away before him till they came out at the thicket-side whereas the hounds had been left, and they were standing there uneasy and whining; so Walter coupled them, while the Lady stayed not, but went away swiftly homeward, and Walter followed.

At last she stayed her swift feet, and turned round on Walter, and said: Squire, come hither.

So did he, and she said: I am weary again; let us sit under this quicken-tree, and rest us.

So they sat down, and she sat looking between her knees a while; and at last she said: Why didst thou not bring the lion's hide?

He said: Lady, I will go back and flay the beast, and bring on the hide.

And he arose therewith, but she caught him by the skirts and drew him down, and said: Nay, thou shalt not go; abide with me. Sit down again.

He did so, and she said: Thou shalt not go from me; for I am afraid: I am not used to looking on the face of death.

She grew pale as she spoke, and set a hand to her breast, and sat so a while without speaking. At last she turned to him smiling, and said: How was it with the aspect of me when I stood before the peril of the Enemy? And she laid a hand upon his.

O gracious one, quoth he, thou wert, as ever, full lovely, but I feared for thee.

She moved not her hand from his, and she said: Good and true Squire, I said ere I entered the thicket e'en now that I would reward thee if thou slewest the quarry. He is dead, though thou hast left the skin behind upon the carcase. Ask now thy reward, but take time to think what it shall be.

He felt her hand warm upon his, and drew in the sweet odour of her mingled with the woodland scents under the hot sun of the afternoon, and his heart was clouded with man-like desire of her. And it was a near thing but he had spoken, and craved of her the reward of the freedom of her Maid, and that he might depart with her into other lands; but as his mind wavered betwixt this and that, the Lady, who had been eyeing him keenly, drew her hand away from him; and therewith doubt and fear flowed into his mind, and he refrained him of speech.

Then she laughed merrily and said: The good Squire is shamefaced; he feareth a lady more than a lion. Will it be a reward to thee if I bid thee to kiss my cheek?

Therewith she leaned her face toward him, and he kissed her well-favouredly, and then sat gazing on her, wondering what should betide to him on the morrow.

Then she arose and said: Come, Squire, and let us home; be not abashed, there shall be other rewards hereafter.

So they went their ways quietly; and it was nigh sunset against they entered the house again. Walter looked round for the Maid, but beheld her not; and the Lady said to him: I go to my chamber, and now is thy service over for this day.

Then she nodded to him friendly and went her ways.

XVI

But as for Walter, he went out of the house again, and fared slowly over the woodlawns till he came to another close thicket or brake; he entered from mere wantonness, or that he might be the more apart and hidden, so as to think over his case. There he lay down under the thick boughs, but could not so herd his thoughts that they would dwell steady in looking into what might come to him within the next days; rather visions of those two women and the monster did but float before him, and fear and desire and the hope of life ran to and fro in his mind.

As he lay thus he heard footsteps drawing near, and he looked between the boughs, and though the sun had just set, he could see close by him a man and a woman going slowly, and they hand in hand; at first he deemed it would be the King's Son and the Lady, but presently he saw that it was the King's Son indeed, but that it was the Maid whom he was holding by the hand. And now he saw of him that his eyes were bright with desire, and of her that she was very pale. Yet when he heard her begin to speak, it was in a steady voice that she said: King's Son, thou hast threatened me oft and unkindly, and now thou threatenest me again, and no less unkindly. But whatever were thy need herein before, now is there no more need; for my Mistress, of whom thou wert weary, is now grown weary of thee, and belike will not now reward me for drawing thy love to me, as once she would have done; to wit, before the coming of this stranger. Therefore I say, since I am but a thrall, poor and helpless, betwixt you two mighty ones, I have no choice but to do thy will.

As she spoke she looked all round about her, as one distraught by the anguish of fear. Walter, amidst of his wrath and grief, had well-nigh drawn his sword and rushed out of his lair upon the King's Son. But he deemed it sure that, so doing, he should undo the Maid altogether, and himself also belike, so he refrained him, though it were a hard matter.

The Maid had stayed her feet now close to where Walter lay, some five yards from him only, and he doubted whether she saw him not from where she stood. As to the King's Son, he was so intent upon the Maid, and so greedy of her beauty, that it was not like that he saw anything.

Now, moreover, Walter looked, and deemed that he beheld something through the grass and bracken on the other side of those two, an ugly brown and yellow body which, if it were not some beast of the foumart kind, must needs be the monstrous dwarf, or one of his kin; and the flesh crept upon Walter's bones with the horror of him. But the King's Son spoke unto the Maid: Sweetling, I shall take the gift thou givest me, neither shall I threaten thee any more, howbeit thou givest it not very gladly or graciously. She smiled on him with her lips alone, for her eyes were wandering and haggard. My lord, she said, is not this the manner of women?

Well, he said, I say that I will take thy love even so given. Yet let me hear again that thou lovest not that vile newcomer, and that thou hast not seen him, save this morning along with my Lady. Nay now, thou shalt swear it.

What shall I swear by? she said.

Quoth he, Thou shalt swear by my body; and therewith he thrust himself close up against her; but she drew her hand from his, and laid it on his breast, and said: I swear it by thy body.

He smiled on her licorously, and took her by the shoulders, and kissed her face many times, and then stood aloof from her, and said: Now have I had hansel: but tell me, when shall I come to thee?

She spoke out clearly: Within three days at furthest; I will do thee to wit of the day and the hour tomorrow, or the day after.

He kissed her once more, and said: Forget it not, or the threat holds good.

And therewith he turned about and went his ways toward the house; and Walter saw the yellow-brown thing creeping after him in the gathering dusk.

As for the Maid, she stood for a while without moving, and looking after the King's Son and the creature that followed him. Then she turned about to where Walter lay and lightly put aside the boughs, and Walter leapt up, and they stood face to face. She said softly but eagerly: Friend, touch me not yet!

He spake not, but looked on her sternly. She said: Thou art angry with me?

Still he spake not; but she said: Friend, this at least I will pray thee; not to play with life and death; with happiness and misery. Dost thou not remember the oath which we swore each to each but a little while ago? And dost thou deem that I have changed in these few days? Is thy mind concerning thee and me the same as it was? If it be not so, now tell me. For now have I the mind to do as if neither thou nor I are changed to each other, whoever may have kissed mine unwilling lips, or whomsoever thy lips may have kissed. But if thou hast changed, and wilt no longer give me thy love, nor crave mine, then shall this steel (and she drew a sharp knife from her girdle) be for the fool and the dastard who hath made thee wroth with me, my friend, and my friend that I deemed I had won. And then let come what will come! But if thou be nought changed, and the oath yet holds, then, when a little while hath passed, may we thrust all evil and guile and grief behind us, and long joy shall lie before us, and long life, and all honour in death: if only thou wilt do as I bid thee, O my dear, and my friend, and my first friend!

He looked on her, and his breast heaved up as all the sweetness of her kind love took hold on him, and his face changed, and the tears filled his eyes and ran over, and rained down before her, and he stretched out his hand toward her.

Then she said exceeding sweetly: Now indeed I see that it is well with me, yea, and with thee also. A sore pain it is to me, that not even now may I take thine hand, and cast mine arms about thee, and kiss the lips that love me. But so it has to be. My dear, even so I were fain to stand here long before thee, even if we spake no more word to each other; but abiding here is perilous; for there is ever an evil spy upon my doings, who has now as I deem followed the King's Son to the house, but who will return when he has tracked him home thither: so we must sunder. But belike there is yet time for a word or two: first, the rede which I had thought on for our deliverance is now afoot, though I durst not tell thee thereof, nor have time thereto. But this much shall I tell thee, that whereas great is the craft of my Mistress in wizardry, yet I also have some little craft therein, and this, which she hath not, to change the aspect of folk so utterly that they seem other than they verily are; yea, so that one may have the aspect of another. Now the next thing is this: whatsoever my Mistress may bid thee, do her will therein with no more nay-saying than thou deemest may please her. And the next thing: wheresoever thou mayst meet me, speak not to me, make no sign to me, even when I seem to be all alone, till I stoop down and touch the ring on my ankle with my right hand; but if I do so, then stay thee, without fail, till I speak. The last thing I will say to thee, dear friend, ere we both go our ways, this it is. When we are free, and thou knowest all that I have done, I pray thee deem me not evil and wicked, and be not wroth with me for my deed; whereas thou wottest well that I am not in like plight with other women. I have heard tell that when the knight goeth to the war, and hath overcome his foes by the shearing of swords and guileful tricks, and hath come back home to his own folk, they praise him and bless him, and crown him with flowers, and boast of him before God in the minster for his deliverance of friend and folk and city. Why shouldst thou be worse to me than this? Now is all said, my dear and my friend; farewell, farewell!

Therewith she turned and went her ways toward the house in all speed, but making somewhat of a compass. And when she was gone, Walter knelt down and kissed the place where her feet had been, and arose thereafter, and made his way toward the house, he also, but slowly, and staying oft on his way.

XVII

On the morrow morning Walter loitered a while about the house till the morn was grown old, and then about noon he took his bow and arrows and went into the woods to the northward, to get him some venison. He went somewhat far ere he shot him a fawn, and then he sat him down to rest under the shade of a great chestnut tree, for it was not far past the hottest of the day. He looked around thence and saw below him a little dale with a pleasant stream running through it, and he bethought him of bathing therein, so he went down and had his pleasure of the water and the willowy banks; for he lay naked a while on the grass by the lip of the water, for joy of the flickering shade, and the little breeze that ran over the down-long ripples of the stream.

Then he did on his raiment, and began to come his ways up the bent, but had scarce gone three steps ere he saw a woman coming towards him from down-stream. His heart came into his mouth when he saw her, for she stooped and reached down her arm, as if she would lay her hand on her ankle, so that at first he deemed it had been the Maid, but at the second eye-shot he saw that it was the Mistress. She stood still and looked on him, so that he deemed she would have him come to her. So he went to meet her, and grew somewhat shamefaced as he drew nigher, and wondered at her, for now was she clad but in one garment of some dark grey silky stuff, embroidered with, as it were, a garland of flowers about the middle, but which was so thin that, as the wind drifted it from side and limb, it hid her no more, but for the said garland, than if water were running over her: her face was full of smiling joy and content as she spake to him in a kind, caressing voice, and said: I give thee good day, good Squire, and well art thou met. And she held out her hand to him. He knelt down before her and kissed it, and abode still upon his knees, and hanging down his head.

But she laughed outright, and stooped down to him, and put her hand to his arms, and raised him up, and said to him: What is this, my Squire, that thou kneelest to me as to an idol?

He said faltering: I wot not; but perchance thou art an idol; and I fear thee.

What! she said, more than yesterday, whenas thou sawest me afraid?

Said he: Yea, for that now I see thee unhidden, and meseemeth there hath been none such since the old days of the Gentiles.

She said: Hast thou not yet bethought thee of a gift to crave of me, a reward for the slaying of mine enemy, and the saving of me from death?

O my Lady, he said, even so much would I have done for any other lady, or, forsooth, for any poor man; for so my manhood would have bidden me. Speak not of gifts to me then. Moreover (and he reddened therewith, and his voice faltered), didst thou not give me my sweet reward yesterday? What more durst I ask?

She held her peace awhile, and looked on him keenly; and he reddened under her gaze. Then wrath came into her face, and she reddened and knit her brows, and spake to him in a voice of anger, and said: Nay, what is this? It is growing in my mind that thou deemest the gift of me unworthy! Thou, an alien, an outcast; one endowed with the little wisdom of the World without the Wood! And here I stand before thee, all glorious in my nakedness, and so fulfilled of wisdom, that I can make this wilderness to any whom I love more full of joy than the kingdoms and cities of the world... and thou!... Ah, but it is the Enemy that hath done this, and made the guileless guileful! Yet will I have the upper hand at least, though thou suffer for it, and I suffer for thee.

Walter stood before her with hanging head, and he put forth his hands as if praying off her anger, and pondered what answer he should make; for now he feared for himself and the Maid; so at last he looked up to her, and said boldly: Nay, Lady, I know what thy words mean, whereas I remember thy first welcome of me. I wot, forsooth, that thou wouldst call me base-born, and of no account, and unworthy to touch the hem of thy raiment; and that I have been over-bold, and guilty towards thee; and doubtless this is sooth, and I have deserved thine anger: but I will not ask thee to pardon me, for I have done but what I must needs. She looked on him calmly now, and without any wrath, but rather as if she would read what was written in his inmost heart. Then her face changed into joyousness again, and she smote her palms together, and cried out: This is but foolish talk; for yesterday did I see thy valiancy, and today I have seen thy goodliness; and I say, that though thou mightest not be good enough for a fool woman of the earthly baronage, yet art thou good enough for me, the wise and the mighty, and the lovely. And whereas thou sayest that I gave thee but disdain when first thou camest to us, grudge not against me therefor, because it was done but to prove thee; and now thou art proven.

Then again he knelt down before her, and embraced her knees, and again she raised him up, and let her arm hang down over his shoulder, and her cheek brush his cheek; and she kissed his mouth and said: Hereby is all forgiven, both thine offence and mine; and now cometh joy and merry days.

Therewith her smiling face grew grave, and she stood before him looking stately and gracious and kind at once, and she took his hand and said: Thou mightest deem my chamber in the Golden House of the Wood over queenly, since thou art no masterful man. So now hast thou chosen well the place wherein to meet me today, for hard by on the other side of the stream is a bower of pleasance, which, forsooth, not everyone who cometh to this land may find; there shall I be to thee as one of the up-country damsels of thine own land, and thou shalt not be abashed.

She sidled up to him as she spoke, and would he, would he not, her sweet voice tickled his very soul with pleasure, and she looked aside on him happy and well-content.

So they crossed the stream by the shallow below the pool wherein Walter had bathed, and within a little they came upon a tall fence of flake-hurdles, and a simple gate therein. The Lady opened the same, and they entered thereby into a close all planted as a most fair garden, with hedges of rose and woodbine, and with linden-trees a-blossom, and long ways of green grass betwixt borders of lilies and clove-gilliflowers, and other sweet garland-flowers. And a branch of the stream which they had crossed erewhile wandered through that garden; and in the midst was a little house built of post and pan, and thatched with yellow straw, as if it were new done.

Then Walter looked this way and that, and wondered at first, and tried to think in his mind what should come next, and how matters would go with him; but his thought would not dwell steady on any other matter than the beauty of the Lady amidst the beauty of the garden; and withal she was now grown so sweet and kind, and even somewhat timid and shy with him, that scarce did he know whose hand he held, or whose fragrant bosom and sleek side went so close to him.

So they wandered here and there through the waning of the day, and when they entered at last into the cool dusk house, then they loved and played together, as if they were a pair of lovers guileless, with no fear for the morrow, and no seeds of enmity and death sown betwixt them.

XVIII

Now on the morrow, when Walter was awake, he found there was no one lying beside him, and the day was no longer very young; so he arose, and went through the garden from end to end, and all about, and there was none there; and albeit that he dreaded to meet the Lady there, yet was he sad at heart and fearful of what might betide. Howsoever, he found the gate whereby they had entered yesterday, and he went out into the little dale; but when he had gone a step or two he turned about, and could see neither garden nor fence, nor any sign of what he had seen thereof but lately. He knit his brow and stood still to think of it, and his heart grew the heavier thereby; but presently he went his ways and crossed the stream, but had scarce come up on to the grass on the further side, ere he saw a woman coming to meet him, and at first, full as he was of the tide of yesterday and the wondrous garden, deemed that it would be the Lady; but the woman stayed her feet, and, stooping, laid a hand on her right ankle, and he saw that it was the Maid. He drew anigh to her, and saw that she was nought so sad of countenance as the last time she had met him, but flushed of cheek and bright-eyed.

As he came up to her she made a step or two to meet him, holding out her two hands, and then refrained her, and said smiling: Ah, friend, belike this shall be the last time that I shall say to thee, touch me not, nay, not so much as my hand, or it were but the hem of my raiment.

The joy grew up in his heart, and he gazed on her fondly, and said: Why, what then hath befallen of late?

O friend, she began, this hath befallen.

But as he looked on her, the smile died from her face, and she became deadly pale to the very lips; she looked askance to her left side, whereas ran the stream; and Walter followed her eyes, and deemed for one instant that he saw the misshapen yellow visage of the dwarf peering round from a grey rock, but the next there was nothing. Then the Maid, though she were as pale as death, went on in a clear, steady, hard voice, wherein was no joy or kindness, keeping her face to Walter and her back to the stream: This hath befallen, friend, that there is no longer any need to refrain thy love nor mine; therefore I say to thee, come to my chamber (and it is the red chamber over against thine, though thou knewest it not) an hour before this next midnight, and then thy sorrow and mine shall be at an end: and now I must needs depart. Follow me not, but remember!

And therewith she turned about and fled like the wind down the stream.

But Walter stood wondering, and knew not what to make of it, whether it were for good or ill: for he knew now that she had paled and been seized with terror because of the upheaving of the ugly head; and yet she had seemed to speak out the very thing she had to say. Howsoever it were, he spake aloud to himself: Whatever comes, I will keep tryst with her.

Then he drew his sword, and turned this way and that, looking all about if he might see any sign of the Evil Thing; but nought might his eyes behold, save the grass, and the stream, and the bushes of the dale. So then, still holding his naked sword in his hand, he clomb the bent out of the dale; for that was the only way he knew to the Golden House; and when he came to the top, and the summer breeze blew in his face, and he looked down a fair green slope beset with goodly oaks and chestnuts, he was refreshed with the life of the earth, and he felt the good sword in his fist, and knew that there was might and longing in him, and the world seemed open unto him.

So he smiled, if it were somewhat grimly, and sheathed his sword and went on toward the house.

XIX

He entered the cool dusk through the porch and, looking down the pillared hall, saw beyond the fountain a gleam of gold, and when he came past the said fountain he looked up to the high-seat, and lo! – the Lady sitting there clad in her queenly raiment. She called to him, and he came; and she hailed him, and spake graciously and calmly, yet as if she knew nought of him save as the leal servant of her, a high Lady. Squire, she said, we have deemed it meet to have the hide of the servant of the Enemy, the lion to wit, whom thou slewest yesterday, for a carpet to our feet; wherefore go now, take thy wood-knife and flay the beast, and bring me home his skin. This shall be all thy service for this day, so mayst thou do it at thine own leisure, and not weary thyself. May good go with thee.

He bent the knee before her, and she smiled on him graciously, but reached out no hand for him to kiss, and heeded him but little. Wherefore, in spite of himself, and though he knew somewhat of her guile, he could not help marvelling that this should be she who had lain in his arms night-long but of late.

Howso that might be, he took his way toward the thicket where he had slain the lion, and came thither by then it was afternoon, at the hottest of the day. So he entered therein, and came to the very place whereas the Lady had lain, when she fell down before the terror of the lion; and there was the mark of her body on the grass where she had lain that while, like as it were the form of a hare. But when Walter went on to where he had slain that great beast – lo! – he was gone, and there was no sign of him; but there were Walter's own footprints, and the two shafts which he had shot, one feathered red and one blue. He said at first: Belike someone hath been here, and hath had the carcase away. Then he laughed in very despite, and said: How may that be, since there are no signs of dragging away of so huge a body, and no blood or fur on the grass if they had cut him up, and moreover no trampling of feet, as if there had been many men at the deed. Then was he all abashed, and again laughed in scorn of himself, and said: Forsooth I deemed I had done manly; but now forsooth I shot nought, and nought there was before the sword of my father's son. And what may I deem now, but that this is a land of mere lies, and that there is nought real and alive therein save me. Yea, belike even these trees and the green grass will presently depart from me, and leave me falling down through the clouds.

Therewith he turned away, and gat him to the road that led to the Golden House, wondering what next should befall him, and going slowly as he pondered his case. So came he to that first thicket where they had lost their quarry by water; so he entered the same, musing, and bathed him in the pool that was therein, after he had wandered about it awhile, and found nothing new.

So again he set him to the homeward road, when the day was now waning, and it was near sunset that he was come nigh unto the house, though it was hidden from him as then by a low bent that rose before him; and there he abode and looked about him.

Now as he looked, over the said bent came the figure of a woman, who stayed on the brow thereof and looked all about her, and then ran swiftly down to meet Walter, who saw at once that it was the Maid.

She made no stay then till she was but three paces from him, and then she stooped down and made the sign to him, and then spake to him breathlessly, and said: Hearken! But speak not till I have done: I bade thee tonight's meeting because I saw that there was one anigh whom I must needs beguile. But by thine oath, and thy love, and all that thou art, I adjure thee come not unto me this night as I bade thee! But be hidden in the hazel-copse outside the house, as it draws toward midnight, and abide me there. Dost thou hearken, and wilt thou? Say yes or no in haste, for I may not tarry a moment of time. Who knoweth what is behind me?

Yes, said Walter hastily; but friend and love...

No more, she said; hope the best; and turning from him she ran away swiftly, not by the way she had come, but sideways, as though to reach the house by fetching a compass.

But Walter went slowly on his way, thinking within himself that now at that present moment there was nought for it but to refrain him from doing, and to let others do; yet deemed he that it was little manly to be as the pawn upon the board, pushed about by the will of others.

Then, as he went, he bethought him of the Maiden's face and aspect, as she came running to him, and stood before him for that minute; and all eagerness he saw in her, and sore love of him, and distress of soul, all blent together.

So came he to the brow of the bent whence he could see lying before him, scarce more than a bow-shot away, the Golden House, now gilded again and reddened by the setting sun. And even therewith came a gay image toward him, flashing back the level rays from gold and steel and silver; and lo! There was come the King's Son. They met presently, and the King's Son turned to go beside him, and said merrily: I give thee good even, my Lady's Squire! I owe thee something of courtesy, whereas it is by thy means that I shall be made happy, both tonight, and tomorrow, and many tomorrows; and sooth it is, that but little courtesy have I done thee hitherto.

His face was full of joy, and the eyes of him shone with gladness. He was a goodly man, but to Walter he seemed an ill one; and he hated him so much, that he found it no easy matter to answer him; but he refrained himself, and said: I can thee thank, King's Son; and good it is that someone is happy in this strange land.

Art thou not happy then, Squire of my Lady? said the other.

Walter had no mind to show this man his heart, nay, nor even a corner thereof; for he deemed him an enemy. So he smiled sweetly and somewhat foolishly, as a man luckily in love, and said: O yea, yea, why should I not be so? How might I be otherwise?

Yea then, said the King's Son, why didst thou say that thou wert glad someone is happy? Who is unhappy deemest thou? And he looked on him keenly.

Walter answered slowly: Said I so? I suppose then that I was thinking of thee; for when first I saw thee, yea, and afterwards, thou didst seem heavy-hearted and ill-content.

The face of the King's Son cleared at this word, and he said: Yea, so it was; for look you, both ways it was: I was unfree, and I had sown the true desire of my heart whereas it waxed not. But now I am on the brink and verge of freedom, and presently shall my desire be blossomed. Nay now, Squire, I deem thee a good fellow, though it may be somewhat of a fool; so I will no more speak riddles to thee. Thus it is: the Maid hath promised me all mine asking, and is mine; and in two or three days, by her helping also, I shall see the world again.

Quoth Walter, smiling askance on him: And the Lady? What shall she say to this matter?

The King's Son reddened, but smiled falsely enough, and said: Sir Squire, thou knowest enough not to need to ask this. Why should I tell thee that she accounteth more of thy little finger than of my whole body? Now I tell thee hereof freely; first, because this my fruition of love, and my freeing from thralldom, is, in a way, of thy doing. For thou art become my supplanter, and hast taken thy place with yonder lovely tyrant. Fear not for me! She will let me go. As for thyself, see thou to it! But again I tell thee hereof because my heart is light and full of joy, and telling thee will pleasure me, and cannot do me any harm. For if thou say: How if I carry the tale to my Lady? I answer, thou wilt not. For I know that thine heart hath been somewhat set on the jewel that my hand holdeth; and thou knowest well on whose head the Lady's wrath would fall, and that would be neither thine nor mine.

Thou sayest sooth, said Walter; neither is treason my wont.

So they walked on silently a while, and then Walter said: But how if the Maiden had nay-said thee; what hadst thou done then?

By the heavens! said the King's Son fiercely, she should have paid for her nay-say; then would I... But he broke off, and said quietly, yet somewhat doggedly: Why talk of what might have been? She gave me her yea-say pleasantly and sweetly.

Now Walter knew that the man lied, so he held his peace thereon; but presently he said: When thou art free wilt thou go to thine own land again?

Yea, said the King's Son; she will lead me thither.

And wilt thou make her thy lady and queen when thou comest to thy father's land? said Walter.

The King's Son knit his brow, and said: When I am in mine own land I may do with her what I will; but I look for it that I shall do no otherwise with her than that she shall be well-content.

Then the talk between them dropped, and the King's Son turned off toward the wood, singing and joyous; but Walter went soberly toward the house. Forsooth he was not greatly cast down, for besides that he knew that the King's Son was false, he deemed that under this double tryst lay something which was a-doing in his own behalf. Yet was he eager and troubled, if not down-hearted, and his soul was cast about betwixt hope and fear.

XX

So came he into the pillared hall, and there he found the Lady walking to and fro by the high-seat; and when he drew nigh she turned on him, and said in a voice rather eager than angry: What hast thou done, Squire? Why art thou come before me?

He was abashed, and bowed before her and said: O gracious Lady, thou badest me service, and I have been about it.

She said: Tell me then, tell me, what hath betided?

Lady, said he, when I entered the thicket of thy swooning I found there no carcase of the lion, nor any sign of the dragging away of him.

She looked full in his face for a little, and then went to her chair, and sat down therein; and in a little while spake to him in a softer voice, and said: Did I not tell thee that some enemy had done that unto me? and lo! now thou seest that so it is.

Then was she silent again, and knit her brows and set her teeth; and thereafter she spake harshly and fiercely: But I will overcome her, and make her days evil, but keep death away from her, that she may die many times over; and know all the sickness of the heart, when foes be nigh and friends afar, and there is none to deliver!

Her eyes flashed, and her face was dark with anger; but she turned and caught Walter's eyes, and the sternness of his face, and she softened at once, and said: But thou! This hath little to do with thee; and now to thee I speak: now cometh even and night. Go thou to thy chamber, and there shalt thou find raiment worthy of thee, what thou now art, and what thou shalt be; do on the same, and make thyself most goodly, and then come thou hither and eat and drink with me, and afterwards depart whither thou wilt, till the night has worn to its midmost; and then come thou to my chamber, to wit, through the ivory door in the gallery above; and then and there shall I tell thee a thing, and it shall be for the weal both of thee and of me, but for the grief and woe of the Enemy.

Therewith she reached her hand to him, and he kissed it, and departed and came to his chamber, and found raiment therebefore rich beyond measure; and he wondered if any new snare lay therein: yet if there were, he saw no way whereby he might escape it, so he did it on, and became as the most glorious of kings, and yet lovelier than any king of the world.

Sithence he went his way into the pillared hall, when it was now night, and without the moon was up, and the trees of the wood as still as images. But within the hall shone bright with many candles, and the fountain glittered in the light of them, as it ran tinkling sweetly into the little stream; and the silvern bridges gleamed, and the pillars shone all round about.

And there on the dais was a table dight most royally, and the Lady sitting thereat, clad in her most glorious array, and behind her the Maid standing humbly, yet clad in precious web of shimmering gold, but with feet unshod and the iron ring upon her ankle.

So Walter came his ways to the high-seat, and the Lady rose and greeted him, and took him by the hands, and kissed him on either cheek, and sat him down beside her. So they fell to their meat, and the Maid served them; but the Lady took no more heed of her than if she were one of the pillars of the hall; but Walter she caressed oft with sweet words, and the touch of her hand, making him drink out of her cup and eat out of her dish. As to him, he was bashful by seeming, but verily fearful; he took the Lady's caresses with what grace he might, and durst not so much as glance at her Maid. Long indeed seemed that banquet to him, and longer yet endured the weariness of his abiding there, kind to his foe and unkind to his friend; for after the banquet they still sat a while, and the Lady talked much to Walter about many things of the ways of the world, and he answered what he might, distraught as he was with the thought of those two trysts which he had to deal with.

At last spake the Lady and said: Now must I leave thee for a little, and thou wottest where and how we shall meet next; and meanwhile disport thee as thou wilt, so that thou weary not thyself, for I love to see thee joyous.

Then she arose stately and grand; but she kissed Walter on the mouth ere she turned to go out of the hall. The Maid followed her; but or ever she was quite gone, she stooped and made that sign, and looked over her shoulder at Walter, as if in entreaty to him, and there was fear and anguish in her face; but he nodded his head to her in yea-say of the tryst in the hazel-copse, and in a trice she was gone.

Walter went down the hall, and forth into the early night; but in the jaws of the porch he came up against the King's Son, who, gazing at his attire glittering with all its gems in the moonlight, laughed out, and said: Now may it be seen how thou art risen in degree above me, whereas I am but a king's son, and that a king of a far country; whereas thou art a king of kings, or shalt be this night, yea, and of this very country wherein we both are.

Now Walter saw the mock which lay under his words; but he kept back his wrath, and answered: Fair sir, art thou as well contented with thy lot as when the sun went down? Hast thou no doubt or fear? Will the Maid verily keep tryst with thee, or hath she given thee yea-say but to escape thee this time? Or, again, may she not turn to the Lady and appeal to her against thee?

Now when he had spoken these words, he repented thereof, and feared for himself and the Maid, lest he had stirred some misgiving in that young man's foolish heart. But the King's Son did but laugh, and answered nought but to Walter's last words, and said: Yea, yea! this word of thine showeth how little thou wottest of that which lieth betwixt my darling and thine. Doth the lamb appeal from the shepherd to the wolf? Even so shall the Maid appeal from me to thy Lady. What! ask thy Lady at thy leisure what her wont hath been with her thrall; she shall think it a fair tale to tell thee thereof. But thereof is my Maid all whole now by reason of her wisdom in leechcraft, or somewhat more. And now I tell thee again, that the beforesaid Maid must needs do my will; for if I be the deep sea, and I deem not so ill of myself, that other one is the devil; as belike thou shalt find out for thyself later on. Yea, all is well with me, and more than well.

And therewith he swung merrily into the litten hall. But Walter went out into the moonlit night, and wandered about for an hour or more, and stole warily into the hall and thence into his own chamber. There he did off that royal array, and did his own raiment upon him; he girt him with sword and knife, took his bow and quiver, and stole down and out again, even as he had come in. Then he fetched a compass, and came down into that hazel coppice from the north, and lay all hidden there while the night wore, till he deemed it would lack but little of midnight.

XXI

There he abode amidst the hazels, hearkening every littlest sound; and the sounds were nought but the night voices of the wood, till suddenly there burst forth from the house a great wailing cry. Walter's heart came up into his mouth, but he had no time to do aught, for following hard on the cry came the sound of light feet close to him, the boughs were thrust aside, and there was come the Maid, and she but in her white coat, and barefoot. And then first he felt the sweetness of her flesh on his, for she caught him by the hand and said breathlessly: Now, now! there may yet be time, or even too much, it may be. For the saving of breath ask me no questions, but come!

He dallied not, but went as she led, and they were light-foot, both of them.

They went the same way, due south to wit, whereby he had gone a-hunting with the Lady; and whiles they ran and whiles they walked; but so fast they went, that by grey of the dawn they were come as far as that coppice or thicket of the Lion; and still they hastened onward, and but little had the Maid spoken, save here and there a word to hearten up Walter, and here and there a shy word of endearment. At last the dawn grew into early day, and as they came over the brow of a bent, they looked down over a plain land whereas the trees grew scatter-meal, and beyond the plain rose up the land into long green hills, and over those again were blue mountains great and far away.

Then spake the Maid: Over yonder lie the outlying mountains of the Bears, and through them we needs must pass, to our great peril.

Nay, friend, she said, as he handled his sword-hilt, it must be patience and wisdom to bring us through, and not the fallow blade of one man, though he be a good one. But look! below there runs a stream through the first of the plain, and I see nought for it but we must now rest our bodies. Moreover I have a tale to tell thee which is burning my heart; for maybe there will be a pardon to ask of thee moreover; wherefore I fear thee.

Quoth Walter: How may that be?

She answered him not, but took his hand and led him down the bent. But he said: Thou sayest, rest; but are we now out of all peril of the chase?

She said: I cannot tell till I know what hath befallen her. If she be not to hand to set on her trackers, they will scarce happen on us now; if it be not for that one.

And she shuddered, and he felt her hand change as he held it.

Then she said: But peril or no peril, needs must we rest; for I tell thee again, what I have to say to thee burneth my bosom for fear of thee, so that I can go no further until I have told thee.

Then he said: I wot not of this Queen and her mightiness and her servants. I will ask thereof later. But besides the others, is there not the King's Son, he who loves thee so unworthily?

She paled somewhat, and said: As for him, there had been nought for thee to fear in him, save his treason: but now shall he neither love nor hate any more; he died last midnight.

Yea, and how? said Walter.

Nay, she said, let me tell my tale all together once for all, lest thou blame me overmuch. But first we will wash us and comfort us as best we may, and then amidst our resting shall the word be said.

By then were they come down to the stream-side, which ran fair in pools and stickles amidst rocks and sandy banks. She said: There behind the great grey rock is my bath, friend; and here is thine; and – lo! – the uprising of the sun!

So she went her ways to the said rock, and he bathed him, and washed the night off him, and by then he was clad again she came back fresh and sweet from the water, and with her lap full of cherries from a wilding which overhung her bath. So they sat down together on the green grass above the sand, and ate the breakfast of the wilderness: and Walter was full of content as he watched her, and beheld her sweetness and her loveliness; yet were they, either of them, somewhat shy and shamefaced each with the other; so that he did but kiss her hands once and again, and though she shrank not from him, yet had she no boldness to cast herself into his arms.

XXII

Now she began to say: My friend, now shall I tell thee what I have done for thee and me; and if thou have a mind to blame me, and punish me, yet remember first, that what I have done has been for thee and our hope of happy life. Well, I shall tell thee...

But therewithal her speech failed her; and, springing up, she faced the bent and pointed with her finger, and she all deadly pale, and shaking so that she might scarce stand, and might speak no word, though a feeble gibbering came from her mouth.

Walter leapt up and put his arm about her, and looked whitherward she pointed, and at first saw nought; and then nought but a brown and yellow rock rolling down the bent: and then at last he saw that it was the Evil Thing which had met him when first he came into that land; and now it stood upright, and he could see that it was clad in a coat of yellow samite.

Then Walter stooped down and gat his bow into his hand, and stood before the Maid, while he nocked an arrow. But the monster made ready his tackle while Walter was stooping down, and or ever he could loose, his bow-string twanged, and an arrow flew forth and grazed the Maid's arm above the elbow, so that the blood ran, and the Dwarf gave forth a harsh and horrible cry. Then flew Walter's shaft, and true was it aimed, so that it smote the monster full on the breast, but fell down from him as if he were made of stone. Then the creature set up his horrible cry again, and loosed withal, and Walter deemed that he had smitten the Maid, for she fell down in a heap behind him. Then waxed Walter wood-wroth, and cast down his bow and drew his sword, and strode forward towards the bent against the Dwarf. But he roared out again, and there were words in his roar, and he said: Fool! Thou shalt go free if thou wilt give up the Enemy.

And who, said Walter, is the Enemy?

Yelled the Dwarf: She, the pink and white thing lying there; she is not dead yet; she is but dying for fear of me. Yea, she hath reason! I could have set the shaft in her heart as easily as scratching her arm; but I need her body alive, that I may wreak me on her.

What wilt thou do with her? said Walter; for now he had heard that the Maid was not slain he had waxed wary again, and stood watching his chance.

The Dwarf yelled so at his last word, that no word came from the noise a while, and then he said: What will I with her? Let me at her, and stand by and look on, and then shalt thou have a strange tale to carry off with thee. For I will let thee go this while.

Said Walter: But what need to wreak thee? What hath she done to thee?

What need! what need! roared the Dwarf; have I not told thee that she is the Enemy? And thou askest of what she hath done! of what! Fool, she is the murderer! She hath slain the Lady that was our Lady, and that made us; she whom all we worshipped and adored. O impudent fool!

Therewith he nocked and loosed another arrow, which would have smitten Walter in the face, but that he lowered his head in the very nick of time; then with a great shout he rushed up the bent, and was on the Dwarf before he could get his sword out, and leaping aloft dealt the creature a stroke amidmost of the crown; and so mightily he smote, that he drave the heavy sword right through to the teeth, so that he fell dead straightway.

Walter stood over him a minute, and when he saw that he moved not, he went slowly down to the stream, whereby the Maid yet lay cowering down and quivering all over, and covering her face with her hands. Then he took her by the wrist and said: Up, Maiden, up! And tell me this tale of the slaying!

But she shrunk away from him, and looked at him with wild eyes, and said: What hast thou done with him? Is he gone?

He is dead, said Walter; I have slain him; there lies he with cloven skull on the bent-side: unless, forsooth, he vanish away like the lion I slew! Or else, perchance, he will come to life again! And art thou a lie like to the rest of them? let me hear of this slaying.

She rose up, and stood before him trembling, and said: O, thou art angry with me, and thine anger I cannot bear. Ah, what have I done? Thou hast slain one, and I, maybe, the other; and never had we escaped till both these twain were dead. Ah! Thou dost not know! Thou dost not know! O me! What shall I do to appease thy wrath!

He looked on her, and his heart rose to his mouth at the thought of sundering from her. Still he looked on her, and her piteous friendly face melted all his heart; he threw down his sword, and took her by the shoulders, and kissed her face over and over, and strained her to him, so that he felt the sweetness of her bosom. Then he lifted her up like a child, and set her down on the green grass, and went down to the water, and filled his hat therefrom, and came back to her; then he gave her to drink, and bathed her face and her hands, so that the colour came aback to the cheeks and lips of her: and she smiled on him and kissed his hands, and said: O now thou art kind to me.

Yea, said he, and true it is that if thou hast slain, I have done no less, and if thou hast lied, even so have I; and if thou hast played the wanton, as I deem not that thou hast, I full surely have so done. So now thou shalt pardon me, and when thy spirit has come back to thee, thou shalt tell me thy tale in all friendship, and in all loving-kindness will I hearken the same.

Therewith he knelt before her and kissed her feet. But she said: Yea, yea; what thou willest, that will I do. But first tell me one thing. Hast thou buried this horror and hidden him in the earth?

He deemed that fear had bewildered her, and that she scarcely yet knew how things had gone. But he said: Fair sweet friend, I have not done it as yet; but now will I go and do it, if it seem good to thee.

Yea, she said, but first must thou smite off his head, and lay it by his buttocks when he is in the earth; or evil things will happen else. This of the burying is no idle matter, I bid thee believe.

I doubt it not, said he; surely such malice as was in this one will be hard to slay. And he picked up his sword, and turned to go to the field of deed.

She said: I must needs go with thee; terror hath so filled my soul, that I durst not abide here without thee.

So they went both together to where the creature lay. The Maid durst not look on the dead monster, but Walter noted that he was girt with a big ungainly sax; so he drew it from the sheath, and there smote off the hideous head of the fiend with his own weapon. Then they twain together laboured the earth, she with Walter's sword, he with the ugly sax, till they had made a grave deep and wide enough; and therein they thrust the creature, and covered him up, weapons and all together.

XXIII

Thereafter Walter led the Maid down again, and said to her: Now, sweetling, shall the story be told.

Nay, friend, she said, not here. This place hath been polluted by my craven fear and the horror of the vile wretch, of whom no words may tell his vileness. Let us hence and onward. Thou seest I have once more come to life again.

But, said he, thou hast been hurt by the Dwarf's arrow.

She laughed, and said: Had I never had greater hurt from them than that, little had been the tale thereof: yet whereas thou lookest dolorous about it, we will speedily heal it.

Therewith she sought about, and found nigh the stream-side certain herbs; and she spake words over them, and bade Walter lay them on the wound, which, forsooth, was of the least, and he did so, and bound a strip of his shirt about her arm; and then would she set forth. But he said: Thou art all unshod; and but if that be seen to, our journey shall be stayed by thy foot-soreness: I may make a shift to fashion thee brogues.

She said: I may well go barefoot. And in any case, I entreat thee that we tarry here no longer, but go away hence, if it be but for a mile.

And she looked piteously on him, so that he might not gainsay her.

So then they crossed the stream, and set forward, when amidst all these haps the day was worn to mid-morning. But after they had gone a mile, they sat them down on a knoll under the shadow of a big thorn tree, within sight of the mountains. Then said Walter: Now will I cut thee the brogues from the skirt of my buff-coat, which shall be well meet for such work; and meanwhile shalt thou tell me thy tale.

Thou art kind, she said; but be kinder yet, and abide my tale till we have done our day's work. For we were best to make no long delay here; because, though thou hast slain the King-dwarf, yet there be others of his kindred, who swarm in some parts of the wood as the rabbits in a warren. Now true it is that they have but little understanding, less, it may be, than the very brute beasts; and that, as I said afore, unless they be set on our slot like to hounds, they shall have no inkling of where to seek us, yet might they happen upon us by mere misadventure. And moreover, friend, quoth she, blushing, I would beg of thee some little respite; for though I scarce fear thy wrath any more, since thou hast been so kind to me, yet is there shame in that which I have to tell thee. Wherefore, since the fairest of the day is before us, let us use it all we may, and, when thou hast done me my new foot-gear, get us gone forward again.

He kissed her kindly and yea-said her asking: he had already fallen to work on the leather, and in a while had fashioned her the brogues; so she tied them to her feet, and arose with a smile and said: Now am I hale and strong again, what with the rest, and what with thy loving-kindness, and thou shalt see how nimble I shall be to leave this land, for as fair as it is. Since forsooth a land of lies it is, and of grief to the children of Adam.

So they went their ways thence, and fared nimbly indeed, and made no stay till some three hours after noon, when they rested by a thicket-side, where the strawberries grew plenty; they ate thereof what they would: and from a great oak hard by Walter shot him first one culver, and then another, and hung them to his girdle to be for their evening's meat; sithence they went forward again, and nought befell them to tell of, till they were come, whenas it lacked scarce an hour of sunset, to the banks of another river, not right great, but bigger than the last one. There the Maid cast herself down and said: Friend, no further will thy friend go this even; nay, to say sooth, she cannot. So now we will eat of thy venison, and then shall my tale be, since I may no longer delay it; and thereafter shall our slumber be sweet and safe as I deem.

She spake merrily now, and as one who feared nothing, and Walter was much heartened by her words and her voice, and he fell to and made a fire, and a woodland oven in the earth, and sithence dighted his fowl, and baked them after the manner of woodmen. And they ate, both of them, in all love, and in good-liking of life, and were much strengthened by their supper. And when they were done, Walter eked his fire, both against the chill of the midnight and dawning, and for a guard against wild beasts, and by that time night was come, and the moon arisen. Then the Maiden drew up to the fire, and turned to Walter and spake.

XXIV

Now, friend, by the clear of the moon and this firelight will I tell what I may and can of my tale. Thus it is: If I be wholly of the race of Adam I wot not; nor can I tell thee how many years old I may be. For there are, as it were, shards or gaps in my life, wherein are but a few things dimly remembered, and doubtless many things forgotten. I remember well when I was a little child, and right happy, and there were people about me whom I loved, and who loved me. It was not in this land; but all things were lovely there; the year's beginning, the happy mid-year, the year's waning, the year's ending, and then again its beginning. That passed away, and then for a while is more than dimness, for nought I remember save that I was. Thereafter I remember again, and am a young maiden, and I know some things, and long to know more. I am nowise happy; I am amongst people who bid me go, and I go; and do this, and I do it: none loveth me, none tormenteth me; but I wear my heart in longing for I scarce know what. Neither then am I in this land, but in a land that I love not, and a house that is big and stately, but nought lovely. Then is a dim time again, and sithence a time not right clear; an evil time, wherein I am older, well-nigh grown to womanhood. There are a many folk about me, and they foul, and greedy, and hard; and my spirit is fierce, but my body feeble; and I am set to tasks that I would not do, by them that are unwiser than I; and smitten I am by them that are less valiant than I; and I know lack, and stripes, and divers misery. But all that is now become but a dim picture to me, save that amongst all these unfriends is a friend to me; an old woman, who telleth me sweet tales of other life, wherein all is high and goodly, or at the least valiant and doughty, and she setteth hope in my heart and learneth me, and maketh me to know much... O much... so that at last I am grown wise, and wise to be mighty if I durst. Yet am I nought in this land all this while but, as me seemeth, in a great and a foul city.

And then, as it were, I fall asleep; and in my sleep is nought, save here and there a wild dream, somedeal lovely, somedeal hideous: but of this dream is my Mistress a part, and the monster, withal, whose head thou didst cleave today. But when I am awaken from it, then am I verily in this land, and myself, as thou seest me today. And the first part of my life here is this, that I am in the pillared hall yonder, half-clad and with bound hands; and the Dwarf leadeth me to the Lady, and I hear his horrible croak as he sayeth: Lady, will this one do? And then the sweet voice of the Lady saying: This one will do; thou shalt have thy reward: now, set thou the token upon her. Then I remember the Dwarf dragging me away, and my heart sinking for fear of him; but for that time he did me no more harm than the rivetting upon my leg this iron ring which here thou seest.

So from that time forward I have lived in this land, and been the thrall of the Lady; and I remember my life here day by day, and no part of it has fallen into the dimness of dreams. Thereof will I tell thee but little: but this I will tell thee, that in spite of my past dreams, or it may be because of them, I had not lost the wisdom which the old woman had erst learned me, and for more wisdom I longed. Maybe this longing shall now make both thee and me happy, but for the passing time it brought me grief. For at first my Mistress was indeed wayward with me, but as any great lady might be with her bought thrall, whiles caressing me, and whiles chastising me, as her mood went; but she seemed not to be cruel of malice, or with any set purpose. But so it was (rather little by little than by any great sudden uncovering of my intent), that she came to know that I also had some of the wisdom whereby she lived her queenly life. That was about two years after I was first her thrall, and three weary years have gone by since she began to see in me the enemy of her days. Now why or wherefore I know not, but it seemeth that it would not avail her to slay me outright, or suffer me to die; but nought withheld her from piling up griefs and miseries on my head. At last she set her servant, the Dwarf, upon me, even he whose head thou clavest today. Many things I bore from him whereof it wereunseemly for my tongue to tell before thee; but the time came when he exceeded, and I could bear no more; and then I showed him this sharp knife (wherewith I would have thrust me through to the heart if thou hadst not pardoned me e'en now), and I told him that if he forbore me not, I would slay, not him, but myself; and this he might not away with because of the commandment of the Lady, who had given him the word that in any case I must be kept living. And her hand, withal, fear held somewhat hereafter. Yet was there need to me of all my wisdom; for with all this her hatred grew, and whiles raged within her so furiously that it overmastered her fear, and at such times she would have put me to death if I had not escaped her by some turn of my lore.

Now further, I shall tell thee that somewhat more than a year ago hither to this land came the King's Son, the second goodly man, as thou art the third, whom her sorceries have drawn hither since I have dwelt here. Forsooth, when he first came, he seemed to us, to me, and yet more to my Lady, to be as beautiful as an angel, and sorely she loved him; and he her, after his fashion: but he was light-minded and cold-hearted, and in a while he must needs turn his eyes upon me and offer me his love, which was but foul and unkind as it turned out; for when I nay-said him, as maybe I had not done save for fear of my Mistress, he had no pity upon me, but spared not to lead me into the trap of her wrath, and leave me without help, or a good word. But, O friend, in spite of all grief and anguish, I learned still, and waxed wise and wiser, abiding the day of my deliverance, which has come, and thou art come.

Therewith she took Walter's hands and kissed them; but he kissed her face, and her tears wet her lips. Then she went on: But sithence, months ago, the Lady began to weary of this dastard, despite of his beauty; and then it was thy turn to be swept into her net; I partly guess how. For on a day in broad daylight, as I was serving my Mistress in the hall, and the Evil Thing, whose head is now cloven, was lying across the threshold of the door, as it were a dream fell upon me, though I strove to cast it off for fear of chastisement; for the pillared hall wavered and vanished from my sight, and my feet were treading a rough stone pavement instead of the marble wonder of the hall, and there was the scent of the salt sea and of the tackle of ships, and behind me were tall houses and before me the ships indeed, with their ropes beating and their sails flapping and their masts wavering; and in mine ears was the hale and how of mariners; things that I had seen and heard in the dimness of my life gone by.

And there was I, and the Dwarf before me and the Lady after me, going over the gangway aboard of a tall ship, and she gathered way and was gotten out of the haven, and straightway I saw the mariners cast abroad their ancient.

Quoth Walter: What then! Sawest thou the blazon thereon, of a wolf-like beast ramping up against a maiden? And that might well have been thou.

She said: Yea, so it was; but refrain thee, that I may tell on my tale! The ship and the sea vanished away, but I was not back in the hall of the Golden House; and again were we three in the street of the self-same town which we had but just left; but somewhat dim was my vision thereof, and I saw little save the door of a goodly house before me, and speedily it died out, and we were again in the pillared hall, wherein my thralldom was made manifest.

Maiden, said Walter, one question I would ask thee; to wit, didst thou see me on the quay by the ships?

Nay, she said, there were many folk about, but they were all as images of the aliens to me. Now hearken further: three months thereafter came the dream upon me again, when we were all three together in the Pillared Hall; and again was the vision somewhat dim. Once more we were in the street of a busy town, but all unlike to that other one, and there were men standing together on our right hands by the door of a house.

Yea, yea, quoth Walter; and, forsooth, one of them was who but I.

Refrain thee, beloved! she said; for my tale draweth to its ending, and I would have thee hearken heedfully: for maybe thou shalt once again deem my deed past pardon. Some twenty days after this last dream, I had some leisure from my Mistress's service, so I went to disport me by the Well of the Oak tree (or forsooth she might have set in my mind the thought of going there, that I might meet thee and give her some occasion against me); and I sat thereby, nowise loving the earth, but sick at heart, because of late the King's Son had been more than ever instant with me to yield him my body, threatening me else with casting me into all that the worst could do to me of torments and shames day by day. I say my heart failed me, and I was well-nigh brought to the point of yea-saying his desires, that I might take the chance of something befalling me that were less bad than the worst. But here must I tell thee a thing, and pray thee to take it to heart. This, more than aught else, had given me strength to nay-say that dastard, that my wisdom both hath been, and now is, the wisdom of a wise maid and not of a woman, and all the might thereof shall I lose with my maidenhead. Evil wilt thou think of me then, for all I was tried so sore, that I was at point to cast it all away, so wretchedly as I shrank from the horror of the Lady's wrath.

But there as I sat pondering these things, I saw a man coming, and thought no otherwise thereof but that it was the King's Son, till I saw the stranger drawing near, and his golden hair and his grey eyes; and then I heard his voice, and his kindness pierced my heart, and I knew that my friend had come to see me; and O, friend, these tears are for the sweetness of that past hour!

Said Walter: I came to see my friend, I also. Now have I noted what thou badest me; and I will forbear all as thou commandest me, till we be safe out of the desert and far away from all evil things; but wilt thou ban me from all caresses?

She laughed amidst of her tears, and said: O, nay, poor lad, if thou wilt be but wise.

Then she leaned toward him, and took his face betwixt her hands and kissed him oft, and the tears started in his eyes for love and pity of her.

Then she said: Alas, friend! Even yet mayst thou doom me guilty, and all thy love may turn away from me, when I have told thee all that I have done for the sake of thee and me. O, if then there might be some chastisement for the guilty woman and not mere sundering!

Fear nothing, sweetling, said he; for indeed I deem that already I know partly what thou hast done.

She sighed, and said: I will tell thee next, that I banned thy kissing and caressing of me till today because I knew that my Mistress would surely know if a man, if thou, hadst so much as touched a finger of mine in love. It was to try me herein that on the morning of the hunting she kissed and embraced me, till I almost died thereof, and showed thee my shoulder and my limbs; and to try thee withal, if thine eye should glister or thy cheek flush thereat; for indeed she was raging in jealousy of thee. Next, my friend, even whiles we were talking together at the Well of the Rock, I was pondering on what we should do to escape from this land of lies. Maybe thou wilt say: Why didst thou not take my hand and flee with me as we fled today? Friend, it is most true, that were she not dead we had not escaped thus far. For her trackers would have followed us, set on by her, and brought us back to an evil fate. Therefore I tell thee that from the first I did plot the death of those two, the Dwarf and the Mistress. For no otherwise mightest thou live, or I escape from death in life. But as to the dastard who threatened me with a thrall's pains, I heeded him nought to live or die, for well I knew that thy valiant sword, yea, or thy bare hands, would speedily tame him. Now first I knew that I must make a show of yielding to the King's Son; and somewhat how I did therein, thou knowest. But no night and no time did I give him to bed me, till after I had met thee as thou wentest to the Golden House, before the adventure of fetching the lion's skin; and up to that time I had scarce known what to do, save ever to bid thee, with sore grief and pain, to yield thee to the wicked woman's desire. But as we spake together there by the stream, and I saw that the Evil Thing (whose head thou clavest e'en now) was spying on us, then amidst the sickness of terror which ever came over me whensoever I thought of him, and much more when I saw him (ah! he is dead now!), it came flashing into my mind how I might destroy my enemy. Therefore I made the Dwarf my messenger to her, by bidding thee to my bed in such wise that he might hear it. And wot thou well, that he speedily carried her the tidings. Meanwhile I hastened to lie to the King's Son, and all privily bade him come to me and not thee. And thereafter, by dint of waiting and watching, and taking the only chance that there was, I met thee as thou camest back from fetching the skin of the lion that never was, and gave thee that warning, or else had we been undone indeed.

Said Walter: Was the lion of her making or of thine then?

She said: Of hers: why should I deal with such a matter?

Yea, said Walter, but she verily swooned, and she was verily wroth with the Enemy.

The Maid smiled, and said: If her lie was not like very sooth, then had she not been the crafts-master that I knew her: one may lie otherwise than with the tongue alone: yet indeed her wrath against the Enemy was nought feigned; for the Enemy was even I, and in these latter days never did her wrath leave me. But to go on with my tale.

Now doubt thou not, that, when thou camest into the hall yester eve, the Mistress knew of thy counterfeit tryst with me, and meant nought but death for thee; yet first would she have thee in her arms again, therefore did she make much of thee at table (and that was partly for my torment also), and therefore did she make that tryst with thee, and deemed doubtless that thou wouldst not dare to forgo it, even if thou shouldst go to me thereafter.

Now I had trained that dastard to me as I have told thee, but I gave him a sleepy draught, so that when I came to the bed he might not move toward me nor open his eyes: but I lay down beside him, so that the Lady might know that my body had been there; for well had she wotted if it had not. Then, as there I lay, I cast over him thy shape, so that none might have known, but that thou wert lying by my side, and there, trembling, I abode what should befall. Thus I passed through the hour whenas thou shouldest have been at her chamber, and the time of my tryst with thee was come as the Mistress would be deeming; so that I looked for her speedily, and my heart well-nigh failed me for fear of her cruelty.

Presently then I heard a stirring in her chamber, and I slipped from out the bed, and hid me behind the hangings, and was like to die for fear of her; and lo, presently she came stealing in softly, holding a lamp in one hand and a knife in the other. And I tell thee of a sooth that I also had a sharp knife in my hand to defend my life if need were. She held the lamp up above her head before she drew near to the bedside, and I heard her mutter: She is not there then! But she shall be taken. Then she went up to the bed and stooped over it, and laid her hand on the place where I had lain; and therewith her eyes turned to that false image of thee lying there, and she fell a-trembling and shaking, and the lamp fell to the ground and was quenched (but there was bright moonlight in the room, and still I could see what betid). But she uttered a noise like the low roar of a wild beast, and I saw her arm and hand rise up, and the flashing of the steel beneath the hand, and then down came the hand and the steel, and I went nigh to swooning lest perchance I had wrought over well, and thine image were thy very self. The dastard died without a groan: why should I lament him? I cannot. But the Lady drew him toward her, and snatched the clothes from off his shoulders and breast, and fell a-gibbering sounds mostly without meaning, but broken here and there with words. Then I heard her say: I shall forget; I shall forget; and the new days shall come. Then was there silence of her a little, and thereafter she cried out in a terrible voice: O no, no, no! I cannot forget; I cannot forget; and she raised a great wailing cry that filled all the night with horror (didst thou not hear it?), and caught up the knife from the bed and thrust it into her breast, and fell down a dead heap over the bed and on to the man whom she had slain. And then I thought of thee, and joy smote across my terror; how shall I gainsay it? And I fled away to thee, and I took thine hands in mine, thy dear hands, and we fled away together. Shall we be still together?

He spoke slowly, and touched her not, and she, forbearing all sobbing and weeping, sat looking wistfully on him. He said: I think thou hast told me all; and whether thy guile slew her, or her own evil heart, she was slain last night who lay in mine arms the night before. It was ill, and ill done of me, for I loved not her but thee, and I wished for her death that I might be with thee. Thou wottest this, and still thou lovest me, it may be over-weeningly. What have I to say then? If there be any guilt of guile, I also was in the guile; and if there be any guilt of murder, I also was in the murder. Thus we say to each other; and to God and his Hallows we say: We two have conspired and slain the woman who tormented one of us, and would have slain the other; and if we have done amiss therein, then shall we two together pay the penalty; for in this have we done as one body and one soul.

Therewith he put his arms about her and kissed her, but soberly and friendly, as if he would comfort her. And thereafter he said to her: Maybe tomorrow, in the sunlight, I will ask thee of this woman, what she verily was; but now let her be. And thou, thou art over-wearied, and I bid thee sleep.

So he went about and gathered of bracken a great heap for her bed, and did his coat thereover, and led her thereto, and she lay down meekly, and smiled and crossed her arms over her bosom, and presently fell asleep. But as for him, he watched by the fire-side till dawn began to glimmer, and then he also laid him down and slept.

XXV

When the day was bright Walter arose, and met the Maid coming up from the river-bank, fresh and rosy from the water. She paled a little when they met face to face, and she shrank from him shyly. But he took her hand and kissed her frankly; and the two were glad, and had no need to tell each other of their joy, though much else they deemed they had to say, could they have found words thereto.

So they came to their fire and sat down, and fell to breakfast; and ere they were done, the Maid said: My Master, thou seest we be come nigh unto the hill country, and today about sunset, belike, we shall come into the Land of the Bear-folk; and both it is, that there is peril if we fall into their hands, and that we may scarce escape them. Yet I deem that we may deal with the peril by wisdom.

What is the peril? said Walter; I mean, what is the worst of it?

Said the Maid: To be offered up in sacrifice to their God.

But if we escape death at their hands, what then? said Walter.

One of two things, said she; the first, that they shall take us into their tribe.

And will they sunder us in that case? said Walter.

Nay, said she.

Walter laughed and said: Therein is little harm then. But what is the other chance?

Said she: That we leave them with their goodwill, and come back to one of the lands of Christendom.

Said Walter: I am not all so sure that this is the better of the two choices, though, forsooth, thou seemest to think so. But tell me now, what like is their God, that they should offer up newcomers to him?

Their God is a woman, she said, and the Mother of their nation and tribes (or so they deem) before the days when they had chieftains and Lords of Battle.

That will be long ago, said he; how then may she be living now?

Said the Maid: Doubtless that woman of yore agone is dead this many and many a year; but they take to them still a new woman, one after other, as they may happen on them, to be in the stead of the Ancient Mother. And to tell thee the very truth right out, she that lieth dead in the Pillared Hall was even the last of these; and now, if they knew it, they lack a God. This shall we tell them.

Yea, yea! said Walter, a goodly welcome shall we have of them then, if we come amongst them with our hands red with the blood of their God!

She smiled on him and said: If I come amongst them with the tidings that I have slain her, and they trow therein, without doubt they shall make me Lady and Goddess in her stead.

This is a strange world, said Walter; but if so they do, how shall that further us in reaching the kindreds of the world, and the folk of the Holy Church?

She laughed outright, so joyous was she grown, now that she knew that his life was yet to be a part of hers. Sweetheart, she said, now I see that thou desirest wholly what I desire; yet in any case, abiding with them would be living and not dying, even as thou hadst it e'en now. But, forsooth, they will not hinder our departure if they deem me their God; they do not look for it, nor desire it, that their God should dwell with them daily. Have no fear. Then she laughed again, and said: What! Thou lookest on me and deemest me to be but a sorry image of a goddess; and me with my scanty coat and bare arms and naked feet! But wait! I know well how to array me when the time cometh. Thou shalt see it! And now, my Master, were it not meet that we took to the road?

So they arose, and found a ford of the river that took the Maid but to the knee, and so set forth up the greensward of the slopes whereas there were but few trees; so went they faring toward the hill country.

At the last they were come to the feet of the very hills, and in the hollows betwixt the buttresses of them grew nut and berry trees, and the greensward round about them was both thick and much flowery. There they stayed them and dined, whereas Walter had shot a hare by the way, and they had found a bubbling spring under a grey stone in a bight of the coppice, wherein now the birds were singing their best.

When they had eaten and had rested somewhat, the Maid arose and said: Now shall the Queen array herself, and seem like a very goddess.

Then she fell to work, while Walter looked on; and she made a garland for her head of eglantine where the roses were the fairest; and with mingled flowers of the summer she wreathed her middle about, and let the garland of them hang down to below her knees; and knots of the flowers she made fast to the skirts of her coat, and did them for arm-rings about her arms, and for anklets and sandals for her feet. Then she set a garland about Walter's head, and then stood a little off from him and set her feet together, and lifted up her arms, and said: Lo now! Am I not as like to the Mother of Summer as if I were clad in silk and gold? And even so shall I be deemed by the folk of the Bear. Come now, thou shalt see how all shall be well.

She laughed joyously; but he might scarce laugh for pity of his love. Then they set forth again, and began to climb the hills, and the hours wore as they went in sweet converse; till at last Walter looked on the Maid, and smiled on her, and said: One thing I would say to thee, lovely friend, to wit: wert thou clad in silk and gold, thy stately raiment might well suffer a few stains, or here and there a rent maybe; but stately would it be still when the folk of the Bear should come up against thee. But as to this flowery array of thine, in a few hours it shall be all faded and nought. Nay, even now, as I look on thee, the meadow-sweet that hangeth from thy girdle-stead has waxen dull, and welted; and the blossoming eyebright that is for a hem to the little white coat of thee is already forgetting how to be bright and blue. What sayest thou then?

She laughed at his word, and stood still, and looked back over her shoulder, while with her fingers she dealt with the flowers about her side like to a bird preening his feathers. Then she said: Is it verily so as thou sayest? Look again!

So he looked, and wondered; for lo! beneath his eyes the spires of the meadow-sweet grew crisp and clear again, the eyebright blossoms shone once more over the whiteness of her legs; the eglantine roses opened, and all was as fresh and bright as if it were still growing on its own roots.

He wondered, and was even somedeal aghast; but she said: Dear friend, be not troubled! Did I not tell thee that I am wise in hidden lore? But in my wisdom shall be no longer any scathe to any man. And again, this my wisdom, as I told thee erst, shall end on the day whereon I am made all happy. And it is thou that shall wield it all, my Master. Yet must my wisdom needs endure for a little season yet. Let us on then, boldly and happily.

XXVI

On they went, and before long they were come up on to the down-country, where was scarce a tree, save gnarled and knotty thorn bushes here and there, but nought else higher than the whin. And here on these upper lands they saw that the pastures were much burnt with the drought, albeit summer was not worn old. Now they went making due south toward the mountains, whose heads they saw from time to time rising deep blue over the bleak greyness of the downland ridges. And so they went, till at last, hard on sunset, after they had climbed long over a high bent, they came to the brow thereof and, looking down, beheld new tidings.

There was a wide valley below them, greener than the downs which they had come over, and greener yet amidmost, from the watering of a stream which, all beset with willows, wound about the bottom. Sheep and neat were pasturing about the dale, and moreover a long line of smoke was going up straight into the windless heavens from the midst of a ring of little round houses built of turfs and thatched with reed. And beyond that, toward an eastward-lying bight of the dale, they could see what looked like to a doom-ring of big stones, though there were no rocky places in that land. About the cooking fire amidst of the houses, and here and there otherwhere, they saw, standing or going to and fro, huge figures of men and women, with children playing about betwixt them.

They stood and gazed down at it for a minute or two, and though all were at peace there, yet to Walter, at least, it seemed strange and awful. He spake softly, as though he would not have his voice reach those men, though they were, forsooth, out of earshot of anything save a shout: Are these then the children of the Bear? What shall we do now?

She said: Yea, of the Bear they be, though there be other folks of them far and far away to the northward and eastward, near to the borders of the sea. And as to what we shall do, let us go down at once, and peacefully. Indeed, by now there will be no escape from them; for – lo you! – they have seen us.

Forsooth, some three or four of the big men had turned them toward the bent whereon stood the twain, and were hailing them in huge, rough voices, wherein, howsoever, seemed to be no anger or threat. So the Maid took Walter by the hand, and thus they went down quietly, and the Bear-folk, seeing them, stood all together, facing them, to abide their coming. Walter saw of them, that though they were very tall and bigly made, they were not so far above the stature of men as to be marvels. The carles were long-haired, and shaggy of beard, and their hair all red or tawny; their skins, where their naked flesh showed, were burned brown with sun and weather, but to a fair and pleasant brown, nought like to blackamoors. The queans were comely and well-eyed; nor was there anything of fierce or evil-looking about either the carles or the queans, but somewhat grave and solemn of aspect were they. Clad were they all, saving the young men-children, but somewhat scantily, and in nought save sheep-skins or deer-skins.

For weapons they saw amongst them clubs, and spears headed with bone or flint, and ugly axes of big flints set in wooden handles; nor was there, as far as they could see, either now or afterward, any bow amongst them. But some of the young men seemed to have slings done about their shoulders.

Now when they were come but three fathom from them, the Maid lifted up her voice and spake clearly and sweetly: Hail, ye folk of the Bears! We have come amongst you, and that for your good and not for your hurt: wherefore we would know if we be welcome.

There was an old man who stood foremost in the midst, clad in a mantle of deer-skins worked very goodly, and with a gold ring on his arm, and a chaplet of blue stones on his head, and he spake: Little are ye, but so goodly, that if ye were but bigger, we should deem that ye were come from the Gods' House. Yet have I heard, that how mighty soever may the Gods be, and chiefly our God, they be at whiles nought so bigly made as we of the Bears. How this may be, I wot not. But if ye be not of the Gods or their kindred, then are ye mere aliens; and we know not what to do with aliens, save we meet them in battle, or give them to the God, or save we make them children of the Bear. But yet again, ye may be messengers of some folk who would bind friendship and alliance with us: in which case ye shall at the least depart in peace, and whiles ye are with us shall be our guests in all good cheer. Now, therefore, we bid you declare the matter unto us.

Then spake the Maid: Father, it were easy for us to declare what we be unto you here present. But, me seemeth, ye who be gathered round the fire here this evening are less than the whole tale of the children of the Bear.

So it is, Maiden, said the elder, that many more children hath the Bear.

This then we bid you, said the Maid, that ye send the tokens round and gather your people to you, and when they be assembled in the Doom-ring, then shall we put our errand before you; and according to that, shall ye deal with us.

Thou hast spoken well, said the elder; and even so had we bidden you ourselves. Tomorrow, before noon, shall ye stand in the Doom-ring in this Dale, and speak with the children of the Bear.

Therewith he turned to his own folk and called out something, whereof those twain knew not the meaning; and there came to him, one after another, six young men, unto each of whom he gave a thing from out his pouch, but what it was Walter might not see, save that it was little and of small account: to each, also, he spake a word or two, and straight they set off running, one after the other, turning toward the bent which was over against that whereby the twain had come into the Dale, and were soon out of sight in the gathering dusk.

Then the elder turned him again to Walter and the Maid, and spake: Man and woman, whatsoever ye may be, or whatsoever may abide you tomorrow, tonight, ye are welcome guests to us; so we bid you come eat and drink at our fire.

So they sat all together upon the grass round about the embers of the fire, and ate curds and cheese, and drank milk in abundance; and as the night grew on them they quickened the fire, that they might have light. This wild folk talked merrily amongst themselves, with laughter enough and friendly jests, but to the newcomers they were few-spoken, though, as the twain deemed, for no enmity that they bore them. But this found Walter, that the younger ones, both men and women, seemed to find it a hard matter to keep their eyes off them; and seemed, withal, to gaze on them with somewhat of doubt or, it might be, of fear.

So when the night was wearing a little, the elder arose and bade the twain to come with him, and led them to a small house or booth, which was amidmost of all, and somewhat bigger than the others, and he did them to wit that they should rest there that night, and bade them sleep in peace and without fear till the morrow. So they entered, and found beds thereon of heather and ling, and they laid them down sweetly, like brother and sister, when they had kissed each other. But they noted that four brisk men lay without the booth, and across the door, with their weapons beside them, so that they must needs look upon themselves as captives.

Then Walter might not refrain him, but spake: Sweet and dear friend, I have come a long way from the quay at Langton, and the vision of the Dwarf, the Maid and the Lady; and for this kiss wherewith I have kissed thee e'en now, and the kindness of thine eyes, it was worth the time and the travail. But tomorrow, meseemeth, I shall go no further in this world, though my journey be far longer than from Langton hither. And now may God and All Hallows keep thee amongst this wild folk, whenas I shall be gone from thee.

She laughed low and sweetly, and said: Dear friend, dost thou speak to me thus mournfully to move me to love thee better? Then is thy labour lost; for no better may I love thee than now I do; and that is with mine whole heart. But keep a good courage, I bid thee; for we be not sundered yet, nor shall we be. Nor do I deem that we shall die here, or tomorrow; but many years hence, after we have known all the sweetness of life. Meanwhile, I bid thee goodnight, fair friend!

XXVII

So Walter laid him down and fell asleep, and knew no more till he awoke in bright daylight with the Maid standing over him. She was fresh from the water, for she had been to the river to bathe her, and the sun through the open door fell streaming on her feet close to Walter's pillow. He turned about and cast his arm about them, and caressed them, while she stood smiling upon him; then he arose and looked on her, and said: How thou art fair and bright this morning! And yet… and yet… were it not well that thou do off thee all this faded and drooping bravery of leaves and blossoms, that maketh thee look like to a jongleur's damsel on a morrow of Mayday?

And he gazed ruefully on her.

She laughed on him merrily, and said: Yea, and belike these others think no better of my attire, or not much better; for yonder they are gathering small wood for the burnt-offering; which, forsooth, shall be thou and I, unless I better it all by means of the wisdom I learned of the old woman, and perfected betwixt the stripes of my Mistress, whom a little while ago thou lovedst somewhat.

And as she spake her eyes sparkled, her cheek flushed and her limbs and her feet seemed as if they could scarce refrain from dancing for joy. Then Walter knit his brow, and for a moment a thought half-framed was in his mind. Is it so, that she will bewray me and live without me? And he cast his eyes on to the ground. But she said: Look up, and into mine eyes, friend, and see if there be in them any falseness toward thee! For I know thy thought; I know thy thought. Dost thou not see that my joy and gladness is for the love of thee, and the thought of the rest from trouble that is at hand?

He looked up, and his eyes met the eyes of her love, and he would have cast his arms about her; but she drew aback and said: Nay, thou must refrain thee awhile, dear friend, lest these folk cast eyes on us, and deem us over lover-like for what I am to bid them deem me. Abide a while, and then shall all be in me according to thy will. But now I must tell thee that it is not very far from noon, and that the Bears are streaming into the Dale, and already there is an host of men at the Doom-ring and, as I said, the bale for the burnt-offering is well-nigh dight, whether it be for us, or for some other creature. And now I have to bid thee this, and it will be a thing easy for thee to do, to wit, that thou look as if thou wert of the race of the Gods, and not to blench, or show sign of blenching, whatever betide: to yea-say both my yea-say and my nay-say: and lastly this, which is the only hard thing for thee (but thou hast already done it before somewhat), to look upon me with no masterful eyes of love, nor as if thou wert at once praying me and commanding me; rather thou shalt so demean thee as if thou wert my man all simply, and nowise my master.

O friend beloved, said Walter, here at least art thou the master, and I will do all thy bidding, in certain hope of this, that either we shall live together or die together.

But as they spoke, in came the elder, and with him a young maiden, bearing with them their breakfast of curds and cream and strawberries, and he bade them eat. So they ate, and were not unmerry; and the while of their eating the elder talked with them soberly, but not hardly, or with any seeming enmity: and ever his talk gat on to the drought, which was now burning up the down-pastures; and how the grass in the watered dales, which was no wide spread of land, would not hold out much longer unless the God sent them rain. And Walter noted that those two, the elder and the Maid, eyed each other curiously amidst of this talk; the elder intent on what she might say, and if she gave heed to his words; while on her side the Maid answered his speech graciously and pleasantly, but said little that was of any import: nor would she have him fix her eyes, which wandered lightly from this thing to that; nor would her lips grow stern and stable, but ever smiled in answer to the light of her eyes, as she sat there with her face as the very face of the gladness of the summer day.

XXVIII

At last the old man said: My children, ye shall now come with me unto the Doom-ring of our folk, the Bears of the Southern Dales, and deliver to them your errand; and I beseech you to have pity upon your own bodies, as I have pity on them; on thine especially, Maiden, so fair and bright a creature as thou art; for so it is, that if ye deal us out light and lying words after the manner of dastards, ye shall miss the worship and glory of wending away amidst of the flames, a gift to the God and a hope to the people, and shall be passed by the rods of the folk, until ye faint and fail amongst them, and then shall ye be thrust down into the flow at the Dale's End, and a stone-laden hurdle cast upon you, that we may thenceforth forget your folly.

The Maid now looked full into his eyes, and Walter deemed that the old man shrank before her; but she said: Thou art old and wise, O great man of the Bears, yet nought I need to learn of thee. Now lead us on our way to the Stead of the Errands.

So the elder brought them along to the Doom-ring at the eastern end of the Dale; and it was now all peopled with those huge men, weaponed after their fashion, and standing up, so that the grey stones thereof but showed a little over their heads. But amidmost of the said Ring was a big stone, fashioned as a chair, whereon sat a very old man, long-hoary and white-bearded, and on either side of him stood a great-limbed woman clad in war-gear, holding, each of them, a long spear, and with a flint-bladed knife in the girdle; and there were no other women in all the Mote.

Then the elder led those twain into the midst of the Mote, and there bade them go up on to a wide, flat-topped stone, six feet above the ground, just over against the ancient chieftain; and they mounted it by a rough stair, and stood there before that folk; Walter in his array of the outward world, which had been fair enough, of crimson cloth and silk and white linen, but was now travel-stained and worn; and the Maid with nought upon her, save the smock wherein she had fled from the Golden House of the Wood beyond the World, decked with the faded flowers which she had wreathed about her yesterday. Nevertheless, so it was, that those big men eyed her intently, and with somewhat of worship.

Now did Walter, according to her bidding, sink down on his knees beside her, and drawing his sword, hold it before him, as if to keep all interlopers aloof from the Maid. And there was silence in the Mote, and all eyes were fixed on those twain.

At last the old chief arose and spake: Ye men, here are come a man and a woman, we know not whence; whereas they have given word to our folk who first met them, that they would tell their errand to none save the Mote of the People; which it was their due to do, if they were minded to risk it. For either they be aliens without an errand hither, save, it may be, to beguile us, in which case they shall presently die an evil death; or they have come amongst us that we may give them to the God with flint-edge and fire; or they have a message to us from some folk or other, on the issue of which lieth life or death. Now shall ye hear what they have to say concerning themselves and their faring hither. But, meseemeth, it shall be the woman who is the chief and hath the word in her mouth; for – lo you! – the man kneeleth at her feet, as one who would serve and worship her. Speak out then, woman, and let our warriors hear thee.

Then the Maid lifted up her voice, and spake out clear and shrilling, like to a flute of the best of the minstrels: Ye men of the Children of the Bear, I would ask you a question, and let the chieftain who sitteth before me answer it.

The old man nodded his head, and she went on: Tell me, Children of the Bear, how long a time is worn since ye saw the God of your worship made manifest in the body of a woman!

Said the elder: Many winters have worn since my father's father was a child, and saw the very God in the bodily form of a woman.

Then she said again: Did ye rejoice at her coming, and would ye rejoice if once more she came amongst you?

Yea, said the old chieftain, for she gave us gifts, and learned us lore, and came to us in no terrible shape but as a young woman as goodly as thou.

Then said the Maid: Now, then, is the day of your gladness come; for the old body is dead, and I am the new body of your God, come amongst you for your welfare.

Then fell a great silence on the Mote, till the old man spake and said: What shall I say and live? For if thou be verily the God, and I threaten thee, wilt thou not destroy me? But thou hast spoken a great word with a sweet mouth, and hast taken the burden of blood on thy lily hands; and if the Children of the Bear be befooled of light liars, how shall they put the shame off them? Therefore I say, show to us a token; and if thou be the God, this shall be easy to thee? And if thou show it not, then is thy falsehood manifest, and thou shalt dree the weird. For we shall deliver thee into the hands of these women here, who shall thrust thee down into the flow which is hereby, after they have wearied themselves with whipping thee. But thy man that kneeleth at thy feet shall we give to the true God, and he shall go to her by the road of the flint and the fire. Hast thou heard? Then give to us the sign and the token.

She changed countenance no whit at his word; but her eyes were the brighter, and her cheek the fresher; and her feet moved a little, as if they were growing glad before the dance; and she looked out over the Mote, and spake in her clear voice: Old man, thou needest not to fear for thy words. Forsooth it is not me whom thou threatenest with stripes and a foul death, but some light fool and liar, who is not here. Now hearken! I wot well that ye would have somewhat of me, to wit, that I should send you rain to end this drought, which otherwise seemeth like to lie long upon you: but this rain, I must go into the mountains of the south to fetch it you; therefore shall certain of your warriors bring me on my way, with this my man, up to the great pass of the said mountains, and we shall set out thitherward this very day.

She was silent a while, and all looked on her, but none spake or moved, so that they seemed as images of stone amongst the stones.

Then she spake again and said: Some would say, men of the Bear, that this were a sign and a token great enough? But I know you, and how stubborn and perverse of heart ye be; and how that the gift not yet within your hand is no gift to you; and the wonder ye see not, your hearts trow not. Therefore look ye upon me as here I stand, I who have come from the fairer country and the greenwood of the lands, and see if I bear not the summer with me, and the heart that maketh increase and the hand that giveth.

Lo then! As she spake, the faded flowers that hung about her gathered life and grew fresh again; the woodbine round her neck and her sleek shoulders knit itself together and embraced her freshly, and cast its scent about her face. The lilies that girded her loins lifted up their heads, and the gold of their tassels fell upon her; the eyebright grew clean blue again upon her smock; the eglantine found its blooms again, and then began to shed the leaves thereof upon her feet; the meadow-sweet wreathed amongst it made clear the sweetness of her legs, and the mouse-ear studded her raiment as with gems. There she stood amidst of the blossoms, like a great orient pearl against the fretwork of the goldsmiths, and the breeze that came up the valley from behind bore the sweetness of her fragrance all over the Man-mote.

Then, indeed, the Bears stood up, and shouted and cried, and smote on their shields and tossed their spears aloft. Then the elder rose from his seat, and came up humbly to where she stood, and prayed her to say what she would have done; while the others drew about in knots, but durst not come very nigh to her. She answered the ancient chief, and said, that she would depart presently toward the mountains, whereby she might send them the rain which they lacked, and that thence she would away to the southward for a while; but that they should hear of her or, it might be, see her, before they who were now of middle age should be gone to their fathers.

Then the old man besought her that they might make her a litter of fragrant green boughs, and so bear her away toward the mountain pass amidst a triumph of the whole folk. But she leapt lightly down from the stone, and walked to and fro on the greensward, while it seemed of her that her feet scarce touched the grass; and she spake to the ancient chief where he still kneeled in worship of her, and said: Nay; deemest thou of me that I need bearing by men's hands, or that I shall tire at all when I am doing my will, and I, the very heart of the year's increase? So it is, that the going of my feet over your pastures shall make them to thrive, both this year and the coming years: surely will I go afoot.

So they worshipped her the more, and blessed her; and then first of all they brought meat, the daintiest they might, both for her and for Walter. But they would not look on the Maid whiles she ate, or suffer Walter to behold her the while. Afterwards, when they had eaten, some twenty men, weaponed after their fashion, made them ready to wend with the Maiden up into the mountains, and anon they set out thitherward all together. Howbeit, the huge men held them ever somewhat aloof from the Maid; and when they came to the resting place for that night, where was no house, for it was up amongst the foothills before the mountains, then it was a wonder to see how carefully they built up a sleeping place for her, and tilted it over with their skin cloaks, and how they watched night-long about her. But Walter they let sleep peacefully on the grass, a little way aloof from the watchers round the Maid.

XXIX

Morning came, and they arose and went on their ways, and went all day till the sun was nigh set, and they were come up into the very pass; and in the jaws thereof was an earthen howe. There the Maid bade them stay, and she went up on to the howe, and stood there and spake to them, and said: O men of the Bear, I give you thanks for your following, and I bless you, and promise you the increase of the earth. But now ye shall turn aback, and leave me to go my ways; and my man with the iron sword shall follow me. Now, maybe, I shall come amongst the Bear-folk again before long, and yet again, and learn them wisdom; but for this time it is enough. And I shall tell you that ye were best to hasten home straightway to your houses in the downland dales, for the weather which I have bidden for you is even now coming forth from the forge of storms in the heart of the mountains. Now this last word I give you, that times are changed since I wore the last shape of God that ye have seen, wherefore a change I command you. If so be aliens come amongst you, I will not that ye send them to me by the flint and the fire; rather, unless they be baleful unto you and worthy of an evil death, ye shall suffer them to abide with you; ye shall make them become children of the Bears, if they be goodly enough and worthy, and they shall be my children as ye be; otherwise, if they be ill-favoured and weakling, let them live and be thralls to you, but not join with you, man to woman. Now depart ye with my blessing.

Therewith she came down from the mound, and went her ways up the pass so lightly, that it was to Walter, standing amongst the Bears, as if she had vanished away. But the men of that folk abode standing and worshipping their God for a little while, and that while he durst not sunder him from their company. But when they had blessed him and gone on their way backward, he betook him in haste to following the Maid, thinking to find her abiding him in some nook of the pass.

Howsoever, it was now twilight or more, and, for all his haste, dark night overtook him, so that perforce he was stayed amidst the tangle of the mountain ways. And, moreover, ere the night was grown old, the weather came upon him on the back of a great south wind, so that the mountain nooks rattled and roared, and there was the rain and the hail, with thunder and lightning, monstrous and terrible, and all the huge array of a summer storm. So he was driven at last to crouch under a big rock and abide the day.

But not so were his troubles at an end. For under the said rock he fell asleep, and when he awoke it was day indeed; but as to the pass, the way thereby was blind with the driving rain and the lowering lift; so that, though he struggled as well as he might against the storm and the tangle, he made but little way.

And now once more the thought came on him, that the Maid was of the fays, or of some race even mightier; and it came on him now not as erst, with half fear and whole desire, but with a bitter oppression of dread, of loss and misery; so that he began to fear that she had but won his love to leave him and forget him for a newcomer, after the wont of fay-women, as old tales tell.

Two days he battled thus with storm and blindness, and wanhope of his life; for he was growing weak and fordone. But the third morning the storm abated, though the rain yet fell heavily, and he could see his way somewhat as well as feel it: withal he found that now his path was leading him downwards. As it grew dusk, he came down into a grassy valley with a stream running through it to the southward, and the rain was now but little, coming down but in dashes from time to time. So he crept down to the stream-side, and lay amongst the bushes there; and said to himself, that on the morrow he would get him victual, so that he might live to seek his Maiden through the wide world. He was of somewhat better heart: but now that he was laid quiet, and had no more for that present to trouble him about the way, the anguish of his loss fell upon him the keener, and he might not refrain him from lamenting his dear Maiden aloud, as one who deemed himself in the empty wilderness: and thus he lamented for her sweetness and her loveliness, and the kindness of her voice and her speech, and her mirth. Then he fell to crying out concerning the beauty of her shaping, praising the parts of her body, as her face and her hands and her shoulders and her feet, and cursing the evil fate which had sundered him from the friendliness of her, and the peerless fashion of her.

XXX

Complaining thus-wise, he fell asleep from sheer weariness, and when he awoke it was broad day, calm and bright and cloudless, with the scent of the earth refreshed going up into the heavens, and the birds singing sweetly in the bushes about him: for the dale whereunto he was now come was a fair and lovely place amidst the shelving slopes of the mountains, a paradise of the wilderness, and nought but pleasant and sweet things were to be seen there, now that the morn was so clear and sunny.

He arose and looked about him, and saw where, a hundred yards aloof, was a thicket of small wood, as thorn and elder and whitebeam, all wreathed about with the bines of wayfaring tree; it hid a bight of the stream, which turned round about it, and betwixt it and Walter was the grass short and thick, and sweet, and all beset with flowers; and he said to himself that it was even such a place as wherein the angels were leading the Blessed in the great painted paradise in the choir of the big church at Langton on Holm. But lo! As he looked he cried aloud for joy, for forth from the thicket on to the flowery grass came one like to an angel from out of the said picture, white-clad and barefoot, sweet of flesh, with bright eyes and ruddy cheeks; for it was the Maid herself. So he ran to her, and she abode him, holding forth kind hands to him, and smiling, while she wept for joy of the meeting. He threw himself upon her, and spared not to kiss her, her cheeks and her mouth, and her arms and her shoulders, and wheresoever she would suffer it. Till at last she drew aback a little, laughing on him for love, and said: Forbear now, friend, for it is enough for this time, and tell me how thou hast sped.

Ill, ill, said he.

What ails thee? she said.

Hunger, he said, and longing for thee.

Well, she said, me thou hast; there is one ill-quenched; take my hand, and we will see to the other one.

So he took her hand, and to hold it seemed to him sweet beyond measure. But he looked up, and saw a little blue smoke going up into the air from beyond the thicket; and he laughed, for he was weak with hunger, and he said: Who is at the cooking yonder?

Thou shalt see, she said; and led him therewith into the said thicket and through it, and – lo! – a fair little grassy place, full of flowers, betwixt the bushes and the bight of the stream; and on the little sandy ere, just off the green-sward, was a fire of sticks, and beside it two trouts lying, fat and red-flecked.

Here is the breakfast, said she; when it was time to wash the night off me e'en now, I went down the strand here into the rippling shallow, and saw the bank below it, where the water draws together yonder, and deepens, that it seemed like to hold fish; and, whereas I looked to meet thee presently, I groped the bank for them, going softly; and lo thou! Help me now, that we cook them.

So they roasted them on the red embers, and fell to and ate well, both of them, and drank of the water of the stream out of each other's hollow hands; and that feast seemed glorious to them, such gladness went with it.

But when they were done with their meat, Walter said to the Maid:

And how didst thou know that thou shouldst see me presently?

She said, looking on him wistfully: This needed no wizardry. I lay not so far from thee last night, but that I heard thy voice and knew it.

Said he, Why didst thou not come to me then, since thou heardest me bemoaning thee?

She cast her eyes down, and plucked at the flowers and grass, and said: It was dear to hear thee praising me; I knew not before that I was so sore desired, or that thou hadst taken such note of my body, and found it so dear.

Then she reddened sorely, and said: I knew not that aught of me had such beauty as thou didst bewail.

And she wept for joy. Then she looked on him and smiled, and said: Wilt thou have the very truth of it? I went close up to thee, and stood there hidden by the bushes and the night. And amidst thy bewailing, I knew that thou wouldst soon fall asleep, and in sooth I out-waked thee.

Then was she silent again; and he spake not, but looked on her shyly;

and she said, reddening yet more: Furthermore, I must needs tell thee that I feared to go to thee in the dark night, and my heart so yearning towards thee.

And she hung her head adown; but he said: Is it so indeed, that thou fearest me? Then doth that make me afraid... afraid of thy nay-say. For I was going to entreat thee, and say to thee: Beloved, we have now gone through many troubles; let us now take a good reward at once, and wed together, here amidst this sweet and pleasant house of the mountains, ere we go further on our way; if indeed we go further at all. For where shall we find any place sweeter or happier than this?

But she sprang up to her feet, and stood there trembling before him, because of her love; and she said: Beloved, I have deemed that it were good for us to go seek mankind as they live in the world, and to live amongst them. And as for me, I will tell thee the sooth, to wit, that I long for this sorely. For I feel afraid in the wilderness, and as if I needed help and protection against my Mistress, though she be dead; and I need the comfort of many people, and the throngs of the cities. I cannot forget her: it was but last night that I dreamed (I suppose as the dawn grew a-cold) that I was yet under her hand, and she was stripping me for the torment; so that I woke up panting and crying out. I pray thee be not angry with me for telling thee of my desires; for if thou wouldst not have it so, then here will I abide with thee as thy mate, and strive to gather courage.

He rose up and kissed her face, and said: Nay, I had in sooth no mind to abide here forever; I meant but that we should feast a while here, and then depart: sooth it is, that if thou dreadest the wilderness, somewhat I dread the city.

She turned pale, and said: Thou shalt have thy will, my friend, if it must be so. But bethink thee! We be not yet at our journey's end, and may have many things and much strife to endure, before we be at peace and in welfare. Now shall I tell thee... did I not before?... that while I am a maid untouched, my wisdom, and somedeal of might, abideth with me, and only so long. Therefore I entreat thee, let us go now, side by side, out of this fair valley, even as we are, so that my wisdom and might may help thee at need. For, my friend, I would not that our lives be short, so much of joy as hath now come into them.

Yea, beloved, he said, let us on straightway then, and shorten the while that sundereth us.

Love, she said, thou shalt pardon me one time for all. But this is to be said, that I know somewhat of the haps that lie a little way ahead of us;

partly by my lore, and partly by what I learned of this land of the wild folk whiles thou wert lying asleep that morning.

So they left that pleasant place by the water, and came into the open valley, and went their ways through the pass; and it soon became stony again, as they mounted the bent which went up from out the dale. And when they came to the brow of the said bent, they had a sight of the open country lying fair and joyous in the sunshine, and amidst of it, against the blue hills, the walls and towers of a great city.

Then said the Maid: O, dear friend, lo you! Is not that our abode that lieth yonder, and is so beauteous? Dwell not our friends there, and our protection against uncouth wights, and mere evil things in guileful shapes? O city, I bid thee hail!

But Walter looked on her, and smiled somewhat; and said: I rejoice in thy joy. But there be evil things in yonder city also, though they be not fays nor devils, or it is like to no city that I wot of. And in every city shall foes grow up to us without rhyme or reason, and life therein shall be tangled unto us.

Yea, she said; but in the wilderness amongst the devils, what was to be done by manly might or valiancy? There hadst thou to fall back upon the guile and wizardry which I had filched from my very foes. But when we come down yonder, then shall thy valiancy prevail to cleave the tangle for us. Or at the least, it shall leave a tale of thee behind, and I shall worship thee.

He laughed, and his face grew brighter: Mastery mows the meadow, quoth he, and one man is of little might against many. But I promise thee I shall not be slothful before thee.

XXXI

With that they went down from the bent again, and came to where the pass narrowed so much, that they went betwixt a steep wall of rock on either side; but after an hour's going, the said wall gave back suddenly and, ere they were ware almost, they came on another dale like to that which they had left, but not so fair, though it was grassy and well watered, and not so big either. But here indeed befell a change to them; for – lo! – tents and pavilions pitched in the said valley, and amidst of it a throng of men, mostly weaponed and with horses ready saddled at hand. So they stayed their feet, and Walter's heart failed him, for he said to himself: Who wotteth what these men may be, save that they be aliens? It is most like that we shall be taken as thralls; and then, at the best, we shall be sundered; and that is all one with the worst.

But the Maid, when she saw the horses, and the gay tents, and the pennons fluttering, and the glitter of spears, and gleaming of white armour, smote her palms together for joy, and cried out: Here now are come the folk of the city for our welcoming, and fair and lovely are they, and of many things shall they be thinking, and a many things shall they do, and we shall be partakers thereof. Come then, and let us meet them, fair friend!

But Walter said: Alas! thou knowest not: would that we might flee! But now is it over late; so put we a good face on it, and go to them quietly, as erewhile we did in the Bear-country.

So did they; and there sundered six from the men-at-arms and came to those twain, and made humble obeisance to Walter, but spake no word. Then they made as they would lead them to the others, and the twain went with them wondering, and came into the ring of men-at-arms, and stood before an old hoar knight, armed all, save his head, with most goodly armour, and he also bowed before Walter, but spake no word. Then they took them to the master pavilion, and made signs to them to sit, and they brought them dainty meat and good wine. And the while of their eating arose up a stir about them; and when they were done with their meat, the ancient knight came to them, still bowing in courteous wise, and did them to wit by signs that they should depart: and when they were without, they saw all the other tents struck, and men beginning to busy them with striking the pavilion, and the others mounted and ranked in good order for the road; and there were two horse-litters before them, wherein they were bidden to mount, Walter in one, and the Maid in the other, and no otherwise might they do. Then presently was a horn blown, and all took to the road together; and Walter saw betwixt the curtains of the litter that men-at-arms rode on either side of him, albeit they had left him his sword by his side.

So they went down the mountain-passes, and before sunset were gotten into the plain; but they made no stay for nightfall, save to eat a morsel and drink a draught, going through the night as men who knew their way well. As they went, Walter wondered what would betide, and if peradventure they also would be for offering them up to their Gods; whereas they were aliens for certain, and belike also Saracens. Moreover there was a cold fear at his heart that he should be sundered from the Maid, whereas their masters now were mighty men of war, holding in their hands that which all men desire, to wit, the manifest beauty of a woman. Yet he strove to think the best of it that he might. And so at last, when the night was far spent and dawn was at hand, they stayed at a great and mighty gate in a huge wall. There they blew loudly on the horn thrice, and thereafter the gates were opened, and they all passed through into a street, which seemed to Walter in the glimmer to be both great and goodly amongst the abodes of men. Then it was but a little ere they came into a square, wide-spreading, one side whereof Walter took to be the front of a most goodly house. There the doors of the court opened to them or ever the horn might blow, though, forsooth, blow it did loudly three times; all they entered therein, and men came to Walter and signed to him to alight. So did he, and would have tarried to look about for the Maid, but they suffered it not, but led him up a huge stair into a chamber, very great, and but dimly lighted because of its greatness. Then they brought him to a bed dight as fair as might be, and made signs to him to strip and lie therein. Perforce he did so, and then they bore away his raiment, and left him lying there. So he lay there quietly, deeming it no avail for him, a mother-naked man, to seek escape thence; but it was long ere he might sleep, because of his trouble of mind. At last, pure weariness got the better of his hopes and fears, and he fell into slumber just as the dawn was passing into day.

XXXII

When he awoke again the sun was shining brightly into that chamber, and he looked, and beheld that it was peerless of beauty and riches amongst all that he had ever seen: the ceiling done with gold and over-sea blue; the walls hung with arras of the fairest, though he might not tell what was the history done therein. The chairs and stools were of carven work well be-painted, and amidmost was a great ivory chair under a cloth of estate, of bawdekin of gold and green, much be-pearled; and all the floor was of fine work alexandrine.

He looked on all this, wondering what had befallen him, when – lo! – there came folk into the chamber, to wit, two serving-men well-bedight, and three old men clad in rich gowns of silk. These came to him and (still by signs, without speech) bade him arise and come with them; and when he bade them look to it that he was naked, and laughed doubtfully, they neither laughed in answer, nor offered him any raiment, but still would have him arise, and he did so perforce. They brought him with them out of the chamber, and through certain passages pillared and goodly, till they came to a bath as fair as any might be; and there the serving-men washed him carefully and tenderly, the old men looking on the while. When it was done, still they offered not to clothe him, but led him out, and through the passages again, back to the chamber. Only this time he must pass between a double hedge of men, some weaponed, some in peaceful array, but all clad gloriously, and full chieftain-like of aspect, either for valiancy or wisdom.

In the chamber itself was now a concourse of men, of great estate by deeming of their array; but all these were standing orderly in a ring about the ivory chair aforesaid. Now said Walter to himself: Surely all this looks toward the knife and the altar for me; but he kept a stout countenance despite of all.

So they led him up to the ivory chair, and he beheld on either side thereof a bench, and on each was laid a set of raiment from the shirt upwards; but there was much diversity betwixt these arrays. For one was all of robes of peace, glorious and be-gemmed, unmeet for any save a great king; while the other was war-weed, seemly, well-fashioned but little adorned; nay rather, worn and bestained with weather, and the pelting of the spear-storm.

Now those old men signed to Walter to take which of those raiments he would, and do it on. He looked to the right and the left, and when he had looked on the war-gear, the heart arose in him, and he called to mind the array of the Goldings in the forefront of battle, and he made one step toward the weapons, and laid his hand thereon. Then ran a glad murmur through that concourse, and the old men drew up to him smiling and joyous, and helped him to do them on; and as he took up the helm, he noted that over its broad brown iron sat a golden crown.

So when he was clad and weaponed, girt with a sword and a steel axe in his hand, the elders showed him to the ivory throne, and he laid the axe on the arm of the chair, and drew forth the sword from the scabbard, and sat him down, and laid the ancient blade across his knees; then he looked about on those great men, and spake: How long shall we speak no word to each other, or is it so that God hath stricken you dumb?

Then all they cried out with one voice: All hail to the King, the King of Battle!

Spake Walter: If I be king, will ye do my will as I bid you?

Answered the elder: Nought have we will to do, lord, save as thou biddest.

Said Walter: Thou then, wilt thou answer a question in all truth?

Yea, lord, said the elder, if I may live afterward.

Then said Walter: The woman that came with me into your Camp of the Mountain, what hath befallen her?

The elder answered: Nought hath befallen her, either of good or evil, save that she hath slept and eaten and bathed her. What, then, is the King's pleasure concerning her?

That ye bring her hither to me straightway, said Walter.

Yea, said the elder; and in what guise shall we bring her hither? shall she be arrayed as a servant, or a great lady?

Then Walter pondered a while, and spake at last: Ask her what is her will herein, and as she will have it, so let it be. But set ye another chair beside mine, and lead her thereto. Thou wise old man, send one or two to bring her in hither, but abide thou, for I have a question or two to ask of thee yet. And ye, lords, abide here the coming of my she-fellow, if it weary you not.

So the elder spake to three of the most honourable of the lords, and they went their ways to bring in the Maid.

XXXIII

Meanwhile the King spake to the elder, and said: Now tell me whereof I am become king, and what is the fashion and cause of the king-making; for wondrous it is to me, whereas I am but an alien amidst of mighty men.

Lord, said the old man, thou art become king of a mighty city, which hath under it many other cities and wide lands, and havens by the sea-side, and which lacketh no wealth which men desire. Many wise men dwell therein, and of fools not more than in other lands. A valiant host shall follow thee to battle when needs must thou wend afield; an host not to be withstood, save by the ancient God-folk, if any of them were left upon the earth, as belike none are. And as to the name of our said city, it hight the City of the Stark-wall, or more shortly, Stark-wall. Now as to the fashion of our king-making: If our king dieth and leaveth an heir male, begotten of his body, then is he king after him; but if he die and leave no heir, then send we out a great lord, with knights and sergeants, to that pass of the mountain whereto ye came yesterday; and the first man that cometh unto them, they take and lead to the city, as they did with thee, lord. For we believe and trow that of old time our forefathers came down from the mountains by that same pass, poor and rude, but full of valiancy, before they conquered these lands, and builded the Stark-wall. But now furthermore, when we have gotten the said wanderer, and brought him home to our city, we behold him mother-naked, all the great men of us, both sages and warriors; then if we find him ill-fashioned and counterfeit of his body, we roll him in a great carpet till he dies; or whiles, if he be but a simple man, and without guile, we deliver him for thrall to some artificer amongst us, as a shoemaker, a wright or what not, and so forget him. But in either case we make as if no such man had come to us, and we send again the lord and his knights to watch the pass; for we say that such an one the Fathers of old time have not sent us. But again, when we have seen to the newcomer that he is well-fashioned of his body, all is not done; for we deem that never would the Fathers send us a dolt or a craven to be our king. Therefore we bid the naked one take to him which he will of these raiments, either the ancient armour, which now thou bearest, lord, or this golden raiment here; and if he take the war-gear, as thou takedst it, King, it is well; but if he take the raiment of peace, then hath he the choice either to be thrall of some good-man of the city, or to be proven how wise he may be, and so fare the narrow edge betwixt death and kingship; for if he fall short of his wisdom, then shall he die the death. Thus is thy question answered, King, and praise be to the Fathers that they have sent us one whom none may doubt, either for wisdom or valiancy.

XXXIV

Then all they bowed before the King, and he spake again: What is that noise that I hear without, as if it were the rising of the sea on a sandy shore, when the south-west wind is blowing.

Then the elder opened his mouth to answer; but before he might get out the word, there was a stir without the chamber door, and the throng parted, and lo! amidst of them came the Maid, and she yet clad in nought save the white coat wherewith she had won through the wilderness, save that on her head was a garland of red roses, and her middle was wreathed with the same. Fresh and fair she was as the dawn of June; her face bright, red-lipped and clear-eyed, and her cheeks flushed with hope and love. She went straight to Walter where he sat, and lightly put away with her hand the elder who would lead her to the ivory throne beside the King; but she knelt down before him, and laid her hand on his steel-clad knee, and said: O my lord, now I see that thou hast beguiled me, and that thou wert all along a king-born man coming home to thy realm. But so dear thou hast been to me; and so fair and clear, and so kind withal do thine eyes shine on me from under the grey war-helm, that I will beseech thee not to cast me out utterly, but suffer me to be thy servant and handmaid for a while. Wilt thou not?

But the King stooped down to her and raised her up, and stood on his feet, and took her hands and kissed them, and set her down beside him, and said to her: Sweetheart, this is now thy place till the night cometh, even by my side.

So she sat down there meek and valiant, her hands laid in her lap, and her feet one over the other; while the King said: Lords, this is my beloved, and my spouse. Now, therefore, if ye will have me for King, ye must worship this one for Queen and Lady; or else suffer us both to go our ways in peace.

Then all they that were in the chamber cried out aloud: The Queen, the Lady! The beloved of our lord!

And this cry came from their hearts, and not their lips only; for as they looked on her and the brightness of her beauty, they saw also the meekness of her demeanour and the high heart of her, and they all fell to loving her. But the young men of them, their cheeks flushed as they beheld her, and their hearts went out to her, and they drew their swords and brandished them aloft, and cried out for her as men made suddenly drunk with love: The Queen, the Lady, the lovely one!

XXXV

But while this betid, that murmur without, which is aforesaid, grew louder; and it smote on the King's ear, and he said again to the elder: Tell us now of that noise withoutward, what is it?

Said the elder: If thou, King, and the Queen, wilt but arise and stand in the window, and go forth into the hanging gallery thereof, then shall ye know at once what is this rumour, and therewithal shall ye see a sight meet to rejoice the heart of a king new come into kingship.

So the King arose and took the Maid by the hand, and went to the window and looked forth; and – lo! – the great square of the place all thronged with folk as thick as they could stand, and the more part of the carles with a weapon in hand, and many armed right gallantly. Then he went out into the gallery with his Queen, still holding her hand, and his lords and wise men stood behind him. Straightway then arose a cry and a shout of joy and welcome that rent the very heavens, and the great place was all glittering and strange with the tossing up of spears and the brandishing of swords, and the stretching forth of hands.

But the Maid spake softly to King Walter and said: Here then is the wilderness left behind a long way, and here is warding and protection against the foes of our life and soul. O blessed be thou and thy valiant heart!

But Walter spake nothing, but stood as one in a dream; and yet, if that might be, his longing toward her increased manifold.

But down below, amidst of the throng, stood two neighbours somewhat anigh to the window; and quoth one to the other: See thou! The new man in the ancient armour of the Battle of the Waters, bearing the sword that slew the foeman king on the Day of the Doubtful Onset! Surely this is a sign of good luck to us all.

Yea, said the second, he beareth his armour well, and the eyes are bright in the head of him; but hast thou beheld well his she-fellow, and what the like of her is?

I see her, said the other, that she is a fair woman; yet somewhat worse clad than simply. She is in her smock, man, and were it not for the balusters I deem ye should see her barefoot. What is amiss with her?

Dost thou not see her, said the second neighbour, that she is not only a fair woman, but yet more, one of those lovely ones that draw the heart out of a man's body, one may scarce say for why? Surely Stark-wall hath cast a lucky net this time. And as to her raiment, I see of her that she is clad in white and wreathed with roses, but that the flesh of her is so wholly pure and sweet that it maketh all her attire but a part of her body, and halloweth it, so that it hath the semblance of gems. Alas, my friend! Let us hope that this Queen will fare abroad unseldom amongst the people.

Thus, then, they spake; but after a while the King and his mate went back into the chamber, and he gave command that the women of the Queen should come and fetch her away, to attire her in royal array. And thither came the fairest of the honourable damsels, and were fain of being her waiting-women. Therewithal the King was unarmed, and dight most gloriously, but still he bore the Sword of the King's Slaying: and sithence were the King and the Queen brought into the great hall of the palace, and they met on the dais, and kissed before the lords and other folk that thronged the hall. There they ate a morsel and drank a cup together, while all beheld them; and then were they brought forth, and a white horse of the goodliest, well bedight, brought for each of them, and thereon they mounted, and went their ways together, by the lane which the huge throng made for them, to the great church, for the hallowing and the crowning; and they were led by one squire alone, and he unarmed; for such was the custom of Stark-wall when a new king should be hallowed: so came they to the great church (for that folk was not miscreant, so to say), and they entered it, they two alone, and went into the choir: and when they had stood there a little while wondering at their lot, they heard how the bells fell a-ringing tunefully over their heads; and then drew near the sound of many trumpets blowing together, and thereafter the voices of many folk singing; and then were the great doors thrown open, and the bishop and his priests came into the church with singing and minstrelsy, and thereafter came the whole throng of the folk, and presently the nave of the church was filled by it, as when the water follows the cutting of the dam, and fills up the dyke. Thereafter came the bishop and his men into the choir, and came up to the King, and gave him and the Queen the kiss of peace. Then was mass sung gloriously; and thereafter was the King anointed and crowned, and great joy was made throughout the church. Afterwards they went back afoot to the palace, they two alone together, with none but the esquire going before to show them the way. And as they went, they passed close beside those two neighbours, whose talk has been told of afore, and the first one, he who had praised the King's war-array, spake and said: Truly, neighbour, thou art in the right of it; and now the Queen has been dight duly, and hath a crown on her head, and is clad in white samite done all over with pearls, I see her to be of exceeding goodliness; as goodly, maybe, as the Lord King.

Quoth the other: Unto me she seemeth as she did e'en now; she is clad in white, as then she was, and it is by reason of the pure and sweet flesh of her that the pearls shine out and glow, and by the holiness of her body is her rich attire hallowed; but, forsooth, it seemed to me as she went past as though paradise had come anigh to our city, and that all the air breathed of it. So I say, praise be to God and His Hallows who hath suffered her to dwell amongst us!

Said the first man: Forsooth, it is well; but knowest thou at all whence she cometh, and of what lineage she may be?

Nay, said the other, I wot not whence she is; but this I wot full surely, that when she goeth away, they whom she leadeth with her shall be well bestead. Again, of her lineage nought know I; but this I know, that they that come of her, to the twentieth generation, shall bless and praise the memory of her, and hallow her name little less than they hallow the name of the Mother of God.

So spake those two; but the King and Queen came back to the palace, and sat among the lords and at the banquet which was held thereafter, and long was the time of their glory, till the night was far spent and all men must seek to their beds.

XXXVI

Lomg it was, indeed, till the women, by the King's command, had brought the Maid to the King's chamber; and he met her, and took her by the shoulders and kissed her, and said: Art thou not weary, sweetheart? Doth not the city, and the thronging folk, and the watching eyes of the great ones... doth it not all lie heavy on thee, as it doth upon me?

She said: And where is the city now? Is not this the wilderness again, and thou and I alone together therein?

He gazed at her eagerly, and she reddened, so that her eyes shone light amidst the darkness of the flush of her cheeks.

He spake trembling and softly, and said: Is it not in one matter better than the wilderness? Is not the fear gone, yea, every whit thereof?

The dark flush had left her face, and she looked on him exceeding sweetly, and spoke steadily and clearly: Even so it is, beloved. Therewith she set her hand to the girdle that girt her loins, and did it off, and held it out toward him, and said: Here is the token; this is a maid's girdle, and the woman is ungirt.

So he took the girdle and her hand withal, and cast his arms about her: and amidst the sweetness of their love and their safety, and assured hope of many days of joy, they spake together of the hours when they fared the razor-edge betwixt guile and misery and death, and the sweeter yet it grew to them because of it; and many things she told him ere the dawn, of the evil days bygone, and the dealings of the Mistress with her, till the grey day stole into the chamber to make manifest her loveliness; which, forsooth, was better even than the deeming of that man amidst the throng whose heart had been so drawn towards her. So they rejoiced together in the new day.

But when the full day was, and Walter arose, he called his thanes and wise men to the council; and first he bade open the prison doors, and feed the needy and clothe them, and make good cheer to all men, high and low, rich and unrich; and thereafter he took counsel with them on many matters, and they marvelled at his wisdom and the keenness of his wit; and so it was, that some were but half pleased thereat, whereas they saw that their will was like to give way before his in all matters. But the wiser of them rejoiced in him, and looked for good days while his life lasted.

Now of the deeds that he did, and his joys and his griefs, the tale shall tell no more; nor of how he saw Langton again, and his dealings there.

In Stark-wall he dwelt, and reigned a King, well beloved of his folk, sorely feared of their foemen. Strife he had to deal with, at home and abroad; but therein he was not quelled, till he fell asleep fair and softly, when this world had no more of deeds for him to do. Nor may it be said that the needy lamented him; for no needy had he left in his own land. And few foes he left behind to hate him.

As to the Maid, she so waxed in loveliness and kindness, that it was a year's joy for any to have cast eyes upon her in street or on field. All wizardry left her since the day of her wedding; yet of wit and wisdom she had enough left and to spare; for she needed no going about, and no guile, any more than hard commands, to have her will done. So loved she was by all folk, forsooth, that it was a mere joy for any to go about her errands. To be short, she was the land's increase, and the city's safeguard, and the bliss of the folk.

Somewhat, as the days passed, it misgave her that she had beguiled the Bear-folk to deem her their God; and she considered and thought how she might atone it.

So the second year after they had come to Stark-wall, she went with certain folk to the head of the pass that led down to the Bears; and there she stayed the men-at-arms, and went on further with a two score of husbandmen whom she had redeemed from thralldom in Stark-wall; and when they were hard on the dales of the Bears, she left them there in a certain little dale, with their wains and horses, and seed-corn, and iron tools, and went down all bird-alone to the dwelling of those huge men, unguarded now by sorcery, and trusting in nought but her loveliness and kindness. Clad she was now, as when she fled from the Wood beyond the World, in a short white coat alone, with bare feet and naked arms; but the said coat was now embroidered with the imagery of blossoms in silk and gold, and gems, whereas now her wizardry had departed from her.

So she came to the Bears, and they knew her at once, and worshipped and blessed her, and feared her. But she told them that she had a gift for them, and was come to give it; and therewith she told them of the art of tillage, and bade them learn it; and when they asked her how they should do so, she told them of the men who were abiding them in the mountain dale, and bade the Bears take them for their brothers and sons of the ancient Fathers, and then they should be taught of them. This they behight her to do, and so she led them to where her freedmen lay, whom the Bears received with all joy and loving kindness, and took them into their folk.

So they went back to their dales together; but the Maid went her ways back to her men-at-arms and the city of Stark-wall.

Thereafter she sent more gifts and messages to the Bears, but never again went herself to see them; for as good a face as she put on it that last time, yet her heart waxed cold with fear, and it almost seemed to her that her Mistress was alive again, and that she was escaping from her and plotting against her once more.

As for the Bears, they throve and multiplied; till at last strife arose great and grim betwixt them and other peoples; for they had become mighty in battle: yea, once and again they met the host of Stark-wall in fight, and overthrew and were overthrown. But that was a long while after the Maid had passed away.

Now of Walter and the Maid is no more to be told, saving that they begat between them goodly sons and fair daughters; whereof came a great lineage in Stark-wall; which lineage was so strong, and endured so long a while that by then it had died out, folk had clean forgotten their ancient custom of king-making; so that after Walter of Langton there was never another king that came down to them poor and lonely from out of the Mountains of the Bears.

THE SOUL OF THE GREAT BELL

• • • • •

LAFCADIO HEARN

She hath spoken, and her words still resound in his ears.

Hao-Khieou-Tchouan: c. ix.

The water-clock marks the hour in the *Ta-chung sz'*—in the Tower of the Great Bell: now the mallet is lifted to smite the lips of the metal monster—the vast lips inscribed with Buddhist texts from the sacred *Fa-hwa-King*, from the chapters of the holy *Ling-yen-King*! Hear the great bell responding!—How mighty her voice, though tongueless!—*KO-NGAI!* All the little dragons on the high-tilted eaves of the green roofs shiver to the tips of their gilded tails under that deep wave of sound; all the porcelain gargoyles tremble on their carven perches; all the hundred little bells of the pagodas quiver with desire to speak. *KO-NGAI!*—All the green-and-gold tiles of the temple are vibrating; the wooden goldfish above them are writhing against the sky; the uplifted finger of Fo shakes high over the heads of the worshippers through the blue fog of incense! *KO-NGAI!*—What a thunder tone was that! All the lacquered goblins on the palace cornices wriggle their fire-colored tongues! And after each huge shock, how wondrous the multiple echo and the great golden moan and, at last, the sudden sibilant sobbing in the ears when the immense tone faints away in broken whispers of silver—as though a woman should whisper, "*Hiai!*" Even so the great bell hath sounded every day for well-nigh five hundred years—*Ko-Ngai*: first with stupendous clang, then with immeasurable moan of gold, then with silver murmuring of "*Hiai!*" And there is not a child in all the many-colored ways of the old Chinese city who does not know the story of the great bell—who cannot tell you why the great bell says *Ko-Ngai* and *Hiai*!

Now, this is the story of the great bell in the Ta-chung sz', as the same is related in the *Pe-Hiao-Tou-Choue*, written by the learned Yu-Pao-Tchen, of the City of Kwang-tchau-fu.

Nearly five hundred years ago the Celestially August, the Son of Heaven, Yong-Lo, of the "Illustrious" or Ming Dynasty, commanded the worthy official Kouan-Yu that he should have a bell made of such size that the sound thereof might be heard for one hundred *li*. And he further ordained that the voice of the bell should be strengthened with brass, and deepened with gold, and sweetened with silver; and that the face and the great lips of it should be graven with blessed sayings from the sacred books, and that it should be suspended in the centre of the imperial capital, to sound through all the many-colored ways of the City of Peking.

Therefore the worthy mandarin Kouan-Yu assembled the master-molders and the renowned bellsmiths of the empire, and all men of great repute and cunning in foundry work; and they measured the materials for the alloy, and treated them skilfully, and prepared the molds, the fires, the instruments, and the monstrous melting-pot for fusing the metal. And they labored exceedingly, like giants—neglecting only rest and sleep and the comforts of life; toiling both night and day in obedience to Kouan-Yu, and striving in all things to do the behest of the Son of Heaven.

But when the metal had been cast, and the earthen mold separated from the glowing casting, it was discovered that, despite their great labor and ceaseless care, the result was void of worth; for the metals had rebelled one against the other—the gold had scorned alliance with the brass, the silver would not mingle with the molten iron. Therefore the molds had to be once more prepared, and the fires rekindled, and the metal remelted, and all the work tediously and toilsomely repeated. The Son of Heaven heard, and was angry, but spake nothing.

A second time the bell was cast, and the result was even worse. Still the metals obstinately refused to blend one with the other; and there was no uniformity in the bell, and the sides of it were cracked and fissured, and the lips of it were slagged and split asunder; so that all the labor had to be repeated even a third time, to the great dismay of Kouan-Yu. And when the Son of Heaven heard these things, he was angrier than before; and sent his messenger to Kouan-Yu with a letter, written upon lemon-colored silk, and sealed with the seal of the Dragon, containing these words:—

> *From the Mighty Yong-Lo, the Sublime Tait-Sung, the Celestial and August—whose reign is called "Ming,"—to Kouan-Yu the Fuh-yin: twice thou hast betrayed the trust we have deigned graciously to place in thee; if thou fail a third time in fulfilling our command, thy head shall be severed from thy neck. Tremble, and obey!*

Now, Kouan-Yu had a daughter of dazzling loveliness, whose name—Ko-Ngai—was ever in the mouths of poets, and whose heart was even more beautiful than her face. Ko-Ngai loved her father with such love that she had refused a hundred worthy suitors rather than make his home desolate by her absence; and when she had seen the awful yellow missive, sealed with the Dragon-Seal, she fainted away with fear for her father's sake. And when her senses and her strength returned to her, she could not rest or sleep for thinking of her parent's danger, until she had secretly sold some of her jewels, and with the money so obtained had hastened to an astrologer, and paid him a great price to advise her by what means her father might be saved from the peril impending over him. So the astrologer made observations of the heavens, and marked the aspect of the Silver Stream (which we call the Milky Way), and examined the signs of the Zodiac—the *Hwang-tao*, or Yellow Road—and consulted the table of the Five *Hin*, or Principles of the Universe, and the mystical books of the alchemists. And after a long silence, he made answer to her, saying: "Gold and brass will never meet in wedlock, silver and iron never will embrace, until the flesh of a maiden be melted in the crucible; until the blood of a virgin be mixed with the metals in their fusion." So Ko-Ngai returned home sorrowful at heart; but she kept secret all that she had heard, and told no one what she had done.

At last came the awful day when the third and last effort to cast the great bell was to be made; and Ko-Ngai, together with her waiting-woman, accompanied her father to the foundry, and they took their places upon a platform overlooking the toiling of the molders and the lava of liquefied metal. All the workmen wrought their tasks in silence; there was no sound heard but the muttering of the fires. And the muttering deepened into a roar like the roar of typhoons approaching, and the blood-red lake of metal slowly brightened like the vermilion of a sunrise, and the vermilion was transmuted into a radiant glow of gold, and the gold whitened blindingly, like the silver face of a full moon. Then the workers ceased to feed the raving flame, and all fixed their eyes upon the eyes of Kouan-Yu; and Kouan-Yu prepared to give the signal to cast.

But ere ever he lifted his finger, a cry caused him to turn his head; and all heard the voice of Ko-Ngai sounding sharply sweet as a bird's song above the great thunder of the fires—"*For thy sake, O my Father!*" And even as she cried, she leaped into the white flood of metal; and the lava of the furnace roared to receive her, and spattered monstrous flakes of flame to the roof, and burst over the verge of the earthen crater, and cast up a whirling fountain of many-colored fires, and subsided quakingly, with lightnings and with thunders and with mutterings.

Then the father of Ko-Ngai, wild with his grief, would have leaped in after her, but that strong men held him back and kept firm grasp upon him until he had fainted away and they could bear him like one dead to his home. And the serving-woman of Ko-Ngai, dizzy and speechless for pain, stood before the furnace, still holding in her hands a shoe, a tiny, dainty shoe, with embroidery of pearls and flowers—the shoe of her beautiful mistress that was. For she had sought to grasp Ko-Ngai by the foot as she leaped, but had only been able to clutch the shoe, and the pretty shoe came off in her hand; and she continued to stare at it like one gone mad.

But in spite of all these things, the command of the Celestial and August had to be obeyed, and the work of the molders to be finished, hopeless as the result might be. Yet the glow of the metal seemed purer and whiter than before; and there was no sign of the beautiful body that had been entombed therein. So the ponderous casting was made; and lo! when the metal had become cool, it was found that the bell was beautiful to look upon, and perfect in form, and wonderful in color above all other bells. Nor was there any trace found of the body of Ko-Ngai; for it had been totally absorbed by the precious alloy, and blended with the well-blended brass and gold, with the intermingling of the silver and the iron. And when they sounded the bell, its tones were found to be deeper and mellower and mightier than the tones of any other bell—reaching even beyond the distance of one hundred *li*, like a pealing of summer thunder; and yet also like some vast voice uttering a name, a woman's name—the name of Ko-Ngai!

And still, between each mighty stroke there is a long low moaning heard; and ever the moaning ends with a sound of sobbing and of complaining, as though a weeping woman should murmur, "*Hiai!*" And still, when the people hear that great golden moan they keep silence; but when the sharp, sweet shuddering comes in the air, and the sobbing of "*Hiai!*" then, indeed, all the Chinese mothers in all the many-colored ways of Peking whisper to their little ones: "*Listen! That is Ko-Ngai crying for her shoe! That is Ko-Ngai calling for her shoe!*"

THE RETURN OF YEN-TCHIN-KING

• • • • •

LAFCADIO HEARN

Before me ran, as a herald runneth, the Leader of the Moon;
And the Spirit of the Wind followed after me—quickening his flight.
Li-Sao

In the thirty-eighth chapter of the holy book, *Kan-ing-p'ien*, wherein the Recompense of Immortality is considered, may be found the legend of Yen-Tchin-King. A thousand years have passed since the passing of the good Tchin-King; for it was in the period of the greatness of Thang that he lived and died.

Now, in those days when Yen-Tchin-King was Supreme Judge of one of the Six August Tribunals, one Li-hi-lié, a soldier mighty for evil, lifted the black banner of revolt, and drew after him, as a tide of destruction, the millions of the northern provinces. And learning of these things, and knowing also that Hi-lié was the most ferocious of men, who respected nothing on earth save fearlessness, the Son of Heaven commanded Tchin-King that he should visit Hi-lié and strive to recall the rebel to duty, and read unto the people who followed after him in revolt the Emperor's letter of reproof and warning. For Tchin-King was famed throughout the provinces for his wisdom, his rectitude, and his fearlessness; and the Son of Heaven believed that if Hi-lié would listen to the words of any living man steadfast in loyalty and virtue, he would listen to the words of Tchin-King. So Tchin-King arrayed himself in his robes of office, and set his house in order; and, having embraced his wife and his children, mounted his horse and rode away alone to the roaring camp of the rebels, bearing the Emperor's letter in his bosom. "I shall return; fear not!" were his last words to the gray servant who watched him from the terrace as he rode.

And Tchin-King at last descended from his horse, and entered into the rebel camp and, passing through that huge gathering of war, stood in the presence of Hi-lié. High sat the rebel among his chiefs, encircled by the wave-lightning of swords and the thunders of ten thousand gongs: above him undulated the silken folds of the Black Dragon, while a vast fire rose bickering before him. Also Tchin-King saw that the tongues of that fire were licking human bones, and that skulls of men lay blackening among the ashes. Yet he was not afraid to look upon the fire, nor into the eyes of Hi-lié; but drawing from his bosom the roll of perfumed yellow silk upon which the words of the Emperor were written, and kissing it, he made ready to read, while the multitude became silent. Then, in a strong, clear voice he began:

"The words of the Celestial and August, the Son of Heaven, the Divine Ko-Tsu-Tchin-Yao-ti, unto the rebel Li-Hi-lié and those that follow him."

And a roar went up like the roar of the sea—a roar of rage, and the hideous battle-moan, like the moan of a forest in storm—"*Hoo! Hoo-oo-oo-oo!*"—and the sword-lightnings brake loose, and the thunder of the gongs moved the ground beneath the messenger's feet. But Hi-lié waved his gilded wand, and again there was silence. "Nay!" spake the rebel chief; "Let the dog bark!" So Tchin-King spake on:

> *Knowest thou not, O most rash and foolish of men, that thou leadest the people only into the mouth of the Dragon of Destruction? Knowest thou not, also, that the people of my kingdom are the first-born of the Master of Heaven? So it hath been written that he who doth needlessly subject the people to wounds and death shall not be suffered by Heaven to live! Thou who wouldst subvert those laws founded by the wise—those laws in obedience to which may happiness and prosperity alone be found—thou art committing the greatest of all crimes—the crime that is never forgiven!*
>
> *O my people, think not that I your Emperor, I your Father, seek your destruction. I desire only your happiness, your prosperity, your greatness; let not your folly provoke the severity of your Celestial Parent. Follow not after madness and blind rage; hearken rather to the wise words of my messenger.*

"*Hoo! Hoo-oo-oo-oo-oo!*" roared the people, gathering fury. "*Hoo! Hoo-oo-oo-oo!*"—till the mountains rolled back the cry like the rolling of a typhoon; and once more the pealing of the gongs paralyzed voice and hearing. Then Tchin-King, looking at Hi-lié, saw that he laughed, and that the words of the letter would not again be listened to. Therefore he read on to the end without looking about him, resolved to perform his mission in so far as lay in his power. And having read all, he would have given the letter to Hi-lié; but Hi-lié would not extend his hand to take it. Therefore Tchin-King replaced it in his bosom, and folding his arms, looked Hi-lié calmly in the face, and waited. Again Hi-lié waved his gilded wand; and the roaring ceased, and the booming of the gongs, until nothing save the fluttering of the Dragon-banner could be heard. Then spake Hi-lié, with an evil smile—

"Tchin-King, O son of a dog! If thou dost not now take the oath of fealty, and bow thyself before me, and salute me with the salutation of Emperors—even with the *luh-kao*, the triple prostration—into that fire thou shalt be thrown."

But Tchin-King, turning his back upon the usurper, bowed himself a moment in worship to Heaven and Earth; and then rising suddenly, ere any man could lay hand upon him, he leaped into the towering flame, and stood there, with folded arms, like a God.

Then Hi-lié leaped to his feet in amazement, and shouted to his men; and they snatched Tchin-King from the fire, and wrung the flames from his robes with their naked hands, and extolled him, and praised him to his face. And even Hi-lié himself descended from his seat, and spoke fair words to him, saying: "O Tchin-King, I see thou art indeed a brave man and true, and worthy of all honor; be seated among us, I pray thee, and partake of whatever it is in our power to bestow!"

But Tchin-King, looking upon him unswervingly, replied in a voice clear as the voice of a great bell—

"Never, O Hi-lié, shall I accept aught from thy hand, save death, so long as thou shalt continue in the path of wrath and folly. And never shall it be said that Tchin-King sat him down among rebels and traitors, among murderers and robbers."

Then Hi-lié in sudden fury, smote him with his sword; and Tchin-King fell to the earth and died, striving even in his death to bow his head toward the South—toward the place of the Emperor's palace—toward the presence of his beloved Master.

Even at the same hour the Son of Heaven, alone in the inner chamber of his palace, became aware of a Shape prostrate before his feet; and when he spake, the Shape arose and stood before him, and he saw that it was Tchin-King. And the Emperor would have questioned him; yet ere he could question, the familiar voice spake, saying:

"Son of Heaven, the mission confided to me I have performed; and thy command hath been accomplished to the extent of thy humble servant's feeble power. But even now must I depart, that I may enter the service of another Master."

And looking, the Emperor perceived that the Golden Tigers upon the wall were visible through the form of Tchin-King; and a strange coldness, like a winter wind, passed through the chamber; and the figure faded out. Then the Emperor knew that the Master of whom his faithful servant had spoken was none other than the Master of Heaven.

Also at the same hour the gray servant of Tchin-King's house beheld him passing through the apartments, smiling as he was wont to smile when he saw that all things were as he desired. "Is it well with thee, my lord?" questioned the aged man. And a voice answered him: "It is well"; but the presence of Tchin-King had passed away before the answer came.

So the armies of the Son of Heaven strove with the rebels. But the land was soaked with blood and blackened with fire; and the corpses of whole populations were carried by the rivers to feed the fishes of the sea; and still the war prevailed through many a long red year. Then came to aid the Son of Heaven the hordes that dwell in the desolations of the West and North—horsemen born, a nation of wild archers, each mighty to bend a two-hundred-pound bow until the ears should meet. And as a whirlwind they came against rebellion, raining raven-feathered arrows in a storm of death; and they prevailed against Hi-lié and his people. Then those that survived destruction and defeat submitted, and promised allegiance; and once more was the law of righteousness restored. But Tchin-King had been dead for many summers.

And the Son of Heaven sent word to his victorious generals that they should bring back with them the bones of his faithful servant, to be laid with honor in a mausoleum erected by imperial decree. So the generals of the Celestial and August sought after the nameless grave and found it, and had the earth taken up, and made ready to remove the coffin.

But the coffin crumbled into dust before their eyes; for the worms had gnawed it, and the hungry earth had devoured its substance, leaving only a phantom shell that vanished at touch of the light. And lo! as it vanished, all beheld lying there the perfect form and features of the good Tchin-King. Corruption had not touched him, nor had the worms disturbed his rest, nor had the bloom of life departed from his face. And he seemed to dream only—comely to see as upon the morning of his bridal, and smiling as the holy images smile, with eyelids closed, in the twilight of the great pagodas.

Then spoke a priest, standing by the grave: "O my children, this is indeed a Sign from the Master of Heaven; in such wise do the Powers Celestial preserve them that are chosen to be numbered with the Immortals. Death may not prevail over them, neither may corruption come nigh them. Verily the blessed Tchin-King hath taken his place among the divinities of Heaven!"

Then they bore Tchin-King back to his native place, and laid him with highest honors in the mausoleum which the Emperor had commanded; and there he sleeps, incorruptible forever, arrayed in his robes of state. Upon his tomb are sculptured the emblems of his greatness and his wisdom and his virtue, and the signs of his office, and the Four Precious Things: and the monsters which are holy symbols mount giant guard in stone about it; and the weird Dogs of Fo keep watch before it, as before the temples of the gods.

THE TALE OF THE PORCELAIN-GOD

LAFCADIO HEARN

It is written in the Fong-ho-chin-tch'ouen *that whenever the artist Thsang-Kong was in doubt, he would look into the fire of the great oven in which his vases were baking, and question the Guardian-Spirit dwelling in the flame. And the Spirit of the Oven-fires so aided him with his counsels, that the porcelains made by Thsang-Kong were indeed finer and lovelier to look upon than all other porcelains. And they were baked in the years of Khang-hí—sacredly called Jin Houang-tí.*

Who first of men discovered the secret of the *Kao-ling*, of the *Pe-tun-tse*—the bones and the flesh, the skeleton and the skin, of the beauteous Vase? Who first discovered the virtue of the curd-white clay? Who first prepared the ice-pure bricks of *tun*: the gathered hoariness of mountains that have died for age; blanched dust of the rocky bones and the stony flesh of sun-seeking Giants that have ceased to be? Unto whom was it first given to discover the divine art of porcelain?

Unto Pu, once a man, now a god, before whose snowy statues bow the myriad populations enrolled in the guilds of the potteries. But the place of his birth we know not; perhaps the tradition of it may have been effaced from remembrance by that awful war which in our own day consumed the lives of twenty millions of the Black-haired Race, and obliterated from the face of the world even the wonderful City of Porcelain itself—the City of King-te-chin, that of old shone like a jewel of fire in the blue mountain-girdle of Feou-liang.

Before his time indeed the Spirit of the Furnace had being; had issued from the Infinite Vitality; had become manifest as an emanation of the Supreme Tao. For Hoang-ti, nearly five thousand years ago, taught men to make good vessels of baked clay; and in his time all potters had learned to know the God of Oven-fires, and turned their wheels to the murmuring of prayer. But Hoang-ti had been gathered unto his fathers for thrice ten hundred years before that man was born destined by the Master of Heaven to become the Porcelain-God.

And his divine ghost, ever hovering above the smoking and the toiling of the potteries, still gives power to the thought of the shaper, grace to the genius of the designer, luminosity to the touch of the enamellist. For by his heaven-taught wisdom was the art of porcelain created; by his inspiration were accomplished all the miracles of Thao-yu, maker of the *Kia-yu-ki*, and all the marvels made by those who followed after him—

All the azure porcelains called *You-kouo-thien-tsing*; brilliant as a mirror, thin as paper of rice, sonorous as the melodious stone *Khing*, and colored, in obedience to the mandate of the Emperor Chi-tsong, "blue as the sky is after rain, when viewed through the rifts of the clouds." These were, indeed, the first of all porcelains, likewise called *Tchai-yao*, which no man, howsoever wicked, could find courage to break, for they charmed the eye like jewels of price;

And the *Jou-yao*, second in rank among all porcelains, sometimes mocking the aspect and the sonority of bronze, sometimes blue as summer waters, and deluding the sight with mucid appearance of thickly floating spawn of fish;

And the *Kouan-yao*, which are the Porcelains of Magistrates, and third in rank of merit among all wondrous porcelains, colored with colors of the morning—skyey blueness, with the rose of a great dawn blushing and bursting through it, and long-limbed marsh-birds flying against the glow;

Also the *Ko-yao*—fourth in rank among perfect porcelains—of fair, faint, changing colors, like the body of a living fish, or made in the likeness of opal substance, milk mixed with fire; the work of Sing-I, elder of the immortal brothers Tchang;

Also the *Ting-yao*—fifth in rank among all perfect porcelains—white as the mourning garments of a spouse bereaved, and beautiful with a trickling as of tears—the porcelains sung of by the poet Son-tong-po;

Also the porcelains called *Pi-se-yao*, whose colors are called "hidden," being alternately invisible and visible, like the tints of ice beneath the sun—the porcelains celebrated by the far-famed singer Sin-in;

Also the wondrous *Chu-yao*—the pallid porcelains that utter a mournful cry when smitten—the porcelains chanted of by the mighty chanter, Thou-chao-ling;

Also the porcelains called *Thsin-yao*, white or blue, surface-wrinkled as the face of water by the fluttering of many fins... And ye can see the fish!

Also the vases called *Tsi-hong-khi*, red as sunset after a rain; and the *T'o-t'ai-khi*, fragile as the wings of the silkworm-moth, lighter than the shell of an egg;

Also the *Kia-tsing*—fair cups pearl-white when empty, yet, by some incomprehensible witchcraft of construction, seeming to swarm with purple fish the moment they are filled with water;

Also the porcelains called *Yao-pien*, whose tints are transmuted by the alchemy of fire; for they enter blood-crimson into the heat, and change there to lizard-green, and at last come forth azure as the cheek of the sky;

Also the *Ki-tcheou-yao*, which are all violet as a summer's night; and the *Hing-yao* that sparkle with the sparklings of mingled silver and snow;

Also the *Sieouen-yao*—some ruddy as iron in the furnace, some diaphanous and ruby-red, some granulated and yellow as the rind of an orange, some softly flushed as the skin of a peach;

Also the *Tsoui-khi-yao*, crackled and green as ancient ice is; and the *Tchou-fou-yao*, which are the Porcelains of Emperors, with dragons wriggling and snarling in gold; and those *yao* that are pink-ribbed and have their angles serrated as the claws of crabs are;

Also the *Ou-ni-yao*, black as the pupil of the eye, and as lustrous; and the *Hou-tien-yao*, darkly yellow as the faces of men of India; and the *Ou-kong-yao*, whose color is the dead-gold of autumn leaves;

Also the *Long-kang-yao*, green as the seedling of a pea, but bearing also paintings of sun-silvered cloud, and of the Dragons of Heaven;

Also the *Tching-hoa-yao*—pictured with the amber bloom of grapes and the verdure of vine-leaves and the blossoming of poppies, or decorated in relief with figures of fighting crickets;

Also the *Khang-hi-nien-ts'ang-yao*, celestial azure sown with star-dust of gold; and the *Khien-long-nien-thang-yao*, splendid in sable and silver as a fervid night that is flashed with lightnings.

Not indeed the *Long-Ouang-yao*—painted with the lascivious *Pi-hi*, with the obscene *Nan-niu-ssé-sie*, with the shameful *Tchun-hoa*, or "Pictures of Spring"; abominations created by command of the wicked Emperor Moutsong, though the Spirit of the Furnace hid his face and fled away;

But all other vases of startling form and substance, magically articulated, and ornamented with figures in relief, in cameo, in transparency—the vases with orifices belled like the cups of flowers, or cleft like the bills of birds, or fanged like the jaws of serpents, or pink-lipped as the mouth of a girl; the vases flesh-colored and purple-veined and dimpled, with ears and with earrings; the vases in likeness of mushrooms, of lotus-flowers, of lizards, of horse-footed dragons woman-faced; the vases strangely translucid, that simulate the white glimmering of grains of prepared rice, that counterfeit the vapory lace-work of frost, that imitate the efflorescences of coral;

Also the statues in porcelain of divinities: the Genius of the Hearth; the Long-pinn who are the Twelve Deities of Ink; the blessed Lao-tseu, born with silver hair; Kong-fu-tse, grasping the scroll of written wisdom; Kouan-in, sweetest Goddess of Mercy, standing snowy-footed upon the heart of her golden lily; Chi-nong, the god who taught men how to cook; Fo, with long eyes closed in meditation, and lips smiling the mysterious smile of Supreme Beatitude; Cheou-lao, god of Longevity, bestriding his aërial steed, the white-winged stork; Pou-t'ai, Lord of Contentment and of Wealth, obese and dreamy; and that fairest Goddess of Talent, from whose beneficent hands eternally streams the iridescent rain of pearls.

And though many a secret of that matchless art that Pu bequeathed unto men may indeed have been forgotten and lost forever, the story of the Porcelain-God is remembered; and I doubt not that any of the aged *Jeou-yen-liao-kong*, any one of the old blind men of the great potteries, who sit all day grinding colors in the sun, could tell you Pu was once a humble Chinese workman, who grew to be a great artist by dint of tireless study and patience and by the inspiration of Heaven. So famed he became that some deemed him an alchemist, who possessed the secret called *White-and-Yellow*, by which stones might be turned into gold; and others thought him a magician, having the ghastly power of murdering men with horror of nightmare, by hiding charmed effigies of them under the tiles of their own roofs; and others, again, averred that he was an astrologer who had discovered the mystery of those Five Hing which influence all things—those Powers that move even in the currents of the star-drift, in the milky *Tien-ho*, or River of the Sky. Thus, at least, the ignorant spoke of him; but even those who stood about the Son of Heaven, those whose hearts had been strengthened by the acquisition of wisdom, wildly praised the marvels of his handicraft, and asked each other if there might be any imaginable form of beauty which Pu could not evoke from that beauteous substance so docile to the touch of his cunning hand.

And one day it came to pass that Pu sent a priceless gift to the Celestial and August: a vase imitating the substance of ore-rock, all aflame with pyritic scintillation—a shape of glittering splendor with chameleons sprawling over it; chameleons of porcelain that shifted color as often as the beholder changed his position. And the Emperor, wondering exceedingly at the splendor of the work, questioned the princes and the mandarins concerning him that made it. And the princes and the mandarins answered that he was a workman named Pu, and that he was without equal among potters, knowing secrets that seemed to have been inspired either by gods or by demons. Whereupon the Son of Heaven sent his officers to Pu with a noble gift, and summoned him unto his presence.

So the humble artisan entered before the Emperor, and having performed the supreme prostration—thrice kneeling, and thrice nine times touching the ground with his forehead—awaited the command of the August.

And the Emperor spake to him, saying: "Son, thy gracious gift hath found high favor in our sight; and for the charm of that offering we have bestowed upon thee a reward of five thousand silver *liang*. But thrice that sum shall be awarded thee so soon as thou shalt have fulfilled our behest. Hearken, therefore, O matchless artificer! It is now our will that thou make for us a vase having the tint and the aspect of living flesh, but—mark well our desire!—*of flesh made to creep by the utterance of such words as poets utter—flesh moved by an Idea, flesh horripilated by a Thought!* Obey, and answer not! We have spoken."

Now Pu was the most cunning of all the *P'ei-se-kong*—the men who marry colors together; of all the *Hoa-yang-kong*, who draw the shapes of vase-decoration; of all the *Hoei-sse-kong,* who paint in enamel; of all the *T'ien-thsai-kong*, who brighten color; of all the *Chao-lou-kong*, who watch the furnace-fires and the porcelain-ovens. But he went away sorrowing from the Palace of the Son of Heaven, notwithstanding the gift of five thousand silver *liang* which had been given to him. For he thought to himself: "Surely the mystery of the comeliness of flesh, and the mystery of that by which it is moved, are the secrets of the Supreme Tao. How shall man lend the aspect of sentient life to dead clay? Who save the Infinite can give soul?"

Now Pu had discovered those witchcrafts of color, those surprises of grace, that make the art of the ceramist. He had found the secret of the *feng-hong*, the wizard flush of the Rose; of the *hoa-hong*, the delicious incarnadine; of the mountain-green called *chan-lou*; of the pale soft yellow termed *hiao-hoang-yeou*; and of the *hoang-kin*, which is the blazing beauty of gold. He had found those eel-tints, those serpent-greens, those pansy-violets, those furnace-crimsons, those carminates and lilacs, subtle as spirit-flame, which our enamellists of the Occident long sought without success to reproduce. But he trembled at the task assigned him, as he returned to the toil of his studio, saying: "How shall any miserable man render in clay the quivering of flesh to an Idea—the inexplicable horripilation of a Thought? Shall a man venture to mock the magic of that Eternal Moulder by whose infinite power a million suns are shapen more readily than one small jar might be rounded upon my wheel?"

Yet the command of the Celestial and August might never be disobeyed; and the patient workman strove with all his power to fulfil the Son of Heaven's desire. But vainly for days, for weeks, for months, for season after season, did he strive; vainly also he prayed unto the gods to aid him; vainly he besought the Spirit of the Furnace, crying: "O thou Spirit of Fire, hear me, heed me, help me! How shall I—a miserable man, unable to breathe into clay a living soul—how shall I render in this inanimate substance the aspect of flesh made to creep by the utterance of a Word, sentient to the horripilation of a Thought?"

For the Spirit of the Furnace made strange answer to him with whispering of fire: "*Vast thy faith, weird thy prayer! Has Thought feet, that man may perceive the trace of its passing? Canst thou measure me the blast of the Wind?*"

Nevertheless, with purpose unmoved, nine-and-forty times did Pu seek to fulfil the Emperor's command; nine-and-forty times he strove to obey the behest of the Son of Heaven. Vainly—alas!—did he consume his substance; vainly did he expend his strength; vainly did he exhaust his knowledge: success smiled not upon him; and Evil visited his home, and Poverty sat in his dwelling, and Misery shivered at his hearth.

Sometimes, when the hour of trial came, it was found that the colors had become strangely transmuted in the firing, or had faded into ashen pallor, or had darkened into the fuliginous hue of forest-mold. And Pu, beholding these misfortunes, made wail to the Spirit of the Furnace, praying: "O thou Spirit of Fire, how shall I render the likeness of lustrous flesh, the warm glow of living color, unless thou aid me?"

And the Spirit of the Furnace mysteriously answered him with murmuring of fire: "*Canst thou learn the art of that Infinite Enameller who hath made beautiful the Arch of Heaven—whose brush is Light; whose paints are the Colors of the Evening?*"

Sometimes, again, even when the tints had not changed, after the pricked and labored surface had seemed about to quicken in the heat, to assume the vibratility of living skin—even at the last hour all the labor of the workers proved to have been wasted; for the fickle substance rebelled against their efforts, producing only crinklings grotesque as those upon the rind of a withered fruit, or granulations like those upon the skin of a dead bird from which the feathers have been rudely plucked. And Pu wept, and cried out unto the Spirit of the Furnace: "O thou Spirit of Flame, how shall I be able to imitate the thrill of flesh touched by a Thought, unless thou wilt vouchsafe to lend me thine aid?"

And the Spirit of the Furnace mysteriously answered him with muttering of fire: "*Canst thou give ghost unto a stone? Canst thou thrill with a Thought the entrails of the granite hills?*"

Sometimes it was found that all the work indeed had not failed; for the color seemed good, and all faultless the matter of the vase appeared to be, having neither crack nor wrinkling nor crinkling; but the pliant softness of warm skin did not meet the eye; the flesh-tinted surface offered only the harsh aspect and hard glimmer of metal. All their exquisite toil to mock the pulpiness of sentient substance had left no trace; had been brought to nought by the breath of the furnace. And Pu, in his despair, shrieked to the Spirit of the Furnace: "O thou merciless divinity! O thou most pitiless god!—thou whom I have worshiped with ten thousand sacrifices!—for what fault hast thou abandoned me? For what error hast thou forsaken me? How may I—most wretched of men!—ever render the aspect of flesh made to creep with the utterance of a Word, sentient to the titillation of a Thought, if thou wilt not aid me?"

And the Spirit of the Furnace made answer unto him with roaring of fire: "*Canst thou divide a Soul? Nay!... Thy life for the life of thy work!—Thy soul for the soul of thy Vase!*"

And hearing these words Pu arose with a terrible resolve swelling at his heart, and made ready for the last and fiftieth time to fashion his work for the oven.

One hundred times did he sift the clay and the quartz, the *kao-ling* and the *tun*; one hundred times did he purify them in clearest water; one hundred times with tireless hands did he knead the creamy paste, mingling it at last with colors known only to himself. Then was the vase shapen and reshapen, and touched and retouched by the hands of Pu, until its blandness seemed to live, until it appeared to quiver and to palpitate, as with vitality from within, as with the quiver of rounded muscle undulating beneath the integument. For the hues of life were upon it and infiltrated throughout its innermost substance, imitating the carnation of blood-bright tissue, and the reticulated purple of the veins; and over all was laid the envelope of sun-colored *Pe-kia-ho*, the lucid and glossy enamel, half diaphanous, even like the substance that it counterfeited—the polished skin of a woman. Never since the making of the world had any work comparable to this been wrought by the skill of man.

Then Pu bade those who aided him that they should feed the furnace well with wood of *tcha*; but he told his resolve unto none. Yet after the oven began to glow, and he saw the work of his hands blossoming and blushing in the heat, he bowed himself before the Spirit of Flame, and murmured: "O thou Spirit and Master of Fire, I know the truth of thy words! I know that a Soul may never be divided! Therefore my life for the life of my work!—My soul for the soul of my Vase!"

And for nine days and for eight nights the furnaces were fed unceasingly with wood of *tcha*; for nine days and for eight nights men watched the wondrous vase crystallizing into being, rose-lighted by the breath of the flame. Now upon the coming of the ninth night, Pu bade all his weary comrades retire to rest, for that the work was well-nigh done, and the success assured. "If you find me not here at sunrise," he said, "fear not to take forth the vase; for I know that the task will have been accomplished according to the command of the August." So they departed.

But in that same ninth night Pu entered the flame, and yielded up his ghost in the embrace of the Spirit of the Furnace, giving his life for the life of his work—his soul for the soul of his Vase.

And when the workmen came upon the tenth morning to take forth the porcelain marvel, even the bones of Pu had ceased to be; but lo! the Vase lived as they looked upon it: seeming to be flesh moved by the utterance of a Word, creeping to the titillation of a Thought. And whenever tapped by the finger it uttered a voice and a name—the voice of its maker, the name of its creator: PU.

And the son of Heaven, hearing of these things, and viewing the miracle of the vase, said unto those about him: "Verily, the Impossible hath been wrought by the strength of faith, by the force of obedience! Yet never was it our desire that so cruel a sacrifice should have been; we sought only to know whether the skill of the matchless artificer came from the Divinities or from the Demons—from heaven or from hell. Now, indeed, we discern that Pu hath taken his place among the gods." And the Emperor mourned exceedingly for his faithful servant. But he ordained that god-like honors should be paid unto the spirit of the marvelous artist, and that his memory should be revered forevermore, and that fair statues of him should be set up in all the cities of the Celestial Empire, and above all the toiling of the potteries, that the multitude of workers might unceasingly call upon his name and invoke his benediction upon their labors.

THE DREAM OF AKINOSUKE

LAFCADIO HEARN

In the district called Toichi of Yamato Province, there used to live a *goshi* named Miyata Akinosuke... (Here I must tell you that in Japanese feudal times there was a privileged class of soldier-farmers—freeholders—corresponding to the class of yeomen in England; and these were called *goshi*.)

In Akinosuke's garden there was a great and ancient cedar tree, under which he was wont to rest on sultry days. One very warm afternoon he was sitting under this tree with two of his friends, fellow-*goshi*, chatting and drinking wine, when he felt all of a sudden very drowsy—so drowsy that he begged his friends to excuse him for taking a nap in their presence. Then he lay down at the foot of the tree, and dreamed this dream:

He thought that as he was lying there in his garden, he saw a procession, like the train of some great *daimyo* descending a hill nearby, and that he got up to look at it. A very grand procession it proved to be—more imposing than anything of the kind which he had ever seen before; and it was advancing toward his dwelling. He observed in the van of it a number of young men richly appareled, who were drawing a great lacquered palace-carriage, or *gosho-guruma*, hung with bright blue silk. When the procession arrived within a short distance of the house it halted; and a richly dressed man—evidently a person of rank—advanced from it, approached Akinosuke, bowed to him profoundly, and then said:

"Honored Sir, you see before you a *kerai* [vassal] of the Kokuo of Tokoyo. My master, the King, commands me to greet you in his august name, and to place myself wholly at your disposal. He also bids me inform you that he augustly desires your presence at the palace. Be therefore pleased immediately to enter this honorable carriage, which he has sent for your conveyance."

Upon hearing these words Akinosuke wanted to make some fitting reply; but he was too much astonished and embarrassed for speech—and in the same moment his will seemed to melt away from him, so that he could only do as the *kerai* bade him. He entered the carriage; the *kerai* took a place beside him, and made a signal; the drawers, seizing the silken ropes, turned the great vehicle southward—and the journey began.

In a very short time, to Akinosuke's amazement, the carriage stopped in front of a huge two-storied gateway (*romon*), of a Chinese style, which he had never before seen. Here the *kerai* dismounted, saying, "I go to announced the honorable arrival,"—and he disappeared. After some little waiting, Akinosuke saw two noble-looking men, wearing robes of purple silk and high caps of the form indicating lofty rank, come from the gateway. These, after having respectfully saluted him, helped him to descend from the carriage, and led him through the great gate and across a vast garden, to the entrance of a palace whose front appeared to extend, west and east, to a distance of miles. Akinosuke was then shown into a reception room of wonderful size and splendor. His guides conducted him to the place of honor, and respectfully seated themselves apart; while serving-maids, in costume of ceremony, brought refreshments. When Akinosuke had partaken of the refreshments, the two purple-robed attendants bowed low before him, and addressed him in the following words— each speaking alternately, according to the etiquette of courts:

"It is now our honorable duty to inform you... as to the reason of your having been summoned hither... Our master, the King, augustly desires that you become his son-in-law;... and it is his wish and command that you shall wed this very day... the August Princess, his maiden-daughter... We shall soon conduct you to the presence-chamber... where His Augustness even now is waiting to receive you... But it will be necessary that we first invest you... with the appropriate garments of ceremony." Having thus spoken, the attendants rose together, and proceeded to an alcove containing a great chest of gold lacquer. They opened the chest, and took from it various robes and girdles of rich material, and a *kamuri*, or regal headdress. With these they attired Akinosuke as befitted a princely bridegroom; and he was then conducted to the presence-room, where he saw the Kokuo of Tokoyo seated upon the *daiza*, wearing a high black cap of state, and robed in robes of yellow silk. Before the *daiza*, to left and right, a multitude of dignitaries sat in rank, motionless and splendid as images in a temple; and Akinosuke, advancing into their midst, saluted the king with the triple prostration of usage. The king greeted him with gracious words, and then said: "You have already been informed as to the reason of your having been summoned to Our presence. We have decided that you shall become the adopted husband of Our only daughter—and the wedding ceremony shall now be performed."

As the king finished speaking, a sound of joyful music was heard; and a long train of beautiful court ladies advanced from behind a curtain to conduct Akinosuke to the room in which the bride awaited him.

The room was immense; but it could scarcely contain the multitude of guests assembled to witness the wedding ceremony. All bowed down before Akinosuke as he took his place, facing the King's daughter, on the kneeling-cushion prepared for him. As a maiden of heaven the bride appeared to be, and her robes were, beautiful as a summer sky. And the marriage was performed amid great rejoicing.

Afterwards the pair were conducted to a suite of apartments that had been prepared for them in another portion of the palace; and there they received the congratulations of many noble persons, and wedding gifts beyond counting.

Some days later Akinosuke was again summoned to the throne-room. On this occasion he was received even more graciously than before; and the King said to him:

"In the south-western part of Our dominion there is an island called Raishu. We have now appointed you Governor of that island. You will find the people loyal and docile; but their laws have not yet been brought into proper accord with the laws of Tokoyo; and their customs have not been properly regulated. We entrust you with the duty of improving their social condition as far as may be possible; and We desire that you shall rule them with kindness and wisdom. All preparations necessary for your journey to Raishu have already been made."

So Akinosuke and his bride departed from the palace of Tokoyo, accompanied to the shore by a great escort of nobles and officials; and they embarked upon a ship of state provided by the king. And with favoring winds they safety sailed to Raishu, and found the good people of that island assembled upon the beach to welcome them.

Akinosuke entered at once upon his new duties; and they did not prove to be hard. During the first three years of his governorship he was occupied chiefly with the framing and the enactment of laws; but he had wise counselors to help him, and he never found the work unpleasant. When it was all finished, he had no active duties to perform, beyond attending the rites and ceremonies ordained by ancient custom. The country was so healthy and so fertile that sickness and want were unknown; and the people were so good that no laws were ever broken. And Akinosuke dwelt and ruled in Raishu for twenty years more—making in all twenty-three years of sojourn, during which no shadow of sorrow traversed his life.

But in the twenty-fourth year of his governorship, a great misfortune came upon him; for his wife, who had borne him seven children—five boys and two girls—fell sick and died. She was buried, with high pomp, on the summit of a beautiful hill in the district of Hanryoko; and a monument, exceedingly splendid, was placed upon her grave. But Akinosuke felt such grief at her death that he no longer cared to live.

Now when the legal period of mourning was over, there came to Raishu, from the Tokoyo palace, a *shisha*, or royal messenger. The *shisha* delivered to Akinosuke a message of condolence, and then said to him:

"These are the words which our august master, the King of Tokoyo, commands that I repeat to you: 'We will now send you back to your own people and country. As for the seven children, they are the grandsons and granddaughters of the King, and shall be fitly cared for. Do not, therefore, allow you mind to be troubled concerning them.'"

On receiving this mandate, Akinosuke submissively prepared for his departure. When all his affairs had been settled, and the ceremony of bidding farewell to his counselors and trusted officials had been concluded, he was escorted with much honor to the port. There he embarked upon the ship sent for him; and the ship sailed out into the blue sea, under the blue sky; and the shape of the island of Raishu itself turned blue, and then turned grey, and then vanished forever... And Akinosuke suddenly awoke—under the cedar tree in his own garden!

For a moment he was stupefied and dazed. But he perceived his two friends still seated near him—drinking and chatting merrily. He stared at them in a bewildered way, and cried aloud: "How strange!"

"Akinosuke must have been dreaming," one of them exclaimed, with a laugh. "What did you see, Akinosuke, that was strange?"

Then Akinosuke told his dream—that dream of three-and-twenty years' sojourn in the realm of Tokoyo, in the island of Raishu—and they were astonished, because he had really slept for no more than a few minutes.

One *goshi* said:

"Indeed, you saw strange things. We also saw something strange while you were napping. A little yellow butterfly was fluttering over your face for a moment or two; and we watched it. Then it alighted on the ground beside you, close to the tree; and almost as soon as it alighted there, a big, big ant came out of a hole and seized it and pulling it down into the hole. Just before you woke up, we saw that very butterfly come out of the hole again, and flutter over your face as before. And then it suddenly disappeared: we do not know where it went."

"Perhaps it was Akinosuke's soul," the other *goshi* said; "certainly I thought I saw it fly into his mouth... But, even if that butterfly was Akinosuke's soul, the fact would not explain his dream."

"The ants might explain it," returned the first speaker. "Ants are queer beings—possibly goblins... Anyhow, there is a big ant's nest under that cedar tree."

"Let us look!" cried Akinosuke, greatly moved by this suggestion. And he went for a spade.

The ground about and beneath the cedar tree proved to have been excavated, in a most surprising way, by a prodigious colony of ants. The ants had furthermore built inside their excavations; and their tiny constructions of straw, clay, and stems bore an odd resemblance to miniature towns. In the middle of a structure considerably larger than the rest there was a marvelous swarming of small ants around the body of one very big ant, which had yellowish wings and a long black head.

"Why, there is the King of my dream!" cried Akinosuke. "And there is the palace of Tokoyo!... How extraordinary!... Raishu ought to lie somewhere south-west of it—to the left of that big root... Yes!—Here it is!... How very strange! Now I am sure that I can find the mountain of Hanryoko, and the grave of the princess."

In the wreck of the nest he searched and searched, and at last discovered a tiny mound, on the top of which was fixed a water-worn pebble, in shape resembling a Buddhist monument. Underneath it he found—embedded in clay—the dead body of a female ant.

ROKURO-KUBI

LAFCADIO HEARN

Nearly five hundred years ago there was a samurai, named Isogai Heidazaemon Taketsura, in the service of the Lord Kikuji, of Kyushu. This Isogai had inherited, from many warlike ancestors, a natural aptitude for military exercises, and extraordinary strength. While yet a boy he had surpassed his teachers in the art of swordsmanship, in archery, and in the use of the spear, and had displayed all the capacities of a daring and skillful soldier. Afterwards, in the time of the Eikyo war, he so distinguished himself that high honors were bestowed upon him. But when the house of Kikuji came to ruin, Isogai found himself without a master. He might then easily have obtained service under another *daimyo*; but as he had never sought distinction for his own sake alone, and as his heart remained true to his former lord, he preferred to give up the world. So he cut off his hair, and became a traveling priest—taking the Buddhist name of Kwairyo.

But always, under the *koromo* of the priest, Kwairyo kept warm within him the heart of the samurai. As in other years he had laughed at peril, so now also he scorned danger; and in all weathers and all seasons he journeyed to preach the good Law in places where no other priest would have dared to go. For that age was an age of violence and disorder; and upon the highways there was no security for the solitary traveler, even if he happened to be a priest.

In the course of his first long journey, Kwairyo had occasion to visit the province of Kai. One evening, as he was traveling through the mountains of that province, darkness overcame him in a very lonesome district, leagues away from any village. So he resigned himself to pass the night under the stars; and having found a suitable grassy spot by the roadside, he lay down there and prepared to sleep. He had always welcomed discomfort; and even a bare rock was for him a good bed when nothing better could be found, and the root of a pine tree an excellent pillow. His body was iron; and he never troubled himself about dews or rain or frost or snow.

Scarcely had he lain down when a man came along the road, carrying an axe and a great bundle of chopped wood. This woodcutter halted on seeing Kwairyo lying down and, after a moment of silent observation, said to him in a tone of great surprise:

"What kind of a man can you be, good Sir, that you dare to lie down alone in such a place as this? There are haunters about here—many of them. Are you not afraid of Hairy Things?"

"My friend," cheerfully answered Kwairyo, "I am only a wandering priest—a 'Cloud-and-Water-Guest,' as folks call it: *unsui-no-ryokaku*. And I am not in the least afraid of Hairy Things—if you mean goblin-foxes, or goblin-badgers, or any creatures of that kind. As for lonesome places, I like them: they are suitable for meditation. I am accustomed to sleeping in the open air: and I have learned never to be anxious about my life."

"You must be indeed a brave man, Sir Priest," the peasant responded, "to lie down here! This place has a bad name—a very bad name. But, as the proverb has it, *Kunshi ayayuki ni chikayorazu* ['The superior man does not needlessly expose himself to peril']; and I must assure you, Sir, that it is very dangerous to sleep here. Therefore, although my house is only a wretched thatched hut, let me beg of you to come home with me at once. In the way of food, I have nothing to offer you; but there is a roof at least, and you can sleep under it without risk."

He spoke earnestly; and Kwairyo, liking the kindly tone of the man, accepted this modest offer. The woodcutter guided him along a narrow path, leading up from the main road through mountain-forest. It was a rough and dangerous path—sometimes skirting precipices—sometimes offering nothing but a network of slippery roots for the foot to rest upon—sometimes winding over or between masses of jagged rock. But at last Kwairyo found himself upon a cleared space at the top of a hill, with a full moon shining overhead; and he saw before him a small thatched cottage, cheerfully lighted from within. The woodcutter led him to a shed at the back of the house, whither water had been conducted, through bamboo pipes, from some neighboring stream; and the two men washed their feet. Beyond the shed was a vegetable garden, and a grove of cedars and bamboos; and beyond the trees appeared the glimmer of a cascade, pouring from some loftier height, and swaying in the moonshine like a long white robe.

As Kwairyo entered the cottage with his guide, he perceived four persons—men and women—warming their hands at a little fire kindled in the *ro* of the principal apartment. They bowed low to the priest, and greeted him in the most respectful manner. Kwairyo wondered that persons so poor, and dwelling in such a solitude, should be aware of the polite forms of greeting. "These are good people," he thought to himself; "and they must have been taught by someone well acquainted with the rules of propriety."

Then turning to his host—the *aruji*, or house-master, as the others called him—Kwairyo said:

"From the kindness of your speech, and from the very polite welcome given me by your household, I imagine that you have not always been a woodcutter. Perhaps you formerly belonged to one of the upper classes?"

Smiling, the woodcutter answered:

"Sir, you are not mistaken. Though now living as you find me, I was once a person of some distinction. My story is the story of a ruined life—ruined by my own fault. I used to be in the service of a *daimyo*; and my rank in that service was not inconsiderable. But I loved women and wine too well; and under the influence of passion I acted wickedly. My selfishness brought about the ruin of our house, and caused the death of many persons. Retribution followed me; and I long remained a fugitive in the land. Now I often pray that I may be able to make some atonement for the evil which I did, and to reestablish the ancestral home. But I fear that I shall never find any way of so doing. Nevertheless, I try to overcome the karma of my errors by sincere repentance, and by helping as afar as I can, those who are unfortunate."

Kwairyo was pleased by this announcement of good resolve; and he said to the *aruji*:

"My friend, I have had occasion to observe that men, prone to folly in their youth, may in after years become very earnest in right living. In the holy sutras it is written that those strongest in wrong-doing can become, by power of good resolve, the strongest in right-doing. I do not doubt that you have a good heart; and I hope that better fortune will come to you. Tonight I shall recite the sutras for your sake, and pray that you may obtain the force to overcome the karma of any past errors."

With these assurances, Kwairyo bade the *aruji* goodnight; and his host showed him to a very small side room, where a bed had been made ready. Then all went to sleep except the priest, who began to read the sutras by the light of a paper lantern. Until a late hour he continued to read and pray; then he opened a little window in his little sleeping room, to take a last look at the landscape before lying down. The night was beautiful: there was no cloud in the sky: there was no wind; and the strong moonlight threw down sharp black shadows of foliage, and glittered on the dews of the garden. Shrillings of crickets and bell insects made a musical tumult; and the sound of the neighboring cascade deepened with the night. Kwairyo felt thirsty as he listened to the noise of the water; and, remembering the bamboo aqueduct at the rear of the house, he thought that he could go there and get a drink without disturbing the sleeping household. Very gently he pushed apart the sliding-screens that separated his room from the main apartment; and he saw, by the light of the lantern, five recumbent bodies—without heads!

For one instant he stood bewildered—imagining a crime. But in another moment he perceived that there was no blood, and that the headless necks did not look as if they had been cut. Then he thought to himself: "Either this is an illusion made by goblins, or I have been lured into the dwelling of a *rokuro-kubi*... In the book *Soshinki* it is written that if one find the body of a *rokuro-kubi* without its head, and remove the body to another place, the head will never be able to join itself again to the neck. And the book further says that when the head comes back and finds that its body has been moved, it will strike itself upon the floor three times—bounding like a ball—and will pant as in great fear, and presently die. Now, if these be *rokuro-kubi*, they mean me no good—so I shall be justified in following the instructions of the book."

He seized the body of the *aruji* by the feet, pulled it to the window, and pushed it out. Then he went to the back door, which he found barred; and he surmised that the heads had made their exit through the smoke-hole in the roof, which had been left open. Gently unbarring the door, he made his way to the garden, and proceeded with all possible caution to the grove beyond it. He heard voices talking in the grove; and he went in the direction of the voices—stealing from shadow to shadow, until he reached a good hiding-place. Then, from behind a trunk, he caught sight of the heads—all five of them—flitting about, and chatting as they flitted. They were eating worms and insects which they found on the ground or among the trees. Presently the head of the *aruji* stopped eating and said:

"Ah, that traveling priest who came tonight!—How fat all his body is! When we have eaten him, our bellies will be well filled... I was foolish to talk to him as I did—it only set him to reciting the sutras on behalf of my soul! To go near him while he is reciting would be difficult; and we cannot touch him so long as he is praying. But as it is now nearly morning, perhaps he has gone to sleep... One of you go to the house and see what the fellow is doing."

Another head—the head of a young woman—immediately rose up and flitted to the house, lightly as a bat. After a few minutes it came back, and cried out huskily, in a tone of great alarm:

"That traveling priest is not in the house—he is gone! But that is not the worst of the matter. He has taken the body of our *aruji*; and I do not know where he has put it."

At this announcement the head of the *aruji*—distinctly visible in the moonlight—assumed a frightful aspect: its eyes opened monstrously, its hair stood up bristling, and its teeth gnashed. Then a cry burst from its lips and—weeping tears of rage—it exclaimed:

"Since my body has been moved, to rejoin it is not possible! Then I must die!... And all through the work of that priest! Before I die I will get at that priest!—I will tear him!—I will devour him!... AND THERE HE IS—behind that tree!—Hiding behind that tree! See him!—The fat coward!"

In the same moment the head of the *aruji*, followed by the other four heads, sprang at Kwairyo. But the strong priest had already armed himself by plucking up a young tree; and with that tree he struck the heads as they came—knocking them from him with tremendous blows. Four of them fled away. But the head of the *aruji*, though battered again and again, desperately continued to bound at the priest, and at last caught him by the left sleeve of his robe. Kwairyo, however, as quickly gripped the head by its topknot, and repeatedly struck it. It did not release its hold; but it uttered a long moan, and thereafter ceased to struggle. It was dead. But its teeth still held the sleeve; and, for all his great strength, Kwairyo could not force open the jaws.

With the head still hanging to his sleeve he went back to the house, and there caught sight of the other four *rokuro-kubi* squatting together, with their bruised and bleeding heads reunited to their bodies. But when they perceived him at the back door all screamed, "The priest! The priest!"—and fled, through the other doorway, out into the woods.

Eastward the sky was brightening; day was about to dawn, and Kwairyo knew that the power of the goblins was limited to the hours of darkness. He looked at the head clinging to his sleeve—its face all fouled with blood and foam and clay; and he laughed aloud as he thought to himself: "What a *miyage* [souvenir]!—The head of a goblin!" After which he gathered together his few belongings, and leisurely descended the mountain to continue his journey.

Right on he journeyed, until he came to Suwa in Shinano; and into the main street of Suwa he solemnly strode, with the head dangling at his elbow. Then woman fainted, and children screamed and ran away; and there was a great crowding and clamoring until the *torite* (as the police in those days were called) seized the priest and took him to jail. For they supposed the head to be the head of a murdered man who, in the moment of being killed, had caught the murderer's sleeve in his teeth. As for Kwairyo, he only smiled and said nothing when they questioned him. So, after having passed a night in prison, he was brought before the magistrates of the district. Then he was ordered to explain how he, a priest, had been found with the head of a man fastened to his sleeve, and why he had dared thus shamelessly to parade his crime in the sight of people.

Kwairyo laughed long and loudly at these questions; and then he said:

"Sirs, I did not fasten the head to my sleeve: it fastened itself there—much against my will. And I have not committed any crime. For this is not the head of a man; it is the head of a goblin—and if I caused the death of the goblin, I did not do so by any shedding of blood, but simply by taking the precautions necessary to assure my own safety." And he proceeded to relate the whole of the adventure—bursting into another hearty laugh as he told of his encounter with the five heads.

But the magistrates did not laugh. They judged him to be a hardened criminal, and his story an insult to their intelligence. Therefore, without further questioning, they decided to order his immediate execution—all of them except one, a very old man. This aged officer had made no remark during the trial; but, after having heard the opinion of his colleagues, he rose up, and said:

"Let us first examine the head carefully; for this, I think, has not yet been done. If the priest has spoken truth, the head itself should bear witness for him... Bring the head here!"

So the head, still holding in its teeth the *koromo* that had been stripped from Kwairyo's shoulders, was put before the judges. The old man turned it round and round, carefully examined it, and discovered, on the nape of its neck, several strange red characters. He called the attention of his colleagues to these, and also bade them observe that the edges of the neck nowhere presented the appearance of having been cut by any weapon. On the contrary, the line of leverance was smooth as the line at which a falling leaf detaches itself from the stem... Then said the elder:

"I am quite sure that the priest told us nothing but the truth. This is the head of a *rokuro-kubi*. In the book *Nan-ho-i-butsu-shi* it is written that certain red characters can always be found upon the nape of the neck of a real *rokuro-kubi*. There are the characters: you can see for yourselves that they have not been painted. Moreover, it is well known that such goblins have been dwelling in the mountains of the province of Kai from very ancient time... But you, Sir," he exclaimed, turning to Kwairyo, "what sort of sturdy priest may you be? Certainly you have given proof of a courage that few priests possess; and you have the air of a soldier rather than a priest. Perhaps you once belonged to the samurai-class?"

"You have guessed rightly, Sir," Kwairyo responded. "Before becoming a priest, I long followed the profession of arms; and in those days I never feared man or devil. My name then was Isogai Heidazaemon Taketsura of Kyushu: there may be some among you who remember it."

At the mention of that name, a murmur of admiration filled the court-room; for there were many present who remembered it. And Kwairyo immediately found himself among friends instead of judges—friends anxious to prove their admiration by fraternal kindness. With honor they escorted him to the residence of the *daimyo*, who welcomed him, and feasted him, and made him a handsome present before allowing him to depart. When Kwairyo left Suwa, he was as happy as any priest is permitted to be in this transitory world. As for the head, he took it with him—jocosely insisting that he intended it for a *miyage*.

And now it only remains to tell what became of the head.

A day or two after leaving Suwa, Kwairyo met with a robber, who stopped him in a lonesome place, and bade him strip. Kwairyo at once removed his *koromo*, and offered it to the robber, who then first perceived what was hanging to the sleeve. Though brave, the highwayman was startled: he dropped the garment, and sprang back. Then he cried out: "You! What kind of a priest are you? Why, you are a worse man than I am! It is true that I have killed people; but I never walked about with anybody's head fastened to my sleeve... Well, Sir priest, I suppose we are of the same calling; and I must say that I admire you!... Now that head would be of use to me: I could frighten people with it. Will you sell it? You can have my robe in exchange for your *koromo*; and I will give you five *ryo* for the head."

Kwairyo answered:

"I shall let you have the head and the robe if you insist; but I must tell you that this is not the head of a man. It is a goblin's head. So, if you buy it, and have any trouble in consequence, please to remember that you were not deceived by me."

"What a nice priest you are!" exclaimed the robber. "You kill men, and jest about it!... But I am really in earnest. Here is my robe; and here is the money; and let me have the head... What is the use of joking?"

"Take the thing," said Kwairyo. "I was not joking. The only joke—if there be any joke at all—is that you are fool enough to pay good money for a goblin's head." And Kwairyo, loudly laughing, went upon his way.

Thus the robber got the head and the *koromo*; and for some time he played goblin-priest upon the highways. But, reaching the neighborhood of Suwa, he there learned the true story of the head; and he then became afraid that the spirit of the *rokuro-kubi* might give him trouble. So he made up his mind to take back the head to the place from which it had come, and to bury it with its body. He found his way to the lonely cottage in the mountains of Kai; but nobody was there, and he could not discover the body. Therefore he buried the head by itself, in the grove behind the cottage; and he had a tombstone set up over the grave; and he caused a *Segaki*-service to be performed on behalf of the spirit of the *rokuro-kubi.* And that tombstone—known as the Tombstone of the *Rokuro-Kubi*—may be seen (at least so the Japanese story-teller declares) even unto this day.

THE MOON POOL

ABRAHAM MERRITT

I

I am breaking a long silence to clear the name of Dr David Throckmartin and to lift the shadow of scandal from that of his wife and of Dr Charles Stanton, his assistant. That I have not found the courage to do so before, all men who are jealous of their scientific reputations will understand when they have read the facts entrusted to me alone.

I shall first recapitulate what has actually been known of the Throckmartin expedition to the island of Ponape in the Carolines—the Throckmartin Mystery, as it is called.

Dr Throckmartin set forth, you will recall, to make some observations of Nan-Matal, that extraordinary group of island ruins, remains of a high and prehistoric civilization, that are clustered along the east shore of Ponape. With him went his wife to whom he had been wedded less than half a year. The daughter of Professor Frazier-Smith, she was as deeply interested and almost as well informed as he, upon these relics of a vanished race that titanically strew certain islands of the Pacific and form the basis for the theory of a submerged Pacific continent.

Mrs Throckmartin, it will be recalled, was much younger, fifteen years at least, than her husband. Dr Charles Stanton, who accompanied them as Dr Throckmartin's assistant, was about her age. These three and a Swedish woman, Thora Helversen, who had been Edith Throckmartin's nurse in babyhood and who was entirely devoted to her, made up the expedition.

Dr Throckmartin planned to spend a year among the ruins, not only of Ponape, but of Lele—the twin centers of that colossal riddle of humanity whose answer has its roots in immeasurable antiquity; a weird flower of man-made civilization that blossomed ages before the seeds of Egypt were sown; of whose arts we know little and of whose science and secret knowledge of nature nothing.

He carried with him complete equipment for his work and gathered at Ponape a dozen or so natives for laborers. They went straight to Metalanim harbor and set up their camp on the island called Uschen-Tau in the group known as the Nan-Matal. You will remember that these islands are entirely uninhabited and are shunned by the people on the main island.

Three months later Dr Throckmartin appeared at Port Moresby, Papua. He came on a schooner manned by Solomon Islanders and commanded by a Chinese half-breed captain. He reported that he was on his way to Melbourne for additional scientific equipment and whites to help him in his excavations, saying that the superstition of the natives made their aid negligible. He went immediately on board the steamer *Southern Queen*, which was sailing that same morning. Three nights later he disappeared from the *Southern Queen* and it was officially reported that he had met death either by being swept overboard or by casting himself into the sea.

A relief-boat sent with the news to Ponape found the Throckmartin camp on the island Uschen-Tau and a smaller camp on the island called Nan-Tanach. All the equipment, clothing, supplies were intact. But of Mrs Throckmartin, of Dr Stanton, or of Thora Helversen they could find not a single trace!

The natives who had been employed by the archeologist were questioned. They said that the ruins were the abode of great spirits—*ani*—who were particularly powerful when the moon was at the full. On these nights all the islanders were doubly careful to give the ruins wide berth. Upon being employed, they had demanded leave from the day before full moon until it was on the wane and this had been granted them by Dr Throckmartin. Thrice they had left the expedition alone on these nights. On their third return they had found the four white people gone and they "knew that the *ani* had eaten them." They were afraid and had fled.

That was all.

The Chinese half-caste was found and reluctantly testified at last that he had picked Dr Throckmartin up from a small boat about fifty miles off Ponape. The scientist had seemed half mad, but he had given the seaman a large sum of money to bring him to Port Moresby and to say, if questioned, that he had boarded the boat at Ponape harbor.

That is all that has been known to anyone of the fate of the Throckmartin expedition.

Why, you will ask, do I break silence now; and how came I in possession of the facts I am about to set forth?

To the first I answer: I was at the Geographical Club recently and I overheard two members talking. They mentioned the name of Throckmartin and I became an eavesdropper. One said:

"Of course what probably happened was that Throckmartin killed them all. It's a dangerous thing for a man to marry a woman so much younger than himself and then throw her into the necessarily close company of exploration with a man as young and as agreeable as Stanton was. The inevitable happened, no doubt. Throckmartin discovered; avenged himself. Then followed remorse and suicide."

"Throckmartin didn't seem to be that kind," said the other thoughtfully.

"No, he didn't," agreed the first.

"Isn't there another story?" went on the second speaker. "Something about Mrs Throckmartin running away with Stanton and taking the woman, Thora, with her? Somebody told me they had been recognized in Singapore recently."

"You can take your pick of the two stories," replied the other man. "It's one or the other I suppose."

It was neither one nor the other of them. I know—and I will answer now the second question—because I was with Throckmartin when he—vanished. I know what he told me and I know what my own eyes saw. Incredible, abnormal, against all the known facts of our science as it was, I testify to it. And it is my intention, after this is published, to sail to Ponape, to go to the Nan-Matal and to the islet beneath whose frowning walls dwells the mystery that Throckmartin sought and found—and that at the last sought and found Throckmartin!

I will leave behind me a copy of the map of the islands that he gave me. Also his sketch of the great courtyard of Nan-Tanach, the location of the moon door, his indication of the probable location of the moon pool and the passage to it, and his approximation of the position of the shining globes. If I do not return and there are any with enough belief, scientific curiosity, and courage to follow, these will furnish a plain trail.

I will now proceed straightforwardly with my narrative.

For six months I had been on the d'Entrecasteaux Islands gathering data for the concluding chapters of my book upon *Flora of the Volcanic Islands of the South Pacific*. The day before, I had reached Port Moresby and had seen my specimens safely stored on board the *Southern Queen*. As I sat on the upper deck that morning I thought, with homesick mind, of the long leagues between me and Melbourne and the longer ones between Melbourne and New York.

It was one of Papua's yellow mornings, when she shows herself in her most somber, most baleful mood. The sky was a smoldering ocher. Over the island brooded a spirit sullen, implacable, and alien; filled with the threat of latent, malefic forces waiting to be unleashed. It seemed an emanation from the untamed, sinister heart of Papua herself—sinister even when she smiles. And now and then, on the wind, came a breath from unexplored jungles, filled with unfamiliar odors, mysterious, and menacing.

It is on such mornings that Papua speaks to you of her immemorial ancientness and of her power. I am not unduly imaginative but it is a mood that makes me shrink—I mention it because it bears directly upon Dr

Throckmartin's fate. Nor is the mood Papua's alone. I have felt it in New Guinea, in Australia, in the Solomons, and in the Carolines. But it is in Papua that it seems most articulate. It is as though she said: "I am the ancient of days: I have seen the earth in the throes of its shaping; I am the primeval; I have seen races born and die and, lo, in my breast are secrets that would blast you by the telling, you pale babes of a puling age. You and I ought not be in the same world; yet I am and I shall be! Never will you fathom me and you I hate though I tolerate! I tolerate—but how long?"

And then I seem to see a giant paw that reaches from Papua toward the outer world, stretching and sheathing monstrous claws.

All feel this mood of hers. Her own people have it woven in them, part of their web and woof; flashing into light unexpectedly like a soul from another universe; masking itself as swiftly.

I fought against Papua as every white man must on one of her yellow mornings. And as I fought I saw a tall figure come striding down the pier. Behind him came a Kapa-Kapa boy swinging a new valise. There was something familiar about the tall man. As he reached the gangplank he looked up straight into my eyes, stared at me for a moment and waved his hand. It was Dr Throckmartin!

Coincident with my recognition of him there came a shock of surprise that was definitely—unpleasant. It was Throckmartin—but there was something disturbingly different about him and the man I had known so well and had bidden farewell less than a year before. He was then, as you know, just turned forty, lithe, erect, muscular; the face of a student and of a seeker. His controlling expression was one of enthusiasm, of intellectual keenness, of—what shall I say—expectant search. His ever eagerly questioning brain had stamped itself upon his face.

I sought in my mind for an explanation of that which I had felt on the flash of his greeting. Hurrying down to the lower deck I found him with the purser. As I spoke he turned and held out to me an eager hand—and then I saw what the change was that had come over him!

He knew, of course, by my face the uncontrollable shock that my closer look had given me. His eyes filled and he turned briskly to the purser; then hurried off to his stateroom, leaving me standing, half dazed.

At the stair he half turned.

"Oh, Goodwin," he said. "I'd like to see you later. Just now— there's something I must write before we start—"

He went up swiftly.

"'E looks rather queer—eh?" said the purser. "Know 'im well, sir? Seems to 'ave given you quite a start, sir."

I made some reply and went slowly to my chair. I tried to analyze what it was that had disturbed me so; what profound change in Throckmartin that had so shaken me. Now it came to me. It was as though the man had suffered some terrific soul searing shock of rapture and horror combined; some soul cataclysm that in its climax had remolded his face deep from within, setting on it the seal of wedded joy and fear. As though indeed ecstasy supernal and terror infernal had once come to him hand in hand, taken possession of him, looked out of his eyes and, departing, left behind upon him ineradicably their shadow.

Alternately I looked out over the port and paced about the deck, striving to read the riddle; to banish it from my mind. And all the time still over Papua brooded its baleful spirit of ancient evil, unfathomable, not to be understood; nor had it lifted when the *Southern Queen* lifted anchor and steamed out into the gulf.

II

I watched with relief the shores sink down behind us; welcomed the touch of the free sea wind. We seemed to be drawing away from something malefic; something that lurked within the island spell I have described, and the thought crept into my mind, spoke—whispered rather—from Throckmartin's face.

I had hoped—and within the hope was an inexplicable shrinking, an unexpressed dread—that I would meet Throckmartin at lunch. He did not come down and I was sensible of a distinct relief within my disappointment. All that afternoon I lounged about uneasily but still he kept to his cabin. Nor did he appear at dinner.

Dusk and night fell swiftly. I was warm and went back to my deckchair. The *Southern Queen* was rolling to a disquieting swell and I had the place to myself.

Over the heavens was a canopy of cloud, glowing faintly and testifying to the moon riding behind it. There was much phosphorescence. Now and then, before the ship and at the sides, arose those strange little swirls of mist that steam up from the Southern Ocean like the breath of sea monsters, whirl for a moment and disappear. I lit a cigarette and tried once more to banish Throckmartin's face from my mind.

Suddenly the deck door opened and through it came Throckmartin himself. He paused uncertainly, looked up at the sky with a curiously eager, intent gaze, hesitated, then closed the door behind him.

"Throckmartin," I called. "Come sit with me. It's Goodwin."

Immediately he made his way to me, sitting beside me with a gasp of relief that I noted curiously. His hand touched mine and gripped it with tenseness that hurt. His hand was icelike. I puffed up my cigarette and by its glow scanned him closely. He was watching a large swirl of the mist that was passing before the ship. The phosphorescence beneath it illumined it with a fitful opalescence. I saw fear in his eyes. The swirl passed; he sighed; his grip relaxed and he sank back.

"Throckmartin," I said, wasting no time in preliminaries. "What's wrong? Can I help you?"

He was silent.

"Is your wife all right and what are you doing here when I heard you had gone to the Carolines for a year?" I went on.

I felt his body grow tense again. He did not speak for a moment and then:

"I'm going to Melbourne, Goodwin," he said. "I need a few things—need them urgently. And more men—white men."

His voice was low; preoccupied. It was as though the brain that dictated the words did so perfunctorily, half impatiently; aloof, watching, strained to catch the first hint of approach of something dreaded.

"You are making progress then?" I asked. It was a banal question, put forth in a blind effort to claim his attention.

"Progress?" he repeated. "Progress—"

He stopped abruptly; rose from his chair, gazed intently toward the north. I followed his gaze. Far, far away the moon had broken through the clouds. Almost on the horizon, you could see the faint luminescence of it upon the quiet sea. The distant patch of light quivered and shook. The clouds thickened again and it was gone. The ship raced southward, swiftly.

Throckmartin dropped into his chair. He lighted a cigarette with a hand that trembled. The flash of the match fell on his face and I noted with a queer thrill of apprehension that its unfamiliar expression had deepened; become curiously intensified as though a faint acid had passed over it, etching its lines faintly deeper.

"It's the full moon tonight, isn't it?" he asked, palpably with studied inconsequence.

"The first night of full moon," I answered. He was silent again. I sat silent too, waiting for him to make up his mind to speak. He turned to me as though he had made a sudden resolution.

"Goodwin," he said. "I do need help. If ever man needed it, I do. Goodwin—can you imagine yourself in another world, alien, unfamiliar, a world of terror, whose unknown joy is its greatest terror of all; you all alone there; a stranger! As such a man would need help, so I need—"

He paused abruptly and arose to his feet stiffly; the cigarette dropped from his fingers. I saw that the moon had again broken through the clouds, and this time much nearer. Not a mile away was the patch of light that it threw upon the waves. Back of it, to the rim of the sea was a lane of moonlight; it was a gleaming gigantic serpent racing over the rim of the world straight and surely toward the ship.

Throckmartin gazed at it as though turned to stone. He stiffened to it as a pointer does to a hidden covey. To me from him pulsed a thrill of terror—but terror tinged with an unfamiliar, an infernal joy. It came to me and passed away—leaving me trembling with its shock of bitter sweet.

He bent forward, all his soul in his eyes. The moon path swept closer, closer still. It was now less than half a mile away. From it the ship fled; almost it came to me, as though pursued. Down upon it, swift and straight, a radiant torrent cleaving the waves, raced the moon stream. And then—

"Good God!" breathed Throckmartin, and if ever the words were a prayer and an invocation they were.

And then, for the first time—I saw—it!

The moon path, as I have said, stretched to the horizon and was bordered by darkness. It was as though the clouds above had been parted to form a lane—drawn aside like curtains or as the waters of the Red Sea were held back to let the hosts of Israel through. On each side of the stream was the black shadow cast by the folds of the high canopies. And straight as a road between the opaque walls gleamed, shimmered and danced the shining, racing, rapids of moonlight.

Far, it seemed immeasurably far, along this stream of silver fire I sensed, rather than saw, something coming. It drew into sight as a deeper glow within the light. On and on it sped toward us—an opalescent mistiness that swept on with the suggestion of some winged creature in darting flight. Dimly there crept into my mind memory of the Dyak legend of the winged messenger of Buddha—the Akla bird whose feathers are woven of the moon rays, whose heart is a living opal, whose wings in flight echo the crystal clear music of the white stars—but whose beak is of frozen flame and shreds the souls of the unbelievers. Still it sped on, and now there came to me sweet, insistent tinklings—like a pizzicati on violins of glass, crystalline, as purest, clearest glass transformed to sound. And again the myth of the Akla bird came to me.

But now it was close to the end of the white path; close up to the barrier of darkness still between the ship and the sparkling head of the moon stream.

And now it beat up against that barrier as a bird against the bars of its cage. And I knew that this was no mist born of sea and air. It whirled with shimmering plumes, with swirls of lacy light, with spirals of living vapor. It held within it odd, unfamiliar gleams as of shifting mother-of-pearl. Coruscations and glittering atoms drifted through it as though it drew them from the rays that bathed it.

Nearer and nearer it came, borne on the sparkling waves, and less and less grew the protecting wall of shadow between it and us. The crystalline sounds were louder—rhythmic as music from another planet.

Now I saw that within the mistiness was a core, a nucleus of intenser light—veined, opaline, effulgent, intensely alive. And above it, tangled in the plumes and spirals that throbbed and whirled were seven glowing lights.

Through all the incessant but strangely ordered movement of the—thing—these lights held firm and steady. They were seven—like seven little moons. One was of a pearly pink, one of delicate nacreous blue, one of lambent saffron, one of the emerald you see in the shallow waters of tropic isles; a deathly white; a ghostly amethyst; and one of the silver that is seen only when the flying fish leap beneath the moon. There they shone—these seven little varicolored orbs within the opaline mistiness of whatever it was that, poised and expectant, waited to be drawn to us on the light filled waves.

The tinkling music was louder still. It pierced the ears with a shower of tiny lances; it made the heart beat jubilantly—and checked it dolorously. It closed your throat with a throb of rapture and gripped it tight like the hand of infinite sorrow!

Came to me now a murmuring cry, stilling the crystal clear notes, it was articulate—but as though from something utterly foreign to this world. The ear took the cry and translated with conscious labor into the sounds of earth. And even as it compassed, the brain shrank from it irresistibly and simultaneously it seemed, reached toward it with irresistible eagerness.

"Av-o-lo-ha! Av-o-lo-ha!" So the cry seemed to throb.

The grip of Throckmartin's hand relaxed. He walked stiffly toward the front of the deck, straight toward the vision, now but a few yards away from the bow. I ran toward him and gripped him—and fell back. For now his face had lost all human semblance. Utter agony and utter ecstasy—there they were side by side, not resisting each other; unholy inhuman companions blending into a look that none of God's creatures should wear—and deep, deep as his soul! A devil and a god dwelling harmoniously side by side! So must Satan, newly fallen, still divine, seeing heaven and contemplating hell, have looked.

And then—swiftly the moon path faded! The clouds swept over the sky as though a hand had drawn them together. Up from the south came a roaring squall. As the moon vanished what I had seen vanished with it—blotted out as an image on a magic lantern; the tinkling ceased abruptly—leaving a silence like that which follows an abrupt and stupendous thunder clap. There was nothing about us but silence and blackness!

Through me there passed a great trembling as one who had stood on the very verge of the gulf wherein the men of the Louisades say lurks the fisher of the souls of men, and has been plucked back by sheerest chance.

Throckmartin passed an arm around me.

"It is as I thought," he said. In his voice was a new note; of the calm certainty that has swept aside a waiting terror of the unknown. "Now I know! Come with me to my cabin, old friend. For now that you too have seen I can tell you"—he hesitated—"what it was you saw," he ended.

As we passed through the door we came face to face with the ship's first officer. Throckmartin turned quickly, but not soon enough for the mate not to see and stare with amazement. His eyes turned questioningly to me.

With a strong effort of will Throckmartin composed his face into at least a semblance of normality.

"Are we going to have much of a storm?" he asked.

"Yes," said the mate. Then the seaman, getting the better of his curiosity, added, profanely: "We'll probably have it all the way to Melbourne."

Throckmartin straightened as though with a new thought. He gripped the officer's sleeve eagerly.

"You mean at least cloudy weather—for"—he hesitated—"for the next three nights, say?"

"And for three more," replied the mate.

"Thank God!" cried Throckmartin, and I think I never heard such relief and hope as was in his voice.

The sailor stood amazed. "Thank God?" he repeated. "Thank—what d'ye mean?"

But Throckmartin was moving onward to his cabin. I started to follow. The first officer stopped me.

"Your friend," he said, "Is he ill?"

"The sea!" I answered hurriedly. "He's not used to it. I am going to look after him."

I saw doubt and disbelief in the seaman's eyes but I hurried on. For I knew now that Throckmartin was ill indeed—but that it was a sickness neither the ship's doctor nor any other could heal.

III

Throckmartin was sitting on the side of his berth as I entered. He had taken off his coat. He was leaning over, face in hands.

"Lock the door," he said quietly, not raising his head. "Close the portholes and draw the curtains—and—have you an electric flash in your pocket—a good, strong one?"

He glanced at the small pocket flash I handed him and clicked it on. "Not big enough I'm afraid," he said. "And after all"—he hesitated—"it's only a theory."

"What's only a theory?" I asked in astonishment.

"Thinking of it as a weapon against—what you saw," he said, with a wry smile.

"Throckmartin," I cried. "What was it? Did I really see—that thing—there in the moon path? Did I really hear—"

"This for instance," he interrupted.

Softly he whispered: "Av-o-lo-ha!" With the murmur I seemed to hear again the crystalline unearthly music; an echo of it, faint, sinister, mocking, jubilant.

"Throckmartin," I said. "What was it? What are you flying from, man? Where is your wife—and Stanton?"

"Dead!" he said monotonously. "Dead! All dead!" Then as I recoiled in horror—"All dead. Edith, Stanton, Thora—dead—or worse. And Edith in the moon pool—with them—drawn by what you saw on the moon path—and that wants me—and that has put its brand upon me—and pursues me."

With a vicious movement he ripped open his shirt.

"Look at this," he said. I gazed. Around his chest, an inch above his heart, the skin was white as pearl. The whiteness was sharply defined against the healthy tint of the body. He turned and I saw it ran around his back. It circled him. The band made a perfect cincture about two inches wide.

"Burn it!" he said, and offered me his cigarette. I drew back. He gestured—peremptorily. I pressed the glowing end of the cigarette into the ribbon of white flesh. He did not flinch nor was there odor of burning nor, as I drew the little cylinder away, any mark upon the whiteness.

"Feel it!" he commanded again. I placed my fingers upon the band. It was cold—like frozen marble.

He handed me a small penknife.

"Cut!" he ordered. This time, my scientific interest fully aroused, I did so without reluctance. The blade cut into flesh. I waited for the blood to come. None appeared. I drew out the knife and thrust it in again, fully a quarter of an inch deep. I might have been cutting paper so far as any evidence followed that what I was piercing was human skin and muscle.

Another thought came to me and I drew back, revolted.

"Throckmartin," I whispered. "Not leprosy!"

"Nothing so easy," he said. "Look again and find the places you cut."

I looked, as he bade me, and in the white ring there was not a single mark. Where I had pressed the blade there was no trace. It was as though the skin had parted to make way for the blade and closed.

Throckmartin arose and drew his shirt about him.

"Two things you have seen," he said. "It—and its mark—the seal it placed on me that gives it, I think, the power to follow me. Seeing, you must believe my story. Goodwin, I tell you again that my wife is dead—or worse—I do not know; the prey of—what you saw; so, too, is Stanton; so Thora. How—" He stopped for a moment. Then continued:

"And I am going to Melbourne for the things to empty its den and its shrine; for dynamite to destroy it and its lair—if anything made on earth will destroy it; and for white men with courage to use them. Perhaps—perhaps after you have heard, you will be one of these men?" He looked at me a bit wistfully. "And now—do not interrupt me, I beg of you, till I am through—for"—he smiled wanly—"the mate may be wrong. And if he is"—he arose and paced twice about the room—"if he is I may not have time to tell you."

"Throckmartin," I answered, "I have no closed mind. Tell me—and if I can I will help."

He took my hand and pressed it.

"Goodwin," he began, "if I have seemed to take the death of my wife lightly—or rather"—his face contorted—"or rather—if I have seemed to pass it by as something not of first importance to me—believe me it is not so. If the rope is long enough—if what the mate says is so—if there is cloudy weather until the moon begins to wane—I can conquer—that I know. But if it does not—if the dweller in the moon pool gets me—then must you or someone avenge my wife—and me—and Stanton. Yet I cannot believe that God would let a thing like that conquer! But why did He then let it take my Edith? And why does He allow it to exist? Are there things stronger than God, do you think, Goodwin?"

He turned to me feverishly. I hesitated.

"I do not know just how you define God," I said. "If you mean the will to know, working through science—"

He waved me aside impatiently.

"Science," he said. "What is our science against—that? Or against the science of whatever cursed, vanished race that made it—or made the way for it to enter this world of ours?"

With an effort he regained control of himself.

"Goodwin," he said, "do you know at all of the ruins on the Carolines; the cyclopean, megolithic cities and harbors of Ponape and Lele, of Kusaie, of Ruk and Hogolu, and a score of other islets there? Particularly, do you know of the Nan-Matal and Metalanim?"

"Of the Metalanim I have heard and seen photographs," I said. "They call it, don't they, the Lost Venice of the Pacific?"

"Look at this map," said Throckmartin. He handed me the map. "That," he went on, "is Christian's map of Metalanim harbor and the Nan-Matal. Do you see the rectangles marked Nan-Tanach?"

"Yes," I said.

"There," he said, "under those walls is the moon pool and the seven gleaming lights that raise the dweller in the pool and the altar and shrine of the dweller. And there in the moon pool with it lie Edith and Stanton and Thora."

"The dweller in the moon pool?" I repeated half incredulously.

"The thing you saw," said Throckmartin solemnly.

A solid sheet of rain swept the ports, and the *Southern Queen* began to roll on the rising swells. Throckmartin drew another deep breath of relief, and drawing aside a curtain peered out into the night. Its blackness seemed to reassure him. At any rate, when he sat again he was calm.

"There are no more wonderful ruins in the world than those of the island Venice of Metalanim on the east shore of Ponape," he said almost casually. "They take in some fifty islets and cover with their intersecting canals and lagoons about twelve square miles. Who built them? None knows! When were they built? Ages before the memory of present man, that is sure. Ten thousand, twenty thousand, a hundred thousand years ago—the last more likely.

"All these islets, Goodwin, are squared, and their shores are frowning sea-walls of gigantic basalt blocks hewn and put in place by the hands of ancient man. Each inner water-front is faced with a terrace of those basalt blocks which stand out six feet above the shallow canals that meander between them. On the islets behind these walls are cyclopean and time-shattered fortresses, palaces, terraces, pyramids; immense courtyards, strewn with ruins—and all so old that they seem to wither the eyes of those who look on them.

"There has been a great subsidence. You can stand out of Metalanim harbor for three miles and look down upon the tops of similar monolithic structures and walls twenty feet below you in the water.

"And all about, strung on their canals, are the bulwarked islets with their enigmatic giant walls peering through the dense growths of mangroves—dead, deserted for incalculable ages; shunned by those who live near.

"You as a botanist are familiar with the evidence that a vast shadowy continent existed in the Pacific—a continent that was not rent asunder by volcanic forces as was that legendary one of Atlantis in the Eastern Ocean. My work in Java, in Papua, and in the Ladrones had set my mind upon this Pacific lost land. Just as the Azores are believed to be the last high peaks of Atlantis, so evidence came to me steadily that Ponape and Lele and their basalt bulwarked islets were the last points of the slowly sunken western land clinging still to the sunlight, and had been the last refuge and sacred places of the rulers of that race which had lost their immemorial home under the rising waters of the Pacific.

"I believed that under these ruins I might find the evidence of what I sought. Time and again I had encountered legends of subterranean networks beneath the Nan-Matal, of passages running back into the main island itself; basalt corridors that followed the lines of the shallow canals and ran under them to islet after islet, linking them in mysterious chains.

"My—my wife and I had talked before we were married of making this our great work. After the honeymoon we prepared for the expedition. It was to be my monument. Stanton was as enthusiastic as ourselves. We sailed, as you know, last May in fulfilment of our dreams.

"At Ponape we selected, not without difficulty, workmen to help us—diggers. I had to make extraordinary inducements before I could get together my force. Their beliefs are gloomy, these Ponapeans. They people their swamps, their forests, their mountains and shores with malignant spirits—*ani* they call them. And they are afraid—bitterly afraid of the isles of ruins and what they think the ruins hide. I do not wonder—now! For their fear has come down to them, through the ages, from the people 'before their fathers,' as they call them, who, they say, made these mighty spirits their slaves and messengers.

"When they were told where they were to go, and how long we expected to stay, they murmured. Those who, at last, were tempted made what I thought then merely a superstitious proviso that they were to be allowed to go away on the three nights of the full moon. If only I had heeded them and gone, too!"

He stopped and again over his face the lines etched deep.

"We passed," he went on, "into Metalanim harbor. Off to our left—a mile away arose a massive quadrangle. Its walls were all of forty feet high and hundreds of feet on each side. As we passed it our natives grew very silent; watched it furtively, fearfully. I knew it for the ruins that are called Nan-Tanach, the 'place of frowning walls.' And at the silence of my men I recalled what Christian had written of this place; of how he had come upon its 'ancient platforms and tetragonal enclosures of stonework; its wonder of tortuous alleyways and labyrinth of shallow canals; grim masses of stonework peering out from behind verdant screens; cyclopean barricades.' And now, when we had turned into its ghostly shadows, straightaway the merriment of our guides was hushed and conversation died down to whispers. For we were close to Nan-Tanach—the place of lofty walls, the most remarkable of all the Metalanim ruins." He arose and stood over me.

"Nan-Tanach, Goodwin," he said solemnly—"a place where merriment is hushed indeed and words are stifled; Nan-Tanach—where the moon pool lies hidden—lies hidden behind the moon rock, but sends its diabolic soul out—even through the prisoning stone." He raised clenched hands. "Oh, Heaven," he breathed, "grant me that I may blast it from earth!"

He was silent for a little time.

"Of course I wanted to pitch our camp there," he began again quietly, "but I soon gave up that idea. The natives were panic-stricken—threatened to turn back. 'No,' they said, 'too great *ani* there. We go to any other place—but not there.' Although, even then, I felt that the secret of the place was in Nan-Tanach, I found it necessary to give in. The laborers were essential to the success of the expedition, and I told myself that after a little time had passed and I had persuaded them that there was nothing anywhere that could molest them, we would move our tents to it. We finally picked for our base the islet called Uschen-Tau—you see it here—" He pointed to the map. "It was close to the isle of desire, but far enough away from it to satisfy our men. There was an excellent camping-place there and a spring of fresh water. It offered, besides, an excellent field for preliminary work before attacking the larger ruins. We pitched our tents. and in a couple of days the work was in full swing."

IV

"I do not intend to tell you now," Throckmartin continued, "the results of the next two weeks, Goodwin, nor of what we found. Later—if I am allowed I will lay all that before you. It is sufficient to say that at the end of those two weeks

I had found confirmation of many of my theories, and we were well under way to solve a mystery of humanity's youth—so we thought. But enough. I must hurry on to the first stirrings of the inexplicable thing that was in store for us.

"The place, for all its decay and desolation, had not infected us with any touch of morbidity—that is not Edith, Stanton, or myself. My wife was happy—never had she been happier. Stanton and she, while engrossed in the work as much as I, were of the same age, and they frankly enjoyed the companionship that only youth can give youth. I was glad—never jealous.

"But Thora was very unhappy. She was a Swede, as you know, and in her blood ran the beliefs and superstitions of the Northland—some of them so strangely akin to those of this far southern land; beliefs of spirits of mountain and forest and water—werewolves and beings malign. From the first she showed a curious sensitivity to what, I suppose, may be called the 'influences' of the place. She said it 'smelled' of ghosts and warlocks.

"I laughed at her then—but now I believe that this sensitivity of what we call primitive people is perhaps only a clearer perception of the unknown which we, who deny the unknown, have lost.

"A prey to these fears, Thora always followed my wife about like a shadow; carried with her always a little sharp hand-ax, and although we twitted her about the futility of chopping phantoms with such a weapon, she would not relinquish it.

"Two weeks slipped by, and at their end the spokesman for our natives came to us. The next night was the full of the moon, he said. He reminded me of my promise. They would go back to their village next morning; they would return after the third night, as at that time the power of the *ani* would begin to wane with the moon. They left us sundry charms for our 'protection,' and solemnly cautioned us to keep as far away as possible from Nan-Tanach during their absence—although their leader politely informed us that, no doubt, we were stronger than the spirits. Half-exasperated, half-amused, I watched them go.

"No work could be done without them, of course, so we decided to spend the days of their absence junketing about the southern islets of the group. Under the moon the ruins were inexpressibly weird and beautiful. We marked down several spots for subsequent exploration, and on the morning of the third day set forth along the east face of the breakwater for our camp on Uschen-Tau, planning to have everything in readiness for the return of our men the next day.

"We landed just before dusk, tired and ready for our cots. It was only a little after ten o'clock when Edith awakened me.

"'Listen!' she said. 'Lean over with your ear close to the ground!' I did so, and seemed to hear, far, far below, as though coming up from great distances, a faint chanting. It gathered strength, died down, ended; began, gathered volume, faded away into silence.

"'It's the waves rolling on rocks somewhere,' I said. 'We're probably over some ledge of rock that carries the sound.'

"'It's the first time I've heard it,' replied my wife doubtfully. We listened again. Then through the dim rhythms, deep beneath us, another sound came. It drifted across the lagoon that lay between us and Nan-Tanach in little tinkling waves. It was music—of a sort; I won't describe the strange effect it had upon me. You've felt it—"

"You mean on the deck?" I asked. Throckmartin nodded.

"I went to the flap of the tent," he continued, "and peered out. As I did so Stanton lifted his flap and walked out into the moonlight, looking over to the other islet and listening. I called to him.

"'That's the queerest sound!' he said. He listened again. 'Crystalline! Like little notes of translucent glass. Like the bells of crystal on the sistrums of Isis at Dendarah Temple,' he added half-dreamily. We gazed intently at the island. Suddenly, on the gigantic sea-wall, moving slowly, rhythmically, we saw a little group of lights. Stanton laughed.

"'The beggars!' he exclaimed. 'That's why they wanted to get away, is it? Don't you see, Dave, it's some sort of a festival—rites of some kind that they hold during the full moon! That's why they were so eager to have us keep away, too.'

"I felt a curious sense of relief, although I had not been sensible of any oppression. The explanation seemed good. It explained the tinkling music and also the chanting—worshipers, no doubt, in the ruins—their voices carried along passages I now knew honeycombed the whole Nan-Matal.

"'Let's slip over,' suggested Stanton—but I would not.

"'They're a difficult lot as it is,' I said. 'If we break into one of their religious ceremonies they'll probably never forgive us. Let's keep out of any family party where we haven't been invited.'

"'That's so,' agreed Stanton.

"The strange tinkling music, if music it can be called, rose and fell, rose and fell—now laden with sorrow, now filled with joy.

"'There's something—something very unsettling about it,' said Edith at last soberly. 'I wonder what they make those sounds with. They frighten me half to death, and, at the same time, they make me feel as though some enormous rapture was just around the corner.'

"I had noted this effect, too, although I had said nothing of it. And at the same time there came to me a clear perception that the chanting which had preceded it had seemed to come from a vast multitude—thousands more than the place we were contemplating could possibly have held. Of course, I thought, this might be due to some acoustic property of the basalt; an amplification of sound by some gigantic sounding-board of rock; still—

"'It's devilish uncanny!' broke in Stanton, answering my thought.

"And as he spoke the flap of Thora's tent was raised and out into the moonlight strode the old Swede. She was the great Norse type—tall, deep-breasted, molded on the old Viking lines. Her sixty years had slipped from her. She looked like some ancient priestess of Odin." He hesitated. "She knew," he said slowly, "something more far-seeing than my science had given her sight. She warned me—she warned me! Fools and mad that we are to pass such things by without heed!" He brushed a hand over his eyes.

"She stood there," he went on. "Her eyes were wide, brilliant, staring. She thrust her head forward toward Nan-Tanach, regarding the moving lights; she listened. Suddenly she raised her arms and made a curious gesture to the moon. It was—an archaic—movement; she seemed to drag it from remote antiquity—yet in it was a strange suggestion of power. Twice she repeated this gesture and—the tinkling died away! She turned to us.

"'Go,' she said, and her voice seemed to come from far distances. 'Go from here—and quickly! Go while you may. They have called—' She pointed to the islet. 'They know you are here. They wait.' Her eyes widened further. 'It is there,' she wailed. 'It beckons—the—the—'

"She fell at Edith's feet, and as she fell over the lagoon came again the tinklings, now with a quicker note of jubilance—almost of triumph.

"We ran to Thora, Stanton and I, and picked her up. Her head rolled and her face, eyes closed, turned as though drawn full into the moonlight. I felt in my heart a throb of unfamiliar fear—for her face had changed again. Stamped upon it was a look of mingled transport and horror—alien, terrifying, strangely revolting. It was"—he thrust his face close to my eyes—"what you see in mine!"

For a dozen heart-beats I stared at him, fascinated; then he sank back again into the half-shadow of the berth.

"I managed to hide her face from Edith," he went on. "I thought she had suffered some sort of a nervous seizure. We carried her into her tent. Once within the unholy mask dropped from her, and she was again only the kindly, rugged old woman. I watched her throughout the night. The sounds from Nan-Tanach continued until about an hour before moon-set. In the morning Thora awoke, none the worse, apparently. She had had bad dreams, she said. She could not remember what they were—except that they had warned her of danger. She was oddly sullen, and I noted that throughout the morning her gaze returned again half-fascinatedly, half-wonderingly to the neighboring isles.

"That afternoon the natives returned. They were so exuberant in their apparent relief to find us well and intact that Stanton's suspicions of them were confirmed. He slyly told their leader that 'from the noise they had made on Nan-Tanach the night before they must have thoroughly enjoyed themselves.'

"I think I never saw such stark terror as the Ponapean manifested at the remark! Stanton himself was so plainly startled that he tried to pass it over as a jest. He met poor success! The men seemed panic-stricken, and for a time I thought they were about to abandon us—but they did not. They pitched their camp at the western side of the island—out of sight of Nan-Tanach. I noticed that they built large fires, and whenever I awoke that night I heard their voices in slow, minor chant—one of their song 'charms,' I thought drowsily, against evil *ani*. I heard nothing else; the place of frowning walls was wrapped in silence—no lights showed. The next morning the men were quiet, a little depressed, but as the hours wore on they regained their spirits, and soon life at the camp was going on just as it had before.

"You will understand, Goodwin, how the occurrences I have related would excite the scientific curiosity. We rejected immediately, of course, any explanation admitting the supernatural. Why not? Except the curiously disquieting effects of the tinkling music and Thora's behavior there was nothing to warrant any such fantastic theories—even if our minds had been the kind to harbor them.

"We came to the conclusion that there must be a passageway between Ponape and Nan-Tanach, known to the natives—and used by them during their rites. Ceremonies were probably held in great vaults or caverns beneath the ruins.

"We decided at last that on the next departure of our laborers we would set forth immediately to Nan-Tanach. We would investigate during the day, and at evening my wife and Thora would go back to camp, leaving Stanton and me to spend the night on the island, observing from some safe hiding-place what might occur.

"The moon waned; appeared crescent in the west; waxed slowly toward the full. Before the men left us they literally prayed us to accompany them. Their importunities only made us more eager to see what it was that, we were now convinced, they wanted to conceal from us. At least that was true of Stanton and myself. It was not true of Edith. She was thoughtful, abstracted—reluctant. Thora, on the other hand, showed an unusual restlessness, almost an eagerness to go. Goodwin"—he paused—"Goodwin, I know now that the poison was working in Thora—and that women have perceptions that we men lack—forebodings, sensings. I wish to Heaven I had known it then—Edith!" he cried suddenly. "Edith—come back to me! Forgive me!"

I stretched the decanter out to him. He drank deeply. Soon he had regained control of himself.

"When the men were out of sight around the turn of the harbor," he went on, "we took our boat and made straight for Nan-Tanach. Soon its mighty sea-wall towered above us. We passed through the water-gate with its gigantic hewn prisms of basalt and landed beside a half-submerged pier. In front of us stretched a series of giant steps leading into a vast court strewn with fragments of fallen pillars. In the center of the court, beyond the shattered pillars, rose another terrace of basalt blocks, concealing, I knew, still another enclosure.

"And now, Goodwin, for the better understanding of what follows and to guide you, should I—not be able—to accompany you when you go there, listen carefully to my description of this place: Nan-Tanach is literally three rectangles. The first rectangle is the sea-wall, built up of monoliths. Gigantic steps lead up from the landing of the sea-gate through the entrance to the courtyard.

"This courtyard is surrounded by another, inner basalt wall.

"Within the courtyard is the second enclosure. Its terrace, of the same basalt as the outer walls, is about twenty feet high. Entrance is gained to it by many breaches which time has made in its stonework. This is the inner court, the heart of Nan-Tanach! There lies the great central vault with which is associated the one name of living being that has come to us out of the mists of the past. The natives say it was the treasure-house of Chau-te-leur, a mighty king who reigned long 'before their fathers.' As *chau* is the ancient Ponapean word both for sun and king, the name means 'place of the sun king.'

"And opposite this place of the sun king is the moon rock that hides the moon pool.

"It was Stanton who first found what I call the moon rock. We had been inspecting the inner courtyard; Edith and Thora were getting together our lunch. I forgot to say that we had previously gone all over the islet and had found not a trace of a living thing. I came out of the vault of Chau-te-leur to find Stanton before a part of the terrace studying it wonderingly.

"'What do you make of this?' he asked me as I came up, He pointed to the wall. I followed his finger and saw a slab of stone about fifteen feet high and ten wide. At first all I noticed was the exquisite nicety with which its edges joined the blocks about it. Then I realized that its color was subtly different—tinged with gray and of a smooth, peculiar—deadness.

"'Looks more like calcite than basalt,' I said. I touched it and withdrew my hand quickly, for at the contact every nerve in my arm tingled as though a shock of frozen electricity had passed through it. It was not cold as we know cold that I felt. It was a chill force—the phrase I have used—frozen electricity—describes it better than anything else. Stanton looked at me oddly.

"'So you felt it, too,' he said. 'I was wondering whether I was developing hallucinations like Thora. Notice, by the way, that the blocks beside it are quite warm beneath the sun.'

"I felt them and touched the grayish stone again. The same faint shock ran through my hand—a tingling chill that had in it a suggestion of substance, of force. We examined the slab more closely. Its edges were cut as though by an engraver of jewels. They fitted against the neighboring blocks in almost a hair-line. Its base, we saw, was slightly curved, and fitted as closely as top and sides upon the huge stones on which it rested. And then we noted that these stones had been hollowed to follow the line of the gray stone's foot. There was a semicircular depression running from one side of the slab to the other. It was as though the gray rock stood in the center of a shallow cup—revealing half, covering half. Something about this hollow attracted me. I reached down and felt it. Goodwin, although the balance of the stones that formed it, like all the stones of the courtyard, were rough and age-worn—this was as smooth, as even surfaced as though it just left the hands of the polisher.

"'It's a door!' exclaimed Stanton. 'It swings around in that little cup. That's what make the hollow so smooth.'

"'Maybe you're right,' I replied. 'But how the devil can we open it?'

"We went over the slab again—pressing upon its edges, thrusting against its sides. During one of those efforts I happened to look up—and cried out. For a foot above and even each side of the corner of the gray rock's lintel I had seen a slight convexity, visible only from the angle at which my gaze struck it. These bosses on the basalt were circular, eighteen inches in diameter, as we learned later, and at the center extended two inches only beyond the face of the terrace. Unless one looked directly up at them while leaning against the moon rock—for this slab, Goodwin, is the moon rock—they were invisible. And none would dare stand there!

"We carried with us a small scaling-ladder, and up this I went. The bosses were apparently nothing more than chiseled curvatures in the stone. I laid my hand on the one I was examining, and drew it back so sharply I almost threw myself from the ladder. In my palm, at the base of my thumb, I had felt the same shock that I had in touching the slab below. I put my hand back. The impression came from a spot not more than an inch wide. I went carefully over the entire convexity, and six times more the chill ran through my arm. There were, Goodwin, seven circles an inch wide in the curved place, each of which communicated the precise sensation I have described. The convexity on the opposite side of the slab gave precisely the same results. But no amount of touching or of pressing these spots singly or in any combination gave the slightest promise of motion to the slab itself.

"'And yet—they're what open it,' said Stanton positively.

"'Why do you say that?' I asked.

"'I—don't know,' he answered hesitatingly. 'But something tells me so. Throck,' he went on half earnestly, half laughingly, 'the purely scientific part of me is fighting the purely human part of me. The scientific part is urging me to find some way to get that slab either down or open. The human part is just as strongly urging me to do nothing of the sort and get away while I can!'

"He laughed again—shamefacedly.

"'Which will it be?' he asked—and I thought that in his tone the human side of him was ascendant.

"'It will probably stay as it is—unless we blow it to bits.' I said.

"'I thought of that,' he answered, 'and—I wouldn't dare,' he added soberly enough. And even as I had spoken there came to me the same feeling that he had expressed. It was as though something passed out of the gray rock that struck my heart as a hand strikes an impious lip. We turned away—uneasily, and faced Thora coming through a breach in the terrace.

"'Miss Edith wants you quick,' she began—and stopped. I saw her eyes go past me and widen. She was looking at the gray rock. Her body grew suddenly rigid; she took a few stiff steps forward and then ran straight to it. We saw her cast herself upon its breast, hands and face pressed against it; heard her scream as though her very soul was being drawn from her—and watched her fall at its foot. As we picked her up I saw steal from her face the look I had observed when I first heard the crystal music of Nan-Tanach—that unhuman mingling of opposites!"

V

"We carried Thora back, down to where Edith was waiting. We told her what had happened and what we had found. She listened gravely, and as we finished Thora sighed and opened her eyes.

"'I would like to see the stone,' she said. 'Charles, you stay here with Thora.' We passed through the outer court silently—and stood before the rock. She touched it, drew back her hand as I had; thrust it forward again resolutely and held it there. She seemed to be listening. Then she turned to me.

"'David,' said my wife, and the wistfulness in her voice hurt me—'David, would you be very, very disappointed if we went from here—without trying to find out any more about it—would you?'

"Goodwin, I never wanted anything so much in my life as I wanted to learn what that rock concealed. You will understand—the cumulative curiosity that all the happenings had caused; the certainty that before me was an entrance to a place that, while known to the natives—for I still clung to that theory—was utterly unknown to any man of my race; that within, ready for my finding, was the answer to the stupendous riddle of these islands and a lost chapter in the history of humanity. There before me—and was I asked to turn away, leaving it unread!

"Nevertheless, I tried to master my desire, and I answered—'Edith, not a bit if you want us to do it.'

"She read my struggle in my eyes. She looked at me searchingly for a moment and then turned back toward the gray rock. I saw a shiver pass through her. I felt a tinge of remorse and pity!

"'Edith,' I exclaimed, 'we'll go!'

"She looked at me hard. 'Science is a jealous mistress,' she quoted. 'No, after all it may be just fancy. At any rate, you can't run away. No! But, Dave, I'm going to stay too!'

"'You are not!' I exclaimed. 'You're going back to the camp with Thora. Stanton and I will be all right.'

"'I'm going to stay,' she repeated. And there was no changing her decision. As we neared the others she laid a hand on my arm.

"'Dave,' she said, 'if there should be something—well—inexplicable tonight—something that seems—too dangerous—will you promise to go back to our own islet tomorrow, or while we can, and wait until the natives return?'

"I promised eagerly—for the desire to stay and see what came with the night was like a fire within me.

"And would to Heaven I had not waited another moment, Goodwin; would to Heaven I had gathered them all together then and sailed back on the instant through the mangroves to Uschen-Tau!

"We found Thora on her feet again and singularly composed. She claimed to have no more recollection of what had happened after she had spoken to Stanton and to me in front of the gray rock than she had after the seizure on Uschen-Tau. She grew sullen under our questioning, precisely as she had before. But to my astonishment, when she heard of our arrangements for the night, she betrayed a febrile excitement that had in it something of exultance.

"We had picked a place about five hundred feet away from the steps leading into the outer court.

"We settled down just before dusk to wait for whatever might come. I was nearest the giant steps; next to me Edith; then Thora, and last Stanton. Each of us had with us automatic pistols, and all, except Thora, had rifles.

"Night fell. After a time the eastern sky began to lighten, and we knew that the moon was rising; grew lighter still, and the orb peeped over the sea; swam suddenly into full sight. Edith gripped my hand, for, as though the full emergence into the heavens had been a signal, we heard begin beneath us the deep chanting. It came from illimitable depths.

"The moon poured her rays down upon us, and I saw Stanton start. On the instant I caught the sound that had roused him. It came from the inner enclosure. It was like a long, soft sighing. It was not human; seemed in some way—mechanical. I glanced at Edith and then at Thora. My wife was intently listening. Thora sat, as she had since we had placed ourselves, elbows on knees, her hands covering her face.

"And then suddenly from the moonlight flooding us there came to me a great drowsiness. Sleep seemed to drip from the rays and fall upon my eyes, closing them—closing them inexorably. I felt Edith's hand relax in mine, and under my own heavy lids saw her nodding. I saw Stanton's head fall upon his breast and his body sway drunkenly. I tried to rise—to fight against the profound desire for slumber that pressed in on me.

"And as I fought I saw Thora raise her head as though listening; saw her rise and turn her face toward the gateway. For a moment she gazed, and my drugged eyes seemed to perceive within it a deeper, stronger radiance. Thora looked at us. There was infinite despair in her face—and expectancy. I tried again to rise—and a surge of sleep rushed over me. Dimly, as I sank within it, I heard a crystalline chiming; raised my lids once more with a supreme effort, saw Thora, bathed in light, standing at the top of the stairs, and then—sleep took me for its very own—swept me into the very heart of oblivion!

"Dawn was breaking when I wakened. Recollection rushed back on me and I thrust a panic-stricken hand out toward Edith; touched her and felt my heart give a great leap of thankfulness. She stirred, sat up, rubbing dazed eyes. I glanced toward Stanton. He lay on his side, back toward us, head in arms.

"Edith looked at me laughingly. 'Heavens! What sleep!' she said. Memory came to her. Her face paled. 'What happened?' she whispered. 'What made us sleep like that?' She looked over to Stanton, sprang to her feet, ran to him, shook him. He turned over with a mighty yawn, and I saw relief lighten her face as it had lightened my heart.

"Stanton raised himself stiffly. He looked at us. 'What's the matter?' he exclaimed. 'You look as though you've seen ghosts!'

"Edith caught my hands. 'Where's Thora?' she cried. Before I could answer she ran out into the open calling: 'Thora! Thora!'

"Stanton stared at me. 'Taken!' was all I could say. Together we went to my wife, now standing beside the great stone steps, looking up fearfully at the gateway into the terraces. There I told them what I had seen before sleep had drowned me. And together then we ran up the stairs, through the court and up to the gray rock.

"The gray rock was closed as it had been the day before, nor was there trace of its having opened. No trace! Even as I thought this Edith dropped to her knees before it and reached toward something lying at its foot. It was a little piece of gray silk. I knew it for part of the kerchief Thora wore about her hair. Edith took the fragment; hesitated. I saw then that it had been cut from the kerchief as though by a razor-edge; I saw, too, that a few threads ran from it—down toward the base of the slab; ran to the base of the gray rock and—under it! The gray rock was a door! And it had opened and Thora had passed through it!

"I think, Goodwin, that for the next few minutes we all were a little insane. We beat upon that diabolic entrance with our hands, with stones and clubs. At last reason came back to us. Stanton set forth for the camp to bring back blasting powder and tools. While he was gone Edith and I searched the whole islet for any other clue. We found not a trace of Thora nor any indication of any living being save ourselves. We went back to the gateway to find Stanton returned.

"Goodwin, during the next two hours we tried every way in our power to force entrance through the slab. The rock within effective blasting radius of the cursed door resisted our drills. We tried explosions at the base of the slab with charges covered by rock. They made not the slightest impression on the surface beneath, expending their force, of course, upon the slighter resistance of their coverings.

"Afternoon found us hopeless, so far as breaking through the rock was concerned. Night was coming on and before it came we would have to decide our course of action. I wanted to go to Ponape for help. But Edith objected that this would take hours and after we had reached there it would be impossible to persuade our men to return with us that night, if at all. What then was left? Clearly only one of two choices: to go back to our camp and wait for our men to return and on their return try to persuade them to go with us to Nan-Tanach. But this would mean the abandonment of Thora for at least two days. We could not do it; it would have been too cowardly.

"The other choice was to wait where we were for night to come; to wait for the rock to open as it had the night before, and to make a sortie through it for Thora before it could close again. With the sun had come confidence; at least a shattering of the mephitic mists of superstition with which the strangeness of the things that had befallen us had clouded for a time our minds. In that brilliant light there seemed no place for phantoms.

"The evidence that the slab had opened was unmistakable, but might not Thora simply have found it open through some mechanism, still working after ages, and dependent for its action upon laws of physics unknown to us upon the full light of the moon? The assertion of the natives that the *ani* had greatest power at this time might be a far-flung reflection of knowledge which had found ways to use forces contained in moonlight, as we have found ways to utilize the forces in the sun's rays. If so, Thora was probably behind the slab, sending out prayers to us for help.

"But how explain the sleep that had descended upon us? Might it not have been some emanation from plants or gaseous emanations from the island itself? Such things were far from uncommon, we agreed. In some way, the period of their greatest activity might coincide with the period of the moon, but if this were so why had not Thora also slept?

"As dusk fell we looked over our weapons. Edith was an excellent shot with both rifle and pistol. With the idea that the impulse toward sleep was the result either of emanations such as I have described or man made, we constructed rough-and-ready but effective neutralizers, which we placed over our mouths and nostrils. We had decided that my wife was to remain in the hollow spot. Stanton would take up a station on the far side of the stairway and I would place myself opposite him on the side near Edith. The place I picked out was less than five hundred feet from her, and I could reassure myself now as to her safety, as I looked down upon the hollow wherein she crouched. As the phenomena had previously synchronized with the rising of the moon, we had no reason to think they would occur any earlier this night.

"A faint glow in the sky heralded the moon. I kissed Edith, and Stanton and I took our places. The moon dawn increased rapidly; the disk swam up, and in a moment it seemed was shining in full radiance upon ruins and sea.

"As it rose there came as on the night before the curious little sighing sound from the inner terrace. I saw Stanton straighten up and stare intently through the gateway, rifle ready. Even at the distance he was from me, I discerned amazement in his eyes. The moonlight within the gateway thickened, grew stronger. I watched his amazement grow into sheer wonder.

"I arose. 'Stanton, what do you see?' I called cautiously. He waved a silencing hand. I turned my head to look at Edith. A shock ran through me. She lay upon her side. Her face was turned full toward the moon. She was in deepest sleep!

"As I turned again to call to Stanton, my eyes swept the head of the steps and stopped, fascinated. For the moonlight had thickened more. It seemed to be—curdled—there; and through it ran little gleams and veins of shimmering white fire. A languor passed through me. It was not the ineffable drowsiness of the preceding night. It was a sapping of all will to move. I tore my eyes away and forced them upon Stanton. I tried to call out to him. I had not the will to make my lips move! I had struggled against this paralysis and as I did so I felt through me a sharp shock. It was like a blow. And with it came utter inability to make a single motion. Goodwin, I could not even move my eyes!

"I saw Stanton leap upon the steps and move toward the gateway. As he did so the light in the courtyard grew dazzlingly brilliant. Through it rained tiny tinklings that set the heart to racing with pure joy and stilled it with terror.

"And now for the first time I heard that cry 'Av-o-lo-ha! Av-o-lo-ha!'—the cry you heard on deck. It murmured with the strange effect of a sound only partly in our own space—as though it were part of a fuller phrase passing through from another dimension and losing much as it came; infinitely caressing, infinitely cruel!

"On Stanton's face I saw come the look I dreaded—and yet knew would appear; that mingled expression of delight and fear. The two lay side by side as they had on Thora, but were intensified. He walked on up the stairs; disappeared beyond the range of my fixed gaze. Again I heard the murmur—'Av-o-lo-ha!' There was triumph in it now and triumph in the storm of tinklings that swept over it.

"For another heart-beat there was silence. Then a louder burst of sound and ringing through it Stanton's voice from the courtyard—a great cry—a scream—filled with ecstasy insupportable and horror unimaginable! And again there was silence. I strove to burst the invisible bonds that held me. I could not. Even my eyelids were fixed. Within them my eyes, dry and aching, burned.

"Then, Goodwin—I first saw the inexplicable! The crystalline music swelled. Where I sat I could take in the gateway and its basalt portals, rough and broken, rising to the top of the wall forty feet above, shattered, ruined portals—unclimbable. From this gateway an intenser light began to flow. It grew, it gushed, and into it, into my sight, walked Stanton.

"Stanton! But—Goodwin! What a vision!" He ceased. I waited—waited.

VI

"Goodwin," Throckmartin said at last. "I can describe him only as a thing of living light. He radiated light; was filled with light; overflowed with it. Around him was a shining cloud that whirled through and around him in radiant swirls, shimmering tentacles, luminescent, coruscating spirals.

"I saw his face. It shone with a rapture too great to be borne by living men, and was shadowed with insuperable misery. It was as though his face had been remolded by the hand of God and the hand of Satan, working together and in harmony. You have seen it on my face. But you have never seen it in the degree that Stanton bore it. The eyes were wide open and fixed, as though upon some inward vision of hell and heaven! He walked like the corpse of a man damned who carried within him an angel of light.

"The music swelled again. I heard again the murmuring—'Av-o-lo-ha!' Stanton turned, facing the ragged side of the portal. And then I saw that the light that filled and surrounded him had a nucleus, a core—something shiftingly human shaped—that dissolved and changed, gathered itself, whirled through and beyond him and back again. And as this shining nucleus passed through him Stanton's whole body pulsed with light. As the luminescence moved, there moved with it, still and serene always, seven tiny globes of light like seven little moons.

"So much I saw and then swiftly Stanton seemed to be lifted—levitated—up the unscalable wall and to its top. The glow faded from the moonlight, the tinkling music grew fainter. I tried again to move. The spell still held me fast. The tears were running down now from my rigid lids and brought relief to my tortured eyes.

"I have said my gaze was fixed. It was. But from the side, peripherally, it took in a part of the far wall of the outer enclosure. Ages seemed to pass and I saw a radiance stealing along it. Soon there came into sight the figure that was Stanton. Far away he was—on the gigantic wall. But still I could see the shining spirals whirling jubilantly around and through him; felt rather than saw his tranced face beneath the seven lights. A swirl of crystal notes, and he had passed. And all the time, as though from some opened well of light, the courtyard gleamed and sent out silver fires that dimmed the moon-rays, yet seemed strangely to be a part of them.

"Ten times he passed before me so. The luminescence came with the music; swam for a while along the man-made cliff of basalt and passed away. Between times eternities rolled and still I crouched there, a helpless thing of stone with eyes that would not close!

"At last the moon neared the horizon. There came a louder burst of sound; the second, and last, cry of Stanton, like an echo of the first! Again the soft sigh from the inner terrace. Then—utter silence. The light faded; the moon was setting and with a rush life and power to move returned to me, I made a leap for the steps, rushed up them. through the gateway and straight to the gray rock. It was closed—as I knew it would be. But did I dream it or did I hear, echoing through it as though from vast distances a triumphant shouting—'Av-o-lo-ha! Av-o-lo-ha!'?

"I remembered Edith. I ran back to her. At my touch she wakened; looked at me wonderingly; raised herself on a hand.

"'Dave!' she said. 'I slept—after all.' She saw the despair on my face and leaped to her feet. 'Dave!' she cried. 'What is it? Where's Charles?'

"I lighted a fire before I spoke. Then I told her. And for the balance of that night we sat before the flames, arms around each other—like two frightened children.

Suddenly Throckmartin held his hands out to me appealingly.

"Goodwin, old friend!" he cried. "Don't look at me as though I were mad. It's truth, absolute truth. Wait—" I comforted him as well as I could. After a little time he took up his story.

"Never," he said, "did man welcome the sun as we did that morning. As soon as it was light we went back to the courtyard. The basalt walls whereon I had seen Stanton were black and silent. The terraces were as they had been. The gray slab was in its place. In the shallow hollow at its base was—nothing. Nothing—nothing was there anywhere on the islet of Stanton—not a trace, not a sign on Nan-Tanach to show that he had ever lived.

"What were we to do? Precisely the same arguments that had kept us there the night before held good now—and doubly good. We could not abandon these two; could not go as long as there was the faintest hope of finding them—and yet for love of each other how could we remain? I loved my wife, Goodwin—how much I never knew until that day; and she loved me as deeply.

"'It takes only one each night,' she said. 'Beloved, let it take me.'

"I wept, Goodwin. We both wept.

"'We will meet it together,' she said. And it was thus at last that we arranged it."

"That took great courage indeed, Throckmartin," I interrupted. He looked at me eagerly.

"You do believe then?" he exclaimed.

"I believe," I said. He pressed my hand with a grip that nearly crushed it.

"Now," he told me, "I do not fear. If I—fail, you will prepare and carry on the work."

I promised. And—Heaven forgive me—that was three years ago.

"It did take courage," he went on, again quietly. "More than courage. For we knew it was renunciation. Each of us in our hearts felt that one of us would not be there to see the sun rise. And each of us prayed that the death, if death it was, would not come first to the other.

"We talked it all over carefully, bringing to bear all our power of analysis and habit of calm, scientific thought. We considered minutely the time element in the phenomena. Although the deep chanting began at the very moment of moonrise, fully five minutes had passed between its full lifting and the strange sighing sound from the inner terrace. I went back in memory over the happenings of the night before. At least fifteen minutes had intervened between the first heralding sigh and the intensification of the moonlight in the courtyard. And this glow grew for at least ten minutes more before the first burst of the crystal notes.

"The sighing sound—of what had it reminded me? Of course—of a door revolving and swishing softly along its base.

"'Edith!' I cried. 'I think I have it! The gray rock opens five minutes after upon the moonrise. But whoever or whatever it is that comes through it must wait until the moon has risen higher, or else it must come from a distance. The thing to do is not to wait for it, but to surprise it before it passes out the door. We will go into the inner court early. You will take your rifle and pistol and hide yourself where you can command the opening—if the slab does open. The instant it moves I will enter. It's our best chance, Edith. I think it's our only one.

"My wife demurred strongly. She wanted to go with me. But I convinced her that it was better for her to stand guard without, prepared to help me if I were forced from what lay behind the rock again into the open.

"The day passed too swiftly. In the face of what we feared our love seemed stronger than ever. Was it the flare of the spark before extinguishment? I wondered. We prepared and ate a good dinner. We tried to keep our minds from anything but scientific aspect of the phenomena. We agreed that whatever it was its cause must be human, and that we must keep that fact in mind every second. But what kind of men could create such prodigies? We thrilled at the thought of finding perhaps the remnants of a vanished race, living perhaps in cities over whose rocky skies the Pacific rolled; exercising there the lost wisdom of the half-gods of earth's youth.

"At the half-hour before moonrise we two went into the inner courtyard. I took my place at the side of the gray rock. Edith crouched behind a broken pillar twenty feet away, slipped her rifle-barrel over it so that it would cover the opening.

"The minutes crept by. The courtyard was very quiet. The darkness lessened and through the breaches of the terrace I watched the far sky softly lighten. With the first pale flush the stillness became intensified. It deepened—became unbearably—expectant. The moon rose, showed the quarter, the half, then swam up into full sight like a great bubble.

"Its rays fell upon the wall before me and suddenly, upon the convexities I have described, seven little circles of light sprang out. They gleamed, glimmered, grew brighter—shone. The gigantic slab before me turned as though on a pivot, sighing softly as it moved.

"For a moment I gasped in amazement. It was like a conjurer's trick. And the moving slab I noticed was also glowing, becoming opalescent like the little shining circles above.

"Only for a second I gazed and then with a word to Edith flung myself through the opening which the slab had uncovered. Before me was a platform and from the platform steps led downward into a smooth corridor. This passage was not dark, it glowed with the same faint silverly radiance as the door. Down it I raced. As I ran, plainer than ever before, I heard the chanting. The passage turned abruptly, passed parallel to the walls of the outer courtyard and then once more led abruptly downward. Still I ran, and as I ran I looked at the watch on my wrist. Less than three minutes had elapsed.

"The passage ended. Before me was a high vaulted arch. For a moment I paused. It seemed to open into space; a space filled with lambent, coruscating, many-colored mist whose brightness grew even as I watched. I passed through the arch and stopped in sheer awe!

"In front of me was a pool. It was circular, perhaps twenty feet wide. Around it ran a low, softly curved lip of glimmering silvery stone. Its water was palest blue. The pool with its silvery rim was like a great blue eye staring upward.

"Upon it streamed seven shafts of radiance. They poured down upon the blue eye like cylindrical torrents; they were like shining pillars of light rising from a sapphire floor.

"One was the tender pink of the pearl; one of the aurora's green; a third a deathly white; the fourth the blue in mother-of-pearl; a shimmering column of pale amber; a beam of amethyst; a shaft of molten silver. Such are the colors of the seven lights that stream upon the moon pool. I drew closer, awestricken. The shafts did not illumine the depths. They played upon the surface and seemed there to diffuse, to melt into it. The pool drank them!

"Through the water tiny gleams of phosphorescence began to dart, sparkles and coruscations of pale incandescence. And far, far below I sensed a movement, a shifting glow, as of something slowly rising.

"I looked upward, following the radiant pillars to their source. Far above were seven shining globes, and it was from these that the rays poured. Even as I watched their brightness grew. They were like seven moons set high in some caverned heaven. Slowly their splendor increased, and with it the splendor of the seven beams streaming from them. It came to me that they were crystals of some unknown kind set in the roof of the moon pool's vault and that their light was drawn from the moon shining high above them. They were wonderful, those lights—and what must have been the knowledge of those who set them there!

"Brighter and brighter they grew as the moon climbed higher, sending its full radiance down through them. I tore my gaze away and stared at the pool. It had grown milky, opalescent. The rays gushing into it seemed to be filling it; it was alive with sparkling scintillations, glimmerings. And the luminescence I had seen rising from its depths was larger, nearer!

"A swirl of mist floated up from its surface. It drifted within the embrace of the rosy beam and hung there for a moment. The beam seemed to embrace it, sending through it little shining corpuscles, tiny rosy spiralings. The mist absorbed the rays, was strengthened by it, gained substance. Another swirl sprang into the amber shaft, clung and fed there, moved swiftly toward the first and mingled with it. And now other swirls arose, here and there, too fast to be counted, hung poised in the embrace of the light streams; flashed and pulsed into each other.

"Thicker and thicker still they arose until the surface of the pool was a pulsating pillar of opalescent mist; steadily growing stronger; drawing within it life from the seven beams falling upon it; drawing to it from below the darting, red atoms of the pool. Into its center was passing the luminescence I had sensed rising from the far depths. And the center glowed, throbbed—began to send out questing swirls and tendrils.

"There forming before me was that which had walked with Stanton, which had taken Thora—the thing I had come to find!

"With the shock of realization my brain sprang into action. My hand fell to my pistol and I fired shot after shot into its radiance. The place rang with the explosions and there came to me a sense of unforgivable profanation. Devilish as I knew it to be, that chamber of the moon pool seemed also—in some way—holy. As though a god and a demon dwelt there, inextricably commingled.

"As I shot the pillar wavered; the water grew more disturbed. The mist swayed and shook; gathered itself again. I slipped a second clip into the automatic and, another idea coming to me, took careful aim at one of the globes in the roof. From thence I knew came the force that shaped the dweller in the pool. From the pouring rays came its strength. If I could destroy them I could check its forming. I fired again and again. If I hit the globes I did no damage. The little motes in their beams danced with the motes in the mist, troubled. That was all.

"Up from the pool like little bells, like bubbles of crystal notes rose the tinklings. Their notes were higher, had lost their sweetness, were angry, as it were, with themselves.

"And then out from the Inexplicable, hovering over the pool, swept a shining swirl. It caught me above the heart; wrapped itself around me. I felt an icy coldness and then there rushed over me a mingled ecstasy and horror. Every atom of me quivered with delight and at the same time shrank with despair. There was nothing loathsome in it. But it was as though the icy soul of evil and the fiery soul of good had stepped together within me. The pistol dropped from my hand.

"So I stood while the pool gleamed and sparkled; the streams of light grew more intense and the mist glowed and strengthened. I saw that its shining core had shape—but a shape that my eyes and brain could not define. It was as though a being of another sphere should assume what it might of human semblance, but was not able to conceal that what human eyes saw was but a part of it. It was neither man nor woman; it was unearthly and androgynous. Even as I found its human semblance it changed. And still the mingled rapture and terror held me. Only in a little corner of my brain dwelt something untouched; something that held itself apart and watched. Was it the soul? I have never believed—and yet—

"Over the head of the misty body there sprang suddenly out seven little lights. Each was the color of the beam beneath which it rested. I knew now that the dweller was—complete!

"And then—behind me I heard a scream. It was Edith's voice. It came to me that she had heard the shots and followed me. I felt every faculty concentrate into a mighty effort. I wrenched myself free from the gripping tentacle and it swept back. I turned to catch Edith, and as I did so slipped—fell. As I dropped I saw the radiant shape above the pool leap swiftly for me!

"There was the rush past me and as the dweller paused, straight into it raced Edith, arms outstretched to shield me from it!"

He trembled.

"She threw herself squarely within its diabolic splendor," he whispered. "She stopped and reeled as though she had encountered solidity. And as she faltered it wrapped its shining self around her. The crystal tinklings burst forth jubilantly. The light filled her, ran through and around her as it had with Stanton, and I saw drop upon her face—the look. From the pillar came the murmur—'Av-o-lo-ha!' The vault echoed it.

"'Edith!' I cried. 'Edith!' I was in agony. She must have heard me, even through the—thing. I saw her try to free herself. Her rush had taken her to the very verge of the moon pool. She tottered; and in an instant—she fell—with the radiance still holding her, still swirling and winding around and through her—into the moon pool! She sank, Goodwin, and with her went—the dweller!

"I dragged myself to the brink. Far down I saw a shining, many-colored nebulous cloud descending; caught a glimpse of Edith's face, disappearing; her eyes stared up to me filled with supernal ecstasy and horror. And—vanished!

"I looked about me stupidly. The seven globes still poured their radiance upon the pool. It was pale-blue again. Its sparklings and coruscations were gone. From far below there came a muffled outburst of triumphant chanting!

"'Edith!' I cried again. 'Edith, come back to me!' And then a darkness fell upon me. I remember running back through the shimmering corridors and out into the courtyard. Reason had left me. When it returned I was far out at sea in our boat wholly estranged from civilization. A day later I was picked up by the schooner in which I came to Port Moresby.

"I have formed a plan; you must hear it, Goodwin—" He fell upon his berth. I bent over him. Exhaustion and the relief of telling his story had been too much for him. He slept like the dead.

VII

All that night I watched over him. When dawn broke I went to my room to get a little sleep myself. But my slumber was haunted.

The next day the storm was unabated. Throckmartin came to me at lunch. He looked better. His strange expression had waned. He had regained much of his old alertness.

"Come to my cabin," he said. There, he stripped his shirt from him. "Something is happening," he said. "The mark is smaller." It was as he said.

"I'm escaping," he whispered jubilantly. "Just let me get to Melbourne safely, and then we'll see who'll win! For, Goodwin, I'm not at all sure that Edith is dead—as we know death—nor that the others are. There was something outside experience there—some great mystery."

And all that day he talked to me of his plans.

"There's a natural explanation, of course," he said. "My theory is that the moon rock is of some composition sensitive to the action of moon rays; somewhat as the metal selenium is to sun rays. There is a powerful quality in moonlight, as both science and legends can attest. We know of its effect upon the mentality, the nervous system, even upon certain diseases.

"The moon slab is of some material that reacts to moonlight. The circles over the top are, without doubt, its operating agency. When the light strikes them they release the mechanism that opens the slab, just as you can open doors with sunlight by an ingenious arrangement of selenium-cells. Apparently it takes the strength of the full moon to do this. We will first try a concentration of the rays of the nearly full moon upon these circles to see whether that will open the rock. If it does we will be able to investigate the pool without interruption from—from—what emanates.

"Look, here on the chart are their locations. I have made this in duplicate for you in the event of something happening to me."

He worked upon the chart a little more.

"Here," he said, "is where I believe the seven great globes to be. They are probably hidden somewhere in the ruins of the islet called Tau, where they can catch the first moon rays. I have calculated that when I entered I went so far this way—here is the turn; so far this way, took this other turn and ran down this long, curving corridor to the hall of the moon pool. That ought to make lights, at least approximately, here." He pointed.

"They are certainly cleverly concealed, but they must be open to the air to get the light. They should not be too hard to find. They must be found." He hesitated again. "I suppose it would be safer to destroy them, for it is clearly through them that the phenomenon of the pool is manifested; and yet, to destroy so wonderful a thing! Perhaps the better way would be to have some men up by them, and if it were necessary, to protect those below, to destroy them on signal. Or they might simply be covered. That would neutralize them.

To destroy them—" He hesitated again. "No, the phenomenon is too important to be destroyed without fullest investigation." His face clouded again. "But it is *not* human; it can't be," he muttered. He turned to me and laughed. "The old conflict between science and too frail human credulity!" he said.

Again— "We need half a dozen diving suits. The pool must be entered and searched to its depths. That will indeed take courage, yet in the time of the new moon it should be safe, or perhaps better after the dweller is destroyed or made safe."

We went over plans, accepted them, rejected them, and still the storm raged—and all that day and all that night.

I hurry to the end. That afternoon there came a steady lightening of the clouds, which Throckmartin watched with deep uneasiness. Toward dusk they broke away suddenly and soon the sky was clear. The stars came twinkling out.

"It will be tonight," Throckmartin said to me. "Goodwin, friend, stand by me. Tonight it will come, and I must fight."

I could say nothing. About an hour before moonrise we went to his cabin. We fastened the port-holes tightly and turned on the lights. Throckmartin had some queer theory that the electric rays would be a bar to his pursuer. I don't know why. A little later he complained of increasing sleepiness.

"But it's just weariness," he said. "Not at all like that other drowsiness. It's an hour till moonrise still," he yawned at last. "Wake me up a good fifteen minutes before."

He lay upon the berth. I sat thinking. I came to myself with a start. What time was it? I looked at my watch and jumped to the port-hole. It was full moonlight; the orb had been up for fully half an hour. I strode over to Throckmartin and shook him by the shoulder.

"Up, quick, man!" I cried. He rose sleepily. His shirt fell open at the neck and I looked, in amazement, at the white band around his chest. Even under the electric light it shone softly, as though little flecks of light were in it.

Throckmartin seemed only half-awake. He looked down at his breast, saw the glowing cincture, and smiled.

"Oh, yes," he said drowsily, "it's coming—to take me back to Edith! Well, I'm glad."

"Throckmartin," I cried. "Wake up! Fight!"

"Fight!" he said. "No use; keep the maps; come after us."

He went to the port and drowsily drew aside the curtain. The moon traced a broad path of light straight to the ship. Under its rays the band around his chest gleamed brighter and brighter; shot forth little rays; seemed to move.

He peered out intently and, suddenly, before I could stop him, threw open the port. I saw a glimmering presence moving swiftly along the moon path toward us, skimming over the waters.

And with it raced little crystal tinklings and far off I heard a long-drawn murmuring cry.

On the instant the lights went out in the cabin, evidently throughout the ship, for I heard shoutings above. I sprang back into a corner and crouched there. At the port-hole was a radiance: swirls and spirals of living white cold fire. It poured into the cabin and it was filled with dancing motes of light, and over the radiant core of it shone seven little lights like tiny moons. It gathered Throckmartin to it. Light pulsed through and from him. I saw his skin turn to a translucent, shimmering whiteness like illumined porcelain. His face became unrecognizable, inhuman with the monstrous twin expressions. So he stood for a moment. The pillar of light seemed to hesitate and the seven lights to contemplate me. I shrank further down into the corner. I saw Throckmartin drawn to the port. The room filled with murmuring. I fainted.

When I awakened the lights were burning again.

But of Throckmartin there was no trace!

There are some things that we are bound to regret all our lives. I suppose I was unbalanced by what I had seen. I could not think clearly. But there came to me the sheer impossibility of telling the ship's officers what I had seen; what Throckmartin had told me. They would accuse me, I felt, of his murder. At neither appearance of the phenomenon had any save our two selves witnessed it. I was certain of this because they would surely have discussed it. Why none had seen it I do not know.

The next morning when Throckmartin's absence was noted, I merely said that I had left him early in the evening. It occurred to no one to doubt me, or to question me further. His strangeness had caused much comment; all had thought him half-mad. And so it was officially reported that he had fallen or jumped from the ship during the failure of the lights, the cause of which was another mystery of that night.

Afterward, the same inhibition held me back from making his and my story known to my fellow scientists.

But this inhibition is suddenly dead, and I am not sure that its death is not a summons from Throckmartin.

And now I am going to Nan-Tanach to make amends for my cowardice by seeking out the dweller. So sure am I that all I have written here is absolutely true.

THE PEOPLE OF THE PIT

ABRAHAM MERRITT

North of us a shaft of light shot half way to the zenith. It came from behind the ragged mountain toward which we had been pushing all day. The beam drove up through a column of blue haze whose edges were marked as sharply as the rain that streams from the edges of a thunder cloud. It was like the flash of a searchlight through an azure mist and it cast no shadows.

As it struck upward the five summits were outlined hard and black, and we saw that the whole mountain was shaped like a hand. As the light silhouetted it, the gigantic fingers of the peaks seemed to stretch, the bulk that was the palm of the hand to push. It was exactly as though it moved to thrust something back. The shining beam held steady for a moment, then broke into myriads of tiny luminous globes that swung to and fro and dropped gently. They seemed to be searching.

The forest had become very still. Every wood noise held its breath. I felt the dogs pressing against my legs. They, too, were silent; but every muscle in their bodies trembled, their hair was stiff along their backs, and their eyes, fixed on the falling phosphorescent sparks, were filmed with the terror-glaze.

I looked at Starr Anderson. He was staring at the North where once more the beam had pulsed upward.

"'The mountain shaped like a hand!'" I spoke without moving my lips. My mouth was as dry as though Lao T'zai had poured his fear-dust down my throat.

"It's the mountain we've been looking for," he answered in the same tone.

"But that light—what is it? Not the aurora surely," I said.

"Whoever heard of an aurora at this time of the year?"

He voiced the thought that was in my own mind.

"It makes me think something is being hunted up there," he said. "That the lights are seeking—an unholy sort of hunt—it's well for us to be out of range."

"The mountain seems to move each time the shaft shoots up," I said. "What's it keeping back, Starr? It makes me think of the frozen hand of cloud that Shan Nadour set before the Gate of Ghouls to keep them in the lairs that Eblis cut for them."

He raised a hand, listening.

From the north and high overhead there came a whispering. It was not the rustling of the aurora, that rushing crackling sound like ghosts of the winds that blew at Creation, racing through the skeleton leaves of ancient trees that sheltered Lilith. This whispering held in it a demand. It was eager. It called us to come up where the beam was flashing. It—drew!

There was in it a note of inexorable insistence. It touched my heart with a thousand tiny fear-tipped fingers and it filled me with a vast longing to race on and merge myself in the light. It must have been so that Ulysses felt when he strained at the mast and strove to obey the crystal sweet singing of the sirens.

The whispering grew louder.

"What the hell's the matter with those dogs?" cried Starr Anderson savagely. "Look at them!"

The malemiuts, whining, were racing away toward the light. We saw them disappear among the trees. There came back to us a mournful howling. Then that too died away and left nothing but the insistent murmuring overhead.

The glade we had camped in looked straight to the North. We had reached, I suppose, three hundred miles above the first great bend of the Kuskokwim toward the Yukon. Certainly we were in an untrodden part of the wilderness. We had pushed through from Dawson at the breaking of the spring, on a fair lead to a lost mountain between the five peaks of which, so the Athabascan medicine man had told us, the gold streams out like putty from a clinched fist.

Not an Indian were we able to get to go with us. The land of the Hand Mountain was accursed, they said.

We had sighted a mountain the night before, its ragged top faintly outlined against a pulsing glow. And now by the light that had led us, we saw that it was the very place we had sought.

Anderson stiffened. Through the whispering had broken a curious pad-pad and a rustling. It sounded as though a small bear were moving toward us.

I threw a pile of wood on the fire, and as it blazed up, saw something break through the bushes. It walked on all fours, but it did not walk like a bear. All at once it flashed upon me—it was like a baby crawling upstairs. The forepaws lifted themselves in grotesquely infantile fashion. It was grotesque but it was—terrible. It drew closer. We reached for our guns—and dropped them. Suddenly we knew that this crawling thing was a man!

It was a man. Still with that high climbing pad-pad he swayed to the fire. He stopped.

"Safe," whispered the crawling man in a voice that was an echo of the whispering overhead. "Quite safe here. They can't get out of the blue, you know. They can't get you—unless you answer them—"

"He's mad," said Anderson, and then gently to this broken thing that had been a man; "You're all right—there's nothing after you."

"Don't answer them," repeated the crawling man, "the lights, I mean."

"The lights," I cried, startled even out of pity. "What are they?"

"The people of the pit!" he murmured.

He fell upon his side. We ran to him. Anderson knelt.

"God's love!" he cried. "Frank, look at this!" He pointed to the hands. The wrists were covered with torn rags of a heavy shirt. The hands themselves were—stumps! The fingers had been bent in to the palms and the flesh had been worn to the bone. They looked like the feet of a little black elephant! My eyes traveled down the body. Around the waist was a heavy band of yellow metal. From it fell a ring and a dozen links of shining white chain!

"What is he? Where did he come from?" said Anderson. "Look, he's fast asleep—yet even in his sleep his arms try to climb and his feet draw themselves up one after the other! And his knees—how in God's name was he ever able to move on them?"

It was even as he said. In the deep sleep that had come upon the crawler, arms and legs kept raising in a deliberate, dreadful climbing motion. It was as though they had a life of their own—they kept their movement independently of the motionless body. They were semaphoric motions. If you have ever stood at the back of a train and watched the semaphores rise and fall you will know exactly what I mean.

Abruptly the overhead whispering ceased. The shaft of light dropped and did not rise again. The crawling man became still. A gentle glow began to grow around us. The short Alaskan summer night was over. Anderson rubbed his eyes and turned to me a haggard face.

"Man!" he exclaimed. "You look as though you have been sick!"

"No more than you, Starr!" I said. "That was sheer, stark horror! What do you make of it all?"

"I'm thinking our only answer lies there," he answered, pointing to the figure that lay so motionless under the blankets we had thrown over him. "Whatever they were—that's what they were after. There was no aurora about those lights, Frank. It was like the flaring up of some queer hell the preacher folk never frightened us with."

"We'll go no further today," I said. "I wouldn't wake him up for all the gold that runs between the fingers of the five peaks—nor for all the devils that may be behind them."

The crawling man lay in a sleep as deep as the Styx. We bathed and bandaged the pads that had been his hands. Arms and legs were as rigid as though they were crutches. He did not move while we worked over him. He lay as he had fallen, the arms a trifle raised, the knees bent.

I began filing the band that ringed the sleeper's waist. It was gold, but it was like no gold I had ever handled. Pure gold is soft. This was soft too—but it had an unclean, viscid life of its own.

It clung to the file and I could have sworn that it writhed like a live thing when I cut into it. I gashed through it, bent it away from the body and hurled it away. It was—loathsome!

All that day the crawler slept. Darkness came and still he slept. But that night there was no shaft of blue haze from behind the peaks, no questioning globes of light, no whispering. Some spell of horror seemed withdrawn—but not far. Both Anderson and I felt that the menace was there, withdrawn perhaps, but waiting.

It was noon next day when the crawling man awoke. I jumped as the pleasant drawling voice sounded.

"How long have I slept?" he said. His pale blue eyes grew quizzical as I stared at him.

"A night—and almost two days," I said.

"Were there any lights up there last night?" Ho nodded to the North eagerly. "Any whispering?"

"Neither," I answered. His head fell back and he stared up at the sky.

"They've given it up, then?" he said at last.

"Who have given it up?" asked Anderson.

And once more—"The people of the pit!" the crawling man answered.

We stared at him and again faintly I, for one, felt that queer, maddening desire that the lights had brought with them.

"The people of the pit," he repeated. "Things some god of evil made before the Flood and that somehow have escaped the good God's vengeance. They were calling me!" he added simply.

Anderson and I looked at each other, the same thought in both our minds.

"No," said the crawling man, reading what it was, "I'm not insane. Give me a very little to drink. I'm going to die soon. Will you take me as far South as you can before I die? And afterwards will you build a fire and burn me? I want to be in such shape that no hellish wile of theirs can drag my body back to them. You'll do it when I've told you about them," he said as we hesitated.

He drank the brandy and water we lifted to his lips.

"Arms and legs quite dead," he said. "Dead as I'll be soon. Well, they did well for me. Now I'll tell you what's up there behind that hand. Hell!

"Listen. My name is Stanton—Sinclair Stanton. Class 1900, Yale. Explorer. I started away from Dawson last year to hunt for five peaks that rose like a hand in a haunted country and ran pure gold between them. Same thing you were after? I thought so. Late last fall my comrade sickened. I sent him back with some Indians. A little later my Indians found out what I was after. They ran away from me. I decided I'd stick, built a cabin, stocked myself with food and lay down to winter it. Did it not badly—it was a pretty mild winter you'll remember. In the spring I started off again. A little less than two weeks ago I sighted the five peaks. Not from this side though—the other. Give me some more brandy."

"I'd made too wide a detour," he went on. "I'd gotten too far north, I beat back. From this side you see nothing but forest straight up to the base of the hand. Over on the other side—"

He was silent for a moment.

"Over there is forest too. But it doesn't reach so far. *No*! I came out of it. Stretching for miles in front of me was a level plain. It was as worn and ancient looking as the desert around the broken shell of Babylon. At its end rose the peaks. Between me and them—far off—was what looked like a low dike of rocks. Then—I ran across the road!"

"The road!" cried Anderson incredulously.

"The road," said the crawling man. "A fine, smooth, stone road. It ran straight on to the mountain. Oh, it was a road all right—and worn as though millions and millions of feet had passed over it for thousands of years. On each side of it were sand and heaps of stones. After a while I began to notice these stones. They were cut, and the shape of the heaps somehow gave me the idea that a hundred thousand years ago they might have been the ruins of houses. They were as old looking as that. I sensed man about them and at the same time they smelled of immemorial antiquity.

"The peaks grew closer. The heaps of ruins thicker. Something inexpressibly desolate hovered over them, something sinister; something reached from them that struck my heart like the touch of ghosts so old that they could be only the ghosts of ghosts. I went on.

"And now I saw that what 1 had thought to be the low range at the base of the peaks was a thicker litter of ruins. The Hand Mountain was really much farther off. The road itself passed through these ruins and between two high rocks that raised themselves like a gateway."

The crawling man paused. His hands began that sickening pad-pad again. Little drops of bloody sweat showed on his forehead. But after a moment or two he grew quiet. He smiled.

"They were a gateway," he said. "I reached them. I went between them. I sprawled flat, clutching the earth in awe and terror. For I was on a broad stone platform. Before me was—sheer space ! Imagine the Grand Canyon three times as wide, roughly circular and with the bottom dropped out. That would be something like what I was looking into.

"It was like peeping over the edge of a cleft world down into the infinity where the planets roll! On the far side stood the five peaks. They looked like a gigantic warning hand stretched up to the sky. The lips of the abyss curved away on each side of me.

"I could see down perhaps a thousand feet. Then a thick blue haze shut out the eye. It was like the blue you see gather on the high hills at dusk. But the pit—it was awesome! Awesome as the Maori's Gulf of Ranalak, that sinks between the living and the dead and that only the freshly released soul has strength to leap across—but never strength to leap back again.

"I crept back from the verge and stood up, weak, shaking. My hand rested against one of the rocks of the gateway. There was carving upon it. There in sharp outlines was the heroic figure of a man. His back was turned. His arms were stretched above his head and between them he carried something that looked like a sun disk with radiating lines of light. There were symbols on the disk that reminded me of Chinese. But they were not Chinese. No! They had been made by hands, dust ages before the Chinese stirred in the womb of time.

"I looked at the opposite rock. It bore an exactly similar figure. There was an odd peaked headdress on both. The rocks themselves were triangular and the carvings were on the side closest the pit. The gesture of the men seemed to be that of holding something back—of barring. I looked closer. Behind the outstretched hands and the disks I seemed to see a host of vague shapes and, plainly a multitude of globes.

"I traced them out vaguely. Suddenly I felt unaccountably sick. There had come to me an impression—I can't call it sight—an impression of enormous upright slugs. Their swollen bodies seemed to dissolve, then swim into sight, then dissolve again—all except the globes which were their heads and that remained clear. They were; unutterably loathsome. Overcome by an inexplicable and overpowering nausea, I stretched myself upon the slab. And then—I saw the stairway that led down into the pit!"

"A stairway!" we cried.

"A stairway," repeated the crawling man as patiently as before. "It seemed not so much carved out of the rock as built into it. Each slab was perhaps twenty feet long and five feet wide. They ran down from the platform and vanished into the blue haze."

"A stairway," said Anderson incredulously, "built into the wall of a precipice and leading down into a bottomless pit—"

"Not bottomless," interrupted the crawling man. "There was a bottom. Yes. I reached it," he went on dully. "Down the stairway—down the stairway."

He seemed to grip his mind.

"Yes," he went on firmly. "I went down the stairway. But not that day. I made my camp back of the gates. At dawn I filled my knapsack with food, my two canteens with water from a spring that wells up there by the gateway, walked between the carved monoliths and stepped over the edge of the pit.

"The steps run along the side of the pit at a forty degree pitch. As I went down and down I studied them. They were of a greenish rock quite different from the granitic porphyry that formed the wall of the pit. At first I thought that the builders had taken advantage of an outcropping stratum, and had carved the gigantic flight from it. But the regularity of the angle at which it fell made me doubtful of this theory.

"After I had gone down perhaps half a mile I stepped out upon a landing. From this landing the stairs made a V-shaped turn and again ran on downward, clinging to the cliff at the same angle as the first flight. After I had made three of these turns I knew that the steps dropped straight down to wherever they went in a succession of angles. No strata could be so regular as that. No, the stairway was built by hands! But whose? And why? The answer is in those ruins around the edge of the pit—never I think to be read.

"By noon I had lost sight of the lip of the abyss. Above me, below me, was nothing but the blue haze. Beside me, too, was nothingness, for the further breast of rock had long since vanished in the same haze. I felt no dizziness, and no fear; only a vast curiosity. What was I to discover? Some ancient and wonderful civilization that had ruled when the poles were tropical gardens? A new world? The key to the mystery of man himself? Nothing living, I felt sure—all was too old for life. Still, a work so wonderful must lead to something quite as wonderful I knew. What was it? I went on.

"At regular intervals I had passed the mouths of small caves. There would be three thousand steps and then an opening, three thousand steps more and an opening—and so on and on. Late that afternoon I stopped before one of these clefts. I suppose I had gone then three miles down the pit, although the angles were such that I had walked in all fully ten miles. I examined the entrance. On each side was carved the same figures as on the great portals at the lip of the pit. But now they were standing face forward, the arms outstretched with their disks, as though holding something back from the shaft itself. Now, too, their faces were covered with veils and there were no hideous shapes behind them.

"I went inside the cave. It ran back for twenty yards like a burrow. It was dry and perfectly light. I could see, outside, the blue haze rising upward like a column. I felt an extraordinary sense of security, although I had not been conscious of any fear. I felt that the figures at the entrance were guardians—but against what? I felt so secure that even curiosity on this point was dulled.

"The blue haze thickened and grew faintly luminescent. I fancied that it was dusk above. I ate and drank a little and slept. When I awoke the blue had lightened again, and I fancied it was dawn above. I went on. I forgot the gulf yawning at my side. I felt no fatigue and little hunger or thirst, although I had drunk and eaten sparingly. That night I spent within another of the caves. And at dawn I descended again.

"It was late that day when I first saw the city—"

He was silent for a time.

"The city," he said at last, "the city of the pit! But not such a city as you have ever seen—nor any other man who has lived to tell of it. The pit, I think, must be shaped like a bottle; the opening before the five peaks is the neck. But how wide the bottom is I do not know—thousands of miles, maybe. And what may lie behind the city—I do not know.

"I had begun to catch little glints of light far down in the blue. Then I saw the tops of—trees, I suppose they are. But not our kind of trees—unpleasant, reptilian trees. They reared themselves on high, thin trunks and their tops were nests of thick tendrils with ugly little leaves like narrow heads—or snake heads.

"The trees were red, a vivid, angry red. Here and there I began to glimpse spots of shining yellow. I knew these were water because I could see things breaking through their surface—or at least I could see the splash and ripple but what it was that disturbed them I never saw.

"Straight beneath me was the city. Mile after mile of closely packed cylinders that lay upon their sides in pyramids of three, of five—of dozens—piled upon each other. It is so hard to make you see what that city is like—look, suppose you have water pipes of a certain length and first you lay three of them side by side and on top of them you place two and on these two one; or suppose you take five for a foundation and place on these four and then three, then two and then one. Do you see? That was the way they looked.

"And they were topped by towers, by minarets, by flares, by fans and twisted monstrosities. They gleamed as though coated with pale rose flame. Beside them the venomous red trees raised themselves like the heads of hydras guarding nests of gigantic jeweled and sleeping worms!

"A few feet beneath me the stairway jutted out into a titanic arch, unearthly as the span that bridges Hell and leads to Asgard. It curved out and down straight through the top of the highest pile of carven cylinders and then—it vanished through it. It was appalling—it was demoniac—"

The crawling man stopped. His eyes rolled up into his head. He trembled and again his arms and legs began their horrible crawling movement. From his lips came a whispering. It was an echo of the high murmuring we had heard the night he came to us. I put my hands over his eyes. He quieted.

"The thing's accursed!" he said. "The People of the Pit! Did I whisper? Yes—but they can't get me now—they can't!"

After a time he began as quietly as before.

"I crossed that span. I went down through the top of that—building. Blue darkness shrouded me for a moment and I felt the steps twist into a spiral. I wound down and then I was standing high up in—I can't tell you what. I'll have to call it a room. We have no images for what is in the pit. A hundred feet below me was the floor. The walls sloped down and out from where I stood in a series of widening crescents. The place was colossal—and it was filled with a curious mottled red light. It was like the light inside a green and gold-flecked fire opal. The spiral stairs wound below me. I went down to the last step. Far in front of me rose a high columned altar. Its pillars were carved in monstrous scrolls—like mad octopuses with a thousand drunken tentacles; they rested on the backs of shapeless monstrosities carved in crimson stone. The altar front was a gigantic slab of purple covered with carvings.

"I can't describe these carvings! No human being could—the human eye cannot grasp them any more than it can grasp shapes that haunt the fourth dimension. Only a subtle sense in the back of the brain grasped them vaguely. They were formless things that gave no conscious image, yet pressed into the mind like small hot seals—ideas of hate—of combat between unthinkable monstrous things—victories in a nebulous hell of steaming, obscene jungles—aspirations and ideals immeasurably loathsome—

"And as I stood I grew aware of something that lay behind the lip of the altar fifty feet above me. I *knew* it was there—I felt it with every hair and every tiny bit of my skin. Something infinitely malignant, infinitely horrible, infinitely ancient. It lurked, it brooded, it saw me, it threatened and it—was invisible!

"Behind me was a circle of blue light. Something urged me to turn back, to climb the stairs and make away. It was impossible. Terror of that unseen watching thing behind the altar raced me onward like a whirlwind. I passed through the circle. I was in a way that stretched on into dim distance between the rows of carven cylinders.

"Here and there the red trees arose. Between them rolled the stone burrows. And now I could take in the amazing ornamentation that clothed them. They were like the trunks of smooth skinned trees that had fallen and had been clothed with high reaching fantastic orchids. Yes—those cylinders were like that—and more. They should have gone out with the dinosaurs. They were—monstrous! They struck the eyes like a blow and they passed across the nerves like a rasp. And nowhere was there sight or sound of a living thing.

"There were circular openings in the cylinders like the opening in the temple of the stairway through which I had run. I passed through one of them. I was in a long bare vaulted room whose curving sides half closed twenty feet over my head, leaving a wide slit that opened into another vaulted chamber above. I saw nothing in the room save the same mottled reddish light of the temple.

"I stumbled. Still I could see nothing, but—my skin prickled and my heart stopped! There was something on the floor over which I had tripped!

"I reached down—and my hand touched a—thing —cold and smooth—that moved under it—I turned and ran out of that place. I was filled with a sick loathing that had in it something of madness—I ran on and on—blindly—wringing my hands—weeping with horror—

"When I came to myself I was still among the stone cylinders and red trees. I tried to retrace my steps, to find the temple; for now I was more than afraid. I was like a new soul panic-stricken with the first terrors of hell. But I could not find the temple! And the haze began to thicken and glow; the cylinders to shine more brightly.

"Suddenly I knew that it was dusk in my own world above and that the thickening of the haze was the signal for the awakening of whatever things lived in the pit.

"I scrambled up the sides of one of the burrows. I hid behind a twisted nightmare of stone. Perhaps, I thought, there was a chance of remaining hidden until the blue lightened, the peril passed, and I could escape. There began to grow around me a murmur. It was everywhere—and it grew and grew into a great whispering. I peeped from the side of the stone down into the street.

"I saw lights passing and repassing. More and more lights—they swam out of the circular doorways and they thronged the street. The highest were eight feet above the pave; the lowest perhaps two. They hurried, they sauntered, they bowed, they stopped and whispered—and there was *nothing* under them!"

"Nothing under them!" breathed Anderson.

"No," he went on, "that was the terrible part of it—there was nothing under them. Yet certainly the lights were living things. They had consciousness, volition—what else I did not know. They were nearly two feet across, the largest. Their center was a bright nucleus—red, blue, green. This nucleus faded off gradually into a misty glow that did not end abruptly. It, too, seemed to fade off into nothingness—but a nothingness that had under it a—somethingness.

"I strained my eyes trying to grasp this body into which the lights merged and which one could only feel was there, but could not see.

"And all at once I grew rigid. Something cold, and thin like a whip, had touched my face. I turned my head. Close behind were three of the lights. They were a pale blue. They looked at me—if you can imagine lights that are eyes.

"Another whiplash gripped my shoulder. Under the closest light came a shrill whispering. I shrieked. Abruptly the murmuring in the street ceased.

"I dragged my eyes from the pale-blue globe that held them and looked out; the lights in the streets were rising by myriads to the level of where I stood! There they stopped and peered at me. They crowded and jostled as though they were a crowd of curious people on Broadway.

"That was the horrible part of it. I felt a score of the lashes touch me—I shrieked again. Then—darkness and a sensation of falling through vast depths.

"When I awoke to consciousness I was again in the great place of the stairway, lying at the foot of the altar. All was silent. There were no lights—only the mottled red glow.

"I jumped to my feet and ran toward the steps. Something jerked me back to my knees. And then I saw that around my waist had been fastened a yellow ring of metal. From it hung a chain, and this chain passed up over the lip of the high ledge.

"I reached into my pockets for my knife to cut through the ring. It was not there! I had been stripped of everything except one of the canteens that I had hung around my neck, and which I suppose they had thought was part of me.

"I tried to break the ring. It seemed alive. It writhed in my hands and drew itself closer around me!

"I pulled at the chain. It was immovable. There came over me in a flood consciousness of the unseen thing above the altar, and I groveled at the foot of the slab. Think—alone in that place of strange light with the brooding ancient horror above me—a monstrous thing, a thing unthinkable—an unseen thing that poured forth horror—

"After a while I gripped myself. Then I saw beside one of the pillars a yellow bowl filled with a thick, white liquid. I drank it. If it killed me I did not care. But its taste was pleasant, and as I drank strength came back to me with a rush. Clearly I was not to be starved. The people of the pit, whatever they were, had a conception of human needs.

"And now once more the reddish mottled gleam began to deepen. Again outside arose the humming, and through the circle that was the entrance to the temple came streaming the globes. They ranged themselves in ranks until they filled the temple. Their whispering grew into a chant, a cadenced whispering chant that rose and fell, rose and fell, while to its rhythm the globes lifted and sank, lifted and sank.

"All the night the lights came and went; and all that night the chant sounded as they rose and fell. At the last I felt myself only an atom of consciousness in the sea of that whispering; an atom that rose and fell with the bowing globes.

"I tell you that even my heart pulsed in unison with them! And the red glow faded, the lights streamed out; the whispering died. I was again alone, and I knew that again day had begun in my own world.

"I slept. When I awoke I found beside the pillar another bowl of the white liquid. I scrutinized the chain that held me to the altar. I began to rub two of the links together. I did this for hours. When the red began to thicken there was a ridge worn in the links. Hope rushed up within me. There was, then, a chance to escape.

"With the thickening the lights came again. All through that night the whispering chant sounded, and the globes rose and fell. The chant seized me. It pulsed through me until every nerve and muscle quivered to it. My lips began to quiver. They strove like a man trying to cry out in a nightmare. And at last they, too, were whispering—whispering the evil chant of the people of the pit. My body bowed in unison with the lights.

"I was—God forgive me!—in movement and sound, one with these nameless things, while my soul sank back sick with horror, but powerless. And as I whispered I—saw them!

"Saw the things under the lights. Great transparent snail-like bodies—dozens of waving tentacles stretching from them; little round gaping mouths under the luminous, seeing globes. They were like specters of inconceivably monstrous slugs! And as I stared, still bowing and whispering, the dawn came, and they streamed to and through the entrance. They did not crawl or walk—they floated! They floated and were—gone!

"I did not sleep. I worked all that day at my chain. By the thickening of the red I had worn it a sixth through. And all that night, under their spell, I whispered and bowed with the pit people, joining in their chant to the thing that brooded above me!

"Twice again the red thickened and lessened, and the chant held me. And then, on the morning of the fifth day, I broke the worn links. I was free! I ran to the stairway. With eyes closed I rushed up and past the unseen horror behind the altar-ledge and was out upon the bridge. I crossed the span and began the ascent of the stairway.

"Can you think what it is to climb straight up the verge of a cleft-world—with hell behind you? Well—worse than hell was behind me, and terror rode.

"The city of the pit had long been lost in the blue haze before I knew that I could climb no more. My heart beat upon my ears like a sledge. I fell before one of the little caves, feeling that here at last was sanctuary. I crept far back within it and waited for the haze to thicken. Almost at once it did so, and from far below me came a vast and angry murmur. Crouching at the back of the cave, I saw a swift light go shooting up through the blue haze, then die down and break, and as it dimmed and broke I saw myriads of the globes that are the eyes of the pit people swing downward into the abyss. Again and again the light pulsed, and the globes rose with it and fell.

"They were hunting me! They knew I must be somewhere still on the stairway, or, if hiding below, I must some time take to the stairway to escape. The whispering grew louder, more insistent.

"There began to pulse through me a dreadful desire to join in the whispering as I had done in the temple. Something told me that if I did, the sculptured figures could no longer save me; that I would go out and down again into the temple forever! I bit my lips through and through to still them, and all that night the beam shot up through the abyss, the globes swung, and the whispering sounded—and I prayed to the power of the caves and the sculptured figures that still had power to guard them."

He paused—his strength was going.

Then almost in a whisper: "I thought, what were the people who had carved them? Why had they built their city around the verge, and why had they set that stairway in the pit? What had they been to the things that dwelt at the bottom, and what use had the things been to them that they should live beside their dwelling-place? That there had been some purpose was certain. No work so prodigious as the stairway would have been undertaken otherwise. But what was the purpose? And why was it that those who had dwelt about the abyss had passed away ages gone and the dwellers in the abyss still lived?"

He looked at us: "I could find no answer. I wonder if even when I am dead I shall know? I doubt it.

"Dawn came as I wondered, and with it—silence. I drank what was left of the liquid in my canteen, crept from the cave, and began to climb again. That afternoon my legs gave out. I tore off my shirt and made from it pads for my knees and coverings for my hands. I crawled upward. I crawled up and up. And again I crept into one of the caves and waited until again the blue thickened, the shaft of light shot through it, and the whispering came.

"But now there was a new note in the whispering. It was no longer threatening. It called and coaxed. It—drew.

"A terror gripped me. There had come upon me a mighty desire to leave the cave and go out where the lights swung; to let them do with me what they pleased, carry me where they wished. The desire grew. It gained fresh impulse with every rise of the beam, until at last I vibrated with the desire as I had vibrated to the chant in the Temple.

"My body was a pendulum. Up would go the beam, and I would swing toward it! Only my soul kept steady. It held me fast to the floor of the cave, and it placed a hand over my lips to still them. And all that night I fought with my body and lips against the spell of the pit people.

"Dawn came. Again I crept from the cave and faced the stairway. I could not rise. My hands were torn and bleeding, my knees an agony. I forced myself upward step by step.

"After a while my hands became numb, the pain left my knees. They deadened. Step by step my will drove my body upward upon them. And time after time I would sink back within myself to oblivion—only to wake again and find that all the time I had been steadily climbing upward.

"And then—only a dream of crawling up infinite stretches of steps—memories of dull horror while hidden within caves, with thousands of lights pulsing without, and whisperings that called and called me—memory of a time when I awoke to find that my body was obeying the call and had carried me half-way out between the guardians of the portals, while thousands of gleaming globes rested in the blue haze and watched me. Glimpses of bitter fights against sleep, and always—a climb up and up along infinite distances of steps that led from a lost Abaddon to a paradise of the blue sky and open world!

"At last a consciousness of clear sky close above me, the lip of the pit before me. Memory of passing between the great portals of the pit and of steady withdrawal from it. Dreams of giant men with strange, peaked crowns and veiled faces who pushed me onward and onward and onward, and held back pulsing globules of light that sought to draw me back to a gulf wherein planets swam between the branches of red trees that had snakes for crowns.

"And then a long, long sleep—how long God alone knows—in a cleft of rocks; an awakening to see far in the north the beam still rising and falling, the lights still hunting, the whispering high above me calling—and knowledge that no longer had they power to draw me.

"Again crawling on dead arms and legs that moved—that moved—like the Ancient Mariner's ship—without volition of mine. And then—your fire—and this—safety."

The crawling man smiled at us for a moment, then quickly fell asleep.

That afternoon we struck camp and, carrying the crawling man, started back south. For three days we carried him, and still he slept. And on the third day, still sleeping, he died. We built a great pile of wood and we burned his body, as he had asked. We scattered his ashes about the forest with the ashes of the trees that had consumed him.

It must be a great magic, indeed, that can disentangle those ashes and draw them back in a rushing cloud to the pit he called accursed. I do not think that even the people of the pit have such a spell. No.

But Anderson and I did not return to the five peaks to see. And if the gold does stream out between the five peaks of the Hand Mountain, like putty from a clenched fist—there it may remain for all of us.

THE GREAT GOD PAN

ARTHUR MACHEN

I

"I am glad you came, Clarke; very glad indeed. I was not sure you could spare the time."

"I was able to make arrangements for a few days; things are not very lively just now. But have you no misgivings, Raymond? Is it absolutely safe?"

The two men were slowly pacing the terrace in front of Dr Raymond's house. The sun still hung above the western mountain-line, but it shone with a dull red glow that cast no shadows, and all the air was quiet; a sweet breath came from the great wood on the hillside above, and with it, at intervals, the soft murmuring call of the wild doves. Below, in the long lovely valley, the river wound in and out between the lonely hills and, as the sun hovered and vanished into the west, a faint mist, pure white, began to rise from the hills. Dr Raymond turned sharply to his friend.

"Safe? Of course it is. In itself the operation is a perfectly simple one; any surgeon could do it."

"And there is no danger at any other stage?"

"None; absolutely no physical danger whatsoever, I give you my word. You are always timid, Clarke, always; but you know my history. I have devoted myself to transcendental medicine for the last twenty years. I have heard myself called quack and charlatan and impostor, but all the while I knew I was on the right path. Five years ago I reached the goal, and since then every day has been a preparation for what we shall do tonight."

"I should like to believe it is all true." Clarke knit his brows, and looked doubtfully at Dr Raymond. "Are you perfectly sure, Raymond, that your theory is not a phantasmagoria – a splendid vision, certainly, but a mere vision after all?"

Dr Raymond stopped in his walk and turned sharply. He was a middle-aged man, gaunt and thin, of a pale yellow complexion, but as he answered Clarke and faced him, there was a flush on his cheek.

"Look about you, Clarke. You see the mountain, and hill following after hill, as wave on wave, you see the woods and orchard, the fields of ripe corn, and the meadows reaching to the reed-beds by the river. You see me standing here beside you, and hear my voice; but I tell you that all these things – yes, from that star that has just shone out in the sky to the solid ground beneath our feet – I say that all these are but dreams and shadows; the shadows that hide the real world from our eyes. There is a real world, but it is beyond this glamour and this vision, beyond these 'chases in Arras, dreams in a career', beyond them all as beyond a veil. I do not know whether any human being has ever lifted that veil; but I do know, Clarke, that you and I shall see it lifted this very night from before another's eyes. You may think this all strange nonsense; it may be strange, but it is true, and the ancients knew what lifting the veil means. They called it seeing the god Pan."

Clarke shivered; the white mist gathering over the river was chilly.

"It is wonderful indeed," he said. "We are standing on the brink of a strange world, Raymond, if what you say is true. I suppose the knife is absolutely necessary?"

"Yes; a slight lesion in the grey matter, that is all; a trifling rearrangement of certain cells, a microscopical alteration that would escape the attention of ninety-nine brain specialists out of a hundred. I don't want to bother you with 'shop', Clarke; I might give you a mass of technical detail which would sound very imposing, and would leave you as enlightened as you are now. But I suppose you have read, casually, in out-of-the-way corners of your paper, that immense strides have been made recently in the physiology of the brain. I saw a paragraph the other day about Digby's theory, and Browne Faber's discoveries. Theories and discoveries! Where they are standing now, I stood fifteen years ago, and I need not tell you that I have not been standing still for the last fifteen years. It will be enough if I say that five years ago I made the discovery that I alluded to when I said that ten years ago I reached the goal. After years of labour, after years of toiling and groping in the dark, after days and nights of disappointments and sometimes of despair, in which I used now and then to tremble and grow cold with the thought that perhaps there were others seeking for what I sought, at last, after so long, a pang of sudden joy thrilled my soul, and I knew the long journey was at an end. By what seemed then and still seems a chance, the suggestion of a moment's idle thought followed up upon familiar lines and paths that I had tracked a hundred times already, the great truth burst upon me, and I saw, mapped out in lines of sight, a whole world, a sphere unknown; continents and islands, and great oceans in which no ship has sailed (to my belief) since a Man first lifted up his eyes and beheld the sun, and the stars of heaven, and the quiet earth beneath. You will think this all high-flown language, Clarke, but it is hard to be literal. And yet; I do not know whether what I am hinting at cannot be set forth in plain and lonely terms. For instance, this world of ours is pretty well girded now with the telegraph wires and cables; thought, with something less than the speed of thought, flashes from sunrise to sunset, from north to south, across the floods and the desert places. Suppose that an electrician of today were suddenly to perceive that he and his friends have merely been playing with pebbles and mistaking them for the foundations of the world; suppose that such a man saw uttermost space lie open before the current, and words of men flash forth to the sun and beyond the sun into the systems beyond, and the voice of articulate-speaking men echo in the waste void that bounds our thought. As analogies go, that is a pretty good analogy of what I have done; you can understand now a little of what I felt as I stood here one evening; it was a summer evening, and the valley looked much as it does now; I stood here, and saw before me the unutterable, the unthinkable gulf that yawns profound between two worlds, the world of matter and the world of spirit; I saw the great empty deep stretch dim before me, and in that instant a bridge of light leapt from the earth to the unknown shore, and the abyss was spanned. You may look in Browne Faber's book, if you like, and you will find that to the present day men of science are unable to account for the presence, or to specify the functions of a certain group of nerve-cells in the brain. That group is, as it were, land to let, a mere waste place for fanciful theories. I am not in the position of Browne Faber and the specialists, I am perfectly instructed as to the possible functions of those nerve-centers in the scheme of things. With a touch I can bring them into play, with a touch, I say, I can set free the current, with a touch I can complete the communication between this world of sense and – we shall be able to finish the sentence later on. Yes, the knife is necessary; but think what that knife will effect. It will level utterly the solid wall of sense, and probably, for the first time since man was made, a spirit will gaze on a spirit-world. Clarke, Mary will see the god Pan!"

"But you remember what you wrote to me? I thought it would be requisite that she—"

He whispered the rest into the doctor's ear.

"Not at all, not at all. That is nonsense. I assure you. Indeed, it is better as it is; I am quite certain of that."

"Consider the matter well, Raymond. It's a great responsibility. Something might go wrong; you would be a miserable man for the rest of your days."

"No, I think not, even if the worst happened. As you know, I rescued Mary from the gutter, and from almost certain starvation, when she was a child; I think her life is mine, to use as I see fit. Come, it's getting late; we had better go in."

Dr Raymond led the way into the house, through the hall, and down a long dark passage. He took a key from his pocket and opened a heavy door, and motioned Clarke into his laboratory. It had once been a billiard-room, and was lighted by a glass dome in the centre of the ceiling, whence there still shone a sad grey light on the figure of the doctor as he lit a lamp with a heavy shade and placed it on a table in the middle of the room.

Clarke looked about him. Scarcely a foot of wall remained bare; there were shelves all around laden with bottles and phials of all shapes and colours, and at one end stood a little Chippendale bookcase. Raymond pointed to this.

"You see that parchment Oswald Crollius? He was one of the first to show me the way, though I don't think he ever found it himself. That is a strange saying of his: 'In every grain of wheat there lies hidden the soul of a star.'"

There was not much furniture in the laboratory. The table in the centre, a stone slab with a drain in one corner, the two armchairs on which Raymond and Clarke were sitting; that was all, except an odd-looking chair at the furthest end of the room. Clarke looked at it, and raised his eyebrows.

"Yes, that is the chair," said Raymond. "We may as well place it in position." He got up and wheeled the chair to the light, and began raising and lowering it, letting down the seat, setting the back at various angles, and adjusting the foot-rest. It looked comfortable enough, and Clarke passed his hand over the soft green velvet, as the doctor manipulated the levers.

"Now, Clarke, make yourself quite comfortable. I have a couple hours' work before me; I was obliged to leave certain matters to the last."

Raymond went to the stone slab, and Clarke watched him drearily as he bent over a row of phials and lit the flame under the crucible. The doctor had a small hand-lamp, shaded as the larger one, on a ledge above his apparatus, and Clarke, who sat in the shadows, looked down at the great shadowy room, wondering at the bizarre effects of brilliant light and undefined darkness contrasting with one another. Soon he became conscious of an odd odour, at first the merest suggestion of odour, in the room, and as it grew more decided he felt surprised that he was not reminded of the chemist's shop or the surgery. Clarke found himself idly endeavouring to analyse the sensation, and half conscious, he began to think of a day, fifteen years ago, that he had spent roaming through the woods and meadows near his own home. It was a burning day at the beginning of August, the heat had dimmed the outlines of all things and all distances with a faint mist, and people who observed the thermometer spoke of an abnormal register, of a temperature that was almost tropical. Strangely that wonderful hot day of the fifties rose up again in Clarke's imagination; the sense of dazzling all-pervading sunlight seemed to blot out the shadows and the lights of the laboratory, and he felt again the heated air beating in gusts about his face, saw the shimmer rising from the turf, and heard the myriad murmur of the summer.

"I hope the smell doesn't annoy you, Clarke; there's nothing unwholesome about it. It may make you a bit sleepy, that's all."

Clarke heard the words quite distinctly, and knew that Raymond was speaking to him, but for the life of him he could not rouse himself from his lethargy. He could only think of the lonely walk he had taken fifteen years ago; it was his last look at the fields and woods he had known since he was a child, and now it all stood out in brilliant light, as a picture, before him. Above all there came to his nostrils the scent of summer, the smell of flowers mingled, and the odour of the woods, of cool shaded places, deep in the green depths, drawn forth by the sun's heat; and the scent of the good earth, lying as it were with arms stretched forth, and smiling lips, overpowered all. His fancies made him wander, as he had wandered long ago, from the fields into the wood, tracking a little path between the shining undergrowth of beech trees; and the trickle of water dropping from the limestone rock sounded as a clear melody in the dream. Thoughts began to go astray and to mingle with other thoughts; the beech alley was transformed to a path between ilex trees, and here and there a vine climbed from bough to bough, and sent up waving tendrils and drooped with purple grapes, and the sparse grey-green leaves of a wild olive tree stood out against the dark shadows of the ilex. Clarke, in the deep folds of dream, was conscious that the path from his father's house had led him into an undiscovered country, and he was wondering at the strangeness of it all, when suddenly, in place of the hum and murmur of the summer, an infinite silence seemed to fall on all things, and the wood was hushed, and for a moment in time he stood face to face there with a presence, that was neither man nor beast, neither the living nor the dead, but all things mingled, the form of all things but devoid of all form. And in that moment, the sacrament of body and soul was dissolved, and a voice seemed to cry "Let us go hence," and then the darkness of darkness beyond the stars, the darkness of everlasting.

When Clarke woke up with a start he saw Raymond pouring a few drops of some oily fluid into a green phial, which he stoppered tightly.

"You have been dozing," he said; "the journey must have tired you out. It is done now. I am going to fetch Mary; I shall be back in ten minutes."

Clarke lay back in his chair and wondered. It seemed as if he had but passed from one dream into another. He half expected to see the walls of the laboratory melt and disappear, and to awake in London, shuddering at his own sleeping fancies. But at last the door opened, and the doctor returned, and behind him came a girl of about seventeen, dressed all in white. She was so beautiful that Clarke did not wonder at what the doctor had written to him. She was blushing now over face and neck and arms, but Raymond seemed unmoved.

"Mary," he said, "the time has come. You are quite free. Are you willing to trust yourself to me entirely?"

"Yes, dear."

"Do you hear that, Clarke? You are my witness. Here is the chair, Mary. It is quite easy. Just sit in it and lean back. Are you ready?"

"Yes, dear, quite ready. Give me a kiss before you begin."

The doctor stooped and kissed her mouth, kindly enough. "Now shut your eyes," he said. The girl closed her eyelids, as if she were tired, and longed for sleep, and Raymond placed the green phial to her nostrils. Her face grew white, whiter than her dress; she struggled faintly, and then with the feeling of submission strong within her, crossed her arms upon her breast as a little child about to say her prayers. The bright light of the lamp fell full upon her, and Clarke watched changes fleeting over her face as the changes of the hills when the summer clouds float across the sun. And then she lay all white and still, and the doctor turned up one of her eyelids. She was quite unconscious. Raymond pressed hard on one of the levers and the chair instantly sank back. Clarke saw him cutting away a circle, like a tonsure, from her hair, and the lamp was moved nearer. Raymond took a small glittering instrument from a little case, and Clarke turned away shudderingly. When he looked again the doctor was binding up the wound he had made.

"She will awake in five minutes." Raymond was still perfectly cool. "There is nothing more to be done; we can only wait."

The minutes passed slowly; they could hear a slow, heavy, ticking. There was an old clock in the passage. Clarke felt sick and faint; his knees shook beneath him, he could hardly stand.

Suddenly, as they watched, they heard a long-drawn sigh, and suddenly did the colour that had vanished return to the girl's cheeks, and suddenly her eyes opened. Clarke quailed before them. They shone with an awful light, looking far away, and a great wonder fell upon her face, and her hands stretched out as if to touch what was invisible; but in an instant the wonder faded, and gave place to the most awful terror. The muscles of her face were hideously convulsed, she shook from head to foot; the soul seemed struggling and shuddering within the house of flesh. It was a horrible sight, and Clarke rushed forward, as she fell shrieking to the floor.

Three days later Raymond took Clarke to Mary's bedside. She was lying wide-awake, rolling her head from side to side, and grinning vacantly.

"Yes," said the doctor, still quite cool, "it is a great pity; she is a hopeless idiot. However, it could not be helped; and, after all, she has seen the Great God Pan."

II

Mr Clarke, the gentleman chosen by Dr Raymond to witness the strange experiment of the god Pan, was a person in whose character caution and curiosity were oddly mingled; in his sober moments he thought of the unusual and eccentric with undisguised aversion, and yet, deep in his heart, there was a wide-eyed inquisitiveness with respect to all the more recondite and esoteric elements in the nature of men. The latter tendency had prevailed when he accepted Raymond's invitation, for though his considered judgment had always repudiated the doctor's theories as the wildest nonsense, yet he secretly hugged a belief in fantasy, and would have rejoiced to see that belief confirmed. The horrors that he witnessed in the dreary laboratory were to a certain extent salutary; he was conscious of being involved in an affair not altogether reputable, and for many years afterwards he clung bravely to the commonplace, and rejected all occasions of occult investigation. Indeed, on some homeopathic principle, he for some time attended the seances of distinguished mediums, hoping that the clumsy tricks of these gentlemen would make him altogether disgusted with mysticism of every kind, but the remedy, though caustic, was not efficacious. Clarke knew that he still pined for the unseen, and little by little, the old passion began to reassert itself, as the face of Mary, shuddering and convulsed with an unknown terror, faded slowly from his memory. Occupied all day in pursuits both serious and lucrative, the temptation to relax in the evening was too great, especially in the winter months, when the fire cast a warm glow over his snug bachelor apartment, and a bottle of some choice claret stood ready by his elbow. His dinner digested, he would make a brief pretence of reading the evening paper, but the mere catalogue of news soon palled upon him, and Clarke would find himself casting glances of warm desire in the direction of an old Japanese bureau, which stood at a pleasant distance from the hearth. Like a boy before a jam-closet, for a few minutes he would hover indecisive, but lust always prevailed, and Clarke ended by drawing up his chair, lighting a candle, and sitting down before the bureau. Its pigeon-holes and drawers teemed with documents on the most morbid subjects, and in the well reposed a large manuscript volume, in which he had painfully entered the gems of his collection. Clarke had a fine contempt for published literature; the most ghostly story ceased to interest him if it happened to be printed; his sole pleasure was in the reading, compiling, and rearranging what he called his *Memoirs to prove the Existence of the Devil*, and engaged in this pursuit the evening seemed to fly and the night appeared too short.

On one particular evening, an ugly December night, black with fog, and raw with frost, Clarke hurried over his dinner, and scarcely deigned to observe his customary ritual of taking up the paper and laying it down again. He paced two or three times up and down the room, and opened the bureau, stood still a moment, and sat down. He leant back, absorbed in one of those dreams to which he was subject, and at length drew out his book, and opened it at the last entry. There were three or four pages densely covered with Clarke's round, set penmanship, and at the beginning he had written in a somewhat larger hand:

> *Singular Narrative told me by my Friend, Dr Phillips. He assures me that all the facts related therein are strictly and wholly True, but refuses to give either the Surnames of the Persons Concerned, or the Place where these Extraordinary Events occurred.*

Mr Clarke began to read over the account for the tenth time, glancing now and then at the pencil notes he had made when it was told him by his friend. It was one of his humours to pride himself on a certain literary ability; he thought well of his style, and took pains in arranging the circumstances in dramatic order. He read the following story:

> The persons concerned in this statement are Helen V., who, if she is still alive, must now be a woman of twenty-three, Rachel M., since deceased, who was a year younger than the above, and Trevor W., an imbecile, aged eighteen. These persons were, at the period of the story, inhabitants of a village on the borders of Wales, a place of some

importance in the time of the Roman occupation, but now a scattered hamlet, of not more than five hundred souls. It is situated on rising ground, about six miles from the sea, and is sheltered by a large and picturesque forest.

Some eleven years ago, Helen V. came to the village under rather peculiar circumstances. It is understood that she, being an orphan, was adopted in her infancy by a distant relative, who brought her up in his own house until she was twelve years old. Thinking, however, that it would be better for the child to have playmates of her own age, he advertised in several local papers for a good home in a comfortable farmhouse for a girl of twelve, and this advertisement was answered by Mr R., a well-to-do farmer in the above-mentioned village. His references proving satisfactory, the gentleman sent his adopted daughter to Mr R., with a letter, in which he stipulated that the girl should have a room to herself, and stated that her guardians need be at no trouble in the matter of education, as she was already sufficiently educated for the position in life which she would occupy. In fact, Mr R. was given to understand that the girl be allowed to find her own occupations and to spend her time almost as she liked. Mr R. duly met her at the nearest station, a town seven miles away from his house, and seems to have remarked nothing extraordinary about the child except that she was reticent as to her former life and her adopted father. She was, however, of a very different type from the inhabitants of the village; her skin was a pale, clear olive, and her features were strongly marked, and of a somewhat foreign character. She appears to have settled down easily enough into farmhouse life, and became a favourite with the children, who sometimes went with her on her rambles in the forest, for this was her amusement. Mr R. states that he has known her to go out by herself directly after their early breakfast, and not return till after dusk, and that, feeling uneasy at a young girl being out alone for so many hours, he communicated with her adopted father, who replied in a brief note that Helen must do as she chose. In thc winter, when the forest paths are impassable, she spent most of her time in her bedroom, where she slept alone, according to the instructions of her relative. It was on one of these expeditions to the forest that the first of the singular incidents with which this girl is connected occurred, the date being about a year after her arrival at the village. The preceding winter had been remarkably severe, the snow drifting to a great depth, and the frost continuing for an unexampled period, and the summer following was as noteworthy for its extreme heat. On one of the very hottest days in this summer, Helen V. left the farmhouse for one of her long rambles in the forest, taking with her, as usual, some bread and meat for lunch. She was seen by some men in the fields making for the old Roman Road, a green causeway which traverses the highest part of the wood, and they were astonished to observe that the girl had taken off her hat, though the heat of the sun was already tropical. As it happened, a labourer, Joseph W. by name, was working in the forest near the Roman Road, and at twelve o'clock his little son, Trevor, brought the man his dinner of bread and cheese. After the meal, the boy, who was about seven years old at the time, left his father at work, and, as he said, went to look for flowers in the wood, and the man, who could hear him shouting with delight at his discoveries, felt no uneasiness. Suddenly, however, he was horrified at hearing the most dreadful screams, evidently the result of great terror, proceeding from the direction in which his son had gone, and he hastily threw down his tools and ran to see what had happened. Tracing his path by the sound, he met the little boy, who was running headlong, and was evidently terribly frightened, and on questioning him the man elicited that after picking a posy of flowers he felt tired, and lay down on the grass and fell asleep. He was suddenly awakened, as he stated, by a peculiar noise, a sort of singing he called it, and on peeping through the branches he saw Helen V. playing on the grass with a "strange naked man", who he seemed unable to describe more fully. He said he felt dreadfully frightened and ran away crying for his father. Joseph W. proceeded in the direction indicated by his son, and found Helen V. sitting on the grass in the middle of a glade or open space left by charcoal burners. He angrily charged her with frightening his little boy, but she entirely denied the accusation and laughed at the child's story of a "strange man", to which he himself did not attach much credence. Joseph W. came to the conclusion that the boy had woke up with a sudden fright, as children sometimes do, but Trevor persisted in his story, and continued in such evident distress that at last his father took him home, hoping that his mother would be able to soothe him. For many weeks, however, the boy gave his parents much anxiety; he became nervous and strange in his manner, refusing to leave the cottage by himself, and constantly alarming the household by waking in the night with cries of "The man in the wood! Father! Father!"

In course of time, however, the impression seemed to have worn off, and about three months later he accompanied his father to the home of a gentleman in the neighborhood, for whom Joseph W. occasionally did work. The man was shown into the study, and the little boy was left sitting in the hall, and a few minutes later, while the gentleman was giving W. his instructions, they were both horrified by a piercing shriek and the sound of a fall, and rushing out they found the child lying senseless on the floor, his face contorted with terror. The doctor was immediately summoned, and after some examination he pronounced the child to be suffering form a kind of fit, apparently produced by a sudden shock. The boy was taken to one of the bedrooms, and after some time recovered consciousness, but only to pass into a condition described by the medical man as one of violent hysteria. The doctor exhibited a strong sedative, and in the course of two hours pronounced him fit to walk home, but in passing through the hall the paroxysms of fright returned and with additional violence. The father perceived that the child was pointing at some object, and heard the old cry, "The man in the wood!" and, looking in the direction indicated, saw a stone head of grotesque appearance, which had been built into the wall above one of the doors. It seems the owner of the house had recently made alterations in his premises, and on digging the foundations for some offices, the men had found a curious head, evidently of the Roman period, which had been placed in the manner described. The head is pronounced by the most experienced archeologists of the district to be that of a faun or satyr. [Dr Phillips tells me that he has seen the head in question, and assures me that he has never received such a vivid presentment of intense evil.]

From whatever cause arising, this second shock seemed too severe for the boy Trevor, and at the present date he suffers from a weakness of intellect, which gives but little promise of amending. The matter caused a good deal of sensation at the time, and the girl Helen was closely questioned by Mr R., but to no purpose, she steadfastly denying that she had frightened or in any way molested Trevor.

The second event with which this girl's name is connected took place about six years ago, and is of a still more extraordinary character.

At the beginning of the summer of 1882, Helen contracted a friendship of a peculiarly intimate character with Rachel M., the daughter of a prosperous farmer in the neighbourhood. This girl, who was a year younger than Helen, was considered by most people to be

> the prettier of the two, though Helen's features had to a great extent softened as she became older. The two girls, who were together on every available opportunity, presented a singular contrast, the one with her clear, olive skin and almost Italian appearance, and the other of the proverbial red and white of our rural districts. It must be stated that the payments made to Mr R. for the maintenance of Helen were known in the village for their excessive liberality, and the impression was general that she would one day inherit a large sum of money from her relative. The parents of Rachel were therefore not averse from their daughter's friendship with the girl, and even encouraged the intimacy, though they now bitterly regret having done so. Helen still retained her extraordinary fondness for the forest, and on several occasions Rachel accompanied her, the two friends setting out early in the morning, and remaining in the wood until dusk. Once or twice after these excursions Mrs M. thought her daughter's manner rather peculiar; she seemed languid and dreamy, and as it has been expressed, "different from herself", but these peculiarities seem to have been thought too trifling for remark. One evening, however, after Rachel had come home, her mother heard a noise which sounded like suppressed weeping in the girl's room, and on going in found her lying, half undressed, upon the bed, evidently in the greatest distress. As soon as she saw her mother, she exclaimed, "Ah, mother, mother, why did you let me go to the forest with Helen?" Mrs M. was astonished at so strange a question, and proceeded to make inquiries. Rachel told her a wild story. She said—

Clarke closed the book with a snap, and turned his chair towards the fire. When his friend sat one evening in that very chair, and told his story, Clarke had interrupted him at a point a little subsequent to this, had cut short his words in a paroxysm of horror. "My God!" he had exclaimed, "think, think what you are saying. It is too incredible, too monstrous; such things can never be in this quiet world, where men and women live and die, and struggle, and conquer, or maybe fail, and fall down under sorrow, and grieve and suffer strange fortunes for many a year; but not this, Phillips, not such things as this. There must be some explanation, some way out of the terror. Why, man, if such a case were possible, our earth would be a nightmare."

But Phillips had told his story to the end, concluding:

"Her flight remains a mystery to this day; she vanished in broad sunlight; they saw her walking in a meadow, and a few moments later she was not there."

Clarke tried to conceive the thing again, as he sat by the fire, and again his mind shuddered and shrank back, appalled before the sight of such awful, unspeakable elements enthroned as it were, and triumphant in human flesh. Before him stretched the long dim vista of the green causeway in the forest, as his friend had described it; he saw the swaying leaves and the quivering shadows on the grass, he saw the sunlight and the flowers, and far away, far in the long distance, the two figures moved towards him. One was Rachel, but the other?

Clarke had tried his best to disbelieve it all, but at the end of the account, as he had written it in his book, he had placed the inscription:

ET DIABOLUS INCARNATE EST. ET HOMO FACTUS EST.

III

"Herbert! Good God! Is it possible?"

"Yes, my name's Herbert. I think I know your face, too, but I don't remember your name. My memory is very queer."

"Don't you recollect Villiers of Wadham?"

"So it is, so it is. I beg your pardon, Villiers, I didn't think I was begging of an old college friend. Goodnight."

"My dear fellow, this haste is unnecessary. My rooms are close by, but we won't go there just yet. Suppose we walk up Shaftesbury Avenue a little way? But how in heaven's name have you come to this pass, Herbert?"

"It's a long story, Villiers, and a strange one too, but you can hear it if you like."

"Come on, then. Take my arm, you don't seem very strong."

The ill-assorted pair moved slowly up Rupert Street; the one in dirty, evil-looking rags, and the other attired in the regulation uniform of a man about town, trim, glossy and eminently well-to-do. Villiers had emerged from his restaurant after an excellent dinner of many courses, assisted by an ingratiating little flask of Chianti, and, in that frame of mind which was with him almost chronic, had delayed a moment by the door, peering round in the dimly-lighted street in search of those mysterious incidents and persons with which the streets of London teem in every quarter and every hour. Villiers prided himself as a practised explorer of such obscure mazes and byways of London life, and in this unprofitable pursuit he displayed an assiduity which was worthy of more serious employment. Thus he stood by the lamp-post surveying the passers-by with undisguised curiosity, and with that gravity known only to the systematic diner, had just enunciated in his mind the formula, "London has been called the city of encounters; it is more than that, it is the city of Resurrections," when these reflections were suddenly interrupted by a piteous whine at his elbow, and a deplorable appeal for alms. He looked around in some irritation, and with a sudden shock found himself confronted with the embodied proof of his somewhat stilted fancies. There, close beside him, his face altered and disfigured by poverty and disgrace, his body barely covered by greasy ill-fitting rags, stood his old friend Charles Herbert, who had matriculated on the same day as himself, with whom he had been merry and wise for twelve revolving terms. Different occupations and varying interests had interrupted the friendship, and it was six years since Villiers had seen Herbert; and now he looked upon this wreck of a man with grief and dismay, mingled with a certain inquisitiveness as to what dreary chain of circumstances had dragged him down to such a doleful pass. Villiers felt together with compassion all the relish of the amateur in mysteries, and congratulated himself on his leisurely speculations outside the restaurant.

They walked on in silence for some time, and more than one passer-by stared in astonishment at the unaccustomed spectacle of a well-dressed man with an unmistakable beggar hanging on to his arm, and, observing this, Villiers led the way to an obscure street in Soho. Here he repeated his question.

"How on earth has it happened, Herbert? I always understood you would succeed to an excellent position in Dorsetshire. Did your father disinherit you? Surely not?"

"No, Villiers; I came into all the property at my poor father's death; he died a year after I left Oxford. He was a very good father to me, and I mourned his death sincerely enough. But you know what young men are; a few months later I came up to town and went a good deal into society. Of course I had excellent introductions, and I managed to enjoy myself very much in a harmless sort of way. I played a little, certainly, but never for heavy stakes, and the few bets I made on races brought me in money – only a few pounds, you know, but enough to pay for cigars and such petty pleasures. It was in my second season that the tide turned. Of course you have heard of my marriage?"

"No, I never heard anything about it."

"Yes, I married, Villiers. I met a girl, a girl of the most wonderful and most strange beauty, at the house of some people whom I knew. I cannot tell you her age; I never knew it, but, so far as I can guess, I should think she must have been about nineteen when I made her acquaintance. My friends had come to know her in Florence; she told them she was an orphan, the child of an English father and an Italian mother, and she charmed them as she charmed me. The first time I saw her was at an evening party. I was standing by the door talking to a friend, when suddenly above the hum and babble of conversation I heard a voice which seemed to thrill to my heart. She was singing an Italian song. I was introduced to her that evening, and in three months I married Helen. Villiers, that woman, if I can call her woman, corrupted my soul. The night of the wedding I found myself sitting in her bedroom in the hotel, listening to her talk. She was sitting up in bed, and I listened to her as she spoke in her beautiful voice, spoke of things which even now I would not dare whisper in the blackest night, though I stood in the midst of a wilderness. You, Villiers, you may think you know life, and London, and what goes on day and night in this dreadful city; for all I can say you may have heard the talk of the vilest, but I tell you you can have no conception of what I know, not in your most fantastic, hideous dreams can you have imaged forth the faintest shadow of what I have heard – and seen. Yes, seen. I have seen the incredible, such horrors that even I myself sometimes stop in the middle of the street and ask whether it is possible for a man to behold such things and live. In a year, Villiers, I was a ruined man, in body and soul – in body and soul."

"But your property, Herbert? You had land in Dorset."

"I sold it all; the fields and woods, the dear old house – everything."

"And the money?"

"She took it all from me."

"And then left you?"

"Yes; she disappeared one night. I don't know where she went, but I am sure if I saw her again it would kill me. The rest of my story is of no interest; sordid misery, that is all. You may think, Villiers, that I have exaggerated and talked for effect; but I have not told you half. I could tell you certain things which would convince you, but you would never know a happy day again. You would pass the rest of your life, as I pass mine, a haunted man, a man who has seen hell."

Villiers took the unfortunate man to his rooms, and gave him a meal. Herbert could eat little, and scarcely touched the glass of wine set before him. He sat moody and silent by the fire, and seemed relieved when Villiers sent him away with a small present of money.

"By the way, Herbert," said Villiers, as they parted at the door, "what was your wife's name? You said Helen, I think? Helen what?"

"The name she passed under when I met her was Helen Vaughan, but what her real name was I can't say. I don't think she had a name. No, no, not in that sense. Only human beings have names, Villiers; I can't say anymore. Goodbye; yes, I will not fail to call if I see any way in which you can help me. Goodnight."

The man went out into the bitter night, and Villiers returned to his fireside. There was something about Herbert which shocked him inexpressibly; not his poor rags nor the marks which poverty had set upon his face, but rather an indefinite terror which hung about him like a mist. He had acknowledged that he himself was not devoid of blame; the woman, he had avowed, had corrupted him body and soul, and Villiers felt that this man, once his friend, had been an actor in scenes evil beyond the power of words. His story needed no confirmation: he himself was the embodied proof of it. Villiers mused curiously over the story he had heard, and wondered whether he had heard both the first and the last of it. "No," he thought, "certainly not the last, probably only the beginning. A case like this is like a nest of Chinese boxes; you open one after the other and find a quainter workmanship in every box. Most likely poor Herbert is merely one of the outside boxes; there are stranger ones to follow."

Villiers could not take his mind away from Herbert and his story, which seemed to grow wilder as the night wore on. The fire seemed to burn low, and the chilly air of the morning crept into the room; Villiers got up with a glance over his shoulder and, shivering slightly, went to bed.

A few days later he saw at his club a gentleman of his acquaintance, named Austin, who was famous for his intimate knowledge of London life, both in its tenebrous and luminous phases. Villiers, still full of his encounter in Soho and its consequences, thought Austin might possibly be able to shed some light on Herbert's history, and so after some casual talk he suddenly put the question:

"Do you happen to know anything of a man named Herbert – Charles Herbert?"

Austin turned round sharply and stared at Villiers with some astonishment.

"Charles Herbert? Weren't you in town three years ago? No; then you have not heard of the Paul Street case? It caused a good deal of sensation at the time."

"What was the case?"

"Well, a gentleman, a man of very good position, was found dead, stark dead, in the area of a certain house in Paul Street, off Tottenham Court Road. Of course the police did not make the discovery; if you happen to be sitting up all night and have a light in your window, the constable will ring the bell, but if you happen to be lying dead in somebody's area, you will be left alone. In this instance, as in many others, the alarm was raised by some kind of vagabond; I don't mean a common tramp, or a public-house loafer, but a gentleman, whose business or pleasure, or both, made him a spectator of the London streets at five o'clock in the morning. This individual was, as he said, 'going home', it did not appear whence or whither, and had occasion to pass through Paul Street between four and five a.m. Something or other caught his eye at Number 20; he said, absurdly enough, that the house had the most unpleasant physiognomy he had ever observed, but, at any rate, he glanced down the area and was a good deal astonished to see a man lying on the stones, his limbs all huddled together, and his face turned up. Our gentleman thought his face looked peculiarly ghastly, and so set off at a run in search of the nearest policeman. The constable was at first inclined to treat the matter lightly, suspecting common drunkenness; however, he came, and after looking at the man's face, changed his tone quickly enough. The early bird, who had picked up this fine worm, was sent off for a doctor, and the policeman rang and knocked at the door till a slatternly servant girl came down looking more than half asleep. The constable pointed out the contents of the area to the maid, who screamed loudly enough to wake up the street, but she knew nothing of the man; had never seen him at the house, and so forth. Meanwhile, the original discoverer had come back with a medical man, and the next thing was to get into the area. The gate was open, so the whole quartet stumped down the steps. The doctor hardly needed a moment's examination; he said the poor fellow had been dead for several hours, and it was then the case began to get interesting. The dead man had not been robbed, and in one of his pockets were papers identifying him as – well, as a man of good family and means, a favourite in society, and nobody's enemy, as far as could be known. I don't give his name, Villiers, because it has nothing to do with the story, and because it's no good raking up these affairs about the dead when there are no relations living. The next curious point was that the medical men couldn't agree as to how he met his death. There were some slight bruises on his shoulders, but they were so slight that it looked as if he had been pushed roughly out of the kitchen door, and not thrown over the railings from the street or even dragged down the steps. But there were positively no other marks of violence about him, certainly none that would account for his death; and when they came to the autopsy there wasn't a trace of poison of any kind. Of course the police wanted to know all about the people at Number 20, and here again, so I have heard from private sources, one or two other very curious points came out. It appears that the occupants of the house were a Mr and Mrs Charles Herbert; he was said to be a landed proprietor, though it struck most people that Paul Street was not exactly the place to look for country gentry. As for Mrs Herbert, nobody seemed to know who or what she was, and, between ourselves, I fancy the divers after her history found themselves in rather strange waters. Of course they both denied knowing anything about the deceased, and in default of any evidence against them they were discharged. But some very odd things came out about them. Though it was between five and six in the morning when the dead man was removed, a large crowd had collected, and several of the neighbours ran to see what was going on. They were pretty free with their comments, by all accounts, and from these it appeared that Number 20 was in very bad odour in Paul Street. The detectives tried to trace down these rumours to some solid foundation of fact, but could not get hold of anything. People shook their heads and raised their eyebrows and thought the Herberts rather 'queer', 'would rather not be seen going into their house', and so on, but there was nothing tangible. The authorities were morally certain the man met his death in some way or another in the house and was thrown out by the kitchen door, but they couldn't prove it, and the absence of any indications of violence or poisoning left them helpless. An odd case, wasn't it? But curiously enough, there's something more that I haven't told you. I happened to know one of the doctors who was consulted as to the cause of death, and some time after the inquest I met him, and asked him about it. 'Do you really mean to tell me,' I said, 'that you were baffled by the case, that you actually don't know what the man died of?' 'Pardon me,' he replied, 'I know perfectly well what caused death. Blank died of fright, of sheer, awful terror; I never saw features so hideously contorted in the entire course of my practice, and I have seen the faces of a whole host of dead.' The doctor was usually a cool customer enough, and a certain vehemence in his manner struck me, but I couldn't get anything more out of him. I suppose the Treasury didn't see their way to prosecuting the Herberts for frightening a man to death; at any rate, nothing was done, and the case dropped out of men's minds. Do you happen to know anything of Herbert?"

"Well," replied Villiers, "he was an old college friend of mine."

"You don't say so? Have you ever seen his wife?"

"No, I haven't. I have lost sight of Herbert for many years."

"It's queer, isn't it, parting with a man at the college gate or at Paddington, seeing nothing of him for years, and then finding him pop up his head in such an odd place. But I should like to have seen Mrs Herbert; people said extraordinary things about her."

"What sort of things?"

"Well, I hardly know how to tell you. Everyone who saw her at the police court said she was at once the most beautiful woman and the most repulsive they had ever set eyes on. I have spoken to a man who saw her, and I assure you he positively shuddered as he tried to describe the woman, but he couldn't tell why. She seems to have been a sort of enigma; and I expect if that one dead man could have told tales, he would have told some uncommonly queer ones. And there you are again in another puzzle; what could a respectable country gentleman like Mr Blank (we'll call him that if you don't mind) want in such a very queer house as Number 20? It's altogether a very odd case, isn't it?"

"It is indeed, Austin; an extraordinary case. I didn't think, when I asked you about my old friend, I should strike on such strange metal. Well, I must be off; good-day."

Villiers went away, thinking of his own conceit of the Chinese boxes; here was quaint workmanship indeed.

IV

A few months after Villiers' meeting with Herbert, Mr Clarke was sitting, as usual, by his after-dinner hearth, resolutely guarding his fancies from wandering in the direction of the bureau. For more than a week he had succeeded in keeping away from the *Memoirs*, and he cherished hopes of a complete self-reformation; but, in spite of his endeavours, he could not hush the wonder and the strange curiosity that the last case he had written down had excited within him. He had put the case, or rather the outline of it, conjecturally to a scientific friend, who shook his head, and thought Clarke getting queer, and on this particular evening Clarke was making an effort to rationalise the story, when a sudden knock at the door roused him from his meditations.

"Mr Villiers to see you sir."

"Dear me, Villiers, it is very kind of you to look me up; I have not seen you for many months; I should think nearly a year. Come in, come in. And how are you, Villiers? Want any advice about investments?"

"No, thanks, I fancy everything I have in that way is pretty safe. No, Clarke, I have really come to consult you about a rather curious matter that has been brought under my notice of late. I am afraid you will think it all rather absurd when I tell my tale. I sometimes think so myself, and that's just why I made up my mind to come to you, as I know you're a practical man."

Mr Villiers was ignorant of the *Memoirs to prove the Existence of the Devil.*

"Well, Villiers, I shall be happy to give you my advice, to the best of my ability. What is the nature of the case?"

"It's an extraordinary thing altogether. You know my ways; I always keep my eyes open in the streets, and in my time I have chanced upon some queer customers, and queer cases too, but this, I think, beats all. I was coming out of a restaurant one nasty winter night about three months ago; I had had a capital dinner and a good bottle of Chianti, and I stood for a moment on the pavement, thinking what a mystery there is about London streets and the companies that pass along them. A bottle of red wine encourages these fancies, Clarke, and I dare say I should have thought a page of small type, but I was cut short by a beggar who had come behind me, and was making the usual appeals. Of course I looked round, and this beggar turned out to be what was left of an old friend of mine, a man named Herbert. I asked him how he had come to such a wretched pass, and he told me. We walked up and down one of those long and dark Soho streets, and there I listened to his story. He said he had married a beautiful girl, some years younger than himself, and, as he put it, she had corrupted him body and soul. He wouldn't go into details; he said he dare not, that what he had seen and heard haunted him by night and day, and when I looked in his face I knew he was speaking the truth. There was something about the man that made me shiver. I don't know why, but it was there. I gave him a little money and sent him away, and I assure you that when he was gone I gasped for breath. His presence seemed to chill one's blood."

"Isn't this all just a little fanciful, Villiers? I suppose the poor fellow had made an imprudent marriage, and, in plain English, gone to the bad."

"Well, listen to this." Villiers told Clarke the story he had heard from Austin.

"You see," he concluded, "there can be but little doubt that this Mr Blank, whoever he was, died of sheer terror; he saw something so awful, so terrible, that it cut short his life. And what he saw, he most certainly saw in that house, which, somehow or other, had got a bad name in the neighbourhood. I had the curiosity to go and look at the place for myself. It's a saddening kind of street; the houses are old enough to be mean and dreary, but not old enough to be quaint. As far as I could see most of them are let in lodgings, furnished and unfurnished, and almost every door has three bells to it. Here and there the ground floors have been made into shops of the commonest kind; it's a dismal street in every way. I found Number 20 was to let, and I went to the agent's and got the key. Of course I should have heard nothing of the Herberts in that quarter, but I asked the man, fair and square, how long they had left the house and whether there had been other tenants in the meanwhile. He looked at me queerly for a minute, and told me the Herberts had left immediately after the unpleasantness, as he called it, and since then the house had been empty."

Mr Villiers paused for a moment.

"I have always been rather fond of going over empty houses; there's a sort of fascination about the desolate empty rooms, with the nails sticking in the walls, and the dust thick upon the windowsills. But I didn't enjoy going over Number 20, Paul Street. I had hardly put my foot inside the passage when I noticed a queer, heavy feeling about the air of the house. Of course all empty houses are stuffy, and so forth, but this was something quite different; I can't describe it to you, but it seemed to stop the breath. I went into the front room and the back room, and the kitchens downstairs; they were all dirty and dusty enough, as you would expect, but there was something strange about them all. I couldn't define it to you, I only know I felt queer. It was one of the rooms on the first floor, though, that was the worst. It was a largish room, and once on a time the paper must have been cheerful enough, but when I saw it, paint, paper and everything were most doleful. But the room was full of horror; I felt my teeth grinding as I put my hand on the door, and when I went in, I thought I should have fallen fainting to the floor. However, I pulled myself together, and stood against the end wall, wondering what on earth there could be about the room to make my limbs tremble, and my heart beat as if I were at the hour of death. In one corner there was a pile of newspapers littered on the floor, and I began looking at them; they were papers of three or four years ago, some of them half torn, and some crumpled as if they had been used for packing. I turned the whole pile over, and amongst them I found a curious drawing; I will show it to you presently. But I couldn't stay in the room; I felt it was overpowering me. I was thankful to come out, safe and sound, into the open air. People stared at me as I walked along the street, and one man said I was drunk. I was staggering about from one side of the pavement to the other, and it was as much as I could do to take the key back to the agent and get home. I was in bed for a week, suffering from what my doctor called nervous shock and exhaustion. One of those days I was reading the evening paper, and happened to notice a paragraph headed: 'Starved to Death'. It was the usual style of thing; a model lodging-house in Marylebone, a door locked for several days, and a dead man in his chair when they broke in. 'The deceased,' said the paragraph, 'was known as Charles Herbert, and is believed to have been once a prosperous country gentleman. His name was familiar to the public three years ago in connection with the mysterious death in Paul Street, Tottenham Court Road, the deceased being the tenant of the house Number 20, in the area of which a gentleman of good position was found dead under circumstances not devoid of suspicion.' A tragic ending, wasn't it? But after all, if what he told me were true, which I am sure it was, the man's life was all a tragedy, and a tragedy of a stranger sort than they put on the boards."

"And that is the story, is it?" said Clarke musingly.

"Yes, that is the story."

"Well, really, Villiers, I scarcely know what to say about it. There are, no doubt, circumstances in the case which seem peculiar, the finding of the dead man in the area of Herbert's house, for instance, and the extraordinary opinion of the physician as to the cause of death; but, after all, it is conceivable that the facts may be explained in a straightforward manner. As to your own sensations, when you went to see the house, I would suggest that they were due to a vivid imagination; you must have been brooding, in a semi-conscious way, over what you had heard. I don't exactly see what more can be said or done in the matter; you evidently think there is a mystery of some kind, but Herbert is dead; where then do you propose to look?"

"I propose to look for the woman; the woman whom he married. She is the mystery."

The two men sat silent by the fireside; Clarke secretly congratulating himself on having successfully kept up the character of advocate of the commonplace, and Villiers wrapped in his gloomy fancies.

"I think I will have a cigarette," he said at last, and put his hand in his pocket to feel for the cigarette-case.

"Ah!" he said, starting slightly, "I forgot I had something to show you. You remember my saying that I had found a rather curious sketch amongst the pile of old newspapers at the house in Paul Street? Here it is."

Villiers drew out a small thin parcel from his pocket. It was covered with brown paper, and secured with string, and the knots were troublesome. In spite of himself Clarke felt inquisitive; he bent forward on his chair as Villiers painfully undid the string, and unfolded the outer covering. Inside was a second wrapping of tissue, and Villiers took it off and handed the small piece of paper to Clarke without a word.

There was dead silence in the room for five minutes or more; the two men sat so still that they could hear the ticking of the tall old-fashioned clock that stood outside in the hall, and in the mind of one of them the slow monotony of sound woke up a far, far memory. He was looking intently at the small pen-and-ink sketch of the woman's head; it had evidently been drawn with great care, and by a true artist, for the woman's soul looked out of the eyes, and the lips were parted with a strange smile. Clarke gazed still at the face; it brought to his memory one summer evening, long ago; he saw again the long lovely valley, the river winding between the hills, the meadows and the cornfields, the dull red sun, and the cold white mist rising from the water. He heard a voice speaking to him across the waves of many years, and saying "Clarke, Mary will see the god Pan!" and then he was standing in the grim room beside the doctor, listening to the heavy ticking of the clock, waiting and watching, watching the figure lying on the green chair beneath the lamplight. Mary rose up, and he looked into her eyes, and his heart grew cold within him.

"Who is this woman?" he said at last. His voice was dry and hoarse.

"That is the woman who Herbert married."

Clarke looked again at the sketch; it was not Mary after all. There certainly was Mary's face, but there was something else, something he had not seen on Mary's features when the white-clad girl entered the laboratory with the doctor, nor at her terrible awakening, nor when she lay grinning on the bed. Whatever it was, the glance that came from those eyes, the smile on the full lips, or the expression of the whole face, Clarke shuddered before it at his inmost soul, and thought, unconsciously, of Dr Phillip's words, "the most vivid presentment of evil I have ever seen". He turned the paper over mechanically in his hand and glanced at the back.

"Good God! Clarke, what is the matter? You are as white as death."

Villiers had started wildly from his chair, as Clarke fell back with a groan, and let the paper drop from his hands.

"I don't feel very well, Villiers, I am subject to these attacks. Pour me out a little wine; thanks, that will do. I shall feel better in a few minutes."

Villiers picked up the fallen sketch and turned it over as Clarke had done.

"You saw that?" he said. "That's how I identified it as being a portrait of Herbert's wife, or I should say his widow. How do you feel now?"

"Better, thanks, it was only a passing faintness. I don't think I quite catch your meaning. What did you say enabled you to identify the picture?"

"This word – 'Helen' – was written on the back. Didn't I tell you her name was Helen? Yes; Helen Vaughan."

Clarke groaned; there could be no shadow of doubt.

"Now, don't you agree with me," said Villiers, "that in the story I have told you tonight, and in the part this woman plays in it, there are some very strange points?"

"Yes, Villiers," Clarke muttered, "it is a strange story indeed; a strange story indeed. You must give me time to think it over; I may be able to help you or I may not. Must you be going now? Well, goodnight, Villiers, goodnight. Come and see me in the course of a week."

V

"Do you know, Austin," said Villiers, as the two friends were pacing sedately along Piccadilly one pleasant morning in May, "do you know I am convinced that what you told me about Paul Street and the Herberts is a mere episode in an extraordinary history? I may as well confess to you that when I asked you about Herbert a few months ago I had just seen him."

"You had seen him? Where?"

"He begged of me in the street one night. He was in the most pitiable plight, but I recognised the man, and I got him to tell me his history, or at least the outline of it. In brief, it amounted to this – he had been ruined by his wife."

"In what manner?"

"He would not tell me; he would only say that she had destroyed him, body and soul. The man is dead now."

"And what has become of his wife?"

"Ah, that's what I should like to know, and I mean to find her sooner or later. I know a man named Clarke, a dry fellow, in fact a man of business, but shrewd enough. You understand my meaning; not shrewd in the mere business sense of the word, but a man who really knows something about men and life. Well, I laid the case before him, and he was evidently impressed. He said it needed consideration, and asked me to come again in the course of a week. A few days later I received this extraordinary letter."

Austin took the envelope, drew out the letter, and read it curiously. It ran as follows:

MY DEAR VILLIERS, I have thought over the matter on which you consulted me the other night, and my advice to you is this. Throw the portrait into the fire, blot out the story from your mind. Never give it another thought, Villiers, or you will be sorry. You will think, no doubt, that I am in possession of some secret information, and to a certain extent that is the case. But I only know a little; I am like a traveller who has peered over an abyss, and has drawn back in terror. What I know is strange enough and horrible enough, but beyond my knowledge there are depths and horrors more frightful still, more incredible than any tale told of winter nights about the fire. I have resolved, and nothing shall shake that resolve, to explore no whit farther, and if you value your happiness you will make the same determination.

Come and see me by all means; but we will talk on more cheerful topics than this.

Austin folded the letter methodically, and returned it to Villiers.

"It is certainly an extraordinary letter," he said, "what does he mean by the portrait?"

"Ah! I forgot to tell you I have been to Paul Street and have made a discovery."

Villiers told his story as he had told it to Clarke, and Austin listened in silence. He seemed puzzled.

"How very curious that you should experience such an unpleasant sensation in that room!" he said at length. "I hardly gather that it was a mere matter of the imagination; a feeling of repulsion, in short."

"No, it was more physical than mental. It was as if I were inhaling at every breath some deadly fume, which seemed to penetrate to every nerve and bone and sinew of my body. I felt racked from head to foot, my eyes began to grow dim; it was like the entrance of death."

"Yes, yes, very strange certainly. You see, your friend confesses that there is some very black story connected with this woman. Did you notice any particular emotion in him when you were telling your tale?"

"Yes, I did. He became very faint, but he assured me that it was a mere passing attack to which he was subject."

"Did you believe him?"

"I did at the time, but I don't now. He heard what I had to say with a good deal of indifference, till I showed him the portrait. It was then that he was seized with the attack of which I spoke. He looked ghastly, I assure you."

"Then he must have seen the woman before. But there might be another explanation; it might have been the name, and not the face, which was familiar to him. What do you think?"

"I couldn't say. To the best of my belief it was after turning the portrait in his hands that he nearly dropped from the chair. The name, you know, was written on the back."

"Quite so. After all, it is impossible to come to any resolution in a case like this. I hate melodrama, and nothing strikes me as more commonplace and tedious than the ordinary ghost story of commerce; but really, Villiers, it looks as if there were something very queer at the bottom of all this."

The two men had, without noticing it, turned up Ashley Street, leading northward from Piccadilly. It was a long street, and rather a gloomy one, but here and there a brighter taste had illuminated the dark houses with flowers, and gay curtains, and a cheerful paint on the doors. Villiers glanced up as Austin stopped speaking, and looked at one of these houses; geraniums, red and white, drooped from every sill, and daffodil-coloured curtains were draped back from each window.

"It looks cheerful, doesn't it?" he said.

"Yes, and the inside is still more cheery. One of the pleasantest houses of the season, so I have heard. I haven't been there myself, but I've met several men who have, and they tell me it's uncommonly jovial."

"Whose house is it?"

"A Mrs Beaumont's."

"And who is she?"

"I couldn't tell you. I have heard she comes from South America, but after all, who she is is of little consequence. She is a very wealthy woman, there's no doubt of that, and some of the best people have taken her up. I hear she has some wonderful claret, really marvellous wine, which must have cost a fabulous sum. Lord Argentine was telling me about it; he was there last Sunday evening. He assures me he has never tasted such a wine, and Argentine, as you know, is an expert. By the way, that reminds me, she must be an oddish sort of woman, this Mrs Beaumont. Argentine asked her how old the wine was, and what do you think she said? 'About a thousand years, I believe.' Lord Argentine thought she was chaffing him, you know, but when he laughed she said she was speaking quite seriously and offered to show him the jar. Of course, he couldn't say anything more after that; but it seems rather antiquated for a beverage, doesn't it? Why, here we are at my rooms. Come in, won't you?"

"Thanks, I think I will. I haven't seen the curiosity-shop for a while."

It was a room furnished richly, yet oddly, where every jar and bookcase and table, and every rug and jar and ornament seemed to be a thing apart, preserving each its own individuality.

"Anything fresh lately?" said Villiers after a while.

"No; I think not; you saw those queer jugs, didn't you? I thought so. I don't think I have come across anything for the last few weeks."

Austin glanced around the room from cupboard to cupboard, from shelf to shelf, in search of some new oddity. His eyes fell at last on an odd chest, pleasantly and quaintly carved, which stood in a dark corner of the room.

"Ah," he said, "I was forgetting, I have got something to show you." Austin unlocked the chest, drew out a thick quarto volume, laid it on the table, and resumed the cigar he had put down.

"Did you know Arthur Meyrick the painter, Villiers?"

"A little; I met him two or three times at the house of a friend of mine. What has become of him? I haven't heard his name mentioned for some time."

"He's dead."

"You don't say so! Quite young, wasn't he?"

"Yes; only thirty when he died."

"What did he die of?"

"I don't know. He was an intimate friend of mine, and a thoroughly good fellow. He used to come here and talk to me for hours, and he was one of the best talkers I have met. He could even talk about painting, and that's more than can be said of most painters. About eighteen months ago he was feeling rather overworked, and partly at my suggestion he went off on a sort of roving expedition, with no very definite end or aim about it. I believe New York was to be his first port, but I never heard from him. Three months ago I got this book, with a very civil letter from an English doctor practising at Buenos Ayres, stating that he had attended the late Mr Meyrick during his illness, and that the deceased had expressed an earnest wish that the enclosed packet should be sent to me after his death. That was all."

"And haven't you written for further particulars?"

"I have been thinking of doing so. You would advise me to write to the doctor?"

"Certainly. And what about the book?"

"It was sealed up when I got it. I don't think the doctor had seen it."

"It is something very rare? Meyrick was a collector, perhaps?"

"No, I think not, hardly a collector. Now, what do you think of these Ainu jugs?"

"They are peculiar, but I like them. But aren't you going to show me poor Meyrick's legacy?"

"Yes, yes, to be sure. The fact is, it's rather a peculiar sort of thing, and I haven't shown it to anyone. I wouldn't say anything about it if I were you. There it is."

Villiers took the book, and opened it at random.

"It isn't a printed volume, then?" he said.

"No. It is a collection of drawings in black and white by my poor friend Meyrick."

Villiers turned to the first page, it was blank; the second bore a brief inscription, which he read:

> *Silet per diem universus, nec sine horrore secretus est; lucet nocturnis ignibus, chorus Aegipanum undique personatur: audiuntur et cantus tibiarum, et tinnitus cymbalorum per oram maritimam.*

On the third page was a design which made Villiers start and look up at Austin; he was gazing abstractedly out of the window. Villiers turned page after page, absorbed, in spite of himself, in the frightful Walpurgis Night of evil, strange monstrous evil, that the dead artist had set forth in hard black and white. The figures of Fauns and Satyrs and Aegipans danced before his eyes, the darkness of the thicket, the dance on the mountain-top, the scenes by lonely shores, in green vineyards, by rocks and desert places, passed before him: a world before which the human soul seemed to shrink back and shudder. Villiers whirled over the remaining pages; he had seen enough, but the picture on the last leaf caught his eye, as he almost closed the book.

"Austin!"

"Well, what is it?"

"Do you know who that is?"

It was a woman's face, alone on the white page.

"Know who it is? No, of course not."

"I do."

"Who is it?"

"It is Mrs Herbert."

"Are you sure?"

"I am perfectly sure of it. Poor Meyrick! He is one more chapter in her history."

"But what do you think of the designs?"

"They are frightful. Lock the book up again, Austin. If I were you I would burn it; it must be a terrible companion even though it be in a chest."

"Yes, they are singular drawings. But I wonder what connection there could be between Meyrick and Mrs Herbert, or what link between her and these designs?"

"Ah, who can say? It is possible that the matter may end here, and we shall never know, but in my own opinion this Helen Vaughan, or Mrs Herbert, is only the beginning. She will come back to London, Austin; depend on it, she will come back, and we shall hear more about her then. I doubt it will be very pleasant news."

VI

Lord Argentine was a great favourite in London Society. At twenty he had been a poor man, decked with the surname of an illustrious family, but forced to earn a livelihood as best he could, and the most speculative of money-lenders would not have entrusted him with fifty pounds on the chance of his ever changing his name for a title, and his poverty for a great fortune. His father had been near enough to the fountain of good things to secure one of the family livings, but the son, even if he had taken orders, would scarcely have obtained so much as this, and moreover felt no vocation for the ecclesiastical estate. Thus he fronted the world with no better armour than the bachelor's gown and the wits of a younger son's grandson, with which equipment he contrived in some way to make a very tolerable fight of it. At twenty-five Mr Charles Aubernon saw himself still a man of struggles and of warfare with the world, but out of the seven who stood before him and the high places of his family three only remained. These three, however, were "good lives", but yet not proof against the Zulu assegais and typhoid fever, and so one morning Aubernon woke up and found himself Lord Argentine, a man of thirty who had faced the difficulties of existence, and had conquered. The situation amused him immensely, and he resolved that riches should be as pleasant to him as poverty had always been. Argentine, after some little consideration, came to the conclusion that dining, regarded as a fine art, was perhaps the most amusing pursuit open to fallen humanity, and thus his dinners became famous in London, and an invitation to his table a thing covetously desired. After ten years of lordship and dinners Argentine still declined to be jaded, still persisted in enjoying life, and by a kind of infection had become recognised as the cause of joy in others, in short, as the best of company. His sudden and tragical death therefore caused a wide and deep sensation. People could scarcely believe it, even though the newspaper was before their eyes, and the cry of "Mysterious Death of a Nobleman" came ringing up from the street. But there stood the brief paragraph: "Lord Argentine was found dead this morning by his valet under distressing circumstances. It is stated that there can be no doubt that his lordship committed suicide, though no motive can be assigned for the act. The deceased nobleman was widely known in society, and much liked for his genial manner and sumptuous hospitality. He is succeeded by..." etc., etc.

By slow degrees the details came to light, but the case still remained a mystery. The chief witness at the inquest was the deceased's valet, who said that the night before his death Lord Argentine had dined with a lady of good position, whose named was suppressed in the newspaper reports. At about eleven o'clock Lord Argentine had returned, and informed his man that he should not require his services till the next morning. A little later the valet had occasion to cross the hall and was somewhat astonished to see his master quietly letting himself out at the front door. He had taken off his evening clothes, and was dressed in a Norfolk coat and knickerbockers, and wore a low brown hat. The valet had no reason to suppose that Lord Argentine had seen him, and though his master rarely kept late hours, thought little of the occurrence till the next morning, when he knocked at the bedroom door at a quarter to nine as usual. He received no answer, and, after knocking two or three times, entered the room, and saw Lord Argentine's body leaning forward at an angle from the bottom of the bed. He found that his master had tied a cord securely to one of the short bedposts and, after making a running noose and slipping it round his neck, the unfortunate man must have resolutely fallen forward, to die by slow strangulation. He was dressed in the light suit in which the valet had seen him go out, and the doctor who was summoned pronounced that life had been extinct for more than four hours. All papers, letters and so forth seemed in perfect order, and nothing was discovered which pointed in the most remote way to any scandal either great or small. Here the evidence ended; nothing more could be discovered. Several persons had been present at the dinner-party at which Lord Augustine had assisted, and to all these he seemed in his usual genial spirits. The valet, indeed, said he thought his master appeared a little excited when he came home, but confessed that the alteration in his manner was very slight, hardly noticeable, indeed. It seemed hopeless to seek for any clue, and the suggestion that Lord Argentine had been suddenly attacked by acute suicidal mania was generally accepted.

It was otherwise, however, when within three weeks, three more gentlemen, one of them a nobleman, and the two others men of good position and ample means, perished miserably in the almost precisely the same manner. Lord Swanleigh was found one morning in his dressing-room, hanging from a peg affixed to the wall, and Mr Collier-Stuart and Mr Herries had chosen to die as Lord Argentine. There was no explanation in either case; a few bald facts; a living man in the evening, and a body with a black swollen face in the morning. The police had been forced to confess themselves powerless to arrest or to explain the sordid murders of Whitechapel; but before the horrible suicides of Piccadilly and Mayfair they were dumbfoundered, for not even the mere ferocity which did duty as an explanation of the crimes of the East End, could be of service in the West. Each of these men who had resolved to die a tortured shameful death was rich, prosperous and to all appearances in love with the world, and not the acutest research should ferret out any shadow of a lurking motive in either case. There was a horror in the air, and men looked at one another's faces when they met, each wondering whether the other was to be the victim of the fifth nameless tragedy. Journalists sought in vain for their scrapbooks for materials whereof to concoct reminiscent articles; and the morning paper was unfolded in many a house with a feeling of awe; no man knew when or where the next blow would light.

A short while after the last of these terrible events, Austin came to see Mr Villiers. He was curious to know whether Villiers had succeeded in discovering any fresh traces of Mrs Herbert, either through Clarke or by other sources, and he asked the question soon after he had sat down.

"No," said Villiers, "I wrote to Clarke, but he remains obdurate, and I have tried other channels, but without any result. I can't find out what became of Helen Vaughan after she left Paul Street, but I think she must have gone abroad. But to tell the truth, Austin, I haven't paid much attention to the matter for the last few weeks; I knew poor Herries intimately, and his terrible death has been a great shock to me, a great shock."

"I can well believe it," answered Austin gravely, "you know Argentine was a friend of mine. If I remember rightly, we were speaking of him that day you came to my rooms."

"Yes; it was in connection with that house in Ashley Street, Mrs Beaumont's house. You said something about Argentine's dining there."

"Quite so. Of course you know it was there Argentine dined the night before – before his death."

"No, I had not heard that."

"Oh, yes; the name was kept out of the papers to spare Mrs Beaumont. Argentine was a great favourite of hers, and it is said she was in a terrible state for sometime after."

A curious look came over Villiers' face; he seemed undecided whether to speak or not. Austin began again.

"I never experienced such a feeling of horror as when I read the account of Argentine's death. I didn't understand it at the time, and I don't now. I knew him well, and it completely passes my understanding for what possible cause he – or any of the others for the matter of that – could have resolved in cold blood to die in such an awful manner. You know how men babble away each other's characters in London, you may be sure any buried scandal or hidden skeleton would have been brought to light in such a case as this; but nothing of the sort has taken place. As for the theory of mania, that is very well, of course, for the coroner's jury, but everybody knows that it's all nonsense. Suicidal mania is not smallpox."

Austin relapsed into gloomy silence. Villiers sat silent, also, watching his friend. The expression of indecision still fleeted across his face; he seemed as if weighing his thoughts in the balance, and the considerations he was resolving left him still silent. Austin tried to shake off the remembrance of tragedies as hopeless and perplexed as the labyrinth of Daedalus, and began to talk in an indifferent voice of the more pleasant incidents and adventures of the season.

"That Mrs Beaumont," he said, "of whom we were speaking, is a great success; she has taken London almost by storm. I met her the other night at Fulham's; she is really a remarkable woman."

"You have met Mrs Beaumont?"

"Yes; she had quite a court around her. She would be called very handsome, I suppose, and yet there is something about her face which I didn't like. The features are exquisite, but the expression is strange. And all the time I was looking at her, and afterwards, when I was going home, I had a curious feeling that very expression was in some way or another familiar to me."

"You must have seen her in the Row."

"No, I am sure I never set eyes on the woman before; it is that which makes it puzzling. And to the best of my belief I have never seen anyone like her; what I felt was a kind of dim far-off memory, vague but persistent. The only sensation I can compare it to, is that odd feeling one sometimes has in a dream, when fantastic cities and wondrous lands and phantom personages appear familiar and accustomed."

Villiers nodded and glanced aimlessly round the room, possibly in search of something on which to turn the conversation. His eyes fell on an old chest somewhat like that in which the artist's strange legacy lay hid beneath a Gothic scutcheon.

"Have you written to the doctor about poor Meyrick?" he asked.

"Yes; I wrote asking for full particulars as to his illness and death. I don't expect to have an answer for another three weeks or a month. I thought I might as well inquire whether Meyrick knew an Englishwoman named Herbert, and if so, whether the doctor could give me any information about her. But it's very possible that Meyrick fell in with her at New York, or Mexico, or San Francisco; I have no idea as to the extent or direction of his travels."

"Yes, and it's very possible that the woman may have more than one name."

"Exactly. I wish I had thought of asking you to lend me the portrait of her which you possess. I might have enclosed it in my letter to Dr Matthews."

"So you might; that never occurred to me. We might send it now. Hark! what are those boys calling?"

While the two men had been talking together a confused noise of shouting had been gradually growing louder. The noise rose from the eastward and swelled down Piccadilly, drawing nearer and nearer, a very torrent of sound; surging up streets usually quiet, and making every window a frame for a face, curious or excited. The cries and voices came echoing up the silent street where Villiers lived, growing more distinct as they advanced, and, as Villiers spoke, an answer rang up from the pavement:

"The West End Horrors; Another Awful Suicide; Full Details!"

Austin rushed down the stairs and bought a paper and read out the paragraph to Villiers as the uproar in the street rose and fell. The window was open and the air seemed full of noise and terror.

> Another gentleman has fallen a victim to the terrible epidemic of suicide which for the last month has prevailed in the West End. Mr Sidney Crashaw, of Stoke House, Fulham, and King's Pomeroy, Devon, was found, after a prolonged search, hanging dead from the branch of a tree in his garden at one o'clock today. The deceased gentleman dined last night at the Carlton Club and seemed in his usual health and spirits. He left the club at about ten o'clock, and was seen walking leisurely up St. James's Street a little later. Subsequent to this his movements cannot be traced. On the discovery of the body medical aid was at once summoned, but life had evidently been long extinct. So far as is known, Mr Crashaw had no trouble or anxiety of any kind. This painful suicide, it will be remembered, is the fifth of the kind in the last month. The authorities at Scotland Yard are unable to suggest any explanation of these terrible occurrences.

Austin put down the paper in mute horror.

"I shall leave London tomorrow," he said; "it is a city of nightmares. How awful this is, Villiers!"

Mr Villiers was sitting by the window quietly looking out into the street. He had listened to the newspaper report attentively, and the hint of indecision was no longer on his face.

"Wait a moment, Austin," he replied, "I have made up my mind to mention a little matter that occurred last night. It stated, I think, that Crashaw was last seen alive in St James's Street shortly after ten?"

"Yes, I think so. I will look again. Yes, you are quite right."

"Quite so. Well, I am in a position to contradict that statement at all events. Crashaw was seen after that; considerably later indeed."

"How do you know?"

"Because I happened to see Crashaw myself at about two o'clock this morning."

"You saw Crashaw? You, Villiers?"

"Yes, I saw him quite distinctly; indeed, there were but a few feet between us."

"Where, in Heaven's name, did you see him?"

"Not far from here. I saw him in Ashley Street. He was just leaving a house."

"Did you notice what house it was?"

"Yes. It was Mrs Beaumont's."

"Villiers! Think what you are saying; there must be some mistake. How could Crashaw be in Mrs Beaumont's house at two o'clock in the morning? Surely, surely, you must have been dreaming, Villiers; you were always rather fanciful."

"No; I was wide awake enough. Even if I had been dreaming as you say, what I saw would have roused me effectually."

"What you saw? What did you see? Was there anything strange about Crashaw? But I can't believe it; it is impossible."

"Well, if you like I will tell you what I saw, or if you please, what I think I saw, and you can judge for yourself."

"Very good, Villiers."

The noise and clamour of the street had died away, though now and then the sound of shouting still came from the distance, and the dull, leaden silence seemed like the quiet after an earthquake or a storm. Villiers turned from the window and began speaking.

"I was at a house near Regent's Park last night, and when I came away the fancy took me to walk home instead of taking a hansom. It was a clear, pleasant night enough, and after a few minutes I had the streets pretty much to myself. It's a curious thing, Austin, to be alone in London at night, the gas-lamps stretching away in perspective, and the dead silence, and then perhaps the rush and clatter of a hansom on the stones, and the fire starting up under the horse's hoofs. I walked along pretty briskly, for I was feeling a little tired of being out in the night, and as the clocks were striking two I turned down Ashley Street, which, you know, is on my way. It was quieter than ever there, and the lamps were fewer; altogether, it looked as dark and gloomy as a forest in winter. I had done about half the length of the street when I heard a door closed very softly, and naturally I looked up to see who was abroad like myself at such an hour. As it happens, there is a street lamp close to the house in question, and I saw a man standing on the step. He had just shut the door and his face was towards me, and I recognised Crashaw directly. I never knew him to speak to, but I had often seen him, and I am positive that I was not mistaken in my man. I looked into his face for a moment, and then – I will confess the truth – I set off at a good run, and kept it up till I was within my own door."

"Why?"

"Why? Because it made my blood run cold to see that man's face. I could never have supposed that such an infernal medley of passions could have glared out of any human eyes; I almost fainted as I looked. I knew I had looked into the eyes of a lost soul, Austin, the man's outward form remained, but all hell was within it. Furious lust, and hate that was like fire, and the loss of all hope and horror that seemed to shriek aloud to the night, though his teeth were shut; and the utter blackness of despair. I am sure that he did not see me; he saw nothing that you or I can see, but what he saw I hope we never shall. I do not know when he died; I suppose in an hour, or perhaps two, but when I passed down Ashley Street and heard the closing door, that man no longer belonged to this world; it was a devil's face I looked upon."

There was an interval of silence in the room when Villiers ceased speaking. The light was failing, and all the tumult of an hour ago was quite hushed. Austin had bent his head at the close of the story, and his hand covered his eyes.

"What can it mean?" he said at length.

"Who knows, Austin, who knows? It's a black business, but I think we had better keep it to ourselves, for the present at any rate. I will see if I cannot learn anything about that house through private channels of information, and if I do light upon anything I will let you know."

VII

Three weeks later Austin received a note from Villiers, asking him to call either that afternoon or the next. He chose the nearer date, and found Villiers sitting as usual by the window, apparently lost in meditation on the drowsy traffic of the street. There was a bamboo table by his side, a fantastic thing, enriched with gilding and queer painted scenes, and on it lay a little pile of papers arranged and docketed as neatly as anything in Mr Clarke's office.

"Well, Villiers, have you made any discoveries in the last three weeks?"

"I think so; I have here one or two memoranda which struck me as singular, and there is a statement to which I shall call your attention."

"And these documents relate to Mrs Beaumont? It was really Crashaw whom you saw that night standing on the doorstep of the house in Ashley Street?"

"As to that matter my belief remains unchanged, but neither my inquiries nor their results have any special relation to Crashaw. But my investigations have had a strange issue. I have found out who Mrs Beaumont is!"

"Who is she? In what way do you mean?"

"I mean that you and I know her better under another name."

"What name is that?"

"Herbert."

"Herbert!" Austin repeated the word, dazed with astonishment.

"Yes, Mrs Herbert of Paul Street, Helen Vaughan of earlier adventures unknown to me. You had reason to recognise the expression of her face; when you go home look at the face in Meyrick's book of horrors, and you will know the sources of your recollection."

"And you have proof of this?"

"Yes, the best of proof; I have seen Mrs Beaumont, or shall we say Mrs Herbert?"

"Where did you see her?"

"Hardly in a place where you would expect to see a lady who lives in Ashley Street, Piccadilly. I saw her entering a house in one of the meanest and most disreputable streets in Soho. In fact, I had made an appointment, though not with her, and she was precise to both time and place."

"All this seems very wonderful, but I cannot call it incredible. You must remember, Villiers, that I have seen this woman, in the ordinary adventure of London society, talking and laughing, and sipping her coffee in a commonplace drawing room with commonplace people. But you know what you are saying."

"I do; I have not allowed myself to be led by surmises or fancies. It was with no thought of finding Helen Vaughan that I searched for Mrs Beaumont in the dark waters of the life of London, but such has been the issue."

"You must have been in strange places, Villiers."

"Yes, I have been in very strange places. It would have been useless, you know, to go to Ashley Street, and ask Mrs Beaumont to give me a short sketch of her previous history. No; assuming, as I had to assume, that her record was not of the cleanest, it would be pretty certain that at some previous time she must have moved in circles not quite so refined as her present ones. If you see mud at the top of a stream, you may be sure that it was once at the bottom. I went to the bottom. I have always been fond of diving into Queer Street for my amusement, and I found my knowledge of that locality and its inhabitants very useful. It is, perhaps, needless to say that my friends had never heard the name of Beaumont, and as I had never seen the lady, and was quite unable to describe her, I had to set to work in an indirect way. The people there know me; I have been able to do some of them a service now and again, so they made no difficulty about giving their information; they were aware I had no communication direct or indirect with Scotland Yard. I had to cast out a good many lines, though, before I got what I wanted, and when I landed the fish I did not for a moment suppose it was my fish. But I listened to what I was told out of a constitutional liking for useless information, and I found myself in possession of a very curious story, though, as I imagined, not the story I was looking for. It was to this effect. Some five or six years ago, a woman named Raymond suddenly made her appearance in the neighbourhood to which I am referring. She was described to me as being quite young, probably not more than seventeen or eighteen, very handsome, and looking as if she came from the country. I should be wrong in saying that she found her level in going to this particular quarter, or associating with these people, for from what I was told, I should think the worst den in London far too good for her. The person from whom I got my information, as you may suppose, no great Puritan, shuddered and grew sick in telling me of the nameless infamies which were laid to her charge. After living there for a year, or perhaps a little more, she disappeared as suddenly as she came, and they saw nothing of her till about the time of the Paul Street case. At first she came to her old haunts only occasionally, then more frequently, and finally took up her abode there as before, and remained for six or eight months. It's of no use my going into details as to the life that woman led; if you want particulars you can look at Meyrick's legacy. Those designs were not drawn from his imagination. She again disappeared, and the people of the place saw nothing of her till a few months ago. My informant told me that she had taken some rooms in a house which he pointed out, and these rooms she was in the habit of visiting two or three times a week and always at ten in the morning. I was led to expect that one of these visits would be paid on a certain day about a week ago, and I accordingly managed to be on the look-out in company with my cicerone at a quarter to ten, and the hour and the lady came with equal punctuality. My friend and I were standing under an archway, a little way back from the street, but she saw us, and gave me a glance that I shall be long in forgetting. That look was quite enough for me; I knew Miss Raymond to be Mrs Herbert; as for Mrs Beaumont she had quite gone out of my head. She went into the house, and I watched it till four o'clock, when she came out, and then I followed her. It was a long chase, and I had to be very careful to keep a long way in the background, and yet not lose sight of the woman. She took me down to the Strand, and then to Westminster, and then up St James's Street, and along Piccadilly. I felt queerish when I saw her turn up Ashley Street; the thought that Mrs Herbert was Mrs Beaumont came into my mind, but it seemed too impossible to be true. I waited at the corner, keeping my eye on her all the time, and I took particular care to note the house at which she stopped. It was the house with the gay curtains, the home of flowers, the house out of which Crashaw came the night he hanged himself in his garden. I was just going away with my discovery, when I saw an empty carriage come round and draw up in front of the house, and I came to the conclusion that Mrs Herbert was going out for a drive, and I was right. There, as it happened, I met a man I know, and we stood talking together a little distance from the carriage-way, to which I had my back. We had not been there for ten minutes when my friend took off his hat, and I glanced round and saw the lady I had been following all day. 'Who is that?' I said, and his answer was 'Mrs Beaumont; lives in Ashley Street.' Of course there could be no doubt after that. I don't know whether she saw me, but I don't think she did. I went home at once, and, on consideration, I thought that I had a sufficiently good case with which to go to Clarke."

"Why to Clarke?"

"Because I am sure that Clarke is in possession of facts about this woman, facts of which I know nothing."

"Well, what then?"

Mr Villiers leaned back in his chair and looked reflectively at Austin for a moment before he answered:

"My idea was that Clarke and I should call on Mrs Beaumont."

"You would never go into such a house as that? No, no, Villiers, you cannot do it. Besides, consider; what result..."

"I will tell you soon. But I was going to say that my information does not end here; it has been completed in an extraordinary manner.

"Look at this neat little packet of manuscript; it is paginated, you see, and I have indulged in the civil coquetry of a ribbon of red tape. It has almost a legal air, hasn't it? Run your eye over it, Austin. It is an account of the entertainment Mrs Beaumont provided for her choicer guests. The man who wrote this escaped with his life, but I do not think he will live many years. The doctors tell him he must have sustained some severe shock to the nerves."

Austin took the manuscript, but never read it. Opening the neat pages at random his eye was caught by a word and a phrase that followed it; and, sick at heart, with white lips and a cold sweat pouring like water from his temples, he flung the paper down.

"Take it away, Villiers, never speak of this again. Are you made of stone, man? Why, the dread and horror of death itself, the thoughts of the man who stands in the keen morning air on the black platform, bound, the bell tolling in his ears, and waits for the harsh rattle of the bolt, are as nothing compared to this. I will not read it; I should never sleep again."

"Very good. I can fancy what you saw. Yes; it is horrible enough; but after all, it is an old story, an old mystery played in our day, and in dim London streets instead of amidst the vineyards and the olive gardens. We know what happened to those who chanced to meet the Great God Pan, and those who are wise know that all symbols are symbols of something, not of nothing. It was, indeed, an exquisite symbol beneath which men long ago veiled their knowledge of the most awful, most secret forces which lie at the heart of all things; forces before which the souls of men must wither and die and blacken, as their bodies blacken under the electric current. Such forces cannot be named, cannot be spoken, cannot be imagined except under a veil and a symbol, a symbol to the most of us appearing a quaint, poetic fancy, to some a foolish tale. But you and I, at all events, have known something of the terror that may dwell in the secret place of life, manifested under human flesh; that which is without form taking to itself a form. Oh, Austin, how can it be? How is it that the very sunlight does not turn to blackness before this thing, the hard earth melt and boil beneath such a burden?"

Villiers was pacing up and down the room, and the beads of sweat stood out on his forehead. Austin sat silent for a while, but Villiers saw him make a sign upon his breast.

"I say again, Villiers, you will surely never enter such a house as that? You would never pass out alive."

"Yes, Austin, I shall go out alive – I, and Clarke with me."

What do you mean? You cannot, you would not dare..."

"Wait a moment. The air was very pleasant and fresh this morning; there was a breeze blowing, even through this dull street, and I thought I would take a walk. Piccadilly stretched before me a clear, bright vista, and the sun flashed on the carriages and on the quivering leaves in the park. It was a joyous morning, and men and women looked at the sky and smiled as they went about their work or their pleasure, and the wind blew as blithely as upon the meadows and the scented gorse. But somehow or other I got out of the bustle and the gaiety, and found myself walking slowly along a quiet, dull street, where there seemed to be no sunshine and no air, and where the few foot-passengers loitered as they walked, and hung indecisively about corners and archways. I walked along, hardly knowing where I was going or what I did there, but feeling impelled, as one sometimes is, to explore still further, with a vague idea of reaching some unknown goal. Thus I forged up the street, noting the small traffic of the milk shop, and wondering at the incongruous medley of penny pipes, black tobacco, sweets, newspapers and comic songs which here and there jostled one another in the short compass of a single window. I think it was a cold shudder that suddenly passed through me that first told me that I had found what I wanted. I looked up from the pavement and stopped before a dusty shop, above which the lettering had faded, where the red bricks of two hundred years ago had grimed to black; where the windows had gathered to themselves the dust of winters innumerable. I saw what I required; but I think it was five minutes before I had steadied myself and could walk in and ask for it in a cool voice and with a calm face. I think there must even then have been a tremor in my words, for the old man who came out of the back parlour, and fumbled slowly amongst his goods, looked oddly at me as he tied the parcel. I paid what he asked, and stood leaning by the counter, with a strange reluctance to take up my goods and go. I asked about the business, and learnt that trade was bad and the profits cut down sadly; but then the street was not what it was before traffic had been diverted, but that was done forty years ago, 'just before my father died,' he said. I got away at last, and walked along sharply; it was a dismal street indeed, and I was glad to return to the bustle and the noise. Would you like to see my purchase?"

Austin said nothing, but nodded his head slightly; he still looked white and sick. Villiers pulled out a drawer in the bamboo table, and showed Austin a long coil of cord, hard and new; and at one end was a running noose.

"It is the best hempen cord," said Villiers, "just as it used to be made for the old trade, the man told me. Not an inch of jute from end to end."

Austin set his teeth hard, and stared at Villiers, growing whiter as he looked.

"You would not do it," he murmured at last. "You would not have blood on your hands. My God!" he exclaimed, with sudden vehemence, "you cannot mean this, Villiers, that you will make yourself a hangman?"

"No. I shall offer a choice, and leave Helen Vaughan alone with this cord in a locked room for fifteen minutes. If when we go in it is not done, I shall call the nearest policeman. That is all."

"I must go now. I cannot stay here any longer; I cannot bear this. Goodnight."

"Goodnight, Austin."

The door shut, but in a moment it was open again, and Austin stood, white and ghastly, in the entrance.

"I was forgetting," he said, "that I too have something to tell. I have received a letter from Dr Harding of Buenos Ayres. He says that he attended Meyrick for three weeks before his death."

"And does he say what carried him off in the prime of life? It was not fever?"

"No, it was not fever. According to the doctor, it was an utter collapse of the whole system, probably caused by some severe shock. But he states that the patient would tell him nothing, and that he was consequently at some disadvantage in treating the case."

"Is there anything more?"

"Yes. Dr Harding ends his letter by saying: 'I think this is all the information I can give you about your poor friend. He had not been long in Buenos Ayres, and knew scarcely anyone, with the exception of a person who did not bear the best of characters, and has since left – a Mrs Vaughan.'"

VIII

[Amongst the papers of the well-known physician Dr Robert Matheson, of Ashley Street, Piccadilly, who died suddenly, of apoplectic seizure, at the beginning of 1892, a leaf of manuscript paper was found, covered with pencil jottings. These notes were in Latin, much abbreviated, and had evidently been made in great haste. The MS was only deciphered with difficulty, and some words have up to the present time evaded all the efforts of the expert employed. The date, "XXV Jul. 1888", is written on the right-hand corner of the MS. The following is a translation of Dr Matheson's manuscript.]

Whether science would benefit by these brief notes if they could be published, I do not know, but rather doubt. But certainly I shall never take the responsibility of publishing or divulging one word of what is here written, not only on account of my oath given freely to those two persons who were present, but also because the details are too abominable. It is probable that, upon mature consideration, and after weighting the good and evil, I shall one day destroy this paper, or at least leave it under seal to my friend D., trusting in his discretion, to use it or to burn it, as he may think fit.

As was befitting, I did all that my knowledge suggested to make sure that I was suffering under no delusion. At first astounded, I could hardly think, but in a minute's time I was sure that my pulse was steady and regular, and that I was in my real and true senses. I then fixed my eyes quietly on what was before me.

Though horror and revolting nausea rose up within me, and an odour of corruption choked my breath, I remained firm. I was then privileged or accursed, I dare not say which, to see that which was on the bed, lying there black like ink, transformed before my eyes. The skin, and the flesh, and the muscles, and the bones, and the firm structure of the human body that I had thought to be unchangeable, and permanent as adamant, began to melt and dissolve.

I know that the body may be separated into its elements by external agencies, but I should have refused to believe what I saw. For here there was some internal force, of which I knew nothing, that caused dissolution and change.

Here too was all the work by which man had been made repeated before my eyes. I saw the form waver from sex to sex, dividing itself from itself, and then again reunited. Then I saw the body descend to the beasts whence it ascended, and that which was on the heights go down to the depths, even to the abyss of all being. The principle of life, which makes organism, always remained, while the outward form changed.

The light within the room had turned to blackness, not the darkness of night, in which objects are seen dimly, for I could see clearly and without difficulty. But it was the negation of light; objects were presented to my eyes, if I may say so, without any medium, in such a manner that if there had been a prism in the room I should have seen no colours represented in it.

I watched, and at last I saw nothing but a substance as jelly. Then the ladder was ascended again... [here the MS is illegible] ...for one instance I saw a Form, shaped in dimness before me, which I will not farther describe. But the symbol of this form may be seen in ancient sculptures, and in paintings which survived beneath the lava, too foul to be spoken of... as a horrible and unspeakable shape, neither man nor beast, was changed into human form, there came finally death.

I who saw all this, not without great horror and loathing of soul, here write my name, declaring all that I have set on this paper to be true.

ROBERT MATHESON, Med. Dr

...Such, Raymond, is the story of what I know and what I have seen. The burden of it was too heavy for me to bear alone, and yet I could tell it to none but you. Villiers, who was with me at the last, knows nothing of that awful secret of the wood, of how what we both saw die, lay upon the smooth, sweet turf amidst the summer flowers, half in sun and half in shadow, and holding the girl Rachel's hand, called and summoned those companions, and shaped in solid form, upon the earth we tread upon, the horror which we can but hint at, which we can only name under a figure. I would not tell Villiers of this, nor of that resemblance, which struck me as with a blow upon my heart, when I saw the portrait, which filled the cup of terror at the end. What this can mean I dare not guess. I know that what I saw perish was not Mary, and yet in the last agony Mary's eyes looked into mine. Whether there can be any one who can show the last link in this chain of awful mystery, I do not know, but if there be anyone who can do this, you, Raymond, are the man. And if you know the secret, it rests with you to tell it or not, as you please.

I am writing this letter to you immediately on my getting back to town. I have been in the country for the last few days; perhaps you may be able to guess in which part. While the horror and wonder of London was at its height – for "Mrs Beaumont", as I have told you, was well known in society – I wrote to my friend Dr Phillips, giving some brief outline, or rather hint, of what happened, and asking him to tell me the name of the village where the events he had related to me occurred. He gave me the name, as he said with the less hesitation, because Rachel's father and mother were dead, and the rest of the family had gone to a relative in the State of Washington six months before. The parents, he said, had undoubtedly died of grief and horror caused by the terrible death of their daughter, and by what had gone before that death. On the evening of the day which I received Phillips' letter I was at Caermaen, and standing beneath the mouldering Roman walls, white with the winters of seventeen hundred years, I looked over the meadow where once had stood the older temple of the "God of the Deeps", and saw a house gleaming in the sunlight. It was the house where Helen had lived. I stayed at Caermaen for several days. The people of the place, I found, knew little and had guessed less. Those whom I spoke to on the matter seemed surprised that an antiquarian (as I professed myself to be) should trouble about a village tragedy, of which they gave a very commonplace version, and, as you may imagine, I told nothing of what I knew. Most of my time was spent in the great wood that rises just above the village and climbs the hillside, and goes down to the river in the valley; such another long lovely valley, Raymond, as that on which we looked one summer night, walking to and fro before your house. For many an hour I strayed through the maze of the forest, turning now to right and now to left, pacing slowly down long alleys of undergrowth, shadowy and chill, even under the midday sun, and halting beneath great oaks; lying on the short turf of a clearing where the faint sweet scent of wild roses came to me on the wind and mixed with the heavy perfume of the elder, whose mingled odour is like the odour of the room of the dead, a vapour of incense and corruption. I stood at the edges of the wood, gazing at all the pomp and procession of the foxgloves towering amidst the bracken and shining red in the broad sunshine, and beyond them into deep thickets of close undergrowth where springs boil up from the rock and nourish the water-weeds, dank and evil. But in all my wanderings I avoided one part of the wood; it was not till yesterday that I climbed to the summit of the hill, and stood upon the ancient Roman road that threads the highest ridge of the wood. Here they had walked, Helen and Rachel, along this quiet causeway, upon the pavement of green turf, shut in on either side by high banks of red earth, and tall hedges of shining beech, and here I followed in their steps, looking out, now and again, through partings in the boughs, and seeing on one side the sweep of the wood stretching far to right and left, and sinking into the broad level, and beyond, the yellow sea, and the land over the sea. On the other side was the valley and the river, and hill following hill as wave on wave, and wood and meadow, and cornfield, and white houses gleaming, and a great wall of mountain, and far blue peaks in the north. And so at last I came to the place. The track went up a gentle slope, and widened out into an open space with a wall of thick undergrowth around it, and then, narrowing again, passed on into the distance and the faint blue mist of summer heat. And into this pleasant summer glade Rachel passed, a girl, and left it, who shall say what? I did not stay long there.

In a small town near Caermaen there is a museum, containing for the most part Roman remains which have been found in the neighbourhood at various times. On the day after my arrival in Caermaen I walked over to the town in question, and took the opportunity of inspecting the museum. After I had seen most of the sculptured stones, the coffins, rings, coins and fragments of tessellated pavement which the place contains, I was shown a small square pillar of white stone, which had been recently discovered in the wood of which I have been speaking, and, as I found on inquiry, in that open space where the Roman road broadens out. On one side of the pillar was an inscription, of which I took a note. Some of the letters have been defaced, but I do not think there can be any doubt as to those which I supply. The inscription is as follows:

> *DEVOMNODENTi*
> *FLAvIVSSENILISPOSSVit*
> *PROPTERNVPtias*
> *quaSVIDITSVBVMra*
> (To the great god Nodens [the god of the Great Deep or Abyss] Flavius Senilis has erected this pillar on account of the marriage which he saw beneath the shade.)

The custodian of the museum informed me that local antiquaries were much puzzled, not by the inscription, or by any difficulty in translating it, but as to the circumstance or rite to which allusion is made.

...And now, my dear Clarke, as to what you tell me about Helen Vaughan, whom you say you saw die under circumstances of the utmost and almost incredible horror. I was interested in your account, but a good deal, nay all, of what you told me I knew already. I can understand the strange likeness you remarked in both the portrait and in the actual face; you have seen Helen's mother. You remember that still summer night so many years ago, when I talked to you of the world beyond the shadows, and of the god Pan. You remember Mary. She was the mother of Helen Vaughan, who was born nine months after that night.

Mary never recovered her reason. She lay, as you saw her, all the while upon her bed, and a few days after the child was born she died. I fancy that just at the last she knew me; I was standing by the bed, and the old look came into her eyes for a second, and then she shuddered and groaned and died. It was an ill work I did that night when you were present; I broke open the door of the house of life, without knowing or caring what might pass forth or enter in. I recollect your telling me at the time, sharply enough, and rightly too, in one sense, that I had ruined the reason of a human being by a foolish experiment, based on an absurd theory. You did well to blame me, but my theory was not all absurdity. What I said Mary would see she saw, but I forgot that no human eyes can look on such a sight with impunity. And I forgot, as I have just said, that when the house of life is thus thrown open, there may enter in that for which we have no name, and human flesh may become the veil of a horror one dare not express. I played with energies which I did not understand, you have seen the ending of it. Helen Vaughan did well to bind the cord about her neck and die, though the death was horrible. The blackened face, the hideous form upon the bed, changing and melting before your eyes from woman to man, from man to beast, and from beast to worse than beast, all the strange horror that you witness, surprises me but little. What you say the doctor whom you sent for saw and shuddered at I noticed long ago; I knew what I had done the moment the child was born, and when it was scarcely five years old I surprised it, not once or twice but several times with a playmate, you may guess of what kind. It was for me a constant, an incarnate horror, and after a few years I felt I could bear it no more, and I sent Helen Vaughan away. You know now what frightened the boy in the wood. The rest of the strange story, and all else that you tell me, as discovered by your friend, I have contrived to learn from time to time, almost to the last chapter. And now Helen is with her companions...

THE INMOST LIGHT

ARTHUR MACHEN

I

One evening in autumn, when the deformities of London were veiled in faint blue mist, and its vistas and far-reaching streets seemed splendid, Mr Charles Salisbury was slowly pacing down Rupert Street, drawing nearer to his favourite restaurant by slow degrees. His eyes were downcast in study of the pavement, and thus it was that as he passed in at the narrow door a man who had come up from the lower end of the street jostled against him.

"I beg your pardon – wasn't looking where I was going. Why, it's Dyson!"

"Yes, quite so. How are you, Salisbury?"

"Quite well. But where have you been, Dyson? I don't think I can have seen you for the last five years?"

"No; I dare say not. You remember I was getting rather hard up when you came to my place at Charlotte Street?"

"Perfectly. I think I remember your telling me that you owed five weeks' rent, and that you had parted with your watch for a comparatively small sum."

"My dear Salisbury, your memory is admirable. Yes, I was hard up. But the curious thing is that soon after you saw me I became harder up. My financial state was described by a friend as 'stony-broke'. I don't approve of slang, mind you, but such was my condition. But suppose we go in; there might be other people who would like to dine – it's a human weakness, Salisbury."

"Certainly; come along. I was wondering as I walked down whether the corner table were taken. It has a velvet back you know."

"I know the spot; it's vacant. Yes, as I was saying, I became even harder up."

"What did you do then?" asked Salisbury, disposing of his hat, and settling down in the corner of the seat, with a glance of fond anticipation at the menu.

"What did I do? Why, I sat down and reflected. I had a good classical education, and a positive distaste for business of any kind: that was the capital with which I faced the world. Do you know, I have heard people describe olives as nasty! What lamentable Philistinism! I have often thought, Salisbury, that I could write genuine poetry under the influence of olives and red wine. Let us have Chianti; it may not be very good, but the flasks are simply charming."

"It is pretty good here. We may as well have a big flask."

"Very good. I reflected, then, on my want of prospects, and I determined to embark in literature."

"Really; that was strange. You seem in pretty comfortable circumstances, though."

"Though! What a satire upon a noble profession. I am afraid, Salisbury, you haven't a proper idea of the dignity of an artist. You see me sitting at my desk – or at least you can see me if you care to call – with pen and ink, and simple nothingness before me, and if you come again in a few hours you will (in all probability) find a creation!"

"Yes, quite so. I had an idea that literature was not remunerative."

"You are mistaken; its rewards are great. I may mention, by the way, that shortly after you saw me I succeeded to a small income. An uncle died, and proved unexpectedly generous."

"Ah, I see. That must have been convenient."

"It was pleasant – undeniably pleasant. I have always considered it in the light of an endowment of my researches. I told you I was a man of letters; it would, perhaps, be more correct to describe myself as a man of science."

"Dear me, Dyson, you have really changed very much in the last few years. I had a notion, don't you know, that you were a sort of idler about town, the kind of man one might meet on the north side of Piccadilly every day from May to July."

"Exactly. I was even then forming myself, though all unconsciously. You know my poor father could not afford to send me to the University. I used to grumble in my ignorance at not having completed my education. That was the folly of youth, Salisbury; my University was Piccadilly. There I began to study the great science which still occupies me."

"What science do you mean?"

"The science of the great city; the physiology of London; literally and metaphysically the greatest subject that the mind of man can conceive. What an admirable *salmi* this is; undoubtedly the final end of the pheasant. Yet I feel sometimes positively overwhelmed with the thought of the vastness and complexity of London. Paris a man may get to understand thoroughly with a reasonable amount of study; but London is always a mystery. In Paris you may say: 'Here live the actresses, here the Bohemians, and the Ratés'; but it is different in London. You may point out a street, correctly enough, as the abode of washerwomen; but, in that second floor, a man may be studying Chaldee roots, and in the garret over the way a forgotten artist is dying by inches."

"I see you are Dyson, unchanged and unchangeable," said Salisbury, slowly sipping his Chianti. "I think you are misled by a too fervid imagination; the mystery of London exists only in your fancy. It seems to me a dull place enough. We seldom hear of a really artistic crime in London, whereas I believe Paris abounds in that sort of thing."

"Give me some more wine. Thanks. You are mistaken, my dear fellow, you are really mistaken. London has nothing to be ashamed of in the way of crime. Where we fail is for want of Homers, not Agamemnons. *Carent quia vate sacro*, you know."

"I recall the quotation. But I don't think I quite follow you."

"Well, in plain language, we have no good writers in London who make a speciality of that kind of thing. Our common reporter is a dull dog; every story that he has to tell is spoilt in the telling. His idea of horror and of what excites horror is so lamentably deficient. Nothing will content the fellow but blood, vulgar red blood, and when he can get it he lays it on thick, and considers that he has produced a telling article. It's a poor notion. And, by some curious fatality, it is the most commonplace and brutal murders which always attract the most attention and get written up the most. For instance, I dare say that you never heard of the Harlesden case?"

"No; no, I don't remember anything about it."

"Of course not. And yet the story is a curious one. I will tell you over our coffee. Harlesden, you know, or I expect you don't know, is quite on the out-quarters of London; something curiously different from your fine old crusted suburb like Norwood or Hampstead, different as each of these is from the other. Hampstead, I mean, is where you look for the head of your great China house with his three acres of land and pine-houses, though of late there is the artistic substratum; while Norwood is the home of the prosperous middle-class family who took the house 'because it was near the Palace', and sickened of the Palace six months afterwards; but Harlesden is a place of no character. It's too new to have any character as yet. There are the rows of red houses and the rows of white houses and the bright green Venetians, and the blistering doorways, and the little backyards they call gardens, and a few feeble shops, and then, just as you think you're going to grasp the physiognomy of the settlement, it all melts away."

"How the dickens is that? The houses don't tumble down before one's eyes, I suppose!"

"Well, no, not exactly that. But Harlesden as an entity disappears. Your street turns into a quiet lane, and your staring houses into elm trees, and the back gardens into green meadows. You pass instantly from town to country; there is no transition as in a small country town, no soft gradations of wider lawns and orchards, with houses gradually becoming less dense, but a dead stop. I believe the people who live there mostly go into the City. I have seen once or twice a laden bus bound thitherwards. But however that may be, I can't conceive a greater loneliness in a desert at midnight than there is there at mid-day. It is like a city of the dead; the streets are glaring and desolate, and as you pass it suddenly strikes you that this too is part of London. Well, a year or two ago there was a doctor living there; he had set up his brass plate and his red lamp at the very end of one of those shining streets, and from the back of the house, the fields stretched away to the north. I don't know what his reason was in settling down in such an out-of-the-way place, perhaps Dr Black, as we call him, was a far-seeing man and looked ahead. His relations, so it appeared afterwards, had lost sight of him for many years and didn't even know he was a doctor, much less where he lived. However, there he was settled in Harlesden, with some fragments of a practice, and an uncommonly pretty wife. People used to see them walking out together in the summer evenings soon after they came to Harlesden and, so far as could be observed, they seemed a very affectionate couple. These walks went on through the autumn, and then ceased, but, of course, as the days grew dark and the weather cold, the lanes near Harlesden might be expected to lose many of their attractions. All through the winter nobody saw anything of Mrs Black, the doctor used to reply to his patients' inquiries that she was a 'little out of sorts, would be better, no doubt, in the spring'. But the spring came, and the summer, and no Mrs Black appeared, and at last people began to rumour and talk amongst themselves, and all sorts of queer things were said at 'high teas', which you may possibly have heard are the only form of entertainment known in such suburbs. Dr Black began to surprise some very odd looks cast in his direction, and the practice, such as it was, fell off before his eyes. In short, when the neighbours whispered about the matter, they whispered that Mrs Black was dead, and that the doctor had made away with her. But this wasn't the case; Mrs Black was seen alive in June. It was a Sunday afternoon, one of those few exquisite days that an English climate offers, and half London had strayed out into the fields, north, south, east and west to smell the scent of the white May, and to see if the wild roses were yet in blossom in the hedges. I had gone out myself early in the morning, and had had a long ramble, and somehow or other as I was steering homeward I found myself in this very Harlesden we have been talking about. To be exact, I had a glass of beer in the 'General Gordon', the most flourishing house in the neighbourhood, and as I was wandering rather aimlessly about, I saw an uncommonly tempting gap in a hedgerow, and resolved to explore the meadow beyond. Soft grass is very grateful to the feet after the infernal grit strewn on suburban pavements, and after walking about for some time I thought I should like to sit down on a bank and have a smoke. While I was getting out my pouch, I looked up in the direction of the houses, and as I looked I felt my breath caught back, and my teeth began to chatter, and the stick I had in one hand snapped in two with the grip I gave it. It was as if I had had an electric current down my spine, and yet for some moment of time which seemed long, but which must have been very short, I caught myself wondering what on earth was the matter. Then I knew what had made my very heart shudder and my bones grind together in an agony. As I glanced up I had looked straight towards the last house in the row before me, and in an upper window of that house I had seen for some short fraction of a second a face. It was the face of a woman, and yet it was not human. You and I, Salisbury, have heard in our time, as we sat in our seats in church in sober English fashion, of a lust that cannot be satiated and of a fire that is unquenchable, but few of us have any notion what these words mean. I hope you never may, for as I saw that face at the window, with the blue sky above me and the warm air playing in gusts about me, I knew I had looked into another world – looked through the window of a commonplace, brand-new house, and seen hell open before me. When the first shock was over, I thought once or twice that I should have fainted; my face streamed with a cold sweat, and my breath came and went in sobs, as if I had been half drowned. I managed to get up at last, and walk round to the street, and there I saw the name 'Dr Black' on the post by the front gate. As fate or my luck would have it, the door opened and a man came down the steps as I passed by. I had no doubt it was the doctor himself. He was of a type rather common in London: long and thin, with a pasty face and a dull black moustache. He gave me a look as we passed each other on the pavement, and though it was merely the casual glance which one foot-passenger bestows on another, I felt convinced in my mind that here was an ugly customer to deal with. As you may imagine, I went my way a good deal puzzled and horrified too by what I had seen; for I had paid another visit to the 'General Gordon', and had got together a good deal of the common gossip of the place about the Blacks. I didn't mention the fact that I had seen a woman's face in the window; but I heard that Mrs Black had been much admired for her beautiful golden hair, and round what had struck me with such a nameless terror, there was a mist of flowing yellow hair, as it were an aureole of glory round the visage of a satyr. The whole thing bothered me in an indescribable manner; and when I got home I tried my best to think of the impression I had received as an illusion, but it was no use. I knew very well I had seen what I have tried to describe to you, and I was morally certain that I had seen Mrs Black. And then there was the gossip of the place, the suspicion of foul play, which I knew to be false, and my own conviction that there was some deadly mischief or other going on in that bright red house at the corner of Devon Road: how to construct a theory of a reasonable kind out of these two elements. In short, I found myself in a world of mystery; I puzzled my head over it and filled up my leisure moments by gathering together odd threads of speculation, but I never moved a step towards any real solution, and as the summer days went on the matter seemed to grow misty and indistinct, shadowing some vague terror, like a nightmare of last month. I suppose it would before long have faded into the background of my brain – I should not have forgotten it, for such a thing could never be forgotten – but one morning as I was looking over the paper my eye was caught by a heading over some two dozen lines of small type. The words I had seen were simply: 'The Harlesden Case', and I knew what I was going to read. Mrs Black was dead. Black had called in another medical man to certify as to cause of death, and something or other had aroused the strange doctor's suspicions and there had been an inquest and post-mortem. And the result? That, I will confess, did astonish me considerably; it was the triumph of the unexpected. The two doctors who made the autopsy were obliged to confess that they could not discover the faintest trace of any kind of foul play; their most exquisite tests and reagents failed to detect the presence of poison in the most infinitesimal quantity. Death, they found, had been caused by a somewhat obscure and scientifically interesting form of brain disease. The tissue of the brain and the molecules of the grey matter had undergone a most extraordinary series of changes; and the younger of the two doctors, who has some reputation, I believe, as a specialist in brain trouble, made some remarks in giving his evidence which struck me deeply at the time, though I did not then grasp their full significance. He said: 'At the commencement of the examination I was astonished to find appearances of a character entirely new to me, notwithstanding my somewhat large experience. I need not specify these appearances at present, it will be sufficient for me to state that as I proceeded in my task I could scarcely believe that the brain before me was that of a human being at all.' There was some surprise at this statement, as you may imagine, and the coroner asked the doctor if he meant that the brain resembled that of an animal. "No," he replied, "I should not put it in that way. Some of the appearances I noticed seemed to point in that direction, but others, and these were the more surprising, indicated a nervous organisation of a wholly different character from that either of man or the lower animals."

It was a curious thing to say, but of course the jury brought in a verdict of death from natural causes and, so far as the public was concerned, the case came to an end. But after I had read what the doctor said I made up my mind that I should like to know a good deal more, and I set to work on what seemed likely to prove an interesting investigation. I had really a good deal of trouble, but I was successful in a measure. Though why – my dear fellow, I had no notion at the time. Are you aware that we have been here nearly four hours? The waiters are staring at us. Let's have the bill and be gone."

The two men went out in silence, and stood a moment in the cool air, watching the hurrying traffic of Coventry Street pass before them to the accompaniment of the ringing bells of hansoms and the cries of the newsboys; the deep far murmur of London surging up ever and again from beneath these louder noises.

"It is a strange case, isn't it?" said Dyson at length. "What do you think of it?"

"My dear fellow. I haven't heard the end, so I will reserve my opinion. When will you give me the sequel?"

"Come to my rooms some evening; say next Thursday. Here's the address. Goodnight; I want to get down to the Strand." Dyson hailed a passing hansom, and Salisbury turned northward to walk home to his lodgings.

II

Mr Salisbury, as may have been gathered from the few remarks which he had found it possible to introduce in the course of the evening, was a young gentleman of a peculiarly solid form of intellect, coy and retiring before the mysterious and the uncommon, with a constitutional dislike of paradox. During the restaurant dinner he had been forced to listen in almost absolute silence to a strange tissue of improbabilities strung together with the ingenuity of a born meddler in plots and mysteries, and it was with a feeling of weariness that he crossed Shaftesbury Avenue, and dived into the recesses of Soho, for his lodgings were in a modest neighbourhood to the north of Oxford Street. As he walked he speculated on the probable fate of Dyson, relying on literature, unbefriended by a thoughtful relative, and could not help concluding that so much subtlety united to a too vivid imagination would in all likelihood have been rewarded with a pair of sandwich-boards or a super's banner. Absorbed in this train of thought, and admiring the perverse dexterity which could transmute the face of a sickly woman and a case of brain disease into the crude elements of romance, Salisbury strayed on through the dimly lighted streets, not noticing the gusty wind which drove sharply round corners and whirled the stray rubbish of the pavement into the air in eddies, while black clouds gathered over the sickly yellow moon. Even a stray drop or two of rain blown into his face did not rouse him from his meditations, and it was only when with a sudden rush the storm tore down upon the street that he began to consider the expediency of finding some shelter. The rain, driven by the wind, pelted down with the violence of a thunderstorm, dashing up from the stones and hissing through the air, and soon a perfect torrent of water coursed along the kennels and accumulated in pools over the choked-up drains. The few stray passengers who had been loafing rather than walking about the street had scuttered away, like frightened rabbits, to some invisible places of refuge, and though Salisbury whistled loud and long for a hansom, no hansom appeared. He looked about him, as if to discover how far he might be from the haven of Oxford Street, but strolling carelessly along, he had turned out of his way, and found himself in an unknown region, and one to all appearance devoid even of a public house where shelter could be bought for the modest sum of twopence. The street lamps were few and at long intervals, and burned behind grimy glasses with the sickly light of oil, and by this wavering glimmer Salisbury could make out the shadowy and vast old houses of which the street was composed. As he passed along, hurrying, and shrinking from the full sweep of the rain, he noticed the innumerable bell-handles, with names that seemed about to vanish of old age graven on brass plates beneath them, and here and there a richly carved penthouse overhung the door, blackening with the grime of fifty years. The storm seemed to grow more and more furious; he was wet through, and a new hat had become a ruin, and still Oxford Street seemed as far off as ever; it was with deep relief that the dripping man caught sight of a dark archway which seemed to promise shelter from the rain if not from the wind. Salisbury took up his position in the driest corner and looked about him; he was standing in a kind of passage contrived under part of a house, and behind him stretched a narrow footway leading between blank walls to regions unknown. He had stood there for some time, vainly endeavouring to rid himself of some of his superfluous moisture, and listening for the passing wheel of a hansom, when his attention was aroused by a loud noise coming from the direction of the passage behind, and growing louder as it drew nearer. In a couple of minutes he could make out the shrill, raucous voice of a woman, threatening and renouncing and making the very stones echo with her accents, while now and then a man grumbled and expostulated. Though to all appearance devoid of romance, Salisbury had some relish for street rows, and was, indeed, somewhat of an amateur in the more amusing phases of drunkenness; he therefore composed himself to listen and observe with something of the air of a subscriber to grand opera. To his annoyance, however, the tempest seemed suddenly to be composed, and he could hear nothing but the impatient steps of the woman and the slow lurch of the man as they came towards him. Keeping back in the shadow of the wall, he could see the two drawing nearer; the man was evidently drunk, and had much ado to avoid frequent collision with the wall as he tacked across from one side to the other, like some bark beating up against a wind. The woman was looking straight in front of her, with tears streaming from her blazing eyes, but suddenly as they went by the flame blazed up again, and she burst forth into a torrent of abuse, facing round upon her companion.

"You low rascal, you mean, comtemptible cur," she went on, after an incoherent storm of curses, "you think I'm to work and slave for you always, I suppose, while you're after that Green Street girl and drinking every penny you've got? But you're mistaken, Sam – indeed, I'll bear it no longer. Damn you, you dirty thief, I've done with you and your master too, so you can go your own errands, and I only hope they'll get you into trouble."

The woman tore at the bosom of her dress, and taking something out that looked like paper, crumpled it up and flung it away. It fell at Salisbury's feet. She ran out and disappeared in the darkness, while the man lurched slowly into the street, grumbling indistinctly to himself in a perplexed tone of voice. Salisbury looked out after him, and saw him maundering along the pavement, halting now and then and swaying indecisively, and then starting off at some fresh tangent. The sky had cleared, and white fleecy clouds were fleeting across the moon, high in the heaven. The light came and went by turns as the clouds passed by and, turning round as the clear, white rays shone into the passage, Salisbury saw the little ball of crumpled paper which the woman had cast down. Oddly curious to know what it might contain, he picked it up and put it in his pocket, and set out afresh on his journey.

III

Salisbury was a man of habit. When he got home, drenched to the skin, his clothes hanging lank about him and a ghastly dew besmearing his hat, his only thought was of his health, of which he took studious care. So, after changing his clothes and encasing himself in a warm dressing gown, he proceeded to prepare a sudorific in the shape of hot gin and water, warming the latter over one of those spirit-lamps which mitigate the austerities of the modern hermit's life. By the time this preparation had been exhibited, and Salisbury's disturbed feelings had been soothed by a pipe of tobacco, he was able to get into bed in a happy state of vacancy, without a thought of his adventure in the dark archway, or of the weird fancies with which Dyson had seasoned his dinner. It was the same at breakfast the next morning, for Salisbury made a point of not thinking of anything until that meal was over; but when the cup and saucer were cleared away, and the morning pipe was lit, he remembered the little ball of paper, and began fumbling in the pockets of his wet coat. He did not remember into which pocket he had put it, and as he dived now into one and now into another, he experienced a strange feeling of apprehension lest it should not be there at all, though he could not for the life of him have explained the importance he attached to what was in all probability mere rubbish. But he sighed with relief when his fingers touched the crumpled surface in an inside pocket, and he drew it out gently and laid it on the little desk by his easy chair with as much care as if it had been some rare jewel. Salisbury sat smoking and staring at his find for a few minutes, an odd temptation to throw the thing in the fire and have done with it struggling with as odd a speculation as to its possible contents, and as to the reason why the infuriated woman should have flung a bit of paper from her with such vehemence. As might be expected, it was the latter feeling that conquered in the end, and yet it was with something like repugnance that he at last took the paper and unrolled it, and laid it out before him. It was a piece of common dirty paper, to all appearance torn out of a cheap exercise book, and in the middle were a few lines written in a queer cramped hand. Salisbury bent his head and stared eagerly at it for a moment, drawing a long breath, and then fell back in his chair gazing blankly before him, till at last with a sudden revulsion he burst into a peal of laughter, so long and loud and uproarious that the landlady's baby in the floor below awoke from sleep and echoed his mirth with hideous yells. But he laughed again and again, and took the paper up to read a second time what seemed such meaningless nonsense.

"Q. has had to go and see his friends in Paris," it began. "Traverse Handel S. 'Once around the grass, and twice around the lass, and thrice around the maple tree.'"

Salisbury took up the paper and crumpled it as the angry woman had done, and aimed it at the fire. He did not throw it there, however, but tossed it carelessly into the well of the desk, and laughed again. The sheer folly of the thing offended him, and he was ashamed of his own eager speculation, as one who pores over the high-sounding announcements in the agony column of the daily paper, and finds nothing but advertisement and trivality. He walked to the window, and stared out at the languid morning life of his quarter; the maids in slatternly print dresses washing doorsteps, the fishmonger and the butcher on their rounds, and the tradesmen standing at the doors of their small shops, drooping for lack of trade and excitement. In the distance a blue haze gave some grandeur to the prospect, but the view as a whole was depressing, and would only have interested a student of the life of London, who finds something rare and choice in its every aspect. Salisbury turned away in disgust, and settled himself in the easy chair, upholstered in a bright shade of green, and decked with yellow gimp, which was the pride and attraction of the apartments. Here he composed himself to his morning's occupation – the perusal of a novel that dealt with sport and love in a manner that suggested the collaboration of a stud groom and a ladies' college. In an ordinary way, however, Salisbury would have been carried on by the interest of the story up to lunch time, but this morning he fidgeted in and out of his chair, took the book up and laid it down again, and swore at last to himself and at himself in mere irritation.

In point of fact the jingle of the paper found in the archway had "got into his head", and do what he would he could not help muttering over and over, "Once around the grass, and twice around the lass, and thrice around the maple tree." It became a positive pain, like the foolish burden of a music-hall song, everlastingly quoted, and sung at all hours of the day and night, and treasured by the street boys as an unfailing resource for six months together. He went out into the streets, and tried to forget his enemy in the jostling of the crowds and the roar and clatter of the traffic, but presently he would find himself stealing quietly aside, and pacing some deserted byway, vainly puzzling his brains, and trying to fix some meaning to phrases that were meaningless. It was a positive relief when Thursday came, and he remembered that he had made an appointment to go and see Dyson; the flimsy reveries of the self-styled man of letters appeared entertaining when compared with this ceaseless iteration, this maze of thought from which there seemed no possibility of escape. Dyson's abode was in one of the quietest of the quiet streets that lead down from the

Strand to the river, and when Salisbury passed from the narrow stairway into his friend's room, he saw that the uncle had been beneficent indeed. The floor glowed and flamed with all the colours of the East; it was, as Dyson pompously remarked, "a sunset in a dream", and the lamplight, the twilight of London streets, was shut out with strangely worked curtains, glittering here and there with threads of gold. In the shelves of an oak *armoire* stood jars and plates of old French china, and the black and white of etchings not to be found in the Haymarket or in Bond Street, stood out against the splendour of a Japanese paper. Salisbury sat down on the settle by the hearth, and sniffed and mingled fumes of incense and tobacco, wondering and dumb before all this splendour after the green rep and the oleographs, the gilt-framed mirror and the lustres of his own apartment.

"I am glad you have come," said Dyson. "Comfortable little room, isn't it? But you don't look very well, Salisbury. Nothing disagreed with you, has it?"

"No; but I have been a good deal bothered for the last few days. The fact is I had an odd kind of – of – adventure, I suppose I may call it, that night I saw you, and it has worried me a good deal. And the provoking part of it is that it's the merest nonsense – but, however, I will tell you all about it, by and by. You were going to let me have the rest of that odd story you began at the restaurant."

"Yes. But I am afraid, Salisbury, you are incorrigible. You are a slave to what you call matter of fact. You know perfectly well that in your heart you think the oddness in that case is of my making, and that it is all really as plain as the police reports. However, as I have begun, I will go on. But first we will have something to drink, and you may as well light your pipe."

Dyson went up to the oak cupboard, and drew from its depths a rotund bottle and two little glasses, quaintly gilded.

"It's Benedictine," he said. "You'll have some, won't you?"

Salisbury assented, and the two men sat sipping and smoking reflectively for some minutes before Dyson began.

"Let me see," he said at last, "we were at the inquest, weren't we? No, we had done with that. Ah, I remember. I was telling you that on the whole I had been successful in my inquiries, investigation or whatever you like to call it, into the matter. Wasn't that where I left off?"

"Yes, that was it. To be precise, I think 'though' was the last word you said on the matter."

"Exactly. I have been thinking it all over since the other night, and I have come to the conclusion that that 'though' is a very big 'though' indeed. Not to put too fine a point on it, I have had to confess that what

I found out, or thought I found out, amounts in reality to nothing. I am as far away from the heart of the case as ever. However, I may as well tell you what I do know. You may remember my saying that I was impressed a good deal by some remarks of one of the doctors who gave evidence at the inquest. Well, I determined that my first step must be to try if I could get something more definite and intelligible out of that doctor. Somehow or other I managed to get an introduction to the man, and he gave me an appointment to come and see him.

"He turned out to be a pleasant, genial fellow; rather young and not in the least like the typical medical man, and he began the conference by offering me whisky and cigars. I didn't think it worthwhile to beat about the bush, so I began by saying that part of his evidence at the Harlesden inquest struck me as very peculiar, and I gave him the printed report, with the sentences in question underlined. He just glanced at the slip, and gave me a queer look.

"'It struck you as peculiar, did it?' said he. 'Well, you must remember that the Harlesden case was very peculiar. In fact, I think I may safely say that in some features it was unique – quite unique.'

"'Quite so,' I replied, 'and that's exactly why it interests me, and why I want to know more about it. And I thought that if anybody could give me any information it would be you. What is your opinion of the matter?'

"It was a pretty downright sort of question, and my doctor looked rather taken aback.

"'Well,' he said, 'as I fancy your motive in inquiring into the question must be mere curiosity, I think I may tell you my opinion with tolerable freedom. So, Mr Dyson, if you want to know my theory, it is this: I believe that Dr Black killed his wife.'

"'But the verdict,' I answered, 'the verdict was given from your own evidence.'

"'Quite so; the verdict was given in accordance with the evidence of my colleague and myself, and, under the circumstances, I think the jury acted very sensibly. In fact, I don't see what else they could have done. But I stick to my opinion, mind you, and I say this also. I don't wonder at Black's doing what I firmly believe he did. I think he was justified.'

"'Justified! How could that be?' I asked. I was astonished, as you may imagine, at the answer I had got. The doctor wheeled round his chair and looked steadily at me for a moment before he answered.

"'I suppose you are not a man of science yourself? No; then it would be of no use my going into detail. I have always been firmly opposed myself to any partnership between physiology and psychology. I believe that both are bound to suffer. No one recognises more decidedly than I do the impassable gulf, the fathomless abyss that separates the world of consciousness from the sphere of matter. We know that every change of consciousness is accompanied by a rearrangement of the molecules in the grey matter; and that is all. What the link between them is, or why they occur together, we do not know, and the most authorities believe that we never can know. Yet, I will tell you that as I did my work, the knife in my hand, I felt convinced, in spite of all theories, that what lay before me was not the brain of a dead woman – not the brain of a human being at all. Of course I saw the face; but it was quite placid, devoid of all expression. It must have been a beautiful face, no doubt, but I can honestly say that I would not have looked in that face when there was life behind it for a thousand guineas, no, nor for twice that sum.'"

"'My dear sir,' I said, 'you surprise me extremely. You say that it was not the brain of a human being. What was it, then?' 'The brain of a devil.' He spoke quite coolly, and never moved a muscle. 'The brain of a devil,' he repeated, 'and I have no doubt that Black found some way of putting an end to it. I don't blame him if he did. Whatever Mrs Black was, she was not fit to stay in this world. Will you have anything more? No? Goodnight, goodnight.'

"It was a queer sort of opinion to get from a man of science, wasn't it? When he was saying that he would not have looked on that face when alive for a thousand guineas, or two thousand guineas, I was thinking of the face I had seen, but I said nothing. I went again to Harlesden, and passed from one shop to another, making small purchases, and trying to find out whether there was anything about the Blacks which was not already common property, but there was very little to hear. One of the tradesmen to whom I spoke said he had known the dead woman well; she used to buy of him such quantities of grocery as were required for their small household, for they never kept a servant, but had a charwoman in occasionally, and she had not seen Mrs Black for months before she died. According to this man Mrs Black was 'a nice lady', always kind and considerate, and so fond of her husband and he of her, as everyone thought. And yet, to put the doctor's opinion on one side, I knew what I had seen. And then after thinking it over, and putting one thing with another, it seemed to me that the only person likely to give me much assistance would be Black himself, and I made up my mind to find him. Of course he wasn't to be found in Harlesden; he had left, I was told, directly after the funeral. Everything in the house had been sold, and one fine day Black got into the train with a small portmanteau, and went, nobody knew where. It was a chance if he were ever heard of again, and it was by a mere chance that I came across him at last. I was walking one day along Gray's Inn Road, not bound for anywhere in particular, but looking about me, as usual, and holding on to my hat, for it was a gusty day in early March, and the wind was making the treetops in the Inn rock and quiver. I had come up from the Holborn end, and I had almost got to Theobald's Road when I noticed a man walking in front of me, leaning on a stick, and to all appearance very feeble. There was something about his look that made me curious, I don't know why, and I began to walk briskly with the idea of overtaking him, when of a sudden his hat blew off and came bounding along the pavement to my feet. Of course I rescued the hat, and gave it a glance as I went towards its owner. It was a biography in itself; a Piccadilly maker's name in the inside, but I don't think a beggar would have picked it out of the gutter. Then I looked up and saw Dr Black of Harlesden waiting for me. A queer thing, wasn't it? But, Salisbury, what a change! When I saw Dr Black come down the steps of his house at Harlesden he was an upright man, walking firmly with well-built limbs; a man, I should say, in the prime of his life. And now before me there crouched this wretched creature, bent and feeble, with shrunken cheeks, and hair that was whitening fast, and limbs that trembled and shook together, and misery in his eyes. He thanked me for bringing him his hat, saying, 'I don't think I should ever have got it, I can't run much now. A gusty day, sir, isn't it?' and with this he was turning away, but by little and little I contrived to draw him into the current of conversation, and we walked together eastward. I think the man would have been glad to get rid of me; but I didn't intend to let him go, and he stopped at last in front of a miserable house in a miserable street. It was, I verily believe, one of the most wretched quarters I have ever seen: houses that must have been sordid and hideous enough when new, that had gathered foulness with every year, and now seemed to lean and totter to their fall. 'I live up there,' said Black, pointing to the tiles, 'not in the front – in the back. I am very quiet there. I won't ask you to come in now, but perhaps some other day—' I caught him up at that, and told him I should be only too glad to come and see him. He gave me an odd sort of glance, as if he were wondering what on earth I or anybody else could care about him, and I left him fumbling with his latch-key. I think you will say I did pretty well when I tell you that within a few weeks I had made myself an intimate friend of Black's. I shall never forget the first time I went to his room; I hope I shall never see such abject, squalid misery again. The foul paper, from which all pattern or trace of a pattern had long vanished, subdued and penetrated with the grime of the evil street, was hanging in mouldering pennons from the wall. Only at the end of the room was it possible to stand upright, and the sight of the wretched bed and the odour of corruption that pervaded the place made me turn faint and sick. Here I found him munching a piece of bread; he seemed surprised to find that I had kept my promise, but he gave me his chair and sat on the bed while we talked. I used to go to see him often, and we had long conversations together, but he never mentioned Harlesden or his wife. I fancy that he supposed me ignorant of the matter, or thought that if I had heard of it, I should never connect the respectable Dr Black of Harlesden with a poor garreteer in the backwoods of London. He was a strange man, and as we sat together smoking, I often wondered whether he were mad or sane, for I think the wildest dreams of Paracelsus and the Rosicrucians would appear plain and sober fact compared with the theories I have heard him earnestly advance in that grimy den of his. I once ventured to hint something of the sort to him. I suggested that something he had said was in flat contradiction to all science and all experience. 'No,' he answered, 'not all experience, for mine counts for something. I am no dealer in unproved theories; what I say I have proved for myself, and at a terrible cost. There is a region of knowledge which you will never know, which wise men seeing from afar off shun like the plague, as well they may, but into that region I have gone. If you knew, if you could even dream of what may be done, of what one or two men have done in this quiet world of ours, your very soul would shudder and faint within you. What you have heard from me has been but the merest husk and outer covering of true science – that science which means death, and that which is more awful than death, to those who gain it. No, when men say that there are strange things in the world, they little know the awe and the terror that dwell always with them and about them.' There was a sort of fascination about the man that drew me to him, and I was quite sorry to have to leave London for a month or two; I missed his odd talk. A few days after I came back to town I thought I would look him up, but when I gave the two rings at the bell that used to summon him, there was no answer. I rang and rang again, and was just turning to go away, when the door opened and a dirty woman asked me what I wanted. From her look I fancy she took me for a plain-clothes officer after one of her lodgers, but when I inquired if Mr Black were in, she gave me a stare of another kind. 'There's no Mr Black lives here,' she said. 'He's gone. He's dead this six weeks. I always thought he was a bit queer in his head, or else had been and got into some trouble or other. He used to go out every morning from ten till one, and one Monday morning we heard him come in, and go into his room and shut the door, and a few minutes after, just as we was a-sitting down to our dinner, there was such a scream that I thought I should have gone right off. And then we heard a stamping, and down he came, raging and cursing most dreadful, swearing he had been robbed of something that was worth millions. And then he just dropped down in the passage, and we thought he was dead. We got him up to his room, and put him on his bed, and I just sat there and waited, while my 'usband he went for the doctor. And there was the winder wide open, and a little tin box he had lying on the floor open and empty, but of course nobody could possible have got in at the winder, and as for him having anything that was worth anything, it's nonsense, for he was often weeks and weeks behind with his rent, and my 'usband he threatened often and often to turn him into the street, for, as he said, we've got a living to myke like other people – and, of course, that's true; but, somehow, I didn't like to do it, though he was an odd kind of a man, and I fancy had been better off. And then the doctor came and looked at him, and said as he couldn't do nothing, and that night he died as I was a-sitting by his bed; and I can tell you that, with one thing and another, we lost money by him, for the few bits of clothes as he had were worth next to nothing when they came to be sold.' I gave the woman half a sovereign for her trouble, and went home thinking of Dr Black and the epitaph she had made him, and wondering at his strange fancy that he had been robbed. I take it that he had very little to fear on that score, poor fellow; but I suppose that he was really mad, and died in a sudden access of his mania. His landlady said that once or twice when she had had occasion to go into his room (to dun the poor wretch for his rent, most likely), he would keep her at the door for about a minute, and that when she came in she would find him putting away his tin box in the corner by the window; I suppose he had become possessed with the idea of some great treasure, and fancied himself a wealthy man in the midst of all his misery. *Explicitly*, my tale is ended, and you see that though I knew Black, I knew nothing of his wife or of the history of her death... That's the Harlesden case, Salisbury, and I think it interests me all the more deeply because there does not seem the shadow of a possibility that I or any one else will ever know more about it. What do you think of it?"

"Well, Dyson, I must say that I think you have contrived to surround the whole thing with a mystery of your own making. I go for the doctor's solution: Black murdered his wife, being himself in all probability an undeveloped lunatic."

"What? Do you believe, then, that this woman was something too awful,too terrible to be allowed to remain on the earth? You will remember that the doctor said it was the brain of a devil?"

"Yes, yes, but he was speaking, of course, metaphorically. It's really quite a simple matter if you only look at it like that."

"Ah, well, you may be right; but yet I am sure you are not. Well, well, it's not good discussing it any more. A little more Benedictine? That's right; try some of this tobacco. Didn't you say that you had been bothered by something – something which happened that night we dined together?"

"Yes, I have been worried, Dyson, worried a great deal. I – but it's such a trivial matter – indeed, such an absurdity – that I feel ashamed to trouble you with it."

"Never mind, let's have it, absurd or not."

With many hesitations, and with much inward resentment of the folly of the thing, Salisbury told his tale, and repeated reluctantly the absurd intelligence and the absurder doggerel of the scrap of paper, expecting to hear Dyson burst out into a roar of laughter.

"Isn't it too bad that I should let myself be bothered by such stuff as that?" he asked, when he had stuttered out the jingle of once, and twice, and thrice.

Dyson had listened to it all gravely, even to the end, and meditated for a few minutes in silence.

"Yes," he said at length, "it was a curious chance, your taking shelter in that archway just as those two went by. But I don't know that I should call what was written on the paper nonsense; it is bizarre certainly but I expect it has a meaning for somebody. Just repeat it again, will you, and I will write it down. Perhaps we might find a cipher of some sort, though I hardly think we shall."

Again had the reluctant lips of Salisbury slowly to stammer out the rubbish that he abhorred, while Dyson jotted it down on a slip of paper.

"Look over it, will you?" he said, when it was done; "It may be important that I should have every word in its place. Is that all right?"

"Yes; that is an accurate copy. But I don't think you will get much out of it. Depend upon it, it is mere nonsense, a wanton scribble. I must be going now, Dyson. No, no more; that stuff of yours is pretty strong. Goodnight."

"I suppose you would like to hear from me, if I did find out anything?"

"No, not I; I don't want to hear about the thing again. You may regard the discovery, if it is one, as your own."

"Very well. Goodnight."

IV

A good many hours after Salisbury had returned to the company of the green rep chairs, Dyson still sat at his desk, itself a Japanese romance, smoking many pipes, and meditating over his friend's story. The bizarre quality of the inscription which had annoyed Salisbury was to him an attraction, and now and again he took it up and scanned thoughtfully what he had written, especially the quaint jingle at the end. It was a token, a symbol, he decided, and not a cipher, and the woman who had flung it away was in all probability entirely ignorant of its meaning; she was but the agent of the "Sam" she had abused and discarded, and he too was again the agent of someone unknown; possibly of the individual styled Q, who had been forced to visit his French friends. But what to make of "Traverse Handel S"? Here was the root and source of the enigma, and not all the tobacco of Virginia seemed likely to suggest any clue here. It seemed almost hopeless, but Dyson regarded himself as the Wellington of mysteries, and went to bed feeling assured that sooner or later he would hit upon the right track. For the next few days he was deeply engaged in his literary labours, labours which were a profound mystery even to the most intimate of his friends, who searched the railway bookstalls in vain for the result of so many hours spent at the Japanese bureau in company with strong tobacco and black tea. On this occasion Dyson confined himself to his room for four days, and it was with genuine relief that he laid down his pen and went out into the streets in quest of relaxation and fresh air. The gas lamps were being lighted, and the fifth edition of the evening papers was being howled through the streets, and Dyson, feeling that he wanted quiet, turned away from the clamorous Strand, and began to trend away to the north-west. Soon he found himself in streets that echoed to his footsteps, and crossing a broad new thoroughfare, and verging still to the west, Dyson discovered that he had penetrated to the depths of Soho. Here again was life; rare vintages of France and Italy, at prices which seemed contemptibly small, allured the passer-by; here were cheeses, vast and rich, here olive oil, and here a grove of Rabelaisian sausages; while in a neighbouring shop the whole Press of Paris appeared to be on sale. In the middle of the roadway a strange miscellany of nations sauntered to and fro, for there cab and hansom rarely ventured; and from window over window the inhabitants looked forth in pleased contemplation of the scene. Dyson made his way slowly along, mingling with the crowd on the cobblestones, listening to the queer babel of French and German, and Italian and English, glancing now and again at the shop windows with their levelled batteries of bottles, and had almost gained the end of the street, when his attention was arrested by a small shop at the corner, a vivid contrast to its neighbours. It was the typical shop of the poor quarter; a shop entirely English. Here were vended tobacco and sweets, cheap pipes of clay and cherry-wood; penny exercise books and pen-holders jostled for precedence with comic songs, and story papers with appalling cuts showed that romance claimed its place beside the actualities of the evening paper, the bills of which fluttered at the doorway. Dyson glanced up at the name above the door, and stood by the kennel trembling, for a sharp pang, the pang of one who has made a discovery, had for a moment left him incapable of motion. The name over the shop was Travers. Dyson looked up again, this time at the corner of the wall above the lamppost, and read in white letters on a blue ground the words "Handel Street, W.C." and the legend was repeated in fainter letters just below. He gave a little sigh of satisfaction, and without more ado walked boldly into the shop, and stared full in the face of the fat man who was sitting behind the counter. The fellow rose to his feet, and returned the stare a little curiously, and then began in stereotyped phrase:

"What can I do for you, sir?"

Dyson enjoyed the situation and a dawning perplexity on the man's face. He propped his stick carefully against the counter and leaning over it, said slowly and impressively:

"Once around the grass, and twice around the lass, and thrice around the maple tree."

Dyson had calculated on his words producing an effect, and he was not disappointed. The vendor of the miscellanies gasped, open-mouthed like a fish, and steadied himself against the counter. When he spoke, after a short interval, it was in a hoarse mutter, tremulous and unsteady.

"Would you mind saying that again, sir? I didn't quite catch it."

"My good man, I shall most certainly do nothing of the kind. You heard what I said perfectly well. You have got a clock in your shop, I see; an admirable timekeeper, I have no doubt. Well, I give you a minute by your own clock."

The man looked about him in a perplexed indecision, and Dyson felt that it was time to be bold.

"Look here, Travers, the time is nearly up. You have heard of Q, I think. Remember, I hold your life in my hands. Now!"

Dyson was shocked at the result of his own audacity. The man shrank and shrivelled in terror, the sweat poured down a face of ashy white, and he held up his hands before him.

"Mr Davies, Mr Davies, don't say that – don't for Heaven's sake. I didn't know you at first, I didn't indeed. Good God! Mr Davies, you wouldn't ruin me? I'll get it in a moment."

"You had better not lose any more time."

The man slunk piteously out of his own shop, and went into a back parlour. Dyson heard his trembling fingers fumbling with a bunch of keys, and the creak of an opening box. He came back presently with a small package neatly tied up in brown paper in his hands, and still, full of terror, handed it to Dyson.

"I'm glad to be rid of it," he said. "I'll take no more jobs of this sort."

Dyson took the parcel and his stick, and walked out of the shop with a nod, turning round as he passed the door. Travers had sunk into his seat, his face still white with terror, with one hand over his eyes, and Dyson speculated a good deal as he walked rapidly away as to what queer chords those could be on which he had played so roughly. He hailed the first hansom he could see and drove home, and when he had lit his hanging lamp, and laid his parcel on the table, he paused for a moment, wondering on what strange thing the lamplight would soon shine. He locked his door, and cut the strings, and unfolded the paper layer after layer, and came at last to a small wooden box, simply but solidly made. There was no lock, and Dyson had simply to raise the lid, and as he did so he drew a long breath and started back. The lamp seemed to glimmer feebly like a single candle, but the whole room blazed with light – and not with light alone, but with a thousand colours, with all the glories of some painted window; and upon the walls of his room and on the familiar furniture, the glow flamed back and seemed to flow again to its source, the little wooden box. For there upon a bed of soft wool lay the most splendid jewel, a jewel such as Dyson had never dreamed of, and within it shone the blue of far skies, and the green of the sea by the shore, and the red of the ruby, and deep violet rays, and in the middle of all it seemed aflame as if a fountain of fire rose up, and fell, and rose again with sparks like stars for drops. Dyson gave a long deep sigh, and dropped into his chair, and put his hands over his eyes to think. The jewel was like an opal, but from a long experience of the shop-windows he knew there was no such thing as an opal one-quarter or one-eighth of its size. He looked at the stone again, with a feeling that was almost awe, and placed it gently on the table under the lamp, and watched the wonderful flame that shone and sparkled in its centre, and then turned to the box, curious to know whether it might contain other marvels. He lifted the bed of wool on which the opal had reclined, and saw beneath no more jewels but a little old pocket-book, worn and shabby with use. Dyson opened it at the first leaf, and dropped the book again appalled. He had read the name of the owner, neatly written in blue ink:

STEVEN BLACK, M.D.,
Oranmore,
Devon Road,
Harlesden.

It was several minutes before Dyson could bring himself to open the book a second time; he remembered the wretched exile in his garret; and his strange talk, and the memory too of the face he had seen at the window, and of what the specialist had said, surged up in his mind, and as he held his finger on the cover, he shivered, dreading what might be written within. When at last he held it in his hand, and turned the pages, he found that the first two leaves were blank, but the third was covered with clear, minute writing, and Dyson began to read with the light of the opal flaming in his eyes.

V

"Ever since I was a young man" – the record began – "I devoted all my leisure and a good deal of time that ought to have been given to other studies to the investigation of curious and obscure branches of knowledge. What are commonly called the pleasures of life had never any attractions for me, and I lived alone in London, avoiding my fellow students, and in my turn avoided by them as a man self-absorbed and unsympathetic. So long as I could gratify my desire of knowledge of a peculiar kind, knowledge of which the very existence is a profound secret to most men, I was intensely happy, and I have often spent whole nights sitting in the darkness of my room, and thinking of the strange world on the brink of which I trod. My professional studies, however, and the necessity of obtaining a degree, for some time forced my more obscure employment into the background, and soon after I had qualified I met Agnes, who became my wife. We took a new house in this remote suburb, and I began the regular routine of a sober practice, and for some months lived happily enough, sharing in the life about me, and only thinking at odd intervals of that occult science which had once fascinated my whole being. I had learnt enough of the paths I had begun to tread to know that they were beyond all expression difficult and dangerous, that to persevere meant in all probability the wreck of a life, and that they led to regions so terrible, that the mind of man shrinks appalled at the very thought. Moreover, the quiet and the peace I had enjoyed since my marriage had wiled me away to a great extent from places where I knew no peace could dwell. But suddenly – I think indeed it was the work of a single night, as I lay awake on my bed gazing into the darkness – suddenly, I say, the old desire, the former longing, returned, and returned with a force that had been intensified ten times by its absence; and when the day dawned and I looked out of the window, and saw with haggard eyes the sunrise in the east, I knew that my doom had been pronounced; that as I had gone far, so now I must go farther with unfaltering steps. I turned to the bed where my wife was sleeping peacefully, and lay down again, weeping bitter tears, for the sun had set on our happy life and had risen with a dawn of terror to us both. I will not set down here in minute detail what followed; outwardly I went about the day's labour as before, saying nothing to my wife. But she soon saw that I had changed; I spent my spare time in a room which I had fitted up as a laboratory, and often I crept upstairs in the grey dawn of the morning, when the light of many lamps still glowed over London; and each night I had stolen a step nearer to that great abyss which I was to bridge over, the gulf between the world of consciousness and the world of matter. My experiments were many and complicated in their nature, and it was some months before I realised whither they all pointed, and when this was borne in upon me in a moment's time, I felt my face whiten and my heart still within me. But the power to draw back, the power to stand before the doors that now opened wide before me and not to enter in, had long ago been absent; the way was closed, and I could only pass onward. My position was as utterly hopeless as that of the prisoner in an utter dungeon, whose only light is that of the dungeon above him; the doors were shut and escape was impossible. Experiment after experiment gave the same result, and I knew, and shrank even as the thought passed through my mind, that in the work I had to do there must be elements which no laboratory could furnish, which no scales could ever measure. In that work, from which even I doubted to escape with life, life itself must enter; from some human being there must be drawn that essence which men call the soul, and in its place (for in the scheme of the world there is no vacant chamber) – in its place would enter in what the lips can hardly utter, what the mind cannot conceive without a horror more awful than the horror of death itself. And when I knew this, I knew also on whom this fate would fall; I looked into my wife's eyes. Even at that hour, if I had gone out and taken a rope and hanged myself, I might have escaped, and she also, but in no other way. At last I told her all. She shuddered, and wept, and called on her dead mother for help, and asked me if I had no mercy, and I could only sigh. I concealed nothing from her; I told her what she would become, and what would enter in where her life had been; I told her of all the shame and of all the horror. You who will read this when I am dead – if indeed I allow this record to survive – you who have opened the box and have seen what lies there, if you could understand what lies hidden in that opal! For one night my wife consented to what I asked of her, consented with the tears running down her beautiful face, and hot shame flushing red over her neck and breast, consented to undergo this for me. I threw open the window, and we looked together at the sky and the dark earth for the last time; it was a fine star-light night, and there was a pleasant breeze blowing: and I kissed her on her lips, and her tears ran down upon my face. That night she came down to my laboratory, and there, with shutters bolted and barred down, with curtains drawn thick and close, so that the very stars might be shut out from the sight of that room, while the crucible hissed and boiled over the lamp, I did what had to be done, and led out what was no longer a woman. But on the table the opal flamed and sparkled with such light as no eyes of man have ever gazed on, and the rays of the flame that was within it flashed and glittered, and shone even to my heart. My wife had only asked one thing of me; that when there came at last what I had told her, I would kill her. I have kept that promise.'

There was nothing more. Dyson let the little pocket-book fall, and turned and looked again at the opal with its flaming inmost light, and then with unutterable irresistible horror surging up in his heart, grasped the jewel, and flung it on the ground, and trampled it beneath his heel. His face was white with terror as he turned away, and for a moment stood sick and trembling, and then with a start he leapt across the room and steadied himself against the door. There was an angry hiss, as of steam escaping under great pressure, and as he gazed, motionless, a volume of heavy yellow smoke was slowly issuing from the very centre of the jewel, and wreathing itself in snake-like coils above it. And then a thin white flame burst forth from the smoke, and shot up into the air and vanished; and on the ground there lay a thing like a cinder, black and crumbling to the touch.

THE TRANSMUTATION OF LING

ERNEST BRAMAH

I

INTRODUCTION

The sun had dipped behind the western mountains before Kai Lung, with twenty li or more still between him and the city of Knei Yang, entered the camphor-laurel forest which stretched almost to his destination. No person of consequence ever made the journey unattended; but Kai Lung professed to have no fear, remarking with extempore wisdom, when warned at the previous village, that a worthless garment covered one with better protection than that afforded by an army of bowmen. Nevertheless, when within the gloomy aisles, Kai Lung more than once wished himself back at the village, or safely behind the mud walls of Knei Yang; and, making many vows concerning the amount of prayer-paper which he would assuredly burn when he was actually through the gates, he stepped out more quickly, until suddenly, at a turn in the glade, he stopped altogether, while the watchful expression into which he had unguardedly dropped at once changed into a mask of impassiveness and extreme unconcern. From behind the next tree projected a long straight rod, not unlike a slender bamboo at a distance but, to Kai Lung's all-seeing eye, in reality the barrel of a matchlock, which would come into line with his breast if he took another step. Being a prudent man, more accustomed to guile and subservience to destiny than to force, he therefore waited, spreading out his hands in proof of his peaceful acquiescence, and smiling cheerfully until it should please the owner of the weapon to step forth. This the unseen did a moment later, still keeping his gun in an easy and convenient attitude, revealing a stout body and a scarred face, which in conjunction made it plain to Kai Lung that he was in the power of Lin Yi, a noted brigand of whom he had heard much in the villages.

"O illustrious person," said Kai Lung very earnestly, "this is evidently an unfortunate mistake. Doubtless you were expecting some exalted Mandarin to come and render you homage, and were preparing to overwhelm him with gratified confusion by escorting him yourself to your well-appointed abode. Indeed, I passed such a one on the road, very richly apparelled, who inquired of me the way to the mansion of the dignified and upright Lin Yi. By this time he is perhaps two or three li towards the east."

"However distinguished a Mandarin may be, it is fitting that I should first attend to one whose manners and accomplishments betray him to be of the Royal House," replied Lin Yi, with extreme affability. "Precede me, therefore, to my mean and uninviting hovel, while I gain more honour than I can reasonably bear by following closely in your elegant footsteps, and guarding your Imperial person with this inadequate but heavily loaded weapon."

Seeing no chance of immediate escape, Kai Lung led the way, instructed by the brigand, along a very difficult and bewildering path, until they reached a cave hidden among the crags. Here Lin Yi called out some words in the Miaotze tongue, whereupon a follower appeared, and opened a gate in the stockade of prickly mimosa which guarded the mouth of the den. Within the enclosure a fire burned, and food was being prepared. At a word from the chief, the unfortunate Kai Lung found his hands seized and tied behind his back, while a second later a rough hemp rope was fixed round his neck, and the other end tied to an overhanging tree.

Lin Yi smiled pleasantly and critically upon these preparations, and when they were complete dismissed his follower.

"Now we can converse at our ease and without restraint," he remarked to Kai Lung. "It will be a distinguished privilege for a person occupying the important public position which you undoubtedly do; for myself, my instincts are so degraded and low-minded that nothing gives me more gratification than to dispense with ceremony."

To this Kai Lung made no reply, chiefly because at that moment the wind swayed the tree, and compelled him to stand on his toes in order to escape suffocation.

"It would be useless to try to conceal from a person of your inspired intelligence that I am indeed Lin Yi," continued the robber. "It is a dignified position to occupy, and one for which I am quite incompetent. In the sixth month of the third year ago, it chanced that this unworthy person, at that time engaged in commercial affairs at Knei Yang, became inextricably immersed in the insidious delights of quail-fighting. Having been entrusted with a large number of taels with which to purchase elephants' teeth, it suddenly occurred to him that if he doubled the number of taels by staking them upon an exceedingly powerful and agile quail, he would be able to purchase twice the number of teeth, and so benefit his patron to a large extent. This matter was clearly forced upon his notice by a dream, in which he perceived one whom he then understood to be the benevolent spirit of an ancestor in the act of stroking a particular quail, upon whose chances he accordingly placed all he possessed. Doubtless evil spirits had been employed in the matter; for, to this person's great astonishment, the quail in question failed in a very discreditable manner at the encounter. Unfortunately, this person had risked not only the money which had been entrusted to him, but all that he had himself become possessed of by some years of honourable toil and assiduous courtesy as a professional witness in law cases. Not doubting that his patron would see that he was himself greatly to blame in confiding so large a sum of money to a comparatively young man of whom he knew little, this person placed the matter before him, at the same time showing him that he would suffer in the eyes of the virtuous if he did not restore this person's savings, which but for the presence of the larger sum, and a generous desire to benefit his patron, he would never have risked in so uncertain a venture as that of quail-fighting. Although the facts were laid in the form of a dignified request instead of a demand by legal means, and the reasoning carefully drawn up in columns of fine parchment by a very illustrious writer, the reply which this person received showed him plainly that a wrong view had been taken of the matter, and that the time had arrived when it became necessary for him to make a suitable rejoinder by leaving the city without delay."

"It was a high-minded and disinterested course to take," said Kai Lung with great conviction, as Lin Yi paused. "Without doubt evil will shortly overtake the avaricious-souled person at Knei Yang."

"It has already done so," replied Lin Yi. "While passing through this forest in the season of Many White Vapours, the spirits of his bad deeds appeared to him in misleading and symmetrical shapes, and drew him out of the path and away from his bowmen. After suffering many torments, he found his way here, where, in spite of our continual care, he perished miserably and in great bodily pain... But I cannot conceal from myself, in spite of your distinguished politeness, that I am becoming intolerably tiresome with my commonplace talk."

"On the contrary," replied Kai Lung, "while listening to your voice I seemed to hear the beating of many gongs of the finest and most polished brass. I floated in the Middle Air, and for the time I even became unconscious of the fact that this honourable appendage, though fashioned, as I perceive, out of the most delicate silk, makes it exceedingly difficult for me to breathe."

"Such a thing cannot be permitted," exclaimed Lin Yi, with some indignation, as with his own hands he slackened the rope and, taking it from Kai Lung's neck, fastened it around his ankle. "Now, in return for my uninviting confidences, shall not my senses be gladdened by a recital of the titles and honours borne by your distinguished family? Doubtless, at this moment many Mandarins of the highest degree are anxiously awaiting your arrival at Knei Yang, perhaps passing the time by outdoing one another in protesting the number of taels each would give rather than permit you to be tormented by fire-brands, or even to lose a single ear."

"Alas!" replied Kai Lung, "Never was there a truer proverb than that which says, 'It is a mark of insincerity of purpose to spend one's time in looking for the sacred Emperor in the low-class teashops.' Do Mandarins or the friends of Mandarins travel in mean garments and unattended? Indeed, the person who is now before you is none other than the outcast Kai Lung, the storyteller, one of degraded habits and no very distinguished or reputable ancestors. His friends are few, and mostly of the criminal class; his wealth is not more than some six or eight *cash*, concealed in his left sandal; and his entire stock-in-trade consists of a few unendurable and badly told stories, to which, however, it is his presumptuous intention shortly to add a dignified narrative of the high-born Lin Yi, setting out his domestic virtues and the honour which he has reflected upon his house, his valour in war, the destruction of his enemies and, above all, his great benevolence and the protection which he extends to the poor and those engaged in the distinguished arts."

"The absence of friends is unfortunate," said Lin Yi thoughtfully, after he had possessed himself of the coins indicated by Kai Lung, and also of a much larger amount concealed elsewhere among the storyteller's clothing. "My followers are mostly outlawed Miaotze, who have been driven from their own tribes in Yun Nan for man-eating and disregarding the sacred laws of hospitality. They are somewhat rapacious, and in this way it has become a custom that they should have as their own, for the purpose of exchanging for money, persons such as yourself, whose insatiable curiosity has led them to this place."

"The wise and all-knowing Emperor Fohy instituted three degrees of attainment: being poor, to obtain justice; being rich, to escape flattery; and being human, to avoid the passions," replied Kai Lung. "To these the practical and enlightened Kâng added yet another, the greatest: being lean, to yield fatness."

"In such cases," observed the brigand, "the Miaotze keep an honoured and very venerable rite, which chiefly consists in suspending the offender by a pigtail from a low tree, and placing burning twigs of hemp-palm between his toes. To this person it seems a foolish and meaningless habit; but it would not be well to interfere with their religious observances, however trivial they may appear."

"Such a course must inevitably end in great loss," suggested Kai Lung; "for undoubtedly there are many poor yet honourable persons who would leave with them a bond for a large number of taels and save the money with which to redeem it, rather than take part in a ceremony which is not according to one's own Book of Rites."

"They have already suffered in that way on one or two occasions," replied Lin Yi; "so that such a proposal, no matter how nobly intended, would not gladden their faces. Yet they are simple and docile persons, and would, without doubt, be moved to any feeling you should desire by the recital of one of your illustrious stories."

"An intelligent and discriminating assemblage is more to a storyteller than much reward of *cash* from hands that conceal open mouths," replied Kai Lung with great feeling. "Nothing would confer more pleasurable agitation upon this unworthy person than an opportunity of narrating his entire stock to them. If also the accomplished Lin Yi would bestow renown upon the occasion by his presence, no omen of good would be wanting."

"The pleasures of the city lie far behind me," said Lin Yi, after some thought, "and I would cheerfully submit myself to an intellectual accomplishment such as you are undoubtedly capable of. But as we have necessity to leave this spot before the hour when the oak leaves change into night moths, one of your amiable stories will be the utmost we can strengthen our intellects with. Select which you will. In the meantime, food will be brought to refresh you after your benevolent exertions in conversing with a person of my vapid understanding. When you have partaken, or thrown it away as utterly unendurable, the time will have arrived, and this person, together with all his accomplices, will put themselves in a position to be subjected to all the most dignified emotions."

II

"The story which I have selected for this gratifying occasion," said Kai Lung, when, an hour or so later, still pinioned, but released from the halter, he sat surrounded by the brigands, "is entitled 'Good and Evil', and it is concerned with the adventures of one Ling, who bore the honourable name of Ho. The first, and indeed the greater, part of the narrative, as related by the venerable and accomplished writer of history Chow-Tan, is taken up by showing how Ling was assuredly descended from an enlightened Emperor of the race of Tsin; but as the no less omniscient Ta-lin-hi proves beyond doubt that the person in question was in no way connected with any but a line of hereditary ape-worshippers, who entered China from an unknown country many centuries ago, it would ill become this illiterate person to express an opinion on either side, and he will in consequence omit the first seventeen books of the story, and only deal with the three which refer to the illustrious Ling himself."

THE STORY OF LING, NARRATED BY KAI LUNG WHEN A PRISONER IN THE CAMP OF LIN YI

Ling was the youngest of three sons, and from his youth upwards proved to be of a mild and studious disposition. Most of his time was spent in reading the sacred books, and at an early age he found the worship of apes to be repulsive to his gentle nature, and resolved to break through the venerable traditions of his family by devoting his time to literary pursuits, and presenting himself for the public examinations at Canton. In this his resolution was strengthened by a rumour that an army of bowmen was shortly to be raised from the Province in which he lived, so that if he remained he would inevitably be forced into an occupation which was even more distasteful to him than the one he was leaving.

Having arrived at Canton, Ling's first care was to obtain particulars of the examinations, which he clearly perceived, from the unusual activity displayed on all sides, to be near at hand. On inquiring from passers-by, he received very conflicting information; for the persons to whom he spoke were themselves entered for the competition, and therefore naturally misled him in order to increase their own chances of success. Perceiving this, Ling determined to apply at once, although the light was past, to a Mandarin who was concerned in the examinations, lest by delay he should lose his chance for the year.

"It is an unfortunate event that so distinguished a person should have selected this day and hour on which to overwhelm us with his affable politeness!" exclaimed the porter at the gate of the Yamen, when Ling had explained his reason for going. "On such a day, in the reign of the virtuous Emperor Hoo Chow, a very benevolent and unassuming ancestor of my good lord the Mandarin was destroyed by treachery, and ever since his family has observed the occasion by fasting and no music. This person would certainly be punished with death if he entered the inner room from any cause."

At these words, Ling, who had been simply brought up, and chiefly in the society of apes, was going away with many expressions of self-reproach at selecting such a time, when the gate-keeper called him back.

"I am overwhelmed with confusion at the position in which I find myself," he remarked, after he had examined his mind for a short time. "I may meet with an ungraceful and objectionable death if I carry out your estimable instructions, but I shall certainly merit and receive a similar fate if I permit so renowned and versatile a person to leave without a fitting reception. In such matters a person can only trust to the intervention of good spirits; if, therefore, you will permit this unworthy individual to wear, while making the venture, the ring which he perceives upon your finger, and which he recognises as a very powerful charm against evil, misunderstandings and extortion, he will go without fear."

Overjoyed at the amiable porter's efforts on his behalf, Ling did as he was desired, and the other retired. Presently the door of the Yamên was opened by an attendant of the house, and Ling bidden to enter. He was covered with astonishment to find that this person was entirely unacquainted with his name or purpose.

"Alas!" said the attendant, when Ling had explained his object. "Well said the renowned and inspired Ting Fo, 'When struck by a thunderbolt it is unnecessary to consult the Book of Dates as to the precise meaning of the omen.' At this moment my noble-minded master is engaged in conversation with all the most honourable and refined persons in Canton, while singers and dancers of a very expert and nimble order have been sent for. The entertainment will undoubtedly last far into the night, and to present myself even with the excuse of your graceful and delicate inquiry would certainly result in very objectionable consequences to this person."

"It is indeed a day of unprepossessing circumstances," replied Ling, and after many honourable remarks concerning his own intellect and appearance, and those of the person to whom he was speaking, he had turned to leave when the other continued:

"Ever since your dignified presence illumined this very ordinary chamber, this person has been endeavouring to bring to his mind an incident which occurred to him last night while he slept. Now it has come back to him with a diamond clearness, and he is satisfied that it was as follows: while he floated in the Middle Air a benevolent spirit in the form of an elderly and toothless vampire appeared, leading by the hand a young man of elegant personality. Smiling encouragingly upon this person, the spirit said, 'O Fou, recipient of many favours from Mandarins and of innumerable taels from gratified persons whom you have obliged, I am, even at this moment, guiding this exceptional young man towards your presence; when he arrives do not hesitate, but do as he desires, no matter how great the danger seems or how inadequately you may appear to be rewarded on earth.' The vision then melted, but I now clearly perceive that with the exception of the embroidered cloak which you wear, you are the person thus indicated to me. Remove your cloak, therefore, in order to give the amiable spirit no opportunity of denying the fact, and I will advance your wishes; for, as the Book of Verses indicates, 'The person who patiently awaits a sign from the clouds for many years, and yet fails to notice the earthquake at his feet, is devoid of intellect.'"

Convinced that he was assuredly under the especial protection of the Deities, and that the end of his search was in view, Ling gave his rich cloak to the attendant, and was immediately shown into another room, where he was left alone.

After a considerable space of time the door opened and there entered a person whom Ling at first supposed to be the Mandarin. Indeed, he was addressing him by his titles when the other interrupted him. "Do not distress your incomparable mind by searching for honourable names to apply to so inferior a person as myself," he said agreeably. "The mistake is, nevertheless, very natural; for, however miraculous it may appear, this unseemly individual, who is in reality merely a writer of spoken words, is admitted to be exceedingly like the dignified Mandarin himself, though somewhat stouter, clad in better garments and, it is said, less obtuse of intellect. This last matter he very much doubts, for he now finds himself unable to recognise by name one who is undoubtedly entitled to wear the Royal Yellow."

With this encouragement Ling once more explained his position, narrating the events which had enabled him to reach the second chamber of the Yamen. When he had finished the secretary was overpowered with a high-minded indignation.

"Assuredly those depraved and rapacious persons who have both misled and robbed you shall suffer bowstringing when the whole matter is brought to light," he exclaimed. "The noble Mandarin neither fasts nor receives guests, for indeed he has slept since the sun went down. This person would unhesitatingly break his slumber for so commendable a purpose were it not for a circumstance of intolerable unavoidableness. It must not even be told in a low breath beyond the walls of the Yamên, but my benevolent and high-born lord is in reality a person of very miserly instinct, and nothing will call him from his natural sleep but the sound of taels shaken beside his bed. In an unexpected manner it comes about that this person is quite unsupplied with anything but thin printed papers of a thousand taels each, and these are quite useless for the purpose."

"It is unendurable that so obliging a person should be put to such inconvenience on behalf of one who will certainly become a public laughing-stock at the examinations," said Ling, with deep feeling; and taking from a concealed spot in his garments a few taels, he placed them before the secretary for the use he had indicated.

Ling was again left alone for upwards of two strokes of the gong, and was on the point of sleep when the secretary returned with an expression of dignified satisfaction upon his countenance. Concluding that he had been successful in the manner of awakening the Mandarin, Ling was opening his mouth for a polite speech, which should contain a delicate allusion to the taels, when the secretary warned him, by affecting a sudden look of terror, that silence was exceedingly desirable, and at the same time opened another door and indicated to Ling that he should pass through.

In the next room Ling was overjoyed to find himself in the presence of the Mandarin, who received him graciously, and paid many estimable compliments to the name he bore and the country from which he came. When at length Ling tore himself from this enchanting conversation, and explained the reason of his presence, the Mandarin at once became a prey to the whitest and most melancholy emotions, even plucking two hairs from his pigtail to prove the extent and conscientiousness of his grief.

"Behold," he cried at length, "I am resolved that the extortionate and many-handed persons at Peking who have control of the examination rites and customs shall no longer grow round-bodied without remark. This person will unhesitatingly proclaim the true facts of the case without regarding the danger that the versatile Chancellor or even the sublime Emperor himself may, while he speaks, be concealed in some part of this unassuming room to hear his words; for, as it is wisely said, 'When marked out by destiny, a person will assuredly be drowned, even though he passes the whole of his existence among the highest branches of a date tree.'"

"I am overwhelmed that I should be the cause of such an engaging display of polished agitation," said Ling, as the Mandarin paused. "If it would make your own stomach less heavy, this person will willingly follow your estimable example, either with or without knowing the reason."

"The matter is altogether on your account, O most unobtrusive young man," replied the Mandarin, when a voice without passion was restored to him. "It tears me internally with hooks to reflect that you, whose refined ancestors I might reasonably have known had I passed my youth in another Province, should be victim to the cupidity of the ones in authority at Peking. A very short time before you arrived there came a messenger in haste from those persons, clearly indicating that a legal toll of sixteen taels was to be made on each printed paper setting forth the time and manner of the examinations, although, as you may see, the paper is undoubtedly marked, 'Persons are given notice that they are defrauded of any sum which they may be induced to exchange for this matter.' Furthermore, there is a legal toll of nine taels on all persons who have previously been examined –"

"I am happily escaped from that," exclaimed Ling with some satisfaction as the Mandarin paused.

"– and twelve taels on all who present themselves for the first time. This is to be delivered over when the paper is purchased, so that you, by reason of this unworthy proceeding at Peking, are required to forward to that place, through this person, no less than thirty-two taels."

"It is a circumstance of considerable regret," replied Ling; "for had I only reached Canton a day earlier, I should, it appears, have avoided this evil."

"Undoubtedly it would have been so," replied the Mandarin, who had become engrossed in exalted meditation. "However," he continued a moment later, as he bowed to Ling with an accomplished smile, "it would certainly be a more pleasant thought for a person of your refined intelligence that had you delayed until tomorrow the insatiable persons at Peking might be demanding twice the amount."

Pondering the deep wisdom of this remark, Ling took his departure; but in spite of the most assiduous watchfulness he was unable to discern any of the three obliging persons to whose efforts his success had been due.

III

It was very late when Ling again reached the small room which he had selected as soon as he reached Canton, but without waiting for food or sleep he made himself fully acquainted with the times of the forthcoming examinations and the details of the circumstances connected with them. With much satisfaction he found that he had still a week in which to revive his intellect on the most difficult subjects. Having become relieved on these points, Ling retired for a few hours' sleep, but rose again very early, and gave the whole day with great steadfastness to contemplation of the sacred classics Y-King, with the exception of a short period spent in purchasing ink, brushes and writing-leaves. The following day, having become mentally depressed through witnessing unaccountable hordes of candidates thronging the streets of Canton, Ling put aside his books, and passed the time in visiting all the most celebrated tombs in the neighbourhood of the city.

Lightened in mind by this charitable and agreeable occupation, he returned to his studies with a fixed resolution, nor did he again falter in his purpose.

On the evening of the examination, when he was sitting alone, reading by the aid of a single light, as his custom was, a person arrived to see him, at the same time manifesting a considerable appearance of secrecy and reserve. Inwardly sighing at the interruption, Ling nevertheless received him with distinguished consideration and respect, setting tea before him, and performing towards it many honourable actions with his own hands. Not until some hours had sped in conversation relating to the health of the Emperor, the unexpected appearance of a fiery dragon outside the city and the insupportable price of opium, did the visitor allude to the object of his presence.

"It has been observed," he remarked, "that the accomplished Ling, who aspires to a satisfactory rank at the examinations, has never before made the attempt. Doubtless in this case a preternatural wisdom will avail much, and its fortunate possessor will not go unrewarded. Yet it is as precious stones among ashes for one to triumph in such circumstances."

"The fact is known to this person," replied Ling sadly, "and the thought of the years he may have to wait before he shall have passed even the first degree weighs down his soul with bitterness from time to time."

"It is no infrequent thing for men of accomplished perseverance, but merely ordinary intellects, to grow venerable within the four walls of the examination cell," continued the other. "Some, again, become afflicted with various malignant evils, while not a few, chiefly those who are presenting themselves for the first time, are so overcome on perceiving the examination paper, and understanding the inadequate nature of their own accomplishments, that they become an easy prey to the malicious spirits which are ever on the watch in those places; and, after covering their leaves with unpresentable remarks and drawings of men and women of distinguished rank, have at length to be forcibly carried away by the attendants and secured with heavy chains."

"Such things undoubtedly exist," agreed Ling; "yet by a due regard paid to spirits, both good and bad, a proper esteem for one's ancestors, and a sufficiency of charms about the head and body, it is possible to be closeted with all manner of demons and yet to suffer no evil."

"It is undoubtedly possible to do so, according to the Immortal Principles," admitted the stranger; "but it is not an undertaking in which a refined person would take intelligent pleasure; as the proverb says, 'He is a wise and enlightened suppliant who seeks to discover an honourable

Mandarin, but he is a fool who cries out, "I have found one."' However, it is obvious that the reason of my visit is understood, and that your distinguished confidence in yourself is merely a graceful endeavour to obtain my services for a less amount of taels than I should otherwise have demanded. For half the usual sum, therefore, this person will take your place in the examination cell, and enable your versatile name to appear in the winning lists, while you pass your moments in irreproachable pleasures elsewhere."

Such a course had never presented itself to Ling. As the person who narrates this story has already marked, he had passed his life beyond the influence of the ways and manners of towns, and at the same time he had naturally been endowed with an unobtrusive high-mindedness. It appeared to him, in consequence, that by accepting this engaging offer he would be placing those who were competing with him at a disadvantage. This person clearly sees that it is a difficult matter for him to explain how this could be, as Ling would undoubtedly reward the services of the one who took his place, nor would the number of the competitors be in any way increased; yet in such a way the thing took shape before his eyes. Knowing, however, that few persons would be able to understand this action, and being desirous of not injuring the estimable emotions of the obliging person who had come to him, Ling made a number of polished excuses in declining, hiding the true reason within himself. In this way he earned the powerful malignity of the person in question, who would not depart until he had effected a number of very disagreeable prophecies connected with unpropitious omens and internal torments, all of which undoubtedly had a great influence on Ling's life beyond that time.

Each day of the examination found Ling alternately elated or depressed, according to the length and style of the essay which he had written while enclosed in his solitary examination cell. The trials each lasted a complete day, and long before the fifteen days which composed the full examination were passed, Ling found himself half regretting that he had not accepted his visitor's offer, or even reviling the day on which he had abandoned the hereditary calling of his ancestors. However, when, after all was over, he came to deliberate with himself on his chances of attaining a degree, he could not disguise from his own mind that he had well-formed hopes; he was not conscious of any undignified errors, and, in reply to several questions, he had been able to introduce curious knowledge which he possessed by means of his exceptional circumstances – knowledge which it was unlikely that any other candidate would have been able to make himself master of.

At length the day arrived on which the results were to be made public; and Ling, together with all the other competitors and many distinguished persons, attended at the great Hall of Intellectual Coloured Lights to hear the reading of the lists. Eight thousand candidates had been examined, and from this number less than two hundred were to be selected for appointments. Amid a most distinguished silence the winning names were read out. Waves of most undignified but inevitable emotion passed over those assembled as the list neared its end, and the chances of success became less at each spoken word. Nevertheless, Ling hoped till the last name was given forth; and then, finding that his was not among them, together with the greater part of those present, he became a prey to very inelegant thoughts, which were not lessened by the refined cries of triumph of the successful persons. Among this confusion the one who had read the lists was observed to be endeavouring to make his voice known, whereupon, in the expectation that he had omitted a name, the tumult was quickly subdued by those who again had pleasurable visions.

"There was among the candidates one of the name of Ling," said he, when no noise had been obtained. "The written leaves produced by this person are of a most versatile and conflicting order, so that, indeed, the accomplished examiners themselves are unable to decide whether they are very good or very bad. In this matter, therefore, it is clearly impossible to place the expert and inimitable Ling among the foremost, as his very uncertain success may have been brought about with the assistance of evil spirits; nor would it be safe to pass over his efforts without reward, as he may be under the protection of powerful but exceedingly ill-advised deities. The estimable Ling is told to appear again at this place after the gong has been struck three times, when the matter will have been looked at from all round."

At this announcement there arose another great tumult, several crying out that assuredly their written leaves were either very good or very bad; but no further proclamation was made, and very soon the hall was cleared by force.

At the time stated Ling again presented himself at the Hall, and was honourably received.

"The unusual circumstances of the matter have already been put forth," said an elderly Mandarin of engaging appearance, "so that nothing remains to be made known except the end of our despicable efforts to come to an agreeable conclusion. In this we have been made successful, and now desire to notify the result. A very desirable and not unremunerative office, rarely bestowed in this manner, is lately vacant, and taking into our minds the circumstances of the event, and the fact that Ling comes from a Province very esteemed for the warlike instincts of its inhabitants, we have decided to appoint him commander of the valiant and blood-thirsty band of archers now stationed at Si-chow, in the Province of Hu-Nan. We have spoken. Let three guns go off in honour of the noble and invincible Ling, now and henceforth a commander in the ever-victorious Army of the Sublime Emperor, brother of the Sun and Moon, and Upholder of the Four Corners of the World."

IV

Many hours passed before Ling, now more downcast in mind than the most unsuccessful student in Canton, returned to his room and sought his couch of dried rushes. All his efforts to have his distinguished appointment set aside had been without avail, and he had been ordered to reach Si-chow within a week. As he passed through the streets, elegant processions in honour of the winners met him at every corner, and drove him into the outskirts for the object of quietness. There he remained until the beating of paper drums and the sound of exulting voices could be heard no more; but even when he returned lanterns shone in many dwellings, for two hundred persons were composing verses, setting forth their renown and undoubted accomplishments, ready to affix to their doors and send to friends on the next day.

Not giving any portion of his mind to this desirable act of behaviour, Ling flung himself upon the floor and, finding sleep unattainable, plunged himself into profound meditation of a very uninviting order.

"Without doubt," he exclaimed, "evil can only arise from evil, and as this person has always endeavoured to lead a life in which his devotions have been equally divided between the sacred Emperor, his illustrious parents and his venerable ancestors, the fault cannot lie with him. Of the excellence of his parents he has full knowledge; regarding the Emperor, it might not be safe to conjecture. It is therefore probable that some of his ancestors were persons of abandoned manner and inelegant habits, to worship whom results in evil rather than good. Otherwise, how could it be that one whose chief delight lies in the passive contemplation of the Four Books and the Five Classics, should be selected by destiny to fill a position calling for great personal courage and an aggressive nature? Assuredly it can only end in a mean and insignificant death, perhaps not even followed by burial."

In this manner of thought he fell asleep, and after certain very base and impressive dreams, from which good omens were altogether absent, he awoke, and rose to begin his preparations for leaving the city.

After two days spent chiefly in obtaining certain safeguards against treachery and the bullets of foe-men, purchasing opium and other gifts with which to propitiate the soldiers under his charge, and in consulting well-disposed witches and readers of the future, he set out, and by travelling in extreme discomfort, reached Si-chow within five days. During his journey he learned that the entire Province was engaged in secret rebellion, several towns, indeed, having declared against the Imperial army without reserve. Those persons to whom Ling spoke described the rebels, with respectful admiration, as fierce and unnaturally skilful in all methods of fighting, revengeful and merciless towards their enemies, very numerous and above the ordinary height of human beings, and endowed with qualities which made their skin capable of turning aside every kind of weapon. Furthermore, he was assured that a large band of the most abandoned and best trained was at that moment in the immediate neighbourhood of Si-chow.

Ling was not destined long to remain in any doubt concerning the truth of these matters, for as he made his way through a dark cypress wood, a few li from the houses of Si-chow, the sounds of a confused outcry reached his ears, and on stepping aside to a hidden glade some distance from the path, he beheld a young and elegant maiden of incomparable beauty being carried away by two persons of most repulsive and undignified appearance, whose dress and manner clearly betrayed them to be rebels of the lowest and worst-paid type. At this sight, Ling became possessed of feelings of a savage yet agreeable order, which until that time he had not conjectured to have any place within his mind, and without even pausing to consider whether the planets were in favourable positions for the enterprise to be undertaken at that time, he drew his sword and ran forward with loud cries. Unsettled in their intentions at this unexpected action, the two persons turned and advanced upon Ling with whirling daggers, discussing among themselves whether it would be better to kill him at the first blow or to take him alive, and, when the day had become sufficiently cool for the full enjoyment of the spectacle, submit him to various objectionable tortures of so degraded a nature that they were rarely used in the army of the Emperor except upon the persons of barbarians. Observing that the maiden was not bound, Ling cried out to her to escape and seek protection within the town, adding, with a magnanimous absence of vanity:

"Should this person chance to fall, the repose which the presence of so lovely and graceful a being would undoubtedly bring to his departing spirit would be out-balanced by the unendurable thought that his commonplace efforts had not been sufficient to save her from the two evilly disposed individuals who are, as he perceives, at this moment, neglecting no means within their power to accomplish his destruction."

Accepting the discernment of these words, the maiden fled, first bestowing a look upon Ling which clearly indicated an honourable regard for himself, a high-minded desire that the affair might end profitably on his account, and an amiable hope that they should meet again, when these subjects could be expressed more clearly between them.

In the meantime Ling had become at a disadvantage, for the time occupied in speaking and in making the necessary number of bows in reply to her entrancing glance had given the other persons an opportunity of arranging their charms and sacred written sentences to greater advantage, and of occupying the most favourable ground for the encounter. Nevertheless, so great was the force of the new emotion which had entered into Ling's nature that, without waiting to consider the dangers or the best method of attack, he rushed upon them, waving his sword with such force that he appeared as though surrounded by a circle of very brilliant fire. In this way he reached the rebels, who both fell unexpectedly at one blow, they, indeed, being under the impression that the encounter had not commenced in reality, and that Ling was merely menacing them in order to inspire their minds with terror and raise his own spirits. However much he regretted this act of the incident which he had been compelled to take, Ling could not avoid being filled with intellectual joy at finding that his own charms and omens were more distinguished than those possessed by the rebels, none of whom, as he now plainly understood, he need fear.

Examining these things within his mind, and reflecting on the events of the past few days, by which he had been thrown into a class of circumstances greatly differing from anything which he had ever sought, Ling continued his journey, and soon found himself before the southern gate of Si-chow. Entering the town, he at once formed the resolution of going before the Mandarin for Warlike Deeds and Arrangements, so that he might present, without delay, the papers and seals which he had brought with him from Canton.

"The noble Mandarin Li Keen?" replied the first person to whom Ling addressed himself. "It would indeed be a difficult and hazardous conjecture to make concerning his sacred person. By chance he is in the strongest and best-concealed cellar in Si-chow, unless the sumptuous attractions of the deepest dry well have induced him to make a short journey;" and, with a look of great unfriendliness at Ling's dress and weapons, this person passed on.

"Doubtless he is fighting single-handed against the armed men by whom the place is surrounded," said another; "or perhaps he is constructing an underground road from the Yamên to Peking, so that we may all escape when the town is taken. All that can be said with certainty is that the Heaven-sent and valorous Mandarin has not been seen outside the walls of his well-fortified residence since the trouble arose; but, as you carry a sword of conspicuous excellence, you will doubtless be welcome."

Upon making a third attempt Ling was more successful, for he inquired of an aged woman, who had neither a reputation for keen and polished sentences to maintain, nor any interest in the acts of the Mandarin or of the rebels. From her he learned how to reach the Yamên, and accordingly turned his footsteps in that direction.

When at length he arrived at the gate, Ling desired his tablets to be carried to the Mandarin with many expressions of an impressive and engaging nature, nor did he neglect to reward the porter. It was therefore with the expression of a misunderstanding mind that he received a reply setting forth that Li Keen was unable to receive him. In great doubt he prevailed upon the porter, by means of a still larger reward, again to carry in his message, and on this occasion an answer in this detail was placed before him.

"Li Keen," he was informed, "is indeed awaiting the arrival of one Ling, a noble and valiant Commander of Bowmen. He is given to understand, it is true, that a certain person claiming the same honoured name is standing in somewhat undignified attitudes at the gate, but he is unable in any way to make these two individuals meet within his intellect. He would further remind all persons that the refined observances laid down by the wise and exalted Board of Rites and Ceremonies have a marked and irreproachable significance when the country is in a state of disorder, the town surrounded by rebels, and every breathing-space of time of more than ordinary value."

Overpowered with becoming shame at having been connected with so unseemly a breach of civility, for which his great haste had in reality been accountable, Ling hastened back into the town, and spent many hours endeavouring to obtain a chair of the requisite colour in which to visit the

Mandarin. In this he was unsuccessful, until it was at length suggested to him that an ordinary chair, such as stood for hire in the streets of Si-chow, would be acceptable if covered with blue paper. Still in some doubt as to what the nature of his reception would be, Ling had no choice but to take this course, and accordingly he again reached the Yamen in such a manner, carried by two persons whom he had obtained for the purpose. While yet hardly at the residence a salute was suddenly fired; all the gates and doors were, without delay, thrown open with embarrassing and hospitable profusion, and the Mandarin himself passed out, and would have assisted Ling to step down from his chair had not that person, clearly perceiving that such a course would be too great an honour, evaded him by an unobtrusive display of versatile dexterity. So numerous and profound were the graceful remarks which each made concerning the habits and accomplishments of the other that more than the space of an hour was passed in traversing the small enclosed ground which led up to the principal door of the Yamen. There an almost greater time was agreeably spent, both Ling and the Mandarin having determined that the other should enter first. Undoubtedly Ling, who was the more powerful of the two, would have conferred this courteous distinction upon Li Keen had not that person summoned to his side certain attendants who succeeded in frustrating Ling in his high-minded intentions, and in forcing him through the doorway in spite of his conscientious protests against the unsurmountable obligation under which the circumstance placed him.

Conversing in this intellectual and dignified manner, the strokes of the gong passed unheeded; tea had been brought into their presence many times, and night had fallen before the Mandarin allowed Ling to refer to the matter which had brought him to the place, and to present his written papers and seals.

"It is a valuable privilege to have so intelligent a person as the illustrious Ling occupying this position," remarked the Mandarin, as he returned the papers; "and not less so on account of the one who preceded him proving himself to be a person of feeble attainments and an unendurable deficiency of resource."

"To one with the all-knowing Li Keen's mental acquisitions, such a person must indeed have become excessively offensive," replied Ling delicately; "for, as it is truly said, 'Although there exist many thousand subjects for elegant conversation, there are persons who cannot meet a cripple without talking about feet.'"

"He to whom I have referred was such a one," said Li Keen, appreciating with an expression of countenance the fitness of Ling's proverb. "He was totally inadequate to the requirements of his position; for he possessed no military knowledge, and was placed in command by those at Peking as a result of his taking a high place at one of the examinations. But more than this, although his three years of service were almost completed, I was quite unsuccessful in convincing him that an unseemly degradation probably awaited him unless he could furnish me with the means with which to propitiate the persons in authority at Peking. This he neglected to do with obstinate pertinacity, which compelled this person to inquire within himself whether one of so little discernment could be trusted with an important and arduous office. After much deliberation, this person came to the decision that the Commander in question was not a fit person, and he therefore reported him to the Imperial Board of Punishment at Peking as one subject to frequent and periodical eccentricities, and possessed of less than ordinary intellect. In consequence of this act of justice, the Commander was degraded to the rank of common bowman, and compelled to pay a heavy fine in addition."

"It was a just and enlightened conclusion of the affair," said Ling, in spite of a deep feeling of no enthusiasm, "and one which surprisingly bore out your own prophecy in the matter."

"It was an inspired warning to persons who should chance to be in a like position at any time," replied Li Keen. "So grasping and corrupt are those who control affairs in Peking that I have no doubt they would scarcely hesitate in debasing even one so immaculate as the exceptional Ling, and placing him in some laborious and ill-paid civil department should he not accede to their extortionate demands."

This suggestion did not carry with it the unpleasurable emotions which the Mandarin anticipated it would. The fierce instincts which had been aroused within Ling by the incident in the cypress wood had died out, while his lamentable ignorance of military affairs was ever before his mind. These circumstances, together with his naturally gentle habits, made him regard such a degradation rather favourably than otherwise. He was meditating within himself whether he could arrange such a course without delay when the Mandarin continued:

"That, however, is a possibility which is remote to the extent of at least two or three years; do not, therefore, let so unpleasing a thought cast darkness upon your brows or remove the unparalleled splendour of so refined an occasion… Doubtless the accomplished Ling is a master of the art of chess-play, for many of our most thoughtful philosophers have declared war to be nothing but such a game; let this slow-witted and cumbersome person have an opportunity, therefore, of polishing his declining facilities by a pleasant and dignified encounter."

V

On the next day, having completed his business at the Yamên, Ling left the town, and without desiring any ceremony quietly betook himself to his new residence within the camp, which was situated among the millet fields some distance from Si-chow. As soon as his presence became known all those who occupied positions of command, and whose years of service would shortly come to an end, hastened to present themselves before him, bringing with them offerings according to the rank they held, they themselves requiring a similar service from those beneath them. First among these, and next in command to Ling himself, was the Chief of Bowmen, a person whom Ling observed with extreme satisfaction to be very powerful in body and possessing a strong and dignified countenance which showed unquestionable resolution and shone with a tiger-like tenaciousness of purpose.

"Undoubtedly," thought Ling, as he observed this noble and prepossessing person, "here is one who will be able to assist me in whatever perplexities may arise. Never was there an individual who seemed more worthy to command and lead; assuredly to him the most intricate and prolonged military positions will be an enjoyment; the most crafty stratagems of the enemy as the full moon rising from behind a screen of rushes. Without making any pretence of knowledge, this person will explain the facts of the case to him and place himself without limit in his hands."

For this purpose he therefore detained the Chief of Bowmen when the others departed, and complimented him, with many expressive phrases, on the excellence of his appearance, as the thought occurred to him that by this means, without disclosing the full measure of his ignorance, the person in question might be encouraged to speak unrestrainedly of the nature of his exploits, and perchance thereby explain the use of the appliances employed and the meaning of the various words of order, in all of which details the Commander was as yet most disagreeably imperfect. In this, however, he was disappointed, for the Chief of Bowmen, greatly to Ling's surprise, received all his polished sentences with somewhat foolish smiles of great self-satisfaction, merely replying from time to time as he displayed his pigtail to greater advantage or rearranged his gold-embroidered cloak:

"This person must really pray you to desist; the honour is indeed too great."

Disappointed in his hope, and not desiring after this circumstance to expose his shortcomings to one who was obviously not of a highly refined understanding, no matter how great his valour in war or his knowledge of military affairs might be, Ling endeavoured to lead him to converse of the bowmen under his charge. In this matter he was more successful, for the Chief spoke at great length and with evilly inspired contempt of their inelegance, their undiscriminating and excessive appetites, and the frequent use which they made of low words and gestures. Desiring to become acquainted rather with their methods of warfare than with their domestic details, Ling inquired of him what formation they relied upon when receiving the foe-men.

"It is a matter which has not engaged the attention of this one," replied the Chief, with an excessive absence of interest. "There are so many affairs of intelligent dignity which cannot be put aside, and which occupy one from beginning to end. As an example, this person may describe how the accomplished Li-Lu, generally depicted as the Blue-eyed Dove of Virtuous and Serpent-like Attitudes, has been scattering glory upon the Si-chow Hall of Celestial Harmony for many days past. It is an enlightened display which the high-souled Ling should certainly endeavour to dignify with his presence, especially at the portion where the amiable Li-Lu becomes revealed in the appearance of a Peking sedan-chair bearer and describes the manner and likenesses of certain persons – chiefly high-priests of Buddha, excessively round-bodied merchants who feign to be detained within Peking on affairs of commerce, maidens who attend at the tables of tea-houses, and those of both sexes who are within the city for the first time to behold its temples and open spaces – who are conveyed from place to place in the chair."

"And the bowmen?" suggested Ling, with difficulty restraining an undignified emotion.

"Really, the elegant Ling will discover them to be persons of deficient manners, and quite unworthy of occupying his well-bred conversation," replied the Chief. "As regards their methods – if the renowned Ling insists – they fight by means of their bows, with which they discharge arrows at the foe-men, they themselves hiding behind trees and rocks. Should the enemy be undisconcerted by the cloud of arrows, and advance, the bowmen are instructed to make a last endeavour to frighten them back by uttering loud shouts and feigning the voices of savage beasts of the forest and deadly snakes."

"And beyond that?" inquired Ling.

"Beyond that there are no instructions," replied the Chief. "The bowmen would then naturally take to flight, or, if such a course became impossible, run to meet the enemy, protesting that they were convinced of the justice of their cause, and were determined to fight on their side in the future."

"Would it not be of advantage to arm them with cutting weapons also?" inquired Ling; "so that when all their arrows were discharged they would still be able to take part in the fight, and not be lost to us?"

"They would not be lost to us, of course," replied the Chief, "as we would still be with them. But such a course as the one you suggest could not fail to end in dismay. Being as well armed as ourselves, they would then turn upon us and, having destroyed us, proceed to establish leaders of their own."

As Ling and the Chief of Bowmen conversed in this enlightened manner, there arose a great outcry from among the tents, and presently there entered to them a spy who had discovered a strong force of the enemy not more than ten or twelve li away, who showed every indication of marching shortly in the direction of Si-chow. In numbers alone, he continued, they were greatly superior to the bowmen, and all were well armed. The spreading of this news threw the entire camp into great confusion, many protesting that the day was not a favourable one on which to fight, others crying that it was their duty to fall back on Si-chow and protect the women and children. In the midst of this tumult the Chief of Bowmen returned to Ling, bearing in his hand a written paper which he regarded in uncontrollable anguish.

"Oh, illustrious Ling," he cried, restraining his grief with difficulty, and leaning for support upon the shoulders of two bowmen, "how prosperous indeed are you! What greater misfortune can engulf a person who is both an ambitious soldier and an affectionate son, than to lose such a chance of glory and promotion as only occurs once within the lifetime, and an affectionate and venerable father upon the same day? Behold this mandate to attend, without a moment's delay, at the funeral obsequies of one whom I left, only last week, in the fullness of health and power. The occasion being an unsuitable one, I will not call upon the courteous Ling to join me in sorrow; but his own devout filial piety is so well known that I can conscientiously rely upon an application for absence to be only a matter of official ceremony."

"The application will certainly be regarded as merely official ceremony," replied Ling, without resorting to any delicate pretence of meaning, "and the refined scruples of the person who is addressing me will be fully met by the official date of his venerated father's death being fixed for a more convenient season. In the meantime, the unobtrusive Chief of Bowmen may take the opportunity of requesting that the family tomb be kept unsealed until he is heard from again."

Ling turned away, as he finished this remark, with a dignified feeling of not inelegant resentment. In this way he chanced to observe a large body of soldiers which was leaving the camp accompanied by their lesser captains, all crowned with garlands of flowers and creeping plants. In spite of his very inadequate attainments regarding words of order, the Commander made it understood by means of an exceedingly short sentence that he was desirous of the men returning without delay.

"Doubtless the accomplished Commander, being but newly arrived in this neighbourhood, is unacquainted with the significance of this display," said one of the lesser captains pleasantly. "Know then, O wise and custom-respecting Ling, that on a similar day many years ago this valiant band of bowmen was engaged in a very honourable affair with certain of the enemy. Since then it has been the practice to commemorate the matter with music and other forms of delight within the large square at Si-chow."

"Such customs are excellent," said Ling affably. "On this occasion, however, the public square will be so insufferably thronged with the number of timorous and credulous villagers who have pressed into the town that insufficient justice would be paid to your entrancing display. In consequence of this, we will select for the purpose some convenient spot in the neighbourhood. The proceedings will be commenced by a display of arrow-shooting at moving objects, followed by racing and dancing, in which this person will lead. I have spoken."

At these words many of the more courageous among the bowmen became destructively inspired, and raised shouts of defiance against the enemy, enumerating at great length the indignities which they would heap upon their prisoners. Cries of distinction were also given on behalf of Ling, even the more terrified exclaiming:

"The noble Commander Ling will lead us! He has promised, and assuredly he will not depart from his word. Shielded by his broad and sacred body, from which the bullets glance aside harmlessly, we will advance upon the enemy in the stealthy manner affected by ducks when crossing the swamp. How altogether superior a person our Commander is when likened unto the leaders of the foe-men – they who go into battle completely surrounded by their archers!"

Upon this, perceiving the clear direction in which matters were turning, the Chief of Bowmen again approached Ling.

"Doubtless the highly favoured person whom I am now addressing has been endowed with exceptional authority direct from Peking," he remarked with insidious politeness. "Otherwise this narrow-minded individual would suggest that such a decision does not come within the judgment of a Commander."

In his ignorance of military matters it had not entered the mind of Ling that his authority did not give him the power to commence an attack without consulting other and more distinguished persons. At the suggestion, which he accepted as being composed of truth, he paused, the enlightened zeal with which he had been inspired dying out as he plainly understood the difficulties by which he was enclosed. There seemed a single expedient path for him in the matter; so, directing a person of exceptional trustworthiness to prepare himself for a journey, he inscribed a communication to the Mandarin Li Keen, in which he narrated the facts and asked for speedy directions, and then despatched it with great urgency to Si-chow.

VI

When these matters were arranged, Ling returned to his tent, a victim to feelings of a deep and confused doubt, for all courses seemed to be surrounded by extreme danger, with the strong possibility of final disaster. While he was considering these things attentively, the spy who had brought word of the presence of the enemy again sought him. As he entered, Ling perceived that his face was the colour of a bleached linen garment, while there came with him the odour of sickness.

"There are certain matters which this person has not made known," he said, having first expressed a request that he might not be compelled to stand while he conversed. "The bowmen are as an inferior kind of jackal, and they who lead them are pigs, but this person has observed that the Heaven-sent Commander has internal organs like steel hardened in a white fire and polished by running water. For this reason he will narrate to him the things he has seen – things at which the lesser ones would undoubtedly perish in terror without offering to strike a blow."

"Speak," said Ling, "without fear and without concealment."

"In numbers the rebels are as three to one with the bowmen, and are, in addition, armed with matchlocks and other weapons; this much I have already told," said the spy. "Yesterday they entered the village of Ki without resistance, as the dwellers there were all peaceable persons, who gain a living from the fields, and who neither understood nor troubled about the matters between the rebels and the army. Relying on the promises made by the rebel chiefs, the villagers even welcomed them, as they had been assured that they came as buyers of their corn and rice. Today not a house stands in the street of Ki, not a person lives. The men they slew quickly, or held for torture, as they desired at the moment; the boys they hung from the trees as marks for their arrows. Of the women and children this person, who has since been subject to several attacks of fainting and vomiting, desires not to speak. The wells of Ki are filled with the bodies of such as had the good fortune to be warned in time to slay themselves. The cattle drag themselves from place to place on their forefeet; the fish in the Heng-Kiang are dying, for they cannot live on water thickened into blood. All these things this person has seen."

When he had finished speaking, Ling remained in deep and funereal thought for some time. In spite of his mild nature, the words which he had heard filled him with an inextinguishable desire to slay in hand-to-hand fighting. He regretted that he had placed the decision of the matter before Li Keen.

"If only this person had a mere handful of brave and expert warriors, he would not hesitate to fall upon those savage and barbarous characters, and either destroy them to the last one, or let his band suffer a like fate," he murmured to himself.

The return of the messenger found him engaged in reviewing the bowmen, and still in this mood, so that it was with a commendable feeling of satisfaction, no less than virtuous contempt, that he learned of the Mandarin's journey to Peking as soon as he understood that the rebels were certainly in the neighbourhood.

"The wise and ornamental Li Keen is undoubtedly consistent in all matters," said Ling, with some refined bitterness. "The only information regarding his duties to which this person obtained from him chanced to be a likening of war to skilful chess-play, and to this end the accomplished person in question has merely availed himself of a common expedient which places him at the remote side of the divine Emperor. Yet this act is not unwelcome, for the responsibility of deciding what course is to be adopted now clearly rests with this person. He is, as those who are standing by may perceive, of under the usual height, and of no particular mental or bodily attainments. But he has eaten the rice of the Emperor, and wears the Imperial sign embroidered upon his arm. Before him are encamped the enemies of his master and of his land, and in no way will he turn his back upon them. Against brave and skilful men, such as those whom this person commands, rebels of a low and degraded order are powerless and are, moreover, openly forbidden to succeed by the Forty-second Mandate in the Sacred Book of Arguments. Should it have happened that into this assembly any person of a perfidious or uncourageous nature has gained entrance by guile, and has not been detected and driven forth by his outraged companions (as would certainly occur if such a person were discovered), I, Ling, Commander of Bowmen, make an especial and well-considered request that he shall be struck by a molten thunderbolt if he turns to flight or holds thoughts of treachery."

Having thus addressed and encouraged the soldiers, Ling instructed them that each one should cut and fashion for himself a graceful but weighty club from among the branches of the trees around, and then return to the tents for the purpose of receiving food and rice spirit.

When noon was passed, allowing such time as would enable him to reach the camp of the enemy an hour before darkness, Ling arranged the bowmen in companies of convenient numbers, and commenced the march, sending forward spies, who were to work silently and bring back tidings from every point. In this way he penetrated to within a single li of the ruins of Ki, being informed by the spies that no outposts of the enemy were between him and that place. Here the first rest was made to enable the more accurate and bold spies to reach them with trustworthy information regarding the position and movements of the camp. With little delay there returned the one who had brought the earliest tidings, bruised and torn with his successful haste through the forest, but wearing a complacent and well-satisfied expression of countenance. Without hesitation or waiting to demand money before he would reveal his knowledge, he at once disclosed that the greater part of the enemy were rejoicing among the ruins of Ki, they having discovered there a quantity of opium and a variety of liquids, while only a small guard remained in the camp with their weapons ready. At these words Ling sprang from the ground in gladness, so great was his certainty of destroying the invaders utterly. It was, however, with less pleasurable emotions that he considered how he should effect the matter, for it was in no way advisable to divide his numbers into two bands. Without any feeling of unendurable conceit, he understood that no one but himself could hold the bowmen before an assault, however weak. In a similar manner, he determined that it would be more advisable to attack those in the village first. These he might have reasonable hopes of cutting down without warning the camp or, in any event, before those from the camp arrived. To assail the camp first would assuredly, by the firing, draw upon them those from the village, and in whatever evil state these might arrive, they would, by their numbers, terrify the bowmen, who without doubt would have suffered some loss from the matchlocks.

Waiting for the last light of day, Ling led on the men again, and sending forward some of the most reliable, surrounded the place of the village silently and without detection. In the open space, among broken casks and other inconsiderable matters, plainly shown by the large fires at which burned the last remains of the houses of Ki, many men moved or lay, some already dull or in heavy sleep. As the darkness dropped suddenly, the signal of a peacock's shriek, three times uttered, rang forth, and immediately a cloud of arrows, directed from all sides, poured in among those who feasted. Seeing their foe-men defenceless before them, the archers neglected the orders they had received, and throwing away their bows they rushed in with uplifted clubs, uttering loud shouts of triumph. The next moment a shot was fired in the wood, drums beat, and in an unbelievably short space of time a small but well-armed band of the enemy was among them. Now that all need of caution was at an end, Ling rushed forward with raised sword, calling to his men that victory was certainly theirs, and dealing discriminating and inspiriting blows whenever he met a foe-man. Three times he formed the bowmen into a figure emblematic of triumph, and led them against the line of matchlocks. Twice they fell back, leaving mingled dead under the feet of the enemy. The third time they stood firm, and Ling threw himself against the waving rank in a noble and inspired endeavour to lead the way through. At that moment, when a very distinguished victory seemed within his hand, his elegant and well-constructed sword broke upon an iron shield, leaving him defenceless and surrounded by the enemy.

"Chief among the sublime virtues enjoined by the divine Confucius," began Ling, folding his arms and speaking in an unmoved voice, "is an intelligent submission—" but at that word he fell beneath a rain of heavy and unquestionably well-aimed blows.

VII

Between Si-chow and the village of Ki, in a house completely hidden from travellers by the tall and black trees which surrounded it, lived an aged and very wise person whose ways and manner of living had become so distasteful to his neighbours that they at length agreed to regard him as a powerful and ill-disposed magician. In this way it became a custom that all very unseemly deeds committed by those who, in the ordinary course, would not be guilty of such behaviour, should be attributed to his influence, so that justice might be effected without persons of assured respectability being put to any inconvenience. Apart from the feeling which resulted from this just decision, the uncongenial person in question had become exceedingly unpopular on account of certain definite actions of his own, as that of causing the greater part of Si-chow to be burned down by secretly breathing upon the seven sacred water-jugs to which the town owed its prosperity and freedom from fire. Furthermore, although possessed of many taels, and able to afford such food as is to be found upon the tables of Mandarins, he selected from choice dishes of an objectionable nature; he had been observed to eat eggs of unbecoming freshness, and the Si-chow Official Printed Leaf made it public that he had, on an excessively hot occasion, openly partaken of cow's milk. It is not a matter for wonder, therefore, that when unnaturally loud thunder was heard in the neighbourhood of Si-chow the more ignorant and credulous persons refused to continue in any description of work until certain ceremonies connected with rice spirit, and the adherence to a reclining position for some hours, had been conscientiously observed as a protection against evil.

Not even the most venerable person in Si-chow could remember the time when the magician had not lived there, and as there existed no written record narrating the incident, it was with well-founded probability that he was said to be incapable of death. Contrary to the most general practice, although quite unmarried, he had adopted no son to found a line which would worship his memory in future years, but had instead brought up and caused to be educated in the most difficult varieties of embroidery a young girl, to whom he referred, for want of a more suitable description, as the daughter of his sister, although he would admit without hesitation, when closely questioned, that he had never possessed a sister, at the same time, however, alluding with some pride to many illustrious brothers, who had all obtained distinction in various employments.

Few persons of any high position penetrated into the house of the magician, and most of these retired with inelegant haste on perceiving that no domestic altar embellished the great hall. Indeed, not to make concealment of the fact, the magician was a person who had entirely neglected the higher virtues in an avaricious pursuit of wealth. In that way all his time and a very large number of taels had been expended, testing results by means of the four elements, and putting together things which had been inadequately arrived at by others. It was confidently asserted in Si-chow that he possessed every manner of printed leaf which had been composed in whatsoever language, and all the most precious charms, including many snake-skins of more than ordinary rarity, and the fang of a black wolf which had been stung by seven scorpions.

On the death of his father, the magician had become possessed of great wealth, yet he contributed little to the funeral obsequies nor did any suggestion of a durable and expensive nature conveying his enlightened name and virtues down to future times cause his face to become gladdened. In order to preserve greater secrecy about the enchantments which he certainly performed, he employed only two persons within the house, one of whom was blind and the other deaf. In this ingenious manner he hoped to receive attention and yet be unobserved, the blind one being unable to see the nature of the incantations which he undertook, and the deaf one being unable to hear the words. In this, however, he was unsuccessful, as the two persons always contrived to be present together, and to explain to one another the nature of the various matters afterwards; but as they were of somewhat deficient understanding, the circumstance was unimportant.

It was with more uneasiness that the magician perceived one day that the maiden whom he had adopted was no longer a child. As he desired secrecy above all things until he should have completed the one important matter for which he had laboured all his life, he decided with extreme unwillingness to put into operation a powerful charm towards her, which would have the effect of diminishing all her attributes until such time as he might release her again. Owing to his reluctance in the matter, however, the magic did not act fully, but only in such a way that her feet became naturally and without binding the most perfect and beautiful in the entire province of Hu Nan, so that ever afterwards she was called Pan Fei Mian, in delicate reference to that Empress whose feet were so symmetrical that a golden lily sprang up wherever she trod. Afterwards the magician made no further essay in the matter, chiefly because he was ever convinced that the accomplishment of his desire was within his grasp.

The rumours of armed men in the neighbourhood of Si-chow threw the magician into an unendurable condition of despair. To lose all, as would most assuredly happen if he had to leave his arranged rooms and secret preparations and take to flight, was the more bitter because he felt surer than ever that success was even standing by his side. The very subtle liquid, which would mix itself into the component parts of the living creature which drank it, and by an insidious and harmless process so work that, when the spirit departed, the flesh would become resolved into a figure of pure and solid gold of the finest quality, had engaged the refined minds of many of the most expert individuals of remote ages. With most of these inspired persons, however, the search had been undertaken in pure-minded benevolence, their chief aim being an honourable desire to discover a method by which one's ancestors might be permanently and effectively preserved in a fit and becoming manner to receive the worship and veneration of posterity. Yet, in spite of these amiable motives, and of the fact that the magician merely desired the possession of the secret to enable him to become excessively wealthy, the affair had been so arranged that it should come into his possession.

The matter which concerned Mian in the dark wood, when she was only saved by the appearance of the person who is already known as Ling, entirely removed all pleasurable emotions from the magician's mind, and on many occasions he stated in a definite and systematic manner that he would shortly end an ignoble career which seemed to be destined only to gloom and disappointment. In this way an important misunderstanding arose, for when, two days later, during the sound of matchlock firing, the magician suddenly approached the presence of Mian with an uncontrollable haste and an entire absence of dignified demeanour, and fell dead at her feet without expressing himself on any subject whatever, she deliberately judged that in this manner he had carried his remark into effect, nor did the closed vessel of yellow liquid which he held in his hand seem to lead away from this decision. In reality, the magician had fallen owing to the heavy and conflicting emotions which success had engendered in an intellect already greatly weakened by his continual disregard of the higher virtues; for the bottle, indeed, contained the perfection of his entire life's study, the very expensive and three-times purified gold liquid.

On perceiving the magician's condition, Mian at once called for the two attendants, and directed them to bring from an inner chamber all the most effective curing substances, whether in the form of powder or liquid. When these proved useless, no matter in what way they were applied, it became evident that there could be very little hope of restoring the magician, yet so courageous and grateful for the benefits which she had received from the person in question was Mian that, in spite of the uninviting dangers of the enterprise, she determined to journey to Ki to invoke the assistance of a certain person who was known to be very successful in casting out malicious demons from the bodies of animals, and from casks and barrels, in which they frequently took refuge, to the great detriment of the quality of the liquid placed therein.

Not without many hidden fears, Mian set out on her journey, greatly desiring not to be subjected to an encounter of a nature similar to the one already recorded; for in such a case she could hardly again hope for the inspired arrival of the one whom she now often thought of in secret as the well-formed and symmetrical young sword user. Nevertheless, an event of equal significance was destined to prove the wisdom of the well-known remark concerning thoughts which are occupying one's intellect and the unexpected appearance of a very formidable evil spirit; for as she passed along, quickly yet with so dignified a motion that the moss received no impression beneath her footsteps, she became aware of a circumstance which caused her to stop by imparting to her mind two definite and greatly dissimilar emotions.

In a grassy and open space, on the verge of which she stood, lay the dead bodies of seventeen rebels, all disposed in very degraded attitudes, which contrasted strongly with the easy and becoming position adopted by the eighteenth – one who bore the unmistakable emblems of the Imperial army. In this brave and noble-looking personage Mian at once saw her preserver, and not doubting that an inopportune and treacherous death had overtaken him, she ran forward and raised him in her arms, being well assured that however indiscreet such an action might appear in the case of an ordinary person, the most select maiden need not hesitate to perform so honourable a service in regard to one whose virtues had by that time undoubtedly placed him among the Three Thousand Pure Ones. Being disturbed in this providential manner, Ling opened his eyes, and faintly murmuring, "Oh, sainted and adorable Koon Yam, Goddess of Charity, intercede for me with Buddha!" he again lost possession of himself in the Middle Air. At this remark, which plainly proved Ling to be still alive, in spite of the fact that both the maiden and the person himself had thoughts to the contrary, Mian found herself surrounded by a variety of embarrassing circumstances, among which occurred a remembrance of the dead magician and the wise person at Ki whom she had set out to summon; but on considering the various natural and sublime laws which bore directly on the alternative before her, she discovered that her plain destiny was to endeavour to restore the breath in the person who was still alive rather than engage on the very unsatisfactory chance of attempting to call it back to the body from which it had so long been absent.

Having been inspired to this conclusion – which, when she later examined her mind, she found not to be repulsive to her own inner feelings – Mian returned to the house with dexterous speed, and calling together the two attendants, she endeavoured by means of signs and drawings to explain to them what she desired to accomplish. Succeeding in this after some delay (for the persons in question, being very illiterate and narrow-minded, were unable at first to understand the existence of any recumbent male person other than the dead magician, whom they thereupon commenced to bury in the garden with expressions of great satisfaction at their own intelligence in comprehending Mian's meaning so readily) they all journeyed to the wood, and bearing Ling between them, they carried him to the house without further adventure.

VIII

It was in the month of Hot Dragon Breaths, many weeks after the fight in the woods of Ki, that Ling again opened his eyes to find himself in an unknown chamber, and to recognise in the one who visited him from time to time the incomparable maiden whose life he had saved in the cypress glade. Not a day had passed in the meanwhile on which Mian had neglected to offer sacrifices to Chang-Chung, the deity interested in drugs and healing substances, nor had she wavered in her firm resolve to bring Ling back to an ordinary existence even when the attendants had protested that the person in question might without impropriety be sent to the Restoring Establishment of the Last Chance, so little did his hope of recovering rest upon the efforts of living beings.

After he had beheld Mian's face and understood the circumstances of his escape and recovery, Ling quickly shook off the evil vapours which had held him down so long, and presently he was able to walk slowly in the courtyard and in the shady paths of the wood beyond, leaning upon Mian for the support he still required.

"Oh, graceful one," he said on such an occasion, when little stood between him and the full powers which he had known before the battle, "there is a matter which has been pressing upon this person's mind for some time past. It is as dark after light to let the thoughts dwell around it, yet the thing itself must inevitably soon be regarded, for in this life one's actions are for ever regulated by conditions which are neither of one's own seeking nor within one's power of controlling."

At these words all brightness left Mian's manner, for she at once understood that Ling referred to his departure, of which she herself had lately come to think with unrestrained agitation.

"Oh, Ling," she exclaimed at length, "most expert of sword users and most noble of men, surely never was a maiden more inelegantly placed than the one who is now by your side. To you she owes her life, yet it is unseemly for her even to speak of the incident; to you she must look for protection, yet she cannot ask you to stay by her side. She is indeed alone. The magician is dead, Ki has fallen, Ling is going, and Mian is undoubtedly the most unhappy and solitary person between the Wall and the Nan Hai."

"Beloved Mian," exclaimed Ling, with inspiring vehemence, "and is not the utterly unworthy person before you indebted to you in a double measure that life is still within him? Is not the strength which now promotes him to such exceptional audacity as to aspire to your lovely hand, of your own creating? Only encourage Ling to entertain a well-founded hope that on his return he shall not find you partaking of the wedding feast of some wealthy and exceptionally round-bodied Mandarin, and this person will accomplish the journey to Canton and back as it were in four strides."

"Oh, Ling, reflection of my ideal, holder of my soul, it would indeed be very disagreeable to my own feelings to make any reply save one," replied Mian, scarcely above a breath-voice. "Gratitude alone would direct me, were it not that the great love which fills me leaves no resting place for any other emotion than itself. Go if you must, but return quickly, for your absence will weigh upon Mian like a dragon-dream."

"Violet light of my eyes," exclaimed Ling, "even in surroundings which with the exception of the matter before us are uninspiring in the extreme, your virtuous and retiring encouragement yet raises me to such a commanding eminence of demonstrative happiness that I fear I shall become intolerably self-opinionated towards my fellow men in consequence."

"Such a thing is impossible with my Ling," said Mian, with conviction. "But must you indeed journey to Canton?"

"Alas!" replied Ling. "Gladly would this person decide against such a course did the matter rest with him, for as the Verses say, 'It is needless to apply the ram's head to the unlocked door.' But Ki is demolished, the unassuming Mandarin Li Keen has retired to Peking, and of the fortunes of his bowmen this person is entirely ignorant."

"Such as survived returned to their homes," replied Mian, "and Si-chow is safe, for the scattered and broken rebels fled to the mountains again; so much this person has learned."

"In that case Si-chow is undoubtedly safe for the time, and can be left with prudence," said Ling. "It is an unfortunate circumstance that there is no Mandarin of authority between here and Canton who can receive from this person a statement of past facts and give him instructions for the future."

"And what will be the nature of such instructions as will be given at Canton?" demanded Mian.

"By chance they may take the form of raising another company of bowmen," said Ling, with a sigh, "but, indeed, if this person can obtain any weight by means of his past service, they will tend towards a pleasant and unambitious civil appointment."

"Oh, my artless and noble-minded lover!" exclaimed Mian, "assuredly a veil has been before your eyes during your residence in Canton, and your naturally benevolent mind has turned all things into good, or you would not thus hopefully refer to your brilliant exploits in the past. Of what commercial benefit have they been to the sordid and miserly persons in authority, or in what way have they diverted a stream of taels into their insatiable pockets? Far greater is the chance that had Si-chow fallen many of its household goods would have found their way into the Yamens of Canton. Assuredly in Li Keen you will have a friend who will make many delicate allusions to your ancestors when you meet, and yet one who will float many barbed whispers to follow you when you have passed; for you have planted shame before him in the eyes of those who would otherwise neither have eyes to see nor tongues to discuss the matter. It is for such a reason that this person distrusts all things connected with the journey, except your constancy, oh, my true and strong one."

"Such faithfulness would alone be sufficient to assure my safe return if the matter were properly represented to the supreme Deities," said Ling. "Let not the thin curtain of bitter water stand before your lustrous eyes any longer, then, the events which have followed one another in the past few days in a fashion that can only be likened to thunder following lightning are indeed sufficient to distress one with so refined and swan-like an organisation, but they are now assuredly at an end."

"It is a hope of daily recurrence to this person," replied Mian, honourably endeavouring to restrain the emotion which openly exhibited itself in her eyes; "for what maiden would not rather make successful offerings to the Great Mother Kum-Fa than have the most imposing and verbose Triumphal Arch erected to commemorate an empty and unsatisfying constancy?"

In this amiable manner the matter was arranged between Ling and Mian, as they sat together in the magician's garden drinking peach tea, which the two attendants – not without discriminating and significant expressions between themselves – brought to them from time to time. Here Ling made clear the whole manner of his life from his earliest memory to the time when he fell in dignified combat, nor did Mian withhold anything, explaining in particular such charms and spells of the magician as she had knowledge of, and in this graceful manner materially assisting her lover in the many disagreeable encounters and conflicts which he was shortly to experience.

It was with even more objectionable feelings than before that Ling now contemplated his journey to Canton, involving as it did the separation from one who had become as the shadow of his existence, and by whose side he had an undoubted claim to stand. Yet the necessity of the undertaking was no less than before, and the full possession of all his natural powers took away his only excuse for delaying in the matter. Without any pleasurable anticipations, therefore, he consulted the Sacred Flat and Round Sticks, and learning that the following day would be propitious for the journey, he arranged to set out in accordance with the omen.

When the final moment arrived at which the invisible threads of constantly passing emotions from one to the other must be broken, and when Mian perceived that her lover's horse was restrained at the door by the two attendants, who with unsuspected delicacy of feeling had taken this opportunity of withdrawing, the noble endurance which had hitherto upheld her melted away, and she became involved in very melancholy and obscure meditations until she observed that Ling also was quickly becoming affected by a similar gloom.

"Alas!" she exclaimed. "How unworthy a person I am thus to impose upon my lord a greater burden than that which already weighs him down! Rather ought this one to dwell upon the happiness of that day, when, after successfully evading or overthrowing the numerous bands of assassins which infest the road from here to Canton, and after escaping or recovering from the many deadly pestilences which invariably reduce that city at this season of the year, he shall triumphantly return. Assuredly there is a highly polished surface united to every action in life, no matter how funereal it may at first appear. Indeed, there are many incidents compared with which death itself is welcome, and to this end Mian has reserved a farewell gift." Speaking in this manner the devoted and magnanimous maiden placed in Ling's hands the transparent vessel of liquid which the magician had grasped when he fell. "This person," she continued, speaking with difficulty, "places her lover's welfare incomparably before her own happiness, and should he ever find himself in a situation which is unendurably oppressive, and from which death is the only escape – such as inevitable tortures, the infliction of violent madness, or the subjection by magic to the will of some designing woman

– she begs him to accept this means of freeing himself without regarding her anguish beyond expressing a clearly defined last wish that the two persons in question may be in the end happily reunited in another existence."

Assured by this last evidence of affection, Ling felt that he had no longer any reason for internal heaviness; his spirits were immeasurably raised by the fragrant incense of Mian's great devotion, and under its influence he was even able to breathe towards her a few words of similar comfort as he left the spot and began his journey.

IX

On entering Canton, which he successfully accomplished without any unpleasant adventure, the marked absence of any dignified ostentation which had been accountable for many of Ling's misfortunes in the past, impelled him again to reside in the same insignificant apartment that he had occupied when he first visited the city as an unknown and unimportant candidate. In consequence of this, when Ling was communicating to any person the signs by which messengers might find him, he was compelled to add, "the neighbourhood in which this contemptible person resides is that officially known as 'the mean quarter favoured by the lower class of those who murder by treachery'," and for this reason he was not always treated with the regard to which his attainments entitled him, or which he would have unquestionably received had he been able to describe himself as of "the partly drained and uninfected area reserved to Mandarins and their friends".

It was with an ignoble feeling of mental distress that Ling exhibited himself at the Chief Office of Warlike Deeds and Arrangements on the following day; for the many disadvantageous incidents of his past life had repeated themselves before his eyes while he slept, and the not unhopeful emotions which he had felt when in the inspiring presence of Mian were now altogether absent. In spite of the fact that he reached the office during the early gong strokes of the morning, it was not until the withdrawal of light that he reached any person who was in a position to speak with him on the matter, so numerous were the lesser ones through whose chambers he had to pass in the process. At length he found himself in the presence of an upper one who had the appearance of being acquainted with the circumstances, and who received him with dignity, though not with any embarrassing exhibition of respect or servility.

"'The hero of the illustrious encounter beyond the walls of Si-chow'," exclaimed that official, reading the words from the tablet of introduction which Ling had caused to be carried into him, and at the same time examining the person in question closely. "Indeed, no such one is known to those within this office, unless the words chance to point to the courteous and unassuming Mandarin Li Keen, who, however, is at this moment recovering his health at Peking, as set forth in the amiable and impartial report which we have lately received from him."

At these words Ling plainly understood that there was little hope of the last events becoming profitable on his account.

"Did not the report to which allusion has been made bear reference to one Ling, Commander of the Archers, who thrice led on the fighting men, and who was finally successful in causing the rebels to disperse towards the mountains?" he asked, in a voice which somewhat trembled.

"There is certainly reference to one of the name you mention," said the other; "but regarding the terms – perhaps this person would better protect his own estimable time by displaying the report within your sight."

With these words the upper one struck a gong several times, and after receiving from an inner chamber the parchment in question, he placed it before Ling, at the same time directing a lesser one to interpose between it and the one who read it a large sheet of transparent substance, so that destruction might not come to it, no matter in what way its contents affected the reader. Thereon Ling perceived the following facts, very skilfully inscribed with the evident purpose of inducing persons to believe, without question, that words so elegantly traced must of necessity be truthful also.

> A Benevolent Example of the Intelligent Arrangement by which the most Worthy Persons outlive those who are Incapable.
>
> The circumstances connected with the office of the valuable and accomplished Mandarin of Warlike Deeds and Arrangements at Si-chow have, in recent times, been of anything but a prepossessing order. Owing to the very inadequate methods adopted by those who earn a livelihood by conveying necessities from the more enlightened portions of the Empire to that place, it so came about that for a period of five days the Yamên was entirely unsupplied with the fins of sharks or even with goats' eyes. To add to the polished Mandarin's distress of mind the barbarous and slow-witted rebels who infest those parts took this opportunity to destroy the town and most of its inhabitants, the matter coming about as follows:

> The feeble and commonplace person named Ling who commands the bowmen had but recently been elevated to that distinguished position from a menial and degraded occupation (for which, indeed, his stunted intellect more aptly fitted him); and being in consequence very greatly puffed out in self-gratification, he became an easy prey to the cunning of the rebels, and allowed himself to be beguiled into a trap, paying for this contemptible stupidity with his life. The town of Si-chow was then attacked, and being in this manner left defenceless through the weakness – or treachery – of the person Ling, who had contrived to encompass the entire destruction of his unyielding company, it fell after a determined and irreproachable resistance; the Mandarin Li Keen being told as, covered with the blood of the foe-men, he was dragged away from the thickest part of the unequal conflict by his followers, that he was the last person to leave the town. On his way to Peking with news of this valiant defence, the Mandarin was joined by the Chief of Bowmen, who had understood and avoided the very obvious snare into which the stagnant-minded Commander had led his followers, in spite of disinterested advice to the contrary. For this intelligent perception, and for general nobility of conduct when in battle, the versatile Chief of Bowmen is by this written paper strongly recommended to the dignity of receiving the small metal Embellishment of Valour.
>
> It has been suggested to the Mandarin Li Keen that the bestowal of the Crystal Button would only be a fit and graceful reward for his indefatigable efforts to uphold the dignity of the sublime Emperor; but to all such persons the Mandarin has sternly replied that such a proposal would more fitly originate from the renowned and valuable Office of Warlike Deeds and Arrangements, he well knowing that the wise and engaging persons who conduct that indispensable and well-regulated department are gracefully voracious in their efforts to reward merit, even when it is displayed, as in the case in question, by one who from his position will inevitably soon be urgently petitioning in a like manner on their behalf."

When Ling had finished reading this elegantly arranged but exceedingly misleading parchment, he looked up with eyes from which he vainly endeavoured to restrain the signs of undignified emotion, and said to the upper one:

"It is difficult employment for a person to refrain from unendurable thoughts when his unassuming and really conscientious efforts are represented in a spirit of no satisfaction, yet in this matter the very expert Li Keen appears to have gone beyond himself; the Commander Ling, who is herein represented as being slain by the enemy, is, indeed, the person who is standing before you, and all the other statements are in a like exactness."

"The short-sighted individual who for some hidden desire of his own is endeavouring to present himself as the corrupt and degraded creature Ling, has overlooked one important circumstance," said the upper one, smiling in a very intolerable manner, at the same time causing his head to move slightly from side to side in the fashion of one who rebukes with assumed geniality; and, turning over the written paper, he displayed upon the under side the Imperial vermilion Sign. "Perhaps," he continued, "the omniscient person will still continue in his remarks, even with the evidence of the Emperor's unerring pencil to refute him."

At these words and the undoubted testimony of the red mark, which plainly declared the whole of the written matter to be composed of truth, no matter what might afterwards transpire, Ling understood that very little prosperity remained with him.

"But the town of Si-chow," he suggested, after examining his mind; "if any person in authority visited the place, he would inevitably find it standing and its inhabitants in agreeable health."

"The persistent person who is so assiduously occupying my intellectual moments with empty words seems to be unaccountably deficient in his knowledge of the customs of refined society and of the meaning of the Imperial Signet," said the other, with an entire absence of benevolent consideration. "That Si-chow has fallen and that Ling is dead are two utterly uncontroversial matters truthfully recorded. If a person visited Si-chow, he might find it rebuilt or even inhabited by those from the neighbouring villages or by evil spirits taking the forms of the ones who formerly lived there; as in a like manner, Ling might be restored to existence by magic, or his body might be found and possessed by an outcast demon who desired to revisit the earth for a period. Such circumstances do not in any way disturb the announcement that Si-chow has without question fallen, and that Ling has officially ceased to live, of which events notifications have been sent to all who are concerned in the matters."

As the upper one ceased speaking, four strokes sounded upon the gong, and Ling immediately found himself carried into the street by the current of both lesser and upper ones who poured forth at the signal.

The termination of this conversation left Ling in a more unenviable state of dejection than any of the many preceding misfortunes had done, for with enlarged inducements to possess himself of a competent appointment he seemed to be even further removed from this attainment than he had been at any time in his life. He might, indeed, present himself again for the public examinations; but in order to do even that it would be necessary for him to wait almost a year, nor could he assure himself that his efforts would again be likely to result in an equal success. Doubts also arose within his mind of the course which he should follow in such a case; whether to adopt a new name, involving as it would certain humiliation and perhaps disgrace if detection overtook his footsteps, or still to possess the title of one who was in a measure dead, and hazard the likelihood of having any prosperity which he might obtain reduced to nothing if the fact should become public.

As Ling reflected upon such details he found himself without intention before the house of a wise person who had become very wealthy by advising others on all matters, but chiefly on those connected with strange occurrences and such events as could not be settled definitely either one way or the other until a remote period had been reached. Becoming assailed by a curious desire to know what manner of evils particularly attached themselves to such as were officially dead but who nevertheless had an ordinary existence, Ling placed himself before this person, and after arranging the manner of reward related to him so many of the circumstances as were necessary to enable a full understanding to be reached, but at the same time in no way betraying his own interest in the matter.

"Such inflictions are to no degree frequent," said the wise person after he had consulted a polished sphere of the finest red jade for some time; "and this is in a measure to be regretted, as the hair of these persons – provided they die a violent death, which is invariably the case – constitutes a certain protection against being struck by falling stars, or becoming involved in unsuccessful law cases. The persons in question can be recognised with certainty in the public ways by the unnatural pallor of their faces and by the general repulsiveness of their appearance, but as they soon take refuge in suicide, unless they have the fortune to be removed previously by accident, it is an infrequent matter that one is gratified by the sight. During their existence they are subject to many disorders from which the generality of human beings are benevolently preserved; they possess no rights of any kind, and if by any chance they are detected in an act of a seemingly depraved nature, they are liable to judgment at the hands of the passers-by without any form whatever, and to punishment of a more severe order than that administered to commonplace criminals. There are many other disadvantages affecting such persons when they reach the Middle Air, of which the chief—"

"This person is immeasurably indebted for such a clear explanation of the position," interrupted Ling, who had a feeling of not desiring to penetrate further into the detail; "but as he perceives a line of anxious ones eagerly waiting at the door to obtain advice and consolation from so expert and amiable a wizard, he will not make himself uncongenial any longer with his very feeble topics of conversation."

By this time Ling plainly comprehended that he had been marked out from the beginning – perhaps for all the knowledge which he had to the opposite effect, from a period in the life of a far-removed ancestor – to be an object of marked derision and the victim of all manner of malevolent demons in whatever actions he undertook. In this condition of understanding his mind turned gratefully to the parting gift of Mian whom he had now no hope of possessing; for the intolerable thought of uniting her to so objectionable a being as himself would have been dismissed as utterly inelegant even had he been in a manner of living to provide for her adequately, which itself seemed clearly impossible. Disregarding all similar emotions, therefore, he walked without pausing to his abode, and stretching his body upon the rushes, drank the entire liquid unhesitatingly, and prepared to pass beyond with a tranquil mind entirely given up to thoughts and images of Mian.

X

Upon a certain occasion, the particulars of which have already been recorded, Ling had judged himself to have passed into the form of a spirit on beholding the ethereal form of Mian bending over him. After swallowing the entire liquid, which had cost the dead magician so much to distil and make perfect, it was with a well-assured determination of never again awakening that he lost the outward senses and floated in the Middle Air, so that when his eyes next opened upon what seemed to be the bare walls of his own chamber, his first thought was a natural conviction that the matter had been so arranged either out of a charitable desire that he should not be overcome by a too sudden transition to unparalleled splendour, or that such a reception was the outcome of some dignified jest on the part of certain lesser and more cheerful spirits. After waiting in one position for several hours, however, and receiving no summons or manifestation of a celestial nature, he began to doubt the qualities of the liquid, and applying certain tests, he soon ascertained that he was still in the lower world and unharmed. Nevertheless, this circumstance did not tend in any way to depress his mind, for, doubtless owing to some hidden virtue of the fluid, he felt an enjoyable emotion that he still lived; all his attributes appeared to be purified, and he experienced an inspired certainty of feeling that an illustrious and highly remunerative future lay before one who still had an ordinary existence after being both officially killed and self-poisoned.

In this intelligent disposition thoughts of Mian recurred to him with unreproved persistence, and in order to convey to her an account of the various matters which had engaged him since his arrival at the city, and a well-considered declaration of the unchanged state of his own feelings towards her, he composed and despatched with impetuous haste the following delicate verses:

CONSTANCY

About the walls and gates of Canton
Are many pleasing and entertaining maidens;
Indeed, in the eyes of their friends and of the passers-by
Some of them are exceptionally adorable.
The person who is inscribing these lines, however,
Sees before him, as it were, an assemblage of deformed and unprepossessing hags,
Venerable in age and inconsiderable in appearance;
For the dignified and majestic image of Mian is ever before him,
Making all others very inferior.

Within the houses and streets of Canton Hang many bright lanterns.
The ordinary person who has occasion to walk by night
Professes to find them highly lustrous.
But there is one who thinks contrary facts,
And when he goes forth he carries two long curved poles
To prevent him from stumbling among the dark and hidden places;
For he has gazed into the brilliant and pellucid orbs of Mian,
And all other lights are dull and practically opaque.

In various parts of the literary quarter of Canton
Reside such as spend their time in inward contemplation.
In spite of their generally uninviting exteriors
Their reflections are often of a very profound order.
Yet the unpopular and persistently-abused Ling
Would unhesitatingly prefer his own thoughts to theirs,
For what makes this person's thoughts far more pleasing
Is that they are invariably connected with the virtuous and ornamental Mian.

Becoming very amiably disposed after this agreeable occupation, Ling surveyed himself at the disc of polished metal, and observed with surprise and shame the rough and uninviting condition of his person. He had, indeed, although it was not until some time later that he became aware of the circumstance, slept for five days without interruption, and it need not therefore be a matter of wonder or of reproach to him that his smooth surfaces had become covered with short hair. Reviling himself bitterly for the appearance which he conceived he must have exhibited when he conducted his business, and to which he now in part attributed his ill-success, Ling went forth without delay, and quickly discovering one of those who remove hair publicly for a very small sum, he placed himself in the chair, and directed that his face, arms, and legs should be denuded after the manner affected by the ones who make a practice of observing the most recent customs.

"Did the illustrious individual who is now conferring distinction on this really worn-out chair by occupying it express himself in favour of having the face entirely denuded?" demanded the one who conducted the operation; for these persons have become famous for their elegant and persistent ability to discourse, and frequently assume ignorance in order that they themselves may make reply, and not for the purpose of gaining knowledge. "Now, in the objectionable opinion of this unintelligent person, who has a presumptuous habit of offering his very undesirable advice, a slight covering on the upper lip, delicately arranged and somewhat fiercely pointed at the extremities, would bestow an appearance of – how shall this illiterate person explain himself? – dignity? – matured reflection? – doubtless the accomplished nobleman before me will understand what is intended with a more knife-like accuracy than this person can describe it – but confer that highly desirable effect upon the face of which at present it is entirely destitute… 'Entirely denuded?' Then without fail it shall certainly be so, O incomparable personage… Does the versatile Mandarin now present profess any concern as to the condition of the rice plants?… Indeed, the remark is an inspired one; the subject is totally devoid of interest to a person of intelligence… A remarkable and gravity-removing event transpired within the notice of this unassuming person recently. A discriminating individual had purchased from him a portion of his justly renowned Thrice-extracted Essence of Celestial Herb Oil – a preparation which in this experienced person's opinion, indeed, would greatly relieve the undoubted afflictions from which the one before him is evidently suffering – when after once anointing himself—"

A lengthy period containing no words caused Ling, who had in the meantime closed his eyes and lost Canton and all else in delicate thoughts of Mian, to look up. That which met his attention on doing so filled him with an intelligent wonder, for the person before him held in his hand what had the appearance of a tuft of bright yellow hair, which shone in the light of the sun with a most engaging splendour, but which he nevertheless regarded with a most undignified expression of confusion and awe.

"Illustrious demon," he cried at length, kow-towing very respectfully, "have the extreme amiableness to be of a benevolent disposition, and do not take an unworthy and entirely unremunerative revenge upon this very unimportant person for failing to detect and honour you from the beginning."

"Such words indicate nothing beyond an excess of hemp spirit," answered Ling, with signs of displeasure. "To gain my explicit esteem, make me smooth without delay, and do not exhibit before me the lock of hair which, from its colour and appearance, has evidently adorned the head of one of those maidens whose duty it is to quench the thirst of travellers in the long narrow rooms of this city."

"Majestic and anonymous spirit," said the other, with extreme reverence, and an entire absence of the appearance of one who had gazed into too many vessels, "if such be your plainly expressed desire, this superficial person will at once proceed to make smooth your peach-like skin, and with a carefulness inspired by the certainty that the most unimportant wound would give forth liquid fire, in which he would undoubtedly perish. Nevertheless, he desires to make it evident that this hair is from the head of no maiden, being, indeed, the uneven termination of your own sacred pigtail, which this excessively self-confident slave took the inexcusable liberty of removing, and which changed in this manner within his hand in order to administer a fit reproof for his intolerable presumption."

Impressed by the mien and unquestionable earnestness of the remover of hair, Ling took the matter which had occasioned these various emotions in his hand and examined it. His amazement was still greater when he perceived that – in spite of the fact that it presented every appearance of having been cut from his own person – none of the qualities of hair remained in it; it was hard and wire-like, possessing, indeed, both the nature and the appearance of a metal.

As he gazed fixedly and with astonishment, there came back into the remembrance of Ling certain obscure and little-understood facts connected with the limitless wealth possessed by the Yellow Emperor – of which the great gold life-like image in the Temple of Internal Symmetry at Peking alone bears witness now – and of his lost secret. Many very forcible prophecies and omens in his own earlier life, of which the rendering and accomplishment had hitherto seemed to be dark and incomplete, passed before him, and various matters which Mian had related to him concerning the habits and speech of the magician took definite form within his mind. Deeply impressed by the exact manner in which all these circumstances fitted together, one into another, Ling rewarded the person before him greatly beyond his expectation, and hurried without delay to his own chamber.

XI

For many hours Ling remained in his room, examining in his mind all passages, either in his own life or in the lives of others, which might by any chance have influence on the event before him. In this thorough way he became assured that the competition and its results, his journey to Si-chow with the encounter in the cypress wood, the flight of the incapable and treacherous Mandarin, and the battle of Ki, were all, down to the matter of the smallest detail, parts of a symmetrical and complete scheme, tending to his present condition. Cheered and upheld by this proof of the fact that very able deities were at work on his behalf, he turned his intellect from the entrancing subject to a contemplation of the manner in which his condition would enable him to frustrate the uninventive villainies of the obstinate person Li Keen, and to provide a suitable house and mode of living to which he would be justified in introducing Mian, after adequate marriage ceremonies had been observed between them. In this endeavour he was less successful than he had imagined would be the case, for when he had first fully understood that his body was of such a substance that nothing was wanting to transmute it into fine gold but the absence of the living spirit, he had naturally, and without deeply examining the detail, assumed that so much gold might be considered to be in his possession. Now, however, a very definite thought arose within him that his own wishes and interests would have been better secured had the benevolent spirits who undertook the matter placed the secret within his knowledge in such a way as to enable him to administer the fluid to some very heavy and inexpensive animal, so that the issue which seemed inevitable before the enjoyment of the riches could be entered upon should not have touched his own comfort so closely. To a person of Ling's refined imagination it could not fail to be a subject of internal reproach that while he would become the most precious dead body in the world, his value in life might not be very honourably placed even by the most complimentary one who should require his services. Then came the thought, which, however degraded, he found himself unable to put quite beyond him, that if in the meantime he were able to gain a sufficiency for Mian and himself, even her pure and delicate love might not be able to bear so offensive a test as that of seeing him grow old and remain intolerably healthy – perhaps with advancing years actually becoming lighter day by day, and thereby lessening in value before her eyes – when the natural infirmities of age and the presence of an ever-increasing posterity would make even a moderate amount of taels of inestimable value.

No doubt remained in Ling's mind that the process of frequently making smooth his surfaces would yield an amount of gold enough to suffice for his own needs, but a brief consideration of the matter convinced him that this source would be inadequate to maintain an entire household even if he continually denuded himself to an almost ignominious extent. As he fully weighed these varying chances the certainty became more clear to him with every thought that for the virtuous enjoyment of Mian's society one great sacrifice was required of him. This act, it seemed to be intimated, would without delay provide for an affluent and lengthy future, and at the same time would influence all the spirits – even those who had been hitherto evilly disposed towards him – in such a manner that his enemies would be removed from his path by a process which would expose them to public ridicule, and he would be assured in founding an illustrious and enduring line. To accomplish this successfully necessitated the loss of at least the greater part of one entire member, and for some time the disadvantages of going through an existence with only a single leg or arm seemed more than a sufficient price to pay even for the definite advantages which would be made over to him in return. This unworthy thought, however, could not long withstand the memory of Mian's steadfast and high-minded affection, and the certainty of her enlightened gladness at his return even in the imperfect condition which he anticipated. Nor was there absent from his mind a dimly understood hope that the matter did not finally rest with him, but that everything which he might be inspired to do was in reality only a portion of the complete and arranged system into which he had been drawn, and in which his part had been assigned to him from the beginning without power for him to deviate, no matter how much to the contrary the thing should appear.

As no advantage would be gained by making any delay, Ling at once sought the most favourable means of putting his resolution into practice, and after many skilful and insidious inquiries he learnt of an accomplished person who made a consistent habit of cutting off limbs which had become troublesome to their possessors either through accident or disease.

Furthermore, he was said to be of a sincere and charitable disposition, and many persons declared that on no occasion had he been known to make use of the helpless condition of those who visited him in order to extort money from them.

Coming to the ill-considered conclusion that he would be able to conceal within his own breast the true reason for the operation, Ling placed himself before the person in question, and exhibited the matter to him so that it would appear as though his desires were promoted by the presence of a small but persistent sprite which had taken its abode within his left thigh, and there resisted every effort of the most experienced wise persons to induce it to come forth again. Satisfied with this explanation of the necessity of the deed, the one who undertook the matter proceeded, with Ling's assistance, to sharpen his cutting instruments and to heat the hardening irons; but no sooner had he made a shallow mark to indicate the lines which his knife should take, than his subtle observation at once showed him that the facts had been represented to him in a wrong sense, and that his visitor, indeed, was composed of no common substance. Being of a gentle and forbearing disposition, he did not manifest any indication of rage at the discovery, but amiably and unassumingly pointed out that such a course was not respectful towards himself, and that, moreover, Ling might incur certain well-defined and highly undesirable maladies as a punishment for the deception.

Overcome with remorse at deceiving so courteous and noble-minded a person, Ling fully explained the circumstances to him, not even concealing from him certain facts which related to the actions of remote ancestors, but which, nevertheless, appeared to have influenced the succession of events. When he had made an end of the narrative, the other said:

"Behold now, it is truly remarked that every Mandarin has three hands and every soldier a like number of feet, yet it is a saying which is rather to be regarded as manifesting the deep wisdom and discrimination of the speaker than as an actual fact which can be taken advantage of when one is so minded – least of all by so valiant a Commander as the one before me, who has clearly proved that in time of battle he has exactly reversed the position."

"The loss would undoubtedly be of considerable inconvenience occasionally," admitted Ling, "yet none the less the sage remark of Huai Mei-shan, 'When actually in the embrace of a voracious and powerful wild animal, the desirability of leaving a limb is not a matter to be subjected to lengthy consideration,' is undoubtedly a valuable guide for general conduct. This person has endured many misfortunes and suffered many injustices; he has known the wolf-gnawings of great hopes, which have withered and daily grown less when the difficulties of maintaining an honourable and illustrious career have unfolded themselves within his sight. Before him still lie the attractions of a moderate competency to be shared with the one whose absence would make even the Upper Region unendurable, and after having this entrancing future once shattered by the tiger-like cupidity of a depraved and incapable Mandarin, he is determined to welcome even the sacrifice which you condemn rather than let the opportunity vanish through indecision."

"It is not an unworthy or abandoned decision," said the one whose aid Ling had invoked, "nor a matter in which this person would refrain from taking part, were there no other and more agreeable means by which the same results may be attained. A circumstance has occurred within this superficial person's mind, however: A brother of the one who is addressing you is by profession one of those who purchase large undertakings for which they have not the money to pay, and who thereupon by various expedients gain the ear of the thrifty, enticing them by fair offers of return to entrust their savings for the purpose of paying off the debt. These persons are ever on the watch for transactions by which they inevitably prosper without incurring any obligation, and doubtless my brother will be able to gather a just share of the value of your highly remunerative body without submitting you to the insufferable annoyance of losing a great part of it prematurely."

Without clearly understanding how so inviting an arrangement could be effected, the manner of speaking was exceedingly alluring to Ling's mind, perplexed as he had become through weighing and considering the various attitudes of the entire matter. To receive a certain and sufficient sum of money without his person being in any way mutilated would be a satisfactory but, as far as he had been able to observe, an unapproachable solution to the difficulty. In the mind of the amiable person with whom he was conversing, however, the accomplishment did not appear to be surrounded by unnatural obstacles, so that Ling was content to leave the entire design in his hands, after stating that he would again present himself on a certain occasion when it was asserted that the brother in question would be present.

So internally lightened did Ling feel after this inspiring conversation, and so confident of a speedy success had the obliging person's words made him become, that for the first time since his return to Canton he was able to take an intellectual interest in the pleasures of the city. Becoming aware that the celebrated play entitled *The Precious Lamp of Spotted Butterfly Temple* was in the process of being shown at the Tea Garden of Rainbow Lights and Voices, he purchased an entrance, and after passing several hours in this conscientious enjoyment, returned to his chamber, and passed a night untroubled by any manifestations of an unpleasant nature.

XII

Chang-ch'un, the brother of the one to whom Ling had applied in his determination, was confidently stated to be one of the richest persons in Canton. So great was the number of enterprises in which he had possessions, that he himself was unable to keep an account of them, and it was asserted that upon occasions he had run through the streets, crying aloud that such an undertaking had been the subject of most inferior and uninviting dreams and omens (a custom observed by those who wish a venture ill), whereas upon returning and consulting his written parchments, it became plain to him that he had indulged in a very objectionable exhibition, as he himself was the person most interested in the success of the matter. Far from discouraging him, however, such incidents tended to his advantage, as he could consistently point to them in proof of his unquestionable commercial honourableness, and in this way many persons of all classes, not only in Canton, or in the Province, but all over the Empire, would unhesitatingly entrust money to be placed in undertakings which he had purchased and was willing to describe as "of much good". A certain class of printed leaves – those in which Chang-ch'un did not insert purchased mentions of his forthcoming ventures or verses recording his virtues (in return for buying many examples of the printed leaf containing them) – took frequent occasion of reminding persons that Chang-ch'un owed the beginning of his prosperity to finding a written parchment connected with a Mandarin of exalted rank and a low caste attendant at the Ti-i tea-house among the paper heaps, which it was at that time his occupation to assort into various departments according to their quality and commercial value. Such printed leaves freely and unhesitatingly predicted that the day on which he would publicly lose face was incomparably nearer than that on which the Imperial army would receive its back pay, and in a quaint and gravity-removing manner advised him to protect himself against an obscure but inevitable poverty by learning the accomplishment of chair-carrying – an occupation for which his talents and achievements fitted him in a high degree, they remarked.

In spite of these evilly intentioned remarks, and of illustrations representing him as being bowstrung for treacherous killing, being seized in the action of secretly conveying money from passers-by to himself and other similar annoying references to his private life, Chang-ch'un did not fail to prosper, and his undertakings succeeded to such an extent that without inquiry into the detail many persons were content to describe as "gold-lined" anything to which he affixed his sign, and to hazard their savings for staking upon the ventures. In all other departments of life Chang was equally successful; his chief wife was the daughter of one who stood high in the Emperor's favour; his repast table was never unsupplied with sea-snails, rats' tongues or delicacies of an equally expensive nature, and it was confidently maintained that there was no official in Canton, not even putting aside the Taotai, who dare neglect to fondle Chang's hand if he publicly offered it to him for that purpose.

It was at the most illustrious point of his existence – at the time, indeed, when after purchasing without money the renowned and proficient charm-water Ho-Ko for a million taels, he had sold it again for ten – that Chang was informed by his brother of the circumstances connected with Ling. After becoming specially assured that the matter was indeed such as it was represented to be, Chang at once discerned that the venture was of too certain and profitable a nature to be put before those who entrusted their money to him in ordinary and doubtful cases. He accordingly called together certain persons whom he was desirous of obliging, and informing them privately and apart from business terms that the opportunity was one of exceptional attractiveness, he placed the facts before them. After displaying a number of diagrams bearing upon the matter, he proposed that they should form an enterprise to be called "The Ling (After Death) Without Much Risk Assembly". The manner of conducting this undertaking he explained to be as follows: the body of Ling, whenever the spirit left it, should become as theirs to be used for profit. For this benefit they would pay Ling fifty thousand taels when the understanding was definitely arrived at, five thousand taels each year until the matter ended, and when that period arrived another fifty thousand taels to persons depending upon him during his life. Having stated the figure business, Chang-ch'un put down his written papers, and causing his face to assume the look of irrepressible but dignified satisfaction which it was his custom to wear on most occasions, and especially when he had what appeared at first sight to be evil news to communicate to public assemblages of those who had entrusted money to his ventures, he proceeded to disclose the advantages of such a system. At the extreme, he said, the amount which they would be required to pay would be two hundred and fifty thousand taels; but this was in reality a very misleading view of the circumstance, as he would endeavour to show them. For one detail, he had allotted to Ling thirty years of existence, which was the extreme amount according to the calculations of those skilled in such prophecies; but, as they were all undoubtedly aware, persons of very expert intellects were known to enjoy a much shorter period of life than the gross and ordinary, and as Ling was clearly one of the former, by the fact of his contriving so ingenious a method of enriching himself, they might with reasonable foresight rely upon his departing when half the period had been attained; in that way seventy-five thousand taels would be restored to them, for every year represented a saving of five thousand. Another agreeable contemplation was that of the last sum, for by such a time they would have arrived at the most pleasurable part of the enterprise: a million taels' worth of pure gold would be displayed before them, and the question of the final fifty thousand could be disposed of by cutting off an arm or half a leg. Whether they adopted that course, or decided to increase their fortunes by exposing so exceptional and symmetrical a wonder to the public gaze in all the principal cities of the Empire, was a circumstance which would have to be examined within their minds when the time approached. In such a way the detail of purchase stood revealed as only fifty thousand taels in reality, a sum so despicably insignificant that he had internal pains at mentioning it to so wealthy a group of Mandarins, and he had not yet made clear to them that each year they would receive gold to the amount of almost a thousand taels. This would be the result of Ling making smooth his surfaces, and it would enable them to know that the person in question actually existed, and to keep the circumstances before their intellects.

When Chang-Ch'un had made the various facts clear to this extent, those who were assembled expressed their feelings as favourably turned towards the project, provided the tests to which Ling was to be put should prove encouraging, and a secure and intelligent understanding of things to be done and not to be done could be arrived at between them. To this end Ling was brought into the chamber, and fixing his thoughts steadfastly upon Mian, he permitted portions to be cut from various parts of his body without betraying any signs of ignoble agitation. No sooner had the pieces been separated and the virtue of Ling's existence passed from them than they changed colour and hardened, nor could the most delicate and searching trials to which they were exposed by a skilful worker in metals, who was obtained for the purpose, disclose any particular, however minute, in which they differed from the finest gold. The hair, the nails and the teeth were similarly affected, and even Ling's blood dried into a fine gold powder. This detail of the trial being successfully completed, Ling subjected himself to intricate questioning on all matters connected with his religion and manner of conducting himself, both in public and privately, the history and behaviour of his ancestors, the various omens and remarkable sayings which had reference to his life and destiny, and the intentions which he then possessed regarding his future movements and habits of living. All the wise sayings and written and printed leaves which made any allusion to the existence of and possibility of discovery of the wonderful gold fluid were closely examined, and found to be in agreement, whereupon those present made no further delay in admitting that the facts were indeed as they had been described, and indulged in a dignified stroking of each other's faces as an expression of pleasure and in proof of their satisfaction at taking part in so entrancing and remunerative an affair. At Chang's command many rare and expensive wines were then brought in, and partaken of without restraint by all persons, the repast being lightened by numerous well-considered and gravity-removing jests having reference to Ling and the unusual composition of his person. So amiably were the hours occupied that it was past the time of no light when Chang rose and read at full length the statement of things to be done and things not to be done, which was to be sealed by Ling for his part and the other persons who were present for theirs. It so happened, however, that at that period Ling's mind was filled with brilliant and versatile thoughts and images of Mian, and many-hued visions of the manner in which they would spend the entrancing future which was now before them, and in this way it chanced that he did not give any portion of his intellect to the reading, mistaking it, indeed, for a delicate and very ably composed set of verses which Chang-ch'un was reciting as a formal blessing on parting. Nor was it until he was desired to affix his sign that Ling discovered his mistake, and being of too respectful and unobtrusive a disposition to require the matter to be repeated then, he carried out the obligation without in any particular understanding the written words to which he was agreeing.

As Ling walked through the streets to his chamber after leaving the house and company of Chang-Ch'un, holding firmly among his garments the thin printed papers to the amount of fifty thousand taels which he had received, and repeatedly speaking to himself in terms of general and specific encouragement at the fortunate events of the past few days, he became aware that a person of mean and rapacious appearance, whom he had some memory of having observed within the residence he had but just left, was continually by his side. Not at first doubting that the circumstance resulted from a benevolent desire on the part of Chang-ch'un that he should be protected on his passage through the city, Ling affected not to observe the incident; but upon reaching his own door the person in question persistently endeavoured to pass in also. Forming a fresh judgment about the matter, Ling, who was very powerfully constructed, and whose natural instincts were enhanced in every degree by the potent fluid of which he had lately partaken, repeatedly threw him across the street until he became weary of the diversion. At length, however, the thought arose that one who patiently submitted to continually striking the opposite houses with his head must have something of importance to communicate, whereupon he courteously invited him to enter the apartment and unweigh his mind.

"The facts of the case appear to have been somewhat inadequately represented," said the stranger, bowing obsequiously, "for this unornamental person was assured by the benignant Chang-ch'un that the one whose shadow he was to become was of a mild and forbearing nature."

"Such words are as the conversation of birds to me," replied Ling, not conjecturing how the matter had fallen about. "This person has just left the presence of the elegant and successful Chang-ch'un, and no word that he spoke gave indication of such a follower or such a service."

"Then it is indeed certain that the various transactions have not been fully understood," exclaimed the other, "for the exact communication to this unseemly one was, 'The valuable and enlightened Ling has heard and agreed to the different things to be done and not to be done, one phrase of which arranges for your continual presence, so that he will anticipate your attentions.'"

At these words the truth became as daylight before Ling's eyes, and he perceived that the written paper to which he had affixed his sign contained the detail of such an office as that of the person before him. When too late, more than ever did he regret that he had not formed some pretext for causing the document to be read a second time, as in view of his immediate intentions such an arrangement as the one to which he had agreed had every appearance of becoming of an irksome and perplexing nature. Desiring to know the length of the attendant's commands, Ling asked him for a clear statement of his duties, feigning that he had missed that portion of the reading through a momentary attack of the giddy sickness. To this request the stranger, who explained that his name was Wang, instantly replied that his written and spoken orders were: never to permit more than an arm's length of space to separate them; to prevent, by whatever force was necessary for the purpose, all attempts at evading the things to be done and not to be done, and to ignore as of no interest all other circumstances. It seemed to Ling, in consequence, that little seclusion would be enjoyed unless an arrangement could be effected between Wang and himself; so to this end, after noticing the evident poverty and covetousness of the person in question, he made him an honourable offer of frequent rewards, provided a greater distance was allowed to come between them as soon as Si-chow was reached. On his side, Ling undertook not to break through the wording of the things to be done and not to be done, and to notify to Wang any movements upon which he meditated. In this reputable manner the obstacle was ingeniously removed, and the intelligent nature of the device was clearly proved by the fact that not only Ling but Wang also had in the future a much greater liberty of action than would have been possible if it had been necessary to observe the short-sighted and evidently hastily-thought-of condition which Chang-ch'un had endeavoured to impose.

XIII

In spite of his natural desire to return to Mian as quickly as possible, Ling judged it expedient to give several days to the occupation of purchasing apparel of the richest kinds, weapons and armour in large quantities, jewels and ornaments of worked metals and other objects to indicate his changed position. Nor did he neglect actions of a pious and charitable nature, for almost his first care was to arrange with the chief ones at the Temple of Benevolent Intentions that each year, on the day corresponding to that on which he drank the gold fluid, a sumptuous and well-constructed coffin should be presented to the most deserving poor and aged person within that quarter of the city in which he had resided. When these preparations were completed, Ling set out with an extensive train of attendants; but riding on before, accompanied only by Wang, he quickly reached Si-chow without adventure.

The meeting between Ling and Mian was affecting to such an extent that the blind and deaf attendants wept openly without reproach, notwithstanding the fact that neither could become possessed of more than a half of the occurrence. Eagerly the two reunited ones examined each other's features to discover whether the separation had brought about any change in the beloved and well-remembered lines. Ling discovered upon Mian the shadow of an anxious care at his absence, while the disappointments and trials which Ling had experienced in Canton had left traces which were plainly visible to Mian's penetrating gaze. In such an entrancing occupation the time was to them without hours until a feeling of hunger recalled them to lesser matters, when a variety of very select foods and liquids was placed before them without delay. After this elegant repast had been partaken of, Mian, supporting herself upon Ling's shoulder, made a request that he would disclose to her all the matters which had come under his observation both within the city and during his journey to and from that place. Upon this encouragement, Ling proceeded to unfold his mind, not withholding anything which appeared to be of interest, no matter how slight. When he had reached Canton without any perilous adventure, Mian breathed more freely; as he recorded the interview at the Office of Warlike Deeds and Arrangements, she trembled at the insidious malignity of the evil person Li Keen. The conversation with the wise reader of the future concerning the various states of such as be officially dead almost threw her into the rigid sickness, from which, however, the wonderful circumstance of the discovered properties of the gold fluid quickly recalled her. But to Ling's great astonishment no sooner had he made plain the exceptional advantages which he had derived from the circumstances, and the nature of the undertaking at which he had arrived with Chang-ch'un, than she became a prey to the most intolerable and unrestrained anguish.

"Oh, my devoted but excessively ill-advised lover," she exclaimed wildly, and in tones which clearly indicated that she was inspired by every variety of affectionate emotion, "has the unendurable position in which you and all your household will be placed by the degrading commercial schemes and instincts of the mercenary-souled person Chang-ch'un occupied no place in your generally well-regulated intellect? Inevitably will those who drink our almond tea, in order to have an opportunity of judging the value of the appointments of the house, pass the jesting remark that while the Lings assuredly have 'a dead person's bones in the secret chamber,' at the present they will not have one in the family graveyard by reason of the death of Ling himself. Better to lose a thousand limbs during life than the entire person after death; nor would your adoring Mian hesitate to clasp proudly to her organ of affection the veriest trunk that had parted with all its attributes in a noble and sacrificing endeavour to preserve at least some dignified proportions to embellish the Ancestral Temple and to receive the worship of posterity."

"Alas!" replied Ling, with extravagant humiliation. "It is indeed true; and this person is degraded beyond the common lot of those who break images and commit thefts from sacred places. The side of the transaction which is at present engaging our attention never occurred to this superficial individual until now."

"Wise and incomparable one," said Mian, in no degree able to restrain the fountains of bitter water which clouded her delicate and expressive eyes, "in spite of this person's biting and ungracious words do not, she makes a formal petition, doubt the deathless strength of her affection. Cheerfully, in order to avert the matter in question, or even to save her lover the anguish of unavailing and soul-eating remorse, would she consign herself to a badly constructed and slow-consuming fire or expose her body to various undignified tortures. Happy are those even to whom is left a little ash to be placed in a precious urn and diligently guarded, for it, in any event, truly represents all that is left of the once living person, whereas after an honourable and spotless existence my illustrious but unthinking lord will be blended with a variety of baser substances and passed from hand to hand, his immaculate organs serving to reward murderers for their deeds and to tempt the weak and vicious to all manner of unmentionable crimes."

So overcome was Ling by the distressing nature of the oversight he had permitted that he could find no words with which to comfort Mian, who, after some moments, continued:

"There are even worse visions of degradation which occur to this person. By chance, that which was once the noble-minded Ling may be disposed of, not to the Imperial Treasury for converting into pieces of exchange, but to some undiscriminating worker in metals who will fashion out of his beautiful and symmetrical stomach an elegant food dish, so that from the ultimate developments of the circumstance may arise the fact that his own descendants, instead of worshipping him, use his internal organs for this doubtful if not absolutely unclean purpose, and thereby suffer numerous well-merited afflictions, to the end that the finally despised Ling and this discredited person, instead of founding a vigorous and prolific generation, become the parents of a line of feeble-minded and physically depressed lepers."

"Oh, my peacock-eyed one!" exclaimed Ling, in immeasurable distress. "So proficient an exhibition of virtuous grief crushes this misguided person completely to the ground. Rather would he uncomplainingly lose his pigtail than—"

"Such a course," said a discordant voice, as the unpresentable person Wang stepped forth from behind a hanging curtain, where, indeed, he had stood concealed during the entire conversation, "is especially forbidden by the twenty-third detail of the things to be done and not to be done."

"What new adversity is this?" cried Mian, pressing to Ling with a still closer embrace. "Having disposed of your incomparable body after death, surely an adequate amount of liberty and seclusion remains to us during life."

"Nevertheless," interposed the dog-like Wang, "the refined person in question must not attempt to lose or to dispose of his striking and invaluable pigtail; for by such an action he would be breaking through his spoken and written word whereby he undertook to be ruled by the things to be done and not to be done; and he would also be robbing the ingenious-minded Chang-ch'un."

"Alas!" lamented the unhappy Ling. "That which appeared to be the end of all this person's troubles is obviously simply the commencement of a new and more extensive variety. Understand, O conscientious but exceedingly inopportune Wang, that the words which passed from this person's mouth did not indicate a fixed determination, but merely served to show the unfeigned depth of his emotion. Be content that he has no intention of evading the definite principles of the things to be done and not to be done, and in the meantime honour this commonplace establishment by retiring to the hot and ill-ventilated chamber, and there partaking of a suitable repast which shall be prepared without delay."

When Wang had departed, which he did with somewhat unseemly haste, Ling made an end of recording his narrative which Mian's grief had interrupted. In this way he explained to her the reason of Wang's presence, and assured her that by reason of the arrangement he had made with that person, his near existence would not be so unsupportable to them as might at first appear to be the case.

While they were still conversing together, and endeavouring to divert their minds from the objectionable facts which had recently come within their notice, an attendant entered and disclosed that the train of servants and merchandise which Ling had preceded on the journey was arriving. At this fresh example of her lover's consistent thought for her, Mian almost forgot her recent agitation, and eagerly lending herself to the entrancing occupation of unfolding and displaying the various objects, her brow finally lost the last trace of sadness. Greatly beyond the imaginings of anticipation were the expensive articles with which Ling proudly surrounded her; and in examining and learning the cost of the set jewels and worked metals, the ornamental garments for both persons, the wood and paper appointments for the house – even incenses, perfumes, spices and rare viands had not been forgotten – the day was quickly and profitably spent.

When the hour of sunset arrived, Ling, having learnt that certain preparations which he had commanded were fully carried out, took Mian by the hand and led her into the chief apartment of the house, where were assembled all the followers and attendants, even down to the illiterate and superfluous Wang. In the centre of the room upon a table of the finest ebony stood a vessel of burning incense, some dishes of the most highly-esteemed fruit and an abundance of old and very sweet wine. Before these emblems Ling and Mian placed themselves in an attitude of deep humiliation, and formally expressed their gratitude to the Chief Deity for having called them into existence, to the cultivated earth for supplying them with the means of sustaining life, to the Emperor for providing the numerous safeguards by which their persons were protected at all times, and to their parents for educating them. This adequate ceremony being completed, Ling explicitly desired all those present to observe the fact that the two persons in question were, by that fact and from that time, made as one being, and the bond between them, incapable of severance.

When the ruling night-lantern came out from among the clouds, Ling and Mian became possessed of a great desire to go forth with pressed hands and look again on the forest paths and glades in which they had spent many hours of exceptional happiness before Ling's journey to Canton. Leaving the attendants to continue the feasting and drum-beating in a completely unrestrained manner, they therefore passed out unperceived, and wandering among the trees, presently stood on the banks of the Heng-Kiang.

"Oh, my beloved!" exclaimed Mian, gazing at the brilliant and unruffled water, "greatly would this person esteem a short river journey, such as we often enjoyed together in the days when you were recovering."

Ling, to whom the expressed desires of Mian were as the word of the Emperor, instantly prepared the small and ornamental junk which was fastened near for this purpose, and was about to step in, when a presumptuous and highly objectionable hand restrained him.

"Behold," remarked a voice which Ling had some difficulty in ascribing to any known person, so greatly had it changed from its usual tone, "behold how the immature and altogether too-inferior Ling observes his spoken and written assertions!"

At this low-conditioned speech, Ling drew his well-tempered sword without further thought, in spite of the restraining arms of Mian, but at the sight of the utterly incapable person Wang, who stood near smiling meaninglessly and waving his arms with a continuous and backward motion, he again replaced it.

"Such remarks can be left to fall unheeded from the lips of one who bears every indication of being steeped in rice spirit," he said with unprovoked dignity.

"It will be the plain duty of this expert and uncorruptible person to furnish the unnecessary, but, nevertheless, very severe and self-opinionated Chang-ch'un with a written account of how the traitorous and deceptive Ling has endeavoured to break through the thirty-fourth vessel of the liquids to be consumed and not to be consumed," continued Wang with increased deliberation and an entire absence of attention to Ling's action and speech, "and how by this refined person's unfailing civility and resourceful strategy he has been frustrated."

"Perchance," said Ling, after examining his thoughts for a short space, and reflecting that the list of things to be done and not to be done was to him as a blank leaf, "there may even be some small portion of that which is accurate in his statement. In what manner," he continued, addressing the really unendurable person, who was by this time preparing to pass the night in the cool swamp by the river's edge, "does this one endanger any detail of the written and sealed parchment by such an action?"

"Inasmuch," replied Wang, pausing in the process of removing his outer garments, "as the seventy-ninth – the intricate name given to it escapes this person's tongue at the moment – but the ninety-seventh – exper-Ling-knows-wha-mean – provides that any person, with or without, attempting or not avoiding to travel by sea, lake, or river, or to place himself in such a position as he may reasonably and intelligently be drowned in salt water, fresh water or – or honourable rice spirit, shall be guilty of, and suffer – complete loss of memory." With these words the immoderate and contemptible person sank down in a very profound slumber.

"Alas!" said Ling, turning to Mian, who stood near, unable to retire even had she desired, by reason of the extreme agitation into which the incident had thrown her delicate mind and body. "How intensely aggravating a circumstance that we are compelled to entertain so dissolute a one by reason of this person's preoccupation when the matter was read. Nevertheless, it is not unlikely that the detail he spoke of was such as he insisted, to the extent of making it a thing not to be done to journey in any manner by water. It shall be an early endeavour of this person to get these restraining details equitably amended; but in the meantime we will retrace our footsteps through the wood, and the enraptured Ling will make a well-thought-out attempt to lighten the passage by a recital of his recently composed verses on the subject of 'Exile from the Loved One; or, Farewell and Return'."

XIV

"My beloved lord!" said Mian sadly, on a morning after many days had passed since the return of Ling. "Have you not every possession for which the heart of a wise person searches? Yet the dark mark is scarcely ever absent from your symmetrical brow. If she who stands before you, and is henceforth an integral part of your organisation, has failed you in any particular, no matter how unimportant, explain the matter to her, and the amendment will be a speedy and a joyful task."

It was indeed true that Ling's mind was troubled, but the fault did not lie with Mian, as the person in question was fully aware, for before her eyes as before those of Ling the unevadable compact which had been entered into with Chang-ch'un was ever present, insidiously planting bitterness within even the most select and accomplished delights. Nor with increasing time did the obstinate and intrusive person Wang become more dignified in his behaviour; on the contrary, he freely made use of his position to indulge in every variety of abandonment, and almost each day he prevented, by reason of his knowledge of the things to be done and not to be done, some refined and permissible entertainment upon which Ling and Mian had determined. Ling had despatched many communications upon this subject to Chang-ch'un, praying also that some expert way out of the annoyance of the lesser and more unimportant things not to be done should be arrived at, but the time when he might reasonably expect an answer to these written papers had not yet arrived.

It was about this period that intelligence was brought to Ling from the villages on the road to Peking, how Li Keen, having secretly ascertained that his Yamên was standing and his goods uninjured, had determined to return, and was indeed at that hour within a hundred li of Si-chow. Furthermore, he had repeatedly been understood to pronounce clearly that he considered Ling to be the head and beginning of all his inconveniences, and to declare that the first act of justice which he should accomplish on his return would be to submit the person in question to the most unbearable tortures, and then cause him to lose his head publicly as an outrager of the settled state of things and an enemy of those who loved tranquillity. Not doubting that Li Keen would endeavour to gain an advantage by treachery if the chance presented itself, Ling determined to go forth to meet him, and without delay settle the entire disturbance in one well-chosen and fatally destructive encounter. To this end, rather than disturb the placid mind of Mian, to whom the thought of the engagement would be weighted with many disquieting fears, he gave out that he was going upon an expedition to surprise and capture certain fish of a very delicate flavour, and attended by only two persons, he set forth in the early part of the day.

Some hours later, owing to an ill-considered remark on the part of the deaf attendant, to whom the matter had been explained in an imperfect light, Mian became possessed of the true facts of the case, and immediately all the pleasure of existence went from her. She despaired of ever again beholding Ling in an ordinary state, and mournfully reproached herself for the bitter words which had risen to her lips when the circumstance of his condition and the arrangement with Chang-ch'un first became known to her. After spending an interval in a polished lament at the manner in which things were inevitably tending, the thought occurred to Mian whether by any means in her power she could influence the course and settled method of affairs. In this situation the memory of the person Wang, and the fact that on several occasions he had made himself objectionable when Ling had proposed to place himself in such a position that he incurred some very remote chance of death by drowning or by fire, recurred to her. Subduing the natural and pure-minded repulsion which she invariably experienced at the mere thought of so debased an individual, she sought for him, and discovering him in the act of constructing cardboard figures of men and animals, which it was his custom to dispose skilfully in little-frequented paths for the purpose of enjoying the sudden terror of those who passed by, she quickly put the matter before him, urging him, by some means, to prevent the encounter, which must assuredly cost the life of the one whom he had so often previously obstructed from incurring the slightest risk.

"By no means," exclaimed Wang, when he at length understood the full meaning of the project; "it would be a most unpresentable action for this commonplace person to interfere in so honourable an undertaking. Had the priceless body of the intrepid Ling been in any danger of disappearing, as, for example, by drowning or being consumed in fire, the nature of the circumstance would have been different. As the matter exists, however, there is every appearance that the far-seeing Chang-ch'un will soon reap the deserved reward of his somewhat speculative enterprise, and to that end this person will immediately procure a wooden barrier and the services of four robust carriers, and proceed to the scene of the conflict."

Deprived of even this hope of preventing the encounter, Mian betook herself in extreme dejection to the secret room of the magician, which had been unopened since the day when the two attendants had searched for substances to apply to their master, and there she diligently examined every object in the remote chance of discovering something which might prove of value in averting the matter in question.

Not anticipating that the true reason of his journey would become known to Mian, Ling continued on his way without haste, and passing through Si-chow before the sun had risen, entered upon the great road to Peking. At a convenient distance from the town he came to a favourable piece of ground where he decided to await the arrival of Li Keen, spending the time profitably in polishing his already brilliant sword, and making observations upon the nature of the spot and the condition of the surrounding omens, on which the success of his expedition would largely depend.

As the sun reached the highest point in the open sky the sound of an approaching company could be plainly heard; but at the moment when the chair of the Mandarin appeared within the sight of those who waited, the great luminary, upon which all portents depend directly or indirectly, changed to the colour of new-drawn blood and began to sink towards the earth. Without any misgivings, therefore, Ling disposed his two attendants in the wood, with instructions to step forth and aid him if he should be attacked by overwhelming numbers, while he himself remained in the way. As the chair approached, the Mandarin observed a person standing alone, and thinking that it was one who, hearing of his return, had come out of the town to honour him, he commanded the bearers to pause. Thereupon, stepping up to the opening, Ling struck the deceptive and incapable Li Keen on the cheek, at the same time crying in a full voice, "Come forth, O traitorous and two-stomached Mandarin! For this person is very desirous of assisting you in the fulfilment of your boastful words. Here is a most irreproachable sword which will serve excellently to cut off this person's undignified head; here is a waistcord which can be tightened around his breast, thereby producing excruciating pains over the entire body."

At the knowledge of who the one before him was, and when he heard the words which unhesitatingly announced Ling's fixed purpose, Li Keen first urged the carriers to fall upon Ling and slay him, and then, perceiving that such a course was exceedingly distasteful to their natural tendencies, to take up the chair and save him by flight. But Ling in the meantime engaged their attention, and fully explained to them the treacherous and unworthy conduct of Li Keen, showing them how his death would be a just retribution for his ill-spent life, and promising them each a considerable reward in addition to their arranged payment when the matter in question had been accomplished. Becoming convinced of the justice of Ling's cause, they turned upon Li Keen, insisting that he should at once attempt to carry out the ill-judged threats against Ling, of which they were consistent witnesses, and announcing that, if he failed to do so, they would certainly bear him themselves to a not far distant well of stagnant water, and there gain the approbation of the good spirits by freeing the land of so unnatural a monster.

Seeing only a dishonourable death on either side, Li Keen drew his sword, and made use of every artifice of which he had knowledge in order to disarm Ling or to take him at a disadvantage. In this he was unsuccessful, for Ling, who was by nature a very expert sword user, struck him repeatedly, until he at length fell in an expiring condition, remarking with his last words that he had indeed been a narrow-minded and extortionate person during his life, and that his death was an enlightened act of celestial accuracy.

Directing Wang and his four hired persons, who had in the meantime arrived, to give the body of the Mandarin an honourable burial in the deep of the wood, Ling rewarded and dismissed the chair-bearers, and without delay proceeded to Si-chow, where he charitably distributed the goods and possessions of Li Keen among the poor of the town. Having in this able and conscientious manner completely proved the misleading nature of the disgraceful statements which the Mandarin had spread abroad concerning him, Ling turned his footsteps towards Mian, whose entrancing joy at his safe return was judged by both persons to be a sufficient reward for the mental distress with which their separation had been accompanied.

XV

After the departure of Ling from Canton, the commercial affairs of Chang-ch'un began, from a secret and undetectable cause, to assume an ill-regulated condition. No venture which he undertook maintained a profitable attitude, so that many persons who in former times had been content to display the printed papers setting forth his name and virtues in an easily seen position in their receiving rooms, now placed themselves daily before his house in order to accuse him of using their taels in ways which they themselves had not sufficiently understood, and for the purpose of warning passers-by against his inducements. It was in vain that Chang proposed new undertakings, each of an infallibly more prosperous nature than those before; the persons who had hitherto supported him were all entrusting their money to one named Pung Soo, who required millions where Chang had been content with thousands, and who persistently insisted on greeting the sacred Emperor as an equal.

In this unenviable state Chang's mind continually returned to thoughts of Ling, whose lifeless body would so opportunely serve to dispel the embarrassing perplexities of existence which were settling thickly about him. Urged forward by a variety of circumstances which placed him in an entirely different spirit from the honourable bearing which he had formerly maintained, he now closely examined all the papers connected with the matter, to discover whether he might not be able to effect his purpose with an outward exhibition of law forms. While engaged in this degrading occupation, a detail came to his notice which caused him to become very amiably disposed and confident of success. Proceeding with the matter, he caused a well-supported report to be spread about that Ling was suffering from a wasting sickness which, without in any measure shortening his life, would cause him to return to the size and weight of a newly born child, and being by these means enabled to secure the entire matter of "The Ling (After Death) Without Much Risk Assembly" at a very small outlay, he did so, and then, calling together a company of those who hire themselves out for purposes of violence, journeyed to Si-chow.

Ling and Mian were seated together at a table in the great room, examining a vessel of some clear liquid, when Chang-ch'un entered with his armed ones, in direct opposition to the general laws of ordinary conduct and the rulings of hospitality. At the sight, which plainly indicated a threatened display of violence, Ling seized his renowned sword, which was never far distant from him, and prepared to carry out his spoken vow, that any person overstepping a certain mark on the floor would assuredly fall.

"Put away your undoubtedly competent weapon, O Ling," said Chang, who was desirous that the matter should be arranged if possible without any loss to himself, "for such a course can be honourably adopted when it is taken into consideration that we are as twenty to one, and have, moreover, the appearance of being inspired by law forms."

"There are certain matters of allowed justice which overrule all other law forms," replied Ling, taking a surer hold of his sword grasp. "Explain, for your part, O obviously double-dealing Chang-ch'un, from whom this person only recently parted on terms of equality and courtesy, why you come not with an agreeable face and a peaceful following, but with a countenance which indicates both violence and terror, and accompanied by many whom this person recognises as the most outcast and degraded from the narrow and evil-smelling ways of Canton?"

"In spite of your blustering words," said Chang, with some attempt at an exhibition of dignity, "this person is endowed by every right, and comes only for the obtaining, by the help of this expert and proficient gathering, should such a length become necessary, of his just claims. Understand that in the time since the venture was arranged this person has become possessed of all the property of 'The Ling (After Death) Without Much Risk Assembly', and thereby he is competent to act fully in the matter. It has now come within his attention that the one Ling to whom the particulars refer is officially dead, and as the written and sealed document clearly undertook that the person's body was to be delivered up for whatever use the Assembly decided whenever death should possess it, this person has now come for the honourable carrying out of the undertaking."

At these words the true nature of the hidden contrivance into which he had fallen descended upon Ling like a heavy and unavoidable thunderbolt. Nevertheless, being by nature and by reason of his late exploits fearless of death, except for the sake of the loved one by his side, he betrayed no sign of discreditable emotion at the discovery.

"In such a case," he replied, with an appearance of entirely disregarding the danger of the position, "the complete parchment must be of necessity overthrown; for if this person is now officially dead, he was equally so at the time of sealing, and arrangements entered into by dead persons have no actual existence."

"That is a matter which has never been efficiently decided," admitted Chang-ch'un, with no appearance of being thrown into a state of confusion at the suggestion, "and doubtless the case in question can by various means be brought in the end before the Court of Final Settlement at Peking, where it may indeed be judged in the manner you assert. But as such a process must infallibly consume the wealth of a province and the years of an ordinary lifetime, and as it is this person's unmoved intention to carry out his own view of the undertaking without delay, such speculations are not matters of profound interest."

Upon this Chang gave certain instructions to his followers, who thereupon prepared to advance. Perceiving that the last detail of the affair had been arrived at, Ling threw back his hanging garment, and was on the point of rushing forward to meet them, when Mian, who had maintained a possessed and reliant attitude throughout, pushed towards him the vessel of pure and sparkling liquid with which they had been engaged when so presumptuously broken in upon, at the same time speaking to him certain words in an outside language. A new and Heaven-sent confidence immediately took possession of Ling, and striking his sword against the wall with such irresistible force that the entire chamber trembled and the feeble-minded assassins shrank back in unrestrained terror, he leapt upon the table, grasping in one hand the open vessel.

"Behold the end, O most uninventive and slow-witted Chang-ch'un!" he cried in a dreadful and awe-compelling voice. "As a reward for your faithless and traitorous behaviour, learn how such avaricious-minded incompetence turns and fastens itself upon the vitals of those who beget it. In spite of many things which were not of a graceful nature towards him, this person has unassumingly maintained his part of the undertaking, and would have followed such a course conscientiously to the last. As it is, when he has made an end of speaking, the body which you are already covetously estimating in taels will in no way be distinguishable from that of the meanest and most ordinary maker of commercial ventures in Canton. For – behold! – the fluid which he holds in his hand, and which it is his fixed intention to drain to the last drop, is in truth nothing but a secret and exceedingly powerful counteractor against the virtues of the gold drug; and though but a single particle passed his lips, and the swords of your brilliant and versatile murderers met the next moment in his breast, the body which fell at your feet would be meat for worms rather than for the melting-pot."

It was indeed such a substance as Ling represented it to be, Mian having discovered it during her very systematic examination of the dead magician's inner room. Its composition and distillation had involved that self-opinionated person in many years of arduous toil, for with a somewhat unintelligent lack of foresight he had obstinately determined to perfect the antidote before he turned his attention to the drug itself. Had the matter been more ingeniously arranged, he would undoubtedly have enjoyed an earlier triumph and an affluent and respected old age.

At Ling's earnest words and prepared attitude an instant conviction of the truth of his assertions took possession of Chang. Therefore, seeing nothing but immediate and unevadable ruin at the next step, he called out in a loud and imploring voice that he should desist, and no harm would come upon him. To this Ling consented, first insisting that the followers should be dismissed without delay, and Chang alone remain to have conversation on the matter. By this just act the lower parts of Canton were greatly purified, for the persons in question being driven forth into the woods, mostly perished by encounters with wild animals, or at the hands of the enraged villagers, to whom Ling had by this time become greatly endeared.

When the usual state had been restored, Ling made clear to Chang the altered nature of the conditions to which he would alone agree. "It is a noble-minded and magnanimous proposal on your part, and one to which this misguided person had no claim," admitted Chang, as he affixed his seal to the written undertaking and committed the former parchment to be consumed by fire. By this arrangement it was agreed that Ling should receive only one-half of the yearly payment which had formerly been promised, and that no sum of taels should become due to those depending on him at his death. In return for these valuable allowances, there were to exist no details of things to be done and not to be done, Ling merely giving an honourable promise to observe the matter in a just spirit, while – most esteemed of all – only a portion of his body was to pass to Chang when the end arrived, the upper part remaining to embellish the family altar and receive the veneration of posterity.

******

As the great sky-lantern rose above the trees and the time of no noise fell upon the woods, a flower-laden pleasure junk moved away from its restraining cords and, without any sense of motion, gently bore Ling and Mian between the sweet-smelling banks of the Heng-Kiang. Presently Mian drew from beneath her flowing garment an instrument of stringed wood, and touching it with a quick but delicate stroke, like the flight and pausing of a butterfly, told in well-balanced words a refined narrative of two illustrious and noble-looking persons, and how, after many disagreeable evils and unendurable separations, they entered upon a destined state of earthly prosperity and celestial favour. When she made an end of the verses, Ling turned the junk's head by one well-directed stroke of the paddle, and prepared by using similar means to return to the place of mooring.

"Indeed," he remarked, ceasing for a moment to continue this skilful occupation, "the words which you have just spoken might, without injustice, be applied to the two persons who are now conversing together. For after suffering misfortunes and wrongs beyond an appropriate portion, they have now reached that period of existence when a tranquil and contemplative future is assured to them. In this manner is the sage and matured utterance of the inspired philosopher Nien-tsu again proved: that the life of every person is largely composed of two varieties of circumstances which together build up his existence – the Good and the Evil."

THE END OF THE STORY OF LING

XVI

When Kai Lung, the storyteller, made an end of speaking, he was immediately greeted with a variety of delicate and pleasing remarks, all persons who had witnessed the matter, down even to the lowest type of Miaotze, who by reason of their obscure circumstances had been unable to understand the meaning of a word that had been spoken, maintaining that Kai Lung's accomplishment of continuing for upwards of three hours without a pause had afforded an entertainment of a very high and refined order. While these polished sayings were being composed, together with many others of a similar nature, Lin Yi suddenly leapt to his feet with a variety of highly objectionable remarks concerning the ancestors of all those who were present, and declaring that the story of Ling was merely a well-considered stratagem to cause them to forget the expedition which they had determined upon, for by that time it should have been completely carried out. It was undoubtedly a fact that the hour spoken of for the undertaking had long passed, Lin Yi having completely overlooked the speed of time in his benevolent anxiety that the polite and valorous Ling should in the end attain to a high and remunerative destiny.

In spite of Kai Lung's consistent denials of any treachery, he could not but be aware that the incident tended greatly to his disadvantage in the eyes of those whom he had fixed a desire to conciliate, nor did his well-intentioned offer that he would without hesitation repeat the display for a like number of hours effect his amiable purpose. How the complication would finally have been determined without interruption is a matter merely of imagination, for at that moment an outpost, who had been engaged in guarding the secrecy of the expedition, threw himself into the enclosure in a torn and breathless condition, having run through the forest many li in a winding direction for the explicit purpose of warning Lin Yi that his intentions had become known, and that he and his followers would undoubtedly be surprised and overcome if they left the camp.

At this intimation of the eminent service which Kai Lung had rendered them, the nature of their faces towards him at once changed completely, those who only a moment before had been demanding his death particularly hailing him as their inspired and unobtrusive protector, and in all probability, indeed, a virtuous and benignant spirit in disguise.

Bending under the weight of offerings which Lin Yi and his followers pressed upon him, together with many clearly set out desires for his future prosperity, and assured of their unalterable protection on all future occasions, Kai Lung again turned his face towards the lanterns of Knei Yang. Far down the side of the mountain they followed his footsteps, now by a rolling stone, now by a snapping branch of yellow pine. Once again they heard his voice, cheerfully repeating to himself; "Among the highest virtues of a pure existence—" But beyond that point the gentle forest breath bore him away.

THE STORY OF YUNG CHANG

ERNEST BRAMAH

NARRATED BY KAI LUNG,
IN THE OPEN SPACE OF THE TEASHOP
OF THE CELESTIAL PRINCIPLES,
AT WU-WHEI.

"Ho, illustrious passers-by!" said Kai Lung, the storyteller, as he spread out his embroidered mat under the mulberry tree. "It is indeed unlikely that you would condescend to stop and listen to the foolish words of such an insignificant and altogether deformed person as myself. Nevertheless, if you will but retard your elegant footsteps for a few moments, this exceedingly unprepossessing individual will endeavour to entertain you with the recital of the adventures of the noble Yung Chang, as recorded by the celebrated Pe-ku-hi."

Thus adjured, the more leisurely minded drew near to hear the history of Yung Chang. There was Sing You the fruit-seller, and Li Ton-ti the wood-carver; Hi Seng left his clients to cry in vain for water; and Wang Yu, the idle pipe-maker, closed his shop of "The Fountain of Beauty," and hung on the shutter the gilt dragon to keep away customers in his absence. These, together with a few more shopkeepers and a dozen or so loafers, constituted a respectable audience by the time Kai Lung was ready.

"It would be more seemly if this ill-conditioned person who is now addressing such a distinguished assembly were to reward his fine and noble-looking hearers for their trouble," apologised the storyteller. "But, as the *Book of Verses* says, 'The meaner the slave, the greater the lord;' and it is, therefore, not unlikely that this majestic concourse will reward the despicable efforts of their servant by handfuls of coins till the air appears as though filled with swarms of locusts in the season of much heat. In particular, there is among this august crowd of Mandarins one Wang Yu, who has departed on three previous occasions without bestowing the reward of a single *cash*. If the feeble and covetous-minded Wang Yu will place within this very ordinary bowl the price of one of his exceedingly ill-made pipes, this unworthy person will proceed."

"Vast chasms can be filled, but the heart of man never," quoted the pipe-maker in retort. "Oh, most incapable of storytellers, have you not on two separate occasions slept beneath my utterly inadequate roof without payment?"

But he, nevertheless, deposited three *cash* in the bowl, and drew nearer among the front row of the listeners.

"It was during the reign of the enlightened Emperor Tsing Nung," began Kai Lung, without further introduction, "that there lived at a village near Honan a wealthy and avaricious maker of idols, named Ti Hung. So skilful had he become in the making of clay idols that his fame had spread for many li round, and idol-sellers from all the neighbouring villages, and even from the towns, came to him for their stock. No other idol-maker between Honan and Nanking employed so many clay-gatherers or so many modellers; yet, with all his riches, his avarice increased till at length he employed men whom he called 'agents' and 'travellers', who went from house to house selling his idols and extolling his virtues in verses composed by the most illustrious poets of the day. He did this in order that he might turn into his own pocket the full price of the idols, grudging those who would otherwise have sold them the few *cash* which they would make. Owing to this he had many enemies, and his army of travellers made him still more; for they were more rapacious than the scorpion, and more obstinate than the ox. Indeed, there is still the proverb, 'With honey it is possible to soften the heart of the he-goat; but a blow from an iron cleaver is taken as a mark of welcome by an agent of Ti Hung.' So that people barred the doors at their approach, and even hung out signs of death and mourning.

"Now, among all his travellers there was none more successful, more abandoned, and more valuable to Ti Hung than Li Ting. So depraved was Li Ting that he was never known to visit the tombs of his ancestors; indeed, it was said that he had been heard to mock their venerable memories, and that he had jestingly offered to sell them to anyone who should chance to be without ancestors of his own. This objectionable person would call at the houses of the most illustrious Mandarins, and would command the slaves to carry to their masters his tablets, on which were inscribed his name and his virtues. Reaching their presence, he would salute them with the greeting of an equal, 'How is your stomach?' and then proceed to exhibit samples of his wares, greatly overrating their value. 'Behold!' he would exclaim. 'Is not this elegantly moulded idol worthy of the place of honour in this sumptuous mansion which my presence defiles to such an extent that twelve basins of rose-water will not remove the stain? Are not its eyes more delicate than the most select of almonds? and is not its stomach rounder than the cupolas upon the high temple at Peking? Yet, in spite of its perfections, it is not worthy of the acceptance of so distinguished a Mandarin, and therefore I will accept in return the quarter-tael, which, indeed, is less than my illustrious master gives for the clay alone.'

"In this manner Li Ting disposed of many idols at high rates, and thereby endeared himself so much to the avaricious heart of Ti Hung that he promised him his beautiful daughter Ning in marriage.

"Ning was indeed very lovely. Her eyelashes were like the finest willow twigs that grow in the marshes by the Yang-tse-Kiang; her cheeks were fairer than poppies; and when she bathed in the Hoang Ho, her body seemed transparent. Her brow was finer than the most polished jade; while she seemed to walk, like a winged bird, without weight, her hair floating in a cloud. Indeed, she was the most beautiful creature that has ever existed."

"Now may you grow thin and shrivel up like a fallen lemon; but it is false!" cried Wang Yu, starting up suddenly and unexpectedly. "At Chee Chou, at the shop of 'The Heaven-sent Sugar-cane,' there lives a beautiful and virtuous girl who is more than all that. Her eyes are like the inside circles on the peacock's feathers; her teeth are finer than the scales on the Sacred Dragon; her—"

"If it is the wish of this illustriously endowed gathering that this exceedingly illiterate paper tiger should occupy their august moments with a description of the deformities of the very ordinary young person at Chee Chou," said Kai Lung imperturbably, "then the remainder of the history of the noble-minded Yung Chang can remain until an evil fate has overtaken Wang Yu, as it assuredly will shortly."

"A fair wind raises no storm," said Wang Yu sulkily; and Kai Lung continued:

"Such loveliness could not escape the evil eye of Li Ting, and accordingly, as he grew in favour with Ti Hung, he obtained his consent to the drawing up of the marriage contracts. More than this, he had already sent to Ning two bracelets of the finest gold, tied together with a scarlet thread, as a betrothal present. But, as the proverb says, 'The good bee will not touch the faded flower,' and Ning, although compelled by the second of the Five Great Principles to respect her father, was unable to regard the marriage with anything but abhorrence. Perhaps this was not altogether the fault of Li Ting, for on the evening of the day on which she had received his present, she walked in the rice fields, and sitting down at the foot of a funereal cypress, whose highest branches pierced the Middle Air, she cried aloud:

"'I cannot control my bitterness. Of what use is it that I should be called the "White Pigeon among Golden Lilies," if my beauty is but for the hog-like eyes of the exceedingly objectionable Li Ting? Ah, Yung Chang, my unfortunate lover! What evil spirit pursues you that you cannot pass your examination for the second degree? My noble-minded but ambitious boy, why were you not content with an agricultural or even a manufacturing career and happiness? By aspiring to a literary degree, you have placed a barrier wider than the Whang Hai between us.'

"'As the earth seems small to the soaring swallow, so shall insuperable obstacles be overcome by the heart worn smooth with a fixed purpose,' said a voice beside her, and Yung Chang stepped from behind the cypress tree, where he had been waiting for Ning. 'O one more symmetrical than the chrysanthemum,' he continued, 'I shall yet, with the aid of my ancestors, pass the second degree, and even obtain a position of high trust in the public office at Peking.'

"'And in the meantime,' pouted Ning, 'I shall have partaken of the wedding cake of the utterly unpresentable Li Ting.' And she exhibited the bracelets which she had that day received.

"'Alas!' said Yung Chang, 'there are times when one is tempted to doubt even the most efficacious and violent means. I had hoped that by this time Li Ting would have come to a sudden and most unseemly end; for I have drawn up and affixed in the most conspicuous places notifications of his character, similar to the one here.'

"Ning turned, and beheld fastened to the trunk of the cypress an exceedingly elegantly written and composed notice, which Yung read to her, as follows:

> Beware of Incurring Death from Starvation
> Let the distinguished inhabitants of this district observe the exceedingly ungraceful walk and bearing of the low person who calls himself Li Ting. Truthfully, it is that of a dog in the act of being dragged to the river because his sores and diseases render him objectionable in the house of his master. So will this hunchbacked person be dragged to the place of execution, and be bowstrung, to the great relief of all who respect the five senses; A Respectful Physiognomy, Passionless Reflexion, Soft Speech, Acute Hearing, Piercing Sight.
>
> He hopes to attain to the Red Button and the Peacock's Feather; but the right hand of the Deity itches, and Li Ting will assuredly be removed suddenly.

"'Li Ting must certainly be in league with the evil forces if he can withstand so powerful a weapon,' said Ning admiringly, when her lover had finished reading. 'Even now he is starting on a journey, nor will he return till the first day of the month when the sparrows go to the sea and are changed into oysters. Perhaps the fate will overtake him while he is away. If not—'

"'If not,' said Yung, taking up her words as she paused, 'then I have yet another hope. A moment ago you were regretting my choice of a literary career. Learn, then, the value of knowledge. By its aid (assisted, indeed, by the spirits of my ancestors) I have discovered a new and strange thing, for which I can find no word. By using this new system of reckoning, your illustrious but exceedingly narrow-minded and miserly father would be able to make five taels where he now makes one. Would he not, in consideration for this, consent to receive me as a son-in-law, and dismiss the inelegant and unworthy Li Ting?'

"'In the unlikely event of your being able to convince my illustrious parent of what you say, it would assuredly be so,' replied Ning. 'But in what way could you do so? My sublime and charitable father already employs all the means in his power to reap the full reward of his sacred industry. His "solid household gods" are in reality mere shells of clay; higher-priced images are correspondingly constructed, and his clay gatherers and modellers are all paid on a "profit-sharing system". Nay, further, it is beyond likelihood that he should wish for more purchasers, for so great is his fame that those who come to buy have sometimes to wait for days in consequence of those before them; for my exceedingly methodical sire entrusts none with the receiving of money, and the exchanges are therefore made slowly. Frequently an unnaturally devout person will require as many as a hundred idols, and so the greater part of the day will be passed.'

"'In what way?' inquired Yung tremulously.

"'Why, in order that the countings may not get mixed, of course; it is necessary that when he has paid for one idol he should carry it to a place aside, and then return and pay for the second, carrying it to the first, and in such a manner to the end. In this way the sun sinks behind the mountains.'

"'But,' said Yung, his voice thick with his great discovery, 'if he could pay for the entire quantity at once, then it would take but a hundredth part of the time, and so more idols could be sold.'

"'How could this be done?' inquired Ning wonderingly. 'Surely it is impossible to conjecture the value of so many idols.'

"'To the unlearned it would indeed be impossible,' replied Yung proudly, 'but by the aid of my literary researches I have been enabled to discover a process by which such results would be not a matter of conjecture, but of certainty. These figures I have committed to tablets, which I am prepared to give to your mercenary and slow-witted father in return for your incomparable hand, a share of the profits and the dismissal of the uninventive and morally threadbare Li Ting.'

"'When the earth worm boasts of his elegant wings, the eagle can afford to be silent,' said a harsh voice behind them; and turning hastily they beheld Li Ting, who had come upon them unawares. 'Oh, most insignificant of table-spoilers,' he continued, 'it is very evident that much over-study has softened your usually well-educated brains. Were it not that you are obviously mentally afflicted, I should unhesitatingly persuade my beautiful and refined sword to introduce you to the spirits of your ignoble ancestors. As it is, I will merely cut off your nose and your left ear, so that people may not say that the Dragon of the Earth sleeps and wickedness goes unpunished.'

"Both had already drawn their swords, and very soon the blows were so hard and swift that, in the dusk of the evening, it seemed as though the air were filled with innumerable and many-coloured fireworks. Each was a practised swordsman, and there was no advantage gained on either side, when Ning, who had fled on the appearance of Li Ting, reappeared, urging on her father, whose usually leisurely footsteps were quickened by the dread that the duel must surely result in certain loss to himself, either of a valuable servant, or of the discovery which Ning had briefly explained to him, and of which he at once saw the value.

"'Oh, most distinguished and expert persons,' he exclaimed breathlessly, as soon as he was within hearing distance, 'do not trouble to give so marvellous an exhibition for the benefit of this unworthy individual, who is the only observer of your illustrious dexterity! Indeed, your honourable condescension so fills this illiterate person with shame that his hearing is thereby preternaturally sharpened, and he can plainly distinguish many voices from beyond the Hoang Ho, crying for the Heaven-sent representative of the degraded Ti Hung to bring them more idols. Bend, therefore, your refined footsteps in the direction of Poo Chow, O Li Ting, and leave me to make myself objectionable to this exceptional young man with my intolerable commonplaces.'

"'The shadow falls in such a direction as the sun wills,' said Li Ting, as he replaced his sword and departed.

"'Yung Chang,' said the merchant, 'I am informed that you have made a discovery that would be of great value to me, as it undoubtedly would if it is all that you say. Let us discuss the matter without ceremony. Can you prove to me that your system possesses the merit you claim for it? If so, then the matter of arrangement will be easy.'

"'I am convinced of the absolute certainty and accuracy of the discovery,' replied Yung Chang. 'It is not as though it were an ordinary matter of human intelligence, for this was discovered to me as I was worshipping at the tomb of my ancestors. The method is regulated by a system of squares, triangles and cubes. But as the practical proof might be long, and as I hesitate to keep your adorable daughter out in the damp night air, may I not call at your inimitable dwelling in the morning, when we can go into the matter thoroughly?'

"I will not weary this intelligent gathering, each member of which doubtless knows all the books on mathematics off by heart, with a recital of the means by which Yung Chang proved to Ti Hung the accuracy of his tables and the value of his discovery of the multiplication table, which till then had been undreamt of," continued the storyteller. "It is sufficient to know that he did so, and that Ti Hung agreed to his terms, only stipulating that Li Ting should not be made aware of his dismissal until he had returned and given in his accounts. The share of the profits that Yung was to receive was cut down very low by Ti Hung, but the young man did not mind that, as he would live with his father-in-law for the future.

"With the introduction of this new system, the business increased like a river at flood-time. All rivals were left far behind, and Ti Hung put out this sign:

> NO WAITING HERE!
> Good morning! Have you worshipped one of Ti Hung's refined ninety-nine-*cash* idols?
>
> Let the purchasers of ill-constructed idols at other establishments, where they have grown old and venerable while waiting for the all-thumb proprietors to count up to ten, come to the shop of Ti Hung and regain their lost youth. Our ninety-nine-*cash* idols are worth a tael a set. We do not, however, claim that they will do everything. The ninety-nine-*cash* idols of Ti Hung will not, for example, purify linen, but even the most contented and frozen-brained person cannot be happy until he possesses one. What is happiness? The exceedingly well-educated Philosopher defines it as the accomplishment of all our desires. Everyone desires one of the Ti Hung's ninety-nine-*cash* idols, therefore get one; but be sure that it is Ti Hung's.
>
> Have you a bad idol? If so, dismiss it, and get one of Ti Hung's ninety-nine-*cash* specimens.
>
> Why does your idol look old sooner than your neighbour's? Because yours is not one of Ti Hung's ninety-nine-*cash* marvels.
>
> They bring all delights to the old and the young, the elegant idols supplied by Ti Hung.
>
> NB – The "Great Sacrifice" idol, forty-five *cash*; delivered, carriage free, in quantities of not less than twelve, at any temple, on the evening before the sacrifice.

"It was about this time that Li Ting returned. His journey had been more than usually successful, and he was well satisfied in consequence. It was not until he had made out his accounts and handed in his money that Ti Hung informed him of his agreement with Yung Chang.

"'Oh, most treacherous and excessively unpopular Ti Hung,' exclaimed Li Ting, in a terrible voice, 'this is the return you make for all my entrancing efforts in your services, then? It is in this way that you reward my exceedingly unconscientious recommendations of your very inferior and unendurable clay idols, with their goggle eyes and concave stomachs! Before I go, however, I request to be inspired to make the following remark – that I confidently predict your ruin. And now this low and undignified person will finally shake the elegant dust of your distinguished house from his thoroughly inadequate feet, and proceed to offer his incapable services to the rival establishment over the way.'

"'The machinations of such an evilly disposed person as Li Ting will certainly be exceedingly subtle,' said Ti Hung to his son-in-law when the traveller had departed. 'I must counteract his omens. Herewith I wish to prophecy that henceforth I shall enjoy an unbroken run of good fortune. I have spoken, and assuredly I shall not eat my words.'

"As the time went on, it seemed as though Ti Hung had indeed spoken truly. The ease and celerity with which he transacted his business brought him customers and dealers from more remote regions than ever, for they could spend days on the journey and still save time. The army of clay-gatherers and modellers grew larger and larger, and the work sheds stretched almost down to the river's edge. Only one thing troubled Ti Hung, and that was the uncongenial disposition of his son-in-law, for Yung took no further interest in the industry to which his discovery had given so great an impetus, but resolutely set to work again to pass his examination for the second degree.

"'It is an exceedingly distinguished and honourable thing to have failed thirty-five times, and still to be undiscouraged,' admitted Ti Hung; 'but I cannot cleanse my throat from bitterness when I consider that my noble and lucrative business must pass into the hands of strangers, perhaps even into the possession of the unendurable Li Ting.'

"But it had been appointed that this degrading thing should not happen, however, and it was indeed fortunate that Yung did not abandon his literary pursuits; for after some time it became very apparent to Ti Hung that there was something radically wrong with his business. It was not that his custom was falling off in any way; indeed, it had lately increased in a manner that was phenomenal, and when the merchant came to look into the matter, he found to his astonishment that the least order he had received in the past week had been for a hundred idols. All the sales had been large, and yet Ti Hung found himself most unaccountably deficient in taels. He was puzzled and alarmed, and for the next few days he looked into the business closely. Then it was that the reason was revealed, both for the falling off in the receipts and for the increase in the orders. The calculations of the unfortunate Yung Chang were correct up to a hundred, but at that number he had made a gigantic error – which, however, he was never able to detect and rectify – with the result that all transactions above that point worked out at a considerable loss to the seller. It was in vain that the panic-stricken Ti Hung goaded his miserable son-in-law to correct the mistake; it was equally in vain that he tried to stem the current of his enormous commercial popularity. He had competed for public favour, and he had won it, and every day his business increased till ruin grasped him by the pigtail. Then came an order from one firm at Peking for five million of the ninety-nine-*cash* idols, and at that Ti Hung put up his shutters, and sat down in the dust.

"'Behold!' he exclaimed. 'In the course of a lifetime there are many very disagreeable evils that may overtake a person. He may offend the Sacred Dragon, and be in consequence reduced to a fine dry powder; or he may incur the displeasure of the benevolent and pure-minded Emperor, and be condemned to death by roasting; he may also be troubled by demons or by the disturbed spirits of his ancestors, or be struck by thunderbolts. Indeed, there are numerous annoyances, but they become as Heaven-sent blessings in comparison to a self-opinionated and more than ordinarily weak-minded son-in-law. Of what avail is it that I have habitually sold one idol for the value of a hundred? The very objectionable man in possession sits in my delectable summer-house, and the unavoidable legal documents settle around me like a flock of pigeons. It is indeed necessary that I should declare myself to be in voluntary liquidation, and make an assignment of my book debts for the benefit of my creditors. Having accomplished this, I will proceed to the well-constructed tomb of my illustrious ancestors, and having kowtowed at their incomparable shrines, I will put an end to my distinguished troubles with this exceedingly well-polished sword.'

"'The wise man can adapt himself to circumstances as water takes the shape of the vase that contains it,' said the well-known voice of Li Ting. 'Let not the lion and the tiger fight at the bidding of the jackal. By combining our forces all may be well with you yet. Assist me to dispose of the entirely superfluous Yung Chang and to marry the elegant and symmetrical Ning, and in return I will allot to you a portion of my not inconsiderable income.'

"'However high the tree, the leaves fall to the ground, and your hour has come at last, O detestable Li Ting!' said Yung, who had heard the speakers and crept upon them unperceived. 'As for my distinguished and immaculate father-in-law, doubtless the heat has affected his indefatigable brains, or he would not have listened to your contemptible suggestion. For yourself, draw!'

"Both swords flashed, but before a blow could be struck the spirits of his ancestors hurled Li Ting lifeless to the ground, to avenge the memories that their unworthy descendant had so often reviled.

"'So perish all the enemies of Yung Chang,' said the victor. 'And now, my venerated but exceedingly short-sighted father-in-law, learn how narrowly you have escaped making yourself exceedingly objectionable to yourself. I have just received intelligence from Peking that I have passed the second degree, and have in consequence been appointed to a remunerative position under the Government. This will enable us to live in comfort, if not in affluence, and the rest of your engaging days can be peacefully spent in flying kites.'"

THE PROBATION OF SEN HENG

• • • • •

ERNEST BRAMAH

RELATED BY KAI LUNG, AT WU-WHEI,
AS A REBUKE TO WANG YU AND CERTAIN
OTHERS WHO HAD QUESTIONED THE
PRACTICAL VALUE OF HIS STORIES.

"It is an undoubted fact that this person has not realised the direct remunerative advantage which he confidently anticipated," remarked the idle and discontented pipe-maker Wang Yu, as, with a few other persons of similar inclination, he sat in the shade of the great mulberry tree at Wu-whei, waiting for the evil influence of certain very mysterious sounds, which had lately been heard, to pass away before he resumed his occupation. "When the seemingly proficient and trustworthy Kai Lung first made it his practice to journey to Wu-whei, and narrate to us the doings of persons of all classes of life," he continued, "it seemed to this one that by closely following the recital of how Mandarins obtained their high position, and exceptionally rich persons their wealth, he must, in the end, inevitably be rendered competent to follow in their illustrious footsteps. Yet in how entirely contrary a direction has the whole course of events tended! In spite of the honourable intention which involved a frequent absence from his place of commerce, those who journeyed thither with the set purpose of possessing one of his justly famed opium pipes so perversely regarded the matter that, after two or three fruitless visits, they deliberately turned their footsteps towards the workshop of the inelegant Ming-yo, whose pipes are confessedly greatly inferior to those produced by the person who is now speaking. Nevertheless, the rapacious Kai Lung, to whose influence the falling off in custom was thus directly attributable, persistently declined to bear any share whatever in the loss which his profession caused, and, indeed, regarded the circumstance from so grasping and narrow-minded a point of observation that he would not even go to the length of suffering this much-persecuted one to join the circle of his hearers without on every occasion making the customary offering. In this manner a well-intentioned pursuit of riches has insidiously led this person within measurable distance of the bolted dungeon for those who do not meet their just debts, while the only distinction likely to result from his assiduous study of the customs and methods of those high in power is that of being publicly bowstrung as a warning to others. Manifestedly the pointed finger of the unreliable Kai Lung is a very treacherous guide."

"It is related," said a dispassionate voice behind them, "that a person of limited intelligence, on being assured that he would certainly one day enjoy an adequate competence if he closely followed the industrious habits of the thrifty bee, spent the greater part of his life in anointing his thighs with the yellow powder which he laboriously collected from the flowers of the field. It is not so recorded; but doubtless the nameless one in question was by profession a maker of opium pipes, for this person has observed from time to time how that occupation, above all others, tends to degrade the mental faculties, and to debase its followers to a lower position than that of the beasts of labour. Learn therefrom, O superficial Wang Yu, that wisdom lies in an intelligent perception of great principles, and not in a slavish imitation of details which are, for the most part, beyond your simple and insufficient understanding."

"Such may, indeed, be the case, Kai Lung," replied Wang Yu sullenly – for it was the storyteller in question who had approached unperceived, and who now stood before them – "but it is none the less a fact that, on the last occasion when this misguided person joined the attending circle at your uplifted voice, a Mandarin of the third degree chanced to pass through Wu-whei, and halted at the door-step of 'The Fountain of Beauty,' fully intending to entrust this one with the designing and fashioning of a pipe of exceptional elaborateness. This matter, by his absence, has now passed from him, and today, through listening to the narrative of how the accomplished Yuin-Pel doubled his fortune, he is the poorer by many taels."

"Yet tomorrow, when the name of the Mandarin of the third degree appears in the list of persons who have transferred their entire property to those who are nearly related to them in order to avoid it being seized to satisfy the just claims made against them," replied Kai Lung, "you will be able to regard yourself the richer by so many taels."

At these words, which recalled to the minds of all who were present the not uncommon manner of behaving observed by those of exalted rank, who freely engaged persons to supply them with costly articles without in any way regarding the price to be paid, Wang Yu was silent.

"Nevertheless," exclaimed a thin voice from the edge of the group which surrounded Kai Lung, "it in no wise follows that the stories are in themselves excellent, or of such a nature that the hearing of their recital will profit a person. Wang Yu may be satisfied with empty words, but there are others present who were studying deep matters when Wang Yu was learning the art of walking. If Kai Lung's stories are of such remunerative benefit as the person in question claims, how does it chance that Kai Lung himself who is assuredly the best acquainted with them, stands before us in mean apparel, and on all occasions confessing an unassuming poverty?"

"It is Yan-hi Pung," went from mouth to mouth among the bystanders – "Yan-hi Pung, who traces on paper the words of chants and historical tales, and sells them to such as can afford to buy. And although his motive in exposing the emptiness of Kai Lung's stories may not be Heaven-sent – inasmuch as Kai Lung provides us with such matter as he himself purveys, only at a much more moderate price – yet his words are well considered, and must therefore be regarded."

"O Yan-hi Pung," replied Kai Lung, hearing the name from those who stood about him, and moving towards the aged person, who stood meanwhile leaning upon his staff, and looking from side to side with quickly moving eyelids in a manner very offensive towards the storyteller, "your just remark shows you to be a person of exceptional wisdom, even as your well-bowed legs prove you to be one of great bodily strength; for justice is ever obvious and wisdom hidden, and they who build structures for endurance discard the straight and upright and insist upon such an arch as you so symmetrically exemplify."

Speaking in this conciliatory manner, Kai Lung came up to Yan-hi Pung, and taking between his fingers a disc of thick polished crystal, which the aged and short-sighted chant-writer used for the purpose of magnifying and bringing nearer the letters upon which he was engaged, and which hung around his neck by an embroidered cord, the storyteller held it aloft, crying aloud:

"Observe closely, and presently it will be revealed and made clear how the apparently very conflicting words of the wise Yan-hi Pung, and those of this unassuming but nevertheless conscientious person who is now addressing you, are, in reality, as one great truth."

With this assurance Kai Lung moved the crystal somewhat, so that it engaged the sun's rays, and concentrated them upon the uncovered crown of the unsuspecting and still objectionably engaged person before him. Without a moment's pause, Yan-hi Pung leapt high into the air, repeatedly pressing his hand to the spot thus selected and crying aloud:

"Evil dragons and thunderbolts! But the touch was as hot as a scar left by the uncut nail of the sublime Buddha!"

"Yet the crystal—" remarked Kai Lung composedly, passing it into the hands of those who stood near.

"Is as cool as the innermost leaves of the riverside sycamore," they declared.

Kai Lung said nothing further, but raised both his hands above his head, as if demanding their judgment. Thereupon a loud shout went up on his behalf, for the greater part of them loved to see the manner in which he brushed aside those who would oppose him; and the sight of the aged person

Yan-hi Pung leaping far into the air had caused them to become exceptionally amused, and, in consequence, very amiably disposed towards the one who had afforded them the entertainment.

"The story of Sen Heng," began Kai Lung, when the discussion had terminated in the manner already recorded, "concerns itself with one who possessed an unsuspecting and ingenious nature, which ill-fitted him to take an ordinary part in the everyday affairs of life, no matter how engaging such a character rendered him among his friends and relations. Having at an early age been entrusted with a burden of rice and other produce from his father's fields to dispose of in the best possible manner at a neighbouring mart, and having completed the transaction in a manner extremely advantageous to those with whom he trafficked but very intolerable to the one who had sent him, it at once became apparent that some other means of gaining a livelihood must be discovered for him.

"'Beyond all doubt,' said his father, after considering the matter for a period, 'it is a case in which one should be governed by the wise advice and example of the Mandarin Poo-chow.'

"'Illustrious sire,' exclaimed Sen Heng, who chanced to be present, 'the illiterate person who stands before you is entirely unacquainted with the one to whom you have referred; nevertheless, he will, as you suggest, at once set forth, and journeying with all speed to the abode of the estimable Poo-chow, solicit his experience and advice.'

"'Unless a more serious loss should be occasioned,' replied the father coldly, 'there is no necessity to adopt so extreme a course. The benevolent Mandarin in question existed at a remote period of the Thang dynasty, and the incident to which an allusion has been made arose in the following way: to the public court of the enlightened Poo-chow there came one day a youth of very inferior appearance and hesitating manner, who besought his explicit advice, saying: "The degraded and unprepossessing being before you, O select and venerable Mandarin, is by nature and attainments a person of the utmost timidity and fearfulness. From this cause life itself has become a detestable observance in his eyes, for those who should be his companions of both sexes hold him in undisguised contempt, making various unendurable allusions to the colour and nature of his internal organs whenever he would endeavour to join them. Instruct him, therefore, the manner in which this cowardice may be removed, and no service in return will be esteemed too great." "There is a remedy," replied the benevolent Mandarin, without any hesitation whatever, "which if properly carried out is efficacious beyond the possibility of failure. Certain component parts of your body are lacking, and before the desired result can be obtained these must be supplied from without. Of all courageous things the tiger is the most fearless, and in consequence it combines all those ingredients which you require; furthermore, as the teeth of the tiger are the instruments with which it accomplishes its vengeful purpose, there reside the essential principles of its inimitable courage. Let the person who seeks instruction in the matter, therefore, do as follows: taking the teeth of a full-grown tiger as soon as it is slain, and before the essences have time to return into the body, he shall grind them to a powder, and mixing the powder with a portion of rice, consume it. After seven days he must repeat the observance, and yet again a third time, after another similar lapse. Let him, then, return for further guidance; for the present the matter interests this person no further." At these words the youth departed, filled with a new and inspired hope; for the wisdom of the sagacious Poo-chow was a matter which did not admit of any doubt whatever, and he had spoken with well-defined certainty of the success of the experiment. Nevertheless, after several days industriously spent in endeavouring to obtain by purchase the teeth of a newly-slain tiger, the details of the undertaking began to assume a new and entirely unforeseen aspect; for those whom he approached as being the most likely to possess what he required either became very immoderately and disagreeably amused at the nature of the request, or regarded it as a new and ill-judged form of ridicule, which they prepared to avenge by blows and by base remarks of the most personal variety. At length it became unavoidably obvious to the youth that if he was to obtain the articles in question it would first be necessary that he should become adept in the art of slaying tigers, for in no other way were the required conditions likely to be present. Although the prospect was one which did not greatly tend to allure him, yet he did not regard it with the utterly incapable emotions which would have been present on an earlier occasion; for the habit of continually guarding himself from the onslaughts of those who received his inquiry in an attitude of narrow-minded distrust had inspired him with a new-found valour, while his amiable and unrestrained manner of life increased his bodily vigour in every degree. First perfecting himself in the use of the bow and arrow, therefore, he betook himself to a wild and very extensive forest, and there concealed himself among the upper foliage of a tall tree standing by the side of a pool of water. On the second night of his watch, the youth perceived a large but somewhat ill-conditioned tiger approaching the pool for the purpose of quenching its thirst, whereupon he tremblingly fitted an arrow to his bowstring, and profiting by the instruction he had received, succeeded in piercing the creature to the heart. After fulfilling the observance laid upon him by the discriminating Poo-chow, the youth determined to remain in the forest, and sustain himself upon such food as fell to his weapons, until the time arrived when he should carry out the rite for the last time. At the end of seven days, so subtle had he become in all kinds of hunting, and so strengthened by the meat and herbs upon which he existed, that he disdained to avail himself of the shelter of a tree, but standing openly by the side of the water, he engaged the attention of the first tiger which came to drink, and discharged arrow after arrow into its body with unfailing power and precision. So entrancing, indeed, had the pursuit become that the next seven days lengthened out into the apparent period of as many moons, in such a leisurely manner did they rise and fall. On the appointed day, without waiting for the evening to arrive, the youth set out with the first appearance of light, and penetrated into the most inaccessible jungles, crying aloud words of taunt-laden challenge to all the beasts therein, and accusing the ancestors of their race of every imaginable variety of evil behaviour. Yet so great had become the renown of the one who stood forth, and so widely had the warning voice been passed from tree to tree, preparing all who dwelt in the forest against his anger, that not even the fiercest replied openly, though low growls and mutterings proceeded from every cave within a bow-shot's distance around. Wearying quickly of such feeble and timorous demonstrations, the youth rushed into the cave from which the loudest murmurs proceeded, and there discovered a tiger of unnatural size, surrounded by the bones of innumerable ones whom it had devoured; for from time to time its ravages became so great and unbearable, that armies were raised in the neighbouring villages and sent to destroy it, but more than a few stragglers never returned. Plainly recognising that a just and inevitable vengeance had overtaken it, the tiger made only a very inferior exhibition of resistance, and the youth, having first stunned it with a blow of his closed hand, seized it by the middle, and repeatedly dashed its head against the rocky sides of its retreat. He then performed for the third time the ceremony enjoined by the Mandarin, and having cast upon the cringing and despicable forms concealed in the surrounding woods and caves a look of dignified and ineffable contempt, set out upon his homeward journey, and in the space of three days' time reached the town of the versatile Poo-chow. "Behold," exclaimed that person, when, lifting up his eyes, he saw the youth approaching laden with the skins of the tigers and other spoils, "now at least the youths and maidens of your native village will no longer withdraw themselves from the company of so undoubtedly heroic a person." "Illustrious Mandarin," replied the other, casting both his weapons and his trophies before his inspired adviser's feet, "what has this person to do with the little ones of either sex? Give him rather the foremost place in your ever-victorious company of bowmen, so that he may repay in part the undoubted debt under which he henceforth exists." This proposal found favour with the pure-minded Poo-chow, so that in course of time the unassuming youth who had come supplicating his advice became the valiant commander of his army, and the one eventually chosen to present plighting gifts to his only daughter.'

"When the father had completed the narrative of how the faint-hearted youth became in the end a courageous and resourceful leader of bowmen, Sen looked up, and not in any degree understanding the purpose of the story, or why it had been set forth before him, exclaimed:

"'Undoubtedly the counsel of the graceful and intelligent Mandarin Poo-chow was of inestimable service in the case recorded, and this person would gladly adopt it as his guide for the future, on the chance of it leading to a similar honourable career; but – alas! – there are no tigers to be found throughout this Province.'

"'It is a loss which those who are engaged in commerce in the city of Hankow strive to supply adequately,' replied his father, who had an assured feeling that it would be of no avail to endeavour to show Sen that the story which he had just related was one setting forth a definite precept rather than fixing an exact manner of behaviour. 'For that reason,' he continued, 'this person has concluded an arrangement by which you will journey to that place, and there enter into the house of commerce of an expert and conscientious vendor of moving contrivances. Among so rapacious and keen-witted a class of persons as they of Hankow, it is exceedingly unlikely that your amiable disposition will involve any individual one in an unavoidably serious loss, and even should such an unforeseen event come to pass, there will, at least, be the undeniable satisfaction of the thought that the unfortunate occurrence will in no way affect the prosperity of those to whom you are bound by the natural ties of affection.'

"'Benevolent and virtuous-minded father,' replied Sen gently, but speaking with an inspired conviction; 'from his earliest infancy this unassuming one has been instructed in an inviolable regard for the Five General Principles of Fidelity to the Emperor, Respect for Parents, Harmony between Husband and Wife, Agreement among Brothers, and Constancy in Friendship. It will be entirely unnecessary to inform so pious-minded a person as the one now being addressed that no evil can attend the footsteps of an individual who courteously observes these enactments.'

"'Without doubt it is so arranged by the protecting Deities,' replied the father; 'yet it is an exceedingly desirable thing for those who are responsible in the matter that the footsteps to which reference has been made should not linger in the neighbourhood of the village, but should, with all possible speed, turn in the direction of Hankow.'

"In this manner it came to pass that Sen Heng set forth on the following day, and coming without delay to the great and powerful city of Hankow, sought out the house of commerce known as 'The Pure Gilt Dragon of Exceptional Symmetry', where the versatile King-y-Yang engaged in the entrancing occupation of contriving moving figures, and other devices of an ingenious and mirth-provoking character, which he entrusted into the hands of numerous persons to sell throughout the Province. From this cause, although enjoying a very agreeable recompense from the sale of the objects, the greatly perturbed King-y-Yang suffered continual internal misgivings; for the habit of behaving of those whom he appointed to go forth in the manner described was such that he could not entirely dismiss from his mind an assured conviction that the details were not invariably as they were represented to be. Frequently would one return in a very deficient and unpresentable condition of garment, asserting that on his return, while passing through a lonely and unprotected district, he had been assailed by an armed band of robbers, and despoiled of all he possessed. Another would claim to have been made the sport of evil spirits, who led him astray by means of false signs in the forest, and finally destroyed his entire burden of commodities, accompanying the unworthy act by loud cries of triumph and remarks of an insulting nature concerning King-y-Yang; for the honourable character and charitable actions of the person in question had made him very objectionable to that class of beings. Others continually accounted for the absence of the required number of taels by declaring that at a certain point of their journey they were made the object of marks of amiable condescension on the part of a high and dignified public official, who, on learning in whose service they were, immediately professed an intimate personal friendship with the estimable King-y-Yang, and, out of a feeling of gratified respect for him, took away all such contrivances as remained undisposed of, promising to arrange the payment with the refined King-y-Yang himself when they should next meet. For these reasons King-y-Yang was especially desirous of obtaining one whose spoken word could be received, upon all points, as an assured fact, and it was, therefore, with an emotion of internal lightness that he confidently heard from those who were acquainted with the person that Sen Heng was, by nature and endowments, utterly incapable of representing matters of even the most insignificant degree to be otherwise than what they really were.

Filled with an acute anxiety to discover what amount of success would be accorded to his latest contrivance, King-y-Yang led Sen Heng to a secluded chamber, and there instructed him in the method of selling certain apparently very ingeniously constructed ducks, which would have the appearance of swimming about on the surface of an open vessel of water, at the same time uttering loud and ever-increasing cries, after the manner of their kind. With ill-restrained admiration at the skilful nature of the deception, King-y-Yang pointed out that the ducks which were to be disposed of, and upon which a seemingly very low price was fixed, did not, in reality, possess any of these accomplishments, but would, on the contrary, if placed in water, at once sink to the bottom in a most incapable manner; it being part of Sen's duty to exhibit only a specially prepared creature which was restrained upon the surface by means of hidden cords, and, while bending over it, to simulate the cries as agreed upon. After satisfying himself that Sen could perform these movements competently, King-y-Yang sent him forth, particularly charging him that he should not return without a sum of money which fully represented the entire number of ducks entrusted to him, or an adequate number of unsold ducks to compensate for the deficiency.

"At the end of seven days Sen returned to King-y-Yang, and although entirely without money, even to the extent of being unable to provide himself with the merest necessities of a frugal existence, he honourably returned the full number of ducks with which he had set out. It then became evident that although Sen had diligently perfected himself in the sounds and movements which King-y-Yang had contrived, he had not fully understood that they were to be executed stealthily, but had, in consequence, manifested the accomplishment openly, not unreasonably supposing that such an exhibition would be an additional inducement to those who appeared to be well-disposed towards the purchase. From this cause it came about that although large crowds were attracted by Sen's manner of conducting the enterprise, none actually engaged to purchase even the least expensively-valued of the ducks, although several publicly complimented Sen on his exceptional proficiency, and repeatedly urged him to louder and more frequent cries, suggesting that by such means possible buyers might be attracted to the spot from remote and inaccessible villages in the neighbourhood.

"When King-y-Yang learned how the venture had been carried out, he became most intolerably self-opinionated in his expressions towards Sen's mental attainments and the manner of his bringing up. It was entirely in vain that the one referred to pointed out in a tone of persuasive and courteous restraint that he had not, down to the most minute particulars, transgressed either the general or the specific obligations of the Five General Principles, and that, therefore, he was blameless, and even worthy of commendation for the manner in which he had acted. With an inelegant absence of all refined feeling, King-y-Yang most incapably declined to discuss the various aspects of the controversy in an amiable manner, asserting, indeed, that for the consideration of as many brass *cash* as Sen had mentioned principles he would cause him to be thrown into prison as a person of unnatural ineptitude. Then, without rewarding Sen for the time spent in his service, or even inviting him to partake of food and wine, the insufferable deviser of very indifferent animated contrivances again sent him out, this time into the streets of Hankow with a number of delicately inlaid boxes, remarking in a tone of voice which plainly indicated an exactly contrary desire that he would be filled with an overwhelming satisfaction if Sen could discover any excuse for returning a second time without disposing of anything. This remark Sen's ingenuous nature led him to regard as a definite fact, so that when a passer-by, who tarried to examine the boxes chanced to remark that the colours might have been arranged to greater advantage, in which case he would certainly have purchased at least one of the articles, Sen hastened back, although in a distant part of the city, to inform King-y-Yang of the suggestion, adding that he himself had been favourably impressed with the improvement which could be effected by such an alteration.

"The nature of King-y-Yang's emotion when Sen again presented himself before him – and when by repeatedly applied tests on various parts of his body he understood that he was neither the victim of malicious demons, nor wandering in an insensible condition in the Middle Air, but that the cause of the return was such as had been plainly stated – was of so mixed and benumbing a variety, that for a considerable space of time he was quite unable to express himself in any way, either by words or by signs. By the time these attributes returned there had formed itself within King-y-Yang's mind a design of most contemptible malignity, which seemed to present to his enfeebled intellect a scheme by which Sen would be adequately punished, and finally disposed of, without causing him any further trouble in the matter. For this purpose he concealed the real condition of his sentiments towards Sen, and warmly expressed himself in terms of delicate flattery regarding that one's sumptuous and unfailing taste in the matter of the blending of the colours. Without doubt, he continued, such an alteration as the one proposed would greatly increase the attractiveness of the inlaid boxes, and the matter should be engaged upon without delay. In the meantime, however, not to waste the immediate services of so discriminating and persevering a servant, he would entrust Sen with a mission of exceptional importance, which would certainly tend greatly to his remunerative benefit. In the district of Yun, in the north-western part of the Province, said the crafty and treacherous King-y-Yang, a particular kind of insect was greatly esteemed on account of the beneficent influence which it exercised over the rice plants, causing them to mature earlier, and to attain a greater size than ever happened in its absence. In recent years this creature had rarely been seen in the neighbourhood of Yun, and, in consequence, the earth-tillers throughout that country had been brought into a most disconcerting state of poverty, and would, inevitably, be prepared to exchange whatever they still possessed for even a few of the insects, in order that they might liberate them to increase, and so entirely reverse the objectionable state of things. Speaking in this manner, King-y-Yang entrusted to Sen a carefully prepared box containing a score of the insects, obtained at a great cost from a country beyond the Bitter Water, and after giving him further directions concerning the journey, and enjoining the utmost secrecy about the valuable contents of the box, he sent him forth.

"The discreet and sagacious will already have understood the nature of King-y-Yang's intolerable artifice; but, for the benefit of the amiable and unsuspecting, it is necessary to make it clear that the words which he had spoken bore no sort of resemblance to affairs as they really existed. The district around Yun was indeed involved in a most unprepossessing destitution, but this had been caused, not by the absence of any rare and auspicious insect, but by the presence of vast hordes of locusts, which had overwhelmed and devoured the entire face the country. It so chanced that among the recently constructed devices at 'The Pure Gilt Dragon of Exceptional Symmetry' were a number of elegant representations of rice fields and fruit gardens so skilfully fashioned that they deceived even the creatures, and attracted, among other living things, all the locusts in Hankow into that place of commerce. It was a number of these insects that King-y-Yang vindictively placed in the box which he instructed Sen to carry to Yun, well knowing that the reception which would be accorded to anyone who appeared there on such a mission would be of so fatally destructive a kind that the consideration of his return need not engage a single conjecture.

"Entirely tranquil in intellect – for the possibility of King-y-Yang's intention being in any way other than what he had represented it to be did not arise within Sen's ingenuous mind – the person in question cheerfully set forth on his long but unavoidable march towards the region of Yun. As he journeyed along the way, the nature of his meditation brought up before him the events which had taken place since his arrival at Hankow; and, for the first time, it was brought within his understanding that the story of the youth and the three tigers, which his father had related to him, was in the likeness of a proverb, by which counsel and warning is conveyed in a graceful and inoffensive manner. Readily applying the fable to his own condition, he could not doubt but that the first two animals to be overthrown were represented by the two undertakings which he had already conscientiously performed in the matter of the mechanical ducks and the inlaid boxes, and the conviction that he was even then engaged on the third and last trial filled him with an intelligent gladness so unobtrusive and refined that he could express his entrancing emotions in no other way that by lifting up his voice and uttering the far-reaching cries which he had used on the first of the occasions just referred to.

"In this manner the first part of the journey passed away with engaging celerity. Anxious as Sen undoubtedly was to complete the third task, and approach the details which, in his own case, would correspond with the command of the bowmen and the marriage with the Mandarin's daughter of the person in the story, the noontide heat compelled him to rest in the shade by the wayside for a lengthy period each day. During one of these pauses it occurred to his versatile mind that the time which was otherwise uselessly expended might be well disposed of in endeavouring to increase the value and condition of the creatures under his care by instructing them in the performance of some simple accomplishments, such as might not be too laborious for their feeble and immature understanding. In this he was more successful than he had imagined could possibly be the case, for the discriminating insects, from the first, had every appearance of recognising that Sen was inspired by a sincere regard for their ultimate benefit, and was not merely using them for his own advancement. So assiduously did they devote themselves to their allotted tasks, that in a very short space of time there was no detail in connexion with their own simple domestic arrangements that was not understood and daily carried out by an appointed band. Entranced at this intelligent manner of conducting themselves, Sen industriously applied his time to the more congenial task of instructing them in the refined arts, and presently he had the enchanting satisfaction of witnessing a number of the most cultivated faultlessly and unhesitatingly perform a portion of the well-known gravity-removing play entitled 'The Benevolent Omen of White Dragon Tea Garden; or, Three Times a Mandarin'. Not even content with this elevating display, Sen ingeniously contrived, from various objects which he discovered at different points by the wayside, an effective and life-like representation of a war-junk, for which he trained a crew, who, at an agreed signal, would take up their appointed places and go through the required movements, both of sailing, and of discharging the guns, in a reliable and efficient manner.

"As Sen was one day educating the least competent of the insects in the simpler parts of banner-carriers, gong-beaters, and the like, to their more graceful and versatile companions, he lifted up his eyes and beheld, standing by his side, a person of very elaborately embroidered apparel and commanding personality, who had all the appearance of one who had been observing his movements for some space of time. Calling up within his remembrance the warning which he had received from King-y-Yang, Sen was preparing to restore the creatures to their closed box, when the stranger, in a loud and dignified voice, commanded him to refrain, adding:

"'There is, resting at a spot within the immediate neighbourhood, a person of illustrious name and ancestry, who would doubtless be gratified to witness the diverting actions of which this one has recently been a spectator. As the reward of a tael cannot be unwelcome to a person of your inferior appearance and unpresentable garments, take up your box without delay, and follow the one who is now before you.'

"With these words the richly clad stranger led the way through a narrow woodland path, closely followed by Sen, to whom the attraction of the promised reward – a larger sum, indeed, than he had ever possessed – was sufficiently alluring to make him determined that the other should not, for the briefest possible moment, pass beyond his sight.

"Not to withhold that which Sen was entirely ignorant of until a later period, it is now revealed that the person in question was the official Provider of Diversions and Pleasurable Occupations to the sacred and illimitable Emperor, who was then engaged in making an unusually extensive march through the eight Provinces surrounding his Capital – for the acute and well-educated will not need to be reminded that Nanking occupied that position at the time now engaged with. Until his providential discovery of Sen, the distinguished Provider had been immersed in a most unenviable condition of despair, for his enlightened but exceedingly perverse-minded master had, of late, declined to be in any way amused, or even interested, by the simple and unpretentious entertainment which could be obtained in so inaccessible a region. The well-intentioned efforts of the followers of the Court, who engagingly endeavoured to divert the Imperial mind by performing certain feats which they remembered to have witnessed on previous occasions, but which, until the necessity arose, they had never essayed, were entirely without result of a beneficial order. Even the accomplished Provider's one attainment – that of striking together both the hands and the feet thrice simultaneously, while leaping into the air, and at the same time producing a sound not unlike that emitted by a large and vigorous bee when held captive in the fold of a robe, an action which never failed to throw the illustrious Emperor into a most uncontrollable state of amusement when performed within the Imperial Palace – now only drew from him the unsympathetic, if not actually offensive, remark that the attitude and the noise bore a marked resemblance to those produced by a person when being bowstrung, adding, with unprepossessing significance, that of the two entertainments he had an unevadable conviction that the bowstringing would be the more acceptable and gravity-removing.

"When Sen beheld the size and the silk-hung magnificence of the camp into which his guide led him, he was filled with astonishment, and at the same time recognised that he had acted in an injudicious and hasty manner by so readily accepting the offer of a tael; whereas, if he had been in possession of the true facts of the case, as they now appeared, he would certainly have endeavoured to obtain double that amount before consenting. As he was hesitating within himself whether the matter might not even yet be arranged in a more advantageous manner, he was suddenly led forward into the most striking and ornamental of the tents, and commanded to engage the attention of the one in whose presence he found himself, without delay.

"From the first moment when the inimitable creatures began, at Sen's spoken word, to go through the ordinary details of their domestic affairs, there was no sort of doubt as to the nature of the success with which their well-trained exertions would be received. The dark shadows instantly forsook the enraptured Emperor's select brow, and from time to time he expressed himself in words of most unrestrained and intimate encouragement. So exuberant became the overjoyed Provider's emotion at having at length succeeded in obtaining the services of one who was able to recall his Imperial master's unclouded countenance, that he came forward in a most unpresentable state of haste, and rose into the air uncommanded, for the display of his usually not unwelcome acquirement. This he would doubtless have executed competently had not Sen, who stood immediately behind him, suddenly and unexpectedly raised his voice in a very vigorous and proficient duck cry, thereby causing the one before him to endeavour to turn around in alarm, while yet in the air – an intermingled state of movements of both the body and the mind that caused him to abandon his original intention in a manner which removed the gravity of the Emperor to an even more pronounced degree than had been effected by the diverting attitudes of the insects.

"When the gratified Emperor had beheld every portion of the tasks which Sen had instilled into the minds of the insects, down even to the minutest detail, he called the well-satisfied Provider before him, and addressing him in a voice which might be designed to betray either sternness or an amiable indulgence, said:

"'You, O Shan-se, are reported to be a person of no particular intellect or discernment, and, for this reason, these ones who are speaking have a desire to know how the matter will present itself in your eyes. Which is it the more commendable and honourable for a person to train to a condition of unfailing excellence, human beings of confessed intelligence or insects of a low and degraded standard?'

"To this remark the discriminating Shan-se made no reply, being, indeed, undecided in his mind whether such a course was expected of him. On several previous occasions the somewhat introspective Emperor had addressed himself to persons in what they judged to be the form of a question, as one might say, 'How blue is the unapproachable air canopy, and how delicately imagined the colour of the clouds!' yet when they had expressed their deliberate opinion on the subjects referred to, stating the exact degree of blueness, and the like, the nature of their reception ever afterwards was such that, for the future, persons endeavoured to determine exactly the intention of the Emperor's mind before declaring themselves in words. Being exceedingly doubtful on this occasion, therefore, the very cautious Shan-se adopted the more prudent and uncompromising attitude, and smiling acquiescently, he raised both his hands with a self-deprecatory movement.

"'Alas!' exclaimed the Emperor, in a tone which plainly indicated that the evasive Shan-se had adopted a course which did not commend itself. 'How unendurable a condition of affairs is it for a person of acute mental perception to be annoyed by the inopportune behaviour of one who is only fit to mix on terms of equality with beggars, and low-caste street cleaners...'

"'Such a condition of affairs is indeed most offensively unbearable, illustrious Being,' remarked Shan-se, who clearly perceived that his former silence had not been productive of a delicate state of feeling towards himself.

"'It has frequently been said,' continued the courteous and pure-minded Emperor, only signifying his refined displeasure at Shan-se's really ill-considered observation by so arranging his position that the person in question no longer enjoyed the sublime distinction of gazing upon his benevolent face, 'that titles and offices have been accorded, from time to time, without any regard for the fitting qualifications of those to whom they were presented. The truth that such a state of things does occasionally exist has been brought before our eyes during the past few days by the abandoned and inefficient behaviour of one who will henceforth be a marked official; yet it has always been our endeavour to reward expert and unassuming merit, whenever it is discovered. As we were setting forth, when we were interrupted in a most obstinate and superfluous manner, the one who can guide and cultivate the minds of unthinking, and not infrequently obstinate and rapacious, insects would certainly enjoy an even greater measure of success if entrusted with the discriminating intellects of human beings. For this reason it appears that no more fitting person could be found to occupy the important and well-rewarded position of Chief Arranger of the Competitive Examinations than the one before us – provided his opinions and manner of expressing himself are such as commend themselves to us. To satisfy us on this point let Sen Heng now stand forth and declare his beliefs.'

"On this invitation Sen advanced the requisite number of paces, and not in any degree understanding what was required of him, determined that the occasion was one when he might fittingly declare the Five General Principles which were ever present in his mind. 'Unquestioning Fidelity to the Sacred Emperor—' he began, when the person in question signified that the trial was over.

"'After so competent and inspired an expression as that which has just been uttered, which, if rightly considered, includes all lesser things, it is unnecessary to say more,' he declared affably. 'The appointment which has already been specified is now declared to be legally conferred. The evening will be devoted to a repetition of the entrancing manoeuvres performed by the insects, to be followed by a feast and music in honour of the recognised worth and position of the accomplished Sen Heng. There is really no necessity for the apparently over-fatigued Shan-se to attend the festival.'

"In such a manner was the foundation of Sen's ultimate prosperity established, by which he came in the process of time to occupy a very high place in public esteem. Yet, being a person of honourably minded conscientiousness, he did not hesitate, when questioned by those who made pilgrimages to him for the purpose of learning by what means he had risen to so remunerative a position, to ascribe his success, not entirely to his own intelligent perception of persons and events, but, in part, also to a never-failing regard for the dictates of the Five General Principles, and a discriminating subservience to the inspired wisdom of the venerable Poo-chow, as conveyed to him in the story of the faint-hearted youth and the three tigers. This story Sen furthermore caused to be inscribed in letters of gold and displayed in a prominent position in his native village, where it has since doubtless been the means of instructing and advancing countless observant ones who have not been too insufferable to be guided by the experience of those who have gone before."

THE EXPERIMENT OF THE MANDARIN CHAN HUNG

• • • • •

ERNEST BRAMAH

RELATED BY KAI LUNG AT SHAN TZU, ON THE OCCASION OF HIS RECEIVING A VERY UNEXPECTED REWARD.

"There are certainly many occasions when the principles of the Mandarin Chan Hung appear to find practical favour in the eyes of those who form this usually uncomplaining person's audiences at Shan Tzu," remarked Kai Lung, with patient resignation, as he took up his collecting-bowl and transferred the few brass coins which it held to a concealed place among his garments. "Has the village lately suffered from a visit of one of those persons who come armed with authority to remove by force or stratagem such goods as bear names other than those possessed by their holders? Or is it, indeed – as they of Wu-whei confidently assert – that when the Day of Vows arrives the people of Shan Tzu, with one accord, undertake to deny themselves in the matter of gifts and free offerings, in spite of every conflicting impulse?"

"They of Wu-whei!" exclaimed a self-opinionated bystander, who had by some means obtained an inferior public office, and who was, in consequence, enabled to be present on all occasions without contributing any offering. "Well is that village named 'The Refuge of Unworthiness', for its dwellers do little but rob and ill-treat strangers, and spread evil and lying reports concerning better endowed ones than themselves."

"Such a condition of affairs may exist," replied Kai Lung, without any indication of concern either one way or the other; "yet it is an undeniable fact that they reward this commonplace storyteller's too often underestimated efforts in a manner which betrays them either to be of noble birth, or very desirous of putting to shame their less prosperous neighbouring places."

"Such exhibitions of uncalled-for lavishness are merely the signs of an ill-regulated and inordinate vanity," remarked a Mandarin of the eighth grade, who chanced to be passing, and who stopped to listen to Kai Lung's words. "Nevertheless, it is not fitting that a collection of decaying hovels, which Wu-whei assuredly is, should, in however small a detail, appear to rise above Shan Tzu, so that if the versatile and unassuming Kai Lung will again honour this assembly by allowing his well-constructed bowl to pass freely to and fro, this obscure and otherwise entirely superfluous individual will make it his especial care that the brass of Wu-whei shall be answered with solid copper, and its debased pewter with doubly refined silver."

With these encouraging words the very opportune Mandarin of the eighth grade himself followed the storyteller's collecting-bowl, observing closely what each person contributed, so that, although he gave nothing from his own store, Kai Lung had never before received so honourable an amount.

"O illustrious Kai Lung," exclaimed a very industrious and ill-clad herb-gatherer, who, in spite of his poverty, could not refrain from mingling with listeners whenever the storyteller appeared in Shan Tzu, "a single piece of brass money is to this person more than a block of solid gold to many of Wu-whei; yet he has twice made the customary offering, once freely, once because a courteous and pure-minded individual who possesses certain written papers of his connected with the repayment of some few taels walked behind the bowl and engaged his eyes with an unmistakable and very significant glance. This fact emboldens him to make the following petition: that in place of the not altogether unknown story of Yung Chang which had been announced the proficient and nimble-minded Kai Lung will entice our attention with the history of the Mandarin Chan Hung, to which reference has already been made."

"The occasion is undoubtedly one which calls for recognition to an unusual degree," replied Kai Lung with extreme affability. "To that end this person will accordingly narrate the story which has been suggested, notwithstanding the fact that it has been specially prepared for the ears of the sublime Emperor, who is at this moment awaiting this unseemly one's arrival in Peking with every mark of ill-restrained impatience, tempered only by his expectation of being the first to hear the story of the well-meaning but somewhat premature Chan Hung.

"The Mandarin in question lived during the reign of the accomplished Emperor Tsint-Sin, his Yamên being at Fow Hou, in the Province of Shan-Tung, of which place he was consequently the chief official. In his conscientious desire to administer a pure and beneficent rule, he not infrequently made himself a very prominent object for public disregard, especially by his attempts to introduce untried things, when from time to time such matters arose within his mind and seemed to promise agreeable and remunerative results. In this manner it came about that the streets of Fow Hou were covered with large flat stones, to the great inconvenience of those persons who had, from a very remote period, been in the habit of passing the night on the soft clay which at all seasons of the year afforded a pleasant and efficient resting-place. Nevertheless, in certain matters his engaging efforts were attended by an obvious success. Having noticed that misfortunes and losses are much less keenly felt when they immediately follow in the steps of an earlier evil, the benevolent and humane-minded Chan Hung devised an ingenious method of lightening the burden of a necessary taxation by arranging that those persons who were the most heavily involved should be made the victims of an attack and robbery on the night before the matter became due. By this thoughtful expedient the unpleasant duty of parting from so many taels was almost imperceptibly led up to, and when, after the lapse of some slight period, the first sums of money were secretly returned, with a written proverb appropriate to the occasion, the public rejoicing of those who, had the matter been left to its natural course, would still have been filling the air with bitter and unendurable lamentations, plainly testified to the inspired wisdom of the enlightened Mandarin.

"The well-merited success of this amiable expedient caused the Mandarin Chan Hung every variety of intelligent emotion, and no day passed without him devoting a portion of his time to the labour of discovering other advantages of a similar nature. Engrossed in deep and very sublime thought of this order, he chanced upon a certain day to be journeying through Fow Hou, when he met a person of irregular intellect, who made an uncertain livelihood by following the unassuming and charitably disposed from place to place, chanting in a loud voice set verses recording their virtues, which he composed in their honour. On account of his undoubted infirmities this person was permitted a greater freedom of speech with those above him than would have been the case had his condition been merely ordinary; so that when Chan Hung observed him becoming very grossly amused on his approach, to such an extent indeed, that he neglected to perform any of the fitting acts of obeisance, the wise and noble-minded Mandarin did not in any degree suffer his complacency to be affected, but, drawing near, addressed him in a calm and dignified manner.

"'Why, O Ming-hi,' he said, 'do you permit your gravity to be removed to such an exaggerated degree at the sight of this in no way striking or exceptional person? And why, indeed, do you stand in so unbecoming an attitude in the presence of one who, in spite of his depraved inferiority, is unquestionably your official superior, and could, without any hesitation, condemn you to the tortures or even to bowstringing on the spot?'

"'Mandarin,' exclaimed Ming-hi, stepping up to Chan Hung, and, without any hesitation, pressing the gilt button which adorned the official's body garment, accompanying the action by a continuous muffled noise which suggested the repeated striking of a hidden bell, 'you wonder that this person stands erect on your approach, neither rolling his lowered head repeatedly from side to side, nor tracing circles in the dust of Fow Hou with his submissive stomach? Know then, the meaning of the proverb, "Distrust an inordinate appearance of servility. The estimable person who retires from your presence walking backwards may adopt that deferential manner in order to keep concealed the long double-edged knife with which he had hoped to slay you." The excessive amusement that seized this offensive person when he beheld your well-defined figure in the distance arose from his perception of your internal satisfaction, which is, indeed, unmistakably reflected in your symmetrical countenance. For, O Mandarin, in spite of your honourable endeavours to turn things which are devious into a straight line, the matters upon which you engage your versatile intellect – little as you suspect the fact – are as grains of the finest Foo-chow sand in comparison with that which escapes your attention.'

"'Strange are your words, O Ming-hi, and dark to this person your meaning,' replied Chan Hung, whose feelings were evenly balanced between a desire to know what thing he had neglected and a fear that his dignity might suffer if he were observed to remain long conversing with a person of Ming-hi's low mental attainments. 'Without delay, and with an entire absence of lengthy and ornamental forms of speech, express the omission to which you have made reference; for this person has an uneasy inside emotion that you are merely endeavouring to engage his attention to the end that you may make an unseemly and irrelevant reply, and thereby involve him in an undeserved ridicule.'

"'Such a device would be the pastime of one of immature years, and could have no place in this person's habit of conduct,' replied Ming-hi, with every appearance of a fixed sincerity. 'Moreover, the matter is one which touches his own welfare closely, and, expressed in the fashion which the proficient Mandarin has commanded, may be set forth as follows: By a wise and all-knowing divine system, it is arranged that certain honourable occupations, which by their nature cannot become remunerative to any marked degree, shall be singled out for special marks of reverence, so that those who engage therein may be compensated in dignity for what they must inevitably lack in taels. By this refined dispensation the literary occupations, which are in general the high roads to the Establishment of Public Support and Uniform Apparel, are held in the highest veneration. Agriculture, from which it is possible to wrest a competency, follows in esteem; while the various branches of commerce, leading as they do to vast possessions and the attendant luxury, are very justly deprived of all the attributes of dignity and respect. Yet observe, O justice-loving Mandarin, how unbecomingly this ingenious system of universal compensation has been debased at the instance of grasping and avaricious ones. Dignity, riches and ease now go hand in hand, and the highest rewarded in all matters are also the most esteemed, whereas, if the discriminating provision of those who have gone before and so arranged it was observed, the direct contrary would be the case.'

"'It is a state of things which is somewhat difficult to imagine in general matters of life, in spite of the fair-seemingness of your words,' said the Mandarin thoughtfully; 'nor can this rather obtuse and slow-witted person fully grasp the practical application of the system on the edge of the moment. In what manner would it operate in the case of ordinary persons, for example?'

"'There should be a fixed and settled arrangement that the low-minded and degrading occupations – such as that of following charitable persons from place to place, chanting verses composed in their honour, that of misleading travellers who inquire the way, so that they fall into the hands of robbers, and the like callings – should be the most highly rewarded to the end that those who are engaged therein may obtain some solace for the loss of dignity they experience, and the mean intellectual position which they are compelled to maintain. By this device they would be enabled to possess certain advantages and degrees of comfort which at present are utterly beyond their grasp, so that in the end they would escape being entirely debased. To turn to the other foot, those who are now high in position, and engaged in professions which enjoy the confidence of all persons, have that which in itself is sufficient to insure contentment. Furthermore, the most proficient and engaging in every department, mean or high-minded, have certain attributes of respect among those beneath them, so that they might justly be content with the lowest reward in whatever calling they professed, the least skilful and most left-handed being compensated for the mental anguish which they must undoubtedly suffer by receiving the greatest number of taels.'

"'Such a scheme would, as far as the matter has been expressed, appear to possess all the claims of respect, and to be, indeed, what was originally intended by those who framed the essentials of existence,' said Chan Hung, when he had for some space of time considered the details. 'In one point, however, this person fails to perceive how the arrangement could be amiably conducted in Fow Hou. The one who is addressing you maintains, as a matter of right, a position of exceptional respect, nor, if he must express himself upon such a detail, are his excessively fatiguing duties entirely unremunerative…'

"'In the case of the distinguished and unalterable Mandarin,' exclaimed Ming-hi, with no appearance of hesitation, 'the matter would of necessity be arranged otherwise. Being from that time, as it were, the controller of the destinies and remunerations of all those in Fow Hou, he would, manifestly, be outside the working of the scheme; standing apart and regulating, like the person who turns the handle of the corn-mill, but does not suffer himself to be drawn between the stones, he could still maintain both his respect and his remuneration unaltered.'

"'If the detail could honourably be regarded in such a light,' said Chan Hung, 'this person would, without delay, so rearrange matters in Fow Hou, and thereby create universal justice and an unceasing contentment within the minds of all.'

"'Undoubtedly such a course could be justly followed,' assented Ming-hi, 'for in precisely that manner of working was the complete scheme revealed to this highly-favoured person.'

"Entirely wrapped up in thoughts concerning the inception and manner of operation of this project Chan Hung began to retrace his steps towards the Yamen, failing to observe in his benevolent abstraction of mind, that the unaffectedly depraved person Ming-hi was stretching out his feet towards him and indulging in every other form of low-minded and undignified contempt.

"Before he reached the door of his residence the Mandarin overtook one who occupied a high position of confidence and remuneration in the Department of Public Fireworks and Coloured Lights. Fully assured of this versatile person's enthusiasm on behalf of so humane and charitable a device, Chan Hung explained the entire matter to him without delay, and expressly desired that if there were any details which appeared capable of improvement, he would declare himself clearly regarding them.

"'Alas!' exclaimed the person with whom the Mandarin was conversing, speaking in so unfeignedly disturbed and terrified a voice that several who were passing by stopped in order to learn the full circumstance, 'have this person's ears been made the object of some unnaturally light-minded demon's ill-disposed pastime, or does the usually well-balanced Chan Hung in reality contemplate so violent and un-Chinese an action? What but evil could arise from a single word of the change which he proposes to the extent of a full written book? The entire fixed nature of events would become reversed; persons would no longer be fully accountable to one another; and Fow Hou being thus thrown into a most unendurable state of confusion, the protecting Deities would doubtless withdraw their influence, and the entire region would soon be given over to the malicious guardianship of rapacious and evilly disposed spirits. Let this person entreat the almost invariably clear-sighted Chan Hung to return at once to his adequately equipped and sumptuous Yamên, and barring well the door of his inner chamber, so that it can only be opened from the outside, partake of several sleeping essences of unusual strength, after which he will awake in an undoubtedly refreshed state of mind, and in a condition to observe matters with his accustomed diamond-like penetration.'

"'By no means!' cried one of those who had stopped to learn the occasion of the incident – a very inferior maker of unserviceable imitation pigtails. 'The devout and conscientious-minded Mandarin Chan Hung speaks as the inspired mouthpiece of the omnipotent Buddha, and must, for that reason, be obeyed in every detail. This person would unhesitatingly counsel the now invaluable Mandarin to proceed to his well-constructed residence without delay, and there calling together his entire staff of those who set down his spoken words, put the complete Heaven-sent plan into operation, and beyond recall, before he retires to his inner chamber.'

"Upon this there arose a most inelegant display of undignified emotions on the part of the assembly which had by this time gathered together. While those who occupied honourable and remunerative positions very earnestly entreated the Mandarin to act in the manner which had been suggested by the first speaker, others – who had, in the meantime, made use of imagined figures, and thereby discovered that the proposed change would be greatly to their advantage – raised shouts of encouragement towards the proposal of the pigtail-maker, urging the noble Mandarin not to become small in the face towards the insignificant few who were ever opposed to enlightened reform, but to maintain an unflaccid upper lip, and carry the entire matter through to its destined end. In the course of this very unseemly tumult, which soon involved all persons present in hostile demonstrations towards each other, both the Mandarin and the official from the Fireworks and Coloured Lights Department found an opportunity to pass away secretly, the former to consider well the various sides of the matter, towards which he became better disposed with every thought, the latter to find a purchaser of his appointment and leave Fow Hou before the likelihood of Chan Hung's scheme became generally known.

"At this point an earlier circumstance, which affected the future unrolling of events to no insignificant degree, must be made known, concerning as it does Lila, the fair and very accomplished daughter of Chan Hung. Possessing no son or heir to succeed him, the Mandarin exhibited towards

Lila a very unusual depth of affection, so marked, indeed, that when certain evil-minded ones endeavoured to encompass his degradation, on the plea of eccentricity of character, the written papers which they dispatched to the high ones at Peking contained no other accusation in support of the contention than that the individual in question regarded his daughter with an obvious pride and pleasure which no person of well-balanced intellect lavished on any but a son.

"It was his really conscientious desire to establish Lila's welfare above all things that had caused Chan Hung to become in some degree undecided when conversing with Ming-hi on the detail of the scheme; for, unaffected as the Mandarin himself would have been at the prospect of an honourable poverty, it was no part of his intention that the adorable and exceptionally refined Lila should be drawn into such an existence. That, indeed, had been the essential of his reply on a certain and not far removed occasion, when two persons of widely differing positions had each made a formal request that he might be allowed to present marriage-pledging gifts to the very desirable Lila. Maintaining an enlightened openness of mind upon the subject, the Mandarin had replied that nothing but the merit of undoubted suitableness of a person would affect him in such a decision. As it was ordained by the wise and unchanging Deities that merit should always be fittingly rewarded, he went on to express himself, and as the most suitable person was obviously the one who could the most agreeably provide for her, the two circumstances inevitably tended to the decision that the one chosen should be the person who could amass the greatest number of taels. To this end he instructed them both to present themselves at the end of a year, bringing with them the entire profits of their undertakings between the two periods.

"This deliberate pronouncement affected the two persons in question in an entirely opposite manner, for one of them was little removed from a condition of incessant and most uninviting poverty, while the other was the very highly rewarded picture-maker Pe-tsing. Both to this latter person, and to the other one, Lee Sing, the ultimate conclusion of the matter did not seem to be a question of any conjecture therefore, and, in consequence, the one became most offensively self-confident, and the other leaden-minded to an equal degree, neither remembering the unswerving wisdom of the proverb, 'Wait! all men are but as the black, horn-cased beetles which overrun the inferior cooking-rooms of the city, and even at this moment the heavily-shod and unerring foot of Buddha may be lifted.'

"Lee Sing was, by profession, one of those who hunt and ensnare the brilliantly coloured winged insects which are to be found in various parts of the Empire in great variety and abundance, it being his duty to send a certain number every year to Peking to contribute to the amusement of the dignified Emperor. In spite of the not too intelligent nature of the occupation, Lee Sing took an honourable pride in all matters connected with it. He disdained, with well-expressed contempt, to avail himself of the stealthy and somewhat deceptive methods employed by others engaged in a similar manner of life. In this way he had, from necessity, acquired agility to an exceptional degree, so that he could leap far into the air, and while in that position select from a passing band of insects any which he might desire. This useful accomplishment was, in a measure, the direct means of bringing together the person in question and the engaging Lila; for, on a certain occasion, when Lee Sing was passing through the streets of Fow Hou, he heard a great outcry, and beheld persons of all ranks running towards him, pointing at the same time in an upward direction. Turning his gaze in the manner indicated, Lee beheld, with every variety of astonishment, a powerful and unnaturally large bird of prey, carrying in its talons the lovely and now insensible Lila, to whom it had been attracted by the magnificence of her raiment. The rapacious and evilly inspired creature was already above the highest dwelling-houses when Lee first beheld it, and was plainly directing its course towards the inaccessible mountain crags beyond the city walls. Nevertheless, Lee resolved upon an inspired effort, and without any hesitation bounded towards it with such well-directed proficiency, that if he had not stretched forth his hand on passing he would inevitably have been carried far above the desired object. In this manner he succeeded in dragging the repulsive and completely disconcerted monster to the ground, where its graceful and unassuming prisoner was released, and the presumptuous bird itself torn to pieces amid continuous shouts of a most respectful and engaging description in honour of Lee and of his versatile attainment.

"In consequence of this incident the grateful Lila would often deliberately leave the society of the rich and well-endowed in order to accompany Lee on his journeys in pursuit of exceptionally precious winged insects. Regarding his unusual ability as the undoubted cause of her existence at that moment, she took an all-absorbing pride in such displays, and would utter loud and frequent exclamations of triumph when Lee leaped out from behind some rock, where he had lain concealed, and with unfailing regularity secured the object of his adroit movement. In this manner a state of feeling which was by no means favourable to the aspiring picture-maker Pe-tsing had long existed between the two persons; but when Lee Sing put the matter in the form of an explicit petition before Chan Hung (to which adequate reference has already been made), the nature of the decision then arrived at seemed to clothe the realisation of their virtuous and estimable desires with an air of extreme improbability.

"'Oh, Lee,' exclaimed the greatly disappointed maiden when her lover had explained to her the nature of the arrangement – for in her unassuming admiration of the noble qualities of Lee she had anticipated that Chan Hung would at once have received him with ceremonious embraces and assurances of his permanent affection – 'how unendurable a state of things is this in which we have become involved! Far removed from this one's anticipations was the thought of becoming inalienably associated with that outrageous person Pe-tsing, or of entering upon an existence which will necessitate a feigned admiration of his really unpresentable efforts. Yet in such a manner must the entire circumstance complete its course unless some ingenious method of evading it can be discovered in the meantime. Alas, my beloved one! The occupation of ensnaring winged insects is indeed an alluring one, but as far as this person has observed, it is also exceedingly unproductive of taels. Could not some more expeditious means of enriching yourself be discovered? Frequently has the unnoticed but nevertheless very attentive Lila heard her father and the round-bodied ones who visit him speak of exploits which seem to consist of assuming the shapes of certain wild animals, and in that guise appearing from time to time at the place of exchange within the city walls. As this form of entertainment is undoubtedly very remunerative in its results, could not the versatile and ready-witted Lee conceal himself within the skin of a bear, or some other untamed beast, and in this garb, joining them unperceived, play an appointed part and receive a just share of the reward?'

"'The result of such an enterprise might, if the matter chanced to take an unforeseen development, prove of a very doubtful nature,' replied Lee Sing, to whom, indeed, the proposed venture appeared in a somewhat undignified light, although, with refined consideration, he withheld such a thought from Lila, who had proposed it for him, and also confessed that her usually immaculate father had taken part in such an exhibition. 'Nevertheless, do not permit the dark shadow of an inward cloud to reflect itself upon your almost invariably amiable countenance, for this person has become possessed of a valuable internal suggestion which, although he has hitherto neglected, being content with a small but assured competency, would doubtless bring together a serviceable number of taels if rightly utilised.'

"'Greatly does this person fear that the valuable internal suggestion of Lee Sing will weigh but lightly in the commercial balance against the very rapidly executed pictures of Pe-tsing,' said Lila, who had not fully recalled from her mind a disturbing emotion that Lee would have been well advised to have availed himself of her ingenious and well-thought-out suggestion. 'But of what does the matter consist?'

"'It is the best explained by a recital of the circumstances leading up to it,' said Lee. 'Upon an occasion when this person was passing through the streets of Fow Hou, there gathered around him a company of those who had, on previous occasions, beheld his exceptional powers of hurtling himself through the air in an upward direction, praying that he would again delight their senses by a similar spectacle. Not being unwilling to afford those estimable persons of the amusement they desired, this one, without any elaborate show of affected hesitancy, put himself into the necessary position, and would without doubt have risen uninterruptedly almost into the Middle Air, had he not, in making the preparatory movements, placed his left foot upon an over-ripe wampee which lay unperceived on the ground. In consequence of this really blameworthy want of caution the entire manner and direction of this short-sighted individual's movements underwent a sudden and complete change, so that to those who stood around it appeared as though he were making a well-directed endeavour to penetrate through the upper surface of the earth. This unexpected display had the effect of removing the gravity of even the most aged and severe-minded persons present, and for the space of some moments the behaviour and positions of those who stood around were such that they were quite unable to render any assistance, greatly as they doubtless wished to do so. Being in this manner allowed a period for inward reflection of a very concentrated order, it arose within this one's mind that at every similar occurrence which he had witnessed, those who observed the event had been seized in a like fashion, being very excessively amused. The fact was made even more undoubted by the manner of behaving of an exceedingly stout and round-faced person, who had not been present from the beginning, but who was affected to a most incredible extent when the details, as they had occurred, were made plain to him, he declaring, with many references to the Sacred Dragon and the Seven Walled Temple at Peking, that he would willingly have contributed a specified number of taels rather than have missed the diversion. When at length this person reached his own chamber, he diligently applied himself to the task of carrying into practical effect the suggestion which had arisen in his mind. By an arrangement of transparent glasses and reflecting surfaces – which, were it not for a well-defined natural modesty, he would certainly be tempted to describe as highly ingenious – he ultimately succeeded in bringing about the effect he desired.'

"With these words Lee put into Lila's hands an object which closely resembled the contrivances by which those who are not sufficiently powerful to obtain positions near the raised platform in the Halls of Celestial Harmony are nevertheless enabled to observe the complexions and attire of all around them. Regulating it by means of a hidden spring, he requested her to follow closely the actions of a heavily burdened passerby who was at that moment some little distance beyond them. Scarcely had Lila raised the glass to her eyes than she became irresistibly amused to a most infectious degree, greatly to the satisfaction of Lee, who therein beheld the realisation of his hopes. Not for the briefest space of time would she permit the object to pass from her, but directed it at every person who came within her sight, with frequent and unfeigned exclamations of wonder and delight.

"'How pleasant and fascinating a device is this!' exclaimed Lila at length. 'By what means is so diverting and gravity-removing a result obtained?'

"'Further than that it is the concentration of much labour of continually trying with glasses and reflecting surfaces, this person is totally unable to explain it,' replied Lee. 'The chief thing, however, is that at whatever moving object it is directed – no matter whether a person so observed is being carried in a chair, riding upon an animal, or merely walking – at a certain point he has every appearance of being unexpectedly hurled to the ground in a most violent and mirth-provoking manner. Would not the stout and round-faced one, who would cheerfully have contributed a certain number of taels to see this person manifest a similar exhibition, unhesitatingly lay out that sum to secure the means of so gratifying his emotions whenever he felt the desire, even with the revered persons of the most dignified ones in the Empire? Is there, indeed, a single person between the Wall and the Bitter Waters on the South who is so devoid of ambition that he would miss the opportunity of subjecting, as it were, perhaps even the sacred Emperor himself to the exceptional feat?'

"'The temptation to possess one would inevitably prove overwhelming to any person of ordinary intelligence,' admitted Lila. 'Yet, in spite of this one's unassumed admiration for the contrivance, internal doubts regarding the ultimate happiness of the two persons who are now discussing the matter again attack her. She recollects, somewhat dimly, an almost forgotten, but nevertheless, very unassailable proverb, which declares that more contentment of mind can assuredly be obtained from the unexpected discovery of a tael among the folds of a discarded garment than could, in the most favourable circumstances, ensue from the well-thought-out construction of a new and hitherto unknown device. Furthermore, although the span of a year may seem unaccountably protracted when persons who reciprocate engaging sentiments are parted, yet when the acceptance or refusal of Pe-tsing's undesirable pledging-gifts hangs upon the accomplishment of a remote and not very probable object within that period, it becomes as a breath of wind passing through an autumn forest.'

"Since the day when Lila and Lee had sat together side by side, and conversed in this unrestrained and irreproachable manner, the great sky-lantern had many times been obscured for a period. Only an insignificant portion of the year remained, yet the affairs of Lee Sing were in no more prosperous a condition than before, nor had he found an opportunity to set aside any store of taels. Each day the unsupportable Pe-tsing became more and more obtrusive and self-conceited, even to the extent of throwing far into the air coins of insignificant value whenever he chanced to pass Lee in the street, at the same time urging him to leap after them and thereby secure at least one or two pieces of money against the day of calculating. In a similar but entirely opposite fashion, Lila and Lee experienced the acutest pangs of an ever-growing despair, until their only form of greeting consisted in gazing into each other's eyes with a soul-benumbing expression of self-reproach.

"Yet at this very time, when even the natural and unalterable powers seemed to be conspiring against the success of Lee's modest and inoffensive hopes, an event was taking place which was shortly to reverse the entire settled arrangement of persons and affairs, and involved Fow Hou in a very inextricable state of uncertainty. For, not to make a pretence of concealing a matter which has been already in part revealed, the Mandarin Chan Hung had by this time determined to act in the manner which Ming-hi had suggested; so that on a certain morning Lee Sing was visited by two persons, bearing between them a very weighty sack of taels, who also conveyed to him the fact that a like amount would be deposited within his door at the end of each succeeding seven days. Although Lee's occupation had in the past been very meagrely rewarded, either by taels or by honour, the circumstance which resulted in his now receiving so excessively large a sum is not made clear until the detail of Ming-hi's scheme is closely examined. The matter then becomes plain, for it had been suggested by that person that the most proficient in any occupation should be rewarded to a certain extent, and the least proficient to another stated extent, the original amounts being reversed. When those engaged by Chang Hung to draw up the various rates came to the profession of ensnaring winged insects, however, they discovered that Lee

Sing was the only one of that description in Fow Hou, so that it became necessary in consequence to allot him a double portion, one amount as the most proficient, and a much larger amount as the least proficient.

"It is unnecessary now to follow the not altogether satisfactory condition of affairs which began to exist in Fow Hou as soon as the scheme was put into operation. The full written papers dealing with the matter are in the Hall of Public Reference at Peking, and can be seen by any person on the payment of a few taels to everyone connected with the establishment. Those who found their possessions reduced thereby completely overlooked the obvious justice of the arrangement, and immediately began to take most severe measures to have the order put aside; while those who suddenly and unexpectedly found themselves raised to positions of affluence tended to the same end by conducting themselves in a most incapable and undiscriminating manner. And during the entire period that this state of things existed in Fow Hou the really contemptible Ming-hi continually followed Chan Hung about from place to place, spreading out his feet towards him, and allowing himself to become openly amused to a most unseemly extent.

"Chief among those who sought to have the original manner of rewarding persons again established was the picture-maker, Pe-tsing, who now found himself in a condition of most abject poverty, so unbearable, indeed, that he frequently went by night, carrying a lantern, in the hope that he might discover some of the small pieces of money which he had been accustomed to throw into the air on meeting Lee Sing. To his pangs of hunger was added the fear that he would certainly lose Lila, so that from day to day he redoubled his efforts, and in the end, by using false statements and other artifices of a questionable nature, the party which he led was successful in obtaining the degradation of Chan Hung and his dismissal from office, together with an entire reversal of all his plans and enactments.

"On the last day of the year which Chan Hung had appointed as the period of test for his daughter's suitors, the person in question was seated in a chamber of his new abode – a residence of unassuming appearance but undoubted comfort – surrounded by Lila and Lee, when the hanging curtains were suddenly flung aside, and Pe-tsing, followed by two persons of low rank bearing sacks of money, appeared among them.

"'Chan Hung,' he said at length, 'in the past events arose which compelled this person to place himself against you in your official position. Nevertheless, he has always maintained towards you personally an unchanging affection, and understanding full well that you are one of those who maintain their spoken word in spite of all happenings, he has now come to exhibit the taels which he has collected together, and to claim the fulfilment of your deliberate promise.'

"With these words the commonplace picture-maker poured forth the contents of the sacks, and stood looking at Lila in a most confident and unprepossessing manner.

"'Pe-tsing,' replied Chan Hung, rising from his couch and speaking in so severe and impressive a voice that the two servants of Pe-tsing at once fled in great apprehension, 'this person has also found it necessary, in his official position, to oppose you; but here the similarity ends, for, on his part, he has never felt towards you the remotest degree of affection. Nevertheless, he is always desirous, as you say, that persons should regard their spoken word, and as you seem to hold a promise from the Chief Mandarin of Fow Hou regarding marriage-gifts towards his daughter, he would advise you to go at once to that person. A misunderstanding has evidently arisen, for the one whom you are addressing is merely Chan Hung, and the words spoken by the Mandarin have no sort of interest for him – indeed, he understands that all that person's acts have been reversed, so that he fails to see how anyone at all can regard you and your claim in other than a gravity-removing light. Furthermore, the maiden in question is now definitely and irretrievably pledged to this faithful and successful one by my side, who, as you will doubtless be gracefully overjoyed to learn, has recently disposed of a most ingenious and diverting contrivance for an enormous number of taels, so many, indeed, that both the immediate and the far-distant future of all the persons who are here before you are now in no sort of doubt whatever.'

"At these words the three persons whom he had interrupted again turned their attention to the matter before them; but as Pe-tsing walked away, he observed, though he failed to understand the meaning, that they all raised certain objects to their eyes, and at once became amused to a most striking and uncontrollable degree."

THE CONFESSION OF KAI LUNG

ERNEST BRAMAH

RELATED BY HIMSELF AT WU-WHEI WHEN OTHER MATTER FAILED HIM.

As Kai Lung, the storyteller, unrolled his mat and selected, with grave deliberation, the spot under the mulberry-tree which would the longest remain sheltered from the sun's rays, his impassive eye wandered round the thin circle of listeners who had been drawn together by his uplifted voice, with a glance which, had it expressed his actual thoughts, would have betrayed a keen desire that the assembly should be composed of strangers rather than of his most consistent patrons, to whom his stock of tales was indeed becoming embarrassingly familiar. Nevertheless, when he began there was nothing in his voice but a trace of insufficiently restrained triumph, such as might be fitly assumed by one who has discovered and makes known for the first time a story by the renowned historian Lo Cha.

"The adventures of the enlightened and nobly-born Yuin-Pel..."

"Have already thrice been narrated within Wu-whei by the versatile but exceedingly uninventive Kai Lung," remarked Wang Yu placidly. "Indeed, has there not come to be a saying by which an exceptionally frugal host's rice, having undoubtedly seen the inside of the pot many times, is now known in this town as Kai-Pel?"

"Alas!" exclaimed Kai Lung. "Well was this person warned of Wu-whei in the previous village, as a place of desolation and excessively bad taste, whose inhabitants, led by an evil-minded maker of very commonplace pipes, named Wang Yu, are unable to discriminate in all matters not connected with the cooking of food and the evasion of just debts. They at Shan Tzu hung on to my cloak as I strove to leave them, praying that I would again entrance their ears with what they termed the melodious word-music of this person's inimitable version of the inspired story of Yuin-Pel."

"Truly the story of Yuin-Pel is in itself excellent," interposed the conciliatory Hi Seng; "and Kai Lung's accomplishment of having three times repeated it here without deviating in the particular of a single word from the first recital stamps him as a storyteller of no ordinary degree. Yet the saying 'Although it is desirable to lose persistently when playing at squares and circles with the broadminded and sagacious Emperor, it is none the less a fact that the observance of this etiquette deprives the intellectual diversion of much of its interest for both players,' is no less true today than when the all knowing H'sou uttered it."

"They well said – they of Shan Tzu – that the people of Wu-whei were intolerably ignorant and of low descent," continued Kai Lung, without heeding the interruption; "that although invariably of a timorous nature, even to the extent of retiring to the woods on the approach of those who select bowmen for the Imperial army, all they require in a story is that it shall be garnished with deeds of bloodshed and violence to the exclusion of the higher qualities of well-imagined metaphors and literary style which alone constitute true excellence."

"Yet it has been said," suggested Hi Seng, "that the inimitable Kai Lung can so mould a narrative in the telling that all the emotions are conveyed therein without unduly disturbing the intellects of the hearers."

"O amiable Hi Seng," replied Kai Lung with extreme affability, "doubtless you are the most expert of water-carriers, and on a hot and dusty day, when the insatiable desire of all persons is towards a draught of unusual length without much regard to its composition, the sight of your goat-skins is indeed a welcome omen; yet when in the season of Cold White Rains you chance to meet the belated chair-carrier who has been reluctantly persuaded into conveying persons beyond the limit of the city, the solitary official watchman who knows that his chief is not at hand, or a returning band of those who make a practise of remaining in the long narrow rooms until they are driven forth at a certain gong-stroke, can you supply them with the smallest portion of that invigorating rice spirit for which alone they crave? From this simple and homely illustration, specially conceived to meet the requirements of your stunted and meagre understanding, learn not to expect both grace and thorns from the willow-tree. Nevertheless, your very immature remarks on the art of storytelling are in no degree more foolish than those frequently uttered by persons who make a living by such a practice; in proof of which this person will relate to the select and discriminating company now assembled an entirely new and unrecorded story – that, indeed, of the unworthy, but frequently highly rewarded Kai Lung himself."

"The story of Kai Lung!" exclaimed Wang Yu. "Why not the story of Ting, the sightless beggar, who has sat all his life outside the Temple of Miraculous Cures? Who is Kai Lung, that *he* should have a story? Is he not known to us all here? Is not his speech that of this Province, his food mean, his arms and legs unshaven? Does he carry a sword or wear silk raiment? Frequently have we seen him fatigued with journeying; many times has he arrived destitute of money; nor, on those occasions when a newly appointed and unnecessarily officious Mandarin has commanded him to betake himself elsewhere and struck him with a rod has Kai Lung caused the stick to turn into a deadly serpent and destroy its master, as did the just and dignified Lu Fei. How, then, can Kai Lung have a story that is not also the story of Wang Yu and Hi Seng, and all others here?"

"Indeed, if the refined and enlightened Wang Yu so decides, it must assuredly be true," said Kai Lung patiently; "yet (since even trifles serve to dispel the darker thoughts of existence) would not the history of so small a matter as an opium pipe chain his intelligent consideration? Such a pipe, for example, as this person beheld only today exposed for sale, the bowl composed of the finest red clay, delicately baked and fashioned, the long bamboo stem smoother than the sacred tooth of the divine Buddha, the spreading support patiently and cunningly carved with scenes representing the Seven Joys, and the Tenth Hell of unbelievers."

"Ah!" exclaimed Wang Yu eagerly. "It is indeed as you say, a Mandarin among masterpieces. That pipe, O most unobserving Kai Lung, is the work of this retiring and superficial person who is now addressing you, and, though the fact evidently escaped your all-seeing glance, the place where it is exposed is none other than his shop of 'The Fountain of Beauty', which you have on many occasions endowed with your honourable presence."

"Doubtless the carving is the work of the accomplished Wang Yu, and the fitting together," replied Kai Lung; "but the materials for so refined and ornamental a production must of necessity have been brought many thousand li; the clay perhaps from the renowned beds of Honan, the wood from Peking, and the bamboo from one of the great forests of the North."

"For what reason?" said Wang Yu proudly. "At this person's very door is a pit of red clay, purer and infinitely more regular than any to be found at Honan; the hard wood of Wu-whei is extolled among carvers throughout the Empire, while no bamboo is straighter or more smooth than that which grows in the neighbouring woods."

"O most inconsistent Wang Yu!" cried the storyteller. "Assuredly a very commendable local pride has dimmed your usually penetrating eyesight. Is not the clay pit of which you speak that in which you fashioned exceedingly unsymmetrical imitations of rat-pies in your childhood? How, then, can it be equal to those of Honan, which you have never seen? In the dark glades of these woods have you not chased the gorgeous butterfly, and, in later years, the no less gaily attired maidens of Wu-whei in the entrancing game of Kiss in the Circle? Have not the bamboo trees to which you have referred provided you with the ideal material wherewith to roof over those cunningly constructed pits into which it has ever been the chief delight of the young and audacious to lure dignified and unnaturally stout Mandarins? All these things you have seen and used ever since your mother made a successful offering to the Goddess Kum-Fa. How, then, can they be even equal to the products of remote Honan and fabulous Peking? Assuredly the generally veracious Wang Yu speaks this time with closed eyes and will, upon mature reflection, eat his words."

The silence was broken by a very aged man who arose from among the bystanders.

"Behold the length of this person's pigtail," he exclaimed, "the whiteness of his moustaches and the venerable appearance of his beard! There is no more aged person present – if, indeed, there be such a one in all the Province. It accordingly devolves upon him to speak in this matter, which shall be as follows: the noble-minded and proficient Kai Lung shall relate the story as he has proposed, and the garrulous Wang Yu shall twice contribute to Kai Lung's bowl when it is passed round, once for himself and once for this person, in order that he may learn either to be more discreet or more proficient in the art of aptly replying."

"The events which it is this person's presumptuous intention to describe to this large-hearted and providentially indulgent gathering," began Kai Lung, when his audience had become settled, and the wooden bowl had passed to and fro among them, "did not occupy many years, although they were of a nature which made them of far more importance than all the remainder of his existence, thereby supporting the sage discernment of the philosopher Wen-weng, who first made the observation that man is greatly inferior to the meanest fly, inasmuch as that creature, although granted only a day's span of life, contrives during that period to fulfil all the allotted functions of existence.

"Unutterably to the astonishment and dismay of this person and all those connected with him (for several of the most expensive readers of the future to be found in the Empire had declared that his life would be marked by great events, his career a source of continual wonder, and his death a misfortune to those who had dealings with him) his efforts to take a degree at the public literary competitions were not attended with any adequate success. In view of the plainly expressed advice of his father it therefore became desirable that this person should turn his attention to some other method of regaining the esteem of those upon whom he was dependent for all the necessaries of existence. Not having the means wherewith to engage in any form of commerce, and being entirely ignorant of all matters save the now useless details of attempting to pass public examinations, he reluctantly decided that he was destined to become one of those who imagine and write out stories and similar devices for printed leaves and books.

"This determination was favourably received, and upon learning it, this person's dignified father took him aside, and with many assurances of regard presented to him a written sentence, which, he said, would be of incomparable value to one engaged in a literary career, and should in fact, without any particular qualifications, insure an honourable competency. He himself, he added, with what at the time appeared to this one as an unnecessary regard for detail, having taken a very high degree, and being in consequence appointed to a distinguished and remunerative position under the Board of Fines and Tortures, had never made any use of it.

"The written sentence, indeed, was all that it had been pronounced. It had been composed by a remote ancestor, who had spent his entire life in crystallising all his knowledge and experience into a few written lines, which as a result became correspondingly precious. It defined in a very original and profound manner several undisputable principles, and was so engagingly subtle in its manner of expression that the most superficial person was irresistibly thrown into a deep inward contemplation upon reading it. When it was complete, the person who had contrived this ingenious masterpiece, discovering by means of omens that he still had ten years to live, devoted each remaining year to the task of reducing the sentence by one word without in any way altering its meaning. This unapproachable example of conciseness found such favour in the eyes of those who issue printed leaves that as fast as this person could inscribe stories containing it they were eagerly purchased; and had it not been for a very incapable want of foresight on this narrow-minded individual's part, doubtless it would still be affording him an agreeable and permanent means of living.

"Unquestionably the enlightened Wen-weng was well acquainted with the subject when he exclaimed, 'Better a frugal dish of olives flavoured with honey than the most sumptuously devised puppy-pie of which the greater portion is sent forth in silver-lined boxes and partaken of by others.' At that time, however, this versatile saying – which so gracefully conveys the truth of the undeniable fact that what a person possesses is sufficient if he restrain his mind from desiring aught else – would have been lightly treated by this self-conceited storyteller even if his immature faculties had enabled him fully to understand the import of so profound and well-digested a remark.

"At that time Tiao Ts'un was undoubtedly the most beautiful maiden in all Peking. So frequently were the verses describing her habits and appearances affixed in the most prominent places of the city, that many persons obtained an honourable livelihood by frequenting those spots and disposing of the sacks of written papers which they collected to merchants who engaged in that commerce. Owing to the fame attained by his written sentence, this really very much inferior being had many opportunities of meeting the incomparable maiden Tiao at flower-feasts, melon-seed assemblies, and those gatherings where persons of both sexes exhibit themselves in revolving attitudes, and are permitted to embrace openly without reproach; whereupon he became so subservient to her charms and virtues that he lost no opportunity of making himself utterly unendurable to any who might chance to speak to, or even gaze upon, this Heaven-sent creature.

"So successful was this person in his endeavour to meet the sublime Tiao and to gain her conscientious esteem that all emotions of prudence forsook him, or it would soon have become apparent even to his enfeebled understanding that such consistent good fortune could only be the work of unforgiving and malignant spirits whose ill-will he had in some way earned, and who were luring him on in order that they might accomplish his destruction. That object was achieved on a certain evening when this person stood alone with Tiao upon an eminence overlooking the city and watched the great sky-lantern rise from behind the hills. Under these delicate and ennobling influences he gave speech to many very ornamental and refined thoughts which arose within his mind concerning the graceful brilliance of the light which was cast all around, yet notwithstanding which a still more exceptional and brilliant light was shining in his own internal organs by reason of the nearness of an even purer and more engaging orb. There was no need, this person felt, to hide even his most inside thoughts from the dignified and sympathetic being at his side, so without hesitation he spoke – in what he believes even now must have been a very decorative manner – of the many thousand persons who were then wrapped in sleep, of the constantly changing lights which appeared in the city beneath, and of the vastness which everywhere lay around.

"'O Kai Lung,' exclaimed the lovely Tiao, when this person had made an end of speaking, 'how expertly and in what a proficient manner do you express yourself, uttering even the sentiments which this person has felt inwardly, but for which she has no words. Why, indeed, do you not inscribe them in a book?'

"Under her elevating influence it had already occurred to this illiterate individual that it would be a more dignified and, perhaps, even a more profitable course for him to write out and dispose of, to those who print such matters, the versatile and high-minded expressions which now continually formed his thoughts, rather than be dependent upon the concise sentence for which, indeed, he was indebted to the wisdom of a remote ancestor. Tiao's spoken word fully settled his determination, so that without delay he set himself to the task of composing a story which should omit the usual sentence, but should contain instead a large number of his most graceful and diamond-like thoughts. So engrossed did this near-sighted and superficial person become in the task (which daily seemed to increase rather than lessen as new and still more sublime images arose within his mind) that many months passed before the matter was complete. In the end, instead of a story, it had assumed the proportions of an important and many-volumed book; while Tiao had in the meantime accepted the wedding gifts of an objectionable and excessively round-bodied individual, who had amassed an inconceivable number of taels by inducing persons to take part in what at first sight appeared to be an ingenious but very easy competition connected with the order in which certain horses should arrive at a given and clearly defined spot. By that time, however, this unduly sanguine story-teller had become completely entranced in his work, and merely regarded Tiao-Ts'un as a Heaven-sent but no longer necessary incentive to his success. With every hope, therefore, he went forth to dispose of his written leaves, confident of finding some very wealthy person who would be in a condition to pay him the correct value of the work.

"At the end of two years this somewhat disillusioned but still undaunted person chanced to hear of a benevolent and unassuming body of men who made a habit of issuing works in which they discerned merit, but which, nevertheless, others were unanimous in describing as 'of no good'. Here this person was received with gracious effusion, and being in a position to impress those with whom he was dealing with his undoubted knowledge of the subject, he finally succeeded in making a very advantageous arrangement by which he was to pay one-half of the number of taels expended in producing the work, and to receive in return all the profits which should result from the undertaking. Those who were concerned in the matter were so engagingly impressed with the incomparable literary merit displayed in the production that they counselled a great number of copies being made ready in order, as they said, that this person should not lose by there being any delay when once the accomplishment became the one topic of conversation in tea-houses and yamens. From this cause it came about that the matter of taels to be expended was much greater than had been anticipated at the beginning, so that when the day arrived on which the volumes were to be sent forth this person found that almost his last piece of money had disappeared.

"Alas! How small a share has a person in the work of controlling his own destiny. Had only the necessarily penurious and now almost degraded Kai Lung been born a brief span before the great writer Lo Kuan Chang, his name would have been received with every mark of esteem from one end of the Empire to the other, while taels and honourable decorations would have been showered upon him. For the truth, which could no longer be concealed, revealed the fact that this inopportune individual possessed a mind framed in such a manner that his thoughts had already been the thoughts of the inspired Lo Kuan, who, as this person would not be so presumptuous as to inform this ornamental and well-informed gathering, was the most ingenious and versatile-minded composer of written words that this Empire – and therefore the entire world – has seen, as, indeed, his honourable title of 'The Many-hued Mandarin Duck of the Yang-tse' plainly indicates.

"Although this self-opinionated person had frequently been greatly surprised himself during the writing of his long work by the brilliance and many-sidedness of the thoughts and metaphors which arose in his mind without conscious effort, it was not until the appearance of the printed leaves which make a custom of warning persons against being persuaded into buying certain books that he definitely understood how all these things had been fully expressed many dynasties ago by the all-knowing Lo Kuan Chang, and formed, indeed, the great national standard of unapproachable excellence. Unfortunately, this person had been so deeply engrossed all his life in literary pursuits that he had never found an opportunity to glance at the works in question, or he would have escaped the embarrassing position in which he now found himself.

"It was with a hopeless sense of illness of ease that this unhappy one reached the day on which the printed leaves already alluded to would make known their deliberate opinion of his writing, the extremity of his hope being that some would at least credit him with honourable motives, and perhaps a knowledge that if the inspired Lo Kuan Chan had never been born the entire matter might have been brought to a very different conclusion. Alas! Only one among the many printed leaves which made reference to the venture contained any words of friendship or encouragement. This benevolent exception was sent forth from a city in the extreme Northern Province of the Empire, and contained many inspiring though delicately guarded messages of hope for the one to whom they gracefully alluded as 'this undoubtedly youthful, but nevertheless, distinctly promising writer of books'. While admitting that altogether they found the production undeniably tedious, they claimed to have discovered indications of an obvious talent, and therefore they unhesitatingly counselled the person in question to take courage at the prospect of a moderate competency which was certainly within his grasp if he restrained his somewhat over-ambitious impulses and closely observed the simple subjects and manner of expression of their own Chang Chow, whose 'Lines to a Wayside Chrysanthemum', 'Mongolians who Have' and several other composed pieces they then set forth. Although it became plain that the writer of this amiably devised notice was, like this incapable person, entirely unacquainted with the masterpieces of Lo Kuan Chang, yet the indisputable fact remained that, entirely on its merit, the work had been greeted with undoubted enthusiasm, so that after purchasing many examples of the refined printed leaf containing it, this person sat far into the night continually reading over the one unprejudiced and discriminating expression.

"All the other printed leaves displayed a complete absence of good taste in dealing with the matter. One boldly asserted that the entire circumstance was the outcome of a foolish jest or wager on the part of a person who possessed a million taels; another predicted that it was a cunning and elaborately thought-out method of obtaining the attention of the people on the part of certain persons who claimed to vend a reliable and fragrantly scented cleansing substance. The *Valley of Hoang Rose Leaves* and Sweetness hoped, in a spirit of no sincerity, that the ingenious Kai Lung would not rest on his tea-leaves, but would soon send forth an equally entertaining amended example of the Sayings of Confucius and other sacred works, while the *Pure Essence of the Seven Days' Happenings* merely printed side by side portions from the two books under the large inscription, 'Is there really any Need for Us to express Ourselves more clearly?'

"The disappointment both as regards public esteem and taels – for, after the manner in which the work had been received by those who advise on such productions, not a single example was purchased – threw this ill-destined individual into a condition of most unendurable depression, from which he was only aroused by a remarkable example of the unfailing wisdom of the proverb which says 'Before hastening to secure a possible reward of five taels by dragging an unobservant person away from a falling building, examine well his features lest you find, when too late, that it is one to whom you are indebted for double that amount.' Disappointed in the hope of securing large gains from the sale of his great work, this person now turned his attention again to his former means of living, only to find, however, that the discredit in which he had become involved even attached itself to his concise sentence; for in place of the remunerative and honourable manner in which it was formerly received, it was now regarded on all hands with open suspicion. Instead of meekly kow-towing to an evidently pre-arranged doom, the last misfortune aroused this usually resigned storyteller to an ungovernable frenzy. Regarding the accomplished but at the same time exceedingly over-productive Lo Kuan Chang as the beginning of all his evils, he took a solemn oath as a mark of disapproval that he had not been content to inscribe on paper only half of his brilliant thoughts, leaving the other half for the benefit of this hard-striving and equally well-endowed individual, in which case there would have been a sufficiency of taels and of fame for both.

"For a very considerable space of time this person could conceive no method by which he might attain his object. At length, however, as a result of very keen and subtle intellectual searching, and many well-selected sacrifices, it was conveyed by means of a dream that one very ingenious yet simple way was possible. The renowned and universally-admired writings of the distinguished Lo Kuan for the most part take their action within a few dynasties of their creator's own time: all that remained for this inventive person to accomplish, therefore, was to trace out the entire matter, making the words and speeches to proceed from the mouths of those who existed in still earlier periods. By this crafty method it would at once appear as though the not-too-original Lo Kuan had been indebted to one who came before him for all his most subtle thoughts, and, in consequence, his tomb would become dishonoured and his memory execrated. Without any delay this person cheerfully set himself to the somewhat laborious task before him. Lo Kuan's well-known exclamation of the Emperor Tsing on the battlefield of Shih-ho, 'A sedan-chair! A sedan-chair! This person will unhesitatingly exchange his entire and well-regulated Empire for such an article,' was attributed to an Emperor who lived several thousand years before the treacherous and unpopular Tsing. The new matter of a no less frequently quoted portion ran: 'O nobly intentioned but nevertheless exceedingly morose Tung-shin, the object before you is your distinguished and evilly-disposed-of father's honourably inspired demon,' the change of a name effecting whatever alteration was necessary; while the delicately imagined speech beginning 'The person who becomes amused at matters resulting from double-edged knives has assuredly never felt the effect of a well-directed blow himself' was taken from the mouth of one person and placed in that of one of his remote ancestors. In such a manner, without in any great degree altering the matter of Lo Kuan's works, all the scenes and persons introduced were transferred to much earlier dynasties than those affected by the incomparable writer himself, the final effect being to give an air of extreme unoriginality to his really undoubtedly genuine conceptions.

"Satisfied with his accomplishment, and followed by a hired person of low class bearing the writings, which, by nature of the research necessary in fixing the various dates and places so that even the wary should be deceived, had occupied the greater part of a year, this now fully confident storyteller – unmindful of the well-tried excellence of the inspired saying, 'Money is hundred-footed; upon perceiving a tael lying apparently unobserved upon the floor, do not lose the time necessary in stooping, but quickly place your foot upon it, for one fails nothing in dignity thereby; but should it be a gold piece, distrust all things, and valuing dignity but as an empty name, cast your entire body upon it' – went forth to complete his great task of finally erasing from the mind and records of the Empire the hitherto venerated name of Lo Kuan Chang. Entering the place of commerce of the one who seemed the most favourable for the purpose, he placed the facts as they would in future be represented before him, explained the undoubtedly remunerative fame that would ensue to all concerned in the enterprise of sending forth the printed books in their new form, and, opening at a venture the written leaves which he had brought with him, read out the following words as an indication of the similarity of the entire work:

> Whai-Keng. Friends, Chinamen, labourers who are engaged in agricultural pursuits, entrust to this person your acute and well-educated ears;
>
> He has merely come to assist in depositing the body of Ko'ung in the Family Temple, not for the purpose of making remarks about him of a graceful and highly complimentary nature;
>
> The unremunerative actions of which persons may have been guilty possess an exceedingly undesirable amount of endurance;
>
> The successful and well-considered almost invariably are involved in a directly contrary course;
>
> This person desires nothing more than a like fate to await Ko'ung.

"When this one had read so far, he paused in order to give the other an opportunity of breaking in and offering half his possessions to be allowed to share in the undertaking. As he remained unaccountably silent, however, an inelegant pause occurred which this person at length broke by desiring an expressed opinion on the matter.

"'O exceedingly painstaking, but nevertheless highly inopportune Kai Lung,' he replied at length, while in his countenance this person read an expression of no-encouragement towards his venture, 'all your entrancing efforts do undoubtedly appear to attract the undesirable attention of some spiteful and tyrannical demon. This closely-written and elaborately devised work is in reality not worth the labour of a single stroke, nor is there in all Peking a sender forth of printed leaves who would encourage any project connected with its issue.'

"'But the importance of such a fact as that which would clearly show the hitherto venerated Lo Kuan Chang to be a person who passed off as his own the work of an earlier one!' cried this person in despair, well knowing that the deliberately expressed opinion of the one before him was a matter that would rule all others. 'Consider the interest of the discovery.'

"'The interest would not demand more than a few lines in the ordinary printed leaves,' replied the other calmly. 'Indeed, in a manner of speaking, it is entirely a detail of no consequence whether or not the sublime Lo Kuan ever existed. In reality his very commonplace name may have been simply Lung; his inspired work may have been written a score of dynasties before him by some other person, or they may have been composed by the enlightened Emperor of the period, who desired to conceal the fact, yet these matters would not for a moment engage the interest of any ordinary passer-by. Lo Kuan Chang is not a person in the ordinary expression; he is an embodiment of a distinguished and utterly unassailable national institution. The Heaven-sent works with which he is, by general consent, connected form the necessary unchangeable standard of literary excellence, and remain for ever above rivalry and above mistrust. For this reason the matter is plainly one which does not interest this person.'

"In the course of a not uneventful existence this self-deprecatory person has suffered many reverses and disappointments. During his youth the high-minded Empress on one occasion stopped and openly complimented him on the dignified outline presented by his body in profile, and when he was relying upon this incident to secure him a very remunerative public office, a jealous and powerful Mandarin substituted a somewhat similar, though really very much inferior, person for him at the interview which the Empress had commanded. Frequently in matters of commerce which have appeared to promise very satisfactorily at the beginning this person has been induced to entrust sums of money to others, when he had hoped from the indications and the manner of speaking that the exact contrary would be the case; and in one instance he was released at a vast price from the torture dungeon in Canton – where he had been thrown by the subtle and unconscientious plots of one who could not relate stories in so accurate and unvarying a manner as himself – on the day before that on which all persons were freely set at liberty on account of exceptional public rejoicing. Yet in spite of these and many other very unendurable incidents, this impetuous and ill-starred being never felt so great a desire to retire to a solitary place and there disfigure himself permanently as a mark of his unfeigned internal displeasure, as on the occasion when he endured extreme poverty and great personal inconvenience for an entire year in order that he might take away face from the memory of a person who was so placed that no one expressed any interest in the matter.

"Since then this very ill-clad and really necessitous person has devoted himself to the honourable but exceedingly arduous and in general unremunerative occupation of storytelling. To this he would add nothing save that not infrequently a nobly born and highly cultured audience is so entranced with his commonplace efforts to hold the attention, especially when a story not hitherto known has been related, that in order to afford it an opportunity of expressing its gratification, he has been requested to allow another offering to be made by all persons present at the conclusion of the entertainment."

THE VENGEANCE OF TUNG FEL

ERNEST BRAMAH

For a period not to be measured by days or weeks the air of Ching-fow had been as unrestful as that of the locust plains beyond the Great Wall, for every speech which passed bore two faces, one fair to hear, as a greeting, but the other insidiously speaking behind a screen, of rebellion, violence and the hope of overturning the fixed order of events. With those whom they did not mistrust of treachery persons spoke in low voices of definite plans, while at all times there might appear in prominent places of the city skilfully composed notices setting forth great wrongs and injustices towards which resignation and a lowly bearing were outwardly counselled, yet with the same words cunningly inflaming the minds, even of the patient, as no pouring out of passionate thoughts and undignified threatenings could have done. Among the people, unknown, unseen and unsuspected, except to the proved ones to whom they desired to reveal themselves, moved the agents of the Three Societies. While to the many of Ching-fow nothing was desired or even thought of behind the downfall of their own officials, and, chief of all, the execution of the evil-minded and depraved Mandarin Ping Siang, whose cruelties and extortions had made his name an object of wide and deserved loathing, the agents only regarded the city as a bright spot in the line of blood and fire which they were fanning into life from Peking to Canton, and which would presumably burst forth and involve the entire Empire.

Although it had of late become a plain fact, by reason of the manner of behaving of the people, that events of a sudden and turbulent nature could not long be restrained, yet outwardly there was no exhibition of violence, not even to the length of resisting those whom Ping Siang sent to enforce his unjust demands, chiefly because a well-founded whisper had been sent round that nothing was to be done until Tung Fel should arrive, which would not be until the seventh day in the month of Winged Dragons. To this all persons agreed, for the more aged among them, who, by virtue of their years, were also the formers of opinion in all matters, called up within their memories certain events connected with the two persons in question which appeared to give to Tung Fel the privilege of expressing himself clearly when the matter of finally dealing with the malicious and self-willed Mandarin should be engaged upon.

Among the mountains which enclose Ching-fow on the southern side dwelt a jade-seeker, who also kept goats. Although a young man and entirely without relations, he had, by patient industry, contrived to collect together a large flock of the best-formed and most prolific goats to be found in the neighbourhood, all the money which he received in exchange for jade being quickly bartered again for the finest animals which he could obtain. He was dauntless in penetrating to the most inaccessible parts of the mountains in search of the stone, unfailing in his skilful care of the flock, in which he took much honourable pride, and on all occasions discreet and unassumingly restrained in his discourse and manner of life. Knowing this to be his invariable practice, it was with emotions of an agreeable curiosity that on the seventh day of the month of Winged Dragons those persons who were passing from place to place in the city beheld this young man, Yang Hu, descending the mountain path with unmistakable signs of profound agitation, and an entire absence of prudent care. Following him closely to the inner square of the city, on the continually expressed plea that they themselves had business in that quarter, these persons observed Yang Hu take up a position of unendurable dejection as he gazed reproachfully at the figure of the all-knowing Buddha which surmounted the Temple where it was his custom to sacrifice.

"Alas!" he exclaimed, lifting up his voice, when it became plain that a large number of people was assembled awaiting his words. "To what end does a person strive in this excessively evilly regulated district? Or is it that this obscure and ill-destined one alone is marked out as with a deep white cross for humiliation and ruin? Father, and Sacred Temple of Ancestral Virtues, wherein the meanest can repose their trust, he has none; while now, being more destitute than the beggar at the gate, the hope of honourable marriage and a robust family of sons is more remote than the chance of finding the miracle-working Crystal Image which marks the last footstep of the Pure One. Yesterday this person possessed no secret store of silver or gold, nor had he knowledge of any special amount of jade hidden among the mountains, but to his call there responded four score goats, the most select and majestic to be found in all the Province, of which, nevertheless, it was his yearly custom to sacrifice one, as those here can testify, and to offer another as a duty to the Yamen of Ping Siang, in neither case opening his eyes widely when the hour for selecting arrived. Yet in what an unseemly manner is his respectful piety and courteous loyalty rewarded! Today, before this person went forth on his usual quest, there came those bearing written papers by which they claimed, on the authority of Ping Siang, the whole of this person's flock, as a punishment and fine for his not contributing without warning to the Celebration of Kissing the Emperor's Face – the very obligation of such a matter being entirely unknown to him. Nevertheless, those who came drove off this person's entire wealth, the desperately won increase of a life full of great toil and uncomplainingly endured hardship, leaving him only his cave in the rocks, which even the most grasping of many-handed Mandarins cannot remove, his cloak of skins, which no beggar would gratefully receive, and a bright and increasing light of deep hate scorching within his mind which nothing but the blood of the obdurate extortioner can efficiently quench. No protection of charms or heavily mailed bowmen shall avail him, for in his craving for just revenge this person will meet witchcraft with a Heaven-sent cause and oppose an unsleeping subtlety against strength. Therefore let not the innocent suffer through an insufficient understanding, O Divine One, but direct the hand of your faithful worshipper towards the heart that is proud in tyranny, and holds as empty words the clearly defined promise of an all-seeing justice."

Scarcely had Yang Hu made an end of speaking before there happened an event which could be regarded in no other light than as a direct answer to his plainly expressed request for a definite sign. Upon the clear air, which had become unnaturally still at Yang Hu's words, as though to remove any chance of doubt that this indeed was the requested answer, came the loud beating of many very powerful brass gongs, indicating the approach of some person of undoubted importance. In a very brief period the procession reached the square, the gong-beaters being followed by persons carrying banners, bowmen in armour, others bearing various weapons and instruments of torture, slaves displaying innumerable changes of raiment to prove the rank and consequence of their master, umbrella carriers and fan wavers, and finally, preceded by incense burners and surrounded by servants who cleared away all obstructions by means of their formidable and heavily knotted lashes, the unworthy and deceitful Mandarin Ping Siang, who sat in a silk-hung and elaborately wrought chair, looking from side to side with gestures and expressions of contempt and ill-restrained cupidity.

At the sign of this powerful but unscrupulous person all those who were present fell upon their faces, leaving a broad space in their midst, except Yang Hu, who stepped back into the shadow of a doorway, being resolved that he would not prostrate himself before one whom Heaven had pointed out as the proper object of his just vengeance.

When the chair of Ping Siang could no longer be observed in the distance, and the sound of his many gongs had died away, all the persons who had knelt at his approach rose to their feet, meeting each other's eyes with glances of assured and profound significance. At length there stepped forth an exceedingly aged man, who was generally believed to have the power of reading omens and forecasting futures, so that at his upraised hand all persons became silent.

"Behold!" he exclaimed. "None can turn aside in doubt from the deliberately pointed finger of Buddha. Henceforth, in spite of the well-intentioned suggestions of those who would shield him under the plea of exacting orders from high ones at Peking or extortions practised by slaves under him of which he is ignorant, there can no longer be any two voices concerning the guilty one. Yet what does the knowledge of the cormorant's cry avail the golden carp in the shallow waters of the Yuen-Kiang? A prickly mormosa is an adequate protection against a naked man armed only with a just cause, and a company of bowmen has been known to quench an entire city's Heaven-felt desire for retribution. This person, and doubtless others also, would have experienced a more heartfelt enthusiasm in the matter if the sublime and omnipotent Buddha had gone a step further, and pointed out not only the one to be punished, but also the instrument by which the destiny could be prudently and effectively accomplished."

From the mountain path which led to Yang Hu's cave came a voice, like an expressly devised reply to this speech. It was that of some person uttering the "Chant of Rewards and Penalties":

"How strong is the mountain sycamore!

"Its branches reach the Middle Air, and the eye of none can pierce its foliage;

"It draws power and nourishment from all around, so that weeds alone may flourish under its shadow.

"Robbers find safety within the hollow of its trunk; its branches hide vampires and all manner of evil things which prey upon the innocent;

"The wild boar of the forest sharpen their tusks against the bark, for it is harder than flint, and the axe of the woodsman turns back upon the striker.

"Then cries the sycamore, 'Hail and rain have no power against me, nor can the fiercest sun penetrate beyond my outside fringe;

"'The man who impiously raises his hand against me falls by his own stroke and weapon.

"'Can there be a greater or a more powerful than this one? Assuredly,

> *I* am Buddha; let all things obey me.'
>
> "Whereupon the weeds bow their heads, whispering among themselves, 'The voice of the Tall One we hear, but not that of Buddha. Indeed, it is doubtless as he says.'
>
> "In his musk-scented Heaven Buddha laughs, and not deigning to raise his head from the lap of the Phoenix Goddess, he thrusts forth a stone which lies by his foot.
>
> "Saying, 'A god's present for a god. Take it carefully, O presumptuous Little One, for it is hot to the touch.'
>
> "The thunderbolt falls and the mighty tree is rent in twain. 'They asked for my messenger,' said the Pure One, turning again to repose.
>
> "'Lo, he comes!'"

With the last spoken word there came into the sight of those who were collected together a person of stern yet engaging appearance. His hands and face were the colour of mulberry stain by long exposure to the sun, while his eyes looked forth like two watch-fires outside a wolf-haunted camp. His long pigtail was tangled with the binding tendrils of the forest, and damp with the dew of an open couch. His apparel was in no way striking or brilliant, yet he strode with the dignity and air of a high official, pushing before him a covered box upon wheels.

"It is Tung Fel!" cried many who stood there watching his approach, in tones which showed those who spoke to be inspired by a variety of impressive emotions. "Undoubtedly this is the seventh day of the month of Winged Dragons, and, as he specifically stated would be the case – lo! – he has come."

Few were the words of greeting which Tung Fel accorded even to the most venerable of those who awaited him.

"This person has slept, partaken of fruit and herbs, and devoted an allotted time to inward contemplation," he said briefly. "Other and more weighty matters than the exchange of dignified compliments and the admiration of each other's profiles remain to be accomplished. What, for example, is the significance of the written parchment which is displayed in so obtrusive a manner before our eyes? Bring it to this person without delay."

At these words all those present followed Tung Fel's gaze with astonishment, for conspicuously displayed upon the wall of the Temple was a written notice which all joined in asserting had not been there the moment before, though no man had approached the spot. Nevertheless it was quickly brought to Tung Fel, who took it without any fear or hesitation and read aloud the words which it contained:

"To the Custom-Respecting Persons of Ching-Fow

"Truly the span of existence of any upon this earth is brief and not to be considered; therefore, O unfortunate dwellers of Ching-fow, let it not affect your digestion that your bodies are in peril of sudden and most excruciating tortures and your Family Temples in danger of humiliating disregard.

"Why do your thoughts follow the actions of the noble Mandarin Ping Siang so insidiously, and why after each unjust exaction do your eyes look redly towards the Yamên?

"Is he not the little finger of those at Peking, obeying their commands and only carrying out the taxation which others have devised? Indeed, he himself has stated such to be the fact. If, therefore, a terrible and unforeseen fate overtook the usually cautious and well-armed Ping Siang, doubtless – perhaps after the lapse of some considerable time – another would be sent from Peking for a like purpose, and in this way, after a too-brief period of Heaven-sent rest and prosperity, affairs would regulate themselves into almost as unendurable a condition as before.

"Therefore ponder these things well, O passer-by. Yesterday the only man-child of Huang the wood-carver was taken away to be sold into slavery by the emissaries of the most just Ping Siang (who would not have acted thus, we are assured, were it not for the insatiable ones at Peking), as it had become plain that the very necessitous Huang had no other possession to contribute to the amount to be expended in coloured lights as a mark of public rejoicing on the occasion of the moonday of the sublime Emperor. The illiterate and prosaic-minded Huang, having in a most unseemly manner reviled and even assailed those who acted in the matter, has been effectively disposed of, and his wife now alternately laughs and shrieks in the Establishment of Irregular Intellects.

"For this reason, gazer, and because the matter touches you more closely than, in your self-imagined security, you are prone to think, deal expediently with the time at your disposal. Look twice and lingeringly tonight upon the face of your first-born, and clasp the form of your favourite one in a closer embrace, for he by whose hand the blow is directed may already have cast devouring eyes upon their fairness, and tomorrow he may say to his armed men: 'The time is come; bring her to me.'"

"From the last sentence of the well-intentioned and undoubtedly moderately framed notice this person will take two phrases," remarked Tung Fel, folding the written paper and placing it among his garments, "which shall serve him as the title of the lifelike and accurately represented play which it is his self-conceited intention now to disclose to this select and unprejudiced gathering. The scene represents an enlightened and well-merited justice overtaking an arrogant and intolerable being who – need this person add? – existed many dynasties ago, and the title is: "THE TIME IS COME! By Whose Hand?"

Delivering himself in this manner, Tung Fel drew back the hanging drapery which concealed the front of his large box, and disclosed to those who were gathered round, not, as they had expected, a passage from the Record of the Three Kingdoms, or some other dramatic work of undoubted merit, but an ingeniously constructed representation of a scene outside the walls of their own Ching-fow. On one side was a small but minutely accurate copy of a wood-burner's hut, which was known to all present, while behind stood out the distant but nevertheless unmistakable walls of the city. But it was nearest part of the spectacle that first held the attention of the entranced beholders, for there disported themselves, in every variety of guileless and attractive attitude, a number of young and entirely unconcerned doves. Scarcely had the delighted onlookers fully observed the pleasing and effective scene, or uttered their expressions of polished satisfaction at the graceful and unassuming behaviour of the pretty creatures before them, than the view entirely changed, and, as if by magic, the massive and inelegant building of Ping Siang's Yamên was presented before them. As all gazed, astonished, the great door of the Yamên opened stealthily, and without a moment's pause a lean and ill-conditioned rat, of unnatural size and rapacity, dashed out and seized the most select and engaging of the unsuspecting prey in its hungry jaws. With the expiring cry of the innocent victim the entire box was immediately, and in the most unexpected manner, involved in a profound darkness, which cleared away as suddenly and revealed the forms of the despoiler and the victim lying dead by each other's side.

Tung Fel came forward to receive the well-selected compliments of all who had witnessed the entertainment.

"It may be objected," he remarked, "that the play is, in a manner of expressing one's self, incomplete; for it is unrevealed by whose hand the act of justice was accomplished. Yet in this detail is the accuracy of the representation justified, for though the time has come, the hand by which retribution is accorded shall never be observed."

In such a manner did Tung Fel come to Ching-fow on the seventh day of the month of Winged Dragons, throwing aside all restraint, and no longer urging prudence or delay. Of all the throng which stood before him scarcely one was without a deep offence against Ping Siang, while those who had not as yet suffered feared what the morrow might display.

A wandering monk from the Island of Irredeemable Plagues was the first to step forth in response to Tung Fel's plainly understood suggestion.

"There is no necessity for this person to undertake further acts of benevolence," he remarked, dropping the cloak from his shoulder and displaying the hundred and eight scars of extreme virtue; "nor," he continued, holding up his left hand, from which three fingers were burnt away, "have greater endurances been neglected. Yet the matter before this distinguished gathering is one which merits the favourable consideration of all persons, and this one will in no manner turn away, recounting former actions, while he allows others to press forward towards the accomplishment of the just and divinely inspired act."

With these words the devout and unassuming person in question inscribed his name upon a square piece of rice-paper, attesting his sincerity to the fixed purpose for which it was designed by dipping his thumb into the mixed blood of the slain animals and impressing this unalterable seal upon the paper also. He was followed by a seller of drugs and subtle medicines, whose entire stock had been seized and destroyed by order of Ping Siang, so that no one in Ching-fow might obtain poison for his destruction. Then came an overwhelming stream of persons, all of whom had received some severe and well-remembered injury at the hands of the malicious and vindictive Mandarin. All these followed a similar observance, inscribing their names and binding themselves by the Blood Oath. Last of all Yang Hu stepped up, partly from a natural modesty which restrained him from offering himself when so many more versatile persons of proved excellence were willing to engage in the matter, and partly because an ill-advised conflict was taking place within his mind as to whether the extreme course which was contemplated was the most expedient to pursue. At last, however, he plainly perceived that he could not honourably withhold himself from an affair that was in a measure the direct outcome of his own unendurable loss, so that without further hesitation he added his obscure name to the many illustrious ones already in Tung Fel's keeping.

When at length dark fell upon the city and the cries of the watchmen, warning all prudent ones to bar well their doors against robbers, as they themselves were withdrawing until the morrow, no longer rang through the narrow ways of Ching-fow, all those persons who had pledged themselves by name and seal went forth silently, and came together at the place whereof Tung Fel had secretly conveyed them knowledge. There Tung Fel, standing somewhat apart, placed all the folded papers in the form of a circle, and having performed over them certain observances designed to insure a just decision and to keep away evil influences, submitted the selection to the discriminating choice of the Sacred Flat and Round Sticks. Having in this manner secured the name of the appointed person who should carry out the act of justice and retribution, Tung Fel unfolded the paper, inscribed certain words upon it, and replaced it among the others.

"The moment before great deeds," began Tung Fel, stepping forward and addressing himself to the expectant ones who were gathered round, "is not the time for light speech, nor, indeed, for sentences of dignified length, no matter how pleasantly turned to the ear they may be. Before this person stand many who are undoubtedly illustrious in various arts and virtues, yet one among them is pre-eminently marked out for distinction in that his name shall be handed down in imperishable history as that of a patriot of a pure-minded and uncompromising degree. With him there is no need of further speech, and to this end I have inscribed certain words upon his name-paper. To everyone this person will now return the paper which has been entrusted to him, folded so that the nature of its contents shall be an unwritten leaf to all others. Nor shall the papers be unfolded by any until he is within his own chamber, with barred doors, where all, save the one who shall find the message, shall remain, not venturing forth until daybreak. I, Tung Fel, have spoken, and assuredly I shall not eat my word, which is that a certain and most degrading death awaits any who transgress these commands."

It was with the short and sudden breath of the cowering antelope when the stealthy tread of the pitiless tiger approaches its lair, that Yang Hu opened his paper in the seclusion of his own cave; for his mind was darkened with an inspired inside emotion that he, the one doubting among the eagerly proffering and destructively inclined multitude, would be chosen to accomplish the high aim for which, indeed, he felt exceptionally unworthy. The written sentence which he perceived immediately upon unfolding the paper, instructing him to appear again before Tung Fel at the hour of midnight, was, therefore, nothing but the echo and fulfilment of his own thoughts, and served in reality to impress his mind with calmer feelings of dignified unconcern than would have been the case had he not been chosen. Having neither possessions nor relations, the occupation of disposing of his goods and making ceremonious and affectionate leave-takings of his family, against the occurrence of any unforeseen disaster, engrossed no portion of Yang Hu's time. Yet there was one matter to which no reference has yet been made, but which now forces itself obtrusively upon the attention, which was in a large measure responsible for many of the most prominent actions of Yang Hu's life, and, indeed, in no small degree influenced his hesitation in offering himself before Tung Fel.

Not a bowshot distance from the place where the mountain path entered the outskirts of the city lived Hiya-ai-Shao with her parents, who were persons of assured position, though of no particular wealth. For a period not confined to a single year it had been the custom of Yang Hu to offer to this elegant and refined maiden all the rarest pieces of jade which he could discover, while the most symmetrical and remunerative she-goat in his flock enjoyed the honourable distinction of bearing her incomparable name. Towards the almond garden of Hiya's abode Yang Hu turned his footsteps upon leaving his cave, and standing there, concealed from all sides by the white and abundant flower-laden foliage, he uttered a sound which had long been an agreed signal between them. Presently a faint perfume of choo-lân spoke of her near approach, and without delay Hiya herself stood by his side.

"Well-endowed one," said Yang Hu, when at length they had gazed upon each other's features and made renewals of their protestations of mutual regard, "the fixed intentions of a person have often been fitly likened to the seed of the tree-peony, so ineffectual are their efforts among the winds of constantly changing circumstance. The definite hope of this person had long pointed towards a small but adequate habitation, surrounded by sweet-smelling olive-trees and not far distant from the jade cliffs and pastures which would afford a sufficient remuneration and a means of living. This entrancing picture has been blotted out for the time, and in its place this person finds himself face to face with an arduous and dangerous undertaking, followed, perhaps, by hasty and immediate flight. Yet if the adorable Hiya will prove the unchanging depths of her constantly expressed intention by accompanying him as far as the village of Hing where suitable marriage ceremonies can be observed without delay, the exile will in reality be in the nature of a triumphal procession, and the emotions with which this person has hitherto regarded the entire circumstance will undergo a complete and highly accomplished change."

"Oh, Yang!" exclaimed the maiden, whose feelings at hearing these words were in no way different from those of her lover when he was on the point of opening the folded paper upon which Tung Fel had written. "What is the nature of the mission upon which you are so impetuously resolved? And why will it be followed by flight?"

"The nature of the undertaking cannot be revealed by reason of a deliberately taken oath," replied Yang Hu; "and the reason of its possible consequence is a less important question to the two persons who are here conversing together than of whether the amiable and graceful Hiya is willing to carry out her often-expressed desire for an opportunity of displaying the true depths of her emotions towards this one."

"Alas!" said Hiya, "the sentiments which this person expressed with irreproachable honourableness when the sun was high in the heavens and the probability of secretly leaving an undoubtedly well-appointed home was engagingly remote, seem to have an entirely different significance when recalled by night in a damp orchard, and on the eve of their fulfilment. To deceive one's parents is an ignoble prospect; furthermore, it is often an exceedingly difficult undertaking. Let the matter be arranged in this way: that Yang leaves the ultimate details of the scheme to Hiya's expedient care, he proceeding without delay to Hing, or, even more desirable, to the further town of Liyunnan, and there awaiting her coming. By such means the risk of discovery and pursuit will be lessened, Yang will be able to set forth on his journey with greater speed, and this one will have an opportunity of getting together certain articles without which, indeed, she would be very inadequately equipped."

In spite of his conscientious desire that Hiya should be by his side on the journey, together with an unendurable certainty that evil would arise from the course she proposed, Yang was compelled by an innate feeling of respect to agree to her wishes, and in this manner the arrangement was definitely concluded. Thereupon Hiya, without delay, returned to the dwelling, remarking that otherwise her absence might be detected and the entire circumstance thereby discovered, leaving Yang Hu to continue his journey and again present himself before Tung Fel, as he had been instructed.

Tung Fel was engaged with brush and ink when Yang Hu entered. Round him were many written parchments, some venerable with age, and a variety of other matters, among which might be clearly perceived weapons, and devices for reading the future. He greeted Yang with many tokens of dignified respect, and with an evidently restrained emotion led him towards the light of a hanging lantern, where he gazed into his face for a considerable period with every indication of exceptional concern.

"Yang Hu," he said at length, "at such a moment many dark and searching thoughts may naturally arise in the mind concerning objects and reasons, omens, and the moving cycle of events. Yet in all these, out of a wisdom gained by deep endurance and a hardly-won experience beyond the common lot, this person would say, Be content. The hand of destiny, though it may at times appear to move in a devious manner, is ever approaching its appointed aim. To this end were you chosen."

"The choice was openly made by wise and proficient omens," replied Yang Hu, without any display of uncertainty of purpose, "and this person is content."

Tung Fel then administered to Yang the Oath of Buddha's Face and the One called the Unutterable (which may not be further described in written words) thereby binding his body and soul, and the souls and repose of all who had gone before him in direct line and all who should in a like manner follow after, to the accomplishment of the design. All spoken matter being thus complete between them, he gave him a mask with which he should pass unknown through the streets and into the presence of Ping Siang, a variety of weapons to use as the occasion arose, and a sign by which the attendants at the Yamên would admit him without further questioning.

As Yang Hu passed through the streets of Ching-fow, which were in a great measure deserted owing to the command of Tung Fel, he was aware of many mournful and foreboding sounds which accompanied him on all sides, while shadowy faces, bearing signs of intolerable anguish and despair, continually formed themselves out of the wind. By the time he reached the Yamên a tempest of exceptional violence was in progress, nor were other omens absent which tended to indicate that matters of a very unpropitious nature were about to take place.

At each successive door of the Yamên the attendant stepped back and covered his face, so that he should by no chance perceive who had come upon so destructive a mission, the instant Yang Hu uttered the sign with which Tung Fel had provided him. In this manner Yang quickly reached the door of the inner chamber upon which was inscribed: "Let the person who comes with a doubtful countenance, unbidden, or meditating treachery, remember the curse and manner of death which attended Lai Kuen, who slew the one over him; so shall he turn and go forth in safety." This unworthy safeguard at the hands of a person who passed his entire life in altering the fixed nature of justice, and who never went beyond his outer gate without an armed company of bowmen, inspired Yang Hu with so incautious a contempt, that without any hesitation he drew forth his brush and ink, and in a spirit of bitter signification added the words, "'Come, let us eat together,' said the wolf to the she-goat."

Being now within a step of Ping Siang and the completion of his undertaking, Yang Hu drew tighter the cords of his mask, tested and proved his weapons, and then, without further delay, threw open the door before him and stepped into the chamber, barring the door quickly so that no person might leave or enter without his consent.

At this interruption and manner of behaving, which clearly indicated the nature of the errand upon which the person before him had come, Ping Siang rose from his couch and stretched out his hand towards a gong which lay beside him.

"All summonses for aid are now unavailing, Ping Siang," exclaimed Yang, without in any measure using delicate or set phrases of speech; "for, as you have doubtless informed yourself, the slaves of tyrants are the first to welcome the downfall of their lord."

"The matter of your speech is as emptiness to this person," replied the Mandarin, affecting with extreme difficulty an appearance of no concern. "In what manner has he fallen? And how will the depraved and self-willed person before him avoid the well-deserved tortures which certainly await him in the public square on the morrow, as the reward of his intolerable presumptions?"

"O Mandarin," cried Yang Hu, "the fitness and occasion for such speeches as the one to which you have just given utterance lie as far behind you as the smoke of yesterday's sacrifice. With what manner of eyes have you frequently journeyed through Ching-fow of late, if the signs and omens there have not already warned you to prepare a coffin adequately designed to receive your well-proportioned body? Has not the pungent vapour of burning houses assailed your senses at every turn, or the salt tears from the eyes of forlorn ones dashed your peach-tea and spiced foods with bitterness?"

"Alas!" exclaimed Ping Siang. "This person now certainly begins to perceive that many things which he has unthinkingly allowed would present a very unendurable face to others."

"In such a manner has it appeared to all Ching-fow," said Yang Hu; "and the justice of your death has been universally admitted. Even should this one fail there would be an innumerable company eager to take his place. Therefore, O Ping Siang, as the only favour which it is within this person's power to accord, select that which in your opinion is the most agreeable manner and weapon for your end."

"It is truly said that at the Final Gate of the Two Ways the necessity for elegant and well-chosen sentences ends," remarked Ping Siang with a sigh, "otherwise the manner of your address would be open to reproach.

By your side this person perceives a long and apparently highly tempered sword, which, in his opinion, will serve the purpose efficiently. Having no remarks of an improving but nevertheless exceedingly tedious nature with which to imprint the occasion for the benefit of those who come after, his only request is that the blow shall be an unhesitating and sufficiently well-directed one."

At these words Yang Hu threw back his cloak to grasp the sword-handle, when the Mandarin, with his eyes fixed on the naked arm, and evidently inspired by every manner of conflicting emotions, uttered a cry of unspeakable wonder and incomparable surprise.

"The Serpent!" he cried, in a voice from which all evenness and control were absent. "The Sacred Serpent of our Race! O mysterious one, who and whence are you?"

Engulfed in an all-absorbing doubt at the nature of events, Yang could only gaze at the form of the serpent which had been clearly impressed upon his arm from the earliest time of his remembrance, while Ping Siang, tearing the silk garment from his own arm and displaying thereon a similar form, continued:

"Behold the inevitable and unvarying birthmark of our race! So it was with this person's father and the ones before him; so it was with his treacherously stolen son; so it will be to the end of all time."

Trembling beyond all power of restraint, Yang removed the mask which had hitherto concealed his face.

"Father or race has this person none," he said, looking into Ping Siang's features with an all-engaging hope, tempered in a measure by a soul-benumbing dread; "nor memory or tradition of an earlier state than when he herded goats and sought for jade in the southern mountains."

"Nevertheless," exclaimed the Mandarin, whose countenance was lightened with an interest and a benevolent emotion which had never been seen there before, "beyond all possibility of doubting, you are this person's lost and greatly desired son, stolen away many years ago by the treacherous conduct of an unworthy woman, yet now happily and miraculously restored to cherish his declining years and perpetuate an honourable name and race."

"Happily!" exclaimed Yang, with fervent indications of uncontrollable bitterness. "Oh, my illustrious sire, at whose venerated feet this unworthy person now prostrates himself with well-merited marks of reverence and self-abasement, has the errand upon which an ignoble son entered – the every memory of which now causes him the acutest agony of the lost, but which nevertheless he is pledged to Tung Fel by the Unutterable Oath to perform – has this unnatural and eternally cursed thing escaped your versatile mind?"

"Tung Fel!" cried Ping Siang. "Is, then, this blow also by the hand of that malicious and vindictive person? Oh, what a cycle of events and interchanging lines of destiny do your words disclose!"

"Who, then, is Tung Fel, my revered Father?" demanded Yang.

"It is a matter which must be made clear from the beginning," replied Ping Siang. "At one time this person and Tung Fel were, by nature and endowments, united in the most amiable bonds of an inseparable friendship. Presently Tung Fel signed the preliminary contract of a marriage with one who seemed to be endowed with every variety of enchanting and virtuous grace, but who was, nevertheless, as the unrolling of future events irresistibly discovered, a person of irregular character and undignified habits. On the eve of the marriage ceremony this person was made known to her by the undoubtedly enraptured Tung Fel, whereupon he too fell into the snare of her engaging personality, and putting aside all thoughts of prudent restraint, made her more remunerative offers of marriage than Tung Fel could by any possible chance overbid. In such a manner – for after the nature of her kind riches were exceptionally attractive to her degraded imagination – she became this person's wife, and the mother of his only son. In spite of these great honours, however, the undoubted perversity of her nature made her an easy accomplice to the duplicity of Tung Fel, who, by means of various disguises, found frequent opportunity of uttering in her presence numerous well-thought-out suggestions specially designed to lead her imagination towards an existence in which this person had no adequate representation. Becoming at length terrified at the possibility of these unworthy emotions, obtruding themselves upon this person's notice, the two in question fled together, taking with them the one who without any doubt is now before me. Despite the most assiduous search and very tempting and profitable offers of reward, no information of a reliable nature could be obtained, and at length this dispirited and completely changed person gave up the pursuit as unavailing. With his son and heir, upon whose future he had greatly hoped, all emotions of a generous and high-minded nature left him, and in a very short space of time he became the avaricious and deservedly unpopular individual against whose extortions the amiable and long-suffering ones of Ching-fow have for so many years protested mildly. The sudden and not altogether unexpected fate which is now on the point of reaching him is altogether too lenient to be entirely adequate."

"Oh, my distinguished and really immaculate sire!" cried Yang Hu, in a voice which expressed the deepest feelings of contrition. "No oaths or vows, however sacred, can induce this person to stretch forth his hand against the one who stands before him."

"Nevertheless," replied Ping Siang, speaking of the matter as though it were one which did not closely concern his own existence, "to neglect the Unutterable Oath would inevitably involve not only the two persons who are now conversing together, but also those before and those who are to come after in direct line, in a much worse condition of affairs. That is a fate which this person would by no means permit to exist, for one of his chief desires has ever been to establish a strong and vigorous line, to which end, indeed, he was even now concluding a marriage arrangement with the beautiful and refined Hiya-ai-Shao, whom he had at length persuaded into accepting his betrothal tokens without reluctance."

"Hiya-ai-Shao!" exclaimed Yang. "She has accepted your silk-bound gifts?"

"The matter need not concern us now," replied the Mandarin, not observing in his complicated emotions the manner in which the name of Hiya had affected Yang, revealing as it undoubtedly did the treachery of his beloved one. "There only appears to be one honourable way in which the full circumstances can be arranged, and this person will in no measure endeavour to avoid it."

Yang Hu looked at him inquiringly, and Ping Siang, crossing the room, opened an inlaid cabinet and drew from a hidden part a closed vessel in which gold-leaf floated in a sweet-scented oil.

"Such an end is neither ignoble nor painful," he said, in an unchanging voice; "nor will this one in any way shrink from so easy and honourable a solution."

"The affairs of the future do not exhibit themselves in delicately coloured hues to this person," said Yang Hu; "and he would, if the thing could be so arranged, cheerfully submit to a similar fate in order that a longer period of existence should be assured to one who has every variety of claim upon his affection."

"The proposal is a graceful and conscientious one," said Ping Siang, "and is, moreover, a gratifying omen of the future of our race, which must of necessity be left in your hands. But, for that reason itself, such a course cannot be pursued. Nevertheless, the events of the past few hours have been of so exceedingly prosperous and agreeable a nature that this short-sighted and frequently desponding person can now pass beyond with a tranquil countenance and every assurance of divine favour."

With these words Ping Siang indicated that he was desirous of setting forth the Final Expression, and arranging the necessary matters upon the table beside him, he stretched forth his hands over Yang Hu, who placed himself in a suitable attitude of reverence and abasement.

"Yang Hu," began the Mandarin, "undoubted son, and, after the accomplishment of the intention which it is our fixed purpose to carry out, fitting representative of the person who is here before you, engrave well within your mind the various details upon which he now gives utterance. Regard the virtues; endeavour to pass an amiable and at the same time not unremunerative existence; and on all occasions sacrifice freely, to the end that the torments of those who have gone before may be made lighter, and that others may be induced in turn to perform a like benevolent charity for yourself. Having expressed himself upon these general subjects, this person now makes a last and respectfully considered desire, which it is his deliberate wish should be carried to the proper deities as his final expression of opinion: that Yang Hu may grow as supple as the dried juice of the bending-palm, and as straight as the most vigorous bamboo from the forests of the North; that he may increase beyond the prolificness of the white-necked crow and cover the ground after the fashion of the binding grass; that in battle his sword may be as a vividly coloured and many-forked lightning flash, accompanied by thunderbolts as irresistible as Buddha's divine wrath – in peace his voice as resounding as the rolling of many powerful drums among the Khingan Mountains; that when the kindled fire of his existence returns to the great Mountain of Pure Flame the earth shall accept again its component parts, and in no way restrain the divine essence from journeying to its destined happiness. These words are Ping Siang's last expression of opinion before he passes beyond, given in the unvarying assurance that so sacred and important a petition will in no way be neglected."

Having in this manner completed all the affairs which seemed to be of a necessary and urgent nature, and fixing his last glance upon Yang Hu with every variety of affectionate and estimable emotion, the Mandarin drank a sufficient quantity of the liquid, and placing himself upon a couch in an attitude of repose, passed in this dignified and unassuming manner into the Upper Air.

After the space of a few moments spent in arranging certain objects and in inward contemplation, Yang Hu crossed the chamber, still holding the half-filled vessel of gold-leaf in his hand, and drawing back the hanging silk, gazed over the silent streets of Ching-fow and towards the great sky-lantern above.

"Hiya is faithless," he said at length in an unspeaking voice; "this person's mother a bitter-tasting memory, his father a swiftly passing shadow that is now for ever lost." His eyes rested upon the closed vessel in his hand. "Gladly would—" his thoughts began, but with this unworthy image a new impression formed itself within his mind. "A clearly expressed wish was uttered," he concluded, "and Tung Fel still remains." With this resolution he stepped back into the chamber and struck the gong loudly.

THE CAREER OF THE CHARITABLE QUEN-KI-TONG

ERNEST BRAMAH

FIRST PERIOD: THE PUBLIC OFFICIAL

"The motives which inspired the actions of the devout Quen-Ki-Tong have long been ill-reported," said Kai Lung the storyteller, upon a certain occasion at Wu-whei, "and, as a consequence, his illustrious memory has suffered somewhat. Even as the insignificant earthworm may bring the precious and many coloured jewel to the surface, so has it been permitted to this obscure and superficially educated one to discover the truth of the entire matter among the badly arranged and frequently really illegible documents preserved at the Hall of Public Reference at Peking. Without fear of contradiction, therefore, he now sets forth the credible version.

"Quen-Ki-Tong was one who throughout his life had been compelled by the opposing force of circumstances to be content with what was offered rather than attain to that which he desired. Having been allowed to wander over the edge of an exceedingly steep crag, while still a child, by the aged and untrustworthy person who had the care of him, and yet suffering little hurt, he was carried back to the city in triumph, by the one in question, who, to cover her neglect, declared amid many chants of exultation that as he slept a majestic winged form had snatched him from her arms and traced magical figures with his body on the ground in token of the distinguished sacred existence for which he was undoubtedly set apart. In such a manner he became famed at a very early age for an unassuming mildness of character and an almost inspired piety of life, so that on every side frequent opportunity was given him for the display of these amiable qualities. Should it chance that an insufficient quantity of puppy-pie had been prepared for the family repast, the undesirable but necessary portion of cold dried rat would inevitably be allotted to the uncomplaining Quen, doubtless accompanied by the engaging but unnecessary remark that he alone had a Heaven-sent intellect which was fixed upon more sublime images than even the best constructed puppy-pie. Should the number of sedan-chairs not be sufficient to bear to the Exhibition of Kites all who were desirous of becoming entertained in such a fashion, inevitably would Quen be the one left behind, in order that he might have adequate leisure for dignified and pure-minded internal reflection.

"In this manner it came about that when a very wealthy but unnaturally avaricious and evil-tempered person who was connected with Quen's father in matters of commerce expressed his fixed determination that the most deserving and enlightened of his friend's sons should enter into a marriage agreement with his daughter, there was no manner of hesitation among those concerned, who admitted without any questioning between themselves that Quen was undeniably the one referred to.

"Though naturally not possessing an insignificant intellect, a continuous habit, together with a most irreproachable sense of filial duty, subdued within Quen's internal organs whatever reluctance he might have otherwise displayed in the matter, so that as courteously as was necessary he presented to the undoubtedly very ordinary and slow-witted maiden in question the gifts of irretrievable intention, and honourably carried out his spoken and written words towards her.

"For a period of years the circumstances of the various persons did not in any degree change, Quen in the meantime becoming more pure-souled and inward-seeing with each moon-change, after the manner of the sublime Lien-ti, who studied to maintain an unmoved endurance in all varieties of events by placing his body to a greater extent each day in a vessel of boiling liquid. Nevertheless, the good and charitable deities to whom Quen unceasingly sacrificed were not altogether unmindful of his virtues; for a son was born, and an evil disease which arose from a most undignified display of uncontrollable emotion on her part ended in his wife being deposited with becoming ceremony in the Family Temple.

"Upon a certain evening, when Quen sat in his inner chamber deliberating upon the really beneficent yet somewhat inexplicable arrangement of the all-seeing ones to whom he was very amiably disposed in consequence of the unwonted tranquillity which he now enjoyed, yet who, it appeared to him, could have set out the entire matter in a much more satisfactory way from the beginning, he was made aware by the unexpected beating of many gongs, and by other signs of refined and deferential welcome, that a person of exalted rank was approaching his residence. While he was still hesitating in his uncertainty regarding the most courteous and delicate form of self-abasement with which to honour so important a visitor – whether to rush forth and allow the chair-carriers to pass over his prostrate form, to make a pretence of being a low-caste slave, and in that guise doing menial service, or to conceal himself beneath a massive and overhanging table until his guest should have availed himself of the opportunity to examine at his leisure whatever the room contained – the person in question stood before him. In every detail of dress and appointment he had the undoubted appearance of being one to whom no door might be safely closed.

"'Alas!' exclaimed Quen. 'How inferior and ill-contrived is the mind of a person of my feeble intellectual attainments. Even at this moment, when the near approach of one who obviously commands every engaging accomplishment might reasonably be expected to call up within it an adequate amount of commonplace resource, its ill-destined possessor finds himself entirely incapable of conducting himself with the fitting outward marks of his great internal respect. This residence is certainly unprepossessing in the extreme, yet it contains many objects of some value and of great rarity; illiterate as this person is, he would not be so presumptuous as to offer any for your acceptance, but if you will confer upon him the favour of selecting that which appears to be the most priceless and unreplaceable, he will immediately, and with every manifestation of extreme delight, break it irredeemably in your honour, to prove the unaffected depth of his gratified emotions.'

"'Quen-Ki-Tong,' replied the person before him, speaking with an evident sincerity of purpose, 'pleasant to this one's ears are your words, breathing as they do an obvious hospitality and a due regard for the forms of etiquette. But if, indeed, you are desirous of gaining this person's explicit regard, break no articles of fine porcelain or rare inlaid wood in proof of it, but immediately dismiss to a very distant spot the three-score gong-beaters who have enclosed him within two solid rings, and who are now carrying out their duties in so diligent a manner that he greatly doubts if the unimpaired faculties of hearing will ever be fully restored. Furthermore, if your exceedingly amiable intentions desire fuller expression, cause an unstinted number of vessels of some uninflammable liquid to be conveyed into your chrysanthemum garden and there poured over the numerous fireworks and coloured lights which still appear to be in progress. Doubtless they are well-intentioned marks of respect, but they caused this person considerable apprehension as he passed among them, and, indeed, give to this unusually pleasant and unassuming spot the by no means inviting atmosphere of a low-class tea-house garden during the festivities attending the birthday of the sacred Emperor.'

"'This person is overwhelmed with a most unendurable confusion that the matters referred to should have been regarded in such a light,' replied Quen humbly. 'Although he himself had no knowledge of them until this moment, he is confident that they in no wise differ from the usual honourable manifestations with which it is customary in this Province to welcome strangers of exceptional rank and titles.'

"'The welcome was of a most dignified and impressive nature,' replied the stranger, with every appearance of not desiring to cause Quen any uneasy internal doubts; 'yet the fact is none the less true that at the moment this person's head seems to contain an exceedingly powerful and well-equipped band; and also, that as he passed through the courtyard an ingeniously constructed but somewhat unmanageable figure of gigantic size, composed entirely of jets of many-coloured flame, leaped out suddenly from behind a dark wall and made an almost successful attempt to embrace him in its ever-revolving arms. Lo Yuen greatly fears that the time when he would have rejoiced in the necessary display of agility to which the incident gave rise has for ever passed away.'

"'Lo Yuen!' exclaimed Quen, with an unaffected mingling of the emotions of reverential awe and pleasurable anticipation. 'Can it indeed be an uncontroversial fact that so learned and ornamental a person as the renowned Controller of Unsolicited Degrees stands beneath this inelegant person's utterly unpresentable roof! Now, indeed, he plainly understands why this ill-conditioned chamber has the appearance of being filled with a Heaven-sent brilliance, and why at the first spoken words of the one before him a melodious sound, like the rushing waters of the sacred Tien-Kiang, seemed to fill his ears.'

"'Undoubtedly the chamber is pervaded by a very exceptional splendour,' replied Lo Yuen, who, in spite of his high position, regarded graceful talk and well-imagined compliments in a spirit of no-satisfaction; 'yet this commonplace-minded one has a fixed conviction that it is caused by the crimson-eyed and pink-fire-breathing dragon which, despite your slave's most assiduous efforts, is now endeavouring to climb through the aperture behind you. The noise which still fills his ears also, resembles rather the despairing cries of the Ten Thousand Lost Ones at the first sight of the Pit of Liquid and Red-hot Malachite, yet without question both proceed from the same cause. Laying aside further ceremony, therefore, permit this greatly over-estimated person to disclose the object of his inopportune visit. Long have your amiable virtues been observed and appreciated by the high ones at Peking, O Quen-Ki-Tong. Too long have they been unrewarded and passed over in silence. Nevertheless, the moment of acknowledgement and advancement has at length arrived; for, as the Book of Verses clearly says, "Even the three-legged mule may contrive to reach the agreed spot in advance of the others, provided a circular running space has been selected and the number of rounds be sufficiently ample." It is this otherwise uninteresting and obtrusive person's graceful duty to convey to you the agreeable intelligence that the honourable and not ill-rewarded office of Guarder of the Imperial Silkworms has been conferred upon you, and to require you to proceed without delay to Peking, so that fitting ceremonies of admittance may be performed before the fifteenth day of the month of Feathered Insects.'

"Alas! How frequently does the purchaser of seemingly vigorous and exceptionally low-priced flower-seeds discover, when too late, that they are, in reality, fashioned from the root of the prolific and valueless tzu-ka, skilfully covered with a disguising varnish! Instead of presenting himself at the place of commerce frequented by those who entrust money to others on the promise of an increased repayment when certain very probable events have come to pass (so that if all else failed he would still possess a serviceable number of taels), Quen-Ki-Tong entirely neglected the demands of a most ordinary prudence, nor could he be induced to set out on his journey until he had passed seven days in public feasting to mark his good fortune, and then devoted fourteen more days to fasting and various acts of penance, in order to make known the regret with which he acknowledged his entire unworthiness for the honour before him. Owing to this very conscientious, but nevertheless somewhat short-sighted manner of behaving, Quen found himself unable to reach Peking before the day preceding that to which Lo Yuen had made special reference. From this cause it came about that only sufficient time remained to perform the various ceremonies of admission, without in any degree counselling Quen as to his duties and procedure in the fulfilment of his really important office.

"Among the many necessary and venerable ceremonies observed during the changing periods of the year, none occupy a more important place than those for which the fifteenth day of the month of Feathered Insects is reserved, conveying as they do a respectful and delicately-fashioned petition that the various affairs upon which persons in every condition of life are engaged may arrive at a pleasant and remunerative conclusion. At the earliest stroke of the gong the versatile Emperor, accompanied by many persons of irreproachable ancestry and certain others, very elaborately attired, proceeds to an open space set apart for the occasion. With unassuming dexterity the benevolent Emperor for a brief span of time engages in the menial occupation of a person of low class, and with his own hands ploughs an assigned portion of land in order that the enlightened spirits under whose direct guardianship the earth is placed may not become lax in their disinterested efforts to promote its fruitfulness. In this charitable exertion he is followed by various other persons of recognized position, the first being, by custom, the Guarder of the Imperial Silkworms, while at the same time the amiably disposed Empress plants an allotted number of mulberry trees, and deposits upon their leaves the carefully reared insects which she receives from the hands of their Guarder. In the case of the accomplished Emperor an ingenious contrivance is resorted to by which the soil is drawn aside by means of hidden strings as the plough passes by, the implement in question being itself constructed from paper of the highest quality, while the oxen which draw it are, in reality, ordinary persons cunningly concealed within masks of cardboard. In this thoughtful manner the actual labours of the sublime Emperor are greatly lessened, while no chance is afforded for an inauspicious omen to be created by the rebellious behaviour of a maliciously inclined ox, or by any other event of an unforeseen nature. All the other persons, however, are required to make themselves proficient in the art of ploughing, before the ceremony, so that the chances of the attendant spirits discovering the deception which has been practised upon them in the case of the Emperor may not be increased by its needless repetition. It was chiefly for this reason that Lo Yuen had urged Quen to journey to Peking as speedily as possible, but owing to the very short time which remained between his arrival and the ceremony of ploughing, not only had the person in question neglected to profit by instruction, but he was not even aware of the obligation which awaited him. When, therefore, in spite of every respectful protest on his part, he was led up to a massively constructed implement drawn by two powerful and undeniably evilly-intentioned-looking animals, it was with every sign of great internal misgivings, and an entire absence of enthusiasm in the entertainment, that he commenced his not too well understood task. In this matter he was by no means mistaken, for it soon became plain to all observers – of whom an immense concourse was assembled – that the usually self-possessed Guarder of the Imperial Silkworms was conducting himself in a most undignified manner; for though he still clung to the plough-handles with an inspired tenacity, his body assumed every variety of base and uninviting attitude. Encouraged by this inelegant state of affairs, the evil spirits which are ever on the watch to turn into derision the charitable intentions of the pure-minded entered into the bodies of the oxen and provoked within their minds a sudden and malignant confidence that the time had arrived when they might with safety break into revolt and throw off the outward signs of their dependent condition. From these various causes it came about that Quen was, without warning, borne with irresistible certainty against the majestic person of the sacred Emperor, the inlaid box of Imperial silkworms, which up to that time had remained safely among the folds of his silk garment, alone serving to avert an even more violent and ill-destined blow.

"'Well,' said the wise and deep-thinking Ye-te, in his book entitled *Proverbs of Everyday Happenings*, 'Should a person on returning from the city discover his house to be in flames, let him examine well the change which he has received from the chair-carrier before it is too late; for evil never travels alone.' Scarcely had the unfortunate Quen recovered his natural attributes from the effect of the disgraceful occurrence which has been recorded (which, indeed, furnished the matter of a song and many unpresentable jests among the low-class persons of the city), than the magnanimous Empress reached that detail of the tree-planting ceremony when it was requisite that she should deposit the living emblems of the desired increase and prosperity upon the leaves. Stretching forth her delicately proportioned hand to Quen for this purpose, she received from the still greatly confused person in question the Imperial silkworms in so unseemly a condition that her eyes had scarcely rested upon them before she was seized with the rigid sickness, and in that state fell to the ground. At this new and entirely unforeseen calamity a very disagreeable certainty of approaching evil began to take possession of all those who stood around, many crying aloud that every omen of good was wanting, and declaring that unless something of a markedly propitiatory nature was quickly accomplished, the agriculture of the entire Empire would cease to flourish, and the various departments of the commerce in silk would undoubtedly be thrown into a state of most inextricable confusion. Indeed, in spite of all things designed to have a contrary effect, the matter came about in the way predicted, for the Hoang-Ho seven times overcame its restraining barriers, and poured its waters over the surrounding country, thereby gaining for the first time its well-deserved title of 'The Sorrow of China', by which dishonourable but exceedingly appropriate designation it is known to this day.

"The manner of greeting which would have been accorded to Quen had he returned to the official quarter of the city, or the nature of his treatment by the baser class of the ordinary people if they succeeded in enticing him to come among them, formed a topic of such uninviting conjecture that the humane-minded Lo Yuen, who had observed the entire course of events from an elevated spot, determined to make a well-directed effort towards his safety. To this end he quickly purchased the esteem of several of those who make a profession of their strength, holding out the hope of still further reward if they conducted the venture to a successful termination. Uttering loud cries of an impending vengeance, as Lo Yuen had instructed them in the matter, and displaying their exceptional proportions to the astonishment and misgivings of all beholders, these persons tore open the opium-tent in which Quen had concealed himself, and, thrusting aside all opposition, quickly dragged him forth. Holding him high upon their shoulders, in spite of his frequent and ill-advised endeavours to cast himself to the ground, some surrounded those who bore him – after the manner of disposing his troops affected by a skilful leader when the enemy begin to waver – and crying aloud that it was their unchanging purpose to submit him to the test of burning splinters and afterwards to torture him, they succeeded by this stratagem in bringing him through the crowd; and hurling back or outstripping those who endeavoured to follow, conveyed him secretly and unperceived to a deserted and appointed spot. Here Quen was obliged to remain until other events caused the recollection of the many to become clouded and unconcerned towards him, suffering frequent inconveniences in spite of the powerful protection of Lo Yuen, and not at all times being able to regard the most necessary repast as an appointment of undoubted certainty. At length, in the guise of a wandering conjurer who was unable to display his accomplishments owing to an entire loss of the power of movement in his arms, Quen passed undetected from the city, and safely reaching the distant and unimportant town of Lu-Kwo, gave himself up to a protracted period of lamentation and self-reproach at the unprepossessing manner in which he had conducted his otherwise very inviting affairs.

SECOND PERIOD: THE TEMPLE BUILDER

"Two hand-counts of years passed away and Quen still remained at Lu-Kwo, all desire of returning either to Peking or to the place of his birth having by this time faded into nothingness. Accepting the inevitable fact that he was not destined ever to become a person with whom taels were plentiful, and yet being unwilling to forego the charitable manner of life which he had always been accustomed to observe, it came about that he spent the greater part of his time in collecting together such sums of money as he could procure from the amiable and well-disposed, and with them building temples and engaging in other benevolent works. From this cause it arose that Quen obtained around Lu-Kwo a reputation for high-minded piety, in no degree less than that which had been conferred upon him in earlier times, so that pilgrims from far distant places would purposely contrive their journey so as to pass through the town containing so unassuming and virtuous a person.

"During this entire period Quen had been accompanied by his only son, a youth of respectful personality, in whose entertaining society he took an intelligent interest. Even when deeply engaged in what he justly regarded as the crowning work of his existence – the planning and erecting of an exceptionally well-endowed marble temple, which was to be entirely covered on the outside with silver paper, and on the inside with gold-leaf – he did not fail to observe the various conditions of Liao's existence, and the changing emotions which from time to time possessed him. Therefore, when the person in question, without displaying any signs of internal sickness, and likewise persistently denying that he had lost any considerable sum of money, disclosed a continuous habit of turning aside with an unaffected expression of distaste from all manner of food, and passed the entire night in observing the course of the great sky-lantern rather than in sleep, the sage and discriminating Quen took him one day aside, and asked him, as one who might aid him in the matter, who the maiden was, and what class and position her father occupied.

"'Alas!' exclaimed Liao, with many unfeigned manifestations of an unbearable fate. 'To what degree do the class and position of her entirely unnecessary parents affect the question? Or how little hope can this sacrilegious one reasonably have of ever progressing as far as earthly details of a pecuniary character in the case of so adorable and far-removed a Being? The uttermost extent of this wildly hoping person's ambition is that when the incomparably symmetrical Ts'ain learns of the steadfast light of his devotion, she may be inspired to deposit an emblematic chrysanthemum upon his tomb in the Family Temple. For such a reward he will cheerfully devote the unswerving fidelity of a lifetime to her service, not distressing her gentle and retiring nature by the expression of what must inevitably be a hopeless passion, but patiently and uncomplainingly guarding her footsteps as from a distance.'

"Being in this manner made aware of the reason of Liao's frequent and unrestrained exclamations of intolerable despair, and of his fixed determination with regard to the maiden Ts'ain (which seemed, above all else, to indicate a resolution to shun her presence) Quen could not regard the immediately following actions of his son with anything but an emotion of confusion. For when his eyes next rested upon the exceedingly contradictory Liao, he was seated in the open space before the house in which Ts'ain dwelt, playing upon an instrument of stringed woods, and chanting verses into which the names of the two persons in question had been skilfully introduced without restraint, his whole manner of behaving being with the evident purpose of attracting the maiden's favourable attention. After an absence of many days, spent in this graceful and complimentary manner, Liao returned suddenly to the house of his father, and, prostrating his body before him, made a specific request for his assistance.

"'As regards Ts'ain and myself,' he continued, 'all things are arranged, and but for the unfortunate coincidence of this person's poverty and of her father's cupidity, the details of the wedding ceremony would undoubtedly now be in a very advanced condition. Upon these entrancing and well-discussed plans, however, the shadow of the grasping and commonplace Ah-Ping has fallen like the inopportune opium-pipe from the mouth of a person examining substances of an explosive nature; for the one referred to demands a large and utterly unobtainable amount of taels before he will suffer his greatly-sought-after daughter to accept the gifts of irretrievable intention.'

"'Grievous indeed is your plight,' replied Quen, when he thus understood the manner of obstacle which impeded his son's hopes; 'for in the nature of taels the most diverse men are to be measured through the same mesh. As the proverb says, "'All money is evil,' exclaimed the philosopher with extreme weariness, as he gathered up the gold pieces in exchange, but presently discovering that one among them was such indeed has he had described, he rushed forth without tarrying to take up a street garment; and with an entire absence of dignity traversed all the ways of the city in the hope of finding the one who had defrauded him." Well does this person know the mercenary Ah-Ping, and the unyielding nature of his closed hand; for often, but always fruitlessly, he has entered his presence on affairs connected with the erecting of certain temples. Nevertheless, the matter is one which does not admit of any incapable faltering, to which end this one will seek out the obdurate Ah-Ping without delay, and endeavour to entrap him by some means in the course of argument.'

"From the time of his earliest youth Ah-Ping had unceasingly devoted himself to the object of getting together an overwhelming number of taels, using for this purpose various means which, without being really degrading or contrary to the written law, were not such as might have been cheerfully engaged in by a person of high-minded honourableness. In consequence of this, as he grew more feeble in body, and more venerable in appearance, he began to express frequent and bitter doubts as to whether his manner of life had been really well arranged; for, in spite of his great wealth, he had grown to adopt a most inexpensive habit on all occasions, having no desire to spend; and an ever-increasing apprehension began to possess him that after he had passed beyond, his sons would be very disinclined to sacrifice and burn money sufficient to keep him in an affluent condition in the Upper Air. In such a state of mind was Ah-Ping when Quen-Ki-Tong appeared before him, for it had just been revealed to him that his eldest and favourite son had, by flattery and by openly praising the dexterity with which he used his brush and ink, entrapped him into inscribing his entire name upon certain unwritten sheets of parchment, which the one in question immediately sold to such as were heavily indebted to Ah-Ping.

"'If a person can be guilty of this really unfilial behaviour during the lifetime of his father,' exclaimed Ah-Ping, in a tone of unrestrained vexation, 'can it be prudently relied upon that he will carry out his wishes after death, when they involve the remitting to him of several thousand taels each year? O estimable Quen-Ki-Tong, how immeasurably superior is the celestial outlook upon which you may safely rely as your portion! When you are enjoying every variety of sumptuous profusion, as the reward of your untiring charitable exertions here on earth, the spirit of this short-sighted person will be engaged in doing menial servitude for the inferior deities, and perhaps scarcely able, even by those means, to clothe himself according to the changing nature of the seasons.'

"'Yet,' replied Quen, 'the necessity for so laborious and unremunerative an existence may even now be averted by taking efficient precautions before you pass to the Upper Air.'

"'In what way?' demanded Ah-Ping, with an awakening hope that the matter might not be entirely destitute of cheerfulness, yet at the same time preparing to examine with even unbecoming intrusiveness any expedient which Quen might lay before him. 'Is it not explicitly stated that sacrifices and acts of a like nature, when performed at the end of one's existence by a person who to that time has professed no sort of interest in such matters, shall in no degree be entered as to his good, but rather regarded as examples of deliberate presumptuousness, and made the excuse for subjecting him to more severe tortures and acts of penance than would be his portion if he neglected the custom altogether?'

"'Undoubtedly such is the case,' replied Quen; 'and on that account it would indicate a most regrettable want of foresight for you to conduct your affairs in the manner indicated. The only undeniably safe course is for you to entrust the amount you will require to a person of exceptional piety, receiving in return his written word to repay the full sum whenever you shall claim it from him in the Upper Air. By this crafty method the amount will be placed at the disposal of the person in question as soon as he has passed beyond, and he will be held by his written word to return it to you whenever you shall demand it.'

"So amiably impressed with this ingenious scheme was Ah-Ping that he would at once have entered more fully into the detail had the thought not arisen in his mind that the person before him was the father of Liao, who urgently required a certain large sum, and that for this reason he might with prudence inquire more fully into the matter elsewhere, in case Quen himself should have been imperceptibly led aside, even though he possessed intentions of a most unswerving honourableness. To this end, therefore, he desired to converse again with Quen on the matter, pleading that at that moment a gathering of those who direct enterprises of a commercial nature required his presence. Nevertheless, he would not permit the person referred to depart until he had complimented him, in both general and specific terms, on the high character of his life and actions, and the intelligent nature of his understanding, which had enabled him with so little mental exertion to discover an efficient plan.

"Without delay Ah-Ping sought out those most skilled in all varieties of law-forms, in extorting money by devices capable of very different meanings, and in expedients for evading just debts; but all agreed that such an arrangement as the one he put before them would be unavoidably binding, provided the person who received the money alluded to spent it in the exercise of his charitable desires, and provided also that the written agreement bore the duty seal of the high ones at Peking, and was deposited in the coffin of the lender. Fully satisfied, and rejoicing greatly that he could in this way adequately provide for his future and entrap the avaricious ones of his house, Ah-Ping collected together the greater part of his possessions, and converting it into pieces of gold, entrusted them to Quen on the exact understanding that has already been described, he receiving in turn Quen's written and thumb-signed paper of repayment, and his assurance that the whole amount should be expended upon the silver-paper and gold-leaf Temple with which he was still engaged.

"It is owing to this circumstance that Quen-Ki-Tong's irreproachable name has come to be lightly regarded by many who may be fitly likened to the latter person in the subtle and experienced proverb, 'The wise man's eyes fell before the gaze of the fool, fearing that if he looked he must cry aloud, "Thou hopeless one!" "There," said the fool to himself, "behold this person's power!"' These badly educated and undiscriminating persons, being entirely unable to explain the ensuing train of events, unhesitatingly declare that Quen-Ki-Tong applied a portion of the money which he had received from Ah-Ping in the manner described to the object of acquiring Ts'ain for his son Liao. In this feeble and incapable fashion they endeavour to stigmatise the pure-minded Quen as one who acted directly contrary to his deliberately spoken word, whereas the desired result was brought about in a much more artful manner; they describe the commercially successful Ah-Ping as a person of very inferior prudence, and one easily imposed upon; while they entirely pass over, as a detail outside the true facts, the written paper preserved among the sacred relics in the Temple, which announces, among other gifts of a small and uninviting character, 'Thirty thousand taels from an elderly ginseng merchant of Lu-Kwo, who desires to remain nameless, through the hand of Quen-Ki-Tong.' The full happening in its real and harmless face is now set forth for the first time.

"Some weeks after the recorded arrangement had been arrived at by Ah-Ping and Quen, when the taels in question had been expended upon the Temple and were, therefore, infallibly beyond recall, the former person chanced to be passing through the public garden in Lu-Kwo when he heard a voice lifted up in the expression of every unendurable feeling of dejection to which one can give utterance. Stepping aside to learn the cause of so unprepossessing a display of unrestrained agitation, and in the hope that perhaps he might be able to use the incident in a remunerative manner, Ah-Ping quickly discovered the unhappy being who, entirely regardless of the embroidered silk robe which he wore, reclined upon a raised bank of uninviting earth, and waved his hands from side to side as his internal emotions urged him.

"'Quen-Ki-Tong!' exclaimed Ah-Ping, not fully convinced that the fact was as he stated it in spite of the image clearly impressed upon his imagination; 'to what unpropitious occurrence is so unlooked-for an exhibition due? Are those who traffic in gold-leaf demanding a high and prohibitive price for that commodity, or has some evil and vindicative spirit taken up its abode within the completed portion of the Temple, and by its offensive but nevertheless diverting remarks and actions removed all semblance of gravity from the countenances of those who daily come to admire the construction?'

"'O thrice unfortunate Ah-Ping,' replied Quen when he observed the distinguishing marks of the person before him, 'scarcely can this greatly overwhelmed one raise his eyes to your open and intelligent countenance; for through him you are on the point of experiencing a very severe financial blow, and it is, indeed, on your account more than on his own that he is now indulging in these outward signs of a grief too far down to be expressed in spoken words.' And at the memory of his former occupation, Quen again waved his arms from side to side with untiring assiduousness.

"'Strange indeed to this person's ears are your words,' said Ah-Ping, outwardly unmoved, but with an apprehensive internal pain that he would have regarded Quen's display of emotion with an easier stomach if his own taels were safely concealed under the floor of his inner chamber. 'The sum which this one entrusted to you has, without any pretence been expended upon the Temple, while the written paper concerning the repayment bears the duty seal of the high ones at Peking. How, then, can Ah-Ping suffer a loss at the hands of Quen-Ki-Tong?'

"'Ah-Ping,' said Quen, with every appearance of desiring that both persons should regard the matter in a conciliatory spirit, 'do not permit the awaiting demons, which are ever on the alert to enter into a person's mind when he becomes distressed out of the common order of events, to take possession of your usually discriminating faculties until you have fully understood how this affair has come about. It is no unknown thing for a person of even exceptional intelligence to reverse his entire manner of living towards the end of a long and consistent existence; the far-seeing and not lightly moved Ah-Ping himself has already done so. In a similar, but entirely contrary manner, the person who is now before you finds himself impelled towards that which will certainly bear a very unpresentable face when the circumstances become known; yet by no other means is he capable of attaining his greatly-desired object.'

"'And to what end does that trend?' demanded Ah-Ping, in no degree understanding how the matter affected him.

"'While occupied with enterprises which those of an engaging and complimentary nature are accustomed to refer to as charitable, this person has almost entirely neglected a duty of scarcely less importance – that of establishing an unending line, through which his name and actions shall be kept alive to all time,' replied Quen. 'Having now inquired into the matter, he finds that his only son, through whom alone the desired result can be obtained, has become unbearably attached to a maiden for whom a very large sum is demanded in exchange. The thought of obtaining no advantage from an entire life of self-denial is certainly unprepossessing in the extreme, but so, even to a more advanced degree, is the certainty that otherwise the family monuments will be untended, and the temple of domestic virtues become an early ruin. This person has submitted the dilemma to the test of omens, and after considering well the reply, he has decided to obtain the price of the maiden in a not very honourable manner, which now presents itself, so that Liao may send out his silk-bound gifts without delay.'

"'It is an unalluring alternative,' said Ah-Ping, whose only inside thought was one of gratification that the exchange money for Ts'ain would so soon be in his possession, 'yet this person fails to perceive how you could act otherwise after the decision of the omens. He now understands, moreover, that the loss you referred to on his part was in the nature of a figure of speech, as one makes use of thunderbolts and delicately scented flowers to convey ideas of harsh and amiable passions, and alluded in reality to the forthcoming departure of his daughter, who is, as you so versatilely suggested, the comfort and riches of his old age.'

"'O venerable, but at this moment somewhat obtuse, Ah-Ping,' cried Quen, with a recurrence to his former method of expressing his unfeigned agitation, 'is your evenly balanced mind unable to grasp the essential fact of how this person's contemplated action will affect your own celestial condition? It is a distressing but entirely unavoidable fact, that if this person acts in the manner which he has determined upon, he will be condemned to the lowest place of torment reserved for those who fail at the end of an otherwise pure existence, and in this he will never have an opportunity of meeting the very much higher placed Ah-Ping, and of restoring to him the thirty-thousand taels as agreed upon.'

"At these ill-destined words, all power of rigidness departed from Ah-Ping's limbs, and he sank down upon the forbidding earth by Quen's side.

"'O most unfortunate one who is now speaking,' he exclaimed, when at length his guarding spirit deemed it prudent to restore his power of expressing himself in words, 'happy indeed would have been your lot had you been content to traffic in ginseng and other commodities of which you have actual knowledge. O amiable Quen, this matter must be in some way arranged without causing you to deviate from the entrancing paths of your habitual virtue. Could not the very reasonable Liao be induced to look favourably upon the attractions of some low-priced maiden, in which case this not really hard-stomached person would be willing to advance the necessary amount, until such time as it could be restored, at a very low and unremunerative rate of interest?'

"'This person has observed every variety of practical humility in the course of his life,' replied Quen with commendable dignity, 'yet he now finds himself totally unable to overcome an inward repugnance to the thought of perpetuating his honoured name and race through the medium of any low-priced maiden. To this end has he decided.'

"Those who were well acquainted with Ah-Ping in matters of commerce did not hesitate to declare that his great wealth had been acquired by his consistent habit of forming an opinion quickly while others hesitated. On the occasion in question he only engaged his mind with the opposing circumstances for a few moments before he definitely fixed upon the course which he should pursue.

"'Quen-Ki-Tong,' he said, with an evident intermingling of many very conflicting emotions, 'retain to the end this well-merited reputation for unaffected honourableness which you have so fittingly earned. Few in the entire Empire, with powers so versatilely pointing to an eminent position in any chosen direction, would have been content to pass their lives in an unremunerative existence devoted to actions of charity. Had you selected an entirely different manner of living, this person has every confidence that he, and many others in Lu-Kwo, would by this time be experiencing a very ignoble poverty. For this reason he will make it his most prominent ambition to hasten the realisation of the amiable hopes expressed both by Liao and by Ts'ain, concerning their future relationship. In this, indeed, he himself will be more than exceptionally fortunate should the former one prove to possess even a portion of the clear-sighted sagaciousness exhibited by his engaging father.'

"Verses Composed by a Musician of Lu-Kwo,
on the Occasion of the Wedding Ceremony of Liao And Ts'ain

"Bright hued is the morning, the dark clouds have fallen;
At the mere waving of Quen's virtuous hands they melted away.
Happy is Liao in the possession of so accomplished a parent,
Happy also is Quen to have so discriminating a son.

"The two persons in question sit, side by side, upon an embroidered couch,
Listening to the well-expressed compliments of those who pass to and fro.
From time to time their eyes meet, and glances of a very significant amusement pass between them;
Can it be that on so ceremonious an occasion they are recalling events of a gravity-removing nature?

"The gentle and rainbow-like Ts'ain has already arrived,
With the graceful motion of a silver carp gliding through a screen of rushes, she moves among those who are assembled.
On the brow of her somewhat contentious father there rests the shadow of an ill-repressed sorrow;
Doubtless the frequently-misjudged Ah-Ping is thinking of his lonely hearth, now that he is for ever parted from that which he holds most precious.

"In the most commodious chamber of the house the elegant wedding-gifts are conspicuously displayed; let us stand beside the one which we have contributed, and point out its excellence to those who pass by.
Surely the time cannot be far distant when the sound of many gongs will announce that the very desirable repast is at length to be partaken of."

THE VISION OF YIN, THE SON OF YAT HUANG

ERNEST BRAMAH

When Yin, the son of Yat Huang, had passed beyond the years assigned to the pursuit of boyhood, he was placed in the care of the hunchback Quang, so that he might be fully instructed in the management of the various weapons used in warfare, and also in the art of stratagem, by which a skilful leader is often enabled to conquer when opposed to an otherwise overwhelming multitude. In all these accomplishments Quang excelled to an exceptional degree; for although unprepossessing in appearance he united matchless strength to an untiring subtlety. No other person in the entire Province of Kiang-si could hurl a javelin so unerringly while uttering sounds of terrifying menace, or could cause his sword to revolve around him so rapidly, while his face looked out from the glittering circles with an expression of ill-intentioned malignity that never failed to inspire his adversary with irrepressible emotions of alarm. No other person could so successfully feign to be devoid of life for almost any length of time, or by his manner of behaving create the fixed impression that he was one of insufficient understanding, and therefore harmless. It was for these reasons that Quang was chosen as the instructor of Yin by Yat Huang, who, without possessing any official degree, was a person to whom marks of obeisance were paid not only within his own town, but for a distance of many li around it.

At length the time arrived when Yin would in the ordinary course of events pass from the instructorship of Quang in order to devote himself to the commerce in which his father was engaged, and from time to time the unavoidable thought arose persistently within his mind that although Yat Huang doubtless knew better than he did what the circumstances of the future required, yet his manner of life for the past years was not such that he could contemplate engaging in the occupation of buying and selling porcelain clay with feelings of an overwhelming interest. Quang, however, maintained with every manifestation of inspired assurance that Yat Huang was to be commended down to the smallest detail, inasmuch as proficiency in the use of both blunt and sharp-edged weapons, and a faculty for passing undetected through the midst of an encamped body of foe-men, fitted a person for the everyday affairs of life above all other accomplishments.

"Without doubt the very accomplished Yat Huan is well advised on this point," continued Quang, "for even this mentally short-sighted person can call up within his understanding numerous specific incidents in the ordinary career of one engaged in the commerce of porcelain clay when such attainments would be of great remunerative benefit. Does the well-endowed Yin think, for example, that even the most depraved person would endeavour to gain an advantage over him in the matter of buying or selling porcelain clay if he fully understood the fact that the one with whom he was trafficking could unhesitatingly transfix four persons with one arrow at the distance of a hundred paces? Or to what advantage would it be that a body of unscrupulous outcasts who owned a field of inferior clay should surround it with drawn swords by day and night, endeavouring meanwhile to dispose of it as material of the finest quality, if the one whom they endeavoured to ensnare in this manner possessed the power of being able to pass through their ranks unseen and examine the clay at his leisure?"

"In the cases to which reference has been made, the possession of those qualities would undoubtedly be of considerable use," admitted Yin; yet, in spite of his entire ignorance of commercial matters, this one has a confident feeling that it would be more profitable to avoid such very doubtful forms of barter altogether rather than spend eight years in acquiring the arts by which to defeat them. "That, however, is a question which concerns this person's virtuous and engaging father more than his unworthy self, and his only regret is that no opportunity has offered by which he might prove that he has applied himself diligently to your instruction and example, O amiable Quang."

It had long been a regret to Quang also that no incident of a disturbing nature had arisen whereby Yin could have shown himself proficient in the methods of defence and attack which he had taught him. This deficiency he had endeavoured to overcome, as far as possible, by constructing life-like models of all the most powerful and ferocious types of warriors and the fiercest and most relentless animals of the forest, so that Yin might become familiar with their appearance and discover in what manner each could be the most expeditiously engaged.

"Nevertheless," remarked Quang, on an occasion when Yin appeared to be covered with honourable pride at having approached an unusually large and repulsive-looking tiger so stealthily that had the animal been really alive it would certainly have failed to perceive him, "such accomplishments are by no means to be regarded as conclusive in themselves. To steal insidiously upon a destructively included wild beast and transfix it with one well-directed blow of a spear is attended by difficulties and emotions which are entirely absent in the case of a wickerwork animal covered with canvas-cloth, no matter how deceptive in appearance the latter may be."

To afford Yin a more trustworthy example of how he should engage with an adversary of formidable proportions, Quang resolved upon an ingenious plan. Procuring the skin of a grey wolf, he concealed himself within it, and in the early morning, while the mist-damp was still upon the ground, he set forth to meet Yin, who had on a previous occasion spoken to him of his intention to be at a certain spot at such an hour. In this conscientious enterprise, the painstaking Quang would doubtless have been successful, and Yin gained an assured proficiency and experience, had it not chanced that on the journey Quang encountered a labourer of low caste who was crossing the enclosed ground on his way to the rice field in which he worked. This contemptible and inopportune person, not having at any period of his existence perfected himself in the recognised and elegant methods of attack and defence, did not act in the manner which would assuredly have been adopted by Yin in similar circumstances, and for which Quang would have been fully prepared. On the contrary, without the least indication of what his intention was, he suddenly struck Quang, who was hesitating for a moment what action to take, a most intolerable blow with a formidable staff which he carried. The stroke in question inflicted itself upon Quang upon that part of the body where the head becomes connected with the neck, and would certainly have been followed by others of equal force and precision had not Quang in the meantime decided that the most dignified course for him to adopt would be to disclose his name and titles without delay. Upon learning these facts, the one who stood before him became very grossly and offensively amused, and having taken from Quang everything of value which he carried among his garments, went on his way, leaving Yin's instructor to retrace his steps in unendurable dejection, as he then found that he possessed no further interest whatever in the undertaking.

When Yat Huang was satisfied that his son was sufficiently skilled in the various arts of warfare, he called him to his inner chamber, and having barred the door securely, he placed Yin under a very binding oath not to reveal, until an appointed period, the matter which he was going to put before him.

"From father to son, in unbroken line for ten generations, has such a custom been observed," he said, "for the course of events is not to be lightly entered upon. At the commencement of that cycle, which period is now fully fifteen score years ago, a very wise person chanced to incur the displeasure of the Emperor of that time, and being in consequence driven out of the capital, he fled to the mountains. There his subtle discernment and the pure and solitary existence which he led resulted in his becoming endowed with faculties beyond those possessed by ordinary beings. When he felt the end of his earthly career to be at hand he descended into the plain, where, in a state of great destitution and bodily anguish, he was discovered by the one whom this person has referred to as the first of the line of ancestors. In return for the care and hospitality with which he was unhesitatingly received, the admittedly inspired hermit spent the remainder of his days in determining the destinies of his rescuer's family and posterity. It is an undoubted fact that he predicted how one would, by well-directed enterprise and adventure, rise to a position of such eminence in the land that he counselled the details to be kept secret, lest the envy and hostility of the ambitious and unworthy should be raised. From this cause it has been customary to reveal the matter fully from father to son, at stated periods, and the setting out of the particulars in written words has been severely discouraged. Wise as this precaution certainly was, it has resulted in a very inconvenient state of things; for a remote ancestor – the fifth in line from the beginning – experienced such vicissitudes that he returned from his travels in a state of most abandoned idiocy, and when the time arrived that he should, in turn, communicate to his son, he was only able to repeat over and over again the name of the pious hermit to whom the family was so greatly indebted, coupling it each time with a new and markedly offensive epithet. The essential details of the undertaking having in this manner passed beyond recall, succeeding generations, which were merely acquainted with the fact that a very prosperous future awaited the one who fulfilled the conditions, have in vain attempted to conform to them. It is not an alluring undertaking, inasmuch as nothing of the method to be pursued can be learned, except that it was the custom of the early ones, who held the full knowledge, to set out from home and return after a period of years. Yet so clearly expressed was the prophecy, and so great the reward of the successful, that all have eagerly journeyed forth when the time came, knowing nothing beyond that which this person has now unfolded to you."

When Yat Huang reached the end of the matter which it was his duty to disclose, Yin for some time pondered the circumstances before replying. In spite of a most engaging reverence for everything of a sacred nature, he could not consider the inspired remark of the well-intentioned hermit without feelings of a most persistent doubt, for it occurred to him that if the person in question had really been as wise as he was represented to be, he might reasonably have been expected to avoid the unaccountable error of offending the enlightened and powerful Emperor under whom he lived. Nevertheless, the prospect of engaging in the trade of porcelain clay was less attractive in his eyes than that of setting forth upon a journey of adventure, so that at length he expressed his willingness to act after the manner of those who had gone before him.

This decision was received by Yat Huang with an equal intermingling of the feelings of delight and concern, for although he would have by no means pleasurably contemplated Yin breaking through a venerable and esteemed custom, he was unable to put entirely from him the thought of the degrading fate which had overtaken the fifth in line who made the venture. It was, indeed, to guard Yin as much as possible against the dangers to which he would become exposed, if he determined on the expedition, that the entire course of his training had been selected. In order that no precaution of a propitious nature should be neglected, Yat Huang at once despatched written words of welcome to all with whom he was acquainted, bidding them partake of a great banquet which he was preparing to mark the occasion of his son's leave-taking. Every variety of sacrifice was offered up to the controlling deities, both good and bad; the ten ancestors were continuously exhorted to take Yin under their special protection, and sets of verses recording his virtues and ambitions were freely distributed among the necessitous and low-caste who could not be received at the feast.

The dinner itself exceeded in magnificence any similar event that had ever taken place in Ching-toi. So great was the polished ceremony observed on the occasion, that each guest had half a score of cups of the finest apricot-tea successively placed before him and taken away untasted, while Yat Huang went to each in turn protesting vehemently that the honour of covering such pure-minded and distinguished persons was more than his badly designed roof could reasonably bear, and wittingly giving an entrancing air of reality to the spoken compliment by begging them to move somewhat to one side so that they might escape the heavy central beam if the event which he alluded to chanced to take place. After several hours had been spent in this congenial occupation, Yat Huang proceeded to read aloud several of the sixteen discourses on education which, taken together, form the discriminating and infallible example of conduct known as the Holy Edict. As each detail was dwelt upon Yin arose from his couch and gave his deliberate testimony that all the required tests and rites had been observed in his own case. The first part of the repast was then partaken of, the nature of the ingredients and the manner of preparing them being fully explained, and in a like manner through each succeeding one of the four-and-forty courses. At the conclusion Yin again arose, being encouraged by the repeated uttering of his name by those present, and with extreme modesty and brilliance set forth his manner of thinking concerning all subjects with which he was acquainted.

Early on the morning of the following day Yin set out on his travels, entirely unaccompanied, and carrying with him nothing beyond a sum of money, a silk robe, and a well-tried and reliable spear. For many days he journeyed in a northerly direction, without encountering anything sufficiently unusual to engage his attention. This, however, was doubtless part of a pre-arranged scheme so that he should not be drawn from a destined path, for at a small village lying on the southern shore of a large lake, called by those around Silent Water, he heard of the existence of a certain sacred island, distant a full day's sailing, which was barren of all forms of living things, and contained only a single gigantic rock of divine origin and majestic appearance. Many persons, the villagers asserted, had sailed to the island in the hope of learning the portent of the rock, but none ever returned, and they themselves avoided coming even within sight of it; for the sacred stone, they declared, exercised an evil influence over their ships, and would, if permitted, draw them out of their course and towards itself. For this reason Yin could find no guide, whatever reward he offered, who would accompany him; but having with difficulty succeeded in hiring a small boat of inconsiderable value, he embarked with food, incense, and materials for building fires, and after rowing consistently for nearly the whole of the day, came within sight of the island at evening. Thereafter the necessity of further exertion ceased, for, as they of the village had declared would be the case, the vessel moved gently forward, in an unswerving line, without being in any way propelled, and reaching its destination in a marvellously short space of time, passed behind a protecting spur of land and came to rest. It then being night, Yin did no more than carry his stores to a place of safety, and after lighting a sacrificial fire and prostrating himself before the rock, passed into the Middle Air.

In the morning Yin's spirit came back to the earth amid the sound of music of a celestial origin, which ceased immediately he recovered full consciousness. Accepting this manifestation as an omen of Divine favour, Yin journeyed towards the centre of the island where the rock stood, at every step passing the bones of innumerable ones who had come on a similar quest to his, and perished. Many of these had left behind them inscriptions on wood or bone testifying their deliberate opinion of the sacred rock, the island, their protecting deities, and the entire train of circumstances, which had resulted in their being in such a condition. These were for the most part of a maledictory and unencouraging nature, so that after reading a few, Yin endeavoured to pass without being in any degree influenced by such ill-judged outbursts.

"Accursed be the ancestors of this tormented one to four generations back!" was prominently traced upon an unusually large shoulder-blade. "May they at this moment be simmering in a vat of unrefined dragon's blood, as a reward for having so undiscriminatingly reared the person who inscribes these words only to attain this end!" "Be warned, O later one, by the signs around!" Another and more practical-minded person had written: "Retreat with all haste to your vessel, and escape while there is yet time. Should you, by chance, again reach land through this warning, do not neglect, out of an emotion of gratitude, to burn an appropriate amount of sacrifice paper for the lessening of the torments of the spirit of Li-Kao," to which an unscrupulous one, who was plainly desirous of sharing in the benefit of the requested sacrifice, without suffering the exertion of inscribing a warning after the amiable manner of Li-Kao, had added the words, "and that of Huan Sin."

Halting at a convenient distance from one side of the rock which, without being carved by any person's hand, naturally resembled the symmetrical countenance of a recumbent dragon (which he therefore conjectured to be the chief point of the entire mass), Yin built his fire and began an unremitting course of sacrifice and respectful ceremony. This manner of conduct he observed conscientiously for the space of seven days. Towards the end of that period a feeling of unendurable dejection began to possess him, for his stores of all kinds were beginning to fail, and he could not entirely put behind him the memory of the various well-intentioned warnings which he had received, or the sight of the fleshless ones who had lined his path. On the eighth day, being weak with hunger and, by reason of an intolerable thirst, unable to restrain his body any longer in the spot where he had hitherto continuously prostrated himself nine-and-ninety times each hour without ceasing, he rose to his feet and retraced his steps to the boat in order that he might fill his water-skins and procure a further supply of food.

With a complicated emotion, in which was present every abandoned and disagreeable thought to which a person becomes a prey in moments of exceptional mental and bodily anguish, he perceived as soon as he reached the edge of the water that the boat, upon which he was confidently relying to carry him back when all else failed, had disappeared as entirely as the smoke from an extinguished opium pipe. At this sight Yin clearly understood the meaning of Li-Kao's unregarded warning, and recognized that nothing could now save him from adding his incorruptible parts to those of the unfortunate ones whose unhappy fate had, seven days ago, engaged his refined pity. Unaccountably strengthened in body by the indignation which possessed him, and inspired with a virtuous repulsion at the treacherous manner of behaving on the part of those who guided his destinies, he hastened back to his place of obeisance, and perceiving that the habitually placid and introspective expression on the dragon face had imperceptibly changed into one of offensive cunning and unconcealed contempt, he snatched up his spear and, without the consideration of a moment, hurled it at a score of paces distance full into the sacred but nevertheless very unprepossessing face before him.

At the instant when the presumptuous weapon touched the holy stone the entire intervening space between the earth and the sky was filled with innumerable flashes of forked and many-tongued lightning, so that the island had the appearance of being the scene of a very extensive but somewhat badly-arranged display of costly fireworks. At the same time the thunder rolled among the clouds and beneath the sea in an exceedingly disconcerting manner. At the first indication of these celestial movements a sudden blindness came upon Yin, and all power of thought or movement forsook him; nevertheless, he experienced an emotion of flight through the air, as though borne upwards upon the back of a winged creature. When this emotion ceased, the blindness went from him as suddenly and entirely as if a cloth had been pulled away from his eyes, and he perceived that he was held in the midst of a boundless space, with no other object in view than the sacred rock, which had opened, as it were, revealing a mighty throng within, at the sight of whom Yin's internal organs trembled as they would never have moved at ordinary danger, for it was put into his spirit that these in whose presence he stood were the sacred Emperors of his country from the earliest time until the usurpation of the Chinese throne by the devouring Tartar hordes from the North.

As Yin gazed in fear-stricken amazement, a knowledge of the various Pure Ones who composed the assembly came upon him. He understood that the three unclad and commanding figures which stood together were the Emperors of the Heaven, Earth and Man, whose reigns covered a space of more than eighty thousand years, commencing from the time when the world began its span of existence. Next to them stood one wearing a robe of leopard-skin, his hand resting upon a staff of a massive club, while on his face the expression of tranquillity which marked his predecessors had changed into one of alert wakefulness; it was the Emperor of Houses, whose reign marked the opening of the never-ending strife between man and all other creatures. By his side stood his successor, the Emperor of Fire, holding in his right hand the emblem of the knotted cord, by which he taught man to cultivate his mental faculties, while from his mouth issued smoke and flame, signifying that by the introduction of fire he had raised his subjects to a state of civilised life.

On the other side of the boundless chamber which seemed to be contained within the rocks were Fou-Hy, Tchang-Ki, Tcheng-Nung and Huang, standing or reclining together. The first of these framed the calendar, organised property, thought out the eight Essential Diagrams, encouraged the various branches of hunting and the rearing of domestic animals, and instituted marriage. From his couch floated melodious sounds in remembrance of his discovery of the property of stringed woods. Tchang-Ki, who manifested the property of herbs and growing plants, wore a robe signifying his attainments by means of embroidered symbols. His hand rested on the head of the dragon, while at his feet flowed a bottomless canal of the purest water. The discovery of written letters by Tcheng-Nung, and his ingenious plan of grouping them after the manner of the constellations of stars, was emblemised in a similar manner, while Huang, or the Yellow Emperor, was surrounded by ores of the useful and precious metals, weapons of warfare, written books, silks and articles of attire, coined money and a variety of objects all testifying to his ingenuity and inspired energy.

These illustrious ones, being the greatest, were the first to take Yin's attention, but beyond them he beheld an innumerable concourse of Emperors who not infrequently outshone their majestic predecessors in the richness of their apparel and the magnificence of the jewels which they wore. There Yin perceived Hung-Hoang, who first caused the chants to be collected, and other rulers of the Tcheon dynasty; Yong-Tching, who compiled the Holy Edict; Thang rulers whose line is rightly called "the golden," from the unsurpassed excellence of the composed verses which it produced; renowned Emperors of the versatile Han dynasty; and, standing apart, and shunned by all, the malignant and narrow-minded Tsing-Su-Hoang, who caused the Sacred Books to be burned.

Even while Yin looked and wondered in great fear, a rolling voice, coming from one who sat in the midst of all, holding in his right hand the sun and in his left the moon, sounded forth, like the music of many brass instruments playing in unison. It was the First Man who spoke.

"Yin, son of Yat Huang, and creature of the Lower Part," he said, "listen well to the words I speak, for brief is the span of your tarrying in the Upper Air, nor will the utterance I now give forth ever come unto your ears again, either on the earth, or when, blindly groping in the Middle Distance, your spirit takes its nightly flight. They who are gathered around, and whose voices I speak, bid me say this: Although immeasurably above you in all matters, both of knowledge and of power, yet we greet you as one who is well-intentioned, and inspired with honourable ambition. Had you been content to entreat and despair, as did all the feeble and incapable ones whose white bones formed your pathway, your ultimate fate would have in no wise differed from theirs. But inasmuch as you held yourself valiantly, and, being taken, raised an instinctive hand in return, you have been chosen; for the day to mute submission has, for the time or for ever, passed away, and the hour is when China shall be saved, not by supplication, but by the spear."

"A state of things which would have been highly unnecessary if I had been permitted to carry out my intention fully, and restore man to his prehistoric simplicity," interrupted Tsin-Su-Hoang. "For that reason, when the voice of the assemblage expresses itself, it must be understood that it represents in no measure the views of Tsin-Su-Hoang."

"In the matter of what has gone before, and that which will follow hereafter," continued the Voice dispassionately, "Yin, the son of Yat-Huang, must concede that it is in no part the utterance of Tsin-Su-Hoang – Tsin-Su-Hoang who burned the Sacred Books."

At the mention of the name and offence of this degraded being a great sound went up from the entire multitude – a universal cry of execration, not greatly dissimilar from that which may be frequently heard in the crowded Temple of Impartiality when the one whose duty it is to take up, at a venture, the folded papers, announces that the sublime Emperor, or some mandarin of exalted rank, has been so fortunate as to hold the winning number in the Annual State Lottery. So vengeance-laden and mournful was the combined and evidently preconcerted wail, that Yin was compelled to shield his ears against it; yet the inconsiderable Tsin-Su-Hoang, on whose account it was raised, seemed in no degree to be affected by it, he, doubtless, having become hardened by hearing a similar outburst, at fixed hours, throughout interminable cycles of time.

When the last echo of the cry had passed away the Voice continued to speak.

"Soon the earth will again receive you, Yin," it said, "for it is not respectful that a lower one should be long permitted to gaze upon our exalted faces. Yet when you go forth and stand once more among men this is laid on you: that henceforth you are as a being devoted to a fixed and unchanging end, and whatever moves towards the restoring of the throne of the Central Empire the outcast but unalterably sacred line of its true sovereigns shall have your arm and mind. By what combination of force and stratagem this can be accomplished may not be honourably revealed by us, the all-knowing. Nevertheless, omens and guidance shall not be lacking from time to time, and from the beginning the weapon by which you have attained to this distinction shall be as a sign of our favour and protection over you."

When the Voice made an end of speaking the sudden blindness came upon Yin, as it had done before, and from the sense of motion which he experienced, he conjectured that he was being conveyed back to the island. Undoubtedly this was the case, for presently there came upon him the feeling that he was awakening from a deep and refreshing sleep, and opening his eyes, which he now found himself able to do without any difficulty, he immediately discovered that he was reclining at full length on the ground, and at a distance of about a score of paces from the dragon head. His first thought was to engage in a lengthy course of self-abasement before it, but remembering the words which had been spoken to him while in the Upper Air, he refrained, and even ventured to go forward with a confident but somewhat self-deprecatory air, to regain the spear, which he perceived lying at the foot of the rock. With feelings of a reassuring nature he then saw that the very undesirable expression which he had last beheld upon the dragon face had melted into one of encouraging urbanity and benignant esteem.

Close by the place where he had landed he discovered his boat, newly furnished with wine and food of a much more attractive profusion than that which he had purchased in the village. Embarking in it, he made as though he would have returned to the south, but the spear which he held turned within his grasp, and pointed in an exactly opposite direction. Regarding this fact as an express command on the part of the Deities, Yin turned his boat to the north, and in the space of two days' time – being continually guided by the fixed indication of the spear – he reached the shore and prepared to continue his travels in the same direction, upheld and inspired by the knowledge that henceforth he moved under the direct influence of very powerful spirits.

THE ILL-REGULATED DESTINY OF KIN YEN, THE PICTURE-MAKER

• • • • •

ERNEST BRAMAH

AS RECORDED BY HIMSELF BEFORE HIS SUDDEN DEPARTURE FROM PEKING, OWING TO CIRCUMSTANCES WHICH ARE MADE PLAIN IN THE FOLLOWING NARRATIVE.

There are moments in the life of a person when the saying of the wise Ni-Hyu that "Misfortune comes to all men and to most women" is endowed with double force. At such times the faithful child of the Sun is a prey to the whitest and most funereal thoughts, and even the inspired wisdom of his illustrious ancestors seems more than doubtful, while the continued inactivity of the Sacred Dragon appears for the time to give colour to the scoffs of the Western barbarian. A little while ago these misgivings would have found no resting-place in the bosom of the writer. Now, however... but the matter must be made clear from the beginning.

The name of the despicable person who here sets forth his immature story is Kin Yen, and he is a native of Kia-Lu in the Province of Che-Kiang. Having purchased from a very aged man the position of Hereditary Instructor in the Art of Drawing Birds and Flowers, he gave lessons in these accomplishments until he had saved sufficient money to journey to Pekingg. Here it was his presumptuous intention to learn the art of drawing figures in order that he might illustrate printed leaves of a more distinguished class than those which would accept what true politeness compels him to call his exceedingly unsymmetrical pictures of birds and flowers. Accordingly, when the time arrived, he disposed of his Hereditary Instructorship, having first ascertained in the interests of his pupils that his successor was a person of refined morals and great filial piety.

Alas! It is well written, "The road to eminence lies through the cheap and exceedingly uninviting eating-houses." In spite of this person's great economy, and of his having begged his way from Kia-Lu to Pekingg in the guise of a pilgrim, journeying to burn incense in the sacred Temple of Truth near that city, when once within the latter place his taels melted away like the smile of a person of low class when he discovers that the mandarin's stern words were not intended as a jest. Moreover, he found that the story-makers of Peking, receiving higher rewards than those at Kia-Lu, considered themselves bound to introduce living characters into all their tales, and in consequence the very ornamental drawings of birds and flowers which he had entwined into a legend entitled "The Last Fight of the Heaven-sent Tcheng" – a story which had been entrusted to him for illustration as a test of his skill – was returned to him with a communication in which the writer revealed his real meaning by stating contrary facts. It therefore became necessary that he should become competent in the art of drawing figures without delay, and with this object he called at the picture-room of Tieng Lin, a person whose experience was so great that he could, without discomfort to himself, draw men and women of all classes, both good and bad. When the person who is setting forth this narrative revealed to Tieng Lin the utmost amount of money he could afford to give for instruction in the art of drawing living figures, Tieng Lin's face became as overcast as the sky immediately before the Great Rains, for in his ignorance of this incapable person's poverty he had treated him with equality and courtesy, nor had he kept him waiting in the mean room on the plea that he was at that moment closeted with the Sacred Emperor. However, upon receiving an assurance that a rumour would be spread in which the number of taels should be multiplied by ten, and that the sum itself should be brought in advance, Tieng Lin promised to instruct this person in the art of drawing five characters, which, he said, would be sufficient to illustrate all stories except those by the most expensive and highly rewarded story-tellers – men who have become so proficient that they not infrequently introduce a score or more of living persons into their tales without confusion.

After considerable deliberation, this unassuming person selected the following characters, judging them to be the most useful, and the most readily applicable to all phases and situations of life:

1. A bad person, wearing a long dark pigtail and smoking an opium pipe. His arms to be folded, and his clothes new and very expensive.
2. A woman of low class. One who removes dust and useless things from the rooms of the over-fastidious and of those who have long nails; she to be carrying her trade-signs.
3. A person from Pe-ling, endowed with qualities which cause the beholder to be amused. This character to be especially designed to go with the short sayings which remove gravity.
4. One who, having incurred the displeasure of the sublime Emperor, has been decapitated in consequence.
5. An ordinary person of no striking or distinguished appearance. One who can be safely introduced in all places and circumstances without great fear of detection.

After many months spent in constant practice and in taking measurements, this unenviable person attained a very high degree of proficiency, and could draw any of the five characters without hesitation. With renewed hope, therefore, he again approached those who sit in easy-chairs, and concealing his identity (for they are stiff at bending, and when once a picture-maker is classed as "of no good" he remains so to the end, in spite of change), he succeeded in getting entrusted with a story by the elegant and refined Kyen Tal. This writer, as he remembered with distrust, confines his distinguished efforts entirely to the doings of sailors and of those connected with the sea, and this tale, indeed, he found upon reading to be the narrative of how a Hang-Chow junk and its crew, consisting mostly of aged persons, were beguiled out of their course by an exceedingly ill-disposed dragon, and wrecked upon an island of naked barbarians. It was, therefore, with a somewhat heavy stomach that this person set himself the task of arranging his five characters as so to illustrate the words of the story.

The sayings of the ancient philosopher Tai Loo are indeed very subtle, and the truth of his remark, "After being disturbed in one's dignity by a mandarin's foot it is no unusual occurrence to fall flat on the face in crossing a muddy street," was now apparent. Great as was the disadvantage owing to the nature of the five characters, this became as nothing when it presently appeared that the avaricious and clay-souled Tieng Lin, taking advantage of the blindness of this person's enthusiasm, had taught him the figures so that they all gazed in the same direction. In consequence of this it would have been impossible that two should be placed as in the act of conversing together had not the noble Kyen Tal been inspired to write that "his companions turned from him in horror". This incident the ingenious person who is recording these facts made the subject of three separate drawings, and having in one or two other places effected skilful changes in the writing, so similar in style to the strokes of the illustrious Kyen Tal as to be undetectable, he found little difficulty in making use of all his characters. The risks of the future, however, were too great to be run with impunity; therefore it was arranged, by means of money – for this person was fast becoming acquainted with the ways of Peking – that an emissary from one who sat in an easy-chair should call upon him for a conference, the narrative of which appeared in this form in the *Pekingg Printed Leaves of Thrice-distilled Truth:*

> The brilliant and amiable young picture-maker Kin Yen, in spite of the immediate and universal success of his accomplished efforts, is still quite rotund in intellect, nor is he, if we may use a form of speaking affected by our friends across the Hoang Hai, "suffering from swollen feet". A

> person with no recognised position, but one who occasionally does inferior work of this nature for us, recently surprised Kin Yen without warning, and found him in his sumptuously appointed picture-room, busy with compasses and tracing-paper. About the place were scattered in elegant confusion several of his recent masterpieces. From the subsequent conversation we are in a position to make it known that in future this refined and versatile person will confine himself entirely to illustrations of processions, funerals, armies on the march, persons pursued by others, and kindred subjects which appeal strongly to his imagination. Kin Yen has severe emotions on the subject of individuality in art, and does not hesitate to express himself forcibly with reference to those who are content to degrade the names of their ancestors by turning out what he wittily describes as "so much of varied mediocrity."

The prominence obtained by this pleasantly-composed notice – for it was copied by others who were unaware of the circumstance of its origin – had the desired effect. In future, when one of those who sit in easy-chairs wished for a picture after the kind mentioned, he would say to his lesser one: "Oh, send to the graceful and versatile Kin Yen; he becomes inspired on the subject of funerals," or persons escaping from prison, or families walking to the temple, or whatever it might be. In that way this narrow-minded and illiterate person was soon both looked at and rich, so that it was his daily practice to be carried, in silk garments, past the houses of those who had known him in poverty, and on these occasions he would puff out his cheeks and pull his moustaches, looking fiercely from side to side.

True are the words written in the elegant and distinguished Book of Verses: "Beware lest when being kissed by the all-seeing Emperor, you step upon the elusive banana-peel." It was at the height of eminence in this altogether degraded person's career that he encountered the being who led him on to his present altogether too lamentable condition.

Tien Nung is the earthly name by which is known she who combines all the most illustrious attributes which have been possessed of women since the days of the divine Fou-Hy. Her father is a person of very gross habits, and lives by selling inferior merchandise covered with some of good quality. Upon past occasions, when under the direct influence of Tien, and in the hope of gaining some money benefit, this person may have spoken of him in terms of praise, and may even have recommended friends to entrust articles of value to him, or to procure goods on his advice. Now, however, he records it as his unalterable decision that the father of Tien Nung is by profession a person who obtains goods by stratagem, and that, moreover, it is impossible to gain an advantage over him on matters of exchange.

The events that have happened prove the deep wisdom of Li Pen when he exclaimed, "The whitest of pigeons, no matter how excellent in the silk-hung chamber, is not to be followed on the field of battle." Tien herself was all that the most exacting of persons could demand, but her opinions on the subject of picture-making were not formed by heavy thought, and it would have been well if this had been borne in mind by this person. One morning he chanced to meet her while carrying open in his hands four sets of printed leaves containing his pictures.

"I have observed," said Tien, after the usual personal inquiries had been exchanged, "that the renowned Kin Yen, who is the object of the keenest envy among his brother picture-makers, so little regards the sacredness of his accomplished art that never by any chance does he depict persons of the very highest excellence. Let not the words of an impetuous maiden disarrange his digestive organs if they should seem too bold to the high-souled Kin Yen, but this matter has, since she has known him, troubled the eyelids of Tien. Here," she continued, taking from this person's hand one of the printed leaves which he was carrying, "in this illustration of persons returning from extinguishing a fire, is there one who appears to possess those qualities which appeal to all that is intellectual and competitive within one? Can it be that the immaculate Kin Yen is unacquainted with the subtle distinction between the really select and the vastly ordinary? Ah, undiscriminating Kin Yen! Are not the eyelashes of the person who is addressing you as threads of fine gold to junk's cables when compared with those of the extremely commonplace female who is here pictured in the art of carrying a bucket? Can the most refined lack of vanity hide from you the fact that your own person is infinitely rounder than this of the evilly-intentioned-looking individual with the opium pipe? O blind Kin Yen!"

Here she fled in honourable confusion, leaving this person standing in the street, astounded, and a prey to the most distinguished emotions of a complicated nature.

"Oh, Tien," he cried at length, "inspired by those bright eyes, narrower than the most select of the three thousand and one possessed by the sublime Buddha, the almost fallen Kin Yen will yet prove himself worthy of your esteemed consideration. He will, without delay, learn to draw two new living persons, and will incorporate in them the likenesses which you have suggested."

Returning swiftly to his abode, he therefore inscribed and despatched this letter, in proof of his resolve:

> "To the Heaven-sent human chrysanthemum, in whose body reside the Celestial Principles and the imprisoned colours of the rainbow.
>
> "From the very offensive and self-opinionated picture-maker.
>
> "Henceforth this person will take no rest, nor eat any but the commonest food, until he shall have carried out the wishes of his one Jade Star, she whose teeth he is not worthy to blacken.
>
> "When Kin Yen has been entrusted with a story which contains a being in some degree reflecting the character of Tien, he will embellish it with her irreproachable profile and come to hear her words. Till then he bids her farewell."

From that moment most of this person's time was necessarily spent in learning to draw the two new characters, and in consequence of this he lost much work, and, indeed, the greater part of the connection which he had been at such pains to form gradually slipped away from him. Many months passed before he was competent to reproduce persons resembling Tien and himself, for in this he was unassisted by Tieng Lin and his progress was slow.

At length, being satisfied, he called upon the least fierce of those who sit in easy-chairs, and requested that he might be entrusted with a story for picture-making.

"We should have been covered with honourable joy to set in operation the brush of the inspired Kin Yen," replied the other with agreeable condescension; "only at the moment, it does not chance that we have before us any stories in which funerals, or beggars being driven from the city, form the chief incidents. Perhaps if the polished Kin Yen should happen to be passing this ill-constructed office in about six months' time..."

"The brush of Kin Yen will never again depict funerals, or labourers arranging themselves to receive pay or similar subjects," exclaimed this person impetuously, "for, as it is well said, 'The lightning discovers objects which the paper-lantern fails to reveal.' In future none but tales dealing with the most distinguished persons shall have his attention."

"If this be the true word of the dignified Kin Yen, it is possible that we may be able to animate his inspired faculties," was the response. "But in that case, as a new style must be in the nature of an experiment, and as our public has come to regard Kin Yen as the great exponent of Art Facing in One Direction, we cannot continue the exceedingly liberal payment with which we have been accustomed to reward his elegant exertions."

"Provided the story be suitable, that is a matter of less importance," replied this person.

"The story," said the one in the easy-chair, "is by the refined Tong-king, and it treats of the high-minded and conscientious doubts of one who would become a priest of Fo. When preparing for this distinguished office he discovers within himself leanings towards the religion of Lao-Tse. His illustrious scruples are enhanced by his affection for Wu Ping, who now appears in the story."

"And the ending?" inquired this person, for it was desirable that the two should marry happily.

"The inimitable stories of Tong-king never have any real ending, and this one, being in his most elevated style, has even less end than most of them. But the whole narrative is permeated with the odour of joss-sticks and honourable high-mindedness, and the two characters are both of noble birth."

As it might be some time before another story so suitable should be offered, or one which would afford so good an opportunity of wafting incense to Tien, and of displaying her incomparable outline in dignified and magnanimous attitudes, this was eagerly accepted, and for the next week this obscure person spent all his days and nights in picturing the lovely Tien and his debased self in the characters of the nobly born young priest of Fo and Wu Ping. The pictures finished, he caused them to be carefully conveyed to the office, and then, sitting down, spent many hours in composing the following letter, to be sent to Tien, accompanying a copy of the printed leaves wherein the story and his drawing should appear:

"When the light has for a period been hidden from a person, it is no uncommon thing for him to be struck blind on gazing at the sun; therefore, if the sublime Tien values the eyes of Kin Yen, let her hide herself behind a gauze screen on his approach.

"The trembling words of Tien have sunk deep into the inside of Kin Yen and become part of his being. Never again can he depict persons of the quality and in the position he was wont to do.

"With this he sends his latest efforts. In each case he conceives his drawings to be the pictures of the written words; in the noble Tien's case it is undoubtedly so, in his own he aspires to it. Doubtless the unobtrusive Tien would make no claim to the character and manner of behaving of the one in the story, yet Kin Yen confidently asserts that she is to the other as the glove is to the hand, and he is filled with the most intelligent delight at being able to exhibit her in her true robes, by which she will be known to all who see her, in spite of her dignified protests. Kin Yen hopes; he will come this evening after sunset."

The week which passed between the finishing of the pictures and the appearance of the eminent printed leaves containing them was the longest in this near-sighted person's ill-spent life. But at length the day arrived, and going with exceedingly mean haste to the place of sale, he purchased a copy and sent it, together with the letter of his honourable intention, on which he had bestowed so much care, to Tien.

Not till then did it occur to this inconsiderable one that the impetuousness of his action was ill-judged; for might it not be that the pictures were evilly-printed, or that the delicate and fragrant words painting the character of the one who now bore the features of Tien had undergone some change?

To satisfy himself, scarce as taels had become with him, he purchased another copy.

There are many exalted sayings of the wise and venerable Confucious constructed so as to be of service and consolation in moments of strong mental distress. These for the greater part recommend tranquillity of mind, a complete abnegation of the human passions and the like behaviour. The person who is here endeavouring to bring this badly constructed account of his dishonourable career to a close pondered these for some moments after twice glancing through the matter in the printed leaves, and then, finding the faculties of speech and movement restored to him, procured a two-edged knife of distinguished brilliance and went forth to call upon the one who sits in an easy-chair.

"Behold," said the lesser one, insidiously stepping in between this person an the inner door, "my intellectual and all-knowing chief is not here today. May his entirely insufficient substitute offer words of congratulation to the inspired Kin Yen on his effective and striking pictures in this week's issue?"

"His altogether insufficient substitute," answered this person, with difficulty mastering his great rage, "may and shall offer words of explanation to the inspired Kin Yen, setting forth the reason of his pictures being used, not with the high-minded story of the elegant Tong-king for which they were executed, but accompanying exceedingly base, foolish and ungrammatical words written by Klan-hi, the Peking remover of gravity – words which will evermore brand the dew-like Tien as a person of light speech and no refinement"; and in his agony this person struck the lacquered table several times with his elegant knife.

"O Kin Yen," exclaimed the lesser one, "this matter rests not here. It is a thing beyond the sphere of the individual who is addressing you. All he can tell is that the graceful Tong-king withdrew his exceedingly tedious story for some reason at the final moment, and as your eminent drawings had been paid for, my chief of the inner office decided to use them with this story of Klan-hi. But surely it cannot be that there is aught in the story to displease your illustrious personality?"

"Judge for yourself," this person said, "first understanding that the two immaculate characters figuring as the personages of the narrative are exact copies of this dishonoured person himself and of the willowy Tien, daughter of the vastly rich Pe-li-Chen, whom he was hopeful of marrying."

Selecting one of the least offensive of the passages in the work, this unhappy person read the following immature and inelegant words:

"This well-satisfied writer of printed leaves had a highly distinguished time last night. After Chow had departed to see about food, and the junk had been fastened up at the lock of Kilung, on the Yang-tse-Kiang, he and the round-bodied Shang were journeying along the narrow path by the riverside when the right leg of the graceful and popular person who is narrating these events disappeared into the river. Suffering no apprehension in the dark, but that the vanishing limb was the left leg of Shang, this intelligent writer allowed his impassiveness to melt away to an exaggerated degree; but at that moment the circumstance became plain to the round-bodied Shang, who was in consequence very grossly amused at the mishap and misapprehension of your good lord, the writer, at the same time pointing out the matter as it really was. Then it chanced that there came by one of the maidens who carry tea and jest for small sums of money to the sitters at the little tables with round white tops, at which this remarkable person, the confidant of many mandarins, ever desirous of displaying his priceless power of removing gravity, said to her:

"'How much of gladness, Ning-Ning? By the Sacred Serpent this is plainly your night out.'

"Perceiving the true facts of the predicament of this commendable writer, she replied:

"'Suffer not your illustrious pigtail to be removed, venerable Wang; for in this maiden's estimation it is indeed your night in.'

"There are times when this valued person wonders whether his method of removing gravity be in reality very antique or quite new. On such occasions the world, with all its schools, and those who interfere in the concerns of others, continues to revolve around him. The wondrous sky-lanterns come out silently two by two like to the crystallised music of stringed woods. Then, in the mystery of no-noise, his head becomes greatly enlarged with celestial and highly profound thoughts; his groping hand seems to touch matter which may be written out in his impressive style and sold to those who print leaves, and he goes home to write out such."

When this person looked up after reading, with tears of shame in his eyes, he perceived that the lesser one had cautiously disappeared. Therefore, being unable to gain admittance to the inner office, he returned to his home.

Here the remark of the omniscient Tai Loo again fixes itself upon the attention. No sooner had this incapable person reached his house than he became aware that a parcel had arrived for him from the still adorable Tien. Retiring to a distance from it, he opened the accompanying letter and read:

"When a virtuous maiden has been made the victim of a heartless jest or a piece of coarse stupidity at a person's hands, it is no uncommon thing for him to be struck blind on meeting her father. Therefore, if the degraded and evil-minded Kin Yen values his eyes, ears, nose, pigtail, even his dishonourable breath, let him hide himself behind a fortified wall at Pe-li-Chen's approach.

"With this Tien returns everything she has ever accepted from Kin Yen. She even includes the brace of puppies which she received anonymously about a month ago, and which she did not eat, but kept for reasons of her own – reasons entirely unconnected with the vapid and exceedingly conceited Kin Yen."

As though this letter, and the puppies of which this person now heard for the first time, making him aware of the existence of a rival lover, were not enough, there almost immediately arrived a letter from Tien's father:

"This person has taken the advice of those skilled in extorting money by means of law forms, and he finds that Kin Yen has been guilty of a grave and highly expensive act. This is increased by the fact that Tien had conveyed his seemingly distinguished intentions to all her friends, before whom she now stands in an exceedingly ungraceful attitude. The machinery for depriving Kin Yen of all the necessaries of existence shall be put into operation at once."

At this point, the person who is now concluding his obscure and commonplace history, having spent his last piece of money on joss-sticks and incense-paper, and being convinced of the presence of the spirits of his ancestors, is inspired to make the following prophecies: that Tieng Lin, who imposed upon him in the matter of picture-making, shall come to a sudden end, accompanied by great internal pains, after suffering extreme poverty; that the one who sits in an easy-chair, together with his lesser one and all who make stories for them, shall, while sailing to a rice feast during the Festival of Flowers, be precipitated into the water and slowly devoured by sea monsters, Klan-hi in particular being tortured in the process; that Pel-li-Chen, the father of Tien, shall be seized with the dancing sickness when in the presence of the august Emperor, and being in consequence suspected of treachery, shall, to prove the truth of his denials, be submitted to the tests of boiling tar, red-hot swords, and of being dropped from a great height on to the Sacred Stone of Goodness and Badness, in each of which he shall fail to convince his judges or to establish his innocence, to the amusement of all beholders.

These are the true words of Kin Yen, the picture-maker, who, having unweighed his mind and exposed the avaricious villainy of certain persons, is now retiring by night to a very select and hidden spot in the Khingan Mountains.

THE REPAIRER OF REPUTATIONS

ROBERT W. CHAMBERS

I

Ne raillons pas les fous; leur folie dure plus longtemps que la nôtre... Voila toute la différence.

Towards the end of the year 1920 the Government of the United States had practically completed the programme, adopted during the last months of President Winthrop's administration. The country was apparently tranquil. Everybody knows how the Tariff and Labour questions were settled. The war with Germany, incident on that country's seizure of the Samoan Islands, had left no visible scars upon the republic, and the temporary occupation of Norfolk by the invading army had been forgotten in the joy over repeated naval victories, and the subsequent ridiculous plight of General Von Gartenlaube's forces in the State of New Jersey. The Cuban and Hawaiian investments had paid one hundred per cent and the territory of Samoa was well worth its cost as a coaling station. The country was in a superb state of defence. Every coast city had been well supplied with land fortifications; the army under the parental eye of the General Staff, organised according to the Prussian system, had been increased to 300,000 men, with a territorial reserve of a million; and six magnificent squadrons of cruisers and battleships patrolled the six stations of the navigable seas, leaving a steam reserve amply fitted to control home waters. The gentlemen from the West had at last been constrained to acknowledge that a college for the training of diplomats was as necessary as law schools are for the training of barristers; consequently we were no longer represented abroad by incompetent patriots. The nation was prosperous; Chicago, for a moment paralysed after a second great fire, had risen from its ruins, white and imperial, and more beautiful than the white city which had been built for its plaything in 1893. Everywhere good architecture was replacing bad, and even in New York, a sudden craving for decency had swept away a great portion of the existing horrors. Streets had been widened, properly paved and lighted, trees had been planted, squares laid out, elevated structures demolished and underground roads built to replace them. The new government buildings and barracks were fine bits of architecture, and the long system of stone quays which completely surrounded the island had been turned into parks which proved a godsend to the population. The subsidizing of the state theatre and state opera brought its own reward. The United States National Academy of Design was much like European institutions of the same kind. Nobody envied the Secretary of Fine Arts, either his cabinet position or his portfolio. The Secretary of Forestry and Game Preservation had a much easier time, thanks to the new system of National Mounted Police. We had profited well by the latest treaties with France and England; the exclusion of foreign-born Jews as a measure of self-preservation, the settlement of the new independent negro state of Suanee, the checking of immigration, the new laws concerning naturalisation, and the gradual centralisation of power in the executive all contributed to national calm and prosperity. When the Government solved the Indian problem and squadrons of Indian cavalry scouts in native costume were substituted for the pitiable organisations tacked on to the tail of skeletonized regiments by a former Secretary of War, the nation drew a long sigh of relief. When, after the colossal Congress of Religions, bigotry and intolerance were laid in their graves and kindness and charity began to draw warring sects together, many thought the millennium had arrived, at least in the new world, which after all is a world by itself.

But self-preservation is the first law, and the United States had to look on in helpless sorrow as Germany, Italy, Spain and Belgium writhed in the throes of Anarchy, while Russia, watching from the Caucasus, stooped and bound them one by one.

In the city of New York the summer of 1899 was signalled by the dismantling of the Elevated Railroads. The summer of 1900 will live in the memories of New York people for many a cycle; the Dodge Statue was removed in that year. In the following winter began that agitation for the repeal of the laws prohibiting suicide which bore its final fruit in the month of April, 1920, when the first Government Lethal Chamber was opened on Washington Square.

I had walked down that day from Dr Archer's house on Madison Avenue, where I had been as a mere formality. Ever since that fall from my horse, four years before, I had been troubled at times with pains in the back of my head and neck, but now for months they had been absent, and the doctor sent me away that day saying there was nothing more to be cured in me. It was hardly worth his fee to be told that; I knew it myself. Still I did not grudge him the money. What I minded was the mistake which he made at first. When they picked me up from the pavement where I lay unconscious, and somebody had mercifully sent a bullet through my horse's head, I was carried to Dr Archer, and he, pronouncing my brain affected, placed me in his private asylum where I was obliged to endure treatment for insanity. At last he decided that I was well, and I, knowing that my mind had always been as sound as his, if not sounder, "paid my tuition" as he jokingly called it, and left. I told him, smiling, that I would get even with him for his mistake, and he laughed heartily, and asked me to call once in a while. I did so, hoping for a chance to even up accounts, but he gave me none, and I told him I would wait.

The fall from my horse had fortunately left no evil results; on the contrary it had changed my whole character for the better. From a lazy young man about town, I had become active, energetic, temperate, and above all – oh, above all else – ambitious. There was only one thing which troubled me, I laughed at my own uneasiness, and yet it troubled me.

During my convalescence I had bought and read for the first time, *The King in Yellow*. I remember after finishing the first act that it occurred to me that I had better stop. I started up and flung the book into the fireplace; the volume struck the barred grate and fell open on the hearth in the firelight. If I had not caught a glimpse of the opening words in the second act I should never have finished it, but as I stooped to pick it up, my eyes became riveted to the open page, and with a cry of terror, or perhaps it was of joy so poignant that I suffered in every nerve, I snatched the thing out of the coals and crept shaking to my bedroom, where I read it and reread it, and wept and laughed and trembled with a horror which at times assails me yet. This is the thing that troubles me, for I cannot forget Carcosa where black stars hang in the heavens; where the shadows of men's thoughts lengthen in the afternoon, when the twin suns sink into the lake of Hali; and my mind will bear forever the memory of the Pallid Mask. I pray God will curse the writer, as the writer has cursed the world with this beautiful, stupendous creation, terrible in its simplicity, irresistible in its truth – a world which now trembles before the King in Yellow. When the French Government seized the translated copies which had just arrived in Paris, London, of course, became eager to read it. It is well known how the book spread like an infectious disease, from city to city, from continent to continent, barred out here, confiscated there, denounced by Press and pulpit, censured even by the most advanced of literary anarchists. No definite principles had been violated in those wicked pages, no doctrine promulgated, no convictions outraged. It could not be judged by any known standard, yet, although it was acknowledged that the supreme note of art had been struck in *The King in Yellow*, all felt that human nature could not bear the strain, nor thrive on words in which the essence of purest poison lurked. The very banality and innocence of the first act only allowed the blow to fall afterwards with more awful effect.

It was, I remember, the 13th day of April, 1920, that the first Government Lethal Chamber was established on the south side of Washington Square, between Wooster Street and South Fifth Avenue. The block, which had formerly consisted of a lot of shabby old buildings, used as cafés and restaurants for foreigners, had been acquired by the Government in the winter of 1898. The French and Italian cafés and restaurants were torn down; the whole block was enclosed by a gilded iron railing, and converted into a lovely garden with lawns, flowers and fountains. In the centre of the garden stood a small, white building, severely classical in architecture, and surrounded by thickets of flowers. Six Ionic columns supported the roof, and the single door was of bronze. A splendid marble group of the "Fates" stood before the door, the work of a young American sculptor, Boris Yvain, who had died in Paris when only twenty-three years old.

The inauguration ceremonies were in progress as I crossed University Place and entered the square. I threaded my way through the silent throng of spectators, but was stopped at Fourth Street by a cordon of police. A regiment of United States lancers were drawn up in a hollow square round the Lethal Chamber. On a raised tribune facing Washington Park stood the Governor of New York, and behind him were grouped the Mayor of New York and Brooklyn, the Inspector-General of Police, the Commandant of the state troops, Colonel Livingston, military aid to the President of the United States, General Blount, commanding at Governor's Island, Major-General Hamilton, commanding the garrison of New York and Brooklyn, Admiral Buffby of the fleet in the North River, Surgeon-General Lanceford, the staff of the National Free Hospital, Senators Wyse and Franklin of New York, and the Commissioner of Public Works. The tribune was surrounded by a squadron of hussars of the National Guard.

The Governor was finishing his reply to the short speech of the Surgeon-General. I heard him say: "The laws prohibiting suicide and providing punishment for any attempt at self-destruction have been repealed. The Government has seen fit to acknowledge the right of man to end an existence which may have become intolerable to him, through physical suffering or mental despair. It is believed that the community will be benefited by the removal of such people from their midst. Since the passage of this law, the number of suicides in the United States has not increased. Now the Government has determined to establish a Lethal Chamber in every city, town and village in the country, it remains to be seen whether or not that class of human creatures from whose desponding ranks new victims of self-destruction fall daily will accept the relief thus provided." He paused, and turned to the white Lethal Chamber. The silence in the street was absolute. "There a painless death awaits him who can no longer bear the sorrows of this life. If death is welcome let him seek it there." Then quickly turning to the military aid of the President's household, he said, "I declare the Lethal Chamber open," and again facing the vast crowd he cried in a clear voice: "Citizens of New York and of the United States of America, through me the Government declares the Lethal Chamber to be open."

The solemn hush was broken by a sharp cry of command, the squadron of hussars filed after the Governor's carriage, the lancers wheeled and formed along Fifth Avenue to wait for the commandant of the garrison, and the mounted police followed them. I left the crowd to gape and stare at the white marble Death Chamber and, crossing South Fifth Avenue, walked along the western side of that thoroughfare to Bleecker Street. Then I turned to the right and stopped before a dingy shop which bore the sign:

HAWBERK, ARMOURER

I glanced in at the doorway and saw Hawberk busy in his little shop at the end of the hall. He looked up, and catching sight of me cried in his deep, hearty voice, "Come in, Mr Castaigne!" Constance, his daughter, rose to meet me as I crossed the threshold, and held out her pretty hand, but I saw the blush of disappointment on her cheeks, and knew that it was another Castaigne she had expected, my cousin Louis. I smiled at her confusion and complimented her on the banner she was embroidering from a coloured plate. Old Hawberk sat riveting the worn greaves of some ancient suit of armour, and the ting! ting! ting! of his little hammer sounded pleasantly in the quaint shop. Presently he dropped his hammer, and fussed about for a moment with a tiny wrench. The soft clash of the mail sent a thrill of pleasure through me. I loved to hear the music of steel brushing against steel, the mellow shock of the mallet on thigh pieces and the jingle of chain armour. That was the only reason I went to see Hawberk. He had never interested me personally, nor did Constance, except for the fact of her being in love with Louis. This did occupy my attention, and sometimes even kept me awake at night. But I knew in my heart that all would come right, and that I should arrange their future as I expected to arrange that of my kind doctor, John Archer. However, I should never have troubled myself about visiting them just then, had it not been, as I say, that the music of the tinkling hammer had for me this strong fascination. I would sit for hours, listening and listening, and when a stray sunbeam struck the inlaid steel, the sensation it gave me was almost too keen to endure. My eyes would become fixed, dilating with a pleasure that stretched every nerve almost to breaking, until some movement of the old armourer cut off the ray of sunlight, then, still thrilling secretly, I leaned back and listened again to the sound of the polishing rag, swish! swish! rubbing rust from the rivets.

Constance worked with the embroidery over her knees, now and then pausing to examine more closely the pattern in the coloured plate from the Metropolitan Museum.

"Who is this for?" I asked.

Hawberk explained, that in addition to the treasures of armour in the Metropolitan Museum of which he had been appointed armourer, he also had charge of several collections belonging to rich amateurs. This was the missing greave of a famous suit which a client of his had traced to a little shop in Paris on the Quai d'Orsay. He, Hawberk, had negotiated for and secured the greave, and now the suit was complete. He laid down his hammer and read me the history of the suit, traced since 1450 from owner to owner until it was acquired by Thomas Stainbridge. When his superb collection was sold, this client of Hawberk's bought the suit, and since then the search for the missing greave had been pushed until it was, almost by accident, located in Paris.

"Did you continue the search so persistently without any certainty of the greave being still in existence?" I demanded.

"Of course," he replied coolly.

Then for the first time I took a personal interest in Hawberk.

"It was worth something to you," I ventured.

"No," he replied, laughing, "my pleasure in finding it was my reward."

"Have you no ambition to be rich?" I asked, smiling.

"My one ambition is to be the best armourer in the world," he answered gravely.

Constance asked me if I had seen the ceremonies at the Lethal Chamber. She herself had noticed cavalry passing up Broadway that morning, and had wished to see the inauguration, but her father wanted the banner finished, and she had stayed at his request.

"Did you see your cousin, Mr Castaigne, there?" she asked, with the slightest tremor of her soft eyelashes.

"No," I replied carelessly. "Louis' regiment is manoeuvring out in

Westchester County." I rose and picked up my hat and cane.

"Are you going upstairs to see the lunatic again?" laughed old Hawberk. If Hawberk knew how I loathe that word 'lunatic', he would never use it in my presence. It rouses certain feelings within me which I do not care to explain. However, I answered him quietly: "I think I shall drop in and see Mr Wilde for a moment or two."

"Poor fellow," said Constance, with a shake of the head, "it must be hard to live alone year after year poor, crippled and almost demented. It is very good of you, Mr Castaigne, to visit him as often as you do."

"I think he is vicious," observed Hawberk, beginning again with his hammer. I listened to the golden tinkle on the greave plates; when he had finished, I replied:

"No, he is not vicious, nor is he in the least demented. His mind is a wonder chamber, from which he can extract treasures that you and I would give years of our life to acquire."

Hawberk laughed.

I continued a little impatiently: "He knows history as no one else could know it. Nothing, however trivial, escapes his search, and his memory is so absolute, so precise in details, that were it known in New York that such a man existed, the people could not honour him enough."

"Nonsense," muttered Hawberk, searching on the floor for a fallen rivet.

"Is it nonsense," I asked, managing to suppress what I felt, "is it nonsense when he says that the tassets and cuissards of the enamelled suit of armour commonly known as the 'Prince's Emblazoned' can be found among a mass of rusty theatrical properties, broken stoves and ragpicker's refuse in a garret in Pell Street?"

Hawberk's hammer fell to the ground, but he picked it up and asked, with a great deal of calm, how I knew that the tassets and left cuissard were missing from the "Prince's Emblazoned".

"I did not know until Mr Wilde mentioned it to me the other day. He said they were in the garret of 998 Pell Street."

"Nonsense," he cried, but I noticed his hand trembling under his leathern apron.

"Is this nonsense too?" I asked pleasantly, "is it nonsense when Mr Wilde continually speaks of you as the Marquis of Avonshire and of Miss Constance—"

I did not finish, for Constance had started to her feet with terror written on every feature. Hawberk looked at me and slowly smoothed his leathern apron.

"That is impossible," he observed, "Mr Wilde may know a great many things—"

"About armour, for instance, and the 'Prince's Emblazoned'," I interposed, smiling.

"Yes," he continued, slowly, "about armour also – maybe – but he is wrong in regard to the Marquis of Avonshire, who, as you know, killed his wife's traducer years ago, and went to Australia where he did not long survive his wife."

"Mr Wilde is wrong," murmured Constance. Her lips were blanched, but her voice was sweet and calm.

"Let us agree, if you please, that in this one circumstance Mr Wilde is wrong," I said.

II

I climbed the three dilapidated flights of stairs, which I had so often climbed before, and knocked at a small door at the end of the corridor. Mr Wilde opened the door and I walked in.

When he had double-locked the door and pushed a heavy chest against it, he came and sat down beside me, peering up into my face with his little light-coloured eyes. Half a dozen new scratches covered his nose and cheeks, and the silver wires which supported his artificial ears had become displaced. I thought I had never seen him so hideously fascinating. He had no ears. The artificial ones, which now stood out at an angle from the fine wire, were his one weakness. They were made of wax and painted a shell pink, but the rest of his face was yellow. He might better have revelled in the luxury of some artificial fingers for his left hand, which was absolutely fingerless, but it seemed to cause him no inconvenience, and he was satisfied with his wax ears. He was very small, scarcely higher than a child of ten, but his arms were magnificently developed, and his thighs as thick as any athlete's. Still, the most remarkable thing about Mr Wilde was that a man of his marvellous intelligence and knowledge should have such a head. It was flat and pointed, like the heads of many of those unfortunates whom people imprison in asylums for the weak-minded. Many called him insane, but I knew him to be as sane as I was.

I do not deny that he was eccentric; the mania he had for keeping that cat and teasing her until she flew at his face like a demon, was certainly eccentric. I never could understand why he kept the creature, nor what pleasure he found in shutting himself up in his room with this surly, vicious beast. I remember once, glancing up from the manuscript I was studying by the light of some tallow dips, and seeing Mr Wilde squatting motionless on his high chair, his eyes fairly blazing with excitement, while the cat, which had risen from her place before the stove, came creeping across the floor right at him. Before I could move she flattened her belly to the ground, crouched, trembled and sprang into his face. Howling and foaming they rolled over and over on the floor, scratching and clawing, until the cat screamed and fled under the cabinet, and Mr Wilde turned over on his back, his limbs contracting and curling up like the legs of a dying spider. He *was* eccentric.

Mr Wilde had climbed into his high chair and, after studying my face, picked up a dog-eared ledger and opened it.

"Henry B. Matthews," he read, "book-keeper with Whysot Whysot and Company, dealers in church ornaments. Called April 3rd. Reputation damaged on the racetrack. Known as a welcher. Reputation to be repaired by August 1st. Retainer Five Dollars." He turned the page and ran his fingerless knuckles down the closely written columns.

"P. Greene Dusenberry, Minister of the Gospel, Fairbeach, New Jersey. Reputation damaged in the Bowery. To be repaired as soon as possible. Retainer $100."

He coughed and added, "Called, April 6th."

"Then you are not in need of money, Mr Wilde," I inquired.

"Listen," he coughed again.

"Mrs C. Hamilton Chester, of Chester Park, New York City. Called April 7th. Reputation damaged at Dieppe, France. To be repaired by October 1st Retainer $500.

"Note – C. Hamilton Chester, Captain USS *Avalanche*, ordered home from South Sea Squadron October 1st."

"Well," I said, "the profession of a Repairer of Reputations is lucrative."

His colourless eyes sought mine, "I only wanted to demonstrate that I was correct. You said it was impossible to succeed as a Repairer of Reputations; that even if I did succeed in certain cases it would cost me more than I would gain by it. Today I have five hundred men in my employ, who are poorly paid, but who pursue the work with an enthusiasm which possibly may be born of fear. These men enter every shade and grade of society; some even are pillars of the most exclusive social temples; others are the prop and pride of the financial world; still others, hold undisputed sway among the 'Fancy and the Talent'. I choose them at my leisure from those who reply to my advertisements. It is easy enough, they are all cowards. I could treble the number in twenty days if I wished. So you see, those who have in their keeping the reputations of their fellow-citizens, I have in my pay."

"They may turn on you," I suggested.

He rubbed his thumb over his cropped ears, and adjusted the wax substitutes. "I think not," he murmured thoughtfully, "I seldom have to apply the whip, and then only once. Besides they like their wages."

"How do you apply the whip?" I demanded.

His face for a moment was awful to look upon. His eyes dwindled to a pair of green sparks.

"I invite them to come and have a little chat with me," he said in a soft voice.

A knock at the door interrupted him, and his face resumed its amiable expression.

"Who is it?" he inquired.

"Mr Steylette," was the answer.

"Come tomorrow," replied Mr Wilde.

"Impossible," began the other, but was silenced by a sort of bark from Mr Wilde.

"Come tomorrow," he repeated.

We heard somebody move away from the door and turn the corner by the stairway.

"Who is that?" I asked.

"Arnold Steylette, Owner and Editor in Chief of the great New York daily."

He drummed on the ledger with his fingerless hand adding: "I pay him very badly, but he thinks it a good bargain."

"Arnold Steylette!" I repeated amazed.

"Yes," said Mr Wilde, with a self-satisfied cough.

The cat, which had entered the room as he spoke, hesitated, looked up at him and snarled. He climbed down from the chair and squatting on the floor, took the creature into his arms and caressed her. The cat ceased snarling and presently began a loud purring which seemed to increase in timbre as he stroked her. "Where are the notes?" I asked. He pointed to the table, and for the hundredth time I picked up the bundle of manuscript entitled *THE IMPERIAL DYNASTY OF AMERICA*.

One by one I studied the well-worn pages, worn only by my own handling, and although I knew all by heart, from the beginning, "When from Carcosa, the Hyades, Hastur and Aldebaran," to "Castaigne, Louis de Calvados, born December 19th, 1877," I read it with an eager, rapt attention, pausing to repeat parts of it aloud, and dwelling especially on "Hildred de Calvados, only son of Hildred Castaigne and Edythe Landes Castaigne, first in succession," etc., etc.

When I finished, Mr Wilde nodded and coughed.

"Speaking of your legitimate ambition," he said, "how do Constance and Louis get along?"

"She loves him," I replied simply.

The cat on his knee suddenly turned and struck at his eyes, and he flung her off and climbed on to the chair opposite me.

"And Dr Archer! But that's a matter you can settle any time you wish," he added.

"Yes," I replied, "Dr Archer can wait, but it is time I saw my cousin Louis."

"It is time," he repeated. Then he took another ledger from the table and ran over the leaves rapidly. "We are now in communication with ten thousand men," he muttered. "We can count on one hundred thousand within the first twenty-eight hours, and in forty-eight hours the state will rise *en masse*. The country follows the state, and the portion that will not, I mean California and the Northwest, might better never have been inhabited. I shall not send them the Yellow Sign."

The blood rushed to my head, but I only answered, "A new broom sweeps clean."

"The ambition of Caesar and of Napoleon pales before that which could not rest until it had seized the minds of men and controlled even their unborn thoughts," said Mr Wilde.

"You are speaking of the King in Yellow," I groaned, with a shudder.

"He is a king whom emperors have served."

"I am content to serve him," I replied.

Mr Wilde sat rubbing his ears with his crippled hand. "Perhaps Constance does not love him," he suggested.

I started to reply, but a sudden burst of military music from the street below drowned my voice. The twentieth dragoon regiment, formerly in garrison at Mount St. Vincent, was returning from the manoeuvres in Westchester County, to its new barracks on East Washington Square. It was my cousin's regiment. They were a fine lot of fellows, in their pale blue, tight-fitting jackets, jaunty busbys and white riding breeches with the double yellow stripe, into which their limbs seemed moulded. Every other squadron was armed with lances, from the metal points of which fluttered yellow and white pennons. The band passed, playing the regimental march, then came the colonel and staff, the horses crowding and trampling, while their heads bobbed in unison, and the pennons fluttered from their lance points. The troopers, who rode with the beautiful English seat, looked brown as berries from their bloodless campaign among the farms of Westchester, and the music of their sabres against the stirrups, and the jingle of spurs and carbines was delightful to me. I saw Louis riding with his squadron. He was as handsome an officer as I have ever seen. Mr Wilde, who had mounted a chair by the window, saw him too, but said nothing. Louis turned and looked straight at Hawberk's shop as he passed, and I could see the flush on his brown cheeks. I think Constance must have been at the window. When the last troopers had clattered by, and the last pennons vanished into South Fifth Avenue, Mr Wilde clambered out of his chair and dragged the chest away from the door.

"Yes," he said, "it is time that you saw your cousin Louis."

He unlocked the door and I picked up my hat and stick and stepped into the corridor. The stairs were dark. Groping about, I set my foot on something soft, which snarled and spit, and I aimed a murderous blow at the cat, but my cane shivered to splinters against the balustrade, and the beast scurried back into Mr Wilde's room.

Passing Hawberk's door again I saw him still at work on the armour, but I did not stop, and stepping out into Bleecker Street, I followed it to Wooster, skirted the grounds of the Lethal Chamber, and crossing Washington Park went straight to my rooms in the Benedick. Here I lunched comfortably, read the *Herald* and the *Meteor*, and finally went to the steel safe in my bedroom and set the time combination. The three and three-quarter minutes which it is necessary to wait, while the time lock is opening, are to me golden moments. From the instant I set the combination to the moment when I grasp the knobs and swing back the solid steel doors, I live in an ecstasy of expectation. Those moments must be like moments passed in Paradise. I know what I am to find at the end of the time limit. I know what the massive safe holds secure for me, for me alone, and the exquisite pleasure of waiting is hardly enhanced when the safe opens and I lift, from its velvet crown, a diadem of purest gold, blazing with diamonds. I do this every day, and yet the joy of waiting and at last touching again the diadem, only seems to increase as the days pass. It is a diadem fit for a King among kings, an Emperor among emperors. The King in Yellow might scorn it, but it shall be worn by his royal servant.

I held it in my arms until the alarm in the safe rang harshly, and then tenderly, proudly, I replaced it and shut the steel doors. I walked slowly back into my study, which faces Washington Square, and leaned on the window sill. The afternoon sun poured into my windows, and a gentle breeze stirred the branches of the elms and maples in the park, now covered with buds and tender foliage. A flock of pigeons circled about the tower of the Memorial Church; sometimes alighting on the purple tiled roof, sometimes wheeling downward to the lotus fountain in front of the marble arch. The gardeners were busy with the flower beds around the fountain, and the freshly turned earth smelled sweet and spicy. A lawn mower, drawn by a fat white horse, clinked across the green sward, and watering-carts poured showers of spray over the asphalt drives. Around the statue of Peter Stuyvesant, which in 1897 had replaced the monstrosity supposed to represent Garibaldi, children played in the spring sunshine, and nurse girls wheeled elaborate baby carriages with a reckless disregard for the pasty-faced occupants, which could probably be explained by the presence of half a dozen trim dragoon troopers languidly lolling on the benches. Through the trees, the Washington Memorial Arch glistened like silver in the sunshine, and beyond, on the eastern extremity of the square the grey stone barracks of the dragoons, and the white granite artillery stables were alive with colour and motion.

I looked at the Lethal Chamber on the corner of the square opposite. A few curious people still lingered about the gilded iron railing, but inside the grounds the paths were deserted. I watched the fountains ripple and sparkle; the sparrows had already found this new bathing nook, and the basins were covered with the dusty-feathered little things. Two or three white peacocks picked their way across the lawns, and a drab coloured pigeon sat so motionless on the arm of one of the "Fates" that it seemed to be a part of the sculptured stone.

As I was turning carelessly away, a slight commotion in the group of curious loiterers around the gates attracted my attention. A young man had entered, and was advancing with nervous strides along the gravel path which leads to the bronze doors of the Lethal Chamber. He paused a moment before the "Fates", and as he raised his head to those three mysterious faces, the pigeon rose from its sculptured perch, circled about for a moment and wheeled to the east. The young man pressed his hand to his face, and then with an undefinable gesture sprang up the marble steps, the bronze doors closed behind him, and half an hour later the loiterers slouched away, and the frightened pigeon returned to its perch in the arms of Fate.

I put on my hat and went out into the park for a little walk before dinner. As I crossed the central driveway a group of officers passed, and one of them called out, "Hello, Hildred," and came back to shake hands with me. It was my cousin Louis, who stood smiling and tapping his spurred heels with his riding-whip.

"Just back from Westchester," he said; "been doing the bucolic; milk and curds, you know, dairy-maids in sunbonnets, who say 'haeow' and 'I don't think' when you tell them they are pretty. I'm nearly dead for a square meal at Delmonico's. What's the news?"

"There is none," I replied pleasantly. "I saw your regiment coming in this morning."

"Did you? I didn't see you. Where were you?"

"In Mr Wilde's window."

"Oh, hell!" he began impatiently, "that man is stark mad! I don't understand why you—"

He saw how annoyed I felt by this outburst, and begged my pardon.

"Really, old chap," he said, "I don't mean to run down a man you like, but for the life of me I can't see what the deuce you find in common with Mr Wilde. He's not well bred, to put it generously; he is hideously deformed; his head is the head of a criminally insane person. You know yourself he's been in an asylum..."

"So have I," I interrupted calmly.

Louis looked startled and confused for a moment, but recovered and slapped me heartily on the shoulder. "You were completely cured," he began; but I stopped him again.

"I suppose you mean that I was simply acknowledged never to have been insane."

"Of course that – that's what I meant," he laughed.

I disliked his laugh because I knew it was forced, but I nodded gaily and asked him where he was going. Louis looked after his brother officers who had now almost reached Broadway.

"We had intended to sample a Brunswick cocktail, but to tell you the truth I was anxious for an excuse to go and see Hawberk instead. Come along, I'll make you my excuse."

We found old Hawberk, neatly attired in a fresh spring suit, standing at the door of his shop and sniffing the air.

"I had just decided to take Constance for a little stroll before dinner," he replied to the impetuous volley of questions from Louis. "We thought of walking on the park terrace along the North River."

At that moment Constance appeared and grew pale and rosy by turns as Louis bent over her small gloved fingers. I tried to excuse myself, alleging an engagement uptown, but Louis and Constance would not listen, and I saw I was expected to remain and engage old Hawberk's attention. After all it would be just as well if I kept my eye on Louis, I thought, and when they hailed a Spring Street horse-car, I got in after them and took my seat beside the armourer.

The beautiful line of parks and granite terraces overlooking the wharves along the North River, which were built in 1910 and finished in the autumn of 1917, had become one of the most popular promenades in the metropolis. They extended from the battery to 190th Street, overlooking the noble river and affording a fine view of the Jersey shore and the Highlands opposite. Cafés and restaurants were scattered here and there among the trees, and twice a week military bands from the garrison played in the kiosks on the parapets.

We sat down in the sunshine on the bench at the foot of the equestrian statue of General Sheridan. Constance tipped her sunshade to shield her eyes, and she and Louis began a murmuring conversation which was impossible to catch. Old Hawberk, leaning on his ivory headed cane, lit an excellent cigar, the mate to which I politely refused, and smiled vacantly. The sun hung low above the Staten Island woods, and the bay was dyed with golden hues reflected from the sun-warmed sails of the shipping in the harbour.

Brigs, schooners, yachts, clumsy ferry-boats, their decks swarming with people, railroad transports carrying lines of brown, blue and white freight cars, stately sound steamers, déclassé tramp steamers, coasters, dredgers, scows, and everywhere pervading the entire bay impudent little tugs puffing and whistling officiously – these were the craft which churned the sunlight waters as far as the eye could reach. In calm contrast to the hurry of sailing vessel and steamer a silent fleet of white warships lay motionless in midstream.

Constance's merry laugh aroused me from my reverie.

"What *are* you staring at?" she inquired.

"Nothing – the fleet," I smiled.

Then Louis told us what the vessels were, pointing out each by its relative position to the old Red Fort on Governor's Island.

"That little cigar shaped thing is a torpedo boat," he explained; "there are four more lying close together. They are the *Tarpon*, the *Falcon*, the *Sea Fox* and the *Octopus*. The gun-boats just above are the *Princeton*, the *Champlain*, the *Still Water* and the *Erie*. Next to them lie the cruisers *Faragut* and *Los Angeles*, and above them the battle ships *California*, and *Dakota*, and the *Washington*, which is the flagship. Those two squatty looking chunks of metal which are anchored there off Castle William are the double-turreted monitors *Terrible* and *Magnificent*; behind them lies the ram *Osceola*."

Constance looked at him with deep approval in her beautiful eyes. "What loads of things you know for a soldier," she said, and we all joined in the laugh which followed.

Presently Louis rose with a nod to us and offered his arm to Constance, and they strolled away along the river wall. Hawberk watched them for a moment and then turned to me.

"Mr Wilde was right," he said. "I have found the missing tassets and left cuissard of the 'Prince's Emblazoned,' in a vile old junk garret in Pell Street."

"998?" I inquired, with a smile.

"Yes."

"Mr Wilde is a very intelligent man," I observed.

"I want to give him the credit of this most important discovery," continued Hawberk. "And I intend it shall be known that he is entitled to the fame of it."

"He won't thank you for that," I answered sharply; "please say nothing about it."

"Do you know what it is worth?" said Hawberk.

"No, fifty dollars, perhaps."

"It is valued at five hundred, but the owner of the 'Prince's Emblazoned' will give two thousand dollars to the person who completes his suit; that reward also belongs to Mr Wilde."

"He doesn't want it! He refuses it!" I answered angrily. "What do you know about Mr Wilde? He doesn't need the money. He is rich – or will be – richer than any living man except myself. What will we care for money then – what will we care, he and I, when – when..."

"When what?" demanded Hawberk, astonished.

"You will see," I replied, on my guard again.

He looked at me narrowly, much as Doctor Archer used to, and I knew he thought I was mentally unsound. Perhaps it was fortunate for him that he did not use the word lunatic just then.

"No," I replied to his unspoken thought, "I am not mentally weak; my mind is as healthy as Mr Wilde's. I do not care to explain just yet what I have on hand, but it is an investment which will pay more than mere gold, silver and precious stones. It will secure the happiness and prosperity of a continent – yes, a hemisphere!"

"Oh," said Hawberk.

"And eventually," I continued more quietly, "it will secure the happiness of the whole world."

"And incidentally your own happiness and prosperity as well as Mr Wilde's?"

"Exactly," I smiled. But I could have throttled him for taking that tone.

He looked at me in silence for a while and then said very gently, "Why don't you give up your books and studies, Mr Castaigne, and take a tramp among the mountains somewhere or other? You used to be fond of fishing. Take a cast or two at the trout in the Rangelys."

"I don't care for fishing any more," I answered, without a shade of annoyance in my voice.

"You used to be fond of everything," he continued; "athletics, yachting, shooting, riding..."

"I have never cared to ride since my fall," I said quietly.

"Ah, yes, your fall," he repeated, looking away from me.

I thought this nonsense had gone far enough, so I brought the conversation back to Mr Wilde; but he was scanning my face again in a manner highly offensive to me.

"Mr Wilde," he repeated, "do you know what he did this afternoon? He came downstairs and nailed a sign over the hall door next to mine; it read:

MR WILDE,
REPAIRER OF REPUTATIONS.
Third Bell.

"Do you know what a Repairer of Reputations can be?"

"I do," I replied, suppressing the rage within.

"Oh," hc said again.

Louis and Constance came strolling by and stopped to ask if we would join them. Hawberk looked at his watch. At the same moment a puff of smoke shot from the casemates of Castle William, and the boom of the sunset gun rolled across the water and was re-echoed from the Highlands opposite. The flag came running down from the flag-pole, the bugles sounded on the white decks of the warships, and the first electric light sparkled out from the Jersey shore.

As I turned into the city with Hawberk I heard Constance murmur something to Louis which I did not understand; but Louis whispered "My darling," in reply; and again, walking ahead with Hawberk through the square I heard a murmur of "sweetheart," and "my own Constance," and I knew the time had nearly arrived when I should speak of important matters with my cousin Louis.

III

One morning early in May I stood before the steel safe in my bedroom, trying on the golden jewelled crown. The diamonds flashed fire as I turned to the mirror, and the heavy beaten gold burned like a halo about my head. I remembered Camilla's agonised scream and the awful words echoing through the dim streets of Carcosa. They were the last lines in the first act, and I dared not think of what followed – dared not, even in the spring sunshine, there in my own room, surrounded with familiar objects, reassured by the bustle from the street and the voices of the servants in the hallway outside. For those poisoned words had dropped slowly into my heart, as death-sweat drops upon a bed-sheet and is absorbed. Trembling, I put the diadem from my head and wiped my forehead, but I thought of Hastur and of my own rightful ambition, and I remembered Mr Wilde as I had last left him, his face all torn and bloody from the claws of that devil's creature, and what he said – ah, what he said. The alarm bell in the safe began to whirr harshly, and I knew my time was up; but I would not heed it, and replacing the flashing circlet upon my head I turned defiantly to the mirror. I stood for a long time absorbed in the changing expression of my own eyes. The mirror reflected a face which was like my own, but whiter, and so thin that I hardly recognised it. And all the time I kept repeating between my clenched teeth, "The day has come! The day has come!" while the alarm in the safe whirred and clamoured, and the diamonds sparkled and flamed above my brow. I heard a door open but did not heed it. It was only when I saw two faces in the mirror – it was only when another face rose over my shoulder, and two other eyes met mine. I wheeled like a flash and seized a long knife from my dressing-table, and my cousin sprang back very pale, crying: "Hildred! For God's sake!" then as my hand fell, he said: "It is I, Louis, don't you know me?" I stood silent. I could not have spoken for my life. He walked up to me and took the knife from my hand.

"What is all this?" he inquired, in a gentle voice. "Are you ill?"

"No," I replied. But I doubt if he heard me.

"Come, come, old fellow," he cried, "take off that brass crown and toddle into the study. Are you going to a masquerade? What's all this theatrical tinsel anyway?"

I was glad he thought the crown was made of brass and paste, yet I didn't like him any the better for thinking so. I let him take it from my hand, knowing it was best to humour him. He tossed the splendid diadem in the air, and catching it, turned to me smiling.

"It's dear at fifty cents," he said. "What's it for?"

I did not answer, but took the circlet from his hands, and placing it in the safe shut the massive steel door. The alarm ceased its infernal din at once. He watched me curiously, but did not seem to notice the sudden ceasing of the alarm. He did, however, speak of the safe as a biscuit box. Fearing lest he might examine the combination I led the way into my study. Louis threw himself on the sofa and flicked at flies with his eternal riding-whip. He wore his fatigue uniform with the braided jacket and jaunty cap, and I noticed that his riding boots were all splashed with red mud.

"Where have you been?" I inquired.

"Jumping mud creeks in Jersey," he said. "I haven't had time to change yet; I was rather in a hurry to see you. Haven't you got a glass of something? I'm dead tired; been in the saddle twenty-four hours."

I gave him some brandy from my medicinal store, which he drank with a grimace.

"Damned bad stuff," he observed. "I'll give you an address where they sell brandy that is brandy."

"It's good enough for my needs," I said indifferently. "I use it to rub my chest with." He stared and flicked at another fly.

"See here, old fellow," he began, "I've got something to suggest to you. It's four years now that you've shut yourself up here like an owl, never going anywhere, never taking any healthy exercise, never doing a damn thing but poring over those books up there on the mantelpiece."

He glanced along the row of shelves. "Napoleon, Napoleon, Napoleon!" he read. "For heaven's sake, have you nothing but Napoleons there?"

"I wish they were bound in gold," I said. "But wait, yes, there is another book, *The King in Yellow*." I looked him steadily in the eye.

"Have you never read it?" I asked.

"I? No, thank God! I don't want to be driven crazy."

I saw he regretted his speech as soon as he had uttered it. There is only one word which I loathe more than I do lunatic and that word is crazy. But I controlled myself and asked him why he thought *The King in Yellow* dangerous.

"Oh, I don't know," he said, hastily. "I only remember the excitement it created and the denunciations from pulpit and Press. I believe the author shot himself after bringing forth this monstrosity, didn't he?"

"I understand he is still alive," I answered.

"That's probably true," he muttered; "bullets couldn't kill a fiend like that."

"It is a book of great truths," I said.

"Yes," he replied, "of 'truths' which send men frantic and blast their lives. I don't care if the thing is, as they say, the very supreme essence of art. It's a crime to have written it, and I for one shall never open its pages."

"Is that what you have come to tell me?" I asked.

"No," he said, "I came to tell you that I am going to be married."

I believe for a moment my heart ceased to beat, but I kept my eyes on his face.

"Yes," he continued, smiling happily, "married to the sweetest girl on earth."

"Constance Hawberk," I said mechanically.

"How did you know?" he cried, astonished. "I didn't know it myself until that evening last April, when we strolled down to the embankment before dinner."

"When is it to be?" I asked.

"It was to have been next September, but an hour ago a despatch came ordering our regiment to the Presidio, San Francisco. We leave at noon tomorrow. Tomorrow," he repeated. "Just think, Hildred, tomorrow I shall be the happiest fellow that ever drew breath in this jolly world, for Constance will go with me."

I offered him my hand in congratulation, and he seized and shook it like the good-natured fool he was – or pretended to be.

"I am going to get my squadron as a wedding present," he rattled on. "Captain and Mrs Louis Castaigne, eh, Hildred?"

Then he told me where it was to be and who were to be there, and made me promise to come and be best man. I set my teeth and listened to his boyish chatter without showing what I felt, but—

I was getting to the limit of my endurance, and when he jumped up, and, switching his spurs till they jingled, said he must go, I did not detain him.

"There's one thing I want to ask of you," I said quietly.

"Out with it, it's promised," he laughed.

"I want you to meet me for a quarter of an hour's talk tonight."

"Of course, if you wish," he said, somewhat puzzled. "Where?"

"Anywhere, in the park there."

"What time, Hildred?"

"Midnight."

"What in the name of—" he began, but checked himself and laughingly assented. I watched him go down the stairs and hurry away, his sabre banging at every stride. He turned into Bleecker Street, and I knew he was going to see Constance. I gave him ten minutes to disappear and then followed in his footsteps, taking with me the jewelled crown and the silken robe embroidered with the Yellow Sign. When I turned into Bleecker Street, and entered the doorway which bore the sign –

MR WILDE,
REPAIRER OF REPUTATIONS.
Third Bell.

I saw old Hawberk moving about in his shop, and imagined I heard Constance's voice in the parlour; but I avoided them both and hurried up the trembling stairways to Mr Wilde's apartment. I knocked and entered without ceremony. Mr Wilde lay groaning on the floor, his face covered with blood, his clothes torn to shreds. Drops of blood were scattered about over the carpet, which had also been ripped and frayed in the evidently recent struggle.

"It's that cursed cat," he said, ceasing his groans, and turning his colourless eyes to me; "she attacked me while I was asleep. I believe she will kill me yet."

This was too much, so I went into the kitchen, and, seizing a hatchet from the pantry, started to find the infernal beast and settle her then and there. My search was fruitless, and after a while I gave it up and came back to find Mr Wilde squatting on his high chair by the table. He had washed his face and changed his clothes. The great furrows which the cat's claws had ploughed up in his face he had filled with collodion, and a rag hid the wound in his throat. I told him I should kill the cat when I came across her, but he only shook his head and turned to the open ledger before him. He read name after name of the people who had come to him in regard to their reputation, and the sums he had amassed were startling.

"I put on the screws now and then," he explained.

"One day or other some of these people will assassinate you," I insisted.

"Do you think so?" he said, rubbing his mutilated ears.

It was useless to argue with him, so I took down the manuscript entitled *Imperial Dynasty of America*, for the last time I should ever take it down in Mr Wilde's study. I read it through, thrilling and trembling with pleasure. When I had finished Mr Wilde took the manuscript and, turning to the dark passage which leads from his study to his bed-chamber, called out in a loud voice, "Vance." Then for the first time, I noticed a man crouching there in the shadow. How I had overlooked him during my search for the cat, I cannot imagine.

"Vance, come in," cried Mr Wilde.

The figure rose and crept towards us, and I shall never forget the face that he raised to mine, as the light from the window illuminated it.

"Vance, this is Mr Castaigne," said Mr Wilde. Before he had finished speaking, the man threw himself on the ground before the table, crying and grasping, "Oh, God! Oh, my God! Help me! Forgive me! Oh, Mr Castaigne, keep that man away. You cannot, you cannot mean it! You are different – save me! I am broken down – I was in a madhouse and now – when all was coming right – when I had forgotten the King – the King in Yellow and – but I shall go mad again – I shall go mad..."

His voice died into a choking rattle, for Mr Wilde had leapt on him and his right hand encircled the man's throat. When Vance fell in a heap on the floor, Mr Wilde clambered nimbly into his chair again, and rubbing his mangled ears with the stump of his hand, turned to me and asked me for the ledger. I reached it down from the shelf and he opened it. After a moment's searching among the beautifully written pages, he coughed complacently, and pointed to the name Vance.

"Vance," he read aloud, "Osgood Oswald Vance." At the sound of his name, the man on the floor raised his head and turned a convulsed face to Mr Wilde. His eyes were injected with blood, his lips tumefied. "Called April 28th," continued Mr Wilde. "Occupation, cashier in the Seaforth National Bank; has served a term of forgery at Sing Sing, from whence he was transferred to the Asylum for the Criminal Insane. Pardoned by the Governor of New York, and discharged from the Asylum, January 19, 1918. Reputation damaged at Sheepshead Bay. Rumours that he lives beyond his income. Reputation to be repaired at once. Retainer $1,500.

"Note – Has embezzled sums amounting to $30,000 since March 20, 1919, excellent family, and secured present position through uncle's influence. Father, President of Seaforth Bank."

I looked at the man on the floor.

"Get up, Vance," said Mr Wilde in a gentle voice. Vance rose as if hypnotised. "He will do as we suggest now," observed Mr Wilde, and opening the manuscript, he read the entire history of the *Imperial Dynasty of America*. Then in a kind and soothing murmur he ran over the important points with Vance, who stood like one stunned. His eyes were so blank and vacant that I imagined he had become half-witted, and remarked it to Mr Wilde who replied that it was of no consequence anyway. Very patiently we pointed out to Vance what his share in the affair would be, and he seemed to understand after a while. Mr Wilde explained the manuscript, using several volumes on Heraldry, to substantiate the result of his researches. He mentioned the establishment of the Dynasty in Carcosa, the lakes which connected Hastur, Aldebaran and the mystery of the Hyades. He spoke of Cassilda and Camilla, and sounded the cloudy depths of Demhe, and the Lake of Hali. "The scolloped tatters of the King in Yellow must hide Yhtill forever," he muttered, but I do not believe Vance heard him. Then by degrees he led Vance along the ramifications of the Imperial family, to Uoht and Thale, from Naotalba and Phantom of Truth, to Aldones, and then tossing aside his manuscript and notes, he began the wonderful story of the Last King. Fascinated and thrilled I watched him. He threw up his head, his long arms were stretched out in a magnificent gesture of pride and power, and his eyes blazed deep in their sockets like two emeralds. Vance listened stupefied. As for me, when at last Mr Wilde had finished, and pointing to me, cried, "The cousin of the King!" my head swam with excitement.

Controlling myself with a superhuman effort, I explained to Vance why I alone was worthy of the crown and why my cousin must be exiled or die. I made him understand that my cousin must never marry, even after renouncing all his claims, and how that least of all he should marry the daughter of the Marquis of Avonshire and bring England into the question. I showed him a list of thousands of names which Mr Wilde had drawn up; every man whose name was there had received the Yellow Sign, which no living human being dared disregard. The city, the state, the whole land, were ready to rise and tremble before the Pallid Mask.

The time had come, the people should know the son of Hastur, and the whole world bow to the black stars which hang in the sky over Carcosa.

Vance leaned on the table, his head buried in his hands. Mr Wilde drew a rough sketch on the margin of yesterday's *Herald* with a bit of lead pencil. It was a plan of Hawberk's rooms. Then he wrote out the order and affixed the seal, and shaking like a palsied man I signed my first writ of execution with my name: *Hildred-Rex*.

Mr Wilde clambered to the floor and unlocking the cabinet, took a long square box from the first shelf. This he brought to the table and opened. A new knife lay in the tissue paper inside and I picked it up and handed it to Vance, along with the order and the plan of Hawberk's apartment. Then Mr Wilde told Vance he could go; and he went, shambling like an outcast of the slums.

I sat for a while watching the daylight fade behind the square tower of the Judson Memorial Church and finally, gathering up the manuscript and notes, took my hat and started for the door.

Mr Wilde watched me in silence. When I had stepped into the hall I looked back. Mr Wilde's small eyes were still fixed on me. Behind him, the shadows gathered in the fading light. Then I closed the door behind me and went out into the darkening streets.

I had eaten nothing since breakfast, but I was not hungry. A wretched, half-starved creature, who stood looking across the street at the Lethal Chamber, noticed me and came up to tell me a tale of misery. I gave him money, I don't know why, and he went away without thanking me. An hour later another outcast approached and whined his story. I had a blank bit of paper in my pocket, on which was traced the Yellow Sign, and I handed it to him. He looked at it stupidly for a moment, and then with an uncertain glance at me, folded it with what seemed to me exaggerated care and placed it in his bosom.

The electric lights were sparkling among the trees, and the new moon shone in the sky above the Lethal Chamber. It was tiresome waiting in the square; I wandered from the Marble Arch to the artillery stables and back again to the lotus fountain. The flowers and grass exhaled a fragrance which troubled me. The jet of the fountain played in the moonlight, and the musical splash of falling drops reminded me of the tinkle of chained mail in Hawberk's shop. But it was not so fascinating, and the dull sparkle of the moonlight on the water brought no such sensations of exquisite pleasure, as when the sunshine played over the polished steel of a corselet on Hawberk's knee. I watched the bats darting and turning above the water plants in the fountain basin, but their rapid, jerky flight set my nerves on edge, and I went away again to walk aimlessly to and fro among the trees.

The artillery stables were dark, but in the cavalry barracks the officers' windows were brilliantly lighted, and the sallyport was constantly filled with troopers in fatigue, carrying straw and harness and baskets filled with tin dishes.

Twice the mounted sentry at the gates was changed while I wandered up and down the asphalt walk. I looked at my watch. It was nearly time. The lights in the barracks went out one by one, the barred gate was closed, and every minute or two an officer passed in through the side wicket, leaving a rattle of accoutrements and a jingle of spurs on the night air. The square had become very silent. The last homeless loiterer had been driven away by the grey-coated park policeman, the car tracks along Wooster Street were deserted, and the only sound which broke the stillness was the stamping of the sentry's horse and the ring of his sabre against the saddle pommel. In the barracks, the officers' quarters were still lighted, and military servants passed and repassed before the bay windows. Twelve o'clock sounded from the new spire of St Francis Xavier, and at the last stroke of the sad-toned bell a figure passed through the wicket beside the portcullis, returned the salute of the sentry, and crossing the street entered the square and advanced toward the Benedick apartment house.

"Louis," I called.

The man pivoted on his spurred heels and came straight toward me.

"Is that you, Hildred?"

"Yes, you are on time."

I took his offered hand, and we strolled toward the Lethal Chamber.

He rattled on about his wedding and the graces of Constance, and their future prospects, calling my attention to his captain's shoulder straps, and the triple gold arabesque on his sleeve and fatigue cap. I believe I listened as much to the music of his spurs and sabre as I did to his boyish babble, and at last we stood under the elms on the Fourth Street corner of the square opposite the Lethal Chamber. Then he laughed and asked me what I wanted with him. I motioned him to a seat on a bench under the electric light, and sat down beside him. He looked at me curiously, with that same searching glance which I hate and fear so in doctors. I felt the insult of his look, but he did not know it, and I carefully concealed my feelings.

"Well, old chap," he inquired, "what can I do for you?"

I drew from my pocket the manuscript and notes of the *Imperial Dynasty of America*, and looking him in the eye said:

"I will tell you. On your word as a soldier, promise me to read this manuscript from beginning to end, without asking me a question. Promise me to read these notes in the same way, and promise me to listen to what I have to tell later."

"I promise, if you wish it," he said pleasantly. "Give me the paper, Hildred."

He began to read, raising his eyebrows with a puzzled, whimsical air, which made me tremble with suppressed anger. As he advanced, his eyebrows contracted, and his lips seemed to form the word "rubbish".

Then he looked slightly bored, but apparently for my sake read, with an attempt at interest, which presently ceased to be an effort. He started when in the closely written pages he came to his own name, and when he came to mine he lowered the paper, and looked sharply at me for a moment. But he kept his word, and resumed his reading, and I let the half-formed question die on his lips unanswered. When he came to the end and read the signature of Mr Wilde, he folded the paper carefully and returned it to me. I handed him the notes, and he settled back, pushing his fatigue cap up to his forehead, with a boyish gesture, which I remembered so well in school. I watched his face as he read, and when he finished I took the notes with the manuscript, and placed them in my pocket. Then I unfolded a scroll marked with the Yellow Sign. He saw the sign, but he did not seem to recognise it, and I called his attention to it somewhat sharply.

"Well," he said, "I see it. What is it?"

"It is the Yellow Sign," I said angrily.

"Oh, that's it, is it?" said Louis, in that flattering voice, which Doctor Archer used to employ with me, and would probably have employed again, had I not settled his affair for him.

I kept my rage down and answered as steadily as possible, "Listen, you have engaged your word?"

"I am listening, old chap," he replied soothingly.

I began to speak very calmly.

"Dr Archer, having by some means become possessed of the secret of the Imperial Succession, attempted to deprive me of my right, alleging that because of a fall from my horse four years ago, I had become mentally deficient. He presumed to place me under restraint in his own house in hopes of either driving me insane or poisoning me. I have not forgotten it. I visited him last night and the interview was final."

Louis turned quite pale, but did not move. I resumed triumphantly, "There are yet three people to be interviewed in the interests of Mr Wilde and myself. They are my cousin Louis, Mr Hawberk, and his daughter Constance."

Louis sprang to his feet and I arose also, and flung the paper marked with the Yellow Sign to the ground.

"Oh, I don't need that to tell you what I have to say," I cried, with a laugh of triumph. "You must renounce the crown to me, do you hear, to *me*."

Louis looked at me with a startled air, but recovering himself said kindly, "Of course I renounce the – what is it I must renounce?"

"The crown," I said angrily.

"Of course," he answered, "I renounce it. Come, old chap, I'll walk back to your rooms with you."

"Don't try any of your doctor's tricks on me," I cried, trembling with fury. "Don't act as if you think I am insane."

"What nonsense," he replied. "Come, it's getting late, Hildred."

"No," I shouted, "you must listen. You cannot marry, I forbid it. Do you hear? I forbid it. You shall renounce the crown, and in reward I grant you exile, but if you refuse you shall die."

He tried to calm me, but I was roused at last, and drawing my long knife barred his way.

Then I told him how they would find Dr Archer in the cellar with his throat open, and I laughed in his face when I thought of Vance and his knife, and the order signed by me.

"Ah, you are the King," I cried, "but I shall be King. Who are you to keep me from Empire over all the habitable earth! I was born the cousin of a king, but I shall be King!"

Louis stood white and rigid before me. Suddenly a man came running up Fourth Street, entered the gate of the Lethal Temple, traversed the path to the bronze doors at full speed, and plunged into the death chamber with the cry of one demented, and I laughed until I wept tears, for I had recognised Vance, and knew that Hawberk and his daughter were no longer in my way.

"Go," I cried to Louis, "you have ceased to be a menace. You will never marry Constance now, and if you marry anyone else in your exile, I will visit you as I did my doctor last night. Mr Wilde takes charge of you tomorrow." Then I turned and darted into South Fifth Avenue, and with a cry of terror Louis dropped his belt and sabre and followed me like the wind. I heard him close behind me at the corner of Bleecker Street, and I dashed into the doorway under Hawberk's sign. He cried, "Halt, or I fire!" but when he saw that I flew up the stairs leaving Hawberk's shop below, he left me, and I heard him hammering and shouting at their door as though it were possible to arouse the dead.

Mr Wilde's door was open, and I entered crying, "It is done, it is done! Let the nations rise and look upon their King!" But I could not find

Mr Wilde, so I went to the cabinet and took the splendid diadem from its case. Then I drew on the white silk robe, embroidered with the Yellow Sign, and placed the crown upon my head. At last I was King, King by my right in Hastur, King because I knew the mystery of the Hyades, and my mind had sounded the depths of the Lake of Hali. I was King! The first grey pencillings of dawn would raise a tempest which would shake two hemispheres. Then as I stood, my every nerve pitched to the highest tension, faint with the joy and splendour of my thought, without, in the dark passage, a man groaned.

I seized the tallow dip and sprang to the door. The cat passed me like a demon, and the tallow dip went out, but my long knife flew swifter than she, and I heard her screech, and I knew that my knife had found her. For a moment I listened to her tumbling and thumping about in the darkness, and then when her frenzy ceased, I lighted a lamp and raised it over my head. Mr Wilde lay on the floor with his throat torn open. At first I thought he was dead, but as I looked, a green sparkle came into his sunken eyes, his mutilated hand trembled, and then a spasm stretched his mouth from ear to ear. For a moment my terror and despair gave place to hope, but as I bent over him his eyeballs rolled clean around in his head, and he died. Then while I stood, transfixed with rage and despair, seeing my crown, my empire, every hope and every ambition, my very life, lying prostrate there with the dead master, *they* came, seized me from behind, and bound me until my veins stood out like cords, and my voice failed with the paroxysms of my frenzied screams. But I still raged, bleeding and infuriated among them, and more than one policeman felt my sharp teeth. Then when I could no longer move they came nearer; I saw old Hawberk, and behind him my cousin Louis' ghastly face, and farther away, in the corner, a woman, Constance, weeping softly.

"Ah! I see it now!" I shrieked. "You have seized the throne and the empire. Woe! Woe to you who are crowned with the crown of the King in Yellow!"

[EDITOR'S NOTE – Mr Castaigne died yesterday in the Asylum for Criminally Insane.]

THE MASK

ROBERT W. CHAMBERS

Camilla: You, sir, should unmask.
Stranger: Indeed?
Cassilda: Indeed it's time. We all have laid aside disguise but you.
Stranger: I wear no mask.
Camilla: (Terrified, aside to Cassilda.) No mask? No mask!

The King in Yellow, Act I, Scene 2.

I

Although I knew nothing of chemistry, I listened fascinated. He picked up an Easter lily which Geneviève had brought that morning from Notre Dame, and dropped it into the basin. Instantly the liquid lost its crystalline clearness. For a second the lily was enveloped in a milk-white foam, which disappeared, leaving the fluid opalescent. Changing tints of orange and crimson played over the surface, and then what seemed to be a ray of pure sunlight struck through from the bottom where the lily was resting. At the same instant he plunged his hand into the basin and drew out the flower. "There is no danger," he explained, "if you choose the right moment. That golden ray is the signal."

He held the lily towards me, and I took it in my hand. It had turned to stone, to the purest marble.

"You see," he said, "it is without a flaw. What sculptor could reproduce it?"

The marble was white as snow, but in its depths the veins of the lily were tinged with palest azure, and a faint flush lingered deep in its heart.

"Don't ask me the reason of that," he smiled, noticing my wonder. "I have no idea why the veins and heart are tinted, but they always are. Yesterday I tried one of Geneviève's goldfish – there it is."

The fish looked as if sculptured in marble. But if you held it to the light the stone was beautifully veined with a faint blue, and from somewhere within came a rosy light like the tint which slumbers in an opal. I looked into the basin. Once more it seemed filled with clearest crystal.

"If I should touch it now?" I demanded.

"I don't know," he replied, "but you had better not try."

"There is one thing I'm curious about," I said, "and that is where the ray of sunlight came from."

"It looked like a sunbeam true enough," he said. "I don't know, it always comes when I immerse any living thing. Perhaps," he continued, smiling, "perhaps it is the vital spark of the creature escaping to the source from whence it came."

I saw he was mocking, and threatened him with a mahl-stick, but he only laughed and changed the subject.

"Stay to lunch. Geneviève will be here directly."

"I saw her going to early mass," I said, "and she looked as fresh and sweet as that lily – before you destroyed it."

"Do you think I destroyed it?" said Boris gravely.

"Destroyed, preserved, how can we tell?"

We sat in the corner of a studio near his unfinished group of the "Fates". He leaned back on the sofa, twirling a sculptor's chisel and squinting at his work.

"By the way," he said, "I have finished pointing up that old academic Ariadne, and I suppose it will have to go to the Salon. It's all I have ready this year, but after the success the 'Madonna' brought me I feel ashamed to send a thing like that."

The "Madonna", an exquisite marble for which Geneviève had sat, had been the sensation of last year's Salon. I looked at the Ariadne. It was a magnificent piece of technical work, but I agreed with Boris that the world would expect something better of him than that. Still, it was impossible now to think of finishing in time for the Salon that splendid terrible group half shrouded in the marble behind me. The "Fates" would have to wait.

We were proud of Boris Yvain. We claimed him and he claimed us on the strength of his having been born in America, although his father was French and his mother was a Russian. Everyone in the Beaux Arts called him Boris. And yet there were only two of us whom he addressed in the same familiar way – Jack Scott and myself.

Perhaps my being in love with Geneviève had something to do with his affection for me. Not that it had ever been acknowledged between us. But after all was settled, and she had told me with tears in her eyes that it was Boris whom she loved, I went over to his house and congratulated him. The perfect cordiality of that interview did not deceive either of us, I always believed, although to one at least it was a great comfort. I do not think he and Geneviève ever spoke of the matter together, but Boris knew.

Geneviève was lovely. The Madonna-like purity of her face might have been inspired by the Sanctus in Gounod's Mass. But I was always glad when she changed that mood for what we called her "April Manoeuvres". She was often as variable as an April day. In the morning grave, dignified and sweet, at noon laughing, capricious, at evening whatever one least expected. I preferred her so rather than in that Madonna-like tranquillity which stirred the depths of my heart. I was dreaming of Geneviève when he spoke again.

"What do you think of my discovery, Alec?"

"I think it wonderful."

"I shall make no use of it, you know, beyond satisfying my own curiosity so far as may be, and the secret will die with me."

"It would be rather a blow to sculpture, would it not? We painters lose more than we ever gain by photography."

Boris nodded, playing with the edge of the chisel.

"This new vicious discovery would corrupt the world of art. No, I shall never confide the secret to any one," he said slowly.

It would be hard to find any one less informed about such phenomena than myself; but of course I had heard of mineral springs so saturated with silica that the leaves and twigs which fell into them were turned to stone after a time. I dimly comprehended the process, how the silica replaced the vegetable matter, atom by atom, and the result was a duplicate of the object in stone. This, I confess, had never interested me greatly, and as for the ancient fossils thus produced, they disgusted me. Boris, it appeared, feeling curiosity instead of repugnance, had investigated the subject, and had accidentally stumbled on a solution which, attacking the immersed object with a ferocity unheard of, in a second did the work of years. This was all I could make out of the strange story he had just been telling me. He spoke again after a long silence.

"I am almost frightened when I think what I have found. Scientists would go mad over the discovery. It was so simple too; it discovered itself. When I think of that formula, and that new element precipitated in metallic scales..."

"What new element?"

"Oh, I haven't thought of naming it, and I don't believe I ever shall. There are enough precious metals now in the world to cut throats over."

I pricked up my ears. "Have you struck gold, Boris?"

"No, better – but see here, Alec!" he laughed, starting up. "You and I have all we need in this world. Ah! how sinister and covetous you look already!" I laughed too, and told him I was devoured by the desire for gold, and we had better talk of something else; so when Geneviève came in shortly after, we had turned our backs on alchemy.

Geneviève was dressed in silvery grey from head to foot. The light glinted along the soft curves of her fair hair as she turned her cheek to Boris; then she saw me and returned my greeting. She had never before failed to blow me a kiss from the tips of her white fingers, and I promptly complained of the omission. She smiled and held out her hand, which dropped almost before it had touched mine; then she said, looking at Boris –

"You must ask Alec to stay for luncheon." This also was something new. She had always asked me herself until today.

"I did," said Boris shortly.

"And you said yes, I hope?" She turned to me with a charming conventional smile. I might have been an acquaintance of the day before yesterday. I made her a low bow. "*J'avais bien l'honneur, madame*," but refusing to take up our usual bantering tone, she murmured a hospitable commonplace and disappeared. Boris and I looked at one another.

"I had better go home, don't you think?" I asked.

"Hanged if I know," he replied frankly.

While we were discussing the advisability of my departure Geneviève reappeared in the doorway without her bonnet. She was wonderfully beautiful, but her colour was too deep and her lovely eyes were too bright. She came straight up to me and took my arm.

"Luncheon is ready. Was I cross, Alec? I thought I had a headache, but I haven't. Come here, Boris;" and she slipped her other arm through his. "Alec knows that after you there is no one in the world whom I like as well as I like him, so if he sometimes feels snubbed it won't hurt him."

"*À la bonheur*!" I cried. "Who says there are no thunderstorms in April?"

"Are you ready?" chanted Boris. "Aye ready;" and arm-in-arm we raced into the dining room, scandalising the servants. After all we were not so much to blame; Geneviève was eighteen, Boris was twenty-three, and I not quite twenty-one.

II

Some work that I was doing about this time on the decorations for Geneviève's boudoir kept me constantly at the quaint little hotel in the Rue Sainte-Cécile. Boris and I in those days laboured hard but as we pleased, which was fitfully, and we all three, with Jack Scott, idled a great deal together.

One quiet afternoon I had been wandering alone over the house examining curios, prying into odd corners, bringing out sweetmeats and cigars from strange hiding-places, and at last I stopped in the bathing room. Boris, all over clay, stood there washing his hands.

The room was built of rose-coloured marble excepting the floor, which was tessellated in rose and grey. In the centre was a square pool sunken below the surface of the floor; steps led down into it, sculptured pillars supported a frescoed ceiling. A delicious marble Cupid appeared to have just alighted on his pedestal at the upper end of the room. The whole interior was Boris' work and mine. Boris, in his working clothes of white canvas, scraped the traces of clay and red modelling wax from his handsome hands, and coquetted over his shoulder with the Cupid.

"I see you," he insisted, "don't try to look the other way and pretend not to see me. You know who made you, little humbug!"

It was always my rôle to interpret Cupid's sentiments in these conversations, and when my turn came I responded in such a manner, that Boris seized my arm and dragged me toward the pool, declaring he would duck me. Next instant he dropped my arm and turned pale. "Good God!" he said, "I forgot the pool is full of the solution!"

I shivered a little, and dryly advised him to remember better where he had stored the precious liquid.

"In Heaven's name, why do you keep a small lake of that gruesome stuff here of all places?" I asked.

"I want to experiment on something large," he replied.

"On me, for instance?"

"Ah! That came too close for jesting; but I do want to watch the action of that solution on a more highly organized living body; there is that big white rabbit," he said, following me into the studio.

Jack Scott, wearing a paint-stained jacket, came wandering in, appropriated all the Oriental sweetmeats he could lay his hands on, looted the cigarette case, and finally he and Boris disappeared together to visit the Luxembourg Gallery, where a new silver bronze by Rodin and a landscape of Monet's were claiming the exclusive attention of artistic France. I went back to the studio, and resumed my work. It was a Renaissance screen, which Boris wanted me to paint for Geneviève's boudoir. But the small boy who was unwillingly dawdling through a series of poses for it, today refused all bribes to be good. He never rested an instant in the same position, and inside of five minutes I had as many different outlines of the little beggar.

"Are you posing, or are you executing a song and dance, my friend?" I inquired.

"Whichever monsieur pleases," he replied, with an angelic smile.

Of course I dismissed him for the day, and of course I paid him for the full time, that being the way we spoil our models.

After the young imp had gone, I made a few perfunctory daubs at my work, but was so thoroughly out of humour, that it took me the rest of the afternoon to undo the damage I had done, so at last I scraped my palette, stuck my brushes in a bowl of black soap, and strolled into the smoking room. I really believe that, excepting Geneviève's apartments, no room in the house was so free from the perfume of tobacco as this one. It was a queer chaos of odds and ends, hung with threadbare tapestry. A sweet-toned old spinet in good repair stood by the window. There were stands of weapons, some old and dull, others bright and modern, festoons of Indian and Turkish armour over the mantel, two or three good pictures, and a pipe rack. It was here that we used to come for new sensations in smoking. I doubt if any type of pipe ever existed which was not represented in that rack. When we had selected one, we immediately carried it somewhere else and smoked it; for the place was, on the whole, more gloomy and less inviting than any in the house. But this afternoon, the twilight was very soothing, the rugs and skins on the floor looked brown and soft and drowsy; the big couch was piled with cushions – I found my pipe and curled up there for an unaccustomed smoke in the smoking room. I had chosen one with a long flexible stem, and lighting it fell to dreaming. After a while it went out, but I did not stir. I dreamed on and presently fell asleep.

I awoke to the saddest music I had ever heard. The room was quite dark, I had no idea what time it was. A ray of moonlight silvered one edge of the old spinet, and the polished wood seemed to exhale the sounds as perfume floats above a box of sandalwood. Someone rose in the darkness, and came away weeping quietly, and I was fool enough to cry out "Geneviève!"

She dropped at my voice, and I had time to curse myself while I made a light and tried to raise her from the floor. She shrank away with a murmur of pain. She was very quiet, and asked for Boris. I carried her to the divan, and went to look for him, but he was not in the house, and the servants were gone to bed. Perplexed and anxious, I hurried back to Geneviève. She lay where I had left her, looking very white.

"I can't find Boris nor any of the servants," I said.

"I know," she answered faintly, "Boris has gone to Ept with Mr Scott. I did not remember when I sent you for him just now."

"But he can't get back in that case before tomorrow afternoon, and – are you hurt? Did I frighten you into falling? What an awful fool I am, but I was only half awake."

"Boris thought you had gone home before dinner. Do please excuse us for letting you stay here all this time."

"I have had a long nap," I laughed, "so sound that I did not know whether I was still asleep or not when I found myself staring at a figure that was moving toward me, and called out your name. Have you been trying the old spinet? You must have played very softly."

I would tell a thousand more lies worse than that one to see the look of relief that came into her face. She smiled adorably, and said in her natural voice: "Alec, I tripped on that wolf's head, and I think my ankle is sprained. Please call Marie, and then go home."

I did as she bade me, and left her there when the maid came in.

III

At noon next day when I called, I found Boris walking restlessly about his studio.

"Geneviève is asleep just now," he told me, "the sprain is nothing, but why should she have such a high fever? The doctor can't account for it; or else he will not," he muttered.

"Geneviève has a fever?" I asked.

"I should say so, and has actually been a little light-headed at intervals all night. The idea! Gay little Geneviève, without a care in the world – and she keeps saying her heart's broken, and she wants to die!"

My own heart stood still.

Boris leaned against the door of his studio, looking down, his hands in his pockets, his kind, keen eyes clouded, a new line of trouble drawn "over the mouth's good mark, that made the smile". The maid had orders to summon him the instant Geneviève opened her eyes. We waited and waited, and Boris, growing restless, wandered about, fussing with modelling wax and red clay. Suddenly he started for the next room. "Come and see my rose-coloured bath full of death!" he cried.

"Is it death?" I asked, to humour his mood.

"You are not prepared to call it life, I suppose," he answered. As he spoke he plucked a solitary goldfish squirming and twisting out of its globe. "We'll send this one after the other – wherever that is," he said. There was feverish excitement in his voice. A dull weight of fever lay on my limbs and on my brain as I followed him to the fair crystal pool with its pink-tinted sides; and he dropped the creature in. Falling, its scales flashed with a hot orange gleam in its angry twistings and contortions; the moment it struck the liquid it became rigid and sank heavily to the bottom. Then came the milky foam, the splendid hues radiating on the surface and then the shaft of pure serene light broke through from seemingly infinite depths. Boris plunged in his hand and drew out an exquisite marble thing, blue-veined, rose-tinted and glistening with opalescent drops.

"Child's play," he muttered, and looked wearily, longingly at me – as if I could answer such questions! But Jack Scott came in and entered into the "game", as he called it, with ardour. Nothing would do but to try the experiment on the white rabbit then and there. I was willing that Boris should find distraction from his cares, but I hated to see the life go out of a warm, living creature and I declined to be present. Picking up a book at random, I sat down in the studio to read. Alas! I had found *The King in Yellow*. After a few moments, which seemed ages, I was putting it away with a nervous shudder, when Boris and Jack came in bringing their marble rabbit. At the same time the bell rang above, and a cry came from the sick room. Boris was gone like a flash, and the next moment he called, "Jack, run for the doctor; bring him back with you. Alec, come here."

I went and stood at her door. A frightened maid came out in haste and ran away to fetch some remedy. Geneviève, sitting bolt upright, with crimson cheeks and glittering eyes, babbled incessantly and resisted Boris' gentle restraint. He called me to help. At my first touch she sighed and sank back, closing her eyes, and then – then – as we still bent above her, she opened them again, looked straight into Boris' face – poor fever-crazed girl! – and told her secret. At the same instant our three lives turned into new channels; the bond that held us so long together snapped forever and a new bond was forged in its place, for she had spoken my name, and as the fever tortured her, her heart poured out its load of hidden sorrow. Amazed and dumb I bowed my head, while my face burned like a live coal, and the blood surged in my ears, stupefying me with its clamour. Incapable of movement, incapable of speech, I listened to her feverish words in an agony of shame and sorrow. I could not silence her, I could not look at Boris. Then I felt an arm upon my shoulder, and Boris turned a bloodless face to mine.

"It is not your fault, Alec; don't grieve so if she loves you—" but he could not finish; and as the doctor stepped swiftly into the room, saying, "Ah, the fever!" I seized Jack Scott and hurried him to the street, saying, "Boris would rather be alone." We crossed the street to our own apartments, and that night, seeing I was going to be ill too, he went for the doctor again. The last thing I recollect with any distinctness was hearing Jack say, "For Heaven's sake, doctor, what ails him, to wear a face like that?" and I thought of *The King in Yellow* and the Pallid Mask.

I was very ill, for the strain of two years which I had endured since that fatal May morning when Geneviève murmured, "I love you, but I think I love Boris best," told on me at last. I had never imagined that it could become more than I could endure. Outwardly tranquil, I had deceived myself. Although the inward battle raged night after night and I, lying alone in my room, cursed myself for rebellious thoughts unloyal to Boris and unworthy of Geneviève, the morning always brought relief, and I returned to Geneviève and to my dear Boris with a heart washed clean by the tempests of the night.

Never in word or deed or thought while with them had I betrayed my sorrow even to myself.

The mask of self-deception was no longer a mask for me, it was a part of me. Night lifted it, laying bare the stifled truth below; but there was no one to see except myself, and when the day broke the mask fell back again of its own accord. These thoughts passed through my troubled mind as I lay sick, but they were hopelessly entangled with visions of white creatures, heavy as stone, crawling about in Boris' basin – of the wolf's head on the rug, foaming and snapping at Geneviève, who lay smiling beside it. I thought, too, of the King in Yellow wrapped in the fantastic colours of his tattered mantle, and that bitter cry of Cassilda, "Not upon us, oh King, not upon us!" Feverishly I struggled to put it from me, but I saw the lake of Hali, thin and blank, without a ripple or wind to stir it, and I saw the towers of Carcosa behind the moon. Aldebaran, the Hyades, Alar, Hastur, glided through the cloud-rifts which fluttered and flapped as they passed like the scolloped tatters of the King in Yellow. Among all these, one sane thought persisted. It never wavered, no matter what else was going on in my disordered mind, that my chief reason for existing was to meet some requirement of Boris and Geneviève. What this obligation was, its nature, was never clear; sometimes it seemed to be protection, sometimes support, through a great crisis. Whatever it seemed to be for the time, its weight rested only on me, and I was never so ill or so weak that I did not respond with my whole soul. There were always crowds of faces about me, mostly strange, but a few I recognised, Boris among them. Afterwards they told me that this could not have been, but I know that once at least he bent over me. It was only a touch, a faint echo of his voice, then the clouds settled back on my senses, and I lost him, but he *did* stand there and bend over me *once* at least.

At last, one morning I awoke to find the sunlight falling across my bed, and Jack Scott reading beside me. I had not strength enough to speak aloud, neither could I think, much less remember, but I could smile feebly, as Jack's eye met mine, and when he jumped up and asked eagerly if I wanted anything, I could whisper, "Yes – Boris." Jack moved to the head of my bed, and leaned down to arrange my pillow: I did not see his face, but he answered heartily, "You must wait, Alec; you are too weak to see even Boris."

I waited and I grew strong; in a few days I was able to see whom I would, but meanwhile I had thought and remembered. From the moment when all the past grew clear again in my mind, I never doubted what I should do when the time came, and I felt sure that Boris would have resolved upon the same course so far as he was concerned; as for what pertained to me alone, I knew he would see that also as I did. I no longer asked for anyone. I never inquired why no message came from them; why during the week I lay there, waiting and growing stronger, I never heard their name spoken. Preoccupied with my own searchings for the right way, and with my feeble but determined fight against despair, I simply acquiesced in Jack's reticence, taking for granted that he was afraid to speak of them, lest I should turn unruly and insist on seeing them. Meanwhile I said over and over to myself, how would it be when life began again for us all? We would take up our relations exactly as they were before Geneviève fell ill. Boris and I would look into each other's eyes, and there would be neither rancour nor cowardice nor mistrust in that glance. I would be with them again for a little while in the dear intimacy of their home, and then, without pretext or explanation, I would disappear from their lives for ever. Boris would know; Geneviève – the only comfort was that she would never know. It seemed, as I thought it over, that I had found the meaning of that sense of obligation which had persisted all through my delirium, and the only possible answer to it. So, when I was quite ready, I beckoned Jack to me one day, and said –

"Jack, I want Boris at once; and take my dearest greeting to Geneviève..."

When at last he made me understand that they were both dead, I fell into a wild rage that tore all my little convalescent strength to atoms. I raved and cursed myself into a relapse, from which I crawled forth some weeks afterwards a boy of twenty-one who believed that his youth was gone for ever. I seemed to be past the capability of further suffering, and one day when Jack handed me a letter and the keys to Boris' house, I took them without a tremor and asked him to tell me all. It was cruel of me to ask him, but there was no help for it, and he leaned wearily on his thin hands, to reopen the wound which could never entirely heal. He began very quietly:

"Alec, unless you have a clue that I know nothing about, you will not be able to explain any more than I what has happened. I suspect that you would rather not hear these details, but you must learn them, else I would spare you the relation. God knows I wish I could be spared the telling. I shall use few words.

"That day when I left you in the doctor's care and came back to Boris, I found him working on the 'Fates.' Geneviève, he said, was sleeping under the influence of drugs. She had been quite out of her mind, he said. He kept on working, not talking any more, and I watched him. Before long, I saw that the third figure of the group – the one looking straight ahead, out over the world – bore his face; not as you ever saw it, but as it looked then and to the end. This is one thing for which I should like to find an explanation, but I never shall.

"Well, he worked and I watched him in silence, and we went on that way until nearly midnight. Then we heard the door open and shut sharply, and a swift rush in the next room. Boris sprang through the doorway and I followed; but we were too late. She lay at the bottom of the pool, her hands across her breast. Then Boris shot himself through the heart." Jack stopped speaking, drops of sweat stood under his eyes, and his thin cheeks twitched. "I carried Boris to his room. Then I went back and let that hellish fluid out of the pool, and turning on all the water, washed the marble clean of every drop. When at length I dared descend the steps, I found her lying there as white as snow. At last, when I had decided what was best to do, I went into the laboratory, and first emptied the solution in the basin into the waste-pipe; then I poured the contents of every jar and bottle after it. There was wood in the fireplace, so I built a fire, and breaking the locks of Boris' cabinet I burnt every paper, notebook and letter that I found there. With a mallet from the studio I smashed to pieces all the empty bottles, then loading them into a coal-scuttle, I carried them to the cellar and threw them over the red-hot bed of the furnace. Six times I made the journey, and at last not a vestige remained of anything which might again aid in seeking for the formula which Boris had found. Then at last I dared call the doctor. He is a good man, and together we struggled to keep it from the public. Without him I never could have succeeded. At last we got the servants paid and sent away into the country, where old Rosier keeps them quiet with stories of Boris' and Geneviève's travels in distant lands, from whence they will not return for years. We buried Boris in the little cemetery of Sèvres. The doctor is a good creature, and knows when to pity a man who can bear no more. He gave his certificate of heart disease and asked no questions of me."

Then, lifting his head from his hands, he said, "Open the letter, Alec; it is for us both."

I tore it open. It was Boris' will dated a year before. He left everything to Geneviève, and in case of her dying childless, I was to take control of the house in the Rue Sainte-Cécile, and Jack Scott the management at Ept. On our deaths the property reverted to his mother's family in Russia, with the exception of the sculptured marbles executed by himself. These he left to me.

The page blurred under our eyes, and Jack got up and walked to the window. Presently he returned and sat down again. I dreaded to hear what he was going to say, but he spoke with the same simplicity and gentleness.

"Geneviève lies before the Madonna in the marble room. The Madonna bends tenderly above her, and Geneviève smiles back into that calm face that never would have been except for her."

His voice broke, but he grasped my hand, saying, "Courage, Alec." Next morning he left for Ept to fulfil his trust.

IV

The same evening I took the keys and went into the house I had known so well. Everything was in order, but the silence was terrible. Though I went twice to the door of the marble room, I could not force myself to enter. It was beyond my strength. I went into the smoking room and sat down before the spinet. A small lace handkerchief lay on the keys, and I turned away, choking. It was plain I could not stay, so I locked every door, every window, and the three front and back gates, and went away. Next morning Alcide packed my valise, and leaving him in charge of my apartments I took the Orient Express for Constantinople. During the two years that I wandered through the East, at first, in our letters, we never mentioned Geneviève and Boris, but gradually their names crept in. I recollect particularly a passage in one of Jack's letters replying to one of mine:

"What you tell me of seeing Boris bending over you while you lay ill, and feeling his touch on your face, and hearing his voice, of course troubles me. This that you describe must have happened a fortnight after he died. I say to myself that you were dreaming, that it was part of your delirium, but the explanation does not satisfy me, nor would it you."

Towards the end of the second year a letter came from Jack to me in India so unlike anything that I had ever known of him that I decided to return at once to Paris. He wrote: "I am well, and sell all my pictures as artists do who have no need of money. I have not a care of my own, but I am more restless than if I had. I am unable to shake off a strange anxiety about you. It is not apprehension, it is rather a breathless expectancy – of what, God knows! I can only say it is wearing me out. Nights I dream always of you and Boris. I can never recall anything afterwards, but I wake in the morning with my heart beating, and all day the excitement increases until

I fall asleep at night to recall the same experience. I am quite exhausted by it, and have determined to break up this morbid condition. I must see you. Shall I go to Bombay, or will you come to Paris?"

I telegraphed him to expect me by the next steamer.

When we met I thought he had changed very little; I, he insisted, looked in splendid health. It was good to hear his voice again, and as we sat and chatted about what life still held for us, we felt that it was pleasant to be alive in the bright spring weather.

We stayed in Paris together a week, and then I went for a week to Ept with him, but first of all we went to the cemetery at Sèvres, where Boris lay.

"Shall we place the 'Fates' in the little grove above him?" Jack asked, and I answered:

"I think only the 'Madonna' should watch over Boris' grave." But Jack was none the better for my homecoming. The dreams of which he could not retain even the least definite outline continued, and he said that at times the sense of breathless expectancy was suffocating.

"You see I do you harm and not good," I said. "Try a change without me." So he started alone for a ramble among the Channel Islands, and I went back to Paris. I had not yet entered Boris' house, now mine, since my return, but I knew it must be done. It had been kept in order by Jack; there were servants there, so I gave up my own apartment and went there to live. Instead of the agitation I had feared, I found myself able to paint there tranquilly. I visited all the rooms – all but one. I could not bring myself to enter the marble room where Geneviève lay, and yet I felt the longing growing daily to look upon her face, to kneel beside her.

One April afternoon, I lay dreaming in the smoking room, just as I had lain two years before, and mechanically I looked among the tawny Eastern rugs for the wolf-skin. At last I distinguished the pointed ears and flat cruel head, and I thought of my dream where I saw Geneviève lying beside it. The helmets still hung against the threadbare tapestry, among them the old Spanish morion, which I remembered Geneviève had once put on when we were amusing ourselves with the ancient bits of mail. I turned my eyes to the spinet; every yellow key seemed eloquent of her caressing hand, and I rose, drawn by the strength of my life's passion to the sealed door of the marble room. The heavy doors swung inward under my trembling hands. Sunlight poured through the window, tipping with gold the wings of Cupid, and lingered like a nimbus over the brows of the Madonna. Her tender face bent in compassion over a marble form so exquisitely pure that I knelt and signed myself. Geneviève lay in the shadow under the Madonna, and yet, through her white arms, I saw the pale azure vein, and beneath her softly clasped hands the folds of her dress were tinged with rose, as if from some faint warm light within her breast.

Bending, with a breaking heart, I touched the marble drapery with my lips, then crept back into the silent house.

A maid came and brought me a letter, and I sat down in the little conservatory to read it; but as I was about to break the seal, seeing the girl lingering, I asked her what she wanted.

She stammered something about a white rabbit that had been caught in the house, and asked what should be done with it. I told her to let it loose in the walled garden behind the house, and opened my letter. It was from Jack, but so incoherent that I thought he must have lost his reason. It was nothing but a series of prayers to me not to leave the house until he could get back; he could not tell me why, there were the dreams, he said – he could explain nothing, but he was sure that I must not leave the house in the Rue Sainte-Cécile.

As I finished reading I raised my eyes and saw the same maid-servant standing in the doorway holding a glass dish in which two goldfish were swimming: "Put them back into the tank and tell me what you mean by interrupting me," I said.

With a half-suppressed whimper she emptied water and fish into an aquarium at the end of the conservatory, and turning to me asked my permission to leave my service. She said people were playing tricks on her, evidently with a design of getting her into trouble; the marble rabbit had been stolen and a live one had been brought into the house; the two beautiful marble fish were gone, and she had just found those common live things flopping on the dining-room floor. I reassured her and sent her away, saying I would look about myself. I went into the studio; there was nothing there but my canvases and some casts, except the marble of the Easter lily. I saw it on a table across the room. Then I strode angrily over to it. But the flower I lifted from the table was fresh and fragile and filled the air with perfume.

Then suddenly I comprehended, and sprang through the hallway to the marble room. The doors flew open, the sunlight streamed into my face, and through it, in a heavenly glory, the Madonna smiled, as Geneviève lifted her flushed face from her marble couch and opened her sleepy eyes.

IN THE COURT OF THE DRAGON

. . . . .

ROBERT W. CHAMBERS

"Oh, thou who burn'st in heart for those who burn
In Hell, whose fires thyself shall feed in turn;
How long be crying – 'Mercy on them.' God!
Why, who art thou to teach and He to learn?"

In the Church of St Barnabé vespers were over; the clergy left the altar; the little choirboys flocked across the chancel and settled in the stalls. A Suisse in rich uniform marched down the south aisle, sounding his staff at every fourth step on the stone pavement; behind him came that eloquent preacher and good man, Monseigneur C—.

My chair was near the chancel rail, I now turned towards the west end of the church. The other people between the altar and the pulpit turned too. There was a little scraping and rustling while the congregation seated itself again; the preacher mounted the pulpit stairs, and the organ voluntary ceased.

I had always found the organ playing at St Barnabé highly interesting. Learned and scientific it was, too much so for my small knowledge, but expressing a vivid if cold intelligence. Moreover, it possessed the French quality of taste: taste reigned supreme, self-controlled, dignified and reticent.

Today, however, from the first chord I had felt a change for the worse, a sinister change. During vespers it had been chiefly the chancel organ which supported the beautiful choir, but now and again, quite wantonly as it seemed, from the west gallery where the great organ stands, a heavy hand had struck across the church at the serene peace of those clear voices. It was something more than harsh and dissonant, and it betrayed no lack of skill. As it recurred again and again, it set me thinking of what my architect's books say about the custom in early times to consecrate the choir as soon as it was built, and that the nave, being finished sometimes half a century later, often did not get any blessing at all: I wondered idly if that had been the case at St Barnabé, and whether something not usually supposed to be at home in a Christian church might have entered undetected and taken possession of the west gallery. I had read of such things happening, too, but not in works on architecture.

Then I remembered that St Barnabé was not much more than a hundred years old, and smiled at the incongruous association of mediaeval superstitions with that cheerful little piece of eighteenth-century rococo.

But now vespers were over, and there should have followed a few quiet chords, fit to accompany meditation, while we waited for the sermon. Instead of that, the discord at the lower end of the church broke out with the departure of the clergy, as if now nothing could control it.

I belong to those children of an older and simpler generation who do not love to seek for psychological subtleties in art; and I have ever refused to find in music anything more than melody and harmony, but I felt that in the labyrinth of sounds now issuing from that instrument there was something being hunted. Up and down the pedals chased him, while the manuals blared approval. Poor devil! whoever he was, there seemed small hope of escape!

My nervous annoyance changed to anger. Who was doing this? How dare he play like that in the midst of divine service? I glanced at the people near me: not one appeared to be in the least disturbed. The placid brows of the kneeling nuns, still turned towards the altar, lost none of their devout abstraction under the pale shadow of their white head-dress. The fashionable lady beside me was looking expectantly at Monseigneur C—. For all her face betrayed, the organ might have been singing an Ave Maria.

But now, at last, the preacher had made the sign of the cross, and commanded silence. I turned to him gladly. Thus far I had not found the rest I had counted on when I entered St Barnabé that afternoon.

I was worn out by three nights of physical suffering and mental trouble: the last had been the worst, and it was an exhausted body, and a mind benumbed and yet acutely sensitive, which I had brought to my favourite church for healing. For I had been reading *The King in Yellow*.

"The sun ariseth; they gather themselves together and lay them down in their dens." Monseigneur C— delivered his text in a calm voice, glancing quietly over the congregation. My eyes turned, I knew not why, toward the lower end of the church. The organist was coming from behind his pipes, and passing along the gallery on his way out, I saw him disappear by a small door that leads to some stairs which descend directly to the street. He was a slender man, and his face was as white as his coat was black. "Good riddance!" I thought. "With your wicked music! I hope your assistant will play the closing voluntary."

With a feeling of relief – with a deep, calm feeling of relief, I turned back to the mild face in the pulpit and settled myself to listen. Here, at last, was the ease of mind I longed for.

"My children," said the preacher, "one truth the human soul finds hardest of all to learn: that it has nothing to fear. It can never be made to see that nothing can really harm it."

"Curious doctrine!" I thought, "for a Catholic priest. Let us see how he will reconcile that with the Fathers."

"Nothing can really harm the soul," he went on, in his coolest, clearest tones, "because—"

But I never heard the rest; my eye left his face, I knew not for what reason, and sought the lower end of the church. The same man was coming out from behind the organ, and was passing along the gallery *the same way*. But there had not been time for him to return, and if he had returned, I must have seen him. I felt a faint chill, and my heart sank; and yet, his going and coming were no affair of mine. I looked at him: I could not look away from his black figure and his white face. When he was exactly opposite to me, he turned and sent across the church straight into my eyes, a look of hate, intense and deadly: I have never seen any other like it; would to God I might never see it again! Then he disappeared by the same door through which I had watched him depart less than sixty seconds before.

I sat and tried to collect my thoughts. My first sensation was like that of a very young child badly hurt, when it catches its breath before crying out.

To suddenly find myself the object of such hatred was exquisitely painful: and this man was an utter stranger. Why should he hate me so? Me, whom he had never seen before? For the moment all other sensation was merged in this one pang: even fear was subordinate to grief, and for that moment I never doubted; but in the next I began to reason, and a sense of the incongruous came to my aid.

As I have said, St Barnabé is a modern church. It is small and well lighted; one sees all over it almost at a glance. The organ gallery gets a strong white light from a row of long windows in the clerestory, which have not even coloured glass.

The pulpit being in the middle of the church, it followed that, when I was turned toward it, whatever moved at the west end could not fail to attract my eye. When the organist passed it was no wonder that I saw him: I had simply miscalculated the interval between his first and his second passing. He had come in that last time by the other side door. As for the look which had so upset me, there had been no such thing, and I was a nervous fool.

I looked about. This was a likely place to harbour supernatural horrors! That clear-cut, reasonable face of Monseigneur C—, his collected manner and easy, graceful gestures, were they not just a little discouraging to the notion of a gruesome mystery? I glanced above his head, and almost laughed.

That flyaway lady supporting one corner of the pulpit canopy, which looked like a fringed damask tablecloth in a high wind, at the first attempt of a basilisk to pose up there in the organ loft, she would point her gold trumpet at him, and puff him out of existence! I laughed to myself over this conceit, which, at the time, I thought very amusing, and sat and chaffed myself and everything else, from the old harpy outside the railing, who had made me pay ten centimes for my chair, before she would let me in (she was more like a basilisk, I told myself, than was my organist with the anaemic complexion): from that grim old dame, to, yes – alas! – Monseigneur C— himself. For all devoutness had fled. I had never yet done such a thing in my life, but now I felt a desire to mock.

As for the sermon, I could not hear a word of it for the jingle in my ears of:

The skirts of St Paul has reached.
Having preached us those six Lent lectures,
More unctuous than ever he preached,

keeping time to the most fantastic and irreverent thoughts.

It was no use to sit there any longer: I must get out-of-doors and shake myself free from this hateful mood. I knew the rudeness I was committing, but still I rose and left the church.

A spring sun was shining on the Rue St Honoré, as I ran down the church steps. On one corner stood a barrow full of yellow jonquils, pale violets from the Riviera, dark Russian violets, and white Roman hyacinths in a golden cloud of mimosa. The street was full of Sunday pleasure-seekers. I swung my cane and laughed with the rest. Someone overtook and passed me. He never turned, but there was the same deadly malignity in his white profile that there had been in his eyes. I watched him as long as I could see him. His lithe back expressed the same menace; every step that carried him away from me seemed to bear him on some errand connected with my destruction.

I was creeping along, my feet almost refusing to move. There began to dawn in me a sense of responsibility for something long forgotten. It began to seem as if I deserved that which he threatened: it reached a long way back – a long, long way back. It had lain dormant all these years: it was there, though, and presently it would rise and confront me. But I would try to escape; and I stumbled as best I could into the Rue de Rivoli, across the Place de la Concorde and on to the Quai. I looked with sick eyes upon the sun, shining through the white foam of the fountain, pouring over the backs of the dusky bronze river-gods, on the faraway Arc, a structure of amethyst mist, on the countless vistas of grey stems and bare branches faintly green. Then I saw him again coming down one of the chestnut alleys of the Cours la Reine.

I left the river-side, plunged blindly across to the Champs Elysées and turned towards the Arc. The setting sun was sending its rays along the green sward of the Rond-point: in the full glow he sat on a bench, children and young mothers all about him. He was nothing but a Sunday lounger, like the others, like myself. I said the words almost aloud, and all the while I gazed on the malignant hatred of his face. But he was not looking at me. I crept past and dragged my leaden feet up the Avenue. I knew that every time I met him brought him nearer to the accomplishment of his purpose and my fate. And still I tried to save myself.

The last rays of sunset were pouring through the great Arc. I passed under it, and met him face to face. I had left him far down the Champs Elysées, and yet he came in with a stream of people who were returning from the Bois de Boulogne. He came so close that he brushed me. His slender frame felt like iron inside its loose black covering. He showed no signs of haste, nor of fatigue, nor of any human feeling. His whole being expressed one thing: the will, and the power to do me evil.

In anguish I watched him where he went down the broad crowded Avenue, that was all flashing with wheels and the trappings of horses and the helmets of the Garde Republicaine.

He was soon lost to sight; then I turned and fled. Into the Bois, and far out beyond it – I know not where I went, but after a long while as it seemed to me, night had fallen, and I found myself sitting at a table before a small café. I had wandered back into the Bois. It was hours now since I had seen him. Physical fatigue and mental suffering had left me no power to think or feel. I was tired, so tired! I longed to hide away in my own den. I resolved to go home. But that was a long way off.

I live in the Court of the Dragon, a narrow passage that leads from the Rue de Rennes to the Rue du Dragon.

It is an *impasse*; traversable only for foot passengers. Over the entrance on the Rue de Rennes is a balcony, supported by an iron dragon. Within the court, tall old houses rise on either side, and close the ends that give on the two streets. Huge gates, swung back during the day into the walls of the deep archways, close this court, after midnight, and one must enter then by ringing at certain small doors on the side. The sunken pavement collects unsavoury pools. Steep stairways pitch down to doors that open on the court. The ground floors are occupied by shops of second-hand dealers, and by iron workers. All day long the place rings with the clink of hammers and the clang of metal bars.

Unsavoury as it is below, there is cheerfulness, and comfort, and hard, honest work above.

Five flights up are the ateliers of architects and painters, and the hiding-places of middle-aged students like myself who want to live alone. When I first came here to live I was young, and not alone.

I had to walk a while before any conveyance appeared, but at last, when I had almost reached the Arc de Triomphe again, an empty cab came along and I took it.

From the Arc to the Rue de Rennes is a drive of more than half an hour, especially when one is conveyed by a tired cab horse that has been at the mercy of Sunday fête-makers.

There had been time before I passed under the Dragon's wings to meet my enemy over and over again, but I never saw him once, and now refuge was close at hand.

Before the wide gateway a small mob of children were playing. Our concierge and his wife walked among them, with their black poodle, keeping order; some couples were waltzing on the pavement. I returned their greetings and hurried in.

All the inhabitants of the court had trooped out into the street. The place was quite deserted, lighted by a few lanterns hung high up, in which the gas burned dimly.

My apartment was at the top of a house, halfway down the court, reached by a staircase that descended almost into the street, with only a bit of passage-way intervening, I set my foot on the threshold of the open door, the friendly old ruinous stairs rose before me, leading up to rest and shelter. Looking back over my right shoulder, I saw *him,* ten paces off. He must have entered the court with me.

He was coming straight on, neither slowly, nor swiftly, but straight on to me. And now he was looking at me. For the first time since our eyes encountered across the church they met now again, and I knew that the time had come.

Retreating backwards, down the court, I faced him. I meant to escape by the entrance on the Rue du Dragon. His eyes told me that I never should escape.

It seemed ages while we were going, I retreating, he advancing, down the court in perfect silence; but at last I felt the shadow of the archway, and the next step brought me within it. I had meant to turn here and spring through into the street. But the shadow was not that of an archway; it was that of a vault. The great doors on the Rue du Dragon were closed. I felt this by the blackness which surrounded me, and at the same instant I read it in his face. How his face gleamed in the darkness, drawing swiftly nearer! The deep vaults, the huge closed doors, their cold iron clamps were all on his side. The thing which he had threatened had arrived: it gathered and bore down on me from the fathomless shadows; the point from which it would strike was his infernal eyes. Hopeless, I set my back against the barred doors and defied him.

There was a scraping of chairs on the stone floor, and a rustling as the congregation rose. I could hear the Suisse's staff in the south aisle, preceding Monseigneur C— to the sacristy.

The kneeling nuns, roused from their devout abstraction, made their reverence and went away. The fashionable lady, my neighbour, rose also, with graceful reserve. As she departed her glance just flitted over my face in disapproval.

Half dead, or so it seemed to me, yet intensely alive to every trifle, I sat among the leisurely moving crowd, then rose too and went towards the door.

I had slept through the sermon. Had I slept through the sermon? I looked up and saw him passing along the gallery to his place. Only his side I saw; the thin bent arm in its black covering looked like one of those devilish, nameless instruments which lie in the disused torture-chambers of mediaeval castles.

But I had escaped him, though his eyes had said I should not. *Had* I escaped him? That which gave him the power over me came back out of oblivion, where I had hoped to keep it. For I knew him now. Death and the awful abode of lost souls, whither my weakness long ago had sent him – they had changed him for every other eye, but not for mine. I had recognised him almost from the first; I had never doubted what he was come to do; and now I knew while my body sat safe in the cheerful little church, he had been hunting my soul in the Court of the Dragon.

I crept to the door: the organ broke out overhead with a blare. A dazzling light filled the church, blotting the altar from my eyes. The people faded away, the arches, the vaulted roof vanished. I raised my seared eyes to the fathomless glare, and I saw the black stars hanging in the heavens: and the wet winds from the lake of Hali chilled my face.

And now, far away, over leagues of tossing cloud-waves, I saw the moon dripping with spray; and beyond, the towers of Carcosa rose behind the moon.

Death and the awful abode of lost souls, whither my weakness long ago had sent him, had changed him for every other eye but mine. And now I heard *his voice*, rising, swelling, thundering through the flaring light, and as I fell, the radiance increasing, increasing, poured over me in waves of flame. Then I sank into the depths, and I heard the King in Yellow whispering to my soul: "It is a fearful thing to fall into the hands of the living God!"

THE YELLOW SIGN

ROBERT W. CHAMBERS

"Let the red dawn surmise
What we shall do,
When this blue starlight dies
And all is through."

I

There are so many things which are impossible to explain! Why should certain chords in music make me think of the brown and golden tints of autumn foliage? Why should the Mass of Sainte Cécile bend my thoughts wandering among caverns whose walls blaze with ragged masses of virgin silver? What was it in the roar and turmoil of Broadway at six o'clock that flashed before my eyes the picture of a still Breton forest where sunlight filtered through spring foliage and Sylvia bent, half curiously, half tenderly, over a small green lizard, murmuring: "To think that this also is a little ward of God!"

When I first saw the watchman his back was towards me. I looked at him indifferently until he went into the church. I paid no more attention to him than I had to any other man who lounged through Washington Square that morning, and when I shut my window and turned back into my studio I had forgotten him. Late in the afternoon, the day being warm, I raised the window again and leaned out to get a sniff of air. A man was standing in the courtyard of the church, and I noticed him again with as little interest as I had that morning. I looked across the square to where the fountain was playing and then, with my mind filled with vague impressions of trees, asphalt drives, and the moving groups of nursemaids and holiday-makers, I started to walk back to my easel. As I turned, my listless glance included the man below in the churchyard. His face was towards me now, and with a perfectly involuntary movement I bent to see it. At the same moment he raised his head and looked at me. Instantly I thought of a coffin worm. Whatever it was about the man that repelled me I did not know, but the impression of a plump white grave worm was so intense and nauseating that I must have shown it in my expression, for he turned his puffy face away with a movement which made me think of a disturbed grub in a chestnut.

I went back to my easel and motioned the model to resume her pose. After working a while I was satisfied that I was spoiling what I had done as rapidly as possible, and I took up a palette knife and scraped the colour out again. The flesh tones were sallow and unhealthy, and I did not understand how I could have painted such sickly colour into a study which before that had glowed with healthy tones.

I looked at Tessie. She had not changed, and the clear flush of health dyed her neck and cheeks as I frowned.

"Is it something I've done?" she said.

"No – I've made a mess of this arm, and for the life of me I can't see how I came to paint such mud as that into the canvas," I replied.

"Don't I pose well?" she insisted.

"Of course, perfectly."

"Then it's not my fault?"

"No. It's my own."

"I am very sorry," she said.

I told her she could rest while I applied rag and turpentine to the plague spot on my canvas, and she went off to smoke a cigarette and look over the illustrations in the *Courrier Français*.

I did not know whether it was something in the turpentine or a defect in the canvas, but the more I scrubbed the more that gangrene seemed to spread. I worked like a beaver to get it out, and yet the disease appeared to creep from limb to limb of the study before me. Alarmed, I strove to arrest it, but now the colour on the breast changed and the whole figure seemed to absorb the infection as a sponge soaks up water. Vigorously I plied palette knife, turpentine and scraper, thinking all the time what a *séance* I should hold with Duval who had sold me the canvas; but soon I noticed that it was not the canvas which was defective nor yet the colours of Edward. "It must be the turpentine," I thought angrily, "or else my eyes have become so blurred and confused by the afternoon light that I can't see straight." I called Tessie, the model. She came and leaned over my chair blowing rings of smoke into the air.

"What *have* you been doing to it?" she exclaimed

"Nothing," I growled, "it must be this turpentine!"

"What a horrible colour it is now," she continued. "Do you think my flesh resembles green cheese?"

"No, I don't," I said angrily; "did you ever know me to paint like that before?"

"No, indeed!"

"Well, then!"

"It must be the turpentine, or something," she admitted.

She slipped on a Japanese robe and walked to the window. I scraped and rubbed until I was tired, and finally picked up my brushes and hurled them through the canvas with a forcible expression, the tone alone of which reached Tessie's ears.

Nevertheless she promptly began: "That's it! Swear and act silly and ruin your brushes! You have been three weeks on that study, and now look! What's the good of ripping the canvas? What creatures artists are!"

I felt about as much ashamed as I usually did after such an outbreak, and I turned the ruined canvas to the wall. Tessie helped me clean my brushes, and then danced away to dress. From the screen she regaled me with bits of advice concerning whole or partial loss of temper until, thinking, perhaps, I had been tormented sufficiently, she came out to implore me to button her waist where she could not reach it on the shoulder.

"Everything went wrong from the time you came back from the window and talked about that horrid-looking man you saw in the churchyard," she announced.

"Yes, he probably bewitched the picture," I said, yawning. I looked at my watch.

"It's after six, I know," said Tessie, adjusting her hat before the mirror.

"Yes," I replied, "I didn't mean to keep you so long." I leaned out of the window but recoiled with disgust, for the young man with the pasty face stood below in the churchyard. Tessie saw my gesture of disapproval and leaned from the window.

"Is that the man you don't like?" she whispered.

I nodded.

"I can't see his face, but he does look fat and soft. Some way or other," she continued, turning to look at me, "he reminds me of a dream – an awful dream I once had. Or," she mused, looking down at her shapely shoes, "was it a dream after all?"

"How should I know?" I smiled.

Tessie smiled in reply.

"You were in it," she said, "so perhaps you might know something about it."

"Tessie! Tessie!" I protested. "Don't you dare flatter by saying that you dream about me!"

"But I did," she insisted; "shall I tell you about it?"

"Go ahead," I replied, lighting a cigarette.

Tessie leaned back on the open windowsill and began very seriously.

"One night last winter I was lying in bed thinking about nothing at all in particular. I had been posing for you and I was tired out, yet it seemed impossible for me to sleep. I heard the bells in the city ring ten, eleven and midnight. I must have fallen asleep about midnight because I don't remember hearing the bells after that. It seemed to me that I had scarcely closed my eyes when I dreamed that something impelled me to go to the window. I rose and, raising the sash, leaned out. Twenty-fifth Street was deserted as far as I could see. I began to be afraid; everything outside seemed so – so black and uncomfortable. Then the sound of wheels in the distance came to my ears, and it seemed to me as though that was what I must wait for. Very slowly the wheels approached and, finally, I could make out a vehicle moving along the street. It came nearer and nearer, and when it passed beneath my window I saw it was a hearse. Then, as I trembled with fear, the driver turned and looked straight at me. When I awoke I was standing by the open window shivering with cold, but the black-plumed hearse and the driver were gone. I dreamed this dream again in March last, and again awoke beside the open window. Last night the dream came again. You remember how it was raining; when I awoke, standing at the open window, my night-dress was soaked."

"But where did I come into the dream?" I asked.

"You – you were in the coffin; but you were not dead."

"In the coffin?"

"Yes."

"How did you know? Could you see me?"

"No; I only knew you were there."

"Had you been eating Welsh rarebits, or lobster salad?" I began, laughing, but the girl interrupted me with a frightened cry.

"Hello! What's up?" I said, as she shrank into the embrasure by the window.

"The – the man below in the churchyard – he drove the hearse."

"Nonsense," I said, but Tessie's eyes were wide with terror. I went to the window and looked out. The man was gone. "Come, Tessie," I urged, "don't be foolish. You have posed too long; you are nervous."

"Do you think I could forget that face?" she murmured. "Three times I saw the hearse pass below my window, and every time the driver turned and looked up at me. Oh, his face was so white and – and soft? It looked dead – it looked as if it had been dead a long time."

I induced the girl to sit down and swallow a glass of Marsala. Then I sat down beside her, and tried to give her some advice.

"Look here, Tessie," I said, "you go to the country for a week or two, and you'll have no more dreams about hearses. You pose all day, and when night comes your nerves are upset. You can't keep this up. Then again, instead of going to bed when your day's work is done, you run off to picnics at Sulzer's Park, or go to the Eldorado or Coney Island, and when you come down here next morning you are fagged out. There was no real hearse. There was a soft-shell-crab dream."

She smiled faintly.

"What about the man in the churchyard?"

"Oh, he's only an ordinary unhealthy, everyday creature."

"As true as my name is Tessie Reardon, I swear to you, Mr Scott, that the face of the man below in the churchyard is the face of the man who drove the hearse!"

"What of it?" I said. "It's an honest trade."

"Then you think I *did* see the hearse?"

"Oh," I said diplomatically, "if you really did, it might not be unlikely that the man below drove it. There is nothing in that."

Tessie rose, unrolled her scented handkerchief, and taking a bit of gum from a knot in the hem, placed it in her mouth. Then drawing on her gloves she offered me her hand, with a frank, "Goodnight, Mr Scott," and walked out.

II

The next morning, Thomas, the bellboy, brought me the *Herald* and a bit of news. The church next door had been sold. I thanked Heaven for it, not that being a Catholic I had any repugnance for the congregation next door, but because my nerves were shattered by a blatant exhorter, whose every word echoed through the aisle of the church as if it had been my own rooms, and who insisted on his r's with a nasal persistence which revolted my every instinct. Then, too, there was a fiend in human shape, an organist, who reeled off some of the grand old hymns with an interpretation of his own, and I longed for the blood of a creature who could play the doxology with an amendment of minor chords which one hears only in a quartet of very young undergraduates. I believe the minister was a good man, but when he bellowed: "And the Lorrrrd said unto Moses, the Lorrrd is a man of war; the Lorrrd is his name. My wrath shall wax hot and I will kill you with the sworrrrd!" I wondered how many centuries of purgatory it would take to atone for such a sin.

"Who bought the property?" I asked Thomas.

"Nobody that I knows, sir. They do say the gent wot owns this 'ere 'Amilton flats was lookin' at it. 'E might be a bildin' more studios."

I walked to the window. The young man with the unhealthy face stood by the churchyard gate, and at the mere sight of him the same overwhelming repugnance took possession of me.

"By the way, Thomas," I said, "who is that fellow down there?"

Thomas sniffed. "That there worm, sir? 'Es night-watchman of the church, sir. 'E maikes me tired a-sittin' out all night on them steps and lookin' at you insultin' like. I'd a punched 'is 'ed, sir – beg pardon, sir..."

"Go on, Thomas."

"One night a comin' 'ome with 'Arry, the other English boy, I sees 'im a sittin' there on them steps. We 'ad Molly and Jen with us, sir, the two girls on the tray service, an' 'e looks so insultin' at us that I up and sez: 'Wat you looking hat, you fat slug?' – beg pardon, sir, but that's 'ow I sez, sir. Then 'e don't say nothin' and I sez: 'Come out and I'll punch that puddin' 'ed.' Then I hopens the gate an' goes in, but 'e don't say nothin', only looks insultin' like. Then I 'its 'im one, but, ugh! 'Is 'ed was that cold and mushy it ud sicken you to touch 'im."

"What did he do then?" I asked curiously.

"'Im? Nawthin'."

"And you, Thomas?"

The young fellow flushed with embarrassment and smiled uneasily.

"Mr Scott, sir, I ain't no coward, an' I can't make it out at all why I run. I was in the 5th Lawncers, sir, bugler at Tel-el-Kebir, an' was shot by the wells."

"You don't mean to say you ran away?"

"Yes, sir; I run."

"Why?"

"That's just what I want to know, sir. I grabbed Molly an' run, an' the rest was as frightened as I."

"But what were they frightened at?"

Thomas refused to answer for a while, but now my curiosity was aroused about the repulsive young man below and I pressed him. Three years' sojourn in America had not only modified Thomas' cockney dialect but had given him the American's fear of ridicule.

"You won't believe me, Mr Scott, sir?"

"Yes, I will."

"You will lawf at me, sir?"

"Nonsense!"

He hesitated. "Well, sir, it's Gawd's truth that when I 'it 'im 'e grabbed me wrists, sir, and when I twisted 'is soft, mushy fist one of 'is fingers come off in me 'and."

The utter loathing and horror of Thomas' face must have been reflected in my own, for he added:

"It's orful, an' now when I see 'im I just go away. 'E maikes me hill."

When Thomas had gone I went to the window. The man stood beside the church railing with both hands on the gate, but I hastily retreated to my easel again, sickened and horrified, for I saw that the middle finger of his right hand was missing.

At nine o'clock Tessie appeared and vanished behind the screen with a merry "Good morning, Mr Scott." When she had reappeared and taken her pose upon the model-stand I started a new canvas, much to her delight. She remained silent as long as I was on the drawing, but as soon as the scrape of the charcoal ceased and I took up my fixative she began to chatter.

"Oh, I had such a lovely time last night. We went to Tony Pastor's."

"Who are 'we'?" I demanded.

"Oh, Maggie, you know, Mr Whyte's model, and Pinkie McCormick – we call her Pinkie because she's got that beautiful red hair you artists like so much – and Lizzie Burke."

I sent a shower of spray from the fixative over the canvas, and said: "Well, go on."

"We saw Kelly and Baby Barnes the skirt-dancer and – and all the rest. I made a mash."

"Then you have gone back on me, Tessie?"

She laughed and shook her head.

"He's Lizzie Burke's brother, Ed. He's a perfect gen'l'man."

I felt constrained to give her some parental advice concerning mashing, which she took with a bright smile.

"Oh, I can take care of a strange mash," she said, examining her chewing gum, "but Ed is different. Lizzie is my best friend."

Then she related how Ed had come back from the stocking mill in Lowell, Massachusetts, to find her and Lizzie grown up, and what an accomplished young man he was, and how he thought nothing of squandering half-a-dollar for ice-cream and oysters to celebrate his entry as clerk into the woollen department of Macy's. Before she finished I began to paint, and she resumed the pose, smiling and chattering like a sparrow. By noon I had the study fairly well rubbed in and Tessie came to look at it.

"That's better," she said.

I thought so too, and ate my lunch with a satisfied feeling that all was going well. Tessie spread her lunch on a drawing table opposite me and we drank our claret from the same bottle and lit our cigarettes from the same match. I was very much attached to Tessie. I had watched her shoot up into a slender but exquisitely formed woman from a frail, awkward child. She had posed for me during the last three years, and among all my models she was my favourite. It would have troubled me very much indeed had she become "tough" or "fly", as the phrase goes, but I never noticed any deterioration of her manner, and felt at heart that she was all right. She and I never discussed morals at all, and I had no intention of doing so, partly because I had none myself, and partly because I knew she would do what she liked in spite of me. Still I did hope she would steer clear of complications, because I wished her well, and then also I had a selfish desire to retain the best model I had. I knew that mashing, as she termed it, had no significance with girls like Tessie, and that such things in America did not resemble in the least the same things in Paris. Yet, having lived with my eyes open, I also knew that somebody would take Tessie away some day, in one manner or another, and though I professed to myself that marriage was nonsense, I sincerely hoped that, in this case, there would be a priest at the end of the vista. I am a Catholic. When I listen to high mass, when I sign myself, I feel that everything, including myself, is more cheerful, and when I confess, it does me good. A man who lives as much alone as I do, must confess to somebody. Then, again, Sylvia was Catholic, and it was reason enough for me. But I was speaking of Tessie, which is very different. Tessie also was Catholic and much more devout than I, so, taking it all in all, I had little fear for my pretty model until she should fall in love. But *then* I knew that fate alone would decide her future for her, and I prayed inwardly that fate would keep her away from men like me and throw into her path nothing but Ed Burkes and Jimmy McCormicks, bless her sweet face!

Tessie sat blowing rings of smoke up to the ceiling and tinkling the ice in her tumbler.

"Do you know that I also had a dream last night?" I observed.

"Not about that man," she laughed.

"Exactly. A dream similar to yours, only much worse."

It was foolish and thoughtless of me to say this, but you know how little tact the average painter has. "I must have fallen asleep about ten o'clock," I continued, "and after a while I dreamt that I awoke. So plainly did I hear the midnight bells, the wind in the tree branches, and the whistle of steamers from the bay, that even now I can scarcely believe I was not awake. I seemed to be lying in a box which had a glass cover. Dimly I saw the street lamps as I passed, for I must tell you, Tessie, the box in which I reclined appeared to lie in a cushioned wagon which jolted me over a stony pavement. After a while I became impatient and tried to move, but the box was too narrow. My hands were crossed on my breast, so I could not raise them to help myself. I listened and then tried to call. My voice was gone. I could hear the trample of the horses attached to the wagon, and even the breathing of the driver. Then another sound broke upon my ears like the raising of a window sash. I managed to turn my head a little, and found I could look, not only through the glass cover of my box, but also through the glass panes in the side of the covered vehicle. I saw houses, empty and silent, with neither light nor life about any of them excepting one. In that house a window was open on the first floor, and a figure all in white stood looking down into the street. It was you."

Tessie had turned her face away from me and leaned on the table with her elbow.

"I could see your face," I resumed, "and it seemed to me to be very sorrowful. Then we passed on and turned into a narrow black lane. Presently the horses stopped. I waited and waited, closing my eyes with fear and impatience, but all was silent as the grave. After what seemed to me hours, I began to feel uncomfortable. A sense that somebody was close to me made me unclose my eyes. Then I saw the white face of the hearse driver looking at me through the coffin-lid—"

A sob from Tessie interrupted me. She was trembling like a leaf. I saw I had made an ass of myself and attempted to repair the damage.

"Why, Tess," I said, "I only told you this to show you what influence your story might have on another person's dreams. You don't suppose I really lay in a coffin, do you? What are you trembling for? Don't you see that your dream and my unreasonable dislike for that inoffensive watchman of the church simply set my brain working as soon as I fell asleep?"

She laid her head between her arms, and sobbed as if her heart would break. What a precious triple donkey I had made of myself! But I was about to break my record. I went over and put my arm about her.

"Tessie dear, forgive me," I said; "I had no business to frighten you with such nonsense. You are too sensible a girl, too good a Catholic to believe in dreams."

Her hand tightened on mine and her head fell back upon my shoulder, but she still trembled and I petted her and comforted her.

"Come, Tess, open your eyes and smile."

Her eyes opened with a slow languid movement and met mine, but their expression was so queer that I hastened to reassure her again.

"It's all humbug, Tessie; you surely are not afraid that any harm will come to you because of that."

"No," she said, but her scarlet lips quivered.

"Then, what's the matter? Are you afraid?"

"Yes. Not for myself."

"For me, then?" I demanded gaily.

"For you," she murmured in a voice almost inaudible. "I – I care for you."

At first I started to laugh, but when I understood her, a shock passed through me, and I sat like one turned to stone. This was the crowning bit of idiocy I had committed. During the moment which elapsed between her reply and my answer I thought of a thousand responses to that innocent confession. I could pass it by with a laugh, I could misunderstand her and assure her as to my health, I could simply point out that it was impossible she could love me. But my reply was quicker than my thoughts, and I might think and think now when it was too late, for I had kissed her on the mouth.

That evening I took my usual walk in Washington Park, pondering over the occurrences of the day. I was thoroughly committed. There was no back out now, and I stared the future straight in the face. I was not good, not even scrupulous, but I had no idea of deceiving either myself or Tessie. The one passion of my life lay buried in the sunlit forests of Brittany. Was it buried for ever? Hope cried "No!" For three years I had been listening to the voice of Hope, and for three years I had waited for a footstep on my threshold. Had Sylvia forgotten? "No!" cried Hope.

I said that I was no good. That is true, but still I was not exactly a comic opera villain. I had led an easy-going reckless life, taking what invited me of pleasure, deploring and sometimes bitterly regretting consequences. In one thing alone, except my painting, was I serious, and that was something which lay hidden if not lost in the Breton forests.

It was too late for me to regret what had occurred during the day. Whatever it had been, pity, a sudden tenderness for sorrow or the more brutal instinct of gratified vanity, it was all the same now, and unless I wished to bruise an innocent heart, my path lay marked before me. The fire and strength, the depth of passion of a love which I had never even suspected, with all my imagined experience in the world, left me no alternative but to respond or send her away. Whether because I am so cowardly about giving pain to others, or whether it was that I have little of the gloomy Puritan in me, I do not know, but I shrank from disclaiming responsibility for that thoughtless kiss, and in fact had no time to do so before the gates of her heart opened and the flood poured forth. Others who habitually do their duty and find a sullen satisfaction in making themselves and everybody else unhappy, might have withstood it. I did not. I dared not. After the storm had abated I did tell her that she might better have loved Ed Burke and worn a plain gold ring, but she would not hear of it, and I thought perhaps as long as she had decided to love somebody she could not marry, it had better be me. I, at least, could treat her with an intelligent affection, and whenever she became tired of her infatuation she could go none the worse for it. For I was decided on that point although I knew how hard it would be. I remembered the usual termination of Platonic liaisons, and thought how disgusted I had been whenever I heard of one. I knew I was undertaking a great deal for so unscrupulous a man as I was, and I dreamed of the future, but never for one moment did I doubt that she was safe with me. Had it been anybody but Tessie I should not have bothered my head about scruples. For it did not occur to me to sacrifice Tessie as I would have sacrificed a woman of the world. I looked the future squarely in the face and saw the several probable endings to the affair. She would either tire of the whole thing, or become so unhappy that I should have either to marry her or go away. If I married her we would be unhappy. I with a wife unsuited to me, and she with a husband unsuitable for any woman. For my past life could scarcely entitle me to marry. If I went away she might either fall ill, recover, and marry some Eddie Burke, or she might recklessly or deliberately go and do something foolish. On the other hand, if she tired of me, then her whole life would be before her with beautiful vistas of Eddie Burkes and marriage rings and twins and Harlem flats and Heaven knows what. As I strolled along through the trees by the Washington Arch, I decided that she should find a substantial friend in me, anyway, and the future could take care of itself. Then I went into the house and put on my evening dress, for the little faintly perfumed note on my dresser said, "Have a cab at the stage door at eleven," and the note was signed "Edith Carmichel, Metropolitan Theatre".

I took supper that night, or rather we took supper, Miss Carmichel and I, at Solari's, and the dawn was just beginning to gild the cross on the Memorial Church as I entered Washington Square after leaving Edith at the Brunswick. There was not a soul in the park as I passed along the trees and took the walk which leads from the Garibaldi statue to the Hamilton Apartment House, but as I passed the churchyard I saw a figure sitting on the stone steps. In spite of myself a chill crept over me at the sight of the white puffy face, and I hastened to pass. Then he said something which might have been addressed to me or might merely have been a mutter to himself, but a sudden furious anger flamed up within me that such a creature should address me. For an instant I felt like wheeling about and smashing my stick over his head, but I walked on, and entering the Hamilton went to my apartment. For some time I tossed about the bed trying to get the sound of his voice out of my ears, but could not. It filled my head, that muttering sound, like thick oily smoke from a fat-rendering vat or an odour of noisome decay. And as I lay and tossed about, the voice in my ears seemed more distinct, and I began to understand the words he had muttered. They came to me slowly as if I had forgotten them, and at last I could make some sense out of the sounds. It was this:

"Have you found the Yellow Sign?"

"Have you found the Yellow Sign?"

"Have you found the Yellow Sign?"

I was furious. What did he mean by that? Then with a curse upon him and his I rolled over and went to sleep, but when I awoke later I looked pale and haggard, for I had dreamed the dream of the night before, and it troubled me more than I cared to think.

I dressed and went down into my studio. Tessie sat by the window, but as I came in she rose and put both arms around my neck for an innocent kiss. She looked so sweet and dainty that I kissed her again and then sat down before the easel.

"Hello! Where's the study I began yesterday?" I asked.

Tessie looked conscious, but did not answer. I began to hunt among the piles of canvases, saying, "Hurry up, Tess, and get ready; we must take advantage of the morning light."

When at last I gave up the search among the other canvases and turned to look around the room for the missing study I noticed Tessie standing by the screen with her clothes still on.

"What's the matter," I asked, "don't you feel well?"

"Yes."

"Then hurry."

"Do you want me to pose as – as I have always posed?"

Then I understood. Here was a new complication. I had lost, of course, the best nude model I had ever seen. I looked at Tessie. Her face was scarlet. Alas! Alas! We had eaten of the tree of knowledge, and Eden and native innocence were dreams of the past – I mean for her.

I suppose she noticed the disappointment on my face, for she said: "I will pose if you wish. The study is behind the screen here where I put it."

"No," I said, "we will begin something new;" and I went into my wardrobe and picked out a Moorish costume which fairly blazed with tinsel. It was a genuine costume, and Tessie retired to the screen with it enchanted. When she came forth again I was astonished. Her long black hair was bound above her forehead with a circlet of turquoises, and the ends, curled about her glittering girdle. Her feet were encased in the embroidered pointed slippers and the skirt of her costume, curiously wrought with arabesques in silver, fell to her ankles. The deep metallic blue vest embroidered with silver and the short Mauresque jacket spangled and sewn with turquoises became her wonderfully. She came up to me and held up her face smiling. I slipped my hand into my pocket, and drawing out a gold chain with a cross attached, dropped it over her head.

"It's yours, Tessie."

"Mine?" she faltered.

"Yours. Now go and pose," Then with a radiant smile she ran behind the screen and presently reappeared with a little box on which was written my name.

"I had intended to give it to you when I went home tonight," she said, "but I can't wait now."

I opened the box. On the pink cotton inside lay a clasp of black onyx, on which was inlaid a curious symbol or letter in gold. It was neither Arabic nor Chinese, nor, as I found afterwards, did it belong to any human script.

"It's all I had to give you for a keepsake," she said timidly.

I was annoyed, but I told her how much I should prize it, and promised to wear it always. She fastened it on my coat beneath the lapel.

"How foolish, Tess, to go and buy me such a beautiful thing as this," I said.

"I did not buy it," she laughed.

"Where did you get it?"

Then she told me how she had found it one day while coming from the Aquarium in the Battery, how she had advertised it and watched the papers, but at last gave up all hopes of finding the owner.

"That was last winter," she said, "the very day I had the first horrid dream about the hearse."

I remembered my dream of the previous night but said nothing, and presently my charcoal was flying over a new canvas, and Tessie stood motionless on the model stand.

III

The day following was a disastrous one for me. While moving a framed canvas from one easel to another my foot slipped on the polished floor, and I fell heavily on both wrists. They were so badly sprained that it was useless to attempt to hold a brush, and I was obliged to wander about the studio, glaring at unfinished drawings and sketches, until despair seized me and I sat down to smoke and twiddle my thumbs with rage. The rain blew against the windows and rattled on the roof of the church, driving me into a nervous fit with its interminable patter. Tessie sat sewing by the window, and every now and then raised her head and looked at me with such innocent compassion that I began to feel ashamed of my irritation and looked about for something to occupy me. I had read all the papers and all the books in the library, but for the sake of something to do I went to the bookcases and shoved them open with my elbow. I knew every volume by its colour and examined them all, passing slowly around the library and whistling to keep up my spirits. I was turning to go into the dining room when my eye fell upon a book bound in serpent skin, standing in a corner of the top shelf of the last bookcase. I did not remember it, and from the floor could not decipher the pale lettering on the back, so I went to the smoking room and called Tessie. She came in from the studio and climbed up to reach the book.

"What is it?" I asked.

"*The King in Yellow.*"

I was dumfounded. Who had placed it there? How came it in my rooms? I had long ago decided that I should never open that book, and nothing on earth could have persuaded me to buy it. Fearful lest curiosity might tempt me to open it, I had never even looked at it in book stores. If I ever had had any curiosity to read it, the awful tragedy of young Castaigne, whom I knew, prevented me from exploring its wicked pages. I had always refused to listen to any description of it, and indeed, nobody ever ventured to discuss the second part aloud, so I had absolutely no knowledge of what those leaves might reveal. I stared at the poisonous mottled binding as I would at a snake.

"Don't touch it, Tessie," I said; "come down."

Of course my admonition was enough to arouse her curiosity, and before I could prevent it she took the book and, laughing, danced off into the studio with it. I called to her, but she slipped away with a tormenting smile at my helpless hands, and I followed her with some impatience.

"Tessie!" I cried, entering the library, "listen, I am serious. Put that book away. I do not wish you to open it!" The library was empty. I went into both drawing-rooms, then into the bedrooms, laundry, kitchen and finally returned to the library and began a systematic search. She had hidden herself so well that it was half-an-hour later when I discovered her crouching white and silent by the latticed window in the storeroom above. At the first glance I saw she had been punished for her foolishness. *The King in Yellow* lay at her feet, but the book was open at the second part. I looked at Tessie and saw it was too late. She had opened *The King in Yellow*. Then I took her by the hand and led her into the studio. She seemed dazed, and when I told her to lie down on the sofa she obeyed me without a word. After a while she closed her eyes and her breathing became regular and deep, but I could not determine whether or not she slept. For a long while I sat silently beside her, but she neither stirred nor spoke, and at last I rose and, entering the unused storeroom, took the book in my least injured hand. It seemed heavy as lead, but I carried it into the studio again, and sitting down on the rug beside the sofa, opened it and read it through from beginning to end.

When, faint with excess of my emotions, I dropped the volume and leaned wearily back against the sofa, Tessie opened her eyes and looked at me...

We had been speaking for some time in a dull monotonous strain before I realised that we were discussing *The King in Yellow*. Oh the sin of writing such words – words which are clear as crystal, limpid and musical as bubbling springs, words which sparkle and glow like the poisoned diamonds of the Medicis! Oh the wickedness, the hopeless damnation of a soul who could fascinate and paralyse human creatures with such words – words understood by the ignorant and wise alike, words which are more precious than jewels, more soothing than music, more awful than death!

We talked on, unmindful of the gathering shadows, and she was begging me to throw away the clasp of black onyx quaintly inlaid with what we now knew to be the Yellow Sign. I never shall know why I refused, though even at this hour, here in my bedroom as I write this confession, I should be glad to know *what* it was that prevented me from tearing the Yellow Sign from my breast and casting it into the fire. I am sure I wished to do so, and yet Tessie pleaded with me in vain. Night fell and the hours dragged on, but still we murmured to each other of the King and the Pallid Mask, and midnight sounded from the misty spires in the fog-wrapped city. We spoke of Hastur and of Cassilda, while outside the fog rolled against the blank window panes as the cloud waves roll and break on the shores of Hali.

The house was very silent now, and not a sound came up from the misty streets. Tessie lay among the cushions, her face a grey blot in the gloom, but her hands were clasped in mine, and I knew that she knew and read my thoughts as I read hers, for we had understood the mystery of the Hyades and the Phantom of Truth was laid. Then as we answered each other, swiftly, silently, thought on thought, the shadows stirred in the gloom about us, and far in the distant streets we heard a sound. Nearer and nearer it came, the dull crunching of wheels, nearer and yet nearer, and now, outside before the door it ceased, and I dragged myself to the window and saw a black-plumed hearse. The gate below opened and shut, and I crept shaking to my door and bolted it, but I knew no bolts, no locks, could keep that creature out who was coming for the Yellow Sign. And now I heard him moving very softly along the hall. Now he was at the door, and the bolts rotted at his touch. Now he had entered. With eyes starting from my head I peered into the darkness, but when he came into the room I did not see him. It was only when I felt him envelope me in his cold soft grasp that I cried out and struggled with deadly fury, but my hands were useless and he tore the onyx clasp from my coat and struck me full in the face. Then, as I fell, I heard Tessie's soft cry and her spirit fled: and even while falling I longed to follow her, for I knew that the King in Yellow had opened his tattered mantle and there was only God to cry to now.

I could tell more, but I cannot see what help it will be to the world. As for me, I am past human help or hope. As I lie here, writing, careless even whether or not I die before I finish, I can see the doctor gathering up his powders and phials with a vague gesture to the good priest beside me, which I understand.

They will be very curious to know the tragedy – they of the outside world who write books and print millions of newspapers, but I shall write no more, and the father confessor will seal my last words with the seal of sanctity when his holy office is done. They of the outside world may send their creatures into wrecked homes and death-smitten firesides, and their newspapers will batten on blood and tears, but with me their spies must halt before the confessional. They know that Tessie is dead and that I am dying. They know how the people in the house, aroused by an infernal scream, rushed into my room and found one living and two dead, but they do not know what I shall tell them now; they do not know that the doctor said as he pointed to a horrible decomposed heap on the floor – the livid corpse of the watchman from the church: "I have no theory, no explanation. That man must have been dead for months!"

I think I am dying. I wish the priest would—

THE SHADOWS

GEORGE MACDONALD

Old Ralph Rinkelmann made his living by comic sketches, and all but lost it again by tragic poems. So he was just the man to be chosen king of the fairies, for in Fairyland the sovereignty is elective."

"They did not mean to insist on his residence; for they needed his presence only on special occasions. But they must get hold of him somehow, first of all, in order to make him king. Once he was crowned, they could get him as often as they pleased; but before this ceremony, there was a difficulty. For it is only between life and death that the fairies have power over grown-up mortals, and can carry them off to their country. So they had to watch for an opportunity.

"Nor had they to wait long. For old Ralph was taken dreadfully ill; and while hovering between life and death, they carried him off, and crowned him king of Fairyland. But after he was crowned, it was no wonder, considering the state of his health, that he should not be able to sit quite upright on the throne of Fairyland; or that, in consequence, all the gnomes and goblins, and ugly, cruel things that live in the holes and corners of the kingdom, should take advantage of his condition and run quite wild, playing him, king as he was, all sorts of tricks; crowding about his throne, climbing up the steps, and actually scrambling and quarrelling like mice about his ears and eyes, so that he could see and think of nothing else. But I am not going to tell anything more about this part of his adventures just at present. By strong and sustained efforts, he succeeded, after much trouble and suffering, in reducing his rebellious subjects to order. They all vanished to their respective holes and corners; and King Ralph, coming to himself, found himself in his bed, half propped up with pillows.

"But the room was full of dark creatures, which gambolled about in the firelight in such a strange, huge but noiseless fashion, that he thought at first that some of his rebellious goblins had not been subdued with the rest, and had followed him beyond the bounds of Fairyland into his own private house in London. How else could these mad, grotesque hippopotamus calves make their ugly appearance in Ralph Rinkelmann's bedroom? But he soon found out, that although they were like the underground goblins, they were very different as well, and would require quite different treatment. He felt convinced that they were his subjects too, but that he must have overlooked them somehow at his late coronation – if indeed they had been present; for he could not recollect that he had seen anything just like them before. He resolved, therefore, to pay particular attention to their habits, ways and characters; else he saw plainly that they would soon be too much for him; as indeed this intrusion into this chamber, where Mrs Rinkelmann, who must be queen if he was king, sat taking some tea by the fireside, plainly indicated. But she, perceiving that he was looking about him with a more composed expression than his face had worn for many days, started up, and came quickly and quietly to his side, and her face was bright with gladness. Whereupon the fire burned up more cheerily; and the figures became more composed and respectful in their behaviour, retreating towards the wall like well-trained attendants. Then the king of Fairyland had some tea and dry toast, and leaning back on his pillows, nearly fell asleep; but not quite, for he still watched the intruders.

"Presently the queen left the room to give some of the young princes and princesses their tea; and the fire burned lower; and behold, the figures grew as black and as mad in their gambols, as ever! Their favourite games seemed to be Hide and Seek; Touch and Go; Grin and Vanish; and many other such; and all in the king's bedchamber, too; so that it was quite alarming. It was almost as bad as if the house had been haunted by certain creatures, which shall be nameless in a fairystory, because with them Fairyland will not willingly have much to do.

"'But it is a mercy that they have their slippers on!' said the king to himself; for his head ached.

"As he lay back, with his eyes half-shut and half-open, too tired to pay longer attention to their games but, on the whole, considerably more amused than offended with the liberties they took, for they seemed good-natured creatures, and more frolicsome than positively ill-mannered, he became suddenly aware that two of them had stepped forward from the walls, upon which, after the manner of great spiders, most of them preferred sprawling, and now stood in the middle of the floor, at the foot of his majesty's bed, becking and bowing, and ducking in the most grotesquely obsequious manner; while every now and then they turned solemnly round upon one heel, evidently considering that motion the highest token of homage they could show.

"'What do you want?' said the king.

"'That it may please your majesty to be better acquainted with us,' answered they. 'We are your majesty's subjects.'

"'I know you are: I shall be most happy,' answered the king.

"'We are not what your majesty takes us for, though. We are not so foolish as your majesty thinks us.'

"'It is impossible to take you for anything that I know of,' rejoined the king, who wished to make them talk, and said whatever came uppermost; 'for soldiers, sailors or anything: you will not stand still long enough. I suppose you really belong to the fire brigade; at least, you keep putting its light out.'

"'Don't jest, please your majesty.' And as they said the words, for they both spoke at once throughout the interview, they performed a grave somersault, towards the king.

"'Not jest!' retorted he; 'and with you? Why, you do nothing but jest. What are you?'

"'The Shadows, sire. And when we do jest, sire, we always jest in earnest. But perhaps your majesty does not see us distinctly.'

"'I see you perfectly well,' replied the king.

"'Permit me, however,' rejoined one of the Shadows; and as he spoke, he approached the king, and lifting a dark forefinger, drew it lightly but carefully across the ridge of his forehead, from temple to temple. The king felt the soft gliding touch go, like water, into every hollow, and over the top of every height of that mountain-chain of thought. He had involuntarily closed his eyes during the operation, and when he unclosed them again, as soon as the finger was withdrawn, he found that they were opened in more senses than one. The room appeared to have extended itself on all sides, till he could not exactly see where the walls were; and all about it stood the Shadows motionless. They were tall and solemn; rather awful, indeed, in their appearance, notwithstanding many remarkable traits of grotesqueness, looking, in fact, just like the pictures of Puritans drawn by Cavaliers, with long arms and very long, thin legs, from which hung large loose feet, while in their countenances length of chin and nose predominated. The solemnity of their mien, however, overcame all the oddity of their form, so that they were very eerie indeed to look at, dressed as they all were in funereal black. But a single glance was all that the king was allowed to have; for the former operator waved his dusky palm across his vision, and once more the king saw only the fire-lighted walls, and dark shapes flickering about upon them. The two who had spoken for the rest seemed likewise to have vanished. But at last the king discovered them, standing one on each side of the fireplace. They kept close to the chimney wall, and talked to each other across the length of the chimneypiece; thus avoiding the direct rays of the fire, which, though light is necessary to their appearing to human eyes, do not agree with them at all – much less give birth to them, as the king was soon to learn. After a few minutes, they again approached the bed, and spoke thus:

"'It is now getting dark, please your majesty. We mean out of doors in the snow. Your majesty may see, from where he is lying, the cold light of its great winding sheet – a famous carpet for the Shadows to dance upon, your majesty. All our brothers and sisters will be at church now, before going to their night's work.'

"'Do they always go to church before they go to work?'

"'They always go to church first.'

"'Where is it?'

"'In Iceland. Would your majesty like to see it?'

"'How can I go and see it when, as you know very well, I am ill in bed? Besides I should be sure to take cold in a frosty night like this, even if I put on the blankets and took the feather bed for a muff.'

"A sort of quivering passed over their faces, which seemed to be their mode of laughing. The whole shape of the face shook and fluctuated as if it had been some dark fluid; till by slow degrees of gathering calm, it settled into its former rest. Then one of them drew aside the curtains of the bed and, the window curtains not having been yet drawn, the king beheld the white glimmering night outside, struggling with the heaps of darkness that tried to quench it; and the heavens full of stars, flashing and sparkling like live jewels. The other Shadow went towards the fire and vanished in it.

"Scores of Shadows immediately began an insane dance all about the room; disappearing, one after the other, through the uncovered window, and gliding darkly away over the face of the white snow; for the window looked at once on a field of snow. In a few moments, the room was quite cleared of them; but instead of being relieved by their absence, the king felt immediately as if he were in a dead house, and could hardly breathe for the sense of emptiness and desolation that fell upon him. But as he lay looking out on the snow, which stretched blank and wide before him, he spied in the distance a long dark line which drew nearer and nearer, and showed itself at last to be all the Shadows, walking in a double row, and carrying in the midst of them something like a bier. They vanished under the window, but soon reappeared, having somehow climbed up the wall of the house; for they entered in perfect order by the window, as if melting through the transparency of the glass.

"They still carried the bier or litter. It was covered with richest furs and skins of gorgeous wild beasts, whose eyes were replaced by sapphires and emeralds that glittered and gleamed in the fire- and snow-light. The outermost skin sparkled with frost, but the inside ones were soft and warm and dry as the down under a swan's wing. The Shadows approached the bed, and set the litter upon it. Then a number of them brought a huge fur robe, and wrapping it round the king, laid him on the litter in the midst of the furs. Nothing could be more gentle and respectful than the way in which they moved him; and he never thought of refusing to go. Then they put something on his head and, lifting the litter, carried him once round the room, to fall into order. As he passed the mirror, he saw that he was covered with royal ermine, and that his head wore a wonderful crown of gold set with none but red stones: rubies and carbuncles and garnets, and others whose names he could not tell, glowed gloriously around his head, like the salamandrine essence of all the Christmas fires over the world. A sceptre lay beside him – a rod of ebony, surmounted by a cone-shaped diamond which, cut in a hundred facets, flashed all the hues of the rainbow and threw coloured gleams on every side, that looked like shadows more etherial than those that bore him. Then the Shadows rose gently to the window, passed through it, and sinking slowly upon the field of outstretched snow, commenced an orderly gliding rather than march along the frozen surface. They took it by turns to bear the king, as they sped with the swiftness of thought, in a straight line towards the north. The polestar rose above their heads with visible rapidity; for indeed they moved quite as fast as the sad thoughts, though not with all the speed of happy desires. England and Scotland slid past the litter of the king of the Shadows. Over rivers and lakes they skimmed and glided. They climbed the high mountains, and crossed the valleys with an unfelt bound; till they came to John o'Groat's house and the northern sea. The sea was not frozen; for all the stars shone as clear out of the deeps below as they shone out of the deeps above; and as the bearers slid along the blue-grey surface, with never a furrow in their track, so clear was the water beneath, that the king saw neither surface, bottom, nor substance to it, and seemed to be gliding only through the blue sphere of heaven, with the stars above him and the stars below him, and between the stars and him nothing but an emptiness, where, for the first time in his life, his soul felt that it had room enough.

"At length they reached the rocky shores of Iceland, where they landed, still pursuing their journey. All this time the king felt no cold; for the red stones in his crown kept him warm, and the emerald and sapphire eyes of the wild beasts kept the frosts from settling upon his litter.

"Oftentimes upon their way, they had to pass through forests, caverns and rock-shadowed paths, where it was so dark that at first the king feared he would lose his Shadows altogether. But as soon as they entered such places, the diamond in his sceptre began to shine and glow and flash, sending out streams of light of all the colours that a painter's soul could dream of; in which light the Shadows grew livelier and stronger than ever, speeding through the dark ways with an all but blinding swiftness. In the light of the diamond, too, some of their forms became more simple and human, while others seemed only to break out into a yet more untamable absurdity. Once, as they passed through a cave, the king actually saw some of their eyes – strange shadow-eyes: he had never seen any of their eyes before. But at the same moment when he saw their eyes, he knew their faces too, for they turned them full upon him for an instant; and the other Shadows, catching sight of these, shrank and shivered, and nearly vanished. Lovely faces they were; but the king was very thoughtful after he saw them, and continued rather troubled all the rest of the journey. He could not account for those faces being there, and the faces of Shadows too, with living eyes."

"At last they climbed up the bed of a little stream, and then passing through a narrow rocky defile, came out suddenly upon the side of a mountain, overlooking a blue frozen lake in the very heart of mighty hills. Overhead the aurora borealis was shivering and flashing like a battle of ten thousand spears. Underneath, its beams passed faintly over the blue ice and the sides of the snow-clad mountains, whose tops shot up like huge icicles all about, with here and there a star sparkling on the very tip of one. But as the northern lights in the sky above, so wavered and quivered and shot hither and thither the Shadows on the surface of the lake below; now gathering in groups, and now shivering asunder; now covering the whole surface of the lake, and anon condensed into one dark knot in the centre. Every here and there on the white mountains, might be seen two or three shooting away towards the tops, and vanishing beyond them. Their number was gradually, though hardly visibly, diminishing.

"'Please your majesty,' said the Shadows, 'this is our church – the Church of the Shadows.'

"And so saying, the king's bodyguard set down the litter upon a rock, and mingled with the multitudes below. They soon returned, however, and bore the king down into the middle of the lake. All the Shadows came crowding round him, respectfully but fearlessly; and sure never such a grotesque assembly revealed itself before to mortal eyes. The king had seen all kind of gnomes, goblins and kobolds at his coronation; but they were quite rectilinear figures, compared with the insane lawlessness of form in which the Shadows rejoiced; and the wildest gambols of the former, were orderly dances of ceremony, beside the apparently aimless and wilful contortions of figure, and metamorphoses of shape, in which the latter indulged. They retained, however, all the time, to the surprise of the king, an identity, each of his own type, inexplicably perceptible through every change. Indeed this preservation of the primary idea of each form, was quite as wonderful as the bewildering and ridiculous alterations to which the form itself was every moment subjected.

"'What are you?' said the king, leaning on his elbow, and looking around him.

"'The Shadows, your majesty,' answered several voices at once.

"'What Shadows?'

"'The human Shadows. The Shadows of men, and women, and their children.'

"'Are you not the shadows of chairs and tables, and poker and tongs, just as well?'

"At this question a strange jarring commotion went through the assembly with a shock. Several of the figures shot up as high as the aurora, but instantly settled down again to human size, as if overmastering their feelings, out of respect to him who had roused them. One who had bounded to the highest visible icy peak, and as suddenly returned, now elbowed his way through the rest, and made himself spokesman for them during the remaining part of the dialogue.

"'Excuse our agitation, your majesty,' said he. 'I see your majesty has not yet thought proper to make himself acquainted with our nature and habits.'

"'I wish to do so now,' replied the king.

"'We are the Shadows,' repeated the Shadow, solemnly.

"'Well?' said the king.

"'We do not often appear to men.'

"'Ha!' said the king.

"'We do not belong to the sunshine at all. We go through it unseen, and only by a passing chill do men recognise an unknown presence.'

"'Ha!' said the king, again.

"'It is only in the twilight of the fire, or when one man or woman is alone with a single candle, or when any number of people are all feeling the same thing at once, making them one, that we show ourselves, and the truth of things.

"'Can that be true that loves the night?' said the king.

"'The darkness is the nurse of light,' answered the Shadow.

"'Can that be true which mocks at forms?' said the king.

"'Truth rides abroad in shapeless storms,' answered the Shadow.

"'Ha! Ha!' thought Ralph Rinkelmann. 'It rhymes. The shadow caps my questions with his answers – very strange!' And he grew thoughtful again.

"The Shadow was the first to resume.

"'Please your majesty, may we present our petition?'

"'By all means,' replied the king. 'I am not well enough to receive it in proper state.'

"'Never mind, your majesty. We do not care for much ceremony; and indeed none of us are quite well at present. The subject of our petition weighs upon us.'

"'Go on,' said the king.

"'Sire,' began the Shadow, 'our very existence is in danger. The various sorts of artificial light, both in houses and in men, women and children, threaten to end our being. The use and the disposition of gaslights, especially high in the centres, blind the eyes by which alone we can be perceived. We are all but banished from towns. We are driven into villages and lonely houses, chiefly old farmhouses, out of which even our friends the fairies are fast disappearing. We therefore petition our king, by the power of his art, to restore us to our rights in the house itself, and in the hearts of its dwellers.'

"'But,' said the king, 'you frighten the children.'

"'Very seldom, your majesty; and then only for their good. We seldom seek to frighten anybody. We only want to make people silent and thoughtful; to awe them a little, your majesty.'

"'You are much more likely to make them laugh,' said the king.

"'Are we?' said the Shadow.

"And approaching the king one step, he stood quite still for a moment. The diamond of the king's sceptre shot out a vivid flame of violet light, and the king stared at the Shadow in silence, and his lip quivered."

"'It is only,' resumed the Shadow, 'when our thoughts are not fixed upon any particular object, that our bodies are subject to all the vagaries of elemental influences. Generally amongst worldly men and frivolous women, we only attach ourselves to some article of furniture or of dress; and they never doubt that we are mere foolish and vague results of the dashing of the waves of the light against the solid forms of which their houses are full. We do not care to tell them the truth, for they would never see it. But let the worldly man – or the frivolous woman – and then—'

"At each of the pauses indicated, the mass of Shadows throbbed and heaved with emotion, but soon settled again into comparative stillness. Once more the Shadow addressed himself to speak. But suddenly they all looked up, and the king, following their gaze, saw that the aurora had begun to pale.

"'The moon is rising,' said the Shadow. 'As soon as she looks over the mountains into the valley, we must be gone, for we have plenty to do by the moon: we are powerful in her light. But if your majesty will come here tomorrow night, your majesty may learn a great deal more about us, and judge for himself whether it be fit to accord our petition; for then will be our grand annual assembly, in which we report to our chiefs the deeds we have attempted, and the good or bad success we have had.'

"'If you send for me,' replied the king, 'I will come.'

"Ere the Shadow could reply, the tip of the moon's crescent horn peeped up from behind an icy pinnacle, and one slender ray fell on the lake. It shone upon no Shadows. Ere the eye of the king could again seek the earth after beholding the first brightness of the moon's resurrection, they had vanished; and the surface of the lake glittered cold and blue in the pale moonlight.

"There the king lay, alone in the midst of the frozen lake, with the moon staring at him. But at length he heard from somewhere a voice that he knew.

"'Will you take another cup of tea, dear?' said Mrs Rinkelmann; and Ralph, coming slowly to himself, found that he was lying in his own bed.

"'Yes, I will,' he answered; 'and rather a large piece of toast, if you please; for I have been on a long journey since I saw you last.'

"'He has not come to himself quite,' said Mrs Rinkelmann, between her and herself.

"'You would be rather surprised,' continued Ralph, 'if I told you where I had been, and all about it.'

"'I daresay I should,' responded his wife.

"'Then I will tell you,' rejoined Ralph.

"But at that moment, a great Shadow bounced out of the fire with a single huge leap, and covered the whole room. Then it settled in one corner, and Ralph saw it shaking its fist at him from the end of a preposterous arm. So he took the hint, and held his peace. And it was as well for him. For I happen to know something about the Shadows too; and I know that if he had told his wife all about it just then, they would not have sent for him the following evening.

"But as the king, after taking his tea and toast, lay and looked about him, the dancing shadows in his room seemed to him odder and more inexplicable than ever. The whole chamber was full of mystery. So it generally was, but now it was more mysterious than ever. After all that he had seen in the Shadow-church, his own room and its shadows were yet more wonderful and unintelligible than those.

"This made it the more likely that he had seen a true vision; for, instead of making common things look common place, as a false vision would have done, it made common things disclose the wonderful that was in them.

"'The same applied to all true art,' thought Ralph Rinkelmann.

"The next afternoon, as the twilight was growing dusky, the king lay wondering whether or not the Shadows would fetch him again. He wanted very much to go, for he had enjoyed the journey exceedingly, and he longed, besides, to hear some of the Shadows tell their stories. But the darkness grew deeper and deeper, and the Shadows did not come. The cause was, that Mrs Rinkelmann sat by the fire in the gloaming; and they could not carry off the king while she was there. Some of them tried to frighten her away, by playing the oddest pranks on the walls, and floor, and ceiling; but altogether without effect: the queen only smiled, for she had a good conscience. Suddenly, however, a dreadful scream was heard from the nursery, and Mrs Rinkelmann rushed upstairs to see what was the matter. No sooner had she gone, than the two warders of the chimney corners stepped out into the middle of the room, and said, in a low voice:

"'Is your majesty ready?'

"'Have you no hearts?' said the king. 'Or are they as black as your faces? Did you not hear the child scream? I must know what is the matter with her before I go.'

"'Your majesty may keep his mind easy on that point,' replied the warders. 'We had tried everything we could think of, to get rid of her majesty the queen, but without effect. So a young madcap Shadow, half against the will of the older ones of us, slipped up stairs into the nursery; and has, no doubt, succeeded in appalling the baby, for he is very lithe and long-legged... Now, your majesty.'

"'I will have no such tricks played in my nursery,' said the king, rather angrily. 'You might put the child beside itself.'

"'Then there would be twins, your majesty. And we rather like twins.'

"'None of your miserable jesting! You might put the child out of her wits.'

"'Impossible, sire; for she has not got into them yet.'

"'Go away,' said the king.

"'Forgive us, your majesty. Really, it will do the child good; for that Shadow will, all her life, be to her a symbol of what is ugly and bad. When she feels in danger of hating or envying anyone, that Shadow will come back to her mind, and make her shudder.'

"'Very well,' said the king. 'I like that. Let us go.'

"The Shadows went through the same ceremonies and preparations as before; during which the young Shadow before mentioned contrived to make such grimaces as kept the baby in terror, and the queen in the nursery, till all was ready. Then with a bound that doubled him up against the ceiling, and a kick of his legs six feet out behind him, he vanished through the nursery door, and reached the king's bedchamber just in time to take his place with the last who were melting through the window in the rear of the litter, and settling down upon the snow beneath. Away they went, a gliding blackness over the white carpet, as before. And it was Christmas Eve.

"When they came in sight of the mountain lake, the king saw that it was crowded over its whole surface with a changeful intermingling of Shadows. They were all talking and listening alternately, in pairs, trios and groups of every size. Here and there, large companies were absorbed in attention to one elevated above the rest, not in a pulpit or on a platform, but on the stilts of his own legs, elongated for the nonce. The aurora, right overhead, lighted up the lake and the sides of the mountains, by sending down from the zenith, nearly to the surface of the lake, great folded vapours, luminous with all the colours of a faint rainbow.

"Many, however, as the words were that passed on all sides, not a whisper of a sound reached the ears of the king: their shadow speech could not enter his corporeal organs. One of his guides, however, seeing that the king wanted to hear and could not, went through a strange manipulation of his head and ears; after which he could hear perfectly, though still only the voice to which, for the time, he directed his attention. This, however, was a great advantage, and one which the king longed to carry back with him to the world of men.

"The king now discovered that this was not merely the church of the Shadows, but their news exchange at the same time. For, as the Shadows have no writing or printing, the only way in which they can make each other acquainted with their doings and thinkings, is to meet and talk at this word mart and parliament of shades. And as, in the world, people read their favourite authors, and listen to their favourite speakers, so here the Shadows seek their favourite Shadows, listen to their adventures, and hear generally what they have to say.

"Feeling quite strong, the king rose and walked about amongst them, wrapped in his ermine robe, with his red crown on his head and his diamond sceptre in his hand. Every group of Shadows to which he drew near, ceased talking as soon as they saw him approach; but at a nod they went on again directly, conversing and relating and commenting, as if no one was there of other kind or of higher rank than themselves. So the king heard a good many stories, at some of which he laughed and at some of which he cried. But if the stories that the Shadows told were printed, they would make a book that no publisher could produce fast enough to satisfy the buyers. I will record some of the things that the king heard, for he told them to me soon after. In fact, I was for some time his private secretary, and that is how I come to know all about his adventures.

"'I made him confess before a week was over,' said a gloomy old Shadow.

"'But what was the good of that?' said a pert young one; 'that could not undo what was done.'

"'Yes, it might.'

"'What! bring the dead to life?'

"'No; but comfort the murderer. I could not bear to see the pitiable misery he was in. He was far happier with the rope round his neck, than he was with the purse in his pocket. I saved him from killing himself too.'

"'How did you make him confess?'

"'Only by wallowing on the wall a little.'

"'How could that make him tell?'

"'He knows.'

"He was silent; and the king turned to another.

"'I made a fashionable mother repent.'

"'How?' broke from several voices, in whose sound was mingled a touch of incredulity.

"'Only by making a little coffin on the wall,' was the reply.

"'Did the fashionable mother then confess?'

"'She had nothing more to confess than everybody knew.'

"'What did everybody know then?'

"'That she might have been kissing a living child, when she followed a dead one to the grave – the next will fare better.'

"'I put a stop to a wedding,' said another.

"'Horrid shade!' remarked a poetic imp.

"'How?' said others. 'Tell us how.'

"'Only by throwing a darkness, as if from the branch of a sconce, over the forehead of a fair girl – they are not married yet, and I do not think they will be. But I loved the youth who loved her. How he started! It was a revelation to him.'

"'But did it not deceive him?'

"'Quite the contrary.'

"'But it was only a shadow from the outside, not a shadow coming through from the soul of the girl.'

"'Yes. You may say so. But it was all that was wanted to let the meaning of her forehead come out – yes, of her whole face, which had now and then, in the pauses of his passion, perplexed the youth. All of it, curled nostrils, pouting lips, projecting chin, instantly fell into harmony with that darkness between her eyebrows. The youth understood it in a moment, and went home miserable. And they're not married yet.'

"'I caught a toper alone, over his magnum of port,' said a very dark Shadow; 'and didn't I give it him! I made delirium tremens first; and then I settled into a funeral, passing slowly along the whole of the dining room wall. I gave him plenty of plumes and mourning coaches. And then I gave him a funeral service, but I could not manage to make the surplice white, which was all the better for such a sinner. The wretch stared till his face passed from purple to grey, and actually left his fifth glass only, unfinished, and took refuge with his wife and children in the drawing room, much to their surprise. I believe he actually drank a cup of tea; and although I have often looked in again, I have never seen him drinking alone at least.'

"'But does he drink less? Have you done him any good?'

"'I hope so; but I am sorry to say I can't feel sure about it.'

"'Humph! Humph! Humph!' grunted various shadow throats.

"'I had such fun once!' cried another. 'I made such game of a young clergyman!'

"'You have no right to make game of any one.'

"'Oh yes, I have – when it is for his good. He used to study his sermons – where do you think?'

"'In his study, of course.'

"'Yes and no. Guess again.'

"'Out amongst the faces in the streets.'

"'Guess again.'

"'In still green places in the country?'

"'Guess again.'

"'In old books?'

"'Guess again.'

"'No, no. Tell us.'

"'In the looking glass. Ha! Ha! Ha!'

"'He was fair game; fair shadow-game.'

"'I thought so. And I made such fun of him one night on the wall! He had sense enough to see that it was himself, and very like an ape. So he got ashamed, turned the mirror with its face to the wall, and thought a little more about his people, and a little less about himself. I was very glad; for, please your majesty,' – and here the speaker turned towards the king – 'we don't like the creatures that live in the mirrors. You call them ghosts, don't you?'

"Before the king could reply, another had commenced. But the mention of the clergyman made the king wish to hear one of the shadow-sermons. So he turned him towards a long Shadow, who was preaching to a very quiet and listening crowd. He was just concluding his sermon.

"Therefore, dear Shadows, it is the more needful that we love one another as much as we can, because that is not much. We have no excuse for not loving as mortals have, for we do not die like them. I suppose it is the thought of that death that makes them hate so much. Then again, we go to sleep all day, most of us, and not in the night, as men do. And you know that we forget everything that happened the night before; therefore, we ought to love well, for the love is short. Ah! Dear Shadow, whom I love now with all my shadowy soul, I shall not love thee tomorrow eve, I shall not know thee; I shall pass thee in the crowd and never dream that the Shadow whom I now love is near me then. Happy Shades! for we only remember our tales until we have told them here, and then they vanish in the shadow-churchyard, where we bury only our dead selves. Ah! brethren, who would be a man and remember? Who would be a man and weep? We ought indeed to love one another, for we alone inherit oblivion; we alone are renewed with eternal birth; we alone have no gathered weight of years. I will tell you the awful fate of one Shadow who rebelled against his nature, and sought to remember the past. He said, 'I will remember this eve.' He fought with the genial influences of kindly sleep when the sun rose on the awful dead day of light; and although he could not keep quite awake, he dreamed of the foregone eve, and he never forgot his dream. Then he tried again the next night, and the next and the next; and he tempted another Shadow to try it with him. At last their awful fate overtook them; and, instead of being Shadows any longer, they began to have shadows sticking to them; and they thickened and thickened till they vanished out of our world; and they are now condemned to walk the earth, a man and a woman, with death behind them and memories within them. Ah, brother Shades! Let us love one another, for we shall soon forget. We are not men, but Shadows.'

"The king turned away, and pitied the poor Shadows far more than they pitied men.

"'Oh! How we played with a musician one night!' exclaimed one of another group, to which the king had directed a passing thought. He stopped to listen. – 'Up and down we went, like the hammers and dampers on his piano. But he took his revenge on us. For after he had watched us for half an hour in the twilight, he rose and went to his instrument, and played a shadow-dance that fixed us all in sound forever. Each could tell the very notes meant for him; and as long as he played, we could not stop, but went on dancing and dancing after the music, just as the magician – I mean the musician – pleased. And he punished us well; for he nearly danced us all off our legs and out of shape, into tired heaps of collapsed and palpitating darkness. We won't go near him for some time again, if we can only remember it. He had been very miserable all day, he was so poor; and we could not think of any way of comforting him except making him laugh. We did not succeed, with our best efforts; but it turned out better than we had expected after all; for his shadow-dance got him into notice, and he is quite popular now, and making money fast – if he does not take care, we shall have other work to do with him by and by, poor fellow!'

"'I and some others did the same for a poor playwright once. He had a Christmas piece to write, and not being an original genius, he could think of nothing that had not been done already twenty times. I saw the trouble he was in, and collecting a few stray Shadows, we acted, in dumb show of course, the funniest bit of nonsense we could think of; and it was quite successful. The poor fellow watched every motion, roaring with laughter at us, and delight at the ideas we put into his head. He turned it all into words and scenes and actions; and the piece came off "with a success unprecedented in the annals of the stage" – at least so said the reporter of the *Punny Palpitator*.'

"'But how long we have to look for a chance of doing anything worth doing!' said a long, thin, especially lugubrious Shadow. 'I have only done one deed worth telling, ever since we met last. But I am proud of that.'

"'What was it? What was it?' rose from twenty voices.

"'I crept into a dining room, one twilight, soon after last Christmas Day. I had been drawn thither by the glow of a bright fire through red window-curtains. At first I thought there was no one there, and was on the point of leaving the room, and going out again into the snowy street, when I suddenly caught the sparkle of eyes, and saw that they belonged to a little boy who lay very still on a sofa. I crept into a dark corner by the sideboard, and watched him. He seemed very sad, and did nothing but stare into the fire. At last he sighed out: 'I wish mamma would come home.' 'Poor boy!' thought I. 'There is no help for that but mamma.' Yet I would try to while away the time for him. So out of my corner I stretched a long shadow arm, reaching all across the ceiling, and pretended to make a grab at him. He was rather frightened at first; but he was a brave boy, and soon saw that it was all a joke. So when I did it again, he made a clutch at me; and then we had such fun! For though he often sighed, and wished mamma would come home, he always began again with me; and on we went with the wildest game. At last his mother's knock came to the door and, starting up in delight, he rushed into the hall to meet her, and forgot all about poor black me. But I did not mind that in the least; for when I glided out after him into the hall, I was well repaid for my trouble, by hearing his mother say to him: 'Why, Charlie, my dear, you look ever so much better since I left you!' At that moment I slipped through the closing door, and as I ran across the snow, I heard the mother say: 'What shadow can that be, passing so quickly?' And Charlie answered with a merry laugh: 'Oh! mamma, I suppose it must be the funny shadow that has been playing such games with me, all the time you were out.' As soon as the door was shut, I crept along the wall, and looked in at the dining-room window. And I heard his mamma say, as she led him into the room: 'What an imagination the boy has!' Ha! ha! ha! Then she looked at him very earnestly for a minute, and the tears came in her eyes; and as she stooped down over him, I heard the sounds of a mingling kiss and sob.'"

"'I always look for nurseries full of children,' said another; 'and this winter I have been very fortunate. I am sure we belong especially to children. One evening, looking about in a great city, I saw through the window into a large nursery, where the odious gas had not yet been lighted. Round the fire sat a company of the most delightful children I had ever seen. They were waiting patiently for their tea. It was too good an opportunity to be lost. I hurried away, and gathering together twenty of the best Shadows I could find, returned in a few moments to the nursery. There we began on the walls one of our best dances. To be sure it was mostly extemporized; but I managed to keep it in harmony by singing this song, which I made as we went on. Of course the children could not hear it; they only saw the motions that answered to it. But with them they seemed to be very much delighted indeed, as I shall presently show you. This was the song:

Swing, swang, swingle, swuff,
Flicker, flacker, fling, fluff!
Thus we go,
To and fro;
Here and there,
Everywhere,
Born and bred;
Never dead,
Only gone.

On! Come on.
Looming, glooming,
Spreading, fuming,
Shattering, scattering,
Parting, darting,
All our life,
Is a strife,
And a wearying for rest
On the darkness' friendly breast.

Joining, splitting,
Rising, sitting,
Laughing, shaking,
Sides all aching,
Grumbling, grim and gruff.
Swingle, swangle, swuff!

Now a knot of darkness;
Now dissolved gloom;
Now a pall of blackness
Hiding all the room.
Flicker, flacker, fluff!
Black and black enough!

Dancing now like demons;
Lying like the dead;
Gladly would we stop it,
And go down to bed!

But our work we still must do,
Shadow men, as well as you.

Rooting, rising, shooting,
Heaving, sinking, creeping;
Hid in corners crooning;
Splitting, poking, leaping,
Gathering, towering, swooning.
When we're lurking,
Yet we're working,
For our labour we must do,
Shadow men, as well as you.
Flicker, flacker, fling, fluff!
Swing, swang, swingle, swuff!

"'How thick the Shadows are!' said one of the children – a thoughtful little girl.

"'I wonder where they come from?' said a dreamy little boy.

"'I think they grow out of the wall,' answered the little girl; 'for I have been watching them come; first one and then another, and then a whole lot of them. I am sure they grow out of the walls.'

"'Perhaps they have papas and mammas,' said an older boy, with a smile.

"'Yes, yes; the doctor brings them in his pocket,' said another consequential little maiden.

"'No; I'll tell you,' said the older boy. 'They're ghosts.'

"'But ghosts are white.'

"'Oh! these have got black coming down the chimney.'

"'No,' said a curious-looking, white-faced boy of fourteen, who had been reading by the firelight, and had stopped to hear the little ones talk; 'they're body-ghosts; they're not soul-ghosts.'

"A silence followed, broken by the first, the dreamy-eyed boy, who said:

"'I hope they didn't make me;' at which they all burst out laughing, just as the nurse brought in their tea. When she proceeded to light the gas, we vanished.

"'I stopped a murder,' cried another.

"'How? How? How?'

"'I will tell you: I had been lurking about a sickroom for some time, where a miser lay, apparently dying. I did not like the place at all, but I felt as if I was wanted there. There were plenty of lurking places about, for it was full of all sorts of old furniture – especially cabinets, chests and presses. I believe he had in that room every bit of the property he had spent a long life in gathering. And I knew he had lots of gold in those places; for one night, when his nurse was away, he crept out of bed, mumbling and shaking, and managed to open one of his chests, though he nearly fell down with the effort. I was peeping over his shoulder, and such a gleam of gold fell upon me, that it nearly killed me. But hearing his nurse coming, he slammed the lid down, and I recovered. I tried very hard, but I could not do him any good. For although I made all sorts of shapes on the walls and ceiling, representing evil deeds that he had done, of which there were plenty to choose from, I could make no shapes on his brain or conscience. He had no eyes for anything but gold. And it so happened that his nurse had neither eyes nor heart for anything else either.

"'One day as she was seated beside his bed, but where he could not see her, stirring some gruel in a basin to cool it from him, I saw her take a little phial from her bosom, and I knew by the expression of her face both what it was and what she was going to do with it. Fortunately the cork was a little hard to get out, and this gave me one moment to think.

"'The room was so crowded with all sorts of things, that although there were no curtains on the four-poster bed to hide from the miser the sight of his precious treasures, there was yet but one spot on the ceiling suitable for casting myself upon in the shape I wished to assume. And this spot was hard to reach. But I discovered that upon this very spot there was a square gleam of firelight thrown from a strange old dusty mirror that stood away in some corner, so I got in front of the fire, spied where the mirror was, threw myself upon it, and bounded from its face upon the square pool of dim light on the ceiling, assuming, as I passed, the shape of an old stooping hag, pouring something from a phial into a basin. I made the handle of the spoon with my own nose, ha! Ha!'

"And the shadow-hand caressed the shadow tip of the shadow-nose, before the shadow-tongue resumed.

"'The old miser saw me. He would not taste the gruel that night, although his nurse coaxed and scolded till they were both weary. She pretended to taste it, and to think it very good; and at last retired into a corner, and made as if she were eating it herself; but I saw that she took good care to pour it all out.'

"'But she must either succeed, or starve him, at last.'

"'I will tell you.'

"'But,' interposed another, 'he was not worth saving.'

"'He might repent,' said another more benevolent Shadow.

"'No chance of that,' returned the former. 'Misers never do. The love of money has less in it to cure itself than any other wickedness into which wretched men can fall. What a mercy it is to be born a Shadow! Wickedness does not stick to us. What do we care for gold – rubbish!'

"'Amen! Amen! Amen!' came from a hundred shadow-voices.

"'You should have let her murder him, and so have had done with him.'

"'And besides, how was he to escape at last? He could never get rid of her – could he?'

"'I was going to tell you,' resumed the narrator, 'only you had so many shadow-remarks to make, that you would not let me.'

"'Go on; go on.'

"'There was a little grandchild who used to come and see him sometimes – the only creature the miser cared for. Her mother was his daughter; but the old man would never see her, because she had married against his will. Her husband was now dead, but he had not forgiven her yet. After the shadow he had seen, however, he said to himself, as he lay awake that night – I saw the words on his face – 'How shall I get rid of that old devil? If I don't eat I shall die. I wish little Mary would come tomorrow. Ah! Her mother would never serve me so, if I lived a hundred years more.' He lay awake, thinking such things over and over again all night long, and I stood watching him from a dark corner; till the day spring came and shook me out. When I came back next night, the room was tidy and clean. His own daughter, a sad-faced, still beautiful woman, sat by his bedside; and little Mary was curled up on the floor, by the fire, imitating us, by making queer shadows on the ceiling with her twisted hands. But she could not think how ever they got there. And no wonder, for I helped her to some very unaccountable ones.'

"'I have a story about a granddaughter, too,' said another, the moment that speaker ceased.

"'Tell it. Tell it.'

"'Last Christmas Day,' he began, 'I and a troop of us set out in the twilight, to find some house where we could all have something to do; for we had made up our minds to act together. We tried several, but found objections to them all. At last we espied a large lonely country house, and hastening to it, we found great preparations making for the Christmas dinner. We rushed into it, scampered all over it, and made up our minds in a moment that it would do. We amused ourselves in the nursery first, where there were several children being dressed for dinner. We generally do go to the nursery first, your majesty. This time we were especially charmed with a little girl about five years old, who clapped her hands and danced about with delight at the antics we performed; and we said we would do something for her if we had a chance. The company began to arrive; and at every arrival, we rushed to the hall and cut wonderful capers of welcome. Between times, we scudded away to see how the dressing went on. One girl about eighteen was delightful. She dressed herself as if she did not care much about it, but could no help doing it prettily. When she took her last look of the phantom in the glass, she half smiled to it – but we do not like those creatures that come into the mirrors at all, your majesty. We don't understand them. They are dreadful to us – she looked rather sad and pale, but very sweet and hopeful. We wanted to know all about her, and soon found out that she was a distant relation and a great favourite of the gentleman of the house, an old man, with an expression of benevolence mingled with obstinacy and a deep shade of the tyrannical. We could not admire him much; but we would not make up our minds all at once: Shadows never do.

"'The dinner bell rang, and down we hurried. The children all looked happy, and we were merry. There was one cross fellow among the servants waiting, and didn't we plague him! And didn't we get fun out of him! When he was bringing up dishes, we lay in wait for him at every corner, and sprung upon him from the floor, and from over the banisters, and down from the cornices. He started and stumbled and blundered about, so that his fellow servants thought he was tipsy. Once he dropped a plate, and had to pick up the pieces, and hurry away with them. Didn't we pursue him as he went! It was lucky for him his master did not see him; but we took care not to let him get into any real scrape, though his eyes were quite dazed with the dodging of the unaccountable shadows. Sometimes he thought the walls were coming down upon him; sometimes that the floor was gaping to swallow him; sometimes that he would be knocked in pieces by the hurrying to and fro, or be smothered in the black crowd.

"'When the blazing plum pudding was carried in, we made a perfect shadow-carnival about it, dancing and mumming in the blue flames, like mad demons. And how the children screamed with delight!

"'The old gentleman, who was very fond of children, was laughing his heartiest laugh, when a loud knock came to the hall door. The fair maiden started, turned paler, and then red as the Christmas fire. I saw it, and flung my hands across her face. She was very glad, and I know she said in her heart, "You kind Shadow!" which paid me well. Then I followed the rest into the hall, and found there a jolly, handsome, brown-faced sailor, evidently a son of the house. The old man received him with tears in his eyes, and the children with shouts of joy. The maiden escaped in the confusion, just in time to save herself from fainting. We crowded about the lamp to hide her retreat, and nearly put it out. The butler could not get it to burn up before she had glided into her place again, delighted to find the room so dark. The sailor only had seen her go, and now he sat down beside her and, without a word, got hold of her hand in the gloom. But now we all scattered to the walls and the corners; and the lamp blazed up again, and he let her hand go.

"'During the rest of the dinner, the old man watched them both, and saw that there was something between them, and was very angry. For he was an important man in his own estimation – and they had never consulted him. The fact was, they had never known their own minds till the sailor had gone upon his last voyage; and had learned each other's only this moment – we found out all this by watching them, and then talking together about it afterwards. The old gentleman saw too that his favourite, who was under such obligation to him for loving her so much, loved his son better than him; and this made him so jealous, that he soon overshadowed the whole table with his morose looks and short answers. That kind of shadowing is very different from ours; and the Christmas dessert grew so gloomy that we Shadows could not bear it, and were delighted when the ladies rose to go to the drawing room. The gentlemen would not stay behind the ladies, even for the sake of the well-known wine. So the moddy host, notwithstanding his hospitality, was left alone at the table, in the great silent room. We followed the company upstairs to the drawing room, and thence to the nursery for snap-dragon. While they were busy with this most shadowy of games, nearly all the Shadows crept downstairs again to the dining room, where the old man still sat, gnawing the bone of his own selfishness. They crowded into the room, and by using every kind of expansion – blowing themselves out like soap-bubbles, they succeeded in heaping up the whole room with shade upon shade. They clustered thickest about the fire and the lamp, till at last they almost drowned them in hills of darkness.

"'Before they had accomplished so much, the children, tired with fun and frolio, were put to bed. But the little girl of five years old, with whom we had been so pleased when first we arrived, could not go to sleep. She had a little room of her own; and I had watched her to bed, and now kept her awake by gambolling in the rays of the night-light. When her eyes were once fixed upon me, I took the shape of her grandfather, representing him on the wall, as he sat in his chair, with his head bent down, and his arms hanging listlessly by his sides. And the child remembered that that was just as she had seen him last; for she had happened to peep in at the dining-room door, after all the rest had gone up stairs. "What if he should be sitting there still," thought she, "all alone in the dark!" She scrambled out of bed and crept down.

"'Meantime the others had made the room below so dark, that only the face and white hair of the old man could be dimly discerned in the shadowy crowd. For he had filled his own mind with shadows, which we Shadows wanted to draw out of him. Those shadows are very different from us, your majesty knows. He was thinking of all the disappointments he had had in life, and of all the ingratitude he had met with. He thought far more of the good he had done, than the good others had got. "After all I have done for them," said he, with a sigh of bitterness, "not one of them cares a straw for me. My own children will be glad when I am gone!" At that instant he lifted up his eyes and saw, standing close by the door, a tiny figure in a long night-gown. The door behind her was shut. It was my little friend who had crept in noiselessly. A pang of icy fear shot to the old man's heart – but it melted away as fast, for we made a lane through us for a single ray from the fire to fall on the face of the little sprite; and he thought it was a child of his own that had died when just the age of her little niece, who now stood looking for her grandfather among the Shadows. He thought she had come out of her grave in the old darkness, to ask why her father was sitting alone on Christmas Day. And he felt he had no answer to give his little ghost, but one he would be ashamed for her to hear. But the little girl saw him now. She walked up to him with a childish stateliness – stumbling once or twice on what seemed her long shroud. Pushing through the crowded shadows, she reached him, climbed upon his knee, laid her little long-haired head on his shoulders, and said: "Ganpa! you goomy? Isn't it your Kismass-day, too, ganpa?"

"'A new fount of love seemed to burst from the clay of the old man's heart. He clasped the child to his bosom, and wept. Then, without a word, he rose with her in his arms, carried her up to her room, and laying her down in her bed, covered her up, kissed her sweet little mouth unconscious of reproof, and then went to the drawing room.

"'As soon as he entered, he saw the culprits in a quiet corner alone. He went up to them, took a hand of each, and joining them in both his, said, "God bless you!" Then he turned to the rest of the company, and "Now," said he, "let's have a Christmas carol." And well he might; for though I have paid many visits to the house, I have never seen him cross since; and I am sure that must cost him a good deal of trouble.'

"'We have just come from a great palace,' said another, 'where we knew there were many children, and where we thought to hear glad voices, and see royally merry looks. But as soon as we entered, we became aware that one mighty Shadow shrouded the whole; and that Shadow deepened and deepened, till it gathered in darkness about the reposing form of a wise prince. When we saw him, we could move no more, but clung heavily to the walls, and by our stillness added to the sorrow of the hour. And when we saw the mother of her people weeping with bowed head for the loss of him in whom she had trusted, we were seized with such a longing to be Shadows no longer, but winged angels, which are the white shadows cast in heaven from the Light of Light, so to gather around her, and hover over her with comforting, that we vanished from the walls and found ourselves floating high above the towers of the palace, where we met the angels on their way; and knew that our service was not needed.'

"By this time there was a glimmer of approaching moonlight, and the king began to see several of those stranger Shadows, with human faces and eyes, moving about amongst the crowd. He knew at once that they did not belong to his dominion. They looked at him, and came near him, and passed slowly, but they never made any obeisance, or gave sign of homage. And what their eyes said to him, the king only could tell. And he did not tell.

"'What are those other Shadows that move through the crowd?' said he to one of his subjects near him.

"The Shadow started, looked round, shivered slightly, and laid his finger on his lips. Then leading the king a little aside, and looking carefully about him once more,

"'I do not know,' said he, in a low tone, 'what they are. I have heard of them often, but only once did I ever see any of them before. That was when some of us one night paid a visit to a man who sat much alone, and was said to think a great deal. We saw two of those sitting in the room with him, and he was as pale as they were. We could not cross the threshold, but shivered and shook, and felt ready to melt away. Is not your majesty afraid of them too?'

"But the king made no answer; and before he could speak again, the moon had climbed above the mighty pillars of the church of the Shadows, and looked in at the great window of the sky.

"The shapes had all vanished; and the king, again lifting up his eyes, saw but the wall of his own chamber, on which flickered the Shadow of a Little Child. He looked down, and there, sitting on a stool by the fire, he saw one of his own little ones, waiting to say goodnight to his father, and go to bed early, that he might rise as early, and be very good and happy all Christmas Day.

"And Ralph Rinkelmann rejoiced that he was a man, and not a Shadow."

THE GOLDEN KEY

GEORGE MACDONALD

There was a boy who used to sit in the twilight and listen to his great-aunt's stories.

She told him that if he could reach the place where the end of the rainbow stands he would find there a golden key.

"And what is the key for?" the boy would ask. "What is it the key of? What will it open?"

"That nobody knows," his aunt would reply. "He has to find that out."

"I suppose, being gold," the boy once said, thoughtfully, "that I could get a good deal of money for it if I sold it."

"Better never find it than sell it," returned his aunt.

And the the boy went to bed and dreamed about the golden key.

Now all that his great-aunt told the boy about the golden key would have been nonsense, had it not been that their little house stood on the borders of Fairyland. For it is perfectly well known that out of Fairyland nobody ever can find where the rainbow stands. The creature takes such good care of its golden key, always flitting from place to place, lest anyone should find it! But in Fairyland it is quite different. Things that look real in this country look very thin indeed in Fairyland, while some of the things that here cannot stand still for a moment, will not move there. So it was not in the least absurd of the old lady to tell her nephew such things about the golden key.

"Did you ever know anybody find it?" he asked, one evening.

"Yes. Your father, I believe, found it."

"And what did he do with it, can you tell me?"

"He never told me."

"What was it like?"

"He never showed it to me."

"How does a new key come there always?"

"I don't know. There it is."

"Perhaps it is the rainbow's egg."

"Perhaps it is. You will be a happy boy if you find the nest."

"Perhaps it comes tumbling down the rainbow from the sky."

"Perhaps it does."

One evening, in summer, he went into his own room and stood at the lattice window, and gazed into the forest which fringed the outskirts of Fairyland. It came close up to his great-aunt's garden and, indeed, sent some straggling trees into it. The forest lay to the east, and the sun, which was setting behind the cottage, looked straight into the dark wood with his level red eye. The trees were all old and had few branches below, so that the sun could see a great way into the forest and the boy, being keen-sighted, could see almost as far as the sun. The trunks stood like rows of red columns in the shine of the red sun, and he could see down aisle after aisle in the vanishing distance. And as he gazed into the forest he began to feel as if the trees were all waiting for him and had something they could not go on with till he came to them. But he was hungry and wanted his supper. So he lingered.

Suddenly, far among the trees, as far as the sun could shine, he saw a glorious thing. It was the end of a rainbow, large and brilliant. He could count all seven colours and could see shade after shade beyond the violet; while before the red stood a colour more gorgeous and mysterious still. It was a colour he had never seen before. Only the spring of the rainbow arch was visible. He could see nothing of it above the trees.

"The golden key!" he said to himself, and darted out of the house and into the wood.

He had not gone far before the sun set. But the rainbow only glowed the brighter. For the rainbow of Fairyland is not dependent upon the sun as ours is. The trees welcomed him. The bushes made way for him. The rainbow grew larger and brighter, and at length he found himself within two trees of it.

It was a grand sight, burning away there in silence, with its gorgeous, its lovely, its delicate colours, each distinct, all combining. He could now see a great deal more of it. It rose high into the blue heavens, but bent so little that he could not tell how high the crown of the arch must reach. It was still only a small portion of a huge bow.

He stood gazing at it till he forgot himself with delight – even forgot the key which he had come to seek. And as he stood it grew more wonderful still. For in each of the colours, which was as large as the column of a church, he could faintly see beautiful forms slowly ascending as if by the steps of a winding stair. The forms appeared irregularly – now one, now many, now several, now none – men and women and children – all different, all beautiful.

He drew nearer to the rainbow. It vanished. He started back a step in dismay. It was there again, as beautiful as ever. So he contented himself with standing as near it as he might and watching the forms that ascended the glorious colours towards the unknown height of the arch, which did not end abruptly but faded away in the blue air so gradually that he could not say where it ceased.

When the thought of the golden key returned, the boy very wisely proceeded to mark out in his mind the space covered by the foundation of the rainbow, in order that he might know where to search should the rainbow disappear. It was based chiefly upon a bed of moss.

Meantime it had grown quite dark in the wood. The rainbow alone was visible by its own light. But the moment the moon rose the rainbow vanished. Nor could any change of place restore the vision to the boy's eyes. So he threw himself down upon the mossy bed to wait till the sunlight would give him a chance of finding the key. There he fell fast asleep.

When he woke in the morning the sun was looking straight into his eyes. He turned away from it, and the same moment saw a brilliant little thing lying on the moss within a foot of his face. It was the golden key. The pipe of it was of plain gold, as bright as gold could be. The handle was curiously wrought and set with sapphires. In a terror of delight he put out his hand and took it, and had it.

He lay for a while, turning it over and over and feeding his eyes upon its beauty. Then he jumped to his feet, remembering that the pretty thing was of no use to him yet. Where was the lock to which the key belonged? It must be somewhere, for how could anybody be so silly as make a key for which there was no lock? Where should he go to look for it? He gazed about him, up into the air, down to the earth, but saw no keyhole in the clouds, in the grass, or in the trees.

Just as he began to grow disconsolate, however, he saw something glimmering in the wood. It was a mere glimmer that he saw, but he took it for a glimmer of rainbow, and went towards it... And now I will go back to the borders of the forest.

Not far from the house where the boy had lived, there was another house, the owner of which was a merchant, who was much away from home. He had lost his wife some years before and had only one child, a little girl, whom he left to the charge of two servants, who were very idle and careless. So she was neglected and left untidy, and was sometimes ill-used besides.

Now it is well known that the little creatures commonly known as fairies, though there are many different kinds of fairies in Fairyland, have an exceeding dislike to untidiness. Indeed, they are quite spiteful to slovenly people. Being used to all the lovely ways of the trees and flowers, and to the neatness of the birds and all woodland creatures, it makes them feel miserable, even in their deep woods and on their grassy carpets, to think that within the same moonlight lies a dirty, uncomfortable, slovenly house. And this makes them angry with the people that live in it, and they would gladly drive them out of the world if they could. They want the whole earth nice and clean. So they pinch the maids black and blue and play them all manner of uncomfortable tricks.

But this house was quite a shame, and the fairies in the forest could not endure it. They tried everything on the maids without effect, and at last resolved upon making a clean riddance, beginning with the child. They ought to have known that it was not her fault, but they have little principle and much mischief in them, and they thought that if they got rid of her the maids would be sure to be turned away.

So one evening, the poor little girl having been put to bed early, before the sun was down, the servants went off to the village, locking the door behind them. The child did not know she was alone and lay contentedly looking out of her window towards the forest, of which, however, she could not see much, because of the ivy and other creeping plants which had straggled across her window. All at once she saw an ape making faces at her out of the mirror and the heads carved upon a great old wardrobe grinning fearfully. Then two old spider-legged chairs came forward into the middle of the room and began to dance a queer, old-fashioned dance. This set her laughing and she forgot the ape and the grinning heads. So the fairies saw they had made a mistake, and sent the chairs back to their places. But they knew that she had been reading the story of Silverhair all day. So the next moment she heard the voices of the three bears upon the stair, big voice, middle voice and little voice, and she heard their soft, heavy tread, as if they had stockings over their boots, coming nearer and nearer to the door of her room till she could bear it no longer. She did just as Silverhair did and as the fairies wanted her to do; she darted to the window, pulled it open, got upon the ivy and so scrambled to the ground. She then fled to the forest as fast as she could run.

Now, although she did not know it, this was the very best way she could have gone, for nothing is ever so mischievous in its own place as it is out of it; and besides, these mischievous creatures were only the children of Fairyland, as it were, and there are many other beings there as well. And if a wanderer gets in among them, the good ones will always help him more than the evil ones will be able to hurt him.

The sun was now set and the darkness coming on, but the child thought of no danger but the bears behind her. If she had looked round, however, she would have seen that she was followed by a very different creature from a bear. It was a curious creature, made like a fish, but covered, instead of scales, with feathers of all colours, sparkling like those of a hummingbird. It had fins, not wings, and swam through the air as a fish does through the water. Its head was like the head of a small owl.

After running a long way and as the last of the light was disappearing, she passed under a tree with drooping branches. It dropped its branches to the ground all about her and caught her as in a trap. She struggled to get out, but the branches pressed her closer and closer to the trunk. She was in great terror and distress when the air-fish, swimming into the thicket of branches, began tearing them with its beak. They loosened their hold at once and the creature went on attacking them till at length they let the child go. Then the air-fish came from behind her and swam on in front, glittering and sparkling all lovely colours; and she followed.

It led her gently along till all at once it swam in at a cottage door. The child followed still. There was a bright fire in the middle of the floor, upon which stood a pot without a lid, full of water that boiled and bubbled furiously. The air-fish swam straight to the pot and into the boiling water, where it lay quiet. A beautiful woman rose from the opposite side of the fire and came to meet the girl. She took her up in her arms, and said:

"Ah, you are come at last! I have been looking for you a long time."

She sat down with her on her lap, and there the girl sat staring at her. She had never seen anything so beautiful. She was tall and strong, with white arms and neck and a delicate flush on her face. The child could not tell what was the colour of her hair, but could not help thinking it had a tinge of dark green. She had not one ornament upon her, but she looked as if she had just put off quantities of diamonds and emeralds. Yet here she was in the simplest, poorest little cottage, where she was evidently at home. She was dressed in shining green.

The girl looked at the lady, and the lady looked at the girl.

"What is your name?" asked the lady.

"The servants always called me Tangle."

"Ah, that was because your hair was so untidy. But that was their fault, the naughty women! Still it is a pretty name, and I will call you Tangle too. You must not mind my asking you questions, for you may ask me the same questions, every one of them, and any others that you like. How old are you?"

"Ten," answered Tangle.

"You don't look like it," said the lady.

"How old are you, please?" returned Tangle.

"Thousands of years old," answered the lady.

"You don't look like it," said Tangle.

"Don't I? I think I do. Don't you see how beautiful I am!"

And her great blue eyes looked down on the little Tangle as if all the stars in the sky were melted in them to make their brightness.

"Ah! But," said Tangle, "when people live long they grow old. At least I always thought so."

"I have no time to grow old," said the lady. "I am too busy for that. It is very idle to grow old – but I cannot have my little girl so untidy. Do you know I can't find a clean spot on your face to kiss!"

"Perhaps," suggested Tangle, feeling ashamed, but not too much so to say a word for herself – "perhaps that is because the tree made me cry so."

"My poor darling!" said the lady, looking now as if the moon were melted in her eyes, and kissing her little face, dirty as it was, "the naughty tree must suffer for making a girl cry."

"And what is your name, please?" asked Tangle.

"Grandmother," answered the lady.

"Is it really?"

"Yes, indeed. I never tell stories, even in fun."

"How good of you!"

"I couldn't if I tried. It would come true if I said it, and then I should be punished enough." And she smiled like the sun through a summer shower.

"But now," she went on, "I must get you washed and dressed, and then we shall have some supper."

"Oh! I had supper long ago," said Tangle.

"Yes, indeed you had," answered the lady – "three years ago. You don't know that it is three years since you ran away from the bears. You are thirteen and more now."

Tangle could only stare. She felt quite sure it was true.

"You will not be afraid of anything I do with you – will you?" said the lady.

"I will try very hard not to be; but I can't be certain, you know," replied Tangle.

"I like your saying so, and I shall be quite satisfied," answered the lady.

She took off the girl's nightgown, rose with her in her arms and, going to the wall of the cottage, opened a door. Then Tangle saw a deep tank, the sides of which were filled with green plants, which had flowers of all colours. There was a roof over it like the roof of the cottage. It was filled with beautiful clear water, in which swam a multitude of such fishes as the one that had led her to the cottage. It was the light their colours gave that showed the place in which they were.

The lady spoke some words Tangle could not understand, and threw her into the tank.

The fishes came crowding about her. Two or three of them got under her head and kept it up. The rest of them rubbed themselves all over her, and with their wet feathers washed her quite clean. Then the lady, who had been looking on all the time, spoke again; whereupon some thirty or forty of the fishes rose out of the water underneath Tangle, and so bore her up to the arms the lady held out to take her. She carried her back to the fire and, having dried her well, opened a chest and, taking out the finest linen garments, smelling of grass and lavender, put them upon her, and over all a green dress, just like her own, shining like hers and soft like hers, and going into just such lovely folds from the waist, where it was tied with a brown cord to her bare feet.

"Won't you give me a pair of shoes too, Grandmother?" said Tangle.

"No, my dear; no shoes. Look here. I wear no shoes."

So saying she lifted her dress a little, and there were the loveliest white feet but no shoes. Then Tangle was content to go without shoes too. And the lady sat down with her again, and combed her hair and brushed it, and then left it to dry while she got the supper.

First she got bread out of one hole in the wall, then milk out of another, then several kinds of fruit out a third; and then she went to the pot on the fire, and took out the fish, now nicely cooked, and, as soon as she had pulled off its feathered skin, ready to be eaten.

"But," exclaimed Tangle. And she stared at the fish, and could say no more.

"I know what you mean," returned the lady. "You do not like to eat the messenger that brought you home. But it is the kindest return you can make. The creature was afraid to go until it saw me put the pot on and heard me promise it should be boiled the moment it returned with you. Then it darted out of the door at once. You saw it go into the pot of itself the moment it entered, did you not?"

"I did," answered Tangle, "and I thought it very strange, but then I saw you and forgot all about the fish."

"In Fairyland," resumed the lady, as they sat down to the table, "the ambition of the animals is to be eaten by the people, for that is their highest end in that condition. But they are not therefore destroyed. Out of that pot comes something more than the dead fish, you will see."

Tangle now remarked that the lid was on the pot. But the lady took no further notice of it till they had eaten the fish, which Tangle found nicer than any fish she had ever tasted before. It was as white as snow and as delicate as cream. And the moment she had swallowed a mouthful of it, a change she could not describe began to take place in her. She heard a murmuring all about her, which became more and more articulate, and at length, as she went on eating, grew intelligible. By the time she had finished her share, the sounds of all the animals in the forest came crowding through the door to her ears; for the door still stood wide open, though it was pitch-dark outside; and they were no longer sounds only, they were speech, and speech that she could understand. She could tell what the insects in the cottage were saying to each other too. She had even a suspicion that the trees and flowers all about the cottage were holding midnight communications with each other, but what they said she could not hear.

As soon as the fish was eaten, the lady went to the fire and took the lid off the pot. A lovely little creature in human shape, with large white wings, rose out of it, and flew round and round the roof of the cottage then dropped, fluttering, and nestled in the lap of the lady. She spoke to it some strange words, carried it to the door and threw it out into the darkness. Tangle heard the flapping of its wings die away in the distance.

"Now have we done the fish any harm?" she said, returning.

"No," answered Tangle, "I do not think we have. I should not mind eating one every day."

"They must wait their time, like you and me too, my little Tangle."

And she smiled a smile which the sadness in it made more lovely.

"But," she continued, "I think we may have one for supper tomorrow.

So saying, she went to the door of the tank and spoke, and now Tangle understood her perfectly.

"I want one of you," she said – "the wisest."

Thereupon the fishes got together in the middle of the tank, with their heads forming a circle above the water and their tails a larger circle beneath it. They were holding a council, in which their relative wisdom should be determined. At length one of them flew up into the lady's hand, looking lively and ready.

"You know where the rainbow stands?" she asked.

"Yes, mother, quite well," answered the fish.

"Bring home a young man you will find there, who does not know where to go."

The fish was out of the door in a moment. Then the lady told Tangle it was time to go to bed, and, opening another door in the side of the cottage, showed her a little arbour, cool and green, with a bed of purple heath growing in it, upon which she threw a large wrapper made of the feathered skins of the wise fishes, shining gorgeous in the firelight. Tangle was soon lost in the strangest, loveliest dreams. And the beautiful lady was in every one of her dreams.

In the morning she woke to the rustling of leaves over her head and the sound of running water. But, to her surprise, she could find no door – nothing but the moss-grown wall of the cottage. So she crept through an opening in the arbour and stood in the forest. Then she bathed in a stream that ran merrily through the trees, and felt happier – for having once been in her grandmother's pond, she must be clean and tidy ever after – and, having put on her green dress, felt like a lady.

She spent that day in the wood, listening to the birds and beasts and creeping things. She understood all that they said, though she could not repeat a word of it; and every kind had a different language, while there was a common though more limited understanding between all the inhabitants of the forest. She saw nothing of the beautiful lady, but she felt that she was near her all the time and she took care not to go out of sight of the cottage. It was round, like a snow-hut or a wigwam, and she could see neither door nor window in it. The fact was, it had no windows, and though it was full of doors, they all opened from the inside and could not even be seen from the outside.

She was standing at the foot of a tree in the twilight, listening to a quarrel between a mole and a squirrel in which the mole told the squirrel that the tail was the best of him and the squirrel called the mole Spade-fists, when, the darkness having deepened around her, she became aware of something shining in her face and, looking round, saw that the door of the cottage was open and the red light of the fire flowing from it like a river through the darkness. She left Mole and Squirrel to settle matters as they might, and darted off to the cottage. Entering, she found the pot boiling on the fire, and the grand, lovely lady sitting on the other side of it.

"I've been watching you all day," said the lady. "You shall have something to eat by-and-by, but we must wait till our supper comes home."

She took Tangle on her knee, and began to sing to her – such songs as made her wish she could listen to them for ever. But at length in rushed the shining fish, and snuggled down in the pot. It was followed by a youth who had outgrown his worn garments. His face was ruddy with health, and in his hand he carried a little jewel, which sparkled in the firelight.

The first words the lady said were:

"What is that in your hand, Mossy?"

Now Mossy was the name his companions had given him, because he had a favourite stone covered with moss on which he used to sit whole days reading, and they said the moss had begun to grow upon him too.

Mossy held out his hand. The moment the lady saw that it was the golden key, she rose from her chair, kissed Mossy on the forehead, made him sit down on her seat and stood before him like a servant. Mossy could not bear this and rose at once. But the lady begged him, with tears in her beautiful eyes, to sit and let her wait on him.

"But you are a great, splendid, beautiful lady," said Mossy.

"Yes, I am. But I work all day long – that is my pleasure; and you will have to leave me so soon!"

"How do you know that, if you please, madam?" asked Mossy.

"Because you have got the golden key."

"But I don't know what it is for. I can't find the keyhole. Will you tell me what to do?"

"You must look for the keyhole. That is your work. I cannot help you. I can only tell you that if you look for it you will find it."

"What kind of box will it open? What is there inside?"

"I do not know. I dream about it, but I know nothing."

"Must I go at once?"

"You may stop here tonight and have some of my supper. But you must go in the morning. All I can do for you is to give you clothes. Here is a girl called Tangle, whom you must take with you."

"That *will* be nice," said Mossy.

"No, no!" said Tangle. "I don't want to leave you, please, grandmother."

"You must go with him, Tangle. I am sorry to lose you, but it will the best thing for you. Even the fishes, you see, have to go into the pot, and then out into the dark. If you fall in with the Old Man of the Sea, mind you ask him whether he has not got some more fishes ready for me. My tank is getting thin."

So saying, she took the fish from the pot and put the lid on as before. They sat down and ate the fish, and then the winged creature rose from the pot, circled the roof and settled on the lady's lap. She talked to it, carried it to the door, and threw it out into the dark. They heard the flap of its wings die away in the distance.

The lady then showed Mossy into just such another chamber as that of Tangle, and in the morning he found a suit of clothes laid beside him. He looked very handsome in them. But the wearer of Grandmother's clothes never thinks about how he or she looks, but thinks always how handsome other people are.

Tangle was very unwilling to go.

"Why should I leave you? I don't know the young man," she said to the lady.

"I am never allowed to keep my children long. You need not go with him unless you please to, but you must go some day; and I should like you to go with him, for he has the golden key. No girl need be afraid to go with a youth that has the golden key. You will take care of her, Mossy, will you not?"

"That I will," said Mossy.

And Tangle cast a glance at him, and thought she should like to go with him.

"And," said the lady, "if you should lose each other as you go through the – the – I never can remember the name of that country – do not be afraid, but go on and on."

She kissed Tangle on the mouth and Mossy on the forehead, led them to the door and waved her hand eastward. Mossy and Tangle took each other's hand and walked away into the depth of the forest. In his right hand Mossy held the golden key.

They wandered thus a long way, with endless amusement from the talk of the animals. They soon learned enough of their language to ask them necessary questions. The squirrels were always friendly, and gave them nuts out of their own hoards; but the bees were selfish and rude, justifying themselves on the ground that Tangle and Mossy were not subjects of their queen and charity must begin at home, though indeed they had not one drone in their poorhouse at the time. Even the blinking moles would fetch them an earth-nut or a truffle now and then, talking as if their mouths, as well as their eyes and ears, were full of cotton wool or their own velvety fur. By the time they got out of the forest they were very fond of each other, and Tangle was not in the least sorry that her grandmother had sent her away with Mossy.

At length the trees grew smaller and stood farther apart, and the ground began to rise, and it got more and more steep till the trees were all left behind, and the two were climbing a narrow path with rocks on each side. Suddenly they came upon a rude doorway, by which they entered a narrow gallery cut in the rock. It grew darker and darker, till it was pitch dark and they had to feel their way. At length the light began to return, and at last they came out upon a narrow path on the face of a lofty precipice. This path went winding down the rock to a wide plain, circular in shape, and surrounded on all sides by mountains. Those opposite to them were a great way off and towered to an awful height, shooting up sharp, blue, ice-enamelled pinnacles. An utter silence reigned where they stood. Not even the sound of water reached them.

Looking down, they could not tell whether the valley below was a grassy plain or a great still lake. They had never seen any place look like it. The way to it was difficult and dangerous, but down the narrow path they went, and reached the bottom in safety. They found it composed of smooth, light-coloured sandstone, undulating in parts but mostly level. It was no wonder to them now that they had not been able to tell what it was, for this surface was everywhere crowded with shadows. It was a sea of shadows. The mass was chiefly made up of the shadows of leaves innumerable, of all lovely and imaginative forms, waving to and fro, floating and quivering in the breath of a breeze whose motion was unfelt, whose sound was unheard. No forests clothed the mountainsides, no trees were anywhere to be seen and yet the shadows of the leaves, branches and stems of all various trees covered the valley as far as their eyes could reach. They soon spied the shadows of flowers mingled with those of the leaves, and now and then the shadow of a bird with open beak and throat distended with song. At times would appear the forms of strange, graceful creatures, running up and down the shadow-boles and along the branches, to disappear in the wind-tossed foliage. As they walked they waded knee-deep in the lovely lake. For the shadows were not merely lying on the surface of the ground but heaped up above it like substantial forms of darkness as if they had been cast upon a thousand different planes of the air. Tangle and Mossy often lifted their heads and gazed upwards to descry whence the shadows came; but they could see nothing more than a bright mist spread above them, higher than the tops of the mountains, which stood clear against it. No forests, no leaves, no birds were visible.

After a while, they reached more open spaces, where the shadows were thinner, and came even to portions over which shadows only flitted, leaving them clear for such as might follow. Now a wonderful form, half bird-like half human, would float across on outspread sailing pinions. Anon an exquisite shadow group of gambolling children would be followed by the loveliest female form, and that again by the grand stride of a Titanic shape, each disappearing in the surrounding press of shadowy foliage. Sometimes a profile of unspeakable beauty or grandeur would appear for a moment and vanish. Sometimes they seemed lovers that passed linked arm in arm, sometimes father and son, sometimes brothers in loving contest, sometimes sisters entwined in gracefullest community of complex form. Sometimes wild horses would tear across, free, or bestrode by noble shadows of ruling men. But some of the things which pleased them most they never knew how to describe.

About the middle of the plain they sat down to rest in the heart of a heap of shadows. After sitting for a while, each, looking up, saw the other in tears: they were each longing after the country whence the shadows fell.

"We *must* find the country from which the shadows come," said Mossy.

"We must, dear Mossy," responded Tangle. "What if your golden key should be the key to it?"

"Ah! that would be grand," returned Mossy. "But we must rest here for a little, and then we shall be able to cross the plain before night."

So he lay down on the ground, and about him on every side, and over his head, was the constant play of the wonderful shadows. He could look through them, and see the one behind the other, till they mixed in a mass of darkness. Tangle, too, lay admiring, and wondering, and longing after the country whence the shadows came. When they were rested they rose and pursued their journey.

How long they were in crossing this plain I cannot tell, but before night Mossy's hair was streaked with grey and Tangle had got wrinkles on her forehead.

As evening drew on, the shadows fell deeper and rose higher. At length they reached a place where they rose above their heads and made all dark around them. Then they took hold of each other's hand, and walked on in silence and in some dismay. They felt the gathering darkness, and something strangely solemn besides, and the beauty of the shadows ceased to delight them. All at once Tangle found that she had not a hold of Mossy's hand, though when she lost it she could not tell.

"Mossy, Mossy!" she cried aloud in terror.

But no Mossy replied.

A moment after, the shadows sank to her feet, and down under her feet, and the mountains rose before her. She turned towards the gloomy region she had left, and called once more upon Mossy. There the gloom lay tossing and heaving, a dark stormy, foamless sea of shadows, but no Mossy rose out of it or came climbing up the hill on which she stood. She threw herself down and wept in despair.

Suddenly she remembered that the beautiful lady had told them, if they lost each other in a country of which she could not remember the name, they were not to be afraid but to go straight on.

"And besides," she said to herself, "Mossy has the golden key, and so no harm will come to him, I do believe."

She rose from the ground and went on.

Before long she arrived at a precipice, in the face of which a stair was cut. When she had ascended halfway, the stair ceased, and the path led straight into the mountain. She was afraid to enter, and turning again towards the stair, grew giddy at the sight of the depth beneath her, and was forced to throw herself down in the mouth of the cave.

When she opened her eyes she saw a beautiful little creature with wings standing beside her, waiting.

"I know you," said Tangle. "You are my fish."

"Yes. But I am a fish no longer. I am an aëranth now."

"What is that?" asked Tangle.

"What you see I am," answered the shape. "And I am come to lead you through the mountain."

"Oh! Thank you, dear fish – aëranth, I mean," returned Tangle, rising.

Thereupon the aëranth took to his wings and flew on through the long narrow passage, reminding Tangle very much of the way he had swum on before her when he was a fish. And the moment his white wings moved, they began to throw off a continuous shower of sparks of all colours, which lit up the passage before them. All at once he vanished, and Tangle heard a low, sweet sound, quite different from the rush and crackle of his wings. Before her was an open arch, and through it came light, mixed with the sound of sea waves.

She hurried out, and fell, tired and happy, upon the yellow sand of the shore. There she lay, half asleep with weariness and rest, listening to the low plash and retreat of the tiny waves, which seemed ever enticing the land to leave off being land and become sea. And as she lay, her eyes were fixed upon the foot of a great rainbow standing far away against the sky on the other side of the sea. At length she fell fast asleep.

When she awoke, she saw an old man with long white hair down to his shoulders, leaning upon a stick covered with green buds and so bending over her.

"What do you want here, beautiful woman?" he said.

"Am I beautiful? I am so glad!" answered Tangle, rising. "My grandmother is beautiful."

"Yes. But what do you want?" he repeated, kindly.

"I think I want you. Are not you the Old Man of the Sea?"

"I am."

"Then grandmother says, have you any more fishes ready for her?"

"We will go and see, my dear," answered the old man, speaking yet more kindly than before. "And I can do some thing for you, can I not?"

"Yes – show me the way up to the country from which the shadows fall," said Tangle. For there she hoped to find Mossy again.

"Ah! Indeed, that would be worth doing," said the old man. "But I cannot, for I do not know the way myself. But I will send you to the Old Man of the Earth. Perhaps he can tell you. He is much older than I am."

Leaning on his staff, he conducted her along the shore to a steep rock, that looked like a petrified ship turned upside down. The door of it was the rudder of a great vessel, ages ago at the bottom of the sea. Immediately within the door was a stair in the rock, down which the old man went, and Tangle followed. At the bottom, the old man had his house, and there he lived.

As soon as she entered it, Tangle heard a strange noise, unlike anything she had ever heard before. She soon found that it was the fishes talking. She tried to understand what they said; but their speech was so old-fashioned, and rude, and undefined, that she could not make much of it.

"I will go and see about those fishes for my daughter," said the Old Man of the Sea.

And moving a slide in the wall of his house, he first looked out and then tapped upon a thick piece of crystal that filled the round opening. Tangle came up behind him, and peeping through the window into the heart of the great deep green ocean, saw the most curious creatures, some very ugly, all very odd, and with especially queer mouths, swimming about everywhere, above and below, but all coming towards the window in answer to the tap of the Old Man of the Sea. Only a few could get their mouths against the glass; but those who were floating miles away yet turned their heads towards it. The Old Man looked through the whole flock carefully for some minutes, and then turning to Tangle, said:

"I am sorry, I have not got one ready yet. I want more time than she does. But I will send some as soon as I can."

He then shut the slide.

Presently a great noise arose in the sea. The old man opened the slide again and tapped on the glass, whereupon the fishes were all as still as sleep.

"They were only talking about you," he said. "And they do speak such nonsense! Tomorrow," he continued, "I must show you the way to the Old Man of the Earth. He lives a long way from here."

"Do let me go at once," said Tangle.

"No. That is not possible. You must come this way first."

He led her to a hole in the wall, which she had not observed before. It was covered with the green leaves and white blossoms of a creeping plant.

"Only white-blossoming plants can grow under the sea," said the old man. "In there you will find a bath, in which you must lie till I call you."

Tangle went in, and found a smaller room or cave, in the further corner of which was a great basin hollowed out of a rock and half full of the clearest sea water. Little streams were constantly running into it from cracks in the wall of the cavern. It was polished quite smooth inside and had a carpet of yellow sand in the bottom of it. Large green leaves and white flowers of various plants crowded up and over it, draping and covering it almost entirely.

No sooner was she undressed and lying in the bath than she began to feel as if the water were sinking into her, and she was receiving all the good of sleep without undergoing its forgetfulness. She felt the good coming all the time. And she grew happier and more hopeful than she had been since she lost Mossy. But she could not help thinking how very sad it was for a poor old man to live there all alone and have to take care of a whole sea full of stupid and riotous fishes.

After about an hour, as she thought, she heard his voice calling her, and rose out of the bath. All the fatigue and aching of her long journey had vanished. She was as whole and strong and well as if she had slept for seven days.

Returning to the opening that led into the other part of the house, she started back with amazement, for through it she saw the form of a grand man, with a majestic and beautiful face, waiting for her.

"Come," he said; "I see you are ready."

She entered with reverence.

"Where is the Old Man of the Sea?" she asked, humbly.

"There is no one here but me," he answered, smiling. "Some people call me the Old Man of the Sea. Others have another name for me and are terribly frightened when they meet me taking a walk by the shore. Therefore I avoid being seen by them, for they are so afraid that they never see what

I really am. You see me now. But I must show you the way to the Old Man of the Earth."

He led her into the cave where the bath was and there she saw, in the opposite corner, a second opening in the rock.

"Go down that stair, and it will bring you to him," said the Old Man of the Sea.

With humble thanks Tangle took her leave. She went down the winding stair till she began to fear there was no end to it. Still down and down it went, rough and broken, with springs of water bursting out of the rocks and running down the steps beside her. It was quite dark about her, and yet she could see. For after being in that bath, people's eyes always give out a light they can see by. There were no creeping things in the way. All was safe and pleasant though so dark and damp and deep.

At last there was not one step more, and she found herself in a glimmering cave. On a stone in the middle of it sat a figure with its back towards her – the figure of an old man bent double with age. From behind she could see his white beard spread out on the rocky floor in front of him. He did not move as she entered, so she passed round that she might stand before him and speak to him. The moment she looked in his face, she saw that he was a youth of marvellous beauty. He sat entranced with the delight of what he beheld in a mirror of something like silver, which lay on the floor at his feet, and which from behind she had taken for his white beard. He sat on, heedless of her presence, pale with the joy of his vision. She stood and watched him. At length, all trembling, she spoke. But her voice made no sound. Yet the youth lifted up his head. He showed no surprise, however, at seeing her – only smiled a welcome.

"Are you the Old Man of the Earth?" Tangle had said.

And the youth answered, and Tangle heard him, though not with her ears:

"I am. What can I do for you?"

"Tell me the way to the country whence the shadows fall."

"Ah! That I do not know. I only dream about it myself. I see its shadows sometimes in my mirror: the way to it I do not know. But I think the Old Man of the Fire must know. He is much older than I am. He is the oldest man of all."

"Where does he live?"

"I will show you the way to his place. I never saw him myself."

So saying, the young man rose, and then stood for a while gazing at Tangle.

"I wish I could see that country too," he said. "But I must mind my work."

He led her to the side of the cave, and told her to lay her ear against the wall.

"What do you hear?" he asked.

"I hear," answered Tangle, "the sound of a great water running inside the rock."

"That river runs down to the dwelling of the oldest man of all – the Old Man of the Fire. I wish I could go to see him. But I must mind my work. That river is the only way to him."

Then the Old Man of the Earth stooped over the floor of the cave, raised a huge stone from it, and left it leaning. It disclosed a great hole that went plumb down.

"That is the way," he said.

"But there are no stairs."

"You must throw yourself in. There is no other way."

She turned and looked him full in the face – stood so for a whole minute, as she thought: it was a whole year – then threw herself headlong into the hole.

When she came to herself, she found herself gliding down fast and deep. Her head was under water, but that did not signify for, when she thought about it, she could not remember that she had breathed once since her bath in the cave of the Old Man of the Sea. When she lifted up her head a sudden and fierce heat struck her, and she sank it again instantly and went sweeping on.

Gradually the stream grew shallower. At length she could hardly keep her head under. Then the water could carry her no farther. She rose from the channel, and went step by step down the burning descent. The water ceased altogether. The heat was terrible. She felt scorched to the bone, but it did not touch her strength. It grew hotter and hotter. She said, "I can bear it no longer." Yet she went on.

At the long last the stair ended at a rude archway in an all-but-glowing rock. Through this archway Tangle fell exhausted into a cool mossy cave. The floor and walls were covered with moss – green, soft and damp. A little stream spouted from a rent in the rock and fell into a basin of moss. She plunged her face into it and drank. Then she lifted her head and looked around. Then she rose and looked again. She saw no one in the cave. But the moment she stood upright she had a marvellous sense that she was in the secret of the earth and all its ways. Everything she had seen, or learned from books; all that her grandmother had said or sung to her; all the talk of the beasts, birds and fishes; all that had happened to her on her journey with Mossy, and since then in the heart of the earth with the Old man and the Older man – all was plain: she understood it all, and saw that everything meant the same thing, though she could not have put it into words again.

The next moment she descried, in a corner of the cave, a little naked child sitting on the moss. He was playing with balls of various colours and sizes, which he disposed in strange figures upon the floor beside him. And now Tangle felt that there was something in her knowledge which was not in her understanding. For she knew there must be an infinite meaning in the change and sequence and individual forms of the figures into which the child arranged the balls, as well as in the varied harmonies of their colours, but what it all meant she could not tell. He went on busily, tirelessly, playing his solitary game, without looking up or seeming to know that there was a stranger in his deep-withdrawn cell. Diligently as a lace-maker shifts her bobbins, he shifted and arranged his balls. Flashes of meaning would now pass from them to Tangle, and now again all would be not merely obscure, but utterly dark. She stood looking for a long time, for there was fascination in the sight; and the longer she looked the more an indescribable vague intelligence went on rousing itself in her mind. For seven years she had stood there watching the naked child with his coloured balls, and it seemed to her like seven hours, when all at once the shape the balls took, she knew not why, reminded her of the Valley of Shadows, and she spoke:

"Where is the Old Man of the Fire?" she said.

"Here I am," answered the child, rising and leaving his balls on the moss. "What can I do for you?"

There was such an awfulness of absolute repose on the face of the child that Tangle stood dumb before him. He had no smile, but the love in his large grey eyes was deep as the centre. And with the repose there lay on his face a shimmer as of moonlight, which seemed as if any moment it might break into such a ravishing smile as would cause the beholder to weep himself to death. But the smile never came, and the moonlight lay there unbroken. For the heart of the child was too deep for any smile to reach from it to his face.

"Are you the oldest man of all?" Tangle at length, although filled with awe, ventured to ask.

"Yes, I am. I am very, very old. I am able to help you, I know. I can help everybody."

And the child drew near and looked up in her face so that she burst into tears.

"Can you tell me the way to the country the shadows fall from?" she sobbed.

"Yes. I know the way quite well. I go there myself sometimes. But you could not go my way; you are not old enough. I will show you how you can go."

"Do not send me out into the great heat again," prayed Tangle.

"I will not," answered the child.

And he reached up and put his little cool hand on her heart.

"Now," he said, "you can go. The fire will not burn you. Come."

He led her from the cave, and following him through another archway, she found herself in a vast desert of sand and rock. The sky of it was of rock, lowering over them like solid thunderclouds; and the whole place was so hot that she saw, in bright rivulets, the yellow gold and white silver and red copper trickling molten from the rocks. But the heat never came near her.

When they had gone some distance, the child turned up a great stone, and took something like an egg from under it. He next drew a long curved line in the sand with his finger, and laid the egg in it. He then spoke something Tangle could not understand. The egg broke, a small snake came out and, lying in the line in the sand, grew and grew till he filled it. The moment he was thus full-grown, he began to glide away, undulating like a sea wave.

"Follow that serpent," said the child. "He will lead you the right way."

Tangle followed the serpent. But she could not go far without looking back at the marvellous Child. He stood alone in the midst of the glowing desert, beside a fountain of red flame that had burst forth at his feet, his naked whiteness glimmering a pale rosy red in the torrid fire. There he stood, looking after her, till, from the lengthening distance, she could see him no more. The serpent went straight on, turning neither to the right nor left.

Meantime Mossy had got out of the lake of shadows and, following his mournful, lonely way, had reached the seashore. It was a dark, stormy evening. The sun had set. The wind was blowing from the sea. The waves had surrounded the rock within which lay the Old Man's house. A deep water rolled between it and the shore, upon which a majestic figure was walking alone.

Mossy went up to him and said:

"Will you tell me where to find the Old Man of the Sea?"

"I am the Old Man of the Sea," the figure answered.

"I see a strong kingly man of middle age," returned Mossy.

Then the Old Man looked at him more intently, and said:

"Your sight, young man, is better than that of most who take this way. The night is stormy: come to my house and tell me what I can do for you."

Mossy followed him. The waves flew from before the footsteps of the Old Man of the Sea, and Mossy followed upon dry sand.

When they had reached the cave, they sat down and gazed at each other.

Now Mossy was an old man by this time. He looked much older than the Old Man of the Sea and his feet were very weary.

After looking at him for a moment, the Old Man took him by the hand and led him into his inner cave. There he helped him to undress and laid him in the bath. And he saw that one of his hands Mossy did not open.

"What have you got in that hand?" he asked.

Mossy opened his hand, and there lay the golden key.

"Ah!" said the Old Man. "That accounts for your knowing me. And I know the way you have to go."

"I want to find the country whence the shadows fall," said Mossy.

"I dare say you do. So do I. But meantime, one thing is certain – what is that key for, do you think?"

"For a keyhole somewhere. But I don't know why I keep it. I never could find the keyhole. And I have lived a good while, I believe," said Mossy, sadly. "I'm not sure that I'm not old. I know my feet ache."

"Do they?" said the Old Man, as if he really meant to ask the question; and Mossy, who was still lying in the bath, watched his feet for a moment before he replied.

"No, they do not," he answered. "Perhaps I am not old either."

"Get up and look at yourself in the water."

He rose and looked at himself in the water, and there was not a grey hair on his head or a wrinkle on his skin.

"You have tasted of death now," said the Old Man. "Is it good?"

"It is good," said Mossy. "It is better than life."

"No," said the Old Man, "it is only more life. Your feet will make no holes in the water now."

"What do you mean?"

"I will show you that presently."

They returned to the outer cave, and sat and talked together for a long time. At length the Old Man of the Sea rose, and said to Mossy:

"Follow me."

He led him up the stair again, and opened another door. They stood on the level of the raging sea, looking towards the east. Across the waste of waters, against the bosom of a fierce black cloud, stood the foot of a rainbow, glowing in the dark.

"This indeed is my way," said Mossy, as soon as he saw the rainbow, and stepped out upon the sea. His feet made no holes in the water. He fought the wind and climbed the waves, and went on towards the rainbow.

The storm died away. A lovely day and a lovelier night followed. A cool wind blew over the wide plain of the quiet ocean. And still Mossy journeyed eastward. But the rainbow had vanished with the storm.

Day after day he held on, and he thought he had no guide. He did not see how a shining fish under the waters directed his steps. He crossed the sea and came to a great precipice of rock, up which he could discover but one path. Nor did this lead him farther than half-way up the rock, where it ended on a platform. Here he stood and pondered – it could not be that the way stopped here, else what was the path for? It was a rough path, not very plain, yet certainly a path. He examined the face of the rock. It was smooth as glass. But as his eyes kept roving hopelessly over it, something glittered and he caught sight of a row of small sapphires. They bordered a little hole in the rock.

"The keyhole!" he cried.

He tried the key. It fitted. It turned. A great clang and clash, as of iron bolts on huge brazen caldrons, echoed thunderously within. He drew out the key. The rock in front of him began to fall. He retreated from it as far as the breadth of the platform would allow. A great slab fell at his feet. In front was still the solid rock, with this one slab fallen forward out of it. But the moment he stepped upon it, a second fell, just short of the edge of the first, making the next step of a stair, which thus kept dropping itself before him as he ascended into the heart of the precipice. It led him into a hall fit for such an approach – irregular and rude in formation, but floor, sides, pillars and vaulted roof, all one mass of shining stones of every colour that light can show. In the centre stood seven columns, ranged from red to violet. And on the pedestal of one of them sat a woman, motionless, with her face bowed upon her knees. Seven years had she sat there waiting. She lifted her head as Mossy drew near. It was Tangle. Her hair had grown to her feet, and was rippled like the windless sea on broad sands. Her face was beautiful, like her grandmother's, and as still and peaceful as that of the Old Man of the Fire. Her form was tall and noble. Yet Mossy knew her at once.

"How beautiful you are, Tangle!" he said, in delight and astonishment.

"Am I?" she returned. "Oh, I have waited for you so long! But you, you are the Old Man of the Sea. No. You are like the Old Man of the Earth. No, no. You are like the oldest man of all. You are like them all. And yet you are my own old Mossy! How did you come here? What did you do after I lost you? Did you find the keyhole? Have you got the key still?"

She had a hundred questions to ask him, and he a hundred more to ask her. They told each other all their adventures and were as happy as man and woman could be. For they were younger and better, and stronger and wiser, than they had ever been before.

It began to grow dark. And they wanted more than ever to reach the country whence the shadows fall. So they looked about them for a way out of the cave. The door by which Mossy entered had closed again, and there was half a mile of rock between them and the sea. Neither could Tangle find the opening in the floor by which the serpent had led her thither. They searched till it grew so dark that they could see nothing, and gave it up.

After a while, however, the cave began to glimmer again. The light came from the moon, but it did not look like moonlight, for it gleamed through those seven pillars in the middle and filled the place with all colours. And now Mossy saw that there was a pillar beside the red one, which he had not observed before. And it was of the same new colour that he had seen in the rainbow when he saw it first in the fairy forest. And on it he saw a sparkle of blue. It was the sapphires round the keyhole.

He took his key. It turned in the lock to the sounds of Aeolian music. A door opened upon slow hinges, and disclosed a winding stair within. The key vanished from his fingers. Tangle went up. Mossy followed. The door closed behind them. They climbed out of the earth; and, still climbing, rose above it. They were in the rainbow. Far abroad, over ocean and land, they could see through its transparent walls the earth beneath their feet. Stairs beside stairs wound up together, and beautiful beings of all ages climbed along with them.

They knew that they were going up to the country whence the shadows fall.

And by this time I think they must have got there.